Confessions
of a Taoist
on Wall Street

By David Payne

Confessions of a Taoist on Wall Street
Early from the Dance

Confessions of a Taoist on Wall Street

A Chinese American Romance

David Payne

BALLANTINE BOOKS • NEW YORK

All rights reserved under International and Pan-American Copyright Conventions. Published in the United States by Ballantine Books, a division of Random House, Inc., New York, and simultaneously in Canada by Random House of Canada Limited, Toronto.

The author is grateful for permission to quote from the following sources:

The I Ching or Book of Changes, the Richard Wilhelm translation rendered into English by Cary F. Baynes. Bollingen Series XIX. Copyright © 1950, 1967 by Princeton University Press. Copyright renewed © 1977 by Princeton University Press. Selected quotations reprinted by permission of Princeton University Press.

The Way and Its Power, by Arthur Waley. Reprinted by permission of Grove Press, Inc.

The Way of the White Clouds, by Lama Anagarika-Govinda. Published by Hutchinsons (London).

"The Way of Life" from *The Chinese Translations* by Witter Bynner. Copyright © 1944 by Witter Bynner, renewed © 1972 by Dorothy Chauvenet and Paul Horgan. Published by Farrar, Straus & Giroux.

http://www.randomhouse.com

Library of Congress Catalog Card Number: 96-96614

ISBN: 345-41038-6

First published by Houghton Mifflin Company
Reprinted by permission of Houghton Mifflin Company

Manufactured in the United States of America

First Ballantine Books Mass Market Edition: December 1985
First Ballantine Books Trade Edition: August 1996

10 9 8 7 6 5 4 3 2 1

For my mother,
Margaret Leah Rose Payne Long —
A first installment on the debt I can never repay

Contents

Preface

I have called this tale a Romance in the sense which Hawthorne delineates in his preface to *The House of the Seven Gables,* where he is at pains to distinguish that form from the Novel. Whereas the Novel strives for an effect of verisimilitude, the Romance is pure, unrepentant mental theater. One expects, even comes to demand, a degree of stylization — conventions of staging, altered effects of light . . . sleight of hand. All this, of course, is present in the Novel too, only less apparent, as the Novelist takes pains to hide the seams, the scars. Despite his chivalric loyalty to material reality, however (which he cherishes as the walrus cherishes the oyster, even as he violates it), the Novelist is an illusionist, a magician, too. In the final analysis, he and the writer of Romance are equally guilty in the Great Deceit which art is. Like all the passionate and disreputable bedfellows in the great bordello of the arts, they are liars in the service of the truth. The writer of Romance is only less sentimental about the facts. A pirate, a buccaneer, he is ready at a moment's notice to weigh anchor from the safe harbor of material and historical certainty. Setting out on the high seas of imagination with his conscripted crew of facts, he doesn't balk at tyranny, but makes them swab his decks, or perch for hours in his crow's nest crying whales, dance a sailor's hornpipe for his pleasure, or even, in extremity, walk the plank. Which is to say, he is always ready to sacrifice reality to the high truth of art, to what Hawthorne so beautifully and succinctly calls "the truth of the human heart." Romance must be judged by its fidelity to this, not to "the facts."

Whether such Machiavellian tactics are as dangerous in art as in politics, I leave to others better qualified than I — the philosophers and critics — to decide, and go merrily on my way. As a precaution, however, I leave Hawthorne — my champion, my chevalier — to defend my rear (which is to say, my tale). I picture him, vigilant ghost, stalking restlessly through the gloomy chambers of his great seven-gabled edifice, built from "materials long in use for constructing castles in the air," having set up housekeeping there for the duration. The House of the Seven Gables is in a little town called Salem by the seaside — not Salem, Massachusetts, where Novelists and others of a doggedly literal turn of mind have always searched for it, but in another Salem, across the border in the country of Romance, the Imagi-Nation, which is on the seacoast too — the seacoast of Bohemia (one short hop from Kansas by tornado).

All this is merely a fanciful way of saying that the "facts" presented in the following pages, while tangentially connected with reality (at least suggested by it), are none of them completely circumscribed within its radius. While none intentionally contravenes either the real or the possible, the truth of my facts should be judged, not as in life, by conformity to history or nature, but only by the extent that they help to localize and authenticate the illusion, establishing themselves harmoniously within the cosmos of the work. The brand of Taoism offered here for public consumption, if not precisely a nostrum, has certainly been doctored for the occasion (though studiously . . . and living Taoism was never a rigid system; in fact its deepest inspiration militates against scholastic formalism, that rigor mortis which has set in at Western universities). The same applies to my treatment of the rituals of high finance and, to a lesser degree, to my presentation of the Flying Tigers. It was never my intention to portray their activities literally, but merely to borrow a little of their mythic luster, to gather a few drops of the sparkling dew time has distilled out of their sweat and blood to make my garden grow. China and Wall Street as presented here are regions that exist nowhere finally except in the author's mind (and yours, Reader, if you choose to let them). They are the imaginary gardens in which I have endeavored (and in which you must now endeavor) to locate this real toad . . . or prince, as the case may prove. (Toad *and* prince, perhaps.)

—D.P.

> *Over that art*
> *Which you say adds to nature, is an art*
> *That nature makes.*
> — Shakespeare, *The Winter's Tale*

PART ONE

Tao (China)

Chapter 1

My first exposure to him was through a photograph, one the monks found tucked in with the wadding of the pillow I lay on when I came to them. In it he appears about the same age I am now, perhaps even younger. Wearing a silk Chinese robe like a smoking jacket over his civilian clothes, a highball glass in one hand, the other stuffed nonchalantly in the pocket of a pair of baggy khaki pants, he stands beside his plane, whose nose is painted with the famous emblem of the AVG — the red, gaping tiger jaws with their pointed rows of abstract, bloody teeth. I notice further he is wearing two-toned shoes. She is with him. Clutching awkwardly at his arm, my mother stands under the propeller, one blade of which is poised above her head like a sword caught freeze-frame in the act of falling. Dressed in Western clothes — a pleated skirt, saddle shoes, white bobby-socks turned down above the ankle — she wears his officer's cap thrust backward on her head, tilted at a jaunty angle. Too big though, it's begun to slip down toward her eyes, leaving her face indistinct — the more so since she does not look squarely at the camera, but off to the side, as though distracted by something just beyond the border of the photograph, something the camera failed to capture.

In contrast to hers, his features are icily sharp. His crop of dark hair bristles straight up on his head, tilted to the side as he looks into the camera, flashing a quizzical smile for the folks back home, or for the photographer, or for me — a smile I could never quite pin down, but which nevertheless (and maybe for that very reason) charms me fatally. Perhaps the ambiguity results less from the smile than from the dark glasses that loom above it, concealing the expression of his eyes. They're the kind worn by aviators and policemen, with the black-green tear-shaped lens.

The cool, anonymous melancholy of those glasses above the puckish smile — the one a modern mask that seems to hide some immemorial, standard human suffering; the other, the smile, largely innocent, perhaps incapable of the suffering the mask implies — the juxtaposition always struck me as impertinent, almost monstrous . . . and at the same time, wonderful. How can I explain? Years of lingering over it with an orphan's hungry fondness worked my longing to a strained, exquisite pitch. When I gazed too long and too hard at that photograph, my imagination grew degenerate with surfeit, dreaming of him. But dreaming was my only recourse. For I never saw my father. Except once . . . perhaps . . . at the very end, after it was too late, standing on the gallery of the New York Stock Exchange. But that is the end of my story, not the beginning.

•

Here and there in the outlying regions of postrevolutionary China, tenuously rooted in the drab exterior of our Great Wall of progress, one still finds an occasional vestige of the old ways. Like columbine among the bricks, eternal China flowers in the cracks along the fault line of our modern age. I know this to be true, as I passed my childhood wandering among the splendid glooms of that forbidden past.

Known immemorially as "the heavenly land," Szechwan province is a place of mists and flowers, high up near the sky. Legend grows in that spectacular ground, where crags yaw out over abysses so deep a man can fall, they say, for nine days straight without hitting bottom. The rocks writhe like strange beasts "tagged" by God and frozen in the throes of pristine vigor for some sin of presumption — a rebellion put down long before Wu Ting, the Illustrious Ancestor, subdued the Devil's Country and gave government to men. In Szechwan's cloud-forest, bamboo and rhododendron grow to rheumy, dripping giants forty feet high, watered by the mountain torrents as they race toward the fall line. Plunging a thousand feet, those torrents fan to iridescent sprays before they reach the pools below — pools still inhabited by their ancient lords, the dragons, who leap and somersault, stirring the waters to froth in an access of diluvial joy. Masters of their lonely world, at night they sit in state accepting the homage of the other animals who come to drink there, reverently lowering their heads to lap the cold, pure water and blinking their phosphorescent eyes.

Szechwan has always supplied China, if not with her finest poets, then certainly with her finest dreamers, supplied them, and been their refuge when she turned the face of wrath. Here in isolated spots, if you are very still and listen in the proper spirit, you may hear the eerie piping of a Taoist flute, played by some hermit or magician, one of those of whom it is said, "He walks among the animals unfeared, speaking their languages, sustaining himself on the dew of the air."

According to a popular story, it was here, to Szechwan, that all the gods withdrew — the dark-visaged gods of thunder as well as smiling, benignant bodhisattvas and Immortals — before the righteous fury of Chairman Mao and his Red Guards during that sad, shameful interlude in our history known as the Cultural Revolution. Distant from Peking by a thousand miles and a thousand years in time, Szechwan has always been, and remains today, largely untouched by history or progress.

To explain this, superstition, though appealing, is unnecessary; simple geography will do: mountains and rivers. In the west rise the Himalayas, the highest range in the world, its peaks glinting blue-black with the glacial permafrost which even the toxic sunlight of that rarest altitude has never melted and can never melt. The massif cuts us off. Likewise the river. For though the Yangtze in the main is a great unifying artery linking the remote interior to the cities on the coast, it becomes unnavigable on the very doorstep of the region. A swift, turbid stream, complex with rapids, it rages uninterrupted from the time it plunges off the plateau of Tibet until it passes through the San-hsia Gorges east of Chungking on its way to Shanghai and the China Sea. In Szechwan the river is a silver thread that tantalizes only, cutting off what it should bind.

It was there, then, on a remote headstream of the Yangtze in southwestern Szechwan, only a stone's throw from the poppy fields of Yunnan Province, that I grew up. But who am I?

Sun I's the name, pronounced "Soon Ye." At least that's what I'm called. My sobriquet . . . As to my true name, well, to cite Lao Tzu's celebrated aphorism from the *Tao Te Ching,* "The name that can be named is not the True Name." In my case this applies with a vengeance.

You see, Sun I is a pun. That's what the monks, my "elder brothers," fixed on as a designation, showing no mercy for me when I came to them, a bawling, blinking infant. Unfortunately the joke — which has inclined me less to laugh than weep — caught on.

I must explain myself. *Sun* and *I* are the transliterated forms of two Chinese characters which mean, literally, "decrease" *(Sun)* and "increase" *(I),* otherwise, "profit and loss." Since, at the time in question, the monks could have formed only the most rudimentary opinion of my character, this cannot be construed as an allusion to some ambiguity in my personality or in my prospects for the future — not a deliberate allusion, anyway. You see, the monks did not arrive at my name themselves, either calculatedly, with malice aforethought, or through some happy (for them) stroke of blind serendipity. They were guided by occult inspiration. *Sun* and *I* are also the names of the forty-first and forty-second hexagrams in the *I Ching,* or *Book of Changes.* This was the reading the oracle returned when the monks consulted it on my behalf for the first time: *Sun,* or "Loss," disintegrating into its opposite, or mirror image, *I,* "Gain." (*Sun* is also the name of one of the eight fundamental trigrams: "The Gentle.")

Before going on, let me pause to say a word about the *I Ching,* for more than once it has made some canny thrust which proved prophetic, or in itself altered the course of my destiny.

The *Changes* might be described as a work combining the virtues of the Christian Bible with those of the *Farmer's Almanac* — intensely religious, even mystical, and at the same time thoroughly pragmatic, like the Chinese soul it mirrors. With layer upon layer of wisdom piled up in its pages over time like geologic strata, it can be a regimen for spiritual development — much as Ignatius Loyola's *Exercises* has been for Jesuits in the West — or, equally well, a peasant may consult the oracle concerning the proper date for planting rice or barley. More pointedly, gamblers can use it to predict the roll of the dice, though in their case the odds are longer, since the one condition the oracle requires of its petitioner is *ling,* which, loosely translated, means "purity of heart." It is said: "To those who are not in contact with the Tao, the oracle does not return an intelligible answer, since it would be of no avail." But this purity is not easily ascertained: a gambler may possess it and a priest may not.

Perhaps the best description of the *I Ching* I've ever heard was given by my master, Chung Fu, who said it is like a well whose bricks were laid by human workmen, but in which brim the cold, transparent waters of the Tao, drawn up from the pure reservoir of Being, which has no bottom that man can sound. His definition captures the idea of a primitive force (*the* primitive force, Tao), ethically neutral in itself and indifferent to man, obeying no laws but its own — always following the line of least resistance and seeking its own level — but which, nevertheless, can be channeled toward a human end and used for good. This end, this good, is wisdom, which the sage who studies the *I Ching* may hope to gain, drinking long, cool, satisfying draughts from the bucket which he draws up heavy, spilling over, from the darkness of the human heart.

The way it works is this: The *I Ching* is based on the Taoist concept of the Great Primal Opposition, familiar to the West in the *T'ai Chi* symbol — the Wheel of Life (sometimes called the Egg of Chaos) in which the light and dark, *yang* and *yin,* cleave together like two great beasts grappling in mortal combat, or embracing in intercourse. All things arise from this ongoing war, and love, between the opposites, which alternate cyclically, each regenerating from the disintegration of the other, which it carries in its womb like a fatal embryo and nourishes at the expense of its own life. All the Taoist arts, the "one hundred paths" of meditation, of which the study of the *I Ching* is only one, are intended to unify these opposites within the self, to recover the wholeness which existed before the One, Tao, splintered into multiplicity. The primal wound of self-division healed, the practitioner reaches back to the still source of Being and achieves at-onement with the world. Thus, by letting go the fragile ambitions and desires of ego, he becomes as irresistible as a force of nature, able to conquer even death.

But to return to the *I Ching.* To understand the principles on which it's based, one may imagine a continuum — say, the spectrum of visible light. In place of blue and red at the extremes would be *yin* and *yang:* this is the spectrum of the Tao, both physical and metaphysical. Just as different colors are made up of varying proportions of red and blue, so life itself — its disposition at a given moment, rather — is determined by the precise proportions of *yin* and *yang* (the dark, yielding, female principle and the light, creative, male principle) in the chemistry of that moment. The spectrum of light breaks into the identifiable ranges of the colors; life breaks down into certain primal situations, equivalent to the "colors" of the Tao, which recur again and again in the eternal oscillation between the extremes of *yin* and *yang*. The *I Ching* identifies sixty-four of these, the various combinations of the eight trigrams. Using yarrow stalks or coins, the Taoist may read — as precisely as a chemist measuring quantities of basic elements in some solution — the composition of his fate. For the Taoist is the universal chemist, and Tao the universal solution which he analyzes — the "elemental soup," the plasma, out of which the "ten thousand things" of created nature were spawned, and into which they must dissolve again at last.

But let me return to the joke my name involves, since as yet I've explained only the first level of it.

Had it not been for a certain detail in my appearance, I might have lived a fairly normal life in China. As a male I possessed some value and might have been sold to a childless couple to continue their line. Girls in my position had a harder time of it. Searching for herbs in the forest outside the monastery, I once found a baby girl lying near the stream as though asleep, only her dumbness had a bluer tint. Despite the advantage my gender conferred, my first exposure to the world might have been an equally unhappy one had it not been for the monks. For this, I forgive their little joke at my expense.

Let me tell you then that I was born with what is referred to euphemistically in China as "a slight deformity of the visual organ": my eyes had "too much white." This is how the Chinese describe someone who lacks the epicanthic fold over the inside corner of his eye. I quote a passage on the trigram *Sun* from the *Changes:*

> The Gentle . . . is advance and retreat, the undecided, odor. Among men it means the gray-haired; it means those with broad foreheads; *it means those with much white in their eyes;* it means those close to gain so that in the market they get threefold value. Finally, it is the sign of vehemence.

There you have it then, the punch line which has left me black and blue. But there's more. Westerners in China are sometimes baited with the derogatory epithet "white eyes." As the Caucasian race universally lacks an epicanthus, its members possess relatively more "white" than their Oriental counterparts, a fact which the Chinese — at least the cruder, more provincial sort — never cease to find hilarious. If you can't understand this, think of the Sambo in old Hollywood films, with his electric, rolling eyes. There *is* something funny about it. I certainly received enough ribbing over it. When I went with Wu to buy rice from the peasants, I frequently got into rows with the snot-nosed little savages who followed us around, ogling me, sniffing out my difference like animals.

Much later, after I had come to America, the *Sun* pun cropped up in an unexpected way, tying back to something in my earliest childhood. There is a ritual in China called "giving sign." An infant is allowed to choose from among several symbolic objects placed around it by its parents, in my case, by the monks. The child's preference is thought to provide an infallible clue to the destiny of the adult. For me the fateful object was a small stone egg in which the features of a monkey, curled innocently like a fetus, but with uplifted head and "fiery eyes," were carved. This was the infamous Monkey, whose Chinese name, meaning "Great Sage, Equal to Heaven," I later found rendered in English as *Sun* Wu K'ung! Happening on Arthur Waley's translation of Wu Ch'eng-en's famous tale, *Journey to the West,* I discovered that the pun had followed me across the linguistic barrier into English, where, incidentally, it proliferated in many new and wonderful forms.

To understand the aptness of my association with Monkey — besides the "fiery eyes" — you must know that after being hatched from his stone egg, he spent his youth, much as I spent mine, frolicking about the Mountain of Fruits and Flowers engaging in various pranks and high jinks in the normal monkey line. At length, however, growing melancholy at the thought of his mortality, Monkey set out over the Western Ocean to find a sage who could teach him to master the Seventy-Two Transformations. This accomplished, he was promoted into the lower echelons of the Heavenly Bureaucracy, serving the Jade Emperor in the capacity of groom. But Monkey felt his talents were wasted in the stables. So on the eve of the Great Peach Banquet he rebelled, drinking toasts to his own health until he'd quaffed off the best part of the reserves of heaven. He then went on a three-day drunk of heroic proportions, stealing vast quantities of Lao Tzu's Gold-Cinnabar Elixir, filching the Peaches of Immortality, and perpetrating other outrages for which, the gods determined, the only fitting punishment was death, a slow roasting in Lao Tzu's alchemical alembic. The only problem was that, having drunk the wine and the elixir, and having stuffed himself with the Peaches of Immortality (not to mention the fact that he was made of stone to begin with), Monkey had become invulnerable. The groom had caroused himself into the enjoyment of not one immortality, but several, and could in no wise be dispatched. When Lao Tzu's apparatus was opened, he emerged cocky as ever. No damage was apparent, except that his eyes were permanently red from smoke. He immediately went back on the warpath. As a last resort, Buddha himself had to be called in. At this point Monkey was imprisoned beneath a stone mountain for five hundred years.

This, as I said, was his youth. His real story begins only later, with his release. The Bodhisattva of Mercy, Kuan Yin, let him out on the condition that he'd behave himself, becoming the disciple and protector of a monk named Tripitaka, a rather hapless fellow, who was on his way to India to retrieve the Mahayana scriptures. This is the westward journey referred to in the title of Wu Ch'eng-en's book. After seventeen years and many perilous adventures, Monkey, along with Pigsy, Sandy, the white dragon-horse, and their lachrymose master Tripitaka, reached heaven at last, acquired the texts, and brought them home to China. As a reward for their great labor of compassion, they were granted enlightenment, each according to his degree.

Monkey's story, which I made Wu tell me over and over during my childhood, filled me with delight, but also with chagrin. While I cherished Monkey, I didn't relish the idea of such a close association. For though lovable, he was scurrilous. Yet associate I was by virtue of the sign I'd given. Waley's transliteration — Sun Wu K'ung — provided the final, most degenerate blossom of the pun.

I suppose it was inevitable that my volatile temper and tendency to brawl should have been christened by the brothers "Monkey Nature," a term which, in their inbred cant, suggested willfulness, rabidity of imagination, mischievousness, and a restless, vehement heart. As he caned me for my transgressions, Wu often emphasized this last quality particularly — vehemence. Hadn't the oracle, with disconcerting prescience, pegged this as an attribute of my character at the same time that it described my eyes?

Bowing to *force majeure*, I took the perceived insult with the blows, then stole away to console myself with silent weeping. In the aftermath, Wu, who was sentimental and big hearted, was invariably stricken with remorse. He would come to console me, offering sweets in his rough hands. Then he always said I was too tenderhearted, too "gentle." Wasn't *Sun* the sign of gentleness?

Yes, even Wu, my best friend, indulged in occasional gibes (though, it's true, with more tenderness and humor than the rest). It was he who told me that when I heard my name pronounced for the first time, I opened my eyes so wide that, though it was past midnight and black as pitch, the cock crowed in the yard thinking it was day.

Finally, however — as you may have guessed already — my "deformity" consisted in this and nothing else: that I had an American father. The truth is — to use another of those exasperatingly polite circumlocutions so typical of my people (conditioned under the pernicious influence of Confucianism, with its "thirty-three hundred rules" of etiquette) — I am a "child of war." In plain English, a bastard.

My father's name was Eddie Love. He was a pilot who came to China in 1941 with the AVG, the American Volunteer Group, better known as the Flying Tigers. This much I knew from an early age, for the abbot, Chung Fu, once had occasion to offer Love the monastery's hospitality, under circumstances I will allude to later. What little Chung Fu picked up of my father's story he passed on to me. It wasn't much. Only later did I discover that Love was the only child of a father who possessed one of the greatest capitalist fortunes in America. Arthur Love, my grandfather, yielded the active management of his inherited assets due to certain "temperamental indispositions," becoming a reclusive dilettante and patron of the arts. This discovery made me wonder if Eddie Love hadn't been a kind of refugee in China, fleeing from the world of debilitating privilege which his parents tenanted, if he hadn't sought out danger as a restorative against his father's insipid presence. I never knew for sure . . . about this, or anything having to do with his character. For my father was an almost magically elusive being, a phantom. And when I tried to close with him, to draw him into my embrace, he always staged a disappearing act and left me holding nothing but thin air.

Of course, I did know some things. The general outline of his portrait was not so difficult to trace. Like the other pilots in the AVG, he had a reputation for being footloose, brave, undisciplined, high-strung. Like them, he had followed General Claire Chennault to China, whether on principle, for adventure, for the money (though that seemed unlikely), or simply to escape the routine of regular service, I never knew. Not a select fraternity he had enrolled in. And yet, for seven months before America officially entered the war, committing troops to the China-Burma-India theater, with a hundred largely obsolete Curtiss P-40 Tomahawks, the Flying Tigers single-handedly defended China from the combined air might of Japan.

Their efforts kept open the "back door" of the Burma Road, the last major overland supply route from the west. Kunming and, ultimately, Chungking itself — the provisional capital, where Chiang Kai-shek and his embattled Kuomintang government had retreated to make their final stand — depended on that lifeline. Had it been severed, China would have probably fallen. That the Flying Tigers were able to operate effectively against an air force that was superior both technologically and numerically was remarkable in itself. It verged on the miraculous that they did so without suffering a single defeat in fifty major air battles. This is why, along with the RAF during the Battle of Britain, they are widely considered the finest air-strike team ever to fly, and why they have undergone a virtual apotheosis, entering the realm of military legend.

My father's apotheosis was something more than "virtual" for me. As a child I literally considered him a god. In moments of melancholy, I often dreamed that one day he would rescue me, diving from the sun in his P-40 to spirit me away to the West. Then I would be happy. It was a desperate fantasy, I know, but I dreamed too with vehemence. Looking back now it seems that I was happy past belief there as a child, and that only when he entered my life did I learn what sorrow truly was.

Chapter 2

The monastery where I grew up was called Ken Kuan, which means literally "mountain" *(ken)* "view" *(kuan).* For Taoists however (who love such things), there is a further layer of implication. By extrapolation *ken* comes to mean "keeping still," *kuan,* "contemplation." This alludes to the form of meditation known as *tso-wang,* or "sitting with blank mind."

On both counts Ken Kuan was well named. It was aeried in a rocky nest of cliffs carved out of the lower Himalayas by the headstreams of the Yangtze, which race down from the hidden source high in the Tanglha Range; and for long ages past, the mountain had been a retreat for Taoist monks who came there, leaving behind their attachments in the "marketplace" of the defiled world, to embark on the arduous journey back to Tao — a journey which is called Return to the Source.

That ultimate end is single, but the approaches to it are many. Just as a number of spokes converge in the hub of a wheel, so the many ways of meditation — the "one hundred paths" — converge in the one Way, which is Tao. Four such paths were followed at Ken Kuan.

The first was the study of the sacred texts, primarily the *I Ching,* but also the *Tao Te Ching* of Lao Tzu, the *Chuang Tzu,* the *Lieh Tzu,* and other lesser works. This training was mnemonic and exegetical.

The second was *tso-wang.* Some of my earliest memories are of playing among the monks as they sat ranged in the temple, practicing their "sitting." By Chung Fu's order I was allowed to come and go as I pleased, with the single condition that I be absolutely quiet. At the least peep, Wu was summoned and I was sent on my way, boxed ears flapping in the wind. Yet strange as it may seem, this expedient was rarely necessary. Though my attention span was short and I was mischievous as any child (more perhaps), I almost never misbehaved in their company. Fear was a factor, I suppose. But there was something else. . . . Often I would gaze at the faces of the brothers — some deeply furrowed with the effort of concentration, breaking out in beads of sweat, others calm and smiling, suffused with the gentle light of inward bliss — trying to puzzle out the mystery of their stillness. Sometimes I even mimicked their breathing and posture, doing my best to focus my concentration in the Mysterious Pass of the Precious Square Inch, that spot in the middle of the forehead between and just above the eyes (site of the pineal gland, that rudimentary eye) where one sees the first glimmerings of the Ineffable, like an aurora borealis in the soul.

Of course, my "meditation" was partly no more than a child's playful emulation of his elders; but, once again, there was more to it. Often when I sat among the meditating brothers, particularly when Chung Fu was present, I felt curious intimations. My body tingled with a sense of imminence, as though somewhere deep within a door had opened on another world, letting through a blast of icy wind which made the hair rise on my arms; or I was suddenly buoyed up on a wave of inexplicable joy, which crested, broke, and tumbled, flooding my brain with a mysterious effluent, cold and rank as winter seawater, which ebbed with a diastolic motion (like some mystic heart relaxing) only to surge again. These experiences left an afterglow of several hours' duration. I know of no other way to explain my sensations except as the electric overflow of the monks' deep-searching bliss flowing into me, something I was able to receive because of the unobstructed innocence of my childish heart. This was my first taste of the profound well-being which quiescence brings — sinking into the clear pool of the Self, to rise invigorated and refreshed — and it made me thirst for more.

I've often thought the Tao afforded me this solace in lieu of the security other children take from the mother's breast, something I never knew. More than any other this thought of what I'd missed, what I'd been deprived of, brought on the fits of melancholy I experienced as a child (and the bouts of temper that followed as inevitably as thunder and lightning out of brooding clouds). But as I grew older I reflected that I had had pacifiers of a more extraordinary sort. Had I not been given "Simplicity to look at . . . the Uncarved Block to hold . . . selflessness and fewness of desires"? Did not Lao Tzu call these "the sustenance that comes from the Mother's breast"? For Tao is a greater mother than any, the Great Mother of all. Bastard though I was, she had not disdained me. On that breast I was nursed with the sweet milk of eternal life, the food of gods and the Immortal Sages. Who, after all, could claim a more exalted lineage?

Why then was I still at times disconsolate, at times bitter? And why, over and over, did I return to that photograph of my father with his cryptic smile and his dark glasses, like an ambassador from another world?

•

The third "path" was the recitation of the *Ten Ox-Herding Songs,* familiarly called *Ten Bulls.* This method involved some textual exegesis, like the study of the sacred books, but also, like *tso-wang,* a certain amount of physical yoga, in particular the "regulation of the breaths" necessary to the proper vocalization of syllables. In its strenuousness and complexity, this method bears an analogy to operatic training in the West.

The *Songs* are so old their author is unknown, which is no doubt as it should be. In their oral transmission over many centuries, like all the artifacts time preserves, they were rubbed down and polished by all the hands through which they passed, until they transcended the personality of any single maker. Purified to the last degree of whiteness and simplicity, they became a fit expression of the universal heart of China.

In the ox herd's songs, he describes his simple work — searching for a lost bull, finding him, riding him home, resting at the end of the day. Thus the first:

> In the world's meadow, I part the high grasses
> searching for my bull.
> Tracking nameless rivers, lost in the tree-walled labyrinth
> of a mountain trail,
> My eyes blur with exhaustion, and my heart begins to falter;
> I cannot find him.
> I listen, defeated, to the soulless chirring of cicadas
> in the moonless wood.

Beneath the literal meaning, there are esoteric undercurrents. The cicada, for example, symbolizes the distractions of the world of sense, the dreary, obsessive buzzing of the "marketplace" from which the novice cannot free his mind. In *tso-wang,* beginners often experience a literal ringing in the ears, not unlike the insect's "soulless chirring." This is the first threshold that must be crossed.

The search for the bull itself is a metaphor for something larger. The bull is Tao, "darker than any mystery, / The Doorway whence issued all Secret Essences." And the stages of the pursuit — looking for him, finding him, taming, using, finally freeing him — are the steps one climbs in the ascent toward attainment, or realization; for actually there is nothing to be attained, only the realization of what was always so from the beginning, but to which we were blind because of our bondage to the world of False Appearances, which the Buddhists call "Samsara." It is said that Samsara equals Nirvana. Taoists express the idea more concretely in the famous *fan-yen,* or paradox, which says that "the search for enlightenment is like looking for a bull while riding on its back." The *hsien,* or Taoist Immortals, are often pictured riding on the backs of bulls.

There is an urgency and poignance in *Ten Bull* meditation which attaches to no other. For the *Songs* are most perfectly suited to the high, sweet clarity of a young boy's voice (with its ineffable melancholy). Adolescence steals that haunting timbre even as it lends the emotional maturity indispensable to the singer who would convey the *Songs'* full range. A classic dilemma: the young possess an instrument which only their elders have the discernment to use and appreciate properly. It is rare to find someone in whom the two combine, at least by nature. This was a very real factor in the creation of the court *castrati* who plagued China from Chou times down into the present century. No doubt their disappearance constitutes a "great leap forward" out of feudal darkness; and yet the *Songs,* and the contemplative life in general, have sadly languished since. Aficionados are always on the lookout for the "precocious boy" who can do them justice.

If I have lingered too long over this, perhaps vanity is to blame. You see, for a time I enjoyed celebrity ("notoriety" might be more accurate) for my singing of *Ten Bulls.* Until my voice changed, that is — a rite of passage which affected me profoundly (though I suppose that's something of a bromide as regards the life of boys). Often in the resin-scented depth of the forest, I sat alone and sang. The sundrift filtered through the pines, wavering on my face and hands as I performed my solitary meditation, accompanied only by the wind's susurrus in the branches. Pleasure lent facility; facility led to pride, pride to ostentation. I flaunted my gift in the public spaces of the monastery. Jealousy brewed among the monks. In addition to the well-seasoned epithets in their offensive arsenal, they conscripted this: "the young cockerel."

I remember an incident, one of many. Humming to myself while Wu and I hauled water one day, I heard someone whisper this name maliciously behind my back. I don't know why it set me off just then, but I flew into such a rage that Wu had to douse me with one of the buckets of water to cool me down. I couldn't have been much more than ten years old. I remember standing on the cold stones of the kitchen floor shivering as he toweled me off.

"Why must you always get yourself into these predicaments?" he scolded, drying me brusquely. Shaking his head, he answered his own question. "Don't tell me, I already know. You have a wild hair. Didn't the oracle say so? It's the *Sun* in you, your Monkey Nature. If you don't watch out, you're going to come to grief by it."

"What makes you so smart?" I challenged, even as I let him wipe my runny nose.

Wu stopped drying and stared at me gravely. "I know the signs," he said with a sigh, "too well. . . . I can see them in your eyes."

•

But there was one last form of meditation, the most arcane and difficult of the Taoist arts — alchemy. Like its medieval Western counterpart, the object of Taoist alchemy is the transmutation of base elements — specifically, white lead (or mercury) and cinnabar — into gold. The popular schools construe this as a literal process whose end is wealth. Among true initiates, however, it is understood as a metaphor for a transformation of a different sort, one that occurs wholly within.

White lead and cinnabar represent the terms of the primal opposition: multiplicity in its simplest and most elegant form. This opposition exists not only in the world, but in each person, and must be reconciled to accomplish wholeness and heal the mortal wound that every human being carries in his heart from birth until the day it finally kills him. White lead is *yang,* the male principle, and corresponds to semen; cinnabar is *yin,* the female, its pigmentation suggesting menstrual blood. These elements are resolved through the decoction of the Gold-Cinnabar Pill (or Elixir), which is to Taoists what the philosophers' stone was to Western magi. Its successful distillation guarantees eternal life.

The so-called dual-cultivation school founded by Sun Ssu-mo Tzu represents an interesting variation on this theme. For the fusion of white lead and cinnabar, the technique practitioners of this alchemy employ is rigorous and unremitting, though highly disciplined, sexual intercourse. The male permanently defers ejaculation to prevent the loss of vital *yang* fluid, which, unlike *yin,* is limited and irreplaceable. By this means — by unconsummated sex — the inner reservoir of this precious, life-prolonging essence, drop by drop, is filled. Called White Tiger/Green Dragon yoga, this school was abhorrent even to many Taoists and has died out due to suppression by the authorities. And yet, who knows? Is it so impossible to think that in a ruined temple somewhere in a remote corner of the kingdom a pair of ancient adepts with toothless, withered faces, but bright, youthful eyes, are going at it, religiously, in hope of saving their immortal souls?

However that may be, at Ken Kuan it was not part of the curriculum. In fact, chastity was the rule of the order — an unwritten rule, but strictly obeyed. At least as far as I know, for my knowledge of the rites was at second and third hand. Alchemy was practiced only by the mature adepts, and even then always under the watchful eye of the master, Chung Fu (who was said to have already distilled the liquor of eternal life). For there were dangers associated with its practice. Poisoning primarily. Attempting to transform the corruptible parts of their natures, some monks (those of a more literal turn of mind) resorted to the direct ingestion of mercury and cinnabar, small quantities at first, but gradually building up the dosage as the body's tolerance increased — an alchemical mithridatism. As one imagines, this had a disastrous effect on the liver, and, in fact, generally proved fatal. Nevertheless, its adherents (the survivors) pointed with a certain satisfaction to the indisputable success of their technique in preserving the body in the grave. As a method of embalming, metal poisoning surpasses even the Egyptian arts and vies with the tar pits of the Mesozoic age.

But there were dangers of another order. I remember the story of a monk who, through some carelessness or misuse of the techniques, lost his soul, which flew out from between the ribs of his body like a songbird from an opened cage. For two days he could hear it singing in a treetop near his window. Then it disappeared into the blackness of the forest, and he wasted away and died of sorrow. Others that I heard of were incarcerated in the bodies of animals for their crimes. Some fell headlong into hell.

I must admit I relished these stories. And Wu spewed them forth like an inexhaustible fountain. Once while gathering *mo-erh* ("cloud-ear" or black tree fungus), I discovered a ruined fox shrine hidden among leaves on the side of a hill. There Wu told me the story of the beautiful anchoress Hu Li, who was "standing on the doorsill" of enlightenment — at the last threshold where utmost concentration is required — when she was violently abducted by imperial troops and commanded to compound the Elixir for the Son of Heaven. In vengeance for her disappointment, on the day the emperor had appointed for his apotheosis, Hu Li bade him dismiss his guards and servants, then served him the "Heavenly Banquet" she'd prepared by her own hand — a banquet whose main course, served in a covered dish, was the still-smoking head of the emperor's baby son with its boiled, staring eyes. For this enormity the gods imprisoned her in the body of a fox, where she remains for all eternity, only allowed to assume human form at certain seasons, when she becomes a lovely maiden who wanders the countryside at night preying on unwary travelers whom she seduces and then devours. The fox shrines, where offerings of raw meat or live chickens are often left, are intended to appease Hu Li and the other Fox Fairies of whom she is the queen.

From the time I was very young, with the same dark, illicit craving with which a Western boy fantasizes about sex, I looked forward to the day when Chung Fu would initiate me into these forbidden rites. It was perhaps the source of my keenest regret that, on leaving China, I had still not begun my training. Time after time the master put me off, telling me I wasn't ready. Wu said that Chung Fu would never teach me until I learned to control my own spirit, that it was my "wild hair" that made the master hesitate. Perhaps he was right, though I certainly didn't think so at the time. I had a tendency to dismiss Wu's counsel out of hand, especially in this matter, since he himself had never been initiated into the mysteries.

•

Since I've mentioned him so often, let me tell you a little about Wu, my master, employer, slave, nurse, surrogate mother, oppressor, defender, and one great boyhood friend. Wu was a peasant whose love of food and drink had left him, at mid-life (where I found him), about as broad as he was tall. He wasn't fat, however. His belly, though tremendous, was as hard as a stone Buddha's. It didn't tremble over rough terrain, but rigidly jounced above the ill-matched shock absorbers of his spindly legs. Wu's natural talent for the culinary arts had landed him a job as cook in the kitchen at Ken Kuan. As soon as I was old enough to work, I was assigned to be his helper, a position which placed me alongside him on the lowest rung of the social ladder.

I never regretted it. Wu's good-natured company was compensation enough. As he sprang about the kitchen, his arms gesticulating wildly, bringing order out of a chaos of knives and vegetables and pans, he would tell me his wonderful stories, embroidering endlessly on simple themes, his invention never running dry. Thinking back, this was one of the chief joys of my childhood.

But it wasn't all fun and games. You see, it had also fallen to Wu's lot to implement punitive and corrective measures in my behalf. He was infinitely faithful, sometimes even inspired, in executing this duty. One example: Wu had a rather heavy beard for a Chinese, which he shaved every few days at most (except for a tuft in the hollow between his bottom lip and chin which he retained out of vanity). As a result his lower jaw was perennially overcast by a dim blue shadow, like the floor of an evergreen forest. Whenever I succeeded in exasperating him to the point of retaliation, he would bend close to me, as though to impart some secret, then rub these bristles against my tender head like a malevolent porcupine. This was coarse punishment indeed, but richly deserved, I'm sure. For Wu was always fair. He had a good heart. And his earthiness was the perfect antidote to the unworldliness of the other monks, who, unlike him, generally came from the upper strata of society.

Wu was not religious by nature, possessing little if any of the anguished sensitivity of the devout. He wasn't given to meditating on the deception of the senses or the vanity of wealth and place. In fact, to my knowledge he never meditated at all. I certainly never caught him at it, unless cooking could be considered a form of meditation, in which case he must have been very close indeed to beatitude. For, as I mentioned, he applied himself with exemplary devotion to the gastronomic arts. His pains weren't properly appreciated in all quarters, however, I'm sorry to say. Most of the other monks considered Wu a glutton and a libertine. And so he was, I suppose, at least by monkish standards, which were the only ones relevant to his case.

Wu took a vacation annually at New Year's. During his absence the hungry monks would vilify him mercilessly, inspiring one another to awesome heights of virtuosity in inventing ingenious and perverse new forms of character assassination. They said he went on a week-long spree, gambling all night at the Mah-Jongg tables in Chungking, hiring prostitutes (man, woman, or child, they said, to Wu it made no difference) to engage with him in unspeakable acts, during which time he was never sober for so much as half an hour. There was not the slightest evidence for any of this, except, of course, that which malice could supply. (I did, however, once see Wu brought back unconscious in the bed of a manure cart.)

But assuming the rumors had some basis in fact, however slight, I've often wondered where Wu got the money for his binges. Hard cash was in short supply at Ken Kuan. Some of the more cynical monks hinted that Chung Fu himself subsidized Wu's annual revels, and what's more, that the money was diverted out of the slender reserves we set aside to purchase what we couldn't grow or make ourselves. As a child I disbelieved these tales. Our abbot willingly contribute to the delinquency of one of his charges? Unthinkable! Now I'm not so sure. The subtlety and power of the master's mind sliced through conventional wisdom like the prow of a ship through the amorphous, level ocean. The only thing I can say with certainty is that whatever Chung Fu's reason for indulging Wu (if indeed he did indulge him), it must have been calculated to bring a rich return on the investment (spiritually speaking, of course). Perhaps it was by this concession that he won Wu's confidence. For won it he had, by fair means or foul. In his loyalty, Wu was like a great-hearted mongrel dog who would fight to the death defending his master.

Still, he sometimes wavered in his faithfulness. There was that irascible side to Wu. When extraordinary labors were required, he often grumbled. One such time was at the Great Spring Festival, when, praying and importuning in an all-night vigil like a team of anxious midwives, we helped nature deliver her flaming burden, the sun, into the northern hemisphere. The chanters worked in shifts, and Wu and I were kept busy in the kitchen round the clock, napping when we could. I ran back and forth gathering herbs — ginger root, garlic, green chilies — and drawing water from the stream which danced at the base of the cliffs, plunging level upon level in a series of short falls to pools of foam and rock. In moments of crisis Wu would accompany me. Our chore was particularly exhausting since we had to carry the filled buckets up a steep incline over a series of narrow, chiseled steps. Wu would come up puffing and blowing, his face tinged rose through the blue stubble on his cheeks and throat. Often he scolded me as my buckets had invariably sloshed out the better part of their contents by the time we reached the top.

"*Aiya!*" he would shout. "Are the rocks thirsty that you give them so much of our precious water to drink? Look at my buckets! How much have I spilled?"

It was true. By some extraordinary luck or skill Wu never seemed to lose a drop, though he hurried along the treacherous stair at twice my pace. (I tried to cut my losses by moving slowly, plotting my course in advance and picking each footrest with deliberate care.)

"I don't understand it," I confessed to him. "You must know some kind of trick. Explain your method."

Clucking his tongue with disapproval, Wu would shake his head. "Wild Hair," he said, "you haven't yet caught on. It's precisely this — excess of method — that confounds you, leaves the bucket nearly empty, and may yet force my foot to castigate your honorable behind." He roared at his joke. "Why is it necessary for you to make two trips to every one of mine? Will you never learn? You are too scrupulous. You must not try to calculate each step. As if your puny brain were smart enough to outwit this big mountain!"

"All right," I rejoined sullenly, "if you're so smart, how do you do it then?"

"How do I do it?" He stared over the edge into the abyss. "I close my eyes and think of nothing. My mind is somewhere else. My legs find their way without me, even over the most uneven ground."

Unaccustomed to such prolonged bouts of philosophic disquisition, he became uneasy under my suspicious look.

"How can I tell you how I do it?" he shouted defensively, looking around as though the answer might materialize from the air.

Then an idea seemed to strike him, and he let out an ebullient, incomprehensible belly laugh. "I can't even remember myself!" He then waddled off, his sack-belly bounding and rebounding between the two unmoving buckets.

Though I doubt it ever occurred to him, Wu was an accomplished man in his own way. At the time, I was too young to appreciate this. Perhaps cooking really was a form of meditation for him though. I mean this. For isn't anything to which a man gives himself with the whole force of his being — making himself its satellite, relying on its gravity as a form of discipline to compel him toward that fierce, last orbit of perfection — a form of meditation? It is in my book. Meditation is what leads to Tao, and Tao, in one of its countless avatars, is also called "the Perfect."

I think the water-carrying episode demonstrates that Wu's acts were in accordance with the Tao. He had learned the art of *wu-wei*, or "actionless activity" (motion that has stillness at its heart), and practiced it with a degree of skill which few, if any, of the more unworldly brothers had achieved. Of course, they scorned him as a coarse peasant occupied with the undignified business of providing nourishment for the body, while they sought higher sustenance. To a large extent, and without bitterness, Wu shared their opinion. But I'm convinced that Chung Fu secretly understood and approved the situation. By his own subtle methods the master was providing his disciple with an appropriate spiritual regimen, teaching Wu to ebb and flow with the unseen tides of *yin* and *yang*.

This theory was implicitly confirmed by Wu himself, who, in the relaxed intimacy attending the successful conclusion of one of the great feasts I mentioned earlier, told me a little of his personal story.

"Were you born here, Wu, like me?" I had asked with a child's naiveté (still too young to know the truth).

My fat friend laughed. "How often is a monkey hatched from a stone egg? Certainly no more than once in a thousand years." He shook his head. "No, Sun I, Wu was produced in the regular manner. I grew up on the outside and came late to the Way."

"What made you choose this life?"

"Choose?" He snickered. "I didn't choose it, it chose *me.*" Pausing over his chopping block, Wu wiped his hands on the grubby apron tied around his waist. Everyone else had gone off to bed, and now, as a special reward for the two of us, he was slicing turnips for the sweet pancakes I loved.

"What did you do before?" I asked.

He gave me a searching look, then glanced off into space as though trying to remember.

"I came from a farming village near Chungking," he said, beginning to chop again. "My whole family — grandparents, aunts and uncles, cousins — lived nearby. We raised vegetables and chickens for the market in the city."

"Why did you leave? Were you unhappy there?"

Wu continued staring at the block. "Not always," he replied after a moment in a subdued voice. "The work was hard, but it was not a bad life. My parents even pampered me a little, especially my mother, for I was her last son, her 'baby,' and there was small likelihood she would ever have another. But when I fell in love and desired to marry, something changed in her. She looked at me with strange eyes. Our familiarity ceased. She withdrew and rarely spoke except to utter some scathing remark about my future bride. I couldn't understand this, for Chai was a simple, modest girl, even bashful. Pretty too, Sun I. I loved her. The day of our wedding was the happiest of my life.

"But when I brought her home to my father's house, my mother set herself against her. She was merciless, treating Chai like a servant, making her scrub the floors from one end of the house to the other, even rooms which were the responsibility of other wives. And if she found a speck of dirt, Chai was obliged to start over. This is only one example. There were many. It was unfair, but within my mother's rights, and Chai bore it patiently. Only her natural modesty turned to tongue-tied diffidence, and her appearance grew peaked, as though her spirit was being crushed within her. My heart broke to see it, but there was little I could do. I always thought my mother would show pity in the end.

"One day when I came from the fields, I found Chai sobbing. At first she wouldn't even look at me, but when I pressed, she broke down and told me what had happened. Then I saw the ugly swelling at the side of her mouth and the black bruises across her back and ribs. She had asked a question which my mother considered impertinent, and been beaten with a bamboo rod. I was in a rage and stormed off to ask my father's permission to move. Out of the question, he said. It was close to harvest; they were getting old and couldn't do without us. 'Have patience,' he said. 'When you have a son, she will relent.'

"So we staked all our hopes on this. And sure enough that first winter she became pregnant. I was elated, and Chai seemed livelier than she had in months. We began eagerly making plans for the future. My father, too, was pleased. When I first told him the news, he momentarily dropped his brusque formality and laughed aloud, clapping me on the shoulder like a boon companion. Then he sent me off to tell my mother.

"I came before her blushing with pleasure. Giving me a curious, appraising glance, she asked me what I wanted. As I spilled out my news, to my surprise she remained aloof, her eyes cold with a dead light. She dismissed me with a nod of her head.

"This is something I never understood, Sun I. Perhaps it was because she was old and stooped. Her dugs were shriveled with the nursing of many children, and now dry forever. Perhaps the presence of a young, healthy woman with new life growing big inside her reminded her of her own barrenness, and her mortality, galling her to a kind of madness. However it was, instead of sharing our joy, my mother became even more spiteful from that time. She made Chai work as hard as ever, though before long Chai began to tire easily under the weight of the child. Eventually, in despair, I tried to speak to my mother, asked her to understand our position. Never in my life had I seen her grow so angry. She trembled and grew pale. Then she began to scream at me and beat her breast, saying if I didn't approve of the way she ran her household, I could find some other place to live. How I wanted to take her at her word! But still my father withheld consent. He asked me to remain until the birth of the child to see if my mother would not experience a change of heart. I had no choice but to obey.

"One day in autumn near the end of her term while she was climbing the garden fence with a load of kindling, Chai stumbled and fell. She began to hemorrhage and went into labor. One of my aunts heard her screaming and ran out of the house. She delivered the child right there, in the stubble of the sunflower harvest, dead. There was nothing she could do to stop the bleeding. By the time I arrived, Chai was dead, too."

Wu paused, his face crimson with deep humiliation. He appeared to be choking — literally — on this impalpable morsel regurgitated from memory.

"It was a boy," he said finally, with an anger time had not diminished.

I thought perhaps he had said all he was going to, when after a long silence he abruptly began again.

"After that I hated my mother with the deepest passion of my heart. I knew I was damned in it, but I couldn't help myself. Every time I saw her I wanted to take her withered neck in my hands and wring it like a chicken's. One morning after an argument with her, I left for the fields and simply kept on going. I never looked back. Since that day I've never seen either her or my father. By now, I suppose, they're both long dead."

"Is that when you came here?" I resumed, after a respectful pause.

Wu shook his head. "No. I went to the city after that. For a while I worked in the markets loading and hauling crates for the vendors. Once I stumbled on my brother there, but he quickly shifted his gaze, pretending not to see me. Around that time I fell in with a bad crowd, addicts some of them. They introduced me to opium. I was sick in my heart, Wild Hair. The drug cost money. Things led to things. My creditor, the owner of the opium den, was a loan shark too, with ties to the local tong. No business was transacted in that neighborhood without a hefty slice for them. They allowed us to buy the mud on credit until we were hooked, then they began to squeeze. Before long my health began to fail. Too broken down to work, I resorted to gambling to pay them off. But they owned the tables too, and they rigged them. It's almost funny, but even then I had an inkling how it was. But by that time it didn't matter anymore. There was a kind of fatal joy in it, Sun I, you know? Like a creeping vine, gambling wound its tendrils around my heart and took possession. Beyond even opium, it was the worst addiction. And not me only — there were hundreds, thousands perhaps, just like me. I learned something in those long, feverish nights as I watched the dice eat everything I had, and more. . . ."

Even now I can see Wu's eyes as they looked at me then.

"As a people we may seem skeptical, our passions sluggish, but there is something reckless in us which the dice trick out. We are a race of gamblers, Sun I. Never forget that. I did, and it was my downfall." He shook his head.

"You see, after a time it became apparent that I would never come up with the money. They sent one of their 'collectors' to see me. He bashed my face against the kitchen table until I couldn't see for blood, all the while begging me to be 'reasonable.' I had cheated them on purpose, he said. All they wanted was justice, some form of equal compensation. But the only thing I had left to pay them was my life, and I knew they had no qualms about taking it. So again I fled.

"By that time I was half crazy. My nerves were shot. I was suffering withdrawal symptoms. I don't know why, but I remembered a story I had heard as a boy about a sage who lived in the mountains, a great wizard who knew the art of turning lead to gold. With no more than this to go on, I set out in search of him, inquiring at temples along the way. The plan I'd hatched in my distempered brain was to induce this fellow, by hook or crook, to teach me alchemy. Once I'd mastered the techniques, I'd return to the city loaded, and have my day of vengeance. The tables would be turned, they'd have to crawl to me. You see, I still had the craving. Ha! What a fool I was!

"It took me many days to get here. When I finally arrived I was at the end of my strength — thin (would you believe it?), diseased, my clothes hanging off me in shreds, the hair matted on top of my head. I looked like a beggar, worse than a beggar. Worse than a leper even! For two days I stood at the entrance and begged admittance. The monks laughed in my face. 'What does a scarecrow like you have to do with a great man like Chung Fu?' Finally the master heard me howling and told them to let me in.

"I'll never forget that first meeting. He peered at me so intently I almost felt the fiber of my heart unraveling. I couldn't bring myself to meet that look. In fact, I almost wept.

" 'What do you want with me, Shifty Eyes?' he demanded, teasing me for my cowardice.

"Prostrating myself three times as I'd been told, I launched into the flowery speech I'd been rehearsing in my mind for days, stumbling frequently over the big words.

" 'You want to become a great alchemist and transmute lead into gold, is that it?' he summarized when I'd finished.

" 'If you please, sir.'

"He burst out laughing. 'Whatever put that idea in your head?'

"I hesitated, then stammered, 'You see, sir, I'm seriously in debt.' I grinned sheepishly.

"But Chung Fu did not see the humor in it. He stopped laughing abruptly and looked me up and down. 'Beat it!' he said finally. 'You're a disgrace.'

"Some of the monks began to snigger. Throwing myself at the master's feet, I howled in protest. 'Give me a chance to prove myself! I'll do anything! Only tell me what's required.'

"Chung Fu had already started to leave the room, but paused and turned back. I screwed up all my courage and I looked directly in his eyes. Like an arm wrestler testing his opponent's grip, he took my measure visually. Then a faint smile appeared on his lips. 'Anything?'

" 'Yes! Yes!' I cried ecstatically. 'Only promise you'll help me.'

"He stroked his chin and narrowed his eyes, letting me squirm.

" 'Please!' I implored. 'Teach me.'

" 'Teach you what?' he asked thickheadedly.

" 'Why, the Way, of course.'

"He shook his head. 'The Way cannot be taught.'

" 'Then simply point me in the right direction. Give me a nudge, I'll do the rest.'

" 'You are persistent,' he admitted, 'though that's not necessarily in your favor.' He gave me an appraising squint.

" 'Well?'

"Whether in exasperation or acquiescence, I don't know, but the master sighed. Interpreting it in my favor, I let out a whoop of joy.

" 'All right then,' he conceded. 'In your case, as a first step toward this exalted goal, I suggest a good dinner.' At that moment I detected for the first time the undertone of laughter that is never quite absent from the master's voice, the gaiety in his eyes.

"He led me on to the kitchen. At the doorway, he looked around in dismay. Piles of unwashed wooden trenchers and bowls lay scattered everywhere, and batallions of ants were carrying away the spoils.

" 'Several months ago we had the great misfortune to lose our cook,' he explained with a sigh. 'Things haven't been the same since.'

" 'I'm sorry to hear it,' I commiserated. 'What happened to him?'

" 'A chicken bone,' Chung Fu replied, puffing out his cheeks and rolling his eyes up in his head to signify a violent conclusion.

"I should have kept my mouth respectfully shut, but I couldn't restrain myself. 'I thought you were vegetarians here.'

"Chung Fu nodded gravely. 'Precisely the point. It has been suggested that it was a form of retribution.'

"Though he spoke in the most serious tones, this pronouncement struck me as hilarious. I burst out laughing despite myself. I was sure he'd be shocked, perhaps throw me out in the road again. To my surprise, he joined in.

" 'Yes, yes, there is something funny about it after all,' he admitted, wiping tears from his eyes. 'But come, though I'm embarrassed to offer you hospitality in such conditions, you're welcome to whatever you find here.'

"Thanking him profusely, I started a fire and set some water on for rice. In my coat pockets I happened to have some morels and pine nuts which I'd found in the forest while scrounging for food the previous night. These I sliced and fried up in a little oil with some peppers from the garden.

"Chung Fu, meanwhile, remained in the doorway, staring off in space.

Though at first he paid me no attention, his presence made me feel uncomfortable. After a while, however, I noticed he'd begun to watch me like a hawk. 'I see you have a certain talent for this kind of thing,' he remarked with false casualness. Self-consciously I poured the rice in with the vegetables and stirred it all together in the oil. As I was about to dish it out, he suddenly slapped his forehead and uttered a shout so abrupt I nearly dropped my dinner in the fire. 'That's it!' I stared at him in amazement. 'I've lighted on the perfect course of training for you!'

" 'You have?'

"He pointed to my hand. I looked down at it. I was still holding the pot. Confused, I looked back up at his face. He nodded enthusiastically.

" 'I don't understand,' I confessed, ashamed of my own stupidity.

" 'You're to stay here and become our cook!' Emitting a small, distinctly unmonastic, shriek of glee, he bolted from the room.

"I must admit, at first I had my reservations. But I wanted to learn alchemy, and if this was the required sacrifice, well then, I would do it! At least until something better came along. It beat working in the fields, and it was certainly an improvement over vagrancy.

"So time passed, and I stayed on. At intervals I would approach the master and ask him when he was going to begin my instruction in the secret arts.

" 'Continue cooking,' he would say. 'You're making progress toward your goal.'

"I'd let several months elapse, then go to him again. 'Venerable Master,' I would say, 'I'm ready to receive your teaching in the principles of alchemy.'

" 'Don't bother yourself!' he would tell me. 'You're striding ahead by leaps and bounds. Continue cooking. You've found your true vocation.'

"Eventually I gave up and stopped asking. Today I'm no closer to making lead out of gold than I was twenty years ago."

On this disappointing note, Wu's narrative came to a conclusion, or rather, I should say, fizzled out and died ignobly. I felt a pang of sympathy for my friend. But to my complete surprise, he burst out laughing, not with chagrin or bitterness, but in apparent joy. He seemed like a man who has just heard the best joke of his life, and who has the added satisfaction of having told that joke himself, from his own experience and at his own expense.

At the time I couldn't understand his attitude, which seemed vaguely half-witted, or worse. In hindsight, however, Wu's story took on increasing resonance, until it echoed in my mind like prophecy — indeed, a kind of prophecy of my own fate. I've often asked myself if this was pure coincidence, or if Wu possessed, in incipient form perhaps, the deep wisdom of a sage.

Whatever the answer, it cannot diminish the debt I owe him. In the rubble of my childhood, he stands alone, the only landmark. Except, of course, for Chung Fu. But the master's influence was rarer, more intangible. Like a spectacular epiphany, he always seemed to materialize at the crucial junctures in my life. An hour with Chung Fu was like a holiday affair, but Wu was present day in and day out, my scourge and solace. Some of the other monks taught me to read and write, to count the stalks, to sing, and other learned matters, but Wu taught me what I know of life.

It seems appropriate, then, that it was Wu who came to me that morning and, in subdued tones, told me to prepare myself for an audience with Chung Fu. A stranger had arrived, he said, and the rumor was he'd come to speak with me.

Chapter 3

This was a startling development. Visitors were the rarest of beasts at Ken Kuan, encountered almost as infrequently as the dragons said to inhabit the stream beyond the walls. And, like the dragons, visitors were considered harbingers of a change in fortune, sometimes for the better, but more often than not for the worse. People avoided us out of fear of some unspecified retaliation by the authorities. This subverted the social function of the monastery and left us unable to fulfill the mandate of Compassion for All Created Things, which is the first and greatest of Taoism's Three Treasures, which all initiates must vow to protect and uphold. (The second is Frugality, which is tied to it. Willingly embraced, Poverty is a form of compassion toward the inanimate world, a gesture of respect and deference to things. The third treasure is Humility, or Lowliness, which involves the promise to refrain from active power over men.)

But to return to our isolation. Actually, there was a bright side. As they say here in America, "Every cloud has a silver lining." (The Chinese version goes: "Shit makes the corn grow.") Frequent intercourse with the outside can distract the quietist from his true purpose. As is well known, if little understood, the marketplace of the defiled world has a way of inciting riot and rebellion in the human heart. Escaping this temptation, we rested a little more easily under our restriction.

Thus it was that in twenty-one years of monastic life, I almost could count on my fingers the number of guests we had received at Ken Kuan, and in all that time not a single one to visit me. That might seem distressing, but I took it totally for granted. Who would have bothered, anyway? I had no name, no family — at least none that would have cared to recognize me. The only possible exception was my mother. But for some reason — I can't say why, precisely — I had always presumed that she was dead. I think perhaps it was the photograph. For the camera had taken her unawares, revealing how vulnerable she was, how tenuously in the world. And there was more than that

. . . an intuition, call it. The world, even the tiny, unthreatening corner of it I'd explored, seemed too harsh for the woman I had dreamed. She might have lived here once, for a brief span of time, but not for long. I nowhere found the radiance that must be hers, which, though impalpable, my soul would recognize, relying on its deepest sense. No, she was dead to me, if not in fact, in memory.

And as for my father, assuming he was alive (and with the same instinct I felt he was), he was far away, across the ocean, on another continent. After all these years, could it be he? The thought filled me with such dread (and longing!) that I grew nauseated and began to sweat.

Yet, besides the infrequency of visitors, and besides the existence in me of that primitive emotional vacuum which had never been disturbed and which, try as I might, I could not imagine filled, one other factor added to my trepidation at Wu's announcement. That I should receive a visitor, my first ever, on this of all days in the year (in my life!) seemed too much to attribute to coincidence. For it was my birthday: I was twenty-one years old. Somehow this made the whole thing seem uncanny, as though the visit were a gift, some valuable bit of flotsam (the remnant of some sunken distress) which, out of its inconceivable depths, the Tao had heaved up at my feet in honor of the occasion. But what?

•

My feet left moist prints on the slate flags as I crossed the inner courtyard toward the south side of the monastery where the master kept his cell. There was a peach tree in the center there, twisted and old, yet full of pith and bearing, as we used to say, "one peach for every monk" each year. As I stooped beneath its branches, I noticed with a feeling like chagrin that the blossoms had already been succeeded by the fruit. Mostly green and small, the peaches hung from the knotted, crusty branches like driblets of water along a blackened gutter's edge after the rain.

Earlier that morning I had consulted the oracle, receiving a reading which I couldn't remember ever turning up before: *Chia Jen,* "The Family." This hexagram is built from the two basic trigrams, *Sun,* "Wind," over *Li,* or "Fire," suggesting to me incitement to some frenzied, perhaps destructive act, as in a conflagration, the fanning of flame by wind.

The judgment said:

> The family is society in embryo; it is the native soil on which
> performance of moral duty is made easy through natural affection, so
> that within a small circle a basis of moral practice is created. . . .
> This is later widened to include human relationships in general.

Did this not point to me? Having been reared without the beneficent influence of familial ties, did I lack some fundamental shoring in my moral instincts? Though oblique, the inference was difficult to avoid. This interpretation was reinforced by the fact that the first line of the hexagram was a moving line, old *yang* disintegrating into *yin,* light into darkness. The comment was:

> If we begin too late to enforce order, when the will of the child has already been overindulged, the whims and passions, grown stronger with the years, offer resistance and give cause for remorse.

Thus, it was with a sense of foreboding that I knocked at Chung Fu's door. High and sweet, his voice rang out. "Come!" Bowing low on entering, I saluted the master first, then turned to the guest and bowed again more formally.

He was an elderly Chinese, remarkably like Chung Fu in certain particulars (they might have suggested a study of difference in sameness), except that he wore the elegant but long-outmoded garb of a Confucian gentleman, or *chün-tzu,* the traditional class of bureaucrats and scholars. At that time the *chün-tzu* had disappeared from the ranks of society almost as completely as Taoist masters like Chung Fu. In traditional China, the masters were the *chün-tzu's* alter egos, disdaining the Confucians' rigid observance of outward form and ritual to follow the inner, intuitive promptings of the Way. The old Confucian wore the scholar's cap and long silk robe, and in his hand he held an ivory-headed cane of great beauty and antiquity, which glistened down the length of its black-lacquered shaft. Chung Fu, on the other hand, was dressed in the simple sackcloth garment of a monk (though as abbot he might have arrayed himself elaborately). Beneath his cap the visitor was scrupulously bald, the sides of his shaved head shining with the rubbed-wax luster of antique furniture. Chung Fu's silver hair was pegged up in the traditional Taoist topknot. Their hands, though, were similar, gnarled like the roots of venerable forest trees that have weathered many storms, hands stained with spots of melanin, indicative of age. Each had the white mustache and goatee of the mandarin. Each had the bright eyes of the wise, though in Chung Fu's eyes that brightness shed a hint of warmth, while in the visitor's it was like the glint of winter sunlight on the ice. (Indeed, a most suggestive subject for a study of sameness in difference.)

"Join us, little brother," Chung Fu invited. "An old acquaintance has come to call on you."

I looked at the visitor. Though there was something remotely familiar in the old man's features, I couldn't place it. The master's remark confused me. "An old acquaintance?"

Chung Fu's eyes were twinkling. "Have you forgotten? Why it was only yesterday!"

Once more I gazed at the stranger, who watched me as intently as I watched him. "I'm sorry, Master," I said, "but you must be mistaken. We've never met."

Chung Fu roared with laughter. "Never, Sun I? Tell me — are you sure?"

I began to feel flustered. What was it about his face that chafed so strangely at remembrance?

The master saw my perplexity, and his obstreperousness subsided into tender, almost sad amusement. "Sun I," he said, "this is the man who brought you here to us so many years ago."

The visitor nodded. "Although this is not a first meeting between us, it should be characterized as 'old acquaintances at first sight.' My name is Hsiao. I am your uncle." Suddenly his features resolved in heightened clarity. What had seemed familiarity revealed itself as likeness. "Your mother was my sister."

My head began to reel as though I had been struck. I looked wildly around the room to see if there were not some legend there to help me break the indecipherable code in which he spoke — "uncle," "sister," "mother" — the easy concepts caved in all at once and I was like one congenitally blind to whom a blow reveals the terrifying brilliance of the world.

"Sun I," the stranger (my uncle!) continued, "this must be very hard for you, to have a relative materialize after all these years. Perhaps you'll feel resentful. But let me tell you why I've come. Contrary to what you may think, it has little to do with your mother."

He hesitated, reconsidering his words. "Well, that's not precisely true. Actually it has everything to do with her — how could it be otherwise? But only indirectly. It was at the request of a man named Eddie Love that I came here today. Love was your father." Apparently expecting this revelation to evoke a strong reaction, and finding it didn't, Hsiao drew the inference. "So you know. . . ." His tone expressed a mixture of surprise and fatalism. "Many years ago I made a promise to him, a promise I'm only able to fulfill today. It was his intention to present you with a gift on the occasion of your passage into manhood."

"What gift?" I asked, my excitement tinged with dread.

"The most important gift there is. The gift of your own history."

Drawing in my breath, I regarded him with a rapt stare. It was as though fate had just stepped from the shadows and laid its hand on me. At that moment I realized I'd been waiting my whole life for him to appear.

"You've come to tell me who I am," I said, not even knowing what I meant, the words welling up from somewhere deep inside me.

Chung Fu shook his head. "Who can tell you that, Sun I? Such knowledge is not in the power of any man to bestow on another, though it is that alone which matters. The discovery of who you are, of your Authentic Self — beside this, what is 'history'? A superfluous detail."

Hsiao coldly blinked his eyes. "A superfluous detail, indeed. What is a self without a history, without a past?"

Chung Fu smiled. "There is a Zen *koan* in which the master exhorts his disciple to show him his Original Face before his parents were born. If this Original Face, which is the same as the Authentic Self of which we speak, exists before the birth of one's parents (that is, eternally, out of time), what need of history?"

"And yet," Hsiao retorted, "didn't Confucius himself say, 'He who does not tread in the tracks cannot expect to find his way into the Inner Room'? You know, of course, whose tracks these are?"

"Of course!" Chung Fu cried, feigning earnest zeal. "The Taoist Bull's!" Snorting happily, he turned to me and winked. "I always said old Master Kung, under all those layers of Confucian mendacity, was a true Taoist."

"Preposterous!" Hsiao exclaimed. He turned away disdainfully. "The tracks are those of the ancestors, Sun I." Pausing, he tried a different tack. "I am a humble scholar. My life has been devoted to the Four Pursuits."

"Let me see," the master mused. "Are they not a dependence on plagiarism, a wandering mind, an overindulgence in spicy foods, and an unnatural affection for little boys?"

"No, Chung Fu, I mean the lute, chess, literature, and painting. But let us cease this 'Dharma combat' and get on with the task at hand." My uncle turned to me. "Actually, there is a certain justice in your master's previous words. In the final analysis, all I can do is give you certain information — who your parents were, how they met, what happened to them, why you were brought here. . . . What value such information has — whether it is crucial to your knowledge of yourself, as I maintain, or, as he suggests, 'superfluous' — neither he nor I can tell you. You must decide this for yourself."

He searched my features with a look of evident pain. "But prior to this decision there is another. Your father instructed me to leave this option open to you: *not to know*. Foreseeing that you might prefer to remain in ignorance, he charged me to tell you these things *only should you wish to hear them*. It's not a pleasant story, Sun I. In the end, who can say? Perhaps you would be better off not knowing."

He turned to Chung Fu and they bowed to one another gravely, like adversaries acquiescing in a point of honor.

I too turned in that direction, searching frantically for support. But though there was a hint of pity in the master's eye, his face betrayed no clue. Like a cold wind blowing through me, I felt a surge of hatred for this man Hsiao, who had so suddenly appeared in my life, pressing his huge, irrevocable gifts on me.

"How can I say no?" I asked bitterly. "You've destroyed my peace already."

"But not as it may be destroyed, Sun I," the master interjected, coming to the defense of the man with whom he had so recently locked horns. "Take heed. You must not throw caution to the winds. What your uncle has spoken, he has spoken out of duty. It would be wrong to deny you such a choice. You must not blame him. From this point on, however, the responsibility is strictly yours. Choose carefully, with the gentleness and penetration your name implies, not the impulsive vehemence which is its darker complement, and which you've given rein to far too often in the past. Today you are a man, and you must act accordingly."

I reached desperately inside myself for something to hold on to, like a panicked swimmer thrashing out for a low-hanging branch along the bank as the foaming current sweeps him on. But there was nothing there.

Swiftly, decisively, "Tell me," I said.

"Ah!" my uncle moaned, impulsively clasping his hands.

Abruptly the master rose to go. He bowed to Hsiao, then me — bows equally weighted. I was not too distraught to recognize what was implicit in that gesture. It overwhelmed me. But it left me feeling anxious too, enfranchised and dispossessed. It was a sudden, ruthless weaning from the past, and I was like a fledgling pushed over the edge of the nest to fly, or drop, and nothing to help me find my wings but some presumed, yet still-untried instinctual resource.

Chapter 4

For a long time my uncle and I sat gazing at one another. His face was stern, but curious, perhaps a little sad as well. Glimmerings of sympathy, and vulnerability, appeared through his composure like human eyes staring through the slits in a wooden mask. What he saw in my face, in my eyes, I can't imagine, unless it were a kind of hunger, and a grim resolve to suffer without crying out.

"I'm not sure how much of this you know already," he began. "It's a long story, but let me tell it from the start so nothing is omitted.

"I suppose the obvious place to commence is with my father . . . my respected father. . . ." Between these terms Hsiao hesitated slightly, bowing his head in reverence. At the same time a change occurred in his expression. I might have been mistaken (this happened almost instantaneously), but I thought I saw him wince, like a man swallowing a dose of medicine — therapeutic, but a trifle bitter. "For in some sense he was the cultivator of the soil from which this luxuriant growth sprang forth."

Emphasizing the word "luxuriant," my uncle's lips curled again with that faint suggestion of distaste, disconcertingly like a smile. Yet the mask retained its air of grave serenity. Was this irony? I couldn't tell.

"He — your grandfather, Sun I — was a forward-looking man, a 'progressive.' Unlike myself, he was, as he put it, 'unencumbered by the prejudices of the past.' This was not because he was uneducated, though he was, but because he was ambitious. I mean no disrespect by either term, for on both counts Father prided himself.

"He was an entrepreneurial 'jack-of-all-trades' — primarily a speculator in commodities — one of a new breed which arose in China during the years of foreign (that is to say, Western) influence after Sun Yat-sen came to power, possessing international (that is to say, Western) connections, and understanding the methods of modern (yes, Western) business. As he used to say, he had given up the abacus for the double-entry ledger. (Though it was not widely recognized, Father had a sense of humor.) While I was growing up we had to struggle, but by the time your mother was born he had amassed a fortune. For there was money to be made in those days, a great deal of it, by quick-witted, serviceable men. And Father was both. Though he had a finger in every pie, the commodity in which he made himself was opium. Besides a permanent home in Chungking, he maintained an estate in Yunnan Province outside Kunming from which he supervised the sowing and harvest of the crop. Not long after the bombing of Chungking began in thirty-nine, he moved my mother and sister there for the duration of the war. I followed shortly.

"Our mother came from an aristocratic family, fallen in means, though not in prestige. It was a good match for him: though poor, she brought him as dowry something he needed more desperately than money: legitimacy in the eyes of the world. Your grandmother, Sun I, was in every sense a great lady. If she lacked anything, it was only a certain toughness of character — something she might not have needed under different circumstances, and whose possibility my father crushed in her. Reared in the old way, to be submissive but not servile, she possessed grace, charm, wit — qualities he did not appreciate, preferring the coarse vivacity of peasant women, their easy yielding. To a man of his tastes, our mother's refinement no doubt seemed a little recherché. And yet she was the product of a thousand years of breeding, a thousand years of leisure, so delicate, so fragile, with her bound feet, her 'golden lilies,' moving with tiny, mincing steps about the house, pausing every little bit to rest and fan herself. Her kind has vanished from the earth. She didn't understand the modern ways, Sun I. To her they seemed ungracious, vulgar, overhasty. Completely at sea in all that concerned my father's business initiatives, she distrusted them instinctively. Yet she dared not interfere, having been taught to defer to her husband's will in everything, a lesson reinforced by Father's temperament. As I said, he was ambitious, and this trait brought out a certain ferocity in his character. He did not brook contradiction easily; from his family, not at all. In the end he had his way with her. Proud conquest.

"I was the eldest. Your mother was nearly twenty years younger than I, a child they never expected. She fell from my mother's tired loins 'like an autumn leaf from an old tree' — that's what my father used to say. That's how she got her name, Ch'iu-yeh, 'Autumn Leaf.' In many ways it was appropriate, for she was a vivid, colorful child, and yet — I don't know quite how to put it — it seemed the vividness of expiring life, an outward flush which signals fever in the body, not health overflowing on itself. Her periods of breathless rapture were blooms of short duration. Afterward she wilted and collapsed, consumed with her own burning. Malaise followed, some indeterminate illness whose roots were perhaps as much spiritual as physical, a kind of melancholia, haunting in one so young.

"Because of the great disparity in our ages, and because my father, with the coming of prosperity, began to feel disdain for the 'provincial attitudes' of our neighbors, your mother passed her childhood in relative seclusion. Not to say she was neglected; if anything, the opposite was true. They doted on her. When she was sick, my mother secretly fed her sweets and expensive medicines — ginseng and bird's nest — prescribed by white-haired elders, practitioners of the old healing, who had attended her as a girl. My father pampered her as well. She was his favorite, his 'treasure.' I think he understood her loneliness. For despite his social ubiquity, his plenitude of 'contacts,' he was lonely, too, distrusted and disliked among his peers, who served the power not the man. And Ch'iu-yeh, in large measure, was the creature of his folly . . . or genius . . . his small human consolation prize. He spared no expense in buying her the finest playthings, articles imported from Europe: German music boxes, bonbons from France, white 'china' dolls from Austria. In a battle of influence fought with such weapons, my mother could not compete. Father hired an English governess for Ch'iu-yeh, and she grew up speaking that language fluently, better, in fact, than she spoke her native dialect, Szechwanese.

"Despite these attentions, Ch'iu-yeh spent the greater part of her time alone, dreaming mostly, I suppose. The single traditional skill my mother managed to impart to her was sewing. Ch'iu-yeh became quite skilled in embroidery, and I think a good part of her fantasy life was channeled into that art. But much more of it was undirected and amorphous. She picked up new enthusiasms by the hour and sloughed them carelessly, like gowns worn once and thrown away. Reading English novels and romances, she believed them true. Her mind was ravished with thoughts of faraway places — England, but even more America, which her governess (who had children there) described to her in the most glowing terms. Such exotic thoughts would have been innocuous in a Western girl, but in a Chinese they were inappropriate. The time had not yet come. Women's feet were still bound. I think it aggravated her already fragile sensibilities. Sometimes she would put her book away and weep for no reason at all. I advised discipline, but my father was too fond, too proud of her accomplishments to take the necessary measures.

"When Chiang Kai-shek made Chungking the wartime capital of China in 1937, your mother was barely sixteen years old, too young to appreciate the seriousness of the situation. On market days when her nurse took her to town, they would spend hours walking along the streets, melting into the ceaseless stream of activity, admiring the surge of life as refugees teemed in from the more cosmopolitan regions near the coast.

"Wealth poured into the city as the rich, fearful of confiscation, ran on before the leading edge of the Japanese army. Within a few months of the Generalissimo's arrival, the price of land had doubled and trebled. Soon no one kept track anymore. (My father grew fatter by the minute.) And at the same time slums sprang up out of bamboo, tin, banana leaf, cardboard — whatever could be scraped up — held together with caked mud and bits of string. Like houses of cards, the wind blew them down, the rain washed them away. And overnight, like mildew, they were back. The most terrible was at the edge of the city on the site of a landfill, a few meager inches of soil bulldozed over a hundred years of breeding filth. Mosquitoes spawned; disease was rampant — cholera, dysentery, trachoma, and of course, syphilis. The only water came through a single filthy ditch which had to serve for everything. Women would dump their family's night soil, then, when the excrement had flowed downstream and the water looked clear, wash out the same buckets and fill them with drinking water. A commendable precaution! But most unnecessary, since upstream twenty yards away another was doing the same thing. It was wretched. The whole city reeked with it, that and the smell of greasy pork dumplings from the fry shops, sputtering in cauldrons of deep fat.

"The streets of the city proper were all commotion and uproar. Men argued in every dialect, women haggled in the open markets, babies cried, chickens squawked, coolies chanted mesmeric songs as they hauled loads up from the junks along the Yangtze docks, braziers jangled their wares — toothpicks and teaspoons, cat-bell Buddhas, back scratchers, earrings and amulets — calico peddlers thwacked blocks of wood together to advertise their stuffs, fortune-tellers beat on tortoises like tom-toms and rattled yarrow stalks. It was a fine confusion, and a great temptation for the young. And mixed with these evocations of eternal China was an even stranger sound: the sound of white men speaking European languages, 'blue-eyed devils from the Western Ocean,' as they were sometimes called.

"This fecund effervescence bubbled through the city until 1939, when the bombardment commenced. Within two years the voluptuous flesh of the romance had rotted off, leaving exposed the terrible bones of war. After the long summers of relentless bombing, the people walked hollow eyed in the streets, gaunt with chronic anxiety and lack of sleep. A grim solidarity existed, but it was like that among the damned, with no pretense of hope. Morale reached a low point following the bombing of the Red Cross hospital. The wind wafted the smell of burning flesh all over the city (there is no smell more horrible than this). Running through the streets on their way to the shelters in the caves, many heard the screams of the dying trapped inside, heard them even as the heat of the flames broke in waves against them, singeing their hair and eyebrows hundreds of feet away, knocking the breath out of them.

"Fortunately, long before things had come to this pass, my mother and sister had been sent to the countryside near Kunming, out of harm's way — at least the obvious harm."

My uncle's gaze drifted past my face, and again he smiled that telltale, disconcerting smile. "It was there that the Americans appeared. Ah, what a glorious epiphany! That group of magnificent young flyers under General Chennault. Exhausted, hungry for hope in any shape, we took them as gods, as saviors . . . even I, who had reason to know better." He laughed.

"The Americans found our devotion not at all objectionable. They believed themselves God's commissioned officers, bearing orders directly from the Chief of Staff. Their attitude toward the Chinese was always patronizing at best, that of the missionary toward the benighted heathen. At their worst they were tyrannous, thinking no more of slapping around the boys who served them in the camps than some men think of beating dogs.

"Their American creed could be reduced to this: clean living, clean thinking, and 'pep'! As if such hygiene — soap and water — could wash away the terrible sins of the human heart, which after centuries of festering had at last come to a head and burst, oozing a putrid discharge over the world. Oh, believe me, they had no idea what they were confronting — the accumulated ills of humanity, in which *they too* were implicated. The Americans believed themselves a new race, exempt from the collective guilt of mankind. What use had they for what was past? They were all future. And yet they should have come to China as suppliants, seeking our aid in acquiring a knowledge of the human verities, the true morality taught by all our sages — Confucian *and* Taoist — which begins with understanding, and ends with taming, the dark urges of the heart. But the Americans had no stomach for being tamed, even by themselves. To them, the word 'morality' referred to a national trait, masking an unexamined assumption of their own privileged relation to God. They were so innocent. But it was a terrible innocence, like that of wild animals, dangerous to themselves and others. Technological predators, that is what they were, so skilled in the art of killing and imposing their will through force that they believed the other, harder morality had become obsolete. Among the many spiritual tragedies of the war, not the least was the apparent corroboration it lent this belief. No, Sun I, they — not the Japanese, certainly not we — were the infidels, the barbarians, each American male a pioneer, heading west into the virgin wilderness of his own soul, carrying a rifle and a knife.

"If I seem bitter it's because I've had many years to ponder the matter. Once I was infatuated with the ways of the West myself. Direct exposure made me reconsider. While I was still a relatively young man, my father sent me to business school in America, to better myself, as he put it. This program of 'self-improvement' ran directly counter to my natural bent. But my father was too self-absorbed to notice this, or, if he noticed it, to care, so dazzled was he with the prospect of modernizing his operations with my help. It has always been a source of pride to me that, in accordance with my filial obligation, I was able to master my rebellious instincts and obey him. I say this even though it was a living hell for me.

"After two years there I became convinced that such studies could be pursued only at the expense of whatever there is of true value in human life. I saw the young men around me throwing away the ballast of their principles broadcast, stripping themselves down to animal leanness for the Hunt, the pursuit of the fleet, elusive quarry of outrageous gain. Distilled into its simplest form, the whole of existence was reduced to this, to gain. Money, or rather profit, was God in America. When I realized this, it sickened me. The word 'modernization' sounded in my ears like a disease, not a panacea. After a violent inner struggle, my course became clear. I saw that I had to return to China, apologize to my father for disappointing him, explain my position, and devote my life to the Confucian values which have sponsored the sane and civilized existence we as a people have enjoyed so long. I thought he'd understand."

My uncle stopped speaking. His face was gorged with blood, the veins swelling and pulsing in his throat. At that moment he did not seem old. A young man's harsh, fanatical conviction glowed in his eyes, making his pain seem ageless and no different from my own. But, as his next words showed, Hsiao did not sense my sympathy.

"You probably regard me as an old-fashioned reactionary, out of step with the times, a stale curmudgeon." He smiled with visible effort as he tried to alter the momentum. "And to an extent, I suppose I am. But let me emphasize that it was not the uncouthness of the Americans' manners and habits that offended me. Great latitude must be observed in such matters, which differ widely among peoples. Though I must say, tolerance for a race which goes whole months together without eating so much as a mouthful of rice is difficult. Instead they consume the flesh of swine and cattle in intemperate quantities, bringing it to table in an appalling condition, huge slabs barely singed by the flame, still oozing blood. There they dismember the sad carcass, gouging and slashing it with kitchen implements — huge knives and triple-tined prongs called forks. I never met one dexterous enough to wield a pair of chopsticks. I for one felt quite nervous at such dinners, like a shipwrecked mariner at a feast of cannibals, fearing to be 'barbecued' myself at any moment!

"But more than this, it was a certain blankness in their eyes that worried me. They took no delight in contemplating what was around them, their thoughts fixed on some receding target, accelerating away from them into the future as they approached it, a thing which they called (and the pathos of this is inexpressible) 'happiness.' Nature had no power to make them glad." He gestured toward the open window as he spoke. In the distance the solemn ranges of the massif could be seen, receding row by row into a sky of lapis lazuli. A fresh wind was blowing through the pine forest, bringing us the odor of uncooked turpentine. And from the ravine below, barely audible, came the crystal rush and clacking of the stream as it coursed through its pebbled bed. My uncle sighed. "They looked upon these gifts with unappreciative eyes, seeing them only as objects to be tamed and appropriated for their own use, ready to torture the last bit of inoffensive beauty out of the natural earth to guarantee a good return on their investments.

"But I have said enough, and more than I intended. Let me return to the main theme of my story. . . .

"As I said, the Chinese deified the Americans for their heroic efforts against the Japanese. And they *were* brave. Unquestionably. I too was inspired by their courage and resolution. But I was alone in my assessment of their limitations as a people, their egoism and arrogance, their dangerously simplistic views of history and morality. My father became furious at the mere suggestion of reproach. He was fond of the Americans, as he said, 'this side idolatry.' This side and beyond, far, far beyond, it seemed to me.

"Our home became a favored retreat of the officers of the AVG during their off-duty hours. They were flattered by my father's solicitude as he vied with the other prominent families to woo their good opinion. This I considered an undignified game of one-upmanship and told my father so in no uncertain terms; silence, I felt, would have been the greater disloyalty. Didn't Confucius himself say that a man may remonstrate gently with his parents if the occasion warrants? Perhaps I wasn't gentle, or not gentle enough. I only know my father became enraged. He said I was a shame and a burden to him when I should have been his staff and support. Rebuking me with 'defection from the cause' (by which, I assume, he meant Business), he called me a drone, a disgrace, and worse. I was mortified, Sun I. When he said he had no further use for me, I proudly took him at his word, and left the house. I moved to Kunming, took a scholar's garret, and nursed my grievance, immersing myself deeply in the classics and dreaming forlornly of the Golden Age of Yao and Shun. Still, I was kept posted on the goings-on by my mother and the servants, who pitied me and instinctively resisted the unfamiliar conduct they saw around them.

"The American flyers were taken with the 'quaintness' of our home, finding its setting 'charming' — which it certainly was, though without the ironic emphasis expressed in their acknowledgment of those qualities. In the central courtyard was a pool, filled with goldfish and lotus pads. This was spanned by an intricately carved and painted humpback bridge. Around this pool the house spread out in concentric circles, like rings in water expanding from a stone, each connected to the next by a beautiful moon gate. But despite the beauty of the place, the Americans secretly laughed up their sleeves to see that we drew water from a well, had rudimentary electric power, and, most damnably, used an outhouse. Not the shelves of classics, the embroidered silks, nor even the priceless lacquerware my mother had brought as her only dowry — the likes of which had not been dreamed of in America — could convince them that they were treading civilized ground.

"Your mother was allowed to participate to her heart's content in the entertainment of these guests. To demonstrate his advanced ideas, my father lifted all restrictions on her. Though my mother wept and pleaded, he pooh-poohed the ancient proprieties concerning the conduct of unmarried women. 'Medieval prejudice,' he called it. Your mother circulated freely among the young officers, offering them the hospitality of the house. Engaging them in converstion, she inquired about the practices of women in the West (she often said she considered herself to be one, only born in exile — a comment that consistently delighted our guests). When they brooded on the danger they faced and on their isolation in our land, she took it on herself to lift their spirits. This became a kind of mission for your mother. With the coming of the Americans, she blossomed, and the intractable melancholy she had struggled with so long all but disappeared." My uncle seemed to lose himself briefly in this memory, smiling a vague, wistful smile. Then an ominous focus returned to his expression.

"One of their number was a young man named Eddie Love. From the first he was an enigma to me, though I was drawn to him. I met him at my father's house shortly before our severance, at a cocktail party given in the Americans' honor. 'Met,' I say, but only in a manner of speaking. Meeting implies some kind of meaningful exchange between beings of the same order, a mutual weighing and reckoning. That is not what occurred between us. I met Love only as you might be said to meet one of those fabulous performing animals which are sometimes brought in from the hinterlands or from abroad and paraded through the streets. Perhaps you've seen them. Most familiar are the dancing bears and organ-grinders' monkeys which can be found in any city in the world. But I am thinking of a 'dancing tiger' I once saw. This animal, captured and transported overland from Burma, measured his stout-ribbed bamboo cage with a single lengthy padded stride, pacing back and forth, or rather around and around, and never lost his balance as the cage jolted over the cobblestones. He was like a swirl of black and orange gases fuming in a stoppered bottle, primitive energies pining to return to nature from which they had been unlawfully extracted. As he paced, the tiger turned his terrible, huge head from side to side and glared at the passersby, his green, vertical eyes bright with a curious, impersonal fury, not at all like human hatred, and somehow beautiful.

"The trainer's 'trick' was pathetically shallow, aiming at that submerged but ineradicable human instinct for cruelty and violence. He would very carefully climb to the top of the cage, which was quite tall and, all the while smiling his odious, self-deprecatory smile and bowing to the crowd with false humility, dangle scraps of red, dripping meat over the tiger's head. The animal, which had obviously been starved and aggravated past endurance, sat back on his haunches and pawed the air like a house cat, occasionally leaping in extreme exasperation for the meat, and dashing his head against the top of the cage, as the trainer, with wrists like rubber bands, snapped back the bait, scarcely able to conceal his glee. The tiger then fell to the floor of the cage where he lay panting on his belly. But presently he roused himself to try again, knowing, perhaps, that it was hopeless, but unable to resist his appetite. And thus the 'dance' went on.

"Why this image, with its undercurrent of repressed violence, occurs to me in connection with Eddie Love, I've never been quite sure, though I never think of him without awakening the memory. In many ways he was the incarnation of the opposite principle, jubilant, free-spirited, liberal. But there was something else in him, some element of danger. In a strange way he always reminded me of one of the members of the Greek pantheon — Hermes in a tuxedo, with aviator glasses and that slightly canine smile, some gay thief with a rose between his teeth, charming even as he spoils.

"But there's a simpler explanation: Love too was a 'tiger,' though of the flying rather than the dancing variety. When I think about it, though, I'm not so sure he wasn't closer to the trainer than the tiger. Perhaps there was a little bit of both in Love. And when I first saw him, he was performing tricks.

"I had come home late and found guests assembled in the courtyard near the pool. Love, in tie and tails, was standing at the crown of the arched bridge doing magic tricks, emceeing his own act in an authentic barker's voice.

" 'Here to perform tonight, for your pleasure, ladies and gentlemen (the ladies in particular), several unparalleled feats of pres-ti-di-gi-TAY-shun never before seen in China, guaranteed to make your hearts leap . . .' — he painted a glowing circle in the air, his fingers glittering like sparklers, sputtering colored fire — 'through the flaming hoop! Acts imported straight from the Great Midway of America!'

"Unbuttoning his white gloves at the wrist, he tossed them nonchalantly into his black beaver top hat, then collapsed it against his knee. Two bewildered doves fluttered forth, lighting briefly on the garden wall before flying away into the dusk. General applause followed, even a few scattered oohs and ahs — my sister's included. I spotted Ch'iu-yeh sitting at the foot of the bridge next to our mother. Leaning forward in her chair, hands folded tensely in her lap (as if at any moment they might fly off too), your mother was hanging on Love's every move with an intensity in her expression which I couldn't help noticing. Her cheeks were flushed, and this high color added radiance to her good looks, making her seem, even to a brother's dull, accustomed eye, beautiful.

"By now Love had punched open the hat and tapped the brim down rakishly over one eye, like the American actor Fred Astaire. Suddenly a look of exaggerated wonder — eyes open wide, lips pursed into a tiny o — lit up his face. Lifting the hat, he searched gingerly on top of his head, discovering (with the mime's smile of childlike, innocent delight) a tiny speckled egg. Balancing it on the tips of his fingers as in an eggcup, he turned at the waist, inviting perusal by the audience. Whether by accident or design I never knew, but as he made his bow, he dropped the egg, spilling its rich, yellow yolk across the planks of the bridge, through which it dripped into the dark waters of the pool. For an instant your father seemed to falter and lose his self-assurance. But as the audience only howled with pleasure, Love immediately launched into fresh buffoonery.

"Thoroughly pleased with the way the evening was progressing, my father stood off in a corner smoking a big cigar. He had collared one of the young Americans and chatted with him in the demotic English he was so proud of, speaking no doubt of his plans to further the 'commercial intercourse' between East and West. To me, he seemed a little like a magician himself as he waved his stogy, wandlike, in the air, and favored the assembly with a smile so benign that God himself, had he been caught effecting it, must have felt a little foolish. The poor soldier who was the immediate recipient of this largesse was all too obviously on his best behavior and would no doubt have preferred to drink a little more and be edified a little less." I thought I detected a note of grudging affection in Hsiao's voice as he reminisced about his father, playing counterpoint against the more obvious chagrin.

"Most of Love's tricks were from the standard repertory, but had I known him even slightly I might have guessed that he had something special up his sleeve. He had an outrageous fancy, immensely attractive and at the same time thoroughly exasperating. Something drove him on to acts that, when on the mark, were superb, unique — some irritant, perhaps, like the grain of sand around which the oyster builds its pearl. At times, though, his fancy failed, produced grotesqueries, like the gray, deformed miscarriages one finds more commonly in the shell. I didn't know it at the time, but I was about to be treated to my first example of that fancy. Whether successful or no, I leave to you to judge.

"The audience cheered your father on as he neared the grand finale. An endless and bewildering array of objects, some precious, some trivial, appeared from the beaver top hat, an inexhaustible well brimming with the stuff of earthly desire. Costly embroidered silk handkerchiefs were tossed carelessly to the crowd and left for whoever wished to pick them up, followed by soiled socks and underwear. A tiny scale-model P-40, complete down to the tiger jaws painted on its nose, buzzed out and executed several dizzying loops and rolls before crashing headlong into the pool. Producing paper flowers and American flags out of his hat, Love buried it at sea with full military honors. Then he began to scatter horns and party favors, candy corn and Hershey's Kisses. A Roman candle launched itself into the darkening sky.

"At last, running out of steam, he drew his sleeve up, put his arm into the hat, searched around, shrugged his shoulders, and seemed ready to give it up. He walked away (all eyes still on him), then hesitated and turned back. Reaching in 'one last time, just to make sure,' he pulled out a furry little foot, and after it a plump, sarcastic-looking rabbit, which sniffed the air suspiciously and rotated its ears. Ordinarily parlor magic's most incorrigible cliché, in the context of this mad barrage the rabbit was completely unexpected, a hilarious anticlimax. The audience exploded laughing. One man actually rolled on the ground. Others had tears in their eyes.

"With this catharsis, hardly noticed by his public, your father the magician reached into his hat and produced a hand grenade. There was an audible gasp, then perfect silence. Smiling, flushed with triumph, Love extracted the pin and lobbed it into the crowd. The man who had been groveling uproariously a moment earlier curled up on his belly and covered his head. Somewhere near the back, I heard a woman sob one brief, hysterical bleat. Most sat stock still and gaped at it. All our terrors rose before our eyes, the threat of violent death which never left us in those days. Each in the privacy of his heart told over his secret fears. Then it exploded . . . with a ridiculous noise, clearly intended to suggest a fart. For one long minute no one laughed.

"No one except Love. Standing on the bridge, elevated several feet above the rest of us, he threw back his head with a high, wild whinny, like a rearing mustang, exuberantly pummeling the air. But there was more than pride and high spirits in that laugh, some note I'd never heard before, unless in a dream. In my mind I associate it with the sadness old women say is in the gaiety of elves and fairies, gods and demons too — all those weir creatures powerful beyond the most extravagant imaginings of men, but impotent to grant their own most urgent wish, which is to die. As I listened to his laugh, a chill crept over me, and the idea flitted through my brain that he was mad.

"These portents must have gone unremarked by the rest. Following the lead of the Americans (who were completely under Love's spell), the whole crowd had erupted into raucous laughter. I was astonished to see happy faces around me for the first time in months. Relief had broken over the assembly like a wave, sweeping everyone away in the mood of manic gaiety Love had inspired. It seemed less your father than the world itself which had gone mad.

"So it blew over. The man who had bit the dust got up and brushed off his jacket, smiling. He seemed genuinely pleased.

" 'That Love!' I heard an American say.

" 'What a character!'

" 'He's crazy!' (This in tones of highest admiration.)

" 'What a sense of humor!'

"Perhaps of everyone, your mother was the most taken with this display. I saw her standing alone at the foot of the bridge, waiting for Love to descend. To use the American expression, she seemed 'dying to meet him.' " My uncle descended momentarily to some fathomless depth of introspection, and when he came up his smile had become urbane and cynical.

"Love came down with the rabbit perched precariously on one arm, like a falcon, stroking its ears with his free hand. When he noticed Ch'iu-yeh beaming at him, he stopped short and stared at her inquisitively, opening his eyes wide. It was a rather lordly pose, but Ch'iu-yeh didn't falter in the least. I made a study of her face, for I saw something there I never had before. Beyond the pride, the flush of mild ecstasy, like a denser element which supported both, there was a vulnerability so resolute it verged on power — not verged on, *was*.

"In Love's expression there was curiosity and readiness, and perhaps a trace of amusement, too, evident in the way his lips repeatedly worked themselves to the brink of a smile before desisting.

" 'What did you think?' he asked her finally.

" 'I think you are a true magician, Mr. Love,' Ch'iu-yeh replied, a little coyly, yet with a thrilling overtone in her voice which reminded me of the nervous jingling of chandelier prisms when a door opens somewhere and a draft sweeps through the house.

Extremely handsome, extremely dangerous, Love bowed from the waist acknowledging her compliment, never for an instant taking his eyes from her face.

Ch'iu-yeh smiled playfully. 'But tell me, is your magic real, or only sleight of hand?'

"He matched her smile. 'There's a difference?'

" 'Of course!'

"Love shrugged with a vaguely sullen sangfroid. 'I make no promises.'

"Surprised by the sudden chill, Ch'iu-yeh blushed. 'I liked the show anyway.' Her tone betrayed a quaver.

" 'It's nice of you to say so,' he replied. 'I enjoy doing it. It's great fun, while it lasts.'

"She opened her eyes inquisitively. 'While it lasts?'

" 'Afterward certain complications arise — you know, *responsibilities.*' His emphasis expressed mock horror. She waited. 'I mean, of course . . .' (he paused, and his manner reversed itself again) '. . . what's one to do with all the frigging bunnies?' Abandoning his suave reticence, he became bumptious, bawdy. 'Over the course of a few nights they really mount up, I can tell you. The damn things multiply like, well . . .' Beside him, a companion burst out laughing. Substantiating his claims, Love lifted the rabbit by the scruff of its neck. 'Exhibit A, the murder weapon,' he said wryly.

"The animal's legs began to work rhythmically, loping in the air. This was both hilarious and pathetic, more pathetic perhaps as the rabbit suddenly let out a piercing scream. Most people have never heard this sound, Sun I, for it is usually only at the point of death that these timid creatures break their silence. I remembered it from my boyhood, when it would sometimes wake me at night and I would know an owl had swept down on the warren and snatched up one of the inhabitants by the throat. That scream is the more chilling as it bears a resemblance to the cry of a human child.

"Without changing his grip, Love lifted the rabbit to his face and stared into its stupid eyes, which were dilated with terror. 'What's wrong with you?' he addressed it, laughing gaily. He seemed unaware of or indifferent to its fear, though not, I think, deliberately cruel.

" 'You're not holding it right,' Ch'iu-yeh chided, taking it from behind. 'Like *this.*' She demonstrated, cradling it like a baby. 'Its little heart is thumping away.' She looked at him reproachfully. 'It's nearly frightened to death.' The animal grew calm in her embrace. 'You have to be more gentle,' she counseled, offering it back.

" 'You're very good at that,' Love noted with a shrewd nod. 'It must be the maternal instinct. Perhaps you'd like to take it off my hands?'

"Ch'iu-yeh hesitated. 'You mean keep it?'

"He nodded.

"She glanced from him to it, then back at him. 'Oh yes! May I really?'

" 'Please do.'

" 'What shall I call . . .' She regarded the rabbit doubtfully.

"Love hesitated, then deftly reached out and lifted the animal's hind leg. He pretended to gasp. '*Him,*' he said, raising his eyebrows significantly. Ch'iu-yeh turned bright crimson. 'As to the name,' he went on, pretending not to notice her discomfiture, 'normally I call them "Bugs," or "Junior," something in that line. But in the case of, uhmm' — he cleared his throat — 'so magnificent a specimen — and he truly is a buck. Is that right, buck? Or is it bull? Or gander? I really don't know in the case of rabbits. At any rate, the choice is obvious.'

"Confused by his banter, Ch'iu-yeh regarded him timidly. Her lower lip trembled slightly. 'Yes?'

" 'Why, *Peter,* of course!' he cried merrily.

"To this day I've never known if it were genuine naiveté on her part, or the most brilliant repartee. Her face betrayed no clue. But after she regarded him for some time in apparent confusion, her face quickly brightened. 'Peter Rabbit?' she queried sweetly. 'I know that fairy tale.'

"Love looked like a man who has just received a blow in the stomach (or even lower down). From a pallid moon of a face, he regarded Ch'iu-yeh curiously, as though seeing her for the first time. There was a tinge of shame in his expression, and, underlying it, a confused new tenderness. Then he burst out wholeheartedly in appreciative laughter. I nearly fell in love with him myself, Sun I."

•

"That was when I introduced myself. Love was in high spirits, and we chatted jovially while Ch'iu-yeh stood by, petting the rabbit with forced concentration. I watched her sympathetically out of the corner of my eye, remembering an American girl I had seen once at an amusement park who clung to a stuffed animal which her boyfriend had won for her in some game of chance. Only in Ch'iu-yeh's case, the animal was alive.

"Love expressed amazement at my command of English, and at Ch'iu-yeh's, which was even better than mine. He spoke a smattering of demotic Cantonese which he had picked up from a succession of Chinese cooks and houseboys — much in demand among the upper classes in New York at one time. He asked how we'd learned the language, and I gave him a brief account of my father's enthusiasm for Western 'culture' — i.e., business — culminating in his decision to send me abroad. At the mention of the word 'business,' I was intrigued to note a change in your father's expression, rather like a cloud passing before the sun. At the time, of course, I had no idea what deep personal resonance the subject had for him. I pressed him for his views, but he evaded me.

" 'Business?' he said. 'Reminds me of a joke. How is business like a Chinese laundry?' He offered me no opportunity to reply. 'Full of stuffed shirts. Or is it starched shirts? I can't remember. My father told me that one.'

"Detecting a note of false nonchalance, I regarded him closely. 'And who is your father?'

"Love turned away as if I had suddenly become invisible, resuming his conversation with Ch'iu-yeh. Having been, as it were, dismissed, I moved off to a distance and struck up a conversation with someone else. But my curiosity was piqued, especially since your father seemed so interested in Ch'iu-yeh. I found myself gradually gravitating back. Though I didn't participate in their conversation, I was close enough to overhear bits and pieces of it.

" 'Is that a chrysanthemum in your lapel, Mr. Love?' she asked. 'I've never seen one quite that color.' She blushed, embarrassed by the simplicity of her remark, and by the transparency of her embarrassment.

" 'Call me Eddie,' Love said. He gazed in her eyes with a musing, almost drunken expression, as if forgetting the question entirely. Then, starting, he looked down at his chest.

" 'This thing?' He shrugged. 'I don't know. I suppose it must be. It's like the ones you give the girls at football games.' He grinned at her boyishly, shy and impetuous at once. 'Do you like it? It has a lovely smell.' Thumbing it out, he stepped toward her. She stepped back.

" 'Chrysanthemums are bitter,' she said. 'Everyone knows that.'

" 'Not this one.'

"She gazed at him in doubtful appraisal, then, conceding to his smile, smiled back. Slipping her fingers trustfully under his lapel, she closed her eyes and bent close to his chest, as though to rest her head there for a dance, drawing the flower toward her.

"Reaching for his handkerchief in the breast pocket of his tuxedo, Love accidentally caught my eye and winked confidentially. I was embarrassed to be caught eavesdropping so shamelessly, but that wasn't why he'd winked.

"Ch'iu-yeh suddenly uttered a tiny cry and drew back, blinking her eyes and sputtering. She looked up at Love in amazement. I then noticed a drop of water tracking down her cheek and realized the flower was a fake, part of the magician's bag of tricks, that he had squirted her with it. From the expression on her face, however, I might have easily believed it was a tear. It beaded on her chin an instant, but Love dabbed it with his handkerchief before it had a chance to drip.

" 'You tricked me!' she cried petulantly. She seemed to vacillate a minute between umbrage and a childlike desire to be won over by the joke.

"Patting dry her face, Love smiled sympathetically. 'I never promised,' he said for the second time. 'Besides, I owed you that one for the rabbit.'

"The balance tipped. Your mother blushed and smiled. Love smiled back. And as I watched I saw their eyes grow bright with recognition, so bright they seemed to light up the dusk. It was like flint and steel, Sun I, and in that moment I saw the innocent spark struck between them which would mount into this conflagration, never guessing then how hot a hell would burn."

•

The familiar gong reverberated strangely, summoning the monks from labor in the garden to afternoon meditation in the dim recesses of the temple. Its appeal seemed listless and irrelevant in the supercharged, burning summer air. I glanced aside impatiently through the window at the glowing, sweaty figures of the brothers filing silently through the courtyard, then back at my uncle's face.

Chapter 5

"From that time on a day never passed that Love didn't send Ch'iu-yeh fresh-cut flowers — roses, irises, orchids sometimes, but most often chrysanthemums. Each morning they appeared in a shallow wicker basket outside her door, a dozen or thirteen, carefully wrapped in newspaper. For a long time no one knew how they got there, or who brought them. They appeared 'as if by magic.' This became an inside joke among the servants, and to my mother a matter of concern. My father, who was away at Chungking most of the time, was never told.

"Yet it was innocent enough. Love didn't deliver them personally; he had recruited a loyal ally from within our ranks, a servant in our father's house to whom your father had formed a strange attachment. Perhaps I should say a word about this, for it illuminates an aspect of his character which, as yet, I haven't touched on.

"You see, besides the manic gaiety which animated him the night he met Ch'iu-yeh — that problematic but compelling charm — your father had another side entirely. Other sides, I should say. For despite his reputation as an extrovert ('the life of the party' was the phrase then current among the Americans) — a reputation I believe he cultivated willfully and not without distaste, and even pain — I'm convinced Love shared only the crumbs of his inner life with others, passionately guarding the rest. In such secrecy he concealed the fact of his own constitutional susceptibility to depression. This formed the basis of his relation to the servant I mentioned earlier, a young man named Chiang Po, who was apprenticed to our gardener.

"Now Chiang Po, as far as I know, had nothing but peasant blood in his veins, muddy as the waters of the Yellow River. Yet he was one of those rare individuals of the lower classes who seem to possess the instincts of a prince. He was a beautiful man, tall, dark, and spare, with the gravely handsome face one finds nowhere else except among the descendants of the Khans. Chiang Po was of Mongolian extraction, yet he lacked their sturdy health and hardihood entirely. He was of slight build, delicate, even frail. I have an idea his health was ruined by a serious bout of fever as a child, scarlatina probably, for he carried the terrible signature in the pockmarks on his face, a disfigurement that only enhanced his beauty, like the chance scars time inflicts in antique ivory. Some of the servants suggested another interpretation of his delicacy, physical and otherwise. It was whispered that Po was, or had been, an opium addict. Whether this was true or not, I made no effort to ascertain. In either case, it is irrelevant to his association with your father.

"Chiang Po was proud with the fierce pride of his race, a pride which his dependency seemed to aggravate into an almost pathological intensity. Aloof and difficult, he never spoke except when spoken to, and then only in the tersest manner. He seemed to resent any attempts at intimacy, or even civility, as patronizing. Several times my father had been on the point of dismissing him for insolence, but each time my sister offered such a spirited defense, timidly seconded by my mother, that he backed down. (Eventually though, when Chi'iu-yeh was no longer there to defend him, father acted on this threat. But that was much later.) Ch'iu-yeh's motive, I assumed, was simple pity for the hardship of his life. My mother, however, had become quite dependent on Po, who, with unerring taste, supplied her table with lovely arrangements of flowers which expressed the tense, whippetlike elegance of his mind.

"I had little contact with Po, but I had noticed him. Whenever I met his eyes, fine flashes of anger leapt forth at me like lightnings from a thunderhead. I respected this in him. The fellow lived as though under siege, allowing himself only two pleasures: his flowers, which he tended with an almost religious devotion, and music. Po played the *erh-hu,* that peculiar two-stringed Mongolian fiddle whose timbre bears such an uncanny resemblance to the human voice, especially in the expression of melancholy.

"Across the barriers of class, of culture, even language (though your father made rapid progress bridging this gap), Chiang Po and Love gravitated toward one another. The servant's soul was like a perfectly notched key whose blade matched the wards of your father's personality and cleanly clicked them open. Some of the other servants told me how sometimes when he was in a certain mood, especially after his injury, Love would sit hour after hour on the bridge in the courtyard of our house, dangling his legs over the edge, looking down into the dark mirror of the pool, while behind him Chiang Po played his fiddle with the horsehair bow and sang. This Po would do for no one else. Sometimes he sang gay, virtuosic tunes, the *erh-hu* imitating the neighing of horses and the rhythm of the race (Mongolians are the greatest horsemen in the world), but mostly the songs were sad, the songs of peasant women whose men have gone away to war, rising to shrill heights of anger, then falling off into a sound like wailing — low, level stretches, like days of inconsolable sorrow end on end. This music touched your father, soothed some pain whose source was hidden deep within, shrouded, as I said, in secrecy.

"Had it not been for the chattering of the servants, I might have remained in the dark about these episodes until much later, when, purely by accident, I witnessed one myself. But more of that later. Here let it suffice to say that these rumors served to pique even further my already considerable interest in your father.

"I cultivated him, and he responded in some measure, seeking my advice in the procurement of certain Chinese artifacts, textiles primarily. Once we visited the silk farms in Szechwan together. That trip stands deeply etched in memory, for it was the closest I ever came to intimacy with your father. I had asked him why he had volunteered for duty in China. He was silent for a long while, and then, with an odd smile on his lips, he replied, 'a lonely impulse of delight.' When I questioned him further, he recited a poem by the Irish poet Yeats. It's called 'An Irish Airman Foresees His Death':

> I know that I shall meet my fate
> Somewhere among the clouds above;
> Those that I fight I do not hate,
> Those that I guard I do not love;
> My country is Kiltartan's Cross,
> My countrymen Kiltartan's poor,
> No likely end could bring them loss,
> Or leave them happier than before.
> Nor law, nor duty bade me fight,
> Nor public men, nor cheering crowds,
> A lonely impulse of delight
> Drove to this tumult in the clouds;
> I balanced all, brought all to mind,
> The years to come seemed waste of breath,
> A waste of breath the years behind,
> In balance with this life, this death.

" 'A lonely impulse of delight' — I've never forgotten that.

"Something else that struck me was the silence Love maintained on the subject of his family. Considering the enthusiasm the other flyers showed for the subject, this was remarkable. Along with dog tags, a private cache of photographs seemed a standard item of U.S. government issue. These the Americans carried, not next to their hearts like the Chinese, but along with their money in an equally private (though perhaps less sacred) spot. There, close at hand and ready to do service at a moment's notice, were all their 'near and dear ones.' Much time was spent passing these photographs back and forth among themselves, and to anyone else who would look at them, and declaring with patriotic fervor, and sometimes maudlin sentiment, 'I wish I was back home.'

"The strange thing about Love was that he didn't seem to be included in the all but universal embrace of this grand sentiment. His comrades never knew quite what to make of his reticence about his home and family. I think they were a little bit in awe of his reserve, and might well have held it against him had he not compensated in other areas — with his resourcefulness and charm, his 'magic,' products of a breeding they were ignorant of, and whose value they would probably have denied on principle had they known — but most of all in the air, where all were intimate under the cold and watchful eye of Death. There, where no lies were possible, your father showed his heart.

"Love was one of the two or three best pilots in his squadron, the Panda Bears. In combat his style was bold, even a little reckless, but he possessed the fine, nervous reflexes of an athlete and pulled it off every time. (Except once. . . . But it is sheer speculation on my part, and perhaps presumptuous, to assume that he was in any way to blame for his crash. Certainly he was never cashiered, or even, to my knowledge, reprimanded for it. In fact, they decorated him.) Your father's value to the unit, though, consisted in more than nerve or physical skill. He had a knack for strategy which showed itself time and again in small technical matters, and eventually blossomed into a major tactical contribution. Because of this gift, Chennault tried to put him out of harm's way, flying reconnaissance. Love refused. At any rate, in combination with these factors, your father's silence concerning his family, rather than acting to his detriment, actually enhanced his standing among his comrades. They respected it as a point of honor and refused to intrude. They even actively protected him insofar as they could." Hsiao got up and paced toward the window where he paused, looking out. Resuming, he spoke with averted features, clasping and unclasping his hands behind his back.

"Because of this, for a considerable length of time neither I nor anyone else was aware of the fact that Love came from one of the dozen or so richest families in America, a family sired by one of the great industrialists of the nineteenth century, that class which arose like terrible predators out of the ooze and slime of that primeval landscape, devouring their competition until they had increased to such a size that they towered over the treetops and enjoyed an uninterrupted view of the horizon of the world — lords of all they saw — they and a handful of others like them. The Morgans, Mellons, Carnegies, Rockefellers, Vanderbilts, Du Ponts — if the Loves were less well known than these, it was perhaps because they had continued to exercise direct control over their empire long after the others had been turned loose like sacred cattle to manure the green fields of charity. The Loves had not, until comparatively recently, had time to found the great foundations, build the libraries, museums, and universities which had made the others famous. For these are the activities to which great families turn in their decline. Culture, or the *cultivation* of the good and beautiful, is the afterglow of pristine vigor. And beauty, though it alone may finally redeem and make life bearable, in its starkest formulation is no more than this — a gorgeous parasite upon life's body. This terrible truth must never be forgotten.

"The Loves, however, were in no danger of forgetting what they had not learned. They had long escaped this falling off. Power had passed from father to son in an unbroken succession for several generations. Eddie Love's father, Arthur Love, was the first weak link in the chain, forged not of iron or steel, but some more delicate and fragile substance. Through him the Loves had lost control of the great corporation they had made (and which had made them).

"Having studied business, I knew about the scandal Arthur Love had stirred up on Wall Street (which, for your information, Sun I, is the tingling brain of the Western world's financial nervous system). The case of his collapse, or his apostasy, or whatever, was famous. Yet somehow I never quite made the connection between that father and this son. In retrospect it seems so obvious; perhaps it was the very obviousness that threw me off. Why should your father have taken such trouble to conceal a background which most others would have been at pains to advertise? Whatever the reason, as it turned out I didn't have to search for it: *it* found *me*. As they say in America, if it had been a snake, it would have bitten me.

"The whole thing came out quite by accident. One morning I was perusing a mutilated copy of a well-known American magazine called *Time* (flown in 'over the hump' from Burma, six weeks old, in an American cargo plane) when something startling caught my eye. In an insert on the cover, emblazoned in bold letters, was written:

LOVE IS DEAD.

" 'Preposterous!' I thought. Desperate as the situation of mankind seemed at that historical moment, such a metaphysical pronouncement still seemed ridiculously farfetched. Turning to the story, however, I soon discovered that the blurb portended nothing so dramatic, but was simply an obituary. 'Simply,' I say, and yet I realized at once that the deceased must have been someone of the greatest consequence — a president, a Supreme Court justice, a great general, even perhaps a famous Hollywood star — but more likely even than all of these, a rich man, some great mogul from the world of business."

There was a note of stridency in my uncle's voice as he said this, and the same wry, mirthless smile turned up the corners of his lips.

"Listen closely now, Sun I, for the story that follows is instructive, one of the few hopeful precedents for personal conduct ever to arise from the barbarous arena of the American marketplace. Art Love — Arthur Edward Love the Fourth, to be exact, Eddie's father — had been one of the most powerful men in the world in his youth: chairman of the board, principal shareholder and chief executive officer of American Power and Light Corporation. He was perhaps the closest thing to a hereditary monarch America ever produced. But he couldn't hold on to his corporate fiefdom. I'm not sure he even wanted to. That's the point.

"He was known to have been a gentle, sweet-tempered boy, rather frail by nature, but precocious, alive to the 'higher delicacies' of art — characteristics which perhaps did not bode well in a future Caesar of finance, which is what his father, A. E. Love the Third, 'Big Ed,' had marked him out to be, following in the family pattern. A stern education, intended to instill a little 'killer instinct' in the child, had little effect on Arthur Love, except that by the end of it he'd begun to suffer from nervous disorders, and the sweetness and lyricism of his youthful temperament had given way to brooding and morbidity.

"It was only with his father's death, however — Big Ed's, I mean — that the epilepsy which was to plague Art Love throughout his life erupted in its full virulence. The first episode occurred at the funeral. What made matters worse was that Arthur was duty-bound to fill his father's shoes. If his performance during those first few months didn't win him any accolades, he was at least given passing marks by those observers with the knowledge, and presumption, to evaluate it. Many, myself included, were surprised he lasted as long as he did. Perhaps the laudanum his doctors prescribed helped him maintain his equilibrium. The cost was heavy though, for Arthur Love became dependent on it, and remained so for the rest of his life.

"In memory his reign, or his administration, seems a strange one, hushed and portentous somehow. It was as if there was a smell of death on Wall Street. Rare excrescences of pity showed themselves in men who'd lost the taste for it, who'd lost the taste for everything except the Hunt, for blood. And blood had always been their element, the Loves', ever since the original A. E. Love, the terrible patriarch of the clan, had taken over the corporation (still known in that day as American Gas) from 'Jubilee' Jim Fisk, the infamous *âme damné* of Jay Gould. Fisk's assassination at the hands of an outraged husband — whose wife Fisk had allegedly seduced — occurred precisely at the time when he and the original Love were locked in ferocious battle for control of American Gas and further, at just the moment when Love appeared to have exhausted his ammunition. Though speculation ran rampant, the courts accorded it a 'crime of passion' and looked no deeper. The real truth I suppose no one ever knew, except A.E. Love himself — and he was not one to fret with conscience, especially when Fisk's death had opened the door he'd waited his whole life to enter, into the sanctum sanctorum of all earthly power. His great-grandson was a different breed entirely. As I say, from the beginning there was a gut feeling in the financial community that Art Love's rule would be brief. And yet the way it ended . . . no one had expected that.

"Try and picture it, Sun I. At the hands of his father and grandfather, APL had expanded and diversified into a dozen different sectors, including munitions during the First World War. At the time of Arthur Love's accession, American Power and Light had become, on the basis of gross assets, the largest corporation in America, and thus, of course, the world." Hsiao smiled wryly. "Of course! Its performance had earned it a place in the sun on the Dow Jones Industrial Average, undisputed centerpiece of the index. That was the era when investors first christened it 'the APL of America's eye.' " Hsiao smiled again.

"It was this then that Art Love irrecoverably lost, or should I say *threw away*, at that notorious stockholders' meeting at the conclusion of his first year when he announced to the Board of Directors that he was 'washing his hands of the ritual blood' — a phrase which has since become notorious on Wall Street.

"Imagine it, Sun I, before an auditorium packed to overflowing with both high and low — those who had put their humble savings into a few shares and held them with unquestioning faith like relics of the cross, together with the crowned heads of American and international finance — Arthur Love repudiated and anathematized the whole community, called them high priests engaged in a 'Black Mass,' the celebration of the sacrificial mysteries of private enterprise, said it was a new religion, old as sin: self-interest. Then he began to castigate his family, suggesting there was truth to the Wall Street anecdote that Loves were baptized not in holy water but in blood. His great-grandfather's hands were red with murder, he said, and each of them in turn, on coming into his inheritance, had bought into that sin: 'the iniquity of the fathers is visited upon the children, and upon the children's children, unto the third and fourth generation.' He was the fourth in his line, he said, and with him it would stop. He refused to pass this guilt on to his children, prayed someday they'd thank him for it. His great-grandfather, he said, had been guilty of the murder of a single man — that was blood enough. He would not be accessory to the murder of a civilization."

Hsiao nodded. "Yes, Arthur Love was a different breed of man entirely from the common Wall Street type, different, and better, in my opinion, even if less strong." Hsiao met my eyes. "At the end of his speech, Love was taken with an epileptic seizure and collapsed on stage. According to the story, as they wheeled him, writhing and thrashing, down the central aisle of the auditorium, several of the elderly Wall Street statesmen and generals wept openly." Hsiao smiled cynically and added by way of afterthought, "though whether in sympathy for their fallen prince or for themselves, I wouldn't know.

"Within the financial community, the reaction at first was one of universal sadness. For the day following Love's collapse, no APL stock was traded, and by common consent the brokers all wore black. But when with Arthur Love recovered and failed to return to his post, the general appraisal changed from sadness to perplexity, then by slow degrees to open hostility. For it became increasingly apparent that an epoch had occurred in Art Love's life. He'd meant what he said. His condition stabilized by laudanum, the old childhood predilections began to reassert themselves. After his giddy ascent and fall from the pinnacles of power and influence, he retreated into himself, became a shy recluse. He retired to the family estate at Sands Point, Long Island, where he became a patron and philanthropist, insulated from the vicissitudes and heartaches of the world in a paradise of art, like some Art Nouveau Adam or mad King Ludwig of Bavaria. Though he never acted on his intention to dissociate himself totally from the corporation, in point of fact he never attended another stockholders' meeting, leaving the management of his interests to others.

"On Wall Street it was maliciously suggested that the supply of oxygen to his brain had been cut off during his seizure, and that Love was not 'all there.' Some implied that he'd become an addict. The doctors and psychiatrists, however, averred that the trauma had acted on the neurons in his brain in the manner of an electric shock treatment, effecting a 'miracle cure.' Others, less given to ingenious theorizing, simply said that he'd grown happy." Hsiao nodded. "Yes, Sun I, a most hopeful precedent." He sighed. "And now Arthur Love was dead. Yes, I knew the story well, all except the most important part. As my eye ran down the columns to the last paragraph of that article in *Time* magazine I happened on the following, or words to this effect: 'Mr. Love is survived by his wife and their only son, A. E. Love the Fifth (called "Eddie" after his grandfather, "Big Ed" Love). Eddie Love, at last report, was in Kunming, China, serving under General Claire Chennault in the AVG.'

"Now try and imagine if you can, Sun I, the effect this discovery had on me."

Chapter 6

"I was stunned by this revelation of Love's paternity. That this young man, to whom my sister seemed increasingly bound in a grave and serious relation, was the heir apparent of one of the greatest fortunes in America (and thus, of course, the world), caught me totally off guard and filled me with dread. Before, though something in him made me wary, I had rather liked him. He was the West, he was America — eternally young and injudicious, jubilant, charming, audacious, unrepentant — a gay, godlike thief filching the apples of the Hesperides, of the Tree of Life, of American Power and Light, what you will, and doing so with impunity, gorging himself, and stuffing what he couldn't eat into his top hat! One couldn't help but admire, even if one finally disapproved.

"But all thought of his personal qualities paled in the light of my discovery. Now, in my mind's eye, he glittered with a forlorn light, like some cursed jewel (a radioactive isotope, perhaps, which it is death to touch, but which may yet possess the power to save the world). Love was like a tuning fork resonating in the pitch of my obsession. After that, whatever else he might have been, for me he was a symbol of the Loves, who themselves were symbols for the class of men I feared the most, and feared because I knew their power."

Hsiao had begun to pace the floor. From time to time, unconsciously I think, he struck the flags sharply with the ferrule of his cane. As I watched him, among all my other feelings anxiety arose on his account, and pity.

"Yet despite my sense of foreboding, my first reaction to the story of Love's background was sympathetic. I felt a kinship between us which somehow I'd intuited all along — though in what it lay I'm not sure I could say, even now, unless it were simply that we were both the sons of fathers, and in that sense necessarily aggrieved." Hsiao caught my eye, smiling briefly at his own attempt at levity. Almost immediately, however, his face darkened into a frown again, and he recommenced his pacing.

"In accordance with laws of etiquette that are not only Confucian but universal, I realized my first obligation was to offer your father my condolences. It occurred to me that due to the deplorable state of communications, it was even possible I'd have to break the news to him myself. This was an alarming prospect, but I didn't balk at it. For there was another reason I felt I had to see him: Ch'iu-yeh. The disclosure of his heritage had quickened my protective instincts. With this discovery, the possibility that anything might come of their romance seemed effectively annihilated.

"At first I went to the barracks and searched for him there. He wasn't with the group of pilots I found lounging tensely in the 'butt room' waiting for the *ching-pao* air raid alarm to sound, and no one seemed able to tell me where he'd gone. I checked the bars along the strip in Kunming where the Americans sometimes gathered. He was in none of them. Finally I gave up.

"Pensive, at loose ends, I drifted inevitably toward home. When I arrived, my mother was alone in the sewing room, poring over her embroidery. This was a sight I was accustomed to, yet there was something unusual about it. She wasn't 'poring' so much as picking listlessly at the piece. The needlework in her lap lay largely neglected as she attended to some other in her mind, her lips moving silently as she puzzled out some thorny paradox or conundrum. The sight released a flood of tenderness in me — to see this old woman, so helpless, yet still struggling determinedly to come to terms with life.

"When she realized I was in the room, she cast me an imploring glance and hurriedly threw down her work. I opened my mouth to speak, but she interrupted and led me to the sliding rice-paper door which opened onto the garden.

" 'Listen,' she said, putting her finger to my lips.

"As if from far away, the sound of music broke upon my consciousness. I held my breath and strained to hear. From the garden came the strains of a mournful fiddle tune. Someone was singing — a man's voice, untrained, but as deeply moving as any I've ever heard.

"The song was vaguely familiar to me. It was a contemporary ballad called 'The River Flows,' quite popular at the time. From its theme and its simplicity of style, however, one might easily have mistaken it for one of the songs of the *Shih Ching,* which were old even in Confucius's time. It tells the story of a peasant woman whose husband has been conscripted and gone away

> . . . to fight and die
> Over a bit of worthless, barren ground
> Along some distant border,
> When your place was here.
> For though you did not know it,
> I am with child again. . . .

"The woman goes on to complain bitterly of the hardships of life without him. In a frenzy of spite, she taunts him with the offers of assistance other men, 'rich men, and strong young boys,' have made her. Then she breaks into lamentation, ending thus:

But I can never love another man,
Not even if I marry. For you left
This desolation in my flesh, this memory —
Your bright, young body —
And my heart refuses to be wise.

"The music stopped. My eyes were full of tears, yet I was not unhappy. Rather I felt like one waking refreshed after a long sleep. My curiosity as to the meaning of the scene had been mysteriously allayed.

"This sensation lasted only a moment, however. Coming to myself, I gently shook off my mother's hand (she too stood as though enchanted) and slid back the panel of the door.

"There in the courtyard, standing at the base of the bridge, was Chiang Po. He was resting his *erh-hu* lightly on a post. The horsehair bow hung limply in his hand, like the tail of a disspirited animal. Though still under his music's spell, I could not make out for the life of me what he was doing there in the middle of the afternoon, playing sad songs for the fish and birds as though there were no constraints upon his leisure except his own goodwill. Then I heard a whisper and realized he was not alone.

" 'Please don't stop,' a mournful voice petitioned.

"Changing my position slightly, I saw that there was someone with Po in the garden: Love. He was sitting on the bridge, dangling his legs over the edge, gazing absently into the dark mirror of the pool. Ch'iu-yeh was beside him. It was she who had spoken. I had not seen them before because from where I had stood they were blocked from sight by a trellis.

" 'He's been here since noon,' my mother whispered, 'sitting and staring into the water just like that, dropping crumbs to the fish. Ch'iu-yeh tried to comfort him and make him speak, but he just shook his head and asked for Po to play. The music seems to ease his mind. What is it, do you think? Go speak to him.'

"Unable to move, I watched Love in dumb wonder as he listlessly studied his own reflection in the pool. The stillness of the water was broken only by the surfacing of curious carp and goldfish who floated up out of their murky world to gaze at him, as though afflicted with a wonder like my own. Their bubbles broke the surface as they lipped the same dumb o o o, like professional mourners whom he paid with crusts broken off from the stale loaf of bread he'd torn to pieces in his lap.

"Realizing that he'd only heard about his father's death that day, I experienced a pang of sympathy so deep my eyes welled up with tears.

" 'Pull yourself together,' my mother said sternly. 'You're his friend. Go to him.'

"Her admonition shamed me and roused me from my dreamy state. Casting a backward glance at her, I went through the door and pulled it softly to. At the sound, Chiang Po turned to me with an expression of unmistakable hostility. Then he stalked off. Love too looked up briefly, but my appearance did not seem to make an impression on him, if indeed he recognized me. His eyes were all unfocused and seemed to stare through me to something behind or beyond — like an addict's, I'd have thought, if I hadn't known better. After a second he went back to his gloomy occupation. Ch'iu-yeh kept her eyes fixed on my face as I approached.

"Going toward the bridge, I rehearsed in my mind all the things I might say to him in commiseration. Like spavined chargers in rusty armor, all the standard phrases rattled through my head, more dead than alive. At the last moment my courage failed me.

" 'What is it, Eddie?' I asked disingenuously, placing my hand on his shoulder.

"Ch'iu-yeh, who was holding his hand, looked at me imploringly and gestured for me to go away. When I shook my head, her eyes became fierce.

"For several moments Love said nothing, continuing to gaze vacantly at the pool as though trying to penetrate its cloudy depths. I was almost convinced he hadn't heard, when he twisted toward me where I stood above and slightly behind him on the bridge. The sun must have been directly at my back, for your father shaded his eyes and squinted. Then, as if an idea had just struck him, the tense furrow working in his forehead relaxed, making his brow seem transparent, almost luminous. Reaching into the pocket of his uniform, he took out his dark glasses and put them on.

" 'Now I can see again,' he whispered, laughing to himself, as though there were some hidden significance in the words.

" 'Eddie,' I said with gathering dread, 'tell me what's wrong.'

"Love tilted his head quizzically as he looked at me, like an intelligent animal unable to divine its master's wish. 'Wrong?' Suddenly his features contorted in an unnatural smile which he seemed unable to suppress. It was as though his face were being violated by some external force. His lips drew back over his teeth like clay worked by an invisible sculptor's hands in the violence of first inspiration. Then he began to laugh, just as he had that time at his magic show, and the same sick thrill twisted in my bowels. Only now I understood its cause — the undertone of desperation in that laughter, its compulsion, the utter joylessness of it — all this appeared to me in a flash of terrible clarity. In that instant I knew my original intuition had been right. Your father was mad. Before I had a chance to regain my self-possession, he began to speak.

" 'What's wrong?' he mimicked acidly. 'What's wrong?' He looked off in the air, as though some marvel had flashed dimly before his inner eye. 'Didn't you hear?' he cried in a high, breaking voice. 'I've been promoted!' This set off another peal of manic laughter, only this time broken intermittently by sobs.

" 'Eddie,' I said, with as much calm as I could muster. 'Eddie. . . .'

"But he ignored me and began to ramble wildly. I could only follow him with the greatest difficulty. 'Hsiao,' he said, 'do you ever have a dream and then the dream comes true? I had this dream, a month, six weeks ago. In it I was flying. A dream . . . but it was so damn real. I could taste the stale rubber of my oxygen mask, hear the wind whistling in the open gun barrels. I thought I was alone until I heard the second engine. At first I thought it was David, my wingman, but then I heard the sound of bullets whizzing past my head, ricocheting off the cockpit armor. I turned into a power dive, six thousand feet straight down, like a stone, then I looped and rolled. But when I looked back he was still behind me. I tried everything I knew, but I couldn't shake him. Finally in desperation, not knowing what else to do, I pulled the joystick, turned the nose up and began to climb. I held the throttle open for a solid minute. My heart was drumming in my ears. Any moment I expected to stall out or lose the wings or take a hit in my fuel reservoir and find myself in hell. When I realized I couldn't hear his engines anymore, I looked back. Nothing but blue sky below me. *Ting-hao* — exhilaration. And how!

" 'Then the plane appeared beneath my wing, way, way down. For the first time I saw it clearly. Red suns on the wings. A Zero. Only I couldn't figure out why he'd fallen so far back, for Zeroes are lighter, more maneuverable than our planes and they have an edge in climbing speed. Then through the glass panel of the other cockpit I saw the pilot's face. He shaded his eyes with his hand, searching for me, and I realized he'd lost me in the glare. For I was climbing straight toward the sun. It seemed close now, impossibly close. The brilliance dazzled me. It occurred to me that only my dark glasses had saved me. Against the backdrop of the solar disc I was invisible, completely whited out.

" 'Looking down again, I saw the double suns had miraculously kindled into flames. The plane was burning. The pilot had bailed out, free-falling toward the sea. But it wasn't the Japanese pilot anymore; it was my father. I could see his face, and he was dropping through the blue depths of space toward the world's own curve. He pulled the ripcord of his parachute. But when it opened nothing but a skein of silk magician's handkerchiefs flew out, trailing gracefully behind him like a kite's tail. I wanted to save him. But when I tried, I found I could no longer check my own ascent. There was a smell of burning in the air, like wax and feathers, and when I looked up the last time it was not the sun at all, but God's own face that I was flying into, and last of all it was *my* body that I saw free-falling toward the earth.' Your father's voice was hushed, rapt as he related this to me.

" 'What does it mean?' I asked. 'I don't understand you, Eddie. You're talking wildly.' I took his arm gently and tried to draw him up.

" 'No, no,' he said, pulling away. 'I had this dream, and it came true. Listen to me Hsiao. . . .' As he spoke my name, he looked directly in my eyes, and he was sane again.

" 'It worried me for days. I had a feeling there was something in it I had to understand. Then it hit me. . . .'

"He paused, and I braced myself, expecting some acknowledgment — surprise, disbelief — of the dream's clairvoyant intimation of his father's death, something which would suggest a telepathic bond of sympathy between them. But I had missed my mark.

" 'It was a battle strategy, you see?' Love said eagerly, searching my face for corroboration. 'What else? It was a tactical inspiration, a gift from heaven! Of course, it wasn't new. I'd read about it as a boy in books about the First World War — Richthofen and the German aces — "Hun in the Sun" they called it. Chennault had mentioned it in passing, said it was considered obsolete. But the early-warning system gave it a new lease on life. That first morning I didn't mention it to anyone but David, wanted to try it first and see how well it worked. When we heard *ching-pao,* our wild war symphony — pots, pans, cow bells, bugles, sirens, gongs — we scrambled quick and got in the air. But instead of leveling off at eighteen thousand feet, laying for them at their approach altitude like we'd been doing, we climbed higher, twenty-four thousand, twenty-five, and began to circle, keeping our backs to the sun. Directly in the line of sight between them and it, we did a perfect disappearing act. They never even saw us. When they came, we nose dropped, screaming down on them — God, a P-40 in a power dive's an awesome thing — two hundred, three hundred miles per hour. We racked their bones, butchered them, Hsiao. We ate them raw, blood, brains, and all. They never knew what hit them — not until the very last, after it was too late. Jesus, it was so beautiful. So beautiful. . . .' I remember thinking his eyes were like the tiger's, Sun I, gazing past me into some tropical jungle paradise. Then he refocused on my face.

" 'Don't you see? It's perfect. To begin with, there's the natural advantage you have playing defense. The attacker has to bring it to you. He has no choice but to commit himself. The Japs can fool us about a lot of things, but if they want to disable the airstrip at Kunming, they have to run their bombers over, right? So we know where they'll be, first of all. Secondly, we know their probable approach direction through the early-warning system. It gives us a crucial jump in time. We can be ready and waiting when they get here. All that's left is to somehow maximize the leverage these advantages give us. That's what the dream revealed, a blind spot (*literally!*) which I could use against him, a camouflage he couldn't see through, a sleight of hand so quick no eye could pick it out. . . . Now Chennault wants to give me a promotion. It's funny, don't you think? A promotion?'

"The grotesque irony this idea held for him escaped me, until I reflected on it in the context of his father's death. *A promotion!*

"I should note, Sun I, that, for whatever reason, Love never took that promotion (from a simple flight leader to vice squad commander of the Panda Bears). No one could ever tell me why he turned it down. Perhaps he simply preferred to keep a low profile, disliking the high visibility, and corresponding vulnerability, of active command. Among the Flying Tigers, as elsewhere in the armed forces, there was a dual command hierarchy: one legitimate, based on seniority and rank, another covert, based on innate personal qualities

— charisma, intelligence, courage, inventiveness. Your father naturally belonged to the second. Love perhaps felt he had little to gain from a formal promotion — additional headaches and responsibilities without an appreciable increase in real power.

"But to return. . . . At this point I felt I had to show my hand, to own up to what I, perhaps alone of everyone he was acquainted with in China, knew.

" 'Eddie,' I said, taking a deep breath, 'I read about your father's death. I'm sorry for you, very sorry.'

"I could never have anticipated what happened next. An alarming change came over Love as soon as I spoke these words. He stiffened and grew stone-cold sober. His lips twitched violently, then he blushed as deeply as a woman. I could tell some terrible emotion had seized him, that he was struggling to control it. He glared at me with an intensity that almost made me cower. I could feel its heat. But I could only see the superficial, deep-sea glaze of his dark glasses reflecting my own image back to me, nothing of the eyes that watched me from beneath. He held and held that gaze, spitting me. When the blush passed off, his face became unnaturally pale, livid in fact. Then his expression changed to one of malice. I'll never forget it. He leered like a demon. A scathing irony slathered his next question:

" 'Are you sure you haven't mistaken me for someone else?'

"I shook my head sadly. 'Who else could it be?'

" 'You, Hsiao.' His reply was not so much a question as a verdict. Then he burst into derisive laughter. Getting to his feet, he strode past me menacingly, storming through the gate into the road.

"Ch'iu-yeh followed him, I her, intending to ask him what he meant. But by the time we got there he'd disappeared, leaving behind nothing but a trail of crumbs from the loaf, like those the children in the Western fairy tale dropped after them to find their way back out of the enchanted forest to the safety of their parents' hut."

The gravity and portent in my uncle's expression almost made me miss the irony in this. He seemed to be trying to communicate, through sheer force of concentration, some level of the story which did not accommodate itself to words.

"The significance of this episode puzzled me for a long time, Sun I. That grief for his father's death was responsible for his condition that day on the bridge, I didn't doubt. In fact, from what I knew of Arthur Love, your father's susceptibility to depression seemed evidence of a temperamental link between them. And yet, why had Eddie flown into such a rage at my simple, honest attempt to express commiseration?

"My first inclination was to attribute it to madness. Without a doubt, a certain part of what he'd said — particularly the concluding volley he'd fired at me — was somewhat less, or more, than sane. Considering it more deeply, though, another explanation suggested itself. Could it be that his anger was caused by the fact that I had unearthed, by accident, the secret he had guarded so tenaciously from his friends, and had perhaps left America to forget — the secret of his paternity, the source of his greatest shame? Only as this thought struck home did I comprehend his terrible silence when the others talked of home."

Hsiao took a deep breath, sighed, and sat back in his chair. "And how well I understood Love's problem! As a son he loved his father; as a man he was ashamed. This even bore a certain analogy, albeit vague, to my own situation. Could it be that that was what he'd meant by his last cryptic remark? Certainly he wasn't so naive, and couldn't have considered me so, as to believe he could deceive me further in the matter of his true identity. *I knew who he was!* Having discovered the father, I had discovered the son.

"But there was a crucial difference between us. Lacking guidance, Love had struck out blindly against his father, and, through him, against his own heritage, his own history . . . against the whole of the past, running away from what he was, to fight in China. He didn't realize this rebellion was a self-defeating one, that maiming his history, he thereby maimed himself; losing it, he lost himself. With Art Love's death, recouping that loss became impossible. Some internal organ — perhaps his soul itself — had been ripped from your father's side, still warm and bleeding, leaving an open wound he'd have to carry in his flesh forever. It was this, I believe, which eventually drove him across the border into madness, into the witch's forest. Having entered it, he could never leave. For he had destroyed the only way which leads back out: the map which is knowledge of the past.

"I am no psychologist, Sun I, but in my opinion your father's psychic self-mutilation was corroborated at the physical level by the incident of his crash. It occurred less than a week after he'd learned of Art Love's death, and I can't help thinking that there was something more at work than simply the 'chance of war.' While I don't believe there was anything deliberate or premeditated about it, I'd be less hesitant to accept another hypothesis: that some interior conflict which had gone unresolved too long finally erupted, enacting itself in the external world as fate.

"He was on a routine strafing mission with his four-plane element. They were north of Kunming, over the river somewhere on the border between Yunnan and Szechwan, not far from Ken Kuan in fact. They had just attacked several cargo-carrying sampans when they caught sight of a contingent of Japanese planes — long-range bombers escorted by eighteen Zero fighter-interceptors, returning, apparently, from a run over Chungking. Taken by surprise, at a large numerical disadvantage, the Americans were further imperiled by their relative altitude. The Japanese had the 'high ground.' Fortunately, Love's element wasn't seen immediately. The four of them climbed directly into the bomber formation before the Zeroes and, not expecting assault from the ground, were able to regroup and retaliate. Two of the bombers were shot down on the first pass — confirmed hits, one of them your father's. That was where the trouble began. Eddie's wingman, David Bateson, told me that the Zeroes intercepted them at about twenty-two thousand feet — six of them, directly out of the sun. He peeled off to the right, your father to the left, stooping to pick up speed. What happened in between, Bateson said he never knew. When he caught sight of Love again, his plane was spiraling toward the river out of control, trailing a plume of jet-black smoke. As he watched, flames began to dance along the fusilage, then the wings disintegrated. He tried to see a chute, he said, but the smoke had become too thick. He couldn't be sure whether your father had bailed out in time or not.

"When they returned to Kunming, word was radioed to the Chinese ground forces in the area, primarily Communist guerillas, to keep a lookout for a downed American pilot. After a week, when nothing came back, Love was listed Missing In Action and presumed dead.

"He wasn't though, not quite. Apparently he hadn't used up all his nine lives. (Keep count though, Sun I. In the series of near-misses that follows, he must have squandered half a dozen.) Though disoriented and severely burned, he managed to get out in time, doing a flip over the side at the last moment. When he came out of his tuck, he told Bateson later, he saw the vertical stabilizer of his plane swimming toward him like a dark fin through the air. 'Closed my eyes and pissed all over myself.' Bateson laughed his head off, repeating Love's remark. A second later the chute popped open, jolting him in the harness. Floating, safe, your father looked up and saw the Zero plunging toward him. Apparently the Japanese had a nasty way of flying under enemy parachutists and lopping their legs off, not aiming to kill, simply to maim. 'Real precision flying' was the droll gem from your father's lips. A burst of machine-gun fire evaporated his chute. One of the slugs caught him from the back and passed through his abdomen at a skewed angle. Amazingly, it missed all his major arteries and organs and only chipped off a piece of a thoracic vertebra — the spinous process, that delicate little wishbone in the spine. Unconscious at that point, your father plummeted two hundred feet into the Yangtze. A group of Lolo tribesmen who had been watching the dogfight from the bank and had witnessed his spectacular descent fished him from the water.

"The Lolos were traditionally a hunting people, but they had turned to the cultivation of the garden poppy, *Papaver somniferum,* as a cash crop, bartering the mud for guns and notions. Though primitive, they had an enterprising streak, like all Chinese. Love was carrying Chinese currency in his flight jacket as well as a valuable .44 sidearm. Exchanging services for goods, the Lolos appropriated these items and undertook to nurse your father back to health. They used herbal remedies to treat his burns, giving him large quantities of opium to eat as an analgesic.

"Love convalesced with them for two weeks, accompanying them on hunts as his strength returned. Later, absurd rumors sprang up about this episode. Love was said to have received initiation into the tribe. An exchange of vows, a shared cup of blood — I don't know what. Eventually he set out accompanied by a guide. Traveling by night, they crossed the lines to our side, arriving at a remote Communist outpost. During that trek he discovered this monastery, staying, I believe, overnight. His final entry into Kunming was little short of triumphal.

"As we might have expected, Love didn't say much about the incident, mostly jokes like the ones Bateson recounted. I heard a few of them myself, and they disturbed me. His humor had a quality of nihilistic abandon. About the opium, he said, deadpan, 'If I'd known what it was, I wouldn't have eaten it. I just thought it was straight dung.' He also said he suspected the Lolos had some 'Hebrew blood'; after all, they had nursed him back to health on 'chicken soup.' 'Chicken soup?' I asked. 'Sure. Only they have an unusual way of preparing it. They cut the head off a live hen and turn her upside down over a bowl, then sip at leisure. Sounds disgusting, I know, but with a little Worcestershire and black pepper, I think it could grow on you.' " Hsiao shook his head.

"Though your father's adventure made him a popular hero, to me, Sun I, it was resonant with tragic implications. I was uniquely situated to understand Love's guilt at the news of his father's death, and how it might have led him, however unconsciously, straight into the sights of that Japanese pilot. If only he and his father had been able to reconcile their differences, as my father and I, after many false starts, were finally able to do. I believe it was simply a matter of the difference in our social backgrounds. Reared in a wiser, more humane tradition, I was able to put aside my antipathy and accord my father the degree of respect and obedience his position as supreme family head entitled him to. Confucianism enabled me to do this. Few have fully understood that this truth resides at the core of the Master's teaching, illuminating all the rest — that we must honor our parents *regardless of their personal merits,* for they are the sacred vessels which contain the balm of social continuity. It is a lofty and difficult truth. To the uninitiated or undiscerning it may seem repulsive, even fanatical, a form of spiritual servitude, bootlicking, blind devotion. But it is a moral paradox of the highest order. Whatever China is, whatever she has accomplished (and an unbroken cultural tradition of five thousand years is no mean accomplishment), it is inextricably bound up with this paradox, and the social principle which arises from it. Filial piety is the cement which binds the human world together. If it is forgotten or neglected, as the Irish poet whom your father fancied observes, 'Things fall apart; the center cannot hold; Mere anarchy is loosed upon the world.' I learned this late, Sun I. My case is not exemplary. But at least I learned it. I fear your father never did.

"But Love was conditioned by the values of the West — its bravado, its aggressiveness, its unembarrassed worship of power and achievement regardless of the means employed to gain them — and he must have regarded his father as a rather pathetic creature. For my part, Art Love was one of the more hopeful figures in the pantheon of American finance, if for no other reason than that he transcended its grubbing, self-interested values. But your father's disrespect was doubtless only heightened by the American disgust with age, and by the peculiar and disheartening antagonism which exists there between the generations. There it is not as it is here in China, Sun I. The young are not encouraged to set themselves humbly to glean their parents' greater knowledge and experience of the world, but rather to oppose them and depose them if they can. The generations are condemned ceaselessly to make war on one another. What one has labored to build up, the next labors to destroy, constructing its new kingdom on the ruins of the old, its walls made out of bricks in which are hidden, like fossils, charred bits of human bones. This process bears a disconcerting similarity to the 'boom and bust' cycle of American capitalism. This self-destructive behavior is deeply ingrained in the American character, and has been virtually institutionalized, in business, as I said, in their 'democratic' government — where no sooner are leaders installed and given time to establish priorities and initiatives than they are summarily removed by the electorate in favor of something 'new and better' — even in their religion, with its metaphor of death and resurrection. You see, Sun I, it is this eternal dissatisfaction with reality, with what is, that causes the restless yearning so characteristic of America and Americans. This is why she is ceaselessly destroying herself and attempting to rise from the ashes, like the phoenix. This is the central promise of Christianity. But what is it but sleight of hand? It allows the development of no cumulative tradition such as we have in China. To me, Sun I, America is the precise and chilling image of what hell must be, a labor like that of the mythical Sisyphus, who rolled his stone up a steep mountain only to have it fall back each time as he neared the top. The American Sisyphus has reached his peak over and over and undermined the stone himself. The pathos, the futility . . . tragic." Hsiao sighed with hard compassion. "Eddie Love was just this sort of figure."

The genuine regret in these pronouncements only enhanced the respect I felt for my uncle. I could see that he was capable of pity, and had compassion for the thing he hated. But his hatred was something I couldn't share. Its intensity seemed a little skewed. I was frightened and put off. I had never heard America spoken of in such scathing terms before — as a "hell" — only as a kind of paradise; and I couldn't help wondering if his condemnations weren't bound up with a private need. For the most part I had listened to him passively, even credulously; but whenever he'd begun to speak about America, or his father, or my own (especially then), whenever that wry expression of distaste, so like a smile, had disfigured his lips, I'd experienced an uneasiness — an uneasiness which deepened into positive discomfort and even pain as he moved into his final crescendo of declamation. Most of all I bridled at what seemed to me his overly neat synopsis of my father. Its tone of self-congratulation made it suspect. And how could I instantly dismiss twenty years of passionate adulation, even on the basis of disclaimers as authoritative as these? When it came to the narration of the "facts," I had listened eagerly. Hsiao's reminiscences had only strengthened my conviction that my father was an extraordinary being. But these very facts belied, for me, the interpretation he'd made of them.

Why conjure madness to explain my father's actions? Nothing that he'd done seemed particularly mad to me — eccentric perhaps, indelibly marked with his inimitable personal signature — but not mad. I was particularly suspicious of his claim that my father's unconscious self-destructiveness had caused the plane crash. Perhaps it was simply easier for Hsiao to dismiss my father as unbalanced than to face up to the truth Love had obliquely pointed out: that Hsiao viewed the world through the lens of his own preoccupation, his private anguish as a son. This is why he'd misunderstood my father's remark, "Are you sure you haven't mistaken me for someone else? . . . You, Hsiao." It seemed plain enough to me. And I guessed that Hsiao's misunderstanding had more to do with his ambivalance toward his own father than with any so-called madness in mine.

This is why, despite my respect for him, I thought my uncle presumptuous. "*I knew who he was!* Having discovered the father, I had discovered the son." I didn't think so. Perhaps I was guilty of the same sin, of importing a bias into my judgment — a bias as deep and ineradicable as my own fundamental conviction about the world — but I most passionately, most *vehemently* demurred!

Chapter 7

"Now, Sun I," Hsiao broke in on my reverie, "without meaning to sound callous — for I legitimately liked your father, as I think you must know by now — I thought his crash had solved my problems."

My look of disbelief and horror prompted him to qualify his statement. "I mean vis-à-vis Ch'iu-yeh, of course." He shook his head. "It was only a postponement. That day beside the pool it would have been inappropriate to sound out Love's intentions toward her. His grief was paramount and had to be respected. Later, with his return from his sojourn with the Lolos, things became no easier. Love was the hero of the moment; admirers thronged around him. I hesitated to prick the pleasant bubble of his celebrity, however equivocal it seemed to me, with a pin of possibly unfounded suspicion. Nothing unseemly, certainly nothing irrevocable, had occurred between my sister and this man. At least, nothing I knew of then.

"Compounding my difficulties, a cooling off, subtle but unmistakable, occurred in our relations from that time — more precisely, in Love's feelings toward me. I noticed a new formality in his manner, behind which he protected himself from my undesired partnership in his secret. This saddened me, for though I had my doubts about his motives toward Ch'iu-yeh, I wished him well. The man interested me extremely, and my fascination had only been increased by the latest round of incidents, particularly the crash, with its suggestion of submerged psychological distress. I had an almost scientific interest in Love, like some researcher investigating one of nature's rarest breeds, perhaps a monster. Beneath this interest though, I felt a keen personal sympathy for him, more than sympathy, almost identification." Hsiao shrugged sadly. "In spite of it, the distance between us grew. Eddie was useless to me in my campaign to dampen what had kindled between him and Ch'iu-yeh. I had to look elsewhere.

"My staunchest ally, my only ally, was my mother. 'Behind the lines' at home, she was better situated to observe developments. Since Love's return, she told me, almost all his free time had been spent at the house with Ch'iu-yeh. All the signs suggested that the possibility of romance which had piqued and tantalized them at their first encounter was now igniting into something real. Love's idle time contributed; while convalescing, he didn't fly for several weeks. My mother was especially distressed by the license Father gave Ch'iu-yeh to regulate her own activities. She and Love were allowed to take long walks together unchaperoned. When my father saw them holding hands — a sight which would have mortified any other parent in China — he smiled benevolently and nodded his approval. All this upset me greatly. I felt Ch'iu-yeh was being granted freedoms she had not been educated to respect or to defend. Since she had been unable to impress on Father the possible consequences of his liberality, my mother begged me to put away my pride and speak to him. Till then, for reasons I'm sure you can appreciate, I had resolved not to betray Love's secret to anyone. But with Ch'iu-yeh's happiness at stake, I felt it best to tell my father everything. I was confident he'd see the trouble and discourage the relationship before it had a chance to ruin her life.

"But I had left one crucial factor out of my calculations. For that reason my disclosure produced an effect precisely opposite the one I'd hoped. As he listened to my revelation, my father became thoughtful. Sickening with suspicion, I saw as I went on that his eyes grew brighter with a calculating light I knew too well. For all his weakness, I had not expected this. I'm ashamed to say it even now. The business prospects such a matrimonial connection opened proved too much for him.

"So rather than putting an end to their relationship, my father, without letting on that he knew Love's secret, subtly encouraged it. How I despised him." Hsiao drew a deep breath. "Yet later he suffered, later he wept 'tears of blood.' The only good that came out of the whole incident was his eventual reclamation. Father finally disavowed the Westernisms he'd accepted so blindly and uncritically as articles of faith, and which had been responsible for the whole tragedy. But his recantation came too late.

"As I had failed with him, there was only one hope left. Ch'iu-yeh listened patiently to what I had to say, but I could see that it had no effect, except perhaps to strengthen her resolve to persevere and eventually prevail over 'misunderstanding and persecution,' like the heroines of the novels she had read. In her eyes there was a look of unutterable joy in her own love, and pity for me because I couldn't comprehend the deep mystery in which she was immersed.

"It was then that I first noticed the change taking place in her, and silently marveled at it, wondering if it were due solely to the emotion she was feeling or if there were something more involved. She had become unusually taciturn, though not with gloom. It was as though some fine sunset were taking place within her, spilling its warm, rich colors over her soul, a glow I seemed to recognize but couldn't place, like a memory of a past life. A new candor appeared in her expression, and her voice grew deeper, husky at the edges, as if she were undergoing a sea change, being swept out by the tide into the deepest waters of her femininity, away from the safe, shallow bar where she had loitered as a girl.

"It was then that she began to sew. Spinning raw silk to thread, she dyed it bloodred and wove it into damask — a labyrinth meander pattern. When this was done (and she worked quickly), she retired to the privacy of her room and began embroidering. She kept her purpose secret, and yet we knew. . . . For the color red is ritually worn to celebrate two occasions only: marriage and birth. (You may not be aware of it, Sun I, but *Fu,* the 'happy' sign, is the first element of the word 'red' — a sartorial pun deeply embedded in our ritual.) You see, your mother was working on her *p'ao,* the bridal robe she intended to wear to celebrate her wedding to Eddie Love.

"At least that was our assumption at the time. And in part I still believe it. Yet certain things suggest that from the start she knew it would never come to pass. I've often wondered if she wasn't aware, even then, of her condition. All along she may have intended the robe to be a legacy to you, Sun I, your birthright. The simpler explanation may suffice; yet one detail about the robe struck me when I first saw it, much later, and has always seemed significant. Your mother worked in the *Fu* of happiness in several places, but the *Shou* sign, which always accompanies it and means 'long life,' is absent. It is as though she knew that she would not live long, not even long enough to wear it." My uncle's voice faltered and he shielded his face with his hand. When he looked up again it was not directly at me, but off somewhere into the distance, into the past.

"How long things continued in this state I don't really know — two months, perhaps closer to three. In my memory there is a haze upon this time, a sense of weightlessness and drift. For despite ourselves I think we were all intoxicated by their love, and swept away into the dream. Toward the end, even I, briefly, allowed myself to hope.

"But the inevitable came, as it had to. One day I saw a notice posted in the marketplace. I should have anticipated it, but the news took me completely by surprise. For fate to work with such insidious cunning . . . it was too deep for me. The irony was that this should have been an occasion for rejoicing. Reading it, however, my heart sank, thinking of Ch'iu-yeh. The notice announced that America had entered the war. The AVG was being disbanded on July Fourth — Independence Day — to be replaced by the regular air force. After holding out so long and so valiantly, the Flying Tigers, the originals, were going home, or were free to."

•

"As soon as I read this, I set out on foot for my father's house. Ch'iu-yeh had to know. It was still quite early in the morning, and the dew which had settled the dust of the road during the night had not yet burned away. This might have made my walk pleasant, had I been engaged in a more lighthearted mission.

But even then I had taken on the role in which I come to you today, that of messenger of woe — a part I hope to play no more.

"When I reached the top of the long grade which rose away from the paddies on the outskirts of the city, my heart was beating fast. I stopped to catch my breath and looked from that high vantage over the irregular shapes of the fields, spreading like a patchwork quilt in earthen colors — pale green and ocher, honey-gold — down toward the vast expanse of Tien Chih Lake, its muddy waters rippling in an early breeze which presently reached me. Peasants were already at work in the fields, tilling. I could see them, tiny flecks of brilliant color, moving through the somber tones of the winter wheat which rose chest-high around them, or going in tandem with the larger white dots of their oxen, like the sails of boats far out at sea, turning the fallow soil. There was a stillness and a timeless peace in the scene which went far to soothe my heart, a sense of permanence and imperturbability which no vicissitude, not even war it seemed, could alter.

"But even as I stood taking such solace from the contemplation of the far horizon, I heard a rumbling overhead, and looking up I saw Love's squadron, the Panda Bears, flying in tight formation like a flock of geese, high up near the sun. Only terrible geese they were, man-eaters with the barbarous mouths of carnivores, nightmarish creatures out of hell's own bestiary. The peasants too had stopped what they were doing and stood staring dumbly up at the vision passing overhead, shading their eyes. I was like them, a slack-jawed peasant standing in the paddies of the Middle Ages as the terrible epiphany of the future appeared in the skies above our heads, descending on us out of another world beyond our power to comprehend — like magic — in the guise of an American pursuit plane with its ordnance and incendiaries. It was at that moment that it finally dawned on me in full clarity that the Americans who had come to liberate us were our greatest enemies. The human inertia of China was too powerful to be deflected out of its true course for long by an invading army of Japanese; as in the past, we would prevail over our enemies, conquering the conquerors by assimilation. But who would save us from our friends? For somehow the Americans, perhaps without even intending to do so, had bought our complicity in their grand design to remake us in their image. Unlike the Japanese, they worked from the inside, undermining the foundations, restructuring desire itself. And my poor sister was at the threshold of the new dispensation, longing to cross over."

•

"When I arrived home things were just beginning to stir. I passed Chiang Po in the garden, working beneath the eastern hedgerow. Clipping pale yellow chrysanthemums with his bright, stainless shears, he laid them in a shallow wicker basket. He raised his head as I approached and glowered at me an instant, then went back to work. Only then did I finally realize the answer to the question that had puzzled us before. He was Love's secret emissary. A sensation like a bad taste attended this discovery, for it occurred to me that the flowers which Love sent Ch'iu-yeh came from our own garden.

"I went straight to your mother's room, and tapped at the door. Receiving no answer, I made bold to enter. She was lying on her featherbed, the coverlet pulled back, her dark, heavy hair unbound for sleeping. It lay spread around her like a calligraphic figure written in the blackest ink on the white linen of the sheet, an enveloping hieroglyph which held the encoded message of her fate, only written in a language that I couldn't comprehend. For a few minutes I simply stood beside the bed. Beads of perspiration dotted her hairline. Her lids were dancing with the underlife of her eyes as she flitted through the interior landscape of a dream. Shadows and drifts of sunlight crossed her face, and her lips moved silently, as though she were listening to some old, familiar song and mouthing the words.

"When I touched her, she opened her eyes immediately and sat up. I took her hand. 'I have something to tell you,' I said softly. She stared at me as though not comprehending, and then a vertiginous terror crossed her face. She squeezed my hand hard. I nodded, but then to defuse her alarm, which prior mishap had made virtually reflexive, added quickly, 'He's all right.'

"She slumped back on the pillow and closed her eyes. 'The AVG's disbanding,' I told her. 'They're going home, Ch'iu-yeh. There was a notice in the market.' I waited for her to respond, but she said nothing. 'Did you hear?'

"As though making a tremendous effort, your mother opened her eyes and looked at me. There was weariness and frustration in that look, as well as pity. But more than that, there was a kind of . . . what shall I call it? Sad amusement, a wistful distance, as of someone looking down at the world from a great height, after having already left it.

" 'I know,' she whispered, in a tone which intimated, beneath its film of superficial weariness, something akin to rapture, and with the same expression on her face that I had seen the night she first met Love.

"I gaped at her, stupid with disbelief. 'You know!' I was stunned, Sun I, absolutely stunned. 'But how?' I demanded when I finally found my voice. 'How could you know?'

"She shook her head. 'It doesn't matter. I know. I've always known.' She searched my face. 'You still don't see, do you?'

" 'No I don't!' I cried. 'I don't see at all!'

"Your mother sighed and averted her head. With a flick of her hand, as though brushing off a summer fly, she waved me off. As she regarded the open window, her expression became very calm and very distant, like the mountains in that landscape, and like them, very cold. Now I ask myself if somehow she had foreseen the end, and forgiven everything in advance."

•

"Sun I, I cannot reproach myself for having interfered. My intentions were strictly honorable." His voice faltered. "Yet now I can see that in every instance my brokerage made the situation worse, exciting my father's greed, and estranging first Love, then Ch'iu-yeh. Yes, after this incident she too began to shy away from me. Increasingly impotent, increasingly anxious, I found myself looking on helplessly as the entanglements became more passionate and more irreversible.

"Another month went by without external developments. Like a fixture in our midst which had always been there and always would be, the AVG showed no signs of demobilizing.

"The only discernible change in the situation was that taking place within Ch'iu-yeh. Inexorably the transformation proceeded. I don't know when it finally occurred to me that what was happening to her was not merely, or purely, a spiritual change, but a physical one as well, a change excited by the sudden flood of hormones into her bloodstream as her body prepared for the hard, incredible mystery of birth. Perhaps it was that afternoon in the garden; I stumbled on them unwittingly as they met for what must have been the last time, though I doubt either of them knew it.

"It was late, near dusk, as it had been the first time. They were sitting side by side near the spot where Love had stood that day delivering his act. Leaning toward her, his hand lightly touching her bare arm, he whispered in her ear. Ch'iu-yeh's eyes were closed, her throat and cheeks flushed. She was smiling, but diffidently, and the tears of some recent altercation were not yet dry upon her cheeks. With both hands she pressed a flower to her bosom — a chrysanthemum. One by one she broke off the white petals and cast them away into the pool, saying something softly to herself which I could not make out.

"I watched her pluck the final petal, her eyes still closed. Turning the disfigured flower in her hand, she searched it gently with her fingers, as the blind search the faces of those they love. Then her smile disappeared; she grew pale and began to grope and tear at the lifeless stalk. The bright petals had begun to sink into the dark, tannin-stained waters of the pool, like tea leaves to the bottom of a cup. Only now no oracle was required to reveal the future.

"Ch'iu-yeh suddenly sobbed and stood up, almost stumbling as she wrenched herself free from Love's grasp. 'It was only a game,' I heard him cry out, trying to appease her. But she only sobbed again and ran harder. Something in her motion as she ran, some heaviness and languor which made her movements seem like drunken caricatures of themselves, brought home to me the fact that she was pregnant. Beyond all shadow of a doubt, beyond all hope, I knew.

"As she ran past, she caught sight of me and stopped. I have never forgotten her look: like someone waking from a dream. The terror in her eyes was inexpressible and bottomless. I think she had finally realized that he had never loved her, and never would — not in the way she dreamed and had required. I reached out to comfort her, but she ran on. I hesitated, then followed her toward the house. As I entered the door, I turned to cast one final glance at Love. But he had already disappeared."

•

"When my father's eyes were finally opened to the truth — or rather, narrowed sufficiently that he could see things in a realistic light — he became desperate over Ch'iu-yeh's condition. This served as a pretext for our reconciliation.

"One day he summoned me home. Alternately screaming like a maniac, biting his hands in rage, and blubbering like a child, he informed me of Ch'iu-yeh's 'dishonor' — a word which had long been absent from his vocabulary on account of its unfashionableness, its 'retrograde associations.' Love, presuming on her youth and innocence, with all the vicious, premeditated cunning of a practiced seducer, had despoiled her, slaked his lust and cast her off, he said, painting the picture in the most opprobrious, and most obvious, tones, though not necessarily the truest. The fault was all his, he went on, for having such a trusting heart, for expecting others to abide by the same code of honor he himself observed. If only he had had an inkling of the essential duplicity of the man! (My father had conveniently forgotten the warning I had given him.) But Love came from such a good — by which he meant rich — family! Who could have dreamed? And what was wealth without honor? Et cetera, et cetera. That Love was without honor was practically a foregone conclusion now, though Father had not previously sounded out Love's intentions. This, I quickly saw, was where I came in. All my father's hopes of 'saving face,' he said, he pinned on me.

" 'But what a fine son-in-law he would have made!' he moaned finally, capping off half an hour's incessant abuse, most of it shamelessly slanderous, with this lament.

"This farce disgusted me. My initial anger toward Love was dissipated by my disillusionment. Once again unwanted sympathy welled up in me as I was forced to consider the deep chagrin Love's own father's inanity, or perceived inanity, must have caused him, a chagrin made almost unendurable by the ineradicable filial love within his heart. This made your father's grief and loneliness palpable to me, and it was only by calling Ch'iu-yeh's image to mind that I was able to remember where my true allegiance lay.

"Purely out of duty, then, without the slightest expectation of success, I went to the barracks to confront Love. The toll the previous days had taken on him surprised me. His eyes had lost their luster, and there were great blue shadows underneath them, whether from nights spent on alert, or from insomnia caused by guilt, I don't know. He was sitting listlessly in the 'butt room' of the duty shack, smoking idly, playing solitaire. His eyes brightened when he saw me, then the gloom settled back as he realized why I'd come. His face grew strained, and he looked fixedly down at the cards, avoiding my gaze.

" 'Pull up a chair,' he offered.

"Under the circumstances his hospitality was offensive. I continued standing where I was, searching his face in silence.

" 'Come on, Hsiao,' he said in a weary voice. 'Don't be that way.'

"He pulled out a chair for me himself, and I conceded.

"He continued to shuffle and reshuffle the cards. 'Pick one,' he said abruptly, thrusting the deck at me.

"I gave him a reproachful look, but he refused to acknowledge it. He seemed insistent, so I played along.

" 'Want me to tell you what it is?'

" 'I suppose you're going to anyway, right?'

" 'Queen of spades,' he said, ignoring my retort.

"He was right. He took the card back and reinserted it, shuffling and fanning out the deck again. 'Pick another.'

"I made no move to comply.

" 'Pick another!' he ordered, waving the deck importunately in my face.

"I did. Again it was the queen of spades.

"For the first time since we'd begun, Love met my eyes. 'Always comes up the Bitch,' he said.

"Then he laughed, just as he had that afternoon when he'd astounded everyone by pulling the hand grenade from his top hat. The expression on his face, however, was anything but amused — more like a grimace. And the sound that issued from his throat was not the exuberant peal I expected, but rather a high, thin cry, like nothing so much as the scream the rabbit had made that same afternoon as he dangled it in his hand.

"Revulsion turned my stomach. 'That's very clever, Eddie.'

" 'No it isn't, the deck is stacked,' he managed to get out between hysterical contractions. He wiped the tears from his eyes and turned the deck over, spreading it out on the table. Every other card was a black queen.

" 'I had it made up special,' he explained, 'for playing Hearts.'

" 'You're mad,' I told him, wanting to vomit.

"He shrugged indifferently.

"Neither of us spoke. He continued convulsing silently. Regaining control at last, he set out on a new tack.

" 'I guess you heard we're going home.' I looked up and challenged his eyes. With his cigarette hanging from his lip, he leaned forward and took his wallet from his back pocket. 'Let me show you something.'

"To my surprise, he produced a photograph. I thought then that perhaps, finally, he was just like all the rest — only more so . . . yes, more so. This idea gave me pleasure sweeter than any revenge.

" 'This is my fiancée,' he explained, sliding a picture across the table for my inspection, as though dealing another card from his deck.

"The girl was about the same age as my sister, but her hair was long and silken, and yellow as corn tassels, not black like Ch'iu-yeh's, and her eyes were blue and smiling like a summer sky, not dark and full of sorrow.

" 'What do you think?' he asked, smiling irrepressibly.

"My sense of vindication vanished. That 'more so' was too much. At that moment your father seemed the literal incarnation of that exuberant young demigod filching the apples, oblivious to the sorrow he occasioned — a brief regret, then off again to new conquests, new diversions. I was stymied by his naiveté.

" 'She's lovely,' I said honestly, with pain.

" 'Isn't she?' He leaned across to give the picture a closer inspection, pleasurably verifying what he already knew.

" 'But it would be better for her to forget she ever knew you, Eddie,' I told him, forcing myself to recover the initiative.

"He stiffened in his chair.

" 'She'll recover in time,' I continued. 'Ch'iu-yeh, I'm afraid, will not.'

" 'Don't say that, Hsiao. Your little sister is stronger than you know. She'll get over it.'

" 'Let me understand you then,' I retorted formally. 'Your intention is to abandon her?'

"Love sighed and shook his head. 'Try to put yourself in my shoes, Hsiao. You've been to America. You know how it would be viewed there.'

" 'Does honor vary so widely with latitude?' I asked scathingly. I had anticipated the argument and contrived the pun beforehand.

" 'Yeah, yeah, that's all well and good,' he minced, 'but Hsiao, you know as well as I do it wouldn't be approved. In America "mixed marriages" aren't thought of kindly. We'd be ostracized.'

" 'You mean to say people would consider it a debasement of your blood to take a "squaw" wife.' My anger flared despite my resolution to control it.

" 'Now don't take it that way,' he objected. "It's not that *I* feel like that. Others might though.'

" 'What do you care what others think?'

" 'I have to live with them. You don't.'

" 'Why not stay here in China then, since you're so sensitive to public opinion? Here I imagine the only discrimination you'd encounter would be in your favor.'

"From the surprised look with which he greeted this suggestion, I could tell he'd never even seriously considered the possibility.

" 'You could play the Great White Hunter,' I couldn't resist adding vengefully.

"He pondered before replying. 'No,' he said at last, shaking his head sadly, but with conviction, 'I could never be happy here.'

"I laughed bitterly. 'What about my sister's happiness?'

"I handed him back the photograph. 'Think about it, Eddie. Think about it hard. You've wronged them both. But fortunately it's still in your power to undo the greater of those wrongs. I don't need to tell you what you have to do. I will say this, though. If you go back, you wrong this girl a second time, Ch'iu-yeh much more deeply. Everything else you've done can still be forgiven. . . . After that, no redemption.'

"There was an expression of such fierce unhappiness on his face that I almost pitied him. But he said nothing.

" 'Well, Eddie,' I sighed, rising to go, 'who knows? Perhaps, despite yourself, you've saved Ch'iu-yeh from the worst fate of all — the misery of living with a man like you.'

"After that I expected never to see Love again. I imagined that when his discharge came he'd run as far and as fast as his legs could carry him, never pausing so much as to catch his breath until he'd put half the world between him and his shame. Then in the safe, familiar context of his home, he would proceed, by degrees, to forget about it, until it came to seem no more than a bad dream, or a joke in doubtful taste. In the end he'd look back on it with pride as a testament to his virility and charm, his power over women.

"But as he had in so much else, he surprised me in this. He made me realize again how little I really knew him, what he answered to, what moved him. For me, Sun I, your father was always like that top hat I had seen him delving into the first time I laid eyes on him. And I never knew what would come out of it — a rabbit, or a hand grenade."

•

"Just before the Americans left, Chiang Kai-shek declared a holiday in their honor, National Aviation Day. There was a parade through the center of the city, followed by a presentation ceremony in which they were all decorated with the Special Grand Cordon of the Blue Sky and White Sun, the highest military honor a foreigner could receive. The Generalissimo, in his white dress uniform, a heavy saber clanking at his side suspended from a black silk sash, walked along the platform taking each man's hand in turn, bowing formally. He held his hat against his body, pinned beneath his arm, his proud head bowed in deference and gratitude. Mme Chiang followed at a distance, smiling her brilliant, easy smile, chatting with the pilots in her Texan English ('shooting the breeze,' she might have said) as she pinned the medals on their breasts. I watched from somewhere near the middle of the crowd, and when they came to Love I thought, what a strange thing a man's heart is. Immaculate in war, yet he had betrayed the most intimate and compelling trust of all. Who could expound this paradox to me? Surely the gods mock us in such men.

"As Mme Chiang pinned the award on his lapel — right where the trick chrysanthemum that started everything had been — I caught Love's eye. His face was flushed with pride. Though slightly peaked, he seemed to be convalescing nicely from the inner wound I'd tried so hard to sear him with. I turned around and started to push my way through the crowd, suddenly on the verge of tears.

"I hadn't gone very far, however, when I felt a hand on my shoulder: it was Love. He was panting.

" 'I had to run to catch you. Listen to me, Hsiao.' He paused to catch his breath. His face was glowing with exertion and the irrepressible happiness of one returning home after a long absence. He appeared extremely beautiful at that moment, and his beauty was unendurable.

" 'I have nothing to say to you,' I told him as a coldness settled on my heart. Within that coldness though, Sun I, fear prickled; and I knew that fear was for myself, because I cared for him, who should have been my enemy.

" 'This won't take long,' he preempted me. 'I know what you must think of me, Hsiao.'

" 'Do you, Eddie?' I wondered silently. 'Do you really?'

" 'Perhaps you have a right to. I just want you to know I'm truly sorry for what's happened. I never wanted things to turn out this way. I've thought about it though, and I've decided that staying here and marrying Ch'iu-yeh would only make things worse. She'd never forgive me; I'd never forgive myself. No one would be happy.'

" 'Happiness again,' I retorted cynically. 'Why should you expect to be? You act as though you assumed happiness were some kind of basic right.'

"Surprise and doubt, and a flickering of irony to match my own, played about his lips, threatening a smile. But when he saw that I was serious, his look darkened into earnestness.

" 'I do,' he said, with a beautiful, grave smile. 'What else is there?'

"I searched his face for the least trace of impertinence, but it was entirely sober. It came home to me then for the first time how young he was, and his dignity and candor moved me, despite myself. The spectacle of such fine instincts in the service of such awful naiveté about the world struck me as imponderably tragic. Distilled into its essence, I think it was this about America that so exasperated us, the rest of us — the old world, or worlds — and at the same time, paradoxically, inspired us with a vision of redemption.

"But I was too hurt, too combative, to yield to such emotions. 'That's right,' I said scornfully. 'I forgot about the Declaration of Independence. It's guaranteed.'

" 'Hsiao,' he said quietly, ignoring my remark, 'there's no other way.'

" 'Why did you stop me?' I spat out, angry and impatient. 'All this was established before. Does it give you pleasure to repeat the scene?'

"He shook his head sadly. 'No. I came to ask a favor.'

"I stared at him in disbelief. He nodded gravely.

" 'What can you possibly want from me?'

" 'It concerns the child.'

" 'The child!' I was astounded. 'What business is that of yours?'

" 'I want to do what I can,' he explained. 'I feel it's my responsibility.'

" 'You feel a responsibility toward the child, but not the mother? You'll have to excuse my obtuseness, Eddie, but I can't understand that. Explain it to me.'

" 'Forgive me, Hsiao. The child is innocent; Ch'iu-yeh made a choice.'

"I winced at this, but held my tongue. A long pause ensued in which I measured him with silent, tense ferocity.

" 'I've always liked you, Hsiao,' he said at last.

" 'What is this favor?' I coldly cut him off.

"Love sighed. 'I've made arrangements with the abbot of a monastery.'

" 'A monastery! What are you thinking of? This isn't Catholic Europe in the Middle Ages, you know.'

" 'Do you have any better ideas?' His eyes flashed at me for the first time during our conversation.

"To my chagrin, I didn't.

" 'Well?'

"I was silent.

"Love apparently considered my perplexity a vindication. A hint of animation appeared in his face.

" 'Besides, Hsiao' — he switched on the old jovial tone he'd habitually used with me before things had come to such grief — 'this is really a swell place.' He grinned.

" '*Swell!*' I repeated incredulously, groaning with disgust. 'Exactly what do you know about Chinese monasteries, Eddie, if you don't mind my asking?'

" 'Well, I stayed in one in Szechwan after I was shot down over there. Remember?'

" 'This is the first I've heard of it.'

" 'You'd like it there, Hsiao.' He smiled in dreamy remembrance. 'The abbot is a wonderful old guy, a real *rara avis,* if you know what I mean. As a matter of fact, in a strange way he sort of reminded me of my . . .' Your father halted abruptly, but I saw his face darken as his mind, carried by inertia, followed down this train of thought.

" 'What sort of monastery is it?' I asked quietly.

"He roused himself from his abstraction. 'Guess,' he said, smiling.

" 'For God's sake, Eddie, this isn't a game.'

" 'It's obvious,' he hinted, ignoring my reproach. He winked at me.

"I considered his levity in such a matter outrageous. But by this time I'd learned to humor him. 'Buddhist, I imagine.'

" 'Wrong,' he said.

" 'Taoist then.'

"He replied with a playful, exaggerated nod.

" 'Well?' His cheap mysteriousness made me furiously impatient.

" 'I wanted him to be educated in the religion of his forefathers.'

" 'What do you mean? There are no Taoists in our family, and never have been, as far as I know.'

" 'Not *your* family,' said Love, '*mine.*'

" 'What are you saying? That you have Taoist ancestors?' I was extremely exasperated.

" 'Of course. The Loves have always worshipped the Tao.' There was a twinkle, or a mad gleam, in his eye. 'Hell, we practically invented it!'

"I shook my head. 'I'm sorry, Eddie, but you've lost me.'

" 'What's so incomprehensible about it? Look at it this way, Hsiao. He'll be a Taoist from a long line of Taoists. The same but different.'

"A match flared in some dim chamber of my brain. 'You mean . . .'

"He nodded, continuing to bask me in the brazen sunlight of that smile. 'That's right,' he replied. 'Tao — D-O-W' (he spelled it out so there could be no mistake) 'as in the Dow Jones Industrial Average.'

" 'Impossible!' I shouted indignantly. 'You've lost your mind. It's monstrous! Irreverent! Do you have even the vaguest idea what the Tao (that's T-A-O) is? It's the absolute antithesis of the thing *your* family worships.'

"Love shrugged. 'It's the ultimate essence of the universe, isn't it?' He broke into a peal of manic laughter.

" 'Yes,' I said, 'but . . .'

" 'Well then!' he cried peremptorily, cutting me off. 'There you are!' "

"Well, Sun I, after this could there be any further doubt about your father's madness? Though there was a disconcerting semblance of 'method' in it, and though he enjoyed long periods of lucidity, in the general drift of his initiatives your father was out of control. As the expression goes, he was 'mad as a hatter.'

"By the look on your face I can see you bridle at my conclusion. What other explanation is there? The skewed nonchalance with which he made the decision, a decision so consequential to you, whom he had assumed responsibility for, *voluntarily* assumed responsibility for — what name can you suggest for it but madness? To sport with someone's future, his own child's, on the basis of a pun! And such a pun!

"Perhaps the hardest thing to explain is why I went along with it. But what choice did I have, Sun I? I could devise no better plan. And, as I said, there was a kind of method in his madness. In many ways it seemed kindest all around; to Ch'iu-yeh, because it offered the best hope for her to resume a normal life, and to you, my boy, because frankly there was no other hope at all. So I became his minister. As he explained the part he wanted me to play, he was again quite lucid, disconcertingly so. He had thought things out in the most minute detail, as though it were another battle strategy. My responsibility was to see you delivered safely, then after a span of years to come again and do essentially what I've done today — try and give you some idea of your history. To give you that, and something else . . . but let that wait a little longer yet."

•

My uncle paused and sighed with weariness. "This brings me very nearly to the end of what I have to say, Sun I. For the rest, there is only the story of your mother, and it is brief. But this is where the tale grows sad. Remembering her, I always think about the lines from the *Shih Ching*:

In the far country there is a doe;
Among white reeds she lingers . . . forever now.
A young girl's heart was filled with thoughts of springtime;
A handsome traveler's promises contrived her fall.

"What she felt, what thoughts crowded in on her during the months of her confinement, I can only guess. She never talked to me about it, or to anyone — unless to Chiang Po, who grieved as well with Love's departure. In a morbid ritual he continued bringing her the same chrysanthemums as before, until the season ended. Only now the flowers took on a funerary cast, and this appalled me. I wanted to spare her the torture of such associations. But though they made her sad, she appeared to need these visits. I didn't have the heart to order him to stop.

"Perhaps they spoke of Love together, I don't know. Whenever I broached the subject, your mother simply turned toward the window, contemplating the mountains as she had that day I told her Love would leave. What did she see there? Perhaps how powerfully the massif rises in the sunlit, frigid air, and how it looks back without human feeling.

"But only one thing drew her full attention now. The robe. Day and night she applied herself to its embroidery. There was a quality of desperation in the way she worked, a fever in the making. She seemed afraid she wouldn't finish it in time, though to what end she worked now that everything had fallen out against her was unclear to us. My mother said she clung to some hope of Love's return. The pathos in this thought was almost unendurable. But another possibility was worse: that Ch'iu-yeh's mind had come unhinged with grief. Though we never spoke of it, I think this was in all our minds, even Father's, for from this time he gradually began to withdraw from the world. He neglected his interests, ate little, and began to pace the house at night, muttering to himself. Whatever the truth about Ch'iu-yeh (and to this day I still don't know), it's certain that the robe exercised a fearful hold on her imagination. In the end it became an obsession. All her hidden turmoil, all her unspoken grief went into it, and the cruel hope that fed it, tantalizing her to the end. It is a beautiful and frightening thing (you shall see it, Sun I; but not yet), a tapestry crowded with awful symbols and portents. When she put it aside — only two days before she went into labor — a far-off look softened her expression and made me fearful. It was like the look in an athlete's eyes after the race is finished. Her spirit was at peace, but it was the peace of one longing to sink down in the stupor of death, having at last caught sight of the destination."

•

"You were born on the night of the full moon in August when the summer was in its final blaze. Hot as it was, I remember a hint of chill, the year's first, tinkling in the air like chimes. The windows of your mother's room had been thrown open to catch that breath of fall. The old midwife grumbled at this, but the doctor, an American officer who had been brought from the base at my father's request, said it could do no harm. It was a relatively uncomplicated birth, as they tell me. Toward the end though, something peculiar happened, which my mother later described to me. As Ch'iu-yeh lay in bed, propped up on pillows struggling to breathe, in the midst of a powerful contraction, she called your father's name. As she did, the light blinked and a fluttering shadow crossed the bed. Hearing the startled cries of those within, alert to a mischance, I rushed in myself. There I found them all looking up at a huge moth which had flown in through the open window and was circling the bare bulb. The sight sent a chill through my whole body.

"At that moment your mother groaned, and your foot emerged, for you were born backward and came into the world like a swimmer, testing the water before plunging in.

"I am not a superstitious man, Sun I, but the image of that moth has never left me. It came so closely on her cry, as if it were an emanation of some sort, the ghostly emissary of Eddie Love, his proxy at the birth. Yet there is no need to strain the facts. If it wasn't a portent, it might as well have been, for within a day after delivering you, your mother developed an infection in her womb. The doctor said it wasn't anything to be concerned about, a minor complication, very common. But it began to spread uncontrollably, until in the end her womb was eaten up with it. She was in agony for several days, frequently delirious, for she declined the morphine my father procured through his contacts, as though to punish him, or herself, or simply life — the life in her. When she was lucid, she suffered greatly. Finally she sank into unconsciousness, and died without ever waking.

"The young doctor was distraught when he came to tell us she was gone. 'I don't understand it,' he said. 'The antibiotics should have halted it.'

"I pitied his naive faith. For all his intelligence and encyclopedic medical knowledge, he couldn't diagnose the simple fact that Ch'iu-yeh had given up. . . . No, not given up; your mother willed to die. That resolve taken, all his skill, for which he'd paid so high a cost, became irrelevant. Nothing could recall her. Once you were born, Sun I, I think your mother felt her task was finished. She simply let it go. Death must have been a great relief to her. I hope it was."

Chapter 8

Though his voice was steady, large tears were rolling down my uncle's cheeks as he concluded.

My eyes were dry, and had been all along. Throughout the course of his tale, which had lasted several hours, Hsiao had played on my emotions as on an instrument, running them through the gamut, from the sick dread of suspense, to pity, to despair, finally to a kind of frantic happiness. Yes, happiness, like that of a beggar on whom the heavens have opened, showering treasure; for so my history seemed to me — a tiny crèche in ivory, a cameo with a woman's face, a signet initialed with a promise and an obligation, and two dark, tear-shaped emeralds the color of Love's mystery. Like the beggar, with a tactile hunger bred of deprivation, I scooped and fondled my jewels, testing weight and rondure, raising them in the sunlight to count their facets and their flaws. I reveled in possession where possession had been impossible, not realizing, not caring, that the precious windfall life had rained on me — the blessing of a history — was at best equivocal, and possibly a curse. But I had never cried.

Now the excitement had overstimulated my imagination, left it in a state of posttumescent apathy, or not apathy so much as a sad, far-seeing peace, in which I recognized that something in the world, something in me, had changed, and changed forever, that the Sun I who had sat cross-legged at his uncle's feet to hear a tale about the past was gone. Or, if not gone completely, deposed, stripped of his sovereignty, a titular monarch now, replaced by a new one whom I barely knew. As if by alchemical transformation, an emotional mitosis, I had self-divided, and my "immortal fetus," my alter ego, whose seed had always been there, had been born . . . been born, or come into his own inheritance after bitter years of hungry exile. But who was he? Who was *I*? This question, which before had always been self-evident, was problematic now. I no longer knew. Somehow my birthright, my history, had dispossessed me.

More than ever I believed the answer was tied to my father. Who was this man, Eddie Love? His identity seemed even more elusive than my own, but bound up with it so that in finding one, I would find the other. His mystery was my mystery.

This idea enchanted me. As it flitted through my brain, I think I must have smiled like a newborn child who sees the refracted colors of the rainbow glowing in a prism just above his head.

Gradually, though, I came back to my old self. This pacific, almost pleasant wonder evaporated like a vapor, leaving behind it a more lasting, though less welcome, residue: fear. I became aware of a restive chafing in my heart, like the anxious and incessant scratching of an animal or insect in the woodwork of a house, gnawing its way out, or in. This was something I had never known before. And yet, I knew that it had always been there just below the threshold of perception.

Lost in reverie, I didn't notice that my uncle Hsiao had risen and gone to fetch Chung Fu. Returning to myself, I found them both standing over me, looking down with pity and concern.

"Where were you wandering, little brother?" Chung Fu asked in a hushed, mournful voice suggesting (indirectly, as rising mist and a change in temperature suggest the nearness of some great, unsuspected ocean) the presence within him of a deep reservoir of compassion.

As I searched his eyes, in which the light of gaiety was now subdued but not extinguished, I knew he understood my pain and suffered with me. My own eyes filled with tears. The sweet release I'd been unable to surrender to till then swept over me. Bowing my head I wept quietly into the folds of my robe.

The master reached out and touched my forehead with cool fingers, brushing back a lock of hair.

"The heart is a wilderness, Sun I," he said.

My uncle sighed.

Then they were silent, waiting patiently for my tears to subside.

When I had eased my heart with weeping, my uncle gently revived the conversation.

"Sun I," he said, "in accordance with your father's wishes, I have told you these things privately. Had it been my choice, I would have wished your master here throughout. But I understand Love's stipulation, for personal matters such as these require the utmost delicacy and circumspection. Share them if you wish; that is your privilege, not your obligation. We are finished now though, and you probably have questions. I asked Chung Fu to join us because his views may supplement my own, compensating for any bias in them. I hope he can corroborate my assessment of your father's madness, and help to put your mind at rest."

"Madness!" the master echoed, as though astonished. "Is that the conclusion you've drawn? Certainly Love was difficult to figure, at least in the beginning. But mad? I hardly think so."

"Can you explain, Master?" I asked eagerly.

"Do you know the story of Confucius's encounter with Lao Tzu?"

"*Yes,*" said Hsiao pointedly.

I shook my head.

Ignoring Hsiao, the master turned to me. "It was a little like that, Sun I. You see, Confucius made a serious mistake. He applied to Lao Tzu concerning some fine point of ceremonial etiquette. Receiving a rude rebuff (even, according to some versions, a kick in the seat of his pants), he returned in great discouragement to his disciples." The master winked at me. "He was so humiliated he was almost *mad* himself. Fortunately, or unfortunately — you decide — one of his bright-eyed, bowing protégés was nearby with a quill pen to catch old Master Kung's befuddled ravings:

> Heaven has granted the wild beasts of the forest feet on which to run from me; similarly, the fish in the deeps have fins to swim away; birds have their wings to fly out of the path of danger. For wings there are springes; for fins, nets; for feet, traps. But of the dragon — who knows how he rises on the mist and cloud to heaven? Today I have met Lao Tzu, and this man is a dragon."

"That story is obviously apocryphal," Hsiao interrupted, "the work of some malicious Taoist scribe. The dates make it highly unlikely that such a meeting could have taken place."

"The dates?" Chung Fu burst out in exuberant laughter. Despite myself, I think I must have chuckled too.

"Well!" said Hsiao under his breath. He blushed with embarrassment.

"You have to admit, it illustrates a certain point," Chung Fu pointed out in a more conciliatory manner.

"I admit nothing," Hsiao replied.

The master raised his eyebrows.

Hsiao sniffed twice with offended dignity, poked out his chin, primped his robe a little, then magnanimously forgave us, saying, "If we're going to try to reach conclusions in a matter of such importance, gentlemen, I suggest we stick simply to facts."

"Yes, yes," Chung Fu agreed diplomatically, "you're absolutely right, the facts. . . . Well, let me tell you what I remember of Love's arrival.

"Late one afternoon we heard a droning in the sky which quickly intensified into a high-pitched scream. We ran out to the courtyard to see what it was. A plane buzzed low over the roofs, so low the wind from the propeller flattened the rye in the garden plot and stirred up tiny vortices of dust along the path. It was a Japanese plane: we could tell from the double bloodred suns on the undersides of the wings. From the sound of the machine guns, I thought at first we were being attacked. I frantically tried to herd the monks inside.

Almost immediately, though, a second plane passed over, this one identifiable by the grinning jaws painted on the snout, or nose — I don't know the terminology. Anyway, it was American, and in pursuit, so several of the monks began to cheer. I thought it odd to be applauding such a ferocious deity, but I got caught up in the emotion and joined with the rest. The planes rose until they had diminished to the size of birds. Shading our eyes, we watched in awe as they spun and wheeled, cavorting as though in play, performing an elaborate mating ritual, two angelic creatures in the blue silence of space. Then one of them exploded — an enormous ball of orange fire — and an instant later a boom a thousand times louder than thunder shook the mountain. The beauty and horror of it took my breath away — the deceptive gracefulness of the dance, then the vaporization of a human life. As we gaped, the second plane passed beneath the rim of the mountains trailing black smoke from the wings. Deeply chastened after the unholy pleasure of the spectacle, we went inside and prayed that the life of the second pilot might be spared.

"Some days passed. We had almost forgotten about the incident when one morning a small band of Lolo tribesmen appeared at the gate escorting a young American. Very pale and weak, he was exhausted from the journey and mildly disoriented from the opium they'd been feeding him to ease his pain. He slept for almost eighteen hours, until dusk the next day, and when he woke up he was like a new man. I remember him, and our interview, as though it were yesterday. Though peaked, he was tall and very handsome, after the Western fashion. His face was pleasingly animated. He smiled often, and well. His teeth were very white. In addition to such physical charms, and despite a limited command of Chinese, he managed to be an engaging conversationalist, with a knack for pleasantries. He was obviously well-bred. And yet, he had a nervous eye that constantly darted over the surfaces of things in search of something that I fear the surface couldn't give him. I remember thinking that he was like a swallow, flitting from twig to twig of thought and never alighting. I had never seen such restlessness. Even considering his condition and circumstances, a residue of unaccountability remained. I liked him though, liked him a great deal, and felt a certain pity for him too. For as I listened to him speak and watched his mannerisms, I began to suspect that in his deepest heart he was the warder of a great unhappiness beyond any mere physical distress, and I wondered about its cause.

"After he had refreshed himself and we had chatted briefly, I took him on a walking tour of the monastery. When I had shown him the grounds and the cloisters, Sun I, I led him up into the southwest tower where the clepsydra is housed. Love had apparently never seen a water clock before. The ingenious simplicity of its mechanism — the slow dripping of the water, the rings spreading outward in the oaken well — must have set off a resonance in his mind, for he stood as though immobilized, watching the water bleed out of the upper cistern, twist down the long finger of the quill, bead, and break off, falling into the pool below, like tears, it is said. Indeed, these droplets, which raise the float imperceptibly through the minutes and hours, are called 'the tears of time.'

"As it chanced, while we were there the hour struck six." The master turned to Hsiao and explained. "Our clepsydra works on a twelve-hour cycle. At six each morning and six each evening, the well brims full. When it does, the float trips a heavy weight attached by rope to the clapper of the tower bell. By this means the monks are summoned to meditation. The release of the weight also triggers a floodgate in the bottom of the well through which the waters run off into a circular moat. From here they are returned to the cistern, and the cycle recommences."

"I see," said my uncle, who was listening with close attention. "An admirable device. I have come across mention of such instruments in my researches. It must be very old."

"Yes," Chung Fu agreed, "they say it has run without interruption for three hundred years. In its ebb and flow it is like the tides of the sea."

"Only more regular!" Hsiao added, profoundly impressed.

"Yes, more regular," the master said. He smiled coyly. "The tides of *yin* and *yang* then: they never vary."

My uncle frowned.

"At any rate," Chung Fu continued, "Love was deeply affected by the spectacle. As the bell tolled and the waters emptied out, a change came over him. His vivaciousness guttered out like a candle. All that lightheartedness and charm, so in evidence before, vanished as though they had never existed. He simply stood staring down into the darkness of the empty well, where the walls are covered with a coat of hairy slime. His face was nearly vacant, yet there was a hint of pain in it as well.

"When he finally started from his reverie, he regarded me with a curious expression and asked, 'And what are your views on death?' "

The master paused to give us ample time to reflect on the significance of this. "Perhaps I should have mentioned it before, but during our walk from time to time Love had asked me questions about life in the monastery — schedule, diet, activities, and so forth — and something of our beliefs, but very little. I had construed his motive as simple good manners, a desire to express polite interest in our way of life. Thus I could have considered his question a simple continuation of the casual drift of conversation. But I don't think it was. Something in the way he asked it, a peculiar urgency in his tone, and the generality and moment of the question itself, precluded such an interpretation.

"I think I must have hesitated before answering, for Love, apparently embarrassed or alarmed at betraying himself so unguardedly to me, launched into a humorous aside, designed, rather ingeniously, I thought, to lay a false scent over the trail of his emotion. He slapped his forehead with the heel of his palm as though remembering something. 'Wait a minute!' he shouted. 'Never mind. I know that. What am I thinking of? I was catechized just the other day in Kunming by one of your brethren. . . . At least, I think he was a Taoist. He had a tortoise shell, and several dozen magic chopsticks. There were drums and bells and tambourines and incense burning. It was a damn good show. I asked him to tell my fortune, and he said I had been a dog in my previous existence but in the next one with any luck at all I could expect to be a god. I gave him a dollar for his pains, and what was left of my cigar, and told him he had the terms right but the sequence reversed — that I was a god before, but in mortal danger of ending in the kennel on the next go-round.' Your father laughed. 'That's it, isn't it?' he asked. 'What's it called? Transubstantiation? No, that's the Catholic trick. Transmigration! That's it.'

"I smiled appreciatively at his antics. 'I'm afraid you've confused our ideas with the Buddhists', Eddie. Transmigration is *their* trick. We're much too plain to advance such fancy theories.'

"Your father sobered. 'What *do* you believe then?'

" 'About death?'

"He nodded, rocking forward to listen with an unnatural intentness. I noted his clenched fists, and the masseter working in his jaw.

" 'Why, simply that all things return to Tao,' I replied.

"As I spoke these words, Love winced as though in pain and shuddered through the length of his whole body. Then, incongruously, he threw his head back and started laughing, a high, eerie laugh which chilled my heart. . . ."

"Madness!" Hsiao piped in like a shrill raven.

Chung Fu ignored him and went on: " 'Eddie,' I said, 'do you understand me? Do you understand the meaning of "Return"?' His expression was at once desperate and wry. 'Oh yes,' he replied, 'I understand. You mean extinction.' "

"There was no more than this. But for me, Sun I, this brief exchange opened a vista into your father's inmost self. In a light as from a flare at sea, I caught a glimpse of the amorphous form that haunted him, that hunted him, its slick back thrusting upward from the waves, its dead eye catching the light an instant before it disappeared again beneath the surface. Love was not the amusing but trifling boy I had at first been tempted to suspect; he was a man who deserved my respect and pity. I became convinced that afternoon, and remain convinced, Sun I, that your father was one of those whose special destiny it is to bear mortality in consciousness through this life, his own mortality and, beyond that, Mortality itself, the stark, frozen summit which rises at the end of the world.

"What suffering had left this mark on him, I cannot say. But about the mark itself there could be no mistake — not for one like me, who has spent his life among the half-light of the cloisters, passing hourly among the members of that sad elite whose sole distinction lies in the special type and intensity of their unhappiness, which comes from thinking always of the end. It is a rare devotion they are privileged, and condemned, to celebrate with singleness and passion all their lives. And Eddie Love was one of them, of us — I'm almost sure of it. For the mark cannot be hidden from the practiced eye.

"Seen in its proper light, this consciousness is a spiritual accomplishment

— a gift, rather, or can be — for it is the catalyst which leads to the renunciation of the world, pointing up its transitory nature. However, I suspect your
father shared the general opinion in the matter, and would have much more
gladly renounced gift than world. In this, perhaps, lay his peculiar tragedy.

"My first impulse was to disburden him of the misapprehension he labored
under, to tell him hope existed through Return to the Source.

" 'You mean meditation?' he asked. 'The compounding of the Pill?'

"I was surprised he'd heard of it and said so.

"He gave a dismissive shrug. 'Not only have I heard of it, I've tried it.'

" 'Have you indeed?' I asked skeptically.

" 'After a fashion. That, or something just as good.'

" 'What do you mean?'

"His smile became almost impish. 'Opium,' he explained. 'The Lolos introduced me to it.'

"I recoiled from his flippant cynicism. 'Opium is an insidious and ultimately
debilitating parody of the intoxicating bliss of enlightenment,' I lectured him
sternly.

"He shrugged again. 'Maybe. But it has all of the best features of same and
is significantly more cost-effective to produce. Why, it could be turned out on
an assembly line.' He laughed his wild laugh again.

"I realized then that in his state, Love could not understand — or, if he
understood, appreciate — the subtle difference between Tao and extinction. I
could only hope that the suffering this caused him would act as a penance,
mitigating his transgressions and purifying him so that he'd be fit for grace.
Something told me that your father was one of those who must find his own
Way through the world, that there was nothing I could do to help him. For
as I said before, 'Of the dragon — who knows how he rises on the clouds and
mists to heaven?' Your father, Sun I, was a dragon.

"Beyond this, there is little I can tell you. The next morning he left for
Chungking. I've never seen him since. All further business between us was
conducted with your uncle as intermediary. . . . Never seen him, yet thought
of him often enough. . . ." The master smiled. "Each time I've looked into your
eyes, Sun I."

We were silent for a time, each involved in private speculation. I was the
first to speak.

"What has become of him, do you suppose?"

The master sighed. "Who can say? For me, Love was like a wounded animal.
Once, long ago, by accident I came across his spoor where it crossed the level
thoroughfare of my own destiny. I paused on my way, knelt down in the dust
and touched the bright blood welling in the print, sniffed its odor on my hands.
Then with my eye I followed the track until it disappeared in the darkness of
the forest where I dared not go, having neither time, nor inclination, nor the
skill to follow.

"I've often wondered if the wound he carried hurt him till he died, or if it merely crippled him and slowed him down until his tireless adversary closed in and took him from behind. My greatest fear, however, was that it galled him into desperation, until he tore himself apart with his own hands."

The master walked to the window. Outside dusk was falling, swathing the valleys in its gauzy light. But the peaks of the Himalayas were on fire, burning with a pale rose flame, like vesper candles in the churchlight of the afternoon. Looking toward them, the master spoke again.

"And yet, perhaps he made it into the high ranges of the mountains where the hunter cannot go, where the cold air and sunlight, the everlasting snows, and the great panorama of the spreading earth have soothed his spirit, healed him, made him whole again. Perhaps he learned to live with the agony in his flesh, until at last it became his friend and counselor, and his eyes grew bright with that deep sanity which is the only wisdom."

As he spoke, I closed my own eyes and summoned up the image in the photograph. A sweet peace descended on my soul. But when I opened them again, I saw my uncle Hsiao, shaking his head with grim sadness. "I don't think so," he demurred.

I felt a hollow open at the center of my being; the cavity of my body resounded with the beating of my heart.

"Your words have given me a deeper insight into Love," Hsiao said, bowing to Chung Fu. "Perhaps you've understood him better, observing without passion, never having suffered at his hands. Doubtless your capacity for compassion is more highly developed than my own. But in a day, an hour, what can one learn about a man? You were not with him over many months as I was. You did not have a chance to see and tally all that was base and reckless in him, and how he killed what tried to love him. And so I say to you, Chung Fu, your knowledge is one-sided; and beyond this, that the thing that stalked him, what you called 'the adversary,' the Hunter (and that you, knowing him so little, could see this at all amazes me!) was not mortality — it was Love. It was himself."

Hsiao turned to me. His face was flushed. "Now at last I understand the image whose meaning has eluded me so long: tiger and trainer. Do you remember? Your master's thought has given me the clue."

"What do you mean?" Chung Fu asked.

Hsiao kept his eyes fixed fast on mine as he explained. "The tiger — that was the wild creature of his natural filial affection. The trainer was the bitter kernel of his pride that baited that affection and eventually destroyed it. The wound was self-inflicted. Love was the Hunter, stalking himself as prey. You see?" In his excitement, my uncle seemed almost predatory himself. "It could have been my fate as well. So easily. Only I embraced my adversary, where he continued to fight on."

"Forgive me for interrupting," Chung Fu put in, "but since you asked me here to provide the dissenting opinion, I must say I think this preoccupation with Love's estrangement from his father is simply your Confucian bias, a hypertrophied sense of filial piety."

"Indeed?" replied my uncle, with that wry, puckering demi-smile. "For my part, I might have said that your insistence on mortality as the decisive factor was not entirely unconnected with your *Taoist* leanings."

A tense silence fell between them. I struggled to digest the implications of this suggestion, or discovery.

"Well, if he wasn't mad, he was a monster," Hsiao interjected heatedly. "In either case, it's clear you shouldn't encourage the boy's worship."

"A monster!" Chung Fu was incredulous. "Surely you don't believe Love was a bad man, that his actions were false hearted?"

"Bad?" Hsiao rejoined. "What is *bad*? The irresponsibility that destroyed my sister in the flowering of life, that led to the abandonment of an innocent child — what are we to call these things if not 'bad'? Perhaps you would prefer to attribute them to inexperience, or even 'excessive innocence'?" He laughed bitterly.

"No," Chung Fu replied, "Love was not innocent. But he was not entirely guilty either. I see him as a man caught up in circumstances for which he was only partially to blame."

"On whom then falls the rest?" Hsiao demanded in a voice of quiet gravity.

The master bowed his head. When he looked up again tears brimmed in his eyes, though he was smiling. "The world."

"You are too cynical, my friend," Hsiao chided, but gently, with affection and respect. "This is the jaundiced truth of the anchorite and dreamer." He shook his head. "No, Chung Fu, though a scholar, I'm more the realist than you. I've lived in, or closer to, the world of men and things and learned my truths from them. You, I'm afraid, have become intoxicated by the solitude and mountain air. The altitude of your retreat has made you dizzy." He smiled. "It's true, you know, what they say, that Taoists are dreamers."

"And Confucians men of probity without a grain of sense," Chung Fu tacked on.

They both laughed softly.

"Tell me, Chung Fu," my uncle resumed, still in good humor but with a hint of his former passion "if not by madness, how do you explain the impertinence, the monstrous whimsicality with which he casually decided this child's fate?" He pointed to me.

"You mean the play on words, I assume?"

"Precisely! Tao and Dow!" Hsiao regarded me with raised eyebrows, as though I alone could appreciate the preposterousness of this juxtaposition.

The master shrugged. "Without other criteria to apply, what better decision could he have made? He followed the intuitive promptings of his own unconscious nature. Is this madness? I choose to think not. Rather, it is the very essence of our way of life."

"Then Love, I suppose, was a Taoist?" Hsiao narrowed his eyes wryly, as at the mining of an unexpected vein of humor.

"The Tao is broad and deep," said the master with an ambiguous smile.

"Come now, you surprise me, Chung Fu," Hsiao rejoined. "I would have thought you'd have serious objections to the association of your sacred Tao with the ultimate symbol of avarice and self-interest in the West. But perhaps you're unaware of precisely what the Dow — the American one — imports?"

"My ignorance is great," the master replied, "but it was my impression that the Dow is some sort of pulse of economic activity in America."

"Exactly!" cried Hsiao in vindication. " 'Economic.' "

"And in this sense," Chung Fu went on, ignoring him, "is it not analogous to the Tao of the *I Ching,* which is also a pulse?"

"In what sense?" Hsiao testily objected. "Explain that, please."

"Why, the world's own pulse, in which the beating heart of life reveals itself to the listener — he who takes the time to master its secret language, to learn, as it were, by heart, the ceaseless, steady music of its systole and diastole, and within that, the false note which signals disorder, its murmurs and fibrillations."

My uncle pursed his lips, savoring the analogy. "Very neat," he admitted, "unfortunately, specious. You've regaled me with several Taoist anecdotes, Chung Fu; now let me turn the edge on you. Recall the poet's words:

> Businessmen boast of their skill and cunning,
> But in philosophy they are like little children.
> Bragging to each other of successful depredations
> They neglect to consider the ultimate fate of the body.
> What should they know of the Master of Dark Truth
> Who saw the wide world in a jade cup,
> By illumined conception got clear of heaven and earth,
> On the chariot of Mutation entered the Gate of Immutability?

"Tell me, Chung Fu, is it not true that the great Tao of the sages is the Way of self-transcendence? And how is this to be reconciled with the Dow of the Americans, which is above all the way of self-interest?"

" 'Can these men be said to have attained completion?' " the master retorted with a well-known *fan-yen,* or paradox, from Chuang Tzu. " 'If so, then so have all the rest of us. Or can they not be said to have attained completion? If so, then neither we nor anything else have ever attained it.' "

"Nonsense," Hsiao snorted. " 'Tao and Dow' — why this is the most shameless sophistry. They are at odds, eternally, like the great primal opposites of which you Taoists speak so frequently, *yin* and *yang.* Who seeks to conflate them, to resolve their implacable enmity, seeks to subvert the laws which underpin the universe itself!"

"Your reasoning is subtle and attractive," the master conceded, "but only superficially so. I fear at a deeper level, the deepest level of all, you are entirely mistaken."

"I beg you to instruct my error," Hsiao said, with suave, academic irony.

The master bowed, as though to a legitimate petition. "Do you know the story of Chuang Tzu and Tung Kuo?".

"Heavenly Ancestors, not another of your interminable Taoist set pieces, I hope!"

"Tung Kuo asked Chuang, 'Where is Tao?' " the master began, unruffled, "and Chuang replied, 'Where *isn't* it?'

" 'Show it to me,' the pupil rejoined.

"Chuang pointed to an ant.

"Tung Kuo recoiled, but being of a contentious nature, persisted. 'And is it in some lesser thing as well?'

"Chuang pointed to the weeds.

" 'The great Tao in common weeds!' Tung Kuo exclaimed. 'Can it be possible?'

"Chuang nodded emphatically. 'There is even Tao in this bit of turd,' he said, kicking a dusty pile of droppings in the road." Chung Fu surveyed my uncle benignly from the unscalable summit of his triumph.

Hsiao appeared unmoved. "And what are we to conclude from this pythonic utterance?"

"Why simply that Tao is in all things, the high and the low, in what is called the impure no less than in what we call the pure."

My uncle wiped a dust mote from his eye, then sniffed. "I must confess, I've never understood such wisdom. I always shied away from your religion on precisely this account, that it seemed irresponsible to me, even immoral."

"I'm sorry you're displeased with us," the master apologized, his pupils twinkling with suppressed merriment, "yet it is written, 'It was when the Great Way declined that human kindness and morality arose.' " He shifted his regard to me. "To you, Sun I, I say, remember: Tao, too, is in the 'marketplace,' no whit less than in the temple, and each of us must pursue his own path where it leads."

As he spoke, something dammed in me burst loose, like the sea through a retaining wall. I looked from him — the sadness and compassion in his eyes beneath the flickering of irony (like the blue arc at the center of a candle flame where it is most intense) — to my uncle Hsiao, the old Confucian, with his masklike face, which now wore an expression of such monitory sternness . . . and something else. Was it defeat? But how could he have anticipated any other outcome in a battle of influence in which I was the implicit prize? Twenty-one years of education, dependency, affection were weighted in the scales against him. Despite the impression he'd made on me, he could not have hoped to prevail against the inertia of my whole background and rearing in a single afternoon.

Still, I felt a huge affection for him, huge respect. I know now that as I stood diffidently before them, silently noting their similarities and differences, their similarity in difference, I was in the presence of two great emissaries of the past, who, yoked together like the mighty opposites, the *yin* and *yang* themselves, in their love and war had made our culture deathless, alone among the civilizations of the earth.

●

After this, the master rang for Wu, who brought in green gunpowder tea and a basket of the ripest fruit the old peach tree in the courtyard could afford. He and Hsiao refreshed themselves in silence, out of deference to me, I think, and the severe trial my emotions had been subjected to that day. But also, I imagine, they were glad of an opportunity to express their mutual esteem in a more genial fashion than the high-minded and uncompromising moral combat they had waged, politely, all afternoon, pausing now together to perform the humble and affectionate offices of hospitality.

Chung Fu picked the amplest and most promising peach from the basket and pared away the skin in a clean spiral ribbon. Then he cut the meat away in crescents.

"For you, my friend." He passed the choicest morsels to my uncle.

He addressed me with more casual politeness. "Would you care for some, Sun I?"

"Yes, thank you, Master," I replied, reaching out to receive it.

Balking on delivering it, he laughed sweetly. "Answer me this riddle first: What is the stone that bears new life within it?"

His maneuver caught me off guard. I pondered, frowning, but my mind drew a total blank. "I don't know."

"Don't know!" he echoed, as though astonished. He lifted his eyebrows at Hsiao. "Well then, let this be your portion!" With this he deftly launched the peach pit at my head, which it struck soundly with a hollow, wooden *thunk*. The projectile rolled into my lap and lay inert.

Rubbing my hurt, I glared at him ferociously.

"Aren't you going to thank me?" he asked mischievously.

"Thank you for what? The knot on my head?"

The master regarded Hsiao, as though asking him to bear witness to my ingratitude. "Monkey never was overly appreciative of favors rendered." He addressed me again. "I don't think you realize what you're holding in your hand."

"I think I do," I replied sarcastically.

"What then?"

"A pit," I said with a disdainful shrug.

"A stone!" he corrected me.

A dim surmise flashed through my brain.

"Exactly," he said, nodding with satisfaction. "The stone that bears new life within it. And do you know why it is called that, why, according to legend, Chuang Tzu chose one as a headstone for his grave?"

I shook my head.

"Because the pit is the soul of the fruit, out of which it creates its own new body. That is why the peach tree is a symbol of eternal life for Taoists, why the first abbot of this monastery planted one in the courtyard whose stock has been preserved ever since.

"This is my final reminiscence of your father, Sun I. I had almost forgotten until Wu brought this fruit. On the afternoon I've described, after our tour, we too shared tea and peaches. Searching for some way to cheer him after the sad reverie he'd fallen into by the clepsydra, I hit on this. When I tossed the pit at him, just as I have at you, and told him this story, he condescended to repay me with a smile . . ." (the master beamed at me, and I could not disguise my pleasure) "just as you do now. Only he caught it, put it in his pocket, and, as far as I know, carried it away with him."

The amusement that had been playing at my uncle's lips during the first part of this interchange quickly disappeared as the purport of Chung Fu's antics became apparent. He examined his teacup with a furrowed brow.

But as I nursed my cup in silence, taking slow draughts of the steaming liquor, I felt strangely pleased, as though an honor had been conferred on me. Enveloped as I was in the familiar, reassuring ambience of the master's cell where I had spent so many happy hours as a child playing with such simple toys — a fruit stone, a yarrow stalk — my uncle's story, with all its unsettling implications, receded to a distance and took on a kind of unreality, as though completely unconnected with myself. The whole thing read like a story from a book, sad, but with that special sadness that mysteriously refreshes us and makes us glad again, because it is not our pain we are called upon to witness. And indeed, having escaped the fate of the protagonists, we have some reason to be thankful for our own. In addition, such stories, if they are good, lead us into the solemn presence of some truth, which we enjoy illicitly, not having paid the heavy price out of our hearts, in their most secret gleanings, the precious and irredeemable treasure of our dreams.

But even as I savored this sweet respite, phrases and images from the story broke in on me rudely, and my pulse accelerated. These brief intrusions were like the rumblings of distant thunder to one basking in the stuporous heat of a long, dreamy summer afternoon, hoping it might last forever.

•

At last my uncle put his cup away and stretched his arms, clearing his throat as a signal that he was ready to get on with the unfinished business. There was resignation in his manner, as though he realized the day had gone against him. But his dignity was unimpaired, and though he'd lost his battle, the larger war was far from over. I noticed with regret that his face had started to congeal again into the mask that it had been before.

"I'm deeply grateful for your hospitality," he said formally, bowing to Chung Fu, "and for your conversation. But time presses on. I must leave while there is light enough to see me down the mountain. For the 'path' is treacherous . . ." (allowing himself one last gibe, he used the word *tao* ironically) "and I will not feel safe until I reach the highroad."

The master raised his hand to interrupt, but my uncle persevered. "It's no use trying to persuade me. I cannot stay. When I've fulfilled the last article of my commission, I must depart."

He searched my face a long moment — again the man I knew. His expression was full of urgent doubt, some question which his eyes appeared to say meant everything to me. Within that urgency though, a wistfulness too. He must have known that with the shortness of the time and the complexity of the issues, the chances were that he would never know the answer.

Reaching into the folds of his robe, he took out a package wrapped in plain brown paper tied with string. "Open this, it contains a treasure. There isn't a mate to it in the whole world. It is the robe, Sun I. Make it your study and devotion. It is all you will ever really know of her, and of that hidden part of yourself which is her legacy. In it, perhaps better than I have done today, you may pick out and trace the thread of your inheritance and fate, for it was woven over you as you lay in the darkness of the womb. The rhythmic clacking of the loom, the sound of needle piercing silk, the soft hiss of the gliding thread — perhaps in some locked chamber of your deepest memory these resonate still, and will continue to, the ground tone of your being. Perhaps the stitches of that labor more than anything else, more even than the chromosomes in your own cells, which, they tell us now, are the guiding threads of life, made you what you are and may become. Reflect and draw your own conclusions. Only remember: it can never be replaced. Keep it safe. Guard it like your life; perhaps it is."

My uncle handed it to me, and a hush fell over my spirit. I looked down at it, listened to the crepitation of the paper as it settled in my hands, exhaling a faint perfume. It was the scent of some crushed flower expressed into an attar, which itself expressed for me, then and forever afterward, all the unutterable melancholy of the world. For I knew it was my mother's scent, the sweet perfume of loss she breathed with her last sigh, which entered my own body and became my soul.

But there was no time to dream this dream. My uncle hastened on. "And this is your father's gift."

I stared, uncomprehending, at a small black purse he held in his extended hand.

"It came from America years ago," he told me as he pressed it in my palm and closed my fingers over it. "It was the last communication — if you can call it that — I ever had from him." He scrutinized me intently. "Before you open it though, you'd better take a look at this." He handed me a manila envelope with unfamiliar postal markings.

Pinching up the clasp, I took out a copy of *Time* magazine, its front cover only: the rest had been torn away. Grinning, almost large as life, my father's face confronted me. It was a drawing, a caricature, a huge head on a tiny body.

He looked older, fleshier than in the photograph; and he was wearing a business suit instead of the uniform I always saw him in. But there could be no mistake about it. It was Love.

He was squeezed into the cockpit of a miniature plane whose nose was painted with the familiar tiger jaws, only these were grinning lewdly, as though at some obscenity or dirty joke. Despite his parodic intent, the artist had caught my father's smile exactly. As if there could be any further question who it was, Love was wearing aviator glasses with the black-green tear-shaped lenses, that symbol of anonymity which had become for me the mark of his identity. Only now there was a reflection in those glasses, a wonderful reflection, as of another world, one more mysterious than any dream. Crowded on the convex surface of each lens, and so doubled, were huge, glittering structures of glass and steel, tall as the Himalayas, with dark, canyonlike abysses yawning under them. They were buildings of course, but to me they looked more like weird mineral excrescences, stalagmites flecked with jewels or spikes of jagged quartz thrust upward from the earth in its primordial upheaval. It might have been the Hall of Mirrors in some unearthly funhouse, towers reflecting towers reflecting towers, some blunt and rectangular, others peaked with spires, like church steeples rising into heaven, pointing toward the sun behind my father's head. As in eclipse, the white radiance of the solar corona played around Love's features, describing an ambiguous aureole.

"They've shown him flying over the skyline of Manhattan," Hsiao informed me, "more precisely the financial district: Wall Street, also known as Emerald City."

There was an innuendo of amusement in his tone which I caught but didn't understand. "Emerald City, like in the Chinese fairy tale?" I proposed. "Where the Jade Emperor lived?"

"No, Sun I, only a jaded emperor lived in this Emerald City, and the fairy tale is strictly American." The irony in his expression was almost poisonous. "But that's another story, too long to explain now."

I waited, hoping he would continue, but he said nothing.

"What does it say?" I asked, handing the picture back to him.

Hsiao searched my face, then sighed and read me the headline:

"HUN IN THE SUN ON WALL STREET!
AMERICA, AND AMERICAN (P&L),
HAVE A NEW LOVE
EDDIE LOVE
(BUSINESS)MAN OF THE HOUR."

"What does it mean?" I asked, anxious with the suspense.

Hsiao regarded me appraisingly. "I don't know."

"Don't know!" I was incredulous. "You must know! Where did you get this?"

"It was sent from America," he said, "with no return address. As to what it means, the truth is, Sun I, *I don't want to know.* The day I made my promise to your father — that promise which has weighed on me like a burden all these years, and which today I finally cast off — I made another . . . to myself. I swore that I would have no more to do with Eddie Love. I've kept both promises."

"But this is an honor, isn't it?" I asked a little frantically, pointing to the magazine. "At least you can tell me that."

"So it would seem."

I dismissed his portentousness with a laugh. "Well, there you are then! That settles it. If he were mad, as you profess, how could he receive such homage from the world? Look! 'Businessman of the hour.' You said so yourself."

Then for the last time my uncle's lips curled into that familiar smile of distaste. "And what if the world that honored him were mad, Sun I? Have you considered that?"

I stared at him speechlessly, briefly toying with the idea that perhaps *he* was the madman.

"You have yet to open the purse," Chung Fu broke in, in a dispassionate voice. The neutrality of his tone was an immense relief, like a pinprick to a balloon stretched tense with air.

"No," I said gratefully, "I haven't."

"Go ahead."

Dully obedient, as in a trance, I pressed the clasp apart. The purse was so light I wondered if it were empty; but along the bottom seam was a hint of form. Slipping my fingers into the narrow mouth, I touched first on something soft, then on something hard. I drew out an object which I couldn't identify immediately. It resembled a cattail, or twig covered in a felty bark. And indeed it was a limb of sorts, or rather a stump: the stump of a small foot, a bit of shedding fur and gristle, a small protruding nub of bone. Connected to it by a delicate gold chain was a key. A key chain with a charm — a rabbit's foot. I studied it with aversion, the dry, dead meat, the blackened sinews like thongs of leather, the pip of bone. I cast an imploring glance at the master, then at Hsiao.

"There's more," Hsiao said.

Looking in the purse again, I found a note. Putting on his half-spectacles, Hsiao did the honors once more.

> "Happy twenty-first!
> From one Dowist to another,
> A key, a chain, a charm:
> The rabbit's foot for luck;
> The chain, necessity;
> The key, a master key
> (May it serve you well),
> A skeleton, which opens up the grave

Secrets of the heart (what is there, this
Key cannot open?), and to the congregation
Of believers (for we are of the same persuasion,
Aren't we?) a church key, which can make you
Drunk with ecstasy, or else
Unlock the Great Cathedral of the Dow.

Your father,
Love."

As my uncle handed me this, he gazed at me over the rim of his glasses, his brow creased with worry. His eyes were narrowed like some old mariner's, facing windward from a rocky headland, searching in the dismal toil and chaos of the elements for a ship feared lost at sea. Far down in that look there was a lantern burning for me, offering a hope of sanctuary, some deep-water harbor. But he must have known he couldn't save me, that it was a desperate hope, for by that same intermittent light I saw the tears the salt spray burned out of his eyes, and watched them as they turned to ice.

He embraced me then, stiffly but fiercely. His face again became the mask. And as quickly as he had entered my life, he was gone.

Chapter 9

That same night, almost as soon as Hsiao had left, Wu scurried into the cell in his soiled apron, fussing and sweating like an anxious biddy. He shooed me off to the kitchen, where he was preparing the evening meal, needing a recruit to man the bellows and chop vegetables.

He should have conscripted someone else. I was too worked up to attend to my duties properly. Twice I blew out the fire while trying to start it. Then as I honed the paring knife, I accidentally tipped over the jar of oil, spilling it everywhere. My hands were wet with it, so slippery I could barely grip the knife.

"What's the matter with you?" Wu chided. "Watch what you're doing!"

These words had hardly left his mouth when the knife skipped off the stone and almost julienned my index finger. The cut wasn't dangerous, but it bled profusely. I even managed to spatter a few drops into a huge *ting* of cooked rice, which in my agitated state I'd neglected to cover.

"You're doing this on purpose!" Wu screamed, beginning to tear his hair. The rice, enough to feed the entire monastery, of course had to be dedicated and burned. To have eaten it would have been a desecration of the highest order, violating our vegetarian precepts, even smacking of cannibalism. (Such niceties, however, did not deter the gods from savoring the sacrifice.)

All the while muttering obscenities under his breath, Wu washed and dressed my wound, his pudgy hands pressing mine with the firm, efficient tenderness of an old mother. When he'd finished tying the gauze bandage, he dismissed me from the kitchen and forbade me to show my face again that night. I was only too happy to oblige.

Out of the wilderness of my tangled impressions and emotions, one thing had seized me with obsessive force: the robe. It tantalized me, exciting all the passion and enthusiasm of a lover — the palpitating tenderness, the diffidence and desire, the irresistible compulsion to pursue and simultaneous dread of the encounter. There was an element of reverence in my feeling; but it was compounded with, perhaps confounded by, something of a very different sort. Part of me wanted to retire and dwell on it in privacy, like an animal skulking away to the darkness of its lair with a savory bone.

Perhaps I was merely overstimulated by the day's events. At any rate, a little light-headed from loss of blood, and with a thrilling, intermittent flutter of anticipation in my belly, I went to the temple, which I knew would be deserted at that hour, carrying the wrapped package Hsiao had given me and my guilty kitchen knife to cut the string. There I lit a prayer lamp, the better to examine my secret prize, my new — and first — possession.

•

In the deep stillness of that place, by the light of the flame which hovered on its reservoir of oil like a white-robed angel walking on the water, I sat and pondered. Solid and reassuring, the slate flags pressed up coolly from underneath me. Yet I was a little afraid to open my mother's gift. In the stillness, I heard a nightingale singing somewhere out in the night. Its music provided a pleasant excuse for procrastination.

Listening, I fell into a meditative state. Though neither deep nor restful, the trance was exceedingly delicious, shot through with tremblings of nervous ecstasy unlike anything I'd experienced before. By turns my body burned as with fever and tingled with chills. The bird's song appeared to come from no particular direction, or all directions; as I went deeper, it seemed to come from within myself.

It was an ethereal strain, now sad, now touched with joy; yet it was neither joy nor sorrow really, not in the common understanding of those words. For though beautiful, the melody was as cold as starlight and lacked a human meaning . . . or else, perhaps, contained a meaning too deep for the heart to fathom. Lost in myself, I forgot the bird and almost believed it was my own soul singing in an unknown tongue, for the robe and for my mother. I had to surface to reassure myself. Opening my eyes, I saw nothing at first. Then, through the window that opened on the courtyard, a slight stir, a fluttering of darkness against the silver horn of the new moon, convinced me that I had been deluded. The real bird had lighted in the upper branches of the peach tree where it performed its serenade.

I crossed to the window casement and leaned out, listening with pleasure. Outside the stars were winking into life. They hung in the branches like the lusters of a chandelier, shivering in the ecstatic crystal darkness of the universe. As my eyes adjusted, I made out the true fruit, the peaches, tiny, opaque globules against the blue-dark evening sky — fruits of darkness counterpoised against the fruits of light.

Finally, I took the paring knife out of the sleeve of my robe where I'd secreted it as I left the kitchen. Neatly severing the twine around the package, I began meticulously unfolding the paper.

The rich material tumbled out in heavy folds as I lifted it into the light. To my surprise, a moth fluttered up past my face. Like a grave robber rifling a vault, I had waked this mummy from its long, slumberous feeding in the silk tomb of the robe. As the moth emerged, a cloud of the same scent which had evoked my pleasurable sadness in the afternoon rose with it. But where the scent had piqued with a suggestion then, now it cloyed oppressively.

Perhaps it was this that disturbed me. Perhaps I was only tired. Or perhaps what distressed me was the complication of the scent I now discovered, the smell of dust and cedar lingering in the perfume. No doubt the robe had lain for years in a dark chest in an attic; but my mind produced the image of a coffin. Just as this association flashed through my brain, I became aware of a low static sound, a drone or whirring, as from a tiny engine. The moth was circling the flame of the prayer lamp. I cringed remembering Hsiao's account of the fluttering shadow which had crossed my mother's bed as she lay laboring to give birth. I tried to catch the insect and crush it against my nail, but with the instinct of a somnambulist, it eluded me. The monotonous droning of its wings — like the noise of an airplane passing high above the mountain, I fancied — continued as I proceeded to inspect the robe. It formed an odd subliminal counterpoint to the song of the nightingale.

As my uncle Hsiao had said, the robe was of a bloodred color. And yet, the color was not sanguine, not like the oxygen-rich blood the heart jets out into the arteries; in the twilight of the temple, it looked more like venous blood, darkened and contaminated with its load of wastes. (Later I would find the shade changed with the light, and with the temperament and mood of the observer.)

As I held the fabric in my hands, my fingertips discovered the raised pattern in the silk, what Hsiao had called the "labyrinth meander." Following that lead, my eye wandered casually into the maze of the brocade, its twisting corridors and alleyways. Once in, I found that I could not retreat. The way closed up behind me, and I could only go deeper toward the labyrinth's heart, into the sanctum of its hidden meaning.

In the central panel on the back, the rim of the sun was resting on the black edge of the world in a scarlet dawn or sunset; which, it was impossible to tell. The only landmark was a tree, gaunt and dead, except for one branch in leaf high up, from which a single piece of fruit depended, green and indeterminate. For me, inevitably, it evoked the peach tree in the courtyard, which earlier that day the master had informed me was a symbol of eternal life, and where the nightingale was singing even then. Whether inspired by these coincidences or by some deeper instinct, forever after I would think of the image this way.

What did it mean? Was it a hopeful vision, or infinitely bitter, this unripe fruit hanging in the branches of a nuded tree of life? I couldn't tell. And there was so much more. . . . The eye passed quickly beyond this scene into the rare regions of my mother's art. High above the earth, two great beasts wheeled vertiginously in the air, their talons hooking as they crushed together, whether to kill or copulate, one couldn't say. Teeth bared, jaws clamped tight together, each appeared to suck the life-breath from the other's mouth, and then resuscitate him with a savage kiss.

These monsters were, respectively, the Dragon and the Tiger: the first with eyes like fulgid emeralds and a golden body flecked with blue-black satin scales; the second, the Tiger, pure, ghastly white, except its mouth, dripping blood from its opponent's throat, or from its own broken heart. The Tiger's eyes were blue, as blue as space, the color the sky should have been.

The blood streaming from the monsters' wounds converged in a single torrent flowing down the sky, washing the dawn (or sunset) with its hue, falling to earth as drops of bitter rain, a rain of blood, under which the whole of nature had been blighted — all except the green peach ripening miraculously in the limbs of the dead tree. What was that fruit? Some last poisonous excrescence growing in the ashes of the holocaust? Or the precious fruit of human hope, whose growth redeemed for her the destruction of the rest? The rainfall reminded me of the beasts' symbolic meaning as primitive forces, cloud and wind: the one swirling and transmogrifying in the heavens, assuming fantastical shapes at will, as the Dragon allegedly can; the other, silent, invisible, swift, like the Tiger springing out of ambush. These two elements, warring, or mating, breed the rain which nourishes the earth. And indeed, there is an expression still current in China, "the play of wind and clouds," which is a euphemism for intercourse. This revealed for me in the robe the hidden legend of my mother's private anguish. For the Dragon and the Tiger, as every Chinese knows, also symbolize the love between man and woman. These primal beasts cleaving in their equivocal embrace were my mother's images of herself and Eddie Love.

With this recognition, I understood that, in a sense not far from the literal, my mother had sewn herself into the robe, and that the robe was her, as surely as if the silk were her flayed skin, her needle, the tattooer's, inseminating an indelible dye. Yet how I might have wished that needle to have served her like a surgeon's, her thread the sutures sewing up the pieces of her wounded life. This futile wish sparked an observation. There was an odd detail about the robe. In life, Love had destroyed my mother; in the robe the outcome of the battle between the Dragon and the Tiger was still undecided, and would remain so. Theirs was a dead heat for eternity.

As I pondered this, my imagination traced a new design in the whorls of the meander: a bloody fingerprint. Could it be that for my mother the long, patient labor of the robe was the working out of a slow-burning but remorseless vengeance? Did she want it to be known that his escape was an illusion only, that she would never let him go, but pursue him like a Fury through the world, polluting everything he touched and loved forever? This thought made me shudder, and at the same time brought me a vindictive satisfaction. . . . But perhaps she only meant to say that in such a war there are no winners, and never can be. Whatever else it might have meant, the standoff in the robe told me one thing with certainty: that in her heart she never conceded.

My father's image as it appeared in the caricature — heavy faced, dark glasses crowded with that apparition — floated through my mind then, and I felt a cold burning in my heart — hatred. This lasted only a moment. How could it last? Fascination, hope, love itself conspired against it, three rivers of balm flowing into the troubled ocean of my soul, dissolving the intolerable salts and acids of my bitterness with their sweet water. But for that moment, while in its grip, I felt a shudder pass through all Creation. The firm foundation of the world trembled beneath me; trembled, but did not collapse.

As I sat flushed and perspiring, my heart still beating violently at the thought of him — Eddie Love and the far world mirrored in the lenses — an unaccountable impulse seized me, and I looked up. For the third time that night I saw the moth. The ghostly blur of wings, the ceaseless whirr it made as it kept up its doleful vigil around the flame — these things made me cringe involuntarily.

My mind leapt to the image of the women tending silkworms in the valley. Waiting until just before the white mulberry puts out its first leaves in April, they then take down from the walls of the storage houses the rolled papers of the previous year's eggs, and put them in the folds of their padded robes, brooding them like hens until they hatch. Afterward they place them in trays of chopped leaves for feeding. When sated, the worms rise erect and begin to ejaculate the silk out of their heads, artfully weaving their gism into a winding-sheet, moving in a figure eight, tracing the ritual hex sign of infinity. I had heard those women singing at their work and stopped to listen many times. The song was beautiful and strange, but I could remember only disconnected bits and pieces . . . "The satin coffin where the silkworm dies is the womb from which the moth emerges."

Perhaps this unlovely thing now hovering in the halo of the lamp, like a dead planet orbiting the sun of its youthful passion, was once itself a silkworm. Resurrected from the grave of its cocoon, impelled by the gravity of memory, it had come back filled with an unclean craving to devour what it had once created, ravaging the silk to sustain the mindless buzz of its existence. I realized then that the lugubrious ritual, the wake and deathwatch it was celebrating there so joylessly, was for itself. How sad. How gruesome.

And yet sadder and more gruesome still, the words that floated up to me then out of the abyss of memory, ". . . The silkworm is the father of the moth."

•

I said before that Dragon and Tiger symbolize the love between the sexes. This formula was designed for popular consumption. Originally their intercourse alluded to an esoteric Taoist ritual, which only superficially resembled sentimental erotic love: White Tiger/Green Dragon yoga. My mother must have had some exposure to the mysteries of "dual cultivation" even if only through reading or conversation. For the robe conjured the rites too pointedly to have done so accidentally.

What I know about White Tiger/Green Dragon technique I learned from the master, who was knowledgeable about all the schools of Taoism, ancient and modern, and their clandestine practices. (I sometimes wondered if he had perhaps participated in the sexual mysteries himself as a young man.)

This yoga is related to alchemy and attempts the compounding of the Gold-Cinnabar Pill, the fusion of *yin* and *yang,* through a regimen of rigorous, highly formalized sexual intercourse, undertaken at certain times and seasons in accordance with astrological configurations and the advice of the oracle. The object of this intercourse is for the male, while maintaining strict seminal continence (by artificial means if necessary: a tight-fitting jade ring placed at the base of the penis, strangulating the ejaculation, inducing the "backward flow"), to excite his partner to repeated climax, absorbing the *yin*-fluid she expends with each orgasm for his own use. This fluid, mixed with his own sperm, is drawn back into the body and heated as in a crucible, the breath acting as a kind of bellows, until at last it begins to rise through two channels parallel to the spine to the *ni-wan* center in the top of the head. This is a distillation process in which all impurities are removed. Out of the residue, which is allowed to condense and drip back down, the Gold-Cinnabar Pill is compounded.

The technique was obviously designed by males for their own use. Since their store of *yang*-fluid is, supposedly, small and easily depleted, they need to supplement it with the *yin*-fluid which all women possess in inexhaustible quantities. The women, generally speaking, have little to gain from the practice (except perhaps some pleasurable sexual activity in a charitable cause), but willingly subordinate themselves in an act of sexual noblesse oblige.

This willing subordination, and the idea that the woman would allow herself to be thus used by the man in his quest to elude death, very poignantly suggested to me my mother's doomed affection. Perhaps even more than her exploitation, the idea of her huge, passive *power,* the inexhaustibility of her feminine vital essence, excited my attention. As I toyed with that notion, a startling thought occurred to me.

There is a subtle and insidious variation on the theme of White Tiger/Green Dragon yoga in which the woman sets out to subvert the man's intention, attempting to excite him to that pitch of passion where self-control becomes impossible, making him spill his load in her vagina, thus garnering his *yang*-fluid to enhance her own longevity. It was by this means that Hsi Wang Mu, the Royal Mother of the Western Heaven, attained her immortality, in the process using up a thousand young men's lives. Incongruous as it may seem, this is what flitted through my brain as I contemplated the handiwork my mother wrought, stories of young men who had been seduced out of their self-interest by powerful, conniving women, young men who had spent themselves for love, ejaculating load after load of their sweet sexual albumen into the hungry darkness, until their lovers' bodies were replete with it.

Such tales resonated for me. Only in my parents' case, it was the woman who had been seduced and given everything. *Or was it?* Certain things made me wonder. Though Hsiao's veracity was unimpeachable, I knew full well that his perception of events was colored. If his portrayal of my mother were correct, how could I explain the equality of the two great adversaries in the robe? Certainly to Hsiao such equality must have appeared preposterous, at best a pathetic dream, at worst a dangerous delusion. But if she were simply the defeated and abused party, Love's victim, what was the meaning of her reply to Hsiao's revelation of Love's impending departure: "I know. . . . I've always known"?

I now began to suspect that Hsiao had not fully sounded my mother's mystery, any more than he had sounded Love's. Perhaps, unknown to Hsiao, passion and the prospect of maternity had transformed her from the child she was into a woman, touched off a sudden flowering of the spirit in her, enabled her to send a taproot down to the water table of instinct and nourish herself on the combined experience of the race. My uncle, so many years her elder and accustomed to thinking of my mother as an overindulged child, may have been unable, finally, to comprehend the changes he saw taking place in her, changes he noted, puzzled over, and eventually dismissed as physiological in origin. Perhaps in the same way he had misread my father, he had misread her; certainly it was less threatening to him to dismiss my mother as temporarily insane than to acknowledge the great passion of her life.

Not that he was *necessarily* wrong; only that he *might* have been. As I studied the robe and speculated on the woman who made it, I realized that there must have been depths in her he hadn't glimpsed or even suspected, hidden treasure troves of character, full of complexity, richness, ambiguity, as there always are in those we love and think we know. My uncle Hsiao had left a great deal out — not by design, but because he didn't know, couldn't have known. Finally his narrative was no more than his own interpretation of events. To reconstruct the bare skeleton of material circumstance, I might rely on it uncritically. For the rest, for the total morphology, I was left to my own devices, to invent, or choose (as the case might be) my history, my self . . . indeed, the world.

This prospect was vertiginous, but it stimulated new associations in the robe. I considered the detail of the Tiger's eyes. Were these blue eyes my father's, the eyes beneath the black-green tear-shaped lenses? Could it be that my mother had known him, known Love, after all . . . better than Hsiao, better than anyone had dreamed? Could it be that she alone had glimpsed what lay beneath the shades of the man, had seen into his nakedness, because she loved him?

If this is right, I imagine that each time her eyes met his, offering him her pity and her hope, they seared his heart like brands, and a mysterious rankling rose in him together with the sulphured whiff of burning flesh. For such knowledge is power and can destroy as well as save. So long in the cold hell of his solitude and secrecy, Love might well have regarded the spring she offered him with a distempered sensibility, smelling carrion on the warm wind, instead of the healthy odors of the fecund earth. Fear then, rather than satiety and indifference, might have made him run, the wild animal's fear of capture. Yes, perhaps my mother was the hunter; not mortality, not filial anguish — *she*. I suddenly saw it. She had hunted Love with innocent faith and adoration, with eyes opened to his ambivalence toward existence. She had seen the best and worst in him and accepted both, accepted all; and this was more terrible to my father than any of the bêtes noires Hsiao and Chung Fu had dredged up from the darkness of their private hearts to account for what he was.

I saw too that Love had betrayed himself through his own efforts at evasion; for in the end she had captured him anyway. . . . Here, in the robe. Captured, but not tried to tame. This Tiger was not trained to dance. It was given free rein to mate and slay in accordance with its instincts. I believe my mother knew a man like Love cannot be tamed except by killing. This was the final message of the robe, addressed to him, but read only by me: "See, I wanted only to love, not to possess you. This was my love — a battle I would have risen to each day, high-hearted, knowing I could never win, not wanting to (but not lose either). Now I am forsaken. What did you want that I witheld? What more precious than what I offered you — life's choicest fruit? You left it here untasted, hanging in the tree to fall of its own weight."

•

So much arose for me from the robe's allusion to White Tiger/Green Dragon yoga that it was some time before I realized my mother's Dragon wasn't green at all, but yellow. Yet I made no pretense at scientific analysis; when has the heart ever yielded to the importunings of science? The fact is, far from disqualifying my intuition, the Dragon's color reinforced it, even added a new dimension to my understanding of the *p'ao*. Here I saw the ring spread outward from the stone, incorporating a larger area of meaning than before, expanding my mother's statement to include possibilities beyond the merely personal. As I contemplated them, the White Tiger and the Yellow Dragon became not my father and mother only, but the Caucasian and Mongoloid races themselves (more specifically, the Americans and the Chinese), suspiciously in love with one another, as all things are in love with their antitheses, awkwardly leaping into one another's arms, as though uncertain whether to attack or make passionate love. This conclusion became irresistible when I reflected that the *I Ching* identifies the Dragon and the Tiger with specific compass points: the east and west, respectively.

Was my mother proposing her affair with Love as a paradigm and precedent for the conjugation, or foreplay, then beginning to take place between East and West? If so, a most perilous one! Yet fruitful . . . perilously fruitful, fruitfully perilous.

But there was one final association which the robe suggested to me, and I must include it in the catalogue. This concerned the Chinese zodiac, whose signs embrace whole years, not merely months, reflecting, I think, the vastly different pace of Oriental life, my people's surer grasp of the immensity of time. (Later it would indeed seem to me as if a month in America were like a year in China.)

The Tiger and the Dragon are the two most powerful denizens of the Chinese zodiac. To avoid the eventuality my mother had depicted in the robe — their clash — these animals are wisely separated by a buffer zone, a celestial DMZ. Glaring suspiciously and longingly at one another, they face off in the heavens across the neutral territory of a single year, whose patron deity and genius is the weakest in this bestiary/pantheon: the Rabbit, which, night after night, as in a spotlight, can be seen bounding across the sky in the face of the moon, running for its life, then diving into the black hole of its burrow, to emerge timidly again with the new month. (To Oriental eyes, it is a rabbit, not a man's face, which appears in the full moon.) The Rabbit is the cosmic refugee, displaced from its native country by the aggression of two great superpowers which collide on its home ground. Each night it skulks in the darkness of the universe, foraging for existence, fleeing every time the sentry sweeps it with the hot light of the floods, fixing its silhouette in that crisp aureole which marks it as "fair game."

This Rabbit disturbed me. It recalled the rabbit Love gave my mother on the occasion of their first meeting, that tremulous creature whose cry, my uncle had said, bore such an uncanny resemblance to the cry of a human child.

Laying the robe aside, having exhausted its possibilities, I felt, and myself in the bargain, I began to pace the floor. The nightingale was still singing, and had been all along. Its song drew me back to the casement.

As I sat listening, Wu's story came to my mind, the one about the monk whose injured soul flew out from between the ribs of his body "like a songbird from an opened cage," lighting in a tree to cry its grievance to the world and sing its master a long, sorrowful farewell, then disappeared into the forest forever.

At just that moment the branch quivered like a bowstring as the bird stopped singing and sprang off into the night. With my eye I followed the trajectory of its flight across the sky until it darkened the bright horn of the new moon and disappeared, as though swallowed up in the concavity. Exactly in the place where it had entered, or had appeared to enter, there was a blue discoloration in the crescent, like a shadow, an adumbration of emergent form. I recognized this blemish as the foot of the celestial Rabbit. Against the silver whiteness of the rim, it was issuing, as from the pearly silk interior of a black top hat.

And in the stillness which ensued on the departure of the nightingale, I heard the whirring of the moth behind me.

Chapter 10

When I finally stumbled off to bed that night, I was saturated, *water-sick,* with new impressions and possessions: love, dread, guilt, hope, madness — multiple cross-purposes. A ragtag history of my own mooned next to me like a lost planet come home at last, attracted by my heart's gravity. I was like everyone now, I had a pedigree. I was human; I was mortal. As to what that meant, I wouldn't have dared venture an opinion, too newly initiated into the mysteries. I doubt I could have, had I tried. The truth is, that night I was unfit for much of anything, virtually delirious. Wu later told me that as I passed him in the cloisters on my way to bed, in response to his greeting and concerned inquiry about my injured hand, I merely grinned a madcap Monkey grin at him, muttered something witless, then fell into vacancy and trudged off. Arriving at my cell, I collapsed face down on my pallet and plunged into a deep abyss of sleep.

Not so deep or dark, however, that it was dreamless. As though I hadn't had enough excitement for one day, I was beset that night by the first episode of a recurring dream, which though perhaps banal, disturbed me.

Each time the dream opened I would find myself following the footprints of an animal, or animals. Sometimes the spoor was stamped by hooves, at others by a pad and claw. The landscape changed on each occasion, but one element was constant: always in the background was the sound of running water, sometimes nearer, sometimes farther off; sometimes percolating like a brook or rivulet, sometimes a hellish torrent railing down its course. Through high meadows thick with uncut grasses, starred by the blue mountain gentian, or in cloud-forests where the sun shone like a huge, pale gas lamp floating in the mist and the sound of water droplets pattering on the leaves of rhododendrons drifted to my ears; sometimes through snow fields, sometimes in sultry heat through the slick clay of a rice paddy; sometimes in deserts, sometimes over an interminable plain, through salt marsh and estuary, into remote caverns underground, I followed, arriving at last, always, at the sea, where the sound of running water merged with the sighing of the waves. There on a beach of packed volcanic sand, I squatted on my haunches in the damp margin of the tidal apron and inspected the last prints even as the incoming tide erased them. The sun was setting into the ocean, running like a silent tear of blood down the blue face of heaven. There was a feeling of perplexity and frustration at having lost the game, and yet the sea, its broad expanse spreading out and out, soothed me with its monumental impassivity, its complete lack of all complexity, all detail. That gray, somber peace, as of the end, or the beginning, distracted my mind from the failed chase, compensated me somehow.

Whether connected with the first occurrence of this dream, I don't know, but the morning after Hsiao's departure I awoke with a vague, low-grade anxiety, and (unaccountably, in light of all I had acquired from my uncle both materially and spiritually) with a conviction of indefinable loss, as of a possession whose existence I had not suspected until I found it missing from my life. For the first time I experienced the oppression of something at the same time hollow and extremely heavy at the center of my being, which would rarely leave me after that, except in sleep, and, for a while, in meditation. I couldn't explain it to myself, but a change had come. I was no longer happy.

Even my meditation was affected. I ceased to pass at once into the state of restful intensity I'd become accustomed to after so many years of practice. Instead I experienced a regression, and was distracted by a certain sound. It was a little like the running water from my dream, though closer to the humming of a kettle just before it bursts into a rolling boil; better yet, like a radio stuck between channels, blaring in a distant room of the house, hissing and sputtering with a low, static roar. The image from the first of the *Ten Ox-Herding Songs* describes it best, I think:

> My eyes blur with exhaustion and my heart begins to falter;
> I cannot find the bull.
> I listen, defeated, to the soulless chirring of cicadas
> in the moonless wood.

The cicada is the symbol of a restless, yearning mind, a heart still passionately attached to the world of sense, the marketplace, afraid to let it go and plummet like a stone (a feather!) into the immaculate, shining Void. Besides its onomatopoeic aptness, the image is appropriate in other ways. For the dreary, mechanical whine of male cicadas in the forest of a summer night, keening the cravings of the flesh, that monotonous, obsessive music of a diseased appetite which can never be satisfied and so must be appeased, or mortified — in this pathetic image is adumbrated the carnal hell of man. Meditation, the return to the still source of being, is an attempt to allay this music, to quiet the cicada that is always singing "in the temple of the heart."

As I sat on my prayer cushion struggling to dive beneath the inflamed layer of my consciousness, to sink down to the cold currents running swift and silent underneath, an image of my younger self flashed through my mind.

I was standing in the temple, holding a broom which I had picked up from a quiet corner and was bandying about with a military flourish, trying to rout a cicada — an actual cicada — which had flown in through the open window during the morning meditation period and, with unmitigated insolence, had started up a stream of strident, uninspired profanity, unmindful of the deep sanctity of the place and the solemn activity going on within it. I caught sight of him at once, disappearing into the shrine of Kwan Ti, the fierce, cross-eyed warrior deity with the unwashed face, blackened not with dirt, presumably, but the smoke and grime of battle. Affronted at this unprecedented invasion, the bloodshot eyes of the image of Kwan Ti bulged in their sockets, as if they might pop from his head at any moment. I probed as respectfully as possible, trying to spook the irreverent insect from his bivouac. All at once the creature let fly a deafening volley and buzzed forth brazenly before my face. I wheeled violently to swat it from the air, but only managed to dislodge a prayer lamp, which clattered across the floor with the sound of a *ching-pao* air raid alarm.

The brothers, who until this time had been sitting quietly, oblivious to the labors I was undertaking on their behalf, now opened their eyes and stared about like men starting from sleep, visited by a premonition of danger. Petrified with terror and chagrin, blushing to the roots of my hair, I stood there naked, imbecilic, as they sized up the situation. Some shook their heads, others nodded knowingly, some leaned toward their neighbors, shielding their mouths with their hands, whispering venomous, hissing syllables. Their eyes said "guilty."

Wu, who had heard the racket from the kitchen and guessed its cause, appeared in the doorway with his big bamboo stick. Catching sight of me cowering pitifully, he sighed, then set grimly about the performance of his duty. He had just seized me by the wrist and whipped me around to apply the stick when the master's voice rang out.

"Bring him to me."

His tone was neither kindly nor severe, yet I quaked with terror as Wu dragged me across the floor.

"Now you've had it," he said under his breath, half spiteful, half pitying.

I didn't doubt it. Though Chung Fu had never punished me, I feared him vastly more than Wu with all his instruments of torture (and his big, easily melting heart). At that young age, I was firmly convinced that Chung Fu was a wizard and might work a fearful metamorphosis on me. Had I not heard that the fresh, unpolluted blood of children was always in demand among alchemists — an essential ingredient in compounding the Gold-Cinnabar Pill? Some of the monks had been so cruel as to tell me that this was why they had kept and fed me so many years, like a sort of Chinese Christmas turkey. Perhaps Chung Fu would have me suspended by hooks and grapples over a lurid cobalt flame to cook out my my vital essence, as the sap is drawn from maple trees, then distill it into an alembic and quaff it off heartily like a wassail cup or a jigger of spirits, belching and wiping his mouth on the sleeve of his robe. This or a similar scenario seemed not at all improbable.

"I thought you wished to sit with us," the master said.

"I do," I desperately implored, "but . . ."

"But what?"

"He's got a wild hair, that's what," Wu chimed in. "It's the *Sun* in him, his Monkey Nature. He can't help himself."

The monks tittered. Chung Fu did not acknowledge the remark.

"I heard a ci-ca-ca-cada ch-ch-chirring," I stammered. "It was so loud I c-couldn't c-c-concentrate."

He opened his eyes wide. "Actually saw it, did you?"

I nodded.

"Where?"

"There!" I pointed to the shrine. Catching sight of Kwan Ti lowering at me malevolently, I realized my breach of etiquette and quickly dropped to my knees before the image, performing a vehement kowtow.

"And you thought you'd silence this disrespectful creature as a service to the rest of us?"

I nodded.

Chung Fu smiled fractionally. "Hmm. Most laudable. But didn't it occur to you that if you sat still it would inevitably reveal its whereabouts to you, in due course possibly even go away by itself?"

Such a development struck me as extremely dubious, but fearing to press my luck, I said nothing, instead simply poking my cheek out with my tongue and rolling my eyes up casually toward the ceiling.

"Do you doubt it?" Chung Fu asked, laughing. "Your faith in Tao is weak, little brother. Don't you know that for those like yourself with chronically restless souls there is always a cicada singing in the temple of the heart?"

The master's sudden leap into metaphor was too strenuous for my young mind to follow. All I could make of it was that he was subtly suggesting that the cicada was a hallucination.

"But it was real!" I cried, passionately protesting this misconstruction, which was both humiliating and unjust. "I saw it!"

"Of course you did," Chung Fu said soothingly. He laid his open hand over my heart as if to calm it. "Where is it now, do you suppose?" he asked in a hushed voice.

I held my breath and strained to hear, but there was nothing . . . only the sound of my heartbeat in my ears. I sighed. "It's gone."

With a motion so swift it almost startled me out of my wits, the master clenched his hand into a fist, where he'd laid it on the front of my robe.

"Listen," he said, raising it to my ear as though there were something in it.

To my amazement, from within the closed confine of his hand came a muted, distant hissing, a sibilance not unlike the roaring of the sea within the twisted volutes of a conch shell, which his old hand in fact resembled.

Before I'd had a chance fully to puzzle out this wonder, Chung Fu burst out laughing. He opened his hand again, and a cicada fluttered upward from his fingertips and flew away through the open window.

•

As I sat that morning in the temple, distracted from meditation by these reminiscences, I considered how the master's gentle sleight of hand had worked its magic on my youthful heart. I had worshipped and adored Chung Fu after that episode and set myself to follow in his footsteps, puzzling with deep seriousness over his slightest word and gesture as though these were oracular and contained the key to transcendent wisdom. This was the process of my education, worked not through coercion but through kindness and through awe, planting the seeds of hope and wonder in the disciple's heart, offering him a dipper full of that mysterious, limpid water which alone can slake the intolerable, acid thirst of earthly craving.

After three years of diligent self-application, I had finally crossed the threshold and entered the illimitable silence. But my concentration at that time was too imperfect to maintain the state for long. Within five years I had improved to the point where I experienced distraction no more than once a week. By the time I was nineteen I could enter into a deep, pure trance at will and remain in it almost indefinitely. By then I had learned to emulate the action of water, percolating down through the seemingly impermeable soil of Appearance to the cold, pure reservoir of Tao.

Two years had passed since then, and truly I thought never to be bothered with the cicada in the temple of the heart again. Thus I was understandably distressed that morning in the temple when the baleful music which I knew so well struck up within my heart. I decided to consult the oracle.

I was directed to the hexagram *Hsü,* the fifth in the *Book of Changes,* "Waiting," or "Nourishment," in English. *Hsü* is made up of the trigram *K'an,* ==, "The Abysmal," positioned above *Ch'ien,* ==, "The Creative." *K'an*'s image is water, its attribute danger. *Ch'ien*'s image is heaven, its attribute strength.

The commentary read:

> All beings have need of nourishment from above. But the gift of food comes in its own time, and for this one must wait. This hexagram shows the clouds in the heavens, giving rain to refresh all that grows and to provide mankind with food and drink. The rain will come in its own time. We cannot make it come; we have to wait for it. The idea of waiting is further suggested by the attributes of the two trigrams — strength within, danger in front. Strength in the face of danger does not plunge ahead but bides its time, whereas weakness in the face of danger grows agitated and has not the patience to wait.

At the reference to "danger," I pricked up my ears. I did not know what it meant specifically, but it set a tuning fork resonating within me. A chill of premonition passed down my spine, intensified by what I found in the judgment, where it was written: "It furthers one to cross the great water." I knew very well that "to cross the great water" was a metaphorical usage and could refer to any decisive action. But the literal significance of the phrase lodged in my mind, and an image from my dream flashed before my inner eye: I saw myself squatting in the sand, as though in an attitude of deference, staring toward the horizon over the expanse of the ocean, as the sun sank into it to be extinguished.

The commentary on *Hsü* went on:

> One is faced with a danger that has to be overcome. Weakness and impatience can do nothing. Only a strong man can stand up to his fate, for his inner security enables him to endure to the end. This strength shows itself in uncompromising truthfulness (with himself). It is only when we have the courage to face things exactly as they are, without any sort of self-deception or illusion, that a light will develop out of events by which the path to success may be recognized.

The first, or bottom line of my reading was a "moving" one, a nine. Turning to the explication of the lines I read:

> Nine at the beginning means:
> Waiting in the meadow.
> It furthers one to abide in what endures. . . .

> The danger is not yet close. One is still waiting on the open plain. Conditions are simple, yet there is a feeling of something impending. One must continue to lead a regular life as long as possible.

Though the repeated reference to danger alarmed me somewhat, and perhaps titillated me a little too, I was determined not to court it. I would follow the oracle's advice and "continue to lead a regular life as long as possible." It was in keeping with this resolve that, later that same afternoon, I attended the master's lecture on the subject of the yearly retreat which was almost upon us, my first since coming of age. It had special significance for me, since, at the end of the six days of solitude and fasting, I would take my vows and receive final initiation into the order.

"Bits of sentient jetsam floating on the ocean of this life, destined for disintegration and remaking — bobbing corks, bits of tattered and uprooted kelp, pieces of driftwood floating, sinking," the master began, "in such things we find the image of ourselves. But even so we have a meaning and are indispensable in the larger order. It is our purpose to enrich the solution of the Tao and assure the future. Should the least grain of sand be lost, the world would end. Tao itself would be sucked into the ensuing vacuum.

"But this is inconceivable; for Tao is the vacuum too. There can be no loss and no destruction, only the Return, the journey back to Tao, which you embark on in this retreat. Embrace it eagerly and with glad hearts. Learn to know and to accept yourself and your place in the scheme. This is the only path to harmony, which, sooner or later, if you persevere, you will achieve. All else is pain, futility — a self-defeating struggle to circumvent the Way of Life, which cannot be circumvented. Each of us must travel down that road and face its terrors. There is no other Way.

"Go to meet it resolutely then, each in your own way, by your own private path. No further guidance is possible, for no single path is like another, except that at the horizon, as in a vanishing perspective, they all converge upon the highroad, disappearing in the darkness we call death. Then perhaps, from that high vantage, we will see the whole and understand. Until that time, though, each in privacy apart from all the rest, toiling and obscure."

A weird, unmoored sensation came over me with this echo of the morning's reading. The master's "private path" recalled the "path to success" mentioned in the hexagram *Hsü*. "It is only when we have the courage to face things exactly as they are, without any sort of self-deception or illusion, that a light will develop out of events by which the path to success may be recognized." Unsettling to think that this might be the same as the "private path" of every mortal creature, which converge upon the "highroad" the master spoke of.

That night I dreamed again of the footprints, again stood on the strip of beach peering away over the wide expanse of water, listening to the melancholy rhythm of the waves.

On the first day of the retreat, I consulted the oracle once more. To my surprise, it directed me back to *Hsü*. The moving line had risen one notch to the second place.

> Nine in the second place means:
> Waiting on the sand. . . .
>
> The danger gradually comes closer. Sand is near the bank of the river, and the water means danger. . . . He who stays calm will succeed in making things go well in the end.

The recurrence of the dream and the mirroring of its imagery in the oracle a second time convinced me that more was at work than mere coincidence, that I was witnessing something dark and mysterious unfolding in my life, like a faded parchment scroll on which was written in beautiful, archaic characters, difficult to make out or understand, the high sentence of inalterable fate. The idea that it was crucial for me to penetrate the meaning of the dream took hold of me. I tried to calm myself as the oracle suggested, but all through that day I was anxious. I tried to meditate, but the chirring of the cicada had grown louder.

•

On the third day there was no surprise forthcoming, no reprieve. With the morbid insistence of a wandering mendicant carrying his ghastly message like a lantern through the world, his illuminated text, memento mori, a bleached human skull, the oracle pointed me back once more to *Hsü.* "Danger," "waiting," an impending "recognition" — all as before. Only now the moving line had ascended yet another degree:

> Nine in the third place means:
> Waiting in the mud
> Brings about the arrival of the enemy.

"Waiting in the mud" — indeed this was appropriate. For on that day a part of me gave way within, like the planks of an old bridge I had walked across each day of my life, never dreaming it might rot, that it *was* rotting even as I used it. Gave way, plunging me back into the fetid sink of nature, the life-mire, all the squalor and the beauty I had not partaken of and thought to have no part in. . . . But from it I had arisen, and back to it — after the respite my peculiar destiny afforded me, my youth, that brief sojourn in the immaculate sanctuary of the Tao — I would return.

That day, despite my resolve to ban all worldly thoughts, my mind wandered to my parents. I recalled Hsiao's words for my mother — "In the far country there is a doe; Among white reeds she lingers . . . forever now" — and broke down in a fit of weeping. This passed as quickly as a cloudburst but did not relieve my heart. Instead it left it heavier, heavy with an impalpable grief, which was not grief only, but contained within it seeds of bitterness and hatred. My father's face rose before me once again, a pennant flying from the masthead of the ship of fate which had now sailed into the tranquil harbor of my life. His grin was the Jolly Roger's grin, his glasses, the dark, hollow eye wells of the skull . . . but so sad, too, the downward-curving lenses, sad with the formal sadness of a mask, or of a clown, who paints the domino of grief across his private pain, and laughs. There was beauty and mystery in that face, a secret which I had to know. My mother, even with the enigma of the robe, was not so strange. A sense of common cause, of shared humanity, made her fate intelligible to me. But Love I could not understand.

Yet I wanted to. I'd loved him too much to let go, loved him with a love as strong and as unquestioning as my love of Tao, the pristine faith. Not even Hsiao's revelations — which I could not choose but believe — could change that or diminish it. In fact, in a subtle chiaroscuro, the play of shadows Hsiao had sketched in my father's portrait only brought the highlights out, made the brightness brighter — *yin* embracing, giving definition to, completing, *yang.* And *yin* was not evil, no more so than the night, which ceaselessly follows day in the ebb and flow of time, part of nature's cycle in the changing, changeless universe. Perhaps my father was as blameless as the night. . . . But I could not believe that anymore. The hatred had emerged full-blown and moored uneasily beside the love, bumping hulls like two huge ships at harbor mouth, vying for a single berth, waiting for the flood tide to cross over.

Who was this man? I had to know. Was he mad, as Hsiao asserted? Or was he Chung Fu's dragon, an "unimproved" Immortal, a bodhisattva in the rough? Maybe a different species entirely — unique, unprecedented — a species even their experience had not prepared them to identify: a magic fish, leviathan, slumbering away a hundred million years at the bottom of the sea, or some mutant thing still slimy with the amniotic fluid of creation, too new to have been classified, which had breached into their nets, tearing them like gossamer . . . a creature they had seen but couldn't capture, couldn't hold, which had slipped back into the sea and was last seen heading westward in the direction of America and the New World.

If Chung Fu and Hsiao didn't know what to make of him, what hope was there for me? Where did Love fit into the general scheme of what I knew? By what accident or chance (or according to what unknown law) had he arisen out of nature? Was he a fluke, or were there others like him — an entire civilization, perhaps, made up of such men, worshipping their barbarous god, a god whose name was . . . what? What did they call their fierce divinity, what name whisper in their prayers?

As if in answer to this query, the crucial pun recurred to me, and in a brilliant mental starburst all my questions, all my doubts and fears, resolved themselves into that single word, that syllable, itself a question and the answer all at once, a shibboleth which I repeated over and over to myself, feeling that somehow it was the key to everything, *the key* "which opens up the grave secrets of the heart . . . a church key, which can . . . unlock the Great Cathedral. . . ." That was it! The word. "Dow." "The other one," the American Dow, my father's Dow, "the same but different." What was this mysterious entity? I had no idea. But the pun charmed me, fatally. The pun — that was the thing. What was its relation to the Tao I knew? Where was the point of confluence where that turgid, foaming stream flowed back into the calm, abiding ocean of the Tao? For back it had to flow. Everything came back. It had to.

I reined in, pulled up short on the brink of an awful precipice. It was a good move, but it didn't save me. The seed of doubt had been implanted, much earlier perhaps . . . pressed into the soft furrow of my fontanel as I lay forming in the womb. But when the insemination occurred is insignificant. What matters is that the machinery had now been set in motion, the question proposed, the journey commenced that would lead me here. Sometimes I think that from then on everything that happened was pure necessity.

•

After a sleepless night spent pacing my cell and listening to the cicadas droning their dire prophecy outside in the darkness, I turned again to the oracle, but now with a sense of inevitability and dread, like a guilty man awaiting the sentence of the court — a sentence which, in his heart, he already knows. *Hsü* again:

> Six in the fourth place means:
> Waiting in blood.
> Get out of the pit.
>
> The situation is extremely dangerous. It is of utmost gravity now — a matter of life and death. . . . There is no going forward or backward; we are cut off as if in a pit. Now we must simply stand fast and let fate take its course.

I resumed my troubled pacing. I could not sit still, much less meditate. The world was throbbing, one vast hive of sound around me. What was wrong? Already the retreat was half over, and my heart, rather than letting go, rather than becoming still and pure like the mirror unstained by any image, was growing increasingly restless, wandering farther and farther afield. The reflection which usurped that mirror's surface was not growing dimmer, but more vivid, as though composed of laser light — the whiteness of the sun focused through prisms or a burning glass, etching my father's image indelibly in the silvering. Because I couldn't meditate, I resorted to the expedient of reciting the Great Vow over and over simply to keep my thoughts from following their unruly and precipitous descent:

> Tao gave birth to the One;
> The One gave birth successively to two things,
> Three things, up to ten thousand.
> I, a pilgrim in this life, an exile
> Embarking on the journey Home,
> Returning to the Source,
> Elect from the ten thousand things, these
> Three Treasures to sustain me
> In my weakness on the first leg of the voyage —
> Humility, Frugality, Compassion —
> Until, in time, when I've grown stronger
> And they become superfluous — a hindrance
> To me in my search — I renounce them
> In their turn, reducing the number
> Of my needs, my baggages, to two,
> *Yin* and *Yang,*
> The terms of the Great Primal Opposition,
> Which, in myself, through unstinting effort,
> I hope to reconcile into the One,
> Restoring the Unity, the Harmony, the Way
> That was and is, thus returning
> To my final destination

TAO

Mother of the manifold existences
We see around us, this
Kaleidoscopic pageant of Appearances:

TAO

The One within this seething
Multiplicity, itself
Immutable and giving
Rise to all the changes.

This is my faith —
That Reality is One,
And Tao is Reality —
Which I declare
Is whole and true
On pain of my perdition.

Therefore:
I cast away the world forever
In order to improve it.
I cast myself away
To find myself.
Let me not turn from this resolve
Till hell give solace to the damned
And my soul turn to ashes.

But the words coursed through my mind like water over stones. Again and again I found that I had drifted back to thoughts of him, like a compass needle swinging to true north, an arrow shooting through the universe unerringly toward Polaris, the dim lodestar of my fate. Then I quickly caught myself up and began to murmur piously, hoping the vow might loosen me from the gravity of love, release me from the compulsion of his spell.

But it was the vow itself which finally undid me. All in a second, cleanly, efficiently, a part of me snapped, or was severed, as though in some perfidious surgery, my heart, my liver, some internal organ, snipped and discarded. Under local anesthesia, I was awake and watched it go dispassionately. Only later, when I divined the change within myself, the lack, did I surmise the magnitude of what I'd lost.

I can point with precision to the moment it occurred:

> This is my faith —
> That Reality is One,
> And Tao is Reality.

Just as I recited this affirmation, I experienced a hallucinogenic clarity in which the familiar features of the world I knew were changed forever, and the words of the vow turned to ashes on my lips. I suddenly knew that I did not believe it, or at least was no longer sure. I doubted. And I knew then that I would never take the vow. To do so falsely would be to invite damnation. Yet I was damned in either case, lost in either case.

The recognition which the oracle had spoken of had occurred. I recognized that my faith had been damaged, possibly irreparably, by my uncle's story and its intimations of another world, another order of experience quite outside my own, finally irreconcilable with it. That was what had gnawed at me, working its slow attrition on the shoring of my certainty through the days of the retreat — the seeming *irreconcilability* of that world, the world I'd seen reflected in my father's glasses, a world impossibly exotic, glittering, beautiful, malign, a place of magic, madness, power, pelf, desire, where all the certainties were turned upon their heads, where dishonor was not incompatible with highest courage, and the way of self-interest led not to destruction but to giddy peaks of ecstasy and power where every dream came true! What was it about this vision that so fascinated and at the same time so appalled me? Was it that a part of me (was this the "new" Sun I?), some volatile essence passed through my father's genes, longed, with the homing instinct of a migratory fowl, to Return to that Source, *his* source — not Tao at all, but *Dow*? The "old" Sun I despised this longing, considered it heretical and blasphemous, a betrayal of the faith.

But was it really? Was this pun a monstrous hoax of nature, two heads on a single pair of shoulders, or did it reflect a real identity between the two? Were they finally one? If what I had been taught was true, they had to be: "That Reality is One, and Tao is Reality." On the truth of that proposition I was staking my future, and beyond that, the salvation of my immortal soul. But what if it weren't so? And how could it be! I was about to wed myself indissolubly, on pain of hell, to a faith which I saw mocked by the smile of mischief on my father's lips, a faith shattered in a million fragments in the glittering, malignant, multifaceted reflection of the skyline of Manhattan!

It was over. Here the road divided, and both forks led to perdition. Either I renounced my childhood faith and so lost all I'd ever had or known, or else I held it falsely and so damned myself forever. Images of my childhood flooded back to me like ledger after ledger of outstanding debts, and below each one, my name, the only security I'd been asked to pledge (my name, that tender unrecognized by any law, that floating currency, now thoroughly debased). I was filled with despair and self-recrimination.

The fear of hell arose in me. I thought of Yen Lo-Wang, the Dark Lord of Death, reading out the tally of my sins and virtues to the busy scribes and bureaucrats in hell — my life a blank page with one dark character, one blot, the sin of this apostasy, this betrayal — then handing me over to the demon lictors who scrapped and bickered for my living heart like vultures for a piece of meat, and threw my gutted carcass into the deep lake of excrement where it rotted for eternity amid the slithering of the great pink worms.

Yet in the intervals between the throes of my despair, a deathlike peace stole over me. I was like a man calmly witnessing his own demise in the general holocaust at the end of the world. The great slow-rolling cloud unfolded before my eyes, petal by petal, like a vast black lotus blooming silently at the heart of space. "Even in the midst of danger there come intervals of peace." *Hsü* — the moving line in the fifth place.

For the whole of the next day until the cell began to dim and I knew dusk had come, I lay on the cold stones, staring at the wall, seeing nothing, neither moving nor thinking. Finally I began to revive a little. I got up and took a dipperful of water, drinking some and using the rest to wash my face. I experienced a surge of hope. Though I could not take the vow in good faith now, in time I might . . . in a year maybe . . . if I devoted myself each day to meditation, immersing myself completely in the Way. This was a setback, doubtless, but it did not have to be an insuperable one. Life might give me a second chance.

But outside the cicadas kept up their interminable keening in the darkness. And that night I dreamed the dream again. Only this time there was a variation. As I stood listlessly surveying the gray expanse of the sea, I was seized by a premonition. Turning around, I looked back over the ground I'd covered, and, for a disoriented moment, got the incongruous impression that the footsteps were following *me,* as though an invisible beast was on *my* trail and had been all along. They closed in, crunching in the sand, and I backed terrified into the water. I was in up to my waist before I realized what was happening. Wheeling violently, I screamed as a gigantic wave crested over me and broke, sweeping me under.

After a while I rose mechanically, and taking down the cypress box in which I kept my stalks, opened it and took them out. Then for the final time I tallied up my fate. Like a voice ascending through the scale toward high C, its crisis and apotheosis, the moving line had risen upward through the *Hsü* hexagram one step each day. Now it could go no higher. It had come to rest:

> Six at the top means:
> One falls into the pit. . . .
>
> The waiting is over; the danger can no longer be averted. One falls into the pit and must yield to the inevitable. Everything seems to have been in vain. But precisely in this extremity things take an unforeseen turn. Without a move on one's part, there is outside intervention. At first one cannot be sure of its meaning: is it rescue or is it destruction?

Closing the book, I got up and, violating the protocol of the retreat, left my cell. Having no idea what I meant to do or say, I went instinctively to the master.

Chung Fu was sitting on a prayer mat at the far end of his cell, legs folded underneath him in the lotus, hands clenched into fists lying palm upward in his lap, left thumb grasped in his right hand. I thought he hadn't noticed my entrance, but without opening his eyes, he said softly, "Welcome, Sun I. I've been expecting you."

Slowly his eyes opened. As his irises expanded, I saw eternity recede before me, farther and farther, like a landscape seen through the wrong end of a telescope, extended section by section in the hand, until it was no larger than a needle's eye. His pupils resembled the tiny spots of darkness floating silently at the heart of the kaleidoscope, serene and still amid the feverish, ever-changing spectacle, like truth. Gradually the radiance of the other world began to leave his face. He was pale, his skin almost translucent. His breathing was barely perceptible, and he looked at me with an impassive expression which bore no trace of familiarity or emotion . . . unless far down, far, far down, there was a spark, a memory, of pity.

"So," he murmured, measuring me in a glance; and at this word, the floodgates of my grief burst open. Covering my face with my hands, I wept.

"Don't cry, Sun I," he said, but his voice quavered, and, looking up, I noticed tears in his eyes, too.

At this I lost all hope. "It's over, over," I moaned softly to myself, to him, to no one.

The master sighed. "Poor Monkey. Now you begin to understand the difficulties of the Way. It is hard, Sun I, hard. But over? What is over?"

"Master, I've betrayed you. I'm unworthy."

"How have you betrayed me?"

Then I told him everything: about the footprints leading me night after night back to the edge of that gray, somber ocean into which the sun was falling like a tear of blood. I told him of the oracle, its remorseless and uncanny repetition of the sign of danger, of the cicada and my crippled meditation, finally of my blasted faith, my doubt, my intuition of a fugitive, disparate truth the Tao could not accommodate — the ten-thousand-and-first thing, equal and coeval of the Tao, but separate and unassimilable — the trail of crumbs my father left behind him, leading back not to the Source, but into some alien, inhospitable terrain of which I knew nothing but the name: Dow.

"Ah," he said. "So it has come to pass." He fell silent, pondering; only the soft, mournful sound of my own whimpering could be heard in the cell.

"Stop crying now," he said at last. "Your tears cannot wash away this sentence. It is fate. Better to accept it." He shook his head. "Perhaps it's for the best."

"How can you say so?" I protested. "I've betrayed you, shamed myself, and lost my faith, all in a stroke. And you ask why I say it's over?" I wept bitterly.

"As for your debt to me," he replied, "and to the others, anything you owed us you have long ago repaid. You gave freely of your youth and joy, your innocent enthusiasms, your gentleness, your vehemence, your life — and these things were leaven to our tired bread. The other charges are more serious. But

I can neither judge you, nor exonerate. That I must leave to you. Justice or mercy, these you must mete out as your heart commands. . . . But tell me, is it possible that the Way has vanished so completely from your heart, that in a few days' time you've discovered to be false what twenty years of life had taught was true?"

I didn't answer immediately, weighing his question.

"Deep down I still believe in Tao," I replied at last. "But I've had a vision of another reality which I think I believe in too. According to the vow, the world is One. If Tao is only partial, Tao is false. If what I've seen is real, then Tao must be an illusion."

"Ah!" he said. "Now I begin to understand. You have not rejected faith out-of-hand, but merely begun to doubt. Doubt is not incompatible with conviction, though it may seem so. It is the *yin,* faith is the *yang.* Doubt is the dark net with which we seine for faith. But both doubt and faith are only stages on the way back to the certainty which comes, not from faith, but from direct experience of the unity of nature and of the world, the truth that 'Reality is One, and Tao is Reality.' The fact is, what you've lost was never yours by right, Sun I. Your faith was borrowed from the rest of us, as you were too young to pay the price yourself. But now the time has come. If you would have it back, then you must earn it."

"Only teach me how!"

He shook his head sadly. "Would that I could. But as I've said before, there are some types of knowledge — the final, highest truths — that no man can ever give another."

"What must I do?"

Chung Fu searched deeply in my eyes. "I think you know already."

I stared at him, uncomprehending. "What do you mean?"

"You must leave the monastery."

I felt a stabbing at my heart. My lips began to tremble. This hurt me more than all the rest. "But why? This is my home. I have nowhere else. After all these years, do I deserve to be thrown out so cruelly? Did you not say that I had been an asset here? Haven't I worked hard and cheerfully? I promise in the future I'll try twice as hard. Only let me stay! Don't cast me out!" Overwhelmed by grief, chagrin, I pleaded without dignity or restraint.

"Take hold of yourself," the master commanded. "What ideas! As if there could be any question of 'throwing out.' Are you a load of garbage or a pail of dirty water that we should throw you out? You are free to remain. Your right is as real as any of the others'. But do not be deceived, Sun I. This is not your home, any more than it is mine or that of any of the brothers. Ken Kuan is but a station on the way. Let me warn you. The heart outgrows a place. You've been happy here. But now a change has come, and things will never be the same again. You may remain, but remember, one may stay too long in the safe sanctuary of his dreams; like an infant who drowses in its mother's womb and so fails to be born, his destiny goes crying through the world unmastered. Staying past our time, we may poison even the sweet well of memory. So doing, we lose all. Sometimes it is only in giving up a thing that we are able to retain it."

"This is just," I thought in a sad ecstasy of self-abasement. Aloud, in tones of quiet resignation, I asked, "Where will I go?"

"I think you know the answer to that question too."

I waited.

"Don't you see, Sun I? You've caught a glimpse of destiny, and it leads out beyond these gates into the world. You must not tarry, or the trail will grow cold."

At these words an association clicked in my brain. The words of the oracle returned to me: "It is only when we have the courage to face things exactly as they are, without any sort of self-deception or illusion, that a light will develop out of events by which the path to success may be recognized."

"Heed the signs," said the master. "You must follow the footsteps of your dream."

A faint exhilarated shiver passed over me as he spoke. Then almost immediately despair surged back.

"But where?" I asked. "Where do they lead?"

"Who can tell? If we knew this . . ." He pursed his lips and shrugged.

I looked at him imploringly.

"The final destination is a mystery which only you can unveil."

"So you say," I retorted with disspirited bitterness. "But how?"

"The secret is locked within you. Seek it there. *Heed the signs.* The clues are in your dream and in the oracle. Where do the footprints lead? Always back to the same strip of beach, the sand on which you wait, gazing away over the wide, spreading water. As you yourself divined, this is the 'great water' the oracle has said that you must cross."

"But is it a real sea, or a threshold in myself? You said before that the answer was locked within my heart. If so, why go into the marketplace of the defiled world, exposing myself to the contagion of lust and greed, if the answer lies within and can be retrieved through meditation?"

"You must be like the lotus," the master said, "which grows in mud and yet retains its purity. Take with you your Three Treasures, Frugality, Humility, and Compassion, and you will need no others."

Inspired by desperation, I persevered in resisting this stern mandate. "But Lao Tzu himself says:

> Without leaving his door
> He knows everything under heaven.
> Without looking out of his window
> He knows all the ways of heaven.
> For the farther one travels
> The less one knows.
> Therefore the Sage arrives without going,

Sees all without looking,
Does nothing, yet achieves everything."

The master laughed loudly. "Would that there were more sages! Unfortunately for the rest of us, the way is often far more devious and convoluted. There are no hard-and-fast rules, no dogmas to rely on. Remember, Lao Tzu also said — as a commentary on his own sententious utterances — 'He who speaks does not know; he who knows does not speak.' And again, 'To remain whole, be twisted!' and 'The more you clean it, the dirtier it becomes.'

"The Way is water, Sun I, not stone. Like water,

It flows on and on, and merely fills up all the places through which it flows; it does not shrink from any dangerous spot nor from any plunge, and nothing can make it lose its own essential nature. . . . Thus likewise, if one is sincere when confronted with difficulties, the heart can penetrate the meaning of the situation. And once we have gained inner mastery of a problem, it will come about naturally that the action we take will succeed. In danger all that counts is really carrying out all that has to be done — thoroughness — and going forward, in order not to perish through tarrying in the danger.

" 'It is only when we have the courage to face things exactly as they are . . .' " said the master. He smiled, and on the instant, taking a deep breath, I forced my heart to open to his terrifying initiative.

"What is the water in my dream?" I asked.

"You said yourself, it is the sea."

"But . . ."

He cut me off. "Tell me again — you said the sun was setting there; does this not tell you something?"

I thought a moment. "The West?"

The master nodded, and again I felt the tingle of impending revelation in my spine.

"But the animal?"

"That!" he exclaimed. "I'm surprised it hasn't occurred to you already."

"You mean you know?"

Smiling cryptically, he tilted back his head and began to sing. His high, clear voice lilted through the cell, a strain of jubilation:

"Under the willows beside the stream, I come upon the spoor.
Footprints are everywhere now, even beneath the velvet depth of the
    grass.
They lead toward the distant mountains; my course is clear,
Clear as the nose on my face as I stare laughing into heaven."

An ecstasy of revelation flooded my heart. I suddenly recognized the shadowy presence that had been hovering so close to me in the night, felt but unperceived. The song he was singing was "Discovering the Footprints," the second in the series of *Ten Bulls!*

" 'Understanding the teaching, I can see the footprints of the Bull,' " the master said, quoting from the commentary.

"Is it possible? Can it be that this beast I've followed now so many nights through the wilderness of my dreams, only to realize in the end that it was following me, is the Bull?"

"Did you not mention hooves?"

A ghostly chill of doubt crept over me. "But sometimes it was pad and claw."

"The way of doubt is the same as the way of faith," he said, "and both lead back to the one destination."

I stared at him as at a prodigy, as I had that day he plucked the cicada from my heart.

"You begin to understand," he told me.

A peal of joyous, bell-clear laughter rose out of my heart. I felt the first pale tints of dawn begin to break inside me, a promise of warmth and comfort to one drenched through and shivering alone in the night.

"Master," I said, "if only this is true."

"Believe it," he replied, "and it will be." He winked at me. "So you see, Sun I, nothing's over. Rather I should say it's just begun. 'Not yet having entered the gate, nevertheless I have discerned the path.' You have not failed, or betrayed us, Sun I. You've found the way, your 'private path' back to the Source, to Tao."

"And it leads westward," I said murmurously to no one, whispering with awe, "through Dow."

"Indeed!" the master agreed in tones of high hilarity. "The part was written for you, and you've rehearsed it all your life. For again you will play Monkey in his journey to the West. Only this time you must be Tripitaka too, setting out to retrieve the sacred texts of revelation."

I smiled, not so much at the master's joke as at what was taking place within me. Like a ray of sunlight breaking in a storm at sea, a sense of wonder, and of recognition, had broken in my heart. Suddenly I knew that this was right, that I had glimpsed my fate, the jewel in the lotus, which had been waiting since the beginning of the world for me to rise and claim it. And the vague conviction of an indefinable lack inside myself, which I had been aware of as long as I could remember, left me, vanished on the instant, evaporating like a cold dew in the light of this new morning.

"Once long ago there was a tradition of religious pilgrimage among us," Chung Fu said. "For there have always been a few for whom, due to a quirk of fate or temperament, the 'hundred paths' were not sufficient, men who through some curse, or spiritual distinction, could not journey in the wagon ruts of tried and traveled ways. For these the journey inward led out into the world. Your father, I sensed, was temperamentally aligned with these. Seeing it in the father, I could not help but seek it in the son. I always expected that one day you too would leave us and go out into the world. That day has come. Sun I, all the hundred paths are hard. All require risk-taking and sacrifice. But this is the hardest. In the hundred paths at least there is the comfort and support of fellowship, a community of like-minded seekers who can share their enthusiasms, their doubts, and so find some degree of solace. In the monastery too there is a relative absence of temptation. But the way that leads back into the world is a lonely and dangerous one. The people of the world will not understand your passion, or if they do they will be frightened by its implications for their lives, and so despise you for it. And the risk is greater. For the unredeemed world of the marketplace is rife with dangerous passions, circulating in the air invisible and virulent as the germs of pestilence. It is difficult to go into the cities of the plague and not receive contagion oneself. Of those who leave, some few return, but many more find the world too succulent, too beautiful and rich, and prefer to spend themselves upon the acquisition of what, by its very nature, diminishes contentment the more of it they acquire. This is not to be condemned. For these men too are inextricably involved in Tao. As it says in the *Tao Te Ching:*

> . . . whether a man dispassionately
> Sees to the core of life
> Or passionately
> Sees the surface,
> The core and the surface
> Are essentially the same,
> Words making them seem different
> Only to express appearance.
> If name be needed, wonder names them both:
> From wonder into wonder
> Existence opens.

"This is why it is said, 'Tao too is in the marketplace.'

"There is a distinction to be made though. As I said before, what is true for the sage is often more ambiguous in its application to the lives of ordinary men. Though from birth all of us — the fool no whit less than the sage — are castaways adrift in the great ocean of the Tao, not all of us cope with the rigors of that fate with equal merit or success. There is a distinction between being *in* Tao and being *with* Tao. Some persevere in trying to make their way against the current all their lives. They are in it, but not with it — to their peril. The Tao is too strong, too remorseless; in the end they drown. Do not be like them. Regard your journey, not as an evasion of your principles, but as an affirmation, not as an opportunity for license, but as the great test of your true sincerity, your purity of heart. For only the man who maintains his integrity, who is true to himself and what he believes in the face of seductive opportunities to do otherwise, knows that those beliefs have a true and lasting foundation in his soul. For him the journey out into the world is not a fall, but a sacrament."

After this, we fell silent. I felt happy, but terribly sober. My soul was numb with the wasting anguish of the long vigil. The new self I had felt emerging as my uncle spoke had now skidded forth from the womb into the world, squinting and blinking in the sunlight, unsure whether to smile or bawl. Within my mind the sun had momentarily appeared from the clouds at the zenith of a windy sky. It shone full and dazzling for a moment, then the high-blown cumuli swept over it again and covered up its face. The sun was revelation; the clouds were doubt. Shivers of cold alternated with delicious intimations of warm sun on my neck and cheeks as I sat in the green, savage spring of Chung Fu's revelation, surrounded by unnamed flowers blooming out of the sodden, muddy earth.

I was afraid to make the decision to leave, to commit myself irrevocably to such a desperate course. But all the signs seemed to sanction it as the way, my way, my path. There was only one further assurance I required.

"Master," I said, "I would like to consult the *Changes.*"

"You are willing to abide by its decision?"

I nodded. "Only . . ."

Chung Fu looked at me quizzically. "Only?"

"Only could you make the consultation for me? Your mastery is so much greater than my own, and your *ling.* You may be able to elicit a more telling response."

"I see that the ways of the fortune-tellers have crept in even here in this sanctuary of erudition," Chung Fu remarked wryly. "Is this what you've been taught, Sun I? Well then, we must have a purge like the Communists!" He grew earnest. "True, we may aid those who are less experienced in interpreting their readings. But we must never presume to cull the stalks themselves on behalf of another. If they are to answer our questions, they must be exposed to our touch. There is a vast quantity of information in the touch. One man holds the stalks in such and such a way, with gentleness, or force, his hands moist with nervous perspiration, or cool with unshakable composure. These things are not arbitrary and unimportant; they are the flower of a human personality, and through them, the sticks have the power to trace that flower back to its root. What we do at any given moment is a product of all our history. It is a definite consequence of intelligible causes. We have arrived at the present by a series of events which is precise and unbroken, a great organic chain stretching backward into the dim recesses of the past just as far as the beginning, and forward into the future, into eternity itself. Just as each act of any given person flowers out of his whole individual history, his personality, so personality itself is the flower of a longer history, human history, and could not have come to be precisely as it is had history been in the least bit different. Thus by a careful investigation of the specific acts of specific individuals, we are led ultimately to an understanding of the whole of life. It is on this principle that the separation of the sticks is based. Everything we do, even the questions we ask, forges a new link in the chain. These are joined in a sequence so vast that it quickly daunts and overwhelms the conscious intellect; nevertheless it exists and can be traced using a different, more powerful sort of knowledge, a scientific intuition which uses the *I Ching* as its instrument. Thus everything is consequential in the manner in which the stalks are manipulated — nothing more so than that if we wish to approach the oracle, we must do so in person, not by proxy. No man should presume to take the measure of another's fate."

So saying, he handed me the sticks. Bidding me close my eyes and formulate my question very precisely, he told me to rub my hands over the yarrow so that my life could flow into the wood, animating and informing it.

"Should I heed the signs and follow my dream toward the West, toward America," I asked, "or remain and seek to still the passion these discoveries have aroused in me through meditation and the monastic life?"

I looked at Chung Fu, and he nodded for me to begin. First I randomly divided the forty-nine stalks into two piles. Then I took one stalk from the right-hand pile and put it between the little and ring fingers of my left hand. Next placing the left-hand pile in my left hand, I proceeded to count away bundles of four until there were only four remaining. These I placed between the ring and middle fingers of my left hand. Taking the right-hand pile, I likewise counted it off by fours until there were again four remaining, which I placed between the middle and index fingers of my holding hand. Adding up the number of stalks I had amassed in this, my left, hand, I found that there were nine. In the first counting it is customary to disregard the single stick (the one originally placed between the little and ring fingers), so my final total was eight. This gave me the bottom line of the hexagram: *yin*. From this point I repeated the procedure five more times, deriving the following hexagram: ☲☶. *Ken*, ☶, "Mountain," below *Li*, ☲, "Fire," with a moving line, a nine, in the top place.

A spark of fire danced in Chung Fu's eyes when he saw this.

"The oracle has spoken to you most directly, Sun I," he said. "See how, beneath, the Mountain stays in place, while above the Fire leaps up and will not stay? You have drawn *Lü*, Sun I, the sign of the Wanderer."

I felt a tingling in my belly, the feeling one has when a wonderful and inexplicable event has come to pass.

"So be it then," I said in my heart. "So be it."

Yet even as I reconciled myself to this resolve, the master's face darkened over the hexagram. "Look closely, Sun I," he said. "The last line you have cast is a moving line, old *yang* disintegrating into *yin*. 'Nine at the top means: The bird's nest burns up,' he said, reciting from memory.

> "The wanderer laughs at first,
> Then must needs lament and weep.

   Through carelessness he loses his cow.
   Misfortune."

I felt a creeping nausea.

The master's face was grave and searching. "Remember, Sun I, these portents are always of what may be, not what must inevitably come to pass. The burnt nest is a symbol of the destruction of one's home, the place to which one retires for rest and protection. From this it comes to mean the loss of one's spiritual sanctuary. Such misfortune is the result of the way the nest is built. It has been improperly constructed. This is a great misfortune, but perhaps it can be rectified, and if not rectified, compensated somehow. At any cost, however, the Wanderer must not resort to levity or vehemence, for if he loses control of himself and his desires, he is lost. He may laugh now, but in the end he will surely weep."

"And the cow?" I asked. "Does this mean I will never find the Bull?"

"Not necessarily," he replied. "The cow and the Bull are the *yin* and *yang* of the one Tao, the same but different. She is his female counterpart, the earth beneath his heaven, passively accepting and absorbing what he, in his exigence, aggressively creates and purveys. Whereas the Bull is powerful, tempestuous, the cow is mild and docile. She represents Humility, or Lowliness, the third of the Three Treasures, the ability to take the buffetings of fate with a reed's resiliency, rather than growing rigid, swelling in pride and anger, only to be broken. Yet she is barren without the seed of fire, the heavenly spark he carries in his body, galling him into an ecstasy of rage which only she can relieve. This is why, when the fury is in full force, the breeder puts the cow into the pen beside the Bull to soothe and calm him. For in the rage of pride of power he may go too high, aspiring to the heaven which in mortal form he may glimpse but never know, and, losing connection with the earth, inflict damage on himself or others. No, one may lose his cow and yet find the Bull, but it would be a dark discovery indeed. In breeding as in the inner life, both are necessary to the conception and fruition of happiness."

As I listened, the sickness deepened.

"This portent is unpropitious," Chung Fu said. "But I suggest you take it as a warning, not a prophecy. For the oracle has unmistakably sanctioned your journey. Don't lose heart. For look — there is something further in the reading. As the moving lines change, do you see the new hexagram which comes into being?"

Afraid to encounter further bad news, I could hardly bring myself to look. But then I noticed that a sweet light of hope had broken in Chung Fu's face. I looked at the altered configuration of the brush strokes on the paper he was holding, and yes, the new hexagram formed out of the transformation of the lines, was *Hsieh*, "Deliverance."

•

Thus it was that on the day of the Great Festival, amid the frenzied din of celebration — the thunderous rolling of the kettledrums, the crashing of cymbals, the dissonant blaring of clarinets, the reverberation of the gong, all sounding close at hand in the main courtyard of the monastery — I stole away, unnoted by the others. The master, looking a bit awkward and constrained in his ceremonial robes, like a little American boy stuffed into a Sunday suit, yet conscious of his own fatuity and highly delighted by it, along with Wu, who seemed depressed and sad, though trying to conceal it, accompanied me to the rear gate. Slung over my shoulder tied in a roll were my few possessions: a blanket, a second pair of good bast sandals like the ones I wore, a bowl for begging, my *I Ching* and yarrow stalks, a small supply of rice, and, carefully folded away at the bottom, my mother's robe, into which I had sewn the key, the note, the photographs and purse — my trove of memorabilia.

The master's mien was gay, his face flushed, his eyes as clear and happy as a child's. I could tell that he was in one of his endearingly rambunctious moods.

"*Hai!*" he shouted. "I envy you, Sun I. Compared with this" — he indicated the festive cacophony arising from the courtyard with a slight backward jerk of his head — "the world must seem a quiet haven for the weary, a contemplative retreat!" He laughed cheerfully. "Is your heart as light as a feather?"

"Master," I said, "today is the festival of life, and yet I feel a part of me is dying." Standing there on the threshold, I once again covered my face with my hands and wept.

"The festival of life, indeed," Chung Fu said in a gentle voice, "and of the year's rebirth. But to be reborn, Sun I, first we have to die."

"I am afraid."

"So much the better! It shows that you are not entirely devoid of sense! Do not fight this fear. It serves a purpose. Let your heart melt and flow. Remember the words of the *I Ching*. Commit them to memory:

> Water sets the example for the right conduct under such
> circumstances. It flows on and on, and merely fills up all the places
> through which it flows; it does not shrink from any dangerous spot
> nor from any plunge, and nothing can make it lose its own essential
> nature. It remains true to itself under all conditions.

"But I don't even know the way," I protested.

"Follow the river," Wu said, looking up for the first time.

Chung Fu nodded. "That's right, Sun I. Remember your dream. Never get too far out of earshot of the sound of running water. Follow the river and it will lead you to the sea."

I pondered these instructions silently.

"I must hurry back before I'm missed," the master said, breaking in on my reverie. "But first, it is traditional to give the pilgrim gifts on his departure, something which will speed him on his way."

So saying, he pulled from the voluminous folds of his robe a staff. "Here!" he shouted, throwing it to me lengthwise. I had to snap quickly to attention to keep from getting a good rap on the chin.

"What is a wanderer without a staff?" he laughed. "This one I cut with my own hands. It is from the second growth of a wild white mulberry which I found growing in the woods nearby. There is no wood tougher or more resilient. That is why the sages said to 'anchor one's hopes to the mulberry tree.' Except for the iron ferrule at the end, it is simple and unadorned. Leave it so. It represents the 'Uncarved Block' of your pristine nature, unspoiled by education or improvement."

I bowed gratefully before him. When I arose, Wu came up to me in silence and, slipping off the strap of a leather wineskin he was carrying on his shoulder, transferred it to my own.

"So!" the master cried. "Let these serve you as the staff of your high purpose and the wineskin of your true desire! Now, if your heart harbors any lingering doubts or regrets, speak them, for the time has come for us to part."

I took a deep breath. "I am resolved," I said. "There are only two things I regret."

"What are these?"

"First, that I have lost forever my opportunity for initiation into the rites of alchemy; second, that I am losing you forever too, that we will never meet again."

"Never meet again!" he repeated, as though astonished. "Is not our destination one and the same? Keep the appointment and we'll be reunited — you may be sure of that! And as for alchemy, ask your great gloomy friend here. Wu can tell you as well as I: the truest alchemy occurs only in the alembic of the wise man's heart."

With this, he placed his old twisted hand over my breast, lightly, modestly, as he had that day so long before, and I felt some eternally young, invigorating power flowing into me. Then quite abruptly, he turned away and hurried off back to the festival, laughing gaily, holding his robes up from the ground and stepping comically, like an old woman lifting her skirts to run through puddles of spring rain.

Wu stood by, shuffling his feet, looking at the ground, refusing to meet my eyes, embarrassed. I walked up to him and put my arms around his neck. His scruffy beard prickled against my cheek as it had so many times before, only now his warm tears wet my face.

"Hurry up!" he said, pushing me away brusquely. "The sun will be setting if you keep on at this rate."

I looked at him and then broke down myself.

"Little Hair!" he cried piteously.

Then we commenced to bray and bawl together, like two asses, accompanied by the din of festive music. The humorousness of this struck us both at once, and just as suddenly we began to laugh.

"Poor Monkey, what chance will you have out there in the wide world?"

Wiping my eyes on the sleeve of my robe, I sniffled and replied with dignity, "I am a man now, Wu."

"What good is that?" he moaned. "That only means that you have twice as many vices as before, twice as many ways of straying from the path." He looked at me in mournful assessment. "You'll be an easy target for prostitutes and thieves."

"But what could they steal from me?" I asked. "I have no money."

"Ah! That is what I once said," he lamented. "But it is better to be rich. That way you could buy them off with cash. But when they find that you are poor, it will be with you as it was with me. Having nothing else to take from you, they'll steal your heart."

I wanted to laugh, but he spoke in such lugubrious tones that my rising mirth popped like a balloon. Yet I refused to leave him on so sad a note.

"Well certainly you are wrong about the women!" I contradicted, attempting levity with a wink.

Wu put both hands on my shoulders and searched deeply in my eyes. "No, perhaps you're right," he admitted, chuckling despite himself. "With that face I doubt you're in too great danger from that quarter." Almost immediately he was back on the attack. "But I warn you, beware the dice! I've seen it in your face and temperament these many years. Gambling will be your downfall if you don't watch your step."

I couldn't help laughing at his final insistence on airing this old, dusty warning. Though I had never had the least desire to indulge in games of chance, Wu never lost an opportunity to admonish me.

"And you, Wu," I joked, "stay out of the rice wine, and stop trying to credit other people with vices which are no one's but your own."

Wu shook his head. "You are too smart for your own good, Sun I. One day you'll remember what I've said. Take care that it isn't only after it's too late."

And so, with his humorous apocalyptic vision to amuse me, I set out. Settling my pack on my shoulders, I strode boldly forth through the gates, planting my staff firmly with each step. As I made my way down the steep path, the cacophony of carnival was gradually lost to hearing, drowned out by the roaring of the stream, rushing tumultuously at the base of the cliffs, full of rabid froth and madness, and seeking its unimaginable consummation in the sea.

The Link

Chapter 1

Of the long trek seaward, what am I to say? The rest of that first summer was consumed in the journey to Shanghai, a journey which, under different circumstances, might have been accomplished in a few weeks, or even days. Yet I've never regretted the time. Blue depths of summer sky, slow-drifting cumuli, the Milky Way, the dew of morning shimmering on stalks of grass, ox carts and wagons, the dust of the road, the river, now impetuous, adolescent, shrill, whipping itself to livid curds, now anciently resigned, burnished silver in the turnings, but always searching, always unsatisfied — my days and nights melted together in an effulgence compounded of impressions such as these. With my freedom came a new seeing, a physical change. It was like stepping from a sepia photograph into three dimensions and full color, or putting on a pair of glasses for the first time after years of partial vision, the pale watercolor wash of ignorant myopia dissolving and the edges resolving. The air itself grew sharp, and space and depth receded, leaving behind a roaring vacuum into which I stepped trembling with fear and delight. Strange that only as I left it did I reach out to embrace the land of my birth, come to know its staggering diversity and more staggering sameness. Those days were like a single day, and it was one long ecstasy of greeting and departure.

At certain moments, however, the vividness and immediacy of the landscape dissipated and I experienced a sensation of déjà vu. Like a double exposure, dimly remembered scenes would superimpose themselves on the face of the visible world. At such times I had to rub my eyes to make sure I was awake, for I seemed to see the landscape of my dream before me. I experienced this once at twilight, standing on the crest of a high ridge peering down into a gorge, where the black cord of the river unraveled, falling two hundred feet over a broken scarp, blooming white in the half-light, like mad banks of rhododendrons shot in time-lapse, exhausting years of life in seconds, sending up a muted thunder and a fine mist of spray on the updrafts; and again one day at noon, as I lay beneath a shade tree on the bank, picking my teeth with a blade of sweet-grass. An ox appeared from the trees on the opposite side of the river and came lumbering down to drink. Collapsing its front legs first, it flopped down whole in the slick clay, anchoring its weight against the incline, looking impassively at the water rushing past, calmly drinking in the flux with its black-purple eyes, which had no whites, except at the corners, and then not white so much as yellow flecked with red, like fertile eggs — eyes so deep, so patient, like two black holes indifferently absorbing the river, the trees, everything around, until history, the world itself vanished into them, or became only an inflection in the vastness of their knowledge, which encompassed everything, and nothing. It looked up at me an instant as I sat chewing my spear of grass, took me in too, absorbed me in its gaze as into one of its seven stomachs, which might have been the realms of all existence, itself a Brahma. Then it swiveled its heavy head around and gazed into the trees, a silver thread falling from its lips caught by the sunlight, shimmering like gossamer from the web of Creation. Having banished such visions from my sleep, now I awoke to find that they had taken life beneath the sun and that my dream had become the world.

Though each hour brought some new wonder to one so long sheltered, so naive and inexperienced, as I was then, I fear the telling might prove a tedious chronicle. Therefore, insofar as possible, I intend to spare the reader a monotonous reconstruction of my journey, replete with place names, treatises on local commerce and agriculture, botanical and ornithological embellishment — all the dreary bric-a-brac so highly prized by professional travelers, so boring to the world at large. This resolve is strengthened by the consideration that, in any case, what befell me during the course of my overland passage falls outside the strict circumference of this narrative, which only resumes with my arrival in New York. Yet there is one incident from that time which I cannot forbear relating. For if my departure from Ken Kuan was a kind of birth — my delivery, or expulsion, from the womb of childhood — then this occurrence marked my harsh baptism into life.

•

I had been traveling southward for days toward Yunnan province, into opium country, along a tributary stream feeding the upper reaches of the Yangtze, a rock-filled torrent swollen with the run-off from the glacier, melted down in the spring thaw. There were no signs of human habitation there, except an occasional efflorescence of pale white or purple blooms of poppies on the steep slopes, where obscure tribal peoples grew their crop of *Papaver somniferum* for the opium lords of Burma and Thailand. Occasionally these had fallen and the unripe heads had been wounded with a knife, oozing a white latex that turned brown and hardened in the sun. It was wild, capricious country, boulder strewn, filled with cataracts which bounded down the steep sides of wooded mountains and leapt off into the stream. The air was filled with soft thunder, like the distant rolling of drums. Sometimes I would sit and gaze into the water until my eyes blurred and I became aware of a faint, ghostly music in the stream, a sound within a sound, as of voices chanting an almost articulate melody contrapuntally above the mindless din of waters, expressly sad, like a universal chorus of lament. Wu once told me that these were the voices of the river dead crying out for burial, those men and women forcibly impressed into the service of the god to augment his flow of waters with their tears.

In this erratic landscape, islands of lushness caused by accretions of wind-blown topsoil alternated with bald crowns of rock, stretches of eroded, skeletal terrain. There was an eerie, inhuman beauty in the place: rust-streaked canyon walls, ash and amber-colored stones, deep twilight lakes of shadow, and screaming plenitudes of open sky above, blue and unattainable. In places whole mountains had been cloven by the stream. One could see the stratified layers of compressed sediment, the tree rings of the earth, each marking out a geologic age; and against that static backdrop, the river, like the ceaseless present, a silver blade dissecting the dead body of the earth in its urgent, ruthless autopsy, sinking ever deeper into the past as it flowed toward the future.

Trekking through this wilderness, I had been forced to rely almost exclusively on the small store of rice I had brought with me from the monastery. By the time I reached the confluence with the main channel of the Yangtze, which in that place is called the Gold Sand River, I had already been traveling for two days without food. There, where the milky, caramel-colored waters of the tributary swirled into the darker water of the mother stream, already beginning its chromatic metamorphosis to the color of the sea, I came late one afternoon upon a small river town — a collection of huts, some made of river-shingle and mud receding up the face of a wooded slope away from the flood, others of bamboo closer to the water, perched on stilts above a wide white spur of sandy beach. One of the latter sported a tin roof, which seemed a mark of affluence amidst so much thatch, an impression confirmed by the transistor radio I heard blaring away within. On the porch of this house, a woman with a small girl tagging at her skirts was hanging out laundry in a desultory, holiday fashion. She was dressed in an embroidered yellow silk cheongsam which seemed a little gaudy and inappropriate to the mundane task she was performing. From time to time she and the little girl ventured up to the rail to steal a glance at the scene transpiring below them on the beach.

Hauled up there amidst several primitive, canoelike vessels, over which lengths of net had been spread to dry, looking grossly disproportionate and fantastical in such company, was a flat-bottomed junk with a high poop, batten sails, and a hull of pitch-black wood. This vessel was of moderate size, just large enough to accommodate a small, makeshift cabin in the stern. Silhouetted figures were scurrying antlike back and forth across the sand loaded down with great bundles, which others lifted from their backs and stowed inside the hold. Standing in the prow, waving his arms in a maniacal semaphore and barking orders in a voice that vied with the radio in volume, was a large man, whom I took to be the captain of the boat.

Resting briefly on the high ground from which I viewed this scene, I fished my begging bowl from my pack, then started to thread my way down the slope. As I approached, I became increasingly excited by the hum of activity and by the sight of human faces, which, no matter how wizened or unkempt, appeared rare and beautiful after my long sojourn in the wilderness.

Passing the tin-roofed house, I stoke a glance at the woman, who eyed me boldly and smiled, as I thought, with lascivious suggestion. Attributing this to my own sinful nature, I quickly looked away. She beckoned me with a *"hist,"* pointing with her chin; but remembering Wu's advice, I kept moving and pretended not to hear.

To my chagrin, my appearance among my fellows did not inspire them with a reciprocal delight. As I planted my staff and jumped from the short rock ledge into the sand, a silence fell over the beach, broken only by the anxious flapping of the sails in the stiff breeze that funneled down the gorge. The coolies straightened under their loads and peered at me cannily from the shadows beneath their pointed, woven hats. The huge, ugly man in the prow lowered his thick fist from the air, where it had been directing traffic, and stared at me through narrowed lids, his eyes the color of river slime. I noticed he had a revolver tucked into his belt. The clumps of men standing about talking cast furtive, suspicious glances at me over their shoulders, and in response to my broad, friendly grin, scowled and spat, then turned away resuming their conference, as though already satisfied that I was not worth their attention. Deeply abashed by this reception I stood apart, shuffling nervously.

"Hist," I heard again. Looking up, I saw the woman nodding me over with a rolling motion of her head and a coy smile.

At a loss for other employment, I approached, bowing respectfully at the base of the deck.

"I haven't seen you here before," she said, with an attempt at nonchalance through which eagerness glinted like the edge of a knife. "You're a handsome boy — and manners too! What have you brought to trade?" She leaned over the rail, calculatedly displaying the dark cleavage of her breasts. "Do you have opium? Where is it? In the hills? How much? Confide in me, I can help you."

Not knowing what to say, I blushed and turned to the little girl, who resembled her, but as opposites resemble one another — in reverse: an incarnation of her mother's lost innocence, perhaps. She was a lovely child, with big, star-struck eyes, clean and still. Yet somehow her gaze disconcerted me more than the woman's. I averted my eyes.

"Don't tell me, then," her mother said petulantly. "Have it your way. Men . . ." she scowled. "You must speak to my husband. Do you know him? There he is, the old fox." She pointed to the beach where the men were engaged in frenzied, conspiratorial trading, centering around a thin, elderly man, distinguishable not only by his relative refinement of dress, but by the lines of his face, an ethnic Haw Chinese amidst the brutish tribal physiognomies. He was running from place to place, wearing a worried, despairing expression, arguing with various characters in a high-pitched, irritating voice, almost a whine, shrill and obsequious at once. I watched as he took inventory, weighed merchandise, made a few swift calculations on an abacus, then with a mournful air and great reluctance paid out small sums from the purse he carried on his belt. He was accompanied by a young assistant, who in all respects resembled nothing so much as a ten-year-old scale model of himself. This young protégé attended to the bargaining with an air of poker-faced sobriety, never batting an eye. His duties consisted of carrying the abacus and scales and presenting them on demand with a show of exaggerated piety, like hieratic implements in a High Mass of commerce, which he and the elder man — acolyte and high priest, respectively — were celebrating there at the far ends of the earth.

"Your son?" I asked, glancing at the woman.

She nodded, and drawing herself up with an air of enhanced dignity and self-importance, said, "We buy."

The beach was littered with stacks of exotic merchandise, most of it raw material of one sort or another, gathered from the remotest crannies of the mountains to be sold for exorbitant prices far downriver. From what she said, I gathered that two convoys were assembling there, one headed overland to Burma, the second downriver to Chungking and beyond to Shanghai and the coast. The Burma convoy consisted of a single product: opium. The Shanghai cargo was of a more miscellaneous nature. The woman chatted blithely on, inventorying it for my edification, half her words lost in the roar of the river. There were crates of birds' eggs carefully wrapped in leaves, some freckled, delicate, small, others large as a baby's head, grotesque, unappetizing; heaps of pelts of every color and description, some no bigger than the palm of the hand, with soft, downy fur for the tips of calligraphic brushes. There were baskets of peculiar plants, roots shaped like genitals, mosses which grew only under the eaves of cliffs. There were lumps of uncut jade and river pearls, sacks of brittle, sun-dried bats' wings gathered by spelunkers in caves beneath the earth, live bats too, in cages, rustlingly somnolent in the sunlight, clinging upside down on perches underneath their shrouds, squalling and shitting when disturbed. There was tung oil, ramie, silk, tobacco, tea, and medicinal herbs.

Most wonderful of all, though, was the *pai hsiung,* the giant panda muzzled and pacing heavily in its cage, which was mounted in the bed of a crude wagon with rough wooden wheels whose yoke lay empty in the sand. Periodically the bear stopped and stared through the bars with ferocious, melancholy eyes the color of mountain honey as it bubbles out from a broken comb into the sunlight. By the singleness of its concentration, it almost seemed to be memorizing the faces of the crowd through a resolve of vengeance. It marked me in the tally too, or so I thought.

Its stare rested most fixedly on someone I might have overlooked completely had the animal not, as it were, directed my attention to him. He was sitting in the rear of the wagon, his back turned to the crowd, curiously indifferent to the spectacle raging around him on the beach. His apathy, which, nonetheless had an element of faded tension in it, some rusted ferrous core, was in such striking contrast to the rabid passion of the others that it lent him an air of mystery, enhanced by the invisibility of his face. He was wearing a tattered military uniform whose make was unfamiliar to me: it was not Communist, for that I should have recognized. Beside him, propped against the side of the wagon, was an automatic rifle and, oddly, a curved Japanese sword, like those carried by officers of the Imperial Japanese Army in the Second World War, a proud relic of their samurai heritage. Beyond this, his sole distinguishing feature was a bone-white scar rising vertically through the stubble of his hair, which was cropped to within a quarter-inch of his skull. This ran straight to the crown of his head and then, like a road vanishing over the horizon, disappeared into the unknown country of his face. I noticed too a wisp of milky white smoke curling upward over his shoulder from a small pipe, whose contents he emptied periodically, tapping out the ash against the side of the wagon so that the wind scattered it across the sand.

"Who is he?" I asked, daring a look at the woman's face.

"That is Tsin," she replied, "the soldier. . . . At least he was a soldier once — a mercenary now for the opium lords of Burma, though he also works for us on this end." She stopped, having thus exhausted the subject.

My look petitioned her. She shrugged. "I don't know much about him really. Only what I've heard. They say he was a personal favorite of the Generalissimo during the war. But then they say so many things, and most of them are lies. Something happened to him. I'm not sure what. I don't think anyone really knows. Certainly no one here. I've heard he murdered someone — but then half the men down there have murdered someone, or would like the rest to think they have. At any rate, he was disgraced for something, cashiered and banished to this godforsaken place, then caught here when the Communists overran the region in fifty. He escaped over the border to the Shan states along with what remained of the Nationalist Army, where they went to work guarding the caravans along the new Burma Road — opium trafficking I mean. Tsin is special, though. He is the only one who dares to cross the border into Yunnan to take the mud across. The KMT picks it up on the other side. It's dangerous work, and very lucrative. He makes the trip once a year at harvest, hiring a few Lolos to help him. On this side, while waiting for the crop, he traps for my husband to make the trip pay both ways. A clever man. Though a smoker, he's reliable — not like the coolies, who wallow in it. Just a little here and there sprinkled in with his tobacco. It's the only thing you could point to, the only clue. They say he took to it after his disgrace." She shook her head. "There are some tasks we can trust to no one else. The bear, for instance. See it down there? It's for a zoo in America. People will pay money to come and observe its misery. Can you imagine? A strange idea. But people will pay for anything, I suppose, as long as it's hard enough to get. It's worth more than all the rest of the Shanghai cargo put together. Tsin told my husband that after he first came upon its spoor, it took him nine days to find the lair. They are so stealthy, so cunning, those animals, not at all the maudlin, pacifistic creatures they're made out to be. What animal is? Look at the size of it. Those paws! He could maul a man, eat him too. Yes, for all the talk of bamboo shoots, you think he'd turn his nose up at human flesh? Especially a big male like that one! I tell you, I wouldn't stop to pat and cuddle if I came across one in the forest.

"But Tsin, he's just the man for such a task. All the others said it was impossible. Know how he did it? Opium and red meat. Extremely clever, as I say. Not a man to trifle with either. See that sword? He never lets it out of reach. It's the very same which made the scar across his head. Or so the rumor goes. It was taken from a Japanese officer during the retreat from Shanghai. According to the story, this officer was leading the pursuit. Outdistancing the others in his reckless Bonzai enthusiasm, he got separated from his troops. Tsin was in the rear guard, protecting the retreating Chinese army, but he lingered and was cut off too. And so they met on neutral ground between the armies, both exhausted, having spent their ammunition in the previous battle. They fought for hours, far into the dusk, sword to sword, and then hand to hand, and finally Tsin prevailed. As he lay on his back bleeding out his life, the Japanese officer passed Tsin the sword, which had been in his family since the Middle Ages, handed down from father to son. It's a fine story, don't you think? Even if it's only hearsay like the rest. But what else is there to go on? No one knows him really. What makes him tick, I don't know. Personally I don't want to. A man like that, who lives alone without a woman, like a rogue animal, who knows no one, and whom no one knows — there's always something wrong inside him, who knows what? All I can say with certainty is that he's different from the others. There is no meanness in him. No kindness either, perhaps. But no meanness."

This man, Tsin, was accompanied by a huge dog of indeterminate breed, which sat rigidly erect on muscular haunches between him and the crowd, as though relieving its master of the burden of vigilance. Its color and total impassivity made it look like it had been hewn from a solid block of granite. It never moved at all except to blink its eyes — or eye, rather, for one of its sockets contained nothing but an orb of cloudy glass, which in its very deadness, its complete lack of all expression, chilled my heart. Once, however, at the sound of the soldier tapping out his pipe against the rail, I saw the thick tail beat the sand twice with crude eloquence, and the great stone dog turned its head, staring momentarily at its master. In that instant, even its dead eye glowed with dumb, brute love. This sign of affection went unrequited by the soldier, who continued smoking in silence.

As the woman went on speaking and I observed more and more, the scene began to assume definition. I surmised that this cornucopia of exotic merchandise, assembled by an equally odd gaggle of adventurers and soldiers of fortune, was earmarked for pent-up city dwellers far away in Shanghai and Peking, who, as I had been taught, hungered with some unconscious, vestigial appetite for the natural world which they had destroyed around them. But they were no longer able to digest it, at least not whole, not raw, and could only consume its most recherché excrescences: animals in zoos and plants compounded into medicinal doses by apothecaries — aphrodisiacs and cordials, restoratives, emetics, diuretics, laxatives — nature premasticated, simmered, filtered, sifted, strained, refined . . . in short, denatured.

That was the function of this bunch of piratical-looking fellows hunkering around me on the sands: to distill life for others, at some risk, but for great profit. And in their ignorant, dangerous faces, I detected the lineaments of rude philosophers, initiated into a privileged intimacy with nature. Who were they but the "natural Taoists" Chung Fu had spoken of so often, those who understood the Way directly, through firsthand experience, unencumbered by the excess baggage of ideas?

In this throng, the captain stood out in high relief, the most audacious presence in a picturesque, and picaresque, assembly. After his cursory appraisal of me, he resumed his bellowing, shouting orders in a booming voice, hurling taunts and insults at the coolies and everyone else in sight. His words were like lashes: the laborers winced and jumped at the command. The others muttered in subdued, resentful tones, clearly intimidated by his presence, keeping him warily in the corners of their eyes, as though he were a gored beast prepared to charge. The man was in a high ecstasy of rage. He had the most ferocious face I've ever seen — eyes glaring, veins swelling in his neck. His anger had an element of drunken, proud abandon, a swilling, belligerent exhilaration — even a reckless, high-flung humor. Whether this was his characteristic manner and he existed perpetually in a state of virtual apoplexy, or whether a particular circumstance had aroused his wrath, I could not have said for sure. From time to time he eyed me with disconcerting intimacy. There was curiosity and malice in his expression, and though he smiled I had the feeling he was searching for some way to make me crawl.

"And that one?" I asked the woman.

"He is the owner and captain of the junk," she said. "He takes our cargo downriver to Chungking. Watch out for him," she advised in a low voice. "At first glance he and Tsin might appear to be opposites, but they are alike in many ways. He is the only captain who dares to bring a vessel this far upriver, even at high water in the spring. He's reckless, and he's no good — a dangerous, violent man. Beware of him." Though her words disparaged, she spoke with wary reverence, in a plaintive, almost idolatrous tone which suggested to me a more than casual acquaintance, as though she knew this man, and to her cost.

"What do you mean?" I asked.

"Just take my word for it," she replied tersely, and smiled a bitter, ragged smile.

With that, as though on cue from her, the captain (who in point of fact could not have heard us, since we were standing at a distance and spoke with lowered voices) eyed me exultingly and cried out to the merchant, "Your wife has found a playmate!"

The old man, who was absorbed in a transaction, started and cupped his hand to his ear. "What's that?"

Apparently he was partially deaf, for his son, tugging at his robe for attention, turned him toward the captain. Seeing who it was, the merchant bowed and simpered with fulsome deference, showing his blackened, rotting teeth.

"I didn't catch that, captain!" he cried officiously, as though it were some great joke upon himself. "What did you say?"

The captain didn't bother to reply, but simply pointed in our direction. Seeing us, the merchant's false smile broke into a thousand pieces strung across his lips, like beads quivering on a thread. Wizened as he was, he blushed. Raising his scrawny arm in the air, he shook his fist.

"Didn't I tell you to stay in the house!" he screamed, in a high, eunuch's voice.

The woman narrowed her eyes with dispassionate contempt. "Did you, husband? I don't think I remember. Anyway, why get yourself worked up? You know you have a heart condition, it's shriveled to the size of a chicken's liver from lack of exercise. What if you died? Where would that leave me? Think how sad we'd be, no one to make us any money."

"Cunt," he lisped witheringly, "crow, viper, slut . . ."

"Ha! ha!" the captain roared, breaking in. "That's right, old man. You've got a whole menagerie there wrapped up in one. I always said you got a bargain on that deal. She's worth every penny you paid for her. How much was it? Let's see. . . . I ought to remember, but I don't. You remember though, don't you, merchant? You never forget a sum."

The merchant turned to him and smiled with impotent hatred. "No need to hash out that old tale again. It's stale enough by now. Everyone here has heard it from your lips at least a dozen times."

"Ha! ha!" laughed the captain again, with a glance at me. "Not everyone. . . . Doesn't seem so long ago, does it? But it must be almost fifteen years. She's changed a bit since then — better dressed." He nodded with approval, then, like an astute consumer, added disparagingly, "Not quite so young." The captain tipped his hat in her direction, a gesture of politeness belied by his ironic smile. "Nice to see you, ma'am! Remember me?"

The woman raised her chin and turned her profile to him, refusing to acknowledge his address.

"Look how proud she is!" the captain cried. "See how she preens and struts! You weren't so proud in those days! You knew me well enough when I found you in that soldiers' brothel in Chungking." Viciousness darkened his features, then disappeared beneath a smile of brilliant malice. "But once a whore, always a whore, that's what I say. Isn't that right, merchant?"

The old man's face was red with shame and fury, but he forced his lips to smile and replied with restrained rage, "The captain jests. Whatever her former ways, my wife has mended them."

The captain laughed once more. "You may know business, but not women. Look at her, how she's done her hair, fixed herself up, how she sidles up to that boy. She's hungry for it, I can tell. Not a withered bag of flab and gristle like you, old man, but something fresh, red meat with real blood in it. You'd better keep an eye on her tonight, or tomorrow you'll wake up in a green hat." The men around the beach began to laugh too. "She may act disdainful, but for all that snort and fussing, I can tell she's dying for it. I ought to know. Ha! ha! It wouldn't be the first time would it, bitch?" He grasped his crotch suggestively and caught my eye. "But I haven't told you yet about that trip, the time I brought her from Chungking. That must have been — what? — the second, third time we did business?"

"Please!" the merchant implored, putting his hands on his son's shoulders as he stood before him. "The boy."

The captain went on, ignoring him, addressing now the merchant, now the crowd at large. "When I left here with the cargo, he told me to keep my eye out for a woman for him. She didn't have to be good-looking, he said, as long as she had a strong back. Ha! ha! How I laughed at that! He paid me well to do it too, and in advance. One of the rare lapses in your business judgment, merchant. You must have been a little nervous. I made quite a profit on that deal. Women could be had for nothing in those days, and I bought the cheapest thing in town. Still, she was strong, as he'd requested, and not so bad really, if you didn't look too hard. Everything was in the right place. Believe me, I can vouch for it. I checked it out beforehand, and after too!" He turned to the merchant. "But maybe not exactly what you had in mind? Ha! ha! A little more than you bargained for? But who's laughing? I hadn't bargained for it either. I didn't realize what a hellcat I'd acquired until I got her on the boat. By the time we got fairly under way she was all over me. I tell you, at the end of the first day I didn't have a hair left on my cock. Later she felt remorse. All that night she wept and tried to scratch my eyes out. I had to lash her to the mast and gag her before I could shut my eyes. That did the trick though. I left her there all night, and in the morning she was tame. The rest of the time she did exactly what I said. That was quite a trip! She was young then, you have to remember. Her tits were firm and high. Not an old sow like she is now. Did she ever tell you how I fucked her right here on the beach the night before you married her?" He spat in the sand as though to commemorate the spot. "She squealed and grunted like a pig, kept crying out for more. Begged me to take her back with me. But I'm no fool. And business is business, right old man? We had a deal. Ha! ha!"

His mirth turned once again. "Mind me, merchant. You'd better keep her under lock and key tonight, and the little one too. There's a lot of men here who wouldn't turn their noses up at it. They get tired of fucking sheep, mountain goats" — he glanced at Tsin — "bears, each other's butt-holes, whatever else they find to stick it in out here. Don't you, friends?"

There were a few sniggers. Some scowled. Tsin registered no reaction.

"You know the old saying: What's one more slice off a cut loaf? I wouldn't mind pumping her myself, just to see if it's spoiled. Ha! ha!"

The woman spat and, drawing the little girl brusquely behind her, stormed into the house. I tried to slink away as inconspicuously as possible, but the captain cried out, "Where are you off to, lover boy? Come back and entertain us. What have you brought to trade? Or did you come to help us load? It's worth a meal, you know."

"I'm a priest," I said, attempting dignity, exaggerating slightly in a small voice.

"A *what?*" he shouted.

"A priest," I repeated, flushing with embarrassment.

He stared at me in disbelief, as though waiting for the punch line, then threw back his head in a horse-laugh. When his hilarity was sated, he began shouting orders again, ignoring me as though I had become invisible.

Bad as it was to be squirming on the hook of his malicious inquiry, it was almost worse to be dropped and left to fend for myself. All of a sudden, I found myself uncomfortably in the limelight. Those who hadn't deigned to notice my existence before, now ogled me shamelessly, some with hostile suspicion. Afraid of betraying my anxiety, I swallowed hard and, assuming a mien of piety, went forward bowl in hand, trusting to meekness as my best defense. My coldest comfort was the reflection that, should my hopes in them prove mistaken, I might at least expect the fabled generosity of thieves. For if these men were not the rustic magi I took them for, then they were surely criminals.

From the outset, the success of my venture appeared unlikely. The first few candidates I approached shooed me away with exorcistic gestures, frowning and hissing. I might have regarded this as an augury and retired discreetly from the field, honor's scutcheon still intact, if slightly smudged. But with the instincts of a bad gambler, I persisted.

As I made the rounds, one fat fellow with a bald head winked and motioned me over with a few quick sideways jerks of the head. Encouraged by his manner, I approached and, stopping before him, bowed respectfully, holding out my bowl.

"Alms for a poor priest," I said, invoking the ritual petition.

In reply I heard a lubricious gurgling followed by a short, curt *quisht.* Looking up in amazement, I found a hurky quid of greenish snot floating like an oyster in the basin of my bowl. The fat man smiled at me with unbelievable brazenness, his eyes reduced to dark slits by the pouches of adipose which puckered together around them, like the lips of a purse when the drawstring is pulled tight.

I felt the blood rush to my face. My hands trembled with rage. The fat man's smile suddenly vanished and was replaced by a look of sober malice. I saw him lay his hand on the hilt of a dagger he had thrust in the leather cummerbund he wore. All eyes regarded us. My opponent gnashed his teeth in eager anticipation of a fight. Mastering myself, I wheeled and stalked off to the edge of the river, where I knelt down and immersed my bowl in the swift current, scouring it with sand. "Humility," I whispered savagely to myself, "Compassion."

This retreat set off a rude chorus of derision among the spectators on the beach. I was hissed at, hooted, jeered. Puffing himself up like a toad, the fat man called after me, "Hey, chicken-heart, you forgot to thank me!"

Closing my ears to the abuse, I marched grimly through the crowd. Possessed by I don't know what inspiration (perhaps because he was the only one who wasn't showing signs of active enmity), I walked up behind the soldier. Standing a few feet from the cart, I addressed him.

At first he appeared not to hear me. Then at the second repetition of my greeting, he turned slowly in his seat and stared at me. A thrill of horror tingled down my nerves at the sight of him. The scar continued running down the right side of his forehead in a jagged line, like a bolt of lightning, cleaving his eyebrow in two, striking in the dead crater of his eye. For, yes, *exactly like the dog's,* it held an orb of cloudy glass, glass the color of the steam and ash that rise from the subterranean pits of tropical volcanoes, or the vapor of dry ice used for mysterious effects upon the stage. But, unlike the animal's eye, the man's seemed partially alive, glowing with a sulphurous light, like a crystal ball, or a dead moon casting back its sun's reflected rays. There was something decidedly hellish in the spectacle — that milky sphere of cold, translucent glass floating in his pale, sepulchral face, like a cadaver's — that made my blood run cold.

"What do you want?" he asked, in a rasping voice, just one degree above a whisper, so soft it took me by surprise.

"I haven't eaten in two days," I said. "If you could spare me something . . ."

The soldier turned and to my horror reached for his sword. Picking it up, however, he merely laid it aside and delved into a pack which was resting underneath it. Taking out two rice cakes, he tossed them to me in swift succession, then turned his back and resumed his smoking.

This small kindness moved me deeply. Prostrating myself in the sand, I thanked him in the most profuse terms. This he acknowledged no more than he had the dog's affectionate tail-wag.

Putting one of these cakes in my pack, I sat down and, composing my mind, proceeded to eat the other, taking small bites, chewing slowly, savoring.

As I ate, the merchant, in the course of his frantic peregrinations, came close to me, shooting me an evil look. Meeting his eye by accident, I tried to brazen it out as best I could.

"Alms!" I cried, grinning foolishly, holding up my bowl in both hands.

"You'll get no alms here, damn you!" he replied petulantly. "We don't believe in charity, or religion either, for that matter. Not even the *government's* authority extends this far upriver." He cackled at his own joke.

Then he scrutinized me briefly, stroking his goatee. "A priest, eh? How do I know you're on the level? What kind of magic can you perform? Can you tell fortunes, change the weather, raise the river? If so, then perhaps we can transact a little business." He smiled at me through narrowed eyes.

"Such feats are beneath the dignity of the true adept," I replied coldly, by rote.

"*Heng!*" he grunted, frowning. "So that's how it is! Something for nothing. Seems that's always the way with priests. But if you ask me, if a man can't perform some useful service in exchange . . ."

A loud voice burst in on our conversation. "Is that priest holding up the show again?" the captain shouted. "Damn him!"

Placing a hand on the gunwale of the boat, he deftly launched himself over the side and landed upright in the sand. Hitching up his pants and thrusting the gun securely in his belt, he walked boldly toward us. Squinting out of one mud-colored eye, he looked me up and down, then spat in the sand.

"You want to eat?"

I nodded.

"Then you can carry a load like the rest."

"I'm not afraid to work," I said, nervously defiant.

With a quick jerk of his head he summoned over a coolie who was bent double under a load of hemp. As the man approached, he continued to probe me. "If you're a priest, how come you haven't shaved your head?"

"I'm a Taoist, not a Buddhist," I replied.

"A Taoist! I thought they'd all died out. More's the pity."

Rolling out from underneath his burden, the man dropped it at my feet.

"Shoulder that," the captain said.

Throwing off my own pack, I reached down and strained to lift it. The hemp was heavier than I expected, but I managed to get it up on top of me. For a second I tottered and came close to falling.

"Around here you don't come begging for handouts and making eyes at the women. Got that, priest? With us, if a man wants to eat, he works — just like Uncle Mao said. We're good Communists. This is a workers' state, remember? But perhaps you aren't a man. . . . I've heard they used to cut them off."

I heard a few snickers from the crowd. The sweat from my forehead ran down into my eyes. I tried to look up, but I could see only ankles and calves. Suddenly I felt him clutch me tightly from behind.

"Let's have a look. What have you got underneath those robes anyway?" I felt him thrust up powerfully against me. Taking advantage of my bent position, he grasped me by the hips and started making crude motions, dry humping me like a puppy for the amusement of the crowd. Something in my heart went wild. With a violent effort, I lurched upright. The load hit him in the chest, knocking him backward. Dropping it in the sand, I wheeled to face him, clenching my fists.

One look at the man's face, however, was enough to chill the heat in my blood. There was a look of insane happiness on his features which short-circuited my anger. The whites of his eyes had turned a shade of pink, as though from drinking, the irises all but disappeared in the flood of adrenalin. His pupils resembled not so much windows on a human soul as tunnels boring back into the darkness of prehistory, a darkness unrelieved by any ray of moral feeling or humanity. There was a nightmare in his eyes — my nightmare, my dream — and its beauty made me gasp for breath even as it threatened to consume me, consume the world, in one great instantaneous conflagration.

I tried to block his fist as it came down, but it crashed through my uplifted arms as if they were paper. His hand smashed into my face like a meteorite smiting the surface of the earth. There was an explosion, a white starburst, and the impact sent me heavily to the ground. The world zoomed in and out of focus, then I lost consciousness completely.

When I opened my eyes again, I was staring directly into the sun, which had begun to set. There was a bitter, brassy taste in my mouth, and when I spat in my hand, a piece of broken tooth came out with the dark blood. I remember thinking the sunset was flowing out of my mouth.

The captain was standing at my feet, legs spread wide, fists on his hips, lowering down at me. "Get up," he said.

As I made no move to comply, he straddled me and, bending down, grasped the front of my robe. Twisting it tourniquetlike, he wrenched me up. As he did so, I saw the soldier standing behind us. His dark, lean form eclipsed the sun briefly, throwing a long shadow over us. His sword was drawn, and with a movement noiseless and precise, he inserted it between my adversary's face and my own, pressing the tip against the captain's forehead, just between his eyes.

"*Aiya!*" he shouted, dropping me.

"Let him alone," Tsin said in his soft, rasping whisper, and with the gentle pressure of the blade he urged him upward inch by inch.

Standing so at his peril, the captain's breast swelled and heaved with an excitement that was part anger, part fear, part surprise.

"Tsin," he said in a low, husky voice, tremulous with suppressed emotion, "I have no quarrel with you."

"Most fortunate for all concerned," the soldier replied. "In that case, you will leave the boy alone."

"Why defend him? What's he to you?"

"That's my affair," Tsin replied curtly, sheathing his sword with a quick, deft motion. He fixed on the captain's face a moment, then turned to depart.

"You filthy addict," the captain spat after him. As the soldier did not respond, he grew bolder. "Who do you think you are? I'll teach you not to interfere." He reached toward his revolver, whether to fire or simply intimidate, I couldn't tell.

"Watch out!" I cried.

But the soldier had wheeled already, drawing as he turned. His eye stared straight ahead in trancelike fixity of concentration. His back was stiff, his pose formal. A glint of light passed along the length of steel, lighting it like the filament of an incandescent bulb, only red. Rising to his toes, he held the sword a moment high above his head parallel to the ground, grasping the long ribbed handle firmly with one hand before the other, tip projecting forward, edge to the sky, his left elbow firmly lodged in his solar plexus. Taking a second step, he came down swiftly and moved ahead, his rear leg describing a crescent in the sand, sweeping inward, then out again. At the same time he brought the blade down before his face perpendicular to the ground, bisecting his eyes, edge forward. In the third position he snapped his wrists sideways so that the tip pointed to his left, the blade again parallel to the earth, but transverse to his direction of motion instead of in its line. As he did this, he drew his rear foot even with his forward one and again went on point, only without rising, coming down instead into a bent-kneed crouch. Though each movement was precise and separate with the severe elegance of dance, the whole transpired in the time it takes to breathe once deeply and exhale. In his final crouch, he was no more than a yard from the captain, who was only then swinging the gun free of his clothes into the firing position.

Exactly what happened next, I can't say precisely. The soldier moved his sword with such speed that it literally disappeared. There was only the *whoosh* the sharp steel made as it sliced the air. Then I heard a click, as of metal against metal. The revolver dropped with a soft crunch in the sand, and along with it, severed as neatly as though by a pair of scissors, the tips of the ring and little fingers of the captain's right hand.

The big man's face turned red as though with embarrassment. He hesitated as if trying to decide what had happened, what to do. Then he began to scream. Falling to his knees, he clutched his maimed hand, gathering it to his belly. Hunching over it with his head down, he began to rock.

Moving with the same relentless speed as before, Tsin deftly speared the revolver where it lay in the sand, threading the tip of his blade through the trigger guard, as through a needle's eye. Whipping it in an arc, he released it above his head. The pressure of the blade against the trigger caused it to fire once in the air. It hovered briefly high above the river before disappearing far out in the water with a small, soundless splash.

The captain looked up, his face livid with a murderous chagrin, and just as he did so, Tsin planted his bare foot on his neck from behind and stomped his face down in the sand.

I watched with disbelieving horror as the soldier raised the sword again into the first position — tip forward, edge to the sky, left elbow firmly lodged in his solar plexus. Uttering a shrill, hawklike cry, he prepared to bring it down.

"No!" the merchant cried, throwing himself at full length over the condemned. "Tsin! Spare him!"

The soldier hesitated without breaking his fixity of gaze. He was hyperventilating. A large vein stood out in his forehead, blue beside the scar, which had turned as white as frosted glass.

"He's hotheaded and an ass, but without him we are ruined," the merchant pleaded. "No one else can take the cargo through the rapids."

"My business is in Burma. What is that to me?" Tsin asked, relaxing slightly without lowering his sword.

"The bear!" the merchant cried. "It's bound for Shanghai, worthless until delivered into the hands of the Americans. Think of all the time you spent stalking it. All for nothing!"

The soldier turned to the old man who groveled before him, holding up his hands, blinking and flinching in terror. "You of all people ask me to show him mercy?" he rasped sternly.

"I hold no grudge against him," the merchant said. "Forget that! There are more important things to think about. This is business."

" 'Business,' " the soldier said contemptuously. "If I spare him now, I'll have to be on my guard against him day and night." He frowned, but lowered his sword. "But I owe you that, old man. Since you've come between him and the sword — even though I know your bravery was motivated only by the thought of profit — I'll let him go . . . this time." He lifted his foot and kicked the captain over in the sand, sheathing his sword disdainfully. "Thank your benefactor, captain," he said. "And heed me well. If ever again on your account I'm forced to draw this sword, you will not live to see it sheathed. I swear it."

With this, the soldier looked directly at me for the first time. His face no longer pale, he seemed years younger. His glass eye glowed with the red light of sunset.

"Come with me," he said, starting off with a deliberate stride.

The merchant followed, bowing and fawning. "A thousand thanks, my friend! Take this young gentleman and attend your leisure. Relax! We'll see to the loading of the bear in your absence."

Deigning no response, Tsin continued walking. As he passed the wagon, he bent down and snapped a chain to the dog's collar. "Stay," he said. At the command, the animal stiffened perceptibly, quivering like a bowstring, as though redoubling its efforts at vigilance.

The soldier walked on past the wagon and started up the path toward the huts. Uncertain what he wanted of me, filled with awe, terrified that I might somehow arouse his wrath myself, I followed at a little distance, staring from time to time at the scar as though it were a geodetic marking, some meridian which might give me bearings in the nightmarish world I had fallen into.

•

When we had gone a little way, the soldier stopped. To my complete astonishment, he laughed and blushed like a young girl. "Why are you walking so far back?" he called behind him.

"I . . . I . . ." I stammered.

"But of course, you disapprove of me! You are a pacifist. Saving your life, I've offended your moral sense." He laughed. "You must show compassion."

Cleaving through his irony, I gravely bowed my head. "I owe you my life."

He shrugged and frowned. "Perhaps I've done you the greater disservice." He studied me. "What's your name?"

"Sun I."

"Well, Sun I, come and walk with me," he said, becoming ebullient again. "I can see that you are green and have small experience of the world. You wouldn't be safe back there on the beach. Such men would eat you alive. But I'll watch over you. Who knows? We may even become friends. At the least, we can kill a few dull hours over a friendly pipe."

"Thank you," I replied, swallowing hard, "but I don't smoke."

He laughed, a short, sharp burst, then suddenly frowned. "You are in my debt," he replied peremptorily, "and that is my pleasure."

So saying, he waited for me to catch up with him, and the two of us continued on in silence toward one of the stone dwellings higher up. Without any previous clue, somehow I knew this was our destination, for alone of all the dwellings in the village, it had a thin wisp of smoke curling above the roof, evidence of a fire within — unusual considering the time of year and the degree of heat. In addition, as we neared it I discerned an odor emanating from the place, a peculiar and equivocal sweetness, as of wildflowers and dung. Sitting listlessly in the dust outside, his back propped against the stone wall, was an emaciated, wraithlike man, who seemed to be suffering from an indeterminate disease. His hands lay inert at his sides, palms up in the dust, and his head dangled on his neck like ripe fruit too heavy for the stalk. As we passed, he twisted his neck without raising his head and looked at us briefly with a glazed expression. Almost immediately, though, his head bobbed back down against his chest and he fell into a stupor.

"Is he ill?" I asked.

Tsin looked at me incredulously, then laughed again in his low, rasping voice. "Ill? On the contrary. He is at the height of felicity!"

Crossing the threshold, we entered a dimly lit room. It took a moment for my eyes to adjust, then by the light of the small cannel fire heaped in a stone well in the center and the forest of oil lamps scattered like a random constellation in the darkness, burning as though in a vigil, I began to make out the scene around me. Everywhere there were men sitting or lying about on the floor, or on the wooden ledges built into the walls, some of them resting their heads on pillows of smooth, white porcelain. A withered old man with dugs like a woman's sat intently roasting a small black pill of something that looked like pitch in the flame of a lamp nearby, regarding it with a fixed stare like a hungry man reverent before a meal. It was spitted on a long needle, the dipper, which he turned slowly and evenly until it began to sag and ooze in a viscous boiling and the smoke began to rise. Placing it in the bowl of a pipe as long and thick as an oboe, he gently inserted the stem between the lips of the reclining man beside him, then went off to service someone else. Some of the men had curled up on their sides like fetuses, as though asleep, only their eyes were open, staring with the same glazed expression as the man we had seen outside. Those in the upper levels were almost invisible, ghostlike in the milky cloud of smoke that hovered near the ceiling. There was no talk, no socializing. No one laughed or smiled. All smoked in silence, oblivious of their neighbors, their surroundings, even themselves it seemed. Except for the occasional flaring of a match, the settling of the coals in the fire, or an interrupted sigh, there was no sound at all.

"You are a Taoist, you said?" Tsin asked.

I nodded.

He smiled and made a sweeping motion with his sheathed sword. "Welcome to the Source, the kingdom of repletion. Here you see *wu-wei* in its most exquisite formulation." His laugh was shrill this time, a little mad.

"They are addicts," I said gravely, reproaching his irreverence. "The pleasure of opium is an insidious and ultimately debilitating parody of the intoxicating bliss of enlightenment, " I said, parroting the master.

"Maybe," he said, "but as they are, so am I."

"How can that be?" I demanded.

He smiled. "You are thinking of what happened on the beach?" He shook his head. "That simply shows your inexperience. Opium doesn't necessarily induce a state of torpor — only in those whose souls are torpid already. The mud makes each man more himself. That's the mystery of it. But you're right — 'ultimately debilitating.' For in the end each man is alike." He pointed with his chin to the man lying nearest us on the floor. "Regard the thing itself. I know one day I'll end like him. If not today, tomorrow. If not tomorrow, ten years hence. The sooner the better, as far as I'm concerned." He laughed and invited me to sit.

As he prepared a pipe, he continued speaking. "Though you do not say so, you are wondering at my mood, why I'm laughing, what has given me such pleasure." He paused, his glance a challenge. "It is the taste of blood, Sun I. It has a tonic effect on me."

Whether he said this only to shock me, I couldn't tell; but I was appalled. Seeing the look on my face, he laughed. "That is what I lived for once, why I became a soldier. Fate brought me to it. From the time I can remember, I cared for nothing else — neither fame nor money, nor power as the world understands it. There is only one true form of absolute and final power for a man, and that is taking life. Giving life is power too, but that is the privilege of women, and their burden. Only in these two activities are the deepest passions of the soul aroused.

"As a boy I hunted deer in the forest with a bow and arrow. I still remember my first kill, how everything in life — the past, the future — paled as I stood before my quarry, the bow drawn in my hand. My heart pounded in my ears, my mouth went dry, but my hand was steady. I saw the liquid eye go bright with panic as it stared at me, and in that instant I first knew the intimacy, deeper than any other, which exists between the hunter and his prey. I let the arrow go, heard it strike the chest with a soft thud, and the crunch of splitting bone as it drove home. A fine spray of blood from the burst heart spurted from its lips. It turned its head heavenward with a dancer's grace, opening its mouth to utter a last cry, some mute appeal, a prayer or imprecation — I don't know what — perhaps to drink the cool blue sky of heaven in to soothe the burning in its heart. I have never been able to express the thing I saw there, the white-hot burst of anguished, elemental life. It was like looking into a woman's eyes as the dam bursts, as you thrust into her for the last time bringing her to climax. Like that, only more intense. Then the deer was lying on its side, its haunches quivering, the huge clouds passing swiftly overhead, the blue sky of the world reflected in its opened eye. The next moment, everything extinguished, the dark eye filling up with rheum. As I stood there alone at the heart of the forest in the heat, all the cries of the birds and insects ceased a moment, the whole world held its breath as though in reverence — an almost uncanny silence. Then I felt the light play of the wind on my cheeks again, like a sign, the gnawing restlessness in my belly already starting up again, though less insistent. I hefted the still-warm body on my shoulder and carried it away for butchering. Ah, Sun I, I was never the same after that. From that time I knew my calling, my purpose in the world, to be a priest like you" — he smiled at me — "and to celebrate the high mystery of death."

In his absorption, Tsin had laid the pipe aside. "But killing an animal is only a pale, poor substitute for the real thing, a shadow exercise. There is so little risk, so little challenge that in the end it becomes almost mechanical. The connoisseurs of my trade know that the intensity of the experience is directly proportional to the risk. Only in the pursuit of an equal adversary does one come into the higher reaches of this mystery. And that means killing men. Not murder, which is done in stealth and from advantage, the lowest form of meanness and dishonor, but in war. In truth, this is why that great sacrament was brought into the world, so that man might come to know himself, his pristine essence. All the platitudes of politics — justice, sovereignty, self-defense — these are just the excuses invented by those not strong enough to stomach the truth (or think the rest of us aren't strong enough to stomach it): that battle is the highest expression of human aspiration, the final truth and end of human life, pushing us beyond our limits into our divinity; that we kill, not out of grim, unwelcome necessity, but because it refreshes and invigorates us, because the spirit craves it, and because only in the moment of taking life are we truly alive ourselves. For the rest of it, we are always half asleep. That dull, gnawing restlessness pervades. If you think I'm joking, or insane, ask any man who's tasted it himself, who's known the savage joy of fighting hand to hand against an enemy in battle. Whatever his nature, you will note that with the passage of the years, after all else has faded, this memory remains. However terrified he might have been, however much he might have loathed what he was forced to do on principle, this experience will necessarily have evoked a searing beauty which try as he may he can never forget. For it is incommensurable with all the other truths and pleasures life affords — even the love of women. Strange that all knowledge should be tied irrevocably to destruction. But there you are.

"I have lived a reasonably long life, at least for one of my profession, and everything I know, the sum of my experience, boils down to this: A man is born, enjoys, perhaps, if he is lucky, a few brief years of illusory happiness as a child in his mother's arms, and then one day, mysteriously, the gnawing in his heart begins. He wakes up to the fact that everything is transitory, that all he loves and knows is slipping out of his control forever even as he knows and loves it. In the shadow of that knowledge, he fills his days with tedious duties, finds some way to trick the hours out until he dies, and only then, just maybe, for a time no longer than the wink of an eye, on the brink of the eternal darkness, does he catch a glimpse of truth — that all he is and does is meaningless in the large scheme of things, that it were better had he not been born. I have carried this knowledge with me since I was a child. That is the ultimate source of the gnawing I have spoken of. And there is only one method of relief. The only moments in my life when I've known respite from the emptiness were in the heat of battle, when I've looked into my adversary's eyes and slain him without malice. Why is this so? You tell me. I cannot tell you.

"But how are you to understand me? What can you know of the ecstasy of combat? Listen, Sun I. There is something in us which responds to the voice of fire roaring uncontrolled, laying waste to villages, the sound of women wailing, cattle lowing in terror, wood hissing and popping in the flames, the intense heat of thatch raging in your face, singeing the eyebrows, cracking the lips, blacking the skin, the smell of burning flesh. There is a sense of something absolutely real and present which obviates the need for gods. It sates and saturates the sensibilities with a conviction of absolute and unequivocal existence. The consolation of religion, life's meaning, the complexion of the future — these problems and dilemmas reveal their specious nature to us and then disappear. The gnawing, the dissatisfaction in the belly, finally vanishes. We cease to be divided with ourselves. This is the consummation of reality, most intense when one comes face to face with a single adversary in the heat of battle, as I've said. It's a funny thing. Have you ever seen dogs fight? Men are not essentially different. They too face off against one another before they spring, direct that final penetrating inquiry into one another's souls as a gesture of respect and challenge, a kind of signature. Volumes of wordless knowledge are exchanged in that eternal instant, the finest in a life. You stand in absolute candor before your enemy, fiercely alive but equally prepared to die. . . . That vulnerability is deeper than love. Such confrontations are the only direct knowledge we can ever have of the eternal, for this prize is granted only to those who are willing to pay for it with life.

"The first man I ever killed — I remember his face with absolute clarity, better than I remember my father's or my wife's. It was during the fall of Shanghai. I surprised him in an alleyway. I'll never forget the surprise, the sadness and fierce determination in his eyes. He was beautiful, complete, transfigured; he might have been an Immortal, and you know? He smiled at me, not in irony, or triumph, or resignation, but out of an impulse of spontaneous joy, I think. Yes, joy. And I smiled back at him. As he appeared to me, so I appeared to him, even as we raised our guns and opened fire. As it happened, I was lucky, a little quicker. I leveled, pulled the trigger. Then for the first time, in a voice I hardly recognized as my own, I heard that shrill, spontaneous shout of primitive triumph (and lamentation too, inseparably mixed) welling out of me, as his body, riddled with bullets, staggered and fell. Breathless, I walked up to him and looked down in his face, saw the white clouds floating in the sea of his dark pupils, as I had seen them in the deer's that day, like petals floating in a well over which a thin pellicle of ice was forming. His life bled out into the street. As I stood savoring each inflection of discovery in his dying eyes, he vanished, escaped with the final sweets across the border of that unknown country where I could not follow him, left me gazing longingly after, filled with a sense of awe and wonder such as I had never known, simply to find myself still there, alive. The unutterable mystery and beauty of the world came home to me in that instant. I came as close to religion, I suppose, as I will ever come, even as I sinned the deepest.

"The sensation carried over into the next day. I woke as from a drunken sleep, every muscle sore, every nerve strained, my mind dazed, my body aching with the hangover of battle. It's an odd throbbing, looming pain, Sun I, like migraine, only not precisely physical; and it sheds a light over everything, illuminating men's faces with the agonizing beauty of transitoriness, which battle, more than any other activity, emphasizes. With this pain I fully realized that, for me, combat is the only reality, that, in the end, the cause, the pretext, doesn't matter, only the thing itself."

The soldier, who had been speaking in a kind of rapture, hesitated. A shadow crossed his face. "A man whom I once loved and killed for told me afterward that I sickened him, that he despised me, that my offering was polluted, that I'd committed a deep and irremissible sin. I felt betrayed and affected not to understand him. What kind of message was this from a great warrior's lips? But even then some part of me glimpsed his meaning, knew that what he said was true. It didn't matter though. Damnation seemed a small enough price to pay for the sweetness of such ecstasy.

"And truly, Sun I, damnation is the price I've paid. But when a man has known the taste of blood, it's not a simple matter to forget. For my part, I've been successful in some measure, substituting one addiction for another, the lesser for the greater, the greatest one of all." He reached for the pipe, then sat back and gazed at me intently. "You know, you remind me of someone I once faced in battle, a young Communist, a boy no older than yourself. As I was about to deliver the coup de grace, I knew from the grave dignity in his expression that, even if he lived another hundred years, he'd never rise above the state of grace he had attained beneath my sword. And so I cut him off, cropped him like a flower before it wilts upon the stalk. I was the wrath of God, Sun I, the angel of beauty and oblivion. I brought him to the final vantage point where everything is clear, and then I set him free from the sick misery of life. . . ." Tsin's voice broke, an incompletely stifled sob escaping his lips as he uttered this last tormented phrase. He placed the bowl over the flame. The opium began to hiss and sputter. As he brought it to his lips, the red light of the coals flashed hellishly in his glass eye. But in his other eye, the living one, a spark of anguished, angry light appeared, a tiny beacon of the sober will, like a swimmer's platform tenuously anchored in the sea of his black pupil.

He took his first puff, inhaled and held it, continuing to speak through his clenched teeth. "But all that is behind me now." There were tears in his eyes, and then . . . the void, the swimmer's platform disappearing underneath a breaking wave of nothingness as he exhaled.

•

Within fifteen minutes all the fineness I'd discerned in Tsin's face was gone. He was again the pale, cadaverous figure I had seen in the wagon earlier. It was as though a ruthless god had swept into and through him, granting him a period of preternatural vitality which consumed the sources of his mortal life with their fierce burning. The transformation was pitiable and horrifying, and it aroused in me a surge of deep resentment against life for the pass that it had brought him to. For even though his talk of the "ecstasy of combat" had sickened me, there had been true passion in his face which now had vanished utterly, succeeded by something indescribably pathetic, almost obscene. The opium allayed the fury in his heart, but truly it was questionable which was worse, the cure or the disease. That the passion with which he'd spoken was an index of the truth of the words themselves, I would have vehemently disputed. The idea was unacceptable. Yet I couldn't dismiss it out of hand. There was a certain justice in the correspondence, the vessel was undoubtedly authentic and appeared to recommend the wine. If nothing else, I understood exactly what he meant by the "gnawing restlessness" in the belly. What else was it but the cicada in the temple of the heart?

He held out the pipe to me, and I took it. Not for the reasons you might expect. There was no threat, no violence in his expression now, nothing that compelled me against my will, only a mute, low-keyed appeal, a request of solidarity in which I intuited a commandment of self-abandon, some fraternal pact between us . . . though in what its basis lay, when sealed, I could not have said.

Taking the thin stem between my lips like the embouchure of a wind instrument, I sucked until the black gum began to crackle and sputter. With the first inhalation, I coughed violently. More cautiously, I drew in a second, smaller breath of smoke. Screwing up my brow in concentration, I waited for the magic to transfigure me. Nothing happened. I inhaled again. Still nothing. I was beginning to wonder if the efficacy of the drug were purely mythical, or if perhaps I were impervious, or doing something wrong, when my brain became enveloped in a cloud of instant warmth and suavity. It was as though a magician had whirled his cape, snapping it in the air; with a burst of intoxicatingly sweet, rainbow-colored smoke — a *puff!* a *pop!* (as of an exploding champagne cork) — a tiny genie materialized, small, green, and muscular, with brass earrings and bracelets on his arms and a topknot on his bald head, black eyes glittering with mischief. Not that I actually beheld any such apparition, but some new element in my consciousness corresponded to his presence. The little devil had a dreadfully prepossessing aspect and did the damnedest tricks. I fell for him at once — the pointed ears, his cute pixie manner.

"I am your servant," he said, with a gallant bow, and therewith transformed the world into a living organism which breathed and glowed. I rode upon the heave and swell of continents, the roiling of the liquid magma beneath the crust became audible to my ear, like the coursing of blood in human veins.

But my genie's exertions tired him. He grew wan and irritable, and I soon discovered he required constant stimulation, constant feeding, else he grew petulant and dull. Then he lay down and began to shiver, staring at me with big, imploring eyes. So, more to appease him than to please myself, I took another puff, which immediately revived him, brought him back to snuff, whereupon he swore with great sincerity and heat to serve me better in the future. This, over and over. Finally I came to dread the inevitable waning of his vigor. I regarded the contents of the pipe with consternation, wondering what I should do when I'd exhausted them. The blank expressions of the other smokers in the den were now full of meaning. I saw directly into their souls, discovering a kind of pity there, though static, lacking the power, or even the desire, to redress what it regretted. With each new inhalation, my little servant's reinvigoration became less and less complete, until in the end he fell into a torpor, shivering and convulsing at the point of death. Then I realized with a shudder that the complexion of the situation had changed — reversed itself to be exact: I now served him. A surge of panic rose from my belly like a white-hot bubble and, bursting on my lips in one last parody of innocent pleasure, became a butterfly, a Monarch, which with a child's delight I reached out smiling to touch. But in my hand it became the moth, the *Bombyx mori*, with hairy legs and a hundred compound eyes aquiver in its head. Then consciousness lapsed, and I fell into a dream.

In it I was serving tea and peaches to the great stone dog, in ritual vessels from the monastery. At a little distance, sitting in silent dignity, the bear was waiting to receive its portion. The little girl was weaving a garland of opium poppies for the bear's head, having already done so for the dog. As I pressed down the lid and poured the tea, the dog looked up at me with a quizzical expression, tilting its head to the side. Curious to ascertain the meaning of that glance, I looked down. From the spout of the pot, not tea, but a thick stream of steaming, viscous blood was pouring. Recoiling with horror and revulsion, I almost dropped the pot. But the animal, noting my distress, said something soothing to me in a human voice, which immediately clarified the situation and relieved my terror — something I could never afterward recall. Then it bowed its great head and began to lap the contents of the cup.

With that I was startled awake by a frenzied baying. At first I could not be sure whether it came from without or had been produced by my own mind, a figment connected with the dream. Opening my eyes, I had a sensation of surfacing from a great ocean depth, coming from the darkness and the pressure out into the light where I could breathe again. I sat up and looked around, partially refreshed by sleep, though far from sober. All was as it had been. The addicts were still lying about, staring with glassy eyes into the golden distance from which I had so recently returned. Only now it was full dark outside, and the soldier had disappeared. This development filled me with alarm at first, until I reflected that he had probably only gone to check about the loading of the bear.

There was a great buzzing stillness over the world, in which I reposed and listened. The baying I had heard, or thought I'd heard, had vanished, so I was forced to conclude that it had been imaginary. Yet the intermittent rumbling of thunder, booming far away over the river and echoing cavernously against the canyon walls, was real enough, as was the strident trill of the cicadas tuning up in the darkness. Occasionally a pulse of heat lightning flashed across the sky, lighting up the outline of the mountains. And once, piercing the din of other sounds, the shrill, plaintive cry of a night bird broke across the hills. Its song was unfamiliar to me, and yet not wholly . . . evocative of something I had known, deeper than memory, almost like a cry for help, but after the damage has been done and is beyond redress.

I can't say why exactly, perhaps it was the drug, but in the stillness and the heat, amid the crying of the bird and the cicadas and the rumbling of thunder, I was filled with an odd sense of imminence. I felt restless and curious. Standing up, I stretched myself, then, taking my belongings, drifted through the door and wandered off, headed vaguely in the direction of the beach.

From the position on the hill where I'd stood earlier that day surveying the scene for the first time, I looked down once again. A flurry of lights moved over the beach, like lightning bugs seen at a great distance in a high, uncut mountain meadow through the silver haze of twilight — torches carried by invisible hands.

Coming onto the beach, I became aware of the buzzing of many voices, whispering excitedly. Above this background, the cries of the bird had risen to a crescendo, assuming a distinctly human cast. I noticed that the bear's cage rested in exactly the same spot it had occupied in the afternoon, a fact which gave me pause, since I had heard the merchant promise to have it loaded. What's more, by the light of the full moon, which cast a swath of rippling light across the river, I could see the door was open. Occasionally, with a gust of wind down the gorge, it creaked on its hinge. This in conjunction with the crying of the bird teased me with a suggested recollection, which I could not pin down. Looking back over my shoulder at this troubling portent as I continued to walk, I tripped on something. Regaining my balance, I saw a huge form, dark in the moonlight, lying in the sand. My first thought was that it was the bear, but drawing close, I recognized it as the dog. Stretched out on the beach, it almost seemed asleep. But its eyes were open, the glass one glittering with an eerie, spectral light beneath the moon, which it resembled. The thought occurred to me that, disdaining any lapse in vigilance, the dog literally 'slept with open eyes.' But as I examined it closer, I noticed that its head was lying in a puddle, not much more than a damp stain in the sand really, with a small residue of standing liquid in it. Shivering with intimation, I knelt down beside the huge beast. With fascinated horror, I dipped my finger in the pool and raised it to my lips. It was sweet and viscous, and by the taste I identified it as blood. Peering closer, I saw a huge rip in the skin above its ear through which the skull glimmered dully. Its head had been crushed open to the brain. Remembering my dream, I leaned down and vomited in the sand.

When the spasms ceased, I rose to my feet and ran frantically to the center of the beach. "What's happened?" I cried out. "Where is Tsin?"

The groups of men holding torches, who until that time had not seen me or simply had taken no notice, stopped what they were doing and turned to stare, their whispers dying on their lips. An eerie silence fell. The wind whipped the torch flames, the cicadas droned, there was the sound of rushing water; but no one answered me. It was like a dream where everyone knew what was going on except myself, but whether out of fear or inability or malice, refused to explain.

Turning from them in exasperation, I looked toward the boat, a great mute opacity against the crystalline transparency of night. My eye lighted on something palely luminous hovering there, wavering above the deck like the flame of a spectral taper. Moving closer, I made out the features of the woman, pacing distractedly over the deck in her cheongsam, wringing her hands. Her hair was disheveled, her eyes wild in the moonlight, and as she paced she wailed in a primitive, ritual cadence which seemed older than the world, a cry which soothed me, even as it bespoke some awful tragedy. I then recognized the source of the curious cries which I'd mistakenly attributed to a rare night bird indigenous to the region, and followed like a ghostly summons to the beach.

Hearing me clattering toward her up the plank, she wheeled skittishly and held her hands up like claws before her face, which she averted slightly, as though to fend off an attack.

"Who is it?" she hissed in a strident, throaty whisper, conveying fright as well as menace.

"Sun I," I said, "the priest."

She lowered her hands and peered at me through the darkness, squinting up her eyes. Satisfied as to my identity, she approached and took my hands. Her eyes grew large. There was a hint of the same wonder in them that had struck me in the little girl's, only its motive was not innocence but terror. By our proximity, I was able to make/out that her robe was spattered and besmirched with something. Was it blood?

She stared at me silently with an imploring expression which made me frantically uncomfortable. For though it was obvious that something serious was wrong, I hadn't the slightest idea what it was or what to do about it.

"What is it?" I asked. "Tell me what's happened."

A tremor started working at her lips, her features puckering as though she were about to weep. She tried to speak, but no sound came. The spasm relaxed briefly, then seized her with redoubled force. She started hyperventilating. Finally it broke, and she began to sob hysterically. Falling to her knees, she buried her face in my robe.

"What is it? What's wrong?" I kept asking, growing more and more alarmed. But she continued weeping, oblivious to my questions, until the spate had exhausted itself. Then as suddenly as it had started, it was over. She looked up at me with clear, tormented eyes.

"Come with me," she said in the rapt voice of a prophetess about to reveal a wonder. Drawing me by both hands, she led me to the gunwale of the boat, facing out into the river.

"I heard it splash there in the river, like a stone," she continued in that uncanny voice, pointing to a spot indistinguishable in the massive flood of roiling water. "There was a dark pit in the river where it fell, then millions of glittering splinters, like a fractured pane of glass."

"What?" I asked, turning her gently toward me, away from the wild spectacle which obsessed her. "What fell?"

Once again her features puckered, but she was able to regain her self-control. Taking me by the hand, she led me across the deck into the stern where the makeshift cabin was erected.

"Where are you taking me?" I asked in alarm, thinking of the captain.

"Are you afraid?" she asked tauntingly.

I bridled at the doorway, refusing to go further.

The woman dropped my hand and faced me. "You asked me what had happened. Go and see for yourself." She raised her arm and pointed across the threshold into the dim interior.

Challenged, I cautiously entered, impelled as much by curiosity as shame or honor. By the dingy glow of a small, smoky lantern mounted on a swivel in the wall, I made out a seaman's table covered with a characteristic clutter: stacks of nautical charts, rough inventory lists, a compass, an ink stone and well, brushes, an abacus. Looming over it on all sides were piles of surplus merchandise together with coils of rigging and miscellaneous odds and ends, which had overflowed the hold and been stowed there. Partially screened by one of these piles was a collapsible canvas cot, which had been erected along the rear wall of the cabin. I couldn't make out the head from where I stood, but at the other end a man's bare legs protruded from behind a wall of hides. They were spread splay, one resting on the cot, the other bent-kneed, dangling over, not quite touching the floor. There was a certain laxness in the body, a degree of torpor which was odd even in a sleeper. My pulse picked up a notch. I turned back to the woman with a questioning glance.

She didn't acknowledge me. Standing stock still, she continued to stare at the bare legs, her brows knitted, her face intense. Slowly she raised her arm again and pointed to the bed.

"Go and look," she said.

At these words, a sick thrill fluttered in my bowels, an intimation of disaster.

I looked at her imploringly, but her face was stern. There was a mandate in it I could not ignore. Taking a deep breath, steeling myself for what I might encounter there, I forced myself to cross the cabin floor.

Rounding the wall of merchandise, I entered the deep umbra of its shadow. At first, mercifully, I was spared the sight of what the bed contained. Then, as my eyes adjusted, I saw the captain's body lying naked in the twisted, greasy sheets. Only his body. The head was severed from the neck — nowhere in sight. The shoulders and the stump lay soaking in a pool of tepid blood, the bluish nub of backbone protruding from a ganglia of veins and arteries in which the clotted gore had already started to congeal like pudding, mottling in the stale air. As I stared at him, at it, my mind beyond horror or disgust, beyond emotion, shocked numb, the woman's voice arose behind me, that same rapt, pythonic intonation.

"I was already in bed. The old man was wheezing next to me through his rotted teeth. Then I heard the whistle outside the house. I didn't want to go to him. I swore I wouldn't. But something broke in me, I couldn't help myself. I began to cry. Like a sleepwalker, I got out of bed and started putting on my clothes. Suddenly I was happy, and I didn't care.

"He was drunk when I came to him. On the way down the hill, he feinted at the dog. It snarled and lunged at him, snapping at the chain. Know what he did? He shot it, laughing. It didn't die at once. Gnashing its teeth, it struggled against the chain, trying to drag itself across the ground to where we stood. Picking up a timber that was lying there, he split its head. Over and over he brought it down. Finally the animal ceased to move. Glutted with the violence of it, he recalled himself and staggered erect. There was a film of slaver on his lips. Swilling from the bottle, he wiped his mouth on the sleeve of his jacket and spat. Pushing me ahead of him toward the boat, he unlatched the bear's cage with the same blood-slopped timber he'd used to bludgeon the dog, using it like an animal trainer's staff to prod and bully it out of its cage. As it came out, it reared on its hind legs and swiped at him, but then fell heavily to all fours and lumbered away, crashing into the undergrowth. Taking another drink, he laughed with satisfaction and pulled me by the hand after him up the gangplank.

"I was afraid. 'What will Tsin do when he finds out?' I asked. But he just laughed and said he'd kill Tsin too.

"We were lying here, him inside me, when the door creaked open.

" 'What is that?' I asked, tensing with alarm.

" 'The wind,' he sighed. 'Nothing.' The flame wavered in the lamp.

"He began to groan and strain on top of me, crying his man-cries. Then just as he began to come, Tsin swept in on us like a whirlwind. Grabbing him from behind by the hair, Tsin wrenched him upward, his come spilling across my belly. Smiling with his teeth, the soldier whispered something in his ear which I could not make out. I heard the blade smack in the flesh, then groan as it labored through the dense meat and snapped the backbone clean in two. The body fell back on top of me, blood spouting from the neck as from a fountain. Tsin lifted the head by the hair. His eyes were still alive," she said, breaking into a hysterical, sobbing laugh. "I could see them rolling with terror and disbelief even as the soldier hefted the head clean from the neck."

She stopped speaking and came up beside me. Laying her hand lightly on my arm, she whispered in my ear.

"Look," she said, pointing, an expression of astonishment on her face that appeared innocent, but was unspeakably obscene. "His cock is still hard." She reached out and touched it gently, as though to verify the fact to herself.

At the sight of this — her tenderness for the mutilation, which she touched as though it were a living thing, a tiny, retiring animal which she was afraid of injuring or frightening away — a hot sob burst upward from my heart. Leaving her standing there beside the bed, I broke and ran from the room, overturning everything in my path. A vial of corrosive acid tipped over in my brain, burning away my sanity. Madness rushed down on me like warm, suffocating fluid, like blood, and I ran aimlessly, like a man whose clothes have caught on fire, who seeks to escape the heat in any way he can, too wild to realize that he carries it with him as he goes and only fans the flames by running. I fell headlong from the gangplank, landing with a dull thud in the sand. The impact crushed the breath out of me. For half a minute I lay dazed, steeping in the hurt, but the fall brought me to my senses. Then the obvious question, which I'd forgotten in the turmoil, recurred to me: where was Tsin?

As I raised my head, I saw the merchant wandering bleary-eyed onto the beach from the direction of the house, rubbing his eyes. The little girl was there already, perhaps had been for some time, unnoted by me or the rest, sitting quietly in the sand, staring about, observing everything with those grave, still eyes. The merchant ran up to her and lifted her by the shoulders, shaking her violently. "Where is your mother?"

Cringing, the child began to weep, though quietly.

"Where is she?" he screamed, infuriated by her passivity.

The girl continued crying softly to herself, making no sign of acknowledgment. Disgusted, he threw her down like a limp rag, then stalked off to question the nearest clump of men.

Hastening across the lighted beach, I stood still in front of her, waiting for her to catch sight of me. She sat scooping handfuls of sand which she let sift through the hole in the bottom of her tiny fist, as through the waist of an hourglass. Her shoulders shook with noiseless sobs. Noticing my feet, she raised her face to me and, wiping her eyes on her sleeve, attempted to stop crying. She hiccupped once, then sniffled, waiting for me to proceed.

I stood speechless, unable to pose my question. Perhaps it was the madness of that night, perhaps an even deeper madness, but I realized I knew her, had always known her, that my fate was linked inseparably with hers. There was a quality in her face I recognized with the absolute confidence one experiences only in examining the mirror, or touching the bones of one's own face. Despite her youth, she possessed the moral presence of extreme old age, as though she had many times gained and lost more than the heart can bear either to keep or part with, and yet survived and been purified through suffering. All that was merely, meanly personal had been eroded out of her, and she lay like a curved bone in the desert whitening beneath the sun of centuries, her ineradicable innocence the single quality, the one essential mineral salt of personality that time had not leached out, but enhanced, enabling her in such extremity of age to preserve her extreme youth. Two tiny full moons floated in the inky blackness of her pupils, like Communion wafers resting on a salver of oblivion. I took that sacrament in my heart and, in all the madness, I felt peace, a peace deeper than any I had sounded in my years of solitary meditation in the monastery. The urgency and rancor, the baptism into the blood-rites of violence I had undergone that afternoon — this and all else faded from consciousness, and I experienced a vigorous healing bliss flooding into me, which I told myself was Tao. Perhaps it was. The intervening years have not tarnished this memory, but buffed it to a high luster, until it has attained an almost talismanic power. When this spell dissolved, I was able to speak at last.

"Where did he go?" I asked her softly. The little girl raised her arm as her mother had, and pointed toward an opening in the forest.

When I reached the edge of the beach, I turned back, intending to say something to her but unable to find the words. Recognizing my quandary, she raised her hand in a gesture of dismissal or farewell, as though to signify there was no need for words, that all was understood between us. She briefly held her hand open there, like a small night flower on the stem of her thin, childish arm, and somehow I knew I wouldn't see her anymore, that it would be my fate to search for her forever and go unappeased. And with this knowledge graved indelibly on my brain, I plunged into the forest, consumed by a feeling of inconsolable remorse.

•

I stumbled out into the night, following a dim moonlit thread of trail into the trees. Within minutes the forest had swallowed me. Every few steps I called the soldier's name and stopped to listen, but no reply came back. My words were lost on the wind, which had begun to pick up now, running through the treetops, rustling the leaves, making the boughs groan and strain. As I trudged on through the darkness, the trail became less and less discernible, until it petered out completely. But I still had the moon to guide me, and the sound of the river drifted to my ears, though farther off. Yet even then the moon was dipping toward the west, soon to set behind the peaks of the high Himalayas, which reached out to embrace it with ferocious longing, like a monstrous child struggling to grasp a pendant glittering on its mother's neck. And even before its setting, the great cloud mass deploying in the west threatened to obscure its light. Wisps and tears of nimbus raced across its face like banshee riders. Drops of rain had started falling, only a few at first, yet each drop splashing as it hit, big enough almost to fill a teacup. A jagged bolt of lightning branched over the mountains, followed by the sound of thunder, as though the world were being rent upon its axis. I kept grimly on, ignoring the signs of the impending falling out in nature. Soon the rain began to fall in earnest. The moon vanished behind a cloud. The wind whipped the treetops. Torrents of driving rain fell around me, pelting the ground. In the commotion I could no longer hear the sound of the river. My last homing mechanism, my last bearing, disappeared. I tramped on through the mud for some time, until I was hopelessly lost. At last, conceding to the elements, I squatted miserably in the lee of a rock, and, huddling on myself, shivering violently, my teeth chattering in my head, waited for the storm to subside. It showed no signs of abating. Tired, lost, discouraged, emotionally ravaged — wretched, in short — I lay down finally in the damp earth, droplets of cold rain dripping down the rock into my face, and fell into a deathlike sleep.

When I awoke it was dawn. The rain had ceased. I was drenched through, cold, empty, shivering, full of aches. Perhaps it was the effect of fever, but despite everything I felt purified, as though I had died and been reborn, reconstituted rather, not as a man, but as some transparent mineral essence, my bowels clear blown glass, frosting over with each wintry breath. The deep-washed dawn light, like gold dredged up from a clear, swift-running river, bathed the forest, glistening in drops of dew which beaded on the dark-green, watermelon-colored leaves of the woody creeper proliferating on the forest floor, pearling like sap in the needles of the pine trees, overflowing the fairy goblets of the bluets sprouting here and there among clumps of moss. To my inestimable delight, the crystal sibilance of running water not far off wafted to my ear. Sitting up, I saw that I had wandered unwittingly upon a rivulet, which would eventually lead me back to the main stream. Growing beside it in the deep secrecy of the wood, as beautiful as anything I'd ever seen, was a purplish flower, almost black, which looked like a cross between an opium poppy and a bird of paradise. Beads of water trembled on its petals. Occasionally they broke and ran, leaving a weblike track over its crisp, delicate face.

A hallucinogenic beauty lay over everything. I drank in the fresh vibrance of the morning until my mind was saturated, reeling drunk.

I must have dozed again, for when I awoke the second time, I felt the sun warm on my face. A rose tinge glowed beneath my eyelids, as through a colored lampshade. For a long time I basked in this gentle early light without opening my eyes, until a shadow crossed my face. Imagining a cloud had passed before the sun, I regretfully recognized an opportunity to repair my indolence and prepared to rise. Sighing, I opened my eyes. Then I saw the bear standing over me, its tawny, molten eyes glowing with subterranean life like magma at the heart of the world, more alive than anything I'd ever seen, God-stoked furnaces which could turn me instantly to ash. I gasped for breath, almost cried out, but managed to stifle the scream in my throat. Its moist nose, like kid leather, was not five inches from my own. The black nostrils dilated and contracted as it sniffed and rooted at me. I could tell it was afraid, excited, just as I was. All in an instant I recalled what Tsin had said about the strange intimacy which exists between the hunter and his prey, the sense of hyper-reality that visits one only at the point of death. I understood it then, as the great animal stood over me glaring down into my soul, its gaze intolerable, as if I were staring straight into the disc of the noonday sun.

The bear was first to break eye contact. Raising its muzzle, it sniffed the wind, as though distracted by a disagreeable scent, something it feared and hated. In the interlude, my mind raced desperately over the possibilities of escape. I could yell, or strike it with my staff and try to make a run for it. But when it looked down again it had begun to pant, its eyes gone deeper than I could read, stern with ferocious justice, like God's own eyes. It opened its red mouth, and a drop of saliva dripped from its tongue, splashing in the middle of my forehead. I took a deep breath, closed my eyes, relaxed, and let it go — opened my heart wide for death. I tried to imagine how it would be, whether it would crush my chest beneath its paw, or if I would feel its hot breath in my face, the slick, suffocating interior of its mouth blanketing my orifices as its jaws clamped tight around my skull, like a sharp vise, crushing it. In the end it didn't matter. I lay there like a young bride nervously excited, waiting for the sense of violation as her lover enters her. The last thing I thought of was the little girl — her grave, still eyes. . . .

When I opened my own eyes again, the bear was trudging off, swaying its ponderous hips side to side. Going to the edge of the stream, it took a drink and sat down on its haunches, looked back, rolled over like a felled tree, and scurried up. To my astonishment, it was playing with me, flirting. Leaning sideways, it cropped the beautiful black flower. As it chewed, it glanced back at me, almost sheepishly. Then it got up and padded delicately through the stream. Reaching the far side, it stopped and sniffed the air again, having completely forgotten my existence. Quickening its pace, it disappeared into the woods.

•

Picking up my things in a daze, I wandered off along the bank of the stream, filled with wonder at the strangeness of existence. Ken Kuan was years away, a vague memory of another lifetime, before the world revealed itself in all its majesty and terror. It seemed like an imaginary kingdom, a fairy realm high up among the everlasting snows, where the pure light of heaven shines undimmed forever, and human sorrow cannot enter in — like one of the retreats set up against the plague in olden days, hermetically sealed off from the world and its contagion. Yet in spite of all precautions, little by little, through some tiny, imperceptible pore or flaw along the seam, life had seeped in, depositing the virulent seed of its infection in my heart, mortality.

Like a young predatory animal on its first hunt, which smells a scent upon the wind, its fated quarry, stops and stiffens, pricking up its ears, nostrils dilating, alert, uncertain what it is — recognizing it not from memory but by instinct alone — I detected the scent which had come to me over and over that day as Hsiao told me his story, making me shiver with the dim thrill of expectation. Now it suddenly came home to me what it was, that scent. It was life. The same wild happiness flooded my heart that I had seen on the soldier's face as he laughed and blushed and spoke of the matchless ecstasy of killing.

I sat down and gazed into the stream, thinking of Tsin, that problematic man, damned in his grace, or graced in his damnation. And with that thought arose another, both on a single tether: the thought of Eddie Love, my father. What he had to do with Tsin, I would have been hard-pressed to specify. But connected they were. I knew this infallibly, instinctually, as the animal knows. The scent had grown stronger. I had come a little farther on my way.

Letting my eyes blur in the white rush of the waters, I sank into a dream of sound. Again I became aware of the thin cry of lamentation rising above the din of waters. Only now there was a new voice in the chorus of the river dead, bellowing piteously, its deep, manly voice shamefully at odds with its pathetic terror. I pitied the captain and was appalled at the hideous irony of his end — losing his head. I thought of the great stone dog, the bear; of the merchant and his wife. But most of all I thought about the little girl. Her image in my mind's eye sent the same shiver through me, set off the primal wailing in my blood. How, through what hidden instrumentality of the heart had this knowledge come to me — that she was my fated quarry, life itself? Was it only an illusion? Did I not already see her bobbing in my wake with Wu and Hsiao, Chung Fu and all the rest, all who had touched me in some way and now were gone, disappearing unreachably into the past? But it was time to push off now, to take my road again and head toward my destination in the sea.

Returning to the main channel, I set out. For the whole of the first day I saw no signs of human life, nor on the morning of the next. But in the afternoon of the second day, as I was walking along a stretch of still, deep-running water, I suddenly heard the sound of laughter and shouting. At first I saw nothing. Then, to my complete astonishment, from around a bend the black-hulled junk appeared, gliding soundlessly toward me over the water, like a dream. I made out the faces of half a dozen of the men I'd seen before on the beach. Even from the bank it was apparent that they were roaring drunk.

Seeing me standing there shading my eyes, they fell silent as they had before on the beach. Then by a common impulse they began to whoop and wave.

"Hey!" they cried. "Come on! Swim for it!" They pantomimed the necessary gestures, putting their hands together palm to palm as though to dive, puffing out their cheeks, holding their noses, swimming through the air.

Seized by an unaccountable joy, I shook off my sandals and, stuffing them in my pack, sprinted toward the water, plunging in amid the sound of cheers. I reached mid-channel just as they were passing. Leaning far out over the side, they fished me up, sopping wet, panting with exertion.

"Well done!" they cried, slapping me on the back. "Excellent priest!"

Winking at the others, one of them teased me saying, "You must have been a fish in your previous incarnation."

"Or a monkey," said a second, rolling his eyes in astute mimicry, making them dissolve in laughter.

"Foolish man!" cried a third. "He's a Taoist, not a Buddhist!" With this, even I burst out laughing.

To my surprise, and mild consternation, the fat man was at the tiller of the boat. I was wary of him at first, but he seemed to have totally forgotten our altercation. He greeted me like an old friend and explained the situation. Discovering the captain's death, the merchant had gone about moaning and tearing his hair for some few minutes, cursing fate and beating his wife. But in the end he had calmed down somewhat. When the body was buried, he began to reckon up his losses like the sober businessman he was, casting about in his mind for ways to extenuate them. At last, he hit on this expedient. Recruiting several experienced volunteers to undertake the journey in the captain's place, he had charged them to sail the cargo as far as the rapids. If the water was high, they were to continue through to Chungking, if not, to portage the boat around to the nearest outpost. Once there, they would either arrange for further transportation or auction the cargo off to the highest bidder. Since he'd been constrained to offer them a percentage as an incentive to undertaking the treacherous voyage, they were all hell-bent on going through, for they reckoned the cargo would bring five times the price in Chungking as in some obscure upriver spot. They looked more like children going on a holiday than men sailing toward one of the most dangerous stretches of white water in the world.

I sailed with them all that afternoon. At night we tied up, ate and drank together. I even told them a little of my story. The next morning at first light we set out again. We had been sailing for two hours, when, as we rounded a bend, a small settlement came into view. One of the men told me that we were now less than an hour above the rapids, and that if I wished to take my leave this was the last convenient place, for from this spot forward the river wound between sheer canyon walls. Until that point I had considered throwing in my lot with theirs. I might still have done so had not something on the bank caught my eye, instantly obliterating my resolve.

"Look!" the fat man cried, pointing over the side. "They've found it!"

There, impaled on a stake of green wood twelve or fourteen feet high, looking out over the water, was the captain's head.

"My God!" I gasped. "Who has permitted this desecration? Why have they put it out like that?"

"It is the custom of the river," he said grimly. "For any who might be searching."

This startled, indeed revolted me; but what appeared as we drew closer was worse yet. The others noticed it at the same instant I did. A furor erupted on the boat.

"What does it mean?" I asked, running from one to another of them. They all shook their heads. Last of all I asked the fat man.

"Tsin," he said. And with that I jumped.

"Goodbye!" I called to them, bobbing up in the current. "Goodbye!"

They waved to me and hove my pack overboard into the stream. I swam to retrieve it, then came ashore some way down the bank. I watched the black-hulled boat sail out of sight around a bend, then walked back toward the gruesome exhibition. The man's head was covered with flies, putrescent, fetid, almost beyond recognition. But it was the other one that drew me more. There, similarly transfixed by a green stake, its jaw hanging slack, its red tongue lolling over the row of bottom teeth, was the head of the bear. It had been eclipsed at first by the captain's profile, then revealed by a kind of parallax as we came abreast. Now I could see it clearly. Its eyes were turned up in its head. They glittered with fierce tears of rheum. Irredeemable. I began to weep.

After a while, I set off in search of Tsin, not really expecting to find him, not sure I wanted to. The scent of life which I had caught so briefly was all mixed up now with the scent of death, this noisome stench of wasteful, needless destruction, like wildflowers and dung. True to form, like the small genie in his cloud of shitten sweetness, Tsin appeared amidst the savor of opium. For here too, as everywhere in China where the authorities cannot enforce the prohibition, was a den, different on the outside but the same within — the same blind faces staring soullessly into the dazzling light, the exquisite mystery of alkaloid disintegration. When I found the soldier, he was lying curled like a fetus, staring toward the wall, his head resting on a porcelain pillow like a corpse's on its headstone. The sword had fallen from his hand and lay abandoned on the floor. I nudged his shoulder, shook it. He looked at me, but with no trace of recognition. Yet I saw myself, reflected in the eye of glass.

Chapter 2

From the time I last saw Tsin until I reached the Yangtze delta above Shanghai, many weeks passed. I was still far upriver from Chungking, and several hundred miles above the head of navigation at I-ch'ang, where I finally shipped aboard a rice barge for the remainder of the journey, agreeing to forego wages in accordance with my vow of poverty, working for board and passage only (a method which would keep me fully employed all the way to the docks of New York City). Since I cannot devote time to a description of each place I visited on my way down to the sea at Shanghai, let me allude to the progress of my journey by recording the gradual transformation I observed in the character of the river, which, like the Tao itself, was "always changing, always the same."

The Yangtze "emerges, in mystery, from the clouds." Thus wrote the traveler Yuan Bin in the sixth century B.C., and it is still as true today. Its source, high in the Tanglha Range, no eye has seen. Yet even as far down as Ken Kuan, located on one of the countless headstreams, unnamed, unmarked on any map, the river remains in its pristine state, untainted by silt, cold, clear, and pure. Here, in its first avatar, the river is a child, tumbling with torrential, heedless joy through steep defiles in a fantastic landscape of evergreens and rainbows, which stray beams of sunlight quarry out of the prismatic mists. Tireless, prodigal of energy, the river flows here with a feral ecstasy, disbelieving in its own mortality. But in time, by imperceptible degrees, this passion moderates as the river approaches adolescence. Its life runs deeper now, growing turbid with complexities of silt. Though it is still temperamental, its outbursts are less frequent, if more violent, than before and bring sober contemplation after, its sense of responsibility increasing in proportion to its own culpability, the burden of its lengthening past. In this guise the Yangtze passes through the San-hsia Gorges on the border of Hupeh and Szechwan, carved out of shale and brick-red sandstone, where in company with the Min and Chia-ling which flow in from the north it disports itself in one last mad debauch, the final tantrum of its youth.

Beyond this point the river enters its life's prime. Great oceangoing vessels begin to appear, chiseling its smooth surface with their bows, casting shavings, white flakes and shards of disturbed water, which quickly melt back down into the polished surface. At last, cloyed with the excess of its delights, sluggish, nearly spent, the Yangtze enters its old age. Swollen with the wealth of its experience, broad and deep, almost inscrutable with the sediment of its accumulated lives, the river's motion becomes virtually imperceptible, except that here and there the tranquil surface is broken by a braid of twisting water, evidence of a swifter current working deep within, drawing it inexorably toward its appointment with the sea. Through rich agricultural lowlands, where rice paddies, vivid green, stretch away on either side as far as the eye can see, not a hill, not a tree to arrest the roving eye, the river flows, prone to floods and other geriatric disorders, the malfunctions of senescence, but leaving behind it rich alluvial deposits, its legacy to earth. Finally at the delta, its embouchure into the sea, the Yangtze is so wide — fifteen miles — the human eye can hardly span it.

I shall never forget the feeling, mingling fulfillment and regret, which came over me as I caught my first whiff of the ocean, the sweet, salt stench of procreation and decay. We chugged across a line of foam into the tidal backwash, teeming with crabs, fish, and shrimp, the black water mackled with white specks of floating gulls. Reckless vendors in their sampans began to cross our bows, screaming out their offers of fresh fruit and roasted duck, fireworks and thousand-year-old eggs, then fell behind us in the slow wake of the barge, still chattering, as we steamed on. The ocean rose before us, making one, not hold his breath and rub his eyes in awe, but simply nod his head as with some long-cherished expectation finally brought to fruition, satisfied in exactly the manner one had foreseen, neither surpassing nor disappointing the anticipation; for all of us, no matter how landlocked an existence we may have led, have some preknowledge of the sea, as of the Tao. Perched on a cargo boom, I looked out at the line of breakers where the black flux of the river met the gray-green water of the China Sea and, after a brief struggle, succumbed to its gentle euthanasia, and was gone. How strange! At the confluence, across that magic threshold, the mighty being vanished with all its secrets, all its sins, its memories and unrequited passions. Having known it in the vehemence of youth, its period of exigence and dashing life, who could have prophesied so soft an exit? There was a mystery there to be discovered. . . . But I have lingered too long over it already.

From Shanghai I made my way down the coast in another cargo vessel to Hsia-men, also called Amoy. Then one moonless night I slipped into the sea, towing my pack after me on a plank of wood. Launching myself into those bitterly contested sea lanes, I swam the two-mile stretch of the Formosa Straits between the mainland and Nationalist-held Quemoy, making my way slowly toward the shoreline I saw looming in the distance: free Taiwan, the other China!

I stayed on that little island world only long enough to refresh myself. After a few days I shipped aboard a steamer bound for Manila, watched the coastline receding into the distance, into the past — my last glimpse of my home, of childhood, a dark scrawl on the horizon, like a brushstroke in an uncompleted character.

•

Manila. It was there that I met my first American, my friend Scottie, who took me under his wing. I traveled with him for more than a year, working on boats of every size and description, trading in all the ports of Indonesia and Malaysia, even once or twice venturing as far as Bangkok and Saigon, as it was then called. It was Scottie who taught me English.

Though I saw him daily over many months, I never quite felt I figured him out. Strong, stocky, nearing fifty, he had a face like an old piece of leather, deeply burned and etched with wrinkles, showing as well the ravages of drink — the fine network of varicose veins on each cheek like necrotic blushes, and the red spot on the end of his nose, which made him look like he'd just raised his face from a dunking in a cup of wine.

Rum, however, not wine, was Scottie's vice, or pleasure, as he alternatively termed it. "Lookit, Sun I," he often said. "Rum for breakfast and ablutions from the self-same bottle before retiring at night — that'll keep a man hell-free, well-heeled, and wired, by cock!" For as long as I knew him, Scottie never deviated from that regimen.

Scottie had a sailor's rough bravura, his fearlessness, his passion for a brawl, his capacity for inspired profanity, all the articles of the trade. Yet this doesn't tell the whole story. There was more to Scottie — a marked curiosity, a hint of trouble, an occasional burst of intellectual ebullition rare in men from that walk of life — marks of an underlying sensitivity and fineness which had been largely ruined, turned to acid by habitual concealment and suppression. Exactly what was eating him, I never learned. For he was reticent on the subject of his past, though garrulous enough in general. Once though, as I was speaking about my mother, he let slip something about his own.

"My old lady resigned from life when she was twenty-five," he said. "Put on a housecoat one day and never took it off again. Wandered through the house day after day, reciting poetry. Emily Dickinson." He laughed, remembering. "Don't remember much about the old lady, really. Just her hands — thin with wringing, almost like claws — and that goddamn poetry. She spouted so much of that shit, she even dinned some of it into me." Scottie spoke disparagingly, but a sad sensitivity glowed through his recollection. "The only one I ever really liked was the one that began, 'My Life had stood — a Loaded Gun.' "

Scottie's general dissatisfaction was obvious from the way he drank, and even more so from his continual harping on the fact of his expatriation. He hadn't set foot in the United States for over twenty years. Exactly how long it had been, I don't remember, but *he* knew, reeling off the figure with a perverse pride.

"How long now, Scottie?" the sailors hazed him to amuse themselves. And looking down at his watch he told you the figure to the hour and the minute with a grin like the dazzle on a blade.

He had a ritual, which he observed on shipboard every night after mess before retiring to his bunk in the forepeak, of X-ing off the date on the calendar, then adding another stave to the many thousands that preceded them in groups of five in the black register he called his "diary" and cultivated as carefully as a miser his account book. Completing this, he tossed off a stiff shot of rum, grunting with approval, then toed off his shoes without unlacing them and fell back in the sack.

Scottie's intellectual qualities showed themselves primarily in his intimacy with celestial phenomena, the stars in particular. The closest thing to joy I ever saw in him was once during a midnight watch off the coast of Java, when, after a few drinks, he suddenly began to whirl like a dervish doing a sailor's horn-pipe, pointing to constellations in every quarter of the sky and reeling off perhaps fifty or sixty names in the space of fifteen minutes, reciting them like a litany, an incantation. Hearing the commotion, the captain stuck his head out of the wheelhouse and told us to pipe down.

Scottie knew not only the names of the constellations but the mythology behind them. Often through the long hours of the watch, in those distant equatorial seas, he entertained me with outlandish stories of the gods and goddesses of classical Greece, amply seasoned with the spice of his own person-ality, his quirky and equivocal "Yankness," as he called it. This was one of the techniques he used to teach me English, and in time, as my comprehension improved, I came to relish these tales as much as I had Wu's. Beyond simple entertainment, however, a few of them affected me profoundly. One haunts me still.

"Lookit, Sun I! That's Orion, Poseidon's bastard boy," he called out to me one night. "He looks a little groggy now, low down on the horizon like that, but he's just climbed out of bed in his old man's palace where he sleeps all day. He's still got cobwebs in his brain. But give him a few minutes! Let him ascend a few degrees and you'll see something. By cock, then he'll be keen! There's not a more dazzling sight in all the heavens than Orion on the chase with his dogs in cry around him."

And he went on to tell me how the Great Hunter, "who was given to venery, in both senses," fell in love with a mortal girl, Merope, and was blinded by her father, Oenopion.

"Orion was an awful mess by then, Sun I. Bellowing pathetically, like one of the many thousand beasts he'd gored, blood dripping from his eyeballs, he staggered down the seacoast of Ionia till he was just across from Lemnos. Over on the island he heard a Cyclops's hammer ringing on the anvils, forging thunderbolts for Zeus. The master blacksmith, Hephaestus, took pity on Orion and lent him the Cyclops Kedalion as a guide. Taking a leave of absence from the forges and a good sword to serve the blind man as a cane, Kedalion set out with Orion on a pilgrimage to the temple of Apollo, god of light. There, fixing his blank gaze on the sun, which blinds a man who can see already, but restores the blind to sight, the Hunter got his vision back. He was tickled pink, ran laughing and whooping down the sky, not even pausing to thank his benefactor. Kedalion raised his hand kind of meek like to ask for the sword back, but in the end simply shrugged and let it go, for he was a drudge, and used to being jerked around. Apollo, however, never forgave the slight."

Scottie then told me how Apollo tricked his sister Artemis, the goddess of the hunt, who loved Orion, into shooting her lover as he was swimming far out at sea, and how in her grief she had the Hunter translated into heaven as a constellation glittering in the night sky.

"See those three bright stars there slanting downward in a line?" he continued. "That's Orion's belt. Just below it there's a smudge of light, which is his sword, the one Kedalion gave him. Its scabbard rather; the sword itself is raised above his head, as you can see, clenched in his fist. The three stars in the belt point downward straight to Sirius, the Dog Star. It's in the constellation Canis Major, which is to say the Larger Dog, and is the brightest star in the sky. Canis Major is Orion's trusty hound."

As Scottie pointed out the brilliant, glassy eye of the Great Dog glimmering low on the horizon, the recollection which had teased my brain all through his story came home to me. Because of Tsin, the tale of the blinded hunter, with his accoutrements, the sword and dog, whose passion for the chase eventually undid him, took on an added resonance for me. I don't know if I can adequately explain this, but it was as though the scene I had so recently lived through and have elsewhere called "my harsh baptism into life" was not simply a chance occurrence peculiar to my experience, but something larger, written long ago and acted many times, perhaps, across the globe in many different tongues, until the Greeks gave it eternal currency in myth, and with the lofty genius of their people looked heavenward and found it there already, written in the stars.

But this was by no means all. The resonance spread out beyond Tsin in a direction I was not then able to follow, not only back to China, but forward to New York.

Scottie's disquisition continued.

"Look there a little higher in the sky, Sun I." He pointed. "That bright star is Aldebaran in the horns of Taurus. It would appear Orion is in danger from that quarter, about to get himself 'impaled on the horns of a dilemma,' if you get my meaning.

"Now I can tell you anything you need to know about Orion, Sun I. But that Bull is a puzzler. I've discussed the matter with authorities the world over, but no one seems to know its true identity. After all, Taurus just means 'bull,' plain bull. That isn't much to go on. I've heard it suggested that it represents the bull Zeus turned into when he abducted Europa, the Phoenician princess, and swam off with her to Crete. 'The rape of Europa' as it's called in the literature. I suppose a respectable case could be made for that interpretation, but in my opinion it's a few fathoms shy the bottom and won't hold flukes.

"Others still say it's the white bull Pasiphaë had the itch for, and while that option seems distasteful, I feel we're getting warmer here. Do you know that story? No, of course not. Well, let me say a few words on the subject. Pasiphaë was the queen of Crete and Minos's wife. As I've said, she developed an unnatural affection for this animal which she saw pawing and snorting in her husband's pasture. Being one sneaky, conniving bitch, she managed to get Daedalus, the Great Artificer, to construct a cow in bronze, which she entered and had wheeled into the pasture. The bull eyed it warily, gave it a few suspicious sniffs then, deciding that all was in order, mounted it and did the deed, to Pasiphaë's great pleasure, and, I imagine, even greater discomfort. (For, lookit, not to linger too long on the crude details, a full-grown bull has a dong that's long as your arm, and that's no cock and bull!) It was the old Trojan bull trick, you see, Sun I. The Greeks got away with that kind of thing more than once. Only in this case, from all appearances, it was the Bull without the Trojan, for Pasiphaë promptly conceived and bore the Minotaur. Which brings me to the point.

"The Minotaur was a hideous monster, half man, half beast. Some say it had a bull's body and a human head, others the reverse — in either case, not exactly nice to look at. And it had a nasty temperament as well, unruly, vindictive, and with a taste for human flesh. Though Minos, showing unusual liberality for a Greek, forgave his wife, he couldn't bring himself to name the Minotaur as his successor. Instead he had Daedalus construct the famous labyrinth, where he confined the monster, throwing him a youth or maiden from time to time to appease his appetite and keep him from breaking loose and stirring up a ruckus. Now, grisly as it sounds, this was no real inconvenience to Crete, for at that time the Athenians were under Minos's dominion, and like the consummate imperialist he was, he wrung the sacrifice from them. Each year a ship set out from Athens with seven youths and seven maidens bound for Crete under black sails. This went on until the king's son Theseus, mad as hell about the whole affair, resolved either to deliver his country or go down in the attempt. Thus, despite Aegeus's protest, the next year he set out, one of the fourteen.

"Now the Gods loved Theseus, which is how the Greeks, with their peculiar terse splendiferousness, expressed the fact that he was lucky. Promptly on his arrival at Crete, Ariadne — Minos and Pasiphaë's daughter — fell in love with him and decided to help him kill the Minotaur. Now I don't mean to carp, for admittedly this adds a love interest to the story, but the fact is this touch is a trifle gratuitous, considering Ariadne's position. Remember, Sun I, the Minotaur was her half-brother — something of a social stigma, to put it mildly. In my opinion she would have helped Theseus anyway. But no matter.

... Ariadne gave him a sword and a clew of thread which he played out behind him as he made his way into the maze in order to find his way back out again. Now exactly what befell Theseus in the labyrinth, no one knows. Up to a point you can visualize the scene — a slice of moon in the sky, the sand crunching under his bare feet, the red light of the torches flickering on the stone walls, the terrific pounding of his heart as he caught a first whiff of that dank air, foul with shit and blood, and heard a distant labored breathing in the labyrinth's heart.... Beyond this, imagination fails. After he emerged, his companions never referred to the incident, treating it sort of like a war injury. And Theseus didn't volunteer any information on the subject either. Perhaps it's better that he didn't.

"At any rate, he was successful, that we know. He slew the monster, broke the girl's heart, and to top it all off, succeeded to the throne of Athens. For either because he was in too damn big a hurry, or because he wasn't thinking straight after the Crete incident, Theseus forgot to strike the black sails and bend a set of white ones, as he'd promised his father beforehand he'd do if he succeeded. Standing on a hill outside the town where he had gone to watch each day, old Aegeus saw the ship returning under 'grievous canvas' and, thinking all was lost, groaned, clutched at his heart, fell into his retainers' arms, and gave up the ghost on the spot. A few of his detractors have suggested that Theseus forgot to change the sail 'accidentally on purpose,' if you know what I mean. And certainly, his grief over his father's death must have been softened a little by inheriting the throne. But beyond that it's all idle speculation, irresponsible and slanderous, as far as I'm concerned.

"At any rate, Sun I, if Orion could be translated to the heavens and live after death, why not the Minotaur? That, at least, is my theory of the Bull's identity." Scottie paused and, tilting up the rear corner of his rain hat, scratched his head. "Of course, if the Bull up there is the Minotaur, then Orion must be Theseus — which throws a goddamn monkey wrench in the whole proceedings! Cock and double cock! See what I mean? That effing bull!"

Reader, perhaps you can imagine what was running through my mind, I who had once enjoyed celebrity (notoriety might be more accurate) for my singing of *Ten Bulls!* Yes, in the horns of Taurus I saw, not the Minotaur, nor his father, not even the white bull that raped Europa — though to my mind that option was most palatable since, after all, at least that bull was an incarnation of Zeus, the father of the gods — no, rather than any or all of these, I saw the Bull of Taoism, that fundamental symbol of enlightenment in my religion, whose footprints had led me to embark on my uncertain pilgrimage into the exotic, uncouth regions of the earth! With a rush of exhilaration, I realized that I had at last perceived him, or at least caught a first fleeting glimpse! I can hardly attempt to convey the excitement I felt. Only let me say that bliss was not unmixed with an element of foreboding. For the Bull, through Scottie's story, had taken on a new and unsettling set of associations. Even beyond the Bull's ambiguous status, though, was the lurid irony of the fact that this

Hunter — Orion, Tsin, whoever he might be — was not engaged in taming the Bull, subduing it to useful labor like the peaceful ox herd of the parable, but, in an unspeakable desecration, had raised his sword to strike it dead!

Of course I said nothing of my thoughts to Scottie, who, after taking a long swallow from his bottle, continued his outlandish monologue.

"But the Bull isn't the only problem old Orion's got on his hands, Sun I." He wiped his mouth on his sleeve and pointed. "Way to the north up there, see that group of stars?"

"Yes," I replied. "In China that is called the Ladle."

"Right you are. Or close enough, at any rate. In English it's called the Dipper. Those stars are in the constellation Ursa Major, or the Great Bear."

At this I pricked my ears up.

"Now it would appear that the Bear cherishes some evil notions toward the Hunter too, and with good reason. See how they've chained him to the Pole and cruelly bait him through the nights? All he can do is fret on the chain, roaring with vexation, pacing around and around Polaris, taking an occasional swipe at Orion's dogs, which lunge in from his blind side with bared teeth and then, before he has a chance to turn, retreat across the Celestial Equator into the safety of the southern hemisphere. It's cruel, ugly sport, Sun I, and Orion's had the best of it till now. But that chain won't hold forever. By cock, some day that Bear's going to break loose and all hell with him.

"Now, Sun I, not everyone sees the same things in the stars. Some don't see anything at all, never having taken time to look. And even among those who do, you might find one or two who would take exception to my interpretations. But on this point I'll stick to my guns. You look up there a minute. I ask you, which way is Orion facing? Front, back, or profile? Oh no, the experts never bother to tell you that. What I mean to say is, is the Hunter facing Taurus, as they would lead you to believe, with his dog *behind* him? I know he was a giant and had long legs, but really — do you think he could outrun his hounds? Or is he facing the other way, toward the Bear (his sword is raised in that direction) with his hounds in hot pursuit? Well these are deep waters, Sun I. But my own personal opinion is that old Orion, whether out of careless-ness or wild bravado, or both, has got himself in a hot spot, between a rock and a hard place as they say, and is beseiged by wild animals on either side — the Bear behind him and the Bull in front! Or vice versa, depending on how you look at it." Carried away by his own improvisation, Scottie burst into a peal of delighted laughter. "Ho-ho! By the flaming cock of Constantinople! Watch out now Orion! Lookit, Sun I. See him turning, now one way, now another, fending them off from both directions!"

By this time Scottie had managed to get himself thoroughly drunk, "half the bay over," as he put it, or "three sheets to the wind" ("decks awash" and "stiff as a ringbolt" were also current expressions). Since the watch was almost over anyway, that ended the lesson for the night. Though this particular discourse was not unrepresentative, as to style and content, of his conversation generally, the references to the Hunter, to the Bull, and to the Bear, as I've said, clicked with my own experience in a way that was not representative at all, but remarkable, almost supernaturally so. When we went below to our bunks, I was in a state of mental ebullition unlike any I'd experienced since the day Hsiao visited Ken Kuan and told me the story of my parents.

•

But I must once again "let water set the right example" and flow onward like the river.

After a year of trading in every nook and cranny of the China Seas with my friend Scottie, one day the two of us shipped aboard a freighter carrying a load of teak up through the Strait of Malacca into the Andaman Sea, arriving in Rangoon, where more than two decades earlier the Dutch pleasure liner the *Jaegersfontaine* had disgorged the first contingent of the AVG, traveling incognito as missionaries, students, big-game hunters, businessmen, explorers, and other delightfully absurd alleged professions, contrived, no doubt, by a repressed Customs official with an imagination shaped by Hollywood. It gave me a pang of empathy and pity to think of those young men — my father among them — with their crew cuts and bright Hawaiian prints, cameras slung around their necks, tanned from weeks of lounging on the decks, weeks spent sipping fresh-squeezed lemonades brought by liveried servants, posing for snapshots, playing cards, writing letters home, cracking jokes ("Oh I say, old bean, I do so hope I bag a Bengal while I'm here in Burma!" and adjusting an imaginary monocle), as though the whole thing were a masquerade. Then standing together silent along the topside rails of the trim Dutch ship, staring with grave faces at the squalor of Rangoon, taking a first whiff of the fetid air, the "omnipresent stench of Asia," after the games, the jokes, the make-believe, getting a first intimation of the measureless distance they had come, and of the overpowering, irreducible reality of the East. They must have realized then that they would not wake up and find the rotting jackfruit turned to carriages, the rats to footmen, that the raging hell they'd come to the brink of they could not wish away, or skirt in the manner of a glib Hollywood director segueing into a new scene, that they would have to pass to the other side through "flames of fire" in order to return to what they knew.

In Rangoon Scottie and I had trouble securing berths. All available work was local, but since I had become reasonably proficient in my command of English, I was ready to push on, either through the Suez to the Mediterranean and then past the Pillars of Hercules into the North Atlantic, or else by way of "the route along the bottom of the world," as Scottie called it, rounding India and Africa. A week went by, ten days. Finally one morning we got word that a Greek vessel, the *Telemachos,* bound for New York via Colombo and Capetown, was loading at the docks. We hurried down to take a look at her.

At first glimpse, she was hardly prepossessing. Standing on the moles, hands in the back pockets of our jeans, heads tilted to the side, we stared up over her rust-streaked sides at the men on deck beneath the cranes. They were swinging large wooden crates on a bull line over the central cargo hatch, then lowering them into the hold. Scottie delivered this apt appraisal: "A dog if I ever saw one, Sun I. I wouldn't be surprised if she was carrying contraband."

On further inspection we discovered that the transom of one of her two lifeboats was stove in and that such life preservers as she had were little more than rags. There were no fire extinguishers aboard, the engine room was black with grease and so slick you could hardly cross the floor without falling on your face, and the mast and topside rigging were caked with soot belched from the smokestack. Worst of all perhaps was the fact that the forepeak had been converted to cargo space and the sailors' quarters relegated to the steerage, which was dank, cluttered, and stank of bilge.

"I wouldn't ride that tub around the block," Scottie declared, "much less around the world."

"I don't blame you," I replied.

He scrutinized me. "You're going anyway, aren't you?"

I shrugged. A pained vulnerability showed in his expression. "I can't stay here forever," I said.

He nodded. "Shit or get off the pot, eh?" Lowering his head as though deliberating with himself, Scottie took a few paces, wheeled, and came back.

"What the hell," he said with a sheepish grin, "I'll go too!" Slapping himself on the thigh for emphasis, he added, "By cock!"

Thus we signed the articles and, after stowing our gear, took our places on deck beside the rest of the crew.

No one seemed to know, or even to evince much curiosity about, the nature of the cargo we were carrying. When we asked, we got the same answer over and over: "misc." (as in "miscellaneous"), uttered in tones which suggested that our interlocutors conceived of it as a distinct commodity. The captain himself, an Englishman, was hardly more informative, adding only that part of it consisted of a quantity of religious artifacts rescued ("heisted," in Scottie's cynical gloss) from a Buddhist temple in Tibet and bound for the Metropolitan Museum in New York City.

This was the extent of our knowledge at the time we steamed out of the Irrawaddy Delta into the Gulf of Martaban and headed southwest toward Sri Lanka. Later, however, Scottie and I did a little investigating of our own, making such discoveries as may be worthy of brief note.

We were some days out of Colombo, in the latitude of the Cape of Good Hope (30° south) but still eastward of it. After a balmy cruise through the tropics in the Indian Ocean, we found ourselves almost overnight in the dead of winter. It was hellish. The seas were mountainous, swells as high as forty feet breaking over the bows and sluicing through the scuppers. The old ship pitched and reared as she drove into a head sea, then shuddered on her keel, ringing like an iron bell, as she fell headlong into the ensuing trough. Nothing was visible above us — neither the sun in the daytime, nor the moon and stars at night — only an ashen-colored pall of cloud moiling in the sky. A sheet of ice covered the deck, augmented by the ceaseless drizzle, sometimes a cold rain, sometimes sleet, most often an indiscriminate slush containing particles of jagged ice.

Compounding our misery, part of the cargo had apparently broken loose in the hold. Night after night as we lay in our bunks trying to get some sleep we heard a continual knocking and sliding sound, as though something were trying to get out, butting with insane fury against the bulkheads. One night after a deep roll, there was a particularly loud crash.

"By cock!" Scottie roared, jumping out of bed in his union suit. "I'm going to find out what that ruckus is if it kills me!"

Whipping on his coat and boots, he snatched up a marlinespike from the corner and headed for the ladder.

"Wait up!" I whispered, hastily slipping my arms into my pea jacket. "I'm going with you."

In a few minutes we were groping our way down the rungs of the steel ladder into a pitch-black hold. At the bottom Scottie struck a match. Holding it cupped in his hand, he peered around.

"You there, Sun I?" he whispered. "I couldn't find my dick to pee in here! Where's that effing light bulb?"

I found it and switched it on.

"Well shit!" he said. "That's what I'd call a damn dim light bulb in a damn dark hold!"

And it was true. The single bulb cast a dingy yellow halo a few feet, then totally capitulated to the darkness. A long extension cord, however, enabled us to take it along as we moved through the head-high rows of wooden crates. In the rear abutting on the steerage bulkhead was a large vacant space where we found what we were looking for. Two tremendous crates had worked their way loose from the cargo chains and toppled over. The first one had been smashed to matchwood. Clearing away a little debris, we discovered a huge gold-fleshed idol with a sword in its right hand lying face down on the floor. Its head was encircled by a halo of fine snow, which had apparently sifted down during the few moments the hatch had been uncovered. Rigging up a block and tackle, we righted it without much trouble. Holding the light to it again, I recognized the figure as Manjusri, the Bodhisattva of Transcendent Wisdom. I knew him by the lotus which he held in his left hand — the Book of Knowledge lying open on the stigma — and by the flaming sword with which he had once cut the Knot of Illusion. Like the rest of the crew, the god was a little the worse for wear. His nose had been knocked completely off his face, and the Third Eye in the middle of his forehead — which, unlike the narrowed, subtle pair beneath, was wide open, trained on the other world — had been cracked. As I was examining Manjusri, the ship lurched sharply.

"Cock and fustian!" Scottie roared, toppling over backward. As he did, the light bulb shattered, its filament glowing palely orange before going out. I heard the grating locomotion of the second crate and leapt. Something cold and hard grazed my ribs, hanging in my clothes. As I smashed against the bulkhead, a tremendous iron clang reverberated through the hold.

Groping around, I discovered what appeared to be a gigantic metal spike on my left-hand side, pinning my coat to the wall. A second spike projected to my right from the broken head of the crate.

"Sun I, darling, are you killed?" Scottie whispered anxiously.

"I'm okay," I replied, wrenching free, leaving a swatch of cloth behind me. "How about you?"

"Oh, a few dozen broken arms and legs. But give me time to catch my breath and I'll be good as new."

A match flared. "Where are you?" he asked.

"Over here. Bring the matches."

"Shit, Sun I, lookit — there's more snow on the floor now. I know we closed the hatch behind us, didn't we? You don't suppose it could be coming down the ventilator, do you?"

I couldn't see what he was talking about.

"Cock!" he cried suddenly. I saw the match fly from his hand and flutter through the air, lighting on the floor. It cast a pale circular aura over the fine white dust of snow and continued burning.

"Pisscock! Fuckit! Wildcat!" Scottie swore, as he jumped and shuffled in the darkness. "If I forget, remind me next time I set out to light myself on fire to do it headfirst and save myself the trouble! Blazing Pinkerton Jesus!"

"Scottie," I said, hardly listening to his bitching, "take a look at that."

"At what, my darling?"

"The match."

Scottie ceased his antics, and we stared at the match as it burned lower and lower. Finally it began to gutter, then flickered out.

"Well, I'll be durned!" Scottie said. He struck another match and threw it down beside the first. "Will you take a look at that!"

The inexplicable fact was that the snow around the match had not begun to melt!

"Shit on my biscuits if I know what it means!" Scottie said. "They say the snow down here is made of steel and gristle, but this beats all!"

But I still had to satisfy my curiosity on the prior point. "Matches, Scottie." Lighting one for himself, he handed me the pack and continued his inspection.

As I lit one of the matches, and as it flared, a smell of sulphur rose to my nostrils. Amidst the darting shadows in the orange, uncertain light, I saw what seemed to be *two tremendous horns* of dark bronze protruding ominously from the head of the broken crate! I gasped and dropped the match. "Scottie!"

"Well I'll be . . ." he said, coming up beside me. "You don't suppose they've tied the devil up and boxed him in this crate, do you?"

"I'm going to open it."

"Before you do, I think you'd better come and take a look at this," he said a little grimly.

We dropped to our knees on the spot where he'd been making his examination. Peering inside the damaged crate as far as the light reached, I could just make out a huge black hand holding what appeared at first to be a drum, but on a closer inspection proved to be an hourglass, as large as the trunk of my body. Sifting slowly from its cracked bell, and augmenting a small pyramid already on the floor, was a fine stream of whitest sand.

"So that's what it is," I said, relieved to have the mystery dispelled.

Without saying a word, Scottie pressed the tips of his index and middle fingers to his tongue, then touched them to the pyramid, collapsing its perfect cone.

"Stick out your tongue," he said.

Compelled by the gravity of his demeanor, I complied. He brushed off the clinging matter, and I tasted something acrid, sulphurous, which dissolved with my saliva, and beneath that, faintly, the salt taste of his fingers. There was a familiar quality in the taste which made it more unpleasant.

"It's heroin," Scottie said.

Instantly the circuit closed across my reminiscence and the current flowed. Though less earthy, it bore a faint but unmistakable resemblance to the savor of the opium, a ghostly, disembodied echo, as of a truth, or falsehood, perceived at a higher level of abstraction.

Scottie rose and crossed to the gilded figure of the god. Striking another match, he held it up and peered closely into its face. "Come here," he said, "lookit."

From the fractured iris in the middle of Manjusri's forehead, an almost imperceptible stream was flowing, singly until it reached the bridge of the broken nose, then branching into two forks, falling down each side of the golden face just past the corners of the lips. Flurrying in the match light, like dust motes in a sunbeam, it settled on the floor. As I watched in stricken silence, it occurred to me that the god was weeping, that from the eye of Transcendental Wisdom in the middle of his forehead chemical tears were falling, tears of dust.

"The damn thing's full of it!" Scottie observed.

The harsh clang of the iron hatch being lifted rang out above our heads. A thick beam of light cut through the darkness. Scottie and I dove behind a wall of boxes.

"Who's down there?" the captain's voice demanded. "Better come out!" He waited for an answer. Then in a lower voice we heard him speaking to the mate. "Probably something's broken loose. See to it in the morning. And tie down the tarpaulin, damn you!"

"Now, sir?" the mate replied.

"What the hell are we running here, a nursery school? Ah well, all right. Leave that till the morning too."

The hatch slid over us and clanged in place. We waited a few minutes, then climbed the ladder and made our escape. Whether the captain saw us, we could not be certain. If he did, he never mentioned it. From that night on, though, for the rest of the voyage, armed guard was posted on the hold. I never found out what was in the second crate — at least not until much later, and then by accident. But I had more than enough to occupy my thoughts and make me nervous. For we were steaming toward America with a desperate cargo underneath us. Cruel irony that after my long pilgrimage I should reach my destination in company with a load of contraband!

•

One morning just before daybreak, Scottie roused me from my bunk.

"What is it?" I asked sleepily.

"Get dressed and come topside," he said, retreating up the ladder before I could ask questions.

Following his instructions in a kind of stupor, I emerged on deck, where he was waiting. A dawn-tinged fog lay on the water, not thick, but reducing the visibility to perhaps a hundred yards, lending the scene a quality of gauzy, dreamlike unreality. I yawned and rubbed my eyes, then stared around grog-gily. "Where are we?"

"These are the banks of the Yellow Sea," he said with a cryptic smile.

"Come on," I said in tones of mild annoyance.

He went on:

> "This — is the land — the Sunset washes —
> These — are the Banks of the Yellow Sea —
> Where it rose — or whither it rushes —
> These — are the Western Mystery!"

"Yellow Sea?" I briefly thought I was dreaming, and that in my dream I'd gone home to China. Then, all of a sudden, a form loomed toward us out of the mist.

"There she is!" Scottie said.

At a distance of eighty yards, floating, as it seemed, unsupported in the mist, I saw the figure of a huge, ferocious angel — Fury perhaps — in the ambigu-ous dawn light it was impossible to make out its aspect, whether of welcome or of prohibition. Not even its sex was obvious. Yet despite a ghostly indistinct-ness in the form, certain features were apparent: its greenish patina, the thin layer of corrosion formed by long exposure to the elements and long neglect. Around its head it wore what seemed to be a crown of thorns, only its barbs were turned outward like a weapon. Like Manjusri, it held a flaming sword upraised in its right hand, in its left hand, a book. Only the sword was broken, and drawing closer, I realized it was not a sword at all, but a torch. The angel's eyes were blind and vacant as it stared out to sea; and as the day broke in the east, throwing black shadows in the sockets, I thought of the Hunter "fixing his blank gaze on the sun" that he might see again. Linked with this image was another — the thought of Eddie Love in his dark glasses.

"Welcome to America!" Scottie cried, breaking in on my reverie. "That's the Statue of Liberty! What do you think?"

As I made no reply, but continued staring silently at the apparition, wrapped in my own thoughts, Scottie took the opportunity to regale me with his own.

"I haven't seen the old girl in over twenty years," he said, clucking his tongue and shaking his head. "The sight's supposed to make you feel all warm and fluttery inside, but by cock it makes my blood run cold! Look at the bitch! A more lonely, cold, forbidding image I never hope to see, Sun I. See what's written on her side?

> Give me your tired, your poor,
> Your huddled masses yearning to breathe free,
> The wretched refuse of your teeming shore.
> Send these, the homeless, tempest-tost to me,
> I lift my lamp beside the golden door.

"At least, that's the official line. Every American kid learns it by heart in school. Don't be so foolish as to think it refers to you though, Sun I. The subtext reads, 'Abandon all hope, ye who enter here.' "

Though more extreme, Scottie's impressions bore comparison with mine. Though at first I was disposed to attribute them to the effect of mist and my abrupt awakening, many times I was to return and pore with urgent curiosity over the expression of the great Muse of Freedom. And though, in time, there was a gradual diminution of intensity, a mellowing, that sense of melancholy portent which I received at my first glimpse would never pass away entirely.

PART TWO

Dow (New York)

Chapter 1

As the sun rose, the mists evaporated almost instantly. The effect was magical, like the rending of a veil. Manhattan sprang to life before my eyes. I saw the spit of tapering land driven like a wedge into the bay, between the East River and the Hudson rolling from its source high in the Adirondacks down through Tarrytown, Sleepy Hollow, Spuyten Duyvil, the rich countryside carved out of the wilderness by the Dutch, who exorcised the primitive spirits and humanized the landscape through their toil; on past the Palisades, beneath the George Washington Bridge, strung like a necklace of incandescent amber beads across the throat of the great lady as she comes homeward from her revels to the sea through the gauzy dawn light. Further (closer), white, blue, and orange fire belched from the smokestacks of Hoboken, lurid in the damp radiance of the morning air. These flames reminded me of the electrical phenomenon known to sailors as St. Elmo's Fire or corposants, which I had first seen off the coast of Africa — bluish-white incandescence mysteriously rising and falling in the rigging, helium balloons of spectral fire. As Manhattan Island resolved itself from the mist, I seemed to be again in those far latitudes at the bottom of the world, the tongue of land sharpening to nothing at the Battery a smaller version of the Cape of Good Hope, the two great rivers mingling there like the oceans of the eastern and western hemispheres. This effect was further enhanced by the glittering spectacle of the enchanted city which rose before me: the enormous towers of glass and steel vaulting in their cruel beauty toward heaven, like icebergs I had seen in the polar seas, white at their sun-tipped edges, turning indigo and darker in the deepest places, black at the heart, glacial remnants, pleasure palaces of ice no summer sun could melt, glowing with scintillant hauteur in the August dawn. . . . Emerald City — now I understood Hsiao's phrase, at least began to. For New York seemed a city cut by God beneath a jeweler's glass.

And around the glittering spires of Wall Street and Midtown higher up, I saw the frenzy at the edges: Manhattan waking, the terrific surge of life. I heard the *whoosh* and hum of distant traffic, the honking of horns across the bay, the intermittent pounding of a jackhammer, rendered almost ethereal by distance and the effect of water. I saw the incessant stream of yellow taxis on FDR Drive, heard them jouncing and jolting over potholes, or rhythmically clacking over spaced seams in the roadbed. I heard the rumbling of the El up on Brooklyn Bridge as it headed out toward Flatbush Avenue and on to Coney Island. I saw the commuters streaming in from Queens across Manhattan Bridge. I saw the cables of the Brooklyn Bridge shining in the sun like strands of silver spiderweb. And all of this evoked in me a nostalgia for a scene I'd never visited before, a nostalgia partially accounted for by the analogy with the Cape of Good Hope, but not entirely. Was it the reflection I'd seen in my father's glasses in the drawing Hsiao had given me? I only know I tingled with a dreamlike sense of dislocation upon learning from Scottie that *Manahatta*, in the original Algonquin, meant "Heavenly Land" — just like *Szechwan!*

As we passed Ellis Island nearing the Battery, the ship veered to starboard heading up into the East River, through the channel known as Hell Gate. We stood along the topside rail observing the spectacle in silence, until finally Scottie spoke.

"Sun I, darling, I know how long you've waited for this moment, and how much it means to you to get ashore. But lookit, you know as well as I do what we're carrying. There's a chance we'll make it through Customs. Who knows? It could well be there's been some palms greased in high places. If that's so, you may be able to slip away while we're unloading and lose yourself in the warrens of the city where the Immigration'll never catch you. It wouldn't be the first time it's been done. On the other hand, if we're detained and searched, and if they find the stuff, as anybody with a pair of eyes in his head is bound to, then the ship'll be impounded and you can kiss it all goodbye. You won't stand a snow cone's chance in hell of getting off. Deported on a slow boat back to China . . . and after all you've been through getting here! It makes me want to cry or commit cold-blooded murder just to think of it! But don't expect sympathy from those unfeeling bastards. As long as they do their bureaucratic duty and get shut of you, they won't give a sailor's damn what happens. Back home the Reds could flay you alive or stick acupuncture needles through your eyelids for all they'd care." Having allowed himself to overheat, Scottie took a deep breath and returned from these higher latitudes of wrath. "Now, Sun I, without more waste of words, I've considered your situation from every angle, and my best advice to you is to grab the bull by the horns and take the plunge."

"You mean . . . ?"

"Jump for it!" he cried. "Swim for your life, to put the matter in plain seaman's English. I mean, it's not as though you'd never done the backstroke. The waters may not be ideal for bathing. They're a little black and oily looking, with an aroma none too pleasant, but they're no whit fouler than the bilge water we've been marinating in, in that damned steerage! By cock, Sun I, if this barrel is the *Telemachos,* then Odysseus's stint as pigherd was no joke! It must have been hereditary! If you've survived a month at sea in this floating latrine, fifteen minutes in the East River isn't going to kill you. Just don't drink it and the worst you'll get is mange. So look sharp now! Go below and get your precious parcel. I know well enough you've had it ready since the day we shipped."

"But Scottie," I said, "what about you?"

"Don't you worry about that, darling. What can they do to me? I'm just a common sailor. I shipped aboard this tub for wages, and if she's carrying contraband, it's not my fault. The worst they can do is send me back to Manila duty free, and I'd consider that a favor. To tell the truth, I'd been sort of ruminating on the idea of going ashore again, but the sight of that damned statue changed my mind. It's been twenty years" — he checked his watch — "two months, twelve hours, and twenty-two minutes since I've set foot in the U.S., and I just think I'll give it another twenty-odd and see how I feel about it then. Now off with you!"

With that, I dove down the hatch, playing the ladder uprights through my hands like a fireman sliding down his pole, then grabbed my pack and scrambled topside again. Despite my overwhelming excitement to be at last so near my destination, not to mention my anxiety over the rigors of the final stretch, I was aware, as I looked at Scottie, of something tugging backward in my heart.

"Well, darling," he said, "this is it. If it suits you we'll just skip the goodbyes. I've had to say too many of 'em in my time, and I've never noticed that it made it any easier, or hastened the reunion, or in fact served any useful purpose whatsoever. So I've forsworn the habit. You've been a good shipmate, and though forced to choose between you and the bottle, I'd take rum, still we've killed a watch or two in memorable fashion, and you never asked to borrow money, so on the whole I'll probably miss you. Here's wishing you smooth sailing." And with that he smiled and offered me his big mitt, then steered me gently to the rail.

"It's a long way down," he said, leaning over. "But just don't think about it. I'll throw your pack down after you bob up."

I looked down at the pitchy waters. "I'm not sure I can," I said, swallowing hard.

Scottie sighed. "I was afraid of that. Okay, darling, I'm going to make it easy for you. Just you do what Scottie says. Take a deep breath and relax." I did as he instructed. "Now close your eyes and count to three real slowly. One . . . two . . . THREE!"

With that, he seized me from behind and tossed me, squirming and clawing like a cat, over the side. I managed to utter a brief, shrill scream of protest, but seeing the dark water rushing up had sense enough to close my mouth before I splashed. Any subtle feelings of chagrin, resentment, sorrow, or anticipation I might have felt were instantly dispelled as I hit the water and went under. With desperate animal energy I scratched and kicked my way toward the surface. Spouting and blowing as I came up, I began to tread water, and just as I did my pack came down heavily on top of me, sending me under again. In my struggle to stay afloat, I hardly noticed the unsavoriness of the element, or the burning of my skin. I did, however, manage to cast a last glimpse up at Scottie, who was leaning over the rail, cheering me on, alternately coaxing and hectoring with a string of phrases no doubt picturesque and worthy of him, but of which I could make out only a few "by cocks" and "darlings." The urgency of his concern was indicated by the fact that he had doffed his hat and was waving it like a battle standard to rouse me to increased exertion. Seeing me out of danger, he quickly put it on again, after running his fingers gingerly once or twice through his thinning hair, as though afraid to find that his hairline had receded further. Then he turned from the rail and disappeared out of my sight for good. Spitting out a mouthful of the putrid water, I set out for the west pile of the Brooklyn Bridge, doing the American crawl.

•

In more sense than one, then, I may say that I emerged in New York City "dripping from the East," or "dripping with the East" — both possibilities have points to recommend them. As I staggered ashore, crawling up the embankment on my hands and knees, I experienced a prickling sensation inside and out that was not entirely attributable to exertion, nor to the joy that overwhelmed me at feeling the soil of America under me for the first time — soil littered, incidentally, with broken glass, bottle caps, beer cans, and a few used condoms — but was due, I think, to a chemistry of another sort. As it happened, my point of disembarkation was about a hundred yards north of the Fulton Street Fish Market in a seedy parking lot tucked away beneath the girders of the elevated roadway. The shadows of FDR Drive lent the place a permanent gloom.

Unknown to me, my progress ashore had been witnessed by the attendants of the lot, two young Italians, whom I saw when I looked up the bank, standing each with one foot propped on the creosote-drenched pylon which marked the perimeter of their jurisdiction and kept the cars from rolling down into the drink. Each had propped an elbow on his lifted knee and held a soiled stack of dollar bills in his hand.

"Hey, Tony, what is it, you think?" one of them asked. "Some kinda fish?"

"Nah," his friend replied. "Prob'ly a wetback from Brooklyn. You know they don't let 'em use the bridges no more. They gotta get a visa."

"Heh, heh. That's good, Tone. Gimme five on that."

"Put it on the tab," said Tone, coolly demurring.

These young men were both wearing blue jeans turned up at the cuff, shirts of slinky rayon acetate opened to the solar plexus, showing quantities of hair and thin gold chains, some plain, others with crucifixes. Both had well-tended dark mustaches and full heads of brushed-back hair, and both were showing the first signs of impending paunches. They looked remarkably alike.

"What's the matter, man?" number one called to me down the embankment. "You miss your train, or what?"

Tony laughed, then, pretending to take up my cause, chided, "He-e-e-y! Show some re*spect*. Maybe he's training for the Olympics or something. Prob'ly the first guy ever to swim the Brooklyn Channel."

" 'Brooklyn Channel' — heh, heh — you kill me Tone. Hey, you don't suppose he jumped, do you?"

Tony shrugged. "Who knows? Can't tell about them WOGs — you know, Wily Oriental Gentlemens."

They glanced at one another significantly.

During this conversation, I had continued on my hands and knees, staring up at them guardedly like a cornered animal, rivulets of water dripping down my face into the dirt. Though their manner was neither friendly nor hostile, and though they probably regarded my appearance as nothing more than a simple break in the monotony of their morning's routine, an opportunity for repartee, still, conscious as I was of the illegality of my act, I was anxious not to be detected and betrayed to the authorities. Keeping silent, I waited for their sport to stale, hoping they would then go away and leave me leisure to take stock of my situation and consider my next move.

"Ma-a-a-n!" number one scolded. "Don't you know that wadda's full of sewage 'n shit?" He turned to Tony. "Know my Uncle Joey in the mob?"

"Yeah, what about him?"

"He told me, ever want to see a guy disappear, just drop him in the river. Melt like an ice cube."

"Yeah," said Tony. "Like the Whizzit of Oz."

"The comic strip?"

"No, stoopit, the book."

"Hey, Tone, you ain't waxin' literary on me, are you?"

Tone looked at him contemptuously. "Don't you remember that bucket Dorothy threw on the Wickit Witch?"

"The which?"

"The Witch, *ass*hole!"

"Oh! The *Witch!* Yeah, so?"

"So it was full of wadda from the East River."

They both laughed.

"Ain't got a whole lot to say for himself, does he?" number one commented. They waited, as though for me to reply. When I didn't, he took his friend by the arm.

"Come on, Tone," he said. "The guy's a fuckin' fruitcake."

"Yeah, man, a real loony-tune."

" 'Loony-tune'! Hey, Tone, you incapacitate me, really."

"Fuckin' asshole Chink. . . ."

The sound of their voices died away. I took a deep breath and rolled over on my back, heaving a sigh of relief. Just above my head a cloudless summer sky stretched toward heaven, the same sky I had known in China, except for a grayish-yellow tinge, and a quivering in the air which I attributed to pollution. Having left it so far back, it had come to find me once again. It was the only thing I recognized.

Over and over I kept repeating to myself, "This is the same world. This is the same world. . . ."

Not to confound great things with small, I felt a little like Columbus must have when he first sighted land and came ashore in the New World, expecting to be greeted by the emissaries of the Son of Heaven, attired in silks and borne in palanquins, only to find instead a few bewildered, half-naked savages, dressed in skins and feathers.

And yet, unfamiliar as it all was, I remembered Chung Fu's words: "Tao, too, is in the marketplace."

"It must be so," I told myself. "Tao must account for this."

The thought calmed my spirit. For the first time in weeks I let myself totally relax and focus inward. I felt cleansed with labor and the sweet monotony of life at sea, work and sleep, sun and sea . . . tanned, healthy, at peace. Faith welled up in me that the New World I'd reached at last and at such cost (for had I not given all?), no less than that from which I'd come, arose from the unfathomable places of the Tao and was no less subject to its laws. Taking a deep breath, I arranged my legs in the lotus and, facing the morning sun now rising over Brooklyn, did *tso-wang* for the first time in many days. Then, gathering my things, I clambered up the bank and set off unafraid, almost blithely, Reader, into the great man-created wilderness of America.

•

Led by chance, or some subliminal homing instinct, like that which calls the salmon from the ocean back upriver to the primal, freshwater spawning ground, I headed southward, wandering with tranquil purposelessness through the vibrant spectacle of the Fulton Street Fish Market like a lazy river meandering on its way, content to reach its destination rather later than sooner, perhaps not even conscious of it. The day was beginning to whiten and shimmer in the August heat, still clean, not yet turned rancid as it would toward midday. Now a delightful ocean freshness exuded from the whitewashed market building and the chicken wire stalls within, a healthy deep-sea stench compounded out of ice and brine. The morning had not penetrated. Entering its magic perimeter, I experienced a faint predawn thrill of bracing coolness, like opening a refrigerator door. The tons and tons of ice exhaled a deep, long sigh of cold tinged slightly with the scent of fish. Hoses ran exuberantly over the concrete floor, no one to tend them. Men walked around in knee-high black or orange boots and oilskins glistening with wet. Huge semis with bright silver corrugated trailers were backed up to the stalls, loading or unloading. A line of men stood around with hand trucks, waiting their turns, some talking, some staring silently up into the dark interior of the refrigerated trailer where two burly, bearded lumpers wearing watchcaps and tattered, grease-blacked yellow slickers loaded large wooden crates of fish four high on the carrier's truck.

As I wandered through the stalls, I read the names of fish scrawled in abbreviated form with a black grease pencil on the rough lids of the blond wooden crates — "whit.," "cod," "blue," "weak.," "had." — and the names of the trawlers that caught them — the *Deborah Kay,* the *Vicki,* the *Ironsides,* the *Mystic Light* from Chatham. Some of the boats hailed from places with strange names — Galilee, Rhode Island, Kill Devil Hills, N.C.

Farther on, I passed a restaurateur dressed in immaculate white clothes, unshaven, a little sleepy, but alert, frowning sternly as he picked through an opened crate, turning a striped bass in his florid palm, testing its firmness with his thumb, a gleam of infinitely subtle gluttony lambent in his practiced eye, the connoisseur's refined appreciation. I saw dark, sea-green flukes, big as banana leaves or woven rattan fans, couched on beds of snow-white ice the color of their own cooked flesh, frowning glumly with their square boxers' jaws; flounders indistinguishable from them except at the lips, which were small and shaped like nipples; live carp milling sluggishly in a tank; soft-shell crabs on beds of grass; periwinkles, mussels, razor clams, long and thin like ladies' fingers; last of all a red-golden noble salmon whose aspect, alone of all the rest, seemed to adumbrate a flickering of consciousness, something anguished, unrequited in the eye. Observing all with patient thoroughness, lingering over nothing, I passed on and out again into the street.

As I exited, I saw an old Chinese man dressed in rags, his fingers clutching the chicken wire as he eyed the goings-on within. Judging by his tattered dress and his look of resignation, I might almost have taken him for a wandering mendicant. But there was a covetous, hungry edge in that resignation, a brokenness, not the ethereality and bliss one looks for in the priest. By this I knew he was a beggar. He caught my eye and stared at me with puzzled intensity.

"A quarter for a cup of coffee?" he petitioned in English, holding out his wrinkled, yellow hand reflexively.

"I'm sorry," I replied in our native tongue, "I have no money."

"You've just arrived," he said in Chinese, as though with a confirmed suspicion.

I nodded.

"Where are you headed?"

I shrugged my shoulders. "I wish I knew."

"Was there something in particular you were looking for?"

For a reason I can't fully explain, thinking he might understand me at a word, I said, "The Tao."

"The Tao," he repeated, drawing out the word, as though savoring its delicate rare essence on his tongue. He peered at me, aghast with suspicion or surmise, then suddenly he laughed insanely, a laugh broken in the middle by a racking, consumptive cough. Stretching out his skinny arm, he pointed his knotted index finger southward.

"You're headed in the right direction," he informed me, going back to English. "Just a little further down."

Then he staggered off in the opposite direction, laughing that mad laugh.

•

Ah, Reader, imagine the intense excitement and trepidation I experienced on turning the corner into Wall Street for the first time! That long, shadowy ravine stretched away before me like the bed of a prehistoric river, carved out between sheer canyon walls. As I stood at the east end near the river surveying all the stolid Beaux Arts buildings, fusty with age and venerability, and the more outlandish modern constructions of steel and glass, the sense of inexplicable nostalgia, of déjà vu, which I'd felt ever since my first glimpse of the city, was rendered even more acute. Was it that the gloomy chasm through which I walked reminded me of the landscape near Ken Kuan, as in some strange Cubist rendering? As the buildings parodied the eternal aspect of the mountains, so the Street itself the river's flux. For though in some sense "prehistoric," Wall Street hardly seemed extinct. If no water flowed between those banks, a great stream of humanity surged there.

As I began to make my way through the morning crowd, I happened to catch the eye of a young secretary who was passing with a jelly doughnut on her way to work. She had large breasts that jiggled as she walked and a certain way of swinging her hips that, while a little frantic and inelegant, even a trifle lewd, I nevertheless admired. I must have given her an imploring look, or seemed particularly helpless, for she stopped and appraised me.

"The Dow?" I asked with a shrug and a sheepish grin, hoping she'd understand me.

Licking a clot of filling from her upper lip with the tip of her pink tongue, she jerked her head backward as though in reference to something behind her. "It's that way. Wo-ul and Bro-id," she said, then jiggled off to her place of employ.

Before long I found myself at the Wall Street entrance to the New York Stock Exchange. Attempting to melt into the stream of traffic flowing through its doors, I was detained by a large black guard, who eyed me briefly with a look of apathetic wariness and barred my way with a large black arm. "Where's your tag?" he asked.

"Tag?" I squeaked.

"Visitors' entrance around the corner," he said.

When I finally found it, I fell in at the tail end of a group of Japanese tourists, whom I might have been construed to resemble only in the most broadly generic sense, lacking moreover the telltale sign of inclusion in their elite economic fraternity: the camera, with its assortment of indispensable attachments, with which they were busily, though with admirable orderliness and efficiency, taking pictures of one another posed before the doors of the Exchange, smiling happily, like the proud proprietors of a new home.

A little stunned with the novelty of it all, I watched the light blink in the elevator panel — 1, 2, 3 — then suddenly, as if by magic, the doors slid open and we debouched into a plush red room: the Visitors' Reception Center, more elegant and luxurious than anything I'd ever seen before.

A young woman speaking a difficult, highly technical language led us through the exhibition. She pointed to a long, narrow electronic screen of a deep bluish-purple color, across which a series of luminous green symbols — letters and numbers scrambled together in weird configurations — were blazing. Underneath it were several machines with keyboards, before which sat a motley variety of characters pressing buttons and waiting for numerical hieroglyphs to flash on the screen. Sometimes they copied figures on the soiled sheets of wrinkled graph paper they held in their hands.

"These are Quotrons, electronic quote machines," the girl explained. "You simply press the three-letter symbol of your stock, and it tells you what it's doing currently, along with daily and yearly high, low, close, last trade, and so on. Do any of you have stocks you'd like to check?" Smiling encouragement, she surveyed the group, blinking her eyes and opening them large with aseptic interest.

No one stirred. The Japanese seemed overcome with feudal modesty, shuffling from one foot to another in an embarrassed silence. One young man finally spoke out. "Toyota?" he asked diffidently, smiling and bowing.

All faces turned to the girl at the counter, who flushed deep red. A few of the more arch members of the group began to chuckle, then as though on cue, they all broke into discreet titters.

"How 'bout Mitsubishi?" one young joker queried, capitalizing further on the joke.

"No," she said coldly, "I'm afraid those stocks aren't listed on the Exchange." Prompted by their embarrassed tour guide, the Japanese continued on their way in haste. I brought up the rear.

At last we were led out onto the Visitors' Gallery overlooking the trading floor of the Exchange. I'd waited a long time to be there, Reader, tried to imagine what the scene would be for me. Even so I was deeply startled, deeply moved. It's one of the impressions I'll carry to my grave. Only the emotion of it though is still fresh and clear; the scene itself is indistinct in memory, indistinct because so enormous, too enormous to take in. I only recall a vast shimmer of energy, like heat waves rising from a desert I looked down on from a precipice, stretching as far as the eye could see in all directions. I had a vague awareness that I would descend from my mountain and cross that desert, would have to. But I had no concrete associations to bring to what I saw, except one so deep, and so pitiful, that I almost hesitate to state it. A desert, yes, but only now, in hindsight. Then it was a prairie for me, all alive, the teeming prairie of the American West, an abstract, indoor version, complete with characters that my imagination lovingly painted as cowboys, Indians, cavalry troops riding to the rescue of besieged wagon trains. I even saw the horses and the buffalo. None of it there, and all of it so true. The wilderness frontier of capitalism. . . . Looking back from such a distance, so changed from what I was, I can allow myself the luxury of pity. And it is pure, this pity, as pure as if it were for another man. It is.

So this was it, I told myself — Dow, "the other one," the American Dow. It appeared to be a microcosm of the whole human world. What did it not contain? As I stood there, it occurred to me that even Eddie Love might be down there somewhere doing whatever they did — striking a bargain, making a bid or an offer, dealing. At that very instant, having cast an idle glance up toward the gallery, he might be watching me, not knowing who I was, yet experiencing an unaccountable tremor of emotion, as I was. I peered earnestly into the multitudes, searching for, half-expecting to find, a man in aviator glasses with black-green tear-shaped lenses. And missing him, realizing the futility of my endeavor, I looked for someone else — an old Chinese wrinkled with years, but with eyes still bright, someone like Chung Fu, who had tasted the sweet peace of Tao and learned to live contentedly with "coarse rice to eat, cold water from the well, the crook of a bent elbow for a pillow" . . . but he was missing too.

"The Dow. . . . What did it not contain?" The thought recurred like a refrain with altered meaning. In the midst of all my wonder, a twinge of the old doubt surfaced. Did it contain the Tao? Where was the Tao in *this*? Was it here at all? I experienced a rush of vertigo, and then the words of the vow came up:

TAO

Mother of the manifold existences
We see around us, this
Kaleidoscopic pageant of appearances,

TAO

The One within this seething
Multiplicity, itself
Immutable and giving
Rise to all the changes.

Only now the words comforted rather than unsettled. Standing on the gallery of the New York Stock Exchange, I closed my eyes and mumbled again the words of the oath I'd rehearsed each day since childhood, and had now given up forever the opportunity to take:

This is my faith —
That Reality is One
And Tao is Reality —
Which I declare

Is whole and true
On pain of my perdition.

Therefore:
I cast away the world forever
In order to improve it.
I cast myself away
To find myself.
Let me not turn from this resolve
Till hell give solace to the damned
And my soul turn to ashes.

And I swore to keep it in my heart. Reconsecrating myself to my origins, I vowed never to forget or to betray them, but to pursue the Tao even here, even into the labyrinth's heart.

Alone now in the shadowy corridor, the Japanese tourists having long ago taken their pictures and departed, I gathered my things soberly together and prepared to leave. Yet I couldn't resist a parting glance over the great panorama. The trading floor was littered with scraps of paper — pink, yellow, powder-blue — like fallen petals or confetti scattered at a New Year's celebration (the newest year that I would ever live), chaff spread by the whirlwind over the great threshing floor of commerce. I noticed that the whole moved in a circle, returning on itself. "What does it mean? Where is it going?" I wondered. The motion suggested much, but revealed nothing. Yet rising from the place, like a roar of the ocean against the continents, or the cry of the crowd from an open stadium — a wild, primitive cry mixed of pain and jubilation, laughter and tears, applause, recrimination, hope, chagrin — I caught the swelling sound of life, human beings celebrating and bewailing their condition, but going . . . no one knew where.

A little dazed and weary, my eyes burning, a ringing in my ears, I wandered out into the sultry heat beneath the glowing overcast that pressed down on the city. Head bowed, gazing at my feet abstractedly, I stumbled into several people in the street, some of whom reacted angrily, others who asked me if I needed help. Before I knew it, I was on Broadway. It was the height of lunch hour. The great artery churned with people streaming toward the Lexington Avenue station at Chase Manhattan Plaza, hailing taxis, ordering Cokes and slices of pizza, ducking into air-conditioned bars with orange neon signs that advertised cold beer.

Subliminally I noted what was going on around me, but my conscious mind was taken up with something else. Emerging from my reverie, lifting my eyes for the first time, I gazed up at the blackened, embattled hulk of Trinity Church, with its grim turrets, its ponderous wrought iron fence, its obscure crochets of English Gothic gimcrackery, its graveyard covered with green summer grass, curiously vivid and alive in the gray wastes of stone. From its position at the top of the gradual acclivity of Wall Street, if for no other reason, the church might well have seemed the fountainhead, the Source "high in the Tanglha Range" of this great Yangtze of finance. (In that case, one might truly have said that the Return to the Source, to Dow, was a short journey, though surely no less difficult for its length.) Presiding over the Financial District, its soul and conscience, Trinity had not remained immaculate, but rather looked as if it had not been washed since the Great Fire, out of whose ashes, like the Phoenix, it arose, carbonized from its long, stoic ministry, teetering on the brink of what one fancifully disposed might have called the Infernal Regions. Judging by appearances, the church might have passed more credibly for a smoked oyster, or one of the "thousand-year-old eggs" one sees in urns in the groceries of Chinatown, than for a soul. And yet, perhaps it was the closest thing to one Wall Street could muster.

Out of the sweltering heat and the carnival riot of noon on lower Broadway, as oppressive as it was exhilarating, I wandered into the cool, dim interior of the church, which, to my surprise, in striking contrast to the scene outside, was completely empty — a cavernous, vast hollow of jeweled, twilit space. Entering the narthex, I blinked my eyes and stared down the long tessellated promenade of the nave. I entered and strolled past rows of varnished hardwood pews, many bearing engraved silver plaques of dedication. The wine-colored velvet prayer cushions were shiny in places with wear. As I passed the carved pulpit, I noted a beautiful King James Bible, bound in Russia leather, lying open on the lectern under a small gold museum lamp; a ribbon of dark purple silk marked the place. Finally I reached the altar, massive and simple, spread with a white linen cloth with a raised design, a floral meander woven cross-grain in the cloth. Two Greek letters, x and ρ, superimposed on one another (a Chi-Rho, as I later learned to call it), had been appliquéd on the linen. A vase of meadow lilies with green fronds and snow-white trumpets of crisp flower stood in the center of the altar as though in preparation for a banquet. Seconding this impression, off to the right in a reliquary recessed in the wall, were objects that resembled eating implements: a small gold plate with a chased pattern worked around the border, a chalice, and a closed silver box which looked like it might have sweets inside, or perhaps cigarettes for distribution after dinner. But where was the food? And who was eating? The golden boy sagging on the cross behind the altar table looked a little faint, as though he'd lost his appetite, and apparently no one else was coming. Personally, I might have readily consented to a bite had it been offered, but unlike the numerous temples I had visited in Asia, where one could always count on getting tea at least, here in this place of Christian worship no hospitality seemed forthcoming.

As I was mulling over these innocent speculations, a startling transformation began to take place in the interior. Whether outside the overcast had parted momentarily, allowing the sun's rays to shine through unobstructed, or, as it touched the zenith and fell the first degree in its descent toward the west, that great luminary had declined to just the proper angle, falling in the slot prepared for it by architect and glazier, I don't know, but suddenly a gleam began to kindle in the upper windows of the clerestory. As I watched, a rain of golden light began to filter from the stained glass into the church — one of the most magnificent sights I've ever seen, almost hallucinogenic. I sat down in a pew and craned my neck, exploring an aspect of the church that had escaped my scrutiny before.

It was like opening the pages of a marvelous storybook and, not knowing how to read, poring fascinated over the pictures, which gave tantalizing hints of the fables, whose meaning finally eluded me. I saw an old man with a white beard, his tear-streaked face turned toward the sky in anguish, a whetted butcher knife glinting in his right hand, raised above his head to strike. A young boy lay strapped beneath him, staring up with disbelief and horror, his arms raised from the elbow in a gesture of rebuff or protest pitifully attenuated by the rope. Behind them a white ram stood furiously bucking in a thicket, its horns tangled in the undergrowth.

There was a night scene depicting a group of drunken revelers dancing over white desert sands around a roaring campfire. Nude women threw back their heads and laughed with contempt, fear, titillation, as leering men pinned them in their laps, manacling the women's wrists with hardened hands. Fierce stars glittered overhead. In their midst, inciting them to riot, a man in priestly robes stood holding a figurine above his head — a golden calf — shouting defiance at the heavens. At the periphery of the scene, standing in the flickering shadows, an old man dressed in white covered his face with his hands, a rubble of stone fragments littering the ground at his feet.

I saw a boy with light down on his cheeks standing in the midst of many gray-bearded patriarchs with black robes, weird hats, and narrowed, calculating eyes. In his left hand he held a coin, its surface incused with the profile of a man of military mien, with clipped bangs, a square jaw, a long aquiline nose, and a crown of bay around his forehead held up by his ears. The young man's other hand was empty, pointing toward the sky.

Another panel showed this same young man on a mountain ledge. With knees drawn up encircled by his arms, he stared gravely at a spreading panorama — fields of wheat, marching armies, white-sailed ships on the blue sea — which an older man of frosty aspect presented to his attention with a sweeping gesture of his arm as though to say, "This could be yours."

These were isolated panels, fine in their own right, but there were others, two triptychs in particular, which showed the same characters in different poses or predicaments, suggesting sequences of narrative. In the first, a pair of happy lovers, he laughing, she demure, gazed at each other with innocent ardor, naked in a green bower. The grass was studded with flowers, and all around the young couple tame beasts lay drowsing in the sunlight, their heads resting on their paws. The scene was uniformly charming, with the exception of one feature. In the background, set off oddly to one side, a little ominous on account of the irrationality of the perspective, stood a tree, which drew my attention because of its resemblance to the one embroidered in my mother's robe. Like hers, this tree was no more than a gaunt, defoliated skeleton; yet it was not completely barren. From its lowest branch a single piece of fruit depended, green and indeterminate. In the second panel, the tree had moved to front-center stage. Only now a jeweled serpent had twined itself around the trunk, its opalescent skin contrasting starkly with the black bark. Forked tongue extruded in a hiss, it stared with menacing subtlety at a scene taking place in the grass beneath the tree. The woman, paler now and frightened, was handing the fruit, scarred with the imprint of her teeth, to the man, who was reaching out to accept. In the third panel, everything had changed. A stern-faced angel in a white garment, holding a flaming sword above his head (like the statue I had seen in New York Bay), was driving the unhappy lovers before him out into a blighted world, not green, but blackish gray and overgrown with thorns. As they fled, they wept and flailed their arms, or one arm, rather, for each carefully used the other to shield his genitals from the angel's eyes. Their knees touched awkwardly too, a piteous touch, as though even as they ran they struggled futilely to hide themselves. Below this triptych, serving, I assumed, as a commentary on the whole, written in a language which I did not recognize, these words were chiseled in the stone: "Memento homo quod cinis es et in cinerem reverteris."

In the first panel of the second sequence (which was in the apse, above the altar, perhaps the most conspicuous place in the whole church) my eye finally lighted on something I recognized — not something, but someone, a pale, bearded man of uncertain age with weary eyes and compressed lips. It was Jesus; even in Szechwan I'd come across that longing, upturned face in cheap devotional paintings supplied by missionaries. I recognized the man, but not the scene. He was standing before a table, spread, like the altar below, with a white cloth. This table, however, bore the elements of a modest feast: a torn loaf of bread, a fiasco of red wine. With Jesus at table was a group of men of various ages and types, one florid, robust, in the prime of life, another a mere boy, pale, sensitive, ethereal. Different as they were, however, they all sat *behind* the table on the same side as their host, eyes trained on him with expressions that ran the gamut of emotion. Alone on the near side, back to the viewer, a hunched, thickly bearded man sat fixing his stare, not on Jesus's face, but on the broken crust he held in his white hand. Visible in profile, this man's eyes bulged from their sockets, his face contorted with inexpressibly horrible surmise. Below the panel, engraved in the wall, was written, "Hoc est corpus meum."

In the second scene of this triptych three crosses stood against the sky on the crown of a bald hill, a man on each. The Crucifixion — even my glancing knowledge of the Christian legends encompassed this. On the shoulder of the man at Christ's right side, a tiny angel was perched, with a human face and white wings like a bird's; on the shoulder of the other in the corresponding place, a twisted, pitch-black devil with pointed teeth and red malicious eyes;

two horns were sprouting from the devil's forehead, and he had legs like a goat's, with cloven hooves. Jesus was in the center, his face averted slightly from a soldier in a horsehair-crested helmet and iron-studded leather wrist guards, who was reaching a sponge up to him on the tip of a lance. Christ's eyes were turned up toward heaven, two white crescents, as he stared at the sun, its black, occluded disc directly overhead, standing still at the zenith of the sky in full eclipse. Below him, at the base of the cross, three soldiers were casting lots, rolling dice from a leather cup into the dirt. Two of them stared disappointedly at the roll, while the third leapt up in excitement, reaching for the stake, a garment of some sort, bloodred, apparently a robe. Below this was inscribed: "Eloi, Eloi, lama sabachthani?"

The third and final panel depicted a sepulcher dug in the side of a hill, its huge stone rolled away, an angel on the stone, apparently invisible to two men below. These men stood on either side of the tomb's mouth, their hands resting on the jamb, as though to support them in a prior moment as they'd leaned in to look; now they peered at one another with wide, wondering expressions. Below them, on a road that ran along the base of the hill, a mourning woman stood raising her tear-stained face from her two hands, looking up with alarm at a stranger in the road before her. Was it Christ? I assumed so; but his appearance was remarkable. His flesh glowed with a lurid opalescence, like bad fish, and though he smiled at her with gentle, loving eyes, his ghastly, elongated palm was raised in an unmistakable gesture of prohibition, the bright stigmatum printed by the nail still red, unhealed. "Noli me tangere," the inscription read.

Having gazed my fill at these stained glass tableaux, I wandered out at last into the graveyard. Sitting down on a stone bench, I became aware again of the ringing in my ears, like the sound of a crystal glass rimmed with a wet finger. My senses were tuned to a high pitch outside the normal range. I peered out through the wrought iron fence at the vibrant, parti-colored hordes moiling in the street and felt choked with emotion, intense delight mixed inexplicably with sadness and regret. A mockingbird was singing in the branches of a weeping willow behind me. I listened to its song, so different from the nightingale's, surveyed the summer flowers growing wild among the graves, noted the rich, golden sunlight running lambent on the silken arches of the grass as it bent over in the breeze, all with the same emotion. As my intoxicated eye tallied these riches, it lighted on a headstone black with time, the headstone of some old, worldly Puritan. The grave had caved in underneath it, leaving the slab perched in the earth at a skewed, precarious angle. The name was now illegible, but one could still make out the death's-head carved in the stone, grinning hideously from its lipless mouth, and the words below it: "Man, remember, dust thou art, and unto dust returnest." As I read this, the answer to the question that had troubled me before as I stood on the gallery of the Exchange occurred to me. Where were they going so blithely, these multitudes, and with what purpose?

"Here," the gravestones whispered. "Here."

Chapter 2

The shadows were beginning to lengthen when I wandered out again into the street. Having no destination, at sea in the welter of the city, I trusted to my instincts, picking a direction at random. Moving up Broadway, at length I found myself following two small, black-haired heads, which bobbed up periodically in the moving ocean of pedestrians, like seabirds I had seen from the deck of the *Telemachos.* The heads belonged to two small Chinese boys playing a game of kick with an empty Coke can, weaving and darting agilely in and out of the crowd, disrupting the steady, sober flow of traffic with their exuberant, unpredictable motions, uttering birdlike cries of delight that lingered hauntingly above the general din of traffic. Once, through miscalculation, they lost control of their ersatz ball. The bright red-and-white can clattered to a halt directly in the path of a young businessman in a dark-blue pin-striped suit, who was walking along rapidly, carrying a leather briefcase. Emerging from his abstraction, he stared at it curiously, then, relaxing from his rigid pose, returned it to them soccer style, with a touching gesture of bravado and élan, a boy himself again for that brief instant. A second time they weren't so lucky. A man not radically different from the first in outward appearance, finding his forward motion similarly impeded, glared at the can with positive ferocity and angrily stomped it flat with the heel of his shoe. The boys stopped in the middle of the street, staring after him with forlorn expressions, as though crushed themselves by the gesture. Soon, however, they recovered themselves, crying out, "*Fang pi,* you ass*hole!*" The man wheeled and shook his fist in outrage. Laughing shrilly with fear and titillation, they ran off in the opposite direction, leaving their small casualty behind them on the field of battle.

Following them, hardly registering my surroundings, some minutes later I realized that the streets were swarming with Chinese. As though through magical transposition I was in Chinatown! Speaking of déjà vu! The business suits and briefcases, the white occidental faces, all the accoutrements of Dow gave way, and, like a fry thrown back by a tenderhearted fisherman, I discovered myself again in my own element, surrounded by almost familiar scenes. How strange! To see those typical Western buildings — square, formalistic, utilitarian — animated from within by the rich flux of Chinese life, colorful, teeming, impenitent chaos! I heard the chatter of countless voices, most of them Cantonese (which, though I spoke only haltingly, I understood almost as well as my own dialect), women haggling at outdoor stalls over fish or bok choy, fresh scallions, ginger. The signs on all the buildings were in characters, and I smiled with delight passing a phone booth with a curved "pagoda" roof, like a Chinese temple. Rows of well-stocked grocery stores and Chinese bakeries denoted a prosperous community. The display windows were full of articles that would have made any Chinese heart glad: bottles of oyster sauce and hoisin ("Food for Connoisseur") packed by the Koon Chun Sauce Factory in Hong Kong. There were bottles of syrups, prune, date, pineapple, "Swallow's Nest" pear; there was arbutus juice and grenadine; ginseng extract; sugar-coated amber, Peking dates; there were dried sardines and cuttlefish; mung beans, black turtle-soup beans, live turtles milling in a crate; waist-high glazed urns of thousand-year-old eggs, still caked with lime from their two-month aging process (during which the yolk turns bottle green, the white a transparent bluish color, almost aquamarine); there was Pearl River Bridge Double-Black Soy Sauce, "recommendable to all restaurants and homes in frying, braising, steaming, boiling, and for appetizing soup or cooked-up food, to which once drops of this soy added, a wonderful flavor will instantly ensue"; there were expensive delicacies — bird's nest, shark's fin, duck's head, fish lips, fruit bat ("Heavenly Rat"), lizard, snake; there was Imported Girl Brand Florida Water, a sort of Chinese Aqua Velva . . . in short, anything the heart could desire, or money buy. As regards the latter condition, however, I was reminded once again of my insolvency, and a note of melancholy crept into my otherwise delighted inventory-taking.

In this mood of mild dejection, while walking down a narrow alleyway, my stomach growling, a swinging door burst open in my face and a rush of spicy, dumpling-scented steam escaped. In the midst of this savory cloud, like a small, yellow genius loci — god of the wok — a middle-aged man in a tall white chef's hat, soiled apron, and a sweat-dampened, sleeveless T-shirt appeared, holding a pail of garbage poised for catapult. Fortunately, catching sight of me, he balked at the last moment, sparing me a further layer in my already rather noisome candy coating. The poor man appeared mortified to have come so near offense. He blushed and bowed, repeating over and over in English, "Excuse please! Excuse please!" Though thin and rather exiguous looking, with a cowed expression which I took, not so much a product of our run-in, as a permanent fixture of his mood, there was something warm and cheerful underneath which came out in his eyes, one of which was blacked. Remembering the old Chinese adage about "a chance encounter in the street," I placed my hands together palm to palm and bowed low in a gesture of priestly courtesy.

"Honored sir, I am a stranger here, alone, without friends or guidance," I began, resorting to laborious, stilted phrases in my ignorance of Cantonese. "Were my condition not so desperate, I would not apply to you, a chance acquaintance, or venture to impose upon your hospitality. Under the circumstances, however, I was hoping you might recommend cheap lodgings where I may situate myself and perhaps procure a meal."

He gaped open-mouthed at my elaborate protestations, as though I were some specimen of life from another planet, or perhaps simply from another, prior age. Then, recalling himself, he suddenly smiled. "You are from Szechwan," he answered me in my own dialect, apparently clued in by my accent. "A priest?"

I bowed low again, signifying assent. "Taoist," I said, to make sure there was no mistake.

"Ah," he said. "A-one! An educated man. I am honored."

"The honor is mine," I replied.

"No, no," he protested.

"Yes, yes," I insisted.

"At any rate, we are well met," he said. "No doubt there is fate in it. For we hail from the same province. Though I have lived here many years, I too was born in the Heavenly Land. Near Chengtu."

The thought of home in the midst of such overwhelming novelty as I had seen that day brought a mist of tears to my eyes. Embarrassed by my emotion, I bowed deeply once more, hiding my face. Showing tact and forbearance, my interlocutor allowed me time to regain my self-control before he spoke again.

"You have arrived only recently?"

"Is it so obvious?" I asked, sniffling and drying my eyes.

He shrugged indulgently and smiled.

"Only today," I said.

He raised his eyebrows.

Just then a wisp of smoke began to seep through the door. He sniffed the air and his eyes grew large with frantic concern.

"Excuse please!" he cried, speaking English again in his confusion and setting off at a sprint. Poking his head briefly back out from behind the swinging door he said, "Wait here."

I heard a burst of recrimination and excuse in rapid, staccato Szechwanese, then a huge sizzling hiss, like new-forged iron plunged red hot in the tank. A flurry of commands ensued.

At last the door swung open. To my surprise, however, it was not my new friend, but a boy about my own age, dressed like the chef only without the hat, and with an expression of guilty chagrin on his features such as one wears after a well-deserved dressing down. Poking out his head, he eyed me glumly.

"He's busy now," he said. "He told me to give you this."

Through the door he passed me a paper napkin stuffed full of hot *dim sum,* transparent in places where the grease had soaked through.

"This too," he added, giving me a scrap of paper. He then disappeared behind the swinging door, which flapped in my face as I stepped forward to protest and call him back.

Sighing, I looked down at the note scribbled on a blank green waiter's ticket in hurried, ill-constructed characters:

> For the hungry young dragon
> Who appeared from the mists
> And wandered up outside our door,
> Please accept:
> Ha-p'i Lo
> P.S. For accommodations inquire at this address:
> 17 Mulberry Street, Mme Chin.

I was touched by this poor and obviously uneducated man's attempt at improvisational verse in the manner of the old Taoist tipplers, Li Po and the Seven Sages of the Bamboo Grove. I wanted to thank him but was afraid to disturb him further. In my quandary, I popped one of his hot, crispy delicacies in my mouth, crunching through the skin of deep-fried batter into the luscious heart, and, vowing to return and thank him later, I set off again in considerably improved spirits, searching for the address he'd given me.

In due time, after making several inquiries, I found what I was looking for. I stood in the street studying the building's aspect before venturing to enter. It had a sort of barrow look about it, its bricks sooted over with age. A noticeable port list made it appear to be in a fairly advanced stage of organic decay, collapsing from the inside, like an ancient invalid whose bones have turned to dust within him. The only thing even vaguely prepossessing about it was the fire escape, a heavy cast-iron affair out of another era, slathered with countless coats of bright fire-engine red enamel paint, as though to foster some illusion of security. A dingy yellow light bulb burned in the vestibule, which had a floor of black and white tesserae arranged in a vortical geometric pattern. Behind it, through the beveled glass panel of the inner door, I could see a narrow stairway ascending steeply into a region of total gloom.

Swallowing anxiously, I tried the door. I admit, I was almost relieved to find it locked. I was about to try my luck elsewhere, when I noticed a small, glowing, orange eye staring out at me from the jamb. Peering closely, I made out a placard above it on which was written: "Ring buzzer for admittance."

I hesitated, then gingerly pressed the button fearing an unpleasant surprise. Nothing happened. Like a curious pup prodding a turtle in the road, growing bolder, I pushed again more confidently. On the third attempt, I felt disposed to sneer. The harsh, nasal catcall which erupted from the wall sent me yelping down the stairs with my tail tucked between my legs.

Shaken, I timidly reascended, clinging to the banister for security. The door was open. I walked on tiptoe down a darkened corridor. To right and left along the hall, dead bolts clicked and doors still chained inside parted just a hair.

Dark eyes peered through the cracks. I approached one door to inquire my way, but it shut swiftly in my face to the rattle of locks and chains. At the far end, beneath another jaundiced light bulb, I found a ponderous door with a weird knob of faceted, prismatic glass. Tacked to its upper half by four tarnished brass thumbtacks was a yellowing sign written in English and Chinese. The print and calligraphy were professionally done, though in a style that was ornate and dated. The whole was surrounded by a border of stars and crescent moons:

MME CHIN
LANDLADY & OCCULTIST
M.D., Ph.D., D.D.S.

FORTUNE-TELLING:
I Ching Consultations
Dowsing
Chiromancy
Geomancy
Feng-shui
Phrenology
Haruspication
& etc.
"You name it"
(Seances Arranged)

HERBAL MEDICINE
CHIROPRACTIC
MARRIAGE COUNSELING
LOVE POTIONS
HOMEOPATHY
(teeth extracted)

ROOMS FOR RENT   PAWN-BROKERAGE
NO CREDIT!!!
Inquire Within.

Tentatively, I rang the bell. After a moment I heard the sound of furniture sliding heavily across the floor within, hurried footsteps. The barrel bolt rocketed backward in its groove. The door parted.

"Who is it?" a strident whisper demanded in Chinese. The voice was a young man's, yet there was something epicene in it, a priggish insistence on precision in the diction, detectable even in so brief a pronouncement, effeminate, if not feminine.

"I was told I might find a room here," I answered.

"Aiyi! Auntie! There's someone here to see you," he called over his shoulder.

I heard a whining and scratching at the base of the door.

"Get down!" he hissed. A young dog's yelp rang out, followed almost instantly by a frantic scuffling, like a skater trying to regain his balance on the ice, as of small claws struggling for traction on a hardwood floor. "Odious animal!"

"Wait here," I was told peremptorily. The door slammed in my face. I stood nervously for several minutes before I heard the night chain slip. "Come in," I was commanded. The great door swung back on its hinges.

Standing in the foyer was a young man with an unnaturally pale face — except for two blushes of high color along his cheekbones — and lips so red that I suspected paint. He was dressed with theatrical elegance, though dated, fastidiously eccentric: an off-white linen jacket with padded shoulders; a black suede flower, a chrysanthemum, pinned to the lapel; a yellow silk foulard — dark-blue quatrefoils with bloodred stigmas; suspenders; pleated trousers; ankle-high black boots of supple, close-grained leather which zipped on the inside of the foot. His coal-black hair was slicked back with glistening pomade. He wore a scent which reminded me of cloves. He eyed me with a peevish expression, bordering on outright hostility. His dark eyes were beautifully lambent and alive, though, magnetic, like a serpent's, full of exquisite sensitivity, and exquisite hatred.

Turning, he magisterially swept aside one panel of a heavy drapery, greenish-blue slubbed silk with tasseled ends, which hung from the lintel of a double doorway. Bracing it behind his arm, he smiled with mocking courtesy, nodding almost imperceptibly in invitation. Brushing past him, close enough to feel his breath warm in my ear, I went in. The curtain dropped behind me. His steps receded. A door opened; closed. I was left alone.

All the shades were drawn. Around one of them, like a rectangle cut in black construction paper, a razor-thin corona of pure light glowed, so brilliant that it was colorless. Otherwise the illumination was all artificial: a brass floor lamp with a white silk shade faded to the color of old parchment; a tarnished silver candlestick placed in the center of a mandala of lace atop a ponderous, serpentine chest of dark mahogany, its white-golden flame floating in the finish like a gibbous moon in water. The wax had dribbled obscenely over the base. A piquant aroma hovered in the air, faint but unmistakable, a peculiar and equivocal sweetness, as of wildflowers and dung. Feeling suddenly nauseated with fear, I dropped down in a chair.

The room was filled with dark, heavy pieces, most notable among them a locked armoire, an ottoman covered with wine-colored velvet, and a love seat with ball-and-claw feet. There was fabric everywhere — stiff lengths of ancient chintz draped over tables, tapestries on the walls. One, a Tibetan *tanka,* depicted a circular labyrinth or mandala — a gigantic web — in the center of which a dark god waited with crazed, bloodshot eyes, a thousand arms, and the subtlest of smiles. On his brow he wore a tiara of the crescent moon, or horns. Most in evidence, however, were the tablecloths and doilies, the dresser scarves and runners of yellowing, delicate lace, draped everywhere like cobweb. Indeed, the room resembled the lair of a decrepit spider, the countless curios and knicknacks — Thai dolls, the Pa Hsien, or Eight Immortals, French confections in farthingales, painted porcelain parrots — like the carcasses of insects suspended in its web, bits of winged, buzzing life gone wrong, waiting helplessly for the spider to return.

As I sank wriggling, so to speak, into this repugnant image, I was startled back to reality by the horrible sensation of some moist, cold thing applying pressure to my leg. Recoiling, I sprang upward like a cat from water. When I landed on the floor again, my heart was pounding violently against my ribs. Gasping for breath, prepared to defend my life if necessary, I peered down into the shadows of the furniture fully expecting to find a creeping, half-vegetable form intent on doing violence to my life.

Instead, I found a puppy, white except for a pair of black, floppy ears, four stocking feet, and one moist, kid-leather nose — the same which had produced the disagreeable sensation. Sitting on its haunches, it tilted its head to the side and arched its refractory ears, which came only partially erect, staring at me quizzically out of soulful puppy eyes. For no apparent reason, it began to whine and wag its tail, which thumped the floor like a fibrillating metronome.

"Come here, *darling!*" I cried in a mild paroxysm of relief, unconsciously imitating Scottie. I squatted on my haunches and clapped my hands, even tried to whistle — *"Wh-r-r-t! Wh-r-r-t!"* — though without much luck.

The dog, however, looking every bit as forlorn and out of context as I felt myself to be, forgave my shortcomings. Scrambling to his feet, he scampered toward me across the floor with loose-jointed bonhomie. Our encounter was memorable and highly gratifying. I patted; he wagged — our activities mutually reinforcing. Licking my hand and apparently finding it to his liking, he even went so far as to teethe upon it vigorously, a familiarity I was forced to rebuff, not from unwillingness, but because his tiny denticles, though barely erupted from the gum, pricked like so many pins.

While engaged in this lighthearted play, I noticed a movement at the periphery of my field of vision. A shadow passed before the candle. Something clutched inside me. Looking up, I saw a figure dressed in black: an old woman standing in the shadows, watching. How long she had been there, I had no idea. I hadn't heard her enter. She was dressed in a traditional cheongsam of jet-black silk, unembroidered, but of the highest quality, with a swastika pattern. Pinned to her bosom — which was large and full, impressive in a woman of her years, as was her waist, which she'd kept small, the ruins of a figure which had once perhaps been "grand" — was a small brooch, a silver crescent moon inlaid with mother of pearl. Dangling beside it in the center of her breast was a heavy ring of keys suspended from her neck by a transparent gossamer of nylon. She was fingering this thoughtfully as she watched, a motion which produced a faint, mechanical clacking, like the beads of an abacus or the shuttle of a loom. On her old, arthritic fingers there were rings with semi-precious stones: moonstone, topaz, lapis, amber, pearl, carnelian, and one large emerald.

She stepped into the aura of the candle where I was able to make out her features clearly. Her yellow face was wrinkled like a piece of old upholstery which has come untacked from the underpinning. It sagged in folds like liquid on her bones. Her hair, which she wore pinned to her head in a loose chignon, was coarse, like a horse's tail, mostly gray, though still shot through with some black threads. Her most remarkable feature, however, was her eyes, two narrow, lashless slits. In each a single spark of pale fire glowed like an ancient firefly, relic of some forgotten summer night, preserved in the dark amber of the rheum. The scleras were not white but ivory, as though with extreme age.

As I stared, she tilted her chin toward her left shoulder just barely in a gesture of acknowledgment, almost coy, then smiled fulsomely, her eyes disappearing altogether in the folds of loose tissue, her lips curling back over a set of stained, ruined teeth, one of which was gold.

"I am Mme Chin," she said.

"My name is Sun I," I replied with a slight squeak.

"Sun I . . . hmm . . ." she mused, "unusual name."

"I've come to see about a room," I said quickly, anxious to parry any overtures toward intimacy from such a creature.

"There is one available."

"How much?"

She smiled. "All in good time. We must become better acquainted first. Your patronymic?"

"I am a priest."

"Ah. You grew up in a monastery then." She gazed at me appraisingly. "I might have known."

I darted a keen glance at her. "How so?"

"Something about your face — the eyes I think." She smiled.

I blushed and fidgeted. Feeling very uncomfortable, as though somehow she knew, or might easily read, my deepest secrets, I attempted a circuitous retreat, belittling my own cause. "I'm afraid I'm wasting your time, Mme Chin. I saw your sign: 'No Credit.' "

She blinked her eyes. "And?"

"Well, I must be frank with you. I have no money now. I'd hoped for a brief period of grace until I could find work."

"Is that all? Don't let it bother you," she replied with surprising amiability. "Let's talk first before we commit ourselves. Who knows, you may have something just as good as cash . . . or better. I see you have a soft spot for animals," she observed, changing the subject. "An admirable trait, and most revealing."

"Who could resist those eyes?" I asked, lifting the pup's chin to examine them. I frisked his ears. "I'd like to have one like him. Where did you find him?"

"We get them from the pound," she said.

I rolled him over playfully, scratching his belly. "What's his name?"

"Name?" She laughed. "Oh, we rarely have them long enough to give them names."

Puzzled, I looked up. "There are others?"

"There were."

I met her eyes, but they told me nothing.

"Fan-ku!" she cried sharply, breaking eye contact. "Fan-ku! Stop listening at the drape and come take away this animal."

The young man entered, his guilt apparent from the violent blushes spreading underneath his powder, yet in all other respects managing an attitude of absolute sangfroid.

"Did you call, Aiyi?" he asked with a show of indifference.

"Where were you?"

"In the bedroom," he coolly replied.

"Painting your toenails, I suppose," she said maliciously, though beaming at his face as though with pride. "Or were you playing with yourself?"

His eyes darkened like velvet brushed against the nap, but he refused the bait.

Mme Chin frowned. "Take the dog," she snapped.

Glowering at me with repressed ferocity, he snatched the puppy brusquely from the floor by the nape of its neck.

"Ar-r-r!" it squealed.

"Shut up," he hissed, cradling it in a stranglehold as he retreated toward the door.

"Wait!" she said.

Very slowly, with gloating deliberateness, she rounded the ottoman and seated herself in the love seat. When she was settled, she looked up at him with the same fulsome smile she had formerly directed at me, but with an expression of cruelty and hunger. Jutting out her chin a fraction, she said in a saccharine voice: "Kiss Aiyi before you go." She didn't look at him, but smiled off to one side, as though suspended in a state of complacent anticipation.

Fan-ku stiffened, shoulders trembling, eyes bulging slightly as he stared at her, the whites visible all the way around. Slowly, as though in a trance, he crossed to her. For a moment he stared wildly at her where she sat, cheek presented for his kiss of homage. The air fairly crackled with tension. I feared some violent outcome. In the end, however, he leaned down and did her bidding, then wheeled around and stormed from the room.

Like a statue kissed magically to life, Mme Chin reanimated with his gesture of subservience. She regarded me with coy challenge, an expression I found absolutely unfathomable, and, moreover, had no wish to understand. "Such a pretty boy," she said, "and so proud."

Knowing nothing else to say, I resorted to a banality. "Your nephew lives with you?"

"Nephew?" She looked at me quizzically, as though not understanding the question. Then she smiled. "You misunderstand, Sun I — Aiyi, that is just a politesse. We are no relation." She lowered her voice. "Though doubtless he would like to be. I am a widow, you see, several times over." Her mood was almost playful now. "You see, I wear black in perpetual mourning." She smoothed her hand seductively over her right breast down to her waist. "I have no children, no family — no one, except myself."

"I'm sorry," I said, thinking I should.

She laughed. "Don't be. It's a full-time job. I couldn't handle more. No, no, I assure you, I keep myself completely occupied."

Confused by her tone and manner, I fell silent, puzzling over the exact nature of their relationship.

"Tsk, tsk," she clucked in an amused tone, as though reading my thoughts. "You are very green, Sun I." Raising her hand, she crooked her finger, beckoning. "Come here."

I ventured as near as the opposite side of the table, grappling the edge with my fingers as though dropping anchor.

"Closer," she whispered.

Unable to resist, I approached, leaning down over her further and further, fixing on her eyes with fascinated horror, like a rabbit mesmerized by a snake.

"You see, Sun I," she whispered, her face so close to mine that I could feel her breath like cobweb on my cheek, smell its faint aroma of corruption, like dust and mothballs emulsified in sickly sweet perfume, "I am a dowager." She pronounced the word seductively.

"You are rich?"

She smiled, her gold tooth glittering obscenely in her mouth. "Filthy."

Coming to my senses, I recoiled and drew erect.

"Don't run away, my pet," she crooned. "I won't eat you. Come and sit by me. Let me tell your fortune."

"I came here to see about a room," I answered coldly. "I am a Taoist priest trained in the use of the *I Ching*. I have no need of fortune-tellers."

"Humor an old woman," she coaxed, pouting. "You may learn something you didn't know."

Reluctantly, I reached for a chair.

"Not there," she said. She patted the velvet cushion of the love seat beside her. "Here."

As I sat down, she deftly whipped the lace cloth up. The octagonal table underneath was made of black wood, buffed to a high luster. In the center was the Egg of Chaos, in the corners, inlaid in ivory marquetry, the eight trigrams. I was facing *Sun*.

At first I was astonished, unpleasantly so. Then it occurred to me that, having told her my name, she might have easily deduced the rest herself. Perhaps it was simply a coincidence. I searched her face for a clue. Her smile told me little. At any rate, I noticed that the dowager, as she had called herself, was seated before the three broken lines: *K'un,* the trigram of the Earth, or Mother.

Taking my palm in both of hers, which were chill and moist, she peered into it intently, as though its surface were transparent, a clouded pool whose botten she was trying to discover.

" 'Sun I,' " she mused. "In your name Gain and Loss are mingled. So, in your palm." She studied my face.

I shifted nervously in my seat. "What do you mean?"

"You have come here recently," she said, ignoring my question, looking down again, "after a long journey undertaken at great risk. Personal sacrifices have been made. . . ."

"My hands are calloused from months of hard work at sea," I conceded. "But it hardly takes a palmist to tell me that."

She looked up. A fateful knowledge glowered in her eyes; old and absolutely certain, it undermined my confidence in the fraudulence of her intent. Ignoring the implied rebuke, she went on: "Personal sacrifices have been made . . . but these are as nothing compared to what is still to come." Her smile was almost gloating. "You have come here in search of something, am I right?"

"Perhaps," I replied, "but it requires no particular astuteness to determine that. Why else would one undertake a difficult journey?"

"Something, or some*one,* " she qualified, smiling cryptically, as though in triumph.

Deep inside me, a locked door opened and a cold gust made the hair rise on my arms. "All right," I said quietly. "But who? Or what?"

"Difficult to tell," she replied with a studious pout. "Your palm is most unusual. See here, how the fate line, cleanly incised, proceeds singly for a term of years, then bifurcates, one fork branching upward, the other down. This signifies a divided nature, one part aspiring up into the realm of spirit, the other drawn by gravity down into the material world. There is an ambiguity in your quest as in your name — Gain and Loss, matter and spirit. I can say only that you have come searching for both worlds and will find only one of them. For the price of the one is the loss of the other."

"I find this all a little vague, Mme Chin," I said, regaining confidence. "It could apply to anyone."

"Let me be more specific then," she said. "You have come searching for someone, and will find only an idea or a belief; or else, seeking an idea, you will find only the person . . . only the *man.* It is a man, isn't it?"

The effect of her specification of gender was undercut by her final question, which I took as implying doubt. "I should tell *you?*" I rejoined with cheerful irony. "Isn't that written in my palm as well?"

She met my eyes and said nothing.

"All this is appropriately cryptic, Mme Chin," I said. "Perhaps it's simply over my head, but I'm afraid, for me, in the end the obscurity becomes opaque."

She shrugged. The light went out in her eyes. "What do you wish to hear?

If you resist me, I can tell you nothing." Her voice became mechanical, dropping into self-parody. "You will become very wealthy. You will fall in love."

"Don't mock me, Mme Chin," I said.

In her expression then I saw something which I thought I knew. "Life is composed of just such banalities," she said. "And it is no less terrifying or profound for that."

Age and immense weariness — that is what I recognized in her expression, in her words, that and a bitterness which had long gone unresolved, growing year by year, like a cancer feeding on the healthy tissues, until gradually it had usurped all the free faculties of life. Now nothing remained but this, a great ingrown malignancy feeding on itself, incapable of cure. Her life had contracted to a single function: feeling pain, and its vicious complement, inflicting pain on others. This was the spider's secret grievance, and relief had become synonymous with death, its own, or the fly's. I saw all this in Mme Chin and, repulsive as it was, I sensed its poignance. I pitied her. That was my first mistake.

"Please continue," I said quietly, offering my hand which I had closed.

"No," she hissed, petulantly flinging it away. "You have broken my concentration." She got up and stalked across the room.

Her wronged tone had its effect. "Please, Mme Chin," I petitioned, certain she wished to be wooed out of her intransigence.

"I have given you all the free counsel I intend to," she replied. "If you wish to learn more, you must pay for it."

"With what?" I asked. "I told you before I have no money."

Sensing my capitulation, she coyly "noticed" my pack on the ottoman. "And I told *you*, you might have something just as good." She pointed with her chin. "What's in that?"

"Only my personal effects," I answered. "Nothing that would interest you. Please continue the reading."

She circled the ottoman. "I have seen as much as I can in your hand. Sometimes one can tell a great deal from memorabilia." She smiled suggestively, grasping the pack's drawstring between her thumb and finger. "May I?"

Feeling slightly sick, I hesitated foolishly; she took advantage and proceeded.

"Mme Chin!"

"Don't worry," she said reassuringly. "You can trust me."

I was defenseless against such brazenness, virtually paralyzed.

"Fan-ku!" she called. "Bring me my spectacles!"

Almost before the words had left her mouth, he entered with her glasses.

"Were you listening again, my pet?" she demanded slyly, as she put them on.

This time he smiled too. Taking up his place behind her chair, he looked on with the tense, hungry patience of a bird of prey.

As Mme Chin shamelessly, with slow-savoring, almost refined gluttony, rifled the small cache of my most intimate possessions, I watched helplessly. It occurred to me why the insect flies into the spider's web. It is not stupidity or error on his part, or deception on the spider's. She lures him with a bait of truth — allows him a brief glimpse into her secret loneliness, the barren ritual of an existence she is doomed to celebrate forever without joy — and, thinking to mitigate, he flies in of his own free will and is devoured.

Her restrained pillage abruptly halted. Drawing out my father's photograph, she held it near the candle and leaned backward frowning, pushing her spectacles lower on her nose.

A sick thrill fluttered in my bowels.

"This is the man you've come to seek," she said without looking at me.

"You know him?" I asked, leaning forward eagerly in my chair, frantic with sudden hope.

She held the photograph above her shoulder for Fan-ku to examine as she met my eye. "What is his name?"

"Eddie Love," I replied, a quaver in my voice betraying my emotion.

"Your father?" she asked, sharply observing my response.

I said nothing.

"An American. . . ." she mused. "Now I begin to understand."

"But do you know him?"

The portentousness which had tantalized me in her manner vanished, replaced by the inscrutable formality of her smile.

"Unfortunately, no," she replied. "He was a soldier? So handsome in his uniform! You have his looks. Such a pretty boy!"

"Will I find him, Mme Chin?" I implored, willing now to believe in her clairvoyance, willing to believe in anything that might help me find my father.

She peered at me intently over the rims of her spectacles. "If I were you," she said, "the question I would ask myself is rather, do I want to?"

"What is that supposed to mean?" The idea jarred me.

"I have told you all you need to know."

Our eyes met on it, then she turned her attention once again to the contents of my pack, drawing out the robe, folded in a rectangle the size of a small book.

"Hold it up," she commanded Fan-ku.

Delicately pinching each shoulder, he flicked his wrists and it fell out into the light.

Mme Chin gasped involuntarily and raised her hand to her breast. Unconsciously she began fingering her keys. The room was completely silent, except for that faint metallic clacking, which might have been the sound of her own thoughts.

"Turn it," she ordered.

With the elegance and disdain of a matador, Fan-ku allowed her the back panel, the sun, the blighted tree, the fruit, the two great beasts wheeling high above the world.

I became absorbed in it as well. It was the first time I had seen it in a while.

I realized the photographic memory of it I carried had faded. Its beauty seemed created new, incommensurable with what I'd known before. Poring over it, I'd memorized each nuance, each turning in the labyrinth, practically each thread; but now the details startled me again. The whole appeared altered somehow, more vivid, purified, as though in the interval it had undergone a further distillation, its physicality enhanced, solidified, until it crossed a magic threshold into immateriality and become pure essence, thought, a vapor.

My wonder was increased by what I saw when I emerged from this brief rapture, which was bittersweet to me. Mme Chin, sitting just as before, from all appearances impassive, eyes narrowed, drowsing like a cat . . . was crying. Two tears had trickled halfway down her cheeks, small quicksilver runnels sparkling as they coursed through the parched deserts of her face.

I was moved. "Mme Chin," I said, "you're crying."

"You seem surprised," she remarked. "What do you think of me? Am I so old and horrible that I may not shed tears? What woman could see this and not weep?"

Not knowing what to say, I was silent.

"Fan-ku, bring the pipe." She turned to me. "I have never seen such work, and I collect — for myself and others."

He carried a tray with a lamp, a dish of black, gooey opium, and a pipe with a chased silver bowl. Breaking off a pellet, he shaped it in his fingers, then spitted it on the dipper and held it to the flame.

"Would you care to join us?" she asked when it was ready, offering me the pipe.

I waved my hand, declining.

We fell silent as they smoked, refilling the bowl twice. When they had finished, Mme Chin rose and crossed to the armoire. Squinting at her keys, she picked one out, a tiny skeleton, and, bending over, applied it to the lock. Standing straight, she swung the door back on its hinge. "Come and look," she said, inviting me with a sweeping gesture of her arm.

Inside I saw a cache of silken treasure: damasks, gauzes, twills, robes of every color, from palest shades of gray and pink to black and red, deep purples, mauves and indigos, a rainbow of vivid, deep-dyed hues, each one surprising and a little strange, as though realized only once.

"This is Japanese," she said, flicking one with her long fingernail, her pride expressed almost disdainfully. "It was worn by a famous courtesan in Tokyo, when that city was called Edo." Her voice had dropped into a rhythmical, incantatory cadence, as though she were reciting poetry, or performing some ritual which she had celebrated many times and mastered long ago. Fan-ku had tiptoed up beside me and was looking on. The morbid passion in his face had drained away, and he seemed almost sweet. There was a look of childish awe on his painted features, like a small boy experiencing a treat he's waited for so long his dreams have made it magical, almost holy.

"This belonged to the abbot of a monastery," she continued, pointing to another. "It is said he wore it on his deathbed, that on the last night of his life, the watchers, exhausted by their vigil, fell asleep. In the morning they awoke and found him gone, and this in the bedclothes."

She touched a third. "This is from the Manchu court. It was worn by a young maid-in-waiting, a noblewoman said to be a favorite of the Dowager Empress, Tzu Hsi. Though well born, she fell in love with a servant in the palace, a boy of common birth. They were discovered. He was executed for his presumption, she locked up to prevent her doing herself harm. But she refused all food and water, committing suicide by means of a remorseless passivity. See the sad-eyed phoenix.

"These are my best pieces," she went on. "But today I've lost my relish for them, seeing this."

I was impressed by the majesty she'd taken on, almost afraid of it. But even as I watched I saw it disappear. Her features hardened. "I must have it," she informed me, picking up my mother's robe again. "Name your price."

I stiffened and appraised her coldly. "It's not for sale."

"Come, come," she cackled, shriveling up before my eyes. "I won't cheat you. I don't scrimp on quality. Chin pays top dollar. I have clients who would kill for this." She smiled cryptically. "I might myself . . . ha-ha! But all joking aside, what is it to you? You are too young to appreciate it. Not to insult you, but in your hands it's like 'a diamond in a sack of rice.' Besides, you have your youth. The world is open to you. For me the scope of pleasure narrows hourly, contracting like the pupil of an eye. The thing itself, life, has become too brilliant for my old eyes to bear directly. I must take it all at second hand, in small, medicinal doses, through such as this . . . or this." She indicated the robe with her first gesture, with her second, Fan-ku. "If for no other reason then, as charity, let me buy it. I won't quibble over price."

"It was my mother's, Mme Chin," I replied. "Some things cannot be bought and sold."

"Tsk, tsk," she said. "That's mere sentiment. Everything has its price, its season. If not today, tomorrow. It's all a matter of timing, circumstance."

"If that is true, it is a worldly truth."

She smiled cynically. "You know another sort?"

"I am a priest," I said.

She shrugged dismissingly. "And I am an old woman."

I shook my head and began to pack away my things. "I'm sorry, Mme Chin. I'm afraid I've wasted your time, and my own."

"And the room?" she reminded me.

"As I said, I have no money."

"And as *I* said, you might have something just as good. I was right." The fulsome smile again spread over her wizened features.

"You would exchange this for a room?" I asked a little savagely.

"No, no," she soothed, "of course not. Only leave it as security. When you pay up, I will return it."

I looked at her mistrustfully, hesitating.

"Come, come," she coaxed, "I'm making an exception to accommodate your situation; accommodate me a little too. Trust me, I'm trusting you. Besides," she added, "what choice do you have? It's getting late. Where else will you go? Who else do you think will take you in, penniless as you are, knowing nothing about you? Don't be a fool. Swallow your pride. Let me help you."

I studied her, trying to fathom her intentions. In her eyes there was a glint of anxious light, like the spider looking on in dismay as the fly struggles against the single gossamer that holds it, almost free. . . .

"Come on," she said, "I'll take you up."

And for some reason which I can't account for fully, I resolved to follow her, or rather, I simply let myself be led.

"Shall I go too?" Fan-ku asked.

"This is business," she informed him curtly. "You stay here."

Unbolting the various chains and latches, she opened the door and hobbled out, bent over, into the corridor, shuffling along. I followed.

It was an interminable climb. She ascended a step at a time, situating one foot carefully, then, clinging to the banister, dragged the other up laboriously to the same level. I felt sorry for her, but she stoutly refused all aid.

"There is an elevator," she wheezed, "but it's temporarily out of order." From the fact that it was boarded up, I surmised that it had been for some time, years perhaps.

The excruciating tedium of the ascent made me realize for the first time how exhausted I really was after my first day. By the time we reached the final landing, I was beginning to drowse a little on my feet.

"This is the top floor," she said at last.

I peered down the hall. "Which door is mine?"

"None of them," she replied.

"None of them?"

"No. There's one last flight of stairs which leads out to the roof. I'm giving you the penthouse."

"Penthouse?"

She frowned. "Well, garret."

Doubling around the final newel, we began the assault on the summit. Above a dented metal door opening on my new domain there was a sign which said Exit.

"Here we are," she announced.

Selecting another key from her collection, she inserted it in the lock, then applied her old, hunched shoulder to the door and heaved against it like a sailor. In the end I had to help her. With one great effort it gave way, precipitating myself and the dowager onto the roof. A flock of startled pigeons fluttered cooing upward, like so many handfuls of slightly soiled confetti, then settled farther off. The roof was covered with dry gravel scattered over tar. It crunched beneath our feet as we walked toward my new home, a small cabana jury-rigged between the blackened skylight and the elevator shaft. All sorts of elbowed, asymmetrical chimney pots with odd bonnets jutted out of the roof at eccentric angles. I could smell supper cooking in a dozen rooms. Emanating from the elevator shaft were disembodied voices: someone singing, the clatter of dishes, a woman bitching at her husband, a small child crying. The building touched several others at various points, forming a dark well, or courtyard. Looking over the side, I could make out mounds of garbage, cracked terra-cotta, gutted refrigerators, furniture smashed to bits, stained, tawdry cushions — a small lost kingdom of abandoned things. On the other side, the river; the great bridge rose into the sky. Beyond, Brooklyn.

"Nice view," I said, charmed.

"Wonderful view!" she agreed.

More pigeons flapped and scattered as we went in. The floor was covered with their lime.

"It needs a little cleaning," she admitted.

"Perhaps I'll grow vegetables," I mused.

"I like your attitude. As you can see, it's very light and airy." She frowned, fingering a broken pane of glass. "There's no hot water, but the plumbing works. The bathroom's there." She pointed to a stained, seatless toilet squatting nakedly at the far end of the room with a guilty look. "The mattress is included." With her shoe she nudged a piece of yellowing foam rubber lying on the floor, its upper side iced with guano.

"How much?"

"Seventy-five a week," she answered, coughing in her hand.

"*How* much?" I asked with emphasis, not because the figure seemed unreasonable — what did I know of rents? — but because I wasn't sure I'd heard correctly.

"Make it fifty. Not a penny lower."

"That seems fair. I'll take it."

She nodded. "It's a steal. Enjoy." She turned to leave.

"What are these?" I pointed to some items scattered in a corner: a faded, sleeveless blue-jean jacket, a black strip of inner tube, a plastic syringe, the crumpled cellophane wrapper of a cigarette pack with a small residue of white powder dusting its bottom, a broken bit of mirror, a rusty razor blade.

"Those belonged to the last tenant," she replied, hurriedly gathering them up. She walked to the well and started to drop them over.

"Wait!" I said. "What if he returns to claim them?"

"I don't think there's much chance of that," she answered with cryptic irony. "Have it your way though." A taunting smile curled her lips as she replaced them. "Perhaps you'll find some use for them. Here are your keys — I'd almost forgotten. Goodbye for now."

I bowed and started to retire.

"Sun I . . ." she called.

I turned around.

The dowager wore the same expression as when she'd asked Fan-ku to kiss her. For a second I feared she might ask me.

"Come and see me," she said, "often!"

I smiled and closed the door.

"Such a pretty boy," I heard her mutter as her footsteps crunched away over the gravel.

Chapter 3

I broke up the crusted guano with a stump of broom which was lying about and swept it out, then tenderly arranged my few possessions in the room. Taking in the view once more, I sighed with satisfaction, then I turned over the foam rubber mattress and fell into a sensuous, exhausted sleep. It must have been midnight or a little before when I awoke (my biological clock was still set to ship time, the rhythm of the watches). I couldn't remember where I was. Missing the pacifying drone of engines, the lazy wallow of the hull washed by languorous waves in tropic latitudes, or bucking and plunging off the tip of Africa in heavy seas — the muted whistling of the wind through the bulkheads, the effervescent hiss and sizzle of flying spray — I was disoriented for a moment. In place of these familiar, almost reassuring sounds were others which I didn't know: the infantile gurgling of roosting pigeons, the liquid *whoosh* of traffic rising from the streets (not unlike the sibilance of waves), horns honking intermittently, now just below me, now farther off, a woman's laughter in the street, growing diffuse and reedy at the level of the rooftops, someone playing an old, scratched recording of the Peking Opera — a woman singing in a high-pitched, birdlike voice about forgotten dynasties and the end of love. These sounds were like tiny paper boats floating on a vast sea of silence, the deep, ringing silence of the night, in which I heard for the first time the ground tone of the city, the subliminal murmuring of all the generators and condensers — air conditioners, refrigerators, fans — all the machines silently at work; and further down, the metabolisms of the sleepers themselves, the silent inner burning, all condensed in that great elemental hum.

I listened with eyes closed until the sound began to trouble me, rising to a roar, becoming inescapable. It intimated something I couldn't place. Suddenly I was wide awake, and restless. I got up and went outside. At this hour from the roof, the city, though beautiful, seemed more alien, like one of the great distant galaxies Scottie had talked to me about, whirring through universal night. I decided to walk to relieve my agitation.

As I was entering the vestibule downstairs, a key turned in the lock and someone entered from the street. To my astonishment, it was Ha-p'i, the chef, looking much as he had looked that afternoon, his grimy apron still tied around his waist. Only now he'd donned a light jacket — big enough for two of him at least — and removed his chef's hat, changes which made him seem even more exiguous than before.

"Mr. Ha-p'i!" I hailed him.

At the sound of my voice he winced. Not even glancing at my face, he huddled on himself and tried to hurry past.

"Wait!" I laid my hand on his shoulder.

He shrieked and fell to the floor in a shivering lump, covering his face with his hands. "Please don't hurt me," he implored in a frantic whisper, "I know I'm late, but I had an unexpected expense this week. It won't happen again, I swear. I'll pay you everything on Friday."

"Mr. Ha-p'i," I said gently, trying to calm him. "You mistake me. I am the priest you met this afternoon and so kindly helped. Remember?"

Tentatively lifting his head from beneath his arms, he peered at me, squinting in the uncertain light. As he recognized me, relief showed in his expression, followed quickly by a horrible chagrin. "Oh shit," he said, "the young dragon."

Leaping to his feet, he began to bow and shuffle apologetically, his blushes visible even in the dingy twilight of the vestibule. "Excuse please! Excuse please!" he cried piteously. "I took you for someone else. Now you know everything. I have lost face forever!"

"I don't know what you mean," I said, trying to ease his embarrassment. "I am in your debt . . ."

"Debt!" he moaned.

". . . for guiding me to Mme Chin, with whom I have concluded a successful arrangement for a room." I bowed deeply. "You are my benefactor."

"No, no," he demurred.

"Yes, yes," I insisted.

He grew somewhat calmer. "You exaggerate," he said, returning my bow, this time with more dignity and restraint. "I am pleased to assist in my insignificant way." He paused, then added with a mild hint of awe, "You have found your own apartment?"

I nodded proudly.

Now that he was standing up, I could see that he had something stuffed beneath his arm which he seemed at pains to conceal. Upon closer scrutiny, this proved to be a rolled newspaper out of which the foot of a skinny chicken was sticking with irrepressible comic joy. He noted the direction of my gaze, and his embarrassment threatened to become acute again.

"And the dumplings," I added hastily, heading him off. "I have not had such fine ones since I left Szechwan, and rarely there!"

He blushed with obvious pleasure and began a little chicken dance of modesty and ritual demurral. "You mustn't flatter an old fool," he said. "He might believe it."

"I'm not," I replied.

"You are," he insisted.

"No, no."

"Yes, yes."

After a few more bows and flourishes for good measure, the equilibrium was sufficiently restored to attempt a conversation.

"Mme Chin has given me the penthouse," I informed him proudly.

"Penthouse?"

"On the roof," I glossed.

"Ah," he said, "you mean the garret." He blushed, this time, I think, on my account. Trying to conceal it, he made a swift elision. "A most appropriate perch for a young dragon!"

I thought I detected a hint of gentle archness in his remark. Now the tables were turned, and *I* was embarrassed, though unsure why. Was there some subtle economic condescension implicit in his attitude? But I swiftly braced myself up, remembering that Poverty was one of my Three Treasures, a badge of honor in a priest. (Yet I had been so pleased!)

I forced myself to smile. We stood shuffling with nervous embarrassment, not knowing what to say to one another, until it occurred to me that he must just have come from work and had been on his feet all day. "Forgive me!" I said. "I am thoughtless. You must be tired. I will not keep you longer."

"For my part," he replied, "I will be unable to sleep for some time. I am too keyed up. Were I not sensible that my hospitality is too poor for a cultivated young man like yourself, I would invite you to partake with me of a small cup of wine before retiring."

Sensing that his invitation was genuine, and realizing that, at any rate, to have turned it down would have been tantamount to corroborating his self-depreciation, I accepted. Remounting the stair to the third floor, I followed him down the corridor to his door. Slipping the key in the lock, he leaned back and whispered, "We must be very quiet. My wife and daughter are asleep."

We entered the kitchen on tiptoe, almost ambushed by a laundry line strung across the room.

"Excuse please!" Lo said, flailing through socks, handkerchiefs, women's panties, brassieres, boxer shorts. A dingy light had been left burning above the sink, gleaming dully in the white enamel finish, scrupulously clean but faded, as though from too frequent and too pious scrubbing. The floor too — a checkerboard of pink and ivory linoleum squares speckled like pigeons' eggs — though bright with fresh wax, looked exhausted by domestic zeal. Everything had a yellowish tint, as though a urine-colored cloud had settled in for the duration on this man's life.

"Welcome to a poor man's house," he said, hurriedly taking down the line.

"I am honored," I replied, bowing low.

"The honor is mine."

"No, no."

"Yes, yes."

He invited me to sit down at a metal table placed against one wall, its surface a shiny swirl of hard pearl-gray Formica circumscribed by a vertical band of corrugated aluminum, the legs, hollow tubes of the same substance, like vacuum cleaner pipes, only thinner, capped with socks of black rubber. Around it were three chairs of similar construction upholstered in red Naugahyde; a fourth was exiled into the cramped space between the refrigerator and the wall. The whole presented an impression of pleasurable, well-ordered confusion.

Though visually this kitchen bore little resemblance to the one I'd grown up in at Ken Kuan, its lingering smells — the smoky aroma of sesame oil, piquant ginger, garlic, cold cabbage, with its sour, slightly loutish flavor — released a flood of pleasurable nostalgia. There were strings of aging chilies hanging from the ceiling too, strung in the same manner Wu had once taught me!

"Ah, the smells!" I said, snuffing a lungful. "It's like coming home again."

"Consider it so!" Ha-p'i beamed at me. "You have the instincts of a cook," he said, tapping his nose.

I laughed. "I should think so! I was practically raised in the monastery kitchen."

"Is that so? A cook as well! The young dragon has many talents!"

"I can hardly call myself a cook," I demurred. "I was never allowed to do more than wash the wok, light fires, chop vegetables. For me it was a big occasion when Wu let me cook the rice!"

I had intended a joke; Lo, however, narrowed his eyes and nodded serious approval. "The old ways are best. Nowadays the young people are too impatient. They will not stand still for discipline. They expect big things immediately. 'Start at the top,' that's my son's philosophy." He sighed and shook his head. "I don't know, perhaps he's right. He's doing very well now, Wo." In contrast to his words, at the mention of his son's name, Lo's expression became dejected. "Like you, he has his own apartment!" He looked at me imploringly, as though his enthusiasm needed corroboration. "When he was with me, though, I couldn't get much out of him. Perhaps I pushed too hard — that's what my wife says. But he whined and carped so, like an old woman. I was afraid he'd never amount to anything. . . . Like that young fellow I have now — all the sensitivity and enthusiasm of a fish! He can find nothing to do unless he's told. Yet he is proud and sulky! After two weeks he thinks he's a great chef! He no longer wants to wash the woks. That's beneath his dignity. It offends him." Lo sneered imitatively. "He wants to cook! What can I do? Maybe Wo is right. Maybe so much menial work is 'stifling,' as he says, and young people need 'challenge, excitement, responsibility.' Even if all the great chefs were apprenticed in the way you have described, entering their vocation, as I did, at ten years old, never allowed even to break an egg till they were fifteen! If nothing else, this fostered the necessary respect. Having to wait so long to crack that egg made it a sacrament, and he became a priest and artist of his own profession. Well, I think, times have changed. I will try the new methods. The boy wants to cook. I will not hold back genius!

"So what happens? Disaster! Twice this week he's ruined my best dish — Leaping Dragons' Blissful Copulation! A tragedy! I could weep! And now, *now,* after this debacle, he declares he's ready to try pork! Beautiful Woman's Rolling Buttocks, he says he's ready for! You know the dish? A triumph!" He kissed his fingertips. "But forgive an old man. How I run on! . . . The wine!"

Reaching into the cabinet above the sink, he gingerly took down a jar, caressing it tenderly in his hands. His eyes glowed with a misty light.

"I have been saving this jar of old Kao Liang for over three years," he said. "Tonight we will drink it together."

I was flattered, though a little uneasy about imbibing.

"It is so seldom that I have the honor to drink with a cultivated man," he went on, "one who has *acquired the taste.* After all, the ancient rites of conviviality were practically invented by your forebears."

Swallowing hard, I began to wonder if I could fulfill his expectations. It occurred to me that he entertained the extravagant popular notion of "tippling Taoists" fostered by Li Po and the poet-dilettantes of the T'ang. I was considering telling him that I knew no more about wine than about "Beautiful Woman's Rolling Buttocks," when he popped the cork and turned to me, beaming.

"Oops," I thought, "too late. Oh well. . . ."

I looked on, smiling nervously as he decanted it into a vase-shaped porcelain crock and set it in a double boiler on the stove. While it heated, he took two cups from the cabinet — diminutive jiggers of gray-blue porcelain, decorated with the *Fu* and *Shou* — and put them before our respective places. When the wine was ready, he filled each cup.

"Like the feuding farmers in the anecdote, to whom the wine revealed the grounds for mutual understanding and appreciation," he said, referring to a famous Chinese tale. He raised his cup to me with a broad smile. Then his face became tense with concentration, like the diver on the cliffs as he looks down at the surf and rocks before he plunges. "*Kan pei!*" he shouted, toasting with the ritual phrase which means "dry cup." With that, he tossed it off at a shot.

Not wanting to give myself away, I followed suit, relying on Monkey's gift for astute mimicry. I almost went over backward in my chair.

My insides cringed with mortification as the liquid went down. It did sweet violence to me. Beneath a candy coating, there was rapine, plunder, bloody murder. It was like taking honey on my tongue then sticking it in an electric outlet. Tears came; I gasped for breath.

Lo leaned back in his chair, cocked his head a little, closed his eyes, and sighed: "Ah, the subtleties of wine." With a tender smile, he raised the crock and filled our cups again, then gazed at me dreamily, blinking his eyes, as though in expectation.

I racked my brain for a toast. "To . . ." Sobriety, temperance, moderation — the perverse possibilities duly suggested themselves. "To the old ways," I hit upon at last, more out of desperation than conviction.

"Kan pei!" he cried wholeheartedly.

This time the violence of the alcohol, meeting less resistance, did less damage. In fact, after the initial shock had passed, a pleasurable glow of warmth began to radiate outward from my traumatized bowels, tingling into the extremities.

"Sui pien!" he announced after this second toast. "As you please!" This signaled the end of the formal drinking. Henceforth we sipped "at leisure," I, nursing my cup as long as possible between each sip, he, barely slacking his pace at all. Strange to say, he seemed to increase in stature as he drank, or else I shrank!

"It is relatively rare to meet a fellow Szechwanese," he said, "especially a man of such accomplishments as yours. The vast majority of people here, as you no doubt have noticed, are Cantonese. For the most part, they regard us as a tribe of woolly barbarians running through the mountains in animal skins, eating raw meat." He laughed, then continued in a tone of resentful pride. "I am a chef. Since I was fifteen, I have set my heart on achieving what we call 'authentic taste.' " (He used the term *zhen wer.*) "Is this a barbarian's desire? I tell you this, not out of pride, but simply to extenuate my faults, which are immeasurable."

"Now *you* exaggerate," I said, belching, "concerning your faults, I mean."

He shook his head grimly. "Unfortunately not." He looked up and met my eyes. "I owe you an explanation for what happened in the vestibule."

"It isn't necessary," I assured him. "Besides, what's to explain? You thought I was an assailant."

"You are kind to give me so much credit," he said, "but the truth lies elsewhere." He gave me a portentous look and shook his head. "No, we have drunk together, Sun I, and that entails an obligation to be frank. Besides," he added, breaking into a sheepish grin and echoing my belch, "as the proverb says, 'Wine must speak.' "

A captive audience, I folded my hands and sat back, acquiescing.

His prologue was a sigh. "Sometimes I ask myself how this has happened — rather, how I have done it to myself. When I first came here, I was not overly ambitious. My passion was single, like a priest's, like yours, my friend. I had no other lives to take into account. I wanted only to perfect my art. As for money, I had more than I'd ever dreamed of, and as much as I desired. There was even a little extra, some of which I saved, some of which I threw away on amusements I considered innocent. Yes, I gambled. But it was venial then, not yet a vice. I had control of my own life, and I felt it was good enough.

"But marriage changed all that. Please don't misconstrue my meaning. My wife and children — they are my one solace. I would change nothing. It's only that in trying to provide for them, little by little — even now I can't explain the process — I felt the tiller slip out of my hands. My wife came from a different social background. She married me for love, when she might have done much better. She was accustomed to a certain style of life that I felt obliged, no, *wanted,* to maintain her in. Because I loved her, I aimed high, hoping to make good. With my small savings, I made a down payment on a restaurant, then took out loans to cover the installments. Sun I, I am happy in the kitchen. I know my place. I go about my work with quiet pleasure, attending to the small details. A fresh carp with a limpid eye and still-resilient flesh, a roast duck properly carved, the first stroke of the knife puncturing the crisp-golden sac of skin, the plume of scented steam arising from the tender flesh inside, the preparation of the sauces, achieving just the proper degree of *xiang* with garlic and chilies in a spicy dish, or *nong* in a rich, slow-simmered casserole" — I use Lo's Chinese terms, as they are untranslatable — *"xien* with shrimp and vegetables barely singed in the wok to make them yield their freshness and their natural essences . . . these things I understand; they bring me happiness. I grudge no effort. I aim above myself. Like a great calligrapher, I know a single stroke can mar the whole, or else express the joys and sorrows of a life. I am not afraid. I take chances. In the kitchen, I am an artist, a commander. I know who I am and what must be. I have no doubts, no hesitations. But on the outside, when I doff my hat and leave my small domain, I enter hostile territory. My self-confidence evaporates. I shrivel up and wait to be insulted. Why this should be, I myself don't know. But so it is — as you saw yourself downstairs.

"Even in the restaurant, in the dining area beyond the kitchen doors, I feel uncomfortable. This was my grief, Sun I. The ten thousand headaches and frustrations of managing a complicated business — I had no understanding of such things, no patience with them. Dealing with the banker and the linen service, carpenters, plumbers, electricians, wholesalers, a broken boiler, paying bills — I found such tasks uncongenial and aggravating. I wanted to retire to the kitchen where alone I felt free. But even there my great unconsidered happiness was poisoned. You see, as cook my heart counseled one thing, as proprietor, another. As cook I knew the extra egg would lend the proper thickening and savor to the dish; as proprietor I knew that cornstarch was much cheaper and would pass. Business was brisk at first. People said the food was good, and our prices were the lowest on the street. As a cook I was contented; as proprietor, I looked through my accounts and saw our profit margin wasn't good enough, that we were actually losing money in some cases. I had to raise my prices. When customers came back a second time, they saw the change and felt they'd been finagled, that I was trying to pull a swift maneuver. They didn't come again; and worse, they whispered. The word of mouth was bad. Business slowed. I cut corners — turned down the heat, compromised further on ingredients. Before long we became another restaurant like all the rest, same prices, same food . . . only they had been there longer. Lacking other criteria, people opted for what they knew. We didn't get a second chance.

"I couldn't meet my payments. I started drinking, paying less and less attention. Sometimes at night I gambled. The excitement took my mind off things. But unlike before, during my bachelor days, it was money I could not afford to lose. And I lost more often than I won. My creditors got nervous. Trying to hold out, I applied to illegitimate sources for money. They obliged me, at ten percent a week. Ah, Sun I, I should have known when I was beaten. But I didn't. Little by little, strand by strand, I wove myself into this web of debt from which, even today, I cannot extricate myself. I was blind. One night I'd been drinking heavily; I started winning. I became exhilarated, thought I couldn't lose. Wild ideas occurred to me. I felt my luck was going to change. I deserved a break, I thought. Life owed it to me. It was my *right!* All seemed possible. Hoping to win big and pay back all my creditors at once, I staked the restaurant." He hesitated, and his face collapsed — a truly lamentable expression if I've ever seen one. "Ah, Sun I, I still believe that game was rigged." He shook his head. "But it doesn't matter. The word went out. The next morning all my creditors called in their loans. And I had nothing — not even the restaurant — to pay them with. I was bankrupt. The bankers had to take what they could get through legal channels. The others were less philosophical about their loss. They took me to a gutted building by the river, stood me on a chair, put a noose around my neck, and told me to say my prayers. Then they tipped me off. I watched the floor rush toward me, thought about my wife and children as I waited for the rope. But it gave way and I fell through my death. A mock execution. They laughed and said they didn't plan to let me off so easily. That was the Italian method. Chinese businessmen and hoodlums are shrewder, less dogmatic, if equally as theatrical. I was more valuable to them alive. They gave me a dispensation. Now I pay them half of everything I make . . . for life."

"How long has this gone on?"

"I have recently begun paying the son of one of the men from whom I originally took the loan."

"But that is intolerable!" I protested. "Who are these men?"

"Don't ask." He returned my glance, then nodded. "Yes, it has been hard. But at least I have my family. My wife has proved her love. She gave up everything for me, sold all her girlhood finery which came as dowry, even took in sewing to help make ends meet. And all without reproach. Had I not known such adversity, I could not have known such love. And, strange to say, in losing all these things, my happiness has been restored to me. I have my kitchen, and my simple mandate there. I consider myself fortunate. In spite of everything, our children have escaped. I have not crippled them through my mistakes. They never knew the things I've told you of. They've all left Chinatown and found their own lives now, all except the youngest, Yin-mi, and she too is beginning to drift beyond our sphere. Wo has a good job and his own apartment. Li, the oldest, has been independent since she was eighteen. She went to college on a scholarship, and has continued on with graduate studies. She's at Columbia now, studying anthropology. In two years she will have her Ph.D."

There was a gentle glow on Lo's face now, which was more than simply alcohol. He looked abstracted, pleased. The wine had made his problem soluble. He had talked and drunk himself into forgetfulness and contentedness. He seemed almost grateful. I felt pity for him, but it was mixed with admiration.

"But I have gone on too long about myself," he said, perking up, his voice a little slurred. "What about you, my young friend? Tell me your story."

Not wanting to seem reticent after the great confidence he had shown in me, I opened up and told him frankly of myself. When I got to the part about the Stock Exchange, he became agitated. Though he stifled the impulse out of courtesy, I could tell he was dying to express some idea my story had aroused. Several times I paused to give him an opportunity to speak, but each time he demurred, drunkenly polite, insisting that I finish first.

Tantalized by his behavior, I hurried through and signaled with my eyes that I had done.

"There is fate in our meeting, Sun I!" he burst out excitedly, leaning forward in his chair, blushing. "I said so from the start. You will scarcely believe the wonderful coincidence I'm going to relate to you! My son, Wo, whom you will meet — he has taken his own apartment." (In his intoxication, he repeated this detail enthusiastically, as though it were a fresh revelation.) "Wo works for the New York Stock Exchange! Perhaps he knows your father. They may be colleagues!"

I was astonished. "What does he do?"

"Oh, I know nothing of such things," Lo deprecated. "I only know he is retained in a high capacity, very high. I have invested money on his advice." He frowned. "But never mind that. . . ."

I imagined an elegantly dressed man, suave and unruffled as he moved through a sea of shouting, red-faced subordinates, granting their petitions with blinks and nods.

"You must meet him as soon as possible!" Lo continued. "I am sure you will become great friends. Every Saturday the whole family comes to lunch — a big affair! — all the aunts and uncles, everyone. Wo has become the star performer, quite respected for his excellent investment advice. One and all are constantly sounding him for tips. You must dine with us if you are free." He beamed at me. "Sun I! Has not fate attended to this matter admirably, showing all the aesthetic subtlety and good taste of a great chef preparing his best dish?"

"Leaping Dragons' Blissful Copulation!" I cried, a little woozy myself. We tossed off an enthusiastic toast.

A drunken inspiration seized me. "You don't suppose he could find work for me, do you?" The wheels turned in my brain.

Lo gave me a surprised look. "You, a priest, would take such work?" He seemed a little shocked.

"Why not? I must do something."

" 'Must'?" he repeated. "But surely you have money?"

I shook my head.

"Broke?"

I nodded.

"But you have your own apartment!" he protested, as though my financial condition were an arguable matter. "I don't mean to pry, but how much did you pay for that?"

"Nothing," I replied.

"Nothing! Preposterous! Since when did Mme Chin start giving credit?"

"You remember the robe I spoke about? I left it as security."

A look of violent alarm appeared on Lo's face. "Oh shit."

"What's wrong?" I regarded him in consternation.

He stared in my direction glassy eyed, but didn't see me. His gaze was focused inward, as though upon a crystal ball in his own mind which showed the future and the past — his past, my future. His face contorted in a look of agony.

I gently touched his elbow. "Lo, are you all right?"

He returned with a shudder. "You must redeem it." He grasped my hand unconsciously.

"I will," I assured him. "As soon as I have money."

"No!" he shouted. "As soon as possible, now, at once!"

"But how?" I was a little taken aback by his vehemence. "With what?"

"How much do you need?"

"Fifty dollars," I told him.

He stared at me with anguished indecision, as though in a quandary.

"I will lend it to you," he offered at last, sighing profoundly.

"But your own debt!"

"Don't remind me!" he moaned, burying his face in his hands.

"Lo," I said, "don't get me wrong, I'm grateful for your offer. But is this necessary? She wouldn't cheat me, would she?"

"Cheat!" he cried. "Dear boy, that's not the question! Would the cat *cheat* the mouse? Would the spider *cheat* the fly, his natural prey? Not at all! Slaughter is the mandate of the predator, the only thing he knows. It is his obligation, his *morality.*"

"But what has this to do with Mme Chin?"

His face darkened. "I am not an educated man like you, Sun I. I am ignorant of the mysteries of divination and the 'thirty-three hundred rules' of ritual observance. But experience has taught me something. I have picked up a few remnants and tag ends of wisdom from the rough trial of living in the world as it is. These things I know, to my cost. We have drunk together. I have been frank with you. Take my word for it. Redeem the robe."

My tipsy exhilaration passed into anxiety. Filled with misgivings, unable to think clearly, I stared down at the table. The amorphous swirl of the Formica was in motion, an accurate reflection of the chaos seething in my mind. I felt stunned, anesthetized by alcohol.

"Wait here," Lo said, pushing back from the table. He stumbled on his chair and it toppled over with a crash. He grimaced. *"Shh."* He put his finger to his lips inanely as he staggered into the hall. I heard him bump one wall, another. *"Shh,"* he said each time. I put my head down on the table. There was an interlude of silence, then a muffled crash, a sound like the patter of raindrops — coins spilling on a carpet.

"Oh shit," he whispered.

I heard the telltale click of a latch bolt retracting as someone turned a knob and cracked a door.

"Father?" a girlish voice called out. Everything went still. Then I heard footsteps padding down the hall.

When I raised my head, I saw a young girl — sixteen, perhaps seventeen — standing on the threshold gazing at me . . . saw, rather, the spectral image of such a girl shimmering and shifting in a miasma of fumes. Her expression was alert but unafraid, even a little curious. She blinked, but otherwise stood motionless, her self-possession unconscious, flawless as an animal's.

She had black, short-clipped boyish hair tousled with sleep, and was wearing a child's white knit pajamas a size too small, riding up at her wrists and ankles, tight over her breasts, which were well developed though not large. They bellied in the cloth with a soft indolence, a bud of nipple pricking up. Her hips were flat and slender like a boy's, and she had long, coltish legs and two sharp wedges of shoulder blade. She appeared to be stranded in between two ages, two conditions, gangly and womanish at once, repudiating neither, like something recently emerged from its cocoon, with the physical memory, the constricted instincts of a pupa and the new body of a butterfly, two great clipper ships of wing.

"Who are you?" she asked.

"I . . ."

"Yin-mi!" Lo interrupted in an imploring, exasperated whisper. She kept her eyes trained on my face. "What are you doing up? Go back to bed."

She turned to him. "What was that noise?"

"Nothing!"

"It sounded like mother's sewing tin."

"All right — why did you ask if you already knew?"

"You were taking money."

"Go to bed Yin-mi! You're not too old for a spanking."

"Did you ask if you could?" she persisted.

Drawing himself up threateningly, Lo turned to her, his eyes flashing. She looked at him calmly, steadily. Her eyes were dark with stillness, depth, transparency. Looking into them, I thought about the nighttime sea I'd slipped into off Quemoy Island and swum through toward my freedom.

Yet something else was brewing underneath. As she stood before her father at cross-purposes, I detected a hint of building trouble and perplexity which had not been there at first, something she was mastering with effort. As I watched, she crossed to Lo and placed her hands lightly on his shoulders, studying his face with deep seriousness. "You've been drinking, haven't you?" Her voice was very quiet.

Lo said nothing.

Pushing up on tiptoe, she silently bussed his cheek. Before she disappeared into the hall, she paused and cast a brief glance back at me over her shoulder, just long enough for me to see the grievance and suspicion in her eyes. That look burned into me, searing my heart like a brand.

At her departure, Lo deflated like a punctured inner tube, his sigh the hiss of escaping air. "Here," he said, pressing a folded stack of dog-eared bills into my palm. "Take it to Mme Chin first thing in the morning."

A spate of confused thoughts and emotions flooded my brain as I looked down at the soiled dollars, the first I'd ever held. The young girl's glance, my vow of poverty — the two things in conjunction spurred a sense of violent self-loathing. The sight of the money filled me with distaste, almost revulsion. Yet I could hardly tear my eyes away from it: the undulating web of intricate green lace with Washington, Sphinx-like, at the center, somehow grave and sybaritic at once; and on the back the strange pyramid with the human eye rising in a blighted plain, below it "Novus Ordo Seclorum." These images stirred me as much as those I'd seen in the stained glass windows of Trinity Church. Yet in the end, the revulsion predominated.

"Lo, please don't be offended, but I can't take this money. It would be against my vow."

"But how will you get by? You can't survive here without money. And didn't you yourself just inquire about a job? And at the New York Stock Exchange!"

In my inebriated condition, the contradiction had escaped me. I frowned over it. "True," I admitted, "but in that case the work would be in the service of a higher purpose, the payment almost incidental. I could reconcile myself to it as a necessary evil. Perhaps I could even make some special arrangement. I have existed on barter till now, maybe I can continue."

"Nonsense!" he said. "High-minded, but hopelessly impractical. You won't last a week nursing such ideals. A very different protocol is operative here than in the monastery, Sun I. But it is no less strict. If you are going to make it, you must quickly accustom yourself to the hard discipline of living in the world as it is."

My resolve faltered. I hesitated. "Nevertheless . . ." I began feebly, not knowing where to take my objection.

"Come, come — what is this, pride? Trust me, Sun I. Your scruple is a hollow one. Or perhaps you feel compunction because the money is my wife's? Listen, my boy, I know her. She wouldn't be offended. On the contrary! She would be more offended if she knew that you had sold away your heritage for a pittance. And if the thought of repayment is worrying you, put it out of your mind!"

"Yes, that too." I grasped eagerly at the straw he offered. "How can I?"

"I was hoping you might ask." He smiled disconcertingly. "I have a scheme which I think may prove mutually advantageous. You will forgive me for plotting, but consider this: why not come and work for me at the restaurant for the remainder of the week — only until Wo has a chance to secure you a more congenial position, mind you. It will be a favor to me, and by Saturday you will have earned more than enough to repay Mrs. Ha-p'i. You can take all your meals there, even earn a little pocket money on the side! An A-one arrangement if I do say so myself! Plus, it will give me the opportunity to retire the fish! What do you say?"

"Well . . ." My capacity for decision had been crippled by alcohol and self-recrimination.

"Now, now," he chided, "don't be reticent. Pride isn't seemly in a priest. Besides, what choice do you have?"

He was right. I sighed and shrugged, signifying acquiescence.

"A-one!" he said, springing from his chair. "You can meet me there tomorrow after you've concluded your business. Be firm with her. Remember where the restaurant is?"

I nodded.

"Perhaps we should have another drink to solemnize our agreement?" He reached for the cabinet.

"I'm afraid I must go."

"Oh," he said with dampened spirits, "I see." He stared at me forlornly, then suddenly brightened. "Well, we must do this often! It's done me worlds of good! You'll be like family from now on, like my own son!"

I was moved by his kindness, and felt profoundly unworthy of it. "Thank you," I said, too drunk for eloquence.

At the threshold we both became embarrassed. Balking our farewell, he extended his hand as I bowed. We both blushed. Then, attempting to make reparations, he bowed as I went for the handshake. Finally we managed to coordinate our efforts, overcompensating for our prior ineptitude by bowing first, next shaking hands, then finally bowing again. On the last of these, I managed to back myself into the hall.

"Goodnight," I said, "and thank you for everything."

"Goodnight!" he echoed enthusiastically, continuing to hold open the door.

I staggered off in the direction of the stairwell. As I swerved unsteadily around the newel and started upward, I saw him, still in the doorway, beaming at me with unabashed drunken sentiment.

•

I tossed in bed, stuporous with drink, craving the sweet oblivion of unconsciousness, yet unable to give in to it, feeling, in my state of alcoholic anesthesia, the interminable vibration of the dentist's drill, conscience trilling the nerve, uncomfortable but never acutely so, through its insistence keeping consciousness focused and intact, unable to dissolve and flow across the magic threshold into sleep. I felt anxious and unclean. The money worried me. I stuffed it underneath the mattress. Occasionally the image of Lo's daughter (Yin-mi, he'd called her) appeared in my mind's eye like a vision of paradise glimpsed through a gaseous, alcoholic haze. That too faded finally, and I listened abjectly to the sounds rising from the elevator shaft — the Well of Sighs. Somewhere far below, as though at the heart of the world, the rhythmic creaking of a bed and the indecipherable moan of a woman rose to me, her voice like nothing I could name. I had never heard such sounds before, and yet I recognized them. Strange to say, they soothed me, like the rocking of a cradle, the primal lullaby of sex. In that cadence I began to drift. The sound merged imperceptibly with the surrounding murmur. Sleep rose before me like a wave: a wall of glittering black water crested with a lip of foam, turning emerald as it reared into the sunlight. As it began to topple over me, I heard her brief, choked cry float up like a seabird above the oceanic roar, so sweet and so forlorn. Almost as an afterthought, it occurred to me that the ground tone of the city, the elemental hum, was like the roar I'd heard that day arising from the floor of the Exchange.

But there was something else, deeper and more primitive than either, a prior noise which they were only echoes of, perceived at increasing removes and with decreasing resolution. What was it? Before I found it, I had lost myself in sleep.

Chapter 4

The next morning when I awoke, my eyes were glued and crusted over with a yellow rheum. I had to spread them open with my fingers. It occurred to me that I'd been crying in my sleep. I gouged them with the knuckles of my index fingers to relieve the itching, twisting my fists back and forth like ratchets. When I opened them again, I saw tiny whitish comets sailing at the periphery of my field of vision, leaving trails. Then I noticed that the sun was already at the level of the rooftops. The air was turning sultry. I had overslept!

Splashing my face with cold, rusty water from the tap, I snatched my keys and bolted. It wasn't until I was turning the key in the lock that I remembered the money and my unpleasant rendezvous with Mme Chin. I went limp at the thought. I racked my brain for some plausible excuse for avoidance or delay: I was late already; it could wait until tomorrow. . . . But no, remembering the look of violent consternation on Lo's face, and what I stood to lose, I heaved a heavy sigh and dutifully returned to get my stake.

Fan-ku eyed me malignantly through the cracked door, insisting the dowager wasn't in. We faced off in tense silence, and from the other room arose a murmurous drone of incantatory speech.

"All right," he whispered with characteristic pettishness, admitting me. "But she has a customer, she can't see you now."

When I told him I had the money, he held his hand out, flicking his thumb over the tips of his fingers, a gesture I'd never seen before, but had no trouble understanding. "Give it to me, I'll see she gets it." His smile was a less accomplished, though promising, version of the dowager's.

At that moment a heartrending yelp pierced the silence. I heard a muted thud, a scrambling; the double drape popped open at the bottom as though filliped from behind, and the pup appeared, nose low to the ground, eyes bugging out, legs sprawling in all directions, body yawing precariously over legs as he turned the corner at full tilt. Seeing me, he barked a desperate salvo and leapt into my arms as I knelt down to receive him. He slurped and rooted at me with his cold nose, frantically affectionate.

A jeweled hand parted the drape, and Mme Chin emerged wearing a strange tiara of peacock feathers in her hair and carrying a white towel and a stainless-steel scissors. I regarded them with queasy intimation. The dowager glowered at me grimly. "Take the dog, Fan-ku," she said, fixing her eye on me, not him.

I didn't want to give my small friend up, but I had no right, and indeed no compelling reason not to. The pup shot me a baleful, accusatory stare in parting from his cramped position in the backward headlock. As Fan-ku swept aside the drape, by the light of a single candle burning on the table where the dowager had read my palm the day before, I saw the silhouetted head and shoulders of a man. My pulse stopped. Too much was happening. I wanted to get out.

"Where did you get it?" the dowager asked peevishly, eyeing the wad of money in my hand. "Did you have to sell yourself?"

I blushed and almost botched my lines. "I had forgotten. I had it the whole time."

"You're lying," she sneered. "Come back later. I'm in the middle of something. I can't trouble with you."

Fan-ku reappeared and stood beside her.

"Now!" I said, ". . . please."

She raised her eyebrows with surprise and affront, then, narrowing her lids, tried to stare me down. I didn't flinch.

Her features curled into the odious smile. "As you wish. Get it!" she snapped viciously at Fan-ku through her smile. "Someone has talked behind my back. Who?"

I dropped my eyes.

"I am strict in business, but not dishonest," she said, taking a righteous and portentous tone. "True, I want the robe, but I would not have stolen it. I had hoped we might be friends, but now I see that will be difficult. Too bad. . . . Such a pretty boy!" She frowned. "Let this be on your head."

Fan-ku emerged with the robe.

"Give it to him! I'll remember this," she said, backing toward the drapery, smiling that smile which I found inestimably more chilling than the look with which she'd tried to intimidate me earlier. Her face vanished behind a terse whip of the drapes. I heard the mumbling recommence in the far room.

Clutching my prize, I issued into the hallway, sweat standing in beads on my forehead. I was glad to have it, yet, when I reflected coolly, I was afraid I'd done her an injustice. What if Lo's allegations were merely paranoic drunken alarms after all? And even if they weren't, how could I justify such exertions, such avidity, with its train of ugly passions, poisoned intercourse, on behalf of a material possession, no matter what its value in sentimental, or other, terms? For the first time, through my own experience, I realized the meaning of the teaching that possession is an encumbrance to the spirit; paradoxically, the inhumanness of the dictum struck me simultaneously — this, too, earned through my own experience. What had appeared self-evident, irrefutable, in the rarefied atmosphere of the monastery was less so here, with something of my own at stake.

Just then a high-pitched, hellish squeal split the air, coming from inside — the pup. The hair prickled on the back of my neck. I turned and faced the inexpressive door with a sensation of sickly horror. What was going on in there? I raised my fist to pound for readmission, but on second thought swallowed hard and went as fast as possible in the opposite direction.

•

Lo occupied the exalted position of Number One Head Chef at Luck Fat's Tea Joy Palace in an obscure back street of Chinatown. The restaurant served superb food in an ambience of slightly seedy, even macabre elegance. The interior was like a catacomb, a series of winding tunnels opening into little cells where private parties congregated, mostly fat Chinese businessmen in polyester suits and ties, sometimes accompanied by loud young women with hard eyes whose garish makeup seemed applied spitefully in a spirit of deliberate self-subversion. These men ate gluttonously, holding their plates close to their mouths, urgently shoveling, pausing occasionally to wash down the feed with straight Courvoisier, which they drank in gulps from their water glasses with as much impunity as if it were weak tea.

Lo ran a tight operation with as little help as possible. From the moment I peeked in from the alley, it was apparent that he had not been kidding the night before when he said his personality was different in the kitchen. Though not rigid or fastidious, neither was he relaxed and jocular like Wu. He couldn't afford to be. There was five times the work. Keeping his head down, absorbed in some deep rhythm of his own, he plowed ahead. Two younger cooks worked under him. They knew their jobs. The pace intimidated me at first, but after watching carefully, I jumped right in. I kept careful note of everything, so that when I had seen them make a dish once, I found some way to make it easier the next time, tossing down plates before they had to ask, oiling the wok, anticipating needs. They rewarded me with grunts and nods, or, when my initiative miscarried, shooed me before them like a frantic chicken pursued by the implacable arbiter of his fate, the poultry farmer. The first day I made stupid mistakes, but by the second I'd begun to get the hang of it. By the third, I'd become an accepted part of the team. Lo had begun to call me "A-One Dragon Assistant."

Even in the short time I worked there, I lost myself once or twice, mesmerized by tasks familiar to me since my childhood. Raising my eyes, I fully expected to see Wu. Not finding him, I surveyed the unfamiliar surroundings, blinking my eyes, not knowing where I was — "the journey of a thousand miles" obliterated momentarily, myself regressed to what I was. Then reality jarred me, and with a sigh I returned to the present.

That third day, a Friday, was my last. The next day was the family dinner.

•

Scrubbed and brushed, wearing my best robe (indeed the one passable robe I had left), I presented myself at the Ha-p'is' apartment promptly at noon. The door was answered by a plump middle-aged woman in traditional dress. Face flushed, wiping her hands on a towel, she leaned over slightly at the waist, looking out from behind the door, blinking her eyes inquisitively. Her stare was abstracted, as though she were thinking of a thousand things, yet when she smiled — reflexively, no doubt — she exuded such modest, good-natured simplicity, such diffidence and jollity, that I felt personally recognized and singled out for favor. I was drawn to her at once. Though plump and double-chinned, her face had the same limpidness as Yin-mi's, and by this I guessed this was her mother. In the older woman this seemed an index of a deep inner modesty, precious in itself. But in the daughter it was that, and something more.

"Mrs. Ha-p'i?" I inquired.

She nodded.

"I'm an acquaintance of your husband's. Sun I's the name."

"Sun I!" she said. "Of course! Please forgive me. Won't you come in?"

Blushing, a little flustered, she opened the door to admit me. We bowed to one another.

"Who is it?" Lo called from the other room.

"The young dragon," she replied.

I blushed.

She beamed and fidgeted.

A young woman in Western clothes stood in a corner of the kitchen, absorbed in conversation with an American companion. This young man fixed on me over her shoulder and allowed his eyes to linger, almost disconcertingly long. Seeing his attention wander, she turned briefly, noted me, then went back to what she was saying. That brief, perfunctory glance unsettled me somehow, even more than his prolonged one.

She was wearing a black silk dress, slit up one leg, with string shoulder straps. It was decorated with a staggered, silk-screened muster of emerald and turquoise-tinted peacocks, their fantails splayed, displaying a myriad of staring, iridescent eyes. Long and close fitting, it suggested a physical litheness beneath that was almost feline — vaguely provocative, but with the same radical innocence (the amorality, rather) as the cat's. She was wearing pendant earrings which showed the nacreous sickle of the crescent moon holding the old moon, cloudy silver, in its arms in an implicit embrace, like the ghostly submarine immensity of an iceberg beneath its sun-kindled tip. I had never seen anyone quite like her. I studied her perhaps a little longer than was polite.

Noting this, Mrs. Ha-p'i made haste to introduce us. "Sun I, there's someone I'd like you to meet," she said, more to attract their attention than mine.

The girl turned.

"This is our elder daughter, Li, and her . . ." she faltered an instant, blushing, " 'friend,' Peter."

Peter nodded and pressed my hand with a soft, lingering pressure, saying nothing but regarding me with an incomprehensibly coy, almost taunting expression — like the one I'd seen the day before in Mme Chin's eyes as she looked at Fan-ku, regarding him as though he were a potential meal. As with his gaze, he maintained his grasp a little longer than I was comfortable with, so that I had almost forcibly to disengage it.

But even more than his unaccountable behavior, the young woman troubled me — her eyes especially, nothing like her sister's or mother's, like nothing else at all, unless it was the bear's eyes, the color of dark mountain honey oozing and bubbling from the comb. I felt an odd visceral flutter when I met them for the first time, and thereafter, insofar as possible, avoided looking. If Yin-mi's eyes, in that brief glimpse, had seemed all clarity and candor, like sunlight on the sea at noon revealing an uninterrupted vista, her sister's eyes were filled with dusk. I caught a glimpse of an interior smoldering, a gauzy, ambivalent light, as from a smoky fire where something green is being seared. She reminded me of a voluptuary returned from a night of secret rites, still incompletely in the world, lingering among the shadows of some candlelit repast, who finds the world mildly amusing in the afterglow of her sublime experience and condescends to it with an easy humor, needing nothing it can offer.

A strange pair. . . . I wasn't entirely sure I liked them. Either of them. They struck me as a younger version of Mme Chin and Fan-ku.

We talked about nothing in particular. She mentioned that she was studying archaeology, but said that she was deeply interested in ethnology as well, and offhandedly proposed a meeting to inquire about my experiences in China. I halfheartedly agreed, partly because she was a member of the family and I wished to appear amenable, partly because her manner suggested that it would never come about.

"Perhaps I could reciprocate," she suggested, with a hint of provocation and amusement in her glance.

I blushed deeply and disproportionately.

She laughed. "I mean, tell you fairy tales for instance, Western ones — tit for tat."

"Oh, I could tell him better fairy tales than you," Peter piped in.

She frowned. Then they excused themselves, saying they were on their way out to an "opening" of some sort in the Village. As they passed through the door, I caught her eyes fixed on me in intense study. It almost made me shudder. Again the troubled, inarticulate pang. I had made up my mind I didn't like her, but the pang grew more intense at their departure.

Oh yes . . . have I mentioned that she was beautiful? Perhaps there's significance in the fact that I've left out, or left till last, what proved for me the most important thing of all. Stunning as she was, I only grudgingly acknowledged her good looks at first. For there was a cold and distant quality to her perfection, like the moon's, something which repelled as much as it attracted.

Lo had still not appeared. Mrs. Ha-p'i and I were left, as before, not knowing what to say to one another, until I remembered what I was carrying in my pocket and had brought specifically for the purpose. The money! I'd almost forgotten.

"Forgive my absentmindedness, Mrs. Ha-p'i," I beseeched. "It doesn't mean I don't appreciate your generosity. I can't tell you how much." I reached into my pocket for it.

"My generosity!" she blushed deeply, placing her hand unconsciously over her breast. "What do you mean?"

Over her shoulder, I saw Lo emerging from the hall. Reading the situation at a glance, he began to signal frantically, shaking his head, tapping his finger to his lips.

But I had already withdrawn the money. Seeing him, I balked on delivery. But it was too late. She regarded me with dismayed simplicity. "What is that for?"

I appealed helplessly to Lo. "I'm sorry," I apologized, shrugging my shoulders, grinning a sheepish, harrowed grin. "I thought . . ."

She pivoted to face him. "Lo?"

He appeared to be in torture. Hanging his head, he blushed so deeply his face turned almost purple.

"What is it?" she asked, taking his hand anxiously. "Lo . . . ?"

"I should have told you," he replied in a pitiful voice. "But it was his mother's bridal robe. He had given it to Mme Chin."

"Mme Chin!" she gasped.

A pregnant cousin, one of the young men's wives, who had followed Lo into the kitchen to fill her glass at the tap, stood appraising the three of us, flabbergasted, the water flowing unheeded over her hand.

Lo pulled his wife aside and began to speak in an earnest whisper.

I stood frozen in my place as they animatedly conferred.

The young woman, recovering her self-possession, started systematically rinsing all the glasses that had collected in the sink, listing, as it seemed to me, rather strongly in an effort not to miss a word of what was said.

As Lo spoke, from time to time Mrs. Ha-p'i blinked at me, or down at the money, which I still held stupidly in my hand, not knowing what to do with it. After perhaps a minute, Lo fell silent. Mrs. Ha-p'i slowly turned her face to her husband, who stood hanging his head like a little boy prepared for censure but hoping to be pardoned. Maternal tenderness surfaced, and, leaning down, she gently kissed the bald spot on the top of his head. Lo sighed and looked up gratefully.

Mrs. Ha-p'i stepped toward me offering her hand, beaming and abashed.

"I'm so sorry . . ." I began.

She spontaneously caressed my cheek, a gesture which might have shocked me had I not been so deeply moved. "No, don't apologize," she said. "I'm glad."

Over her shoulder, I saw Lo mopping his brow with his handkerchief. Catching my eye, he gave me a sly wink which very nearly floored me.

"Come," he said, stepping between us. "We have given the young dragon quite a fright. He's not used to the petty intrigues of domestic life, having spent his time sporting among the clouds. We musn't impose and keep him to ourselves. He came to meet Wo and discuss important matters. They must be introduced at once!"

He took me by the arm, and the three of us started down the hall. Hurriedly drying her hands on a dish towel, the young woman waddled after us.

As we entered the hall, I could hear the hum of conversation coming from the other room.

"You were able to get it back?" Mrs. Ha-p'i inquired as we walked, probing for the sequel of the story. "The robe, I mean."

"Oh yes," I replied. "It was relatively painless. She didn't seem happy to see me, but after a brief spat, she became almost amenable. I was surprised. After what Lo said, I'd expected trouble."

"You're lucky," she said, a touch of incongruous rancor in her voice. "That woman is unscrupulous."

"Yes," chimed in the pregnant woman in an eager whisper. "Some say she has connections with the Triad."

"The Triad?" I asked, turning toward her as we entered the sitting room.

The drone of conversation ceased. I looked up, and half the room was staring at me. There were perhaps a dozen or fifteen people there, all Chinese, all in Western dress, one old woman the sole exception. They ranged in age from this white-haired matriarch, who sat by the left-hand wall in a graceful chair of Chinese cherrywood — the only fine piece in the room — to Yin-mi, seated beside her, poised on the edge of a straight-backed chair with a caned seat, attending politely to the older woman's conversation. She sat wonderfully erect and natural, delicately nursing a teacup and saucer on her knees, which were pressed together. She was wearing a loose white blouse with a round collar and a black ribbon bow tie, a dark skirt, ribbed white kneesocks, and leather pumps. Noticing the silence, she too ceased what she was doing and studied me, blinking her eyes with mild curiosity. Suddenly it occurred to me what it was in her face that was so extraordinary and unsettling: she looked amazingly like the little girl I'd seen in the upriver town where I met Tsin! The association made my heart skip.

"The Triad," a harsh, nasal voice remarked in English. "Don't tell me you still believe in that old bogie?"

Murmurs broke out afresh around the room.

"I mean, sure, it existed at one time — maybe it still does, in name. But it's a token organization. They have about as much influence in Chinatown now as the Ku Klux Klan. The Italians ran them out of business a long time ago."

Recollecting myself in the meantime, I had wheeled about to face the speaker. Sitting sprawled on the sofa at the far end of the room beneath the window was a rotund young man, who bore a disconcerting resemblance to the Buddha, at least in the matter of corporeal magnitude. About my own age, he was wearing a synthetic Hawaiian print shirt, brilliant grenadine with splashes of yellow and electric orange mixed in to relieve the eye. This was stretched tight over his belly, riding up an inch or so above his jeans, showing a fish-white line of adipose and a few black hairs, much the same in thickness and texture as those pasted across his upper lip in feeble imitation of a mustache. A thick black shock of uncombed hair slanted down over his right eye. He regarded me neutrally, then jerked his head to the side, sweeping his bangs out of his way, running his hand behind to reinforce and stabilize the effect.

"But Wo . . ." someone objected.

Wo!

". . . what about the drug traffic — the heroin and opium on the streets of Chinatown?"

"Yes," seconded another, "and the gambling?"

This was Wo? My expectations were utterly confounded. Trying to assimilate the incongruity between the image I'd conceived in my imagination and the present reality, it was only with great difficulty that I attended to the rest of the exchange.

Wo shrugged complacently. "That's all Cosa Nostra," he pronounced casually ex cathedra, flinging his hair back. A corner of his downy lip turned up in a sly smile. "Financed, of course, by an occasional multinational."

Glances were exchanged around the room. No one dared propose any further objections, his reference to "multinationals" lending the final touch of credibility to his papal bull.

With this, he turned back to his audience — comprising the masculine contingent of the room, all clustered tightly around the sofa jockeying for position, like a gaggle of eager courtiers — and resumed the conversation, which I had evidently interrupted. These men were asking questions in English, their grammar displaying varying degrees of competence. Wo's replies were sprinkled liberally with impressive-sounding names — National Semi, Con Ed, Standard Cal, Schlumberger, IBM, and one I recognized with a tingle of suppressed excitement, APL — which were received with little squeals of delight and gratitude. One man was even taking notes. These names Wo dropped with all the hauteur and nonchalance of a monarch dispensing largesse to his subjects; and indeed, as he sat there with his arms spread over the back of the sofa and his chubby leg (in a black high-top basketball sneaker) tucked under him, so that no one else might sit down even if he dared, Wo seemed not unlike a slovenly young prince conducting a levee for an adoring entourage.

"That's Wo!" Lo whispered in my ear enthusiastically and unnecessarily. "Come, I'll introduce you."

Clutching the sleeve of my robe, he cleared a path through the crowd, which gave way only reluctantly.

He cleared his throat. "Excuse please," he said, adopting what appeared to be the de facto official diplomatic language in the presence of the throne.

Wo held up his hand, silencing his interlocutor, and looked at his father. "Hiya Pops," he said. "We're kinda right in the middle of something here. What's up?"

"Excuse please," Lo repeated deferentially. "There's someone here I wish you to meet." He drew me up beside him into the presence.

"This is Sun I." He stepped back, giving me the floor.

I wasn't sure if I should address him by some title, Your Copiousness, perhaps. Opting for informality, I simply made a low bow. "Your father has told me a great deal about you," I said in Chinese, employing our native tongue primarily because I felt more comfortable with it, but also perhaps with an anarchic hint of Monkeyish mischief. "I've looked forward to this meeting."

"I don't speak that shit," Wo replied matter-of-factly in English.

"Wo!" Mrs. Ha-p'i exclaimed, shocked.

He shrugged and flipped his hair. Then with a weary sigh, he sluggishly roused himself from the sofa. Standing up, he offered me his paw, shaking without enthusiasm, or even pressure, scrutinizing me with a mild show of interest. "That's a wild outfit you got there," he commented, brushing my robe with the backs of his fingernails.

Taking this as a compliment, I replied in kind. "Yours too."

"Oh yeah? You like it? Cost me thirty bucks." He slung his hair again, and it occurred to me that, beyond simple functionality, this mannerism expressed a species of self-satisfaction and complacency. "You're the one that's into the Dow, huh?"

"He's a Taoist!" Lo interjected helpfully, in tones meant to convey the singularity and impressiveness of this condition.

"A Dowist!" Wo squealed, doubling over with laughter. "Gee, Pops, you really put your foot in it sometimes when you speak English."

"Excuse please!" Lo said, blushing with mortification.

"A Taoist *priest,*" a voice interjected. Everyone turned to look.

Yin-mi was sitting exactly as before, balancing the teacup on her knees, only now there was a bright gleam in her eyes, and her cheeks were suffused with color.

My heart pounded. The fact that she had troubled to commit to memory even so minuscule and general a fact about me and could recite it filled me with unaccountable happiness.

"Oh, *I* get it," Wo replied. "Taoist like the religion." Pursing his lips, he frowned and nodded. "That's cool." He flipped his hair. "Can you tell fortunes 'n shit?"

I bowed my head in embarrassment.

"Hey, maybe you could use that stuff to forecast the market. . . ." He weighed the suggestion. "Nah," he decided, "that's just asking for trouble, bringing in a bunch of religious hocus-pocus."

I stiffened.

"I'll tell you what's *real* magic though, the IBM SYSTEM 360."

There were grunts of corroboration around the room.

"So, ah . . . Sonny — it was Sonny, wasn't it?"

"Sun I," I corrected with a hint of testiness.

"Yeah, Sonny, like I was saying, what can I do for you?"

Taking advantage of this opening, Lo shoved us down together on the sofa. "You talk," he said, as he began the thankless task of trying to herd the others away. As we waited for the hubbub to die down, I puzzled studiously over Yin-mi's face as she conversed nearby with the old woman, trying to recover the perspective that had suggested the young girl. As I watched, she helped her older interlocutor to her feet, then sat back down, blew into her teacup, and began to sip.

"Ah, Sonny," Wo said in annoyance, "you gonna sit there staring off in space, or you wanna rap?"

"Excuse me," I apologized. "I know how busy you must be. Your father told me of the important position you occupy at the New York Stock Exchange."

Wo tossed his hair back with uncommon vehemence and grandeur. "Yeah, so?"

"I was hoping you could help me." I lowered my eyes deferentially. "I wish to become acquainted with the Dow."

"I thought you were already a Taoist," he remarked with a facetious grin.

"I mean the American Dow."

"The Dow Jones," he glossed professorially. "Listen, Sonny, we gotta keep the two things straight if we're gonna carry on a conversation. There's quite a difference, you know."

"Superficially perhaps," I replied, spurred at last to rebellion by his niggling condescension. "But at a deeper level, the two are one."

"Oh yeah? I'm no philosopher, but you coulda fooled me. You wanna explain that, or should I just let it pass?"

Opening my mouth to respond, I noticed that Yin-mi had looked up from her cup. Holding it a few inches below her lips, she watched me with a look of close attention. I remember thinking that the grave clarity of her expression was like a drink of pure well water after the rich, almost obscene liqueur presented in her sister's face. She didn't avert her glance, but continued observing me with candid interest, as though intent on what I had to say. I dropped my eyes in embarrassment.

"The Tao is the Source," I said quietly, choosing my words with care, as though I were in court, pleading my case before a high tribunal of exacting judges.

"The source of what?" he asked. "The Mississippi?"

"Of everything," I replied. "It is the matrix of existence, the formless womb out of which the ten thousand forms arise, and to which they return at last, as to the grave."

"Whew!" said Wo, shaking his hand limply at the wrist. "Don't spread it on too thick, huh, Sonny? I might have to ask the flight attendant for a paper bag."

Though the specific meaning of this gibe flew past me, I was aware of being ridiculed. I faltered.

"Let him finish, Wo."

We both turned our heads, he in annoyance, I gratefully.

"Butt out, Yin-mi."

"Go ahead," she encouraged in a whisper which ignored him. There was a faint flush on her cheeks.

"Yeah, all right," Wo conceded. "What else? I still can't picture it. What's it like?"

"It is like nothing else," I replied, not to him, but to her. "It is an emptiness, the shining void at the center of existence. It is quiescence, harmony, emancipation from the self."

She flushed, but didn't look away. A brilliance played in her eyes.

"Sounds dull," Wo commented. "Like I said, a bunch of hocus-pocus, totally unreal. At any rate, if nothing else, it for damn sure has nothing to do with the Dow — the other one, *my* Dow. Now *that's* real! All this other stuff sounds good, but it's too theoretical. Experience won't bear it out. The Dow's the exact opposite — not 'emancipation *from* the self' " — he placed a mocking emphasis on my expression — "but emancipation *of* the self — you know? Number One. Me first. Every man for himself, no holds barred, no quarter asked or granted, and the devil take the hindmost. It's dog eat dog. Cat eat mouse. Dog eat cat. Man eat dog. And everybody shake their booty, you understand what I'm saying? That's what the Dow's about. And if you don't think it's real, take it from me." He flipped his hair. "About half a mile from here you can verify it with all five senses if you wanna, cut it with a knife and eat it on a slice of bread. Show me this other Tao of yours so I can see it like *that,* then maybe I'll convert. For now I think I'll just let my money ride where it is."

"The spectacle is vivid and immediate, I don't deny that." I sighed, reaching back in a closed drawer of my mind for the appropriate refutation. "But by its very grossness the Phenomenal World is always more easily captured in the coarse-meshed sieve of the senses. Just because a thing is easily grasped doesn't mean it's real. In fact, illusions are much simpler to apprehend than truths. Your Dow is such an illusion; its reality is the reality of a shadow. Tao is the body which casts that shadow. It casts the shadows of all the 'ten thousand things,' of which the Dow is only one."

"Yeah, but I don't see it, Sonny. A shadow at least has the same shape as the thing that casts it, right? I mean, there's a recognizable resemblance between the two, you know? But Tao and Dow! They're complete opposites as far as I can see. I mean, you ever see a chicken cast the shadow of a hippopotamus, or a Mack truck a Playboy bunny's?"

"Think of it this way," I said, taking encouragement, even inspiration from

Yin-mi's concentrated attention. "Imagine a mountain stream, turbid, reckless, helling down a broken scarp between the rocks. . . ." (She nodded.) "Now follow it in your mind. As it reaches the base of the mountain, the slope becomes more gentle. It slows and broadens, carves a deeper channel. At some point, after a journey of a thousand miles, that river, which was once a foaming torrent on a distant steep, flows into the sea, its rage all spent, absorbed in the greater body like an insignificant detail, brought in as gently as a screaming child raised to its mother's breast to nurse. That swollen mountain stream — that is your Dow. The ocean is mine." Yin-mi clapped her hands delightedly. I was rather pleased with the metaphor myself. It was the first time it had occurred to me, and it arose from my own experience.

"Sounds good," Wo said. "But I'm still not convinced. Metaphors are great as far as they go. But poetry is one thing, logic is another. I want proof. Tell me where the two things run together. Using your own metaphor, tell me where the . . . what's it called? . . . you know, the . . ." — he looked at Yin-mi, snapping his fingers — ". . . the place the river runs into the ocean?"

"The delta," Yin-mi whispered, to me.

"Yeah, the delta," he said. "Where is that?"

I started to respond, but the easy flow of speech had deserted me. I was like a schoolboy at an exam, taking frantic inventory of the items he has filed away in memory and finding nothing corresponding to the teacher's question.

I started to extemporize a glib response, hoping to salvage the argument, but found I could not, impeded by something stern and hopeful in Yin-mi's glance which I feared to shatter. "I don't know," I said. "I haven't seen that place myself."

"Uh-huh, that's what I thought," he replied, as though vindicated.

"Perhaps that's what you came to find?" Yin-mi suggested tentatively, a slight tremor in her voice.

I did not reply; there was no need. A pact was made between us, something wordlessly asked and answered, terms proposed and accepted. She conceded me the whole depth of her being. I had never before seen so much in another human being's face.

"Oh yeah?" said Wo with a quizzical, amused, and mildly derisory tone. "You guys been introduced?"

The spell was broken. Yin-mi peered into her teacup.

"As I was saying, Sonny," he continued, "the delta. . . . You admit it's something you take on faith. Well, that's okay, I guess. I suppose that's what religion's all about. I wouldn't risk money on it though. You take your religion, I'll take mine. . . . But how did we get off on this anyhow? You were saying something about you wanted to get into the Dow, weren't you?"

I nodded.

"Listen, I've just got to ask one question. If it's so unreal and shadowy, and this other one's so great, why bother? Seems like there's a contradiction there somewhere. Don't tell me. . . ." He grinned at me coyly, in a manner suggesting complicity in some not quite aboveboard scheme. "You've got a few bucks you want to invest, right?"

"That would be against my vow of poverty," I informed him coldly.

"No kidding!" He appeared to be astonished. "Making money is against your principles, huh? That's a new one on me."

"I wish merely to study the Dow as a disinterested observer," I explained. "To observe without participating."

"In it but not of it, huh?"

I nodded. "Besides," I added, "I have no money to invest."

"I feel for you, pal, I really do. But what do you expect me to do about it?"

"Well, because of your high position, I was hoping you could find me a job."

Wo recoiled as though the idea caught him off guard and rubbed him the wrong way. "A job, huh? I figured there was something like that under all the philosophy stuff." He considered. "Listen, Sonny, if I wanted, I could probably get you on down there as a squad boy or something, but take my advice, find something else. A religious dude like you . . . it wouldn't agree with you. Stick with the restaurant. You'll be happier there. Pops says you've got a real knack for it. Besides, down at the Exchange they treat you like a coolie, the money's lousy."

"I don't care about that," I interrupted. "Money isn't my object. I want only enough to live."

"Well, I don't know. . . ."

"Listen, Wo," I said desperately, resolving to play my last trump. "There's something I haven't told you. Besides the delta" (I flashed Yin-mi an appreciative, acknowledging glance) "there's another reason for my interest in the Dow. I've come all the way here, to America, to try and find my father. You're my only hope."

"Your father?" He raised his eyebrows. "That's a new twist. I get the feeling now we're finally getting down to the nitty-gritty, past all the metaphor and philosophy." A shadow of perplexity crossed his face. "But what's that got to do with me getting you a job?"

"He's connected with the Dow," I answered. "It's my only clue. I have no other place to look."

"What, you expect just to bump into him down there or something?"

"Perhaps," I replied. "I don't really know. It's an intuition."

"Intuition, huh? Is that the Taoist method? I'm not putting it down or anything, you understand, but isn't it a little old-fashioned? I mean, this is the twentieth century, isn't it? Ever hear of a phone book?"

"Phone book?"

"Sure. Don't you have phones in China?"

"Not at the monastery," I replied.

"Yeah, yeah, everything natural and no preservatives, right? Well, we make things easy over here." Beside the sofa was an end table with a telephone on it, sitting on the Manhattan directory. "Let your fingers do the walking," he said, pulling it out. He winked and flipped back his hair. "Okay, give it to me."

"What?"

"The name, the name."

"Oh," I said, "Love."

He licked his index finger and began to flip. "Law . . . Lee . . . Lie . . . Low . . . Oops, too far. Here it is — Love. Initials?"

"A. E. Or Eddie."

"Eddie Love." He pursed his lips. "Eddie Love. . . . Where have I heard that name? Hey, wasn't he . . ." — he snapped his fingers — "that guy at APL — the one who took it over. That big scandal and everything?"

"You're thinking of his great-great-grandfather," I corrected.

"No, was it that long ago?"

I nodded.

He scrutinized me briefly, then shrugged. "Well, I guess you ought to know. History isn't my strong point. It was definitely before my time, I do know that." The import of it appeared to dawn on him. "But you can't be serious! That guy, or one of his grandsons or whatever — one of the *Loves* is your father?"

I nodded again.

"Come on," he chided. "What is this, a joke? It better not be, 'cause if it is, I'm gonna be really pissed."

"It's not a joke," I assured him.

He stared into space, as though at some magnificent pageant of opportunity unfolding in the air. "Whoa!" he said, drawing out the syllable to tremendous length. "Not bad. Not bad at all. You gonna sue?"

"Wo!" Yin-mi protested.

I think I must have turned bright red.

"Okay, okay," he backed down. "So it's none of my business? Sor-*ry*. Forget I asked."

"What about the name?" Yin-mi reminded him.

"Right: A. E. Love." He scanned the page. "Here's an A. C. Love . . . a D. C. Love . . . no A. E. though."

"How about Eddie?" I asked.

"Nope, no Eddie either. There's an E. E. Love (sounds like a porn star, doesn't it?) How about plain E. Love? There is an E. Love. Wanna try it?"

"Please!"

He tucked the receiver under his chin and dialed. "Hello? May I speak to Mr. Love?" He winked at me. "Hello? Hello? Is this Eddie Love? *Elijah!* What kind of name is that? Well don't take it personal. Yeah? You too buddy, in a pushcart!" He slammed down the receiver.

"Sorry," he said. "No luck. Maybe it's an unlisted number."

He dialed the operator. "Directory assistance? Do you have an A. E. or Eddie Love? Yeah, like it sounds. Check new listings and unpublished numbers, will you? What? I know you can't divulge that information. Did I ask you for the number? All I want to know is if there is a listing in that name. You can tell me that, can't you? I thought so. What? There isn't. No Eddie either? Okay, honey, have a nice weekend. Bye-bye."

Wo cradled the receiver. Flipping back his hair, he shrugged his shoulders and pouted fatalistically. "No such dude," he said. "At least according to N.Y. Tel." His brows knitted in concentration. "Could be he lives in the suburbs though, a guy like that. Probably Westchester or the Hamptons, Connecticut maybe. But hell, if we checked every possibility it could take all day. I'd like to help you, Sonny, I really would. But . . ." Grinning sheepishly, he turned his palms up in the air.

"I could help," Yin-mi volunteered earnestly.

"Would you?"

"Yeah," Wo said, "good idea. But take the phone and plug it in in Mom and Pop's bedroom, will you? We've got business to discuss out here. Try those places I told you first. Then check the towns along the train routes. Maybe you'll get lucky." He reached down and unplugged the telephone. Wrapping the cord around it several times, he thrust it toward me. "See you later."

"And the job?" I asked.

"Still harping on that, huh? Listen, Sonny, scrap it. I'm telling you, it's not a good idea."

"Please," I said in a quiet, supplicating voice.

He compressed his lips in a manner that presaged bad news.

"Wo! He's Father's friend," Yin-mi upbraided. "Why do you hesitate? It's such a small request."

"Oh yeah? You think I just snap my fingers and everybody jumps, huh?"

Some of the courtiers, who for some time had been sidling closer as inconspicuously as possible, exchanged questioning glances, which Wo noticed.

"Not that I couldn't, you understand, if I wanted."

"Why don't you then?" she asked simply.

The entourage directed their attention to him. Wo clearly felt pressured, as though this were a test of his legitimacy. Clenching and unclenching his fists, breathing a little heavily, he confronted Yin-mi in obvious exasperation.

She absorbed his displeasure with the same expression I remembered from the time before when she'd stood up to Lo, neither fear nor malice, only a crystalline earnestness, at the heart of which, like a rare treasure in a museum case, there was a question framed in candor, something absolutely vulnerable, absolutely uncompromising, and requiring candor to be answered.

"All right, all right," Wo capitulated with an angry sigh. "Monday morning, quarter to nine, meet me at Trinity Church."

A murmur of adulation went up among the crowd.

"Thank you!" I cried, overjoyed.

Wo tossed his bangs like a grandee. "Okay, okay," he said. "Just don't bow, all right? I can't take that shit."

"I'll be eternally grateful, Wo," I said, extravagantly, perhaps, but in complete sincerity.

"Yeah," he said, almost wistfully, "I hope so. . . ." He chuckled. "Don't worry, though, I'll get mine back."

"Anything!" I promised.

Immediately I repented of the doubts I'd entertained on my first glimpse of him. I fully believe that if he had offered me his pudgy hand, I would have kissed it then and there as though he were the emperor.

Fortunately, however, the opportunity did not arise. Detaching his glance to signal that our audience was at an end, Wo drew the attention of one of the alert courtiers waiting in the wings, and with an incomparable toss of the head, indicated that he might approach. He then plopped down heavily on the sofa, sending up a minor squall of wind from the cushions. In less than a second, the whole bevy descended eagerly on us, like banished subjects recalled from exile, their appetite for their monarch, their gratitude, only enhanced by his whimsical display of power. Above the rush, I sought out Yin-mi.

"Help! Stampede!" she cried, laughing, reaching out her hand above the crowd. Surprised and charmed by this touch of playfulness, which opened up a side of her I hadn't seen, I took it. But it was she who led me. Her hand was small and cool. It exerted a decisive pressure. In a peristalsis of agitating bodies, inch by inch we passed through the crowd. Guided by her, I experienced a sweet, momentary ecstasy of drift and indecision, which I gave in to willingly. I felt a physical security like a young child's drowsing in its mother's arms, unconsciously, irresponsibly happy. Finally, with one great heave, we were expelled at the far end of the room into a region of outer darkness. There she let go of my hand, and a small desolation opened up inside me.

When she turned and smiled at me, however, flushed, a little breathless, the injury was instantly repaired, and with significant addition.

Chapter 5

The Ha-p'is' bedroom was diminutive and overflowing. There was no place to sit except the bed, which spread out like a sagging plain of open, restful space with chaos impinging at the edges — a well-ordered chaos though, like in the kitchen, as though the clutter had been systematically arranged. The sheets were the color of Scottie's tennis shoes, cirrhosis-gray from too much washing. Yet the thread of the embroidered panel at the head, a lilting pattern of interlocking *Fu*'s and *Shou*'s, was just as red, perhaps, and vivid, as it had been on their wedding day. That the workmanship was Mrs. Ha-p'i's I inferred from the pincushion — a smiling, squint-eyed Chinaman with a fat belly — lying faceup on the far pillow underneath a reading light. He was transfixed by pins and embroidery needles with clipped loops of multicolored thread knotted through their eyes, like gay pennants fluttering from the tips of picadors' lances. Yet he still smiled. Somehow this jolly sufferer reminded me of Wo, imposed on by an inconvenient voodoo curse. No doubt, I told myself, conjuring what Humility I could, the association was gratuitous and inspired by envy of Wo's exalted state. On a hatbox at the same side of the bed was a piece of beautiful black silk with a tasseled fringe, intended as a shawl. A portion of it was stretched across a round embroidery frame, a small tambourine of unfinished wood. Within this circle, petit point, Mrs. H. was embroidering a chrysanthemum, its stem vivid green beneath a golden spray of regal, cloudlike flower. I felt a pang of bittersweet nostalgia — the robe, my mother, Love . . . the trick chrysanthemum that started everything. . . .

"It's beautiful, isn't it?" Yin-mi said, noticing my absorption. "My mother does them for a friend of hers, Mrs. Chen. She has a curio shop on Mott Street and takes them on consignment."

Though I knew the utter futility of it, somehow I wanted her to understand my mood, the wistfulness that had arisen in my heart. But I couldn't bring myself to speak.

"What are you thinking?" she asked gently.

I laughed disparagingly. "More than I could ever say."

"It's your mother's robe, isn't it?"

I was astonished. "How did you know that? You seem to read my thoughts."

"My father," she replied simply.

"He told you about the robe, the money? But he said nothing to your mother. Why is that?"

"*I* asked," she said with a candor that made me blush and turn away.

"Does it embarrass you for me to say that?"

"No," I replied. "Well, yes. . . . I don't know."

She laughed, the same quality of limpidness in her voice as in her eyes.

"I'm afraid I made a stupid blunder today when I came in," I said. "I started to return the money, only your mother didn't know what it was for. I felt like an idiot, or even worse, a criminal. Your father had to explain. I'm afraid it put him in a terrible spot."

"It's all right," she assured me. "He's used to it. He lives that way."

"What do you mean?" I asked, a little taken aback. "What way?"

"Always on the verge of one small disaster or another, full of good intentions, trying to help — himself or others — but generally leaving things in a worse fix than he found them."

"But he did help me."

She smiled. "I know. He likes you. *Admires* you."

"I can't see why," I replied, embarrassed.

"He considers you an educated man."

I laughed. "Oh *that!* Somehow he's gotten the idea that I'm a connoisseur. I can't understand it. Nothing could be further from the truth."

She swayed back, closed her eyes, cocked her head a little. "Ah . . . the subtleties of wine," she sighed. The imitation was perfect.

"That's it!" I cried, delighted.

We both burst out laughing.

"I was too ashamed to confess my ignorance," I admitted.

"It doesn't matter. He probably knows. He only wanted someone to drink with and talk to. He's lonely. All he knows is work."

"Yes," I agreed, chuckling, "I can vouch for *that.*"

She regarded me with a serious look. "I think my father sees a younger self in you. He admires your dreams, your ideals. Most of all your freedom. He no longer has the luxury to dream. Life has deprived him of that consolation. That's why he drinks. It's his only pleasure. He's given everything for us."

"You love him a great deal, don't you?" I asked in a chastened tone.

She nodded. "And admire him."

In this remark I detected a hint of censure, or challenge, or protectiveness . . . an implied comparsion between us, unfavorable to me, though posed unconsciously on her part.

"I wonder what your mother thought?" I asked, realizing even as I spoke that I was really interested in something else, that I was fishing, a little disingenuously perhaps, for her own appraisal.

"She's a soft touch," Yin-mi said. "Compliment her cooking. Watch Father.

He's a past master. All he has to do is tell her that her pressed duck or bird's nest soup is better than his, and instantly she turns to jelly. She blushes, hits him playfully, fusses with him, coddles, and agrees immediately to everything he proposes. He's been using it for years. You'd think she'd catch on." She smiled. "He may not look it, but underneath that mild-mannered exterior, there's a little of the rogue."

I remembered his wink.

"Yin-mi," I said, "the other night in the kitchen . . ."

"Yes?"

"What did you think?"

"Think?"

I nodded.

"I thought Father was lifting Mother's sewing money," she replied. "And I was right." She laughed.

"No," I said, "I mean . . . about me?"

The laughter, which gilded her eyes like sunlight on a pool of water, vanished, revealing still, solemn depths.

"Just before you left the kitchen," I said. "You turned and looked back."

"I remember," she said.

"You had this expression . . ."

She blinked.

"I thought you despised me."

She seemed surprised, and then her voice grew soft. "I didn't know what to think."

"Do you now?" I asked, unable to suppress a quaver in my voice.

"I'm not sure," she said. "I think so. Some."

This small concession brought me disproportionate joy. I felt my heart go weightless, floating off in a blue, cloudless sky like a helium balloon, vanishing. I tried to call it back, but it was no use.

Yin-mi tilted her head and appraised me quizzically. There was a limitless horizon in her face, that great stillness and solemnity one discovers when looking out to sea. Finding the answer to her question, or perhaps, more likely, deferring it until another time, at length she disengaged her eyes.

"I think there are some phone books in that drawer," she said, pointing to a dresser. "I'm not sure what exchanges, or how old they are, but it won't hurt to check. You can do that while I make some calls."

As Wo had suggested, she tried the Hamptons first, then Westchester County. Drawing a blank, she began systematically calling the towns along the Hudson line. Meanwhile I occupied myself thumbing through the assortment of old directories. There were a dozen of these, more or less, a few from New Jersey, most from various places on Long Island. These great Doomsday tomes impressed me. Each book tantalized a moment, promising a secret jewel of revelation. This hope invested the dreary wastelands of homogeneous print with a spark of vitality and interest, suspense even . . . until the disappointment came. Then they became dead inventories, oppressive reams of abstract, empty names.

I appealed to Yin-mi. Cradling the receiver between her chin and shoulder, she shrugged. "No luck yet," she whispered. "I'll try the New Haven line next."

I bent over another book. Another blank. Before long I'd exhausted all but one: Port Washington. Indifferently remarking its cover, I sighed and started to open it. Then something arrested my attention. I turned back. Among the exchanges listed on the front in smaller type below the main one was a name I recognized: Sands Point. Suddenly I remembered: the Love family estate. Hsiao had mentioned it. My heart began to race.

Seeing my excitement, Yin-mi put her hand over the mouthpiece of the receiver and dropped it in her lap. "What is it?"

"I may have found it," I told her as I thumbed. "I remembered something. . . . Just a minute. Loman . . . Lord . . . Losey . . . Love . . . Love . . . Here it is! A. E. Love the Fourth, Twelve Lighthouse Road."

"Okay, calm down," she counseled, equally excited. "Give me the number."

"Three-six-nine . . ." I said.

"Three . . . six . . . nine" she repeated, fingering the dial, which clicked then whined as it returned to place.

"Two-three-two-seven."

"Two . . . three . . . two . . . seven." She raised the receiver to her ear. "It's ringing," she whispered. She held it out to me.

I regarded it dumbly, then observed Yin-mi. She nodded. Suddenly it dawned on me: *this was it — this was the connection —* this twisted, black umbilicus would tie me to him. In a few seconds, at the other end, he would pick up, the circuit would close, the impulse flow between the magnets, his voice a spark of pure electric fire trilling down the line into the live wires of my nerves, into my life. Caught in an updraft of nervous ecstasy, my heart tumbled giddily aloft. Then booming up from underneath, out of the bass register, nameless and unreasoning, the terror came.

"Sun I," she said, "the phone."

I took it. Seas of nothingness streamed in a silent vortex toward my inner ear through the plastic sieve of the receiver, which strained for a response, seined the humming darkness for a gleam of wriggling life.

There was a click; static crackled on the line; a woman's voice came on.

"I'm sorry. The number you have reached, three-six-nine–two-three-two-seven, is not in service. If you feel you have reached this recording in error, please consult your local listings and dial again, or try the operator. This is a recording." Click. White noise. The keening of cicadas.

Slowly I placed the receiver on the hook.

Yin-mi questioned me silently.

"Disconnected," I said abjectly.

"Let me try again." She picked it up. "Maybe I dialed the wrong number."

I watched her apathetically. As she listened to the ring, she explored a portion of the ceiling. Tensing, she became attentive. Then slowly blankness crept into her expression. She put the receiver down and sighed. "I'm sorry."

Turning the phone book toward her, she scanned the column idly. "A. E. Love the Fourth," she mused, reading from her fingertip. She flipped the book shut.

"Wait a minute," I said, reviving slightly as I recalled more precisely what Hsiao had told me. "My father was the Fifth. That was *his* father's name — *Arthur* Love."

"You know something?" she answered, pointing to the cover. "This directory is over ten years old. Maybe they've changed the number. Let's try directory assistance in Port Washington."

But there was no listing now for A. E. Love at all, Fourth or Fifth. The name seemed to have been erased from the roll call of humanity.

"Don't give up yet," Yin-mi said. "Maybe he's moved. There are still a lot of places we haven't tried."

For another ten minutes she bravely kept it up, while I sat by studying her, resigned to the outcome, almost indifferent.

"Don't be sad," she said at last, sighing herself. "Come on. We'll take a break. Let's go to the roof. You haven't showed me where you live."

I submitted, letting myself be led by her again. In the kitchen we passed her mother.

"Where are you going?" she asked, surprised. "Dinner is almost ready."

"We'll eat later," Yin-mi said. "Okay? We're going to the roof."

Mrs. H. regarded us dubiously, but noticing my dejection, relented. "Well, all right. But don't be long."

•

From the stale obscurity of the building with its hint of mossy coolness, we burst into the sunlight and the upper air. There was the semblance of a breath of wind, but it was only the contrast, without to within. The air was humid, with a platinum sheen. My faithful flock of pigeons, accustomed to my peregrinations, barely inconvenienced themselves on our account, making way only under threat of physical coercion, and then with great mutterings and rufflings of outraged dignity.

"You've tamed them," Yin-mi remarked innocently, as though impressed.

"Or vice versa," I replied, more jaded.

She laughed, then observed me soberly, with a hint of pity. "Don't be discouraged," she whispered.

"About what?" I asked disingenuously. "The pigeons? I'm resigned to them."

"You know that's not what I mean. Your father."

I shrugged. "I'm not. I never really expected to find him in that way."

She waited for an explanation.

Another bubble floated up from the well of memory. "I must follow the intuitive promptings of my own unconscious nature," I said, recalling the master's words to Hsiao. "That is the essence of our Way of Life."

"You have great faith," she said. "I admire that."

I did not reply, having caught briefly again, without intending to, the facet of her being which recalled the little girl's. A spark of blue diamond fire struck from her soul danced in the highlight of her pupils, transfixing me.

"Why do you look at me like that?" Her candor was second nature to her, unreflective, fearless. She didn't mean to intimidate me with it; but I was intimidated, a little.

"I feel like we are 'old acquaintances at first sight,' " I said, smiling to myself as Hsiao's remark supplied itself unbidden to my lips. I laughed wistfully, remembering.

" 'Old acquaintances at first sight'?"

"Over and over today, these disconcerting echoes of the past," I mused aloud to her. "It's as though I'd lived all this before. Ever since I came to New York I've had that feeling, but never so much as now. Why is that?"

She waited.

"When I left the monastery, the last direction my master gave me was to follow the river. 'It will lead you to the sea,' he said."

"The delta," she glossed with a sweet curve of smile.

"Yes," I replied, smiling back. "That's what I was thinking of before, that journey, when the metaphor occurred to me — the swollen mountain torrent ripping toward its destination, debouching at last, its rage all spent, into the steady, level ocean, its final act not one of violence or passion, but of acquiescence: Dow into Tao. Strange, I'd never thought of it before. It was there inside me, part of my own life, yet it lay dormant until my argument with Wo. It wasn't so much anything he said that drew it out, I think. Something I discovered in your eyes then brought it home to me. I don't know how it is, but they tutored me to know myself. That's what I meant, 'old acquaintances at first sight.' Maybe we've met before, Yin-mi, somewhere a long, long time ago."

She was flushed; her shoulders trembled slightly as though she were a little out of breath. She didn't look away though, and I found the courage to continue.

"But it's more specific. During my journey, while I was still far upriver, I came to a small town. A convocation was assembling there — traders, trappers, thieves, types I'd never encountered before — among them, strangest of all, a man named Tsin. He was a soldier, a mercenary, rather. Tsin saved my life . . . and took another man's." Then I told her the story: about the soldier and the captain, the opium, the ecstasy of combat, how it had culminated in the murder, the mutilation I'd found lying in the twisted, bloody sheets.

She listened carefully, patiently from the beginning. But as the tale progressed, she warmed to it increasingly. Swept up in the narrative, she lost herself, as in a spell, I, the magician. Entrancing her, I became inspired myself, unearthing delicious kernels of significance that I had missed before, like windfalls in a distant meadow lying undiscovered in the grass. I experienced a sense of exhilarating unburdening, of release, myself the tumid river now, flowing toward her as a sea. I described for her with minute particularity the sensation of opening my eyes and finding the bear standing over me "like looking into God's own eyes." Then returning to the tonic key, I told her of the little girl and that parting look she'd given me, which I had carried in my heart from that far, barbarous outpost all the way across the world, around the Cape of Good Hope, to America, finally, and New York. "And you might be her twin," I said, "her very self in fact, only a few years older." I tried to gauge her reaction.

" 'Old acquaintances at first sight,' " she mused in a soft voice. "Now I think I understand." She smiled, but tremulously. I detected the same hint of trouble and perplexity in that smile which I had seen that night in the kitchen, the underlying compunction she was mastering with effort.

"What is it?" I asked. "What's wrong?"

She shook her head. "Nothing's wrong. Actually, I'm very happy you've confided in me."

"You seem so serious."

"I'm moved," she said. "That's all. Your story was so odd and terrible. You spoke with such excitement, almost rapture. It makes me sad." She frowned as though choosing her tack with care. I was touched by her manner, her ingenuous gravity, these simple remarks delivered so deliberately, as though possessed of great weight and consequence. They exposed an intellectual simplicity, deceptively slow moving, leaving an impression of singleness and momentousness, like the slow drift of a glacier across a continent.

"Especially the part about the soldier," she went on, oblivious to my scrutiny. "That drew you out more than the rest. All that blood-lust and brutality — you were fascinated. Why, Sun I?"

"Fascinated!" I protested. "*Horrified* is more like it."

Her brows knitted with intense study. "But you spoke with such relish that the atrocities seemed almost beautiful." I winced. "I believe you though, Sun I. I could hear the horror underneath the words, almost like an animal wailing. I don't think that was just my imagination." She posed this like a question.

I shook my head, not knowing the answer.

"Why did you tell me this?"

I took her shift in tone as evidence of protest or impatience. "I don't know," I replied, chastened.

"Why do I feel that you've entrusted me with a responsibility?"

"I didn't mean to burden you," I apologized. "I only wanted to explain."

"I know," she said. "It's all right. I'm *glad.*" She touched my hand and smiled unexpectedly. So unexpectedly, that I was left at a loss. Something erupted in my heart which might have passed for bliss, or agony, yet was neither, beyond them both, a pure and irreducible intensity of feeling without content.

"What are you thinking?" she asked. Sensing my bewilderment, she laughed. "*Say* something!"

I was incapable, utterly lost in the contemplation of her face, which altered with her laughter like a kaleidoscope exploding in a new configuration. I noticed that one of her teeth was a fraction crooked, and that skewing — so ridiculous, so unaware of itself, so unrepentantly *factual* — made me want to cry and laugh at once. Her lip drew upward like a curtain, revealing a pink line of gum above her teeth; a tiny starburst scintillated from the sheen of clear saliva, and I was dazzled. The skin beneath her eyes, its fine graininess of texture, its thinness and delicacy, was like the petal of an orchid with its violet flush, hardly flesh at all, too sensitive and fine, as though in transition between two states, evolving toward the pure spirituality of the eye. In her left iris, the color of stained mahogany, I noted a small gold sequin above the pupil, slightly off center, like an inclusion in a semiprecious stone, the flaw which inestimably enhances value. Her lashes, her forehead, the vermilion border of her lip, all appeared with the startling vividness of lunar seas and chasms through the lens of my heightened perception. As her mirth subsided, she wiped a tiny rill from the corner of her eye with the back of her left wrist, and in an uninterrupted motion unconsciously curled a lock of black hair around her ear, tracing the arc with a finger. Following that small unconsidered gesture, I became pliable and entwined with the lock. Most amazing of all, through these physical details, her soul, her *self* shone, like sun through the stained glass windows of the church, giving them warmth and life. Though impalpable, it was entirely vivid to my sense and greeted me familiarly. The experience of it was incommensurable with anything I'd known before, and it made me realize I'd never really *seen* another person, or experienced intimacy, until that moment. The clarity would not last, but consume itself with its own intensity. Even then, the poverty of my experience failed to teach me the true name of what had happened. Had it done so, spiritual Frugality, and all that went with it, would have resisted the knowledge.

"Do you believe in reincarnation?"

Her question meshed oddly with my thoughts. The idea was an obvious corollary of our line of reasoning, but in my condition it struck me as clairvoyant. Unmoored within myself, no longer choosing my direction, I passively allowed another phrase to bubble out of my unconscious mind: "We're much too plain to advance such fancy theories." An ungovernable impulse seized me; I threw back my head and laughed. I could hear the undercurrent of hysteria, but it was like someone else's. It interested me but didn't move me.

Yin-mi gave me an anxious, questioning look.

"It's not a Taoist idea," I told her, forcing myself to regain control, "and yet . . ." I shook my head, at a loss.

"Father Riley spoke to us about reincarnation once at TYA," she said.

"Father Riley?" I asked. "TYA?"

She blushed. "Father Riley is our rector. TYA — that stands for Trinity Young Adults."

"Trinity Church?"

She nodded.

"I've been there!"

She laughed. "So have I! Many times. In fact, I'm a member of the congregation."

"You're a Christian?" I was astonished.

She blushed. "I try to be. An Episcopalian."

" 'Episcopalian,' " I mused, pronouncing the strange word.

"It sounds like a geologic epoch, doesn't it?" she remarked. "That's what I used to think — Silurian, Precambrian, Cretacious, Episcopalian . . ."

"Is it a sect?" I asked.

"Denomination is the preferred term, I think," she replied, with a hint of amused severity.

"How strange!"

"What is?" she asked.

"You, a Christian!"

"Why is that strange?"

"You're *Chinese!*"

"Chinese *American,*" she corrected. "Remember where you are, Sun I. Look there across the rooftops. That spire. That's the steeple of a church — the Church of the Transfiguration on Mott Street. It's Roman Catholic. This city is full of churches, almost all of them Christian. There are no Taoist temples here. *You* are the strange one, maybe the only Taoist in New York City, a minority of one." She smiled. "Except, of course, the other kind, on Wall Street. But they aren't religious. The New York Stock Exchange is not a church." The thought appeared to amuse her.

"What makes a church?" I was a little rankled by her categorical assuredness, yet I asked more in sincerity than perverseness.

She tilted her head at me quizzically. "I don't know," she replied in a softer, slightly chastened tone. "But in the Bible Christ did drive the moneylenders from the temple."

"If he had been a Taoist, he would have made a place for them instead," I speculated. "Either that, or made the countinghouse a church."

She appeared uncertain whether to take me seriously or not, then, deciding, laughed. "What an idea! I probably shouldn't laugh. I think it's blasphemous." She laughed anyway.

"But how could he exclude them?" I was genuinely troubled by the idea.

"Haven't you ever heard that it's easier for a camel to pass through the eye of a needle than for a rich man to enter the kingdom of heaven?"

"Why is that?" I demanded. "Didn't God create rich men and their activities too? On what basis would he repudiate them?"

"I think it's obvious."

"Not to me."

"They defiled his house with their activities," she explained. "They didn't keep the commandments."

I shook my head, unsatisfied. "Is that the Christian Way?"

"Maybe," she said. "I'm not sure what you're getting at."

"Your God excludes; the Tao embraces," I dictated, with a touch of pride and bitterness.

"Embraces even what is bad? What's the virtue in that?"

"It's the whole point, isn't it?"

She shook her head. "I don't understand."

"Remember the delta?"

A slightly troubled expression came into her face. "Perhaps you should talk to Father Riley, I'm not sure I can answer your question."

"I think maybe you already have," I said.

She observed me doubtfully, trying to read my meaning. "May I ask you something?"

"Of course."

"Perhaps it's merely ignorance, but when you say 'Tao,' what exactly do you mean? I have an idea, but I'm not sure. Is it like heaven?"

I smiled unintentionally. "Not exactly. But something like."

"Then you think everyone should go to heaven, regardless of their crimes or merits?"

"I don't believe in heaven as a place we go," I replied. "Heaven is something that exists only in our minds."

"An imaginary place?"

"No. Just an inner one."

Yin-mi's eyes were vulnerable and grave. "I think I believe that too," she said in a soft voice.

"And as to crimes and merits," I continued, sensing a sort of capitulation in her and drawing myself up unconsciously to preach, "they appear only as a result of prejudice, deluded seeing. They are relative, illusory finally."

"Do you honestly believe that?" she asked, with a quaver in her voice that caught me up. I started to say yes but, seeing her fragility and trust, hesitated, holding back the rote response that was ready on my lips, as I had once before that day. "Well, what's true for the sage is often less so for the ordinary man."

By an unstated mutual consent which we found in one another's silence, we decided to terminate our controversy.

"I think you should meet Father Riley," she said. "You'd probably have a lot to talk about. He could give a much better account of the Christian position than I can, I'm sure. And besides, he's very knowledgeable on the subject of Oriental philosophy. The first time I ever heard him speak, at my high school, that was his topic. He concentrated mainly on Zen and Hinduism, but he mentioned Taoism too. He said that when he was in college, before he entered the seminary, he took a course in comparative religion and became fascinated by how the insights of the Sutras and Vedas parallel those of the Scriptures."

"Yes," I agreed, "that's almost a truism, isn't it, that at the highest level all religions are the same, that the realization they promise and aspire to is the same realization?"

"But I don't think he would necessarily agree with you on that," she objected. "That was his ultimate point — that Christianity was different, that it had brought something new into the world, something that changed history and consciousness forever. He said that Christianity had superseded its own origins in Judaism, and with them, all the primitive religions."

"And what is this great revelation?" I asked ironically.

"Love," she earnestly replied.

"Love!" I was incredulous. "That's not exactly a new idea, you know, Yin-mi. After all, Compassion is one of Taoism's Three Treasures, and it's fundamental in Buddhism too. I'd be interested to hear by what route the Christians lay claim to the original patent."

"You'd have to ask him," she said. "I don't think I could reconstruct the argument." She paused. "Perhaps you should."

"Perhaps," I replied ambiguously.

"You could come with me to a meeting of the TYA some night."

I considered.

"Tonight, in fact! Why not?" She became eager. "I know you'd like him. He's wonderfully learned, and intelligent, and sensitive, and kind. Won't you?"

"Not tonight," I replied, feeling a reticence I didn't completely understand. I wanted to please her, yet I felt a conflict of loyalty, and, too, her effusion irked me for some unaccountable reason. "Another time perhaps."

She seemed crestfallen.

"Don't be disappointed. I'd just like to think it over."

"It's all right, I understand."

"I'll go with you another time."

"Promise?"

"Promise."

She smiled happily, and I considered my small concession amply repaid.

"But tell me, Yin-mi," I began again, returning to a point I had still not quite digested, "how did you become an Episcopal in the first place?"

"Episcopalian," she corrected. "Well, it's simple really. The church is only a few blocks away. Chinatown is in Trinity parish. There's a program called the Community Outreach Ministry. Father Riley and some of the other pastoral officers make appearances from time to time at public functions to explain the church, its values and offerings, to members of the community who might not know about it otherwise. I mean, the Episcopal Church is traditionally viewed as such a bastion of Waspish conservatism."

"Waspish?" I asked.

"Wasp — white Anglo-Saxon Protestant. It's difficult to break the ice with other segments of the community, minorities particularly. Father Riley wants to change all that, to make the church serve the whole community, not just Wall Street. A lot of people feel threatened by him. He's come under fire. But he's a very progressive thinker, and stubborn in his principles. It's his Irish blood, he says. Anyway, I heard him speak for the first time at my high school. I told you that. I'd never been exposed to religion at home, or even felt the need for it. I don't think most Chinese are really religious in the Western sense. For them it's more a sort of social thing, though I suppose when they do go in for it, they generally carry it to great heights." She smiled. "Or at least extremes. But it attracted me. I felt a little as if a door had opened and I'd walked into an unexplored room inside myself. I had known it was there, passed it a hundred times maybe, without ever pausing to go in, without even wondering what might be there. When I finally did enter, I found many strange and wonderful objects covered with dust and cobwebs, whose purposes I couldn't guess. Maybe they had no purposes, I thought. But I knew the lack wouldn't diminish their importance; it would make them doubly precious somehow. I can't explain. I suppose at that first lecture I really only got the first peek into the room. Ever since, little by little I've been exploring it. There's still a lot I haven't seen. Maybe you can never see it all — who knows?

"But Father Riley gave me my first glimpse. I'm grateful to him for that. He's very charismatic, a powerful speaker. That day I got carried away in what he was saying, like I did with you this afternoon." She smiled; I blushed. "Having lived here all my life, I'd never once been inside the church. It's odd, isn't it? Well, after hearing him, I decided to go down there some day and take a look. I put it off and put it off, then finally one Saturday I went. There was almost no one there. I'd never dreamt how beautiful it would be. I crept into one of the pews near the back. For a long time I sat staring up at the vault — so high up — examining the stained glass. While I was there, a lady came in. She was middle-aged, rather stout, wearing high heels and one of those stovepipe skirts that hug your legs and make you walk as though your knees are tied together. She had on a stole made out of a fox, or maybe a weasel, looped around biting its own tail, with beady little amber eyes, and black leather gloves with a little pearl button at the wrist — very fine quality, very elegant, I remember them perfectly — an old-fashioned hat, too, with a navy veil, which was lowered. She crossed herself and genuflected, then knelt down at the pew across from mine and started taking off her gloves. Her hands trembled badly. It was pathetic. I was almost shocked to see how bad her hands looked after those beautiful gloves — sickly white, with brown, tobacco-colored stains that looked like melanoma, crisscrossed by huge, bluish-purple veins. I hadn't liked her very much when I first saw her, but all of a sudden I felt sorry for her, the way she struggled with that button, the way her hands trembled. If I hadn't been so embarrassed, I might have offered to help. Finally she managed to get off the second one. Very demurely, almost shy, she lifted her veil up and looked directly at me. I was embarrassed to be caught staring, but there wasn't the least bit of reproach in her expression. She had such sad, gentle eyes, Sun I. There was a moment of odd closeness between us. I smiled at her and she smiled back, nodding her head like this." Yin-mi demonstrated. "Then she turned to pray, resting her elbows on the pew in front of her, clasping her hands almost frantically, as though they were two separate people reaching out to comfort one another. I watched for a while, but, feeling like I was spying on her, I eventually looked away. The incident disturbed me for some reason. I felt a little restless and upset. I was considering getting up to go, when, on an impulse, I reached down instead and lowered the knee rest. I knelt down and clasped my hands in front of me, like her. I don't think I've ever felt more self-conscious or embarrassed in my life. I could feel my cheeks burning. I prayed she wouldn't look around. But that passed. I didn't pray, didn't say any words, but bit by bit a kind of hush settled over my spirit, a tingling almost like a chill. It was as though a ghostly wind were blowing over me. It made my flesh crawl and my eyes mist over. Then I started to cry. Why, I don't know. I'd never experienced anything like it. It only lasted a few minutes; when it was over I felt foolish and depressed, yet at the same time, refreshed and stronger. Does that make sense?"

"I think so," I replied. "Some."

She smiled. "It's changed with time. If it's rarely as emotional, it's more fulfilling now. The only thing I can compare it to is swimming."

"Swimming?"

She nodded. "Something similar happens to me swimming long distances. You're going along, counting off the laps, and suddenly you blank out and lose all track. You aren't aware of it until afterward, of course, when you wake up in the middle of your lane, still swimming along as strong as ever, but for a time you've been somewhere else . . . I don't know how to put it . . . almost as though you were out of your body. You almost stop existing for a few laps, and then you come back. It's scary, but it's wonderful too." She furrowed her brow as though trying to work it out for herself; that effort at concentration, the unembarrassed simplicity of it, elicited my tenderness again. "I don't know why, it just is. There's a sense of something supernatural having occurred, something almost miraculous. That's what it was like that day, or the closest I can come to describing it. I lifted my head, saw where I was, and I knew I'd lost a piece of time. The lady was gone, which made me sad, for somehow I wanted her to be there to share my experience if only by a look. I got up to go and on the way out took some of their literature. At home later I filled in the card and dropped it in the mail.

"The next week I got a call from one of Father Riley's assistants." She laughed. "My mother thought it was some boy from school calling for a date. As she called me to the phone, she started signaling frantically with her hands, mouthing messages with her lips. She was disappointed when I told her who it was. I'm not even sure she believed me." Yin-mi smiled. "At any rate, I went to one of the Sunday morning Inquirer's classes. From there I was invited to the TYA. One thing led to another, and I've been going ever since. After a few weeks, I decided I wanted to be received, so I began to attend Confirmation classes. Last spring I was baptized. That's the story. Not so strange, really, is it? No trumpets, no archangels, no blinding lights . . . I guess it's really kind of bland. You're probably bored." She laughed — at herself, at me, at a great deal, I think. There was a gentle, fulfilled light in her face that I found beautiful but unaccountably irritating. I said nothing.

She waited, expectantly at first, as though anticipating a reaction such as my story had elicited from her, then increasingly with a sense of confusion and even hurt, as though she were pained by my reticence. I felt ashamed. She'd been so generous in her appreciation, so warm. But I didn't know what to say to her.

"I suppose we should go down now and eat," she resumed after a few moments. The note of disappointment and constraint in her voice was agonizing, yet an inner compunction prevented me from doing anything about it.

"I'm not hungry now," I said in an access of boorish introversion, which I despised myself for but was powerless to overrule.

"But Mother will be hurt," she objected. "She was especially counting on you."

"I'm sorry," I replied. "Tell her I'm not feeling well."

"What's wrong, Sun I?" she said imploringly. "Why have you changed? Did I say something?"

"I'm just tired, that's all," I replied, not precisely lying, but giving false weight to a minor circumstance.

She regarded me with concern. "You'll still go with me to TYA sometime, won't you?"

"I promised, didn't I?" I replied, unable to suppress an undertone of peevishness and irritation.

Overlooking it, she smiled. The diffidence and sincerity in her expression shed a radiance which somehow piqued me even more.

"Goodbye, Sun I."

I held out my hand almost grudgingly.

As she took it, to my surprise, she pulled herself toward me and kissed me lightly on the cheek. "Sun I," she whispered in my ear, "I feel I've known you too." Then she hurried toward the door. In an agony of remorse, I watched her go, my heart in riot.

Chapter 6

With great trepidation, great excitement, I loitered near the wrought iron gate of Trinity, eyeing the long line of yellow Checker cabs as, one by one, blinkers flashing, they shunted out of traffic, sidling to the curb, like boxcars disgorging elegant cargoes of spit-shined, pin-striped cattle. With each new arrival, I trotted alongside as the car rolled to a halt, anxiously peering through the side window to catch a glimpse of my impatiently awaited mentor, Wo. This did not endear me to the cabbies, or their patrons either. I was beginning to feel mildly discouraged when, above the general din of men and automobiles, Wo's voice rang out like an abrasive angelus.

"Hey, Sonny! What's *hap*-pening!"

It was music to my ears. Delighted, I sprinted down the line, eagerly searching back seats for the source of the voice. To my confusion, it appeared to be coming from none of them.

"Over *here!*" I turned from the street back to the sidewalk. And there, issuing not from cab or limousine as I'd expected, but driven along with the grayish, lumpen herd from, of all places, the subway station, was Wo! Deus ex machina indeed; but the wrong machine! My expectations — for a second time — were utterly confounded. What was worse, he wasn't even wearing a three-piece suit, but the same Hawaiian shirt I'd seen him in two days before, dubiously improved by a mustard stain on the left pocket which looked like it had been used to transport a dressed hot dog. The sight of his characteristic entourage dancing attendance — all incidentally, wearing Hawaiian shirts in slavish imitation of their master — did little to assuage my misgivings, for such an assortment of cowlicks, bucktoothed grins, and otherwise spavined youth as met my eyes could rarely before have been assembled in one place. They looked like refugees from an itinerant remedial circus. At first I was astonished, then mortified, then deeply impressed. It struck me that such nonchalance in dress was more laudable than the most elegant attire. What monumental disregard for societal convention! It was positively Taoist in inspiration!

Worthy of Chuang Tzu himself! The degree of compassion, the noblesse oblige, implied in his decision to associate with these unfortunates . . . ah, sublime! Perhaps Wo's disconcerting resemblance to Buddha was not fortuitous after all; perhaps it extended beyond the matter of mere physical circumference. I was ashamed for having judged so quickly by externals and felt some slippage from the old days when I would never have been guilty of such an error.

"Take a hike, you guys," Wo said to the others as they approached, so secure in his authority he didn't even need to look to see he was obeyed. Flipping his bangs, he took my arm, smiling a broad, slightly glassy smile.

"So Sonny," he said, "today's the big day! Hey hey hey! Ready to kick ass and take names?"

I nodded enthusiastically.

"Remember now," he said, assuming a cautionary tone, "I'm not guaranteeing anything."

My countenance fell.

"But I don't think there'll be any problem."

My spirits revived. "Thank you, Wo. You don't know how much this means to me. I only wish there were some way I could repay you."

"Actually, I'm glad you brought that up," he said offhandedly. "As it happens, there is something . . ."

"Of course!" I replied, delighted at the prospect. "Anything. What would you like me to do?"

He studied me, all trace of his characteristic smugness vanishing beneath an anxious, almost hunted look. "You'll see," he said with a cryptic, mirthless laugh.

Just then we arrived at the entrance to the Exchange where I had been rejected just a few days earlier. The same black guard barred my way with the same black arm, until Wo stepped forward and smoothed things over.

"It's okay, George," he announced, tossing his hair. "He's with me."

George regarded us both dubiously, then with a shrug allowed us to pass on the strength of Wo's I.D. I was awed by this display of "influence," and, in light of our previous exchange, reassured. Side by side we passed through the doors, compressed like water through the neck of a funnel by the weight of the crowd behind.

Once inside, Wo's behavior began to alter markedly. His slovenly bluster, which had worked on me until it seemed almost endearing, passed off, and he became nervous and agitated. He cast abashed, deferential smiles (in which I saw his first resemblance to his father) at various older men in suits, who either returned them coldly or didn't deign to notice him at all. Holding me rigidly by the elbow, he led me through the crowd to the elevators, thence to the sixteenth floor, where he deposited me before the desk of a secretary or employment clerk, over whom he mumbled a few incantatory phrases, looking for all the world like a quack magician about to perform some mummery and painfully conscious of his own impotence to effect it. Flashing me an apologetic grin, he ducked into the crowd and disappeared. "Back in a flash," I heard him say just as she looked up, an expression of surprise on her face which was not entirely pleasant.

"What was that?" she asked, looking around as though for something to devour. "Did you say that?" She squinted at me out of one eye.

I shook my head. "It was Mr. Ha-p'i," I replied, pointing behind me where Wo had disappeared.

"Mr. *who?*"

"Ha-p'i," I repeated distinctly.

"Well, he can hoppy on out of here till nine o'clock," she said, "and you with him!"

Her indifference to his name excited a belated, yet still half-formed, suspicion.

This clerk, a woman of indeterminate age, somewhere between twenty-five and forty, had blond, cotton candy hair and wore a great deal of makeup applied without benefit of an artist's instincts. Her most remarkable feature, however, was her eyebrows, which intersected above her nose like the cross hairs in a bombardier's sights, giving her a decidedly threatening appearance. Before being interrupted, she had been busily at work filing her nails, an occupation to which she now returned, attending with minute attention to the repair of a damaged cuticle. I cleared my throat to reattract her attention.

As I did so, she fixed a wide, intimidating stare on me, filing all the while with redoubled vigor, effectively transforming a bland, innocuous procedure into a supersubtle conductor of aggression. With a savage thrust of her emery board and corresponding jerks of head and shoulder, she directed my attention to the clock. "I don't start work till nine," she informed me.

It was two minutes before the hour.

Just then a young man burst in frantically, face flushed, briefcase recklessly flailing, jacket flapping behind him. "Sally, get personnel on the phone for me!" he shouted peremptorily, rushing past the desk. "*Right now!*"

Dropping everything in confusion, she picked up the phone and began to dial as fast as her newly burnished fingers could go, in the process chipping off a nail. "Damn!" she whispered furiously under her breath, popping the finger in her mouth. As she waited for someone to answer, she happened to catch my eye and colored violently beneath her rouge, darting me a look of withering contempt, as much as to say, "You should be ashamed!" as though I had shown a lack of gallantry. Hurriedly uttering something into the mouth-piece, she pressed a button and slammed the receiver on the hook.

"*Now,*" she said threateningly, "what can I do for you?" Her eyes said "to you."

"My benefactor, Mr. Ha-p'i . . ." I paused to let the name sink in once again, "suggested I seek here for employment."

"Mr. *who?*" she reiterated in an irritated tone. "Never mind. Don't tell me." She started rummaging through some papers. "Messenger, I assume?"

I stared at her quizzically. "Messenger?"

Groaning, she slapped the papers on the desk and gave me a hopeless look. "Yes, messenger. You know, runner, squad boy, gopher."

"Gopher," I said, partly out of genuine naiveté, partly to irritate her, "isn't that an animal?"

" 'Isn't that an animal?' " she mimicked mincingly. "Cute. Real cute. Yes, it's an animal — has four legs and lives on Wall Street, just like bulls and bears. Only it stays in a hole and keeps its nose low to the ground. Think you can handle it? Right down your line, I'd say. Or were you applying maybe for president of the Exchange?" She smiled at me with vindictive satisfaction.

"Messenger will be fine," I replied, indisposed to further sally.

Having paid me back for witnessing her humiliation, she became more businesslike and tractable. "Okay," she said, "you understand how it works, right?"

I shook my head.

"Wrong. That figures. It's very simple really. You fill out an application here. It goes on file where it will be retained for six months. You'll be called as needed on a chronological basis. If nothing opens up, after that time you'll have to reapply. All right?"

"You mean I won't be able to start today?"

"Today!" She seemed incredulous. "I sincerely doubt it! I've seen boys reapply three and four times before getting on. On such short notice . . ." The light on her phone began flashing. "Just a minute." She picked up. "Yes sir? Right. A shortage? Three places? Yes sir, there's one here now. But shouldn't I call the next one on the list? Yes sir! I'll send him right down!" Hanging up, she scrutinized me suspiciously. "You knew we had an opening, didn't you? Who did you say you knew?"

"Mr. Ha-p'i."

She shrugged. "Happy for you."

"You mean . . . ?"

"You're hired."

I felt a surge of happiness. Wo's stock, which had been severely tested during the course of the interview, instantly rebounded, shooting skyward exponentially.

"Ever work for the Exchange before?" she asked. "No, obviously not. Well, just fill out these forms, and I'll have someone tell you where to go." (Apparently she wouldn't have been averse to telling me herself.) Reaching into a box behind her desk, she handed me a pale blue smock, freshly laundered and starched, folded in a square, with a number in the collar. "Try that on for size."

I slipped my arms in, buttoned up, rotated my shoulders. "It's a little large, I think."

She shrugged. "One size fits all."

Raising the cross hairs, she peered over my shoulder, targeting in on someone new. "Oh you there, boy — yes, *you!* Get over here."

I turned apologetically toward her new victim, chagrined at having caused an innocent bystander to be so ignominiously singled out.

"I've got a job for you. On your way in this morning take him with you and show him the ropes."

Standing there in the middle of the floor red as a beet, wearing a shit-eating grin and a pale blue smock, exactly like the one I'd just been given, over his Hawaiian shirt was . . . yes, Wo! I did a double take and, as the expression goes, nearly croaked!

"Wo!" I cried in dismayed astonishment.

He flipped his hair and shrugged. "You were expecting maybe Keith Funston? I told you I'd be back, didn't I?"

The secretary regarded us suspiciously.

"But . . ."

"Come on," he said. "We've got to punch the clock."

As we walked, Wo looking neither right nor left, he blushed symphonically, indexing undreamt tonalities of red. I shuffled sideways like a crab, gaping at him stupidly.

After a brief march, we stopped to confer. From close up he appeared a little queasy around the edges. "Guess I fooled you, huh?" he bluffed thinly.

"Then it's a joke?" I dubiously inquired.

He rolled in his lips and shook his head. "No joke."

"Then you're a gopher," I said wonderingly, *"just like me!"*

"Hey, no need to get offensive," he replied testily. "Yeah, I'm a runner. So what?"

"But your family — you told them . . ."

"I never lied," he interjected quickly.

"Maybe not overtly."

"Look, Sonny, I know you're a priest and all, but spare me the homily, okay? Who are you to judge? You asked me to get this job for you, and I got it, didn't I?"

"Yes," I said, "and I'm grateful."

"And you said you'd do something for me in return, right?"

I nodded.

"So this is it."

"What?" I asked.

"Keep your mouth shut."

"But Wo," I protested, "they're investing their hard-earned money on the basis of your advice." Thinking of his father, I added, "Money they can't afford to lose."

"Hey, not to worry," he replied, assuming his old air of glib assurance. "Just because I'm a peon in the hierarchy doesn't mean I can't pick stocks. I get my tips from the top. Hell, I've got a better batting average than most of the pros, on paper. And when I get a little capital to work with — man, I'll be out of here! No, listen, that deal last week, that was just an unfortunate screw up. I told Pops it was risky. Nobody bats a thousand." He grinned and shrugged.

"Besides, Sonny" — he returned to a more imploring tone — "it would kill the old man if he knew. Just when we're finally beginning to get our shit together too, you know? I mean, you can't imagine what it was like working for him in that restaurant! I couldn't do anything right, at least as far as he was concerned. I busted balls too. It was *slavery,* man! And then you come along — instantly promoted to A-One Dragon Assistant. Sure it burns my ass. But skip it. He's finally happy now since I've moved out and got this job. He doesn't understand what I'm doing, but at least he doesn't think I'm a total wipeout anymore. I've got my own apartment, and that impresses him. He's never been there of course. It's in the East Village — pretty much a sty, actually. But so what? He thinks I'm making it. So why spoil it for him? Understand what I'm saying?"

I nodded.

"Keep your mouth shut?"

"Yes," I said grudgingly, torn between pity and disapproval, weighing too the feelings of the other members of his family, to whom I felt much closer than I did to him, particularly at that moment.

He heaved a sigh of relief and grinned broadly, almost blithely. "Besides," he said, "I'm in the inside lane for a promo to reporter." He thumbed his lapels and winked. "Black jacket and everything. Come on, or we'll be late."

This disclosure left me with a slightly queasy feeling. At the very least it seemed an inauspicious way to inaugurate my undertaking, christening the journey toward self-knowledge with a lie, though of course the lie was his, not mine. And at that juncture, my thoughts ran more on Wo than on myself. In a moment of not wholly welcome vision, aspects of his character and plight revealed themselves to me, a chain reaction of duplicity proliferating at a dizzy rate, one lie leading to the next, self-compromise to self-compromise, each undertaken in a fruitless attempt to defuse the consequences of his one original self-betrayal and exacerbating them instead. He seemed classically the man in Tao (or *Dow!*) but not *with* it, swimming against the current. I pitied him sincerely, but there was little I could do, except shun his example and vow to learn from his mistakes.

•

No, it was not an auspicious beginning. Nor did I take to the work as naturally as I had at Lo's. This was to be expected, I suppose. But circumstances seemed to conspire against me. I had the bad luck to run up against the same broker several times that first morning, each time bungling the encounter. Among the Aryan hordes of fit, immaculately groomed, brisk-mannered men parading the floor warming up for the "event" the bell would set in motion (the exercise of inherited privilege), this fellow was an oddity, like a member of a different species, and an endangered one at that. In point of fact, this was almost literally the case, since this fellow — "Aaron Kahn," his tag said, "Floor Trader"

— was of the "Jewish persuasion." At the time, however, the intuition of difference I describe was largely subliminal, since I was still at the point where all white faces looked pretty much alike; and of the Jews, those fabulous creatures, my knowledge was sketchy at best, having no scientific basis but derived, such as it was, from mythology. Yes, Kahn was my first Jew.

He had a vaguely lugubrious appearance: a heavy face with sagging jowls, circles underneath his eyes, like a raccoon or a panda bear, two blue poultices of liver. His was the downcast walrus face of someone overweight and permanently depressed. Balding in front, his hair hung in limp curls behind, almost to his collar. Yet his hairline, as it receded, was gradually bringing into view a luminous orb of brow, something monumental, dignified — at least potentially — like an old mountain or the work of a great master lying smothered underneath some contemporary gaucherie. He wore his depression lightly, having broken it in, apparently, to that degree of comfort which even the proverbial hair shirt attains at last, becoming almost like a friend. I don't know quite how to put it, but in his attitude of gloom there was an unmistakable element of self-consciousness, something vaguely parodic, a deadpan glimmer in his eye, if that makes sense, which relieved it, even lent it an equivocal charm.

He sniffled a great deal. His nose was red; his eyes the same, and teary. From time to time he daubed them with his handkerchief, which he withdrew, not from his breast pocket — the spot unanimously designated and approved by his Wasp colleagues — but from the side pocket of his jacket, sewn shut and of a merely ornamental character in the others'. This was stuffed with other odds and ends as well, among them an atomizer of Dristan mist, which he uncorked at frequent intervals and inserted in his proboscis, giving me the opportunity, incidentally, to observe that he wore copper bracelets on his wrists — for bursitis, as I later learned. Appearances to the contrary, however, this man was not a slob, or was a refined one, at least. His clothes were of the finest material and cut, though he had perhaps worn them once too often without benefit of cleaning, so that they had begun to exude a slightly sour smell, rather reassuring in those deserts of cologned asepsis, particularly to my Asiatically indoctrinated nostrils. He had a crumpled elegance, like a corsage worn twice, at the rehearsal dinner and again at the wedding, for purposes of economy. As he would later put it to me in his inimitable way, Kahn expressed in his person the "anal-expulsive sublime" — a concept I am no more able to decoct in words than "Monkey Nature." One either understands immediately, or not at all. At any rate, it was clear that we were made for one another.

When I first caught sight of him, he was eating bonbons from tissue paper he held in his left hand. This was tied at the top with a pink ribbon and bore a seal the color of cloudy silver, the words "Bonwit Teller" printed in burnished roman letters across its surface. From a hole torn in the side, he popped these goodies in his mouth like so much popcorn, his face perfectly bland, showing no emotion whatever, certainly not pleasure. If anything, his expression betokened, at some almost unfathomable remove, a vague anxiety, and, slightly closer to the surface, regret. As I observed him eating, I was struck by his hands, which were quite delicate, with silky excrescences of jet-black hair, better groomed than that on his head, having an almost combed appearance. But there were Band-Aids on almost all his fingertips, and his cuticles, where visible, gave the impression of having been repeatedly gnawed.

"What are you staring at, Confucius?" he twitted, noticing my scrutiny. "Didn't your mother teach you any manners? Or don't you get enough to eat?"

He apparently had not expected me to be so crushed and mortified by this light blow and, repenting his harshness, leaned close confidingly and whispered in my ear, "I can't help myself," a seemly confession, put humbly and with evident sincerity in the best mea culpa style. I wanted to forgive him, and would have, had not a certain indefinable something in his manner convinced me that the whole thing was a spoof.

"Here, have a bonbon," he said, proffering me the tissue, at the same time catapulting another into his mouth from the platform of his thumbnail, as though shooting marbles.

"No?" He shrugged. "I was running low anyway. Damn good though!" he added temptingly. Putting them in his pocket, he stared at me in appraisal. "You know, kid, you remind me of somebody — I can't think who." Waiting for a reaction and not getting one, he shrugged and wandered off, snuffling his nose indifferently, perhaps derisively, I could not tell which. Turning the corner of a trading booth, he vanished into the crowd.

Before long the bell sounded and trading commenced. I was instantly swept up in the great sea of life which I had theretofore merely looked down on from above. The sense of vast perspective, the peculiar nostalgia I'd experienced at my first glimpse of the trading floor, became increasingly vague as I began to fret over personal duties. In my struggle to stay afloat, I found little leisure for abstract theorizing.

Once again, as in my K.P. days with Wu, I found myself at the bottom of the social hierarchy. The runner resides on the lowest rung of the ladder of Exchange personnel. He is always hustling to do the bidding of superiors: reporters, telephone clerks, brokers, specialists (though these last rarely condescend so far from their pinnacles of sublimity as to make use of him, or even to notice his existence). Summarily hied forth by a shouting, red-faced hector the lowly runner is expected to understand his mission by the merest gestures — the frantic waving of a slip of paper before his nose, a convulsive jerk of head and shoulder clamped together over the receiver of a phone (leaving hands free to scribble orders and fondle cups of lukewarm coffee). Into the breach like so much cannon fodder, his is not to question why. And he goes willingly, fired with a sense of duty, as though charged with a high, patriotic trust, though lacking any clear and distinct impression of what that trust might be. Once out of earshot and eyesight, he frantically tries to second-guess his man, inventing strange talismanic ceremonies designed to appease the broker at a distance and immunize the messenger himself from the excoriations of a Mystic Wrath. These generally prove ineffective and a waste of nervous energy, for he continues to be chastised from all quarters at every opportunity.

This, at least, was my experience, on that first morning anyway. It might not have been typical: I'm willing to admit that I was not, perhaps, the most gifted candidate ever to cross that venerable threshold and scud across the floor before the random winds of commerce. Yet even I improved with time. Gradually, with exposure, one begins to develop a sixth sense, a sort of fiscal ESP which enables him to fathom the inscrutable designs of brokers from the thinnest shreds of evidence. This, however, can take days, even weeks! That first morning, as I suggest, I was at sea.

My approach was all wrong, you see. This wasn't entirely my fault either. My training put me at a disadvantage. I was handicapped by a hypertrophied sense of etiquette. Conjured by a broker shaking a bit of paper in my face with wild urgency as though it were Sun Mo Tzu's lost formula of alchemical transmutation, I was unable to countermand the ingrained impulse to bow. By the time I had, someone else had spirited it away to phone booth or teletype. The broker, seeing his number flapping on the annunciator board, was most likely off for some new order, not, however, before giving me a look which damned me categorically, beyond all hope of reprieve, to the forgotten regions of nether hell, populated by those lost souls whose case on earth was classified as "terminally hopeless." These encounters unnerved me, left me anxious and distraught. It happened twice with Kahn, once early on, the second time toward noon. On the first occasion he merely muttered something underneath his breath and turned to someone else; the second time, however, he halted ominously and eyed me with exasperated pity. By that point I was overwhelmed with mortification and chagrin, almost in tears.

"Want some friendly advice, kid?" he asked.

"Master!" I cried impulsively, falling on my knees.

"Hello!" he said in astonishment. Glancing nervously from side to side as though fearful of observation, he leaned over and grasped me by the elbow. "Up! Up!" he said. "Jesus, kid! Where are you from anyway, Kansas?"

"China," I replied.

"China! That's even worse! You aren't one of those boat people are you? Listen, kid, I don't know about back home, but over here it just isn't done. First lesson about Manhattan: never apologize — for *anything. Especially* if you're in the wrong. It's the supreme faux pas. Understand?"

I nodded.

"That's what I was going to tell you before. Know what your problem is? You're too polite. I mean, good manners are one thing, but this is to castrate oneself with good intentions, to coin a phrase. As my uncle, the mad Ashkenazi — without whom I would not be where I am today — used to say: 'No balls, no glory.' So *please* — a little more chutzpah, a little less Oriental Complacency. Otherwise you'll have a short career." He drew his finger across his throat. ". . . One day."

"Help me to amend my faults," I beseeched him humbly, tears of gratitude welling in my eyes. "Teach me this hoo . . . hoo . . . hootspa."

"That's chu . . . chu . . . chutzpah," he gargled from the back of his throat. "Okay, just don't get sentimental about it. If there's one thing I can't stand, it's schmaltz. It's on my Supreme Aversion list, right below gefilte fish." He stared at me with gloomy sympathy. "Here, have a bonbon. It'll calm you down." He reached in his pocket and felt around. "On second thought, take one of these instead. I'm running short. I'll have to stop by Bonwit's on the way home." He handed me something long and thin in a bright wrapper. "I don't like to stoop to this, you know," he informed me gravely, nodding toward his gift — a $100,000 Bar. "But they're okay in a pinch. Listen, kid," he continued, "I'm going to give you another chance." He reached into his pocket and withdrew his wallet, taking out a twenty. "How about going out and getting us some lunch? Bring it to me upstairs in my office, twenty-one oh one. And, ah, kid . . . let me see some change?"

"What would you like?" I asked timidly, having no idea what measures might be necessary to appease an appetite like his, and terrified at the thought of arousing his displeasure.

"Oy!" he cried in exasperation. "Show some initiative! Use your imagination!"

I bowed reflexively, checking myself in mid-motion, and backed away. He sighed and turned back to the trading floor, wheeling about an instant later to call after me, "Only no Whoppers or Italian meatballs!"

From the pay phone in the Members' Lobby I called Lo. "Lo, my whole future is at stake!" I cried breathlessly. "You must help me!"

"What is it?" he shrilly replied, infected by the note of panic in my voice. "You need money?"

"No!" I cried. "*Food!*"

"Food?" He laughed. "No problem. Leave everything to me. How many?"

"Two," I said, "but . . ."

"Excuse please, pick up fifteen minutes."

I had wanted to impress on him the supreme importance of the occasion, the delicacy and discrimination required in filling the order. But it was too late now. Filled with misgivings, I pushed through the door onto the simmering street and started on my way toward Chinatown, moving at a rickshaw dog-trot.

Outside the restaurant beneath the sign which said LUCK FA 'S TEA OY P LACE, like a neon grin missing several teeth, was a chest-high billboard I hadn't seen before, a two-sided tepee of sorts, enticing pedestrians coming from both directions with the Monday Special, A1 DIM SUM TEA LUNCHEON!!!

The foyer, though dimmer than a funeral parlor, as usual, and about as festive, resounded nevertheless with a clatter of dishes and other telltale sounds of conviviality — grunts, laughter, shouting — piped in by circuitous routes from the hidden grottoes in the catacombs.

Lo appeared, towing along the young fish, who had been reelected by default, plus the two cooks, all carrying white paper bags.

"Please forgive this imposition," I said, bowing deeply.

"Excuse please!" he objected, returning my bow with an even deeper one. "No imposition! The young dragon is like family."

"Thank you," I said gratefully, nodding to each of them in turn. "Sounds like you're very busy today."

"No shit!" said the young fish. "It's like a zoo!"

The three gave him stern, silent looks of disapproval, under which he cringed and withdrew into himself.

Lo nodded gravely. "Full."

"Take-out orders too!" I said, pointing to the bags. "Is one of those for me?"

They exchanged looks, then burst into laughter. "All," Lo said.

"All of those for me?" I asked in disbelief. "But, Lo, I have only twenty dollars."

He shook his head. "No problem. On the house."

"I couldn't!"

"You must!"

"No, no!"

"Yes, yes!"

"But how will I carry it all?"

He pointed toward the door. Through the tinted glass I saw a taxi idling at the curb. He flashed me a roguish grin.

"But . . . but . . ."

He waved his hands. "No more objections. We must go back to work."

They started transferring bags into my arms.

"Now this is slivered jellyfish, this one cold sesame noodles . . ." He catalogued eagerly, excited by his own munificence. "Here is the preserved duck, hot and spicy cabbage, thousand-year-old eggs, sliced kidneys in spicy home-style sauce . . . and for the main course, ah!" (he kissed his fingertips) "prepared to rigorous specification from a recipe handed down from the great Ho Ha of the T'ung: Sublime Translation of the Great Bear into Heaven!"

"Lo . . ." I said, breaking in on his rhapsody in a timid whisper, reluctant to dampen his enthusiasm but feeling it necessary under the circumstances, "what exactly is 'Sublime Translation of the Great Bear into Heaven'?"

He stared at me in disbelief. "The young dragon, who has spent so many years acquiring the 'authentic taste,' a paragon among his peers in connoisseurship, has not heard of Sublime Translation of the Great Bear into Heaven, the greatest masterpiece of the greatest chef who ever lived?" He looked almost shocked. Shaking his head, he heaved an exiguous sigh as a commentary on the degraded conditions of modern life, under which even the most promising youths could be reared to manhood in a state of such deplorable ignorance, virtual barbarism. "Paws in broth," he said pathetically.

Recalling the wine, however, he brightened. "A jar of old Mao T'ai," he whispered to me in greedy, conspiratorial tones. "You will appreciate that at least."

I grinned and thanked him nervously.

"And for dessert," he said, warming up again for the finale, "your favorite!"

"Lo!" I protested. "You didn't!"

But he had — fragrant turnip pancakes filled with bits of shrimp and dipped in oyster sauce!

"A banquet fit for the Son of Heaven!" I cried in awe and gratitude.

"Tut, tut," he said, modestly demurring. "The dragon exaggerates." As he spoke, however, he preened himself unconsciously.

"Now go!" he cried shoving me out the door. "Hurry before it gets cold!"

•

Laden down with my cargo, which periodically reshuffled itself — the top bags falling to the floor only to be reinserted at the bottom of the stack, and so on in an arithmetical progression not dissimilar to crop rotation — at last I arrived at 2101, perspiring and out of breath. The name plate on the door, however, gave me pause. Expecting to see "Kahn," I found "Ahasuerus" instead. I hesitated indecisively on the threshold.

"Come in! Come in!" he said impatiently, swinging the door open from within. "What took you so long? I've been waiting thirty seconds."

I teetered into the office, raining bags.

"Jesus, kid," he said, "you plan to feed the whole Exchange, or what? Do I look that fat to you?"

Dropping the whole thing on his desk, I reached in my pocket and handed him the change.

"Change too!" He counted it. "Eighteen dollars! Incredible! What's in there anyway, rolled oats?" He narrowed his eyes and stared at me, nodding approvingly. "You've got promise, kid. What's your name?"

"Sun I," I replied.

"I've got to give it to you, Sonny," he said, confirming beyond all hope of redemption Wo's prior christening — my new Dowist identity — "you may be a little slow on your feet, but executing orders, lunch orders, that is, is a squad boy's most important function, and you seem to have a knack for it. You get high marks, at least with respect to quantity and price. Now, if it's only edible" — he reached for the nearest bag — "this could be the beginning of a long and fruitful association."

"Mr. Kahn, may I ask you a question?"

He paused and looked up, blinking blandly, his arm having disappeared halfway to the elbow in the nearest bag. "Sure, kid, what is it?"

"Ahasuerus — is that your family name?"

He chuckled. "No, no, kid, that's a joke. Actually, he was a famous relative of mine — my uncle."

Though hardly enlightened by this reply, I had no chance to inquire further.

"Hello! What's this?" He took out a piece of jellyfish, sniffing it suspiciously, then removing it to arm's length. He looked up at me with his expressive walrus deadpan, pinching it squeamishly between thumb and forefinger, as with a tweezers. "Chinese antipasto?"

"Pickled jellyfish," I replied.

"Hmm . . . sounds good. Looks like the leftovers from a bris."

"It is!" I cried enthusiastically. "Try some!"

He neighed squeamishly, as though the prospect made him queasy. "I can't even eat *aspic,* kid," he replied mournfully. "Hell, Jell-O gives me the heebie-jeebies. I can't help it. Weak constitution, you see, raised on chicken broth. It's my Hebraic background. I've tried to rise above it, but . . ." (he sighed and shrugged his shoulders fatalistically) "we can't escape our origins. It's fate. The gravity of blood, you know."

"But it's delicious," I protested, "and *very* mild."

"Well," he hedged, "I am rather ravenous." He had the air of an infidel who wants to be converted.

"Go ahead," I encouraged.

"Get me a glass of water," he said, handing me a Styrofoam cup, "just in case. Out in the hall."

When I returned I was astonished to find him laying to with a will, stuffing himself hand over fist, both cheeks bulging. "Na bood," he managed to get out through a full mouth.

I began to assist him, opening bags, cataloguing their contents, tucking his napkin into his collar underneath his chin at his request. Before long he had polished off the appetizers and worked his way to the main course. He patted his lips with a paper napkin, pursing them demurely, then rubbed his hands.

"What's this?" he asked eagerly. "No, don't tell me: stir-fried filigree of fruit bat in ichor, right?"

The witticism flew by me like a misguided missile. "I'm not familiar with that dish," I replied innocently. "But if the ingredients are available, I'm sure my friend Lo could prepare it for you."

"Never mind," he said, blowing his nose loudly in his handkerchief.

"At any rate," I went on, "this particular creation is called Sublime Translation of the Great Bear into Heaven."

"Translation?"

I nodded.

"No," he said, "I mean *translation.*"

"Oh," I replied, "bear paws in broth."

"Good!" he remarked, chewing vigorously. "A little tough, but good."

"It's named for the constellation Ursa Major," I remarked, remembering Scottie's lecture and attempting to quicken his appetite with a little intellectual sauce.

"Entirely bearable!" he said. "Better than usury, in fact!"

Shielded by my ignorance, I was able to conserve a groan.

He pointed with his chopstick. "What's that?"

"The wine!" I cried in dismay. "I'd totally forgotten."

"Wine too!" he remarked. "This gets better all the time!"

I took it out and saw there was a note attached.

"What's that, the bill?" he asked.

"For connoisseurs," it said in Lo's crude script, "the subtlest of wines. Drink deep!" I smiled, my eyes misting over with gratitude for my friend. I read it aloud.

"Let me have some," he said, dumping his water in a plastic potted plant. I poured.

He tested its bouquet. "Hmm . . . interesting." Raising it to his lips, he tossed off a sip. "Jesus!" he cried, spewing it across the desk. "It tastes like bathtub gin!"

"It's an acquired taste," I said, with a touch of hauteur.

"Hu-hu," he mincingly replied. "Aren't we snooty? So where are the egg rolls?" he asked, pushing back from the desk.

"I'm afraid . . ."

"Just kidding, kid. Jesus, don't be so literal! A little more chutzpah."

"Hoo . . . hoo . . ."

"*Chu*tzpah," he said. "Keep trying, you'll get it. So, kid, tell me a little bit about yourself. Make it brief and pithy though, we don't have time to schmooze. When did you arrive, last week sometime?"

I nodded.

"Jesus, you're serious!"

I blinked innocently.

He shook his head. "So what brought you to New York? Don't tell me — the bagels, right?"

"I . . . I . . ."

"Don't stutter, kid. A little more . . ."

"Hootzpah!" I interjected quickly.

He nodded approvingly. "Better."

"I wish to understand the workings of the Dow," I said, returning to his question.

Kahn smiled wryly. "Don't we all. So what else is new? You want to make a quick million and bring Mama and Papa-san over on the *Q.E.* Two, right? Staterooms for all the pigs and chickens?"

"My mother is dead," I replied with dignity. "I've never known my father."

"Sorry, kid," he said. "Nothing personal intended. I see an opening, and . . ." — he shrugged — "I can't help myself. So what do you plan to do with all this putative moola?"

"Moola?" I asked.

"Money."

"I have no interest in making money," I replied.

"Hello!" he said. "No interest in making money! I thought you said you wanted to understand the Dow?"

"I do," I replied. "But not for the purpose of acquiring personal gain. The wealth I seek is of another sort."

"I think I smell an idealist," he remarked drily.

"Idealist?" I asked. "Is that another sect like the Episcopalians?"

"Sort of," he replied.

"I'm not a Christian."

"Neither am I, kid."

"I'm a Taoist."

"And I'm a Jew," he said, mechanically advancing the progression. "Whoa! What? Hello!" he cried suddenly, as what I'd said came home to him. "A *Taoist*? Like *Chinese* Taoism?"

"You know what Taoism is?" I asked, surprised.

"Kid!" he protested. "Look at this face! Do I present the aspect of a total schmo? Regard this parchment." He tapped the glass of a framed document on the wall behind his desk. "See that? Columbia University. Bachelor of Arts. Master's too! This same Kahn whom you now see before you so degraded — or exalted, depending on how you look at it — was once a bona fide member of the academic community. Though my chosen field was lit'ratoor I made an occasional foray across the lines into comparative religion. I know what Taoism is! What I don't know is what business a Taoist, such as you profess to be, has deploying on the floor of the New York Stock Exchange."

"But I told you," I replied. "I wish to understand the workings of the Dow."

"Spell that."

"D-o-w."

"Hello!" he said. "Just as I suspected — a pun!" He pursed his lips, pondering. "Hmm . . . I think I like it. Yes, it's got definite potential as an advertising gimmick — a snapper, as Mark Twain might have said. The Tao within the Dow. What do you think? Maybe we could peddle it to the Exchange for P.R. purposes, to sort of humanize the image. Fifty-fifty. Agreed?"

I shook my head.

"Hey, don't be greedy," he protested. "Sure, the idea is yours, I admit it. But you've got no market. I've got connections in the business, kid. Hell, I was once in advertising myself. That was Phase Two of my career. You see, I was all primed for academia, when . . . ah well, I won't go into that. Suffice it to say, lack of funds. Poor Kahn, a mere nursling in worldly experience, ruthlessly weaned from the institutional pap and forced into the cold real world. Actually, kid, don't let 'em sell you that: it's neither as cold or as real as they make out. Anyway, I did a stint in an advertising agency, from which I was rescued by the seat of my pants, so to speak, by the bequest of my uncle Ahasuerus, the Wandering Jew, whose propensities toward itinerancy I inherited in no small degree."

"*The* Wandering Jew?" I asked, eyes large with awe.

"Well . . ." he hedged, "*a* wandering Jew. At any rate, he left me his seat on the Exchange. Phase Three — or Four, rather — Three being my service to God and country in the OWI. But that's another story."

"So you became a broker?" I asked innocently.

"Kid, please!" he said, drawing himself up with pride and disdain. He thumbed his name tag at me. "I am a floor trader, not a lowly commission slave. I trade independently for my own account. Compared to me, a broker is a mere plebeian." He sighed, deflating to more manageable proportions. "Of course, times are hard. Sometimes I'm reduced to executing the excess orders of the commission house boys. I don't like to stoop to it, of course. But survival takes precedence over dignity, right? You see, floor traders are an endangered species. Actually, I'm one of the last of a dying breed, a lone wolf, so to speak. In the old days, when my uncle Ahasuerus was in his prime, things were different. A floor trader could make a decent living trading eighths and quarters. Besides, he could cheat. No longer! Things have come to a sad pass. We've been systematically hunted down and exterminated. My own particular case is even sadder. You see, though my uncle Ahasuerus made me rich in a single stroke (his stroke), he neglected to provide me with that crucial sine qua non without which the possession of a seat becomes as much a liability as an asset — i.e., cash. I mean, what is a seat without cash? What am I supposed to do, sit in it? It's not even comfortable! One of those grim early American jobs with no cushions, no accessories, no nothing. No self-respecting Jew would be caught dead in one. My predicament, you see, is like that of the old Southern gentry. I'm land poor, or seat poor if you prefer. Though my assets (where my ass sits) are worth close to a quarter of a million, I have to scrounge for money to trade with, at least lately. Reduced to virtual schnorring, kid! It's humiliatin'! My friends cross to the other side of the street when they see me coming. And, as if that weren't bad enough, they're out to get me!"

"Who is?" I asked in alarm.

"You know, the goyim, the SEC — *everybody*. Hell, what with regulations and increased expenses — overhead, clearing fees, transfer taxes, dues — I'm getting eaten alive. It's destroyed my peace of mind. Not to mention my equanimity! See these bags underneath my eyes? I can't sleep nights. They weren't always there, you know. Hell, I wasn't a bad-looking guy before I got into this business. Don't smile! I'm serious. I could get a piece of ass when I wanted to. Now my hair is falling out. I've lost my appetite. Hell, kid, I'm going to pieces. It's this seven-year streak of bad luck that's done it. I don't know how much longer I can take it. I'm serious! At this rate, I've probably only got a few more months to live."

At this point I couldn't repress a smile, which he noticed, switching to a different strategy.

"So you ask the obvious question: Why don't I sell out and get into a more congenial line of work? Yes, I've often asked myself this question. Is it the Protestant Work Ethic, you ask, that detains me? No, kid, Kahn is not a

Protestant. Of course, the Jews have their own endemic version of that delightful institution. It's called guilt. What it boils down to, kid, is simply that Kahn
is afflicted with a masochistic love of the mouth that bites him. It's the call
of the wild, you see. I can't resist it. Never could.

"Hell, kid, all I need is a break, you know? Like a copy of Wednesday's
Wall Street Journal an hour before the market opens Tuesday. Hee, hee! Not
that I care unduly about money, you understand. I'm not materialistic. I only
want to show these Wasps a Jew-boy's got a stinger too." He grasped his crotch
suggestively. "It's the principle of the thing that interests me. Hee, hee! Get
it? Principal? Interest? What can I tell you, kid? Like I said, it's the call of the
wild. The market is the last frontier, a wilderness civilization has created. The
classic struggle for survival. Love it — can't help myself. Always have. So
that's my story, at least the expurgated version." He narrowed his eyes and
scrutinized me thoughtfully. "So you want to get into the Dow as well? A
Taoist no less! Maybe I could give you a little nudge."

"Would you?" I was beside myself with happiness. "That is the pinnacle of
my desires, to become the disciple of so great and deep a student of the Dow
as you!"

"Hold on a minute," he interrupted. "What's this disciple business? Once
again let me remind you, a different protocol is operative over here. We're not
in China."

"But you will teach me?" I asked hopefully. "At least show me how to
begin!"

"What you want to learn cannot be taught," he replied, echoing something
I couldn't quite put my finger on. "Experience is the only way. Of course, in
the beginning I'll keep an eye on you to make sure you don't commit any
obvious blunders in your investments."

"Investments?"

"Sure," he said. "What are we talking about here?"

"But I explained before that I wasn't interested in making money."

"I thought you said you wanted to understand the Dow?"

"I do," I replied, "but . . ."

He shook his head. "Kid," he said in solemn, hieratic tones, "there's only
one way. If you want to understand the Dow, you've got to play the game."

"But that's impossible!" I cried, recoiling. "It would be against my principles. All I desire is objective knowledge. I want to observe without participating."

"Ah-ha," he said, "the academic temperament — I can smell it a mile
away. You want to try the sanitary methods, eh? I don't recommend it, kid.
I think you'll be disappointed." He paused, as though to give me an opportunity to recant. "But everybody's got a right to his own rope. If you're determined to do it the hard way, I'll nose around and see what I can
come up with — providing, that is, you keep supplying me with lunches.
Deal?"

"Oh yes," I agreed. "Absolutely! Thank you!"

"Okay, okay, no schmaltz, all right?"

I folded my hands in my lap and bowed my head.

"Now, I hereby declare this schmooze adjourned! See you on the floor! And remember, kid . . ."

"I know," I cried eagerly. "*Chutzpah!*"

Chapter 7

During the course of the next week or two, I dined nightly with the Ha-p'is. Generally it was just the three of us, Yin-mi, her mother, and myself, Lo being detained at work until quite late. From the very first I felt relaxed around Yin-mi. In her presence a sense of peace welled up in me, its origins utterly mysterious, almost as though it radiated out of her, a benign effluence, an incandescence which her soul shed indiscriminately on everyone around, as prodigal as the sun, imparting to them, in diminished measure, those same qualities of poise and inner stillness which she possessed so greatly, and which, in time, I came to recognize as the filament of her character. Paradoxically, this very sense of peace, whose intensity and depth were incommensurable with any cause I could assign, disquieted me profoundly. Yet it was a delicious unrest and had a quickening effect. Intermittently I felt it thrilling through me like a faint electric shock, a nervous tingle of excitement. Though I dreaded it, I missed it terribly when it was gone, which was when she was.

Mrs. Ha-p'i presented a more mundane, hence tolerable, disturbance. For several days she never relaxed in her attentions, rushing about in a constant fluster, full of smiles, replenishing my teacup after every sip, bringing me things I didn't want. Her unremitting hospitality kept me in a perpetual state of high anxiety, skittish as a bird. I bore up under this barrage as well as I was able, having very little choice in the matter, and realizing, besides, that it was animated by a genuine solicitude in my behalf. Her energy in those first few days was truly admirable, if disspiriting in the extreme to the enemy, among whom I unwillingly numbered myself. She was tireless, unrelenting. I was on the verge of despair. The disease appeared to be chronic and likely to prove fatal — if not to her, to me. Gradually, however, she showed signs of weakening. Reality began to reassert itself. Little efflorescences of charming vulnerability began to sprout in the cracks and fissures which were opening in the concrete wall of her resolve. I was ecstatic. Only then did it occur to me (or rather, I should say, was my wishful surmise confirmed), that there was something slightly disingenuous in her performance, that all this apologetic, ceremonious posturing was undertaken, not out of love, but duty, because etiquette demanded it, that it was not a natural growth. Realizing this, I secretly heaved a sigh of relief and cursed Confucius in my heart for saddling us with such confused, perverted institutions.

I'll never forget the first time she faltered. She had been preparing dinner for us, standing over a hot stove holding a wooden spoon, staring into a column of rising steam at the bottom of which a flounder in garlic-ginger sauce was bubbling to custard, awaiting the critical moment. By signs inscrutable to most, the fish revealed its readiness for sacrifice. (Lo, in explaining the criterion of consistency in this dish, solemnly informed me once that the flounder "winked" at him when it was ready. He refused to elaborate. Several times during my stint at the restaurant I had been caught standing idle, peering into the steamer waiting for the fish to signify, while it stared up at me in glum triumph, refusing all sign. Then one day I was almost sure I saw it. Lo, however, informed me in no uncertain terms that I had been mistaken. Apparently the "authentic" wink is something too quick and subtle to be detected except by those who possess the true *zhen wer*.) At any rate, Mrs. H. — who knew her stuff as well as anyone — rushed to the table with our fish. There was a soggy crunch as the spoon split through the softened backbone, spilling a precious cellule of hot, delicious marrow. Ladling out our portions au jus, she sprinted back and forth fetching side dishes and condiments while Yin-mi and I sat witnessing helplessly. When she'd finally finished, she plopped down heavily in her chair, heaving a huge sigh of fatigue. Her face was red and glowing. With her oven mitt she mopped the perspiration from her forehead, then flung it casually over her shoulder toward the sink.

"Hand me the salt, Sun I." The blessed words escaped somehow through the barbed wire meshes of her censorship, like a carrier pigeon fluttering over the revetments with an olive branch in its beak.

I was so stunned I almost missed my golden opportunity. Yin-mi, however, gave me a timely nudge under the table, and I was up like a flash to retrieve the missing item. By the time I returned, Mrs. H. had recognized her error. She looked up with chagrin, and found us grinning delightedly. I presented the salt to her with effusive ceremony, whereupon Yin-mi burst into laughter. Mrs. H. blushed, hesitated, then joined wholeheartedly in the fun. No more was said about the matter. But after that, subject to brief fits of recidivism, she amended, relapsing into what came to seem to me her characteristic style, which I can only describe as abashed matronly omnipotence. After this I was quickly assimilated, coming to know for the first time the vexing solace of domestic life, becoming for all intents and purposes a bona fide member of the family, which is to say, taken totally for granted. I experienced a happiness unlike any I'd ever known before, and, as I thought then, better.

Sometimes after supper Yin-mi and I would climb up to the roof, where we sat dangling our legs, talking casually, watching the passersby on the street, feeding the pigeons crusts, listening to the well of sighs (which once surprised us with the same sound I'd heard before, the primal lullaby of sex). By these and other means we took casual advantage of those long, gauzy summer twilights, watching the red, bloated sun sink toward the cool, smoke-colored river, disappearing at last behind the dark bluffs of the Palisades into the wilds of Jersey. Something was happening to us which neither she nor I understood — or if we did, only imperfectly. It didn't matter. There was no need for haste. We were contented with the prolonged, lazy dalliance of our relationship, this casual drift toward . . . was it love? At the time I would have vehemently denied it (would have had to, on ideological grounds if no other) had I thought about it, which I didn't. It was enough to follow where the river led; time did not appear to be a factor.

I continued my story by installments, a Chinese *Thousand and One Nights.* And she was my Scheherazade, at least in patience. She endured my telling and even encouraged me to dream beyond it toward the future — so generous hearted, so full of warmth and sympathy (though she could disapprove as well).

The only cloud in the sky, morally speaking, was my enforced reticence on the subject of Wo. On the one or two occasions when Yin-mi inquired about her brother, I found her simple directness of manner, that great solemnity in her eyes, almost unendurable. Each time I was on the point of breaking my promise, but managed to resist the impulse, husbanding Wo's secret, which to my dismay had become mine now as well. Jury-rigging together some feeble device, I put her off. She did not persist. Yet I could tell she wasn't satisfied. That hint of trouble and perplexity appeared in her face, causing me more distress than all the rest.

If Yin-mi let me off the hook, her mother was not about to. Oblivious to my discomfort, Mrs. H. made constant inquiries about her son, feeling, no doubt, quite reasonably, that it was the most natural thing in the world and wholly within her rights. I felt very sorry for her, but this touched a tender nerve, forcing me to lie, or so cunningly to avoid the nub of truth without deliberate falsehood as effectively to lie.

For this and other reasons, Wo and I conscientiously avoided one another at the Exchange, our estimations soured by our partnership in sin. These evasion tactics proved effective there, proceeding by unstated mutual consent. In the differing terrain of 17 Mulberry Street, however, they didn't work so well. Bit by bit, the burden of concealment introduced a subtle constraint in my relations with my adopted family, very small but noticeable, like the cicada which had once disrupted my meditation in the temple — this cicada, conscience. Though still a frequent guest, I began to choose my times and go my own way more often.

•

But while in my domestic situation I was holding more aloof, becoming, in Kahn's phrase, a "lone wolf" of sorts, in my professional capacity the opposite was true. In the market, from the day of our first lunch-hour conversation, I began following at Kahn's heels like a devoted lapdog or a fond disciple (but with as little overt display of "schmaltz" as possible). Aaron Kahn — my new master!

And what a disagreeable one he was! Or at least let on to be. He constantly decried my "Oriental Complacency," exhorting me instead to "chutzpah," the battle cry of Ashkenazi warriors, as he sometimes referred to it. This difficult concept remained largely opaque to me until one day in a flash of insight it revealed itself as the Yiddish counterpart of the Chinese word for "vehemence," the quality ascribed in the Shuo Kua "wing" of the *I Ching* to the trigram *Sun*. As a corollary, Oriental Complacency, which had seemed almost equally as vague, paired itself obligingly with "gentleness." These polarities — gentleness and vehemence — as the reader will remember, constitute the *yin* and *yang* of the *Sun* trigram, which of course is homonymous with my own name. This was the basis for the unfortunate pun which, as I have said, has hounded me remorselessly since birth. Poor name! In an even more befuddled condition than ever since its recent "improvement" at the hands of Wo and Kahn, who had taken it on themselves to translate it from Chinese to English — Taoist to Dowist, so to speak — as Sonny!

The light of this discovery (re: chutzpah) flickered like an uncertain candle in the general darkness of my mind. And the relief was only temporary. Consider the implications! All my life I'd been counseled to act "with the gentleness and penetration your name implies, not the impulsive vehemence which is its darker complement, and which you've given rein to far too often in the past," the master's very words. With my best interests at heart, he and Wu had tirelessly admonished me to mortify my Monkey Nature and cleave to my better lights. Vehemence: chutzpah; gentleness: Oriental Complacency — you begin to see my dilemma. Whereas my former mentors had sought to stifle the former and encourage the latter, my new master, Kahn, coached the reverse. Hello! Candle extinguished!

Yet though Kahn's opinions weighed heavily with me, even he could not balance in the scales against twenty-odd years of training. While severely wrenched and sprained inside, I stuck to my guns. I had no intention of straying from the principles of my upbringing. I would be a Taoist first, a Dowist second — if at all. (But that was the point, wasn't it? I wanted to be both. What's more, I wanted them to be the same. They had to be. "Reality is One, and Tao is Reality." That included Dow, necessarily; in other words, the delta.) Besides, I doubt I could have changed if I had wanted to. If vehemence, or Monkey Nature, through all those long years at the monastery had been a chronic and ineradicable disease, now that it was wanted it was nowhere to be found. I had become as docile as a rabbit! Perhaps the cure was time-released, like Contac capsules, and only beginning to act now. At any rate, it seemed that all the chutzpah had been tutored right out of me in my youth.

But though he constantly complained about my "O.C." (Oriental Complacency) and let on that my dependency imposed on him, his grumbling soon revealed itself as a mode of affection. Ah, Kahn! Secretly I think he was pleased and flattered, being such a loner in that place himself. But he doggedly kept up the facade of distance, even telling me once in exasperation that he was considering turning me over to the World Relief Organization, the refugee arm of the United Nations.

In fact, mention of the U.N. is rather apt. For, acting on my intention to observe without participating, was I not like a neutral observer in the midst of that great battle which commences each day on the floor of the New York Stock Exchange promptly at 10:00 A.M. and rages on till 4:00 when the closing bell (which I could never totally dissociate from the gong of the clepsydra at Ken Kuan) signals the end of another round? Then the combatants retire to more hospitable rounds (of drinks), imbibed together in cool, dim, smoky clubs and bars, where they discuss the day's campaigns. The greatest war games in the world: every man a general, and all the casualties on paper! Like an Elysium of capitalist warriors, where all the armies of the fallen rise to fight again tomorrow, or so it seemed to me with that first heady whiff.

Kahn was like a sort of Jewish Mosby: a will-o'-the-wisp, a demon, popping up out of nowhere when least expected, stopping trains (the Burlington Northern one day, Canadian Pacific the next), robbing banks (Chemical, Chase Manhattan), playing possum at strategic moments when the market wavered, bluffing, masquerading (as himself sometimes, pretending to trade for his own account when he was actually working for another, temporarily a mercenary, only "giving up" the name of his principal when the deal was closed — after the kill, that is). Doggedly I stalked him through the trenches, past the redoubts and demilunes of the eighteen posts, on main floor and garage, into his chosen "crowd." At number two, for instance. . . .

"What's Steel?" he'd carol in his nasal tenor, like a Pavarotti warming up in his greatest role, the lover wooing, transfigured by the joy of his profession.

"Fifty-eight to a quarter," the specialist would retort in his surly baritone (the villain, or the suspicious father).

"Fifty-eight and an eighth for a hundred," Kahn would offer.

A moment of ominous silence, the tension mounting.

Then suddenly, off stage, the pellucid angelus of the soprano, like a crystal vibraphone played with silver mallets, rising above the crowd, announcing, "Take it!"

An acceptance! Sold!

Orchestra, *tutti!* The house explodes in riotous applause. The specialist, reconciled at last, cries out the banns.

The happy lovers plight their troth in a brief lyrical duet expressive of their mutual felicity, not neglecting to mention, as is customary in such courtship rituals, their names, their numbers, and the firms they represent. Kahn at this time "gives up" if not working in his own behalf, like a Paolo to his Francesca, piteously sighing for having thrown away his labors for another.

But in the recondite world of the Exchange, such "matches" are not the only ones. There is the little matter of Rule 72, which states, in essence, that when two bids are simultaneously entered, each equaling or larger than the number of shares being offered at the bid price, the rival bidders flip a coin and the winner of the match takes all. And how Kahn loved a match! I remember the very first I witnessed, which had the unforeseen effect of cementing our relation. In this little scene, the specialist played the croupier, looking on with an indifferent eye, jaded, godlike, handing Kahn his special penny from the waist pocket of his vest.

"What's the matter, William, scared to risk a quarter?" Kahn twitted, an obvious faux pas. The other brokers in the crowd exchanged glances, the specialist peering at him over the rim of his half-spectacles, not deigning a reply.

Kahn didn't care. Full of himself, possessed by his demon, as he sometimes said, he gleefully exhibited his greed, flaunting it in their faces, exultingly defiant. Though I blushed for him, I couldn't help admiring such exuberant bad manners. What chutzpah! What a mensch!

"Come here, little Abraham," he crooned to the coin. Rubbing it between his palms to "warm it up," he began to chant: "Father of the twelve tribes of Israel, this is Aaron calling, son of Ida and Moe. If you're still up there somewhere with your shepherd's crook watching out for us like you're supposed to, look down on your faithless progeny and have mercy. Scatter the enemy! Help me multiply my cattle, chattel, and disposables, not to mention capital! I swear I'll renounce my shegetz ways and marry a nice Jewish girl like Ida said to. . . . What's that?" He cocked his ear and pretended to be listening. "All right, so it's a schmeer! What's nepotism to a Jew? Right, guys?" Smiling ferociously, he looked around at the other brokers in the crowd, all of whom maintained a frigid silence. At such moments Kahn's sense of humor took on a strangely self-destructive cast, almost fanatical. An aura of tragedy surrounded him then, and without his saying it, I knew he couldn't help himself. Such scenes contributed to his ostracism, which in turn supplied new fuel to his underlying desperation.

"Come here, kid," he called over his shoulder, still rubbing. "Blow on this." He extended his palms, pressed together in an attitude of prayer, toward my lips. "Uncle Ahasuerus had a phylactery. But they've gone out of style. I need a luck piece, kid, a four-leaf clover. Maybe you're it."

With that he tossed the coin in the air, far higher than necessary, so that it almost disappeared in the cathedral vault of the Exchange.

"Tails!" the other broker called as it reached its apex and began to plummet downward, pinging on the floor, bouncing off so that the crowd had to scatter to avoid it, spinning on its edge an instant, teetering, then turning over: heads.

I felt a thrill, a tingle shiver through me which I instantly suppressed. Turning to Kahn, whom I'd expected to cry out or jump for joy, I found him instead even more dispassionate than I, staring down mutely at the coin, his expression vacant, almost wistful. He turned to me, twisting the copper brace-let on his wrist.

"That's it," he said. "We've got to stick together, kid. You're my lucky nickel, my rabbit's foot." As I watched him obsessively repeating his nervous gesture, it occurred to me that in the warehouse of his extraordinary personal-ity, among the other items in the inventory, my highly educated friend pos-sessed a streak of superstitiousness as well.

But this scene told me more than that of Kahn. When it was over he was disgusted. He shooed me away and withdrew into himself. Late in the after-noon, when he finally relented and allowed me to approach, I confronted someone I hardly recognized, a different man. Younger looking, more erect, his bearing had taken on an unaccustomed dignity, an intimation of struggle endured and overcome, of suffering transcended. His bleary eyes had cleared and shone with a positively spiritual light, his face transfigured, almost beauti-ful. A hidden nobility had surfaced from the deepest places in his soul. Kahn had become a prince.

What caused this remarkable transformation, I never fully understood, and such light as I was afforded only came much later. After several drinks one night in a bar, he dropped his facade of aloofness and showed me an unmistak-able sign of favor.

"Come on, kid," he said, his speech a little slurred, "let's hit the can." Priest and novice though I was, I recognized in this gesture one of the highest compliments in the masculine vocabulary of comradely affection. (Ah, Wu, you taught me well!)

Kahn slung his arm around my shoulder, steadying himself thereby as well as conferring honor on my person. We got some rude stares, but we were above such mean-spirited aspersions, or beyond them, anyway.

In the tiled bathroom, before the mirrors, under the fluorescent lights, holding our respective schlongs, we released horse-torrents into the gleaming urinals, peering down from time to time to see that everything was proceeding smoothly, or beaming at each other in silent affection, blinking our eyes, feeling under no compulsion to improve the time with speech.

Kahn silently nodded me toward a graffito on the wall.

> To do is to be — Sartre
> To be is to do — Camus
> Scoobie doobie doo — Sinatra

"To be is to suffer, kid," he said without smiling, "if you're a Jew."

"Aaron Kahn," he added wryly, by way of attribution.

But to return to the floor of the Exchange. . . . At the conclusion of a trade, Kahn would hand me the ticket with his name and number and a brief description of the transaction, and I would rush off to the telephone booths to relay the information via the brokerage house back to the customer himself. As I returned, I would watch for the magical materialization of the symbols on the electronic tape flowing like a bluish-purple river, swift and silent above the room, a river filled with little greenish phosphorescent fishes, numerical and alphabetic. It always gave me a tremendous "rush" to see the information thus transferred and, at the speed of light, flashed up on similar screens in brokerage houses all across America. It was as though I had contributed in my own small way to the making of the Averages, to the ebb and flow of Dow.

But as they say in the business, when you've seen one execution, you've pretty much seen them all. Though I profited immensely from such lessons as Kahn gave me on the floor, as I stayed there longer and acquired more of a feel for what was going on, it gradually began to dawn on me that in my quest to understand the Dow, something more would be required.

"Master . . ." I said, approaching Kahn one day.

"All right already! Cut this master shit, okay?" he exploded. "I'm not your master, kid. You're not a slave. This is America, remember? No slaves, no masters. Be a mensch!"

After giving him time to cool down, I continued deferentially. "But surely in the great mystery and art which is the Dow there must be renowned masters . . . sages then," I revised, catching an evil look, "who have penetrated to the truth themselves and so can offer help to others in their quests, just as there are in China in the great religions?"

"Look, kid," he said, taking me aside, "don't take this wrong — I say it for your own good — but you've got to work on your language a little bit. You sound like the Delphic oracle, for Christ's sake! Tone it down! As to your question, it so happens I've been working on something along those lines. I've got a little surprise for you. Got any plans this afternoon at two?"

"I'm working, you know that."

"I spoke to your supervisor," he said with a grin. "You're going to the doctor."

"The doctor?"

"The medicine man!" he informed me cryptically, taking pleasure from my befuddlement.

"But I'm not sick," I protested.

"Jesus, kid, don't be so literal! I'm speaking metaphorically. I mean an *economic* medicine man, someone who purports to explain why the market does what it does. An investment strategist, in other words. Actually, as far as medicine men go, this guy is not exactly avant-garde. Ernie Powers, you might say, is in the vanguard of the rear guard, or old guard as they prefer to think of themselves. He is the foremost living proponent, perhaps the only living proponent, of the Intrinsic Value school — which we might call the antediluvian, or prelapsarian market philosophy — a hard-core Fundamentalist. If you're going to get an education in the market, you may as well start at the beginning. And E. P. is definitely the beginning, a living fossil, atavism of the Prudent Man, a type once famous on the Street but now virtually extinct, a sort of fiduciary Peking Man, if you will. You should identify with that, kid.

At any rate, E. P. — or P. E., as his friends affectionately refer to him — is the chairman of the board and chief executive officer of a small, privately held management firm, Powers and Burden, which handles only the most exclusive clientele, the monied aristocracy, so to speak. I pulled a few strings and managed to get you into the stockholders' meeting this afternoon. You can listen to old Ernie play the bones."

"Thank you, mas- . . . Kahn," I said.

"Don't mention it, kid. Only one thing . . ."

"Yes?"

"Go easy on the O.C. No kowtows, huh? Not everybody is as tolerant as I am. You start pulling that stuff, and these guys'll call the police. I'm not kidding."

I promised, very deferentially, to conform to his wishes in all respects, then retreated as quickly as possible.

As it turned out, the string he had pulled was a rather frayed one. When I arrived, I found a white jacket and black bow tie waiting for me, and I was sneaked in with the catering company and employed serving hors d'oeuvres to the assembled stockholders.

Ernest Powers, Sr., was a tall, fit-looking old man with wispy, snow-white hair as fine as eiderdown and cheeks like two newly burnished apples. He was dignified and affable, but there was something crusty and intransigent in his manner, like one who knows himself to possess a privileged perspective on the truth. A bit of the curmudgeon, in other words, though not a tyrant. He did not appear to be averse to letting others pursue their own strategies, however misguided, if for no other reason than the amusement it afforded him, laughing like an old hand at the consistent folly of mankind. He entered the room familiarly, like a patriarch attending a small family gathering. Along the way he stopped frequently to chat, pressing a hand here and there, inquiring about a husband at home bedridden with gout, or a grandson at Harvard Law. Pausing, he took a piece of rye toast with pâté de foie from the tray I was carrying and, winking, exclaimed, "What, no eggrolls!"

After a few preliminary remarks, the minutes were read and the year's financial statement, prepared no doubt by some suitably Whiggish accountant, handed round, each copy bound in a leather sheath, like a Bible or the menu of a very expensive restaurant. Powers explicated it, elaborating on certain aspects, then opened the floor to questions.

No one raised a hand. Everyone was perfectly contented, perfectly trusting, like a fold of sheep before the shepherd. Powers signaled for a wafer. As I was trotting down the aisle, someone stood up in the rear. "Give us the bottom line, Mr. Powers: how do you account for your success over the years?" The question was asked in a tone of mildly arch appreciation.

A twinkle appeared in the old man's dark blue eyes, which were almost the color of the ocean and no doubt indicated a temperament just as moody. He stood up, leaving me at the base of the podium craning my neck, as though peering up at a high, windy monument.

"Simple, son," he replied. "Stick to fundamentals. Keep a clear head and a strong cash position. And if that's too much to remember, keep the clear head and heave the rest."

There were appreciative chuckles from the audience, composed of men and women who were much like him, but only alloys of the thing he purely was.

"And another thing." His face became severe. "Never speculate!"

"What do you mean by 'speculation,' Mr. Powers? Isn't that what we're paying you to do in our behalf?" the same man asked, taking courage and speaking with more pluck. Except for myself and the other members of the catering crew, he was the youngest person in the room, and he would almost certainly never see the underside of fifty again — not in this life, anyway. Still, he was a youngster in that company and, perhaps to emphasize that fact, was determined to speak for the forces of progress, playing a sort of home team devil's advocate.

"Young man, the fees we charge here are for investing your money, not speculating with it," Powers retorted.

"What's the difference?"

A dark shadow crossed Powers's face, then, mastering himself, he smiled with an air of gentle condescension, as though granting an indulgence to a wayward member of the flock. "Speculation isn't based on Intrinsic Value, investment is," he pontificated.

"Could you elaborate?"

There was an impatient stirring among the other members of the audience.

"Intrinsic Value?" Powers bellowed in distress. "Do you mean to tell me that you're unacquainted with the bedrock of financial theory, the keystone to the arch of sound investment?"

"Why no, Mr. Powers, I don't," the whippersnapper rejoined. "It's simply that I'd like to get it from the horse's mouth, so to speak."

Powers signaled his delight with a high nasal sound, not unlike a whinny. He then ensconced himself on the podium like an occupying army settling in for a long stay. "It's very simple really," he said, "like all great ideas. Intrinsic Value holds that stock prices generally, as measured by the Averages, and in the cases of particular companies as well, are causally related to, and reflect, underlying conditions in the economy. Sounds self-evident, doesn't it? But there are plenty of debunkers, I assure you, who claim that prices fluctuate entirely at random, or perhaps have some design but one which can never be discovered by rational examination. We disagree. We believe there is a reason, and it can be ascertained. Put it this way: The market is a gear in the drive-wheel of America. Its teeth mesh with the cogs of the larger wheel of the economy and are turned by it, the whole thing interlinked rationally like a machine, though specific gear ratios are difficult to calculate." Powers simpered. "According to some skeptics, it's not even obvious which way the motive power is transmitted — from the economy to the market or vice versa. But that's pure balderdash, as any child can see. You can't propel a river with a mill wheel. Yes, over the long haul — note that — the Dow reflects the underlying health or sickness of the economy.

Strong economy: bull market; weak economy: bear market. It can even anticipate the swing by a matter of weeks or months. By the same token, a given
stock's performance reflects the financial health and viability of the company
that issues it. The more solid a company is fundamentally — that is, the higher
its Intrinsic Value — the greater its worth and, in the long run, the higher its
price. This viability can be judged by an astute investor through careful attention to the balance sheet, earnings per share being the single most important,
though far from the only, factor. One must also look at dividends and yields,
assets and liabilities, long-term debt, management quality, market sector, and a
myriad of other factors. And these things in their turn must be considered in the
context of the macrocosm: interest rates, inflation, federal deficit, balance of
trade, GNP, stock and bond yields, construction starts, new orders, inventories,
industrial production, strikes, and so on, not to mention *political* fundamentals,
such as wars, elections, coups. But let's not wax recondite. Personally, I'm a firm
believer in the value of P.E., or the Price/Earnings Ratio — what a stock costs
compared to what it pays, and the lower the better — as a sound indicator of
Intrinsic Value (that is, as long as it's not jimmied around too much by these
'creative accountant' types, such as you see so often today in the cases of
corporate mergers).

"No system is infallible, though. That's why smart investors need professional advice like ours. 'The bottom line, and the line above it' — that's our
motto here. Another reason our service is invaluable is that, though over the
long haul, as I've said, value will out, in the short term all sorts of hocus-pocus
gets thrown in, blurring the outline. Fear and greed, the twin nemeses of the
market, bedazzle the unwary investor with their gorgon stare. . . . Yes, what
is it?"

"Gorgon stare?"

"Well, you know what I mean. They tempt him to speculate, to bet his stake
on illusory value. The man who takes this route is lost. Short term, he may
have limited successes, even brilliant ones, but in the end few prosper by this
mode, be they bulls or bears. This is why a clear head is the paramount
consideration. A speculator is a gambler. He stakes it all on a throw of the dice,
trusting to chance. This is the strategy of desperation, first stage in an irreversible process of moral disintegration which entails, not incidentally, either, but
by necessity, financial ruin in the end. An investor never gambles — and we
are all investors in this room, I dare say, even you, young man, controversial
as you make yourself out to be. You wouldn't be here otherwise. The investor
leaves nothing to chance. His goal is to *conserve capital* and to see it *appreciate.*
Intrinsic Value is the key to this approach. If, as we maintain, there is a reason,
and that reason is Intrinsic Value, then to back that certainty with capital is
not to speculate but to invest in a sure thing. That is the goal of our program.
In the marketplace in the long run, like the action of water over stones, the
ephemeral is leached out and dispersed, and what is solid endures and pros-
pers. Call this Quality, Reality, Truth, what you will — they are all names for
the same thing: Intrinsic Value."

"But in the long run we're all dead anyway, Mr. Powers," the gadfly wryly rejoined.

"Tut, tut," Powers deprecated. "I believe Keynes has priority on that witticism, by several decades, too."

The fellow blushed.

"Look here, young man," Powers continued, "Maynard Keynes was too damn smart for his, yours, mine, and everybody else's own damn good. When it came to implementing socialism, he made Karl Marx himself look like an academic pansy. His policies are directly responsible for the deplorable fix this country is in today, not to mention Great Britain. All this deficit spending, artificial demand stimulation, pump priming, or whatever you care to call it — all government intervention in areas that should be left to market forces to adjudicate. It's all based on fallacious reasoning. It's an attempt to disregard or get around the fundamental law of nature, to conjure the world out of its eternal sequence of cause and effect. It's an attempt to get something for nothing. In other words, it's speculation — a different sort of speculation, granted, but speculation nonetheless. Young man, there is no free lunch." He paused a moment to let this sink in, nibbling a rye toast as he did so. "Every cause produces an effect, and that effect is implicit in and congruent with the cause — is, and must be, even if their congruence is not apparent at first sight. We reap exactly what we sow. Sooner or later, one way or another, you have to pay for what you get. In the East they call it Karma, I believe. Put in another way, there is no ex nihilo creation. What there is, is a way of examining the financial statements of particular companies to discover if they're undervalued or inflated in the marketplace, and investing accordingly. You may have some short-term successes with other methods, as I've said. But if you intend to last, as we have, you'd better get down to basics. There is no magic in this approach, just a lot of damn hard work. But things, the Dow included, behave the way they do for a reason. The world is not arbitrary. The reason is out there and can be ascertained. If you ask me why more people don't ascertain it, it's because they let their emotions get in the way. Remember what I said in the beginning? You've got to keep a clear head."

"Don't forget a strong cash position," someone piped up. There were a few cheers.

"Yes, that too," Powers agreed. "But in the end the clear head's the single most crucial factor. Out there in the jungle of the marketplace it looks like utter chaos. Intrinsic Value is difficult to recognize and sift out from amidst the turmoil and mendacity, the persiflage, the hype. But it's there, believe me. What kind of world would this be if it weren't? Tell me this, young man. Can you imagine a world without Intrinsic Value, a world in which there were no rational discoverable reason for why things behave as they do?"

"I don't think so, Mr. Powers," he replied, chastened.

"Put your mind to it. I think you can."

The fellow fished around a bit, then tentatively suggested, "Do you mean the Third World, Mr. Powers?"

"No."

"I just can't think . . ."

"Oh yes, all of us are familiar with such a world — a world without the redemption of Intrinsic Value — at least by repute, though I sincerely hope that none of us ever has occasion to visit it."

"You mean the Communist bloc, don't you, Mr. Powers?"

"Close, but no cigar. Young man, I mean hell. Where else is the divine justice of cause and effect suspended and everything decreed by fiat, the despotism of pure (that is, impure) chance? Yes, my young friend, a universe without meaning. Purely arbitrary. That is hell. So you see, Intrinsic Value is more than a financial theory, more than a world view even."

The audience jumped to its feet, giving him a standing ovation.

"Could you explain to us then how you've kept your head clear all these years?" the converted sinner humbly petitioned.

"No, son, there isn't any formula for it, though Ben Graham used to claim there was, and to have discovered it himself to boot. Ben was a smart lad with sound principles. His only problem was he lacked a sense of humor, as anyone knows who's tried to read his book. To return to the question though, I'm always ready and willing to discuss business. But I keep my religion private."

•

I emerged from this experience encouraged, if a little bewildered. My mind, whirling with new ideas, was in a state of almost pleasurable confusion. A great deal of Powers's homily had rolled by me "like Huang Ho water off the feathers of a Peking duck," as Kahn would picturesquely phrase it later on examining me for my impressions and discovering the relative paucity thereof. Yet one thing at least remained. Over and over this single phrase kept running through my mind: "There is a reason, and it can be ascertained." I found this highly reassuring. It had an almost talismanic quality for me, like certain Taoist liturgical catenas: "Reality is One, and Tao is Reality." Kahn asseverated that this was because it catered to my particular religious bias, Taoism being inherently teleological. I was quick to put him in his place, however, enjoying, in this one field at least, a superior command of the subject. Taoism had no bias, I categorically informed him. Unscrewing the cap of his pocket atomizer, he took a long, loud snoutful of Dristan Mist, then blew his nose in his handkerchief. This response was somewhat ambiguous I admit, but I was satisfied.

Yet there *were* some remarkable similarities between Taoism and Powers's pet theory. The more I thought about the concept of Intrinsic Value, the more familiar it became, until a startling analogy occurred to me. What, after all, I asked myself, is the substantial being which underlies everyday reality, and at all costs must be discovered, sifted out from the noise and color and panoply — all the manifold distractions of the marketplace? It was Tao, I answered,

> The One within this seething
> Multiplicity, itself
> Immutable and giving
> Rise to all the changes . . .

from the marketplace of the defiled world. But in the other "marketplace" was it not Intrinsic Value? (Strange, too, that the Taoist term for the unredeemed world should coincide precisely with the name of the arena in which the Dow is daily acted out and made incarnate, the marketplace. Another coincidence, like the pun, Tao and Dow? I wondered. . . .)

As great claim as these issues made to my attention, however, they were completely usurped by something else, a seemingly minor consideration, hardly touched on in the lecture. Yet it took sole and undisputed possession of my thoughts. After the meeting I burned with an urgent desire to discover the meaning of the cryptic references Powers had made to "bulls and bears." This was the second time I'd heard these creatures conjured in a similar context. Did they have some symbolic currency in the secular mythology of the stock market? The morning of my hiring I'd been too intimidated to inquire about it from the secretary, but now I was determined to get to the bottom of it. Luckily, the meeting at Powers and Burden adjourned in time for me to make it back to the Exchange before the closing bell. I found Kahn in the Members' Lobby.

"Kahn!" I shouted from across the room, running toward him. "What are bulls and bears?"

Everyone paused and turned to stare. The whole room exploded with laughter.

I planted myself squarely before him, panting like a winded horse.

"Jesus, kid!" he exclaimed. "Take it easy, will you!"

"I have to know!" I cried.

"All right! All right already! It's simple really, nothing to get worked up over. A bear is a guy who speculates on an anticipated fall in prices — a pessimist, in other words. He makes his money on skepticism and disbelief, going short or buying puts. By the same token, a bear market is one that's headed down. Bad times. A bull is the exact opposite — an optimist, who buys in anticipation of an upswing. A long-term bull market is what investors pray for, bears excepted, who prefer to growl and hibernate. It's kind of like *yin* and *yang*, kid. Bull is *yang;* bear is *yin*. Together they make the world go round, and the Dow go up and down. Understand?"

"You mean then," I tentatively posed, "one could say that the bull is the *Dowist* symbol of enlightenment?"

"Yeah, more or less," he conceded.

I walked away like a man in a trance. Over my shoulder I heard Kahn call out, "And, kid — you're making progress on the O.C. problem. It's not exactly chutzpah yet. It still lacks the requisite degree of style and finesse, but you're getting there. Just don't go overboard, okay?"

I wandered out into the sultry afternoon, and found my feet taking me against the flow of traffic down toward the East River. I was in a state of mental overload, virtually stunned, aware only of the ground tone of the city murmuring around me. As I passed out of the shadows into Nassau Street, however, into the warm, honeyed sunlight, catching my first whiff of rank salt air, this mood slipped instantly from me. I felt a little giddy and light-headed, hyperaware of the sensuous texture of the world around me. The sun was mining dazzled silver in the river, which had revealed an unaccustomed tint of blue, like a blush. Its slanted rays struck out medallions and skipped them, Washington-like, across the waves toward Brooklyn, which hovered enveloped in a faint rose-tinted cloud of smog, revealing here and there a touch of summer green. Pigeons gurgled contentedly on ledges above the street. The garbage itself revealed ambiguous beauties.

As I walked, a sweet refrain drifted in and out of consciousness:

> A nightingale warbles in a willow grove beside the stream.
> The sun is mild, a gentle breeze caresses the swaying trees,
>   flipping up the silvered underbellies of the leaves.

What was it from? Over and over it played through my mind, gradually becoming more insistent. So familiar! Yet I couldn't for the life of me remember where it came from, or how the verse continued. As I walked on, I saw a silver airplane rise from the distant runways of La Guardia. Circling in a slow arc above Manhattan, its wings flashed jeweled fire, then it passed directly overhead and disappeared into the sun. Suddenly a dam burst somewhere deep inside me, and the words poured forth:

> Behold the Bull, he cannot hide!
> That swelling chest, that flaring nostril, that steely curve
>   of massive horn,
> What poet could do justice to them?

Yes, it was the third song of *Ten Bulls!* With this realization a fragment of the commentary came back to me: "He trains his ear on the cacophony of ordinary sounds and, suddenly, the clear music of the Source emerges!" Yes, ordinary sounds: the cooing of pigeons, the words of Powers's lecture, the thunderclap of a jet airplane breaking the speed of sound. What difference did it make? "The Tao resides implicitly in common things, like the salt in ocean water, like the binder in a tin of paint. It is the neutral plasma in which the elements of Nature's lifeblood are suspended." Suddenly I remembered my dream: the apparition of those footsteps receding before me, the elusive phantom of my destiny, whose spoor, with the master's help, I had identified but never till this instant seen face to face. Yes, at last it had been granted me — my "First Glimpse of the Bull," symbol of enlightenment not only for Taoists but Dowists as well!

Chapter 8

Though no closer to my father — whom I put off asking Kahn about, filled with some unaccountable misgiving after the disappointment of the phone search, something I avoided articulating, even to myself — at least I was making progress toward my other and somehow, I sensed, related goal of understanding the market. At last! Wasn't the similarity I'd discovered between Tao and Intrinsic Value promising, evidence, albeit circumstantial and inconclusive, of a link between Tao and Dow (the delta, in Yin-mi's clairvoyant phrase)? It certainly seemed so to me.

After P. E. and Intrinsic Value, Kahn said it was imperative that I be served an antidote without delay to "save me," as he put it, "from ossifying in self-complacency." The cure involved exposure to the school of Technical Analysis, whose practitioners are commonly known as Chartists because of their advocacy of, and heavy reliance on, graphs as a predictive tool, plotting, among other things, price and volume fluctuation over time. According to conventional wisdom on the Street, Technical Analysis represents the strategic, and even, in some sense, metaphysical, antithesis of fiduciary Fundamentalism à la Ernie Powers.

As it happened, not long after the meeting at Powers and Burden, Kahn informed me that the International Congress of Consolidated Chartists was in town, holding a convention in an Upper West Side hotel. Though Kahn styled himself an iconoclast, disdaining all "merely theoretical" or "dogmatic" approaches to investment strategy — the so-called sanitary methods — he offered to accompany me on my second expedition, having heard that Clyde Newman, Jr., the rising guru of Technical Analysis, whatever his claims to analytical perspicacity, "put on a damn good show."

"It should provide a few laughs at least," Kahn said, adding, "He's from Topeka, Kansas. That's good enough for me."

That morning, a Friday, Kahn called the hotel from his office and found out that the convention was being conducted as a sort of round-the-clock seminar, with lecturers on the podium continuously from ten in the morning till late at night. Newman was scheduled to speak at six.

"We'll take a cab from work," Kahn said. "My treat."

When the closing bell sounded, I was raring to go. I raced into the street and hailed a cab, practically running it down in my enthusiasm. Kahn followed wheezing after, faking a limp, alternately dropping his briefcase, his umbrella, or his raincoat, then bending down to retrieve them, pausing in the middle of the street to mop the perspiration from his brow and effect a few mysterious chiropractic manipulations in the small of his back before continuing.

As he ducked into the cab and flopped back spread-eagle on the seat, puffing like a beached whale, he told the driver "Bonwit Teller."

I looked at him in surprise.

"I've got to stop off on the way for supplies. Is that all right with you?" he asked in irritation.

"Bonbons, you mean." I pouted with a trace of petulance.

Sensing my disappointment and impatience, he added in more conciliatory tones, "We may need them."

●

Despite the detour, we arrived at the appointed place half an hour early. A lecture was in progress, but the house was almost empty. Those few in attendance were scattered spottily about the floor, some whispering in pairs, some listening, one or two taking notes, a few at the periphery dozing groggily, party hats slightly askew, unshaved faces dropping incrementally toward their chests. Starting awake suddenly, these diehard revelers would stare around disoriented for a moment, then gradually nod off again.

As we seated ourselves, the guard changed and a new lecturer came on, a small man in a dark suit with nervous hands and an expression of conviction that somehow apologized for its own fervor.

He shuffled his papers and blew into the microphone. "No, I'm not Clyde Newman," he said with a timid grin, attempting a joke.

Dead silence.

"Mr. Newman will be on right after I finish," he said, burying his face in his notes. "I won't be long. I promise." From somewhere near the back of the auditorium, the plangent toot of a kazoo. "I'd like to speak to you today about Dow theory . . ." he began.

"Hello!" I thought. "*Dow* theory!"

The rest of the house woke up too. Boos and hisses proliferated. Paper airplanes flew.

The lecturer cleared his throat. ". . . and its relation to Technical Analysis."

Kahn nudged my arm. "Come on, kid," he whispered. "This stuff is prehistoric. We don't have to listen to these second-stringers. Let's take a walk around the block until the main act comes on."

"Hold on, Kahn!" I said. "I want to hear this."

"Ah, youth," he sighed. Folding his arms across his chest, he closed his eyes and reclined in his chair, snoozing as conspicuously as possible.

Despite my predisposition to profit from it, the lecture *was* almost painfully boring. The lecturer did, however, say one or two things which resonated for me. For instance: Charles Dow and his lieutenant at the *Wall Street Journal*, William Hamilton, apparently maintained that the movement of the Dow Averages is like the ebb and flow of the ocean. The primary movement — the long-term momentum of a major bull or bear market — is the tide, within which secondary movements — discernible rallies in bear markets or, conversely, reactions in bull markets that correct excesses in the primary trend without reversing its direction — correspond to waves. Daily fluctuations are the ripples. These Dow and Hamilton dismissed as insignificant. I gathered that this is where Technical Analysis had parted ways with Dow theory. The Chartists maintained that daily fluctuations were the key to everything. But Dow had pioneered the whole concept of plotting price fluctuation in the first place. In attempting to distinguish between the mere backwash of a secondary wave and the ebbing of a primary tide — the moment when the Dow "breaks out" signaling a major turnaround — Dow had been forced to graph daily changes. He had thus, unwittingly, supplied Technical Analysis with its most powerful tool. His interest had been in long-term reversals of momentum, what the lecturer called the Two Hundred Day Moving Average point of view. I tried to ask Kahn exactly what this meant, but he was sound asleep.

"He couldn't see the trees for the forest," the lecturer concluded pithily. "He was like a prehistoric man who has discovered the wheel, but only makes use of it to spin pots. It was left up to us to apply it to the axle of the cart. Still, he was the father of our tribe and deserves to be acknowledged."

A few halfhearted cheers rang out, which the lecturer took as encouragement — mistakenly, as it turned out.

"I believe we're particularly indebted to Dow for giving us the concept of discounting."

"Sit down!" someone cried from the back of the room.

People were filing into the auditorium.

"We want Newman!"

A ground swell started to develop — "New-man! New-man!" — threatening to overwhelm the speaker like a tiny ripple in the midst of a primary movement.

At that moment Newman himself appeared from the wings, a clean-cut, hawk-faced man in a sky-blue suit with a few sequins on the back and the lapels, with a white belt and shoes, looking rather like a country-music star minus the guitar. Smiling, holding his hands above his head for silence (but also, no doubt, to acknowledge the applause), he surveyed the audience with a slightly walleyed stare, which made him look a little bit fanatical.

"We'll cover discounting, brother, and save you the trouble," Newman said, wedging between the lecturer and the lectern.

"In that case, I guess I'm finished," the little man conceded. Gathering his notes in a fluster, he retired, to great jubilation in the peanut gallery. I felt sorry for him.

Kahn, who had by now woken up, leaned over and whispered to me. "Newman's old man was an evangelist for an obscure Midwestern sect — can't recall the name. You know the type, though, one of those groups that splinter off on the basis of some doctrinal quibble. I think the article I read said they believe grape juice is really transubstantiated into wine, emphasize good works, and deny innate depravity in the elect. I only mention it because Clyde Junior grew up in the revival tent and has a reputation for the proselytizing style. Can't help himself, I imagine, evangelism in the blood."

"What is evangelism?" I asked.

"Evangelism?" Kahn leaned back and thought. "Evangelism is that peculiarly American institution in which the national talents for salesmanship and righteousness are so felicitously combined."

Newman then started to speak, beginning by cataloguing his contributions to the field of creative charting and citing several new "formations" he thought should be added to the standard list by point-and-figure enthusiasts. Along with Head and Shoulders, Double Top, Rectangle, Diamond, Rising Wedge, Flag, Pennant, Scallop and Saucer, Exhaustion Gap, Momentum Gap, Island Reversal, Trend Line, Spiral, Whirligig, and Complex Top — ho-hum stuff, the meat and potatoes of the Technician's existence — Newman pointed out some more esoteric configurations which he'd discovered and christened in a characteristic manner. There was the Calvary Cross, for which he cherished a particular fondness. The Latin Cross, he said, indicated too much passion in the marketplace, leading to speculative excesses. The Archepiscopal Cross indicated concerted action on the part of the cartel of powerful Anglican bishops, under the direction of the Most Reverend and Right Honorable Archbishop of Canterbury; the Greek and Jerusalem Crosses indicated ethnic interest in the market on the part of the indicated constituencies. The Chi-Rho, he alleged, foretold a rally in pharmaceuticals. The Tau Cross was particularly bullish. Finally there was the Maltese Cross, which he claimed foreshadowed the entry of unscrupulous elements into the marketplace, bent on manipulation (here he alluded darkly to Cosa Nostra involvement).

"What do you say, kid?" Kahn whispered, leaning toward me. "I begin to detect a certain pattern in his patterns."

And it was true. Though Newman was "objective as a scientist," as he said himself, it was remarkable to see how his discoveries paralleled his personal preoccupations. Newman's charts were emblazoned with the mystic handwriting of his god, and he expounded them to us like some Daniel to a nervous convention of trembling Belshazzars.

At this point, Newman opened the floor to questions. Someone stood up and asked how a particular chart formation could be related to such specific effects in the marketplace.

"Let me understand you, friend," Newman began. "You are asking me 'the reason'?"

There were snickers from a few of the more hard-core Technicians in the room.

The man nodded innocently.

"Let me reply to your question with a question," Newman said with a rhetorical flourish. He paused for effect, then thundered, "Do you believe in the Lord?" As he shouted this, he slapped his hand flat on his pile of lecture notes and leaned far out over the lectern, his walleyes scintillating with fervor, as though inclined to immediate predation.

The questioner looked around like a drowning man searching for a hand to pull him from the water. Those in the vicinity shifted nervously in their seats and avoided his eyes. The kazoos maintained an ominous silence.

"Well, yes, I suppose so," he conceded reluctantly, finding no avenue of honorable withdrawal open to him.

"Good!" said Newman, slapping his notes again and standing upright. "Now, let me ask you if you always understand the Almighty's designs in each and every circumstance of daily life — say, the sudden death of a dearly beloved spouse, or, again, a little child plucked untimely in the spring of his or her young life?"

This obviously touched a personal chord in the questioner. Lowering his eyes to the floor, he sniffled and replied in a contrite voice that seemed on the verge of breaking, "No, I can't understand that kind of thing. I must admit, at times it makes me think He's cruel, or even . . . perhaps . . . doesn't exist at all."

"But you have faith?"

The man hesitated, coughed into his hand. "Yes," he replied grudgingly.

"Praise the Lord!" Newman cried reflexively, bridling himself immediately to resume his Socratic duties.

"And isn't it true, brother, that in spite of the inscrutability of the Lord's designs, deep in your heart you know your duty, what you are called to do as you go about the difficult business of living, bearing your cross every day?"

"I suppose," he said.

"Hallelujah!" Newman cried. "Now do you understand?"

"Frankly, no," the man replied. "I don't."

"Well, that's all right, brother," Newman said. "Don't be discouraged. I'll try and help you see the light. You see," he began, "what I'm pursuing here is an analogy between the attitudes of the True Believer to his God and that of the Technical Analyst to the market, or, more properly, to the Dow. The Believer, while not always understanding the ways of the Lord, which may seem harsh and unreasonable at times, if not downright premeditatedly malicious, *nevertheless* has faith that there *is* . . ." — his voice rose, placing a singing emphasis on this word — "a purpose which *is* being fulfilled, that the Lord *has* a reason for what he does, and that everything we do and suffer, no matter how great or trivial it appears to our purblind organs of vision, is ordained by him for our own ultimate benefit, part of the Master Plan by which our Savior, Jesus Christ, the Divine Architect, will one day build his Heavenly Jerusalem on this perishable earth! Not a sparrow falls, brothers, but that our Heavenly Father sees it and approves!

"Through a study of the sacred documents of the Christian faith, the New Testament in particular, the Believer, following the example of Jesus and his disciples, puts himself into accord with the Plan, even if he doesn't fully understand what it is. In the same way, the Technician, though never for a moment claiming to understand what makes the Dow do what it does — the *reason*, that is — nevertheless, by a diligent application to the scriptures of his religion — i.e., the charts — can extrapolate from past permutations of the Average rules of conduct which will prepare him for the future. It's all a question of faith, brothers. We may not be able to penetrate the sublime mystery of the Dow, any more than the mind of God, but does it really matter? By studying the charts we can put ourselves into accord with its overarching purpose, distilling a practical 'market morality' which will fructify in profits."

"Praise the Lord!" someone shouted.

"Tell it, brother!" Newman responded.

At this point, he took another question from the floor. A young boy, seventeen or eighteen at the oldest, with several recently excavated pimples and a throbbing Adam's apple which balanced on his current of words like a Ping-Pong ball on a jet of water, raised his hand and stood up. "I think I understand you, Mr. Newman," he began. "Only I still don't see how you can dismiss fundamental factors so categorically. Are you claiming that on the basis of looking at the day-to-day fluctuations of a given stock on a piece of graph paper you can somehow divine the underlying financial health of the company concerned?"

"Ah," said Newman, smiling and clasping his hands in a pious attitude. "I see we have a Doubting Thomas in our midst. Young man," he said, leaning out over the podium again, "the 'underlying financial health of the company concerned' — that is, its putative 'Intrinsic Value' — is completely irrelevant. An investor doesn't even need to know the *name* of a company to decide whether to invest in it, though that information is helpful when placing an order with your broker." He simpered. "All he needs are his charts.

"Ah ha! The idea rankles — I can tell by your expression. You balk at it. Son, this is the Gethsemane of every Chartist, the supreme test of faith. I'm very glad you asked this question, for it leads to a consideration of the idea broached by my very worthy predecessor on this podium today. You see, it is the firm belief of every orthodox Technician that the Dow itself, the Mother Index, saves us the trouble of keeping abreast of all the manifold details which the Fundamentalists worry over, too many finally to be collated, each with its appropriate weight and emphasis in the equation, by an organ as fallible and inefficient as the human brain, which, after all, wondrous as it is in some respects, is heir to the corruption inherent in all flesh. And yet, due to the mercy of the Lord, who in his infinite compassion has given man the Dow, this intolerable burden has been lifted from our shoulders. Son, *everything is discounted in the Dow.* Now in case you haven't heard that word before, take heed. 'Discounting' is the central tenet of our faith. . . . All right, what is it?" he asked irritably.

His "worthy predecessor," no doubt encouraged by that flattering reference to himself, was bouncing up and down in his chair, waving his notes in the air in his anxiety to enrich the discussion with some worthy tidbit of information. "I have a quote here from William Hamilton which I think will make the whole thing crystal clear," he said eagerly. "May I read it?"

Newman seemed about to demur, when a short arpeggio from the kazoo section in the gallery, *fortissimo e apassionato,* deterred him. Casting a wrathful glare in that direction, he sanctioned the speaker's interruption with a nod, inflicting it as a penance of his refractory flock.

"Hamilton said," the little man began, " 'The weakness of every other method' of investment strategy 'is that extraneous matters are taken in from their tempting relevance. But it must be obvious that the Averages have already taken these things,' i.e., fundamentals, 'into account, just as a barometer considers everything which affects the weather. The price movement represents the aggregate knowledge of coming events. The market represents everything everybody knows, hopes, believes, anticipates . . .' and, if I may interpolate a passage here from Gerald Loeb, 'the hopes and fears of humanity, . . . greed, ambition, acts of God, invention, financial stress and strain, weather, discovery, fashion, and numberless other causes impossible to be listed without omission . . . with all that knowledge sifted down to . . . the bloodless verdict of the marketplace.' "

"That says it very well," Newman said. "Thank you. You see, son, everything from business inventories to the president's vital signs are absorbed in and reflected by the Dow. It's a collective measure of all the manifold factors which make up the financial condition of this country. A barometer — that's precisely what it is, and not only of financial America, but the nation as a whole. Since the financial is related to everything else, it would not be overweening, I believe, to posit the Dow as the single most critical measurement of the 'state of the Union' of these United States, economically, politically, morally, however you care to view it, at any given moment in time. Son, the Dow is the pulse of America. You are still skeptical, I see. You will say that I am going too far, that I have contradicted myself, that I am out-fundamentalizing the Fundamentalists, who even in their most stiff-necked and uncircumcised worldly arrogance would never claim such universal currency for the Dow, feeling, perhaps, as you do yourself, that a financial index can have no conceivable purchase on matters outside finance. But, remember: everything is discounted. *Everything.* The Dow, like God, is omniscient. That is our faith. I make no claim to understanding how this is so but limit myself to a simple statement of fact, empirically derived. . . .

"Which brings me to the main point of my talk today. Brothers, I have chosen this occasion to unveil a new and wonderful indicator, which I humbly submit will be of great interest to you and your children after you unto the furthest generations. I have christened it the Newman Per Capita Pew Oscillator. Brothers, we have all heard a great deal about how hard times — recession, depression, war, plague, famine, and whatnot — are bullish for religion. Many of you, perhaps, have accepted this assertion uncritically, as I did for many years. But now I have seen the light. Brothers, isn't it clear that this old axiom is blasphemous, a slur on the name of our Redeemer, Jesus Christ? And who had really taken a hard look at the data with an objective, dispassionate eye? No one, I submit, until I took that task humbly on myself for the greater glorification of the Lord. And now, after months of study and research, our team has come up with the gratifying conclusion that there is a *positive* correlation between church attendance in this country and the strength of the Dow Jones Industrial Average. In a study of the last twenty years, I have found a marked and consistent overlapping of HPO — High Pew Occupancy — with the duration of bull markets. Conversely, in periods of religious inclemency, when statistically significant portions of the population have turned their faces away from the radiant smile of our Redeemer, the strength of the market — as measured not only by the Dow but by market breadth, advance/declines, new highs/new lows, and, most significantly, short selling (which shows a consistent inverse correlation with HPO) — has been undermined.

"Now what does all this mean to us as investors? Brothers, I am telling you that religion is good business. Not only Merrill Lynch, but Jesus Christ himself is bullish on America! It behooves us, then, to repent with all due haste. Each and every righteous Christian soldier should put his house in order and spare no pains in converting the heathen, urging his refractory brothers and sisters to reenter the fold before it's too late, not only for the sake of his or her soul, but for the sake of increased profits for you and me!"

"Praise the Lord!" rang out antiphonally around the auditorium.

"I tell you, brothers, some of you might have disbelieved my earlier assertions in the Newman 'Good News' Market Letter that the Dow would one day soon stand at a level undreamt by even the raging bulls of our profession. 'A prophet is not without honor but in his own country, and among his own kin, and in his own house' (Mark six, verse four). Great God Almighty, people! Can you imagine the rally that would ensue should Jesus Christ fulfill his promise to return to earth at the turn of the millennium *as has been prophesied,* not only by me but other respectable persons with impeccable credentials and good track records? Yes, brothers, I have seen the indicators! The day is at hand! Repent! Be ready, for he cometh like a thief in the night. Behold, if I could tell you what my eyes have seen gazing down the corridor of time into the not-too-distant future! Brothers, I am moved to prophesy, to testify and speak in tongues! I see a better day ahead when the labors of the faithful will be rewarded, not with that treasure which moth and rust doth corrupt either, but heavenly tender, which inflation cannot devalue — coin of the realm! As I gaze down that dark corridor and train my ears on what will be, I see bright angels dancing on the floor of the Exchange, I hear joyful hosannas of praise and thanksgiving reverberating in the rafters, rather than the weeping and gnashing of teeth that now rise from that den of iniquity, that combined Sodom and Gomorrah, that hell on earth!"

The kazoos brayed forth like trumpets in clarion tones. The entire audience was in a state of violent agitation, moaning, weeping, thrashing in their seats. Some even rolled in the aisles, foaming at the mouth, their eyes turned up in their heads. An exhilarating force electrified the crowd, touching even Kahn and me with tremors of vicarious ecstasy.

"Maybe we'd better leave," Kahn whispered with a look of exaggerated concern, "before they take it into their heads to 'save' us. We're both heathens here, you know. Speaking for myself, I've escaped baptism so far; I plan to continue to as long as possible. Besides," he added wryly, "I don't know how to swim."

In a daze myself, I let him lead me out.

Chapter 9

"Jesus, could I use a drink! How about you, kid? . . . Kid?"

I was still mildly stunned.

"What, hungry?" Kahn ventured.

"Sort of," I replied.

"Come on then, let's nosh. I heard there's a new French restaurant on Columbus Avenue just above the Circle. I'll buy you dinner."

I mumbled my thanks in a preoccupied tone, sincere but absent, still trying to distill a liquid pearl of clear significance from the heady ferment Newman's lecture had set effervescing in my mind. I followed at Kahn's heels, tame and distracted.

The maître d's lectern stood unguarded at our approach. Through a lattice which partially screened the entrance to the dining room, we saw him standing near the kitchen door talking to a group of waiters. The setting was more elegant than anything I'd seen. A large crystal chandelier hung in the center of the room, and tall white candles in gilt-brass sconces sat on all the tables, throwing dancing highlights up into the prisms of the lusters. These were touched too with green from a small oasis thick with fern and bamboo planted in an island just below it. Down the slick black face of a lichen-covered stone, a sweat of cold, clear water seeped and oozed, coalescing in a rill which purled the length of the garden through a narrow channel in a bed of fine white sand.

Catching sight of us, the maître d' frowned and left off in mid-sentence, hurrying toward his post.

Only then, with that frown, did it occur to me how bedraggled we looked. Kahn had long since shucked his jacket and now carried it draped over his arm. He'd rolled his shirt-sleeves to the elbow, opened his collar, and slipped his tie knot down as far as the second button. His formidable five o'clock shadow was now improved by some three hours. And I was not exactly *bon ton* either in tennis shoes and my blue smock.

"Messieurs?" the man said, with a small, perfunctory nod of supercilious deference. Straightening, he eyed us without enthusiasm.

"A table for two," Kahn said.

"Monsieur has a reservation?"

"A reservation!" Kahn asked incredulously. "What for?" He pointed over the fellow's shoulder. "Look — there are two, three, four, *five* empty tables I can see from here."

He clicked his tongue sympathetically. "I am afraid all these are reserved, monsieur."

"Don't give me that," Kahn snapped.

Like a schoolmaster or a conductor, using his sleek gold pen as a baton, he tapped a small sign on the lectern: "Reservations Only."

"All right, so we'll make a reservation," Kahn said, turning to me with a shrug.

The maître d' bowed and skipped behind the lectern with a small hop-step like a sparrow. "For what time, monsieur?" he asked, flipping open the book.

"What time is it now?" Kahn asked.

He lifted his wrist and deftly pushed back his sleeve with two fingers. "Seven forty-five, monsieur."

"Okay," Kahn said, "make it seven forty-six. I want to go to the can and wash up." He winked at me and grinned.

"Oh la, monsieur!" he chided, tossing his pen down on the opened page and slapping the ledger shut. "Nothing before e-le-*van!*" He clucked his tongue disapprovingly.

"What is this anyway, a private club?" Kahn cracked irately.

The maître d' stiffened with dignity. "We reserve the right to refuse seating to whom we choose, monsieur."

"Yeah, especially Chinks and Jews, right?" He turned to me. "Come on, kid. I know a place close by where they'll be glad to take our money."

As we retreated, he suddenly turned back on his heel. "Hey, monsieur," he called. "You look familiar. Haven't I seen you around someplace?"

The maître d' shrugged. "I have worked many places both in Paris and New York, most recently at *La Fleur de Lys.*"

Kahn shrugged as though to signify it didn't register. "My mistake," he said. "I thought it was Vichy — the ovens. See you later, Pétain."

On the way out he said, "Wish I didn't love the food so much. It's too damn good for them."

"For whom?" I asked.

"The French."

Kahn was not particularly familiar with the neighborhood, so we ended up in an Irish pub farther uptown on Amsterdam. The place was dingy and saturnine, with dim lighting, sawdust scattered over the floor, a smell of dregs and yeasty piss, and a few obsolete trout-fishing implements arranged awkwardly on the wall, all faded to the dead mahogany tone of the panel.

"This is better, isn't it?" Kahn said unconvincingly. "A little local color?"

We flopped down heavily in a booth. I was thankful simply to be off my feet. Wiping his hands on a soiled half-apron, a young man in his middle twenties sauntered toward us from the far end of the bar where he was watching a boxing match on television with an older companion. He was wearing a baseball underjersey with blue three-quarter sleeves, slipped up on his forearms, and down-at-heel running shoes. He walked with a kind of jounce, like a sailor, so that his thick head of loose red curls flattened and rose with every stride.

"Evening gents," he said, surprising us with a brogue. He swabbed the table with a rag. "What can I get far ya?"

"What do you say, kid?" Kahn asked.

"Best Stoat in New Yark," he offered. "The real article. My uncle Mick there" (he indicated the stunned block of flesh sitting anesthetized before the television watching two black bantams peck and sting each other, their grunts vaguely audible, floating to us across the bar) "he's a real artist. Takes six minutes to draw a pint. A head like cream, and so thick and dark you almost need a knife and fark to partake of it. A meal in itself. Quite satisfyin'. I never seen one to beat him, even back in Belfast where I lived."

Kahn seemed unimpressed. "I guess you ferment your own hops right here on the premises and everything?" he said, with an inconspicuous sniff.

The waiter missed the olfactory innuendo. "I wouldn't go so far as that," he said. "But it's prime stuff, I will say that."

"Let me have a Dry Sack," Kahn ordered.

"One Dry Sack." he echoed, jotting it down.

"On the rocks."

"On the rocks." He made a flourish on his ticket book and stabbed a period. "Coming up!"

"With milk," Kahn added.

The waiter gave him an odd look. "With *milk*?"

Kahn smiled sheepishly and put his palm gingerly on his belly. "Dyspepsia, you know," he explained. "Chronic."

"Too bad!" the waiter said. "How about a Pepto-Bismol on the side, as a chaser? Sart of like a digestive bilermaker."

"That's funny," said Kahn with a look of persecution.

"And the other gentleman?"

"I'm still hungry," I said to Kahn.

"Sorry, kid, I forgot." He turned to the waiter. "What's to nosh?"

"Nosh?"

"You know, hors d'oeuvres?"

"Well," he said, "Uncle Mick makes good onion sandwiches."

Kahn cringed as though about to neigh. "Just bring us some crackers."

"And to drink?"

"I don't know," I said. "I . . ."

"Bring him a Dry Sack too," Kahn said. "You'll like it, kid. It's sweet like that Chinese stuff you drink."

"With milk?" the waiter asked. "Or without?"

"Without," Kahn replied, narrowing his eyes.

The waiter started off.

"And don't forget the crackers," Kahn called, adding under his breath, "cracker. 'You almost need a knife and fark to partake of it,' " he mimicked. "I'll say. To cut the smarm. What would you think, kid, if I grew earlocks and a beard, strapped a change purse to my belt, and went around like Shylock, spouting Yiddish aphorisms in a thick accent and occasionally whipping out the old Jew's harp for a musical number on revenge — 'An oy for an oy!' " He darted a look in the direction the waiter had retreated. "The bugger. Did you catch his expression? Belfast. . . . I bet he's in the IRA. On the lam with Uncle Mick in New York City." He pronounced this phrase ironically, like an old movie title.

"What's the matter, Kahn?" I asked, surprised by the unusual vehemence in his tone.

He sighed and slumped back in the booth, rubbing his temples. "It's my sinuses, kid," he said. "They're acting up on me. All this dust. It really gets me. Right here behind my eyes — this continual, unremitting low-grade pain."

"I'm sorry," I sympathized.

The waiter reappeared and served our drinks, tossing down a basket with a paper napkin in it, over which was spread a quantity of loose Captain's Wafers.

"Got any aspirin?" Kahn asked.

"I'll see," he replied.

"L'chayim," Kahn toasted, raising his glass. Taking a long sip, he sighed.

"Kan pei!" I replied, sampling. "That's good. What's it called again?"

"Dry Sack."

"Ummm." I licked the residue from my upper lip. "Delicious!"

The waiter returned and put down an aspirin tablet on the table at Kahn's elbow.

"What's this?" Kahn asked incredulously. "I need three at least. I'm suffering," he added, with an anguished look.

"It'll cost you," the waiter said.

"How much?" Kahn asked, sitting up alertly.

"Twenty-five cents apiece."

"Five for a dollar," Kahn bid.

The waiter reached for the bottle underneath his apron. At the same time, Kahn slouched down for better access to his own pants pocket and drew out a crumpled bill, which he smoothed out on the table and edged across, keeping his hand flattened over it like a vigilant paperweight.

The waiter shook out the tablets one at a time, then snapped the lid back and reached for the money.

"Hey, that's only four!" Kahn accused, retracting his hand defensively.

"I gave you one already," the waiter pointed out. "That makes five."

"I thought that one was on the house," Kahn protested.

"That's what you get far thinkin'," the waiter replied, smiling grimly.

"Jesus, kid, do you believe this guy?"

"No need to bring the Savyar into it," the waiter chided.

In no position to arbitrate, I kept silent, taking it all in.

"But look," Kahn argued. "Five doesn't help me. I need six. Three for now; three for later."

"Another quarter."

Kahn sighed with exasperation and fished out a coin, skipping it across the table.

The waiter scooped it deftly as it dropped off the edge. Uncapping the bottle, he took out another tablet and, skipping it similarly, retreated.

"Have some crackers," Kahn said, pushing the basket toward me. Throwing back his head, he popped the aspirins one at a time, sipping his drink between each.

I took a bite, then let my jaw go slack in mid-chew, putting down the unfinished portion on the table. The crackers were stale, almost soggy.

"Come on, kid, eat up," he said. "I thought you said you were hungry." Picking up one himself, he took a bite and spat out the contents in the sawdust.

The waiter looked around. Kahn motioned him over with a jerk of his head.

"Another round, gents?"

Kahn looked up at him, shrugging his shoulders, palms upturned — a gesture of ironic capitulation, part appeal, part accusation. "So what are these, matzos?" he asked. "Here's a fin." He took out a five-dollar bill. "Go across the street if you have to. But for Christ's sake, bring us some saltines!"

The waiter took the money and was back in two minutes.

"Thank you," Kahn said, with exaggerated courtesy. "Sholem. Sholem aleichem. Now bring us another round and we'll be happy.

"So, kid," he continued, tearing off the end of the box, doling us out a packet apiece, "what did you think of Newman? Quite a show, eh?"

"Fascinating," I replied, taking another sip of my drink of which I was becoming fonder by the minute, "only . . ."

"Only?"

I sighed. "Only I'm more confused now than I was before."

"Good," he said. "That's promising. It's got to get worse before it gets better."

"The thing that gets me is that they seem totally irreconcilable," I continued, thinking aloud.

"What does?"

"Intrinsic Value and Technical Analysis."

"So what else is new?" he remarked cynically.

"On the one hand, Powers says an astute investor must pick through the balance sheet with a fine-tooth comb — sales, earnings, assets, liabilities . . . 'the bottom line and the line above it'; whereas, according to Newman, one doesn't even need to know a company's name to know whether or not to buy. Only the charts are relevant."

"But remember, kid," Kahn cautioned, "they're looking at the problem from very different perspectives. The Fundamentalists are interested in the long haul, growth and income. The Technicians are basically traders, interested in capital gains, quick profits made from daily price fluctuation. They don't categorically deny the importance of Fundamental factors, they just maintain that they're banal. Whatever causative effect they have on daily fluctuations has already been discounted. Something else plays the decisive role. What that something is, they don't say — some ghostly, all-pervading, godlike ether which manifests itself in the repeating wave patterns on their charts, hypothetically appealing, but practically undiscoverable."

" 'If one looks for it, there is nothing solid to see; if one listens for it, there is nothing loud enough to hear. Yet if one uses it, it is inexhaustible,' " I recited musingly.

"Right, kid," Kahn said carelessly, hardly attending, "that's the general idea."

"That's a quote," I told him, "from the *Tao Te Ching.* 'It' is Tao."

"Hmm," Kahn said, taking another sip of his drink. "They sound pretty similar, don't they? Interesting coincidence."

"I think perhaps it's more than that," I replied, serving up the dish that I'd been stewing mentally on the way. "I think Technical Analysis and Taoism share some very fundamental assumptions."

"Such as?"

"Well," I began, "in his lecture on Intrinsic Value, Ernie Powers summed up his position with the statement: 'There is a reason, and it can be ascertained.' I was thinking about it while we walked, and it seems to me that Newman's position can be similarly reduced."

"Oh yeah? So what's the Weltanschauung of Technical Analysis?"

" 'There is a reason, but we can never know it,' " I ventured.

He pursed his lips and nodded. "Okay, I'll grant that . . . as far as it goes. Only add this: though we can never know it, we can *use* it."

"Right," I agreed.

"In other words, ontologically they're identical, insofar as what they allow exists," he said. "Epistemologically, however, insofar as what they allow we can know, they're irreconcilable."

"I'm not sure I understand those words," I said, "but anyway, I think this assumption bears a striking resemblance to that which underlies the *I Ching.* "

He nodded for me to proceed.

"Though the Tao, like the Dow, is alleged to be inaccessible to the intellect, its disposition can be fathomed through the agency of the *Changes,* as can the Dow through the charts, and once fathomed, used. From what I was able to tell, the entire philosophy of Technical Analysis would not be too grossly misrepresented by this quote from the *Tao Te Ching:*

> . . . by seizing on the Way that was,
> You can ride the things that are now.

For to know what once there was, in the Beginning,
That is called the essence of the Way."

I paused, allowing Kahn a chance to comment. Whether it was the mellowing effect of the alcohol, I don't know, but for once he was passive, yielding to my initiative.

"This ties in with the idea of 'discounting,' " I continued. "Though the word is new to me, the idea is familiar. The ability of the *I Ching* to predict the future is based on a similar concept of discounting, only incomparably more vast."

"Come on, you don't mean to tell me you believe that old hocus-pocus about the *I Ching* telling fortunes, do you?" Kahn asked, perking up. "I always thought the *Changes* was more a sort of spiritual guidebook. It can't really predict the future, can it?"

"Oh yes," I replied earnestly. "I've seen it do so many times."

"Hello! No kidding! You actually believe that?"

I nodded.

He slumped back in his chair, his eyes a little glassy with surmise.

"Just as the Dow is 'omniscient,' " I went on, "that is, is affected by and thus reflects conditions far outside the narrow confines of finance, just so the *I Ching* — its purview the whole of universal history. As Newman was lecturing, I recalled something the master once explained to me about the *I Ching*'s ability to foretell the course of coming events: 'We have arrived at the present by a series of events which is precise and unbroken,' he said, 'a great organic chain stretching backward into the dim recesses of the past just as far as the beginning, and forward into the future, into eternity itself. Everything we do forges a new link in the chain. These are joined in a sequence so vast it quickly daunts and overwhelms the conscious intellect; nevertheless, it exists and can be traced using a different and more powerful sort of knowledge, a scientific intuition which uses the *I Ching* as its instrument.' " I studied Kahn for a reaction.

"Well?"

"Well, couldn't this description — the great organic chain — apply equally well to *Dow*, the Average itself?"

He simply looked at me.

"Or conversely," I continued, "isn't it tantamount to saying that everything is *discounted* in the *Changes*?"

Perhaps it was Kahn's uncharacteristic receptivity and pliability, perhaps the exhilaration of discovery, perhaps the condition of my nerves, overwrought after a long day of continuous stimulation and bombardment — most likely a combination of all these — but as I expatiated these ideas to Kahn, I became inspired. Like Newman, I too felt disposed to prophesy and speak in tongues. In the fortuitous manner with which such rapture characteristically seizes on its images, I extrapolated from something Scottie had once told me in connection with the stars. He had said that every act from the Creation onward has produced some momentum, an energy which may be changed in form but never destroyed. Like the light from stars billions of light-years distant in space, which is continually arriving on our planet undiminished after such magnitudes of travel, so the events of universal history continue to make themselves felt, as vibrations, shock waves, traveling forward, like that light, through eternities, not of space, but of time, down to the present moment. The *I Ching* is like an infinitely sensitive psychic instrument which picks up that lingering energy and performs a sort of spiritual spectroscopy on it, breaking it down into its prior components, thus unfolding the hidden secrets of the past and future. And just as the Taoist puts himself into conformity with the Tao through the *I Ching,* so the Dowist — that is, the Technician — rides the Dow through the study of the charts, his own oracle bones." I paused. "Well?"

"Well what?" Kahn asked.

"Do you think all this could be coincidental?"

He shrugged. "More like some sort of large-scale synchronicity, I'd say, synchronicity at the historical level. I mean, after all, the wheel was invented more than once."

"What is synchronicity?" I asked.

"Synchronicity? It just means two events or ideas which appear to be causally related, and in fact to be inexplicable outside the paradigm of cause and effect, and yet demonstrably aren't. 'Mystic connection,' you might say."

"Yes, mystic connection," I agreed, eagerly taking up the phrase.

"But even granting that," he went on, "where does it get you? I mean, so they're mystically connected?" He shrugged.

"Don't you think that's evidence of a delta," I asked, "a confluence between Dow and Tao?"

"I don't know, kid. It's suggestive, I admit. But if you ask me, the delta, as you call it, isn't going to be some mental place you discover by turning inward — intellectually discover, I mean. You've got to find it in the world. Otherwise it doesn't really count. It remains hypothetical."

I pondered this. When I looked up again, I found Kahn scrutinizing me intensely. Propping his elbows on the table, he'd begun to turn and turn the copper bracelet on his wrist, eyeing me the while with an expression that discomfited me, almost predatory, though partly wistful. Surprised in his surveillance, he smiled a smile that almost made me shudder.

"Want to know what really interests me in what you said?" he asked. He leaned toward me over the table, so far out that he was nearly crawling on his belly. Startled, I edged back reflexively against the seat, his face below mine still so close that I could smell the candied liquor on his breath, the chaste sweetness of its original bouquet chemically altered by saliva, less clean now, a shitten sweetness intimating compromise of principle.

"You say the *I Ching* can be used to predict the future," he said in a whisper husky with emotion. "In your opinion, can it be used for picking stocks?"

Seeing the look of revulsion on my face, he recalled himself, retreating from his predatory posture and sitting erect again. "Hypothetically speaking, of course," he added.

"Of course," I replied, partially, but not totally, reassured. I cleared my throat. "In my opinion, yes, it could be so used . . . *if* one approached it in the proper spirit, that is, with the sufficient degree of *ling.*"

"What is *ling?*" he asked.

"Purity of heart."

Kahn winced as though scalded.

"As to whether it *should* be so used," I continued, "that's a different matter entirely. In my opinion, to use the *I Ching* for purposes of personal gain would be a desecration. It would go against the spirit of the Tao. One who engaged in such practices would almost certainly inflict irreparable spiritual damage on himself, squandering such *ling* as was his to begin with and thereby losing his ability to command the oracle. It is written: 'To those who are not in contact with the Tao, the oracle does not return an intelligible answer, since it would be of no avail.' "

"Poetic justice, huh?" Kahn said.

"Exactly."

Kahn seemed to collapse inwardly. With a profound sigh, he sank back in the seat, the fervid light in his eyes extinguished. "You're right, kid," he said. "One hundred percent. I admire your principles. Don't despise me for asking. I couldn't help myself."

"Of course not!" I replied, reassured by his contrition, my devotion to him, if anything, augmented by his confession of weakness.

"Thanks, kid," he said with a slight quaver in his voice. "That means a lot to me. You know, during your spiel, I was thinking — you remind me of somebody. . . ." He examined my face wistfully.

Something clutched inside me. Trembling, almost breathless with excitement, I opened my lips to whisper the shibboleth, the secret name I carried in my heart like a live coal, threatening instantly, with any encouraging breath of wind, to flare up.

"Know who?" he asked.

I shook my head, choked with emotion, unable to reply.

"Myself," he said.

I stared dazed into his eyes.

"That's right," he affirmed, "me. You look surprised. I don't blame you. I don't mean as I am now, but as I once was, when I first came here — not long out of graduate school, ideas and principles still intact, just like yours, the same innocent enthusiasm. I was a virgin then, like you. I still had my cherry, morally speaking, a bing too, not a maraschino. The last time I checked it resembled more a martini olive skewered on an hors d'oeuvre fork. But in those first days, that first year, say, all of it seemed new and fresh, a spectacle worthy of Elizabethan times (I still thought in literary images then), full of pageantry and panoply, lusty, irreverent, feisty, unrepentant, vulgar, but overflowing with life — so different from the university. My head whirled with images, impressions and ideas just as outrageous as those you've been expounding." He shook his head. "I don't know. You saw all that in Newman's lecture, and to me it was just schlock. Maybe I'm wiser, but I envy you, kid. I really do. They say there's no thrill like the high of trading, and I don't know but I believe it. But maybe in the long run it coarsens you. As I listened to you, it made me realize that I don't have ideas like that anymore. And that makes me sad. Somewhere along the way I lost it. Don't you lose it, kid.

"For someone who lists schmaltz right below gefilte fish on his Supreme Aversion List, I'm getting pretty gushy, eh kid?" He tossed off a quarter of his drink at a swallow.

Feeling sorry for him and wanting to derail his self-pity before it had a chance to build up steam, I returned to a question I'd tried to ask earlier. "What did Newman's 'worthy predecessor' mean by a Two Hundred Day Moving Average?"

Kahn was staring down with a look of absorbed concentration at the white serum swirling around the cubes in his glass, making them ring and jingle like icebergs in a frothing polar sea. "Hmm?" he said distractedly. "Oh yes. Two Hundred Day Moving Average. It's basically a trend line, kid. More or less. Same general idea."

"Trend line?"

"A way of identifying some persisting overall momentum underlying the oscillations of the Average. If you look solely at day-to-day fluctuations in a given stock, or in the Dow itself, it's sometimes hard to get a sense of the general drift over the intermediate to long term. The thing hops around like the EKG of a dog in heat. Somewhere underneath it, though, there's a trend, a general momentum. It's the clew of thread you use to guide you through the labyrinth of momentary flux. To find it, all you do is average out the troughs and crests of daily closing prices over, say, a two-week period, plot them and connect the dots to find a smooth line, heading up or down at a more or less precipitous rate, or drifting sideways nowhere in particular, as the case may be. Do that for two hundred trading days, and you've got your Two Hundred Day Moving Average. All it is in essence is a tool for visualizing an invisible momentum, a way of ferreting out the unity within the multiplicity."

"Why two hundred days in particular?" I asked.

"I don't know. It's just a convenient time period, approximately nine months of working days. Anything less than that and you might be in danger of confusing a secondary reaction with a primary trend, as the worthy predecessor said. Actually, I don't suppose there's any reason why you couldn't make it as long as you wanted. A Two Hundred Week Moving Average, or hell, for that matter, why not a Two Hundred Year Moving Average?" As he uttered this last phrase, Kahn suddenly froze.

"Kahn?" I asked.

"Shh, shh!" he commanded, waving his hands frantically for silence. "Don't move. Don't breathe. I think I'm giving birth. Umh . . . umh . . ." he grunted. "It's coming. Yes . . . yes . . . A live one! A real, a bona fide *idea!*"

"What are you talking about?"

"Listen, kid, remember what Newman said about the market, the Dow, being a sort of holistic barometer reading the systemic weather of the nation, reflecting microcosmically, through discounting, all the diverse passions and ambitions which motivate the entire population?"

I nodded uncertainly.

"Well, according to him, the sum total of all those disparate momenta equals — or at least is related to — Dow, or rather its Two Hundred Day Moving Average. Thus his argument for Dow as the central vital sign of the nation, a distillation of America itself, expressing the essence of our culture (or lack of it). By extracting a Two Hundred Day Moving Average from the Dow we get a glimpse of an overall momentum — call it Big Mo. Big Mo is the unity which underlies the dizzying multiplicity of Dow and of our national life, economic, political, social, intellectual, religious, what have you, all discounted in the Average. Once you've penetrated to the point where you can see clearly the nature and direction of Big Mo, you should be capable, theoretically at least, of riding it, as you said, through the changing tides of momentary panic and speculation. Though it changes, it changes very slowly, because its inertia is so huge, as huge as America itself. Only a tremendous effort can produce even the slightest alteration in its direction. Our national life moves in a frantic orbit around the smooth, unhurried progress of Big Mo, like daily fluctuations around some great Two Hundred Day Moving Average. Only Big Mo is more properly a Two Hundred Year Moving Average (here's the tie-in, kid), expressing the historical inertia of this country — the Big Mo of America! Think of it, kid! The possibilities are mind boggling. Overarching, ever-increasing Moving Averages! Beyond the Two Hundred Year Moving Average of America, a Two Thousand Year Moving Average, expressing the cumulative historical inertia of Western man since the birth of Christ. And that Two Thousand Year Moving Average no more than a tiny blip in the great Two Million Year Moving Average of the human race; that, in its turn, subsumed in the Two Billion Year Moving Average of life on earth!"

Undercutting the previous effect, he added with characteristic irony, "Kahn, despite himself, waxes profound." He grinned. "What do you think, kid? Maybe I'm not as incorrigible as we thought. Perhaps old Kahn's not completely dead above the ears?"

Interpreting these questions as rhetorical in nature, I made no reply.

"Right, kid?" he persisted.

"Of course not," I said.

He sighed and shook his head. The brief meteor of speculative bravado he'd dazzled me with had passed, and he relapsed into depression. "I'm not so sure," he said, having begged the question, apparently, simply for the pleasure of self-contradiction.

"Waiter!" he called. "Bring us Sack!"

Chapter 10

By this display of mild obstreperousness, I knew Kahn was getting drunk, a fact which did not cause me undue concern, perhaps because I was fast approaching that condition too.

"Sometimes I wonder what I'm doing here," he lamented.

"If you want to go somewhere else, I'm agreeable," I offered.

"Not in this bar, fundament," he retorted acidly, "I mean the market."

"Oh," I replied, assuming a serious mien.

"I used to have these flashes sometimes. I'd start awake and look around, expecting to find myself back in my carrel at Columbia refreshed after a brief snooze. The faces on the trading floor blurred together, the voices merged into a roar like . . . like . . . the buzzing of millions of insect wings, a swarm of African locusts, or . . ." — his face brightened, as with remembrance — ". . . oh yeah, like that background radiation they discovered at Bell Laboratories. Ever read about it? Part temperature, part sound, as best I could make it out, pervading the whole universe — three degrees Kelvin, I think it was — a lingering echo of the Big Bang right there on Wall Street, somehow appropriate in the midst of so much greed and worldly vanity, like a memento mori (beloved of all students of literature), reminding us of the prospect awaiting us in the end (same as the beginning). In other words, a moment of existential terror. You know what I'm saying, kid?"

"I don't have the slightest idea," I confessed.

"Let me put it another way," he said. "You know Chuang Tzu's dream of the butterfly?"

I nodded.

"Well, correct me if I'm wrong, but after this dream he woke up and couldn't decide if he was a man who had dreamt himself a butterfly, or a butterfly dreaming himself a man, am I right?"

"Yes, that's it," I said.

"Well, it's basically the same thing. Only in my case I couldn't tell (still can't sometimes) whether I was a capitalist pig who had dreamt himself an intellectual, or an intellectual dreaming he was a capitalist pig."

"I see," I said.

"Forget me, though," he continued. "Let me put it to you. Where do you see yourself twenty, thirty years down the line, when you're my age?"

"Back at Ken Kuan," I replied without hesitation.

He nodded. "If you'd asked me that question at your age, sitting in that carrel in the stacks, I would have said the same thing, only it would have been the university instead of a monastery. But in my opinion they're variations on a single theme. If you'd suggested that I'd be hustling profits on the floor of the New York Stock Exchange, I'd have laughed in your face. I wouldn't even have been offended, it would have seemed so preposterous. Take that for what it's worth, kid. I'm not one to put on airs and prate about the wisdom of experience, but it's funny the way things turn out sometimes, you know? 'The best laid plans of mice and men'?" He sighed and took a long sip of his drink, jiggled the ice cubes like some private mnemonic cue.

"As an undergrad, I had a long, beautiful love affair with English literature, especially the Elizabethan period. Shakespeare . . ." His features broke into a spontaneous, boyish smile I'd never seen before, completely inadvertent and quite winning. "*Henry the Fourth Part One.* Hotspur, Hal, 'the fat knight,' Sir John Falstaff (Falstaff most of all!) — boy I loved that play! Maybe it ain't the greatest thing he ever wrote, not as profound as *Lear* or *Hamlet,* but so fucking hilarious! And so fucking sad. So merciful — that at least — as merciful as anything the old boy ever wrote. He rolled the human race up in a ball — 'that trunk of humors, that bolting hutch of beastliness, that swollen parcel of dropsies, that huge bombard of sack, that stuffed cloakbag of guts, that roasted Manningtree ox with the pudding in his belly, that reverend vice, that gray iniquity, that father ruffian, that vanity in years' — in short, Falstaff. And he forgave him, forgave us, forgave everything . . . more, *loved* it. It's hard to know the world like that and still love it in spite of itself, not in pity either, not martyr-love, but with a sense of humor. Maybe that alone explains his stature, that he could look reality in the face and not falter, not die, not hedge, or balk, or jib, or falsify, or color, or equivocate, but see it for what it was, and laugh from the bottom of his heart, laugh at it, with it, for it — and appreciate it, most of all. It seems like such a simple thing. But no one else has ever been able to do it, at least no one who ever wrote. Could be that's why you can't ever get to the bottom of him — because he made his bottom, his Bottom, the world's bottom. And that's why his laugh still echoes like the Big Bang. It's part of it. Three degrees Kelvin." He grinned sheepishly in apology. "Sorry, kid. I guess I must be getting a little drunk or something."

"It's okay," I replied. "I like listening to you. . . . Only, who was Shakespeare?"

He groaned. "Never mind. I deserve it, kid, deserve *you.* It must be some sort of penance for crimes committed in other lives. The point I was trying to make, or at least work my way around to, was that all of it, my literary training as an undergrad, was wonderfully unconnected with my own life — which is maybe exactly why it appealed to me. When I read *The Merchant of Venice,* I identified with Jessica, the daughter of Shylock the Jew. She felt she was hostage to a barbarous and uncongenial heritage and was simply dying to be ravished by Lorenzo and the Christians. Ah, 'that quality of mercy'!" he said, shaking his jowls and waving his finger in the air like Jimmy Durante. "The only difference between her and me was that after four years of high school at Mount Abarim and four more at Columbia, my assimilation had been accomplished. I considered myself deracinated, disinfected, 'cured,' however you want to put it. A shegetz, in other words. You see, kid, I wasn't born a genius. I had to come to it the hard way. I didn't understand back then about the gravity of blood."

"What's that?" I asked.

"Put it this way. Run a Wasp through the refiner's fire of Western liberal education and no matter how much garlic and spices you throw in, it still comes out well-done Yankee pot roast; smoke a Jew and you get lox. No use crying over it, it can't be helped. It's the gravity of blood. An 'assimilated Jew' is like a reformed lush, kid. He never stops being an alcoholic, he just mortifies the craving for the bottle. Same with a Chinese or a nigger. You can educate him, polish the rough edges, throw a coat of whitewash on his manners, but you can't wash away the blackness in his heart. Does that sound racist to you? It isn't. The world might be more peaceful and more tidy, but in my opinion it sure as hell wouldn't be half as interesting if every Jew was a Jessica and every nigger was an Uncle Tom. And if it's the word 'nigger' you object to, then let me tell you, the black man has no monopoly on righteous indignation. The day they disinfect the word 'Jew' of all its unsavory connotations, then we'll be happy little Jews and niggers all together, as cosy as bugs in a rug, using the abusive epithets as terms of endearment. Until then, I'll call him nigger, and he can call me Jew in the old way, business as usual.

"At any rate, maybe that's why in my senior year I gravitated toward American literature, the first step in a gradual drift toward self-definition. That was the candy coating around the bitter bolus of my own ineradicable Jewishness. If I'd had to swallow it all at once I think I might have gagged. I had to come at being a Jew through being an American. I ended writing my thesis on Mark Twain. Pretty far from the Jewish Renaissance, you'll say, but he did once refer to himself as 'the American Sholom Aleichem.' " He grinned again.

"Of course, it's true, I did go through a 'Jewish phase' as a kid. That was the first of my phases. But I left that pretty much behind with my yarmulke after my bar mitzvah. In between that and college — which I guess would constitute Phase Three — came my intro to the stock market. Enter Uncle Schmuel, also known as Hanaël. Did I tell you about him yet?"

"You said you inherited your seat from an uncle," I recounted, "but I thought his name was Ahasuerus, not Schmuel, or Ha-, whatever."

"Schmuel, Hanaël, Ahasuerus . . . same guy. What I gave you before, kid, was only the Cliff's Notes abstract of the Life of Kahn. The sumptuous pleasures of the unexpurgated version are still before you." He smiled wryly. "My first glimpses of Uncle Schmuel (I never called him Hanaël; as far as I know, only his mother did) date from Flatbush Avenue, where he used to come to dinner with us once a year in our flat above my father's pawnshop, towing some dumb blond bombshell type in a mink stole he'd given her, which, incidentally, she wouldn't take off the whole afternoon. She just sat there like a lox while we schmoozed and ate, declining all the nosheri, you know, just kind of sniffing at it and turning up her nose like it was spoiled or something — my mother's piroshki too, which was the ultimate sin, worse than a slap in the face — just sat there in her mink, saying nothing, smiling this hard, glassy smile, knees clamped tight together like a vise, looking for all the world like one of Caesar's greyhounds in her diamond choker, 'Noli me tangere' written all over her. By that point my mother would be on the verge of apoplexy. Moe would cast furtive glances at her, now sheepish, now appealing, now concerned, while he played cards with Uncle Schmuel, who was having a great time himself, oblivious of the social feud — hell, *race war!* — going on between the women, leaning back from time to time to chuck his shiksa under the chin with the grateful, mildly lecherous fondness of middle age, saying, 'Ain't she something, Moe? Look at that figure! Eats like a bird, too, just like a little tweety bird!' The two of them sat in a cloud of smoke from the good cigars my uncle brought over from some tobacconist in Manhattan, drinking his bootleg scotch and playing gin rummy for a nickel a point, Schmuel staking Pops because he thought he couldn't afford it, and, against Pops's protests, wiping out all debts after the last Hollywood and leaving the money as a sort of tip. I know in some ways it was just as trying for him as it was for my mother. But he adored Schmuel.

"They were half-brothers by the same mother. She came from a musical family in Warsaw, very sophisticated, very cosmopolitan, though not particularly wealthy. She fell in love with a young Hungarian nobleman, a baron, I think, who was spending time in Warsaw acquiring 'tone' — the original Hanaël. He must have been pretty dashing, judging by Schmuel, and no doubt something of a rake. She threw herself at him, and he at her, briefly . . . as long as it took.

"On discovering her pregnancy, her family disowned her. It might have been real unpleasant, if my grandfather hadn't seen her and fallen hopelessly in love. He was considerably older than she was, in his forties or fifties. He'd already made his fortune in pawnbrokerage. He took her in, even gave Schmuel his own name and raised him as a son. My grandmother though, who was somewhat embittered — understandably, I suppose — spitefully insisted on calling him Hanaël, and raised him speaking French. My grandfather cheerfully went on calling him Schmuel. They communicated in Yiddish. Strangely, or not so strangely, when he learned English — primarily through Yiddish speakers

— Uncle Schmuel spoke it with a heavy Eastern European accent. It was weird the way he'd sometimes throw a French phrase with perfect accent and intonation into his conversation, like a rich mayonnaise served with lox.

"By the time he was eighteen, Schmuel had conceived a burning passion for the military and wanted to become a hussar — an ambition that might have been particularly difficult to pull off, considering the traditional anti-Semitism of the Poles. But his father — his real father, the original Hanaël — who hadn't done squat for him before, felt guilty and pulled some strings. Schmuel was granted a commission, not, of course, as Schmuel, but as Hanaël. Though this must have greatly chagrined my grandfather (whose only recorded political or intellectual sentiment was a predilection for pacifism), I doubt the deception was that difficult to carry out. Schmuel didn't really look that Jewish as a young man — I've seen pictures — more like a Slav or a gypsy. I guess that was his father's Hungarian blood. Later the bone and cartilage revolted in his face, tectonic realignment, you know, primarily the schnozzle. Pops's first memories were of the dashing officer in his uniform, shako underneath his arm, standing militarily erect in the drawing room of their home in his knee-high riding boots, waxed mustaches, his arm around my grandmother's waist, she flushed and adoring, my grandfather, the pacifist, upstage, a little discountenanced, out-manned by his stepson, who was maybe less appreciative of all his adoptive father had done for him than he should have been. (But then gratitude and tenderness aren't necessarily the qualities one looks for and treasures in an Ahasuerus.)

"Then the war broke out, the First World War, that is. Schmuel was wounded a few months after hostilities began. I'm not sure how it happened, but I like to think of him charging, saber drawn and flashing in the sunlight, horse's hooves thundering over the ground, straight into a battery of artillery. For the glory of God and Poland! Cut down like wheat. Schmuel came home to recuperate. One of the lucky ones, he only took some grapeshot in the shoulder. My father used to take him the paper and his morning tea. Sometimes Schmuel would tell a story of the war, pat my father on the head, and give him a few groszy for a licorice.

"He was there for several months, and when he left to return to the war Pops never heard from him again. . . . Until they met by accident one day on Delancey Street in New York where Pops saw him buying a boutonniere from a flower girl. Schmuel didn't recognize him, but Pops said he knew at once. By that time he'd already made his first fortune and bought his seat on the Exchange. As to what happened in between . . . ? There's only one memento from that time: a photograph of Uncle Schmuel dressed like a hunter, felt crown hat with brim, sheepskin coat, cavalry boots somewhat down at heel, and, strangely, an earring in his ear. With a rifle cradled in the crook of his arm, an ammo belt strapped diagonally across his chest, he's squatting on his haunches in the snow, staring up at the camera with this perfervid grin on his face. With his right hand he's holding open the jaws of a full-grown wolf, pinching back the upper lip to show the teeth. The wolf's eyes are rolled back in its head, and the camera has caught a haunting glimmer from one of them. That photograph has always haunted me. The call of the wild — it's in my blood.

"At the time in question, however, I mean those yearly dinner parties on Flatbush Avenue, Schmuel was still only the rich uncle with the shiksa, whom I resented on my mother's account but tolerated for my father. I admit I was influenced too by the delicious bonbons he brought me from secret treasuries in New York City, the first I'd ever had. Yes, Uncle Schmuel, alias Ahasuerus, was instrumental in implementing all my vices, even that virginal one, first and tenderest, which I suppose may be construed as Kahn's Original Sin. Funny, in those early scenes what stands out most in my memory, far more than Uncle Schmuel, are the shiksas, those snooty secretaries, overdressed, over made-up, putting on airs and not quite able to pull off the class act they aspired to. A different one each year, but always the same.

"At that point, you see, I was still in Phase One, 'exaggerated Jewish Piety,' a brief but urgent flowering, recrudescence of some unconscious racial aspiration, I suppose. Neither of my parents was particularly devout, still it was absolutely de rigueur that I be bar mitzvahed. I mean, no bar mitzvah, no mensch! I was not exactly enthused by the prospect at first, but martyred myself for the sake of the payola. I approached it with the same air of weary resignation one takes to any 'b.m.,' which is how Moishe Lipshitz, who lived on the same block and turned thirteen two weeks ahead of me, and I christened it, hardened cynics even at thirteen." Kahn laughed and shook his head. "Approaching it with that sort of gallows humor, I would never have expected they'd be able to pull it off. But I got brainwashed. . . . No, that's not fair. It was more than that. You see, I hadn't counted on meeting someone like Herschel Liebowicz, our rabbi. Herschel was something special, a young guy, very good looking, athletic, six foot three, a head full of loose, dark curls. He had charisma. There was something in his face, a kind of glow, very warm and human, but a little bit beyond, you know? Like he was listening to some vibration in the air that no one else could hear. He'd found something, you could see it in his face, and he conducted it like electricity to everyone around. He was a beautiful Jew, kid, a David, a throwback to one of those dark, lean-muscled, laughing-eyed warriors who used to run around the deserts of Palestine in their loincloths and sandals, brandishing spears and instilling fear in the hearts of the Gentiles, before the Diaspora, when we were still the chosen people of God. . . ." Kahn's voice broke. Taking out his Dristan mist, he ministered to his grievance, taking a loud snoutful, then sighed and wiped his eyes. "I heard that after the war Herschel took his family and moved to Israel. It really made my day. He was the kind of guy you root for all your life and want to check back on periodically to make sure he's still out there somewhere doing it, you know? Like he was carrying the ball for all of us." His voice cracked again. "I'm sorry, kid. I can't help myself." He took a deep, amphoric breath.

"Anyway, during the indoctrination period, when I was learning to read, or at least parrot, the relevant passages from the Torah, I fell completely under his spell. My discipleship, though brief, was very intense. Everytime I was around him, I got palpitations." He laid his fist over his heart. "This went on for about as long as our sessions lasted, which make me suspect, looking back, that it was more plain animal magnetism on his part than conviction on mine. Hero-worship rather than religion. At the time though, I was deadly serious. It was no laughing matter." (He laughed.) "I was on fire with righteousness. I became a fucking zealot, kid! Piety? I was so pious they used to call me 'Siddurtha.' No kidding, kid.

"I had this aunt — my mother's sister — one day I came back from temple and found her in the apartment. My mother had gone out to the store for something I think. Anyway, noticing my yarmulke, she gives me this arch look and says, 'I see you've taken up the cloth.' Boy, was that a mistake! Oh yes, kid, I made her *pay*! I launched into a long sermon excoriating the Jews for their lax morals, bewailing the lapsed greatness of the tribes, and exhorting them to band together and redeem the lost glory of Israel — a real jeremiad. When I finished, she just sat there with her jaw hanging slack like she'd been slugged. Later on, after my mother came back, through the kitchen door I heard her say, 'So what's with that Aaron of yours? He's like the burning bush — he burns and is not consumed!' It'll give you some idea of my state of mind at the time to tell you that I didn't even laugh. Not even a tiny smile did I crack. This was serious business. No fooling around. Moishe Lipshitz caught the bug as well, not quite as bad as I did, but he still ran a temperature and was seized at inconvenient moments by verbal flux, when he had to run for the nearest audience. We were like a couple of young Jewish Ancient Mariners, kid. Two on a single block — I'll tell you, it was a strain on the community."

Kahn lost himself temporarily in a gale of asthmatic snickers. "Where were we? Oh yeah, the burning bush. Well, it had always been sort of an implicit assumption around the house — insidiously planted and duly fertilized and watered by my mother — that I would become a scholar. Know what the definition of a genius is, kid?"

I shook my head.

"An average child with Jewish parents. In my infrequent moments of lucidity, I was wise enough to resent it. In general though, Ida's clandestine operations were too sophisticated. I never had a chance. I actually believed I could be anything I wanted — you know, steer the hook and ladder, play shortstop for the Brooklyn Dodgers. Under Herschel's influence, my mother's casual seed bore fruit. And with a vengeance. One day I came home from temple and announced in stentorian tones that I was going to devote my life to Talmudic studies. Herschel cautiously encouraged me, started teaching me Hebrew for real. After the bar mitzvah ceremony, he took me aside and gave me this beautiful copy of the Torah bound in leather, with a little ribbon to mark the place. It still makes me weepy when I think of it. He said if I'd just keep it up, one day I'd be able to experience its 'stern beauties' for myself. Stern beauties. . . ." Kahn shook his head. "Kid, the contamination of the world proved too much for me. I succumbed. Plus there was Ahasuerus.

"One day — this was still before my bar mitzvah — my father took me out for lunch in the city. Afterward we stopped by the Exchange. It was my first trip. We stood up in the gallery. All the furor and commotion, the sheer size of the place, left me feeling sort of dazed. While we were up there Pops catches sight of Uncle Schmuel and calls out to him in Yiddish at the top of his lungs. For a minute the place went dead silent. Everybody looked up at us. I wanted to crawl into a hole, kid. Seriously. But Uncle Schmuel lights up like a Christmas tree (maybe I should say a menorah). He waves us down, and Pops pulls me after him through the crowd, sort of examining the cracks in the floor. Pay attention, kid. It's at just this point that Kahn was treated to his first glimpse of the mad Ashkenazi. On the trading floor of the Exchange, Uncle Schmuel was in his element, like a fly in shit. He ceased to be Schmuel and became Ahasuerus! Kid, he acted like he owned the place. What chutzpah! What a mensch! I stared on amazed, uncertain if he was the same guy. He seemed about six inches taller than when I'd seen him before, and ten years younger. There was an ecstatic glow on his face, like a secular — or maybe I should say profane — version of the thing I'd seen in Herschel Liebowicz. All my old assumptions were exploded. While we were there this goy in a fancy suit comes up to him and shakes hands. They schmooze for a few minutes; the guy offers Uncle Schmuel a cigar, lights it for him. Then Uncle Schmuel turns to us.

" 'Jesse,' he says, 'this is my brother, Moe, the meshuggener, and his bar mitzvah, Aaron. Boys, shake hands with Jessie Livermore, the Great Bear.'

"Jessie Livermore! Can you imagine, kid? Of course, at the time I didn't know him from Adam. But Jesus! I shook the guy's hand, and he offered me a cigar. Twelve years old and he offers me a cigar! I only wish I had it now! Ah, kid, giants still walked the earth in those days. That would have been the summer of twenty-eight, just a little over a year before the crash. The market was primed. Everybody, I mean *everybody,* was raking in mazuma to the tune of Eddie Cantor singing 'Making Whoopie' on the radio. My uncle used to say that was the year that all the schlemiels grew wings. Even Pops got the fever and put in money at Uncle Schmuel's direction. He bought RCA at eighty-five. When it hit one hundred he started getting nervous. Poor Pops! He wasn't a schlemiel exactly, certainly no schlimazel, but a little bit of a nebbish maybe. Okay, so what's the matter with you?"

"I'm sorry," I said, "but what's a slm-?"

"That's *schlem-,* kid, *schl*emiel. Put it this way. A schlemiel is the guy who spills hot soup in the schlimazel's lap, and the nebbish is the guy who apologizes and has to wipe it off. That's the classic definition. My uncle used to say that a schlimazel is a schlemiel who hasn't heard the news. I may be a schlemiel, kid, but I'm no schlimazel. That's what *I* say. And you can take it to the bank.

"About RCA though, Pops sells out at a hundred and five, feeling like a millionaire. Within a year it's gone to four-twenty! Four hundred and twenty, kid, can you believe it? It was a Golden Age. Right there that afternoon, even as he shook my uncle's hand, acting so smarmy, handing out cigars, I bet old Livermore was starting to ease out, dropping a few shares short here and there. He was probably one of the only guys who didn't lose his ass on Black (or Shvartz, as my uncle called it) Thursday. Hell, he profited on the fall. They never forgave him for that, making money on other people's misery. Maybe so, but Livermore didn't cause that misery. The assholes brought it on themselves. He just played the game, and played it better than anybody living. He might have been a Wasp, but Uncle Schmuel always said he was a Jew at heart. The only man who ever made a million dollars on despair. Hell, kid, he out-Jewed the Jews. The Great Bear! Talk about a constellation! If I had a hero in the market — besides Ahasuerus — he would be it.

That first glimpse of Uncle Schmuel in the market was a revelation for me. The guy was a mensch. Of course, I was still deeply under Herschel's influence then, but the seed was planted even so early.

"Oddly enough, my bar mitzvah itself marks the crucial threshold between Phase One and Phase Two, or Jewish Piety and Ahasuerus Fever. Strange as it may seem, starting that very day, I began to gravitate away from Herschel toward my uncle. It wasn't the ceremony itself that caused the change. That was just as stirring, solemn, fluttery as one could have hoped. I'm referring to the party afterward.

"Pops and Moishe Lipshitz's father pooled their resources and rented a local dance hall for the afternoon, hiring a band of local minstrels under the direction of Freddie 'the Freeloader' Epstein, who played the Wurlitzer and was sort of the neighborhood tummler. Let's see, besides the organ there was a guy on accordion, a glockenspiel, some aspiring Heifetz on the violin, who seemed to be in pain the whole afternoon and played even the polka with a touch of tremulous melancholy. There was a clarinet, some guy with a snare drum on a stand, who broke one of his sticks and had to schlepp along the rest of the afternoon with one plus a brush. Yeah, it was definitely a barnyard orchestra, but all of them were Jews and so played with feeling, if without much concern for harmonizing with their neighbors. What they lacked in finesse though, they made up for with enthusiasm. The dozen or so bottles of cider Pops had fermented and put up in the attic helped things along too. In fact, it was a right decent party. Not spectacular, but entirely respectable.

"With the arrival of Uncle Schmuel, however, things cranked into a different gear: overdrive. The past lapsed into banality. 'Oy vay!' I hear my mother cry. I look at her, she's holding her jaw like she's got toothache, staring toward the door. I turn and *ecce homo!* Ahasuerus! Entering like a sort of Jewish Gatsby, the trayf Messiah! Kid, I'm telling you, such chutzpah you've never seen. This guy wrote the book. Remember, it's 1928. Ahasuerus is in his prime, maybe fifty-five. Still has his military bearing, broad shoulders, small waist. His suit is custom tailored, really natty. He's got his hair slicked back. He looks like

Valentino in *The Sheik.* On his arm, the obligatory shiksa. Only now she's been incarnated as a flapper — bobbed hair, beads, rolled stockings, short skirt, cigarette holder, lipstick tube, compact — the whole shtick, and hanging loose to boot. All the Jewish matrons, proper in baleen, proceed to drop their teeth. Somebody hits a wrong note and the music just kind of whiffles off into inanity. Uncle Schmuel swaggers up, chest thrown out. The shiksa on his arm bounces and prances, leaning close to whisper something in his ear, breaking out in this high, giddy laugh from time to time, not noticing, or pretending not to notice, that everybody in the place is staring at her. Stopping in the middle of the dance floor, Schmuel looks around with a big grin, then takes out a cigar and lights it. 'Hoy, Moe!' he calls, with a little jerk of the head. 'Come over.' Pops, with a look of timid astonishment, lets go my mother's hand, who's about to sink through the floor, and complies.

" 'I vant you should meet Delores,' he says in his thick Yiddish accent, 'my jazz baby. She's the cat's pajamas. Voilà mon frère, chérie.'

" 'Nerts, Schmooey,' the flapper says. 'You and your frawn-say.' Offering Pops the hand with the cigarette holder (which, incidentally, holds no cigarette), she forgets herself and does a little recidivistic curtsy. 'Pleased I'm shoo-wah,' she says.

"I see my mother bite her fist. 'Oy gevalt!' she moans. 'That I should live so long!'

"At this point Freddie Epstein, showing remarkable presence of mind, strikes up 'Making Whoopie' on the Wurlitzer, and the band recklessly plunges in.

" 'Oh yeah!' says Delores, snapping her fingers to the beat. 'Come on, Schmooey,' she says, tugging at his arm. 'I want to teach you the Black Bottom.'

" 'Dance with the kid,' he says, shoving her in my direction. 'Come on, Moe. I vant to show you somethink. Il y a quelque chose en bas.' He snaps his fingers. 'Vite, vite!'

"They head toward the door and the shiksa takes me by the hand. 'Come on, cutie,' she says with a coy little smile. I feel a lump in my throat and another one in my pocket, and thank Jesus for the Guineas in the fish market (where I was working — my father's brilliant idea) who've taught me half a dozen steps, enough to get by in the emergency. So here I am, kid, dancing on my bar mitzvah with a flapper. I try not to look, but I can't help myself. Yes, it's true, she's got nothing underneath. I mean, I can see them flapping, nipples and all! It almost gives me whiplash just trying to keep up with them! She knows I'm looking too, and she just laughs. Oh Jesus! She's got this long string of beads on, you know, and as she spins they go into orbit, slapping me in the face occasionally. She's going at it so that every so often her skirt comes up and I can see the slip she's wearing underneath, the frilly stuff along the bottom, and her thighs bare all the way to the knee!

" 'You're good,' she says to me, and I become a dervish. I'm whirling her around so fast, and she's leaning back laughing this giddy laugh and giving in to it, inviting me to do it harder. Kid, suddenly I understand what the bar mitzvah's all about. In my heart of hearts I say my broches to Uncle Schmuel, now Ahasuerus for good, who's given me this gift.

"What happens next almost defies belief! The song is over. I'm standing there flushed and panting. The shiksa is a little breathless too. She's excited, blushing. Losing her composure, she looks around anxiously for Uncle Schmuel.

"He appears, and she flutters to his arm.

" 'So, can he dance?' he asks her.

"She giggles and gives me the same coy look. 'He's good, Schmooey,' she says, 'the bee's knees. You could learn a thing or two from him.'

" 'I wish I had his youth!' he says. He winks at me and tilts his head toward her. 'What do you say, kid, you like?'

"I'm overcome with embarrassment. He takes a cigar out of his breast pocket and, leaning over, gives it to me, whispering, 'Such a tuchis, Aaron! Quel cul! You vant her, she's yours.'

"I almost had a heart attack. Fortunately, it wasn't necessary to ravish her on the spot. Clashing cymbals and a one-legged roll on the snare-drum announced the next stage in the proceedings. Uncle Schmuel claps his hands, the door flies open, and half a dozen little shvartzers in livery enter, carrying . . . Such things they were carrying!" Getting excited, Kahn went a little overboard with the Yiddish syntax. "Two dozen bottles of bubbly, the real stuff, imported straight from France without the labels! Similar quantities of gin in Mason jars — hospital quality, too, none of that cheap, denatured industrial dreck. This, for the rank and file. For the family — which is to say, himself and Pops — a half-gallon of real scotch whiskey, brought in at a high premium from the rum fleet lying thirty miles offshore in some Cosa Nostra speedboat. Needless to say, all necessary mixers were included. This big, shiny nigger appears from the street lugging two fifty-pound blocks of clear blue ice, flawless, not a bubble in either, grappling them in tongs, one in each hand, taking staggery, constipated steps, the sweat dripping down his face, the blocks sweating too, as smooth as glass. He drops them in an enamel bathtub brought for the occasion, then, wiping his arm across his forehead and blowing a big sigh, takes his ice pick out of his back pocket and taps it gently into the block with a wooden mallet, so that a tiny white fracture burrows through the block just ahead of the steel tip of the pick. Three or four times he does this, all in the same plane, then he gives a tap and suddenly the glacier calves, splits perfectly in half! Ah, kid, an everyday occurrence, in no way extraordinary. Normally I wouldn't have even noticed, but today I watch and it seems like a miracle. I feel applause is called for. We give the nigger an ovation and a big tip!

"The liquor starts to flow, then come the presents! A few weeks earlier Pops had taken me quietly aside and told me, 'Uncle Schmuel wants to give you something special. So how about it?' Know what I asked for, kid? The complete edition of the Talmud, all sixty-three books! 'So what's your second choice?' my father says. But I'm insistent. I tell him my heart's set on it. He shrugs and says he'll see what he can do, but not to hold my breath. So how do you suppose Ahasuerus interpolates my request? What does he bring the young bar mitzvah?

"After giving us a chance to clear our palates with champagne (partaking liberally of scotch, himself), Schmuel signals the band to desist and casually withdraws something from his pocket. 'Gif me your hand, Aaron,' he says, his eyes a little misty with anticipated grandeur. I comply, and he slips something on my finger. What is it, I wonder, a diamond ring? No, it's too light. I draw it toward me. It's green and made of paper, like the little rings we made at school with dollar bills, folded over and over so that at last the dollar sign ended on the signet. What is this, a joke? I take a closer look. After the one, there is a zero . . . and another . . . and another . . . a thousand dollar bill! I can't believe my eyes. I'm stunned. To me a fin is affluence; a ten is an impressive fortune; a hundred walks a thin line, wobbling drunkenly between plutocracy and myth; but a thousand! A *thousand!* Kid, such things did not exist outside Monopoly games! I throw my arms around his neck. 'So you buy your Talmud if you vant to, Aaron,' he says with a sniffle, a little carried away by his own generosity. 'I didn't have the hot to do this to you. Not on your bar mitzvah!' And he kisses me on the lips. . . .

"Yo!" Kahn called to the waiter. "Bring us another round!"

"After that Uncle Schmuel got drunk and started singing the Polish national anthem with Pops. Ahasuerus calls out for a polonaise and makes a grab at my mother (who's from the Ukraine). 'Keep your hands to yourself, you gonif!' she cries, calling on my father to defend her honor. But the band, not knowing the difference, has broken into a polka anyway! The party degenerates into a free-for-all. The shiksa, by this time thoroughly disgusted with the whole affair, has lapsed into a more characteristic pose and stands in the corner leaning against the wall, arms folded self-consciously over her chest in a gesture of prohibition, looking on at Ahasuerus like Michael at David when he stripped down and danced before the Arc of the Covenent in his shorts, or loincloth — whatever it was — 'despising him in her heart.' Suddenly I don't want her anymore. My heart is filled with love and pity for my uncle. I seek him out. I find him leaning down, talking to this little girl about my own age whose mother, terrified, stands behind her, clutching her shoulders with savage maternal protectiveness.

" 'He's got a schlong like this,' I hear him tell her, referring, presumably, to me. He chops his elbow joint with the blade of his hand. 'Don't ask me how I know. I know. It runs in the family, all right? Don't miss your opportunity!' By that time though Ida had had about all she was going to take. Fuming, she marched me toward the door holding me by the ear, strictly forbidding me ever to associate with Ahasuerus again. Of course, this prohibition (small 'p'), like the greater, only made defiance that much more delicious. For Ahasuerus and me it was only the beginning. The room slow-danced around me, reeling like a merry-go-round, as she shoved me across the floor. The last thing I saw was Herschel Liebowicz standing by the doorway, holding his folded tallith in one hand and in the other my copy of the Torah, which I'd forgotten. He gave it to me with a beautiful, grave smile and raised his hand in goodbye. His eyes were very sad as though he knew it was the end. Oh, we'd see each other. I'd show up for a few Hebrew lessons. But that was our symbolic parting. A stronger gravity was drawing me away from him, and he knew it. There were tears in my eyes as we entered the street. Saying not a word, my mother paraded me home and, pausing only long enough to warm a cup of chicken broth and make me drink it under threat of violence, sent me off to bed at six o'clock — the young bar mitzvah who had that day become a man."

•

"After that, for a period of a year and more Ahasuerus and I were thick as thieves. For the rest of the summer, every afternoon at three when I got off work at the fishmarket, I'd run down to the Exchange and hang around with Uncle Schmuel until the closing bell. It was a continual contact high. Walking out onto the floor, one crossed a magical perimeter into a charmed world. All the brokers seemed drugged with prosperity, full as ticks, a little bloated and obscene maybe. I took it for granted that this was the way it always had been, was, and would be, world without end. But truly, kid, it was the Golden Age. The market had never been so high before, and probably never has been since. Euphoria reigned. When I think back on it now, the whole place is bathed with an eerie light. I suppose I couldn't help but be affected. Unconsciously though. At that time to me it was little more than a context, the background music against which Ahasuerus, my personal Pied Piper of Hamelin, played his solo. Of course, I learned to read the tape and kept up with a few stocks — my father's RCA in particular — but it was really more to please Ahasuerus and win his approval than genuine interest on my part. The numbers were too abstract to really move a child that age. Plus I had nothing of my own invested." He gave me a significant look. "I hadn't caught the disease. This lasted, as I said, about a year, until the fall, or crash, whatever you want to call it. Sometime during that period, without my knowledge or my mother's, Ahasuerus approached Pops and told him he wanted to set up a trust fund for my education. For all his faults, Pops had his pride. He wouldn't hear of it at first. But Schmuel took him aside and asked why he should be denied this pleasure. In his position the money was only a drop in the bucket. What was he to do with all he'd made, die and give it to the government? He wanted to do something worthwhile with it. And I'd become almost like a son to him, he said.

"In the end Pops relented. The next fall I was enrolled in Mount Abarim, a fancy private school in Manhattan for wealthy Jews, most of them of Germanic background, who had been in America since before the Civil War. They looked down on the Ashkenazi, like my parents, like me, of Central and Eastern European stock, who immigrated later, toward the turn of the century. To them I was a 'kike.' " Kahn laughed bitterly. "Oh yeah, kid, Mount Abarim taught me a thing or two about discrimination, primarily this: that the fiercest anti-Semites are the Jews themselves. I have no room to be high and holy about it either. The truth is, I started picking up those attitudes myself. Mount Abarim is where I became a self-ordained member of the Jewish liberal elite, the aristocracy of the assimilated — a shegetz in other words. Of course, it was a gradual process and took a long time to accomplish in all its glory. Only at Columbia would it finally be completed. But even so early did I begin my metamorphosis into an assimmulatto, a simulacrum, a simulator, a simulation, in other words, a Jessica. The grotesque irony, of course, is that my uncle, the mad Ashkenazi, funded the whole thing. His gold subsidized the marvelous transmutation of little Aaron from dark meat into white. And what was the result? I became a snob just like the shiksa and despised him in my heart. I played Jessica to his Shylock and looked down on his vulgar money and his vulgar ways. I suppose I'm partially exonerated by the fact that I never knew Ahasuerus was picking up the tab, not until much later when it was too late to thank him. But to be honest, I wonder if knowing would have made a difference.

"My education though was a subtle, long-term thing, a slow gravitation away from Schmuel toward the mainstream of American culture (as I perceived it), a primary movement, if you will. Within it there were more immediate causes for the distancing, chief among them the crash of twenty-nine. Summer was over; I no longer made my afternoon pilgrimage to Wall Street. I was in school the day it happened — October twenty-fourth, Black Thursday. Pops said he never knew how much Schmuel lost, because he never knew how much he'd had to begin with. But, kid, the ravage was apparent in his face. A year before, that enchanted summer of twenty-eight, he was (I'm guessing) fifty-five and looked ten years younger. By the summer of 1930 he looked like a seventy-year-old wino. I'm not kidding you. Ahasuerus didn't land on his feet that time. Once or twice on holidays from school I went down to the Exchange to visit him like in the old days. I couldn't believe the change — in it or him. The place was like a funeral parlor, and Ahasuerus was the corpse. He was listless, stopped shaving regularly, there was almost always liquor on his breath. The whole thing depressed me. I started going less and less. Then one day Pops told me he was in the hospital. I asked if I could visit, but he said no. I didn't see Uncle Schmuel for almost a year. Whenever I asked what was wrong with him, Pops was evasive. 'Exhaustion,' he said. I never really learned the truth, but I suspect it was a nervous breakdown.

"Ahasuerus was nothing though if not resilient. I guess he'd only used up eight of his nine lives. By the time the recovery began to pick up steam in thirty-four, he was back out on the trading floor, going at it as hard as ever.

He gave it his best shot I'm sure, but you know it must have taken something out of him. He never totally regained his former verve, or his fortune, apparently. Oh, he became moderately wealthy again, but never in the old way.

By this time the distance between us had widened considerably. I was in my first year at Columbia and looked back on those old days packing fish and tagging at his heels at the Exchange with wistful condescension, an 'episode of youth.' I remembered him fondly, but his stature had contracted in my eyes. To me, the cultivated young Jewish intellectual with academic ambitions, he came increasingly to seem an outlandish atavism, an incarnation of the vulgar, slightly comic old-world alter kocker, out of place in modern times. Sure, we still kept in touch. Sometimes he'd call me up and ask me out to dinner, and if I had nothing better to do — studying or girls, that is — I'd go. But the old magic was lacking. Before he'd always been the one who gave, I the beneficiary. Now, however, it was apparent he needed something from me. I was like an emotional talisman, I think, with which he pathetically tried to conjure back his former self. He sought to repair his injured self-esteem with the adoration I'd once given him so freely. And because he needed it so desperately, I couldn't give it. Those dinners were sad for both of us. It made me doubt my memories. I assumed I'd magnified him out of all proportion in my recollections, so now I overcompensated, shrinking him by half. Thus, by an unstated mutual consent, we let it lapse. I'll never forget something he said to me the last time we met for dinner: 'I may be a schlemiel, Aaron, but I'm no schlimazel.' The pathos of it didn't hit me until much later. Maybe I didn't want to understand.

"Ahasuerus died two years later. Thanksgiving 1941. I was in graduate school by then. He and my parents had gone down to Florida. Two weeks of sun and fun in fabulous Miami Beach. Pops calls me and tells me he's had a stroke. Get this, kid. In bed! I don't mean sleeping, either. I'm not lying. The woman is a hooker, not exactly a paragon of social tact. She tells Pops she was sort of flattered by the commotion. She thinks he's coming until he starts turning blue. That's when she starts screaming, and the shamus picks the lock. 'He was a wonderful lover for an old man,' the woman tells Pops by way of eulogy. Sincere homage. Pops says it makes him cry. Of course, at the time of the phone call Ahasuerus has not yet given up the ghost. The doctor has given them the word though: the case is hopeless. But with Ahasuerus, who knows? His eyes are open, a little glazed, but open, Pops says. They aren't sure if he recognizes them, or if he's even conscious. Nevertheless, Pops tells me, 'We thought maybe you'd like to come.'

"Here I am a thousand miles away. It's getting down to the wire in the semester. And this isn't just any semester. I'm staring down at a stack of books yea high which I have to get through before my orals, which are about ten days away. The timing couldn't be worse. I say, 'Pops, if he doesn't even know you . . .'"

" 'We're not sure,' he interjects quickly.

" 'Gee, Pops,' I say, 'I'm really sick about it.'

" 'All right, Aaron,' he says. 'We're not going to pressure you. It's your decision, you decide. You've got to live with it.'

"I did; I didn't — did decide; didn't go (didn't live with it either, at least not well).

"The day after my exam — which I passed, not exactly with flying colors, though not by the skin of my teeth either, somewhere in between, I guess — I get a telegram. Ahasuerus is dead. I pack a bag and take a taxi to the airport. I get aboard an airplane for the first time in my life, right? An Eastern Airlines DC-3. It takes all day and half the night, what with the stops and everything. Pops is all to pieces, kid. Just crying like a baby. We sit up till morning together in the hotel room, drinking scotch. He tells me the whole schmeer — about the money, the trust fund, everything. What can I tell you? I'm sick. Just sick. That trip laid enough guilt on me to last a lifetime. Plus some. To top it all off, Pops tells me Schmuel was lucid for a while near the end and asked for me. Pops could have spared me that at least, don't you think? But no, let's pile it on! Sure! Why not? Just back it up and dump it here! Fuck!" said Kahn viciously, sweeping his drink off the table with his arm. "Bring me another one," he told the waiter.

"Okay, kid. New York City, a few days later. The reading of the will. The trust is bankrupt, I discover. I can't go back to school. Even Pops says he didn't know. It's all gone. Everything. Except the seat. The fucking seat. Which Ahasuerus, of course, bequeaths to me. Get this — with the stipulation that it not be sold before my thirtieth birthday. Can you believe it? He's even paid the dues. Ahasuerus indeed!

"Kid, for about a week I didn't know myself. I sat in that apartment on One hundred and fifteenth alternately pitching fits, throwing things at the wall, and breaking down and blubbering, falling asleep for fifteen hours at a time. Rage, remorse, self-pity, guilt — you name it, I milked it. And it milked me. I drank whiskey. I took cold showers. I drank black coffee. I ate bonbons. Boxes of them, cases! When I was sane I tried to decide what I was supposed to do with my life. Suicide seemed the only rational alternative for ending my misery. But what can I tell you? I'm too irrational to act on it. Besides, I'm afraid of pain." He shrugged and cracked a small, apologetic smile. "So what happens? Fate comes to the rescue. December seventh, 1941. The Japanese bomb Pearl Harbor. What the hell? I think. I'll join the army and go blow things up. If nothing else, at least it should make me feel a little better. So I go to enlist. I fill in the form, right, and go off to have my physical. Guess what? Rejected. Flat feet. I mean, I was maybe a little worried about my weight, but flat feet! It's humiliatin'!

"So, not to torture you with suspense, Kahn spends the next four years eating bonbons when he can get them, which isn't very often, and tabulating statistics on production figures for the OWI — Office of War Information, for your information, kid — which incidentally is why I didn't go with you to

P. E. Powers's lecture on Intrinsic Value: I can't take it anymore. Gun-shy (butter-shy, too). I got enough fundamentals there to last me a lifetime. Several lifetimes. Plus some. Of course, every once in a blue moon, because of my 'literary background,' you understand, they let me write up a press release for Elmer — Davis, that is. It wasn't bad I guess. It gave me time to think. And, more importantly, time not to. After I calmed down, I sort of assumed I'd go back and get my Ph.D. when it was over. I experienced moments of doubt, of course, when I remembered my performance on my orals and wondered if I really had it in me to set the academic community on fire. But these were temporary aberrations. The university was home to me by this time. I mean, what else was I fit for? Ah ah ah! Don't anticipate!

"So anyway, finally we drop Oppenheimer's little toy on the Japanese, and they begin to get the picture. You can't fuck with Bwana. God is on his side. Oh Jesus! So we roll up the carpet down at the OWI, lock the doors, and all go home, back to the real world. I find myself out on the street, a young, wealthy, Jewish derelict, two years left to go in Ahasuerus's sentence before I can sell my seat. I talk to Pops and ask if he can spring for my tuition. He can't, he says. He doesn't have the money. 'Besides,' he tells me, 'you're twenty-eight years old. It's time you turned your education to some account,' by which, of course, he meant converting sense to dollars. 'Get a job for two years,' he says. 'Save. If you still want it after that, it'll still be there.' What could I say to that, kid? I find work with an advertising agency writing copy for Pepsi-Cola and other worthy causes. My old friends at Columbia are horrified and *very* sympathetic. Actually, it's not too bad. Kahn rather likes it. He gets to be a little of the poet. Ah, kid, what a fall was there!

"So two years pass. I've been out of it six years. I've grown a little bit complacent, a little soft around the middle. I'm out of training. Listen up, kid. This is the sad part. I have my two years' savings, right? Enough to last me until I can sell the seat, which should take me through my Ph.D. no problem. Comfortably. Hell, in style! So what happens? I put it in the market. Pepsi-Cola. That's right, kid. I wrote so much copy I finally sold it to myself. Don't ask me how it happened, I'm still not sure. I couldn't help myself. It's still there, kid. So am I.

"What can I say?" He shook his head. "The market is the last frontier, a wilderness civilization has created. It's the last place in this country where the struggle for survival still goes on like it did in the Mesozoic Age. All the great predators still roam free, freely engaging in their ancient privilege of venery and slaughter. You see, kid, that's how I saw Ahasuerus. That's how I see myself. The call of the wild. That's why I've never sold out, I suppose, the bottom line. And the floor trader is the king of the jungle in our world, the purest incarnation of the type. We're an endangered species though. They're trying to legislate us out of existence. Because for all their talk about free enterprise, the self-interest we stand for is so pure and so extreme in nature, most men, even businessmen, can't look the proposition square in the face without flinching. But it's the test-case of the whole free enterprise system, the *reductio,* not *ad absurdum,* but *ad essentiam,* without which the whole rule falls.

"I guess from what I've said to you tonight, you can see I've never totally reconciled myself to this role. It's something I aspire to, part of me. Yet there's an equal and contradictory aspiration drawing me in the opposite direction. Intellectual or capitalist pig?" He shrugged. "Sometimes I'm afraid the warfare of the two will prevent me from really becoming either. That's what I admired, even worshipped, in men like my uncle and Jessie Livermore: in them it was immaculate, the rage. That wildness existed in them unspoiled. All considerations of morality aside, kid, it's a beautiful thing to witness, an organism so completely in harmony with itself, so single, so free of guilt. Maybe my ambivalence is more evolved, who can judge? I only know that thing which the intellectual side rejects can take you to a place the intellect never goes, where all the cold, deliberate arguments seem like pedantic quibbles. In that place all the rules are overruled. The rational stuff is like Newtonian mechanics: it's okay to describe the ordinary world, but take it to the extremes, the realms of the infinitely large or small, and it falls apart; its inapplicability there proves its larger speciousness. Sometimes I think maybe all morality, all law, is merely Newtonian mechanics in the face of the relativity of altered states."

"The ecstasy of combat," I murmured, carried far by his speculations.

"That's it, kid," he said, as if he knew. "On the money."

We were silent for a while, nursing our drinks, both of us completely drunk, but completely sobered. From time to time Kahn would heave a sigh, or I would. But what was there to say?

Finally he looked up. "So that's it, kid, the whole megillah. It's all true too, every word of it." He smiled wryly. ". . . Every other word at least. So say something. What's the verdict?"

"I don't know what to say," I replied. "I'm overwhelmed."

Kahn sighed. "I pardon you, kid. I guess it is a lot to digest at one sitting. As I see it, though, the entire unexpurgated version of the Life of Kahn reduces to a single moral judgment, succinct and pithy, sort of a world view like the Fundamentalists' and Technicians', Kahn's Weltanschauung: 'I may be a schlemiel, but I'm no schlimazel.' Is that asking too much?" This time I knew the question was not merely rhetorical.

I shook my head. "I don't think so."

He sighed. "Thanks, kid. I appreciate it. I guess I should have said that in the beginning, huh, and saved us both the rigors of the story?"

We both laughed.

"Last call!" the bartender cried.

But we had had enough — more than enough. And then some. Pushing open the door into the street, we had to stop and catch our breath. The New York dawn was blood drenched, insane, full of a mournful beauty which seemed to intimate the aftermath of war or famine, a great city burning in the east, consumed by holocaust. Ghostly plumes of steam were rising from the gutters in the humid air, like smoke, as though from some recently completed carnage. There were pools of standing water on the sidewalk, too, pinkish with the sunrise as though with diluted blood. As I walked up into the lurid conflagration of that sky, my eye was caught by the string of traffic lights on Eighty-sixth, discrete nodes of unnatural light, like rubies in a raging fire, glowing without heat; and as I held my breath I watched them, one by one, turn green.

Chapter 11

I opened my eyes and stared around. My head was throbbing. I felt nauseated. I had no idea what day or week it was. The quality of the light, however, suggested dusk. At least I was in my own apartment. That was something. The banging continued.

"All right, all right already!" I shouted. "I'm coming. Who is it?"

Sitting up on my mattress, I saw the tip of Lo's nose pressed flat against my windowpane as he peered in.

"Excuse please!" he said nervously, breaking spontaneously into his little chicken dance of propitiation as I opened the door. "I hadn't thought to find you sleeping at this hour."

"What time is it?" I asked dully.

"Almost six! Had you forgotten? You were to dine with us."

"It's Saturday then?" I asked, beginning to regain my bearings. My God — Yin-mi! It suddenly hit me. I had promised to go with her to TYA tonight.

Lo studied me closely. "The young dragon has perhaps drunk too much wine?"

I groaned. "Lo, do you have an aspirin? Better make it three," I added on second thought. "I'm suffering."

He shook his head. "Excuse please. Aspirin is no use in such conditions. Believe me, I know." He flashed me the roguish grin.

"Help me, Lo," I moaned forlornly, clutching my head between my hands.

He pursed his lips. "In such situations, there is only one solution," he pontificated. "And some say the remedy is worse than the disease."

"I don't care!" I cried. "Just tell me. What is this solution?"

"Have another drink!"

I whinnied and ran for the toilet.

"Don't go 'way!" he said, clapping me on the shoulder as I leaned into the bowl. "I'll be right back!"

True to his word, a moment later he reappeared with a bottle. I was lying on my mattress in a cold sweat, hardly daring to breathe for fear of upsetting the fragile peptic equilibrium my first bout of the heaves had won me.

"The first sip is the worst," he informed me, filling our respective jiggers. "But believe me, after that you'll feel as good as new."

In spite of my condition, I was alert enough to notice and resent the fact that he'd become unusually expansive.

"I don't think I can." I grimaced and reared backward as he urged the cup toward my lips. The bouquet alone was almost enough to make me spew.

"I was afraid of that," he remarked with a frown. "The young dragon must follow my instructions, otherwise . . ." — he shook his head grimly — "no hope."

I gave him a vulnerable, searching look, then acquiesced with a fatalistic sigh.

"Okay, open your mouth . . ." he coached.

I complied.

"And close your eyes . . ."

I didn't have to; they were closed already.

"Better hold your nose too," he added, throwing off his prosody, "just to make sure. . . . Now for the big surprise! Kan pei!"

When I regained consciousness, I felt like someone who has died for a brief instant and been resuscitated on the operating table.

Lo was sitting in a chair beside my bed examining his watch. "You've been out for thirty seconds. I think it's a record. How do you feel?"

I rubbed my temples. "Not bad," I replied. I focused my concentration on my navel: no problem in that quarter either. "Not bad at all. In fact" — I sprang erect in bed — "I feel wonderful! Let's have another drink!"

He beamed at me happily as he poured the wine.

"To . . . the solution!" I proposed.

"Kan pei!" he cried.

"Ah, the subtleties of wine," I said.

Lo laughed with delight. "It has been too long since I have had the pleasure of drinking with the young dragon."

"The pleasure is entirely mine," I contradicted, with a suave bow.

"No, no," he demurred.

"Yes, yes," I insisted.

We both laughed.

"Ah, Sun I, you are sorely missed at the restaurant." His countenance became mildly dejected. "Things haven't been the same since the departure of our A-One Dragon Assistant."

"How is the young fish? Is he still with you?"

"Unfortunately." Lo shrugged. "What can I say? The fish continues as before, leaving a trail of desolation in his wake, destroying everything he touches, floundering and carping. We are all agreed, your brief stay at Luck Fat's was like a Golden Age." He eyed me timidly. "You would not consider returning to us, I suppose?"

"Ah, Lo, you are too kind. Your offer overwhelms me." I sighed. "But what you ask is impossible, at least for the present. I am only beginning to make headway in my quest. As yet I've only scratched the surface of the Dow. There is so much more to learn. I can't turn back now."

"I see," he said, disappointed. "Well, should you ever change your mind . . ."

I smiled at him, and we finished our cups in silence.

Lo reached for the bottle.

"No, no," I said, placing my hand over my cup.

"Yes, yes," he insisted. "We must sharpen our perceptions with another round and then discuss. Last time we were remiss. Neglecting this, we not only forfeited the greatest pleasure of the connoisseur, but were disrespectful to the wine itself. Tonight we must make atonement for our sins."

I swallowed with anxiety, taking the cup he handed me.

"So, what is your opinion?" he asked gravely, after allowing me ample time for reflection.

"Lo" — I put my jigger on the table and bowed my head — "I have deceived you by allowing you to think I am a connoisseur. The truth is, as regards the subtleties of wine, I am the greenest neophyte."

"Your modesty becomes you," he complimented, "but you must not be reticent with me. After all, we have drunk together, and that entails an obligation to be frank. Come, come. Your honest opinion."

My imploring glance had no effect. "Well," I ventured, "it bears comparison with a certain vintage I sampled recently — only last night, in fact."

He sat up with a show of interest. "What vintage is that?"

I cleared my throat. "Dry Sack," I pronounced uneasily.

"Dry Sack." He pursed his lips and nodded. "I have not heard of it. It must be very rare."

"If you have not heard of it . . ." Shrugging, I left him to draw the inference.

"And your opinion?"

He pursed his lips deprecatingly. "Well, it is not a special vintage, certainly no Dry Sack! Though you are kind enough to compare them. Hardly even as good as a K'ao Liang. Personally I find it a bit lazy, a little sluggish on the tongue." He sought my corroboration.

"Yes, a bit syrupy, I think."

"But not too sweet?" he rejoined sharply.

"Oh no!" I cried in alarm, instantly regretting my foolish intrepidity. "Not too sweet at all. I only meant a little . . . thick," I said cautiously.

Lo took a deep breath, almost a sigh, then slowly he began to nod. "Yes, exactly. A bit 'thick,' a little bit lethargic, as though disspirited. But not too far off the mark?" he suggested, with a touching, almost boyish vulnerability.

"No, certainly not!" I agreed.

"Not really . . . mediocre?"

"Rather good actually," I assured him.

"Yes, it is, isn't it?" he agreed with satisfaction. "Indeed, it is a royal-blooded wine, though perhaps not of the highest rank. Not the crown prince, but one of his younger brothers, to whom fate has given great talents without the opportunity to develop them, and who has consequently squandered them in dissipation. A wine of great unhappiness, of tragedy, perhaps."

He regarded me with great solemnity, and it occurred to me that, all unconsciously, my friend was speaking of himself.

"Indeed, a noble wine," I said quietly, with sincerity.

"How long since I have enjoyed the companionship of a man who truly understands the subtleties." His eyes welled with incipient tears. "I can drink with you, Sun I. You are a cultivated man."

"You exaggerate," I demurred, simpering.

"No, no."

"Yes, yes."

"We must go now, though," he reminded me. "We're already late. Yin-mi will be getting anxious."

•

"Open, wife, it's I," he called. "I've brought a visitor."

We heard an excited fumbling at the latch.

"Oh, Sun I!" Mrs. H. exclaimed, beaming at me in her characteristic manner. "Please come in. Where have you been? We were worried about you!"

"I overslept," I muttered with guilty succinctness.

"But we haven't seen you in a week!" she protested. "You've become a perfect stranger."

"Now, wife," Lo admonished with mock sternness, "if you carp and fuss so, you will frighten him away for good. Did you not know that dragons are the shyest of creatures, though in their wrath most terrible and mighty?"

"But what does he eat?" she protested.

"How should I know?" He shrugged. "He is a dragon, isn't he? Perhaps he lives on air!" On the sly he winked at her; she pressed her fingertips to her lips, suppressing a titter.

For the first time, the humor and the gentle reproof implied in Lo's epithet revealed themselves to me. I laughed appreciatively. "I am not so unworldly as you suggest, Lo. Certainly my asceticism is not strong enough to hold out against the prospect of one of Mrs. Ha-p'i's excellent home-cooked meals!"

Mrs. H. blushed, beamed and fluttered, fairly levitating in a paroxysm of delight. Circling her waist with his arm, Lo drew her toward him, patting her fanny in the process with sly affection.

"Lo! Our guest!" she exclaimed in mortification. "What are you thinking of?"

"Surely you don't imagine Sun I is scandalized by such behavior?" he replied. "Can you think that in his wanderings the young dragon has failed to be initiated into the mysteries of the 'play of wind and clouds'? Come now, wife. Though a young dragon, he is also a young man." He shot me his sly wink.

"Look how you've embarrassed him!" Mrs. H. protested sympathetically, cuffing him on the shoulder.

My guilt, or innocence, must have been apparent in my face. Lo seemed genuinely astonished.

She glared at her husband. "You've been drinking, haven't you?"

Pouting, he held his thumb and finger up an inch apart to indicate a dram.

"What's going on here?" Yin-mi asked, emerging from the hall. "That's right, Mother, punch him out! Are they teaming up on you? Beat them both! You should be ashamed — a poor, defenseless woman!" Her easy, limpid laughter infected Lo and me at once. Mrs. H. balked, grew flustered, then, giving over, followed suit. The potential crisis was averted.

"You two certainly seem in good spirits tonight," Yin-mi commented with a trace of her father's archness.

"Royal spirits!" Lo agreed, winking at me.

"They've been drinking," Mrs. H. said reproachfully, but with a grudging smile.

The furrow appeared in Yin-mi's brow. "You mean Father has," she corrected her mother. "Surely not Sun I?"

Her mother regarded her from under arched eyebrows.

Yin-mi turned to me incredulously. "Sun I?"

In her face there was the same curiosity and candor I had seen that first night as she stood in the doorway watching me, even a trace of mild amusement, but running underneath, the solution into which these separate currents all dissolved, that great solemnity which was the central motive and characteristic impulse of her being.

I had to drop my eyes.

Instead of a reproach, however, to my surprise she burst out laughing at the very incongruousness of it — *me* drinking. "Come on." She took me gaily by the arm. "We'll be late if we don't hurry."

"Here, take this parasol," Mrs. H. called after us. "The weather report calls for showers and possible thunderstorms later tonight."

The streets were full of children riding bicycles and playing stickball, neighbors lounging on their stoops and fire escapes conversing genially. Old couples strolled arm-in-arm in the dusky streets. Seeing us, they paused and smiled, bowing slightly at the waist, a gesture which included, or at least invited, us into the age-old mystery their contented faces intimated, the mystery of human continuity, of conjugal fidelity and love, which in its Taoist aspect is called the "willing bondage to the Wheel" (of Sorrow). Despite the moral ambiguity of such inclusion to one in my position, I was touched and grateful. I felt flattered by it, even thrilled. With a shy, gentle pressure, Yin-mi drew closer to my arm, making me almost dare to hope (and yet I could not hope, could not allow myself) that she was experiencing a similar emotion. We continued on in an expansive silence.

"Looks like I got your father into trouble again," I remarked, after we'd walked a way.

She searched my face with an expression of amusement which threatened to bubble over into laughter. "The two of you did seem rather full of yourselves," she commented, adding, "I'm sure he boiled his own hot water though." She said this with a hint of archness, which again reminded me of Lo, but her eyes were very tender, almost sad, as if absorbing our error and forging it.

I should have been grateful perhaps, but a part of me — call it Monkey Nature (fired by wine) — wasn't sure it wanted to be forgiven and resented the presumption on her part. For the second time, I felt the mysterious rankling rising in my heart. Without further aggravation, this might have dispersed by itself, but unfortunately, she followed that solemn look with: "You really shouldn't encourage him, you know."

"Encourage *him*!" I exploded.

"He works so hard, Sun I," she explained gently, "and unlike you he has no spiritual sanctuary to return to when the delights have faded and left him with the shame and sickness, nothing to brake his impulse toward it or buffer its ill effects."

"What is 'it'?" I asked mincingly.

She was grave. "You know."

"You mean drunkenness," I said.

"Yes, if you will, 'drunkenness,' or, more precisely, what you once described to me as 'the exquisite mysteries of disintegration.' "

"That was opium," I objected.

"And this is something just as good," she said, sadly but firmly, "which is to say, as bad."

I was startled by the depth and complexity of her remark, even more so by the haunting echo it bore to Mme Chin's at our first meeting. This pleased me strangely and aroused my admiration, yet without diminishing my resentfulness. "Even if, as you say, he has no sanctuary to return to," I continued, "he has his 'solution.' Perhaps in its way that too is 'something just as good.' "

"What solution?" she asked innocently.

I hesitated before answering. I saw the same fragility and trust in her which several times before had moved me to self-remembrance and compassion when a base impulse had threatened to erupt. These things moved me now, and just as deeply, but I did not desist. In Kahn's too-telling phrase, I couldn't help myself. "Have another drink!" I answered, affecting levity, but feeling instead a sense of heavy sickness and despair, succeeded by an immense, disspirited apathy when I had said it, reminiscent indeed of the dark downside of opium, after the blood has consumed its heady ether and is left with the sludge of the spent fuel.

She continued observing me in silence, that great solemnity in her expression more terrible than any reproach she might have uttered. From underneath the torpor, I felt shame and loathing welling up — primarily against myself but, respecting no boundaries, sweeping her into the vortex too. I tried to draw my arm away, but she refused. Something in my heart went wild. Without thinking, purely by reflex, I raised my other hand as though to strike her, more by way of warning than in actual intention, yet equally unforgivable either way.

"I will," I threatened in a low, boorish voice, "if you don't let me go."

She shook her head resolutely. "I won't," she asserted. "Not when you're like this."

"Like what?" I tugged again, but more halfheartedly, discovering in myself a desire not to be released, and a reciprocal fear she might.

"Drunk," she said.

"I'm not drunk!" I shouted.

"Tipsy then, and foolish!" she shouted back, equaling my volume, though evidently distressed to have to.

Delighted by her answer, I broke out laughing.

She burst into tears.

With a sweet, pained tenderness, I watched her weep. "Yin-mi," I said finally, in a quiet voice, the anger all dissolved, "forgive me. You're right. I am a fool."

Her eyes glowed blissfully through her tears. "Shhh," she said, putting her finger to my lips. "You must never say that, or even think it. Only I can." She laughed and sniffled at once. "Give me your handkerchief." I passively obeyed. She daubed her eyes, then blew her nose obstreperously. "There," she said, handing it back. "Now we're even." She laughed happily, her face radiant as though with physical exertion from the swift emotional reversal.

Once again the hairline seam in the fabric of reality yawned open, and in her face a host of molten, shimmering secrets revealed themselves to me. Her features blurred, each detail too immense, too exhausting for my eye to encompass whole, a world. In her flesh, her eyes and hair, I saw the elemental beauty of uncreated matter restlessly churning and transforming, its voluptuousness overwhelming and unspeakably obscene, intimating decay, the breath of putrefaction inherent in all mortal things. And just as quickly as it had opened, the seam annealed, and she became herself again, Yin-mi, the girl I knew. The sickness in my heart now was not self-loathing but pity and tenderness, the same emotion I'd experienced that first day in New York, sitting on the bench in the graveyard of Trinity Church, looking out through the wrought iron bars at the crowds toiling in the street as the stone revealed its secret.

"What's the matter?" she asked tremulously. "You aren't still angry, are you?"

I shook my head.

"Why are you looking at me like that?"

"I don't know."

"You're crying!" she said in surprise.

"Am I?" I reached up and pressed my lashes with my fingertips.

"You really don't know, do you," she said in a quiet voice.

"Do you?" I asked, taking up the implication.

She smiled. "Oh yes. That is, I think so. Some. I think I've known it all along, since the first night."

I asked the question with my eyes.

Not pausing to resolve the mystery for me, she took my arm, still smiling, and we went off again.

•

"Now you stay here," she ordered, ushering me into a pew at the rear of the church. "There's a special Mass tonight. I have to sing in the choir. I'll come back and get you when it's over."

With that, she disappeared into the vestry.

Once again I was alone in Trinity. After the scene outside, a sense of repose settled over me, and I was grateful. There was something healing here, in the perpetual twilight of the church, the vastness and depth of the interior space filled with its impalpable smoke of gloom, dissolving the salient edges and recesses into one homogeneous solution. The hush was liquid, like the whispering silence of a shell, intimating the tidal movement of some distant ocean. Indeed, Trinity, with its gothic spires and knobs, bore a resemblance to a huge, inverted conch, in which, like undefended creatures of the deep, I and the other members of the congregation had taken temporary refuge. The sibilant reverberation in its acoustic hollow was like a rarefied harmonic of the ebb and flow of mystic waters, Tao. The church was like a physical embodiment of a meditative state, one I'd frequented in the past as easily as tonight I'd entered the building from the street, but now, since Hsiao's visit and my departure from Ken Kuan, found increasingly difficult of access. And connected with this impression was another: that the church, with its splendid glooms, was like a living monument to the expression in Yin-mi's eyes.

Staring up into the clerestory toward the windows, I was disappointed to find them mute and inexpressive, like broad expanses of moonlit water, obscure except for an occasional ripple in the glass, highlights spangled upward from the candles burning in the nave. Compensating for the loss, however, was a sense of imminence which I hadn't noticed on the first occasion, as of a gathering storm. Indeed, the atmosphere, like the interior of a thunderhead, fairly crackled with invisible, electric fire, as though some divine intelligence brooded there, threatening to reveal himself in a terrible epiphany. Knowing so little of the Christian God, I feared his advent and wondered at the avenue it would take. Would he manifest himself in a benignant form, smiling on the world he had created, or with the fangs and bulging, bloodshot eyes of a Mahakala?

With sensuous wonder, I surveyed the props of the Mass, whose function I had guessed at so wildly before and still could not divine: the seven-branched candelabra burning on either side of the altar above the snow-white cloth. "XP" — what did it mean? Some magical alchemical prescription for eternal life, perhaps? I noted the silver pyx in which, unknown to me, the unblessed host awaited consecration by the priest, the paten over which, shortly, he would bless and break it, the chalice for the wine.

Noiselessly, the choir and celebrants began to gather in the vestibule. The organ pealed a thunderous bass run as prelude to the hymn, and the processional began. They filed in, two by two, in their black vestments, hymnals open in their hands, their faces lifted, chins raised, throats extended, singing into the vault. A young man passed my pew bearing the crucifix. The polished brass glimmered in the wavering, uncertain candlelight, the sad boy, with his thin, effeminate body and his drawn face, combining in his person the strengths and weaknesses of man and woman, youth and age, hanging by the cruel nails driven through his feet and hands, above him the legend, INRI.

As she passed, Yin-mi smiled at me demurely. Shifting the hymnal into her left hand, she waved surreptitiously from beneath its cover, a discreet little syncopated finger salute. Riley trailed the procession, walking alone, hands clasped behind his back, holding a book. He was smiling, gazing into the distance as though absorbed in working out some speculative possibility that had just revealed itself to him. I knew him at once from Yin-mi's description.

In his late thirties, though much younger looking, he was tall and broad shouldered, but almost cadaverously thin. He had a large, luminous brow and pale gray-blue eyes, which when unengaged, as now, had a characteristically abstract expression, but could become, as I learned, surprisingly shrewd surprisingly quickly. They had a gemlike, scintillant quality. His wavy red hair rose from the part toward a peak at the opposite side of his head, like a mounting breaker or an unbalanced tongue of Pentecostal flame. His complexion was beautiful, extremely white; his skin had a translucent quality, with a few sandy freckles scattered underneath his eyes like sleep, lending him a charming vulnerability. His face had a certain glow not entirely attributable to the fineness of his complexion; I recognized it well: the clear, ethereal, slightly manic bliss of a man who habitually fasts. I had seen it often in the brothers at Ken Kuan. But whereas among them it had characteristically suggested a quality of interiority and repose, in Riley it portended an ecstasy, something overflowing on itself, his body like a tuning fork resonating at the soul's own frequency, a pitch too high for matter to sustain. About his eyes was an intensity that was difficult to look at without flinching, like the look in the bear's eyes, only rendered more accessible and less frightening by intelligence. As he noted me in passing, that intensity seemed literally to burn into me, suggesting a certainty and conviction as deep as any I had ever seen. He wasn't handsome: despite the mollifying freckles, his features had an unpleasant concentration that destroyed that possibility. Yet the man had a melancholy, fateful beauty, "an outward and visible sign of inward and spiritual grace," and from the first moment I saw him, before we ever spoke, I intuited his sincerity and elevation and understood why Yin-mi had entrusted herself to him, why, indeed, she loved him. And so, in my state of tipsy clairvoyance, amid the confused profusion of other emotions, there was a tinge of jealousy on her account as well — quite unconscious, I might add.

Soothing, mildly soporific, the service flowed around me like a river, a stately pageant of dream imagery bathing and enveloping my consciousness, sweeping me onward toward some unimaginable consummation. Lulled into a state of voluptuous passivity by the gorgeousness of the spectacle, I watched the ritual unfolding in delicate tracery at the altar, understanding nothing, not needing to. Halfway through the service, I was mildly annoyed to find the usher standing abreast of me in the aisle, fixing me with a look of gentle exhortation. Laying his hand on the back of the pew (he wore a signet ring of heavy gold which rapped there ever so lightly, like a tap at the door of my conscience), he nodded to me. Though I had no wish to be roused from my state of pleasing invalidism — preferring in this, as in the market, to observe without participating, yet reared to respect not only the spirit but, insofar as possible, the letter of all religions, a guest in that place as well — I decided it could do no harm to fall in with their requirements. Rising, I followed the others as they filed toward the apse. I was gratified to see how deeply my small concession moved Yin-mi. As I passed her in the choir on my way to the altar, out of the corner of my eye I saw her waving to me, a little too demonstratively perhaps, but no doubt she was thrilled that I should make this gesture freely with no prompting on her part. I waved back.

With Monkey's immemorial gift for astute mimicry, feeling slightly foolish and self-conscious (but under professional obligation, as it were), I observed the others as they genuflected to the crucifix and filed out along the altar rail, following suit myself. Kneeling on cushions of claret-colored plush, worn shiny with the knees of many worshippers, I imitated them as they propped their elbows on the balustrade of polished brass, right palm cupped in left, and bowed their heads. Though I had seen the Christian attitude of prayer before, the position of the hands was new to me. This detail held an academic interest. Each meditation has a different so-called *mudra*. Some form a circle with the thumbs and forefingers: the cosmic mudra of the Buddhists, conjuring infinity, as it were. Taoists grasp the thumb of the left hand in the right palm like the links of a chain, signifying the adept's attempt to integrate himself into the great organic chain of Being through *tso-wang*. I was speculating on the possible significance of the Christian position, when suddenly it was very palpably demonstrated to me. Startled by a light, almost ticklish pressure in my palm and hearing the words, "this do in remembrance of me," I opened my eyes and looked up to see Riley passing along the rail. Pausing briefly before each communicant, he pressed something into their hands, murmuring as he did so, his voice resonant with emotion, its timbre suggesting the luminous twilight of the church. Examining my hand when he had passed me, I found a white paper-thin wafer stamped with a cross. Riley's voice had lapsed into a soothing, inarticulate drone. In remembrance of whom? I wondered. I had no time to speculate, for I observed that my neighbors were pressing their tongues into their hands, then retracting them into their mouths to suck the small disks of bread (not chewing, there was no movement of the jaw — my Monkey eye made careful note of this), letting them dissolve as though savoring the taste too much to quicken it by outright mastication. Personally I found them rather bland and tasteless and was reminded of my experience in the Irish bar the night before with Kahn, but I knew better than to despise the well-meaning hospitality of others, no matter how humble.

By the time this anemic little Christian cookie had disintegrated, I saw Riley returning down the row, this time with the cup. After it touched each drinker's lips, he wiped the rim with a white napkin and turned it slightly for the next. Again all I heard was the "remembrance of me." As he offered me the cup I was once more gratified by that sense of pleasing invalidism. I remembered Wu nursing me as a child when I was feverish, sitting in a chair beside my bed feeding me with his own hands, offering me sweets and soothing drinks, then wiping my lips with a clean cloth. This pleasant memory was enhanced by something else, a coincidence that amused and delighted me. Tasting the wine, I recognized the vintage instantly. No doubt about it. It was Dry Sack!

Despite the attitude of slight condescension with which I endured this ritual, after it was over I was strangely moved. Perhaps in my condition that single sip was all that was required to push me over the edge back into my intoxicated state, but I felt a sweet liquid fire burning not only in my head but in my heart. I rose uncertainly, a little dazed, and returned with the others to my place. It was some consolation to notice that they too all appeared a little drunk. Their faces glowed with a look of stillness and fulfillment. Suddenly I thought of Lo and wished that he were there. A connoisseur like him, I thought, could hardly fail to appreciate the subtleties of such a vintage. On the way back to my pew, I experienced a wonderful surge of exhilaration and wanted to laugh out loud or sprint down the aisles. Restraining myself, I sat back down where I had been before and, still imitating the others, kneeled and clasped my hands.

As I sat in this posture, my hilarity gradually subsided. Little by little a sense of peace and gratitude percolated upward from the tear-well of my deepest being. For some time, as I've noted, my meditation had suffered, had failed to satisfy me, but now I passed swiftly into a state of clear, restful intensity as profound as any I had ever known. The cicada in the temple of the heart gave over, segueing into a gentler music, like the sound of snow falling on the ocean. This in turn eased till it suggested the muted sighing of a conch, then, magically, nothing . . . the perfect silence of the void. How long since I had heard that silence! My soul breathed to its full capacity for the first time in many months. Like rainwater pooling in a hollow in limestone hills, sinking through the capillaries in the rock, I relied on the force of gravity, of Tao, to return me to the water table. Slowly and resistlessly I sank, with that unhurried, inexorable force which erodes the continents. A sense of joy and deep refreshment welled up in me. I felt cleansed, elastic, reinvigorated. I blinked and cool streaks of tears ran down my cheeks.

Standing in the apse on the left side of the altar was a young boy, twelve, perhaps thirteen, his face radiant with delicate health, suffused by two blushes of high color, touching in its self-conscious attempt at gravity of mien. He was reading from a text, raising his eyes from time to time to engage his audience, his voice still unchanged, a pure, sweet soprano (which invoked my childhood for me, and the singing of the *Songs*). For the first time in the service, I actively asserted my concentration and listened to the words:

"Though I speak with the tongues of men and of angels, and have not love, I am become as sounding brass, or a tinkling cymbal.

"And though I have the gift of prophecy, and understand all mysteries, and all knowledge; and though I have all faith, so that I could remove mountains, and have not love, I am nothing.

"And though I bestow all my goods to feed the poor, and though I give my body to be burned, and have not love, it profiteth me nothing.

"Love suffereth long, and is kind; love envieth not; love vaunteth not itself, is not puffed up,

"Doth not behave itself unseemly, seeketh not its own, is not easily provoked, thinketh no evil,

"Rejoiceth not in iniquity, but rejoiceth in the truth;

"Beareth all things, believeth all things, hopeth all things, endureth all things.

"Love never faileth; but whether there be prophecies, they shall fail; whether there be tongues, they shall cease; whether there be knowledge, it shall vanish away.

"For we know in part, and we prophesy in part.

"But when that which is perfect is come, then that which is in part shall be done away.

"When I was a child, I spoke as a child, I understood as a child, I thought as a child; but when I became a man, I put away childish things.

"For now we see through a glass darkly; but then, face to face; now I know in part, but then shall I know even as also I am known.

"And now abideth faith, hope, love, these three; but the greatest of these is love."

With what rapt attention, even awe, I listened! This passage was as powerful and uncanny as anything in the *I Ching*. Never had words seemed more beautiful to me or sounded such deep places in my spirit. I couldn't fully account for it. Though the text was clarity itself, its general meaning as unambiguous as sunlight, it mystified me, as though the words were a diaphanous veil shimmering and fluttering over something behind, beyond, tantalizing me with glimpses of implied form. "Now I know in part, but then shall I know even as also I am known." And particularly these, "For now we see through a glass darkly; but then, face to face." What splendid and imponderable epiphany did those words portend?

At the conclusion of the service, after the departure of the choir, I remained seated in my pew in a state of excited abstraction, puzzling over these wonders.

After a while, becoming aware of another presence, I discovered Yin-mi standing over me, studying my face with deep seriousness, as she had studied her father's face that first night in the kitchen, the same furrow of perplexed concentration working in her brow. She was very pale. Only after a moment did I realize that she was crying, for she made no sound. Misreading this in accordance with my mood, I was overjoyed, more convinced than ever that some clairvoyant bond of sympathy existed between us, that she shared my emotions. Feeling no need to speak, I touched her hand.

To my surprise she shuddered and withdrew it.

"What's the matter?"

"Sun I," she said in a quiet, trembling voice, "do you realize what you've done?"

Her gravity of tone alarmed me. "What do you mean?"

"You've taken Communion."

"Aren't you pleased?" I asked.

"Pleased! Didn't you see me waving you away from the altar?"

"I don't understand," I said, imploring her. "I simply did what all the rest were doing. Did I make some mistake? I swear I didn't chew."

"All the rest were confirmed Christians," she distinguished. "You aren't even baptized. You have no right to take the Sacrament."

I blinked at her stupidly, the serenity and bliss of my meditation instantaneously exploded. I felt hurt, a little vengeful. "So what is this anyway, a private club?" I blurted, bitterly invoking Kahn's phrase.

"It isn't funny," she chided. "Try and understand: for an unbaptized person to take the Sacrament is forbidden . . . even perhaps a deadly sin," she added, after a brief hesitation. "Yes, I'm almost sure."

"Deadly sin?"

"A sin for which there is no redemption, no forgiveness."

"Come on," I replied skeptically, laughing uneasily and attempting to seduce a smile from her. "It can't be as bad as that. As a matter of fact, I rather enjoyed it!"

She burst into tears. "Oh, Sun I, how can you joke about damnation and the death of your soul?"

"Damnation?" I repeated. "The death of my soul?"

"Come with me," she directed resolutely, taking my hand.

"Where are we going?" I asked, feeling tipsy, reckless, a little bit amused, a little bit angry, at the same time enjoying the cool pressure of her hand and the sensation of being led.

"To see Father Riley."

•

We found him alone in the sacristy, standing before a table to which the vessels of the service had been removed. As we entered the door, he was just lifting a white cloth from the paten. I remember this because it occurred to me at that instant, as he pinched the fabric between thumb and forefinger, that he looked exactly like a magician about to perform a trick, reaching into the folds of his handkerchief to produce a dove. Hearing the door open, he spread the napkin back in place and turned to greet us. "Ah, your Taoist friend," he said, smiling and extending his hand. "I've wanted to meet you. Yin-mi tells me you've been staying away out of an inordinate fear of conversion." Taking in the concern and trepidation in her face, he caught himself up. "What is it, Yin-mi?"

She implored him silently, her lips trembling slightly. In that look I saw the depth of trust and respect she reposed in him, and the affection — an intimacy which excluded me, threatened me too somehow. I felt a sharp, unreasoning pang of panic and rebelliousness.

"It's my fault," she said, bowing her head penitentially, falling with unconscious ease into the immemorial rhythm of confession.

He took her hand as though to offer solace. "What have you done?"

"I neglected to tell Sun I about the Sacrament. . . . He's taken it by mistake." A shadow crossed Riley's face. "He isn't even baptized," she continued, bursting into tears again and adding, a little hysterically, "It's a deadly sin!"

"Calm down," he said with gentle authority. "Let's not jump the gun on this. Deadly sin!" To my surprise he grinned, as though the idea amused him. Yin-mi stopped crying. "Isn't it?" she sniffled, appealing to him.

His brow contracted as though in perplexed concentration. "Well, that could be a rather tricky question if one considered all the theological subtleties. Off the top of my head, though, I'd have to ask in what sense deadly sin could apply to Sun I in the first place. I mean, damnation would seem a bit absurd, certainly redundant, for a Taoist, don't you think?"

"What do you mean?" she asked.

"Simply that as a 'heathen and an infidel' " (he pronounced the phrase with a self-ironic emphasis) "Sun I stands condemned already." He winked at me as though asking for indulgence, and I realized that he was joking, trying to relieve the tension with levity.

I was in no mood to be amused. "That can't be true," I challenged, calling his bluff.

"Oh yes it can be," he retorted with chilling curtness, "and is. But my," he continued, attempting to change the subject, "haven't we gotten off to a good start!"

"You mean that all who aren't avowed Christians are automatically condemned to hell?" I persisted.

"Something along those lines," he replied. "The Roman Catholics distinguish and call it 'limbo.' In recent times, infused with the spirit of democracy, we no longer make the discrimination."

"Surely you don't believe that?" I asked, taking up the irony in his tone.

"I do believe it," he said, suddenly earnest. "Though it's highly unfashionable to say so, or even to allude to it in polite conversation. People prefer to avoid the unpleasant corollaries of faith. Such dogmas are something we'd prefer to put away in a dark hole along with the rack and thumbscrews and the rest of the Inquisitorial hardware. But that is the rigor of belief. Accepting the one great premise, I accept everything that follows from it. Christ said, 'I am the way, the truth, and the life; no man cometh unto the Father, but by me.' It's a hard truth. I may not find it to my taste. But I accept it."

"It's despicable," I retorted. "I don't think I like your faith."

He smiled without mirth. "Sometimes I'm not so sure I like it either. But liking it isn't really the point. Salvation is too important to be decided by preference or niceties of taste."

"Presumably then, Jesus has sentenced Lao Tzu and Buddha to the flames with all the rest," I said ironically.

"Presumably, though in the case of such luminaries I'd imagine they've at least been given a room with a view — Elysium, you know." He simpered.

"How can you make light of it?" I reproached him. "The supposed damnation of half the human race? It's a question of belief for others too, you know, for *me!*"

"I'm trying to convert you," he said with that whimsical smile from which it was impossible to distill an unambiguous essence either of earnestness or irony.

"Well then, at least I don't have to worry about my other trespass," I said, "the Communion, I mean. Under the circumstances, that would appear to be moot."

"I wouldn't say that either," he contradicted. "In the Articles of Religion, number twenty-five, it says, concerning the Sacraments, 'They that receive them unworthily, purchase to themselves damnation, as Saint Paul saith.' You have to understand, Sun I, the Eucharist is the central mystery of our religion. Its solace is a privilege which is purchased only by faith in Christ and commitment to the church. You most certainly are not entitled to it. In my exhortation, which you might have heard if you'd been listening, I said, '. . . which being so divine and comfortable a thing to them who receive it worthily, and so dangerous to those who will presume to receive it unworthily; my duty is to exhort you, in the mean season, to consider the dignity of that holy mystery and the great peril of the unworthy receiving thereof.' You're partially exonerated, though, by your ignorance," he added by way of mitigation. "I presume you did this unwittingly?"

Even more enraged by his offer of qualified pardon, "exoneration," I refused to take it up. "I must tell you, I resent your glib assurance of salvation, and your dismissal of all the other paths. What makes you so sure that you, and you alone, are right?"

"I don't like to be prescriptive or academic on the point, Sun I, but again I must refer you to the Articles. Number seventeen says, 'They also are to be had accursed that presume to say, that every man shall be saved by the Law or sect which he professeth, so that he be diligent to frame his life according to that Law, and the light of Nature. For Holy Scripture doth set out unto us only the Name of Jesus Christ whereby men must be saved.' "

"And who took it on themselves to pontificate thus?" I asked scathingly.

"The Convention of the Bishops, Clergy, and Laity of the Protestant Episcopal Church of America."

"Why should I accept their authority?" I demanded.

"Well, if their authority is insufficient for you, let me cite a deeper one. You ask me how I know?" His eyes scintillated with conviction. "Through this." He laid his fist over his heart exactly as Kahn had, and I knew that he was alluding to the *Tao Te Ching:*

> Shadowy it is and dim;
> Yet within it there is a force,
> A force that though rarefied
> Is nonetheless efficacious.
> From the time of old till now
> Its charge has not departed
> But cheers onward the many warriors.
> How do I know that the many warriors are so?
> Through this.

Meaning, of course, intuition, the knowledge of the heart.

I was astonished and oddly moved. I was drawn to him, though I bridled against his magnetism. I began to understand Hsiao's anger and indignation over that pompous, peculiarly Western assumption of righteousness ("and thus, of course, the world") and wondered if it weren't tied to the stern and uncompromising exclusivity of the Christian mandate: "No man cometh unto the Father, but by me." How different from Taoism and Buddhism, which accord validity to all the paths while regarding the spiritual destination as the same, and which are so much more generous, so much richer in ambiguity. Despite his infuriating self-assurance, though, Riley's conviction was beyond mere arrogance, and I couldn't help but recognize it. That conviction troubled me more than all the rest and made him seem particularly dangerous.

"So what is so special about your little ritual that you guard it so jealously?" I asked.

Riley raised his eyebrows. "You mean you don't understand the meaning of the Mass?"

"You mean the Dry Sack and saltines?" I asked maliciously.

"Come over here," he said abruptly, approaching the table where I'd seen him when we first entered. Lifting the napkin, he held up a piece of the uneaten host. "See this?" Turning my hand over, he placed it in the flat of my palm.

A mischievous impulse seized me, and I let the wafer drop back in the pyx. "So what are these, matzos?"

Riley grew stern and took up the wafer. Lifting it to the level of his forehead, he broke it, saying in that same mesmeric tone of voice, "Take, eat; this is my body, which is broken for you: this do in remembrance of me." He closed his eyes and placed it on his tongue.

Raising the chalice similarly in both hands, he continued, "This is my blood of the New Testament, which is shed for you, and for many, for the remission of sins." He turned and stared directly in my eyes, his expression accusatory and portentous.

"Charming symbolism," I commented with an archness I didn't really feel.

He shook his head. "But it isn't symbolic, Sun I."

A light broke in my consciousness. "You mean . . . ?"

He nodded. "You should have listened. I said, 'Grant us therefore, gracious Lord, so to eat the flesh of thy dear son Jesus Christ, and to drink his blood, that our sinful bodies may be made clean by his body, and our souls washed through his most precious blood, and that we may evermore dwell in him, and he in us.' "

"But that's cannibalism!" I cried, revolted.

"Don't be trite," he chided. "It's a great deal deeper than that."

I gaped at Yin-mi, hoping she might contradict him, then turned back to Riley. Each returned my gaze with firmness and resolve, and an undercurrent of curiosity, as though concerned to assess my reaction. I was dumb with astonishment, stunned. I stood like a traveler on a mountain path who, feeling a faint tremor underneath his feet, a distant rumbling as of thunder, pauses, cocking his ear, that attitude of alertness, of curiosity without alarm, a frozen snapshot of his final moment, the avalanche descending on him even then from a thousand feet, silent, swift, and unappealable. As though alive, Tsin materialized before me as he had been in that terrible instant when he looked up from the pipe he was preparing, his face flushed with adrenaline, victory, the "ecstasy of combat," his glass eye glowing with the reflection of the red coals in the fire: "It is the taste of blood, Sun I. It has a tonic effect on me." I was so smitten by the vividness of this apparition that its significance hardly dawned on me. I could actually see him floating there a foot above the ground, that red gleam in his eye baiting and mocking me. As I gaped at it, at him, in a state of numbness and wonder, a litany of phrases played through my mind with no apparent meaning or connection: ". . . this do in remembrance of me. . . ." In remembrance of whom? "For now we see through a glass darkly; but then, face to face . . ." and one other, ". . . and have not love, I am nothing."

"And have not love" — suddenly the lambent glimmer in the soldier's eye became a brilliant starburst, a supernova, a conflagration which consumed the universe and left me dazzled, temporarily blind. When I could see again, the reflection had shrunk to the dimensions of a fingernail, floating like a tiny crescent moon in the sea of a black-green tear-shaped lens. For the briefest instant my father's face loomed before me, head tilted to the side, flashing that quizzical smile, impertinent, almost monstrous, and at the same time, wonderful! "This do in remembrance of me. . . ." Then he vanished in thin air, and darkness overwhelmed me.

Chapter 12

"What does that mean, do you suppose?" I heard Riley ask Yin-mi in a sickbed whisper. Opening my eyes, I saw them indistinctly, as though through cloudy glass, or underwater, two dark blurs of form on either side of me.

"I'm not sure," she replied in the same tone. "Look, he's awake."

"What does what mean?" I asked, sitting up in the chair where they'd placed me, the visual aberration dissipating swiftly like haze touched by sunlight, leaving only a vague burning sensation in my eyes and an unusual sensitivity to light.

"How do you feel?" Yin-mi asked tenderly, squeezing my hand.

"I don't know — all right, I guess. What does what mean?" I persisted.

She cast a pained, inquisitive look at Riley, who in turn regarded me. "You've been unconscious for several moments," he said, "delirious. Over and over you kept repeating a single phrase. We've been trying to puzzle it out."

"What phrase?"

He narrowed his eyes intently. " 'A fitting feast for a Dowist.' "

I blinked in confusion. A dead silence fell over the room.

"What are you thinking?" Yin-mi asked wonderingly. "You have the oddest smile on your lips."

"A fitting feast for a Dowist," I repeated, lingering over each syllable, delighted with the music of the phrase. Then I burst out laughing.

"Sun I," Riley said in a concerned tone that surprised and gratified me, "are you sure you're feeling quite all right? I don't want to alarm you, but what just occurred looked distinctly to me like a mild seizure of some sort. There isn't perhaps a history of epilepsy in your family?"

This remark, which I took as an aspersion, sobered me quickly. "Certainly not," I replied. "It's a reaction to the wine, that's all. I'm not used to drinking."

"A single sip of wine hardly seems sufficient to produce such a reaction," he pointed out quite reasonably.

"He and my father were drinking before we came," Yin-mi said.

"That's right," I corroborated. "And besides, I think you underestimate the efficacy of your Sacrament. After all, the Communion wine is no ordinary vintage, Father, as you yourself have most kindly pointed out. In fact, it's a most potent elixir indeed! Drinking of that vintage, what man could fail to become intoxicated?"

Riley turned to Yin-mi with a fractional smile. "Well, at least he seems to be feeling better," he commented archly. "All right, Sun I, certainly I'm not going to deny the truth of what you say, though your irony is a trifle sophomoric. Nevertheless, the efficacy of the Sacrament is generally confined to the spiritual, or metaphysical, plane."

"Now, don't hedge!" I chided. "You just said a while ago it wasn't symbolic. The next thing you know, you'll be telling me it's only a metaphor after all."

"You're right, Sun I," Riley agreed. "It is more than a metaphor. We do hold that Christ is present in the cup, mystically present, though, not literally or physically present. We don't subscribe to the Catholic idea of transubstantiation. And in my opinion, our belief deepens the significance of the ritual."

"What do you mean?" I asked acerbically.

"I'll explain it sometime."

"Why not now?" I challenged.

He smiled indulgently. "Forgive me, Sun I, but I can't discuss theology with a drunken Taoist. You force me to point out the fact that you're still quite obviously soused — literally soused, and perhaps metaphysically soused as well." His smile became even more condescending and paternal, gayer too. "Let's go downstairs and get a cup of coffee. That should help rectify the situation."

"I don't drink coffee," I said surlily.

"Ah, another Western sacrament you disapprove of!" he continued in an expansive manner. "Well, you won't mind if Yin-mi and I avail ourselves, for it is most potent, and very meet and right that we should do so. You really should, though," he added. "It might help sober you up."

"I'm not drunk," I retorted sullenly.

"Now, now," he condescended, "no need to be embarrassed. After all, I'm a priest, aren't I? And with Irish blood to boot! It's nothing new to me."

"Don't patronize me," I said. "You're skirting the issue."

"Very astute," he said, smiling as he opened the sacristy door for Yin-mi and myself. "I try and make a policy of it. It's called 'strategic retreat,' a trick I picked up at the seminary. Anglicans are famous for it." He winked. "Don't worry though, you'll get another shot."

•

A festive, carnival atmosphere prevailed in the basement of the church where the meeting of the TYA was being held. "Rap sessions" were in progress in several quarters, a raffle was being conducted, the young boy who had read the epistle, in street clothes now, was spinning the drum for bingo, singing out the numbers on the Ping-Pong balls; two young men on electric guitar and saxophone (accompanied by a frowsy parish mother on upright spinet, whose contribution they did not seem to relish, or even particularly to notice) were playing progressive jazz, haltingly, for a group of young girls who sat barefoot on the floor, knees circled with their arms, heads resting on knees, swaying wistfully to the beat, or what could be discerned of one. A "teen bar" had been set up. Out of all the possibilities of recreation, that looked most congenial to me.

"May I get you something?" Riley asked.

I smiled at him maliciously. "I'll take a Dry Sack, with . . ."

"Don't tell me," he said, raising his hand. "On the rocks with venom." He laughed. "I'm afraid we're teetotalers down here, Sun I. The advantage is, there's no admission charge. If you want to get in upstairs where they serve the hard stuff, you have to pay the cover and become a card-carrying member." He winked. "All the more reason for converting. I have to go now, though, and say hello to the flock. Take care of him, Yin-mi. We don't want to lose a potential sheep."

"He likes you," she whispered as he walked off.

I scowled. "I'm not so sure I like him."

"You brought it on yourself," she pointed out, adding, "besides, I think you do."

"What makes you think he likes me anyway?" I asked, ignoring her remark.

"I can just tell. You challenge him. Only I wish you'd try to be a little bit less controversial."

"Me!" I cried in exasperated protest. "What about him?"

She laughed delightedly. "I'm going to get a Coke. Would you like something?"

"Only to be left alone," I replied ill-humoredly.

"You'd better be nice to me," she teased, "or I might take you *literally!*" She laughed.

Frowning, I watched her go. Several times she paused to speak to people she knew, touching hands, exchanging chaste, affectionate kisses, breaking into that easy laughter that I loved. I felt a pang at heart, part tenderness, part resentment. And guilt. What was I doing here, I asked myself, in a Christian church? I had done it for her. But I had no business forming attachments with this girl. Friendship, disinterested compassion — that was one thing. But what if she were to develop expectations of another sort? Inevitably the day would come when I would return to the monastery. My sojourn in her world was for a single purpose only and destined to be brief. When that day came, I didn't want her to be hurt. This was what I told myself. In my heart, however, I think perhaps I knew my real fear was for myself. I seemed to have fallen so far into that world already, and with each step the footing became more perilous. I was terrified of falling so far in I couldn't get back out again, ever. The drinking, for instance — it was shameful! Look what it had brought me to. Yet I couldn't help myself, or rather, I seemed a little too adept at it — helping myself, that is.

At the bar, Riley approached her, said something. They both looked at me and laughed.

I bristled with resentment, withdrawing further into myself. Standing apart, I brooded and plotted.

"Father Riley sends you this, compliments of the house," she said as she returned, handing me a paper cup.

"What is it?" I asked, sniffing the bloodred drink suspiciously and puckering my lips in aversion.

"A Virgin Mary," she laughed.

"A Virgin Mary?"

"Like a Bloody Mary, only without the alcohol."

I lowered at Riley across the room. He raised his Pepsi in a toast.

"I don't want it," I said. "I've had enough of your sacraments for one day. I don't need the menstrual mysteries too."

Yin-mi blushed. "It's just tomato juice," she said in a hurt tone.

"I don't care. Take it away."

"You're being very difficult," she remarked. "Why are you so defensive? You act like Father Riley is going to whip out a sword and forcibly convert you at any minute."

"I'm more afraid of being burnt at the stake," I retorted. "It wouldn't be the first time."

"You've been burnt before?" She laughed. "Try relaxing. This is meant to be a party, not a session of the Inquisition."

"From what I've seen, for Christians a very thin line divides the two. My Uncle Hsiao once told me that at Western dinner parties he always felt like a shipwrecked mariner at a feast of cannibals, fearing any moment to be barbecued himself. You Christians seem to be all right as long as there's plenty to go around. But what if the 'host' runs out? I wouldn't want you to start examining me with hungry eyes."

She smiled quizzically, squinting as though I were far away. "I've never seen you like this, so . . ."

"Vehement?" I asked coyly.

"Yes, vehement. And bitter. You're almost like someone else."

I smiled at her choice of words. "Oh no, it's me all right, an ineradicable part of my nature. I can't help myself," I added, more in tones of defiance than apology.

"Perhaps you shouldn't drink," she counseled quietly. "That seems to bring it out."

"Perhaps I shouldn't," I quipped, "but it's so much fun."

"Glad to hear you're enjoying yourself," Riley said, approaching us again. "I've had a cheering thought myself." He turned to Yin-mi. "Isn't it delightful, and reassuring, to have the power of our mysteries confirmed by an independent observer, recapitulated scientifically, so to speak?" To me, he continued, "Your experience tonight certainly constitutes a more eloquent and compelling argument for conversion than any I might offer, don't you think?"

"No," I said, "I don't. Granting the power of your Sacrament, there's still the question of its morality."

"Ah!" he said. "I can see you've been laying for me, sharpening your weapons." He laughed. "All right then, fire away. What moral objections can you propose to the Sacrament?"

"It's cannibalism," I said. "Pure and simple. You can't deny it, or put me off with a charge of being trite. What's trite about it? Eating flesh and drinking blood — what kind of God does such a mystery invoke? One I'm not particularly sure I'd like to meet in a dark alley, much less worship! It makes me think of ghouls and vampires."

"You forget," he said in a sober tone, "it is God himself who gives his most precious body and blood to redeem mankind."

"Quite right!" I conceded. "Your point's well taken. It is the worshippers themselves who eat. You make your God your victim."

"What you say in scorn is unintentionally profound, Sun I."

"Well, I retract the metaphor," I said. "Your God is innocent, meekly allowing himself to be cannibalized by his constituents. It is the Christians who are the ghouls and vampires."

"Why are you so bitter?" he asked.

"Haven't you sentenced me to hell?"

He nodded. "Yes, but also invited you to the Resurrection."

"I don't believe in your hell, or your Resurrection either," I said. "Or your smarmy, milquetoast God."

"You don't know him. Our 'smarmy, milquetoast God,' as you call him, who underwent crucifixion to redeem our sins — and a greater act of courage I dare you to conceive. . . ."

" 'Your' sins," I qualified, interrupting him.

"No, our sins — the sins of the world. You are included in the general ransom, if only you accept his sacrifice in your heart. This is the kind, forgiving God of mercy, the God of the New Testament, Jesus, the Son. But there is also God the Father, Jehovah, the God of the Old Testament. And you are right indeed to fear him, for he is terrible when provoked, a God of wrath."

"I suspected there was a catch. Not very nice, is he?"

"He has no patience with cynicism, I can tell you that!"

I was unspeakably pleased finally to ruffle his composure.

"But Sun I," he continued, restraining himself, "if I'm not mistaken, Taoism and Buddhism have their dark gods as well: the terrible gods of liberation who attempt to frighten the adept over the precipice into enlightenment — Kwan Ti, Mahakala, Yamantaka. Speaking loosely, perhaps too loosely, I would suggest that the Old Testament God serves a similar function."

"The difference being that our gods are psychological, metaphorical, if you will. They symbolize the secret powers of the heart. Heaven lies within us, and all the gods," I said, looking at Yin-mi, "and hell does also. That's why I'm not afraid of your anathema."

"It's a beautiful idea," he said. "I've toyed with it often enough myself."

"You sound wistful, Father," I observed. "Perhaps in the end it is I who shall convert you."

He smiled and shook his head. "Perhaps, but I don't think so. Persuasive as you are, Sun I, I doubt you can top my own inner Mephistopheles. I've flirted with the idea, but in the end I always come back. Your 'way' dissatisfies me finally."

"Why does it dissatisfy you?"

"Because it's insufficient. It leaves out too much."

"What does it leave out, Father?"

"The world," he said, "the world as it is."

"What do you mean? Taoists live in the world too. Look at me."

"Yes, but according to your teachings the world is a dream, an illusion, all we do and suffer an illusion, too, we ourselves finally no more than a product of 'deluded seeing.' That answer, though superficially enticing, is too easy, almost glib, and at the same time too despairing. I don't believe in it. Not necessarily because I don't want to, but because for me human beings have a primary, irrefutable existential validity which precedes all metaphysics and rules it. They substantiate themselves through what they do and suffer — perhaps primarily through what they suffer. . . ."

"To be is to suffer," I glossed cynically, recalling Kahn.

"Something like that," he said. "By making its agents and patients unreal, you deny the reality of suffering, and thus deny life of its dignity and terror. If there is no external world, no other, then our suffering is an illusion too. And I can't accept that. I see too much of it every day. It has a raw, rank validity no metaphysics can ever have — not for me."

"But you're wrong," I said. "It's not that suffering isn't real, but only that it's self-inflicted and unnecessary."

"I don't believe that. It contradicts my fundamental intuition about the world, my 'this.' Metaphysics aside, though, the thing that finally convinced me of the inadequacy of the Eastern view was that by denying the external world and the reality of suffering you also deny us the one consolation available."

"And what is that?"

"Love," he said, " 'and have not love, I am nothing' — remember the Epistle?" (I noticed that Yin-mi was blushing.) "With no external world, no other, there can be no love. Nor can there be love without suffering."

"You forget, Father," I objected, "Compassion is one of Taoism's Three Treasures."

"It's not the same thing," he replied.

"What are we speaking of then?"

He challenged my eyes. "Living in the world as it is. Love is in the world and suffers. Compassion is a sort of wistful backward glance over the shoulder after we've already left it. It is beyond suffering, immune to it, and for that very reason a bit anemic and contemptible, unimportant finally."

"Why must it always hurt?" I asked.

"If you don't understand, I'm not sure I can tell you."

"Perhaps because attachment to the world — its half-truths and incompletenesses, its transience and contradiction — satisfies an ingrained need to hurt ourselves," I suggested. "Craving a place beyond the vanities and ephemera and not finding one, denied it out of choice or blindness, we must punish ourselves by consequence, finding punishment of the world ineffectual."

Riley became sad. "That is very profound I think, Sun I, though only partially right — a dangerous combination, dangerous primarily to the espouser. It runs so much deeper than that, just as the Mass runs deeper, and more clean. Perhaps John says it best, or rather, Christ through John: 'Verily, verily, I say unto you, Except a grain of wheat fall into the ground and die, it abideth alone; but if it die, it bringeth forth much fruit.' Do you understand that, that we have to be broken to bear? That's why Christ says, 'For whosoever will save his life shall lose it; and whosoever will lose his life for my sake shall find it.'"

Riley was obviously moved; and I was moved by him, humanly, as a man, though I remained unconvinced. "You're very persuasive, Father," I conceded, "and obviously sincere in your beliefs. I respect that. But you've left something out of the tally. Love is not the only consolation. There is also quiescence, the 'joys of the path.' The Return to the Source offers ample rewards to those who are strong enough to bear its rigors and austerities, and at the end of the road, the greatest bliss of all, enlightenment."

"Ah yes, the 'peace which passeth understanding' à la chinoise," he said, returning to an ironic tone. "I'm not sure I buy it."

"You don't have to 'buy it,'" I retorted indignantly. "I'm not trying to convert you. I respect your beliefs, for the most part anyway. Why won't you do me the same courtesy?"

"'No man cometh unto the Father, but by me'; 'one baptism for the remission of sins,'" he reiterated grimly.

> "For God so loved the world that he gave his only begotten Son, that whosoever believeth in him should not perish, but have everlasting life. For God sent not his Son into the world to condemn the world, but that the world through him might be saved. He that believeth on him is not condemned; but he that believeth not is condemned already, because he hath not believed in the name of the only begotten Son of God. And this is the condemnation, that light is come into the world, and men loved darkness rather than light, because their deeds were evil.

"Don't you see, Sun I? If I pull out that plug, the whole dike crumbles after it. A water wall of darkness and error sweeps down behind it and washes away the world."

"You really believe that?" I asked incredulously.

"Yes, I do," he said emphatically. "And you may scoff as much as you like, but that's why I feel an obligation to try and bring you in, though I joke about it. 'Joy shall be in Heaven over one sinner that repenteth, more than over ninety and nine righteous persons who need no repentence.' "

"You consider me a sinner then?" I asked with a hint of archness.

"Of course!" he replied. "A charming one — and ultimately reclaimable, which is even better. You see, I admit my motives are not entirely disinterested. The credit would look good on my heavenly balance sheet. I've got a lot of debits to atone for."

I laughed. "Your faith is too exigent."

"All love is exigent!" he replied.

I felt myself flush, but resisted being charmed out of my opposition. "All this exigence and passion! All this ecstasy! I have a hard time with a religion which images its highest state of sanctity and spiritual accomplishment as one of drunkenness. Your highest mystery reveals itself in a cup of wine. Taoism's sacrament — if it had a sacrament — would reveal its deepest secret in a sip of cold, clear water from a well. My training has taught me that ecstasy distorts rather than reveals. Ecstasy is a form of need, and need sees falsely. Are we not closer to the truth in moments of tranquility, our concentration focused within, judgment unimpaired by passion, by need?"

"Human beings are needy creatures," Riley said.

"Yes, but you are entirely too fatalistic. Need must acquire to appease itself; and acquisition is always a risky business. But there is another 'Way' besides the way of acquisition. There is also the Way of relinquishment. That is what Taoism teaches, and though we don't deny the validity of other paths — even your *tao* of love — the Way of relinquishment is preferable, if for no other reason than the tranquility it promotes, not to mention the spiritual powers it develops in its adepts."

"Such as?"

I shrugged. "The ability to foretell the future, for instance."

"Ah yes, the *I Ching,*" he said. " 'And though I have the gift of prophecy, and understand all mysteries and all knowledge; and though I have all faith so that I could remove mountains, and have not love, I am nothing.' What you call tranquility, the Way of relinquishment, I call the way of resignation and despair. Even if such tranquility is possible, I question if it's worth the price."

"What price?"

"Love, Sun I. For me it always comes back to that. Love is passionate in nature, exigent, needy — all the things you disparage, all the things I cherish. 'Beareth all things, believeth all things, hopeth all things, endureth all things. Love never faileth.' "

"Never, Father?" I asked, turning inward for an instant, to contemplate a private place. "I wonder. I wonder too if love isn't sometimes cruel."

"Yes, of course, to love is to suffer, I've admitted that, but . . ." — he eyed me closely — "you say that in the strangest way. What exactly are you thinking?"

Smiling grimly, I sought Yin-mi. "Nothing, Father," I said. "Nothing."

Our "rap session" continued late into the evening, long after the last weary revelers of the TYA, individually or together, had straggled out into the night. We covered and re-covered much of the same ground broken in these initial forays, but there was at least one new subject interjected into the discussion which I will briefly note, since I found it most suggestive.

As the conversation grew more intimate, Riley began to question me about my motives for coming to New York and involving myself in the Stock Exchange, a move which, he protested, he could find no logic in (for I omitted all mention of my father) until I explained to him the idea of the delta.

When I first invoked the image, he sat back clasping his hands, looking off in the distance.

"Now I begin to understand. That's fascinating, Sun I, absolutely fascinating. . . . And you know, I think it has a rather suggestive Christian parallel."

"Oh?" I responded.

He rocked forward in his chair and regarded me eagerly. "Yes indeed. The attempt to find the Tao within the Dow — or conversely, and more precisely perhaps, to locate the Dow on the schematic map of reality designed by the Taoist philosopher-cartographers — is very much like the Christian attempt to reconcile the existence of evil in the world with a purely benign creator, 'to reconcile the ways of God to man,' as Milton says. That hidden irritant is the seed around which generations of apologists have secreted the pearl of Christian theology. I suppose the impulse for all religion springs from a similar grievance, Taoism included. Though you don't couch the problem in terms of good and evil, yet you might well ask yourself why the Tao precipitated itself into the 'ten thousand things,' why the original harmony self-divided, or broke down, into the chaos of the defiled world, the 'marketplace,' posing man, incidentally, the arduous task of Returning to the Source. I mean, if the Tao was so perfect and harmonious in the beginning, why did it disintegrate? What happened? How did we lose it? I don't know the Taoist answer to that question," he said, as though I might illuminate it for him.

"Tao did not disintegrate," I replied. "It has never been lost. It is immanent within us."

"Ah, 'immanent' . . ." he said. "But that's hedging. Even if it exists here and now and always has, why can't we perceive it? How to account for the error in our minds — there's the rub. We call it the Fall from Grace."

"Well, what's the Christian answer?"

"There are a number of them, some quite ingenious. That formulated in the Exultet, for example: 'O certe necessarium Adae peccatum. . . . O felix culpa.' "

"What does that mean?"

" 'O truly necessary sin of Adam. . . . O fortunate fall.' "

"How fortunate?"

"By bringing sin and death into the world, the Fall also brought about the possibility of redemption."

"Wouldn't it have been better simply to leave well enough alone from the beginning?"

"Perhaps in some crude, quantitative, cost-effective sense. But one must view these things with an artist's eye. Without a Fall, without a splintering into multiplicity, there could have been no love. Love is the gravity of the severed fragments pining for one another in a fallen world. Love is the Physician's attempt to heal himself. When we love one another, we participate in the mystical reintegration of God's body. To which, of course, you can reply that it would have been better if God had never wounded himself in the first place and maintained his wholeness. But that is the point. The process of *achieving* wholeness — love — becomes more important than the end itself. That is the Christian revelation, the new light Christ brought into the world that had never been seen before, that the Fall was not only necessary, but fortunate. Because what we lost — wholeness — is outweighed by what we gained — love. Love is the greatest of all spiritual goods, and in a sense Christianity invented it. It requires incompleteness as a precondition; by that very fact it is unavailable to you as a Taoist, to whom wholeness is all in all. This seems to me the failure of the Eastern religious sense, or obsolescence, rather let me say than failure, for it's more a question of being superseded than proved wrong. It attempts to go *back,* repudiating the salvation that is available to us living in the world as it is, the fallen world. Ostrichlike, burying its head in the sand, Taoism fails to see that the possibility of grace afforded us here and now outweighs the womblike solace of the state we lost, fails to see that the highest good only came to be out of the greatest tragedy, which was the original self-division, the Fall. That's the miracle, you see, that 'Love has pitched his mansion in the place of excrement,' as Yeats says. Taoist wholeness becomes an impediment to the higher salvation offered by Christ, which only comes through loss and suffering. We must be broken to be made whole again through love."

I disagreed, of course, and let him know it in no uncertain terms, adducing my reasons. Beyond this, though, little more of consequence was broached during our conversation, except that at one point, during a lull, Yin-mi brought up the topic of my mother's robe, describing it to Riley in the most glowing terms. He expressed an interest in seeing it, and I reluctantly agreed, suspecting deep down that it was simply a further ploy in their conspiracy to convert me. Then Riley had a brainstorm. Why not bring it to a meeting of the TYA and give a brief talk about it, its construction, symbolism, whatever occurred to me, a sort of "show and tell" using the robe as a springboard to describe my own background, "growing up in a remote Taoist monastery in western China," "daring escape from the mainland," etc.? Secretly I suspected that Riley, despite his good breeding, was a little too taken with the Oriental mystery and intrigue angle and slightly lost his head. In the end he wanted to have handbills printed up and posted all over the Wall Street area, making the thing a real event. I felt patronized a little, but this was more than outweighed by the flattery involved. So, after thumbing through the church calendar and setting a date considerably in advance so that "the word could be spread," as he put it, Riley prevailed on me to accept. I made subtly but unmistakably clear that, for this heathen Taoist, it was an act of condescension, of noblesse oblige. To my delight Riley picked up on this and commented to Yin-mi aside in a stage whisper that they had indeed been hoisted by their own petards. When he wasn't trying to convert me, I rather liked him.

"Well, Sun I, I'm delighted to have met you finally and had this little talk," he said, leading Yin-mi and me out onto the walk. "Is everything settled for the lecture?"

"I think so," I replied.

"Good, then I'll look forward to seeing you then if not before. Yes, before, by all means! Don't be a stranger. Feel free to drop in anytime. Only . . ." — he gave me a coy look of disapproval — "no more chipping at the Sacrament." He laughed. "Until we've converted you, that is. After that, the sky's the limit. It's a continual buffet banquet, 'all you can eat' for the price of the cover and lasting for eternity!"

"The price is too high," I said, allowing myself the merest dregs of a smile.

"Nonsense!" he objected. "Look at what you get, a seven course meal! Five partial sacraments as hors d'oeuvres and appetizers, plus two full-fledged main courses. And for dessert, the hope of heaven — a just desert indeed!"

"And look at what I lose," I retorted.

"What do you lose?"

" 'The Mystery,' " I said, quoting the first chapter of the *Tao Te Ching*, "Or rather the 'Darker than any Mystery, the Doorway whence issued all Secret Essences.' " I shook my head. "No, Father, I prefer my own humble supper to your rich table: coarse rice to eat, cold water from the well, the crook of a bent elbow for a pillow . . . and what goes with it, a quiet heart."

"And love, Sun I?" he asked, all trace of whimsy vanished now, embracing Yin-mi too in his glance. "What of that?"

I blushed, but held his eye. " 'Only he that rids himself forever of desire can see the Secret Essences; he that has never rid himself of desire can see only the Outcomes.' "

" 'Whether a man dispassionately sees to the core of life,' " he replied, " 'or passionately sees the surface, the core and the surface are essentially the same, words making them seem different, only to express appearance.' "

Deeply impressed, I remained silent. For Riley had produced an alternative, and contradictory, rendering of exactly the same passage in the *Tao Te Ching* that I had quoted.

He took Yin-mi's hand and bade her goodnight, then mine, applying a gentle, intimate pressure that embarrassed me slightly. "That is my final question and appeal to you, Sun I," he said. "Think about it: What of love? And this," he added, pressing a small copy of the Book of Common Prayer into my hand. "I want you to have it. Glance through it in an idle hour." He shrugged. "Who knows?"

My last impression of him was as he was standing on the threshold watching us pass through the wrought iron gate to turn up Broadway. There was no trace of whimsicality in his expression then, only a reflection in his eye cast by the streetlight, a scintilla which recalled for an instant the glimmer in the eye of the soldier, the benignant Hunter.

Chapter 13

By this hour, in accordance with Mrs. Ha-p'i's predictions, the sky had indeed begun to brood and lower. Great thunderheads, like towering monuments of ash, pale bluish in color, were massing out at sea and floating toward us over the open water, bringing a whiff of North Atlantic brine. The air had become quite cool, and voices seemed to carry mysteriously over distance. I fancied I could hear the shouts of the longshoremen working the graveyard shift over on the Brooklyn side, and the salvos of the crews of the incoming tankers. Intermittently there was a rumble of thunder, and then I heard the soft, secretive patter of rain on the pavement, heard it before I felt it, smelled it too — an acrid whiff of asphalt-scented steam rising from the street, which almost sighed with relief. Raising her mother's parasol, Yin-mi wordlessly invited me under its protective umbra, and we continued on in the same intimate, slightly abashed silence as before. She held my arm shyly, and though her nearness comforted me, it troubled me too. I couldn't give myself unreservedly to its solace, for it threatened me somehow. This had occasionally troubled me before. Perhaps it was the source of the "mysterious rankling." But it had never been made explicit for me until tonight, through my conversation with Riley. Not that it was a philosophical consideration, some element of dogma; on the contrary. But our discussion had honed my perception. No, what that intimacy threatened in me was much more primitive and fundamental: my sense of my own integrity, in the deepest sense of the word, the inviolable kernel of my inner wholeness. "Except a grain of wheat fall into the ground and die, it abideth alone; but if it die, it bringeth forth much fruit." Christianity advocated that rupture of the shell of self, striking a taproot into the soil of life — attachment. But for Taoism, attachment, desire, was the root of all evil. Of course I refused to let myself be shaken by Riley's persuasive sophistries, but this gentle pressure on my arm, this wordless intimacy, that was something else. . . . "And what of love?"

Just as we passed beneath the Brooklyn Bridge, a flash of lightning hit the nearer tower. For an instant the whole river was illuminated in a pale fluorescence, the dark water seething restlessly in that ghostly light. As it touched the tower and was absorbed into the rods, the lightning resembled a filmstrip of a jagged chalk line scrawled on a blackboard, only run in reverse, the line retreating into its origin. The vivid fluid was drunk into the cable and hurtled down through the chaos of the waters into the dark regions of the earth below the river, brought to consummation there, grounded.

Then it began to pour. We stood under the shelter of the bridge and watched it, intimidated and admiring. After a few minutes Yin-mi said, "It doesn't look like it's going to let up anytime soon. Mother will be worried. What do you think, should we make a dash for it?" Her eyes flashed an eager, provocative challenge.

"I don't know," I said dubiously. "It must be almost half a mile from here."

"Come on," she said, "I dare you." She smiled at me then in a way she never had before, audacious, almost impertinent, tempting me and laughing in my face. I experienced a tingle of surprise and titillated umbrage. Then she was off, sprinting through the downpour. "Last one there's a rotten egg!" she cried. "A rotten thousand-year-old egg!"

I heard her laugh, and I plunged. The cold shock of the rain made me catch my breath. I was instantly drenched through. My toes squished in my socks and shoes, which felt like ten-pound flippers. As I ran uphill against a flume accumulating in a gutter, I fell face down in the torrent. This only quickened my exhilaration. Rising on my forearms, I splashed and flopped like a joyous fish disporting himself in a shallow, warm, primeval sea. I utterly lost myself, stomping and whooping. Then, hearing her taunting laughter out ahead of me, I set out again. I could make out her white blouse through the jagged diamond shower of the rain, and a pang of poignant desperation shot through me. I began to sprint, straining as I never had before. Before I'd gone a hundred yards, I thought my heart would burst with the unreserved exertion, but quickened instinct pushed the pain into insignificance. I was gaining on her all the time, until she took an unfamiliar turn and disappeared into a street I didn't know. Reaching the corner, I stopped and stared into an empty cul-de-sac. Dead end. Where had she gone? My heart was pounding violently, and all of a sudden I was overcome by an impulse to lean down and sniff the stones. The absurdity of the idea made me laugh idiotically. Continuing in pursuit, I discovered several alleys Yin-mi might have turned into. I knew if I made the wrong choice I'd lose her, lose the game. I was on the point of doubling back to the main thoroughfare, hoping to beat her home through sheer speed, when I noticed the ruptured parasol lying in the alley's mouth, the white paper of the underbelly like a blossom pelted to earth in the downpour. Her spoor, a deliberate clue. Without even pausing to pick it up, I set off into the labyrinth.

Twenty or thirty yards from the opening, the alley turned sharply to the left, so that my line of sight into the street was blocked. Opacity ahead and behind me, I slowed down and began to make my way more cautiously. Stretching out my arms, I could feel the walls on either side, covered by a damp, membranous integument of soot and grime, cool and vaguely mossy. Except for the ghostly shine of the clouds in a thin slit above, there was virtually no light. I had to make my way at first almost entirely by the sense of touch. Silhouetted against that cleft of sky were the skeletal forms of fire escapes, out of reach above my head. The soft patter of the rain was quieter here than on the outside, and I could hear the consumptive gurgling of water falling into an indiscernible drain ahead of me in the alley. Despite the darkness, trickles of water down the walls of the buildings glowed with a silvery luminescence, like streaks of phosphorescence in some dripping underground cavern. Occasionally pale boats of garbage drifted by me, awash on the runnel which flowed down one side of the alley near my feet. The smell too suggested the underworld, rain and asphalt, like the smell of ashes, combined with the obscene fecundity of the garbage. Something scurried across my path a few feet ahead of me. I froze and peered into the dark. As it passed, it reared and the light caught its eyes — a rat. It glowered at me with a face that seemed intelligent and full of immemorial malice, then fell to all fours and hurried off.

That apparition finally dissolved my exhilaration, replaced it with foreboding which chilled my excitement but did not extinguish it. An image passed before my mind's eye that made my heart lurch and falter. The parasol lying broken on the pavement briefly suggested another interpretation. What if it weren't a clue left deliberately in play? What if something had happened? What if there had been someone in the alley when she turned? What if . . . ? My sense of dread was so powerful it almost made me nauseated, and the suspense quickened to an unbearable intensity. I started hurrying. As my eyes adjusted, I began to see more rats. They were everywhere, flushed out of the sewers by the rain. The alley kept turning and turning, new branches proliferating off to the side every few yards until I lost all sense of direction. I became desperate, like a man in water so dark he can't see his own bubbles and so has nothing to guide him back into the light and air. More and more convinced that I had taken the wrong fork, I considered turning back at every step. Only I was no more confident of my ability to retrace my way than to proceed.

Just then I turned the angle of a wall and a grayness opened up ahead of me — not light, but an intimation of open space at least. I issued into a strange irregular opening surrounded by the high walls of buildings on all sides, a courtyard of sorts, only filled with heaps of litter: smashed furniture, refrigerators compacted from the fall like the wrecked carcasses of automobiles, their white enamel shining dully, like bones, great green, anonymous sacks of garbage oozing their contents. I recognized it immediately, the small lost kingdom of abandoned things which I had often peered into from my own rooftop. I was relieved to find myself so close, yet had no idea how to proceed. From the roof I had never even seen the alley by which I'd entered, much less a way out to the street. But there had to be one. I began to look, circling the walls, feeling with my hands. A few steps before I reached it, I saw the place the darkness deepened in the wall. Entering it, at last I saw the halo of a streetlight. I began to run. I tripped and scraped my hands, got up again. Then I was beneath the familiar lamp, clutching my knees with stinging, bloody hands as I heaved and panted. In my relief I forgot Yin-mi. When the thought of her returned, I straightened up to look around, and just at that instant something clutched me from behind. I screamed and sprang toward the street. Behind me her excited laughter mocked me as she raced up the steps into the vestibule. Closing the door behind her, she peered at me quickly through the glass before disappearing. I was numb, and then the most violent rage I've ever felt in all my life overcame me. I leapt up the steps three at a time. The door was locked. I shook it several times with idiotic savagery, until it occurred to me I had my key. I jabbed it in. As I turned it, I caught a glimpse of my face in the window, gorged with blood, almost purple, the veins distended in my neck, my eyes almost entirely pupil.

She was leaning against the inner door, her hands behind her butt supporting her, one knee lifted, foot propped vertically flat against the door. Her knee was angled inward in a gesture of instinctive feminine suggestiveness, and denial. Her hair was drenched, but shaken out, its blackness intensely vivid. Her eyes shone, and her whole attitude suggested triumph and coy surrender, that the joke was over, or awaited only my formal acknowledgment to be over. What drew my attention most of all though were her breasts, entirely visible through the soaked blouse, the nipples erect with cold. She made no effort to conceal them. I noticed she was panting slightly too, as I was. I sprang at her without the slightest idea what I meant to do. Seizing her around the waist, I lifted her, locking my arms at the base of her spine, squeezing with all my strength, looking straight into her eyes. She laughed with delight and titillation. I could feel the blood hot in my face as I wound her tighter. After a moment the laughter disappeared. She grimaced slightly with pain, and then with a look of tender sadness, she bent down almost languidly and kissed me on the lips, kissed me deeply with her tongue. In my astonishment, I dropped her to the floor. She came lightly to her feet and backed away a few steps, regarding me with searching, vulnerable eyes. I gazed back at her, aware of nothing but the taste of her mouth, sweetened almost unbearably by the lingering savor of the wine.

"Why did you do that?" I asked in a tremulous voice.

"I don't know," she said. "Do I have to have a reason?"

Suddenly I began to cry. I put my face in my hands and wept uncontrollably, with huge, wrenching sobs.

"Don't," she whispered, coming back to me and putting her arms around my shoulders. "Don't, Sun I." I could feel the soft pressure of her body shyly insinuating itself all down my length, the chill of her wet clothes, and the warmth of her nakedness radiating at the points of contact, so hot it seemed to burn.

I looked up, my face still twitching and puckering involuntarily with sobs.

"Shh," she said. "It's all right. You're cold. Come upstairs and let me fix you tea and get you a warm blanket."

Surrendering, I let her lead me once again.

•

"Look at you!" Mrs. Ha-p'i cried, throwing aside her embroidery and rising from her chair. "You're both drenched to the bone!" In her tone relief and sympathy vied with a more critical impulse. "Yin-mi, go and change at once," she commanded sternly. Abashed and huddling, Yin-mi uttered a timid "Yes ma'am," and shuffled off down the hall.

"Sun I, come with me," she ordered peremptorily. I too obeyed the summons, both of us instantly transformed into deferential children. Mrs. H. led me to the spare bedroom. "Wo left some things here when he found his own apartment," she said, more to herself than me. "Let's see. . . ." Opening the closet, she began to file brusquely through the items on hangers. "Here," she said, picking something at random. Over her shoulder she tossed me a lime and yellow Hawaiian print. "And some pants." She turned to me with a pair of madras Bermuda shorts.

"Well they don't have to match, do they?" she asked pettishly, seeing what must have been a look of mournful protest on my face.

"No ma'am," I said. "These are fine."

"All right. You can change in the bathroom. Better take this too," she added, tossing me a belt. "Wo is rather big-boned, whereas you are . . . thin." She pronounced this with what seemed to me a disparaging emphasis.

"Thin?" I thought silently, looking down at my own body as I turned to leave. I had never thought of myself as particularly thin, but I was so cowed, so overmastered by O.C., that I couldn't help but acquiesce in her judgment. Certainly if Wo's obesity could pass as "big-boned," then I was little better than a rail.

While I was in the bathroom, the lights in the building went out. By the time I emerged, Mrs. H. had already lit candles. Yin-mi had still not made her appearance when I reentered the sitting room. The brusque and merciless maternal efficiency which had animated Mrs. H. softened when she caught sight of me. Observing me so timid, so abashed and vulnerable, swaddled and swallowed in those vulgar warehouses of gaudy, belligerent rayon-acetate, her indignation was appeased. I'd been afraid she might laugh, but instead tenderness and pity appeared in her expression. Lifting her sewing basket from the seat of a soiled pink easy chair beside her own, she patted it, inviting me to sit. My deference was so unconscious and so deep as I obeyed that it must have evoked some memory in her, for with a gesture of maternal solicitude and affection, she brushed my bangs lightly from my forehead with a little flicking motion of her fingers. Then heaving a deep sigh, she turned back to her embroidery.

"Well, did you and Yin-mi have a good time?" she asked.

"Yes ma'am," I said.

She regarded me quizzically. I don't know exactly where I was then, only that I was in a state of deep infantilism, regressed so far into myself that I was incapable of conversation. I think she sensed this. Picking up the piece she was working on, she held it close to her face in the dim light, then rummaged in her basket for a spool of thread. As she worked, she examined me from time to time over her half-spectacles.

When Yin-mi finally padded in, her hair dry and mussed with toweling, in sock-footed pajama bottoms and a long-sleeved crew-neck shirt of dark-blue velour, Mrs. H. cast her a glance, pulling through a thread. "Perhaps Sun I would like a cup of tea, dear. Why don't you go out and put the water on." At her words Yin-mi turned and padded out again as though on remote control.

Mrs. H. studied me. I blushed. An odd smile appeared on her lips, and she plunged deliberately into her work, applying herself with swift, dextrous fingers, becoming absorbed in it at last, seeming almost to forget my presence. Though she said nothing, I didn't feel uncomfortable or out of place, but included and accepted in the cozy atmosphere she radiated, a soiled but comfortable domestic aureole. Gradually I found myself staring more and more fixedly at the intricate workings of her fingers. Her worn hands were traversed by great blue concourses of veins, aqueducts of blood, extremely beautiful in an elemental sense. They seemed to glow with heightened reality. The hairline seam in the surface world parted and closed once again, giving me tantalizing glimpses into the inner life of her hand: the oxygenated blood pulsing in the arteries in the bottom of the wrist and flowing back exhausted through the large veins in the back of the hand; the moist, striated muscle tissue expanding and contracting as she worked her fingers; the tendons, bones, and ligaments.

I became mesmerized by the spectacle. There was magic in it, at once soothing and so melancholy, poignantly evoking the buried memory, that secret, deepest pain. I became aware at last that her fingers had perceptibly slowed, that she was no longer attending. She had begun to examine my face with a deep attention like Yin-mi's. For a brief instant I seemed to see the daughter staring at me from behind her mother's face, as though the older woman were an uncompleted statue, which, freed from its excess, refined by the sculptor's chisel into the spare image of its pristine essence, would reveal, precisely, Yin-mi.

"You were thinking of your mother, weren't you?" she said, as though her heart were touched to the quick.

Though I hadn't been fully conscious of it before, I realized she was right. Her clairvoyance startled me. Our formal relation dissolved in an instant of timeless intimacy. Then we both turned away, she to her work, I to the doorway, impatient for Yin-mi's reappearance.

When she spoke again it was in a more characteristic voice. "You look a little drawn and worried tonight, Sun I," she ventured. "Are you having problems, dear? Money perhaps?" She sighed. "You know how poor we are, but if we can ever help . . ." She smiled. I was touched.

"Or . . ." she added, as though offhand, raising her eyebrows as she took a stitch, "you might speak to Wo. Perhaps he could do something for you." Her show of casualness almost worked, but my practiced eye was too keen. I could detect the maternal deviousness working underneath, following its eternal beeline. I waited, sighed, and sure enough . . . "Tell me, Sun I," she said in a frank, imploring tone, laying aside her work, "is he happy?"

The intimacy we had just experienced, though it had vanished now, powerfully conjured my emotions. Once again I almost faltered in my resolution to protect Wo. Surely it would be a relief to him finally to be able to cast off that burden, I thought. But I couldn't.

"I don't see him often," I said, scrutinizing my hands, "but as far as I know he is."

For a long, uncomfortable interlude I could sense her probing me. Then she sighed and returned to her work. "Yes," she said wearily, as though reciting a litany to herself which she did not believe, "I know he's doing well. He has his own apartment now. But sometimes I worry." With this last phrase, her voice broke slightly, and I saw that she was weeping. It wrung my heart.

She smiled apologetically, snuffling through her tears. "Forgive me, Sun I. Mothers are a terrible nuisance, aren't they?"

In a quiet voice that trembled slightly, I replied, "I don't think so, Mrs. H."

She bit her lip, then reached out spontaneously and touched my cheek. "You poor child!"

Yin-mi appeared from the hall carrying a tray holding a small brown teapot and three china cups trembling in their saucers. "Where's Father?" she asked, oblivious to our interaction.

Mrs. Ha-p'i sighed and started gathering together the things in her lap. "He's been asleep for hours, dear. He went to bed almost as soon as you left. He was exhausted."

"You mean drunk," Yin-mi glossed with unhappy irony.

"Don't be disrespectful." Her mother rebuked her, though patiently, without anger. "You know how hard your father works."

"Yes, I know," Yin-mi said with the same petulance. "But he was."

Neither of them spoke. There was a tension between them I had never witnessed.

"Are you having tea?" Yin-mi finally asked, coldly, but with a hint of grudging remorse.

"No thank you, darling," her mother answered. "You know I never drink at night. I have enough trouble sleeping as it is." Turning to me, she smiled that characteristic smile of abashed matronly omnipotence. "Goodnight, Sun I," she said warmly. "I'm so glad you came to visit us. Please come more often. Anytime. . . . Oh!" she cried, breaking into a nervous titter and falling into her social fluster. "I forgot. I wasn't supposed to mention that. Well, never mind. Lo is asleep. You won't tell him, will you?"

I smiled and shook my head. "No," I promised, "and I'll be sure to come back soon." I offered her my hand.

Using it for support, she leaned over and kissed Yin-mi's cheek. "Don't stay up too late, dear."

Slouching in her chair, arms folded sullenly across her chest in a defensive posture, Yin-mi responded perfunctorily, merely lifting her chin for easier access.

Mrs. H. looked at her, sighed once more, then padded softly down the hall in her silk slippers, entered the bedroom, and closed the door behind her.

With her departure, Yin-mi brightened. I was puzzled and a bit put out. She poured a fragrant stream of the steaming brew into my cup and handed it to me. "What?" she asked, noting my expression.

"Nothing," I said. "I just thought you were a little disrespectful to your mother."

"Oh, Sun I!" she protested in exasperation, letting her saucer drop on the tray with a loud clatter. "What do you know about it? You don't understand. She simply refuses to see."

"See what?"

"The truth."

"Which is?"

"That Father is an alcoholic."

I looked at her incredulously.

"Oh, come on. Surely you've figured that out by now?" She laughed bitterly. "I guess it's just too alien to your experience. Not much of that sort of thing in the monastery, I suppose?" She shook her head. "Sometimes it just makes me so depressed, living here. I can't stand it, seeing them getting so old, hunched over and wasted with all the years of pettiness, all the fears and worries over money. What do they have show for it? Survival?" She laughed dismissingly.

I was astonished to hear her talk that way, and disapproved. "I totally disagree," I retorted. "Seeing them tonight has made me realize more than ever how remarkable they are. What treasures they've amassed through all these years of shared hardship and affection!"

Her bewilderment darkened to umbrage. "How is it that you always manage to turn things on their heads?"

I smiled indulgently. "It's an old trick I picked up at the monastery," I said, invoking Riley's phrase. "Taoists are famous for it."

"You are prematurely wise, Sun I," she replied scornfully. "But your wisdom is like a scholar's, gotten out of books, without loss or risk. You've learned it with your mind, but not with your hands and feet, not with your heart."

I raised my hand to protest.

"Let me finish. I look at my parents and I see meanness, indignity, suffering without hope — the kind of suffering that exhausts a person and eventually crushes him. Yes, my father is an alcoholic, and that's why. Suffering has touched the deepest places in his spirit and withered them. But, do you know, I respect him more than you? Why? Because at least he's lived. You carry your philosophy around with you like a sheath of insulation. It protects you from the world, but it also imprisons you inside yourself — a condom between you and reality. Oh sure, I know you've suffered too, but not in the same way. For you it's all in play. Your suffering is theater, without lasting consequences. Suffering like yours would be a luxury to a man like my father. You can always turn it into an opportunity for growth — the discipline of the gardener's shears, which clip the plant so that it will spring back fuller, more luxurious than before, but never touch the secret nerve of its life. But the real world is a forest, Sun I, not a garden. It's life and death out here. Your philosophy blinds you to that fact. You aren't committed to anything real, you've loved nothing. To you it's all a fatuous illusion, worthy of compassion but not involvement. The admiration you express for my parents' lives is poisoned by the ozone you bring down from the stratosphere in your great condescension. They are no more to you than laboratory animals. But I say again, I respect them more than you and all your philosophy. Because you've never loved something as my father has, so that you'd suffer anything to preserve it, even the death of your own spirit."

I was completely astonished at this outburst of defamation which my casual remark had suddenly released, all the more so in that I had no idea where it came from or what had triggered it. I might have been hurt by it, mortified, but I was too amazed. Besides, Yin-mi's appearance usurped my attention. I had never seen her in such a state, her beautiful eyes terrible to look at now, full of vulnerability and pain, like two great haunted wounds, demanding some restitution from me too deep for me to fathom.

"You're right," I said at last in a soothing voice, attempting to console her without patronizing. "But each of us makes his own choices, your father one way, and I another. Who's to say which is right, or indeed that both aren't right?"

"That's just it!" she said. "You're so far out of touch with the real world that you really believe that — that 'each of us makes his own choices.' Bullshit! My mother and father never had the luxury of choice. They took what they were given and made a life from that. In the best scholastic manner, you ask, 'Who can say which is right?' But I tell you that even if my father is a coolie and a lush, I respect him more than you because he has had the courage to love with all his heart and perish in the attempt, while you with all your precious philosophy always have an escape valve, a loophole in the contract."

She was crying now, almost hysterical. Though her words stung me to the quick, I was more alarmed on her behalf than on my own. I had never seen her like that. Yet it was too painful simply to absorb. I had to defend myself.

"Perhaps I'm wrong," I replied in a quiet, measured tone, "but it seems to me that all of us are free to make our own choices. If we aren't, it's because at some point we've relinquished that freedom in exchange for something else. But that too is a choice. The monasteries were open to all in China. Your father might have entered one. But he chose to come to America, to marry and raise a family. That is his 'way,' and it seems to me a good one. True, the kinds of consolations which detachment brings are not available to him, you're right there. But he has a companion through all the trials of life, a love as solid as the foundations of the world in which to anchor his hopes. That too is a kind of solace. And you must see it's a solace unavailable to me, or anyone who chooses the monastic path."

"But why, Sun I? Why must you deny yourself that solace?" she asked, tenderness and pity welling up from beneath her anger.

Finally I understood, and the realization was very sweet, but agonizing, like the wafted aroma of a feast that I would never eat. "You would have me give up my philosophy, renounce my quest, all the things you disparage, all the things I cherish. . . ."

"Oh no, Sun I!" she interrupted, placing her finger on my lips. "You must not think that. Your search is precious to me. I love your philosophy and what it springs from, your honest faith in your beliefs, your purity of heart, your innocence and courage. . . ."

"But . . ."

"Shh," she whispered. "Don't you see? It doesn't matter what I say. I love these things because I love you."

She took my hands and drew me unresisting toward her, gently turned my head and laid it on her shoulder, and began to stroke my hair. "Ever since that first night," she whispered. "You thought I despised you. . . ." I could hear the smile in her voice, though my head was turned away. "But it wasn't that. I was only looking to make sure."

I felt such a weariness, such a craving for unconsciousness, such a desire to melt myself in her — a weariness I had been carrying around inside myself for years perhaps without ever suspecting its existence. But I opened my eyes and pushed her gently to arm's length. "You musn't love me, Yin-mi," I told her softly, "not in that way. For I can never return it. You ask me for the secret jewel in the casket of my life, and I can't give it. It's already promised."

"How promised?" she asked. "To whom?"

"To my religion. To give you what is owed already would be a perjury so deep that it could never be forgiven."

"You're wrong, Sun I," she said. "I'm only asking for your heart. Your soul I leave to you to do with as you will or must. I wouldn't dream of changing that. You keep your secret jewel, I'll be content with lesser alms."

"But how can they be separate?" I asked, growing confused and losing my composure.

She blinked and smiled. "I don't know how they can be, I only know they are."

"Oh, Yin-mi," I said wearily, "if I could love that way, I'd ask for no one else but you. I swear. But try to understand, my destiny lies along another path."

"You are so young," she said. "How can you know your path?" Her eyes were soft with submission and acceptance. There was an assurance there more profound than any I'd ever seen, except perhaps the master's. But Chung Fu's assurance had that edge of gaiety, something one could cling to so as not to sink, whereas Yin-mi's was vast and low and all-accepting, like a sea, and I felt myself dissolving into it. I panicked, stiffened, and walked to the window.

She didn't follow me. After a while I became aware of the clinking of dishes as she cleared away the tea. The sound was subdued and comforting, as the patter of the rain had been after the tense, ominous rumbling of the thunder. The electricity had still not been restored.

I looked out. The moon shone on the zigzag railings of the fire escapes below me. The sight reminded me of the view from Ken Kuan into the ravine where the river flashed silver-white among the rocks, floating its vigorous clamor upward, where it became dispersed, rarefied, taking on the quality of whispered innuendo. Close up and far away. The difference was like that of a battle observed by the soldiers in the trenches, the lurid, meteoric blaze of shells exploding overhead, and the same sight observed from a great distance by anxious watchers on the walls of well-defended cities, to whom it seems merely sad and a little ominous, like a winter sunset spreading its dying light across the barren fields, evoking a poignant longing in their hearts for summer. ". . . A condom between you and reality . . ." "For now we see through a glass darkly. . . ." "You have loved nothing as he has, so that you would suffer anything to preserve it, even the death of your spirit. . . ." "And what of love, Sun I?" The voices of this night floated back to me like the chorus of the river dead, haunting me. More haunting still, Yin-mi's equivocal embrace, and the taste of her mouth, which I could not forget. For some reason I could not determine, images of war continued to crowd in on me, seeping up like magma through a fissure which a realignment of tectonic plates had opened in my heart on what had once seemed solid ground. I saw myself the conscientious objector assigned to guard the walls, looking down from my great height at the columns of troops deploying in the streets, some of them boys no older than myself, and just as afraid of dying, even if only spiritually dying. I smiled bitterly. "Only." But who was the enemy? What was it? Perhaps no more than what Riley had called "living in the world as it is." As the ranks passed through the gate, one soldier caught my eye, and in his youthful face, drawn by fear and resolution into a taught beauty weighty beyond his years, I saw bitter wisdom and a silent recrimination which searched the secret places in my spirit. It was the same look I had seen in Yin-mi's eyes.

Doubts about the supreme validity of the Way of Life I'd learned under the tutelage of my Taoist mentors had never bothered me before, at least not at this visceral level. I'd assumed that the liberation of the heart from the disruptive influence of unbridled passion, the spirit purified of desire, rather than swollen to bursting with the turbid waters of its pent-up longing, was the ideal to be striven for, that the way of relinquishment was superior to the way of acquisition. And in my heart I still believed these things. Yet something else had made its mark on me that night. Why did I feel this sense of doubt about myself, of shame, as though accused of cowardice? Perhaps because I refused to fight the old battle with the old weapons and had retreated instead into myself, loyal to the conviction that war could only propagate hostility and perpetuate itself. But the look in the eyes of those marching into mortal peril is a terrible reproach to those left standing on the walls. And wasn't it in all their eyes — Yin-mi's, Lo's, her mother's, even Riley's? I might have borne it had I not this night felt an earth-tremor of doubt shudder through me. Like some Atlantis of the spirit, heaving and buckling upward from the bottom of the world, steaming and bubbling with foam, a whole new emotional continent rose before me, an unexpected hemisphere of being, a New World discovered in a quadrant where the mandarin cartographers had failed to look for it. Now there were fertile woods and mountains, grasslands teeming with deer and bison, great river basins draining into inland seas, and waving fields of grain, where before there had been nothing but the amorphous, level oceans, the salty, all-dissolving brine of Tao. This continent was love, and its vast panoramas, its monstrous fecundity, the strangeness of the beasts who grazed and hunted there, made me lose my scale and shrink to nothing against the sky. I wanted the old safety of the world I'd known: a garden landscape tended by devoted monks, not Sequoias and Douglas firs, but *p'en-tsai* trees which grow for generations and never rise above the waist; a place where all the rocks are cunningly arranged for elaborate symbolic and aesthetic effect but never dangerous, never prone to slide; where the diverted rivers burble with a never-varying music, and nightingales, not eagles, perch in the trees to sing. I wanted a garden, not a forest — not this wilderness. A kind of dread came over me as I contemplated this New World with its delights and dangers, for it offered me a glimpse of another Way, a *tao* of love, equal and coeval of the *tao* of quiescence, and its complement, which together formed the irreducible dichotomy of the world, and could never be reconciled or assimilated into one another as long as the world should last. And yet, how could this be true if "Reality is One, and Tao is Reality?" It couldn't. Either this shimmering new continent was an illusion, or . . . Could I even formulate the thought? Tao was an illusion. For if Tao is only partial, Tao is false. Was Riley right when he said there was no place for love within the Tao, or was there some unimaginable . . . "delta," yes, delta, where that impassioned torrent issued in the mystic sea as well? And further, was it possible, or even conceivable, that the delta where love issued to its consummation in quiescence was the same as that where Dow flowed into Tao? It occurred to me that until I had come to America, the Tao I'd known and felt such a comfortable allegiance to had been a bowdlerized version, a laboratory specimen, a hothouse flower. I had known the light and not the darkness. Now it was rising like a fretted sea around me, and I was stranded on the shoreline, watching the storm tide mount, wondering if it would spare the spot of earth where I was standing.

In the midst of these unsettling thoughts, I became aware of Yin-mi's presence behind me.

"Are you there?" I asked without turning.

"Yes," she answered softly.

"Are you ever afraid, Yin-mi?"

"What is there to be afraid of?" she replied, a slight quaver in her voice.

"I don't know," I said. "Something in our hearts."

We both fell silent, until I heard her crying. I turned around.

"What is there to cry about?" I asked, approaching and putting my hand lightly on her shoulder.

"I don't know," she wept, smiling through her tears, "something in my heart."

She took my hand and pressed it to her cheek, closing her eyes. Again I heard the hunter's horn intoning in the distance, the mournful baying of the hounds, felt my heart moved to obey the summons. Again I resisted.

A low, auspicious hum became audible. The lamps began to glow with a brown, feeble light. The buzz quickened and suddenly the room was filled with an incandescent glare, unnatural and lurid after the soothing darkness, like the light of science pitilessly turned into the heart's most intimate regions.

I could see the pale orchid blueness under Yin-mi's lids, irritated from weeping. She looked bruised and hurt, her skin pale, as though she'd dusted it with powder. Yet she had never appeared so lovely to me. I felt naked and ashamed. Nervously I withdrew my hand.

"Well," I said with false ease, "the lights are back on. I wonder what time it is? Very late, I'm sure. I guess I ought to go."

"I could make up the bed in Wo's room," she offered. "Why don't you stay? Please stay."

"I can't, Yin-mi," I said, almost imploringly.

She turned her still eyes, like the little girl's, to me once more, and I fled before her.

"Goodbye," I called as I opened the door, not looking back.

"When will you come again?" I heard her ask, just as the lock clicked shut. But I went on, pretending not to hear.

Chapter 14

The "unexpurgated version" of the Life of Kahn, my forbidden Communion at Trinity, the wild chase through the rain, Yin-mi's declaration — I was astonished, and terrified, by the profusion and fecundity, and the confusion, of the "real world," and of my friends' lives, of my life too, I suppose (guilt by association), though I resisted this conclusion, preferring to think of myself still as an observer, not a participant, believing that such objectivity was possible and could be sustained. I had to count revulsion, too, in the emotional tally I took after the events of that weekend. I was stirred with nostalgia for the monastery, the simplicity, the chaste sweetness of that life, and longed to lose myself in meditation. But I was unable to concentrate and dissolve. The cicada in the temple of the heart keened more insistently than ever. Disquieting thoughts arose: Riley's question, "And what of love, Sun I?"; the apparition of Tsin; the sight of Yin-mi's breasts, like unopened buds which shame the picker's hand; the taste of her mouth. And floating above them all, like the Cheshire cat, my father's mysterious, taunting smile, together with the phrase from the Communion, "This do in remembrance of me." These images resurfaced accompanied by rushes of hot physical shame. *Tso-wang* was hopeless. Even sleep was difficult. When I closed my eyes, this litany of distracting voices floated through my mind, as though rising on the same current of air as the noises from the Well of Sighs, merging into the existential murmur of the city. I arrived at the Exchange on Monday morning exhausted, limp, a twinge of despair in my heart. I craved the immaculate, shining place inside myself I knew was there but could not find my way back to. Perhaps it was related to my lack of sleep, but there was also that odd burning sensation in my eyes which I had first noticed after my blackout at the church. It had not improved appreciably over the weekend.

On top of all this, I was intellectually overtaxed, strained to capacity with unsuccessful attempts to reconcile the two disparate market strategies Kahn had introduced me to. Like the Scarecrow in the *Wizard of Oz,* my temples bulged with information about Intrinsic Value and Technical Analysis, information which, though suggestive, had as yet paid me no dividends in real knowledge and had, in fact, only served to confuse me further. Showing no mercy, Kahn pressed me to a further expedition that very morning.

He had called the Ha-p'is' Sunday evening, leaving word for me to meet him in the little drugstore on Pearl Street we sometimes frequented before the market opening, taking our ablutions, as Scottie might have said, he his coffee, I my morning tea. "Something special has come up" was all the message said, tantalizing me mercilessly as Kahn so frequently did. In spite of this, I was glad of the opportunity to talk with him alone. With everything else, the uncertainty about my father had become intolerable. If anyone could shed some light on the subsequent history of Eddie Love, it had to be Kahn. Who had a more intimate knowledge of the human aspect of the Street, the inner life of the great corporations and the men who ran them? Among his other accomplishments, Kahn was virtually a walking Wall Street scandal sheet. I was finally prepared to overcome my fear of what I might discover.

As I sat in my booth, steeling myself to chutzpah and self-assertion over my cup of steaming tea, Kahn burst in from the street, taking me by surprise.

"Come on, kid," he urged, grabbing my arm and dragging me through the door. "No time to lose. If we hurry, you just might make the eight forty-two."

"The eight forty-two?"

"Yeah, you're going to New Haven."

"New Haven! Where's that?"

"In Connecticut."

"Where in Connecticut?"

"Beside the tracks presumably, you schmo. How should I know? Consult your atlas!"

"But why am I going there?"

"I'm sending you to Dr. J. — Julius Everstat, that is — a buddy of mine from way back, Mount Abarim and again at the OWI. He's a mathematician at Yale, did some work on the application of statistical techniques to the study of the stock market. I want you to get a whiff of academe, the professorial approach to market analysis. Besides, he's got an interesting story to tell."

"But why New Haven?"

"Well, I would have tried to scare up something a little closer to home, at Columbia or NYU, but for some reason the strain doesn't prosper in its purest and most virulent form inside the borders of Manhattan, probably because the purely aseptic environment necessary to its growth can't be maintained here — too much squalor."

"But I need to talk to you."

"That's your problem, kid, too much talk, not enough action."

"But it's important!"

"Important! What could be more important than your education? You've got to be hungry for it, kid. Remember the old saying of the mad Ashkenazi, 'No balls, no glory.' "

"Kahn!" I cried in exasperated reproach, engaging him in a momentary bout of volitional arm wrestling.

"All right, all right already — so we'll talk! But *after* you get back, okay? Just move your tuchis now, for Christ's sake! I called the guy and he's going to pick you up at the station. What is this anyway? Listen to me. I do you a favor, and I'm begging you! I should beg? Here, take this." He shoved something in my hand.

"What is it?" I asked.

"A ticket," he replied. "That's right, I even bought your ticket. See what a nice guy I am? You don't deserve such a friend. And this — his address and phone number. Just in case he doesn't show. Julius is a very sweet guy, but terribly absentminded. Now go! Go!" So saying, he shooed me down the entrance to the Lexington Avenue subway, where I caught the express to Grand Central.

The train to New Haven emerged from the subterranean warrens of the station in the vicinity of Harlem and proceeded along Park to One twenty-fifth. The avenue here bore no relation to its Midtown incarnation. Blackened, fire-gutted tenements lined the street, an occasional potted geranium on a fire escape, or a laundry line spread with colors whose gaudiness became comprehensible against the depressing squalor of the setting. Then came the sterile moonscape of high-rise tenements, the Elysium of public planning, a utopia where children played their games in meadows not of asphodel or even grass but asphalt. Gradually the landscape began to open up. The scale became more human, more intimate. Tightly packed shops on listing streets lined the waterfronts of nameless towns, white-framed, steepled churches, dilapidated factories, high-voltage coils surrounded by chain-link fences, the black stone walls of the tracks bleeding runnels of lime. Then there were forests, and the sea. Passing a low salt marsh in which the green cord grass was beginning to turn to straw, I was surprised and delighted to see thousands of white and yellow butterflies fluttering in the air. Though it was still high summer, a tinge of autumn was in the air, a certain clarity in distances and, despite the heat, a hint of chill, like breathing through crushed ice. Huge cumuli sailed overhead, like full-rigged clipper ships drifting over the Atlantic eastward toward Cathay.

•

Kahn's misgivings proved well founded. Julius didn't make it. Apparently the stresses and responsibilities of mundane, sublunary existence were too much for him to cope with, or too trivial for his attention, so absorbed was he in the pursuit of higher mathematics. Aggravating my problem, the number Kahn had given me was apparently Julius's home phone, for no one answered though I let it ring off the hook. Fortunately I had his office address, so with a sigh

I set out on foot, asking directions as I went. In hindsight I'm able to amuse myself with the reflection that my acquaintance with the Random Walk began at street level and was initiated by the action of my feet — a consolation which, unfortunately, was not available to me at the time.

When I finally reached Everstat's office the door was open. I found the scholar deep in contemplation, leaning over a table spread with computer printouts, pale green and curling at the edges like ancient parchment scrolls, the particular one under consideration weighted by a slide rule, a teacup, and a box of paper clips, one corner winging free. The look of brooding absorption on his face, the way he grunted to himself from time to time and stroked his beard, idly twisting it to dreadlocks, which he idly then raked out, appealed to me. Perhaps here at last, I told myself, was an authentic Western magus, one who could save me from the confusion that was overwhelming me.

At my knock, he looked up slowly, a myopic glaze in his eyes. "Yes?" he asked politely but without enthusiasm.

"Dr. Everstat?"

"Well, what is it?" he said impatiently, glancing at his wristwatch. "Good God! I'm late!" As he leapt from his chair, I noticed that his jeans had a crease from the dry cleaners. His T-shirt boasted: "Statisticians are a better bet." One had the impression that his girlfriend or his mother had dressed him, so out of keeping were these details with his mien, deeply etched and purified by years of solitary thought.

"Excuse me." He sidled past me into the corridor. "I have a very important date. I was supposed to meet someone at the station twenty minutes ago. He's probably left already." He came to a standstill in the hall and stared into space. "I wonder what the odds on that would be?" He hesitated as though absorbed in internal computation, then, bestirring himself, bustled off again.

"Dr. Everstat!" I called after him.

He stopped and wheeled around. "What?" he shouted angrily. A look of realization dawned in his face. He raised his finger slowly, pointing. "You?"

I nodded.

He hit his forehead with the heel of his palm, then laughed. "Of course! I should have guessed at once from your . . . ah . . . physiognomic peculiarities."

"You mean, because I look Chinese," I glossed, smiling.

"Right!" he cried, taking my hand, evidently relieved at my easy acceptance of the ethnic allusion. "So you're Sun I." He pronounced my name correctly in the Chinese manner, which made a favorable impression after his earlier obliviousness to detail. "My friend, Aaron — how is the old devil anyway . . . ?"

"Devilish as ever."

He smiled. ". . . Tells me that you're a student of the market, and that you'd like to see how we operate up here."

I nodded. "I'm trying to distill some knowledge of the Dow from a study of the competing schools of market analysis."

"Perhaps we can save you some time and wasted effort," he replied, simpering. "There are no other 'schools' of market analysis. Ours is the only one that merits that title. True, there are other 'approaches,' but they are like primitive folk religions. Their gurus are no better than medicine men invoking animistic deities, relying on their pathetic little intellectual fetishes to protect them against a power they don't understand."

"Your method is different?"

He shrugged confidently. "They rely on faith, hope, love — what have you — the outmoded tools of religion. We have scientific method. Instead of fetishes and gris-gris, we are backed by the whole arsenal of Space Age high technology."

I was impressed by his confidence. "With all that at your disposal, you must have done quite well in your own investing career. What do you like right now?" I asked casually.

Believe me, Reader, I never dreamt that such an innocuous question — which among students of the market is about as threatening as a question about the weather among meteorologists — could throw him, an acknowledged expert, into such confusion. Everstat blushed, opened his mouth to speak, hesitated, became confused, looked down at his shoes, then managed to stammer, "Ah . . . well . . . you see, Sun I, though I am a diligent student of the market, I . . . so to speak . . . never invest myself." He grinned sheepishly, then, collecting himself, began again in bolder, more assured tones. "No, I am strictly disinterested. One has to be in seeking truth, don't you think? Self-interest is a fatal form of blindness in a field where clarity is essential."

"Then your researches have no practical application?"

"To the extent that we try and counsel others on what they're up against, they do," he answered, "disburdening them of all the propaganda put out by the Fundamentalists and Technicians, all the other specious prophets."

"How specious?" I interrupted.

"Because their advice is tainted with self-interest," he explained, "since, almost to a man, they are brokers who make fat commissions when they can convince their clients to buy and sell. No, though our adversaries insist that it's our greatest weakness, and even that it disqualifies our opinions altogether, the truth is, objectivity is our greatest strength. Because we never invest ourselves, our examinations are as free of bias as is humanly possible."

"Ah!" I sighed, with unspeakable gratification. "You observe without participating."

"You might put it that way," he conceded.

I was tempted to throw my arms around him in fraternal embrace. "How wonderful! At last a man after my own heart! Dr. Everstat, if only you could show me how you and your colleagues have garnered your deep knowledge of the Dow without compromising your objectivity, or incurring any risk, it would be invaluable to me in my own search."

"Always glad to help," he simpered, obviously flattered by my enthusiasm, but adding in a more equivocal tone, "though I'm not sure what I have to tell you will be what you want to hear." He invited me to precede him. "This way. Let me show you the shop."

Through eccentric windings in dingy, ancient corridors, Everstat led the way. At last we came to a dimly lit stone staircase, spiraling downward through one of the many turrets of the building. As we made our laborious way down toward the basement, I had the strange sensation, despite Everstat's ethnic background, that we had entered the labyrinth of the Anglo-Saxon mind, a region of fabulous glooms, full of grotesques and self-mortifying saints, types barely distinguishable from one another in the uncertain light.

Imagine my surprise when, as Everstat applied his key to the lock of the massive oak door, carved with the faces of gargoyles and mitred bishops, I found myself standing, not on the threshold of a dungeon full of engines of torture, nor a pagan altar stained with the blood of human sacrifice, but in a blindingly white room, lit by rows of fluorescent ceiling lamps (there were no windows, of course, since we were several stories underground), and lined with bank after bank of gleaming computers, exuding a variety of hums of different pitches — hardly the Anglican chorale I had expected, more like an electronic barbershop quartet! Men in white lab coats were reading printouts here and there, or in-putting programs at the terminals along the walls. A technician (an electronic technician, mind you, not a Chartist) with a soldering iron was performing delicate open-heart surgery on one of the older members of the computer tribe, which had attained, I was told, the ripe old age of three and was now in its senescence, on a pension, no longer cost-effective, unable to do enough work to cover its enormous electricity bill, but subsidized out of gratitude for its long months of loyal service.

Everstat sighed, and a glow of inner peace and security appeared on his face as we crossed the threshold, entering this little paradise, or womb, of high technology. He regarded me with godlike magnanimity, as though from a great distance, patronizing but not unkind, no doubt pitying my benighted state and the arduous journey I would have to undergo to arrive at the transcendent wisdom he'd already found. We proceeded down a random aisle, the subliminal hum punctuated now and then by the tick of a reel stopping and starting up.

"It's all here, my friend," he said with an expansive gesture. "You know, you're lucky to get in. This place is strictly off limits to worldings." He laughed. "Seriously though, Sun I, when you stepped through that door . . ." (he pointed, but it had disappeared behind a bank of computers) "you effectively entered the future. This is the state of the art. The hardware you see here, and the software you don't, but which is here too nonetheless, like the soul within the body, is revolutionizing the entire world, not least the concept of security investment. Of course, it takes time for these things to 'trickle down' to the man on the street — Wall Street especially." He winked. "I must admit, the capitalist hordes have had a tendency to scoff. But what great discovery has ever been appraised at its true value when it first appeared? Darwin still has his detractors. Yet, like evolution, the Random Walk is destined to outdistance its competitors. Take my word for it, Wall Street will eat its words one day, and soon."

I listened in silent awe as he discoursed on what would be and what would not. Comparing his tools for gathering knowledge with those I'd been given by my Chinese masters, I experienced a tremor of doubt. How could we ever hope to compete against such fabulous magicians? Beside this shining arsenal, what was a dog-eared copy of the *I Ching* and a handful of yarrow stalks? It was like pitting archers against a modern army equipped with heavy artillery, even nuclear weapons.

"Can you explain to me, Dr. Everstat, how these machines have helped you penetrate the secret essence of the Dow?"

" 'Secret essence,' " he chuckled. "You make it sound like a conspiracy to violate a virgin, or break the seventh seal."

I blushed.

"But such metaphors are not entirely inappropriate," he continued, taking a grave tone, embarrassed himself. "I mean this business of 'secret essences.' The Dow has always been one of the most mysterious and elusive formations on the American landscape, smiling its Mona Lisa smile you might say, a smile which portends a riddle. 'What makes me tick?' she seems to ask, and men are instantly magnetized and allured. Once they accept the combat she proposes, though, Sphinx-like she devours those who fail to satisfy her, the Great American Black Widow, brooding at the center of her web, devouring her mates in the anguish of her unfulfilled satiety. How many have entered that labyrinth and returned, Sun I? How many have found the answer? Very few. Perhaps none. . . . Until now. If you'll excuse the graphicness of the metaphor, we have fucked her. We have solved the riddle." His oracular smile soured into a frown. "Unfortunately, as it turns out, the old bitch isn't a very satisfying lay. What is it they say about anticipation always being sweeter than fulfillment?"

"What do you mean?" I asked.

"Well, to answer you, let me backtrack. According to conventional wisdom, the Random Walk theory of stock market price fluctuation is derived from purely logical considerations, an elegant and very beautiful syllogism. Thus: *If* men are rational profit-maximizers, and investors (buyers and sellers, that is) are men; *then* price fluctuation in the market is a random walk."

"But what . . . ?" (I was going to say, "What is a random walk?" but he held up his hand.)

"Don't interrupt," he said. "All things will be revealed to you in their proper places. You must realize that this is only the skeleton of the argument. Between antecedent and consequence there is a very delicate and elaborate chain of reasoning. Or perhaps your question concerns the putative self-evidence of the premises? I must admit that on occasion I have been led to question the assumption that rationality prevails in the marketplace. Sometimes it's difficult to resist the conclusion that obscure and perverse psychological forces — herd behavior, for instance — are at work as well."

I think I must have ogled him a bit. Could there be any question of it? Certainly on the Street it was accepted as a given, too banal even to deserve mention. What marvelous vantage had he attained through his rarefied researches from which he could so confidently dismiss this maxim?

Everstat smirked, continuing on his own track. "I suppose if one wished to indulge in a little wicked quibbling, he might even question the minor premise, that Wall Street traders are men at all. Their behavior certainly smacks of bestiality at times. But seriously, concerning the major premise, after my 'dark night of the soul' I always come around and renounce the heresy. I tell myself that even if you have a weirdo masochist here and there who wants to lose his money and invests accordingly, it isn't a statistically relevant proportion of the investment population. Besides, that kind of thing is unquantifiable." He uttered this last word with a disdainful emphasis, as though it were the ultimate derogation of the value of a thing.

"But all of this, though pertinent, is not what I want to talk to you about. The conventional wisdom — the idea of an unambiguous conclusion logically deduced from self-evident premises — is very flattering to our belief in our capacity for rational behavior and altruism, but the truth is, it is a facade applied in hindsight, a Greek facade, as it were, forthright, sunny, clear, applied over an edifice of a very different sort, a baroque mansion, let us say, filled with secret passages, strange nooks and alcoves, a setting more appropriate for intrigue and betrayal." He lowered his voice. "The story I am going to tell you, Sun I, is known to very few and, I might add, believed by even fewer. I am able to vouch for its veracity, however, because I happened to be one of the participants. In fact, I may as well tell you, I spent over a year of my life working on the project which ultimately led to the application of the Random Walk to stock market analysis, research for which I received neither recognition nor recompense. If I am bitter, I have a right to be. But I'm not the only one who was wronged, and in fact my injury is very slight compared to another's, and I am able to revenge it, whereas my friend is no longer in a position to do either.

"I met Michael Schwartz while we were still schoolboys at Mount Abarim, a pale, timorous boy with a severe speech impediment, deeply troubled, but also deeply gifted. In fact, Michael was a genius, if anyone I've ever met deserved the name. He had the greatest aptitude for mathematics I've ever encountered, and more than this, he loved it, and could work. If ever there was a Pythagorean, it was Michael. For to him the maxim that 'things are numbers' was more than a suggestive hyperbole. It was an article of faith. Consequently his inquiries led him away from the realm of pure mathematics, where I've remained (which he disparaged as no more than an elegant form of chess, a sort of glass-bead game), toward the practical — if you can consider theoretical physics practical, a matter of perspective, I suppose. Michael's was really a religious search. It was his constant obsession to use mathematics to distill experience. He once told me that it was his ambition to derive the garden of the living world in all its splendor and profusion from the dry, brown, unlikely seed of a mathematical equation. Ambitious, no? But isn't that the ambition of all of us finally, the search for eternity in time, infinity in finitude, Nirvana in Samsara?

"He became involved in work on unified-field theory at Princeton's Institute for Advanced Study. What could have been more appropriate — that attempt to deduce the world from a single immutable law, to force the multiplicity of natural phenomena through the bottleneck of the equations? I saw him infrequently during those years. Our paths had diverged. But when we did run into one another, he seemed happier than I had known him, though there was still evidence of the old pain. But with someone like Michael, it can never be healed fully, only controlled. Basically I was happy for him. I thought at least that he was safe.

"That's why the news of his suicide was so shattering. It came as a complete surprise. I was devastated. It seemed so senseless, so wasteful — at least at first. Later though, as I looked into it, it began to resolve itself into one of the purest, most focused acts I've ever beheld. Though it may seem cold to say so, it had all the rigor and inevitability of a demonstration in geometry.

"Now I'm not competent to explain the details of the case. I know little more about physics than you, probably. I only know that he was working in some connection with the problem of mirror symmetry in elementary particle research, which until that time was regarded as a fundamental property of nature. Its elegance and mathematical simplicity must have appealed to him. But as he went deeper into it, he began to discover some puzzling exceptions, which he was attempting to assimilate into the law. I don't know the precise scenario, I only know that it came about with the publication of Mme Wu's experiments on radioactive beta decay, which finally exploded the notion of symmetry and opened up the vertiginous prospect of a fundamental asymmetry in nature. Michael read the article very carefully and dispassionately, did some computations, then went home, took a pistol from the drawer, and shot himself in the head." Everstat fell silent.

"You may disagree with me, Sun I, but in my opinion that is one of the noblest deaths imaginable. *That* was intellectual passion. He lived his idea, and when it failed him — or when he thought it had — he shot himself. That he was wrong, that he misunderstood — if he misunderstood — doesn't matter. The point is that he acted on what he believed. But I don't want to bore you with it. What does Michael's life, and death, have to do with you? You've come to hear about the Random Walk. Well, this is the tie-in. Michael's mother knew that I was also a mathematician (she didn't realize how far apart our fields really were), and having no one else to turn to asked me to go through his papers to see if there was anything of value. Of course I obliged her, though it was an imposition on my time." He glanced at his watch and frowned. "Now there was quite a bit to go through. Michael had kept notebooks of ideas, sort of a mathematical version of Leonardo's sketchbooks. These were filled with the most incredible hodgepodge. He had an immense curiosity. Most of the notebooks consisted of the merest sketches, suggestive, preposterous, and playful by turn. But one idea had been worked out in some detail. In fact, he had filled several binders. What it was, was the gradual evolution of a mathematical model for stock market price fluctuation, more specifically a way to isolate the central law according to which the fluctuation proceeds.

"For him this was apparently simple recreation. There is no evidence that he considered it more than an intriguing pastime. And besides, there was really no way he could have tested his model, for it was for all practical purposes humanly insoluble, not for any theoretical reason, but mechanically. The equations were so complex, with literally hundreds of variables, that it would have taken years to work them out by conventional methods. Now remember, computers were still a relative novelty at that time. FORTRAN was not, as it is today, a language which all scientists and mathematicians speak from birth. I don't think Michael realized that these equations could be managed. I knew they could. From my experience I knew the machines could do the work, primitive as they were. The real problem was going to be the software. I estimated that it could take up to a year, possibly longer, to develop a program to test his model. The equations interested me, but I wasn't sure I wanted to risk that much time on what might well turn out to be a wild-goose chase. Besides, I had my hands full already with my own work.

"So I wrote a brief letter to a prominent journal advising the readership of the existence of the equations and offering them to anyone with the proper credentials who was willing to undertake the work. I got a few tepid inquiries from graduate students looking for original Ph.D. thesis topics. I was about ready to pack them away in the attic, when something interesting occurred. I got a call from a man . . . well, his name doesn't matter, or who he worked for. Suffice it to say he was a statistician in the employ of one of the large corporations. I suppose I was incredibly naive at that time, Sun I. I mean, certainly I had considered the implications of the equations, but intellectually, abstractly, not in terms of the potential power stakes involved — not until I talked to this fellow, that is. 'Do you have any idea what you're sitting on?' he asked me. 'If these equations are correct, we're talking about an economic revolution. A perfectly predictable market! Do you know what that would mean? You're in the same position as Mayer Rothschild at the Battle of Waterloo! It would be like getting a copy of Tuesday's financial page before the market opened Monday. In a single day you could become the richest man on earth, assuming you had adequate capital reserves to invest. Which is one of the incentives I can offer for your letting me and my staff participate, the second being as large a research team as you desire to cut your work load and speed the process. Just think — you could take anything you wanted, and as much as you wanted! And it's all a matter of a single day, or at most a week or two, which is why haste and secrecy are so important. The market couldn't long survive profit-taking on that order, particularly if the word got out. It would precipitate a crash that would make the Great Depression look like May Day,' he told me. 'You could have the country on its knees. You're sitting on a potential economic atom bomb. And we're offering to make you the Oppenheimer of your own Manhattan Project!' Which, I suppose, made him my General Gates, though Mephistopheles might make the nature of his offer more transparent. Well, Sun I, imagine how I felt! I hung up the phone, went home, and agonized over it for several days. Then I called him and refused. The next day I applied for a leave of absence and began to work on the program myself.

"Now don't misunderstand me, Sun I, it wasn't a selfish motive that led to my decision. In fact, the prospect of possessing such power and actually using it terrified me." He raised his finger. "But to have such power, and *refuse* . . . ah! That would be sublime. Well, not to mince words, I plunged into it. Day after day I hammered it out. Of course, my part of the work was basically mechanical. Any number of people could have done what I did. The incommensurable quantity was the equations themselves. Michael, you might say, was the architect, I the carpenter giving a concrete embodiment to his dream. My corporate Mephistopheles continued to try and seduce me — there were considerable sums involved — but after I'd successfully resisted him once, resisted myself, that is, his attacks held no great terrors for me and in the end became perfunctory, even a little pathetic.

"I'd been working for some months and was fairly well on my way. It was summer. I remember I was sitting in my room one evening. It was stiflingly hot. I had my little rotating fan on, blowing from behind me. No shirt. It must have been seven, eight o'clock, still light outside. I decided to take a break, go down to the little Italian grocery on the corner of Elm and buy a Coke and a hero. Now, I suppose every scholar has his own little deskside ritual, like a physician's bedside manner. I have this ceremony I perform. Probably it's a bit absurd, but mathematicians have as much right to be absurd as the population at large, don't they? Well, I drink tea when I work. I drink it all day and all night. Constantly, obsessively. Not to stay awake either. It's not the caffeine. When I'm on vacation I can go two weeks without thinking of a cup of tea. No, it's a nervous need. Having something to fondle, to retreat to, a mute little friend who understands the terrors of pure concentration, reassures me with its warmth. It's a great comfort. I know I drink too much of it, but I console myself with the thought that if it weren't that, it would be something worse, cigarettes probably. I used to try and cut down, but why bother? It doesn't affect me anymore. I can sleep as soundly after half a dozen pots as after none.

"At any rate, I have a special teacup. It's upstairs in my office. Perhaps you saw it? A gift from my mother. I keep it on a cloth napkin at my right so as not to circle the wood. Whenever I leave my desk I use it as a paperweight for what I'm working on. I place it down in a certain way — handle to the right, parallel to the edge of the desk. Nothing profound, that's simply how I hold the cup. Purely second nature. I don't think about it. I wouldn't have thought about it that day either, if something hadn't jarred. I went out, got my grinder, and came back. The door was locked, just as I'd left it. I sat down at the desk, kicked my feet up, unwrapped the white paper wrapper of my sandwich, and started to take a bite, when something unusual caught my eye. The handle of the cup was turned — not much, it's true, just a few degrees, but enough to notice. I put down my sandwich, took a closer look, and on the papers I was working on I saw a double tea-ring from the bottom of my cup! In addition, Michael's notebook was turned to a different page. Now I admit, my rotating fan could perhaps have accounted for that. But the tea-ring? No. I had put it down once, and it had been moved, placed back in a slightly different position. I began to examine things more closely, and then nothing seemed right. My pencils were arranged in an odd way, the papers I was working on looked like they'd been tampered with. Well, you may think all this was my imagination. I tried to dismiss it as that as well. But an interesting thing occurred, Sun I. From that day on, Mephistopheles stopped calling me. That's right. Perhaps he realized the futility of it, you say? Perhaps. Or perhaps he no longer needed me, having pilfered what he wanted himself!

"I've only put this together in hindsight. The incident startled me, made me wary, but I kept on as before, only I began to hide Michael's notebooks when I left my room. Well, let me skip ahead. The program took longer than I'd expected. Almost eighteen months. As I drew near the end, I began to get excited. Finally I went on line with the completed program. I remember that morning. I saw the usual faces, professors drinking cups of coffee and chatting idly, some bit of gossip, some new idea, someone leaning over another's shoulder as he sat at the keyboard, pointing to the printout, asking a question, offering a suggestion. The same as always. But not for me. Though outwardly I behaved as I always did, inwardly I was in a state of virtual mania. I kept thinking about Oppenheimer — that day at Trinity when they tested the bomb, Enrico Fermi taking odds on whether it would incinerate New Mexico. Then the detonation, exultation, awe, finally terror, and Oppenheimer thinking of those lines from the *Bhagavad Gita:* 'I am become Death, destroyer of worlds.' I felt a little like that myself, Sun I. I was so nervous I could hardly type in my commands. Finally I got it all in and sent it up, then I fixed a cup of tea and waited for the printout. Of course I was interested in the specific variable, but first of all I wanted to know simply if the equations worked. . . ." Everstat paused and looked off.

"Well?" I said. "Did they?"

"Hmm?" he dreamily responded.

"Did they work?"

He narrowed his eyes. "Oh yes, Sun I, they worked."

"Well, what was the answer?" I cried in exasperation.

"The answer?" He smiled like a cretin.

"Yes, what was the answer?"

"There is no answer," he replied.

"I thought you said they worked!"

He nodded. "They did, Sun I. That is the answer — that there is no answer."

"But how can that be?" I demanded. "What does it mean?"

"It means that prices in the stock market fluctuate essentially at random. It's one of those weird miasmas in nature where the normal laws are suspended — like the black holes of the astrophysicists — where some fundamental asymmetry between cause and effect applies. Statisticians have their own name for such a phenomenon. We call it a Random Walk."

I stared at him, absolutely flabbergasted, as the import of his words dawned on me. "You mean there is no reason?"

He nodded. "You might put it that way."

"But that's preposterous!" I protested. "How can you account for the success of knowledgeable professionals in picking stocks?"

He shrugged. "Luck, Sun I. The truth is, the most experienced, highly trained professional isn't one iota more enlightened than the greenest neophyte. And the most sophisticated 'system' advanced by the so-called experts has no more to recommend it than the classic technique of throwing darts at the day's financial columns. The savvy professionals like your mentor Aaron — whom I dearly love, don't misunderstand me — are like a group of men sitting before a radio stuck between channels, listening to the roar of static and going to great pains to convince themselves that what they hear is music. Or, to propose another analogy, they are like individuals undergoing psychological examination: the Dow is the Rorschach blot, and their 'systems' are merely the subjective patterns they perceive based on their private conflicts and neuroses. Why can't they see the truth? Because of self-interest, Sun I.

"But you must let me finish my story. Less than two weeks after my discovery, I pick up a copy of *Statistical Forum,* and what do I see? An article on 'The Dow as Random Walk.' No mention of my program, or Michael's equations, of course. The whole thing logically derived, very simple, very elegant. The basic idea is this: A transaction on the stock exchange involves two parties, a buyer and a seller, both rational animals, and consequently self-interested profit-maximizers. Now, they have equal access to the same information about the securities they propose to buy and sell, respectively. The transaction occurs at a price that both consider fair, otherwise they would not engage in it. Well, if the foregoing is true, and one man yet feels impelled to buy, another to sell, then there can be no logical, systematic manner of price fluctuation which both can predict. Stock prices fluctuate at random. Very clean, very pretty. An intellectual virgin birth!" Everstat's features contorted in a look of ugly irony as he said this. "Well, Sun I, at first I was simply stunned. Then I began to put two and two together. You probably see what I'm driving at already?"

I shook my head.

"Perhaps it will make it clearer if I mention that the university in which this wunderkind had tenure enjoyed a very cosy relationship with the aforementioned corporation, Mephistopheles's corporation?"

I still couldn't see.

"They stole it from me, damn it! Then doled it out in the form of largesse to one of their protégés, who wrapped it up in a new package and published it, stealing my thunder!" Everstat kicked a nearby computer pettishly, stubbing his toe in the process. "Damn things," he muttered. "Well, I was hot. I took my story to the dean. He was interested in the program and the equations, though he raised some quibbles — all very minor, very petty — over certain things I'd done, said why not publish them as supplementary to this fellow's work? But when I mentioned the story of the theft, he became very grave, very cautious. What evidence did I have? A double tea-ring? Harumph! Well, Sun I, that was that!"

Everstat continued speaking for some time, but I wasn't listening. His private grievance, real or imaginary, was interesting, but the Random Walk — that was what occupied me. If what he said was true, it struck at the jugular of my intentions to discover the motive force behind the transformations of the Dow, the unity within the multiplicity. If he was right, there was none! Reader, I felt as though he'd dropped the bomb indeed, a metaphysical bomb, and *on me!*

I hardly remember our parting. He offered to take me back to the station, but I declined and staggered out alone. The light of the afternoon sun was in my face all the way back to the station, intensely, blindingly brilliant. It was a great relief to board the train again, the tinted panels of the windows, the cool, air-conditioned interior soothed my eyes, my mind. Not much though. If I had been depressed in the morning, I was doubly so now. All the way in to New York, I thought about the progress of my education in the Dow to that point. The delta seemed palpably receding before me. I felt myself going, not downstream toward the spreading sea of illumination into knowledge, not toward peace, fulfillment, release, but back upriver toward the headstreams, toward confusion, turmoil, and a greater violence. In fact, the whole notion of "progress" in my search mocked the actual state of affairs. For wasn't the process of my education until now a gradual regression from certainty to nihilism, from hope to despair?

First there was Powers. "There is a reason, and it can be ascertained." For him the idea of man as a rational profit-maximizer, or, more specifically, rationality itself ("a clear head") was not an initial assumption, a *terminus a quo,* as it was for the academics, but an ideal, a *terminus ad quem,* toward the realization of which he applied his discipline.

Then Newman. "There is a reason, but we can never know it, though we can use it." The intermediate position.

Finally Everstat. "There is no reason. The Dow is a Random Walk." Was this the final verdict, the summit of knowledge? I refused to accept it. Was it not a progressive plunge into the mire of intellectual cowardice and cynicism, not only about the Dow, but about the universe itself and man's place in it? For what were these market strategies in the final analysis after all if not world views? A scale dropping into the lowest register of despair.

Was this the "wisdom" I had expected to receive at the hands of these market "sages," who were here called "pros" instead? I bridled at the very idea that Everstat's system, the Random Walk, represented the apex of wisdom concerning the Dow. Yet it had begun so hopefully! For of all of them, he alone had started from a position closest to my own, cherishing his objectivity, observing without participating. What was left?

Chapter 15

Kahn sat back against the rail of the gallery, the teeming mitosis of the trading floor like a huge, unfocused backdrop behind his head, lending outline to his features. His expression as he listened to me pouring out my doubts and contradictions was both amused and sad, both stern and sympathetic. He was uncharacteristically quiet throughout, never interrupting. And even when the spate had exhausted itself, he continued staring at me silently, a fierce gleam in his eye, a gleam of both mockery and exhortation.

"So, kid," he said, "you've tried the sanitary methods and they don't work. The fetishes of all the medicine men have proven ineffective, pathetic bits of straw and feathers. And you wanted a magic that could master life." He laughed in scorn and pity. "What does it all boil down to, your 'education' in the market? All the experts have their systems, all final and infallible, all different, all contradictory. Now you come to me and ask me for my talisman. I'm not sure I can give you one, kid. Let me ask you something. Did you really expect that someone else could give you 'the answer,' something you could write down on a slip of paper, memorize, and then apply happily ever after? How easy that would be! And how cheap. Look down there, kid," he said, indicating the floor with a nod while keeping his eyes engaged with mine. "The urgency, the hope, the despair, the immense humanity of it, *all that life* — did you really think all that could be condensed into a paraphrase, some Cliff's Notes version which you could study a semester, master, and exhaust? Uh-uh, kid. There's only the unexpurgated version of the Dow. And for that I'm not sure even one lifetime is enough. The Dow's a mystery, kid, a religion, and like any mystery, there's a price for initiation. 'In this country everyone must pay for everything he gets' — I forget who said that."

"What else can I pay!" I protested. "Haven't I given everything already, left home and journeyed across the world for this?"

He shook his head. "It's not enough. You left your home, it's true. But you carried your assumptions with you." He laughed. "You're like a snail carrying his own house around with him as he goes. I can see them now, your shell and horns. It's slowed you down, kid. You've come a ways, but there's a ways to go. Now you've reached a sort of *nec plus ultra* in your wanderings. There lie the Pillars of Hercules, and beyond . . . who knows? The western cataract maybe, the end of the world? No one can answer that, Sonny. No one can tell you what you'll encounter on the other side. The risk is absolute. But if you want to undertake that voyage, you've got to cast off all your ballast now, strip down to the essential nakedness, like a warrior."

"I'm not sure I understand you, Kahn," I said. "What is this ballast you're talking about, this shell I carry around with me as I go?"

"That little portable altar shrine in your heart, kid, your spiritual Winnebago."

"Don't mock me, Aaron."

"I can't help myself," he said. "Besides, kid, I mean it affectionately, and I'm sincere."

"I believe you are," I conceded.

"Your masters taught you to value and seek out certainty — the power to elude the ravages of time and change — to seek it in a still, shining place inside yourself, a place which meditation opens up and you call Tao."

"Yes," I acknowledged. "So they taught; so I believe."

"Then why are you here?" he asked. "If their answer satisfied you, why did you leave the monastery?"

"Sometimes I wonder," I replied, disspirited and wistful. "It seemed once that my path lay in this direction, through the marketplace, through Dow, but now I'm not so sure. Maybe it was only an illusion. Maybe I should have stayed and continued on the path I knew, cultivating that place inside myself which you describe."

Kahn narrowed his eyes incredulously. "And give up life?" His question pierced me like an arrow, scoring to the quick. "That's my question," he continued. "For my part, if these things prove mutually exclusive — certainty and life — then I choose life. I'd prefer to tempt the worst and live, rather than attain the safe asepsis which your Way holds out as its greatest promise. To take that way, that safety, would be equivalent to a lobotomy, a moral castration, a kind of death. Perhaps the only certainty is death."

"And so the Dow — your Dow — is life?" I asked in wounded irony.

"That's it, kid," he said. "Life as it is, confused, unruly, perilous (we're talking mortal peril here), corrupt perhaps, but overflowing at every pore with the juices of existence. The world as it is." He nodded and made a sweeping gesture toward the floor, as though to say "This could be yours." "Out of the ooze and slime of the life-mire the answer must emerge. Look down there. If the answer isn't here, it isn't. Period."

"And what must I do to find this answer?"

"You've got to give your innocence," he said, "your moral virginity."

"Give it?" I recoiled. "To whom?"

"To life," he replied. "The altar in your heart you've tended so lovingly all these years, washing it down with buckets of clear water from the well, scrubbing it on your hands and knees, sweeping, dusting, keeping it immaculate — now you've got to sully it with a blood sacrifice. What else did you think it was for? The paschal lamb is you, Sonny. You must play Abraham to your own Isaac and slay yourself. Once you've spoiled it, no solvent will ever wash that altar clean again. The stain will remain, but you can at least begin to live."

"But what does all this mean?" I asked despairingly.

"What does it mean?" He regarded me in stern sympathy. "To understand the Dow, you've got to invest, kid — something of yourself. There's no other way. It's the price of initiation. You've got to play the game. That's my mandate and my ultimatum to you."

The commotion from the trading floor rose to me like the sound of crumbling foundations, dynasties falling, worlds in upheaval. "And my vow?" I asked tremulously.

"That is the sacrifice you must make in your heart."

"You realize you're asking me to damn myself?"

He smiled gravely. "That's right, Sonny, it is damnation, damned to life, living in the world as it is, because it's all there is."

"And the Return to the Source?"

He laughed, tilting his head back. "This is the Source, Sonny, and you're already here."

"Perhaps for you the Dow is the Source," I conceded. "But what about the delta, where the two flow into one another? For they must flow into one another, Aaron. You must see that. 'Reality is One, and Tao is Reality.' "

"Sounds good, Sonny, but I'm not sure I believe it. What if Reality isn't — 'One,' I mean? What if there is no delta?"

"There has to be," I said. "If Tao is only partial, Tao is false."

"Maybe it is. You've got to look that in the face. Maybe this is all there is."

"You're wrong!" I contradicted him. "I've seen that place."

"Oh, I don't doubt that you've seen something," he disparaged, "that there's a psychological condition corresponding to that inner void you talk about. Too much fasting, too much silence, too long vigils of bodily discomfort, 'regulation of the breaths,' sexual continence — all that self-mortification — it isn't surprising that it induces some interesting and rather extreme states of mind. But perhaps they're only freaks of consciousness, who can say? And if so, what a tragedy to mistake them for the be-all and end-all of existence. Such a waste."

"Please, Kahn, don't say any more," I begged him. "If you do, I'm afraid I'll hate you."

"Okay, kid. I'm finished anyway." He stared at the tips of his shoes abstractedly, frowning. After a moment he eyed me appraisingly. "You don't look too good," he said. "Let's go for a walk, want to? We've still got half an hour."

I observed him blankly.

"Come on," he coaxed, jerking his chin up in a confidential, reassuring manner. He took my elbow and gently urged me upward.

I followed him.

•

As we left the building and started wending our way, without thinking, drawn by some elemental gravity, down toward the river, I was in a state of great disheartenment. Kahn's "ultimatum" stuck in my craw like some bit of indigestible gristle. I felt the urgent necessity of going forward with my search into the meaning of the Dow, and at the same time, the absolute impossibility of doing so at such a cost as he'd assessed. How could I ever see my way clear to taking up the gauntlet he'd laid down?

"Even if you're right," I said, after a long interlude, playing my thoughts aloud, "not that you *are,* but just for the sake of argument, from a practical viewpoint how could I invest? I have no money."

"Good question," he said, rolling his bottom lip over the top one and nodding his head. "Money is a problem. On your salary, too, I'd say credit was out of the question."

"Exactly," I assented with relief. "So you see, even from that perspective, it's hopeless."

"Not so fast," he said. "That's very clever, but I can't allow you to wallow unopposed in such shameless O.C." He pondered. "I guess monks don't accumulate much in the way of personal possessions over the course of a career, huh? Trinkets, curios, bibelots, Taoist mementos, preferably in gold or silver?"

I gave him a keen, searching glance. "Why do you ask?"

He shrugged. "Oh, I don't know. I was just wondering if there was anything you might sell."

I shrugged back at him. "No, I don't think . . ." I froze in my tracks with a sensation of incipient vertigo, my disheartenment quickening suddenly to panic.

"Kid? What's the matter, kid? Something hit a nerve?"

"My mother's robe," I said in a whisper of dawning realization, not so much to him as to myself.

"Is it nice?"

"Nice!" I protested. "It's irreplaceable!"

He pursed his lips and nodded. "That might be just the thing."

I stared at him in horror. "Never!" I cried. "That would be an apostasy greater even than breaking my vow."

"Well, maybe you could just pawn it," he suggested delicately.

"No!" I shouted. "Absolutely not! Nothing is worth that price!"

"Okay, okay, take it easy, kid. Jesus! What's the alternative? Either that, or you just give up, throw in the towel on the whole deal. Is that what you're going to do, give up?" Sighing with exasperation, he shook his head. "Sometimes I wonder about you, kid. I mean, I admire your principles and everything, but sometimes I don't know if you're going to make it out here. Maybe you're not cut out to live in the world."

"Maybe I'm not," I replied, unable to suppress the quaver in my voice, unaccountably wounded by a judgment which, to a Taoist, might have been construed as a compliment of a high order. "Maybe I should just go back."

"Maybe you should," he agreed. "I'm sorry, kid, but that's the way it is. I've done all I can do. The rest is up to you." He regarded me in mournful assessment. "Just do me one favor, okay? Don't dismiss my proposition out of hand. Give yourself a few days to think it over first before you make your decision. Think about this aspect of it too: parting with the robe doesn't necessarily have to be a sacrilege. It could also be construed as the sacrifice of a material possession — an *attachment* — for the sake of higher knowledge."

"That's sophistry," I said.

"Is it? I'm not so sure. You turn it over in your mind a few days. If you can come up with, say, five hundred, or even better, a thousand, I've got a little deal in the works I maybe could cut you in on. If it works out like I expect it to, you could redeem the robe within the month, six weeks tops, and get yourself a little stake on the side to play around with in the bargain. That way you could have your cake and eat it too. How does that sound?"

"I could redeem it?" I asked.

"Sure!" he said. "Assuming it works out, that is, which I think it will."

"How certain is it?"

"Not that again," he griped. He gave me an arch look. "Kid, you want certainty, you've got to do honest work." He laughed. "In this world redemption is always a risky proposition. No bromide intended. Look, here we are!"

Almost without my knowing it, we had made our way to the waterside.

"Ah," Kahn sighed, snuffing up a chestful of the briny air. "I love that smell. I wish I could bottle it up and take it with me on the job like smelling salts, you know? When the air gets too close and thick with abstraction and the 'stink of mendacity,' just a little something I could take a whiff of now and then to remind me of the real meaning of what we're doing there."

"And what is the 'real meaning'?" I asked, with a twinge of remote aggression, resenting his expansiveness.

We had attained a vantage from which we could look out over the river and simultaneously observe the activity of the Fulton Street Fish Market slightly to the north. Kahn walked up to the edge and propped his foot on the concrete mole, gazing over the water toward Brooklyn. The August sun, like a newly minted coin, shed scraps and shards of superfluous gold into the tussling currents, which at that moment seemed almost blue. "You know, I think better with my eyes on Brooklyn," he mused, as though he hadn't heard my question, almost as though he were alone. He turned to me. "I used to have an urge sometimes to give it all up, come back here and take a job on the docks again, you know, simple, honest work that has some more tangible connection to subsistence. Out here with your arms plunged up to the elbow in a crate of fish you don't have to ask yourself the purpose of what you're doing, the morality of it. It's immediate and unconditional. You're putting food on the tables of America, helping to sustain the collective life. There's a bracing reality in the the work that satisfies a longing in the soul. In comparison, Wall Street can seem so vain, an illusory paper world which contributes nothing solid to the well-being of the country, or the race, or humankind, like these simple folk who deal in the raw stuff of subsistence." He sighed. "I used to think of the economic apparatus of this country, which begins and ends in Wall Street — for all roads lead back there, as to Rome — as a foolish and un-scrupulous way of padding out the links in the economic chain between pro-ducer and consumer, hundreds of middlemen wedging their way in between the fisherman and the housewife who buys her cod or flounder and takes it home for supper, diminishing his rightful profit for his labor and risk, and also taxing her husbandry by making her contribute to the support of the superflu-ous machinery. It seemed unfair, unnatural, vaguely obscene. I guess I was kind of a Taoist myself in those days, kid — socialist, more like." He smiled. "Yet it isn't as simple as all that. The intervening machinery isn't merely parasitic. It provides an original contribution too: a market. Without markets, the intercourse between producers and consumers would be severely curtailed, if not cut off altogether. Complexity requires a division of labor. Beyond production, there must be a mechanism for distribution. Ergo markets and the birth of Commerce.

"Think about it, kid. It's not so horrifying really. Where does all this fish come from? Ninety-nine percent of it is caught by commercial fishermen working off big steel-hulled trawlers, most owned by companies with share-holders, boards of directors, executives, the whole shtick. Even those privately owned are built and bought with loans from banks, banks tied into the system somehow, perhaps even listed on the New York Stock Exchange. That steel is created from iron ore smelted in blast furnaces in Pennsylvania or Ohio by Bethlehem or U.S. Steel. The nylon cordage in the nets is synthetically pro-duced in the textile industry; the engines built of parts manufactured in dozens of industries, not to mention the oil and gasoline they burn — Esso, Shell — each one of those boats a microcosm of corporate America. None of it could exist without the infusion of capital the Dow makes possible. It's the artery into which that vital transfusion is mainlined. Without it, the fisherman would still be paddling around in a bark canoe, using stone-tipped lances to spear his prey, and lucky just to get enough to feed himself and his family, without even considering supplying the needs of others." He paused.

"So you see, free enterprise even promotes communality and social responsi-bility, albeit in the service of self-interest. Supply and demand," he mused, "engaging in their eternal intercourse, practically invisible from the surface, a silent dialogue. You take your need, your wish, however frivolous or commend-able, plug it into the wall socket, and the system supplies it, like electricity swiftly, painlessly, no questions asked. This market, Fulton Street . . ." (he pouted and shrugged) "it's just a local one-twenty-volt outlet. But Dow, kid, Dow is the core of the nuclear reactor. Without that fission — which admittedly has destructive potentialities — things would grind to a halt, the collective life would cease. But how else did life arise anyway? Out of the ooze and slime, quickened by toxic sunlight. What else is the sun, the source of life itself, but a vast, ongoing nuclear holocaust burning in the depths of space, destined to swell and consume us? Wipe out the risk, the danger, and you return to the frigid silence of inanimate being — entropy, kid, the second law of thermodynamics. The Dow is the sun of our economic life, Sonny. Its inexhaustible radiant energy, toxic though it is or may be, irradiates the whole life of the nation, allowing such incredible richness and diversity to arise and flourish. That's what capitalism and the free-market system are all about. By subjecting everything to the discipline of the marketplace, which rewards and punishes, it expands the boundaries within which the consumer may exercise his basic right of free choice, his liberty in the material realm. In order to accomplish this, the system must take on the risk of overcomplexity. Realistically speaking though, there's no way to limit that except by taking measures which in the end deprive the consuming and producing populations of some measure of their freedom. That's the basic trade-off: freedom can't exist without complexity, and complexity by its very nature allows, must allow, the possibility of decadence.

"But what's the alternative? Socialism? But socialism allows in only so much sunlight, just enough to sustain life. Though it produces, at least in theory, a more standard, homogeneous crop, it blights the fecundity of nature. Nature, kid, that's the key. Taoists are big on nature, aren't they? So are Dowists. Capitalism is an attempt to let nature achieve her own homeostasis in the economic sphere.

"I know I'm rambling on, but all this ties back into the stock market, and your decision, Sonny. You ask me about the meaning of the Dow; maybe this is the more appropriate way of telling you. I know the prospect of investing terrifies you. You've been taught that attachment is the root of all evil. You say to yourself, I'm seeking liberation from the material world; isn't it then the height of insanity to seek that liberation by plunging into the material world itself? But that's the paradox. Remember what I said? Out of the ooze and slime of the life-mire the answer must emerge. And you've got to get it on your hands, kid. That's why your attempt to observe without participating has led you nowhere. What else is enlightenment anyway but a refinement of the kind of freedom I've been talking about? Liberation. Liberty. That's the secret, if there is a secret. Freedom can't exist without evil, or at least the possibility of evil. They spring from a single root. In seeking the ultimate enhancement of life in liberation, you've got to risk its ultimate negation in evil. You've got to risk the death of your soul. That's what the marketplace is all about. It's like a great battleground where good and evil are constantly acting out their ancient enmity through individuals — not man against man, but man against himself. Wall Street is the ultimate test of character. The real meaning of investment has nothing to do with money, but with one's self. Wall Street is the great floating crap game of the spirit, and to buy your chips you've got to put down a little piece of your heart."

I stood surveying the river, the play of sunlight on the rippling currents so brilliant it was almost painful. I hadn't followed Kahn's argument in all its turnings. But what I had picked up hinted at a desperate faith, and yet a great and noble one it seemed to me. What he'd said, which resounded most terribly, most finally, in that single phrase, his ultimatum: "To know the Dow, you've got to invest," recalled the master's words to me (so long ago): "Tao, too, is in the marketplace," and these things seemed like flowers growing wild over some deep grave of truth. On the other side was my uncle Hsiao's admonition, the oracles of conventional wisdom: "Tao and Dow — why this is the most shameless sophistry! They are at odds, eternally, like the great primal opposites. . . . Who seeks to conflate them, to resolve their implacable enmity, seeks to subvert the laws which underpin the universe itself!" Which of these was true? The time had come to issue now. I had to make my choice. Strange to say, the prospect filled me not so much with terror as sadness.

"What's the matter, kid?" Kahn asked, breaking in on my reverie. "You keep rubbing your eyes. You got something in them?"

"It's just the glare on the water," I said. "It's so bright out here it hurts my eyes."

"Don't look at it directly then," he advised. "Come on. Let's stop at the drugstore on the way back. I'll buy you a Coke."

I nodded, and we turned away from the river and began to walk.

•

The windows of our customary haunt on Pearl Street were tinted, the interior dim, cool, and murmurous with air-conditioning, which dripped its condensation in an accumulating puddle on the concrete sidewalk. The cool, artificial twilight soothed my eyes, and my spirit. We sat down at the counter, ordered fountain Cokes and slowly sipped them, saying nothing, turning now a little to the left, now a little to the right on our revolving stools, till finally the black ice blanched to its original color and the straws slurred in the bottoms of our cups. Then we rose and prepared to depart. At the cash register I reached into my pocket, but Kahn frowned, knitting his brows.

"Let me get it, kid," he said, putting his hand on mine in gentle prohibition.

I turned away while he dealt with the cashier. Behind the long half-wall of locked cases with their prescription medicines, visible from the shoulders up, the pharmacist in his white coat worked in his private, sterile domain. Three steps up from the floor, mounted as though on a dais, he seemed like a priest or an alchemist, a look of relaxed concentration on his features intimating profound contentment, rocking gently back and forth as he worked, his task a mystery, perhaps compounding a rare potion in his mortar. My eye ranged absently over the terrain of the display cases, lighting at last with quickened interest on something on the counter, virtually under my nose, something I had passed coming and going dozens of times, perhaps, and never noticed, invisible by virtue of its intense banality. It was the hexagonal revolving display rack of Ray-Ban sunglasses. I began to wheel it, catching a stuttered glimpse of myself in the series of cosmetic mirrors. Odd that I should have been so unconscious, but it was not until I saw the actual pair of glasses that I made the association — a pair of aviator glasses with black-green tear-shaped lenses. My pulse quickened perceptibly. With a furtive impulse, as though indulging in some delicious wickedness, I reached out and took them, unfolded the gold arms of tensile wire, raised them, put them on, curled the loops of wire around my ears, and looked into the mirrors of the still-revolving rack. As in a staggered filmstrip, I saw the strange smile spreading incrementally across my lips, a smile which I was at a loss myself to decipher.

"Come on, kid," Kahn said, interrupting my ceremony. In the mirror I saw him counting his change as he turned away from the cashier. Then he caught a glimpse of me in the mirror and started. Our eyes engaged, though he could not see mine through the green opacity of the lenses.

"Jesus!" he said.

I faced him. "What is it?"

He continued staring, then slowly shook his head as though emerging from a mild trance. "Nothing, kid, I just realized something. All this time I've been saying you remind me of somebody? I finally figured who it was."

My stomach fluttered with excitement. "Who?"

"You wouldn't know him," he deprecated, "a guy named Love."

"Eddie Love?" I repeated in a shrill, quavering voice.

"Yeah, ever heard of him? He was a bit before your time, I guess. In those glasses though, I swear you're a dead ringer for him."

My knees went limp and I clutched his arm, thrusting my face up close to his, trying to speak.

"Jesus, kid! What's the matter with you? Let go of me," he said, trying to wriggle his way free.

"Kahn," I said in a rapt whisper, "Love is my father."

"Your father!" Kahn dropped his spare change. It bounced and pinged across the floor, scattering in all directions. He looked down at it, then back at me. "Have you lost your mind?"

"That's what I was trying to tell you before," I continued.

"Tell me when?"

"The other morning, before you sent me to New Haven."

Kahn appeared dazed by this information.

"Do you know him?" I asked eagerly.

"What?" he replied remotely, with a blank expression.

"*Do you know him?*"

"Know him!" He regarded me stupidly. "I knew him — at least knew who he was. Sure. Who didn't?"

"What do you mean 'knew'?" I asked.

"Kid," he said, with an expression of anxiety, laying his hand lightly on my wrist, "let's sit down a minute."

"What is it, Kahn?" I implored as he thrust me into the booth.

"Just hold your horses, first things first." He slid in across from me. "Now to begin with, what makes you think Eddie Love is, was . . . Oh Jesus! . . . your father? How could he be? Love was American; you're Chinese."

"The AVG," I said. "He was in China for seven months."

"Hello! That's true," he whispered to himself, mildly astonished. "The Flying Tigers."

"That's where he met my mother. . . ." And starting from the beginning, I told him the whole story in a frantic, disjointed manner.

As he listened and the weave of detail and incident became denser, more impervious to doubt, his astonishment gradually increased and he grew paler and paler. In the end he looked almost sick.

"So that's it? That's all you know?" he asked me when I'd finished.

"All!" I protested. "What else is there?"

"What else? Everything! That's where the story begins, after he came home from China, at least what I know of it."

"What do you mean? What happened then?"

"Jesus! Let me see if I can reconstruct it for you. They came back in, let's see, late forty-two? Yeah, that's right. After the AVG disbanded and became the Twenty-third, the new commander, this guy named Bissell, refused the original pilots the thirty-day furlough they asked for, tried to strong-arm them into signing up for another tour of duty, beginning immediately, by threatening to have their draft cards waiting for them in their mailboxes when they returned stateside. Not exactly the most brilliant tactic to use in dealing with a group like that, war-tried veterans used to running on a long leash and enjoying an almost fatherly rapport with their commander, Chennault — who incidentally got screwed in the bargain. They resented the hell out of it, rightly, as far as I'm concerned. Most of them told him where he could stick his draft cards and refused induction into the Twenty-third. Anyway, they got a hero's welcome when they came home. Everybody knew who they were. They were the first ones who had really taken it to the Japs, showed that it could be done, that they weren't invincible. I think there was even a ticker-tape parade. I followed it pretty closely down at the news bureau of the OWI. There were a lot of parties and stuff. I remember Love's name cropping up in the social columns a few times. I didn't know who he was then, just a face in the crowd, you know? Then they all scattered and went their separate ways, pretty much dropped out of sight.

"When your father resurfaced, he was flying solo. He made quite a splash." Kahn paused. "That's an unfortunate metaphor, kid, I'm sorry. I saw it on one of the inside pages of the *New York Times,* a feature item. Apparently bored to tears at home, your old man tried to reenlist, but was refused for medical reasons, a back injury, I think. So what did he do? He bought himself a fucking P-40, a trainer they had sitting around, had it overhauled and fitted up, painted with the tiger jaws and everything, and began to tool around in it for kicks. You could see him any given day over the beach at Coney Island. It caused quite a sensation. There was a rash of newspaper articles and editorials decrying his frivolity, his irresponsible exercise of privilege, 'while our boys are out there fighting and dying for their country,' and so on. Of course, to do him justice, he had been there too, and been there first, but people have a way of glossing over the details. I think the consensus was that he was nuts, or just so eccentric as to make the distinction moot. That was pretty much my diagnosis too at the time. The notoriety — odium even, I might say — he gained might have been pretty disheartening to someone who had been through all your father had, annoying at least."

" 'Might' have been?" I interrupted.

"If he hadn't planned it, that is," Kahn said cryptically, "provoked it even."

"Provoked it?"

"Yeah, as a P.R. scam, a diversionary tactic. It's sort of a pet theory of mine. You know your father was an amateur magician, right? Well, I think Love might have been dangling the bauble of his eccentricity before their eyes with one hand while he picked their pockets with the other."

" 'Their' who?"

"The management of American Power and Light." He paused. "You know about the Loves and APL?"

I nodded.

"How the family had lost executive control of the corporation during his father's time?"

"Yes, yes, Arthur Love," I said impatiently. "I know about that."

"Well, no one — especially the board and officers of APL — thought Eddie Love had the slightest interest in business. They wrote him off as the eccentric millionaire playboy, cut from the same mold as Arthur Love, only with slightly different vices. Yet he'd inherited a sizable chunk of stock at his father's death, held temporarily in trust — in fact, the largest single block of outstanding shares. Well, at the same time that he was gadding about in his P-40 making himself Public Enemy Number One in all the women's clubs on Long Island, he was secretly buying more, adding to his trove through purchases made through numbered accounts at banks around the country. Very slick, very slick. He had a real penchant for surprise attack. Late in 1943 he showed up at the shareholders' meeting, apparently the first one he'd ever attended. Nobody even knew who he was.

"Well, they proceeded through the minutes and the various orders of business to the election of the Board of Directors for the coming year. Now you have to understand, since Art Love's time the Loves had always voted their block of shares as management directed. It was taken for granted. Well, Eddie Love had just turned thirty, the age specified in the trust for him to take control over his own affairs. Management was caught with their hands in their pockets, having assumed the 'Love block' would vote, as it always had, at their direction. Eddie Love had a different idea.

"You have to try and visualize the scene. This young guy in dark glasses stands up at the back of the auditorium and moves that he be allowed to propose several candidates of his own. Well, at first they chuckled at his naiveté, and when he persisted they harumphed and coughed in their hands, finally refused outright to entertain the motion. Then he *demands* that they entertain it, and they threaten to throw him out. And suddenly he pulls his *coup de maître:* produces the proxies, enough to control the vote. A furor ensued. You have to understand, takeovers were a relative rarity in those days. There wasn't the same kind of vigilance against them. These guys were caught totally unprepared, blind-sided. To make a long story short, Love appointed his own board. Among the new directors was one of his old buddies from the AVG, highly qualified, as you'll imagine, and, like Love, at loose ends after his return from China and ready to do something new, willing to give business a try. This was David Bateson, his old wing man in the element. At the directors' meeting immediately after, your father had himself officially rubber-stamped chief executive officer, and walked away, having in a single afternoon become chairman of the board and CEO of American Power and Light, the most powerful corporation in America! Not bad for a day's work, huh? Wall Street was stunned, divided about equally between outrage, delight, and slack-jawed amazement. Nothing like that had ever happened before, Sonny. The next week he was on the cover of *Time* magazine, 'Man of the Hour.' 'Hun in the Sun on Wall Street,' they called it. The article was written by this guy named Hackless, a self-appointed chronicler and apologist for the Loves.

"Your father didn't rest on his laurels either. After he got in he really shook things up. APL had diversified considerably since the old days when it was a simple utility, but Love pushed it even further. Under his direction, I guess you could say, American Power and Light became the first 'conglomerate,' though the actual term wasn't coined until much later. They were quite heavily involved in government munitions contracts at the time, but your father — in the middle of a war, right? — decided to push them into an entirely new field. Guess what?" He grinned.

"Kahn!"

"Pharmaceuticals. That's right. What audacity! And what's more, he pulled it off. Within a few months' time he'd practically cornered the market on a particular very important commodity, perhaps the biggest single slice in the whole pie: morphine. APL produced a bid on a government contract to supply the armed forces, not only the Americans, kid, but all the Allies. I don't want to be morbid, but do you have any idea of the size of the demand for anesthesia during a world war? Somehow he was able to produce the stuff at a higher quality and lower price than anyone else in the market. No one could touch him. No one knew how he did it. To tell the truth, no one really cared. I mean, you don't ask to read the fine print when you're bleeding and in pain, right?

Whether you're an individual *or* a country. That was what made him. From there it was nowhere but up. By the end of the war your father was one of the most powerful men on Wall Street, one of the wealthiest too. I remember hearing it said that his name would have appeared on a list of the ten richest men in the world, somewhere near the top.

"But at the same time, his behavior in his private life started growing more and more eccentric. People said he drank. There was a lot of gossip and second-guessing in the social columns. He was regarded as one of the prize catches anywhere. Apparently he went through a lot of women. Never married, though. But as for his eccentricity, the accounts aren't exaggerated. I can vouch for it myself, because I happened to get a personal taste of it — one, incidentally, I could just as well have done without.

"In the old days you used to be able to go up on the roof of the Exchange building, no hassle. Not too many people knew about it, but a few of the brokers would sometimes eat lunch up there when the weather was nice. It wasn't too long after I first came to Wall Street. I went up there with this friend of mine from the floor. We're sitting around with our bag lunches, right? We hear this strange noise, not very loud at first, like it's coming from far away, but getting louder every second. 'What's that?' I ask, wiping my mouth with a paper napkin. 'You hear something?' 'I don't hear anything,' he says. I look around, up, don't see anything, but this noise keeps getting louder and louder until it becomes positively deafening. Everybody's starting to freak. All of a sudden this huge winged shadow sweeps across the roof, like a gigantic bird of prey, a pterodactyl or something, and out of the glare of the sun a plane appears, screaming down at us in a full-throttle power dive. We both throw our lunches in the air and hit the deck. I thought it was a stray kamikaze who hadn't heard the war was over, blown on some trade wind from Japan. At the last moment he does a high-speed pull-out and passes over us, so close the gravel scatters in the slipstream and we can feel the heat of the engine, smell the exhaust fumes. Looking up from under my arms, I see the tiger jaws and know instantly who it is. When he made a second pass, I saw him — wearing aviator glasses, just like those, kid — looking back at us over his shoulder, head thrown back, mouth open as though he's laughing his head off, having the time of his life.

"He buzzed us a couple more times, then seemed to tire of it and dipped off. We see this huge plane disappear beneath the roof line, right? We all get up and run to the edge and look down. Kid, your old man was flying straight down the ravine of Wall Street toward the river. I swear the fit was so close his wing tips almost brushed the buildings. As a matter of fact, at the very end he tilted slightly to get clearance. Down below in the street women were screaming and running for shelter, men were standing there shading their eyes, looking up. Somebody lets out a rebel yell, and a few of the more audacious start to clap and cheer. The janitor is running around frantically trying to remember where the anti-aircraft emplacements are, which had been removed by then anyway. So then he loops the loop and comes back, and this time he strafes us, not with bullets, but with little silken parachutes, all in different colors — plum, pink, emerald, indigo. Most of these airy little cargoes floated to the street. A few, however, got blown back up on the updraft. One landed near us on the roof. We fought to get hold of it. Guess what was attached? Bags of fortune cookies, kid. That's right. And all with the same message. 'Amor vincit omnia,' which is to say, 'Love conquers all.' " Kahn shook his head. "Talk about chutzpah! Maybe he was a little meshuga, but what balls! In the afternoon, purely out of tribute, I think, APL went up two and a half points.

"If he was crazy though, he left it at home: no evidence of it in the way he ran the corporation. Within five years your father had reached the top, gone over it. He shot the moon, kid. No one on Wall Street could stand shoulder to shoulder with him. There hadn't been a presence, a conscious mastery, like his on the Street since the days of the old robber barons. In fact, he was kind of an atavism of the type, Commodore Vanderbilt firing cannonades from the poop deck of his yacht, the *Corsair,* and flying the Jolly Roger. I remember this article Hackless wrote at the time comparing him to Alexander the Great: no more worlds to conquer.

"Well, I guess it must have been 1950 when the scandal broke. Apparently when the Communists pushed into western China and Tibet, consolidating their revolution, to their immense surprise in . . . I guess it would be Yunnan province. Isn't that where they still grow all the poppies? Yeah, that's right. I remember because that was where he crash-landed after that dogfight, the one where he was injured. At any rate, way out there in the sticks, in this remote, inaccessible region unpopulated except by a few primitive tribal peoples, they found what amounted to a little agro-industrial complex, a virtual 'autonomous district' dedicated to the intensive cultivation, harvest, and industrial refinement of the various products of the *Papaver somniferum,* affectionately known as the garden poppy. Hundreds of workers — farmers, laborers, chemists — producing their own food. Even had a little auditorium where they showed Western movies. Apparently the idea had come to Love while he was still over there. He even made a few tentative exploratory gestures, but never acted on it till after he came to power.

"I remember a cartoon that appeared on the editorial page of the *New York Times* around then: A patrol of Communist soldiers is wading through a poppy field. The leader, who looks sort of like a cross between Chiang Kai-shek and the Cowardly Lion, is yawning, unshouldering his rifle. 'Take five, men,' the caption said. 'I think I'll just lie down here a moment and catch forty winks.' In the distance are the spires of a fantastic city that bears a striking resemblance to Wall Street. Well, I think there had been some feeling among the upper echelons of the business establishment that something was not completely on the up-and-up. But no one had suspected anything like that. I mean, the magnitude of it! Paying no taxes (except in the form of huge bribes to the Kuomintang, who were in active complicity), using government land, with an inexhaustible supply of cheap labor, protected by a sophisticated paramilitary organization recruited from the Nationalist Army, but separately administered, and funded by American Power and Light, Love had set up what amounted to a virtual little nation-state, an industrial paradise geared to the production of morphine. Perhaps no one would have minded, except that when they began to break up the refineries it appeared that they were turning out not only high quality morphine but opium and heroin too. And in immense quantities. Apparently there were a few mysterious Sicilians on the premises as well. The leaders of the paramilitary had advance warning and escaped with a few soldiers over the border into the Shan states. The warlords who rule there today are what's left of the commanders of the original opium army.

"The scandal helped to bring down Chiang Kai-shek, though he swore to the end he knew nothing about it. Maybe he was telling the truth: the Kuomintang had become so corrupt by then that central control was more or less a joke. It also contributed to the freeze in relations between the U.S. and China during the fifties. Oh, kid, it was a big stink. I remember the day it broke over the wire. McCarthy wasted no time in having him subpoenaed before the House Committee on Un-American Activities, planning no doubt to carve him up the way he later tried to carve up Dean Acheson and General Marshall, as an 'executioner' of Chiang's regime. Love was criminally indicted too on half a dozen charges, few if any of which I think could have stood up in court, for he'd covered his tracks pretty well. I guess he simply wasn't willing to put it to the test.

"The media made it out to the Love estate in Sands Point about an hour before the FBI. Typical. The paparazzi were there in droves. I guess it must have been one of the first 'media events' on record. Your father was living there alone with his Chinese servant at the time. He met them very calmly, very civilly, sat them down in his little Chinese garden around the pool, among the sculptured rocks, the *pen-t'sai* trees, all of which, he explained, he'd had put in since his return from China. This was all on film, right? Though he was eminently composed, you could tell he was a little off his bean because he kept asking them about the fruit. 'It's just been picked,' he said, and he showed them the tree and explained what an unusual variety it was, and how he'd imported it himself from China. He seemed obsessed with it."

"Fruit?" I asked. "What kind of fruit?"

"I don't know, what difference does it make?" he replied, annoyed at the interruption. "Litchis, kumquats maybe — no, no, come to think of it, it was peaches. I remember now. For whatever it's worth. At any rate, he was wearing a silk Chinese robe over his normal clothes, and his dark glasses. After they'd all been served, he took out a statement and read it to the cameras, taking sole responsibility and exculpating the other directors of any knowledge of what had happened, explaining the whole business, about how it had come to him after his crash and everything. All on film, right? Suddenly, as though far away in the background, you hear this high, piercing wail: the sirens. Love lifts his head like an animal sniffing the wind and cocks his ear. Then quietly he excuses himself and walks unhurriedly across the lawn, his limp just visible, to where the plane is waiting, already idling. About this time the police had made the turn into the circle of the driveway, screeching and skidding and spewing gravel, and started driving wildly across the lawn, hanging out the windows with their pieces like the Keystone Kops, like the good old days with Al Capone. Love hops up on the wing, climbs in, pulls the canopy over him, and just as they screech to a stop, fishtailing and harrowing deep furrows in the grass, taxis off, turns around, and takes off right over their heads, so that they had to duck.

"Kid, he treated them to an aerial sequence that might have been choreographed to Mozart, a ballet full of loops and rolls and Immelmanns, all sorts of fancy stunt flying. In the film you see the FBI agents standing there looking up, shading their eyes, mouths agape, pistol hands hanging limply at their sides, like little kids at the circus. He did a snap roll, then a half-snap into inverted position. The engine stalled out from fuel starvation, and he floated silently over them, hanging by his harness, like a jack-in-the-box, looking up at them and down at the clouds. Popped the canopy too, so that the wind was rushing past his face, like a dog with his head hanging out the window of a car. Crazy, crazy — beautiful-crazy. One of the cameramen said it was one of the weirdest things he'd ever seen, Love hanging there looking at them upside down, eerie and ridiculous at once. It was so quiet, he said, you could hear the wind whistling in the open gun barrels and the thin, high peal of Love's exhilarated laughter. Then suddenly he did another half-snap into normal position, kicked over the engine, and turned into a dive, screaming down at them, opening fire. Later they found the shredded strings of red paper firecrackers scattered over the lawn — one of your father's famous practical jokes. Only this time it backfired, for as they scrambled for cover, the men on the ground returned fire, and they had semi-automatic weapons, some of them. A few rounds apparently hit home. At the last second Love pulled out, turned up almost brushing the tops of the trees, then did an Immelmann — half a loop and half a roll, simultaneously gaining altitude and changing direction — then went into a power climb and disappeared into the sun. In the final seconds of the film you can just make out the tiny streamers of black smoke trailing from the wings, like leash wires trying to hold him down to earth, almost at the point of snapping."

"So what happened?" I implored, sick with unbearable excitement. "Please, Kahn, don't torture me. He got away, didn't he?"

He studied me with sympathy, a portent in his eyes. "Yeah, kid, he got away," he said softly. "Last sighted by a motorcycle cop on the Verrazano-Narrows Bridge — said it was like a meteor in the noonday sky, the plane trailing twin tails of fire from the wings like flagella, spilling black oil on the roadbed as it passed, dripping down the uprights of the bridge. Bathers on the beach at Coney Island said they saw a white flash far out at sea, heard the boom and thought the Russians had dropped the bomb on New York City. The charred, mangled hulk of the fusilage washed ashore on a deserted stretch of beach way up Far Rockaway somewhere, but the currents swept bits and pieces of it as far north as Block Island and as far south as Cape May, New Jersey. People collected them all that summer, like relics, you know?"

"And Love?" I asked, beginning to weep.

Kahn shook his head. "I'm sorry, kid."

I broke down. The cashier stared at us.

"Apparently he bailed out before the plane exploded, because the next day the parachute washed ashore on Coney Island. They found it rippling and swelling on the tide near shore, like a huge jellyfish, or a magician's handkerchief. The greatest trick of all that it was empty, nobody — no body — in the harness. Apparently he took it off, tried to swim, and never made it. The Coast Guard and the local police mounted a massive search. But the plane had gone down almost ten miles out to sea." Kahn sighed. "They never recovered the body. The next day in the *Times* the headlines read: "Love Is Dead — MIA over Wall Street." Byline, Ernest Hackless.

"There was some speculation in the press for a while that the whole thing had been staged, as there had been years before about his father's abdication, that Love had pulled a sleight of hand to throw off his pursuers, made a getaway to Rio or Havana, back to China maybe, taken up a new identity, and started a new life. Others said he'd never left, speculated that he'd had plastic surgery and was still up there somewhere in Wall Street, invisibly pulling the strings of American Power and Light. But with his injury and everything, the chances he could have made it are exceedingly remote. I guess it just goes to show the kind of regard he was held in on the Street. A real myth developed around him, the way I guess they always do around those guys who climb so high so fast, almost beyond the ken of the rest of us, then vanish without trace. Like Whitman said, 'He is most wonderful in that last half-hidden smile or frown, and by the flash of the moment of parting the one that sees it shall be encouraged or terrified for many years.' I guess I'd fall in one of those two camps myself, kid, though I'm not sure exactly which." Kahn sniffed, and took a whiff of Dristan. "He was an Ahasuerus, kid, a Livermore — even if he was a businessman and not a trader. I mean it as the ultimate compliment. Perhaps it's not in the best of taste, but I always sort of admired the way he went out, too. Whatever else they might have said about your old man, he sure knew how to make an exit."

"Yes," I sobbed bitterly, "he was always good at that."

"The best. Ah, kid, give it up," he said as I continued weeping. "It was all so long ago."

"Not for me," I answered. "Not for me."

Acknowledging the justice of this, he sat in silent sympathy, waiting for my sorrow to exhaust itself. Then gently he urged me up. "Come on, kid. Let's go."

As he pushed open the door for me, the cashier called after us, "Hey! What about those glasses? You going to pay for them or not? They're not party favors, you know."

"Sorry," Kahn said to her. "Here, kid, let me put them back." Gently, he slipped them from my face and turned away.

As he did so a strange, vehement impulse seized me and I grabbed his arm. "Give them to me, Kahn," I said. Taking out my wallet as he stared, I counted out the bills one at a time on the glass countertop, refitted my new possession, then pushed open the door and strode ahead of him into the brilliant sunlight of the street. Looking up, I found that I could bear the direct light of the sun, and that its rays revealed a mysterious hint of green.

Chapter 16

All other considerations, even Kahn's ultimatum, went temporarily awash in the emotional upheaval attending the revelation of my father's death. That he was gone, irretrievably gone — my mind dutifully grappled with this fact, but my heart refused to accept it. If it were so, and there could be no doubt it was, the fact changed everything. Precisely how, though, I could not quite grasp, not quite decipher. The truth is, I was in no condition to draw conclusions about anything, only filled with a sense of vague fatality, as though this were the end. My entire initiative had miscarried, and with the failure of my search for my father came the failure of my other search for the meaning of the Dow, the delta, the Tao within the Dow. I continued to perform my duties at the Exchange, but listlessly, perfunctorily. Kahn's pity was not obtrusive, but it was always there, a light in his eyes that I could hardly bear, even through the filters of the black-green tear-shaped lenses.

I wanted to speak to Yin-mi, wanted her to soothe my pain and bitterness with the solemn, secret balm her presence dispensed. But I felt a strange compunction. In my despondency I sensed that everything had changed on that front too, that I had lost her, lost her through her revelation of her feelings for me. I could not forgive her that, the chase through the rain and our equivocal embrace. Twice I went to their apartment to speak with her, but each time turned away on the threshold without knocking.

Finally one day Kahn approached me. "Kid, you can't keep on like this forever. You've got to bear up and live. I've got a suggestion. I don't know if it'll help, but why don't you go up there and look around?"

"Go up where?" I asked.

"Sands Point, the old Love estate. I did some checking up, there's no one living out there now except a caretaker, the old Chinese guy who used to work for Love. Maybe he'd be willing to open up the house and let you nose around. It might do you good, set your mind at rest."

I don't know why precisely, but his idea appealed to me, appealed to me more than anything had in days. I decided to follow up on it.

•

When the train pulled into the station at Port Washington, I found a De Luxe taxi idling at the curb, a sleek black glossy bomber from another era. My driver, a young, but not so young, Italian with a drooping eyelid and a stare that modulated between the frank and the vacuous, was leaning against the hood of the car with his legs crossed and his hands in his pockets.

"Where to?" he asked.

"Do you know the Love estate in Sands Point?"

"That old heap out on Lighthouse Road? Sure. Hop in."

As we pulled away, I noticed him eyeing me in the rearview mirror. "What you wanna go out there for?" he asked, showing a familiarity unthinkable in a Manhattan cabbie, and, from my point of view, not particularly desirable. "You a friend of Bozo's?"

"Bozo?"

"Yeah, Bozo, Bo, the old Chinaman who lives out there in the cottage. I don't know if that's his real name, but that's what we used to call him."

"That must be the caretaker," I mused aloud. "No, I don't know him."

"I'd watch out for him, if I was you. He's a little touched in the head, if you know what I mean. Not to put too fine a point upon it, a fucking lunatic. I don't think he speaks much English either."

"You know him then?" I asked.

He chortled. "In a manner of speaking. When I was in high school sometimes we'd go out there on Friday nights and roll the place."

"Roll?"

"Yeah, you know, throw rolls of toilet paper in the trees, explode M-8os in the pool, sling a few eggs and water balloons at the front door — that kind of stuff, nothing really harmful. But the old guy had no sense of humor. He really let it get to him, like the house was his or something. He started fighting back, setting booby traps and shit. Dug this pit, right? Like he was gonna trap a tiger or something. Covered it over with leaves and grass, Benny Fanoli spent the night at the bottom of it with a broken ankle. After that it became a fucking war zone. Nowadays though they don't hassle him too much. I kind of feel sorry for the old guy now. You say you're a friend of his?"

"No," I reiterated. "I don't know him."

"What you going out there for then?" he asked. "You ain't thinking of buying the place, are you?"

"Is it for sale?"

"Yeah, has been for years. But take my word for it, it's a real dump. Even back then the place was coming apart at the seams. I guess it must have been real nice in its day, but they've let it go all to hell now. Besides, it's got to be expensive. Millions probably. Just the land. Right there on the Sound next to all them other places. You got that kind of money?"

I laughed.

"Yeah, me neither — worth seeing though. . . . Well, here we are. This is the driveway. I'd take you up, but as you see . . ." The road was crossed by a chain from which a sign depended: No Trespassing.

"That's all right, I'll walk."

"Okay," he said. "See you round. Give my regards to Bozo."

He scratched off and left me beside the road. The driveway, covered sparsely with gravel and deeply rutted, disappeared into what looked like a deep wood. Stepping over the chain, I started down, catching glimpses as I went of several other dwellings beyond through the thick foliage. It was dark and cool and very humid there among the trees. Very silent too, except for the twittering of birds, and an occasional stray puff of wind which sighed through the branches overhead. The pocked, irregular pathway resembled a dry river bed much more than a road, and as I proceeded it was much easier to believe that I was trekking into the wilderness than toward a great house. I had walked a ways when I became aware of the low, distant heaving of the surf, like a whisper replying to the trees, and, keening above it like a mournful church bell summoning its congregation to some obsequy, the tolling of a buoy outside on the bar, rocking on the swell.

Around a bend, the woods gave way precipitately onto the grounds. I entered a long circular drive, still deep in gravel and crushed shell which looked like it was freshly raked. There was an island in the center canopied by a single magnificent oak, a hundred feet high at least, thickly clustered with leaves and boughs, and casting its shadow over what must have been an entire acre. Below it, the lawn sloped in a spacious trough down to the water, where a stone wall had been erected demarcating the margin of the beach. Beyond spread the petroleum-colored waters of Long Island Sound, glassy with a vacuous serenity. Across the water in the farthest distance the prospect of a wooded headland reposed in blue, uncertain air. To my right, the trough rose slightly into a stand of pines and firs, but on the left the ascent was steep up to the house, perched above terraced beds of flowers on a high bluff overlooking the water and the rocks.

I had expected a monumental, imposing edifice, but was pleasantly surprised. The house possessed instead a quaint, old-fashioned elegance. Dating from early colonial times, it had the eccentric but not displeasing lines one associates with dwellings from that era, an air of vagary, even whimsy, as though it had been rethought and added to many times by many different owners not totally harmonious in taste, but had survived their caprices to contrive a language and a logic all its own. Perhaps its coherence was accounted for as much as anything by the roof, massive and beautiful, with its imbricated layers of heavy, turquoise-tinted slates, broken here and there by the asymmetrical outcroppings of the dormers. For some reason — maybe it was that darker, vivid blue against the sky — it suggested a fairy castle to my imagination.

The house itself was in a state of advanced disrepair: several shutters fallen, windows broken (some which remained of wavy, hand-blown glass), the white paint faded to a grayish-blue suggestive of Scottie's tennis shoes and peeling off in flakes. Yet its original effect was not entirely lost; rather it was like a beautiful woman who has let herself go in her old age. The salmon geraniums in the planters along the slate walk to the door were glorious, like summer torches lighting the way to an ambiguous repast. The house was like a hazy area of memory in the rich, vivid present of the lawn, something diseased, necrosing, but somehow precious, like a slice of wedding cake wrapped in its napkin and packed away in a dark box in an attic to molder and collapse.

As I approached, no one was in sight, but I could hear a rhythmical clacking, a garden implement, maybe, a spade or hoe, struck in loose soil with comfortable, repetitive effort. A voice was singing in Chinese — a man's voice, clear and poignant, a little ragged around the edges of the highest notes, but wonderfully expressive. It appeared to be coming from around the far side of the house. Following the music, I entered a portal in a high, clipped hedge of English boxwood, immediately debouching in the middle of a long, narrow lawn behind the house. This was raised some four feet above the level of the ground floor and connected to a canvas-canopied terrace (whose awning had candy cane stripes) by a flight of five slate steps. To my right at a distance of fifty yards, this lawn terminated, segueing into an empty swimming pool without a diving board, chaise longues with cushions removed. Beyond, through a thinned stand of trees along the bluff, one caught glimpses of the Sound. To my left, away from the house, the arms of the hedge tapered toward one another in an oval, never touching, veering parallel at the last moment into a narrow corridor connecting with an area of verdant gloom. In the cradle of this oval stood a white marble statue: Venus Anodyemene standing in the shallow salver of a corrugated scallop shell, swaddled from the waist down, bare-breasted, performing her toilet without hands, her eyes blank but nonetheless conveying a wistfulness tinged with ferocity. She recalled the Statue of Liberty, inviting and prohibiting at once.

As I studied this layout, the singing, which had temporarily stopped, commenced again. I looked back toward the pool. On a higher terrace was a vegetable garden, lush and tall with corn and tomatoes, waist-high bushes of snow peas, melons, cantaloupes. It was from there that the singing came. A man who had been kneeling stood up and began to hoe again, his face invisible beneath the circle of a pointed, woven hat. He was tall and lean, stoop shouldered but very graceful in his motions, almost elegant. I proceeded toward him down the lawn, climbed the steps, and stood watching him in silence through the corn, puzzling over an unaccountable sensation of prior acquaintance. Sensing an intruder, he broke off and looked up, leaving the hoe resting in the furrow. An expression of reflexive hostility passed across his features. Then narrowing his eyes to take a closer look at me, he started and gasped as though in distress. Wincing, apparently in pain, he clutched at his heart and began to stagger backward, heedless of the plants he trampled, keel-ing over finally with a thin cry in a row of cabbages, clutching at the sky.

Astonished and dismayed, I raced up and knelt beside him. He appeared to be unconscious, his face livid, his eyes turned up in his head, the lids twitching as though in REM sleep. A thin line of drivel frothed between his lips. Afraid he'd had a heart attack or sunstroke, I loosened his collar, then put his head in my lap and began to fan his face. In spite of my immediate anxiety about his well-being, I could not suppress a fascination with his looks. His delicate, high-boned beauty, the scars on his face, which only enhanced that beauty like . . . like . . . What was it? A phrase teased at recollection. Suddenly I caught it: "like the chance scars time inflicts in antique ivory." That was it. I froze. My God — could it be? Bozo, Bo . . . Po. *Chiang* Po? Hadn't Hsiao said he'd run away after my mother's death? Where else would he have gone, loving my father as he had? Yes, it was he! It had to be! My heart beat wildly as this living fragment from the past — which had so recently seemed irrecoverable — floated up from the well of oblivion, lying even now in my lap, his face between my hands. For several minutes I sat in that position, until gradually his color began to return. His eyelids fluttered.

"Chiang Po," I whispered, anxious to see if his response would corroborate my guess.

He opened his eyes. His pupils were tremendously dilated, even in the brilliant sunlight. His gaze rested on something beyond me, as though I were transparent. There was an odd smile on his lips. His look, in sum, simulated ecstasy, but I attributed it more conservatively to physiological distress.

"I wasn't sure if you were going to open your eyes or not," I said, with the mild, joking reproof one allows oneself with invalids.

He continued staring. Then his eyes came into focus on my face. "I was afraid to," he replied, "afraid to find that it was all a dream and you had gone."

I smiled at him in puzzlement, not wanting to challenge whatever notion he'd contrived for fear of upsetting him.

As we stared into one another's eyes — or I into his, for I was wearing the dark glasses — the light in his face brightened into a kind of bliss, almost like an animal's as it studies its human keeper, full of loyalty and gratitude. His eyes suffused with tears. He reached for my hand, clutched it, pressed it to his lips. "Master . . ." he said.

I recoiled involuntarily, as though walking barefoot in a pleasant garden I had stepped on a grotesque, crawling creature. The nature of his error was only too poignantly apparent to me after my experience with Kahn. He mistook me for my father! But even given the resemblance — at such removes of time? Instantly the cabbie's diagnosis, which I'd considered hyperbolic, flashed through my mind, and I wondered if indeed Chiang Po weren't mad.

Fortunately he didn't register my reaction. Sighing deeply, he closed his eyes. His grasp went limp. "You've come back," he said. There was fulfillment in his tone, but below it, abyss upon abyss of pain.

"You mistake me," I said gently, making an effort to control my revulsion.

"I'm not the man you take me for."

His response was a blissful reproach, almost indulgent. "Aren't you?" he replied. "Have I waited so long not to know you now?"

In the soft glow of his certainty, the sweet condescension implicit in that smile, I felt my moorings almost go awash. I had forcibly to resist my impulse to flow into his dilated pupils, into his madness.

"They told me you were dead," he continued. "But I always knew that you'd come back, as you came back to us in China after the crash when we'd all given you up for dead." He stirred and tried to rise.

"Lie still," I said. "You're not well enough to move."

"No," he said, struggling to free himself. "It isn't seemly." He sat up. "You must come and see the house. Nothing has changed. All is as you left it."

"Po!" I protested helplessly.

"Come," he urged with a smile of glassy remembrance. "We'll go through the garden. You'll see. Everything's the same."

There was something about the way he smiled off in the distance and the mechanical gesture with which he invited me to follow him that gave me the impression that I'd stepped into a daydream, that he was the master of ceremonies leading me on a fantasy tour which he'd rehearsed many times before, but never had the opportunity to perform in life. I rose and followed him down the steps and across the lawn, past the Venus, through the corridor in the hedge. It opened into a landscape where the impression of unreality deepened. I had visited it many times before in imagination. It was the garden of my mother's childhood house.

Everything was there as Hsiao had described it: the dark pool with its dispersed flotillas of lotus and water-hyacinth, its unbroken areas of bright-dark surface mirroring the willows and the sky, all spanned by the wooden humpbacked bridge, intricately carved and painted. Our shoes crunched on a walk of pebbles and crushed shell as we stepped toward its margin, past weird rocks, clumps of moss, phantasmagoric topiaries of nameless beasts, through a stand of twisted, dwarfish fruit trees, one a little larger than the rest, separated off at a distance.

As we passed this larger tree, Po turned to me. "Do you remember this?" His face wore a glow of confidential sentiment, utterly obscure to me.

I gazed at him, at it. In truth, it bore a distinct resemblance to the peach tree in the courtyard of Ken Kuan, though a mere shoot, a bud, compared to that venerable elder, yet scarred and twisted too in its own right, as though old (more like the tree depicted in my mother's robe). Beneath it rested a stone bench.

"It has grown considerably, no doubt, since you last saw it, yet stunted still, still a dwarf. As we suspected, the line does not prosper in this climate, which is too extreme and changeable. Each winter I must wrap it from the ground up to protect the roots from frost and the winds that blow in off the water. Even with such effort, the harvest it produces in the spring is at best equivocal

— half a dozen pieces of sound fruit each year. Yet I have duly planted the stones and tended them with care, as you wished, and so now at last we begin to have an orchard of a kind, not robust of course, but with a beauty all its own. Rather like hers, I think."

"Like whose?"

He gave me an odd look. "Ch'iu-yeh's, of course. . . . Come," he said with a sad smile, inviting me to precede him on the bridge.

My footsteps echoed hollow on the planks, so that I consciously softened them as though in church. As I descended on the other side, I ceased to hear Chiang Po behind me. Turning, I saw he'd paused on the summit. Placing both hands on the rail, he'd begun to stare at himself in the water, his expression dreamy, distracted, a little wistful.

"What is it, Po?" I asked, coming up beside him, looking down at our reflections.

Staring into the mirror of the pool, he raised his hands and gently touched the bones of his face, stretching smooth the fine wrinkles at the corners of his eyes. He faced me, and I saw his eyes were brimming. "I have grown old," he said. "But you . . ." He reached out and brushed my cheeks with the tips of his fingers as though to confirm his own surmise, perhaps simply to assure himself of my reality. "You haven't aged at all." There was no resentment in his tone as he said this; rather he beamed at me as though in pride. "But how could you grow old?" He paused, then in a tone of tremulous gravity asked, "You've found the secret, haven't you?"

"The secret?"

"What you always dreamed of," he replied, "though you never spoke of it except to laugh. Eternal life."

The unintended irony of this remark almost made me sob.

"Chiang Po . . ." I appealed.

But he was already making his way down the bridge, supporting himself on the rail, shaking his head. "How strange it all is," he sighed, as though with an immense fatigue.

Departing from the garden, we rounded the house on the side of my original approach and made our way to the front door. From the rear pocket of his pants, Chiang Po took out a set of keys and fumbled with them while I waited on the stoop. Above the door on either side were two candle-lamps encased in glass and brass, folded like starched dinner napkins into little freestanding houses. The glass was cloudy with salt spray from the Sound, and the brass was turning green. Perched on one of the panes as though asleep was a large brown moth with black spots on its wings. I reached up to brush it off, and it turned to dust beneath my fingers.

The door creaked on the hinge. A breath of stale, musty air exhaled from the interior, a smell a little like wet wool in its unsavoriness, only dry, intensely dry, with the medicinal dryness of the taxidermist's shop, a smell like the sherried breath of old women, giving hints of moth balls and perfumes, teas, digestive biscuits, sachets, crocheted blankets, a smell unpleasant not with age but with disuse and idle preservation.

We entered a long hall proceeding along the breadth of the house, a staircase rising on the left into the second story. Through narrow glass panels on either side of the door at the far end, I made out the terrace, the lawn, the vegetable garden. The ceilings were low and crossed with beams, many of them splitting, warped, or otherwise irregular, showing the vagaries of the carpenter's adz as well as the spontaneous deformations of time. The door swung back against a brass umbrella stand filled with curiously carved walking sticks and parasols whose fabric had moldered on the baleen ribs. This contained an ornamental sword as well, in an extremely old, corroded scabbard. There was an amber tint to everything, like the sheen on polished hardwood floors after the wax has dulled, the stain of time. The floor was covered with fine old Chinese carpets in a tint of oxblood, threadbare in places, but more precious for their hint of transitoriness and frailty. The only significant piece of furniture was a large couch against the right-hand wall, a Victorian "fainting bench" with scroll arms, highly stylized and forbidding, covered in faded bloodred satin. Above it, frescoed in the wall, was an Oriental scene: a large weeping cherry in the foreground dropping a few petals, languidly framing a pavilion in the distance on the margin of a lake, mountains in the background — a scene not unlike the garden outside, only apparently of prior execution. I wondered if someone in the family before Eddie Love had had a taste for chinoiserie, and immediately thought of Arthur Love. This suspicion was strengthened as we wandered by a disproportionate number of Chinese curios and antiquities, mostly porcelains, lamps and vases in famille rose and noire, but also a beautiful selection of blue and white K'ang Hsi bowls and jars which floated luminously in the darkness of an old corner cupboard.

As we proceeded down this hall, I could see through double doors on the left-hand side a dining room with an imperfectly turbaned crystal chandelier, lusters dangling like a drunken diva with her jewels in disarray, and a similarly draped sideboard and table, the latter the size of a small arc. Having almost reached the further door, we took a sudden right and entered a large, similarly low-ceilinged room with a marble fireplace and a grand piano, a great deal of covered furniture, and a row of dark portraits on the walls. These I ached to see, but Po was intent on taking me to the next room. This proved to be a library — and quite a library! Elliptical in shape, it was at least a hundred feet long, perhaps a hundred and twenty, occupying practically the whole wing of the house, the ceiling extraordinarily high, coffered and embossed with parget medallions (evidently it dated from a later time). The walls were lined with books bound in leather, their titles stamped in gold on the spines. Unlike the rest of the house, here the smell of leather was heady and delicious, like the bouquet of fine old Bordeaux. There was a gaming table covered in green leather, a dim, tremendous globe, an abundance of soft couches and chairs arranged deliberately without focus to conduce to privacy, two portable staircases on either side for retrieving volumes from the upper shelves, a bar, a phonograph (a deep-chested console model, the Dumont Balladier). Po opened a door at the end, and the hissing of the surf blew in to us together with a heady whiff of brine, giving the air an intoxicating richness.

Chiang Po stood aside observing me with obvious relish as I explored. After a while, having sated my curiosity, ready to see more, I turned to him.

"So," he said, smiling, "are you ready now?"

"Ready for what?" I asked.

"To go there."

I regarded him in silence, making an effort not to betray my ignorance in hopes he would elaborate.

"Come," he said.

We returned the way we'd come, mounting the stairs in the entry hall to the second floor. At the top we turned left past several closed doors, bedrooms presumably, into a warren of dressing rooms and closets faced with full-length beveled mirrors, giving the place a resemblance to the Hall of Mirrors in a funhouse.

"Wait here," Po said. "I'll go and turn the lights on."

I watched him disappear around a corner, then cautiously followed him into the wilderness of mirrors. As I entered at one end, I simultaneously observed myself exiting at the other, my image flashing out ahead of me in infinite reduplication. Though in a sense I arrived as soon as I set out, this simultaneity produced an effect of temporal retardation, not of speed, for as I walked I seemed to move without progressing, as on a treadmill, running a gauntlet of myself (or selves). Searching for Po at a turning, I stupidly bumped into the cool, unyielding surface of a sheet of silvered glass, and rebounding, set off confidently in another direction only to rebound again. Warier, I paused and turned in a slow circle trying to ascertain the way, and as I did, found myself surrounded by a startling ring of my own images which seemed to taunt me vaguely with my own perplexity and defy my breaking through. Setting out a third time, I bumped myself again, reacting in a fit of rage, which was directed back to me with the perfect symmetry of Karma. Angrily shaking the closet door, I slid it back, creating a dark warp in the illusion. Inside I discovered a black tuxedo and a starched, ruffled shirt. Above them on a shelf was a black beaver top hat. Suddenly the lights came on, and turning I found Po behind me.

"It is still there," he said, as though in vindication. "As I told you, nothing has been touched."

The corridor terminated finally in another staircase, narrow, steep, and winding, which came out on a small landing before a single locked door, unremarkable except for the knob of faceted prismatic glass, like the one at Mme Chin's. Chiang Po rattled through his keys, picking out a skeleton which he inserted in the lock. As the door opened, an unexpected burst of sunlight dazzled us, exploding from within as though compressed; a rush of fresh, sea-scented air swept past, lifting up my hair, the *whoosh* it made like the sound of air escaping from an opened can of tennis balls, or an Egyptian tomb. Gaping around me in astonishment, I entered the most wonderful room I'd ever seen. The walls, which formed the sides of an isosceles triangle, sloping upward to the ridgepole, were covered with dark-green paper mackled with thousands of white flecks, irregularly scattered like paint whisked from a large brush, like snowflakes swirling in the aura of a street lamp or, even more, the spray of stars along the Milky Way seen from earth in a deep-emerald midnight sky. This indeed is what they represented, the ceiling a transcription from a star chart, a zodiac writ large on a green ground. My eye wandered through the wilderness of stars, picking out the constellations Scottie had catechized me with: Orion, Canis Major, Taurus ("that effing bull!"), Ursa Major, the Great Bear chained to the pole — all were there! I can hardly describe the effect of looking up into the nighttime sky, even as broad daylight streamed in through the dormers. Though disorienting, there was something magical about it, uncanny and exhilarating. In a simultaneity like that within the Hall of Mirrors, day and night seemed to have battled to a standstill in that tint of green, and time had ceased. The larger flow of time seemed abrogated too. The years had not entered in that place. A sense of brilliancy and freshness hung palpably over the room like a spell. How different from the dim, funereal complexion of the other rooms! As if in evidence of my conceit, the large grandfather clock beside the mantle at the far end of the room had stopped, both hands unanimous in their intention, raising twelve o'clock high, like straight-backed heliotropes or arrows shooting for the sun, which was painted on the revolving panel in the face, having paused forever at the zenith of the sky. A vase of pale yellow chrysanthemums rested on a doily on a table. Though I might have guessed who put them there, it was as if in that rare, salutory atmosphere they had been there since the day my father disappeared, and suffered nothing, never wilted, never spoiled. My gaze wandered to the dormer, through which I saw away across the lawn in the far distance, rising from a cloud of verdure, the white needle of a church spire gleaming in the sunlight. I felt a rush of happiness, an ecstasy and lightness, as though intoxicated by the lingering savor of the bouquet of some heady wine which had been uncorked there and decanted, the liquor of eternal life. Yes, in that ambience of youth and immortality and joy I might have almost believed my father had indeed distilled and drunk it, and not died, but been translated, apotheosized — one of those constellations glittering so brilliantly above me now in that emerald sky.

For I had a more vivid consciousness of his presence than ever before. It was his room, and he had stamped it with the unmistakable mark of his identity. I was astonished at the things I saw. My father had lived through all his stages there, preserving the most precious artifacts of each and arranging them in a haphazard archipelago, its islands stepping-stones in time from youth to age. The room was like a combination of a men's club and a nursery.

Here in a corner were the trappings of his magic career: the trick decks and coins with both faces alike; the skein of knotted, parti-colored handkerchiefs; the black beaver top hat with the pearl-colored silk interior and false bottom; a trunk festooned with chains and locks, his magic ropes and swords — all the standard tackle. But there was something I'd never seen before as well: a large, black, glossy box, not unlike a coffin, only deeper and not quite so long, out of which protruded at one end, from the neck up, a faceless mannequin in a black wig, and at the other, ankles and a pair of shoes, red-sequined slippers with blunt heels and buckles of bright-colored glass that almost looked like rubies. In the middle a large-toothed ripsaw balanced unsupported in a groove of its own making, pausing momentarily in its dastardly design of "sawing the lady in half." Not far away was a large puppet theater, nearly as tall as I was, with dark-green velvet curtains which had been left open, allowing a peek behind the scenes where Punch and Judy, abandoned by the puppeteer, had fallen asleep in one another's arms, foreheads touching, propping one another up in an exhausted, angular embrace. Along the ridgepole of the roof where the two walls intersected, running the length of the whole room, was a Chinese dragon kite with a ferocious painted paper face and a body sewn from different colored strips of silk. This creature was suspended from wires of varying lengths so that he seemed to undulate and ripple as he sailed, an effect enhanced by the breeze ushering from some as yet undiscovered source. Flying escort through the cosmos, or perhaps attacking, were a dozen model planes of every vintage — Sopwith Camel biplanes, Fokkers, Spads — not of plastic either, but carved balsa with stretched fabric wings and painted with painstaking skill and delicacy. There was a dirigible as well, and a hot-air balloon. There was a shelf of books sporting biographies of Eddie Rickenbacker and Baron von Richthofen; *Night Flight* by Saint-Exupéry and, separated by a parked Sopwith Camel, *The Little Prince* by the same author, next to Machiavelli's *Prince*. There was another book called *The Greatest Escape: Houdini's Return from Death,* as well as *Confessions of an English Opium Eater* by de Quincey, *The Poems of Samuel Taylor Coleridge;* and finally, on a coffee table, in the place of honor as it were, and closest to hand, a well-thumbed, dog-eared copy of *The Wizard of Oz* by L. Frank Baum. Opening it casually to the introduction, I found this sentence: "It aspires to being a modernized fairy tale, in which the wonderment and joy are retained and the heart-aches and nightmares are left out." It might have been the inspiration of the room itself!

I wandered past armies of painted lead toy soldiers drawn up on the field of battle, knights-in-armor on prancing coursers in hood and full caparison deploying blithely in the ranks of Napoleon's grenadiers. I passed a papier-mâché volcano contrived for a school project; on its charred slopes, perched at a precarious angle, a plastic brontosaurus searched for nonexistent fodder, looking up just in time to see Tyrannosaurus Rex, his smile developed at his arms' expense, charging upward from the savanna to devour him. In the shadow of a palm tree, a triceratops observed the spectacle, idly munching on a wad of green shredded paper, apparently a lettuce. There were Erector sets and chemical retorts, alembics, test tubes, an electric Jacob's ladder — all the necessary paraphernalia for a budding young mad scientist.

It was oddly chilling, among these things, suddenly to come upon the hunting bow — a curved and recurved stave of polished wood with carved, elaborate grip, and a sheath of barbed, vicious-looking arrows — hanging on the wall beneath the buck's head, a six pointer, raised at the alert, nostrils dilated, a spark of light reflected in the black glass eyes. As I neared the end of the room, I saw his uniform with the AVG insignia, a Flying Tiger in a top hat leaping from the sun, hanging on a wooden clotheshorse, freshly pressed and brushed as though ready for use, his black G.I. shoes polished beside it on the floor. Nearby on a table, in a Dutch Masters cigar box, cushioned on a folded Chinese flag, was a velvet case in which I found his medal and, rattling loose beside it, something which I decided at last could only be the blunted seven-millimeter slug which he, or someone else, had carved out of the leather seat of his P-40, after it had passed through his whole body, hitting nothing but the spinous process, "that delicate wishbone in his spine." Beside it, to my chagrin, but not really my amazement anymore, was an opium pipe with a chased silver bowl. And with these other trophies, a lock of black hair tied with a thread of bloodred silk, which wrenched my heart. Sitting on the dresser, staring at me in cruel mockery out of his cute button eyes, was the stuffed toy panda. Beside it were two photographs of Love — one of which I knew. It was the original picture: Love beside the plane in the dark glasses, khakis, robe, and two-toned shoes. Only something was missing: my mother. A pair of scissors had neatly snipped her out, banishing her thus easily from his life. But the trick had not quite been successful. Reaching from beyond the border of the photograph, her white, ghostly hand clutched him tightly above the elbow as though refusing to let go, reaching back in vengeance from the other world. The effect was haunting. The second shot showed Love as a little boy, standing beside the pool in a sailor's suit, holding above his shoulder a biplane poised for flight, his head tilted to the side as he looks into the camera, squinting in the sunlight, shading his eyes with his hand. The photograph was poignant and unsettling. The pose of happiness looked faked, as though his arm were tired and some prompter standing behind the photographer were encouraging and hectoring him to maintain his attitude of play.

That was it. There was nothing after China, almost as though his life had stopped. My original mood of euphoria dispersed. There was something here that hurt and finally eluded me, that same bewitching quality of heartlessness that Hsiao had described in his laugh, not cruelty, not unkindness, but heartlessness. Indeed I seemed to hear it all around me now, that laughter, ringing in my ears. The room reminded me in a curious way of Ken Kuan, remote, monastic, though exactly what gave that impression I'd be hard-pressed to say. Certainly there was no flavor of asceticism, for it was rather like a pleasure palace of material delight. But it was as though life had not entered here, banished wholesale by the same spell that excluded time. As I surveyed the items in the room, the child's together with the man's, it occurred to me that the child had remained alive within the man, not crushed beneath the weight of years. That pristine being had been magically preserved within his heart, like a fetus in a bottle, not dead, but using its prenatal gills to breathe the difficult formaldehyde. But at what cost? I examined the second photograph again, and it struck me that he'd been frozen in that attitude for life. I felt a surge of pity for my father. Perhaps so easily the mystery resolved itself: a case of arrested development. Banality. And yet he had been brave and had inspired devotion. He had tasted the world's eminence, he had known sadness, he had sinned. For all these reasons, and because of the old thing in my heart, I could not dismiss him as a child who had never grown up, a wunderkind who had refused the burden of maturity, any more than I could dismiss him on Hsiao's allegations. What was the truth? Was it possible that all the while behind the screen of the dark glasses his eyes were focused inward like a monk's, peering unafraid into the sunlight of a secret revelation, his eyes dazzled by the unbearable radiance of the fission in his heart? Or was it cold and empty there forever in the core, and was he like an invalid, with eyes too weak to bear the common light? Did the glasses signify an impulse toward greater license, greater freedom, or a feeble attempt at self-defense? Was he keeping something in, or out? And could I ever know? There was a great silence at the center of his life which I doubted I should ever break or make resound. Love had eluded his accounting, both with me and with the world. His ambiguity was final. That stroke proved his genius if nothing else had. Perhaps the only thing for it was to give him up as Hsiao had done, admit defeat and return where I had come from. And yet I couldn't. For, not knowing him, I knew that I should never know myself.

As this depressing thought occurred to me, a tap came at the door. Chiang Po entered with a deferential bow and then approached me. He stood in silence studying my face, and then his eyes grew sad.

"The mood has come upon you?" he asked, less as a question than a confirmed suspicion. Sighing deeply, he took me by the elbow like an invalid and led me unresisting to the bed. Turning out the pillows, he fluffed them and propped them against the headboard, then gently guided me up, lifting my legs and taking off my shoes. As I watched, he crossed to a small writing desk and, turning the key in the drawer, took out a box. Then he pulled a small chair up to the bedside table, placed the box on top, and opened it. As he did so, it exhaled a cloud of shitten sweetness, wildflowers and dung. Pinching off a small piece of the black goo, he began to knead and shape it between his thumb and fingers. Then, lighting a small lamp, he pierced the pellet with the dipper and held it spitted over the flame, placing it last in the chased silver bowl of the pipe I'd seen before and inserting the stem obligingly between my lips. Mesmerized by the ritual, I inhaled and held it. He then took it for himself and crossed to the coffee table, taking up the volume lying there. This he placed in my hands, then with a bow, retreated, leaving me alone.

As I flipped open the cover of the *Wizard of Oz*, the pages spontaneously parted, as though through some memory imparted to the spine from frequent repetition. I began to read:

> They walked along listening to the singing of the bright-colored birds and looking at the lovely flowers which now became so thick that the ground was carpeted with them. There were big yellow and white and blue and purple blossoms, besides great clusters of scarlet poppies, which were so brilliant in color they almost dazzled Dorothy's eyes.
>
> "Aren't they beautiful?" the girl asked, as she breathed in the spicy scent of the flowers.
>
> "I suppose so," answered the Scarecrow. "When I have brains I shall probably like them better."
>
> "If only I had a heart I should love them," added the Tin Woodman.
>
> "I always did like flowers," said the Lion; "they seem so helpless and frail. But there are none in the forest so bright as these."
>
> They now came upon more and more of the big scarlet poppies, and fewer and fewer of the other flowers; and soon they found themselves in the midst of a great meadow of poppies. Now it is well known that when there are many of these flowers together their odor is so powerful that anyone who breathes it falls asleep, and if the sleeper is not carried away from the scent of the flowers he sleeps on and on forever. But Dorothy did not know this, nor could she get away from the bright red flowers that were everywhere about; so presently her eyes grew heavy and she felt she must sit down to rest and to sleep.

As I read this passage, I felt my own eyelids beginning to droop.

> "What shall we do?" asked the Tin Woodman.
>
> "If we leave her here she will die," said the Lion. "The smell of the flowers is killing us all. I myself can scarcely keep my eyes open."

I was consumed with languid interest, but unable to keep my eyes focused on the page. They reeled and slipped from line to line, catching occasionally and holding.

> "Run fast," said the Scarecrow to the Lion, "and get out of this deadly flower-bed as soon as you can. We will bring the little girl with us, but if you should fall asleep you are too big to be carried."
>
> So the Lion aroused himself and bounded forward as fast as he could go. In a moment he was out of sight.

"Let us make a chair with our hands and carry her," said the Scarecrow. . . .

On and on they walked, and it seemed that the great carpet of deadly flowers that surrounded them would never end. They followed the bend of the river, and at last came upon their friend the Lion, lying fast asleep among the poppies. The flowers had been too strong for the huge beast and he had given up, at last, and fallen only a short distance from the end of the poppy-bed, where the sweet grass spread in beautiful green fields before them.

"We can do nothing for him," said the Tin Woodman, sadly; "for he is much too heavy to lift. We must leave him here to sleep on forever, and perhaps he will dream that he has found courage at last."

Huge tears began to roll down my cheeks, though I could not say why, for I had never read the story and could form only the vaguest conception of the situation. Taking off my glasses, I turned over on the pillows and continued weeping until I fell asleep.

I woke up with a start, filled with a premonition that there was someone with me in the room. But I saw no one, and my eyes lighted at last on a curtain fluttering in the window of one of the dormer alcoves. A small gilded bird cage which I hadn't noticed before hung from the ceiling in this recess. It was swaying slowly on its chain, twisting and untwisting in the wind. Rising from the bed, I crossed to examine it more closely. The tiny door was slightly ajar, fostering an illusion of recent occupancy, as though the bird had just that moment flown. Exploring further, I discovered that the mysterious breeze which I'd felt earlier was blowing through a broken pane of glass. Throwing open the windows, I saw the light of the afternoon sun glittering across the ripples in the Sound. As I watched the endless variations, a small silver plane flew over the water. The noise of the engines faded; it receded to a small black speck and finally disappeared.

I turned from the window to find Chiang Po confronting me in the doorway. He was holding a tray with refreshments, and though I was hungry I hardly noted what they were. For my attention was completely absorbed in trying to decipher his expression.

"Po?" I queried gently.

He flushed bright red. "Who are you?" he demanded in a scathing, furious tone.

Reaching up, I felt around my eyes, remembering I'd taken off the glasses before I fell asleep.

"Po . . ." I began, as soothingly as possible, "let me explain."

"*Bastard,*" he hissed venemously, "you've broken my heart."

"You don't understand," I protested, at the same time sidling cautiously toward the bed, picking up my shoes and glasses.

"I understand well enough," he retorted, starting to stalk me. "You've deceived me."

"Not intentionally," I remonstrated.

"Get out!" he exploded, becoming livid as he had before in the garden.

Fearing for his safety and my own, I brushed past him onto the landing. Halfway down, I turned and saw him glaring after me, his eyes crackling with angry lightnings, his hands trembling, tears rolling down his cheeks.

"Forgive me, Po."

He raised his arm and peremptorily pointed the way out. "Go," he ordered. "And don't come back. *Bastard!*"

Chapter 17

After this trip my despondency reached its lowest ebb, or rather its high-water mark. To have come so close, felt his presence so palpably, and yet know that he was out of reach forever — the tantalization was merciless and profoundly distressing. I think it undermined my faith in life, even perhaps my sanity. Certainly my health suffered. I took a week's sick leave from the Stock Exchange, my position there indemnified by Kahn, who acted beautifully and without thanks the part of my protector. During that time I rarely left my room, or even, indeed, my bed. Consequently I ate almost nothing. I was too depressed to think of food. I didn't dress. I didn't wash my face or shave. I slept for hours at a time. When I was awake I spent long periods mooning over my image, wearing the dark glasses, in the scrap of mirror left me by the former tenant of the room, a neurotic ceremony which sprang to life full-blown out of the depths of my despair and pacified me curiously, as though the pathetic cheat of this imposture could satisfy me for the loss of him whom I had never had. Deep in my heart I think I was waiting for something, a sign, not consciously waiting, but waiting all the same. Where it would come from, what shape it would take, I hadn't an inkling, yet I waited, and I watched.

In the rare interludes of lucidity granted me, it appeared my choices had come down to two, though perhaps "choices" is a misnomer in this case, for there was no question of a free movement of the spirit in the direction of some hoped fulfillment. Rather, I was presented with the double horns of a dilemma and invited to impale myself on one: pawn the robe, or leave. Though both involved a perhaps irremissible self-compromise, I was leaning toward the latter. For it struck me as more honorable, or rather, less dishonorable, to abandon a quest conceived in pride and probably fatuous anyway — i.e., the search for the delta — cutting my losses, as it were, and heading east — than to betray my mother's memory, a known good. And yet, if I gave up the idea of the delta, what would I be returning to? If Dow and Tao were separate finally and forever, Reality was multiple, and Tao was false. I had grown up under an illusion. There was no point in returning to a discredited way of life (Way of Life). "The bird's nest burns up." Truly, the prophecy had come home. But even this seemed preferable to the alternative of pawning the robe. Though I had not "proved" conclusively that the delta was a mirage, with my father's death, it ceased to matter. My passion, my singleness of purpose, waned from its original pitch. The meaning of the Dow ceased to kindle and inspire me. I became indifferent. Without him the Dow was alien and strange, a cold, inhospitable landscape, like the dark side of the moon, unillumined by the vivifying sunlight of his life and mystery.

Puzzling over this change, I realized that all along my search for the meaning of the Dow, and my attempt to reconcile it with the Tao, had been a search for *him,* an attempt to reconcile his mystery and meaning with my Way of Life, to classify him, Linnaeus-like, among the natural phenomena, the flora and fauna, which my a priori vision of the world had taught me could be possible and to expect. Whether out of ignorance, or whimsy, or precocious instinct, Eddie Love had *been* the Dow for me, its incarnation and embodiment, and with his disappearance it became a hollow symbol, a ruin, a temple from which the gods had all departed. Perhaps if he had been alive I might have steeled myself to it — pawning the robe, I mean — but dead, what was the point? All the more reason to cherish it, not recklessly gambling the only artifact of either of my parents I had left.

I wandered lost in this volitional lacuna several days. One morning I heard a knock at my door.

"May I come in?" Yin-mi asked, pushing her head through the crack.

Fortunately I had made it out of bed and was sitting up, albeit shirtless, unshaven, and uncombed, at my little table over a cup of cold tea brewed the day before and left out overnight. I turned glumly to observe her, then resumed my position without comment.

"Sun I?" she ventured with a note of timid concern.

"What?" I asked gruffly.

"You don't look well. Are you sick?"

"I'm fine."

She sat down in a chair beside me, studying my face diffidently, but with concern, while I sullenly avoided her eyes. She was dressed as though for the beach, in a loose white cotton sun dress, sandals; she carried a canvas satchel.

"Father Riley asked me to check and see if the lecture was still on," she opened timidly.

"The lecture!" I whispered, suddenly remembering.

"It's tomorrow night."

"Shit!" I said under my breath.

"You hadn't forgotten . . . ?"

"As a matter of fact . . ." I shrugged apologetically, leaving her to draw the inference.

"You are going to do it? You won't disappoint him?"

I studied her briefly, agonizing over the entreaty in her voice. "I guess I don't have much choice, do I?" I replied, smiling resentfully.

She appeared relieved. "Well, it might be fun," she suggested.

"Right."

"Have you seen the posters?"

"What posters?"

"They're all over downtown," she informed me, reaching into her bag. "I helped put them up Tuesday afternoon."

"I haven't been downtown."

"Here." With a slight smile, she unrolled one on the table.

I regarded it, frowning. "Where did they get this photograph?"

"Someone at TYA had an Instamatic, didn't you see him? It's a good likeness, don't you think?"

I glanced at her sharply to see if an ironic intention were concealed in this remark.

"Father Riley said he thought you looked like a lion in a den of hungry Christians," she told me, bubbling over with happy laughter. Seeing my scowl, she forced herself to assume gravity of mien. Her amusement, though, welled up from underneath, sparkling ebulliently in her eyes. I couldn't resent it either, for I knew her fun at my expense was sparked by affection, not meanness. Yet I wondered at it, for though I detected a faint subliminal reference in her manner to what had occurred between us at our previous encounter, she seemed to have assimilated and accepted it and passed on without injury or regret. I was impressed, even a little awed, by her courage and resilience, and by her resolute and irrepressible gaiety of heart. I found myself admiring her more than ever and wondering at my trepidation over seeing her again. Her presence had a tonic effect on me. After five minutes I felt measurably better than I had for several days, though nothing, I'm afraid, could have effected a total restoration of my spirits in the condition to which I'd sunk.

The poster was typical of the genre, a handwritten, mimeographed affair, borderline sensational: "A *Rare Glimpse* of Life in a *Secret Taoist Monastery in China* by One Who *Actually Lived There* (!) and *Escaped* to Tell the Story!!! (Including a display of certain rare and valuable artifacts — a ceremonial robe . . . & etc.) Public cordially invited to attend." My photograph, looking like I had recently bitten the head off a live chicken, or was contemplating doing so forthwith, was inset in the upper left-hand corner.

"First step on the road to fame and fortune," she playfully remarked.

I met her wryness with a drier look.

"He also wanted me to show you this." She reached into her bag and rummaged blindly, then, not finding what she wanted, spread it open between her knees and peered in. "Tsch," she clucked in disappointment. "I brought my notes, but I forgot the book." She leaned back in her chair and stretched her feet out, pondering. "Wait," she said, sitting up. "You have a copy."

"A copy of what?"

"The Prayer book. Don't you?"

I pointed toward my makeshift shelf, an upturned fruit crate with bricks for bookends. She fingered out the volume, then leaned over to examine the book next to it. "What's this?"

"The *I Ching.*"

She picked it up and ran her finger through the light film of dust which had accumulated on the cover. "Looks like it hasn't been used for a while," she commented.

Her remark, though casual, stung me.

"I've always wanted to learn how to use it," she mused. "Li gave me a copy for my birthday one year, only in English. I could never figure out about the stalks though, how you do them."

"It isn't hard," I said. "You might start out with coins though. They're even simpler, though a little crass perhaps, not quite so proper."

"Does it matter?"

"Everything matters."

She directed a sweet, vulnerable appeal at me. "Maybe you could teach me how sometime?"

I shrugged. "I suppose so. Why not?"

"You don't sound very enthusiastic," she remarked with a coy frown. "Aren't you anxious to convert me?"

"It's not at the top of my list of priorities."

"You Taoists certainly are lackadaisical. Father Riley is much more conscientious. In proof of which" — she returned to her seat and to business — "he asked me to show you this." She started flipping through the Book of Common Prayer. "It's in the Articles of Religion, number twenty-eight, I think. Yes, here it is. He said this might help explain the meaning of the Mass and perhaps answer your question."

"What question?"

"Don't you remember?"

"I asked a lot of questions. I'm not sure which one specifically you mean."

She read from her pad. " 'If you deny the physicality of such a ritual, what do you have left?' I took notes on what he said to tell you," she explained, nodding to the pad. "Remember now?"

"Yes," I said. "So?"

"May I read it to you?"

"Go ahead."

" 'The Supper of the Lord is not only a sign of the love that Christians ought to have among themselves one to another; but rather it is a Sacrament of our Redemption by Christ's death: insomuch that to such as rightly, worthily, and with faith, receive the same, the Bread which we break is a partaking of the Body of Christ; and likewise the Cup of Blessing is a partaking of the Blood of Christ.

" 'Transubstantiation (or the change of the substance of Bread and Wine) in the Supper of the Lord, cannot be proved by Holy Writ; but it is repugnant to the plain words of Scripture, overthroweth the nature of a Sacrament.' Note that," she said, glancing at me from under raised eyebrows, " 'and hath given occasion to many superstitions.

" 'The Body of Christ is given, taken, and eaten, in the Supper, only after an heavenly and spiritual manner. And the mean whereby the Body of Christ is received and eaten in the Supper, is Faith.' "

Closing the book, she studied me briefly, then scanned her pad again. "Father Riley said to pay careful attention to the difference between a genuine Sacrament and transubstantiation. He said the literal-mindedness of Roman Catholicism in regard to the dogma of transubstantiation is, in his opinion, a vulgarity. Rather than a vitiation of the power of the Eucharist, as you seemed to suggest, he regards the Episcopalian alternative as subtler, more evolved. Transubstantiation is vulgar because it assumes the need for, and attempts to supply, a guarantee of the mingling of the visible and invisible worlds, the literal presence of Christ in the bread and wine. This removes, or at least lightens, the burden of belief in the communicant's heart. The true miracle and efficacy of the Sacrament does not consist in some magical transmutation of the elements themselves into the literal blood and body, but rather in the subtler alchemy which occurs in the believer's heart through faith. Christ is present mystically in the cup. That is the meaning of the Sacrament."

"What was that phrase?" I asked, sitting up with suddenly kindled interest.

"Which?" she asked. " 'Christ is present mystically . . .'?"

"No, before that."

" 'The true miracle and efficacy of the Sacrament does not consist in some magical transmutation of the elements themselves . . .' "

"That's it."

" '. . . into the literal blood and body, but rather in the subtler alchemy which occurs in the believer's heart through faith.' " She searched my face inquisitively. "What?"

"That phrase echoes something the master told me once, one of the last things he said before I left: 'the truest alchemy occurs only in the alembic of the wise man's heart.' "

"Then you understand?"

I nodded. "I think so. 'The Body of Christ is given, taken, and eaten, in the Supper. . . .' How did it go?"

" '. . . only after an heavenly and spiritual manner. And the mean whereby the Body of Christ is received and eaten in the Supper, is Faith.' "

"Faith." I drifted off into inarticulate speculation.

"What are you thinking?"

"Hmm?" I replied, breaking forcibly the inward focus of my reverie. "You know, I'm not really sure."

I wasn't being disingenuous either, for I could not have put my finger on any specific idea this exchange had quickened into being. In fact, my conscious mind was blank. Yet I was aware of what I can only call a faint benign perplexity, something moiling underneath the surface of my mind. I was conscious of this only as a vague irritation, such as perhaps the oyster feels toward the seed, and yet some subliminal train of speculation had been set in motion, my unconscious mind had set to work on it, laving it with the precious latex of its vital fluids, weaving in dark necessity what would shine forth in the light a pearl (or perhaps one of the warped misbirths one finds more commonly within the shell). I only sensed it had to do with faith.

"So," I said at last, nodding toward her clothes and bag, "where are you off to?"

She looked down at her dress as though she weren't quite sure herself and needed to refresh her memory. "Well, I was thinking of taking the train out to Coney Island," she began uncertainly, almost apologetically. "It's probably the last chance I'll have before school starts. My mother said it was all right, only . . ." — she appealed to me diffidently — "she doesn't want me to go alone."

"Coney Island . . ." I mused, remembering the story of the crash.

"What's the matter?" she asked, clueing in on a note of unintended wistfulness in my tone. "Have you been there?"

I shook my head with a sad smile.

She regarded me with perplexity, then became solemn. "It's in Brooklyn," she explained, continuing to scrutinize me. "All the way across. On the ocean."

I nodded.

"There's an amusement park with games and rides, a tremendous Ferris wheel. Have you ever ridden one?"

I shook my head. "A Ferris wheel? What is that?"

"This huge revolving wheel made of steel with little cars they lock you into. It takes you way up high so you can see for miles in all directions, out to sea — ships and sailboats, and if it's clear, back to Manhattan. From up there, the city looks like something you could hold in the palm of your hand, a little piece of computer circuitry or something. There's a beach there, and a boardwalk. It shouldn't be too crowded today either." She paused. "Come with me," she suddenly proposed, half-daring, half-imploring, as though she'd already sounded my intentions and found me indisposed. "What else do you have to do?"

Though tempted to accede, I hesitated.

"Come on!" she coaxed. "I promise I won't attack you."

I laughed. "Perhaps I should," I conceded, thinking of my father, curious to see the place where it had ended. Perhaps that physical proximity would bring me closer to my own spiritual terminus, I thought, perhaps I'd finally find what I was looking for.

"Of course you should!" she continued. "It would do you good to get out."

"You're probably right. Besides" — my mind gravitated back to the inescapable responsibility of my dilemma — "it may be the last time."

"The last time what?" she asked, giving me that look of concern again. I shook my head. "Never mind. I'll go."

"Good!" she cried. "Mother is packing us a lunch."

I chuckled. "So you already counted on persuading me before you asked?" She beamed a coy smile and shrugged her shoulders happily.

"Well, go ahead. I'll meet you downstairs after I've shaved and changed my clothes."

"See you in a minute," she said, rising from the table. On her way to the door, she detoured to the bookshelf and, pointing to my copy of the *Changes*, cast a petitionary glance at me over her shoulder. "May I take this? Maybe you'll have time to show me how to use it while we're there."

"Sure," I replied. "Go ahead."

Placing it gingerly among the other things in the bottom of her bag, she skipped out.

•

We walked together to the bridge and caught the train. As we crossed, I stared wistfully out over the river. Gulls were wheeling above the water, and the sky was clear with a crystal tint that hinted at the end of summer. In the middle distance I could see the Statue of Liberty gazing forlornly seaward toward the span of the Verrazano-Narrows Bridge, hanging like a dark rainbow on the low horizon. The mesmeric rhythm of the train rocked me back into my former gloom, but it was painless now. I felt anesthetized.

Yin-mi continued to study me in silence. Occasionally our eyes met by accident, and I made an effort to smile, then looked away, seeing the anxiety and concern in her expression. Finally she spoke. "You're acting strange today. Something's happened, hasn't it?"

"Yes," I admitted quietly. "Something has."

"You've found your father?" There was a diffident tremor in her voice.

I nodded, noting but hardly surprised by her clairvoyance. "Yes. Found him . . . and lost him."

"He's not . . . ?"

"Right," I interrupted, so as not to hear the word. "He's not."

Her look held such pity and distress that I now felt a pang of sympathy for her. "Oh, Sun I, I'm so sorry," she offered, almost pleading. Then she began to cry.

I was profoundly touched. "I know." I pressed her hand. "Thank you."

For a long while we were silent, I peering out the window, she sitting quietly beside me. Then briefly and matter-of-factly I told her what I'd learned.

"What will you do now?" she asked when I'd done.

"I don't know. Perhaps go back. There doesn't seem much point in staying now." I sought her eyes. "Does there?"

She greeted this in silence.

"If I stay, I'll have to pawn my mother's robe," I continued.

"Why? Are you in need of money?"

"No, not that so much, but I'm stuck, going nowhere."

"I don't think you should."

I turned to her sharply. "Then you think I should leave?"

She shook her head. "No, I don't think that either. But you mustn't pawn your mother's robe in any case." She uttered this with an air of absolute finality. I had expected just such moral certainty from her, just such candor.

"But there's no third option. If I don't, I have to leave. It's as simple as that," I stipulated, suddenly disposed to argue despite the fact that her remarks corroborated my own feelings.

"But why limit yourself to such extreme alternatives?"

"Because to justify prolonging my absence from the monastery, I must continue to explore the Dow, and I can't do that without investing. Kahn has convinced me of that. To invest I must have funds. The robe is the only thing of value I possess."

"I thought investment was against your vows." She was very solemn.

"It is," I said, turning away. I didn't speak again until the train pulled into Coney Island, the last stop.

•

We emerged from the El into the warrens of juice bars and souvenir shops under the trestles, then gradually wandered up the strip, past the fortune-tellers' shops with their proprietresses' cognomens written in cursive letters inside spread neon palms, past pizzerias, clam bars, bail bondsmen's. In the distance I could see the vast white skeleton of the roller coaster, and nearer, looming tremendous over the whole park, illuminated in broad daylight, the Wonder Wheel. It appeared to hover unsupported in the air like a huge hoop of magic fire, and in my despondency it seemed a fitting emblem of the Wheel of Life itself, geared to a machine, metallic and sensational, empty at the heart, tracing gigantic zeroes in the sky. Those zeroes mocked me with the poverty of a discredited Way of Life. No magic tiger would leap through that flaming hoop, I told myself. Not now. It was too late. It was over.

Turning into the park, we wandered past the games: the ring-toss, the darts, the shooting galleries, the string-pull. The banks of furry blue and pink stuffed animals, with their ogling eyes and smiles of febrile gaiety, insinuated shameful complicity in some compromising secret, an attitude the barkers corroborated as best they could, only, as it were, in a minor key, incapable of such sustained exaltation. Burdened with merely human hearts, they seemed weary and about to give up, which is precisely what I felt myself on the verge of doing. Repetitive peals of taunting laughter floated to us from the chambers of the Haunted House — joyless and obsessive, not even frightening — where limp-jointed skeletons on wires and springs leapt out at screaming children passing in the cars. We passed the Wolf Man's Lair, the Bearded Lady; a barker's voice cried out: "Step right up and see Me-THU-se-lah, the world's most ancient infant, or youngest senior citizen. Chronologically five years old according to his birth certificate (on display inside for your perusal), yet afflicted with a rare, incurable disease — pro-GE-ri-a — he displays the gnarled and wizened features of a hundred-year-old man. See him dodder in his cradle in his JU-ve-nile senescence. . . ." His voice became indistinguishable in the general din.

Passing through the rigors of this tawdry gauntlet, we emerged at last onto the boardwalk overlooking the beach. The funhouse clamor thinned behind us, and the smell of chili and machine oil was dispersed by an off-shore breeze. The Atlantic was as quiet as a millpond there, and surprisingly clean, a deep bluish-green with a lace ruffle at the fringe where it rose up against the yellow sand. The beach was almost deserted, but sentineled by rows of orderly garbage barrels and tall signs advertising lists of prohibitions which showed a positively forensic cleverness in their inclusiveness: "No Spitting, Fornicating, Nudity, Defecation, Urination, Obscenity, Alcoholic Beverages, Gambling, Jockeying, Jostling, or Undue Jocularity of Any Sort" (the eight concluding letters of the last term scratched out and replaced with a *y* to read "Joy"). A series of stone jetties perpendicular to the beach appeared at intervals, extending out into deep water. A few beachcombers were gingerly making their way in or out on these, teetering and balancing with their arms like high-wire artists.

Yin-mi went off to the bathhouse to change, and I climbed down the steep concrete stairs onto the sand. Rolling up my cuffs, I tramped along the tidal margin, vaguely making for the rocks. As I wandered, I gradually fell into an elegaic mood. With a sad, fantastical whimsy, I found myself half-searching for charred bits of wreckage from my father's plane washed up along the beach or glimmering untarnished in the shallow water off the jetties, like sand-scoured gold doubloons scattered across the sea floor. Making my way out to the farthest limit of the breakwater, where the noises of the park died away entirely and there was only the patient lapping of the water on the rocks and the whisper of the freshet in my ears, I sat down, circling my knees with my arms and studied the unbroken horizon, the sky so vast, so blue, so empty. From time to time, for no apparent reason, my mind drifted back to Riley's phrase: "the subtler alchemy which occurs in the believer's heart through faith." Why had that seized me? Was it merely the coincidental resemblance to Chung Fu's remark? On the lee side of the rocks the water was glassy, and peering down into it, I once again was confronted by my image in the dark glasses. As I rested my chin on my knees, brooding over it, a second face appeared in the pool and I felt a light touch on my shoulder.

"Hello, Narcissus," Yin-mi said, smiling up at me from the water.

"Who's Narcissus?" I asked.

"He was the Greek who became infatuated with his reflection in a pool of water. When he dove in to embrace it, he drowned."

I pondered this, continuing to contemplate my image. "Maybe he wasn't so much infatuated as distressed by it," I suggested musingly. "Maybe he dove in not to embrace but to shatter the face that mocked him from the depths and ended by destroying himself instead."

She leaned down over my shoulder and regarded with me. "Is that what you see, something which taunts and threatens?"

"I don't know," I replied. "What do you see?"

"Someone struggling to maintain his innocence."

"Is it possible to be innocent and live?"

"Yes," she whispered, "I think so. You must have faith."

"I'm not so sure," I hedged, breaking the intimacy and starting to rise. "Anyway, what is faith?"

We walked along the beach once more, and in the distance saw two children, a little boy and girl perhaps four or five years old, working industriously with plastic pails and shovels. They were almost up to the their armpits in their own excavation. Periodically they sank out of sight then bobbed up again, like pistons alternately firing in a small two-stroke engine. Arcs and rooster tails of sand flew from their shovels. Up the beach a ways, their mother, in a straw hat, sunglasses, and a skirted bathing suit, was lounging in a canvas chair beneath a striped umbrella, reading. From time to time she peered anxiously over the edge of her magazine to make sure they were safe. Both of them had ducked out of sight briefly when an uncommonly audacious wave raced up the strand and overwhelmed them, washing over the lip of their revetment. Their screams and shouts, though primarily occasioned by surprise and liberally mixed with laughter, brought their mother lumbering from her chair like a colossus, running on heavy, quavering thighs to save them. They erupted from the hole giggling and spouting and running frantically in place, practically bumping into our knees in their heedless flight. Laughing, we reached down to catch and fend them off, and to our surprise they suddenly froze and turned to one another blinking big, astonished eyes.

"Kitty!" the little boy exclaimed in a loud whisper that intimated volumes.

She looked at us and bit her bottom lip.

Just then their mother reached us, falling breathless to her knees. The little girl took instant refuge in her arms. "Are you all right?" the woman asked anxiously, pushing her child to arm's length to examine her. "For heaven's sake, don't frighten me like that!" She put her hand over her bosom and sighed.

The little girl nodded demurely, keeping her eyes fixed shyly on our faces.

"Mommy! Mommy!" her brother cried, attacking her from the opposite direction with ecstatic vehemence. "It's true! It's true! Look!" He pointed exultantly at us.

"Don't point, Johnny," she chided, encircling him with her arm to repress his own refractory member. "It's not polite."

"But it's true!" he protested loudly, struggling in her arms.

"Calm down, sweetheart!" she said, in a tone halfway between coaxing and prescription. "What's true?"

"They're Chinese. We made it!"

The nature of his mistake dawned on her. She flushed bright red. "Hush, Johnny!" she scolded. "They're as American as we are." Giving him a shake, she appealed to us apologetically. "I'm so sorry. I told him that if he dug deep enough, he'd eventually come out in China. I had no idea he'd actually believe it."

Yin-mi burst out laughing.

The woman smiled gratefully. "Honestly, what an imagination!" She looked at him with exasperated pride.

I ogled him as though he were a prodigy.

Taking them by the hand, she started off. "Come on," she whispered severely to the little boy, who lingered gaping at us.

"But it's true!" he cried plaintively. As they retreated up the beach, he continued to twist back when he could, the ferocity of conviction in his eyes undiminished.

"*That*'s faith," Yin-mi casually laughed as we walked off.

I stared at her witlessly, thrown profoundly off my bearings by her remark and by the incident itself. The seismic rumblings which she had touched off earlier that morning with the passage from the Prayer book now reached a higher level on the Richter scale of my unconscious.

We bought Cokes at the nearest stand, sat down on a wooden bench in the shadow of the rusted tower of the Parachute Jump, closed down years before after a series of fatalities, and spread out our picnic facing the sea.

"You're not eating," she remarked after a while. "What is it? You seem preoccupied."

"I'm not sure," I replied. "All morning I've had this odd sensation that things were conspiring to speak to me."

She put down her sandwich. "What do you mean?"

"It's as if some invisible presence were hovering just behind the veil of the surface world, whispering in my ear, only too low to make out the words, or in a language which I can't decipher, like an oracle."

"What is it?" she asked. "Do you have a sense?"

"This is where he died," I mused obliquely, gazing out over the dark ocean at the empty horizon. "Out there."

"You think it's him — your father?"

"How could it be? He's dead."

She considered this. "Perhaps the oracle could help," she suggested.

I shrugged.

"Why don't you try?"

"I've thought of it," I said.

"Why haven't you then? You aren't afraid of what it might say?"

I shook my head. "Whatever it is, it could only be a relief."

As though in challenge, she reached in her satchel and took the *I Ching* out. "Here." She offered it to me with a little frown of settled resolve.

"But we forgot to bring the stalks," I temporized.

"Well, we have coins, don't we?"

"I told you before, coins are inappropriate."

"That's just an excuse, isn't it?" she queried, gentle but firm. "It won't matter, as long as you're sincere." She took three pennies from her change purse and placed them in my hand. I conceded with a sigh.

I coached her through the various stages in the consultation, explaining as I went along. With coins it went much faster, yet I couldn't suppress the feeling that they compromised the ritual. The reading which emerged was *Sui,* the seventeenth hexagram, called "Following" in English. There were moving lines in both the second and third places, both sixes: *yin,* or darkness, on the verge of changing into *yang,* or light. The judgment read:

> Following has supreme success.
> Perseverance furthers. No blame.

"Following," I mused silently. Following what? Or whom? As I saw it, there were two roads, one leading back, the other deeper in. Which was indicated?

I examined the main body of the text for a clue:

> If a man would lead, he must first learn how to follow.

This only compounded my perplexity. I turned ahead to the description of the lines. There I found the following:

> Six in the second place means:
> If one clings to the little boy,
> One loses the strong man.

My stomach fluttered. I glanced to the next:

> Six in the third place means:
> If one clings to the strong man,
> One loses the little boy.
> Through following one finds what one seeks.
> It furthers one to remain persevering.

" 'If one clings to the little boy, one loses the strong man,' " Yin-mi repeated meditatively.

" 'If one clings to the strong man, one loses the little boy,' " I countered, unconsciously retorting.

"What do you think it means?" she demanded.

"I don't know. It counsels two contradictory courses of action."

"Or simply hones the implications of them both and then defers to you."

"Oh, I don't need to have it made any plainer," I remarked with a bitter laugh.

"If you know the choices and their implications," she asked, "what's holding you back?"

"I want both."

She laughed, apparently thinking I was joking.

"I'm serious," I insisted, and seeing my face she sobered. "Is it so much to ask, after all," I demanded, "that the child should be preserved within the man, cherished and so spared, that they might coexist together in a single human heart?"

"I don't know," she replied, with a gentle smile. "It does seem a lot. Perhaps life doesn't allow that compromise."

I was silent, weighing the import of her words.

"You know, last year in English class we read this essay," she said. "I don't remember the title or who wrote it, but he was talking about America. He said this country is like a molting snake, casting off the dead skin of the European past. He said that nothing is more natural for a living creature than to slough its old skin and move on to the next stage — nothing more natural, and nothing harder. Because passing across that threshold is very painful, almost like dying. In fact, it is a kind of death. And sometimes the snake falls too much in love with the beautiful patterns on his former body and refuses to abandon it; then he sickens and rots in the old skin. It becomes his tomb."

"What are you saying?"

She shook her head. "I'm not saying anything. They're someone else's words. I can't make the choice for you. I just remembered them and said them."

"Perhaps the robe is the old skin I must slough," I mused.

"Maybe," she replied. "But then again, maybe it's something deeper."

We looked at one another in silence.

"Tell me, Sun I," she said at last, "which is he . . . *was* he — your father, I mean — the strong man or the little boy?"

"That's just it," I replied, "I think he was both. He didn't have to savage innocence to achieve his manhood. He didn't have to choose."

"Or wouldn't."

"Or refused to consciously," I retorted with heat, "repudiating the dilemma with its specious option of one horn or the other." Recalling the bottom line, however, I sighed, deflating. "But he's dead."

"I wonder . . ." she said speculatively, looking off.

I regarded her sharply. "Wonder what? If he's dead? I told you before, the plane went down almost ten miles out."

"Not that," she demurred. "Physically, yes, of course he is. But in another sense, perhaps he's still alive."

"How?"

"In you," she answered. "You always said that he was searching for immortality. Maybe he found it, in your memory, in your heart."

The thought touched me, more with gratitude for her concern, however, than by its intrinsic weight or usefulness. "My heart feels so frail and mortal," I replied, with a weary smile. "It hardly seems enough."

She reached out and grazed my cheek, as her mother had.

"Maybe that's all immortality really is," I speculated, searching halfheartedly for closure where I knew there would be none, "keeping the little boy alive within the man. Maybe in that sense he did achieve it."

We smiled at one another with sad tolerance and affection. She began to clear away the remains of the lunch we hadn't eaten.

"I know what!" she said, suddenly brightening. "I'll take you on the Wonder Wheel! That will cheer you up if anything will."

I blinked at her apathetically.

"Yes," she affirmed determinedly, jumping to her feet and pulling me by the hand. "You're going. It's my party and you have to do what I say. Now *come on.*"

Sluggishly I rose and let her lead me, gravitating backward as she strained ahead.

We bought our tickets at the little booth and handed them to the impassive attendant with his rolled red-bandanna headband and grease-stained T-shirt. He pulled the lever backward and the Wonder Wheel lurched to a halt, the cars trembling like nervous Christmas tree ornaments. Raising the bar, he ushered us in, then clamped it over us. I rolled back my head and looked up through the jointed geometric superstructure, like a giant metal web, and felt a little sick with awe at its stupendousness. Our takeoff was so sudden I gasped and clutched the bar with both hands. Immediately we stopped again to let a second couple board, the car rocking back and forth unsteadily, creaking on its axle.

"It's all right," Yin-mi encouraged, patting my hand.

I stared at her wildly and tensed for the next move. Away we went, fetched up as by the talons of a tremendous bird of prey, a motion swift in itself but seeming slow by virtue of the huge circumference of the circle we were compassing, the slowness an exquisite torture, drawing out the agony. Reaching the zenith of the arch, we passed it wheeling down; my stomach kept on going. I didn't dare look down, but kept my eyes fixed straight ahead. The sky was something of a comfort, its undifferentiated blueness mercifully showing no marks of changing altitude.

"Close your mouth," Yin-mi whispered, leaning toward me. "A pigeon might fly in."

"Pigeon!" I protested, afraid to look at her. "Since when do pigeons fly this high? Try an eagle!"

Her laughter did a giddy Doppler shift as we plummeted toward the ground. "Oh!" she cried. "Look down!"

Like a fool, not thinking, I obeyed her. "Oh, my God," I said in a thin voice, "we're going to die." A dizzy, teetering sensation came over me, accompanied by nausea and panting, dilation of the pupils — panic, in short.

"You don't look so good," she commented, as we wheeled aloft on our second orbit.

Unable to divert even a tiny fraction of my psychic forces from the front line of the battle, I did not reply, or even turn my head.

"Try this," she suggested. "Close your eyes, take a deep breath, and count to ten. It always works for me."

I obeyed instantly, interlarding the count with fervent prayers. The technique gave the impression of success, for when I opened my eyes again we no longer appeared to be in motion, though the wind still whistled past my face. To my complete astonishment, I saw a seagull almost close enough to touch, beating his wings with a slow oaring motion, flying, apparently, in perfect synchrony with us, and, so doing, seeming to stand still. This was quite wonderful to me. I looked at him; he looked back. I think he smiled. Nudging Yin-mi, I pointed him out, grinning at her with idiotic bliss, my discomfiture temporarily forgotten. By way of reply, she pointed down, and the depths of my fatuity yawned wide. We weren't moving after all. The machine had stopped, broken down no doubt, leaving us stranded there (perhaps forever!) at the apogee of the Wonder Wheel! My breathlessness came back; my heart began to race. My panic threatened to return. "We *are* going to die!" I thought.

All at once I began to howl with laughter, my panic alchemized miraculously into exhilaration. I felt the thrill of total uncontrol, a vertigo uncomfortable but delicious. I saw the tiny microbes of the bathers squirming on the yellow beach and, farther out, the water where its color changed from emerald to blue, then black. The whitecaps looked like fingernail parings scattered over the surface of a black marble table. Beyond, the great curve of the world spread itself out with languid, tremendous grandeur. I was like an inexperienced astronaut who, released from the secure cabin of his preconceptions, walks in space, becoming so exhilarated by the sensation of weightlessness, so absorbed in the ineffable beauty of the void, that he forgets its lethalness and refuses to come in, giving himself completely to an orgy of ecstatic seeing.

And that was when it happened. As we perched there in our mobile aerie at the zenith of the world, a low rumbling became audible, like distant thunder, only sustained, and growing louder, proceeding from no discernible direction, but as though from all directions, enveloping us with sound.

"What is it?" I asked, turning to her.

She shrugged and then peered down between her parted knees. "What are they staring at?"

Below us everything had stopped. The park stood still, all the people frozen in their places gazing up.

The noise grew louder.

A solitary hand sprang up in the crowd, followed by another, and another, setting off a chain reaction, like popcorn, staccato bursts of hands from everywhere, now one side, now another, till all the multitudes in a unanimous impulse pointed toward the sky.

"Sun I," she said, swallowing with archetypal social horror, "I think they're pointing at us."

But I was hardly conscious of them, or of her, studying the empty sky with a grim prescience as the noise increased, like a soldier on the ramparts waiting for day to break and the battle to commence. The din grew louder.

Then I saw it. "Look!" I cried, pointing and leaping against the bar in a spontaneous attempt to stand.

"Sit down!" she screamed, grabbing my belt and pulling me backward.

The car lurched wildly, like a ship caught beam-to in a heavy sea.

"Look!" I cried again, more vehemently. "Don't you see it?"

"What?" She squinted into the sunlight, shading her eyes with her hand. "I don't see anything."

She wasn't wearing dark glasses, though; I was. Shielded from the glare, I saw it perfectly as it appeared from the bright disc of the sun — the plane, a silver Piper, such as one often observes in summer flying over crowded beaches, towing an advertising banner. At first I couldn't make out what it said. Then the plane roared over, so close that we could hear the pennant rippling in the slipstream. I pieced it out a letter at a time as it appeared, bloodred letters ten feet tall:

L-O-V-E N-E-V-E-R F-A-I-L-E-T-H

followed by the superscription "CCC" — Community of Christian Churches, as I later learned.

No, there was nothing uncanny about it. I can assert this with complete conviction now. At the time, though, I was sorely tempted to think otherwise. I don't know if I can explain this, Reader, but something happened to me when I saw that plane. Call it synchronicity, "mystic connection," or whatever, but the knot instantly unraveled in my brain. The passage from the Epistle, 1 Corinthians 13 came back to me: "Beareth all things, believeth all things, hopeth all things, endureth all things; Love never faileth." Now it brought a swelling tide of associated images, which it crowned and completed. I remembered Riley's phrase — "the subtler alchemy which occurs in the believer's heart through faith" — and understood why it had struck a chord in me. That thought, in its turn, evoked another, the image of the little boy digging in the sand, believing in accordance with the pristine faith of every American child who's ever played with a spade and bucket beside the sea, that by rooting deep enough into the common soil of his experience, through the granite bedrock of reality itself, he would emerge at last in a fey, enchanted world called China, Never-Never Land, the Kingdom of the Imagi-Nation, unprecedented and exotic, dangerous and benign, peopled by mandarins and demons, where wishes were commands and every dream came true. In him I saw an image of myself — what I had been, rather, what I had lost. I too had once believed that I might kneel down anywhere in Wall Street and, prying up a stone, a piece of pavement, the cornerstone of the New York Stock Exchange itself, begin to scoop the suffocated, light-starved earth with my bare hands, burrowing up eventually like a mole into the courtyard of Ken Kuan, under the spreading branches of the peach tree; believed that by plying diligently at the difficult, unyielding substance of the Dow with the jewel-tipped instrument of my faith, as a criminal scratches at the prison walls with his spoon or ice pick, I might emerge at last to freedom under the blue, spreading skies of China, under the immaculate heaven of the Tao. But faith had yielded first, ground to powder against the diamond substance of my father's being. He had shaken it, and his death, which might conceivably have released me from the challenge of pursuing him into the mystery, instead had given faith its mortal stroke (as though conclusive proof that hell did not exist and Satan was chimerical should shake one's faith in God!). Oh, Reader, I don't pretend to understand it, but only insist as a witness in its truth and ask you to believe. "The heart is a wilderness."

But something happened when I saw that banner. I found what I was looking for; the sign. The final piece of the puzzle fell into place, and I realized Yin-mi was right. *He was alive* — perhaps not in the sense she'd meant, but more profoundly. That was the message of the plane, "Love Never Faileth." He had indeed achieved his immortality, not physically (but that would have been a vulgar transubstantiation anyway, to use Riley's phrase), not in my heart, but in another, truer sense, and I had known it all along. Only the knowledge had receded from consciousness and appeared lost. Love was alive in *it,* in the Dow, and I might still partake of him through it, mystically, as I had partaken of my mother through the robe. Riley's gloss to the passage from the Prayer book was the key: "The true miracle and efficacy of the Sacrament does not consist in some magical transmutation of the elements themselves into the literal blood and body, but rather in the subtler alchemy which occurs in the believer's heart through faith."

Recalling this, I understood the nature of his immortality. He was mystically incarnate in the Dow as Christ is in the elements of bread and wine, and the means whereby I might partake of him was faith. And augmenting this insight was another: if he had been the Dow, embodied somehow its seminal energy and essence, then by the commutative law, the Dow was him! This was the miracle, I suddenly saw, that I must celebrate through the sacrament of my continued search. In that instant faith returned, and with it, hope. I experienced a resurrection in my heart. My protracted, agonizing labor came to crisis and bore this mental child, the little boy of my reconsecrated faith — my father. And it was just such faith my heart required to persevere. "Beareth all things, believeth all things, hopeth all things, endureth all things. . . ." LOVE NEVER FAILETH.

As I read that transcribed across the noonday sky, a revelation exploded in my brain and filled the world with light. Like the the flash a soldier sees from the barrel of his enemy's rifle before the bullet strikes him, I saw my fate and knew that it was futile to resist it. A thrill of fear passed through my heart and then a feeling of profound release, as though some heavy burden had been lifted from my shoulders and I were floating weightlessly in space. A reckless gaiety welled up in me like cold, fresh water from an artesian well whose source is undetected, and I had to laugh — a different kind of laughter than I'd known before, the sound of my own voice surprising, bold and deep, as though it came from some unsounded region at the bottom of my heart. And it was then I knew that this was all I'd ever wanted from the start.

PART THREE

The Tao Within the Dow

Chapter 1

Immediately on our return I took the robe out, wrapped it up in tissue, and went to Mme Chin's. Now that I had made my choice I had to do it quickly. I knew that if I hesitated, or even dared to look at it, my resolution would fail me. In the back of my mind I understood that this would subvert Riley's and Yin-mi's plans, but psychologically I could not afford the luxury of weighing their convenience. It took all the will I could muster simply to do what was required. Strangely, though there was a quality of desperation in my resolve, I acted in an almost trancelike state, like a somnambulist, observing my own feverish activity with a fatalistic coolness.

Outside Mme Chin's apartment a strain of incontinent laughter floated to me, muted by the door: the dowager's.

"Don't touch that! I'll cut it off if you do that again," I heard her threaten incomprehensibly in an unthreatening tone. "You're such a naughty boy, Fan-ku!"

"Give me a little money, Auntie, and I'll be even naughtier," he invited.

Again the laugh.

Gathering up my courage, I knocked.

"Shhh," she hissed. An ominous silence fell. "Go see who it is."

The door parted. Fan-ku eyed me through the crack. "What do you want?"

"I need to speak to Mme Chin."

"It's the priest," he said over his shoulder.

"Tell him we're busy. Go away," she called.

"It's about the robe," I said, similarly bypassing our intermediary.

Silence again.

"Let him in," she directed.

"Aiyi!" he protested.

The door closed, and a heated exchange ensued, strident, venemous whispers I could not decipher. Then the night chain slipped and the door swung open.

"Come in," he hissed, almost spitting the words in my face. He was standing in his stocking feet, a little glassy eyed. His pomaded hair was mussed, his shirt untucked and open halfway down his chest. There was a smear of lipstick on one cheek just below his ear.

One panel of the drape was tied back to the jamb with a tasseled waist cord. In the far room I could see a portion of the love seat and the black octagonal table. A bottle of brandy rested on it, and a half-filled glass, which Mme Chin's hand with its long, insidious nails and bedizened fingers delicately nursed, circling the rim, plinking it with an absent fillip.

"Come in," she invited from her invisible coign of vantage.

I had to make a special effort to control my face.

The dowager was sitting half-dressed on the love seat, the priceless silk *p'ao* of Hsu Tzi's maid-in-waiting — the sad-eyed phoenix — loosely draped over her bare shoulders, a dingy yellow slip beneath, machine embroidered over the breast panel, a nondescript floral pattern which bore a disconcerting resemblance to worms rioting uproariously in the rib cage of a decomposing corpse. Her chignon was partially unpinned at the back of her head and hung on one side in a brittle, untidy festoon. Her lipstick was smeared, and her eyes were glazed and narrowed. They seemed like two flushed toilets slowly filling, not with water, but with rheum. Within the slits the two sparks glowed like feverish matches.

"Don't gape," she chided in a contemptuous tone, both mildly offended and amused. "I saw a peasant once with just such a face climbing off a manure cart in Shanghai."

Fan-ku guffawed coarsely.

"Shut up," she told him. "Come here."

He crossed to her.

"Lean down." Taking a handkerchief, she twisted it and placed it in her mouth, letting it soak in her saliva. Then she brusquely wiped the lipstick from his cheek. "Now get out. And close the drape!"

"So," she said, taking in the package in my hand, then sizing me up in impertinent appraisal, nodding her head slowly, cynically. "I told you, didn't I?" Gloatingly she poured herself a shot and tossed it off, closing her eyes and shivering almost imperceptibly. "Everything has its season and its price."

I regarded her in silent reproach, inviting her scorn, having no weapons to defend myself.

"Let me see it."

I placed the package on the table and she unwrapped it, held it up. The evil, bilious fluid drained out of her eyes, and she became solemn, almost stately. "Yes," she sighed, "it is beautiful. I will give you a fair price."

"I don't want to sell it, Mme Chin."

She glanced at me unguardedly, betraying surprise and disappointment.

"I only want to borrow, using the robe as collateral."

"You mean *pawn* it," she snorted, adding snidely, "you're learning a lot of fancy jargon from your friends downtown."

" 'Pawn' then," I conceded, "if you prefer."

She poured herself another drink and brooded into the glass. "I don't like it. You insulted me before, implying my dishonesty. Why trust me now?"

"It wasn't that I mistrusted . . ."

"Never mind," she interrupted. "I'll tell you why. You're hard up for cash."

"Yes," I admitted, "I need the money."

She cackled gloatingly. "The tables have been turned, haven't they, Sun I? Now you come to me. But tell me this: why should I help you?"

"I'm not asking you to help me, Mme Chin. I'm making you a business proposition. I'm offering to pay."

" 'Pay,' " she scoffed. "What good is that to me? I don't need your petty cash, Sun I. I'm rich — a dowager. What I want is this." She pointed with her chin.

"Besides," she went on, allowing me no chance to demur or retreat, "pawning is too messy. I rarely do it anymore. People used to come to me all the time with their precious 'heirlooms,' some bit of jade or scrap of silk. I gave them cash at interest. My rates were steep, I don't mind telling you. I never did lend by the book. But why should I? It was a personal favor. And I set dates. No equity of redemption here. Patience has limits, Sun I. I'm an old woman, I can't wait forever. It was all up front though. Nothing underhanded. A 'business proposition' all the way, as you so charmingly put it. And they agreed. So then on the last day a woman comes to me weeping and wringing her hands, begs me on her knees to give her more time 'for the sake of her family.' 'How can I face my daughter if I sell away her bridal portion?' she asks. How should I know? I ask you, Sun I, what is that to me, eh? Business is business. A deal is a deal. *Sss,*" she hissed disgustedly. "I put up with it when the money mattered. But now why should I? I don't need the aggravation." She eyed me shrewdly to measure the effect of her delivery. "I'll tell you what though," she said, "despite the insult, I still like you. Perhaps I could make an exception in your case." She smiled fulsomely. "Here's my proposition. I'm willing to lend you money, a generous sum. Only you must make it worth my while."

"How so?" I asked.

"You must allow me at least a sporting chance of getting what I want. We'll set a deadline."

"How long?"

She shrugged. "Say, two months, ten weeks?"

I calculated quickly. "A month" — Kahn had said a month, hadn't he? "All right," I agreed, allowing myself the widest leeway possible, "ten weeks. Only . . . at what rate of interest?"

"Oh, the usual."

"Which is?"

"Ten percent."

"Ten percent per annum or quarterly," I asked, attempting to be shrewd. She laughed. "Why, ten percent a week, my pet."

"Ten percent a week!" I protested. "That's outrageous!"

She shrugged and frowned. "Standard terms. If you don't like them, try elsewhere. Take it to the Jews and see what they'll give you for it." She snickered. "This is a specialty item, not everybody can appreciate it. Besides, I'm offering you real money."

"How much?"

"Say, five hundred?"

"Five hundred! It's worth thousands."

"Umm . . . one, perhaps," she conceded grudgingly. "Remember, it's to your advantage not to be too greedy. The more I lend you, the higher your payments."

"Make it one and a half."

"All right, give me until next week."

"I need the money now."

"What do you think I am, the bank?" she retorted querulously. "I couldn't possibly, not on such short notice. I don't keep that kind of money here."

"All right," I relented in exasperation. "A thousand."

"Done!" she cried, rubbing her hands together in a miserly fashion, like a fly. "Ten percent a week for ten weeks to be paid on Fridays with your rent."

"Couldn't we make it one lump sum payable with the return of the principal?"

She frowned. "You are in no position to dictate terms."

I swallowed hard. "Otherwise no deal."

She glared at me penetratingly, then unexpectedly laughed. "So, you have a little spunk in you after all. I'm delighted to see it. I was beginning to wonder." Abruptly she frowned again, adding admonitorily, "You are hard; I will be too. If you go past your date . . ."

I shook my head. "I won't."

"But if you do," she persisted, "you must promise me there'll be no whimpering and sniveling."

I nodded.

"Then we're agreed."

"Agreed." (A most damnable, pernicious greed!)

"Wait here, I'll go and get it. Fan-ku!" she called, fishing out her keys, which she kept warmed next to her heart.

He appeared at the threshold.

"Keep Sun I company while I'm gone." She gave him a meaningful stare.

He sat down on the ottoman and challenged me with glazed, sullen defiance. I smiled politely, which succeeded only in evoking a blacker look. Blushing, embarrassed, I looked down at the floor.

After a few minutes it occurred to me that my friend and fellow sufferer, the young pup, was nowhere in evidence, his vitality and, albeit embattled, good cheer conspicuously absent in the dreary, sinister surroundings. "Fan-ku," I ventured, hoping thereby to break the ice with my mute interlocutor, "where is the dog?"

He opened his eyes wide returning my stare, evidently a little surprised at my temerity in addressing him. "The dog?" His features registered a blank look, which presently brightened with remembrance. "Oh, you mean the white one with the ears?" He raised his hands and hung them limp-wristed on either side of his face, sketching ears with brief pantomimic expertise.

"Yes," I replied with an appreciative laugh, "him."

"He's gone," he informed me with clipped finality, relapsing into his former inaccessibility.

"Gone?" I asked. "Gone where?"

He said nothing, avoiding my eyes. Then a happy inspiration seemed to strike him. He chuckled to himself. "To a better home," he said.

"A better home?"

He laughed outright. "Don't worry. We already have a replacement. Shall I show you?" He rose and started for the door, pausing at the threshold. "Don't touch anything," he directed, giving me a suspicious look.

When he returned, he was cradling a trembling, mouselike creature with thick black downy fur and a face composed of tweaks of ears, a pointed nose, and two immense, sad eyes, which stared about in timorous appeal.

Fan-ku petted the dog, eyeing me with incomprehensible brazenness, smiling with his teeth. "Well?" he inquired. "What do you think?"

"It's very nice," I said.

"Yes, it is, isn't it?" he agreed. "Much nicer than the other one."

Choked with loyalty, I stubbornly withheld assent.

"Quite intelligent too," he added.

I regarded the shivering lump of fuzz with a mixture of pity and skepticism.

"It can do tricks," he informed me.

"Tricks? What kind of tricks?"

He shrugged and pouted. "Oh, fortune-telling for instance."

I gave him a frankly derisory look.

"You don't believe me?"

Just then Mme Chin reappeared from the far room.

"Aiyi," he appealed to her playfully, "the priest doesn't believe our dogs tell fortunes."

She smiled at him drily, narrowing her eyes, then turned to me. "It's true, Sun I, though they are generally only good for one performance."

Fan-ku guffawed again, and she dismissed him with a toss of her head and a vicious scowl.

"So, my dear," she said officiously, "here it is." She handed me a brown paper bag folded small and wrapped with a red rubber band. "More money than you've ever seen at once, no doubt, perhaps more than you'll ever see again."

I examined it vacantly, aware at some subliminal level of the great disparity between the numbness it evoked and the deep emotion I had felt that other day fondling the wrapping of my mother's robe, listening to the crepitation of the paper in my hands, inhaling its sad, equivocal perfume — a disparity rendered more poignant by the fact that in some sense, in the currency of the real world, at least, this purported to be its equivalent, or "something just as good." I wondered would it prove so.

"Aren't you going to count it?" she inquired.

"What?" I asked absently. I hesitated, then demurred. "I trust you, Mme Chin."

She gave an incredulous snort. "You're a strange boy, Sun I," she said, "dreamy and unworldly. You've wandered here like a somnambulist. Let me give you some advice. You'd better wake up now. This is a world apart from your precious monastery in the mountains of Szechwan. You've been all right so far, but you've had nothing either. You were lean. Now you've added flesh. Not much perhaps, but enough. The wolves will smell it out and stalk you. Beware. You'd better come to quick, or else you're going to make someone a meal."

"Thanks for the advice," I replied sullenly, turning to go.

"Wait."

Looking back, I saw that she was holding something out to me, a slip of paper.

"What's this?" I asked.

"It's your receipt."

•

Immediately on returning to my apartment I fell prey to second thoughts, chafing and writhing internally at the thought of what I'd done. Hot bursts of physical shame throbbed through me with the regularity of a pulse. Unable to bear myself in solitude, I set out for the Ha-p'is', resolving to confess my error to Yin-mi, prepared to accept her censure — needing it perhaps — but secretly hoping to find absolution in her eyes as well.

In retrospect, what happened seems uncanny in its rightness, or wrongness — even now I'm not sure which — like a conclusion following with remorseless logic from the premise of my act. She wasn't there. In fact, no one answered. The door, however, which had been incompletely shut, clicked open at my knock, and I caught the sound of someone speaking, a voice I didn't recognize at once but knew I'd heard before. Checking the number to make sure I hadn't mistaken the apartment, I cautiously inched open the door and peered around. There was no one in the kitchen. At the far end of the hall, however, I saw a young woman standing in diminished profile, cradling the phone between her cheek and shoulder, speaking in a soft, low voice. As she leaned her head, her glossy hair fell in a rich, dark torrent almost to her waist. Li.

My pulse quickened unaccountably.

She had laid her left forearm across her belly, propping her opposite elbow in the palm, casually winding and unwinding a chain of hammered gold as fine as cobweb around her lifted index finger as she spoke.

Watching her there from ambush (which I intended moment by moment to give up, but didn't), I felt a thrill of illicit titillation, a surge of adrenaline, a shortness of breath.

"I'm not judging you," she said. "Just because I accept it theoretically doesn't mean I have to share my bed with it, does it? What? 'Ethnocentric'?" She laughed. "That's very witty, Peter. I think your charm increases in proportion to the indefensibleness of your positions. That's why you're so dangerous. 'Irresistible'? Don't flatter yourself — it only aggravates the insult. And that's something you definitely can't afford. A threat? If you like. What? Damn you, Peter! Don't do this to me again." She placed the receiver hard on the hook and stared straight ahead. "Bastard!" she breathed suddenly in a piercing, icy whisper. Then she crumpled at the waist, leaning forward like an unstrung marionette, hugging her elbows with her hands as though in pain. When she turned around, tears of exasperation welled in the corners of her eyes which were still pressed tightly shut. That look of unrehearsed agony made my heart rise to my mouth.

I had almost forgotten how beautiful she was: the high cheekbones, the lustrous torrent of her hair, her straight white teeth, most of all her twilit eyes, honey colored like the bear's and, like his, molten now with passion. I felt almost traitorous to acknowledge it, but she was unarguably more beautiful than Yin-mi, her beauty, too, somehow less regrettable, an effect of ripeness, perhaps. I only know the sight of her breasts swaying unconstrained beneath the silk affected me strangely (so unlike Yin-mi's, whose fragility and girlish smallness shamed the appetite as unopened buds shame the picker's hand). A tremor of anguished physical excitement such as I had never known trembled through my body, a geyser of repressed sexuality spouting through the crust of my chaste life. I still recall it vividly, that breathlessness, that slight weakness at the knees, the first and purest keening of Eros in the blood, a sensation I vehemently abjured, but out of purely intellectual conviction, without the tincture of visceral remorse I had experienced on recognizing my desire for Yin-mi.

Catching sight of me, she betrayed neither surprise nor chagrin. She appraised me with clinical interest, then suddenly, to my profound amazement, smiled — no more than a tiny up-curve at the corners of her lips, a smile in which I intuited, in place of what was missing there and might have been expected, a hint of subdued provocation. I was astounded at the swift transition from distress to mastery. It was almost sinister.

After regarding me thus for several moments, she turned and walked into the living room. The cool brazenness of this desertion (which I could not resent, being the intruder), her utter lack of curiosity as to what I wanted there, shocked me with the force of a physical blow. At the same time I was piqued.

Again that delicious, anguishing, somatic thrill pulsed through me. I followed her instinctively without even pausing to consider.

She was standing before the window where I had stood observing the fire escapes the night the lights went out. As before, she held her right elbow in her left palm, twisting and untwisting the chain. For a long while she was silent. I wasn't sure she was aware of my presence. Then she spoke.

"Are you in love with her?" she asked.

The blood rushed violently to my face, but she didn't even turn around to witness my discomfiture.

"With whom?" I asked, forcing myself to reply with disingenuous circumspectness.

She darted me a look and smiled reproachfully. "With my little sister, of course. Isn't that whom you've come to fetch?"

"We're friends."

"That isn't what I asked."

"I care for her," I conceded.

"But do you love her?"

"I am a priest," I said. "I am constrained by certain vows . . ." I caught myself up in mid-sentence. Remembering where I'd just been and what I'd done, I experienced a momentary emptiness, then an upwelling of chagrin so powerful it almost made me sob.

She regarded me quizzically, a trace of vague amusement in her expression. "Vows? Are they effective?" She laughed. "Perhaps that's what I ought to try." She came away from the window, taking the seat beside me on the sofa and turning the full force of her attention on me for the first time. "I've been meaning to look you up. I think you've been avoiding me." Her eyes sparkled with a hint of mischief.

"Avoiding you?" I gasped, drawing backward, dazzled by her nearness, this swift assumption of intimacy after previous reserve. It flattered and unnerved me.

"Yes," she replied, "didn't we agree to get together for a chat before?" Her eyes drifted from my face; her smile became a little brighter. "Peter almost called you himself, but I forbade him. He thought you were terribly attractive, in an exotic sort of way. He likes the Oriental mystique." She appraised my features. "But your eyes aren't Chinese. . . . He's right though, you aren't bad-looking."

This pronouncement thrilled and terrified me, particularly since she uttered it with such clinical casualness, as she might pass judgment on a laboratory animal whose exertions and sufferings in her behalf she found pitiable, yet outside the pale of her legitimate sympathies. This attitude communicated itself to me off the edge of her voice, the merest inflection, and I might easily have been mistaken. Yet in that instant I felt again a tremor of poignant desperation as the panorama of an immeasurable, an almost cosmic distance opened up between us, wounded by the remoteness of one who had no reason to be otherwise, as I had none to care.

"I'm interested in learning about your life," she said.

"My life?" I searched back to our previous conversation. "For your studies in ethno- . . . What is it again?"

"Ethnology," she supplied. "You know what that is?"

"Not really."

"It's the study of primitive peoples and cultures," she explained. "Vanishing or vanished systems and values, dead languages, lost religions" (her eyes glinted with surgical precision) "like yours."

"My religion isn't lost," I contradicted her fiercely.

She smiled more softly. "Not to you. That's why I'm interested."

"Do you intend to study me?" I inquired with a nervous laugh.

She smiled and said nothing.

"Why do such things interest you?" I pursued.

She shrugged. "Why not? Who knows what secrets they may contain? A fragment of semantic possibility trapped in the grammar of a dead language like a shining bubble in the ice. Tap your pick into it and it explodes, filling the air with fragrance, a whiff of what the world was like a thousand, or a hundred thousand years ago, when it was new."

"Such discoveries must be very rare."

"Very," she agreed. "But my time is not so precious." Her expression grew a little wistful, I thought.

"You must be very dedicated," I observed.

She shrugged. "Or very bored. Perhaps I merely require very recondite forms of stimulation." The wistfulness became more pronounced as she said this, but she continued smiling with that same hint of remote amusement, as though daring me to attempt an assessment of her exact degree of insincerity.

"It wasn't very gallant of you to eavesdrop on my conversation," she chided almost playfully, changing the subject. "How much did you overhear?"

"Very little," I assured her.

"I don't suppose you would have understood it anyway," she said, frowning and allowing her eyes to drift. I felt a stab, but realized she inflicted it unconsciously. "Or did you?" she challenged, rounding the circumference and coming at me from the opposite direction.

I shook my head.

"Are you interested?" she asked with sudden mischievous inspiration.

I blushed.

"It was Peter — I suppose you gathered that. You've probably gathered, too, that we're lovers . . . sometimes. I was supposed to meet him here tonight. We were going to a play in the Village. I called him up a few minutes ago to see if he'd left his apartment, only to find he wasn't coming, or rather, was. But not with me. Something had come up, he said. And I knew what. *Bastard.* Something between his legs. One of his little friends from Yale arrived in town at the last minute, and he stood me up."

Remembering the flash of pain I'd seen before, I dared a glance at her. "I'm sorry."

"Why should you be? Besides, you don't know the whole story." She regarded me with a curious expression. "It's a man."

"His friend?"

She nodded, smiling mirthlessly. "That's right. Peter's bi. Know what that means? He does it with little boys as well as little girls. Pretty, isn't it?" She challenged me for a response. "Well? You might at least be shocked. I'm disappointed. Are such things so common among Taoist orders that it doesn't even get a rise?"

"I don't know what to say."

She was silent, a look of exasperation in her eyes which threatened to condemn me too in some wholesale, systematic pogrom whose principle I didn't understand.

"He must be a fool," I ventured with a trembling voice.

Tilting her head, she regarded me in quizzical appraisal. "Why?"

I swallowed and plunged blindly. "To risk displeasing you."

"Am I so special?" she fished with a hint of revived coyness.

"You're beautiful," I said with a serious face, striving to be scrupulously honest, though dispassionate.

Missing the innuendo, she flushed and opened her eyes wide. "Do you think so?"

Feeling the blood burn in my face, I looked away.

She brushed my hand lightly, a spark of magical sexual electricity leaping the poles between us, chilling and burning in that place. Involuntarily I shivered.

"I don't know what to do." She resumed her complaint in a softer, remoter tone. "I can't be sexually jealous of another man. That would be penis envy in the extreme." She rose from her chair and walked back toward the window, phasing me out as suddenly as she had tuned me in. "But how can I help it? He makes me feel like some bloody-minded Freudian Fury bent on castrating him, amputating half of his sensual nature. It's unreasonable to be jealous, he says, since his affairs are no threat to me. And it's true, he's monogamous — except with other men. I don't want to play the part of the sex police, or censor his libidinal palette. But I can't just accept it either. One half of his entire life from which I'm to be denied all access forever and ever, a gigantic lacuna into which he disappears for days at a time, where I can't follow, and he won't take me. The dark side of the moon. Sometimes I feel I hardly know him."

"But . . ."

"But what?" she demanded, darting me a quick, dangerous glance, as though remembering my presence under compulsion. "Why continue to see him?" She paused to read the accuracy of her guess from my expression. Seeing a confession in my eyes, she smiled and receded to a great distance. "You take vows," she said cruelly. "You wouldn't understand."

"Maybe I would," I rejoined, unable to suppress the wounded quaver in my voice.

She challenged me silently, as though to test my sincerity. "All right," she relented. "I love the ambiguity in him. It attracts me, even as it repels. Because it comes from such a depth of self-assurance. I've never seen anyone who had it in such a degree. He's the only man I've ever known who had a secret he wouldn't give away even for love. There's a marvelous integrity in that, if you can see it, something very beautiful and pure. Most men are wild to give themselves away. They're looking for a master in a woman, someone to absolve their sins." (I flashed to my reason for seeking out Yin-mi.) "Peter cherishes his. It's not a dogma with him either, but something totally innocent and unconscious, a kind of magnificent animal freedom. He refuses to obey the law — my law, any law. He's the freest person I've ever met because he has the strength to accept the pain of his own doubleness, without murdering either half for the sake of a false peace."

"You care for him a great deal," I said, with anguish.

A pained tenderness appeared in her face, and she smiled with vague weariness and gratitude. "Maybe I was wrong," she conceded. "Maybe you can — understand, I mean. Maybe you do."

Sitting down, she laid her hand on mine again, not taking it away this time. A shadow of the original desolation crossed her features. "I'm sad tonight, Sun I. I don't want to be alone. Come with me to the play."

•

The production, in a dingy experimental theater somewhere in the Village, went by me in a blur of sound and color. I sat dumbly, trying to fathom my mood and emotions, staring from time to time at the woman beside me, wondering who she was and what strange gravity of fate had drawn us into the same orbit for a night, and where it might finally lead. Puzzled and amazed, I watched the incorporeal shimmer of thought and emotion animate her features as the play swept her along on its momentum, or alternately left her stranded on some barren spur of disappointed expectation. When I looked away, her reality, so vivid while I gazed directly, became equivocal. Again and again I returned, refreshing assurance at the feast of vision. I had no idea who she was and didn't care. The charmed circle of the theater spread beyond the stage and enveloped us, as in a warm sac of amniotic unreality. I seemed to breathe a viscous atmosphere of dreams, a twilight world beneath the sea, filled with the stardust glitter of refracted sunlight sparkling through the infinitesimal prisms of suspended salts. I surrendered completely to a sense of drift and wonder. The past lapsed into insignificance. It was as if I had opened a door inside myself and walked into a different universe, or the same one seen with different eyes, eyes sensitive to a different wavelength, some rarer light outside the visible spectrum, which transformed all the old objects and revealed many new ones theretofore undreamt. No compulsion moved me to evaluate the ethical timbre or validity of my mood and inclinations. I felt bewitched or drugged, as though in an opium dream, but it was anodyne to my conscience, raw and tender after my experience at Mme Chin's, blessedly, blessedly painless. That twilight in her eyes portended a twilight in her life — a moral twilight. With her there was only the immediate, a sensual tingling like the sudden flow of blood back into a sleeping limb, or a brief vertigo, breathless, alarming, but not entirely unpleasant; and that undercurrent of despair, despair of ever touching her deep life. Yet even this had a sensuous magic, its poignance rendered sweeter by virtue of its very hopelessness.

I don't know what was happening to me (had happened rather, for even so early it presented itself as accomplished fact, something past and irrevocable), but from the instant the door parted and I saw her, I no longer felt I knew myself or what I was capable of. More important, perhaps, I no longer felt I knew what I wasn't capable of. It was as though some essential integument of my personality had been ruptured and a rich, ambiguous ooze of unsuspected darkness had started to seep forth. I've often wondered how large a part circumstance — my recent return from Mme Chin's — played in my peculiar and doubtless inordinate reaction. Was our meeting at that particular moment coincidental, or was it an effect of destiny, an exaction of that deepest psychological law which ordains that everything we fail to reconcile within ourselves, to do, or to suffer down to its furthest, most exquisite implication must enact itself externally as fate? Did she appear as a consequence of my apostasy, or was my peculiar receptivity to her such a consequence? I still don't know the answers to these questions. Thinking back on it, I feel a shudder of the original terror and exhilaration, everything else suddenly eclipsed. The mooring line of my deepest certainty snapped, I floated into an unknown sea, stretching from horizon to horizon, making me half believe my previous life on shore had been the dream, that there was no shore, no solid land at all, only the sea, this vast, inclusive sea of her.

This was all the more odd in light of what had occurred at Coney Island, that spontaneous remission of my ravaged faith and reconsecration to the original goals of my pilgrimage, the search for the delta, the Tao within the Dow. The pawning of the robe hadn't seemed to compromise that faith; in fact, what other means had I for keeping it intact? Yet it was an ambiguous bargain at best. No rationalization could plausibly explain away the deed as moral. At best it was expedient, a concession to necessity. Yet any hope of salvaging my quest was linked with just such an ambiguous bargain. Chung Fu's image of the lotus growing from the mud returned to me, and for the first time perhaps I truly understood the meaning of the paradox: "To remain whole, be twisted" — for the first time too felt the dark joy of the swimmer, at peril, but brave and confident, hopelessly adrift in life.

•

Of the play, *The Winter's Tale,* I remember almost nothing: a young girl picking flowers, a statue come to life. The language was too dense and convoluted, my distraction too complete. Only one scene absorbed me wholly, and that not so much because of any inherent interest in the staging, but because of private associations it evoked. A man descended from shipboard, as I myself had not so long ago descended, with a swaddled child in his arms, wandering across what appeared to be a desert. Looking about furtively as though in distress or chafing with a guilty conscience, he placed the child on the ground with a show of great reluctance, sighing and making the sign of the cross first over it, then over himself. The child set up a howl. As he made his way off, he kept turning to look back over his shoulder, wrenched by its piteous cries. Paying scant attention to where he was going, he didn't see what the audience did — a large bear which had wandered up and stood observing his approach. As the man drew near, it lumbered heavily erect on its hind legs, and he stumbled backward straight into its arms. Eyes big with surprise, he gingerly felt behind him, pinching the animal's nose unwittingly. It emitted a low, testy growl. He wheeled to face it where it towered above him. It returned his glance. Breaking the dramatic illusion, he coyly winked at the audience, which to my confusion burst out laughing. (I was in a state of nervous terror.) Then, attempting to brazen it out, he led the bear a few measures of a waltz. In the process, he stepped on its toe, and it let out a deafening roar, fell to all fours, and chased him off stage. A bloodcurdling scream signified the upshot of their encounter.

All this, of course, suggested my own encounter with the giant panda at dawn after that fateful afternoon and evening on the Gold Sand River, only enriching (or confusing) the association by linkage with a constellation of images from a more recent past — that of the strong man and the little boy from the *I Ching*. In spite of the literal meaning of the play, which was largely opaque to me, at the level of personal symbolism I saw the strong man carrying the child of his own innocence across the desert of the world, and, after great anguish, renouncing it, leaving it to its fate amidst the elements. In this scenario, which I projected out of naiveté and inner need, the appearance of the bear was a direct consequence of the man's apostasy, his suffering a clear and unambiguous effect of cosmic justice. Was it merely ignorance, or an effect of incipient imbalance, that I should find this pantomime of my own psychic life enacted in the external world? However it was, for me it seemed an omen. Identifying myself with the character I later learned to call Antigonus and the pawning of the robe as the betrayal of the child within myself, I wondered should the rest hold true, and I be slated for a reencounter with the bear, only with a different upshot — not a giant panda, this time, with an ethereal taste for rare wildflowers, but an American grizzly with a taste for blood.

Chapter 2

The air was cool and heavy when we emerged from the theater. Though it was long past dark, a white cloud overhead shimmered with a pale luminescence, reflecting back the city's light. The sky around it held a tint of blue, like afternoon detained beyond its hour and perhaps against its will.

"It's beautiful tonight," Li said, stretching out her arms. She took a deep lungful of air, then walked in a slow circle. "There won't be many more like this." Halting, she turned to me as though deliberating. "How would you like to go on an expedition?"

"An expedition?"

"Sure," she replied. "A sort of ethnological field trip." She smiled to herself.

"Where to?"

"The Upper West Side, where else? It's Friday night. The streets should be delirious. And I'm peculiarly well suited as a cicerone, since it's my own neighborhood."

The play seemed to have lifted her spirits. Charmed by her sudden expansiveness, I readily assented.

"We'll take the train," she directed. "How much money do you have?"

My spoils were at home beneath the mattress, so my best efforts produced only two crumpled bills and odd change.

"Tsch, tsch," she clucked in playful disapproval. "Poor boy, haven't you learned yet? Good looks aren't everything. Or are you simply inexperienced with girls? In any case, you'll find I'm not as easy to afford as my little sister." She laughed. (Her admonition, however, though obviously in play, betrayed a hint of underlying seriousness.) "Tonight it doesn't matter though. In keeping with the spirit of the time, we'll pretend it's Saturnalia, everything turned upside down — boy bishops paddling the bottoms of their bald-pated elders . . ." (her eyes wandered briefly from my own, growing cold) "and exchanging fond caresses with acolytes of the same sex; ladies of the court paying heavy premiums for the privilege of seducing beggars." Her eyes returned to mine, which must have betrayed a hint of mortification, inferring a personal implication from the latter example as she had doubtless exhumed one unintentionally in the former. "No, Sun I," she assured me, shaking her head and threading her arm through mine. "I don't mean you and me. Just a figure of speech." We began to walk.

Suddenly she caught us up again, spinning me toward her. "At twelve o'clock, though, it all ends — I give you fair warning." Her tone was ambiguous, arch as though in play, but again suggesting an earnestness masked by jest. "I become an ugly witch, and you must drive back to the bottom of your well. The spell is broken, and I revert to the real prince, the fairy prince." She smiled unhappily. "And it can never be cast again. You have to understand that. Do you?"

I nodded.

She regarded me doubtfully. "I'm not sure you do," she said, "not sure you can." She continued to probe me with her honey-colored eyes, then sighed and looked away. "But it doesn't matter. Come on, I think I hear a train."

•

The Upper West Side. Apparently Kahn and I hadn't spent long enough, or been far enough uptown, really to get a sense of it. Li was a better guide. As we emerged from the Seventh Avenue express at Broadway and Ninety-sixth, loud Latin dance music met our ears, blaring away from the Casino Havana, where dark forms drifted past an upstairs window, cheek to cheek, briefly illuminated by lurid flashes from the red neon rainbow arches that glared down on the streets. Immediately below at street level was a store window sporting religious statuary, painted porcelain saints with immaculate Castilian features, skins as pale as cloud, eyes uplifted piously toward heaven, though with a hint of proud disdain. One of these lowered threateningly, his brow contracted in a fit of stern didactic rage. As in the stained glass rendering of Christ at Trinity, his arm was crooked at the elbow, finger pointing at the sky. Over this uplifted arm, however, someone had draped a pair of castanets, which dangled from the cord with a mute irony, smug and unconscious as a mussel. A bearded black man, unseasonably dressed in an overcoat a size too large, lounged against the iron railing of the station, taking violent swigs from a pint-sized paper bag, scowling and spitting at the feet of passersby. A young Chicano with a jaunty walk and stylish clothes, but dark rings underneath his eyes, jostled me — accidentally I supposed, until he whispered, coughing in his hand to avoid my eyes, "Smoke, smoke, co-KA-een." Getting no response, he wheeled and disappeared into the crowd.

These first few encounters set the tone of the whole walk. For there was something flitting, insubstantial in all the forms we saw. Passing a pizzeria, I noted a young black dangling two wristwatches over the greasy counter, offering both for a slice, while the proprietor, standing in the street-front window, not even looking, dispassionately ladled a thin red sauce in an expand-

ing spiral, clockwise, over the pale round of dough. His arms, thickly furred
with black hair, like an animal's, were dusted to the shirt-sleeves with a film
of flour, looking bluish, vaguely dead. Shaking his head grimly, turning down
the proposition, he seemed like some Rhadamanthus in the underworld, denying an appeal for grace. Outside a package store a huge black man shook his
fists and bellowed at the sky in inarticulate rage like a baited bear, while wary
Anglos with scoured, frightened faces flitted by like well-groomed wraiths.
And hovering above it all, charming at first, but soon growing stale through
repetition, finally maddening, like a form of psychological torture, the angelus
of the ice-cream truck — " 'Rico Freeze" — droning "Jack and Jill" intermi-
nably, like a stuck recording, sending them uphill on a treadmill, and then
tumbling down again over and over.

"It's always Mardi Gras up here," Li said, smiling to herself as though what
she really saw was some long vista in her heart, "and tomorrow's always Lent.
Lent too at extortionate rates." She glanced at me briefly and dispassionately,
as though to determine whether her epigram had fallen on barren ground or
fertile, not much caring either way perhaps. Taking a deep breath of the rich,
rank air, she slowly turned her head from side to side. "Salo," she said. "A
thousand days of Sodom." And not even knowing what she meant, I could see
the entrapment and despair in her, the protest, the riddled courage, the resignation uncongealed, some failed, exquisite thing. "I won't stay here forever,"
she whispered almost fiercely, like a promise to herself. Then she smiled at me.
In her eyes I saw a hint of the same grievance I had seen in Yin-mi's eyes that
night after our wild chase through the rain when she excoriated me so severely,
only more highly wrought in Li.

"Come on," she urged. "I've changed my mind. This is too depressing. I
don't want to walk. Let's go home."

Entering the recessed courtyard of her building, a cacophony of dissonant
music met our ears: violinists doing scales, saxophonists playing riffs, a soprano keening from an upstairs window, clinging like an angry cat to upper
ledges of the register where she was never meant to tread.

"The music of the spheres," Li glossed, "and squares, and queers, cheerlead-
ers, jeerers — a choir of self-abusing Muses — Jews and Druids, Rosicrucians
— cosmic disharmony made manifest, a symphony of virtuosos with no conductor. Welcome to the Upper West Side, Purgatorio of the Performing Arts.

"Buenos noches, Ramon," she greeted the doorman, who was speaking on
the pay phone in the lobby in vehement Spanish, running a comb through his
slicked-back hair, patting the sides delicately with the heel of his palm. Placing
the comb over the mouthpiece, he smiled dyspeptically in acknowledgment.
"I didn't see your motorcycle outside," she remarked. "What are you doing
here tonight?"

Ramon grinned and shrugged, then went back to his conversation.

"He usually works the day shift," she explained as we approached the
elevator. "Ramon has a Harley Twelve-fifty which he parks in the courtyard.

Every day at approximately three-thirty his unemployed friends and cronies assemble for the big event, when he goes out and kicks it over, revving it for the final thirty minutes before he goes off duty 'to clean de carbón out de engéen' as he says, then zooming off for parts unknown."

"You don't seem particularly happy here," I observed.

Her laugh was practically a guffaw. "How could you tell?"

"If you dislike it so much, why do you stay?"

"Poor boy," she said. "How little you understand."

"You keep saying that. Why don't you give me a chance?"

She shrugged. "What choices do I have? The Lower East Side? Chinatown? As far as I'm concerned those aren't choices at all. I'll never go back to Mulberry Street, you can be sure of that. I'd rather die — or move to Kansas. Preferably die."

"Kansas?"

"Short for the real world," she explained. "New York is Emerald City. Or haven't you heard?" She paused and began again on a new track. "You're wrong about one thing though. Just because I complain doesn't necessarily mean I don't like it here. I guess you haven't been in New York long enough to realize that. New Yorkers like to revel in their degradation. It's a kind of communal ritual made sacred through long observance, like certain primitive tribes who are careful never to show too much satisfaction over what they accomplish or acquire, fearing to excite the envy of the gods. It has ethnic variations — Jewish and Italian, Chinese, Pakistani — ritual formulas and flourishes, like cursing, an art absorbed by osmosis from one's environment, but requiring passion and imagination, too, rewarding the skillful practitioner with heap big wampumpeag. An ethnological field trip I said, remember? Me sabee?" She smiled, stopping before a door and taking out her key. "But come inside," she invited. "Chop-chop. I promise I'll stop bitching and be nice, at least till twelve o'clock."

•

Something thumped in the dark as she opened the door. She switched on the light in the kitchen, and we found ourselves confronting a deranged-looking cat, which stood on the kitchen table glaring at us with wild, glassy eyes, the gray, tattered fur upright along its arched back and neck. Hissing and spitting as though tensed to spring, it suddenly rethought its position and leapt sideways into the next room with paws extended fore and aft as though flying into total void.

"What was that?" I asked, relaxing from my crucified position against the wall.

"That?" Li casually rejoined. "Oh, that was only Jo. Don't pay any attention. She's a little batty."

"I'll say," I inaudibly corroborated, taking a deep breath as my pulse returned to normal.

"How about a glass of wine?" she offered, opening the refrigerator. "Or is that against your vows?"

"Another connoisseur!" I teased her mildly. "Only if you release me from the obligation to discuss the vintage. Your father has already humiliated me more than once."

"It's Gallo," she said, smiling drily, "and you're released on the condition that you refrain from further gallows humor. Go on in, I'll bring it to you."

The main room of her apartment was very simple, very spare, giving the impression of a Japanese rock garden. The hardwood floors were varnished and polished to a high luster, and a black enamel study lamp on a drafting table cast its pale reflection in the maple, like a hazy sun reflected in a blond, wooden sea. Various plants were placed around: an asparagus fern in a hanging pot, trailing its tendrils almost to the floor, a huge elephant-ear philodendron in a brown crockery urn with sleek gold dragons baked into the glaze. There wasn't really much to see. The room was strangely contentless, especially for a Chinese. Yet it seemed neither vague, unfinished, nor impersonal, radiating rather a vivid sense of presence, only presence expressed through nullity and sheen, an impalpable luster, precise and highly wrought, like everything about her. This extreme simplicity, and the brilliance of the floors and their nakedness, which made each step resound, lent it a benign crystal clarity, like an autumn day bottled up and brought inside, its mildness disguising the first chill of winter.

There was a faint music playing somewhere, a plaintive, desultory strain, immediately distinguishable from the cacophony we'd heard without, though, like it, apparently aimless. Yet this was a different sort of aimlessness, soothing, comfortable with its own disorder, not striving for meaning.

"Do you like that?" Li asked, as she entered and handed me a glass.

"What is it?"

"An aeolian harp."

"A what?"

"A wind harp. Come look." Sipping from her glass, she put it down and cranked the window outward. The sound grew louder.

"Aeolus was the god of the winds in Greek mythology."

Coming up beside her, I could see a peculiar instrument fitted on the ledge, a wooden box with strings stretched across its open ends.

" 'And that simplest Lute,' " she said, placing her hand lightly on my forearm for attention, her gaze abstracted slightly as though focused on an inner page:

> "Placed length-wise in the clasping casement, hark!
> How by the desultory breeze caress'd,
> Like some coy maid half yielding to her lover,
> It pours such sweet upbraiding, as must needs
> Tempt to repeat the wrong!"

She laughed and relaxed. "Peter gave it to me. He said it reminded him of me."

"In what way?" I asked. "Because it's coy?"

Her eyes became opaque and vaguely distant. "No," she replied. "Because it's soulless."

She then turned abruptly and started for the kitchen. "I'm going to start cooking," she informed me without looking back. "You can entertain yourself, can't you? Get drunk or invade my privacy or something? Only don't go into my bedroom if you don't mind. I haven't had a chance to get in there and it's a mess."

A second perusal revealed something I hadn't seen before. In front of the window on a block of black, varnished wood which served as a pedestal stood an ivory figurine six inches high, unmistakably female, though, oddly, facing not in toward the room as for display, but away, as though peering through the window into the dark. Her figure was an attenuated backward *S,* the hip thrust out on her left side, her upper body lithely resting in a languorous concave arc. One long, slim hand rested at her side, the fingernails carved with exquisite precision. The other, apparently, was raised to her throat, pinching shut the shawl she'd draped demurely over her face and hair. Unable to resist her allure, I rotated her without lifting. The profile of a fox revealed itself, smiling inside the hood, lips parted slightly in a wry, malicious smile, teeth rendered in the same detail as the nails of the hands.

At just that instant the sound of padded feet scatting across the floor startled me from behind, and Jo bolted from the dark screen of the bedroom door, blazing a trail across the room, bouncing off several walls. Pursuing her at no great distance came a second animal, a cat also, but unlike her in every other respect. He was a sleek, well-muscled male with a glossy, solid black coat, big as a Manx, beautiful. The only thing about him the least imperfect was his right front paw. Not that it was deformed, exactly, only too large for him by half, as though grafted on from some larger cousin in the family *Pantera.* His eyes, too, were strange, though more in the manner of a personal adornment than a flaw, blue like a Siamese's, only darker by a shade, and fulgid like precious stones, vaguely suggestive of the light in a blind man's eyes.

I thought at first they were playing, until, leaping from full stride, he tackled her ferociously, using her to cushion the impact as they smashed into a wall. Undeterred, she spat and thrashed, yowling valiantly, until he knocked her cockeyed with a double love-tap from his built-in cudgel, after which she became more tractable, panting there pinned beneath his forepaws. Straddling her shoulders to hams, he paused to adjust his weight, then licked his lips and leaned down as though to eat her raw starting with the belly. Instead, however, to my great relief, he began to suckle at a vestigial teat. The look on her face as she submitted was truly horrible — mashed sideways against the floor like a human face against a windowpane, eyes bugging out, heart beating frantically and visibly against her skinny rib cage covered with its lint of fur. After a few perfunctory sucks at the dry nipple, the wrestlers uncoupled, and a loud sizzling from the kitchen, accompanied by an explosion of aroma, drew my attention in that direction.

Li was standing over a black iron skillet, stirring with a wooden spoon. On the table a glazed earthenware bowl contained a cauliflower broken into flowerets dotted with small fresh English peas and a handful of Mandarin orange slices. "Come look," she invited. "Do you like Indian food?"

"I don't know," I replied. "I'm not sure I've ever had it."

"This is ghee," she explained, as she continued to stir the simmering liquid, "clarified butter."

Uncorking a small glass canister labeled "turmeric" on a wooden rack above the stove, she spooned out a fine rust-colored powder and tossed it into the bubbling, translucent solution. Another technicolor explosion left an acrid pungence hovering in the room. As I watched, she sprinkled in successive pinches of ocher, clay, and brick-red spices, each producing its own subtle alteration in the smell, which arrived at a deepening complexity. She was like an alchemist compounding rare earths over a pale blue flame; and I like some sailor passing to windward of the Spice Islands, dreaming of the bowers of bliss, sniffed the opened jars: coriander, cumin, mustard seed, white pepper, cardamom, fenugreek, and clove. Dipping in to taste, I found the merest pinches made my forehead bead with sweat and collected beneath my fingernails, encrusted deposits as though from grubbing in the earth — red clay, loess, indelible soils. Somehow at the time, and even more so later, the preparation of that curry, passionate and bitter, seemed a fitting culinary expression of Li's personality, something which evoked a thirst so powerful it turned the very marrow of my bones to dust and uprooted reason. Yet she allayed the thirst she artificially created, serving me smooth, mild *lassis,* yogurt, rose water, honey, and crushed ice swirled in a blender.

For dessert she prepared a grapefruit baked with cinnamon and sherry. In the end perhaps it was a bit too much for my simple tastes. I picked at it, trying to make it appear well used, if not eaten.

"Don't you like it?" she asked.

"Oh yes!" I lied. "It's very good."

She regarded me archly, undeceived. "I know what you'd like," she observed, half-peevish, half-amused. "A bowl of rice with a little black-bean sauce."

I lowered my head in shame. She had hit the mark exactly.

"Or some turnip pancakes dipped in oyster sauce."

"That's my favorite dish!" I cried, astonished.

She winked. "I'm telepathic."

"All the women in your family seem to be."

"Of course! We're all witches. My mother, she's the Good Witch of the South, the really powerful one that keeps the low profile and rules the Quadlings. And Yin-mi is Glinda, the one with the chipmunk voice who comes in a soap bubble. She doesn't soil her didies. And me? I'm the Wicked Witch of the West — or will be . . ." (she checked her watch) "in another hour and a half. If you don't leave before then you'll become a Winkie." She laughed. "But seriously, don't you get tired of 'soul food'? I get within fifteen blocks of Mott Street and I go queasy all over with a Pavlovian MSG buzz, chills and fevers. Just thinking about Chinese cooking makes me sick."

"But your father — both your parents — are such fine chefs!" I protested.

"That's right," she affirmed. "They ate nothing else, talked nothing else, thought nothing else all their lives, all my life. The idea of it almost nauseates me now. I'd rather go hungry than eat *dim sum,* or *moo goo gai pan.* No thank you. This Chinese girl decrare moratorium on quickee take-out, *fo-ev-ah.*" She bowed, raising her hands palm to palm above her head. "Excuse please, thank you very much!"

Though a little shocked at her irreverent parody of her father, I couldn't help smiling at it. I could tell that she was getting tipsy. But then so was I.

"Come on now, Sun I, a toast." She filled her glass and chimed it with her spoon.

"What should we toast?"

"You can't expect me to take you out, cook dinner, and think up the toast as well," she chided, continuing her insistent clatter. "At some point you've got to take the initiative, and the sooner the better. Before you know it, it'll be midnight." Her face was flushed with alcohol, her eyes shining and fixed directly on mine with that expression that combined amusement and provocation.

"All right," I conceded. "To you." I raised my glass.

She would not accept it. Lowering her head and shaking it emphatically with mock childishness, she pressed for qualification, continuing to sound her glass. "To me what?"

"To your cooking!" I proposed, charmed by her disingenuous tantrum.

"Boo! Hiss! I don't like it. Try again."

"All right," I said softly, going breathless with the compliment. "To your beauty."

"Hooray!" she cheered. "I knew you had it in you!" Observing the look of exposed earnestness on my face, she suddenly ceased her obstreperousness. My own mood seemed to infect hers in some degree. Smiling vulnerably, she lifted her glass, then, hesitating, put it down again. "Do you really think I am — beautiful, I mean?"

Touched, I nodded.

"Come here," she said, a low edge of breathlessness in her voice now as well. "Let's clink glasses."

As I stood over her, she looked up at me almost imploringly. "He is a fool, isn't he?"

I felt a shudder of exquisite pain, realizing she was thinking of Peter even then. But I nodded. "Yes."

Attempting to rise, she stumbled slightly, catching herself on me. Placed fortuitously in that position, one of her hands resting on my shoulder, the other pressing her glass of wine against my chest, she regarded me curiously, as though seeing me for the first time. She glanced her fingers through my hair reflexively. "Thank you," she said, her eyes slightly misted over.

Then, changing pace again, she clinked my glass with tipsy recklessness, closed her eyes, and took a large sip. Slipping both arms behind my head, elbows crooked languidly over my shoulders, her glass still in her hand, she laughed soundlessly to herself. Then her face totally relaxed and she kissed me on the lips — shallowly, but warm, moist, and lingering. I watched her intently without responding, but not resisting either.

Separating, she hung there without opening her eyes, lips parted slightly so that I could see her teeth, smiling that same remote interior smile. "I should have done that earlier," she said. She looked at me.

We stood studying one another, her hands still on my shoulders, neither of us making any move to disengage. I trembled a little, weak with nervous energy. Yet this was purely physical, something in my joints. At the center, I was curiously calm. After a moment she leaned forward and kissed me again, this time more deeply, with her tongue. Lingering beneath the savor of the wine, I detected a faint delicious aftertaste of soured milk, her metabolic signature.

"Beautiful enough to make you break your vow?" she whispered in my ear with tactile, caressing syllables.

The trembling became more violent, almost a shiver.

She laughed over my shoulder and collapsed against me. "Or did they provide for that contingency at the monastery?"

I didn't know what she meant, until I felt her hand insinuate itself between my legs into my crotch.

Going suddenly hard, I recoiled violently.

"Oops!" she said. "Nope, it's there all right."

Deeply wounded, shocked in fact, I regarded her with chagrin.

She blinked her eyes wide and rounded her lips, playfully mimicking my outrage. Seeing me intransigent, however, genuinely hurt, she softened. "Don't," she gently implored me, stroking my face with the back of her hand.

My umbrage passed away and the weakness returned, only rawer, more vulnerable with the consciousness of injury, an injury forgiven at great cost. "Poor boy," she said with a sad, sympathetic pout, "come with me." Then taking my hand, she led me toward the bedroom.

•

"Are you really a virgin?" she asked casually over her shoulder, pausing as she unzipped her dress, but not fully turning to face me where I sat on the bed. Letting it fall around her feet, she stepped out, then crossed her arms in front of her and lifted her slip off over her head. Then she wheeled, her white, full breasts swaying slightly with the motion, like two boats at mooring — the first

time I had ever seen a woman's nakedness. Her body was lithe and tight like
an animal's. She was flushed and glowing, partly with a physical shyness she
had fully mastered, partly with conscious pride at her own loveliness. "You're
terrified!" she observed with a surprised laugh, not callously though, but with
an undertone of tenderness, almost maternal, new in her voice. She pursed her
lips sympathetically and fell to her knees in front of me, taking both my hands.
"It's all right," she encouraged, unexceptionably kind, yet unable to suppress
an underlying ebullience and amusement at what must have been, for her, the
extreme novelty of the situation. "Trust me — you've got everything you need.
I checked." She smiled, then, seeing me unrelieved, grew serious again. "It's
okay," she coaxed. "There's no hurry. We've got time. We'll talk. Okay? Tell
me a story."

"Li . . . " I turned a harrowed face to her. "I don't . . ."

"Shhh." She put her finger to my lips. "Relax. Tell me a story."

"I don't know any stories," I replied, in a low, dispirited voice, dropping
my eyes to the floor.

"Tell me about yourself, then," she suggested. "That's the story I really
want to know."

I regarded her uncertainly.

She nodded. "Go ahead," she encouraged. Propping up her pillows against
the wall, she lounged back languidly behind me, sparing me the exquisite
torment of her nakedness, keeping the circuit open, though, with a hand,
which she rested lightly on my shoulder, then let slip smoothly down my back,
hooking a finger casually over my belt inside my pants. At the same time she
propped her long leg on the edge of the bed, sidling it against my arm and
shoulder, tucking her bare foot underneath my thigh as though to keep it
warm. These minor alignments, though completely spontaneous and unconsidered on her part, established a naive tactile intimacy between us which partially disarmed the threat I felt.

After a few false starts that tied themselves in knots of self-disparagement
and apology, I launched forth. By this time the telling had begun to assume
a ritualized format, proceeding by its own momentum. I touched on virtually
everything, sketching in the distant backdrop with a few broad lines — Ken
Kuan, my uncle's visit, the departure, "following the river" — proceeding to
more recent developments, Kahn's ultimatum, the pawning of the robe. In
reply to a question of hers about my original motive for leaving China, I ended
on the keynote of the "delta." A faint subliminal shudder of betrayal and
chagrin unsettled my heart as I conjured Yin-mi's image — her first gift to me
— giving it away as though it were a common thing, and to her sister, to Li.
I hung fire, thinking of her. But where her image had been so vivid only hours
before, now I saw Yin-mi through a haze of distance, like a face staring back
at me out of a sepia photograph in an ornate antique silver frame, cloudy with
oxidation. What burning had darkened it? I only knew the feeling in my heart
was like a requiem, and that it had to do with Li. By the end, though, I had

waxed almost garrulous. I was flushed and inspired, and exhilaration numbed my sense of danger and impropriety.

Li, however, lounging naked as before, had become distant and musing. Biting her thumbnail in concentration, she lay kicking her foot off the edge of the bed and letting it fall slowly back.

Growing conscious of my scrutiny, she stopped, shaking off her trance visibly, as an animal shakes off water.

"What were you thinking?" I asked.

"Hmm? Oh, about the delta, and the play. Remember those lines, 'Over that art which you say adds to nature, is an art that nature makes'? While you were speaking, they flashed through my mind in connection with Peter, and you. I think there's an analogy between your situations. You're both attracted to, in some sense possessed by, an impulse at odds with your beliefs about what the world is, or should be (with him, at odds with what the world is willing to allow about itself). In your case it's Dow, in his, sexual ambivalence ('that art which you say adds to nature'). Only he's accepted the duality in himself, almost in accordance with Shakespeare's insight that the art itself *is* nature. You're still trying to reconcile your contradictions, attempting to raze out the ambivalence in your heart, to murder one of your potential selves, or write it off as specious. The delta . . ." she repeated, laughing softly to herself. "Poor boy, come here." Smiling, she extended me her hand. Using a single arm, she raised herself from the pillows, slipping out one for me and plumping it next to her own. "Lie down beside me."

I submitted to the guiding pressure of her hands, of her will.

"That's right," she whispered. "Now close your eyes. Relax. I have an idea." Rolling toward me, she laid her nearer leg languidly on top of mine, a gesture which, while provocative, did not seem brazen, almost shy in fact, as she refrained from more intimate intrusion, applying no muscular pressure, only weight. She unbuttoned the buttons of my shirt, one by one, starting at the chest and proceeding down. "Why do they have to do it backward?" she protested jokingly, hanging up on one. "I'll never get used to it."

When she had finished, she spread it open to each side, then bent down sweeping her cheek and hair along my belly, like a cat begging for attention, circling my nearer nipple with her tongue, then licking the bud erect. Her tongue had a strange sandpaper roughness. . . . Or perhaps my senses were only preternaturally vivid. The sensation gave me an exquisite, almost unbearable pleasure, not far from torture. Clenching and unclenching my fists, I arched up from the bed under her.

Suddenly she drew away, resting over me with her palms spread on the coverlet, on one hip below, legs drawn up near her body. "You like that," she observed with amusement.

I fell back panting and stared up at her, resenting, a little, her power, and also her curtailment of its exercise.

"You weren't supposed to look."

"Why not? I like to look," I challenged, increasingly swept up in the momentum.

"Close them," she ordered with coy peremptoriness. "Good. Now . . ." She stretched out on her side of the bed. "I'm going to show you something — No, don't open your eyes." She forestalled me with two cool fingertips over my lids. "Make you feel something, rather. Give me your hand." She took it herself, spreading out my palm under her own. She then guided it gently down her face, her neck, over her clavicle to her breast, where she allowed it to linger briefly (her nipples were erect), before prompting it on down the length of her smooth flank, over the dollop of her hipbone, out at last onto the mound of her pubis, with that astounding change in texture.

"Feel that," she crooned, turning her head on the pillow and speaking close into my ear. "Like a wooded knoll, crinkly with fur." Her palm still over mine, fingers over fingers, she exerted pressure, slowly crooking the middle one, pressing it up into her. "Like a dry river bed," she described, "running between wooded hills, 'following the river.' " Hearing her sweet whispered laugh, I opened my eyes. Her head was tilted back, her throat extended as though for sacrifice, inviting the priest's knife. Her eyes were closed, a sliver of white gleaming beneath the lids. Her face was radiant with an unearthly light, like nothing I'd ever seen before, and as I watched her, fascinated, an impulse of tenderness for her, which hardly dared to touch, melded with excruciating hunger.

"I'm going to take you prospecting," she whispered, smiling to herself, "dowsing for water — your finger the forked stick, the mandrake root. You trace along the ravine, dredging gently but insistently." Her hand guided and taught me. "Stop. There. Feel? The damp dirt underneath the brush and scree. You delve there, and suddenly . . . ah!" she cried a little weakly, losing her train and frowning as though in pain or intense concentration. I thought I'd hurt her, until she laughed again. ". . . bubbling up from the deep aquifer . . . water! You've discovered it." She opened her eyes and looked deeply into mine with no transition, smiling, flushed. "Here is the delta, sweet boy," she said, pressing my hand down hard, "the only one that matters. This is where it comes together, where we come together, you and me . . . where we come . . . together."

Her eyes were bright with the wonder and the power of it, its deep deliciousness.

"So," she said, "will you break your vow for me?"

I let my gaze linger a little longer on hers, not from any hesitation, but wanting only to prolong the moment, savoring her beauty, drunk with fatality and happiness. "It's already broken," I replied.

And it was true.

Chapter 3

"I believe that's what they call a shit-eating grin," Li observed with amusement. "Only it's about nine-tenths sugar. If I had a bucket of cold water right now, I'd douse you simply for the pleasure of watching you dissolve in a puddle." She shook her head. "Not good, Sun I. Not good. That's what *I'm* supposed to do."

"I'm very happy," I replied, beaming at her proudly and vulnerably.

She laughed. "And *I* want a cigarette." Pivoting on her ass, she swung her legs over the side and reached for the drawer knob of the bedside table.

"I didn't know you smoked," I remarked, mildly disappointed at the discovery.

"I don't," she answered, as she rummaged, "usually." Finding what she wanted, she slammed the drawer succinctly and spun back onto the bed, sweeping her hair aside with a gesture disconcertingly like Wo's. She let the cigarette hang laxly from the corner of her mouth as she struck the match. "Only after sex," she said, challenging my eyes as she consigned it to the flame.

She took a deep drag, held it, and sighed out the smoke, indicating the drawer with a brief jerk of her head. "There're several cartons in there." Her expression was completely deadpan, and then her laughter bubbled over.

Finally catching the joke, I didn't laugh.

"Oh dear," she fretted. "You aren't going to be morose and saturnine, are you? I hope not, because the Saturnalia's over."

"What do you mean?"

"Have a cigarette," she proposed with brusque evasion.

"I don't smoke."

"Come on, try it. You've already fallen, you may as well go all the way. The experience isn't complete without it. Take my word for it. I ought to know, right?"

I was alarmed by her shift in tone — clipped, aggressive jollity — and as I forced my lips into an uneasy smile of corroboration, I realized how far I was in above my head. Suddenly she frightened me. She seemed powerful, and out of control of her own power, which made my position doubly precarious, since I was clinging onto *her.*

"All right," I said, with a nervous grin, shrugging my shoulders, and taking the cigarette as she offered it, between my index and middle fingers. I wondered silently at the deliberate awkwardness of the gesture, which ignored the thumb — the ritualized inarticulateness of the smoker's grasp.

Amused, Li watched my uncertain fumblings. "It really is easier, you know."

Again the clairvoyance. I looked up, but she had receded into herself, leaning back on the pillow, arms crossed over her stomach.

I inhaled, careful not to draw too much, then lifted my chin as I had seen her do, slowly letting the smoke escape through rounded lips.

"Good, isn't it?" Her voice was languid, sleepy.

"It's milder than opium," I remarked, speaking my thought aloud.

"*You've* smoked opium?" she asked, astonished.

"Twice." I took another puff.

She clucked her tongue. "You're a strange boy, Sun I. Full of surprises." Reaching out her hand, she opened and closed her fingers like a scissors, mutely importuning the cigarette.

"It's my Monkey Nature," I explained as I inserted it.

She took another drag. "This is nice," she said, offering it back.

And suddenly I felt safe again. There was an intimacy in our distance then, which I sensed conversation would only have spoiled.

When the cigarette had burned down close to the filter, I leaned over her and crushed it into the ashtray on the bedside table. Only then did I notice there were several others. The pang this gave me had hardly settled when Li stirred.

"Listen." She raised her finger and turned her eyes up to the side, as though to make out something over her shoulder.

"I don't hear anything," I replied, with a trace of petulance she did not pick up on, returning to my side of the bed.

"That's just it," she whispered, in a tone of rapturous relief. "It's quiet. Blessedly, blessedly quiet."

We both listened.

Finally Li sighed. "This is when it's best. Sometimes late at night when there's nothing else, you catch an echo of the traffic up from the courtyard, a long, low *whoosh,* almost like waves in a conch shell." She smiled. "A deep sea sigh, a sound almost like silence. *Peac-c-ce,*" she whispered. "*Peac-c-c-ce.*"

As though on cue from her, the wind picked up and I heard the steady roll of breakers as I had heard them for the first time off the coast of China as we steamed into the harbor at Shanghai. The harp was driven to a sympathetic frenzy.

" 'And now its strings,' " she recited, lying just as before, arms crossed over her stomach, eyes closed, head tilted back on the pillow,

> "Boldlier swept, the long sequacious notes
> Over delicious surges sink and rise,
> Such a soft floating witchery of sound
> As twilight Elfins make, when they at eve
> Voyage on gentle gales from Faery-Land.

"Fairyland," she whispered. "That's where I want to go. That's where I'm going. I'm fading, Sun I . . . fading. Take me there."

"I will," I promised with urgent, fanciful extravagance.

She smiled, then turned sideways on the pillow to observe me. "Will you, sweet boy? How would you take me there? On a magic carpet woven of good intentions? Or do you have a pair of magic ruby slippers?"

"Yes," I told her, not even knowing what she meant. "Or I could get them."

She laughed. "I know where you'd like to take me. Back to your monastery in China in a little box." A trace of remote pity came into her face, and she lowered her voice. "But that isn't my idea of Fairyland, sweet boy. I'm afraid I wouldn't make a very good monk. I love sin too much." Her smile challenged her credibility, yet somehow I believed her, and I didn't care.

"Besides," she went on. "You can't go back. You've broken your vow. 'Nevermore,' " she said with a portentous intonation. "I made you break it. You must hate me for that."

"I don't hate you," I tenderly contradicted her.

"You will."

I shook my head. "I could never hate you, Li. Never. I . . ."

"Shhh," she said, putting her finger gently to my lips. "Don't say it. If you do I might hate you."

She sighed and lay back on the pillow again. "No," she averred. "Only one man can take me there — my fairy prince." She smiled unhappily.

"Why can't I be your fairy prince?" I asked wistfully.

She laughed outright, almost a guffaw. "Because you're not a fairy."

Though I'd occasioned it, I was hurt by her levity, which seemed to digress unfairly from the main fact of my pain and my desire.

"But I could be a prince at least," I persisted a little pathetically.

"Yes," she agreed. "You could be. You will be. But someone else's prince, sweet boy. Not mine."

A siren went off somewhere in the night but Li did not react. I endured it privately, but it finally grew too tremendous in the silence, usurping everything, until it seemed a scream inside myself, all the anguish of the universe condensed in one hysterical, insistent bleat.

"What *is* that?"

"I can't stay here much longer," she replied in a low, toneless voice, as though speaking to herself. In the partial darkness of the room, I could make out tears beading on her lashes and welling in the corners of her eyes. "God damn it. God damn it," she chanted in that same neutral voice, "I don't think I can stand it." She turned to me with weariness and exasperation. "Sometimes they go on for two days at a stretch."

"What is it?" I asked, more gently this time.

"A car alarm."

"A break-in?"

She nodded. "Once last winter one went off in the next block. It woke me up at four in the morning. It was still going when I went out to catch the bus for class. And in the afternoon when I came home. It's the Die-Hard batteries," she said, laughing a little giddily. "They ought to do a commercial: 'The Sears no-maintenance Die-Hard battery has prompted more residential suicides than the next two competitors combined. Don't settle for less. Buy the best. Buy Sears. It's definitely searing.' After it stopped — and by that time the car was completely totaled, people had smashed out the windows with bricks, kicked in the fenders, stripped the hubcaps — I could still hear it ringing in my ears for days. Days. It literally became a part of me. My brain cells memorized it and repeated it over and over like a mantra, only mindless, invoking Cosmic Buzz — the flip side of Taoist Primal Harmony." She laughed again. "The horrible thing is that after a while you almost come to want it, like a fix, a form of security."

Suddenly it stopped.

"Thank God," she sighed. "Oh, thank you baby Jesus. Thank you very much!"

At that instant I became aware of the black cat standing on the corner of the bed, having already assimilated his leap even before I saw him, poised there motionless as though materialized from thin air, regarding us with perfect self-possession out of those cold, brilliant eyes. At my notice, he twisted his head and licked his shoulder fur vigorously, then languorously stretched out his front paws, yawning sleepily and licking his lips. Coming back up like a dancer from a full split, closing his splayed legs like a scissors, he shook himself with brief violence, springing his tail up in the air.

"Did it wake you up?" Li pouted sympathetically, stirring for the first time in several minutes.

The cat meowed plaintively, then stepped lightly across my foot and crossed the coverlet to her.

"Poor boy," she crooned, holding out her hand.

Arching his back, the cat rubbed under her palm, lifting his face to her with pleasure.

He's beautiful," I remarked, repeating aloud my previous appraisal. "Come here, kitty." I clicked my tongue and rubbed my thumb over my fingers in front of him. "Kitty, kitty."

"He doesn't respond to smarm," she laughed. "He's an aristocrat, royalty in fact." She rolled him, purring, over on his belly, which she then began to stroke. Clutching her wrist between both paws, claws sheathed, he thrust his chin up, purring blissfully.

"He sounds like a little engine," I chuckled.

She leaned over him, shrouding him with her hair and began to purr back, reproducing the sound — a low, stuttered, gutteral, rasping sigh — with such uncanny accuracy it made me shiver.

"What are you doing?" I asked, slightly nervous with her persistence and absorption in the ritual.

She tossed her hair back. "We're talking."

"You understand his language?"

"Of course," she affirmed. "I'm a Siamese, not to mention an ethnologist." She laughed and leaned back down.

"What's his name?"

"Eddie," she answered, continuing her play.

"Eddie!" I repeated with unpleasant shock. "Why Eddie?"

"Eddie-puss," she explained. "Eddie-puss and Jo. They're a couple."

"Isn't Joe a male name? What made you decide to call her that?"

"It's short for Jocasta. Jocasta and Eddie-puss." She darted that amused, taunting smile at me. "Don't you get it?"

"Get what?"

"Oedipus and Jocasta."

Her answer shed no light. I regarded her blankly.

"They're mother and son. Don't you know the story of Oedipus?"

I shook my head. "Tell it to me."

"You like stories, don't you?"

I nodded with a blissful, sheepish smile, sensing her on the verge of a concession.

She sighed. "All right, I'll tell you this one. But only on one condition."

"Okay."

"Aren't you even going to ask me what?"

"All right, what?"

She laughed. "I don't know yet. I'll tell you when I think of it."

"That's a rather open-ended bargain," I commented.

She shrugged. "Take it or leave it. You don't have a choice."

"All right," I agreed. "I take it."

"Okay, it was Greece a long, long time ago," she began. "A town called Thebes in the province of Boeotia, a region chiefly noted for the troglodytic character of its inhabitants — generally swineherds — and its propensity for disaster. Oedipus set the ball rolling and passed it on to his sons, Eteocles and Polynices, who were almost as spectacularly ill-fated as he was himself and did their best to waste the city. What little they left standing was finally finished off by Alexander some time later on his Greek campaign. But that's a sidelight. . . . Oedipus. Well, let me say a word about his father to start with, because otherwise nothing else makes sense. His name was Laius, and he was the king of Thebes. At the birth of his son, Laius piously consulted the oracle at Delphi for luck — sort of the Greek version of handing out cigars — only to learn, to his horror, that the child was fated to jeopardize his throne and life should he be allowed to grow to manhood."

As she spoke, an echo popped into my mind: "If one clings to the little boy, one loses the strong man" — from my own "oracle." I had no leisure to consider the implications of the association, however, as she continued without pausing.

"Unable to do the deed himself, Laius handed the boy over to one of the aforementioned swineherds with orders to 'terminate with extreme prejudice.' "

"Like in the play?"

She nodded. "Right, like in the play. Also like in the play, Laius had the characteristic bad luck to pick the one fellow in the region with some vestigial nubbin of a tender heart. He couldn't handle a literal assassination, but after a long struggle with his conscience, prompted by duty and honor, he was able to steel himself to a dose of infant torture, hanging the bawling baby upside down in a tree by his foot before he left him. It was so swollen by the time they found him that they called him Big Foot — Oedi-pus. That was the original association, right Eddie?" She gave the cat a playful scratch.

"That's part one. A hiatus occurs here. The camera pans. The caption on the screen reads, 'Many Years Later . . .' The scene is set on the road to Delphi. Oedipus is grown. He and Laius meet by accident, not knowing one another. The road is narrow. Laius is in a hurry. He's late for a very important date with the sibyl. Being a king and used to giving orders peremptorily, he orders Oedipus to yield the road. Oedipus, who's inherited a little of the royal fire himself and kept it burning despite his ambience, refuses to obey. Classic confrontation. Laius, of course, flies into a rage, draws his sword, and, for some reason that I've never fully understood, slays Oedipus's horse. What did the horse have to do with it? Maybe he was swinging for Oedipus and simply missed. At any rate, at this point Oedipus flew off the handle too and killed him, killed Laius, his own father — without, of course, the slightest inkling he was committing patricide.

"Second hiatus. Enter the Sphinx. Ever heard of her? Well, she was a particularly diabolical monster in the classical, i.e., misogynistic, mode, with the body of a lion and a woman's face. She was haunting the roads near Thebes, terrorizing passersby with a riddle. Not too impressive by present standards of terrorism? Well, if you couldn't answer it, she ate you — which adds a little spice. At any rate, the riddle was, 'What animal goes on four feet in the morning, two at night, and three in the evening?' "

"Man!" I answered.

"I thought you said you didn't know this story."

"I don't," I replied. "That's an old Chinese riddle."

"You're kidding." She blinked. "Well, anyway, Oedipus knew the answer too. The Sphinx was so chagrined that she offed herself on the spot, throwing herself from a rock. In gratitude the Thebans made Oedipus king, conferring on him as incidental booty the former queen, Laius's widow. That's right, Jocasta, his own mother. Rather piquant, eh? Of course, in their favor one must say that neither had any idea of the enormity they were committing. The Gods knew though. And they weren't having any of *that!* At least among mortals. That was usurping *their* prerogative. So they afflicted Thebes with pestilence and famine, the usual spate of disasters. Oedipus, showing an atavistic trace of his father's superstitiousness, turned to the oracle to find out who was responsible, only to be taunted by his own name by way of answer. That was when it all came out, the double breach of taboo — patricide and incest, mother fucker, father slayer. The news drove Jocasta crazy. She hanged herself. Oedipus went mad with grief and tore out his own eyes."

"Tore out his eyes!"

She nodded. "His eyes." She yawned, patting her mouth with the back of her hand. "So? Did you like my story?"

"Like it!" I cried. "It was horrible, horrible!" I paused. "But, yes, in a way I did."

She laughed. "You're a strange boy, Sun I. What are you thinking? You've got a peculiar look in your eyes, your odd, un-Oriental eyes."

"I was thinking of my father."

She appraised me silently, then smiled. "His name isn't Laius, is it?"

I shook my head. "No," I said. "It's Eddie."

"You are strange," she reiterated. "Perhaps you like stories too well."

"I always did," I replied. "I can't help myself."

"That's okay. It's one of my shortcomings, too. But be careful. They have a way of coming true."

I shook my head wistfully. "It's not a worry for me. My father's dead."

"Oh, I see. I'm sorry."

"So am I," I said with a sad smile.

"But remember what I said?" she inquired, taking a deep breath and a new tack. "In this country everyone must pay for everything he gets. I've given you something, now you must pay up. It's your turn to fulfill your end of the bargain."

"All right. What do you want?"

"My wish is your command, right?"

I nodded.

"Okay, you looked so snug and comfortable while I was telling mine, it made me jealous; I want a story too. Just a short one," she qualified, "before you go."

"But I've already told you one," I protested.

"I know," she conceded. "But that doesn't count. Yours was from real life. I want another kind."

"What kind? All the stories I know are from real life."

"A bedtime story," she stipulated, ignoring my deprecation, "something fanciful and Chinese."

"A fairy tale," I supplied.

She smiled at the allusion. "Exactly. I told you a Western myth; you tell me a Chinese one. A sort of cultural exchange." She sighed and leaned back on the pillows. "Perhaps we could make it a precedent for further intercourse — *cultural* intercourse, I mean. A sort of you-show-me-yours, I'll-show-you-mine arrangement." She laughed and yawned again. "Excuse me. I'm getting punchy. You'd better hurry up before I fall asleep on you."

As she spoke, I suddenly remembered the netsuke in the front room. "The Hu Li. . . ."

"What is that?" she asked sleepily.

Then I told her the story Wu had once told me of the beautiful anchoress, her long solitary vigil in quest of enlightenment, its interruption, and her unconscionable revenge against the man responsible for her disappointment, serving the emperor a banquet with his own son as the centerpiece, like a roast pig with an apple in its mouth.

"At least she spared him the agony of a later Oedipal struggle," Li commented, holding the covers up to her chin and smiling with half-opened eyes. "Laius should have hired her to do his dirty work. The whole thing would never have happened. We all would have been spared a lot of grief."

"But the emperor loved his son," I pointed out.

"True," she admitted. "It reverses the Western version in that particular, doesn't it?"

I nodded.

"But what happened to the girl?"

"Her soul was imprisoned in the body of a fox," I told her.

"A fox?" She tensed with alert gravity.

I nodded. "Forever. She is said to haunt the roads at night in China, disguised as a beautiful woman, seducing unwary young men whom she then devours — not unlike the Sphinx."

"You saw the netsuke in the front room."

"Yes. Where did you get it?"

"A gift," she answered tersely.

I searched her face. "From Peter?"

She smiled and closed her eyes.

"I suppose that reminded him of you, too?"

She shrugged. "Perhaps I'm one of your Fox Fairies too, Sun I, have you considered that?"

I shook my head. "If you were, you wouldn't tell me."

"Wouldn't I?" She regarded me with amused provocation. "Perhaps that would be the most cunning way to disarm your suspicions."

"I don't think I'd mind so much being devoured by you."

She laughed. "Be careful I don't take you up on it."

●

Every so often, out of her sleep, Li uttered small, plaintive cries, distant, high pitched, and mournful, like the upper register of the harp. I stroked her hair to comfort her, but she shook her head and turned away, as though my hand scalded her flesh. It was odd to see her wandering there, lost in a dreamscape where all her beauty and finesse were powerless against whatever shapes of darkness rose before her.

Unable to sleep, I lay through three solemn knells of bells, tolling the hour in a clock tower far away. Periodically the wind rose, stirring the murmurous harp strings to a fit of violent agitation, that music somehow wrenching, like a threnody, the piteous sorrow of a thing born with no power to articulate its grief, or perhaps a god whose language was beyond my ken. It occurred to me that the wind harp bore a resemblance to the *Changes*. Its strings were like the yarrow stalks, an instrument contrived by human ingenuity sensitive enough to catch the subtle galvanic vibrations of the Tao. Its music, with its ever-changing motif, was the incomprehensible melody of life itself — incomprehensible, but perhaps not finally without meaning — which had blown me here on this strange wind tonight.

Li had said that she was like the harp, soulless. But was it soullessness I heard, something totally at random, or was the harp merely vibrating with an impulse too superfine for detection in the coarse-meshed sieve of the senses? I might easily have believed that with her exquisite sensibilities, the clear, unremorseful amorality of her nature, she was in her being like a tuning fork, vibrating invisibly in the key of life, a pitch beyond my accustomed hearing.

As I lay in this sweet, unearthly torpor, she suddenly cried out and sat bolt upright, panting. "Who's there?" she asked in fright. "Peter?"

"It's only me," I said. "Sun I. Don't be afraid."

Hardly heeding, she got up precipitately and went into the bathroom. Flipping on the light, she closed the door behind her. I heard the water begin to run.

I lay there listening to the flow of the shower. As she did not come out for some time, I found myself gradually nodding off. In that pleasurable state of semiconsciousness, I felt the bed sink and rise again beneath her weight as she returned. Smiling contentedly, but without opening my eyes, I drifted off.

I had no idea how long I'd been asleep or what woke me, but when my eyes sprang open the room was almost totally dark, except for a vague starshine through the windows, compounded out of the city's reflected incandescence. For a moment I was uncertain where I was and thought perhaps I was in my own bed back on Mulberry Street. Then I remembered Li with a poignant rush of tender panic. I turned my head in her direction. Beside me on the pillow her eyes were open, studying me in the darkness. In the aura of reflected light they gleamed with the uncanny luminescence of an animal's. Then I heard the toilet flush and gasped as the faint thud of a cat's paws resounded on the floor. I noticed the light still shining underneath the bathroom door. Just then it opened and Li appeared, wearing a towel wrapped around her, her hair pinned in a loose chignon.

"Do you know what time it is?" she demanded brusquely. "After three o'clock," she replied, answering her own question before I had a chance to. "You've overstayed your time. You'll have to go."

"But why?" I sat upright in bed. "What difference . . . ?"

"Please don't make it any harder than it is. I really don't aspire to play the Wicked Witch. I warned you. You said you understood."

"But that was before! I thought you were kidding."

"Well, I wasn't." A trace of pity shone in her eyes. But it was like the bright filament of the crescent moon I'd seen in her earrings, and beneath it, cold and tremendous, loomed a glacial mass of decision and intransigence.

Stunned with the colossal arbitrariness of it, feeling my heart begin to break up inside me into a thousand lacerating fragments, like a heart of glass, I rose slowly and put my clothes on. By the time we'd reached the kitchen door and she had ushered me through into the hall, I was weeping.

"Poor boy," she whispered, "don't cry for me. It isn't worth it."

"I'm in love with you," I said, sobbing uncontrollably into my hands.

"Don't love me," she counseled in a sad, soothing voice. "I'm not good enough for you. Love my little sister. You're alike. She's a good witch."

"But I don't love her, I love you," I answered fiercely through my sobs.

"Shhh," she said, putting her finger to my lips. "I wouldn't be good for you, Sun I. You'd be too delicious. I'd only eat you up and take your ruby slippers."

"You can have them!" I offered. "And anything else."

She smiled with wistful condescension. "But you don't even know what they are, or the nature of their powers."

"What are they then?"

She laid her hand over my heart. "They're what brought you here; and if you don't lose them, they're what's going to take you home, back to Kansas, back to the real world. Don't lose them, Sun I. It's easy to. And don't give them away. Not to me, not to anyone, unless it's her. You can trust Yin-mi."

"But I don't want her," I reiterated. "I want you. I want you to have them."

"Ah, sweet boy," she whispered, "that's my secret, don't you see? I don't really want them. Ruby slippers are only good for a one-way trip — back to Kansas. But I want to go to Fairyland, and you can't take me there."

I started to speak, but again she pressed her finger to my lips. Holding me there a moment in her gaze, she then drew her arm in through the door and closed it in my face.

Chapter 4

The next morning, a Saturday, I was awakened by a knock at the door.

"Sun I?" a voice inquired diffidently and sweetly.

I groaned and rolled over as my heart began to race. It was Yin-mi.

"I didn't mean to wake you," she apologized, putting her head through the door. "I didn't realize you were still asleep. I just wanted to ask if we might walk together to the lecture tonight. I could pick you up around six-thirty. You might need some help carrying things or something?"

Though beneath the covers I was wide awake with terror, almost preternaturally alert, I mumbled something inarticulate and noncommittal.

"Good," she said, interpreting it as an affirmation. "I'll let you go back to sleep then. You probably need it. See you then!" The door closed, and I partially relaxed. Then abruptly it opened again. "I'm really looking forward to it!" she chirped excitedly by way of postscript. "So is everybody!" Then she was gone.

I felt hung over from the wine, but it was nothing compared with the moral hangover I was reeling under. Somehow the previous night did not seem real, like a dream, a nightmare, a terrifying and delicious nightmare. Only there was Li. The thought of her was like an errant star, the great black hole of an imploded sun, which had wandered into my emotional solar system and was drawing me toward some fierce accounting in her depths. Her presence was so immense, so heavy in my heart, that there was room for almost nothing else.

My first, best impulse was to run after Yin-mi and tell her to call it off while there was time. Had I not been so unmanned by lovesickness and depression, I might have mustered the courage to do the right thing by her and Riley. But I couldn't face her. I was afraid of that clairvoyance in her soul, afraid she would know my betrayal had gone deeper than the pawning of the robe, irretrievably far.

So, instead, after dressing and putting on my dark glasses, I skulked out of the building like a thief, tiptoeing past the Ha-p'is' door, resolved to seek refuge in the anonymity of the streets.

All day I wandered, hardly noting where, in a daze of mental and physical numbness through which the pain of my lovelornness broke occasionally like a clarion call, the melancholy note of a hunting horn in the autumn air. Today indeed it seemed like fall, for the first time, in earnest. Toward noon, after walking what must have been miles, the overcast in my brain started to break up too, and I began to drift by some inexplicable but ineluctable emotional gravity back toward the Upper West Side, haunting it as the ghost of a dead soul haunts an abandoned house, site of a remembered happiness whose loss it has not accepted or forgiven.

At around six-thirty, the hour designated for meeting Yin-mi, I wandered into a bar and searched Li's number out in the directory, then called from the pay phone. My hands began to sweat as I listened to the rings. By the time the count reached five I'd given up; then she answered. Her voice was indistinct, a little slurred. There was music playing in the background, laughter.

"Li?"

"Who is this?" she asked curtly.

"It's me," I replied. "Sun I."

"*Who?*" she demanded. "Speak up, we've got a bad connection."

I hesitated a moment too long. "Some crank," I heard her say just before the phone went dead.

When I tried to call a second time, the line was busy.

For an hour or so until dark fell, I wandered in gradually narrowing concentric circles around her building, constrained from enacting my desperate and pitiful resolve, not so much by manfulness as trepidation. Under cover of the gradually deepening obscurity, however, my baser instincts rallied. From across the street, I cased the joint like a would-be burglar. Through the glass double doors of the lobby, I could see Ramon stationed at his usual post beside the pay phone, violently remonstrating with an unseen interlocutor, running his comb through his hair in the intervals. Growing bolder, I wandered to the corner of the building, finally into the courtyard itself, where I stood counting off the lighted squares of the windows, trying to decide which one was hers. Occasionally a form appeared in silhouette, making my pulse accelerate.

While I stood there, straining for a glimpse, a hand closed tightly around my arm, just above the elbow. Ramon regarded me with a brilliant, and not entirely friendly, grin. "Wha's happeneén, mon?"

"I was just . . ."

He closed his eyes and nodded. "Sure, sure, I know. Only she don't huant to see ju, mon. Deeg? Ju better split before I call de cops. Comprende?"

I nodded and started to hurry off.

"Maybée ju deek ain' beeg enough for hair," he taunted as I retreated shamefacedly away.

I went into the first package store I saw and bought a fifth of Dry Sack, then drifted east across the avenues — Amsterdam, Columbus, Central Park West — into the park, where I sat down on a slatted green bench and, after rumpling down the paper bag, uncorked my bottle. I had taken several abandoned swallows when an old, but not so old, black wino with a cane, who was hobbling by on the asphalt path, stopped stock still in front of me and started staring. Ignoring him, I downed another swig.

"You bettuh slow down, brother," he advised. "Gonna be a lawng night tonight." He paused for a reaction and, not getting one, asked, "Kin I set down?"

Taking my indifference as an invitation, he settled himself beside me, putting his cane across his knees. I turned briefly to look. A fairly typical example of the species, I thought: stocking cap, grizzled beard, bloodshot eyes, tattered, baggy coat.

"You lookin' kine 'a down at de mouf," he observed. "Must be a wuhmun in it somewheres." He shook his head pessimistically. "Umh-umh. Seem lack iss always de same thang, doan' it? Honky, Chinaman, Injun, Nigga' — doan' make no diffunce — all got de same disease. De blues is de disease, and wuhmun is responsible. Doan' know 'bout Hong Kong, brother, but I tell you how they sing it down in Santee, South Cah'lina." He paused and cleared his throat, then spat and held out his hand without looking at me. "Lemme have a swalla furs, if you doan' mine."

I handed him the bottle. He tilted it up, took a long sip, then wiped his mouth on the sleeve of his coat. He shoved it to arm's length, squinting as though to read the label through the bag. "Wha's dis?"

"Dry Sack," I replied.

"Umm-hmm. Ain' no Thunderbud, but iss awright." Handing it back, he began to sing in a quivering, raspy, but not unpleasant baritone:

> "I ax de Good Lawd, sen' me an angel down,
> Say I ax de Good Lawd, sen' me an angel down.
> Lawd say, cain' spah you no angel, Murphy,
> But I sen' you Thelma Brown."

He laughed and slapped his thigh. "Yeah, Lawd, doan' know 'bout Hong Kong, but das how we sing it down in Santee." He scrutinized me again. "I believe you got it bad, my frien'. But doan' let it whup ya. Shoot! What you got ta worry 'bout? You young. You healfy. You fine another wuhmun. Shucks, son, I been whah you at, an' I been furder. On de other side now." He shook his head. "Ain' no hope lef' for me. No med'cine in the wurl gonna cure what I got. Wuhmun done it too. Look ahere." He started to lean forward on the bench. "Know what dis is? Got rheumatide otrighteous. Cain' ben' down worf a dawg no mo'. Dat's from sleepin' outside in de cold. Wuhmun threw me out de house. See my shoelace, brother? Sometime it stay untied lack dat fo' a week at a time fo' I loosens up enough to tie it. Gotta wait for spring. Show a little Chrisjun cha'htee. Lemme have another swallow of yo' Sock, den ben' down an' tie it fo' me. I'm axing you, bro. Please."

Moved by this time by his apparent sincerity and the piteousness of his appeal, I leaned over to comply.

And that was when he hit me — crowning my whole evening, as it were. I suppose I should have been alerted by the smarm of his delivery, but I was still too green, and moved besides by the spectacle of a fellow sufferer asking for relief. I think his cane must have been weighted with lead, because when I woke up I had, besides a splitting headache, a knot on the side of my head the size of a small apple. A crust of dried blood had formed, matting my hair. Some hours had apparently elapsed. I was lying facedown in the grass beside the bench. A cold dew had fallen over me. I could see it sparkling on the grass in the glow of a street lamp.

He had taken the little money I had and kindly left me the husk of my looted wallet. The bottle too, of course, was missing, which was a greater tragedy. It was some solace to me that I had left the bulk of my new fortune at home under the mattress. I felt a momentary pang of anxiety as to its safety there, hardly noticeable, however, beneath the weight of my other cares and tribulations. Wobbling on jellied legs, I zigzagged off, not toward the safety of the lighted street, but deeper into the park, wandering first across the drive, then the bridle path, finally up onto the elevated gravel track surrounding the reservoir. I was a little light-headed, feverish perhaps. My teeth chattered as I hung there, fingers sunk in the chain-link fence, peering out across the water toward the stone pump house in the southeast quadrant and Midtown beyond. The night was almost preternaturally clear and vivid. I could see the Milky Way arching overhead, like a swath cut by a brilliant sickle in the fields of darkness. The water was so still I could make out the twinkle of reflected stars, like ice cubes jingling and concussing in some dark punch; and away across the reservoir, looming black against the night, the Midtown towers — Chrysler, Pan Am, the spectral needle of the Empire State — like giant carcinomas flecked with stars. I think that might have been the first time the breathless magic of the city ever touched me, really touched me, with its fatal wand, so deeply that I wondered if I'd ever make it home again.

Retreating back in the direction I'd come, I lay down in a depression in the earth, secluded by a rampart of surrounding boulders from the eyes of any passers who might happen by at that late hour. There I fell asleep again, this time by natural causes, covered by the cold, cold dew.

•

Sunday, again, I spent putting off the inevitable return to responsibility and recrimination, tallying up considerably less mileage than the day before, however, having exhausted my supply of nervous energy, merely apathetic and depressed. From time to time the thought of my unattended stash returned to trouble me. It was late at night when I finally found my way back to Mulberry Street, using the fire escape to reach the rooftop as a final, and ultimately fruitless, precaution against moral ambush.

There was a note pinned to the door of my apartment which I didn't even read until I'd entered and assured myself the money hadn't been tampered with. Breathing a sigh of relief, I caught myself up, experiencing a pang of curiously delayed revulsion at my behavior. Silently I wondered at myself. What was happening to me? Not even trying to ascertain an answer, I sighed and tore open the envelope. It was from Yin-mi:

> Dear Sun I,
>
> If I should happen to miss you, please get in touch with me as soon as you come in. I've been worried sick. Father Riley and I sat up all last night waiting to hear from you. We've tried the police, the hospitals — everywhere. I just know something terrible has happened or we would have heard from you. I pray I'm wrong. It was a fiasco at the church. There was almost a riot. But nothing else matters as long as you're safe. If you're hurt, or in trouble in some way, please let me try and help you. No matter what it is. In any case, let me hear from you as soon as you get this. No matter what time it is. *Please.*
>
> All my love,
Yin-mi

Stifling the sob in my throat, I crumpled the note as soon as I'd read it and threw it in the trash. I couldn't deal with it in the condition I was in. The implications would have broken me, already fractured with a hairline flaw (Wild Hairline, Reader) running between the hemispheres of my brain all the way to my genitals through the chambers of my divided heart.

Beset with paranoid dreams, several times during the night I awoke drenched with sweat, listening breathlessly for the sound of footsteps crunching in the gravel of the roof. Each time I compulsively checked to see the money was still there, arose, tried the door to be certain it was locked and bolted. I counted and recounted the bills several times to ease my mind, then firmly resolved to spend the first dollar of my new wealth to purchase a night chain. Relief, even happiness, surged through me each time, after these bouts of bad dreams, I slipped my hand under the pillow, fondling the paper bag. Its presence reassured me, like a pacifier, a talisman.

Then clarity returned and I realized the money itself was the only conceivable motive a thief could have for breaking in. With profound chagrin, I remembered a quotation: "Hoarded riches are an invitation to the thief." Where was that from? Yes, of course, Lao Tzu. Could I really have forgotten?

Only with daybreak did the dreams and fantasies disperse. I understood for the first time the primitive terror of the animals, and why they sing with such abandon on the coming of the day. Though more exhausted than when I'd lain down, I was thankful to rise. Hoping to get out unobserved, I began to dress immediately, putting on my pants and shirt, and tying my tie before the mirror.

Hardly had the sky begun to lighten over the rooftops, throwing the buildings into silhouette, when Yin-mi appeared. Not even bothering to knock, she threw open the door. In the mirror I caught a glimpse of her expression.

"Thank God," she uttered in a voice of weary relief. Collapsing in a chair, she buried her face in her hands and began to cry.

Surprised by the intensity of it, both moved and shamed, I turned around.

She looked up through streaming eyes, blissfully. "I was so worried. Didn't you get my note?"

"Yes, I got it," I replied.

"You should have waked me. I wanted you to."

"I'm sorry," I said simply.

"It's okay. You were probably just being considerate."

Blushing, I faced the mirror and started knotting my tie again.

"Well?" she demanded finally with an uncharacteristic hint of impatience. Before I could reply she was up and at my side. "What happened?" she asked in distress, gingerly touching my head wound. "*Oo.*" She winced and sucked the air through her teeth. "You're hurt."

"It's nothing," I told her.

"What happened?"

"I got mugged."

"I knew it. I knew something had happened." There was a quaver of triumphant vindication in her tone. "Where were you?"

"The Upper West Side," I replied. "In the park."

"Are you all right?"

"Yes, fine."

"You're sure?"

"Positive."

"Thank God. I told Father Riley you wouldn't just stand us up for no reason, that you must have been hurt, otherwise you would have let us know. Have you seen a doctor?"

"It's really not that bad."

"The skin is broken." She touched it lightly. "Doesn't that hurt? Let me clean it out for you. It's filthy." She went to the faucet, wetting a towel under the stream. Standing on her tiptoes, she began gently swabbing. "Tell me what happened," she petitioned softly, absorbed in her task, not attempting to make eye contact. "Tell me all about it. . . . Maybe we can have the lecture next week," she mused as her mind raced on ahead.

"There isn't going to be a lecture," I said, arresting her hand as it worked.

"What do you mean?" she asked quizzically, gently disengaging her hand. "Why not?"

"Because there isn't any robe."

A hint of distress appeared in her face, then she raised her eyebrows in dawning surmise. "Oh no," she breathed in a loud whisper, "it wasn't stolen?"

The thought of lying briefly crossed my mind, but something in her expression made it impossible, as it always had. I shook my head. "No."

"Then what happened?" She was becoming agitated. "I don't understand. What happened to the robe? What were you doing on the Upper West Side?"

"I went up there after I pawned it," I said, turning back to the mirror again, buttoning my collar button, slipping the knot up to my throat.

"Pawned it!"

I nodded. "Friday afternoon after we came back."

"But you didn't tell me. And when I came by Saturday you said . . ." She stopped short each time, guessing the truth. In the mirror my face seemed sober, pale, funereal, almost like a corpse's. She simply stared at me in wonder. Then her eyes deepened (deep as my betrayal, irretrievably deep). Taking my small burden — the paper bag — I gently moved her aside, mumbling lamely in her ear, "I'm sorry," as I passed. I hurried down the stair into the street, knowing I should never again be able to bear that great solemnity in her eyes, or to forget it.

•

I didn't replay our encounter in my mind, or think about it further as I walked. A numb despair settled over me. My thoughts ran on the same track as the evening before, as though no interruption had occurred. I was a little queasy at the prospect of making my way unescorted through the streets. After yesterday's run-in, it seemed the height of folly to risk another mugging, perhaps even brutal death, for the sake of . . . what? A bag of paper? Yet I reassured myself that the fact that I had money on me today couldn't possibly advertise itself to anyone. Beyond a slight bulge in my pocket, carefully concealed beneath my smock, it couldn't effect any substantial change in my looks. Or could it? I became self-conscious. Was there perhaps a new evasiveness in my gaze, a barely perceptible nervousness in my walk which had not been there the day before, a clue which an experienced thief might use to single me out from the crowd? Was it possible my windfall was "discounted" in my face?

"Preposterous!" I told myself, peering nervously from side to side. "Pure paranoia." And yet, could it be there was some truth in it after all? For I felt as though a change, ever so small, had occurred within me. And was it not part of the teachings that changes in a part, no matter how subtle, eventually translate themselves throughout the whole? Was it not necessarily true that a man's spiritual condition was reflected in his face? In tandem with this suggestion I experienced a revelation of a minor sort. I began to understand the numbness and inscrutability that animate, or rather deaden, the faces that forever circulate through Wall Street from Trinity down to the river. It was the soul's own defensive posture, a way of anesthetizing itself against the harrowing pressures of living under siege. These men and women were obsessed by cares that they might lose what they had spent the better part of life amassing, guarding their hoards with such determined ferocity that the joy in simple pleasures had gone out of their eyes, and their faces, chameleonlike, had begun to assume the color of the cliffs that line both sides of the financial canyon that is Wall Street.

For reasons of my own, I decided to adopt their manner for a day, assuming the Wall Street mask of fear: the glazed, dull, watery eye, the slouching shoulders. Quickening my pace, I stared straight ahead or down at my feet by turns, moving briskly, avoiding the eyes of passersby, pacing the beaten track with an expression now harrowed, now vacant, just like the thousands of others I saw daily pressing through the subway turnstiles, homogenized products off of an assembly line. Only with a difference, since for me it was no more than a temporary disguise, a mask assumed for one day only to throw thieves and muggers off the track. Underneath, my values, my contempt for the whole spectacle, my pity and compassion for the others, remained intact.

And yet . . . and yet . . . somehow this too was Tao, I reminded myself. I despaired of ever laying bare the unimaginable heart of that most awful paradox.

At any rate, I found the role dangerously simple to project. In fact, had I not already donned, unconsciously, what constitutes perhaps the most important article of the whole costume? I mean, of course, the dark glasses: "But if you did not wear spectacles the brightness and glory of the Emerald City would blind you. Even those who live in the City must wear spectacles night and day." This sentence from the *Wizard of Oz,* which I had bought after my return from Sands Point, played through my mind, reinforcing my conviction.

By the time I reached Trinity the elasticity had gone out of my step. I already felt drained and dreaded the prospect of the day. I passed Wo in the lobby on my way in. I hadn't seen him for quite some time.

"Looks like it's starting to get to you, too," he observed. "You're not bouncing around here with the same gung ho enthusiasm as you used to."

His remark aroused unexpected hostility. I distinctly disliked his presumption in lumping me, without my consent, in that hapless, cynical fraternity of time-biders and ne'er-do-wells whose president and major booster he was. I think I must have colored with bitter embarrassment before I mastered myself. Then, shrugging my shoulders with an air of haughty indifference, I walked off without a word.

Alone again, I gloated secretly in the knowledge that I had put myself forever beyond the petty reach of his mean-spirited aspersions by virtue of what I was carrying in my pocket. Then a reciprocal impulse challenged, and I felt shame for harboring such thoughts, priding myself on the possession of something that not five minutes before I had deplored. I made a solemn promise to myself never to forget that what I'd done was for the sake of knowledge, not for wealth, and never in future, even for a single moment, to lose sight of that saving distinction.

In spite of my resolve and my best efforts, as I passed through the corridors of the Exchange, I was soothed by a new and unprecedented complacency as I looked at my fellow runners. I couldn't help myself. A subtle intimation passed through me that somehow I had passed beyond them, that we were no longer of the same class. There was no aversion in this. In fact, I felt an intensified compassion for them and applauded their efforts at self-betterment.

But secretly I wondered how many of them had what it really took to rise out of their position, a position whose indignity had never occurred to me in exactly the same light before. But now I had been elevated beyond their reach, promoted into the big leagues. What made me different? I owned shares. Now I had a piece of the pie, a stake in the future of America. Or soon would have.

When I found Kahn I disburdened myself of all the worries, all the hopes and fears, that the simple overnight possession of so much cold cash had elicited. Putting his arm around my shoulder paternally, he led me off into a corner, away from the roisterous activity of the trading floor, consoling me thus: "You see, kid? It's already started happening." He nodded his head as though satisfied and vindicated.

"What has?" I asked, confused by his ellipsis.

"In one sleepless night you've learned more about the Dow than in all the weeks you'd been here, watching from the sidelines, attending lectures, asking questions. . . . These are the famous 'cares and worries of responsibility.' " His look of hard sympathy reminded me of the look I'd seen in Tsin's eyes as he watched me take the stem between my lips and draw. There was a new intimacy between us, a sense of deeper fraternity than ever before. Gratified as I was, I felt a little uneasy; for it bore traces of the desperate, cynical fellowship that springs up among outlaws and fallen men.

"This is reality, Sonny," he said, "and you've bought a piece."

"Reality?" I asked. "I'm not so sure. Remember, this is only temporary."

He smiled and shook his head. "You'll find it's a whole lot easier to get in than to get out."

"I'm investing my money, Kahn," I informed him, "not my heart."

"Facilis descensus Averno," he said, looking not so much at me as through me.

"Is that Yiddish?"

He smiled. "Almost. It's Latin."

"What does it mean?"

" 'The descent to hell is easy,' " he translated. " 'Night and day the gates of Dis stand open; but to recall our steps and ascend again into the upper air, that is the labor, that is the task.' "

Our eyes met on it.

"So!" he said at last, with a burst of cheer that signaled a change of subject as well as mood. "I suppose we may as well get down to *business,* eh?" Taking me by the arm confidentially, he led me away. "I think I may have just the thing!"

Chapter 5

"Okay kid, I'm going to give you the straight poop," Kahn began as we attacked our lunch. He spewed half a masticated eclair in all directions, succumbing to an attack of unexpected laughter. "Sorry, Sonny. I didn't mean that." He handed me a paper napkin. " 'The straight poop.' That's pretty good. I'll have to tell Norm about that."

"What are you talking about?" I demanded querulously, picking flecks of pastry cream off my smock.

"It'll become clear as I go along," he said. "This is something I've been working on for over a year. I haven't mentioned it because it's still at a very delicate stage, strictly top secret. I have this friend from Mount Abarim, Norman Murdfeld. He's a commodities trader on the Chicago Board of Trade. Corn futures mostly. Because of his connections in the field, so to speak, he was able to get in on the ground floor of this sweet little operation a guy named Hiram Cox cooked up out there. Hiram's a rube, but what the hell? A little short on cash initially, he offered Norm a piece of the action, and Norm talked to me. I jumped on it, even though I had to put myself in hock up to my ears. There are liens against my seat and the building I own now, but we're just on the verge of the payout. And if I'm right, this could make the great Pepsi-Cola score look like penny ante. I'm serious, kid. It could be the masterstroke of my career. If this pans out, I could retire and go on the Grand Tour, set up a stud farm in Palm Beach or Boca Raton. And because I like you, kid, I'm going to cut you in."

"What is it?"

"All right already! Don't be so impatient!" he chided. "All will be revealed to you in time." Rocking back in his swivel chair, he lorded his advantage over me, stuffing his cheeks. Slowly licking his fingertips clean, he extracted them one by one from between his rounded lips with a pert gesture and a sound like a small kiss. "Won't you have one?" he offered with coy politeness.

"Kahn!" I threatened.

"Okay," he relented, leaning forward suddenly and planting his elbows on the desk. "Here it is: long-term heavy farm equipment leasing." He paused, waiting for the applause.

I ogled him blankly.

"You know, tractors, combines, harvesters, that kind of stuff," he elaborated. "Don't you see? It's a really sweet little concept — leasing, I mean. No one had considered it before. It was always you buy it, it's yours, including the headaches. Our idea is better from both ends: for the farmer, because he has no heavy initial load and payments substantially below what he would be paying to own, and, best of all, no maintenance worries; better for the company, because we've discovered that pretty much by simply creating an effective service fleet, we can get the farmer to buy our plant for us, so that at the end of a six- to eight-year lease, we have, free and clear, tractors with only half their effective field-lives used, ready to be leased out again — every dollar they bring in from that point pure gravy. In other words, free tractors."

"What's the name of the company?"

He chuckled. "That's the most beautiful part. You ready? Jane Doe."

I gave him the same blank look.

"Jesus, kid! Wake up! John Deere, don't you see? The leader in the industry? Now is that brilliant or what? Think of the advertising possibilities! 'A more attractive alternative.' 'The better half of the industry.' Picture it." He smoothed his palms out in the air like a magician, opening a curtain and a vista. "This sweet little corn-fed thing appears on your tube: bib overalls, braided pigtails, baseball cap, the works. She's rubbing her toe in the dirt, holding her hands behind her back, looking kind of awkward and embarrassed. The camera closes in and she begins to speak: 'I'm sending him a Dear John letter, America. From here on out it's just you and me.' Suddenly she looks up and grins, half milkmaid, half femme fatale. 'And it doesn't have to last forever either, you know,' she says. Then she flings her cap away, shakes out her hair, and strips into a sequined swimsuit. 'I'm liberated, baby!' she belts out. 'From now on it's pay as you go!' " He paused expectantly. "So what do you think? Is it poetry or what?"

"I don't know, Kahn," I hedged. "It sounds interesting, but . . ."

"Okay, okay," he said testily, a little miffed to have his imaginative flight impeded, "you haven't heard the best part yet. Up to this point Doe has been trading over the counter. It's done quite well too. But we're all agreed — and by 'we' I mean Norm, Hiram, and myself, a few others, our little cartel of insiders — that we need a wider market for the stock. So we're going to list with the Exchange."

"List?"

"Sure. List Doe to be traded on the New York Stock Exchange. Enter the big leagues in other words."

"Isn't that difficult?"

He fluttered his hand. "So-so."

"What are the chances?"

"For us, a shoo-in," he said. "We've already done all the groundwork. That's sort of where I came in. Norm and I spent a lot of time tidying things up on the business end — you know, accounting policies and whatnot — so we could present a pretty package to the boys down in the Stock List Department. Doe had no trouble meeting the net asset and profit criteria demanded by the Exchange. What we didn't have was diversified enough holdings, i.e., enough outstanding shares owned by enough shareholders. So what we did was cut a deal with the boys in Stock List which involves simultaneous listing and a large public issue of common stock: a half-million shares at ten bucks apiece. They've bought it hook, line, and sinker. The rest is a formality. The application simply has to be presented to the Board of Governors. I have it from one of the guys that they're going to review us this coming Thursday. By next week our name should be in lights on the marquee with all the other big boys (and girls), the newest, hottest issue in America! Anyone who hasn't heard of us should prick their ears up pretty quick. If we can only get some momentum rolling behind the offer, it could be a bonanza. We could have a feeding frenzy on our hands."

"And if you can't — get the momentum rolling, I mean?"

"Ah!" He lifted his index finger and leaned back in his chair. "That's a good question, one we've thought of before. But there's an answer!" He rocked forward again, fixing me with an incisive stare. "Now pay close attention, kid, because this is the sweetest part of the whole deal, and the most secret. You see, as a member of the cartel, I can tell you that Doe has its eye on this little company out that way called Sui Generis, not very big, but a real jewel. They have a series of plants that manufacture animal feed and fertilizer, both under the Sui label. Confidentially, I'm prepared to tell you that for the last three weeks we've been involved in top-secret negotiations with the founder and owner of said company, one Olaf Tryggvesson. Now Olaf, though a crochety old son of a bitch, is a genius in his way. He had an idea, and he's made it pay handsomely. Only he's too crabbed and unimaginative to see that it has potential far beyond the two-bit sort of local operation he's developed. He's too stingy and conservative. Norm told me he came to the meeting in his pickup, wearing overalls, with a three-day growth of beard, sat there the whole time picking his teeth, chewing tobacco, and spitting the juice in a Styrofoam coffee cup. Had manure on his boots, too, which he refused to wipe off 'for moral reasons,' pointing out that 'shit had made him vut he vus today.' Kind of touching, don't you think?

"But let me tell you what he's got out there that's so special and that we want so bad. You see, he buys corn from the farmer, then converts it into feed, which he sells back to the farmer at a profit to feed his hogs. Then after it's been, so to speak, reconstituted a second time, he buys it back as manure for virtually nothing, which he converts into fertilizer using a patented process which Bunge has been trying to steal from him for years. Olaf invented it himself. I don't pretend to understand all the nuances, but I know the central feature is a machine he built to facilitate the manure conversion process. It's called the Fecal Dynamo, or more familiarly, the Poop Pump. That's why I cracked up earlier. You see, what old Olaf has got himself out there, quite literally, is a way of making money off of shit. Do you see the implications?"

"I'm not sure," I groped. "Perhaps you'd better elaborate a little further."

"He sells them this high-priced feed, which he then buys back for zip as manure. Chemically speaking, it's just about the same, only pricewise it's dropped out of sight due to a little 'depreciation' in the product. Don't you get it? He makes it at both ends!" Kahn was breaking up now as he spoke. "It's the classic short sale, don't you see, only guaranteed! Olaf sells feed, on the expectation of a drop in price, then buys back cheap, as manure. 'Buy cheap; sell dear' — it could be his motto. Only in a short sale in the market you can never be sure the Dow is going to accommodate your whimsy. Sometimes the stock you expect to drop goes up in price and you get squeezed. Not so Olaf. You see, for him it's guaranteed. His information is infallible. It comes straight from God. It's tied to the cycle of nature itself. As a Taoist you should get into that, kid. He knows that whatever else may screw up on him (on us) in this unreliable, spiteful state of things which we call life on earth, that feed is always, no matter what, going to depreciate in value after going through a pig's intestines. It's classic. On a large scale, the concept could revolutionize agriculture in the corn belt. Only old Olaf's head starts spinning when he thinks about sums larger than five figures and distances beyond the county line. Besides, he's old. He's ready to sell the business and retire with a comfortable income, breeding prize heifers and beauhogs — or whatever you call 'em — in his spare time. He's already agreed in principle to sell the cartel a controlling interest in Sui. He's a smart old bugger, though. Know what one of his conditions was? That he get part of his payment in shares of Doe. He knows a good thing when he sees it. It's all pretty much set. Olaf says he doesn't 'vant to gnaw gnaw-think' about the 'whalings and dalings' of us 'yuunk kids.' As soon as he sees a certified check in his hand though, I've got an idea he'll be ready to start talking turkey.

"Picture the scenario now, kid. A cheap new issue with a hot idea lists on the Exchange. The public is skeptical. People sniff around a bit. It begins to move. Some large blocks are traded." Kahn smiled. (I remember that smile.) "Doe starts to pick up a little mo', if you know what I mean. Then there's an announcement of an impending merger. 'With whom?' people ask. 'Sui Generis,' somebody (me) replies nonchalantly. 'What the hell kind of name is that?' they ask. 'Bunge has been trying to buy them out for years. You see they've got this secret process . . .' 'Bunge? Secret process?' Then psychology takes over. Doe shows up in the Percentage Gainers column of the *Wall Street Journal,* then on the Most Active List. The general public starts to take notice. The hometown boys start to nibble at the edges, and the Technicians note some seismic rumblings in their Odd-Lot Oscillators. By the time it hits fifteen, even

Merrill Lynch has lifted its huge, sleepy head to sniff the air, in which there's a strong aroma of manure. The brass appoints a specialist to research the company and publish a report. Probably Melvin Piper. Who does he come to? That's right, yours truly. 'Hey, Aaron, ever heard of this Jane Doe company?' 'Who me?' I ask. Then I give him the scoop, or poop, laying it on with a trowel. 'It's going to forty,' I say, 'fifty maybe.' 'Holy shit!' he says, rushing out of my office like a madman. The next week there it is in the Merrill Lynch Market Newsletter. Triple-A-plus rating. 'An excellent opportunity for growth. Little or no downside risk.' Twenty million investors, from Moose Lake, Maine, to San Luis Opisbo, pick it up in their mailboxes, and the phones start ringing. The commission house boys can't process the orders fast enough. 'Hey, Aaron, could you help me out a little here?' 'Sure!' I say. 'Always ready to do a favor for a friend.' Then I start making commissions executing orders on my own stock! And there you are, kid. We've shot the moon. It's beautiful, beautiful. Your thousand — that's a hundred shares. If it works out, you should make three grand easy, maybe four or five. Not bad for a beginner, huh? So what do you say? You in?"

I hardly heard his question I was so absorbed in watching the spectacle of his face, flushed, radiant, incisive. He was as happy as I'd ever seen him as he outlined the battle plan. And all I could think about was his identification only a few days earlier of Wall Street as a proving ground for character.

"Kahn," I said, "you know I trust you implicitly. If it weren't for you, well, where would I be?"

"Thanks, kid, I appreciate that."

"But tell me, is this really on the up-and-up?"

He sighed and sat back. "Okay, kid, since you ask, I'm going to be completely candid with you. Sure there are a few things about the operation that aren't entirely kosher. But hell, who ever heard of kosher pork? Right? I mean, you can't let your O.C. get the best of you. Sometimes in the field — even the cornfield — a soldier has to improvise on his orders a little bit, take the initiative into his own hands. We're not contemplating anything here that hasn't been done before, and by the best. But who's going to know? To answer your question though, yes, we'll be trading on the basis of inside information, i.e., the impending Jane Doe–Sui merger, but that kind of thing goes on all the time. You can't let moral quibbles get in the way of really great opportunities. Think big, kid! Think about Napoleon, Caesar, Mayer Rothschild! Hell, if this works out like I expect it to, it could rival anything Ahasuerus ever did here. I could earn my spurs as an authentic latter-day W.J., which is to say, Wandering Jew. And you too, kid. It seems foolish to hesitate now. You've already taken the plunge, why not go all the way? This deal, as I see it, is your best bet. It promises to be lucrative and expeditious. I promise you, we're not doing anything here that hasn't been hallowed by long Wall Street tradition. And remember, I have your best interests at heart. Hell, I'm not even going to charge you a commission. And besides, what's a hundred shares? It's not exactly like your participation is going to float the venture. Sonny, I'm trying to do you a favor. I should justify?"

"All right, Kahn," I yielded. "If you say it's okay, then I believe you."

He mopped his brow. "Jesus, kid! That was the hardest sale I ever made. But thanks. I appreciate it, the vote of . . ." (he grinned) "Kahn-fidence, so to speak." He studied my face. "What's the matter, Sonny?"

"I just thought of something."

"What's that?" he inquired.

"You know the company Sui Generis?"

He nodded. "What about it?"

"Well, a few days ago when I consulted the oracle about what I should do, the hexagram it returned was number seventeen, 'Waiting.' "

"So?"

"Well, its Chinese name is *Sui.*"

"No shit!" he said as though impressed. I noticed he'd touched the bracelet on his wrist. "See what I told you, kid? We ought to use that thing, the *I Ching,* I mean. It's sinful not to!"

•

The listing occurred without a hitch, as Kahn had predicted. What he hadn't predicted, and couldn't reasonably have been expected to foresee, was that the issue of a half-million shares of Jane Doe common would coincide almost exactly with the last gasp of a summer rally which had already run its course. Like an exhausted beast of burden, it lay even then expiring in the dust, only to be kicked superfluously dead by the government, which had the cheek to announce an unexpected downturn in the economy, especially in the agricultural sector, where bumper crops had produced surpluses, driving prices below anticipated levels. This stroke of bad luck, however, had only proved grist to Olaf's mill (so to speak), enabling him to buy his raw materials even cheaper than usual. In the flush of this unwitting coup, he wasn't so sure anymore about retiring.

"Not to worry," Kahn assured me. "It's simply a matter of reopening negotiations and offering him a few additional 'sweeteners.' It'll just take a little more time."

Time. As the Reader knows, that was one commodity which, for me at least, was in precious short supply. Yet there was nothing for it. I had to wait.

During the day it wasn't so bad. I kept busy with my relatively mindless, but consuming, duties as a squad boy. Even there subtle but insidious changes began creeping into my behavior. After the O.C.-induced catatonia of my first few days on the trading floor, I had blossomed into what Kahn asseverated was a "model gopher," always cheerful and polite, never grumbling over unusual requests (such as when a specialist asked me to bring him a length of toilet paper so that the could blow his nose, then gave me the privilege of disposing of the steaming afterbirth). Now, however, I began to take on some of the preoccupations, and mannerisms, of a broker — a dangerous and insufferable presumption in a coolie of my order. Sometimes in the middle of the floor I would go into a trance, mesmerized by the spectacle of the tape running above the room, blazoning its message to the world in hieroglyphs that none but the initiated could decipher, the moving pageant of the future unfolding before my eyes (a minute in retard). Doe, of course, was the legend I hoped to see translated to the world. If I was rarely gratified at first, it became a sort of abstract pleasure. Was Steel going to add an eighth on its next trade, or lose one? Though not remotely interested myself, at least in the material sense, I couldn't resist the temptation to try and second-guess it. When I was wrong I shrugged fatalistically, consoling myself with the timeless wisdom, "Nobody knows what's going to happen in the market; never have, never will." When I was right I shrugged as well. "A lucky guess," I said, but with a flush of color in my cheek, a glow of inner satisfaction, half-believing in my heart that through some special dispensation from fate, whose terms were obscure even to myself, I had been granted the power to predict the future, a power which put me in a different category from "the other guy," exempt from the iron laws of gravity which circumscribed his narrow life. The point was, I suppose, that I felt on new terms of intimacy with the Dow, something totally incommensurable with what I'd experienced before while standing on the sidelines "observing without participating."

Kahn was tolerant of these lapses. At lunch hour in his office as I sat with furrowed brow, punching up the symbol DOE over and over on the Quotron, he tiptoed around like an old matron looking after a pregnant girl whose husband is away at the front fighting in the trenches. I was the young girl, with all my hopes and fears riding on the future; Kahn, the kindly elder, strong, stern, and sympathetic. The analogy evoked a pang of anguish. I wondered if perhaps I hadn't glimpsed my mother's state of mind during the months of her confinement. Suddenly I understood Hsiao's suggestion that the wild alternations between hope and fear — whatever it was in her that produced the enigmatic parable of the robe — must surely have been absorbed by a kind of spiritual osmosis into the being of the child that fed and slumbered in her womb. If this were so, the consciousness of it had lain dormant in me all these years. For until I had invested something of my own, until I'd had something to lose, I had never understood the suffering, sometimes frantic, sometimes merely sad, that is attendant on the heart of longing, irrespective of its nature, the same in hope as fear.

But my longing was linked to something other than the robe, perhaps more powerfully linked: to Li. Tied to this longing, and equally as vivid, were feelings of remorse and guilt centering on Yin-mi. That is why the nights for me were even harder than the days, after the bell had sounded and Wall Street had disgorged its hosts. In some ways I envied the commuters, though they complained most, and with most justice, about the rigors of their schedules: those long, dreary hours in the trains coming and going each day, arriving home exhausted, after dark, to a warmed-over dinner, going over a report, listening to the news, falling asleep, getting up again while everyone else was sleeping, taking a shower, rushing to make the train. Their lives were lonely, disspiriting, empty, but at least, I told myself, for them the night held no such terrors as it held for me. They were insulated by regimentation against the vertigo of being at loose ends, spared the free time in which the soul escapes, by necessity if not by choice, from its habituated rounds, and yet on looking inward finds it has no place to go, having destroyed, or simply lost the way back to, its pristine sanctuary. This was my predicament exactly. That place inside myself, built out of river stones, cool beneath the shadows of the trees, where the sun's mild rays sifted gently down to a floor of pine straw, illuminating motes of dust as they danced on invisible currents of air, that place where I had once retired to sing . . . I looked and it was gone. For such a place does not exist, not in the souls of financiers and traders (which is what I had become in my own modest right by my own choice), or if it does that man is as rare as the "righteous man" whom Abraham sought in Sodom. For such a place is built out of a silent gratitude to life, and of the passions which the Dow excites, perhaps that is the rarest.

I, for one, know I did not feel grateful, but anxious and dissatisfied. I pitied myself. I wanted to see Li, but I knew the desire wasn't mutual. Besides, each time I thought of her, Yin-mi's image rose up before me like a castigating angel. Similarly, when I wanted the solace of her company as in the old days, the thought of Li paralyzed my initiative, that and the thought of how I'd let her down. In the early days of this waiting period, not long after our conversation, Yin-mi once even left a note on my door. "How can I understand if you won't try and explain?" it said. But what explanation could I offer? That was the point. There simply wasn't any. And I couldn't face her under those conditions, totally guilty, totally exposed.

I attempted to get back into meditation. But as I sat my mind was anything but blank. I could not control the swirling cloud of dusty visions which, from some peculiar conversion of high and low emotional pressure systems, sprang from the parched soil of my mind, like tornadoes in Kansas I had read about, lifting houses bodily from their foundations, then splintering them to matchwood when they dropped them. This spinning cloud of grief and frustration hurled smashed bits of furniture and clanging trash can tops against the walls of my brain until I couldn't hear the sound of my own breath, swept up myself into the heart of the disturbance, like Dorothy.

Each morning on my return to Wall Street, I anxiously sought out Kahn in the hope of some good tidings. But each day he simply gave me a sympathetic smile and shrugged his shoulders. "Not yet, kid," he said.

Though we were quickly approaching the autumnal equinox, on the floor the days seemed to be growing longer. The Dow was languishing in the financial doldrums near the equator. Day after day the market prophets prophesied that the wind was bound to pick up soon and send the Averages cleaving mightily once more through the lines of latitude on the charts into more hospitable and invigorating climes. Investors responded with redoubled apathy.

"When, Kahn? When?" I asked continually.

"So what am I supposed to do, kid?" he rejoined, shrugging his shoulders and pouting his lips. "I'm into this a whole lot heavier than you are, remember. But you've got to see, a new issue never thrives in a market like this. But it won't die. It's only dormant kid, believe me. Just be patient. Sui will come through for us. And the portions will be *generous*, or should I say *Generis*." He grinned. "Every once in a while you get a market like this, neither bull nor bear, but something in between, a monstrosity with all the worst qualities of both and none of the good qualities of either, neither fish nor flesh, put nor call. I like to call it a boar market."

"A boar market?"

"Yeah, b-o-r-e," he spelled it out, chuckling.

"Okay, Kahn," I acquiesced. "I just hope something happens soon."

As it turned out, my wish was granted. But perhaps I should have been a little more specific in placing my order. Something happened all right. The market awoke from its lethargy, displaying behavior that was neither bullish nor unduly bearish, nor even boarish, but more like a groundhog emerging from its burrow near the end of winter, rubbing its sleepy eyes with furry little fists, looking around in the bright winter glare, only to start at its own shadow on the snow, then scamper back yelping with fright into its burrow, to remain there a few more weeks. Just so the Dow. On moderately heavy volume, it reared its perverse little head out of its hole and looked back over the long, tedious plain of its recent somnolence, then promptly retreated fifteen points and fell asleep again. No one was happy except the Technicians, who took the opportunity to convene a conference and christen a new formation, which, with uncharacteristic hilarity, they called "The Contrary Prairie Dog" (as opposed, I suppose, to some more tractable sort).

Articles began to appear in all the important journals, with titles like, "Is the Dow Dead (or Only in a Coma)?" and "How Much Common Security Is Too Much?" Commission brokers started to appear in welfare lines. And all over America thousands of housewives returned to their kitchens from their neighborhood Junior League, cowering in disgrace beneath their husbands' supportive, paternalistic smiles and complacent choruses of "I told you so." Specialists began to smuggle backgammon boards onto the trading floor, and there were sometimes ominous silences of several seconds between the punching out of one trade on the Teletype and the advent of the next. Flights to the Bahamas were booked to capacity, and the janitors seemed to be pushing the remains of a lot more bag lunches on their brooms at the end of the day.

And still Olaf was recalcitrant. Things continued in this vein through September and into October. Time kept ticking away toward the deadline, and still Jane Doe had not doubled, which is what it had to do for me to recoup my principal and meet the interest payments. In fact, the hottest new issue in America had eased from 10 to 8¾. Even Kahn was starting to get edgy. I was on the verge of panic.

With two weeks left to go, I resorted to the desperate expedient of paying Mme Chin a visit to ask for an extension. I should have known better. I did know better. It wasn't a rational act.

Shaving after work, splashing a little Florida Water on my cheeks, and putting on a fresh shirt, I did my feeble best to maximize my advantages in anticipation of a grim encounter.

I caught her and Fan-ku on the landing, locking up as they prepared to go out for the evening. Seeing me, a glint of telling light — something old, shrewd, and Sphinx-like, calculating yet indifferent to the outcome (almost indifferent) — scintillated in her pupils. "So, Sun I," she said, "I assume you've brought the money?" She uttered this with a formality and reserve which precluded all pleasantry, prepared to resent it, under the circumstances of our bond, as an impertinence.

"That's just what I wanted to talk to you about," I explained, infusing my tone with as much confidence and ebullience as I could muster, hoping she'd find it infectious.

She stared at me gravely (immunized, apparently, long before). "What is there to talk about? Did we make a deal or not? Then was the time for talk, now is the time for action. Bring me the money first, then we can talk as much as you like. In the meantime we are adversaries. Don't try and persuade me to make an exception for you. I'm hard, Sun I. If you don't know that, learn it now. My word is iron; it will not bend. I make no exceptions. Ever. Where would I be if I'd let every customer who walked through my door with some 'priceless' bibelot squirm out of our agreement? I'll tell you where. Still back in Shanghai reading palms for money and walking the streets selling myself to sailors. Now, however, I wear silk like a gentlewoman" (she lifted her eyebrows and swept her hand down her side, proudly displaying the evidence), "as you can see. Now it is I who can afford to buy." She glanced just slightly in Fan-ku's direction, smiling. "This is what matters in the end, Sun I. And I've gotten it by being hard. It's a lesson you have yet to learn. So don't ask me to alter our agreement. It's a waste of breath. You must excuse me though. We have an engagement and are pressed for time. Do not return until the time is up. You still have two weeks. Perhaps something will materialize. After that consider the robe lost irrecoverably. Then, if you wish, we may be friends again. Or, if you cannot relinquish your possession in your heart, we may be cold and distant neighbors. Or you may leave. It's all the same to me." She threaded her arm through her companion's, and they walked off, the dowager and her queer, pretty boy, that grim, macabre pair, leaving me mooning after them, cowed and dejected, and with a sense of frustration that crystallized in fury, giving off a hint of sulphur before it vaporized into despair.

The next day when I told Kahn about the incident, he patted me on the back and said, "I believe that's what they call 'the discipline of the marketplace.'"

Chapter 6

As fate, or luck, would have it, at just about that point some of the telltales began to flutter in the rigging high up among the shrouds and furled topgallant sails of Wall Street, and feebly, doubtfully at first, but picking up headway as it went along, the Dow weighed anchor. In other words, the market made a cautious advance. Odd-lot traders from out of town and great institutional investors alike lifted their moist muzzles in the wind and sniffed about, some attracted by the innocent fragrance of opening buds of hope, others by the smell of blood, a few, like Kahn and me, willing to settle simply for a whiff of Illinois field patty. Ten days before the deadline, after I had already begun the painful, and perhaps ultimately fruitless, task of weaning myself emotionally from the robe, Jane Doe showed uncharacteristic pluck, opening up a half from its close the day before. Was this a saucy show of nerve portending greater things to come, or merely the final spasmodic fibrillations of an expiring heart? Unfortunately I had no professional cardiologists in consultation to reveal the meaning of this fluctuation in her EKG, which is to say, no Technicians to interpret the charts. I didn't need professional advice, however, to divine the meaning of the figure that flashed by me on the screen:

DOE
10000s 9¼

Ten thousand shares at 9¼! Jane had just achieved a measure of instant notoriety, her name flashed up in blinking lights on the Big Board, like a famous performer on the marquee of a great hotel in Vegas! While brokers all over the country were sipping their second cups of coffee over their *Wall Street Journal*s, idly punching up quotes between the paragraphs, Jane Doe made America stand up and take notice as she brashly exposed herself to the eye of the public, mingling unabashedly with the aristocrats of finance (Ma Bell herself, staid hostess of the fete!), crashing their invitation-only party on the Big Board. Five glorious minutes in the limelight of the Most Active List, before the doorman quietly ushered her back out into the cold!

"Kahn! Kahn!" I shouted, running madly toward the elevators through the crowd of groggy clerks and brokers, who all ogled me as though I were insane. "Did you see?" I cried, bursting through his office door. I stood on the threshold panting.

He was sitting at his desk, not leaning back in his swivel chair puffing a cigar with a jubilant smirk as I'd expected, but hunched forward like a guilty animal expecting a blow at any moment from its master's hand. Staring anxiously at the screen of his Quotron, he appeared to be muttering to himself. On the desk in front of him was a pile of shredded paper, blank trade slips which he'd torn to pieces as though in preparation for a celebration with confetti. Only from his somber mien, it might more appropriately have been the pile of sweepings pushed up by the cleaning crew after the party is over.

"Didn't you see the tape?" I asked. "A block of Doe just went by at a nine and a quarter, up three-quarters from the close."

He looked up with an expression of amusement which had no joy in it, but a splenetic, slightly curdled quality, like soured milk. "You don't say?" he mockingly replied.

"What's the matter, Kahn?" I asked, suddenly deflating with concern over his strange antics. "This is what we've been waiting for, isn't it? I mean, sure, it's only a beginning, and we're still in the red. But you've got to start somewhere, right?"

He continued to fix me with a silent, scathing look.

"What's the matter? Don't you see what it means?"

He laughed bitterly. "Yeah," he said. "It means I'm out another six thousand bucks, more or less."

"Six thousand bucks? What are you talking about?"

"I originally bought those shares at less than three. Yesterday when I sold them they were at eight and five-eighths. And when I bought them back this morning they'd taken on another five-eighths. Multiply that by ten thousand. Six grand, right?"

"You . . . ?" I whispered shrilly, half questioning, half accusing, pointing my finger at him reflexively.

"Don't point the finger," he chided. "It's not polite. I thought I'd taught you that."

I looked at it and put it down.

"Now, if the SEC will only abide by the same rules of etiquette . . ." he quipped with a dry cackle.

"It isn't illegal?"

"What? Selling my own shares and buying them back?" He laughed. "Bona fide manipulation. Outlawed under the Securities Exchange Act of 1934. It's called painting the tape — a wash sale, basically. I've been turning over bits and pieces for days now, but this time I went the whole hog, so to speak." He grinned thinly.

"But why?" I implored him.

"Why? *Why? You* ask me that? Haven't you been running around here the last few weeks asking me ten, twenty times a day, 'When, Kahn? When?' What do you want from me? I couldn't take it anymore!"

"You're not serious?"

"I'm *serious*, kid!"

My lips began to tremble. I felt like I was going to cry.

"Okay, okay — it wasn't only you. Jesus, kid! Don't be such a nebbish. My loans are coming due. My creditors are starting to threaten. If this Sui thing doesn't come through soon, I may lose my building, plus my other assets, which is to say, where my ass sits. Well, I figure since I'm more or less trapped, I may as well go all the way, right? I mean, no balls, no glory. Somebody's got to set the old ball rolling, don't they? With luck without precipitating any heads into similar motion. Actually, come to think of it, balls may not be the most auspicious image in this connection either." He grinned and touched his copper bracelet. "But you know what I mean."

"But what if you get caught?"

"Not to worry," he assured me. "I've been purchasing through a numbered account at Second Jersey Hi-Fidelity. Remember, kid, I may be a schlemiel, but I'm no schlimazel. I know how to cover my tracks. No one's going to know."

"But . . ."

"No more ifs, ands, and buts." He made a cut sign in the air like a director. "Please, a little faith! You want to see our profits materialize, don't you? You want to get your mother's wedding dress, or whatever you said it was, out of hock, right?"

I nodded uncertainly.

"Well, this is the only way. It's as plain as the nose on my face."

I sat staring witlessly at his admittedly impressive proboscis as though somehow within its depths, like the precious spermaceti in the "Heidelberg tun" of the whale's head, the answer lay waiting to be exhumed.

"I know my methods are a little unorthodox," he admitted, "but they'll produce results. Trust me, kid."

Just then a hurried knock sounded at the door. Kahn leaned back in his chair and put on his business face. "Come in," he invited sonorously.

"Sorry to bother you, Aaron," said a bald little man, peeking in. He had a forehead almost as broad — in comparison with his chin and lower face — and luminous as a light bulb. On his tiny, bridgeless nose a pair of heavy horn-rimmed glasses were inching their way downward, so that he gazed at us over them with an air of fatuous archness, fatuous because unintentional and thus self-reflecting. "I was just wondering if you knew anything about this stock, uh . . . what's it called?" He glanced down at his clipboard. "Oh yeah" (he snickered) "Jane Doe. Mike Burnside down at Morgan Guaranty just called up and asked me about it. I said I'd get back to him."

"Jane Doe?" Kahn asked, coolly lighting his cigar. "What kind of name is that?" He caught my eye as he sucked it alight, cheeks collapsing and expanding like a kissing fish, eye just as glum and inexpressive, at least to the casual observer. I, however, could detect a certain well-known deadpan glimmer there.

Our visitor laughed appreciatively. "I think it's kind of original myself," he ventured with a sheepish grin.

"Perhaps it is, perhaps it is," Kahn smoothly agreed, waving out his match. He examined his ash unhurriedly. "You know, Piper, I do seem to remember hearing something about that stock."

"Wonderful!" his interlocutor cried, forcing his way through the door.

"You know Mr. Piper, don't you? From Merrill Lynch?" He emphasized these last words subtly and darted me a meaningful stare.

"Pleased to meet you," I greeted, offering my hand.

"Sure, sure," Piper replied impatiently, making an attenuated nod in my direction.

"You were just leaving, weren't you?" Kahn suggested. "Why don't you go out and bring us a couple coffees?"

Piper took out his pen and sat down eagerly on the edge of the chair beside Kahn's desk.

I played along with Kahn's little performance. "Cream and sugar, Mr. Piper?" I asked suavely.

"Yes, *thank you,*" he affirmed threateningly.

"I'll take mine black," Kahn said, "as usual. Oh, and Sonny," he called after me, "be sure and close the door behind you."

I looked at him cynically; he winked in the most cavalier manner imaginable.

"Okay, Aaron," I heard Piper petition eagerly, "so what's the scoop?"

" 'Poop,' my dear man, 'poop,' " Kahn replied, rocking back in his chair and blowing a smoke ring in the air. "That's the million-dollar word."

I blush to admit it, but outside in the corridor I succumbed to a paroxysm of gleeful hilarity. Bending over, I slapped my knee at the thought of Kahn's fluent bunco. What chutzpah! What a pro! What a Kahn! I apostrophized idolatrously. And what luck on my part to have fallen in with a master so accomplished in his chosen arts! I caught myself up, however, recalling the nature of the business at hand, and my enthusiasm underwent an alchemical transmutation into its opposite, from gold to lead, as it were. What had he done? What was he doing? What was *I* doing? Castigating myself for my momentary dementia, I repudiated all delight and, putting on a somber face, went to get the coffee.

When I returned the bid was up to five-eighths and the ask was seven-eighths. At his post in the garage annex of the trading floor, the specialist was getting a very quick education in Jane Doe.

"How's Doe?" I heard one broker shout as he approached, waving his order in his hand.

Before the specialist could answer, another interrupted, offering, "One hundred Doe at seven-eighths!"

"Sold!" the first cried.

Within moments bigger fish had started nibbling the bait. Another large block blazed across the tape.

DOE
1000s 10

And *voilà!* Doe was back in the black! By the end of the day it had soared to 12, having hit 12½ briefly before falling back. I was elated. Pride? *Pride?* Such a surge of pride shot through me that, taking temporary leave of my senses, I then and there vowed to stand by our doe-eyed darling till death did us part. It was my first experience of "winning," and I began to comprehend the tremendous glamour and satisfaction of it, as though it were an objective, quantifiable sign of divine election. Such a rush! To have that great lady, the Dowager Empress, catch your eye and nod in acknowledgment. I understood how so many men had thrown themselves away, burning their bridges behind them, eschewing all lesser hopes and satisfactions in pursuit of her, the Great Black Widow, and with no more reasonable expectation of success than those uxorious spiders that she would admit them to the eternal sunshine of her favor, making an exception for them out of love, after having satisfied her appetite year after year with their predecessors. In the flush of it, I felt an ecstasy unlike any I'd ever known before, riding on a sense of power that verged on omnipotence. Oddly, this did not diminish the sense of gritty anguish and self-compromise that had overwhelmed me at Kahn's confession of his ploy, nor the strain of increasing complexities in my personal life. All the elements existed there together, like a roaring bonfire in an open place, fed indiscriminately on the most varied fuels.

The sensation became more frequent, its duration longer, as day by day over the next few days, Doe accelerated on the trading floor, rising to 16 by the end of the week. That weekend Olaf, excited apparently by the rise, finally capitulated, giving Kahn and the rest of the cartel the nod. On Monday morning of the final week before the deadline, the merger was announced.

The opening of Doe was delayed over an hour that morning due to the backlog of orders precipitated by the leakage of the news. When the specialist had finally collated his bids and offers, he fixed the price at eighteen dollars. Kahn and I were delirious with joy. Neglecting our respective duties on the floor, we opened champagne in his office and lit cigars, whooping and doing little do-si-dos (do-si-*does*) of mutual admiration. The entire week was a riot. We lived hour to hour. There were moments of mania when all seemed possible, others of despair when profit-taking seemed to suck the lifeblood out of our darling, leaving her wan and apathetic, on the verge of collapse. But she continued to spring back from support and burst through successive lines of resistance, so that on Thursday, the next to last day of my bond, it touched 20 for the first time briefly, before retreating to 19¾ at the close.

"So, Kahn, do you think we'll make it tomorrow?" I asked eagerly as we headed home.

"I think so," he said, stretching out the syllables smugly with a paternal calmness. "At this point I don't think there's anything that can stop us." He scrutinized me briefly. "But that's not even really the question for you, is it, kid?"

I stared at him quizzically.

"What are you going to do?" he asked.

"Why, redeem the robe, of course!" I replied in surprise. "What else would I do? Isn't that the whole point?"

He nodded slowly, with the same paternalistic manner. "Sure, sure, what else," he mused.

"Kahn?"

"Hmmm?"

"There's something on your mind. What?"

He shrugged and pouted. "Oh, I don't know."

"Kahn!"

"All right, kid," he said, becoming acute. "I've just been wondering to myself, say you sell out and redeem the robe, what then?"

"What do you mean?"

"Where does it leave you? Right back where you started, doesn't it?" he continued, obliquely replying. "I mean, sure, you've had your little fling with the Dow, your little one-night stand. But you can't be so naive as to believe you've really mastered it."

"No, of course not," I conceded.

"Well, correct me if I'm wrong, but wasn't that the whole point of the experiment in the first place, 'to understand the Dow' — all that stuff about the delta and everything?"

I regarded him mutely.

"I mean, don't get me wrong, kid. You've made progress. I told you before, the last few weeks have taught you more about the Dow than all the previous time you'd put in together. But the delta — do you really think you're *there*?"

For a moment I turned inward, searching for the truth. It didn't take me long. I shook my head. "No," I said. "If anything, I think I'm further away than when I started."

We studied each other intently.

"I admire your honesty, kid," he said softly. "I hate to spoil the party, but as a friend I felt bound to put it to you."

"You just couldn't let me luxuriate in my O.C.," I glossed with a grudging smile.

He shrugged. "Plus, there's the fact that this is the worst possible time to sell, judged by purely intrinsic factors. Doe is just warming up, riding on her own momentum. It's now that the real profits begin to materialize. Remember the old maxim, 'Cut your losses and let your profits run.' You sell now, you aren't going to see any of that. You've got the robe back, granted, but you're flat broke again, just another schmo. I guess it boils down to which is more important to you, the robe or your career as an investor." He patted me on the back and started off. "I don't want to sway you though. Just let me know tomorrow. If you decide to sell, I'll execute the order. If not . . ." He waved and disappeared into the subway.

As I walked up toward Chinatown, I thought over the problem he'd raised. "What was more important . . . ?" Late into the evening, alone in my room, I pondered. Somehow in the frenzy I'd lost sight of this essential question. Now that it recurred, the answer didn't seem as clear-cut and unequivocal as it once had. At first I'd tended to regard it as a simple choice between a human artifact on the one hand, something endowed with history and meaning, the only relic my mother had left behind her; and on the other hand, money, "specie," "cash." Obviously these were in the highest degree incommensurable. Yet Kahn had put it in a different light: ". . . the robe or your career as an investor." Indeed it was not so simple. For it wasn't only my career as an investor that was riding on the issue, but the larger career I'd come to America to pursue, and had, in fact, been embarked on my whole life. I mean, of course, the proof of faith, the search for the delta, for the Tao within the Dow, which at Coney Island had melded indissolubly with the search for my father, who was the Dow now for me by the commutative law. Already I'd traveled so many miles in that quest. Here again it was abort or go forward, deeper into the web, deeper into the ambiguities. But, in a sense, hadn't the decision been made already? Hadn't I made it that afternoon at Coney Island? Perhaps. But pawning the robe and parting with it for good — and with the full permission of my conscious will — these were two different things.

As I struggled with these questions, Kahn's ultimatum kept playing through my mind: "To understand the Dow, you've got to invest, kid — something of yourself." Wasn't it apt then, terribly apt, that fate should blandly point to this, my most precious possession, as the necessary sacrifice, its desired hecatomb? Kahn had been right before. I hadn't yet given all. And what was more important, steadfastly persevering in my quest until I reached the delta (or it proved itself unambiguously illusory), or clinging to my relic from the past? Indeed the question had taken on a deeper meaning.

Or was this labored construction merely a rationalization to explain away greed and incipient addiction? I could not think clearly about the issue. At one moment I determined that the proper course was to give up my material clinging (to the robe) and proceed with my study. But the irony overwhelmed me! Give up my "material clinging" and sit back idly paring my nails while my profits in Jane Doe doubled and trebled? What hypocrisy! And yet, I reminded myself, any profit I might realize was not intended in and for itself, but only as a means toward the end of deeper knowledge of the Dow. As long as my conscience was clean, I assured myself, I could not go wrong. But was my conscience clean? Of course it was! And yet . . .

What it came down to in the end, unfortunately, was a rather mundane, methodological consideration: timing. As Kahn had pointed out, if I sold out now on the eve of the deadline, I would irrevocably sacrifice all future benefits, educational and spiritual, which would accrue through profit maximization (i.e., I would lose my stake). And when would such another opportunity come around again? How long had Kahn said it had been since his last big score? Seven years of bad luck. I couldn't wait around. I had to ride it while it lasted. I had to do it *now*.

After a restless night tossing and turning in my bed, on waking up and disentangling myself from the sheets, which had wound themselves around me like the tendrils of a parasitic vine, I knew that for better or worse I had decided to stay in and let my mother's robe go by the way. If I became extraordinarily rich, I consoled myself unenthusiastically and with more than a trace of self-reflective irony, perhaps I could buy it back from Mme Chin at an exorbitant rate. (No, Reader, I didn't believe it either.)

•

All morning I felt sick at heart, walking about the trading floor listless and anxious at once, a burden to myself and precious little help to anyone else. At times I almost wished Doe would take a plunge, at least retreat below 20 for the day, so that I could slough off on fate the responsibility for my decision. No such luck, of course. By midafternoon it had tacked on another point. I had no one to blame but myself. I wasn't happy with my decision, but over and over I consoled myself with the reflection that I would have been even more miserable had I sold out and had to abort my career in "enlightened investment." Leaving the irony aside, was this completely candid? I'm still uncertain. Perhaps a great weight of tedious, enervating care would have been lifted from my heart had I gone ahead and sold the stock, relegating myself voluntarily to the sidelines once again where there was no danger of incurring spiritual injuries (i.e., no possibility of becoming tainted with possession). Yet what precisely did it mean to be "tainted with possession"? The question hinted at another turning in the moral labyrinth I had entered. I debated whether in this case *wu-wei*, or actionless activity, consisted in keeping the eye trained on the distance, clear, tranquil, dispassionate, while the hand reached in and groped for what it could; or alternatively, if the hand should hold aloof while the eye and mind actively engaged in trying to understand, to possess *intellectually*? Was such possession any less culpable than actual physical possession? Somehow I felt it was better to dirty the hand than the mind, and yet I wondered if it weren't naive to believe that one might besmirch the one without the other.

Kahn, for all his shrewdness, was no help to me in resolving my dilemma. His patience with such questions in the first place was not the greatest, but he was rendered even less accessible by the passion of the chase. I had never seen him in such high spirits. There was a new terseness in him, in appearance as well as utterance, a honed edge of concentration. He seemed to have dropped pounds and sloughed off all "humors" at the same time, all intellectual extravagance and superfluity, like so much ballast. His sallow complexion had taken on a tint of pink. He stood taller and straighter. At moments I would catch him standing still in the middle of the trading floor, eyes uplifted toward the tape, a subtle, interior smile on his face, a flush on his cheeks, a gleam in his eyes, nostrils dilating with pleasure, like some great predator on the Hunt sniffing the air. It was almost an attitude of worship, or else of the intensest profanation. But what did I expect? Because of who he was and where he came from, he could not choose but lead me as he did. I knew his ultra-American attitude of "no balls, no glory," knew it blinded him to the world of values I was seeking. And still I chose to follow. Why? Out of sloth? Bad faith? Was I simply following the line of least resistance?

I'm not above imputing these, and worse, motives to myself, because I know that at a higher level I persevered through faith, the faith that had been reconsecrated that afternoon at Coney Island, the faith that the disparity between his way of life and mine, between Ken Kuan and Wall Street, was only an apparent one, that this turbulent, impetuous tributary I was riding — Dow — would debouch at last into the Tao. The brine of that sea, I believed, was a universal solvent in which all differences would be dissolved and brought into solution. That was my faith, the faith that I had left China to test and, hopefully, verify, that Reality is One, and Tao is Reality.

Had I not seen with my own eyes the Yangtze resolve itself into the China Sea, which in turn flowed into the great eastern ocean; and again, the Hudson flowing down to the Atlantic? I knew too that somewhere beneath a perilous, stormy cape at the bottom of the world these two great oceans flowed together, just as *yin* and *yang* flowed together. Having rounded it in the external world, it now fell to my lot to round the Cape of Good Hope in myself, to follow the winds and tides of life until they brought me to the place where the American Dow, that river of supreme self-interest, rounded its own promontory and flowed into the great Pacific of the Tao.

I had to see if what I knew and loved could stand the test of America's unintimidated reality, if the general rule, Tao, could accommodate the special case, Dow. If it couldn't, how could I persevere in the endeavor of my early years, knowing its immense and cruel fatuity? How rededicate myself to quiescence as a way of life — sinking down like water through the porous layers of the ego to the abiding water table of the Tao — knowing that water table was merely a sewer? I was like a scientist who had traveled around the world to view the eclipse of the sun, the one momentary exception on which the fate of the rule depends. Dow was the eclipse of Tao, and if I could not ascertain by examining its black, occluded disc that underneath the sun shone brightly as before, then my religious faith was an illusion, a false hope.

If that were true, I would be in the position of the primitive herdsman I had heard about in China, who, seeing the darkening overhead, thought the world had come to an end, and, preferring the vast uncertainty of death to a world he could no longer recognize or trust, committed suicide, hanging himself in a fruit tree while his flock bleated in terror around his dangling feet.

Chapter 7

In spite of everything, I was relieved that afternoon when the bell finally sounded. It was out of my hands now, too late to go back. After work I had an impulse to go by and ask Mme Chin for one last look at my treasure, but I "nixed" it with a brusque, blunt toughness that surprised me in myself, a callousness new in my emotional repertoire. Now I understood, and even to a degree shared, the aversion for "schmaltz" I had heard Kahn express a hundred times before. Not that I relinquished the robe so easily in my heart, but a sense of tremendous weariness combined with the complete futility of the gesture of paying last respects, making the prospect unappealing if not downright repulsive. Kahn said something odd that afternoon as we parted.

"Well, kid, I guess you can consider yourself blooded now." He smiled grimly. "It's appropriate, don't you think? Blooded on the Doe."

I didn't understand exactly what he meant until I looked the word up in the dictionary: "Blood *tr. v.:* to initiate a novice who has successfully followed hounds from find to death by marking his face with the blood of the kill." Suddenly it dawned on me. Pawning was find. But this was death.

On my way back to Chinatown, I stopped before Trinity Church. Behind the iron bars a drift of golden leaves lay scattered over the graves, a few floating down even then from the trees, flipping in silent ecstasies from sun to shadow in the stray beams of sunlight that quarried the chill, blue autumn air. In the soot-crusted, hunched facade of the church I caught a glimpse of something old and very sad, wise too, like one who has lived with a wound for a long time and has learned, through suffering, the hard art of patience, tasted, through the wound itself, the wine of an intenser solace than the healthy know. Rejecting the church's mildly disconcerting offer of refreshment, I passed on, not, however, without a shake of the head and a small sigh.

As prosperity, or prosperity-soon-to-be, became an accustomed way of life, I dwelled more and more on what it would mean for me when it was over. After all, we couldn't ride the passion of the Hunt forever. One day when we had run the doe just as far and fast as she could go, or we could, we would have to make the hard decision to forego the further delights of savored anticipation, and let the arrow fly while she was still in range, or else risk losing her forever. Doe, then, would become simply a trophy on the wall, something to remember and talk about, but not a reason for going on, as she now so vividly was. What would come next? Say the scenario developed exactly according to plan, and I came away stuffed to bursting with the miraculously multiplying loaves baked from our original dough. Where would I be then? *What* would I be then? Richer, certainly, but wiser? What would I have learned? Well, for one thing, Kahn had been right: to know the Dow you had to invest. I conceded it now. How dubious that proposition had once seemed, how unpalatable, and how rudimentary now.

As the days passed and the pot grew richer, a curious corollary of that law became salient. Accepting the premise that exposure was salubrious, it followed that the more contact I had with the Dow, the more chance I would have of understanding it, and that the deeper my understanding penetrated, the closer I would come to the object I was searching for: the delta, the confluence of Tao and Dow. Well and good. It was the next step in the syllogism that startled and disconcerted me. What precisely did more contact with the Dow consist in, and how did one go about obtaining it? Well, not to put too fine a point upon it, money. As I examined it, the self-evidence of the advantages that would accrue to my spiritual well-being and mental health from the accumulation of large capital reserves appeared like a flash of lightning from a dark sky. I recoiled, of course, with aversion. Preposterous! I told myself, laughing scornfully, if also with a hint of mild hysteria. At the second glance the smile melted from my lips. Where was the flaw in the reasoning? Accepting the premise, didn't the conclusion follow with remorseless logic? Perhaps I was beginning to lose perspective, I told myself. On the other hand, I had to consider the chilling possibility that this truth might one day come to seem as elementary as that expressed in Kahn's ultimatum.

One afternoon (after a complacent morning of watching the tape and adjusting my mental balance upward accordingly in increments of eighths and quarters), I was returning to Kahn's office with our lunches. The elevator stopped at the Visitors' Center, and on a whim I decided to take a peek from the gallery, simply for old-times' sake. I surveyed the scene below, sighing with half-grudging satisfaction at the beauty and enormity of the spectacle, sniffing that rich barnyard aroma. After a moment, I noticed what looked like a small riot in progress at one of the posts in the garage. Why, it was the Doe post (the "rolling pin" of sacred memory, as Kahn had christened it)! Trading was frantic, more frantic than I had ever seen it, even after the announcement of the Sui merger. The commotion resembled that within a colony of ants stomped flat by a vicious hiker. Brokers were waving their slips over their heads and shouting at the tops of their lungs. The specialist, holding his hands up as though to fend them off, was shaking his bowed head in sympathetic but stern demurral. But what was he denying them? Were they trying to buy or sell? And where was Kahn? My large friend was conspicuously absent from this obstreperous and remonstrative crowd — "conspicuously," I say, because it was as if the designated victim had had the cheek to stand up his clamoring, impatient public at the scene of a mob lynching. Indeed, the dispensing of vigilante justice seemed at hand. As faithful sidekick of the offending hombre, I was in no hurry to be delegated to serve in my master's stead, so I retreated as swiftly and inconspicuously as possible to his office, where I knocked on the door.

"Go away!" he growled from within.

"Kahn, it's me!" I cried. "Open up. I've got the lunches."

As he made no further reply, I took out my key and let myself in.

As if in keeping with my metaphor from the westerns, Kahn was sitting at his desk contemplating, with a wild, glassy stare, what appeared to be a Colt .44 revolver. Sweeping it into the drawer of his desk, he looked up at me with dilated pupils, a frightened, vulnerable look at odds with the lunatic grin on his lips.

I felt the flesh prickle along my arms. A sickening anticipation gripped me. "Kahn?" I breathed, hardly louder than a whisper.

"It's all over, kid," he said, meeting my eyes. "The cake's all dough — Jane Doe."

"You mean . . .?"

He closed his eyes and nodded. "They've halted trading on the floor."

Unable to speak, I simply gaped at him.

"They've found out, kid. I'm finished."

"Found out?"

He nodded. "Everything — the cartel, the purchases, the inside information, the tape painting — everything. The fucking whole megillah."

I was flabbergasted.

"Okay, so I'm a schlimazel," he shrugged. Then he began to cry.

He took out his handkerchief and blew his nose loudly after a few minutes, apparently somewhat relieved. "Excuse the schmaltz," he apologized with thin irony and a thinner grin.

"But how?" I ventured.

He sighed and shook his head. "I don't know, damn it! Piper must have sold me. From what I can piece together, it started as a fairly routine investigation. They were alerted by the sudden rise and simply wanted to check that everything was on the up-and-up. Then Piper's report appeared. That stimulated a lot of further buying. They went to him, and he gave me to them. The wimp."

" 'They?' "

"The SEC, kid."

I gasped.

"That's right, kid, the big boys. This is blood sport. We're playing for real money."

"What'll happen now?"

He shrugged. "That all depends on how far the Board of Governors wants to push it. I'll be expelled of course."

"From the Exchange? For good?" I cried in dismay.

He nodded. "But losing my seat is the least of my potential problems. You know as well as I do the public perception of the 'unprincipled floor trader.' Well, to fend off the reformist hordes, they're always touting their ability to police their own members." He gave me a significant look.

"So?" I asked.

"So they might just decide to make a scapegoat of me."

"Meaning what?"

"They might call in the law. I don't think my being of the Jewish persuasion would incline them to leniency in this case, either, do you? They've been trying to get rid of me for years. What better pretext?"

The next day they subpoenaed his records. Kahn stopped leaving his office. He bought cartridges for his gun and loaded it. He began twirling it ostentatiously in the halls, like a gunslinger. People noticed and gave him a wide berth. I looked on in dismay, helpless. I was there the afternoon they finally came for him. A knock at the door — "SEC enforcement division." My knees almost collapsed with terror. Only with the greatest difficulty was I able to maintain control over my bowels. Not only the immediate peril — Kahn's peril (in which I too was implicated, no doubt, but to a degree I was incapable of assessing) — but my own residual culpability as an illegal alien flashed through my mind.

To my surprise, Kahn simply smiled wryly as though relieved, and extended his hand toward the door in an ironic gesture of presentation, looking at me from under arched brows as if to say, "You see?"

This was implicit, however. What he actually did say, taking the revolver out of his desk drawer as he did so, was, "Well, kid, there are six bullets in this gun. What do you say? Do we use 'em on ourselves or go for a shoot-out?"

"Kahn!" I cried in vehement protest. "This is no time for kidding!"

He shrugged and smiled grimly. "So who's kidding, kid?"

"Open up!" Fists banged insistently.

A dry smile curled the corners of Kahn's lips. Looking me straight in the eyes, he raised the gun to his temple.

"What are you doing, Aaron?" I implored.

"Ida couldn't live with the disgrace," he said with wry, nihilistic humor, especially chilling in the circumstances.

"Kahn!" I screamed.

He slowly squeezed the trigger; the hammer lifted incrementally from the breech.

Suddenly the door burst open and half a dozen agents overflowed into the room. Two fell on their knees aiming their .38s; the rest fanned out behind, dramatically supporting the wrists of their gun-hands with their free ones. "Freeze!" they shouted.

"Come on in, boys," Kahn invited, smiling sarcastically.

"Don't move or we'll shoot!"

"Be my guest," Kahn said, gesturing toward his own gun with his free hand as though to spell out the precise complexion of the situation for their laggard sensibilities. "Only let the kid go," he stipulated. "He's got nothing to do with this. I only sent him out for lunch."

The nearest agent caught my eye. "Get out of here," he ordered, jerking his head toward the door.

I looked at Kahn helplessly.

He pouted, closing his eyes and nodding reassuringly. "It's okay, kid," he said. "Go ahead."

Not knowing what else to do, I started for the door.

"Oh, Sonny, before you go . . ." he called after me, "light me a cigar, would you? I want to savor my last few moments." He solicited the agents' permission. "A last request, fellows?" The same one who had waved me off now waved me on. "Go ahead," he said brusquely.

Kahn shifted the gun to his left temple as he twirled the stogy in the match I struck, sucking it alight with the familiar bellows motion of his cheeks. From my position in front of the desk, I acted as a screen between him and the agents. As I stood on the verge of tears, performing what seemed likely to prove last offices for him, Kahn turned his eyes up suddenly to my face and silently mouthed the words, "Don't wor-ry. The gun is plas-tic."

I stared at him slack jawed with amazement, until the match burned my fingers and I jumped.

"Now get out of here or I'll shoot!" he grumbled aloud. "You're starting to make me nervous!"

"Hurry! Beat it!" the agents cried, waving their guns in alarm.

I didn't stop to protest or ask questions.

•

When I saw him again later that afternoon in jail, he explained that his antics had been undertaken in an attempt to provide substantiation for an insanity defense. "After all, if Third World types and the spoiled brats of the bourgeoisie can get away with it for murder, rape, arson, political assassination, what have you, why not white-collar criminals for service 'above and beyond the call' in the line of legitimate business? It's discriminatory!"

Poor Kahn, still joking even as they slipped his head into the noose. I don't think it had quite yet come home to him what had happened. He was almost exhilarated — cocky, belligerent, cracking jokes, all of it a little skewed. Within a week though, I would have welcomed even such dubious inspirations as the insanity defense simply to see him relieved from the depression that had settled on his life like a cold gray fog and threatened to break his heart.

I think the humiliation of waiting in the holding cell for his lawyer, then being paraded ignominiously into the docks like some freak-show specimen, began to sober him. After his attorney and the prosecutor had conferred briefly with the judge, the latter invited him to approach the bench. From where I sat in the courtroom, I was able to make out his remarks. "I'm something of a trader myself, Mr. Kahn," he said. "As a matter of fact, my broker recommended Doe to me about two weeks ago."

"Smart broker, Your Honor," Kahn observed in an ill-considered display of chutzpah, grinning. "Treat him right. A good man is hard to find."

The judge frowned and glared at him hard over the rims of his glasses. "In your case I'd say that's especially applicable. Lucky for you I didn't take him up on it. As it is, because of the nature of the crime and the absence of a prior record on your part, I'm releasing you without bond on your own recognizance. For the record though, I think you're a perfect scoundrel."

"I always was a perfectionist," Kahn rejoined. "I can't help myself. I like to be the best at what I do."

By the time we left the courtroom through a crowd of bullying, importunate reporters, the smirk had vaporized from my friend's face, leaving behind a ghostly, haunted absence.

Pausing mechanically at a corner to pick up his afternoon paper, Kahn and I found this headline in the *Daily News:*

SUI-CIDE PACT INTERRUPTS TRADING ON WALL STREET KAHN INDICTED FOR MANIPULATION

Below, in smaller letters, a subhead read:

Son of Love Involved in Scandal

•

It's strange, you know, how quickly things can turn against you, how quickly a situation can become irretrievable. Very strange. I suppose that's one of the real-life lessons the Dow teaches its disciples soonest, something I wouldn't have gotten on the sidelines. It's lose and learn on Wall Street, to alter the old adage, lose and learn. The Unpardonable Sin of trading? The Dowist's supreme faux pas? Equating eggs with chickens, Reader. That is what I did. It's almost funny. I should have been more upset, I suppose. But my predominant feeling was one of relief, and of release, as though things had suddenly been made good — all my lapses — the slate of my transgressions wiped clean. A tremendous weight dropped from my heart, one I'd hardly been aware of till it floated off and the old thing buoyed up from underneath. If it hadn't been for Kahn, I would have felt shamefully blithe about the whole affair.

That was a big "if," however. It nearly destroyed my friend. I felt a large measure of responsibility, as though in importuning him I had contributed to the pressure which had finally pushed him beyond the line to cheat. As it turned out, beyond his financial liabilities, which were considerable (he had to declare bankruptcy, Chapter 13), the legal end of it didn't amount to much. Kahn's lawyer was able to get him off with six months of weekends in an upstate penitentiary teaching hardened criminals — who seemed to have both aptitude and interest — the ins and outs of "principled investing" — the judge emphasized that "principled." I think it was the disgrace more than anything that got to him, not only of the formal sentence of the court, but that meted out to him by his peers, and perhaps most importantly by the Board of Governors. Kahn was indeed expelled from the Exchange, his seat slated to be auctioned off to contribute to the payment of his debts. Worst of all, he was proscribed from ever holding membership again. Kahn took his lumps like a mensch for the most part — everything but that. But to be mercilessly and summarily banned from taking part in that activity which to him was synonymous with life itself! That was the final blow. That was what broke his will. Poor Kahn! How I pitied him! He had been suddenly relegated to the sidelines, condemned to *observe without participating*.

Without intending to be facetious, this was, quite literally for him, the equivalent of hell on earth. If this did not constitute cruel and unusual punishment, what did? It was diabolical! It was sadistic! Standing unarmed at the periphery, panting and straining like a collared hound while the fox flew by, grinning in his face, that was what eventually wore him down to a nub of his former self. (Figuratively speaking. In physical terms his girth increased. He topped 250 on the scales.) Of course, he was still free to armchair quarterback like any other poor sucker from that lusterless fraternity, the General Public. He could open an account with a small-time broker in some retail firm and phone his orders in, to be transferred via several relays to the floor. But the thought of such degradation was intolerable to him, as the Reader may well understand. Not to be able to execute his orders himself, in person, *ipse homo* — it was mortifying, it was unthinkable! If only he could have gotten a job working on the floor as a simple broker with one of the big commission houses. Though infinitely beneath him, at least he could have done it with some dignity, like an aristocrat of old family fallen on hard times, poor, yet at least solvent in self-respect, and, most importantly, still close to the Source, to Dow. But uh-uh, nothing doing. They passed him by — they, who weren't good enough to kiss his feet! His reputation was a stigma he couldn't hide. Office managers shuddered at the fearful brand. Ah, poor Kahn! How my heart bled for him!

And yet, do you know what his attitude was, what he continued to maintain throughout it all?

"I only wish it could have lasted forever," he told me, staring off into the distance with a wistful, smoky light in his eye. His voice was low and husky, a little breathless with passion's telltale demi-quaver, as though he were saying goodbye to the love of his life, to life itself. "It was worth it, kid. Even this." That sad, princely dignity flashed through his pain. "It was so beautiful. So beautiful." He shook his head. "It's all over for me, kid. I know I'll never have another joy that runs so deep. I was there, kid. *There*. You know?" He gave me a significant look.

"Don't be melodramatic, Kahn," I exhorted sternly. "I mean, after all, it's not exactly as though your life were over."

He regarded me appraisingly through narrowed lids, then sighed and shook his head again. "You still don't see, do you?"

"See what?"

"That that's precisely what it does mean. My life *is* over."

"But there are lots of other things you could do," I protested.

He pursed his lips grimly. "I've done too many things already. I've worn out my wandering shoes, kid, my Wandering Jew shoes." He smiled to himself. "My Wandering Jew suede shoes." The tic of wit did not relieve the heaviness. "For me, this was it. I don't want anything else."

It was hard for me to admit — especially to myself — but I spoke what was in my heart. "Perhaps I do see, Aaron. Now."

A sad fraternity shone in his eyes which reminded me somehow of Tsin. "Blooded," was all he said.

"When a man has known the taste of blood, it is not so easy to forget." The soldier's words flitted through my mind. I stared at Kahn gravely, but he smiled to himself and reentered the mothlike orbit of his obsession. "You know, with a little more luck, a little more cash, we could have pulled the most amazing scam since the great Piggly Wiggly corner of twenty-one. Our names in the history books." He looked off into space, then suddenly laughed obstreperously. "And both in pork!" He shook his head. "That reminds me of a saying: 'A bull can make money in Wall Street; a bear can make money in Wall Street; but a pig always gets Sui in the end.' I got it, kid, in the end. In both ends!" He made an obscene gesture. "Fore and aft!" He was laughing so hard tears streamed down his cheeks.

I did my best to disguise my alarm, but the truth is, I was beginning to fear for his sanity. Hoping at least somehow to extenuate the financial burden, I called the members of the now defunct cartel to see if they might not at least take up a subscription for the scapegoat who had been sacrificed for their collective sins, but it was fruitless. Their secretaries took my number, and the calls were never returned.

No, it was clear enough. No one else was going to help. The burden fell on me. And I didn't mind so much. I felt responsible, as I've said, having played an instigative role. Even had I been guiltless, I couldn't have left my old friend in the lurch like that. For he did seem like an old friend by now, though it really hadn't been so long since I first spied him turning the corner of a trading booth, casually popping bonbons. Never again! Somehow I couldn't visualize him in any other landscape. After all, what is an elephant without a savanna, a crocodile without a silt-rich river delta, a bear without his sundry hibernacula, a bull without a meadow or arena? Yes, I too found myself giving way to schmaltz. But I braced up under the thought of my responsibility to relieve his plight. How though? That was the question. And, sadly, I had no answer for it.

When the SEC filed charges and trading was halted, Doe had been at 32. When it reopened, the bid was 3⅞. Olaf, who had been warily guarding his cookies on the sidelines, immediately abjured, in public, all connection with Doe, its owners, and representatives. He even went so far as to suggest that the merger rumors had been circulated without his knowledge or consent by the management of Doe, thus raising the specter of further prosecution on the count of stock fraud. Fortunately, his involvement was too well documented to lend credence to this charge and it was dropped. It didn't help Doe, though. It lost two points on the announcement and continud steadily dwindling thereafter. The company couldn't hold out. Within two weeks Doe appeared on the tape preceded by an ignominious "Q," Wall Street's Scarlet Letter, the mark of Cain, the mark of Kahn. Bankruptcy. Receivership. Chapter 11.

QDOE
2s 13.16

Two hundred shares at 13/16. After that I stopped looking. Not from apathy, either. The sight made me sick to my stomach.

If it had this effect on me, you can imagine what it did to Kahn. He was fading fast. I watched as, bit by bit, he degenerated into a sort of elegant bum. Some fatal gravity (the gravity of blood?) attracted him back day after day to the Exchange, where he was treated as a pariah. Though he had stopped shaving regularly, he still took the trouble to dress, putting on a suit and tie. At least at first. But his expensive clothes began to look more rumpled than ever, as though he slept in them, and they'd started to exude a positively noxious odor, redolent no longer of the aroma of boiled, so much as spoiled, piroshki. When I noticed that he'd stopped wearing socks under his leather lace-ups, I knew that things had proceeded pretty far.

I used to see him standing upstairs in the gallery of the Visitors' Center, hour after hour, like an accusing specter, the wraith of some slain, unrequited soul, levitating on the winds, staring down with bulging, vacant eyes at the scene inhabited in life, mutely anathematizing. How my heart went out to him! I went up as often as I could, taking him little sick-bribes, bonbons and such, gestures of commiseration and appeasement. But he grimly refused all sustenance, implying only too unmistakably what he was really hungry for. Out of an overwhelming impulse toward self-mortification, he took only bread and water. I don't know how he stood it, listening hour after hour to that cheerful tape recording repeating its interminable message, explaining how the market worked. "Say you, the customer, John Q. Public, in Anytown USA decide you want to sell one hundred shares of XYZ Corporation. . . ." How happy the little gnome sounded as he reeled off the links in the transaction: customer to retail broker, broker to telephone clerk, clerk to floor broker via annunciator board, and so on through specialist, reporter, even mentioning the humble squad boy, then back to the customer himself by the same tedious, redundant relay. What torture for him! As if Einstein had been strapped to a chair and forced to listen to a recording of "Newton's Laws" played over and over! Yet he appeared to crave self-punishment. His appetite for that, at least, was insatiable. And, as I've suggested, I was afraid there was only one dish that would satisfy it finally and for good. Suicide. And not the dress rehearsal this time either, but the real thing. Something had to be done.

But what? Try as I might, I could think of nothing that offered legitimate hope of a resolution. Having no other resource, I did as I had done innumerable times before in situations where intellect found itself at a loss; I turned to the *Changes*. Taking out my copy of the book (over which a light film of dust had fallen once again), like the fisherman in the fairy tale conjuring the magic fish, I called to it in my time of need, hoping it would vouchsafe me an answer out of the unfathomable depths of its great heart. My only hesitation in making the consultation was a nagging dread lest it confirm my suspicion that by actions I'd committed, places I'd been, things I'd accepted and allowed, I might have lost the requisite "purity of heart" to command it.

The reading the oracle returned was number 59, *Huan*, "Dispersion," or "Dissolution," with moving lines in the top four places. This hexagram is composed of the trigrams *Sun*, ☴ , or "Wind," above *K'an*, ☵ , or "Water." As the lines arranged themselves, I was struck by something I couldn't quite put my finger on. Wind above Water. What was it? *Sun* above *K'an*. *Sun* above . . . *K'an*? Sun above Kahn! The homophone of my own name, of course, was old hat, but his! It was uncanny! And perhaps the most uncanny thing of all was that it had never even dawned on me before.

When I had gotten over the initial thrill, or shock, I turned immediately to *K'an* in the Shuo Kua wing of the *I Ching*, which discusses in detail the meaning of the trigrams.

> The Abysmal is water, ditches, ambush, bending and straightening out, bow and wheel.
> Among men it means the melancholy, those with sick hearts, those with earache.
> It is the blood sign; it is red.
> Among horses it means those with beautiful backs, those with wild courage, those which let their heads hang, those with thin hoofs, those which stumble.
> Among chariots it means those with many defects.
> It is penetration, the moon.
> It means thieves.
> Among varieties of wood it means those which are firm and have much pith.

I began to cry. It was like a revelation for me. There was so much there! So much. Was it not the man himself? The Abysmal! It certainly seemed appropriate to his condition now.

It began to come together for me. *Sun over K'an:* didn't this corroborate my intuition of responsibility? Suddenly I understood what the oracle had meant at Coney Island: *Sui,* "Following." "If a man would lead he must first learn to follow." "Following" had meant following Kahn's advice, his ultimatum. I'd had to follow him into Doe, into Dow, in order to be able to lead him now, out of his depression. But how? The hexagram suggested an answer.

> The common celebration of the great sacrificial feasts and sacred rites . . . was the means employed by the great rulers to unite men. The sacred music and the splendor of the ceremonies aroused a strong tide of emotion that was shared by all hearts in unison. . . . A further means to the same end is cooperation in great general undertakings that set a high goal for the will of the people; in the common concentration on this goal, all barriers dissolve, just as when a boat is crossing a great stream all hands must unite in a joint task.
>
> But only a man who is himself free of all selfish ulterior considerations, and who perseveres in justice and steadfastness, is capable of so dissolving the hardness of egotism.

"Sacrificial feasts and sacred rites . . . music and the splendor of the ceremonies." Interesting. But what precisely was its connection with my mission? I came up short. After all, the rites and rituals referred to were those celebrated at the Chinese court centuries ago in connection with ancestor worship. What possible contemporary application could they have? And yet, the oracle seemed to prescribe this — whatever it was, some "great general undertaking" — as the proper therapeutic regimen for my heartsick friend. Hoping to shed some light on these matters, I turned to the lines:

> Six in the third place means:
> He dissolves his self. No remorse.

> Under certain circumstances, a man's work may become so difficult that he can no longer think of himself. He must set aside all personal desires and disperse whatever the self gathers about it to serve as a barrier against others. Only on the basis of a great renunciation can he obtain the strength for great achievements. By setting his goal in a great task outside himself, he can attain this standpoint.

Well, certain things at least were clear. I was the subject enjoined to "no longer think of himself" in order to effect a "great task outside himself," i.e., Kahn's rehabilitation. But what was the "great renunciation"? I read on.

> Six in the fourth place . . .

> Dispersion leads in turn to accumulation.
> This is something that ordinary men do not think of.

"Dispersion . . . accumulation . . . a great renunciation." The fog grew thicker.

Nine in the fifth place means:
His loud cries are as dissolving as sweat.
Dissolution! A king abides without blame.

In times of general dispersion and separation, a great idea provides a
focal point for the organization of recovery. Just as an illness reaches
its crisis in a dissolving sweat, so a great and stimulating idea is a
true salvation in times of general deadlock. It gives the people a
rallying point.

"A great and stimulating idea is a true salvation in times of general deadlock." Indeed! But *what was the idea*? Could it have something to do with the
"rites and ceremonies" mentioned earlier, I wondered?

Nine at the top means:
He dissolves his blood.
Departing, keeping at a distance, going out,
Is without blame.

The idea of the dissolving of a man's blood means the dispersion of
that which might lead to bloodshed and wounds, i.e., avoidance of
danger. But here the thought is not that a man avoids difficulties for
himself alone, but rather that he rescues his kin — helps them to get
away before the danger comes, or to keep at a distance from an
existing danger, or to find a way out of a danger that is already upon
them.

Here my prevision of the possibility of suicide seemed grimly corroborated.
Yet the context of taking preventive measures was constructive.

Having reached the end of the reading, I turned back and painstakingly went
over every phrase to try and clarify its intention. It was no use. I only tied
myself in knots. It always came back to those rites and ceremonies whose
identity was so obscure. Everything seemed to hinge on that. Was it the
church, the synagogue? Neither of these suggestions seemed particularly
promising. Giving up at last, I decided to accept the oracle's advice to "depart,
keep at a distance, go out." Depressed and anxious, I continued to thrash my
problem over as I walked the streets.

Letting chance, or my unconscious, guide the way, as was my habit, I found
myself gravitating irresistibly back toward the Financial District. At the head
of Wall Street, however, I felt the homing signal fade, no urge to enter. Turning
instead, I recognized at once in Trinity Church the unconscious destination
of my unconscious search. Again its gravity had drawn me. What gravity
though? What was I seeking there?

Afternoon Mass had already begun. A trickle of latecomers was still entering through the gates, crepe-black, crepitating women, hushed and hurrying.
As inconspicuously as possible, I mingled with that flow. Pausing in the

vestibule, I gazed warily down the nave. An unfamiliar priest was standing on the dais before the altar in his alb and stole, consecrating the elements. That determined me. Stealthily I crossed the rear of the church to the aisle and slipped into a pew in the shadow of one of the great ribbed columns running up into the vault, proliferating into flowerets, stone alveoli in that great breathing space, murmurous with the conch's extended sigh. My sense of being an intruder, of having gained illicit access to forbidden rites, only served to pique further the unaccountable excitement I felt on being there, an excitement that left me virtually breathless. I gazed around, eagerly drinking in sensations I remembered only too vividly and which had, mysteriously, with the passage of time and the accretion of a modest history, taken on an even greater luster in my mind. What was it that had drawn me back? There was something I wanted here.

The priest turned to the congregation and raised his hands shoulder high, palms extended flat, a gesture of invitation, restful, assured, inclusive, an embrace extended invisibly through the air in the manner of a kiss blown from the fingertips.

"Come unto me," he invited in a low, rich, resonant tone, like Riley's, containing the twilight timbre of the church, a voice that belonged to the ritual, not the man, "all ye that labor and are heavy laden, and I will give you rest."

It acted on me like a drug or the incantation of a hypnotist. A great weight of weariness descended over me, not so much physical as spiritual. I became aware of an inner ache, something crying out below the threshold of consciousness, like the siren outside Li's apartment, a wail the genes themselves had memorized. I'd never noticed it before and couldn't even say when it had started. Around me, all the others were rising from their knees, diffidently tiptoeing into the central aisle to approach the altar.

"A fitting feast for a Dowist." The words came back to me and suddenly I knew. That was it. That was the gravity, the gravity of blood. I can't explain it, Reader, but I was seized by a craving so powerful it almost made me crumple up and weep in agony. I began to salivate. I bit my tongue to keep from crying out, bit it so hard it bled. I could taste the bitter, cobrous trickle like pennies in my mouth. It relieved me, but only for a moment. Then the impulse seized me with redoubled force. It was like possession, like delirium tremens, the addict's craving, greater than his will to live. Only a sip — that was all I wanted — to wet my lips with the burning, mystic blood. That would have satisfied me. It would have been enough. Enough, though, was too much. Impossibly much. The greatness of the price was more than I could pay, more than I could even bring myself to measure. The greatness of the price.

How long this lasted, I'm not really sure. Mastering myself at last, I bolted from my seat. I was running so fast when I hit the vestibule that I collided with someone and almost knocked him down. "Excuse me," I said, taking an arm in the shadows. "Forgive . . ." A pair of pale blue eyes transfixed me, so intense they almost scintillated in the twilight.

"Father Riley!"

"Sun I," he returned, nodding. "This is certainly a surprise."

We studied one another silently.

"I have to apologize," I said at last in a tremulous voice, dropping my eyes to the floor.

"About the lecture?" he anticipated, cutting me off. "Don't be silly. I completely understand. I only hope my importunity didn't contribute to the tragedy. At any rate, I commiserate your loss. I regret not having had the chance to see the robe. I'm sorry it had to happen, but since it did, it's a blessing that you weren't more seriously hurt."

Until he mentioned it by name, I hadn't been sure what he was speaking of. What "tragedy" did he mean? Doe? Collecting my wits, however, I realized he was referring to my encounter with the mugger. I almost laughed. Reflecting further, I surmised that Yin-mi had covered for me. In fact, she'd lied to him outright, this man she cared for deeply, even revered, telling him the dispossession had occurred through theft. The thought brought a confused, wrenching pang, part gratitude, part shame, but a warm current of flattery flowed beneath. I think I blushed despite myself. Remembering where she and I stood, however, what had come between us, I was overwhelmed with a poignant sense of irretrievable loss.

"Are you all right, Sun I?" Riley asked.

"Of course. Why?"

"You aren't feverish, are you?"

"No. Why?"

"Your cheeks are flushed," he replied. "There's a glitter in your eyes." He laid his cool hand over my brow. "You do seem a little warm."

"I do?"

He nodded. "Come along. We'll go to my office. I'll brew you a cup of strong hot tea. It's the best thing in the world for a cold." He started off before I could protest, so I had no choice but to follow.

"So, what brought you here this afternoon anyway?" he asked as he rinsed out the cups and put a tea bag in each one. He looked over his shoulder with a hint of archness. "I don't suppose you've decided to convert?"

I laughed at the recollection of the joke and his persistence. "No, Father, I don't suppose so."

"Not yet?"

I shook my head. "Not yet."

He faced me and folded his arms over his chest, appraising me as the water heated in the coffee maker. Behind him the drip-drip of the water into the clear glass pitcher attracted my attention. I thought of the clepsydra at Ken Kuan and the "tears of time." A mournful peace crept over me and I sighed.

"You've changed, you know," Riley remarked.

"What?" I asked, starting from my reverie.

"I said you've changed."

I looked at him. "In what way?"

"That's what I'm trying to figure out. I can't quite put my finger on it."

I smiled. "If you can't tell how, what makes you think I've changed at all?"

"It's written all over you — in your face, your eyes, your whole attitude and manner. For instance, the last time I asked you that question about conversion, you bristled and stiffened up. This time you laughed. Why is that? What's happened in the meantime to make that possible?"

I shrugged. "I haven't any idea. Perhaps it's simply a fantasy of yours, wishful thinking."

He shook his head firmly. "No, I don't think so. It's as if something hard in you had started to break up, like an iceberg touched by warmer currents flowing up from the equator."

He scrutinized me, still trying to ferret it out. "There's almost a kind of glow about you. You haven't found your delta, have you?"

I laughed sadly at the irony of it. "Far from it, Father."

He gave me an acute, searching glance. "What do you mean?"

"I think perhaps I've lost it," I said, discovering the idea even as I spoke.

"Ah!" he said with a little cry of surprise. "It's not the glow of illumination then, but simply mortal tarnish."

His eyes met mine, knowing, wistful-wise.

But the water was ready. He turned around to attend to it. We sipped slowly and by an unstated consent spoke of other things. Indeed, the greater part of the conversation was unspoken, subtext. On the surface we treated trivial, gossipy affairs. I explained about the mugging. He listened and sympathized. He didn't press. A comfortable intimacy had unaccountably sprung up between us where before there had been tension and mistrust. Each of us, I think, privately marveled at it and proceeded gently, afraid we might frighten it away. It resembled the intimacy I had seen between the brothers at Ken Kuan in those rare hours when they took respite from their meditations, sitting quietly together drinking tea or observing the landscape, the shared, appreciative silence of men whose mental lives are congruous, the intimacy of priests.

When I left him, I felt contented and at peace. At moments my conviction of personal blessing mounted almost to exhilaration, only very quiet, very interior. It was as though something had been righted that was wrong. I sensed that it could not have happened before, that the whole debacle — losing the robe, Doe, everything — had made it possible. Walking back toward Chinatown, I laughed, remembering the old adage: indeed, shit did make the corn grow! At least in patches. And if I had mended my fences with Riley, perhaps it was possible with others too. My hope and confidence surged. Bit by bit, my mellow humor became broader, more uproarious. Pausing before the window of a liquor store, my eye glanced over the Dry Sack, lighting on the label of a different bottle, the brandy I'd seen Mme Chin drinking the afternoon I pawned the robe. "What the hell!" I thought, taking out my wallet and counting to see if I had enough. "Just to show her there are no hard feelings."

•

The dowager answered the door herself. Behind her the apartment was totally black.

"Forgive me. I hope I didn't wake you."

"Shhh!" she commanded in a strident whisper. "I have a customer."

"Oh." Silently I wondered, tenant? Spiritual advisee? Some poor fool like me pawning away an irredeemable part of his history or himself in order to pay his monthly bills, or perhaps finance some vicious habit?

"What do you want?" she asked brusquely, suspiciously. I noticed she was wearing the tiara of peacock feathers, and a black lace shawl. Reflecting the light in the hall, the rings on her fingers cast liquid spangles out of the darkness.

"I can come another time."

"If it's the robe, you'd best put it out of your mind," she warned. "It's gone."

"Gone?" I repeated, an involuntary quaver of surprise and disappointment in my voice.

"I've sold it."

I waited, hoping for some extenuation of the sentence. None was offered. I sighed heavily. "Well, if it is, it is," I acquiesced, trying to put the best face on things. "There's nothing to be done."

"Precisely," she agreed, almost with relish. "I mentioned it to one or two of my contacts, and within a week a man showed up willing to meet my price. He didn't even haggle. I probably could have got much more."

We traded looks, confirming the finality of it.

"Well . . ." I reached into my pocket.

Starting, she watched my hand apprehensively as it disappeared into my smock, as though she expected me to produce a gun, a knife, or a blunt instrument.

I proceeded magnanimously, refusing to acknowledge her suspicion, except perhaps through the merest trace of wounded righteousness in my tone. "I brought you a small present." I handed her the bottle in its brown paper bag. "Just to show that there are no hard feelings."

Pulling herself together, she accepted, smiling fulsomely. Extracting it by the neck, she quickly checked the label. "My brand too!" she commented with gratified surprise. She beamed a coy, flirtatious smile at me, effusive with ersatz girlishness, particularly grotesque on her wizened face. "You're learning," she congratulated. "I must confess I had my doubts about you, Sun I. But maybe I was wrong. You have hidden potential. You may make it yet." She basked me with amused approval. "A bottle of booze is a much more serviceable gift for an old woman than a vial of your precious tears," she quipped, barely suppressing a chuckle, "which, after all, is what you seemed on the verge of offering on the occasion of our last meeting. In return, I can assure you that the robe is in the best of hands. The buyer was unmistakably a connoisseur. He handled it with such reverence — it would have eased your heart to see — as though it were a human thing." She mused upon the recollection.

"What was his name?"

She frowned. "I didn't ask. He paid for it in cash."

"Well, what did he look like?" I persisted, with a trace of vehemence.

She shrugged. "He was white, like all the rest, I suppose."

"Is that all you can tell me?" I protested.

"What difference does it make? A business type, well dressed, distinguished, tall. He might have been a banker or an executive. How should I know?"

"What about his face?"

"What about it?" she retorted, her tone becoming increasingly querulous.

"Can you describe it to me? What color were his eyes?"

She shrugged. "I couldn't see his eyes."

"Why not?" I demanded.

"He was wearing dark glasses."

"Dark glasses?" I repeated. "Did you say dark glasses?"

"Yes, dark glasses," she petulantly confirmed. "What's the matter, do I stutter?"

"No, no, I'm sorry," I apologized. "It's just . . ."

"Just what?"

I shook my head. "Nothing. Never mind."

"What's the matter with you?" she asked. "You look pale."

"I'm all right," I contradicted.

She scrutinized me narrowly. "Oh yes, you almost made me forget. He asked me to give you something. It was in the pocket of the robe. 'Tell him he's forgotten something,' he said."

I seemed to hear a strain of ghostly laughter floating down the wind from some unfathomable distance, even as she pressed it in my hand. Yes, Reader, the key: the key chain with the charm, the charming rabbit's foot. It evoked the same aversion as on that first day in the master's cell, only quickened now with a thrill of positive horror. Having put it away for safekeeping during the voyage, somehow in the press and bustle of my life I'd forgotten all about it. As I reexamined it, my father's note once again ran through my mind:

> From one Dowist to another,
> A key, a chain, a charm:
> The rabbit's foot for luck;
> The chain, necessity;
> The key, a master key
> (May it serve you well),
> A skeleton, which opens up the grave
> Secrets of the heart (what is there, this
> Key cannot open?), and to the congregation

Of believers (for we are of the same persuasion,
Aren't we?) a church key, which can make you
Drunk with ecstasy, or else
Unlock the Great Cathedral of the Dow.
                                    Your father,
                                    Love.

The baying of the hounds, which had drifted off almost out of hearing, becoming plaintive, desultory, forlorn, so that I thought they'd lost the scent, that it was over, commenced again, frantic, urgent, closer than ever before. Could it be, I asked myself? Could it? How strange that only after I'd given up all hope of ever finding him he should suddenly appear! The implications of this deepened and spread outward like rings around a stone in a still pool, assuming the proportions of a general truth about life. The master's words came back to me: "Sometimes it is only in giving up a thing that we are able to retain it." I thought about the bear that fey morning on the Gold Sand River, how only after I'd accepted my own death had he turned away and let me live; thought, too, about the Abraham and Isaac window in Trinity Church, which Yin-mi had explicated, how the father had had to relinquish in his heart what he loved most in all the world to sanctify his possession of it and prove himself worthy.

I wrenched myself violently awake from this dream. I dared not let imagination run in that direction. It was a coincidence, suggestive, tantalizing, but nothing more, I told myself. Balanced in the scales against what I knew already — the virtual certainty of Love's death, the dead certainty — it could not stand up. After all, could I reasonably gainsay Kahn's story on the evidence of . . . ? Why, what evidence was there? Mme Chin's description might have applied to practically any man I knew in Wall Street, as well as countless others all over the city. As though there were no other American connoisseurs of Chinese art! Preposterous! And yet, the detail of the glasses. Upon reflection even that seemed hardly decisive. No, weighing it soberly in the balance, I had no choice but to cleave steadfastly to my original position, the one made inevitable by Kahn's relation of the subsequent history and ultimate demise of Eddie Love. Anything else, any theory of some mysterious buyer, was, well, quite simply, vanity and delusion.

But the key itself. I regarded it again. What precisely was it?

Noticing my scrutiny, Mme Chin pursed her lips and raised her eyebrows, throwing out as though offhand, "To a lockbox, isn't it?"

I ogled her witlessly.

"You don't even know, do you?" she asked with scornful pity.

I made no reply.

"Take it to a locksmith," she suggested. Then she closed the door in my face, leaving me standing there in stunned silence.

Chapter 8

I had often passed a small shop near the northern boundary of Chinatown, a locksmith's establishment, down a flight of stairs from a busy Chinese laundry at street level. The proprietor's name, announced in gilded characters on the window, was Mr. Har. Many times on walking by I had seen him bent over in the incandescent halo of his lamp, studying some intricate mechanism with a serene, intense expression, probing its inner life like a surgeon with an array of pointed instruments. As much as his appearance, the proclamation on his window had enchanted me. Keys Made/Locks Opened, it read. The characters, however, could also be construed to mean Solutions Proposed/Problems Resolved.

The day was damp and cool; a light autumn drizzle fell intermittently from a gray, lowering sky. Puddles in the street shone in the silver light. Amid these somber tones, the white, agitated blasts of steam puffing from the exhaust vent of the laundry, big-bellied, billowing cumuli, had a brash, magical appearance, enhanced by the smell of scalded starch that lingered thick and gluey in the humid air. I inhaled its sweet, slightly acrid scent as I went down the gritty concrete steps into Mr. Har's domain.

He was busy with a customer, a young Italian-looking mother in her late twenties with a little boy of three or four, who stood behind her holding one flap of the tail vent of the man's overcoat she wore, sucking his thumb and regarding the proceedings in vulnerable, tongue-tied silence.

Mr. Har, sleeves rolled up over his hairless arms (with muscles like thin, tensile cables, piano wires connected to the hammers of his fingers, playing a searching melody), peered through his black-framed glasses at a wooden box under a powerful light on the counter. The box was constructed of dark, rich fruitwood, cherry perhaps; the cloudy, yellowing wax made it difficult to say. In the center of the lid a blond inlay had been planted, a parquetry chrysanthemum in which a bee was sucking nectar, his black and yellow stripes, his stinger, admirably conveyed by alternating bands of different colored wood.

Mr. Har examined it from above, below, each side. Green felt covered the bottom. No keyhole was visible. They were obviously attempting to open it. He smiled officiously at the woman, inclining his ear slightly toward the box as he probed, like a doctor palpating a patient for a tumor. "Very ord," he said.

"Ord?" she asked.

He beamed and nodded. "Many yee-ah."

"Oh, *old!*" she interpreted. "I found it in the attic the other day with some of Mama's things, letters, dresses. The moths had gotten to most of them and I had to throw a lot out. But I hadn't ever seen this before, and it was locked. I figured maybe there was something valuable inside. Can you open it?"

Mr. Har put it down on the counter, and as he ran his long, pincerlike fingers along the bottom, the lid sprang open and a chime began to hammer out a delicate, airy waltz on the miniature carillon concealed in the mechanism. In the interior two dancers, a bride and groom, wooden faces expressionless but painted in robust, healthy tones of pink, twirled mechanically along a circular track in no particular relation to the music.

The woman's face lit up momentarily. The little boy cooed and clapped his hands. She reached down and picked him up so he could see. Their faces, cheeks touching as they watched, showed delight and fascination, like two children peeping through the banisters at the brilliant, enchanted world of the adults in the ballroom below.

Mr. Har, too, smiled and nodded, tapping his finger on the counter edge in time to the music.

Then with an abrupt violence that startled everyone, the woman reached out and knocked the lid shut. "Mama always was a fool," she pronounced, scorn and pity in her tone. "How much is it worth?"

"I don't want. Why you don't keep?" Mr. Har asked in a reproachful, almost beseeching tone. He looked at it wistfully. "Famiree item. Sentimentar vayoo."

"Keep it," she offered, taking her child's hand, turning brusquely to go.

"Wait!" he called.

She turned back.

Opening the cash register, he took out a five-dollar bill and spread it out on the counter.

"Thanks," she said, with perhaps a trace of irony, as she stuffed it in the pocket of her overcoat. She picked up the little boy. "Come on, Joey. We better get dinner ready before your old man comes home."

The child stared over her shoulder as they left, eyes fixed with longing on the box, the same expression I'd seen in the eyes of the little boy on Coney Island.

Behind the counter, Mr. Har examined his new acquisition, oblivious to my presence.

"That's very nice," I commented, approaching the counter.

He looked up. "Famiree item," he explained, holding it toward me by way of demonstration. He shook his head. "Too bad. Peopre shourdn't serr."

"Shouldn't . . . ?" I asked, trying to catch what he'd said.

"Serr for dorrah," he elaborated.

"Oh, *sell.*"

He appeared to seek corroboration of his pieties.

I obliged him, nodding emphatically.

"Can I herp genterman?"

I laid the key on the counter. "Can you tell me what this is?"

"That key," he replied, smiling and bowing.

I returned his smile politely. "Yes, but to what?"

"Safety-deposit box," he informed me without hesitation. "Frat brade," he explained. "This, box num-bah." He pointed to the numerals engraved on the bow.

"Is there any way of telling what bank?"

He regarded me suspiciously. "Where you get this item?"

I hesitated, but a certain fixity in his expression warned me that equivocation would get me nowhere. "My father left it to me," I said.

He fixed his eyes on mine a moment, as though reading an inner combination, then picked the key up and examined it more closely under the light. He looked at me again through one squinted eye. "You shoo–ah now?"

I nodded.

"I not supposed to do this, you know." He took a heavy, black, vinyl-bound tome from beneath the counter and began to flip through the pages. Apparently finding what he wanted, he picked up the phone and made a call, turning his back and speaking with lowered voice. He then wrote out the following information on a slip of paper: "Box # 1127, Chemicar Bank, Main Office."

I was so happy I almost hugged him. Instead, however, I reached for my wallet. "How much do I owe you?"

He closed his eyes and shook his head. "No charge. Famiree item."

In my excitement an inspiration seized me. "Will you take ten for the box? That's a hundred percent profit in five minutes' time."

He shrugged and pushed it toward me.

I rushed out, paused at the top of the stairs to look in both directions, then sprinted toward the pair of figures I saw receding in the distance toward Little Italy.

When I caught up with them I was panting. "Here," I offered, holding out the box to the little boy, who was still riding on his mother's shoulder. Seeing the wonderful gift, his expression changed to one of disbelieving happiness. "Mama!" he cried.

She started at the shout. Finding me behind her, a shadow of fear crossed her features. "What do you want?" she asked in a low, cautious voice.

I smiled at her with stupid happiness so that the boy had to thrust the box in front of her before she understood. She took it from him, then peered at me again. To my surprise, her expression was even less amenable than before. I watched with helpless horror as she lifted the box above her head with one hand, grimacing and closing her eyes as the child cried and flailed out across her to get at it, then smashed it on the pavement with all her strength. She glared at me with a flushed, angry face, then stormed off, holding the screaming, inconsolable child.

I stood gazing with wistful vacancy at the fragments — the bride and groom lying face up in the rill of water coursing toward the drain — then headed off in the direction of the subway for my expedition to the bank.

•

A starburst scintillated from the lip as the huge steel and chrome door groaned backward on its hinge, revealing for an instant the fabulously bright forbidden realms of money, then clanged to with an iron reverberation as the junior officer emerged. As he walked toward me out of that sea of dazzling light with the long, deep, narrow metal box, all I could think of was the window in Trinity Church depicting the angel of the Lord rolling back the stone and coming forth triumphantly from the tomb with the grave-clothes as a token for the faithful that Christ had indeed risen. It was almost like a transcendental experience, a glimpse into paradise itself.

"Follow me," he said. And I would have, anywhere.

But it was only into a small cubicle with a built-in desk and chair, where one was at liberty to peruse and itemize the contents of his hoard in privacy.

As he closed the door, I sat down and took a deep breath, staring at the box like a child at Christmas with a wrapped present, hoping by a kind of spiritual X-ray vision to ferret out its contents. Now, of course, it's largely a moot point, but I suppose the true question, had I thought to ask it, was not so much what was actually inside the box as what I wished to find there. I was excited, as excited as I'd ever been in my whole life, a hopeful excitement, too, at least predominantly. I must admit though, a slight, queasy undercurrent of foreboding clouded my anticipation.

What would I have asked for? I can't say precisely, only something small and relatively digestible (emotionally and spiritually, I mean), something which would not have disrupted my life any further than it had already been disrupted. You know the sort of thing I mean: a pocket watch, a signet ring, a medal from the war, some implicit token of recognition, showing that he'd thought of me and wished to repair, insofar as reparation was possible, the damage he'd inflicted — unwittingly inflicted — on my life and our relation.

Perhaps, then, you can begin to imagine my surprise when I lifted up the lid and found . . . ah, Reader! I wish to impart this information soberly, but even now, after all this time, it's difficult to control my emotions in the face of an enormity so, well, enormous! Found . . . found . . . Damn it all! I won't be melodramatic. I won't! Found, first of all, to be brief, cash. Not just a few choice bills either, such as even a nest egg of immodest proportions might be expected to contain, but stacks and stacks of it! Fertile plains of green like the lettuce fields of Salinas, the Elysian fields themselves, proliferating with insane, unnatural fecundity. Taking temporary leave of my senses, I laughed hysterically and began to throw handfuls around the cubicle like confetti. I papered the walls with them.

Partially recovering, I lapsed into a prolonged, trancelike meditation on the bills themselves. Though old by normal standards (in the brief half-life of that unstable isotope, wealth), these seemed as crisp and new as on the day of issue, preserved by the rare, immortal air of the vault. With dumb awe I examined the various denominations, completely absorbed, almost mesmerized, in the task. I had never recognized the artistry of a dollar bill before, or the weight and quality of the paper on which it was printed. After careful and dispassionate perusal, however, I felt obliged to admit that on aesthetic grounds alone the dollar deserved its preeminence among the world's currencies. In fact, it was suitable for framing. Licking my fingers, I counted out the crisp, slightly cockled bills as I had seen cashiers do at banks along the Street. "Money," "moola," "bread," "dough," "cash," "tender," "green" — the generic names deployed themselves as Kahn had once recited them to me, followed quick-step by the species — "buck," "smacker," "eight-bit," "greenback," "frog-skin," "lettuce leaf," "shinplaster," "George," "simoleon," "boffo" — all the various American nuances which resolved into that tender note, the universal tonic chord of money, DOLLARS! I examined the faces of the various patron saints of cash: George Washington, Father of the Nation; Abe Lincoln, Emancipator of the Slaves. How appropriate that they should be immortalized on a floating currency, passed hand to hand, interceding in the debts of their posterity. How it must fill every native heart with pride, I thought, to make the symbolic trade-off, selling Lincoln into voluntary slavery in a butcher's till in exchange for a pound of ground chuck or some chitlins!

Only little by little as I made my way through, tenderly collating and stacking my piles, did the thought occur to me: what an educational coup! Not only did the presence of the presidents on the bills serve as a standard, a noble exhortation to financiers and criminals alike not to derogate from the highest principles in their transactions, but at the same time it educated the young, making the practical activity of counting money synonymous with the study of American history! I felt awed and flabbergasted once again before the spectacle of Yankee ingenuity; felt too, for the first time perhaps, the gratifying and ennobling sentiment of patriotic fervor — privileged to be here! — as the vista of America, Land of Golden Opportunity, Home of the Free and the Brave, opened up to me between my stacks of cash. My breast swelled with patriotism. Suddenly I loved my new home. Tears of gratitude welled in my eyes. America! My euphoria was only mildly compromised by the reflection that I was an illegal alien, possessing none of the rights and privileges enjoyed by the inhabitants, and subject to immediate and tyrannical deportation without appeal if apprehended.

As this perhaps suggests, exhilaration and innocent wonder were complicated in my appraisal by an element of something darker and more mordant, a nihilistic ecstasy, I'd call it, which took a cynical pleasure in the irony of my predicament: my sudden windfall coming so close on the heels of my "purgation," my "absolution." "Everything was going to be made right, the slate wiped clean" — my own phrases returned to me accompanied by a lively inner chorus of Bronx cheers. Ha! What a fool I was!

But I had no time to indulge in pratfalls. There was more to see. Below the cold cash were other mysterious instruments, which on closer perusal proved to be war bonds. And in considerable quantity!

Last of all, the stock certificates — even, if possible, more beautiful than money, with their engraved borders and the corporate logo of American Power and Light, the Tree of Life (or was it the Tree of the Knowledge of Good and Evil?) floating in primordial chaos, an enormous, earth-shaped piece of fruit hanging, green and indeterminate, in the branches, and I like some Newton drowsing in its shade, about to be awakened by its fall, not with an idea, but a concussion! One hundred thousand shares endorsed to me! Reader, not to beat around the bush, I was a millionaire! Several times over, in fact! And it had been there *all the time!* I laughed and wept with wild, pathological resentment. Just when everything had been made right and my life had become simple again. The irony was too hideous. I couldn't bear to look at it. I was dazzled, blinded. Luckily the walls were soundproof, for I think I must have screamed a few obscenities. Perhaps it would have helped if they'd been padded too.

Now at last I understood the note. But whereas before I had been tantalized by its ambiguity of reference, now for the first time I detected a flicker of malevolence in its insinuations: "for we are of the same persuasion, aren't we?" Again my thoughts gravitated back to the stained glass windows in Trinity Church. This time the man with frosty, glittering eyes came back to me, the fields of wheat, the marching armies, the white-sailed ships on the blue sea, all presented to his young companion with a sweeping gesture of his arm as though to say "This could be yours." Well, *were* we of the same persuasion, he and I? Was I a Dowist too? In my heart, on the instant, quietly but firmly, I said no. I won't. I won't take it. I would get up that instant, leave the cubicle, close the door behind me, walk away, and not look back. This resolution brought me peace. I would do it. I would.

Then a new battery of associations came at me from another direction. What Kahn couldn't do with such a windfall! It might make all the difference. I shook my head. It couldn't be helped. I knew him too well to think he'd ever swallow his pride so far as to take charity from me.

But perhaps it didn't have to be charity. . . . An echo flitted through my brain, too indistinct on the first pass for me to make it out. But it continued to reverberate, gaining increasing resolution. Suddenly I caught it: "sacrificial feasts and sacred rites . . . music and the splendor of the ceremonies." The oracle. "Under certain circumstances a man's work may become so difficult that he can no longer think of himself." Could it be that that was what it had meant by "a great renunciation"? I felt an electric chill, actually shuddered at this evidence of the oracle's prescience. I turned it over in my mind, examined it from every angle. It had to be. What else could it have meant? "Sacrificial feasts and sacred rites . . . music and the splendor of the ceremonies" — what was that but the market, the rituals of investment as practiced by the priests of high finance? What was the "sacred music" but the rhythmic clacking of the teletype, the hum of the tape, the roar and hubbub of thousands of voices rising from the trading floor, chanting their mesmeric anthem, their ritual invocation of a higher power: Dow! Yes, that was it. That had to be it! What it had taken away, it would restore! And my moral mandate, my mission, the "great task outside myself" was Kahn's rehabilitation, which I was to pursue even at the cost of foregoing my own desire to renounce my windfall; pursue, even, *via* my windfall, by plunging him (and myself along with him, for the ride) back into his element, the marketplace!

In other words, we were to pool our resources — his know-how, my wherewithal — and go into business! On the strength of my "inheritance" could we not purchase a new lease on life, or any damn thing else we pleased, for one melancholic Wandering Jew? Oh, Reader, could we not?

"For Kahn's sake then!" I proposed to myself exactly in the manner of a toast.

•

The next step was to drum up some enthusiasm for the project in the proper quarter, namely Kahn's. I only hoped it wasn't too late. The next day during my lunch hour I set out on his trail. Consisting of a series of empty Dry Sack bottles accompanied by little gutted, waxy half-pint cartons of milk (touching, like something from a schoolchild's lunch tray), it wasn't hard to follow. He had been sighted stalking the remotest corners of the district, trudging along in his unpressed suit, sockless, unshaved, eyes glazed and red with weeping, the raccoon pouches vivid as bruises underneath his eyes. With his briefcase — which he continued to lug long after he had ceased to have a use for it, a pathetic reminder of former glory — he looked like a balding, overgrown Jewish bag lady. I found him at a little bar not far from the Exchange which we had frequented in the old days before things came to grief, the Buttonwood Café.

This establishment, along with several others, purported to be on the site of the legendary tree of the same name, under whose spreading branches that now sainted group of Dutch financiers, the founding fathers of Wall Street, with their round, red-cheeked, beer-bloated faces bobbing on stumpy necks, puffing meerschaums with religious fervor, had once attained enlightenment, Dutch-style, conceiving their financial utopia, the New York Stock Exchange, just as Gautama Buddha had entered Nirvana under the Bodhi tree in India long before. Come to think of it, Newton had received his inspiration similarly.

Perhaps it always happened under trees. But I had been enjoined not to think about myself. I was here for Kahn.

The sad, sorry figure I found slumping in a corner of the bar, under a potted plant that looked distinctly like a Wandering Jew, was going about his beatitude in a very different manner. From the look of it, Kahn was trying to drink himself into Nirvana, though oblivion would no doubt have done just as nicely for his purposes. In his condition, I doubt he'd have noticed the difference. Highball glasses were stacked in a careful pyramid on the table, a monument erected to his own dissipation. At my entrance the cocktail waitress, who had seen us there together before, took me urgently aside.

"I don't know what to do with Mr. Kahn," she complained. "He's been in here all morning, not to mention all day yesterday and the day before. I don't want to have to call the police. He's always been a good customer. But if he doesn't leave soon, I'm afraid I'll have to." She lowered her voice. "I think he's cracked. He won't even let me clear the table, says he's trying to recapitulate the Babylonian captivity and rebuild the pyramids himself, only with cocktail glasses."

Despite the gravity of the situation, I couldn't restrain a smile at this. I tried to reassure her, but nothing worked so well as a crisp fin slipped into her not unwilling palm.

"Okay, Kahn," I opened, attempting a cheerful, inoffensive irony, "the Diaspora is over."

Lifting his head from his arms, he gazed at me with a submerged, underwater look, like a glum fish. "Go away and let me suffer," he mumbled. "It's the only thing that makes me happy."

"Don't be difficult," I chided.

"If there's one thing I can't stand, it's a missionary," he informed me, putting his head back down. "I thought the type didn't exist among the Chinese."

As I made no reply, he looked back up. "You did come here to save me, I assume?"

"What are you having?" I asked pointedly. "Never mind. Waitress! Bring us another round, Dry Sack on the rocks."

"With milk," Kahn added, belching.

"As if I didn't know," she replied, giving me a threatening look.

"So what's all this about the Diaspora being over? Who are you anyway, kid, Moses?" He cackled to himself. "Kid Moses, Moses Tse-tung."

"Diaspora means dispersion, doesn't it?"

"Yeah. So?"

I grinned at him, unable to resist applying the leverage of my secret just a little as he had so often.

"So, so?" he asked, waving his arms in irritated exhortation, as though fanning a refractory flame.

"I consulted the oracle on your behalf and that was the reading it returned, number fifty-nine, 'Dispersion.' 'The sacrificial feasts and sacred rites . . . music and the splendor of the ceremonies.' Remind you of anything?" I gave him a coy look.

"The Seder, right?"

I shook my head.

"No? Okay, I give up. Can the Oriental mystery and intrigue bit will you, kid? I'm a desperate man. If you've got something to tell me, spit it out."

"Okay, Kahn, not to beat around the bush — we're rich!"

"Peachy," he replied with a deadpan expression. "Who's 'we'?"

"Us! You and me." I waited for a sign of rapture. "What's the matter, you don't seem pleased."

"Don't get me wrong, kid. It's not that I'm ungrateful. But would you mind telling me what the fuck you're talking about?"

"I've inherited a million bucks, Kahn! Two million!"

"Don't tell me," he rejoined wryly, "your rich spinster aunt in Cleveland passed away and . . ."

"No, Kahn," I cut him off. "Eddie Love!"

"Eddie Love?" He pricked up his ears, showing signs of taking me seriously for the first time.

I nodded.

"All right already, so tell me!"

And I did, very slowly and carefully, making ample concessions for his inebriation. He seemed to be following, yet as I neared the end his expression still betrayed no trace of encouragement. "What's the matter, don't you believe me?" I asked as I concluded.

"Oh, sure," he said. "Why not? If there's anything I've learned, it's that anything can happen, and probably will, especially if it's unpleasant. There's a statistical correlation there some mathematician ought to investigate."

"Is that all you can say?" I demanded in exasperation.

"I know, I know, if you can't say something nice, don't say anything at all, right? Don't misunderstand me, kid. I'm happy for you. I really am. It's only that, considering the demands of my own self-pity, I don't have a lot of time and energy left over for back patting and general fraternization. That shouldn't be too hard to understand for a smart kid like you, kid."

"But that's just it!" I cried, ignoring his irony. "You don't have to feel sorry for yourself anymore."

"Why not?" he asked bluntly. "Surely you wouldn't deprive me of my one and only consolation in adversity?" A gleam of mockery and admonition appeared in his eye. "Surely you haven't come to offer me the dole?"

Luckily, as the Reader knows, I had foreseen this potential impasse and devised a clever means of skirting it. "Not at all," I replied. "On the contrary, I've come to ask you a favor."

He laughed a lax, incontinent laugh, broken off abruptly by another belch. "Ask *me* a favor! That's rich. What do you need from me? You've got cash.

You know the ropes. What do you need me for? I'm the one that lost the robe for you, remember?"

"No, Kahn," I contradicted. "I lost it by my own decision. You're not responsible for that."

But he was already launched on a jeremiad of self-pity and excoriation. "Haven't you heard the news yet, kid? I'm the one who couldn't beat it honestly. It was too tough. Seven years of bad luck and I panicked. I tried to cheat, and I got caught. Too bad. Tough fucking luck. But you! You came through smelling like clover, four-leaf clover."

"Why not let a little of it rub off on you?" I suggested.

He shook his head. "If I haven't taught you anything else, kid, I might have hoped I'd taught you that. 'Cut your losses and let your profits run,' remember? I'm a loss, kid. A dead loss. Do yourself a favor, don't team up with a loser."

"You also taught me the value of contrary opinion," I rejoined. "When everyone else is selling, that's the time to buy. It looks like everyone else is selling now."

He conceded the point with a brief, unhappy smile. Sighing, he shook his head. "You know, I'm still not sure exactly how it happened. The whole thing is like a dream. Am I wrong, or just a few weeks ago was I not righteously declaiming to you on the marketplace as a 'testing ground for character'? 'The trial by fire,' I think was the choice expression I used?"

I blushed with embarrassment, for him and for myself.

"Am I such a hypocrite?" He shrugged. "I guess I must be. When it came down to it, though, I never thought I'd do it — choose money over . . . whatever, virtue, self-respect, all *that*. But I did. It wasn't even a question. I just leaned over and fucked myself right up the ass. I don't know what happened. It's hard to pin it down. One day I simply woke up and there it was. I didn't even stop to think twice about it. That's what kills me. It was like instinct, you know? I read about this young girl, a hippie type from New York, assigned as a social worker to an Indian reservation somewhere out West. She got a wolf cub, brought it home, house-trained it, tried to domesticate it, the whole doggie obedience school bit. Then one night the wolf saw the full moon through the window rising over the mountains, and he let out this forlorn, haunted wail she'd never heard before. The next day he was gone. Right through the glass. Right through the fucking wall of glass. That's it, kid. You can't make a wolf a pacifist or vegetarian, no matter how principled you may be personally. He simply doesn't have it in him. There's a wall of glass, I think, in all of us — like the one in the gallery looking down on the Exchange. Some people manage to stay behind it safely all their lives, never leave the gallery; something sends others crashing through onto the trading floor, sent me. Something . . ." He smiled with bitter wisdom. "The gravity of blood, that's what it was with me, kid. All my fathers and grandfathers, the Ashkenazi warriors, running pawnshops in Prague and Warsaw — their lifelong hunger, their hunched shoulders, their parched souls and shriveled hearts, their enormous greed like a millstone around their necks — suddenly it all cried out to me across the ages, 'It's yours, little fresser; you've got a right to it; take what you can while you can,' and all my intentions of restraint, circumspection, honesty, altruism, all *that,* scattered on the winds like so much chaff. Ah, Sonny!" he sighed, rubbing his hands together briskly. "Is it cold in here to you or what? My bursitis!"

"All right, Kahn," I exhorted. "Stop feeling sorry for yourself."

"Ah ha!" he cried vehemently. "I knew it. I knew you came in here to preach to me. Why should I stop? It makes me feel better. Want to know a secret about the Jews? My mother told me this and I've never forgotten it. (Did I tell you this already? I can't remember. Okay, so I'm a little shikker. What difference does it make?) We're best when we suffer. It brings out the latent talent in a Jew. It's a product of our history. We've been shit on so long, we've developed a whole repertoire of compensatory techniques. Admit it: no other race has matched us for smarts — soul either, for that matter — with the possible exception of the redoubtable you-know-who. The only problem is, we fall apart in prosperity, get withdrawal symptoms, go cold turkey. Look at Israel. That's why so many Jews have that abrasive manner you've perhaps noticed. It's because at some level, unconscious probably, every Jew knows that to be is to suffer. He craves an insult or a slight, incites you to it if he must, in order to secure a spiritual benefit to himself. It's the only path he knows toward enlightenment. If anyone else but me was saying this I'd accuse him of rabid anti-Semitism. The only problem is, it's true."

"Well," I replied, "from the look of it I'd say you haven't learned the trick. Your suffering doesn't seem to have brought to light any heretofore hidden potentials, except perhaps for dissipation. Would you call that one of the 'compensatory techniques' the Jews, particularly Aaron Kahn, have mastered in order to ennoble themselves through suffering?"

Kahn scowled and made a hissing sound like some slinking night-creature singed by a ray of daylight. "You know, Sonny," he said, "you were such a sweet kid when you first came here, easygoing, diffident, fired by religious curiosity. That's what attracted me to you, your lack of cynicism about the world. It was refreshing." He paused. "What happened?"

"You don't mean my 'Oriental Complacency,' do you?" I inquired ironically, wounded a little by his implication.

"See what I mean?" he retorted. "That's just it. You're becoming jaded, kid, cynical. More and more I see the Wasp in you come out. I don't want to lay any heavy trips on you, but it's obvious, you know. You're changing. That story you told me, about Eddie Love being your father and all? I must admit, I had my doubts at first. Not anymore. The resemblance is only too obvious." He sighed and shook his head. "You're no different, kid. It's the gravity of blood. Sooner or later it rules us all. No way around it. Recidivism. Take me. I never wanted to be a Jew. But little by little, like a tiny pebble, a grain of sand picked up and carried by the advance of a glacier, my own personal wishes unweighted and ignored, I was swept away by racial and historical forces. And you, kid, I pity you more than myself. At least with me those forces were all tending in the same direction, even if it was opposite the one I would have chosen. But you! God help you. Half Wasp, half Chinese, like some mythical beast, a satyr or a merman, man above, beast below, half East, half West, half dragon, half tiger, like your mother's robe, caught between the opposites — what do you call them? My memory is slipping on me. *Yin* and *yang* — yeah, that's it, caught between your *yin* and your *yang*.

Kahn and I exchanged a long look, then each of us turned away, he to the ice cubes floating in the milky residue of his drink, I to the window. In the street many young men, their manner brisk and efficient, their features unambiguously Anglo-Saxon, hurried along the sidewalk, briefcases in hand, trench coats draped across their arms. Would I not do better with one of them, I asked myself — one of those durable young men, energetic, in good health, joggers who ate well and watched their waistlines, and strictly segregated their business and personal lives — would it not make better sense to elect a partner from their ranks? Perhaps. Perhaps. But they did not interest me. They seemed like so many puppets and mannequins compared to this aging Jew with his melancholy eyes circled with rings, like two blue poultices of liver, too blue, true blue. There was an elemental attraction between myself and Kahn, partly I think, because we each came from an old race which had suffered and survived and knew itself. Not like these Americans, still, as my uncle Hsiao had said, brand spanking new, still warm from the mold, unproved, untried. And yet, as Kahn had pointed out, I was half Wasp myself, an alloy, some new metal, some new mettle, half boundless hope and energy and inexperience, half immemorial suffering, stoicism, resignation.

Certainly, I thought, it would be easier for me to deploy my new wealth without so much as a backward glance in Kahn's direction. It seemed especially tempting now, when he was so difficult. But my task was to "set aside all personal desires" and put my goal in "a great task outside myself." After all, what was the money for, if not for Kahn? I etched this fact in memory through vehement rehearsal, realizing that if I lost sight of it I was finished. Besides, despite his whining and carping, I knew Kahn had hit upon a fundamental truth in my regard and uttered it without fear of the consequences. Though I rankled at it, even perhaps hated him a little, at the same time I appreciated his candor. After a moment's sting, of love and hate, the former emotion proved the more enduring. I gently laid my hand on his. "Are you ready to listen now?"

"Sonny, let it go, won't you? I don't care anymore, don't you see?" he implored.

His expression said something else entirely though. "No," I replied, "I don't."

He put his head down on the table and began to weep.

"Let's go. Let's get out of here," he said, controlling himself at length, his heavy face red with shame, his eyes darting about this way and that, avoiding mine.

I paid the tab while he escaped from the cruel curiosity of the management and patrons into the anonymity of the street.

We began to walk, once again, in the direction of the river. Our pace was brisk and we said nothing. At length we came to the Brooklyn Bridge. Walking along the water's edge, we stopped and looked out at its monumental span crossing the water several hundred feet above our heads. With my slow accretion of a personal history, it had come to seem a curious symbol, peculiarly American, with its two great piles plunging ponderously to the bottom, into the ooze and slime of the polluted river, and up above, silver in the sunlight, the cables, like the glistening threads of a spiderweb, or harp strings, an aeolian harp humming in the upper air, or yet again, the barely detectable wires of the puppeteer, holding it all together. That strands so frail and tenuous, so beautiful, should contrive to hold together so much mindless, ugly mass and power never ceased to amaze me, and, as I said, seemed fitting as a symbol of America itself, its gigantic power, and the almost invisible strings which pulled it.

"You know," Kahn said, his voice relaxed now, no longer on the verge of breaking, "my first year at Mount Abarim I used to walk across this bridge every day, over and back. It was a pact between my father and myself. You see, he didn't tell me about Ahasuerus. He led me to believe that the whole thing was contingent on my showing my desire by making that walk day in and day out, in any sort of weather. 'Every privilege requires a sacrifice,' he said. 'You gotta accept responsibility.' I took it to heart. I used to get such a thrill, even on the coldest days, standing up there in the middle looking down at the swirling currents. It gave me a giddy sense of . . . I don't know what — power, special destiny — as though I'd been called to a high task, and proved my worthiness through sacrifice. There was the fatuity of childhood in it, of course, but sometimes I used to cry when I thought about it, my mission in life. Those were the sweetest tears I ever shed. But I never found that mission, that place that had been reserved for me since the beginning of the world. I schlepped around. I tried to be a scholar. That was close. Maybe I should have stuck with it, but it failed to satisfy a certain part of me, a base part, maybe, but a real one. It was a craving to be out there in the thick of things mixing it up, inviting risk and danger, something adventurous.

"You know, I've missed the university often since I came to Wall Street, but the truth is — and I say this even now after everything that's happened — though I'm ashamed of what I did there, and sometimes even question the very principles on which the place is founded, still I never once that I remember felt that restiveness and anxiety, that gnawing hunger, while I worked at the Exchange. Because bad as it may be, something there satisfied my appetite for life." Kahn looked away over the water. "I still couldn't call it by a name. Not even if you paid me." He laughed bitterly, catching the inadvertent irony in his own remark. "No, not even if you paid me." He turned to me with a forced smile. "That's saying something, isn't it, kid?" His spirits seemed to sink. "I guess it's better not to think about it. It's gone, and that's the end of it. What I've got to do now is find something else. I wonder where I'll end up this time. Care to place any bets?"

"I'll tell you what you're going to do," I replied.

He raised his eyebrows in surprise.

I nodded sternly. "You're going to climb back in the saddle and ride."

He laughed. "There's only one problem, kid, they took my saddle."

"A figure of speech, Kahn," I replied caustically.

"You know, kid, I never realized you had a sense of humor before. But that's really funny, 'climb back in the saddle and ride.' I mean it. Take it as a compliment. You may be losing your humanity, but the good news is, it's bringing to light a heretofore untapped potential for comedy." He furrowed his brow, assuming a histrionic pose. "I'll just put on muh chaps 'n spurs, pop a plug between muh cheek and jaw, and mosey on in there. 'Boys,' I'll say, 'you may as well give up 'cause I ain't a-quittin' till I git what I come for.' No, Sonny, I mean it, that's really good. What difference does it make that I don't have a cent to my name, that I've been blackballed by the Board of Governors, that I've lost my reputation and my friends?"

"You still have me," I said.

I could see an acid rejoinder on the tip of his tongue, but he restrained it. Deflating with a sigh, he patted my arm. "No, kid, you're right. And I appreciate it."

"You know, Aaron," I said, "there's an old Taoist paradox that describes the process of seeking enlightenment as searching for a bull while riding on its back. Sometimes what we're looking for is in the most unlikely places, right before our noses."

"That's very profound," he remarked with halfhearted irony.

"Well, profound or not, you say you've got to decide what to do with your life, find a way of picking up the pieces. And, presumptuous or not, I think I know a way. I've heard you complain about the profession from the day I met you, but for all that — and what you said just now reinforces my conviction — I'm convinced that the market is your *tao*, your own private path back to the Source. It's your shot at grace, Kahn. You've suffered a serious setback, granted, but is that any excuse for giving up the journey altogether? In my mind that would be more inexcusable than the original error. Everything else can be forgiven, but not that."

"That's all very easy for you to say," he rejoined heatedly, "but it doesn't alter the facts. How precisely am I to go about climbing back in the saddle, as you put it? I told you, kid, I'm broke. My name is the four-letter word currently favored by investors everywhere. I've lost my influence."

"I've thought about it extensively, Kahn," I cut in, "and I want to propose that we go into business together."

"Business?" he asked. "What kind of business?"

"I don't know. That's what I was hoping you could tell me. Some type of financial service maybe? I'm out of my depth in the business end of it. I leave that totally to you. That's what I need you for. And it's not charity either. My funds, your expertise — a fifty-fifty contribution of resources. What do you say?"

He looked at me sweetly, almost sentimentally. "That's awfully nice of you, kid, trying to give your old mentor a break. But don't be a chump. I've ruined you once, what makes you think I won't again?"

"I've already told you, Kahn, I take responsibility for my own acts. And besides, of the two of us I wronged you more."

"What!" He stared at me incredulously. "You're clever, Sonny, but I want to see how you're going to con that from the data. Precisely how did you wrong *me*?"

"By my importunity," I replied. "By not believing you. In the *Tao Te Ching* it's written, 'By not believing people we turn them into liars.' My exorbitant expectations of you and my disbelief in your ability to fulfill them put an unfair pressure on you that warped you from your original intention, which I still believe was good."

Kahn turned away, stifling a sob. "It was, kid. Believe that!"

"So then," I asked, "is it a deal?"

He looked at me doubtfully once again, then heaved a sigh of heavyhearted acquiescence. "Okay," he agreed, admonitorily. "I only hope you won't live to regret it." He paused. "Or me either."

We both laughed, then set off without further ado.

Chapter 9

Such sweetness attended on this small benevolence! As I walked home through the streets, I felt my cheeks occasionally suffuse with blood at the thought of what I'd done. Proud and happy, I wondered if Riley weren't right after all. Perhaps something in me *was* thawing, loosening, starting to break up and flow toward warmer seas. Was this the *tao* of love?

Having settled this matter so propitiously, I looked with a less jaded eye at my new wealth. There was no disputing the fact: it had served me well. Exhilarated by my little coup, I thought briefly and perfunctorily, if at all, about its irreconcilability with Lowliness, the last of my Three Treasures. If I was actively putting myself forward in Kahn's affairs, it was with an unselfish motive, wasn't it? And hadn't a resort to power been implicitly sanctioned by the *I Ching* itself? No, I would not be deterred from my good offices on the basis of a pedantic quibble. For that is exactly the light in which the dogma of Noninterference presented itself at that moment. What was more important, I asked myself, human life or doctrinal purity? A brief but violent flicker of resentment against my upbringing flared in my consciousness. What was one to infer about a Way of Life under which such a question, such an opposition, such a choice could even arise? Was there not some fundamental inhumanity in it? But what was I saying! This was blasphemy! My emotional weather vane swung 180 degrees, west to east.

Still, rather than abdicate the power my new wealth endowed me with, my thoughts ran on new ways to deploy it. One in particular seized me with the force of inspiration. Indeed, it rivaled my plans for Kahn's rehabilitation in ingeniousness, though perhaps less blamelessly disinterested. On this subject, however, I was not inclined to split hairs. I mean, of course, Li. I recalled an image which had recurred again and again in her conversation. Fairyland. With jittery exhilaration, hope hardly daring to assert its claims against habitual diffidence, I realized I was now in a position to take her there. Not on a carpet woven of good intentions either, but on a *magic* carpet, Reader, made of cloth of gold!

The question was, would she let me. I had no idea if my plan would work. Yet Ahasuerus's maxim, "No balls, no glory," seemed as applicable in this context as that in which it was originally uttered, maybe more so. Perhaps it covered the entire spectrum of American life!

Having made my resolution, I enjoyed a temporary surge of confidence. I eagerly set about making preparations for the encounter. First I bought myself a suit on Canal Street, first-quality double knit, such as I had seen the Chinese swells in Luck Fat's wearing — the ones with the girls. I complemented this with shirt, tie, and new boxer shorts (in honor of my own rebellion!), topping off the whole ensemble with a tasteful pair of red Naugahyde loafers from the Pic 'n Pay which I'd had my eye on since my arrival in the city. In the prodigality of my inspiration, I bought a dozen pairs!

On my way home, moved with another idea for rectifying the sins of the past — this one of omission rather than commission — I stopped at a package store and picked up the bottle of Dry Sack I'd promised Lo at our last tippling session, then swung by Luck Fat's.

When he saw me peeking in through the alley door, surprise and grievance flickered across his features. But he mastered himself instantly. "The young dragon returns from his wanderings at last!" he announced with his characteristic hint of friendly archness, smiling and bowing effusively as I came in.

"I was just going by," I began, "and thought that too long a time had elapsed since I made my promise to you." Smiling, I produced the wine.

He lifted it from the bag and eyed it closely. "The honorable vintage we discussed at our last session?"

I nodded, beaming.

"I am overwhelmed." He made a low bow.

"The pleasure is entirely mine," I insisted.

"No, no," he contradicted.

"Yes, yes," I rejoined.

We both burst out laughing.

"I realize you are too busy to try it now," I deprecated, "but when you have leisure perhaps you will condescend to sample it, and then we may pass a pleasant hour discussing as we used to in the old days."

"Ah, yes, the old days," he sighed. "My wife gives me no rest, you know. 'Where is Sun I?' she asks. 'Why does he never come to visit anymore? Do we have smell in our armpits? Is our conversation dull?' 'It is your tiresome nagging, woman!' I tell her. 'It is enough to frighten anyone away! In fact, if you keep it up, I will be forced to petition the emperor for divorce.'" He laughed. "'But seriously, how should I know? The dragon makes many far flights in his circumnavigation of the globe, flights unimaginable to the likes of simple folk like you and me. All we may be certain of is that one day he will return for rest and sustenance when he is weary. And we will be here when he comes.'"

"Thank you, Lo," I said, responding to the earnest proffer disguised beneath his jovial remarks.

He smiled and bowed.

"Well . . ." I irresolutely marshaled myself to go.

He put his hand on my arm. "Wait just a little. Before you go, we will have a cup together." I started to demur, but he prevented me. "No, no, I insist. Things are slow tonight. What can it hurt? Otherwise you put me in the position of being impolite. Just one."

"Well, all right," I consented hesitantly, "if you think it's okay."

"Perfectly okay. A-one, in fact!"

As he was heating the wine, he turned to me. "You know, Sun I, though she never speaks about it, I think perhaps your visits have been more sorely missed by Yin-mi than anyone. Of course, it's not my place to ask, but I hope no trouble has arisen between you. I know she is fond of you, and I think we had all begun to assume that you were fond of her."

"Oh, I am. It's just that . . . You know, I came by not so long ago," I began again, deciding that skirting the issue would be best. "She wasn't home. In fact, no one was there, except your daughter Li."

"Ah, you met Li!"

I nodded.

"And what did you think of her?"

"I'd seen her before, remember? At the family gathering."

"Oh yes, of course."

"She's very beautiful," I remarked with unintended wistfulness.

He observed me closely, frowning. "Yes, very beautiful."

"I didn't really have a chance to get to know her," I lied, hoping to counteract the previous impression and perhaps draw him out a little. "She seemed very different from Yin-mi."

He laughed. "As different as night and day."

"How so?" I asked.

"Each child has different gifts, of course."

"Of course."

"Since she was a little girl, Li has known exactly what she wanted and gone after it. She hardly needed us to help her find her way. She is like a cat in that respect. It has its own peculiar intelligence and operates on principles that seem strange to us. A cat cannot be trained either. It knows what it knows. Trespass on its nature and you may drive it crazy, even kill it, but change it — that you can never do. It's great quality is independence, as the dog's is loyalty. Yin-mi is like a dog in that respect. She has a noble, generous nature and lives outside herself. She is less canny and more vulnerable than her sister. She loves the clear, the high, the strong, just as Li is attracted to paradox and ambiguity." He interrupted himself to pour the wine. "Kan pei!" he said, clinking cups with me.

"Kan pei," I replied.

"But you must forgive me for going on about my daughters."

"No, no," I objected. "Not at all. I'm interested. Please continue."

"You aren't simply being polite?"

I shook my head.

"Well, if you are interested, I will tell you an image that for me captures the difference precisely. May I?"

I nodded vehemently.

"Do you know the Confucian *Analects*?"

"Not very well," I admitted.

"Well, I too can make no presumption to a thorough acquaintance with the master's sayings, but as a young man, and occasionally since, I have dabbled in them. You will have heard of the Sacred Dances, the Succession Dance and the War Dance?"

"I have heard of them."

"Well, as you probably know, the Succession Dance mimes the accession of Emperor Shun in peaceful conditions. All was in harmony in heaven and earth. The War Dance, on the other hand, depicts the accession of the warlike emperor Wu, who came to the throne by overthrowing the Yin." He paused and sipped his wine. "There is a passage in the third book . . ." — he cleared his throat — " 'Confucius spoke of the Succession Dance as being perfect beauty and at the same time perfect goodness; but of the War Dance as being perfect beauty, but not perfect goodness.' " He regarded me significantly. "Of course, it is the height of presumption for me to speak of my own worthless progeny in the context of the Sacred Dances, but taking that into account, otherwise for me the distinction has always resonated. Do you not think so?"

"I'm sure I don't know," I begged off, not daring to touch it. After a pause, I asked, "Which dynasty did you say Wu overthrew?"

"The Yin," he replied.

•

Thus it was that, treading as bravely as I might in my new loafers, I set out. I took the subway uptown, the local, to give myself more time to collect my thoughts. After stopping at a florist in her neighborhood to purchase a bouquet of chrysanthemums, I hailed a cab to carry me the last few blocks, wanting to make a more impressive entrance. Unfortunately, there was no one in the courtyard to witness it, not even Ramon, whom I could see through the glass doors talking on the lobby phone, back turned to the street. The outer door was unlocked, the inner one propped behind a chair so he wouldn't have to inconvenience himself for the arrival of tenants. I thought I might make it to the elevators before he noticed me, but no such luck; he turned around. "Momento," he said, putting his palm over the receiver. "Hey, mon, whar the fuck ju theenk ju goink?"

I slipped out a bill and dangled it temptingly between my thumb and forefinger, like a flag before a bull, only with the opposite intention, of pacification.

He looked at it, then at me. Suddenly his features broke out in that lean bandito smile. "Oh, sure, mon, no problema. Ju want me to reeng far ju?"

I shook my head as I delivered the bribe, and headed pronto for the elevators as he went back to the interminable dialogue.

When I reached her door, I stared at it hard a moment, then sighed and turned back. I couldn't.

I turned again. I had to! I took a deep breath. It was a foolish plan, I told myself. I should have called first. She would see me through the peephole and call the police. There was no way it could work. Steeling myself to the worst, with a kind of stoic resignation I knocked.

No one answered. I was distinctly relieved. I spun and almost ran to the elevator. Just as the door trundled open, however, I heard the night chain slip. Li's door cracked, and she leaned out, looking first in the opposite direction, then directly at me. Our eyes engaged in silent, mutual study.

She was wearing a robe, pinching it closed at her throat. Her hair fell from her back as she leaned out, hanging in a long perpendicular skein toward the floor. The elevator doors closed again in my face.

"Trying to run away?" she asked, that little flicker of coy amusement in her tone.

I swallowed painfully and shook my head.

"That's good," she said, "because I think you just missed your ride." She laughed and came out in the hall, leaning casually against her jamb, eyeing me inconspicuously, noting and, as I flattered myself, impressed by my new clothes. "So, what brings you up my way? Not that I'm not flattered, but you remember what I said, what we agreed."

"I've come to take you . . ." I balked on delivery of the rest of my prepared line.

She tilted her head quizzically. "Take me where?"

"To Fairyland," I breathed tremulously, the shibboleth fractured and dissolved by the vibrato which nervousness lent my tone.

She regarded me in surprise, then suddenly laughed, showing her straight white teeth and her long, smooth expanse of throat. When she refocused on me, her amusement had become muted by sympathy. "Poor boy," she consoled. She held out her hand.

"So you can afford a night on the town," she commented, once we were inside.

"I can afford a thousand and one nights now," I replied.

"Something's happened — don't tell me. . . . You have a new job?"

I shook my head.

"You're still working on the trading floor?"

I nodded, adding quickly, "Yes, but I could change that anytime."

She raised her eyebrows.

"I can do anything I want, *now*."

"Is that so?" she rejoined. She examined me head to foot. "You might begin by buying some new clothes."

"You don't like my suit?" I asked, wounded.

"It isn't new?"

I nodded.

She bit her lip. "Sorry," she offered. "It really isn't all that bad. Just be careful not to smoke in it. If you drop a spark, you'll be instantly consumed." She chuckled, adding, "The shoes, though, have to go."

"I'm already consumed," I told her, ignoring her disparagements, pulling out all the stops.

She raised her eyebrows, expectant, challenging, coy.

"By you."

She laughed. "Hmm . . . not bad," she conceded. "You've evidently acquired some expertise since the last time we met. Are you going to tell me what's happened, or leave me panting in suspense?"

I gazed at her drunkenly without answering.

"Don't tell me then. Let's see, you've won the lottery?"

I shook my head. "I've come into . . . well . . . call it an inheritance."

"I see."

"But that's not what I want to talk to you about," I tacked. "The money doesn't matter. In fact, it disgusts me. All I really care about is you. I want to make you happy. I want to make you love me. Tell me what I can do."

"Good heavens! You really must be affluent! How much did you make?"

"Does it matter?" I implored.

"I don't know," she said. "It might."

"A lot."

"That doesn't tell me much," she deprecated. "A thousand dollars is a lot, so is a million. It's all relative. Which figure is closer to the mark?"

"A million," I answered, "though that's still a little low."

She opened her eyes wide. "That could definitely make a difference."

"How much of one?"

"That depends."

"Enough to marry me?" I proposed, mad with love, not even pausing to consider what I was doing.

"Don't be a fool. You know I can't do that." There was an edge of disgust in her tone. She eyed me, musing. "Are you telling me the truth?"

I nodded.

"Perhaps we could arrive at a compromise," she suggested.

"I don't want to compromise."

"I know," she replied. "But that's all I'm offering. Sometimes you have to take what you can get." She shrugged. "It's a fact of life."

I took it too, and gladly. And it was good. Unbelievably good. Better even in the issue than the anticipation. That night there was no question of my going home. I lay beside her all night, watching her sleep and breathe, listening to the small cries she uttered out of her dream. She fell off rather quickly after we made love, after we fucked — that was her word, and she used it so naturally, without squalor or self-consciousness. I had feared it before. But it had a fine rankness, like the act itself — "fucking." . . . I was too exhilarated, too ecstatic to close my eyes. I wanted to savor every instant, to wring out each drop of happiness the moment could afford, to fuck it, to fuck my life. For the first time I felt rich, impossibly rich, rich with life, with possibility, drunk on it, reeling, beautifully, vertiginously high. Again resentment flared against my old Way of Life for denying me this pleasure. That I could not have known it sooner seemed a crime, a sin! For this ecstasy soared over anything I'd ever dreamt. The words from the *Tao Te Ching* came back tinged with an unintentional irony: "The savor Tao gives forth . . . how thin, how flavorless!" Truly! Compared to what? Compared to *this*! And it had come so quickly, almost instantaneously. My mind was in such a whirl I could hardly recall the sequence of events. So much had happened since the last time I had lain with her. Precisely what though? What was the crucial difference between then and now? What made possible this impossible happiness?

Money. Wasn't that it? Wasn't that what it all boiled down to? As I reflected on this, my exhilaration gradually ebbed into thoughtfulness, subdued and wistful. As in the Dow, was it not here again the "master key," as my father had so precisely intimated, the prerequisite, the sine qua non which made participation fruitful and even, at the most basic level, possible? But could this really constitute the bottom line? Could knowledge of the Dow, and even more, could love, be bought and sold like a commodity? Perhaps it could in this marketplace, the marketplace of the defiled world.

Was that then all it was, my margin of grace precisely congruous with the size of my bank account? What other conclusion was there? Nothing had changed in me essentially, nor in her. Yet I was here now and secure, whereas before I hadn't been. "A fact of life," that was what she'd called it. The expression rankled. In what sense factual? In what sense life? Life in the world as it is — perhaps that's what the phrase meant. Was it enough, living in the world as it is? Perhaps not, but what if it were all there was? Could I accept that fact, that life, could I *live* with it? I wondered. The recollection of Li's tone of voice as she uttered the phrase — I couldn't get over it, the radical amorality it intimated. A fact of life. There was something strangely pure in it, so confirmed, so limpid, so unapologetic, an intonation which suggested, to my mind, my father's laughter, how I imagined it had been. Lo had hit the mark exactly. She was like a cat. She knew what she wanted and went after it with the predator's purity of appetite. No guilt, no whimpering, no remorse, no walrus tears. And this, which for me would have involved the deepest self-compromise, for her involved no compromise at all. She was like water, shrinking from no plunge, always true to itself, following the line of least resistance and seeking its own level. She was more Taoist than I! I marveled at it. I think the strangeness, the purity — equivocal as it was — the abandon and intensity of her inner life piqued my curiosity more than anything about her, even her beauty, even her sex, yes, even fucking. For these things she was willing to share, but the other, I knew, no matter how rich I was or what I offered her, I could never own. That is why I knew that, appearances to the contrary, I could never buy her. No, in her way she was as pure as Yin-mi. Only how different a purity! I considered Lo's image: the War Dance, perfect beauty without perfect goodness; the emperor Wu who overthrew the Yin. The Yin . . .

My thoughts drifted to Yin-mi, wistfully lingering. The Succession Dance: perfect beauty, perfect goodness. With pained surprise, I realized I didn't want that anymore. It seemed colorless in comparison to what her sister offered. If her graces were less mature, less polished, less alluring than her sister's, in fairness I had to admit that they still possessed a candor and freshness, a delightfully unfinished quality that exposure, cultivation, promiscuity — whatever one chose to call it — had buffed down and polished in Li, refined almost out of existence. Li was beautiful by art, not nature, or rather art had enhanced nature in her. An art that nature made, wasn't that the expression? In comparison, Yin-mi's charms were bland, her light as prosaic and unsubtle as the sun to a man with weak eyes who has acquired a taste for high-ceilinged rooms with dark wainscot and heavy velvet drapes, the perpetual gloom of the manor illumined only by the gleam of candlelight in crystal and heavy silver table settings. Truly, the image is appropriate, for more than anything else I think now I craved the unaccusing twilight of Li's moral life, so different from the searching, uncompromising light of Yin-mi's eyes. I knew the remorseless clarity she would turn upon my contradictions. I had witnessed too many times the power of her great solemnity, that tremendous passive force she wielded against her father, against Wo, against me, finally. I didn't want that now.

Yin-mi was the sole remaining obstruction in the river of my new happiness. Kahn, Riley, Mme Chin, Li, all the restless and accusing ghosts had been appeased, laid to rest; only she was left, churning the waters of my soul to frenzy. Or was she the river and I the rock? Her sense, her perspective seemed incommensurate to her years, as though indeed it had existed for centuries, slowly wearing away the hard, unyielding strength that opposed it. She was one of those rare persons one meets in a life who seems to possess the accumulated force of many ages, many lives.

To some extent Li, too, resembled a being old in ages not in years. But her course through her Karmic reincarnations seemed more desultory, lacked the singleness of purpose which animated Yin-mi, who was like a wave moving through the oceans of time and fate, her heart and eye and brain all trained on the destination, the instant of massing, throwing up its proud white crest, then crashing over the bar into the stillness beyond, the clear, deep waters of eternity. Possessing a genius for procrastination, Li had dallied in the fulfillment of her destiny, loving the sensuous, transitory pleasures of the earth, too well perhaps. She reminded me of a younger incarnation of Mme Chin, one with an appetite, a rage to love. Having learned to pique her sensibilities to yield the most exquisite grace notes of their ranges, tricking out the rarest timbres and bouquets of sense, Li had lost sight of the destination, but found herself.

•

That night I dreamt I was wandering in darkness, not a void, but some localizable space I remembered yet couldn't immediately identify. Walls enclosed me on both sides. I felt my way forward, inching along a convoluted corridor, proceeding as into a labyrinth. Where was I? Was it the maze of alleyways behind the building on Mulberry Street into which I had chased Yin-mi that night in the rain? It might well have been, only the walls didn't have that sooty, membranous texture; they were rough and shaggy like unsanded wood. A reddish light flickered in the distance, and a strange aroma lingered in the air, thick, sweet, slightly sickening, like the smell of opium, but with some additional component. I knew by instinct what it was: shit and blood. "Shit and blood" — where had I heard that phrase? Before I had a chance to reconstruct the memory, the walls dropped by the side, and I emerged into an open space like an arena where the ground was covered by a fine white sand. Suddenly I realized where I was: the hold of the *Telemachos!* Only Scottie wasn't there, and the figure I could make out in the corner dimly glowing in the reddish half-light was not Manjusri, but the Statue of Liberty. By that same light the ruptured crate revealed its contours, only now it bore a distinct resemblance to a coffin. Reaching out, I tried the lid. It yielded. To my unspeakable frustration, just as I was about to satisfy my curiosity as to who, or what, lay inside, something startled me and I woke up.

Eddie. The cat had leapt up between us on the mattress and was padding stealthily across the coverlet to Li, who was sleeping quietly. Shoving him off the bed in annoyance, I tried to find my way back to the dream. It was useless. The next morning I woke up with nothing to show for my efforts except a rekindled curiosity about an incident I'd virtually forgotten. What was in the crate? A vain question, I knew, since I had no hope of ever answering it.

That morning in the shower, however, I began unconsciously to whistle a tune. I paused as the water ran, trying to place it. When I couldn't, I shrugged it off and went on lathering myself. By noon I'd forgotten about it. For days though, it was to keep cropping up at odd moments, insinuating itself onto my lips until I began to be annoyed, even a little spooked by it.

Before going downtown the next day, Li and I staged an exuberant and defiant auto-da-fé on the corner of West End Avenue, making a bonfire of my new polyester suit and loafers. Wistfully, I watched them blaze, then kissed her goodbye as we parted ways, she up toward Columbia, I downtown (wearing a pair of black leather pants and matching accessories lifted from Peter's wardrobe) to my new avatar in Wall Street.

•

Kahn took me to his tailor's and had me measured for half a dozen pin-striped suits in banker's-gray worsted. While we were at it, I picked up a similar quantity of hand-sewn welted calfskin oxfords, thinking regretfully of my dozen pairs of red Naugahyde slip-ons and their premature and unplanned obsolescence. The obligatory ribbed, knee-length socks with garters were acquired also, as well as all other assorted indispensable paraphernalia, shirts, ties, cuff links, etc. Throughout this expedition, Kahn was subdued and deferential, with the inordinate seriousness of a man with a new job who wishes to make a good impression, more like a gentleman's gentleman than the Kahn I knew and loved. Needless to say, this was trying in the extreme — not at all what I'd had in mind.

The next order of business consisted of attending the auction of his seat, which was being brought to the block that morning against his outstanding debts. This threatened to be even more funereal than our sartorial outing. Halfway through the bidding, though, I had an inspiration. I leaned over and whispered a directive in his ear. Kahn looked at me with surprise quickening to joy and promptly made a motion, causing a small furor among the assembled aspirants, a fact which brought him no little satisfaction. While the others winked, pulled their earlobes, looked pointedly over the rims of their glasses, and made other esoteric signs, Kahn discretely signaled his — our — intention to the auctioneer with an ebullient nose salute, which he then generalized to the congregation at large. After this he seemed in distinctly better spirits. When we had leased office space in the Exchange Building — number 2101 (my inspiration also) — he was beginning to look like his old self.

But the pleasures of extravagant, wholesale expenditure only salved the wound. It was like local anesthesia, which makes the pain bearable, but lasts only so long. After it wears off more radical healing is required. What Kahn needed was a victory, something to help restore his confidence. We needed a business coup.

Prior to that, however, we needed a business. Yes, the question arose, what were we going to do? How to marshal my new resources? This is where I hoped to draw him out, and also draw him in. It was the first official "order from the top," my original executive mandate. Only that aspect of the oracle's suggestion still required elucidation. What was the "great idea"?

"Kahn," I said, "bring me an idea."

And he did. I was genuinely surprised at the expeditiousness of the process. I think tragedy and ostracism had dammed up his energy so long that when I offered him a new opportunity, the torrent burst from him of itself in a kind of flash flood of inspiration. It was a little like opening Pandora's box.

One morning not long after, he burst into the office panting, flushed, wild eyed. "Kid, I think I've got it," he said, trembling with excitement.

"Got what?"

"*It,* kid, *it.* The great idea."

I waited for him to continue. As usual, he didn't. "All right already, so tell me," I urged him, waving my hands in irritated exhortation.

"I can hardly believe I didn't think of it before. It's so obvious!" He shook his head and drifted off into inarticulate speculation.

"*What* is?" I reiterated.

"It's something I've thought about for years. Only I never had the capital to float it."

"Kahn!" I cried in exasperation. "Tell me!"

"All right already," he said testily. "Don't get a hard-on. I'm talking about an investment management company, kid."

"An investment management company?" I stared at him blankly.

"Sure, you know, sort of like a financial brain trust, where someone pays you a heavy premium for the privilege of having you invest his money for him."

"Why should anyone want to do that?" I asked.

"Because of your reputation, your proven track record."

At the mention of the word "reputation" I think I must have blanched.

"I know, I know," he anticipated. "You're wondering what kind of sucker would trust me with his money after Doe. But I'm not talking about my reputation, kid. I'm talking about *yours.*" There was a twinkle of mischief in his eye.

"Mine!" I cried. "But that's preposterous, Kahn. I don't even *have* a reputation."

"Now, now, kid," he demurred, "don't be modest. This is no time for O.C. I say to know you is to love you, and who's seen you at closer quarters than I have? If you don't have a reputation, why then we'll just have to manufacture you one, won't we?"

"Manufacture?"

"Sure! Which is not to say 'fabricate,' " he added.

"But how?"

"I'm glad you asked me that. This is where the 'great idea' comes in. You ready?"

"I suppose so."

"You'd better make sure, kid, because this is likely to throw you for a loop. You better sit down." He pulled out a chair and gently lowered me into it by the elbow as though I were a convalescent, or a geriatric case. "Here, let me get you a glass of water." He leaned over the glass cooler and burbled out a paper coneful. "Now," he said, "you're probably wondering what I've got up my sleeve. Why a management company? Aren't there already a surplus of them out there vying for the available clientele, smart guys, brilliant some of them, with excellent, unblemished track records? What can we do to compete? Why should anyone want to turn to a washed-up Wandering Jew with dubious moral credentials and a Taoist monk who got off at the wrong stop on the Shanghai Express and ended up in Wall Street? How can we compete? What have we got that they haven't? Money? That's not enough. Brains? No, there are a lot of dizzier whiz kids out there than the likes of you and me. Integrity? We'll skip over that one. Not doing too good are we, kid? But put your mind to it. What makes us different from the rest?"

"Heart?" I suggested.

He fluttered his hand in the air.

"Courage then?" I proposed.

He shrugged and pouted his lips.

"Okay, then, Kahn, I give up. What?"

"Well, kid, after the Doe fell, so to speak, I had a lot of time to ponder. I played it all over and over in my mind a hundred thousand times. I've looked at it from the bird's-eye perspective, the worm's-eye view (especially that one, kid). I've examined it from every angle in every light at every different magnifying power, and you know what strikes me finally as the most remarkable thing about the whole deal?"

"No, what?"

"*Sui,*" he said.

"Sui Generis?"

He shook his head. "No, *Sui,* number seventeen, kid. The *Changes.*"

A shiver of queasy anticipation sidled down my spine.

"That's what I can't get over. The *I Ching* picked that stock before you even knew it existed. Of course, you interpreted it in your own way. Now if it had been *me* . . ."

"But Kahn!" I protested. "You're forgetting what happened. Doe was an unqualified disaster! Assuming the oracle did intend it as a tip — and I'm far from admitting that — just assuming though, it would have to rank as one of the worst bum steers in Wall Street history."

Kahn chuckled. " 'Bum steer.' That's another animal I'll have to add to my Wall Street bestiary."

"Admit it then," I pursued. "I'm right."

"Hold on there. Not so fast," he objected. "True, the oracle gave us — gave you, to be specific — *Sui,* and it didn't work out. On the other hand, the oracle didn't require us to make hogs of ourselves either, did it? To alter the old maxim slightly, you can lead a pig to *Sui,* but you can't make him stop eating. No, kid, you can't blame the oracle for that. We had a nice profit working there, and we screwed it up by getting greedy."

" 'We'!" I protested.

He furrowed his brows, but passed over it. "What happened wasn't the oracle's fault. It was simple human frailty, kid. We couldn't help ourselves. Or, if you prefer, *I* couldn't help *my*self — or was a little too adept at it, if you want to look at it that way. The important thing is, it proved its capacity for picking stocks. Which brings me back to my original point. Remember? What do we have that the others don't?" He grinned at me triumphantly.

"But Kahn!" I cried. "It would be a desecration of the oracle to use it for acquiring personal gain. Besides, what makes you so sure it wasn't simply a coincidence?"

He became supercilious, as though he'd anticipated my objections and knew exactly how to parry them. "As to your first point," he said, frowning as he inspected- his cuticles, "would the oracle willingly collaborate in its own treasonous misuse? Would the supreme instrument of your religion acquiesce in its own 'desecration'?" he declaimed. "I think the mere suggestion betrays a shocking lack of faith on your part, Sonny," he said, as if wounded. "If the oracle suggests, even invites, its own use as a forecasting technique, I think it would be damned unsporting of us not to take it up.

"As to your second point," he continued, without pausing to give me a chance for rebuttal, "in my opinion coincidence is highly unlikely. Still, I admit I can't rule it out with *absolute* certainty."

"Thank God!" I said. "You're beginning to sound rational again."

He ignored it. "There's only one way to find out."

Uh-oh, I thought to myself, what now? "Well?" I asked aloud.

"Ask again," he explained. "Petition the *I Ching* for another tip. If it works, we're made men. Every investor in the country will be pounding on our doors begging to give us their 'redundant capital.' " He smiled.

I frowned. "And if it doesn't work?"

He winked at me. "That's the beauty of it, kid," he said, lowering his voice to a tone that accommodated both intimacy and rapture. "Even if it doesn't, so long as we can make the G.P. — that's the General Public — *believe* it does, then we've got them by the short hairs. You know what this place is like, kid. You've seen the herd psychology at work. For all its affectations of sobriety, all the talk of 'bloodless verdicts,' the 'calm, dispassionate eye,' Wall Street is the most superstitious place on earth. There's not a broker on the floor that doesn't have a special tie, a key chain, a pair of cuff links or suspenders, some little fetish with which he habitually attempts to suspend the iron laws of gravity and statistics and conjure the great god Success. He'd rather be flayed alive than leave home without it. Everybody laughs at the phenomenon, of course, but everybody also *believes*. That's what we all want, kid. Remember what I said before? A magic that can master life. That's what everybody's looking for. The infallible technique. A talisman. The direct line to the top, the Big Top. Strip away the facade of rationality, and we're all savages conjuring animistic deities. Flay off the three-piece suit, and you'll find matted hair, claws, teeth. It's still a world of blood sacrifice, rituals of propitiation offered to arbitrary, all-powerful gods. I'd never had that feeling so much as toward the end there with Doe. It was like the air was thick and sickening with the stench of it — the drinking of blood from human skulls before the hunt to make ourselves invulnerable to death. Laugh if you want to, kid, but it's not so very far away. The bridge still exists, back to the wilderness. That's why we won't have to try very hard to convince them. Because they'll want to believe. They'll laugh for the first five minutes or the first five months, but eventually the dark ghosts will float up out of the abyss of what we are and where we came from, and they'll come running to us for our spell. Like the wolves, kid, at the wailing of the pack: they won't be able to help themselves." His rapture quickened as he spoke.

"But Kahn," I objected, "if it doesn't work, it would be dishonest. The same thing all over again, like Doe."

He shook his head. "I'm just sketching the contingency, kid, the worst possible scenario. You see, I *do* believe." He unconsciously turned the copper bracelet on his wrist. "It's kind of funny, don't you think?" he remarked with a slight laugh.

"What is?"

"You're the one that has to be convinced about the validity of your own religion."

The irony of this, even if a false one, made me pause to consider with a kind of mournful wonder.

"Well," he said, "what do you say?"

You may believe me or not, Reader, as you choose, but I swear if the decision had been for myself alone, I would have abjured the suggestion, the temptation, on the spot, abjured it utterly and forever. But it wasn't. That was the whole point. It was for him. "The thought is not that a man avoids difficulties for himself, but rather that he rescues his kin — helps them . . . to find their way out of a danger that is already upon them."

"All right," I assented gravely. "I'm not completely comfortable with it, but I'll go along. For your sake, Kahn."

"You won't regret it, kid," he promised, touching my hand, his eyes kindling with gratitude like wind-stoked coals. "So where do we begin?"

I pushed the book toward him across the desk with a grim, portentous expression.

He arranged himself, eyeing it and rubbing his hands in eager anticipation. "What else do we need?"

"Yarrow stalks," I answered, deliberately terse.

"Yarrow stalks?"

"Or coins."

"Coins by all means!" he said ebulliently. "Much more appropriate for our purposes, don't you think? Anything else?"

I hesitated before replying. "Well, there is *ling.*"

"*Ling?*"

"Don't you remember?" I asked. "Purity of heart."

Kahn winced and slid the assembled implements back across the blotter. "You do it, kid, okay?" he petitioned sheepishly. "I'm not sure I trust myself."

Pathetic and touching, the gesture stirred me to an unenthusiastic acquiescence. Though I kept it to myself, I couldn't suppress an inner pang of similar self-mistrust regarding the balance in my own inner bank account of that most precious spiritual commodity. Over and over the admonition kept playing through my mind: "To those who are not in contact with the Tao, the oracle does not return an intelligible answer, since it would be of no avail."

In this case, however, my fears were apparently unfounded. For the answer the oracle returned was most pointedly and poignantly intelligible, at least by my interpretation. The hexagram was number 4, *Meng,* "Youthful Folly," with a nine in the second, and a six in the fourth place. This hexagram consists of the trigram *Ken* ("Keeping Still," "Mountain") above *K'an* ("The Abysmal," "Water"):

> Keeping still is the attribute of the upper trigram; that of the lower is the abyss, danger. Stooping in perplexity on the brink of a dangerous abyss is the symbol of the folly of youth.

Immediately, even at this most elementary level, I saw an unambiguous directive: *Ken* conjured the image of Ken Kuan, symbol of the old Way, Keeping Still, *over K'an* as in Kahn, whose character as water denoted restless movement. Give precedence to the old ways over the new, the oracle seemed to counsel, at the risk of committing Youthful Folly. The judgment said:

> Youthful Folly has success.
> It is not I who seek the young fool;
> It is the young fool who seeks me.
> At the first oracle I inform him.
> If he asks two or three times, it is importunity.
> If he importunes, I give him no information.

> A teacher's answer to the question of a pupil ought to be clear and definite like that expected from an oracle; thereupon it ought to be accepted as a key for resolution of doubts and a basis for decision. If mistrustful or unintelligent questioning is kept up, it serves only to annoy the teacher. He does well to ignore it in silence, just as the oracle gives one answer only and refuses to be tempted by questions implying doubt.

There was little question in my mind. This was the "first oracle." An intelligible answer was forthcoming. If I persisted in my importunity, however, the consequence I dreaded was sure to follow. I would be ignored, since, as I was out of contact with the Tao, "it would be of no avail."

Finally I turned to the lines:

> Nine in the second place means:
> To bear with fools in kindliness brings good fortune.

> These lines picture a man who has . . . enough strength of mind to bear his burden of responsibility. He has the inner superiority and strength that enable him to tolerate with kindliness the shortcomings of human folly.

Up to this point the oracle had seemed unambiguously opposed to the project Kahn had proposed and to which I had reluctantly agreed. Here, however, a crack opened up to doubt. At the mention of "a burden of responsibility," I thought immediately of my obligation to assist in Kahn's rehabilitation, previously mandated by the oracle. In this case, didn't "to bear with fools in kindliness" mean to humor him in his admittedly extravagant design of using the *Changes* as a forecasting technique? I turned to the last moving line in hopes of clarifying this point.

> Six in the fourth place means:
> Entangled folly brings humiliation.
>
> For Youthful Folly it is the most hopeless thing to entangle itself in empty imaginings. The more obstinately it clings to such unreal fantasies, the more certainly will humiliation overtake it.
> Often the teacher, when confronted with such entangled folly, has no other course but to leave the fool to himself for a time, not sparing him the humiliation that results. This is frequently the only means of rescue.

This only increased my perplexity. Was I the teacher indicated here, who "confronted with such entangled folly, has no other course but to leave the fool [i.e., Kahn] to himself" in the hope of eventual "rescue"? Or, on the contrary, was the *Changes* itself the teacher and I the young fool being served fair warning that persistence in an ill-considered project would lead to my eventual abandonment to the corrosive processes of my own folly? Obviously the answer to this question was crucial, since in one case the oracle's advice constituted a license to proceed, in the other a proscription.

All this transpired silently. It was only after several moments that I redirected my attention outward toward Kahn. He was sitting in an attitude that suggested similar intensity of concentration. Elbow propped on the desk, he held his head in the palm of his hand, forming the expression "Youthful Folly" on his lips, repeating it silently over and over. I watched with ominous fascination.

Suddenly he froze. "That's it," he whispered to himself. Dropping his arm, he looked up. "I've got it, kid."

"Well?" I asked.

"What do you think of when you think of Youthful Folly?"

Very briefly I filled him in on the associations the hexagram had conjured and the perplexity the oracle had finally left me in.

"No, no, kid," he said in a tone of tolerant disgust, "you've got it all wrong. You're looking at the thing from the wrong perspective. It's not a personal indictment we're dealing with here, it's a market tip. Don't you see? Youthful Folly. . . . I was reading an article about it the other night in *Forbes.* 'The Sexual Revolution and Its Implications for Corporate Profits.' It got me so excited the pages were all stuck together when I finished." He grinned.

"Kahn!" I protested. "That's preposterous!"

"Hold on. Let me finish. I don't think you realize the new markets that are being opened up by increasing promiscuity in this country. Did you know that there's even a corporate lobby in Washington actively promoting sex education in the schools under the guise of disinterested liberalism? Kid! We're entering a new era! And it's Business's business to be out there in the vanguard thrusting away. Let me give you a for-instance. Ever been in a service station's men's room? Well, you've seen the rubber machines, right? Take your choice: ribbed, reservoir tipped, prelubed with Sensitol, sheepskin (for Talmudic scholars?), not to mention the more exotic types, such as your French Tickler and your multicolored parfait swirl, and all at two bits a shot. (A shot, heh-heh — sorry, kid, no pun intended.) A quarter! Jesus, kid! I mean, how much can your unit production cost be on a Trojan for Christ's sake? About the same as a penny balloon, right? That's a twenty-five hundred percent markup, kid. Now *that's* business! And think of the volume they do!" Kahn cupped his hand to his ear. "I can hear those quarters now, clinking into slots all over America, an unceasing stream of silver, just like slot machines. Hell, better! People may go hungry, but no matter what happens, kid, recession, depression, natural disaster, or nuclear war, you can be sure a man is going to get his twanky. Gotta milk that gland!" He rolled his eyes, shook his finger and his jowls like Jimmy Durante. "And that's just rubbers, kid! We haven't even touched on diaphragms and IUDs, contraceptive foams and jellies, not to mention the Pill! There lies the hope of the future! Look west young man, into the bubbling retorts of our pharmaceutical laboratories! Hell, we've invented more ways to sabotage the natural functions of the body than I can count on my cock hairs! It's wonderful! Then, of course, venereal disease is going to increase in direct proportion to the upsurge in premarital (hell, preadolescent, *juvenile!*) sex. Think of the quantities of penicillin and related antibiotics ingested or intravenously injected via the buttocks weekly in clinics in New York City alone! It boggles the mind! Bread can't go bad fast enough! I'm *serious,* kid! I could go on and on, but I trust I've made my point."

"Well, you've certainly made some point," I conceded, "though I'm not quite sure I know what it is."

"Youthful Folly, kid! You know, fucky-fucky? I wouldn't be surprised if you'd engaged in a little bit of it yourself."

I blushed violently.

"Ah ha! I'm right. There!" he cried in vindication. "No more of your affectations of Taoist prudery. Don't you see, kid? It's a clear sign to buy the pharmaceuticals. I can feel it in my . . ." — he grinned at me slyly and made an obscene gesture — "bone!"

Though a little overwhelmed by his spiel, I managed to point out that it ignored the basis of my original objections.

"If your interpretation were correct, why does it say 'Youthful Folly has success'?" he pointedly rejoined. "Besides, even if you're right, look at the lines: nine in the second place, 'tolerate with kindliness the shortcomings of human folly.' " He grinned sheepishly, turning on an engaging, boyish charm. "Bear with me, kid. Give me a little rope to hang myself. If I'm wrong, it'll all come out in the wash. Just humor me in this one thing, and I swear on the blood of my own martyred prepuce I'll never ask you for a favor again as long as I live or can get it up. I'll even put it in writing if you want it, five years or fifty thousand miles."

I gazed at him with mournful, exasperated affection. Maybe I was a soft touch, but how could I deny him what he asked? His exuberance, his outrageous charm and brio — it was irresistible. Besides, I told myself, wasn't it my duty to set aside all personal desires and put my goal in a great task outside myself? I sighed and let it pass. If I was wrong, it was no skin off my . . . well . . . What could it cost me but a little cash? And there was plenty and to spare of that. I soberly made out a check in his name for fifty thousand dollars and handed it over. In his access, his virtual paroxysm, of joy and excitement, I feared Kahn might kiss me on the cheek. Back in the game, a player once again! I had to smile, despite my reservations. If nothing else, it was obvious that I was succeeding in my mission of rehabilitating him.

On a hunch, Kahn put our stake on a small, aggressive firm, still new and relatively unknown in Wall Street, trading for virtual change. Two days later they announced the introduction of a new product line, a ginseng-based herbal aphrodisiac "compounded from an ancient Chinese recipe," which in "independent experiments at several major universities" had been proven to induce acute satyriasis in mice. The laboratory animals had apparently sacrificed themselves with lemminglike fervor, applying themselves to the act with such abandon that they paused for neither food nor drink and occasionally actually "died in the saddle" after having fought the good fight. There was a rush for the drugstores such as had not been seen since the announcement that the FDA was cracking down on the illegal dispensing of Schedule III controlled substances — Quaaludes and Demerol — and assigning narcotics' numbers to physicians. Almost overnight our fifty thousand dollars became a hundred and fifty. I couldn't help thinking of the passage in the Shuo Kua wing of the *I Ching* relating to the trigram *Sun*. Just below the part about "those with much white in their eyes," it further elaborates the hallmarks of the indicated constituency thus: "those close to gain, so that in the market they get threefold value." It was an impressive performance to say the least. I admit I was perhaps a little titillated by the success. I mean, after all, if Kahn was right, weren't we dealing here with the exact situation Julius Everstat had described in his musings on the Random Walk — what it might have been, had been hoped by some to be before it revealed its sour anticlimax — a financial atom bomb, a perfectly predictable market? Yes, I admit it was exciting. And perhaps I wouldn't have been so utterly distraught to be proved wrong in my misgivings. At any rate, after this I noticed that they nagged with less insistence.

I might point out that this served as a pattern for all future business-oriented consultations of the *Changes.* I was like Hermaphroditus in the *Satyricon,* a sort of freak show demigod, sacrosanct by virtue of the rather dubious distinction of possessing organs of both sexes, who was carried around in a basket by his keepers, the high priests (read Kahn), who interpreted his incoherent blitherings for the eager masses. Which is to say, it was a fruitful combination of my "touch" (rendered sacred by virtue of my putative *ling*) and his interpretative skills, derived from intimate acquaintance with the Fortune 500. A most profitable symbiosis. But I mustn't allow bitterness to anticipate the twistings of the plot, wrenching as they were, dislocated as they left me.

On my expressing some further doubts on the legitimacy of our technique, Kahn eyed me in exasperation and cynically replied, "Yeah, kid, you can cry all the way to the bank."

Chapter 10

Flushed with success, Kahn took charge, issuing orders and operational directives like a general or a top executive. The memos flowed like wine. I looked on in gratified awe at his miraculous recovery.

"Okay, Kahn, so what's next?" I timidly inquired.

"Well, kid," he replied, "as I see it, here's where we stand: We've got our idea — investment management; we've got our personal angle — the *I Ching*. I'm convinced; you're convinced. Now all we have to do is convince the General Public. And that means promotion. What we've got to come up with is a really brilliant advertising campaign. Speaking of which, as a former copywriter I'd like to head that up myself."

I yielded, of course, with utmost deference.

"Before we even think about promotion though, we've got to have a package to promote. As you probably know, what all advertising depends on is a great universal symbol, like a Platonic Form or LCD."

"LCD?"

"Lowest Common Denominator," he glossed. "The advertising man must have the purity of vision to see the eidolons of the consumable floating in that special heaven of desire."

"You mean the id?" I asked.

"Don't be cute," he krechtzed. "It's got to be catchy, it's got to be beautiful, something which satisfies the heart and engages the mind. I know a lot of people look down their noses at it, but in my opinion advertising has a legitimate claim to inclusion in the mainstream of American poetry. What else so well expresses the heart and soul of the people? When an ad is really first-rate it gets you like nothing else can, like a tune you can't get out of your head, playing over and over, a sort of benign tic douloureux. There are certain jingles that get to me in a way that even the most highly wrought conceits in lyric poetry can't touch, things which call up visions of my youth and make me weep for the past and my lost innocence."

"Come on, Kahn," I said skeptically.

"I'm serious, kid! Take, well, take Burma-Shave for example. You've probably never heard them, but there was a time when everybody in America had those jingles on their lips, five- and six-line unrhymed ditties that appeared on signs along the side of the road, one line per sign, always ending with the phrase 'Burma-Shave.'

> IT'S NOT TOASTED
> IT'S NOT DATED
> BUT LOOK OUT
> IT'S IMITATED
> BURMA-SHAVE

"I can never think of them without remembering Pops." Kahn took out his handkerchief and blew his nose. "I'll never forget the first time I saw one. He took us on a weekend trip to the Adirondacks.

> HE PLAYED
> A SAX
> HAD NO B.O.
> BUT HIS WHISKERS SCRATCHED
> SO SHE LET HIM GO
> BURMA-SHAVE

"How he laughed!" Kahn dabbed his eyes. "The inspiring scenery — waterfalls, changing autumn leaves, furry little animals with their cute chubby cheeks stuffed full of nuts and berries — all that has faded, but that jingle remains. Burma-Shave. . . ." He shook his head. "In my opinion it should be enshrined as an endemic national verse form, as quintessentially American as the haiku is Japanese. You can take your 'Many Chambered Nautilus,' give me Burma-Shave! I made a proposal once to that effect in a paper for an American literature course, but the professor was such a snot-nose he wouldn't even look at it.

"You can laugh if you want to, kid, but let me tell you something. The advertising man is not like your common Joe out on the Street hustling for profits. No, others may be interested in money, but he's interested in truth, or something even better. It's acknowledged, too, by anyone who really counts. Believe it or not, though generally kept in the closet, it's as common to find a closet copywriter among the high and mighty of the financial world as to find would-be poets in the academic community. No, kid, take it from me, an advertising man is not like you or me.

"I ask you, was Homer or Dante or Shakespeare — yes, even the Bard himself! — any better able to express the values of his age, to hold a mirror up to mores, so to speak, than the advertising man does ours? Only his is a communal art, like the cathedrals of the Middle Ages, not marred by the overweening pride of the 'artist,' quote unquote, who insists on personal recognition for his work. No, these anonymous creators work only for love and a living wage, not fame, and that's the secret of the purity of their art. I mean, how else come up with such great slogans as . . . well, 'It's the Pepsi generation!' to take another particularly close to my heart? Do you see the magnitude of that? It embraces a whole era, establishes its hue and cry, gives us an image in which to see and know ourselves. I hear that, kid, and suddenly it's summer, under the lights in Yankee Stadium, the second game of a doubleheader. Micky Mantle has just knocked one into the center-field bleachers and is trotting around the bag at third, smiling and tipping his hat. The crowd is on its feet. As he touches home plate his teammates hand him the Pepsi. He upends it, the cold condensation dripping down his sweaty arm, over his chin and batting glove, while the crowd goes wild, cheering, stomping its feet, the stadium delirious with happiness, a thousand bottles raised in a sugar-sweet carbonated toast to the beauty of existence — America at the crest of its postwar boom, before the liberal backlash set in, the greatest nation in the world at the peak of its prosperity, a moment which perhaps comes only once in a thousand years. . . . And all of it crystallized in amber, kid, by some unknown genius — an advertising man!"

Despite my doubts, for just a moment as he spoke I saw what must have been the young Kahn peering out at me, eager and intense, from the prison of his sagging flesh. And though the things he recounted were unfamiliar or unknown to me entirely, I believed. What but the truth could have the power so to transfigure him, I asked myself. The image of Tsin floated ominously before my mind's eye as though by way of reply, followed closely by a second image: my father's smile, which hovered like the Cheshire cat's in space.

"Kid? . . . Kid?" Kahn's voice came to me as though from a great distance.

"Hmm?" I slowly emerged from my reverie, and Kahn's shape resolved itself before my eyes.

"Are you all right?"

"Of course," I replied. "Why?"

"You went into sort of a trance there for a minute."

We studied one another in silence.

"So," he said at last, "are you ready?"

"Ready?"

"To hear my idea."

"Kahn," I replied, "I think I'm ready for anything, *now.*"

He gave me a curious stare, then proceeded. Flipping open his briefcase, he produced a folder full of papers covered with crude diagrams, scribbled comments, doodles with cramped professorial glosses, mementos of inspired lucubration.

"You see, kid, what we need is a name, something to tie all the loose ends together. I racked my brain for a long time trying to come up with something that would perfectly reflect our own unique orientation in the market and yet resonate for the General Public too. We've got to suggest the *I Ching,* that whole constellation of Eastern imagery, and at the same time remain faithful to the internal climate of the marketplace itself, something out of the natural symbolism of the Dow — part Tao, part Dow, like you're always talking about, or used to talk about."

I frowned at this qualification.

He continued. "While I was pondering, two things kept playing through my mind: your comment about getting back in the saddle and riding . . ." I blushed. "No, kid, I mean it, it was inspirational," he assured me.

"What was the second?" I asked.

"The Taoist maxim about the search for enlightenment being like looking for a lost bull while riding on its back." He grinned expectantly.

"Well?" I prompted.

"Don't you see, kid? That's it!"

"What's what?"

"Bull!"

"Bull?"

"Perfect symbol of the interrelatedness of our goals: the bull of prosperity on the one hand, the bull of Dow; on the other, the bull of enlightenment, the bull of Tao and the *I Ching*. You see? It's ideal!" He paused. "What's the matter, kid? You've got the strangest expression on your face. Don't you like it?"

But I was thinking about the tune that had been playing around in my head for days, since my dream of the hold of the *Telemachos*. Suddenly I realized what it was:

> I clutch the rope and cling for dear life!
> The Bull is dangerous and unruly.
> He gallops away toward cloud-wreathed mountain ranges,
> Or confronts me in the valley, snorting and pawing, prepared to
>   charge.
>
> He eluded me in the wild regions of the earth, but today I finally
> seized him. Long indiscipline has produced bad habits: the Bull has
> grown accustomed to a diet of sweet grass and intoxicating wild
> flowers; hay and the bridle are inimical to his tastes. To tame him, I
> must show the whip.

It was the fourth song, "Seizing the Bull"!

"Well, kid?"

"Nothing," I said. "Go on."

"Well, that's about as far as I've taken it," he remarked. "I was hoping for some feedback from you before getting down to the real nuts and bolts. What do you think about calling the company, say, Pure Bull? No, no, make that True Bull. Better yet, Trubull — more contemporary. We could say something like, 'Go for the best. Don't accept anything less than pure, unadulterated Bull!' "

I suppose my reaction must have been apparent from my face.

"Okay, okay," he said in a tone of slight annoyance, "so you don't like it. Just say so. How about this then? Bull Incorporated. Now is that a gas or what? It's simple; it's austere . . ." (he grinned) "au steer. It's got classical lines. It has a certain nobility, don't you think? Wait! Wait a minute! 'Nobility.' . . . That's it! Nobull. 'Come and join the nobility at Nobull Inc.' "

"Kahn," I interposed, alerted by the telltale glitter in his eye that things were about to get out of hand, "perhaps we should just stick with Bull Inc., what do you say?"

"It's your baby," he replied in a tone of mild admonition, shrugging his shoulders as though abjuring all responsibility for any disasters that might result from my feckless conservatism and plain O.C. "So then, we're agreed?"

I nodded. "Agreed."

"Excellent!" He rubbed his hands together. "*Now.* We've got ourselves, if I do say so myself, an eminently promotable package, so how do we promote it?"

Sure that the question was purely rhetorical, I waited.

"Okay, kid, now here's my plan. Listen closely, because it's the capstone of the whole endeavor, the matadorial coup de grace, so to speak." He paused a moment, savoring his advantage.

"Kahn!"

"An ordeal," he proposed.

I looked at him blankly.

"A media ordeal to be specific," he qualified with a grin.

"I don't get it. What's an ordeal?"

"It's a term for a ritual test performed in ancient times to determine the character or integrity of an individual through exposure to some form of stress or danger. It still survives among certain primitive peoples, and even crops up as a mysterious atavism in contexts as progressive as, say, the stock market, for example."

"You've lost me, Kahn."

"In other words, kid, it's a sort of legitimization ceremony, a rite of passage like the bar mitzvah, or like a young man undergoes to prove himself worthy of participating in the hunt and sitting with his elders by the fire — a sort of public trial by fire, in other words, only in this case for an institution rather than an individual. You see what I'm getting at?"

"Frankly, no," I replied.

"Okay, kid, let me spell it out for you. The *Wall Street Journal,* right? A full-page spread." He swept his arm through the air as though setting the rows of boldface capitals:

"Kahn and Sun Enterprises is proud to announce the grand opening of an investment management company with a difference
BULL INCORPORATED
("Willing and Abull to Serve Your Needs")

Trading your redundant capital on the New York Stock Exchange,
AMEX, NASDAQ, and other regional exchanges around the country,
on the basis of an exciting new SECRET WEAPON
The *I CHING*
book of ancient Chinese prophecy, tried and proved to work with 100%
accuracy in forecasting stocks *when wielded by the right person*. We have
that person!
SONNY, son of EDDIE LOVE
the preeminent authority in America today in the forecasting technique
of *I Ching* Prognostication.
SKEPTICAL?
Good.
We're going to put our money where our mouth is,
ONE MILLION DOLLARS CASH!!
to be wagered on a single consultation of the oracle as manipulated by
Sonny and interpreted by his associate, Aaron Kahn.
INTERESTED, AMERICA?
You're invited to come along for the ride. Bring your rotten apples and
tomatoes if you want to, *but bring your checkbooks too, America!* It's
going to be a real
STAMPEDE!!!

"Something to that effect," he suggested. "So, what do you think?"

"A million dollars?" I asked.

He shrugged. "It won't do to be skimpy, kid. We're trying to establish an
image. I mean, after all, what's the magic number, the sweetest sum to American ears? You got it, kid. A cool mill, a hundred thousand Hamiltons. No
doubt about it. If we're going to do it, we may as well go all the way, right?
No balls, no glory, as Ahasuerus used to say. Wait a minute! That's it! I've got
it! Our motto!"

"No balls, no glory?"

"No *bulls*, no glory, kid." He grinned with an almost obscene pleasure.
"Admit it, it's brilliant."

"Incredible," I conceded.

"Incredi-*bull!*" he corrected.

•

As Kahn had anticipated, the announcement of the ordeal produced a measur-
able response on Wall Street. If it cannot be described as a furor, it's simply
because the majority tended to see it as a joke, or an instance of mental
aberrancy. After all, Kahn had his reputation. It clung to his neck with fond
ferocity, like an albatross, even after he had, with the community's approval,
been spiritually garroted. In any case, our initiative presented a rare opportunity for fun and games, an opportunity that otherwise serious and somber crew

was determined to take advantage of. Whenever we were spotted on sidewalks or in the elevators on our way to the offices of Kahn and Sun Enterprises, salvos of only nominally surreptitious semaphore were passed in the form of winks and elbow digs, suppressed coughs, eye rolls, and taps against the old bean. But behind the hilarity, I sensed a residue of gratitude and affection for providing such a rare and badly needed entertainment in that sober place.

The scoffers got their first taste of the comeuppance to come at 8:00 A.M. of the fateful morning Kahn and I appeared with the rented P.R. system and the rolling T.V. cameras in Chase Manhattan Plaza, along with the grim-faced representative of the bank with the million-dollar cashier's check, all made out except the top line, "Pay to the Order of." As the crowds moiled along the street toward their offices, Kahn entertained them with a nonstop P.R. spiel, like an on-site radio broadcaster advertising some "grand opening" — which is precisely what it was, only on a larger scale. And in accordance with the protocol of that great American advertising ritual, the drawing for the door prize was announced for noon, during lunch hour, in other words, to draw the greatest possible attendance and also to quicken the suspense. It was our hope and firm intention that our little "happening" would provide the topic of conversation in every office in the financial district for the next four hours. *Bzz. Bzz.* "Did you hear?" "No! You're kidding!" "Would I shit you?" "Are they for real?" "Who knows?" "Let's check it out." "You got it! See you there!"

Our ploy was so successful that the city had to delegate a detachment of mounted police to the area for crowd control. It was like a festival. And Kahn had foreseen it all, down to the most minute detail! He'd even had balloons printed up with the name of the company and our new motto, No Bulls, No Glory. As a matter of fact, in his capacity as emcee, he had delegated me to hand them out among the crowd. I wasn't resentful, either. No, on the contrary, I was happy to be associated with him. My only prayer was that the *Changes* wouldn't let us down, but show a prescience as impressive as his own. I had my doubts. Kahn, though, was drunk with confidence. Before the spectacle of his faith, I almost felt ashamed. What was there to lose? Only a million dollars. I contemplated the loss with a brave show of resignation, my most Taoist act in months.

At exactly 12:15 Kahn solemnly summoned me to the front. The sound of my name over the loudspeakers startled me so severely I let go the strings of the balloons. They buoyed off lighthearted into the blue vista between the buildings. I watched them wistfully, wishing I could similarly escape. My progress through the crowd was accompanied by the roll of a snare drum which Kahn had also produced for the occasion, perhaps remembering his own bar mitzvah party.

When I reached the dais, he called for silence over the mike and solemnly helped me into the new robe he'd insisted I wear for the occasion in order to give the spectacle an "authentic touch." I felt like a monstrosity from another culture and another age on display before a wondering crowd hungry for novelty. A hush fell. The crowd had overflowed into the street and extended out of sight in both directions. Traffic was gridlocked. All those eyes on me! Behind me on the dais, Kahn, in his own robe, solemnly attempted to compose himself in the lotus, settling, after several vain attempts, for simply crossing his ankles "Injun style." He closed his eyes and took on a very solemn expression. I gazed at him, at the expectant faces in the crowd. The ludicrousness, the cheap imposture of it, the compromise of principle — so fatuous as to be more pathetic than damnable — struck me all at once, and I could hardly keep from laughing. Helpless trills of giggles rippled through me from the belly upward. Perhaps I was hysterical. I held my breath and tried to contain it. My face turned red. Luckily, all that escaped was an ambiguous blast of air, which might easily have been interpreted as a meditative sigh or a deep-breathing exercise. Having survived this paroxysm, I suddenly had the sensation of waking from a dream. What was happening here? What was I doing?

The pressure of a hundred thousand pairs of eyes upon me, however, gave me no leisure to pause for long over moral quibbles. It was perform or face the consequences. My nervous hysteria intensified as I reflected that, if I disappointed them in their impatience for a spectacle, they were likely to tear me apart and feed me to the pigeons instead. Thus it was with the greatest imaginable feelings of self-compromise, disgrace, embarrassment, chagrin, resentment, shame, and self-loathing of every conceivable variety that I began the consultation. As I tumbled the coins in my sweaty hands like a gambler, an association flashed through my mind that made me want to weep and mortify my flesh right there before that audience to make good all that I had done. The image was of the dancing tiger from Hsiao's story! "Tiger and trainer — perhaps there was a little bit of both in Love." Wasn't I his own true son then? Wincing, I put on my dark glasses. Then, blowing in my cupped palms for luck, I shook the silver dollars and let them fall.

The reading the oracle returned was number 48, *Ching,* "The Well," with a moving line in the second place. Immediately I saw the reply was to be as pointed as the last had been, for The Well consists of the trigram *K'an,* The Abysmal, over *Sun.* There it was again! Only reversed, showing Kahn in the position of ascendency. I sighed with relief. Didn't this suggest that I was right in following his lead? Or was the pronouncement merely descriptive? The judgment said:

> The town may be changed,
> But the well cannot be changed.
> It neither decreases nor increases.
> They come and go and draw from the well.
> If one gets down almost to the water
> And the rope does not go all the way,
> Or the jug breaks, it brings misfortune.

An old association sprang immediately to mind: Chung Fu's image of the *Changes* itself as a well whose bricks were laid by human workmen, but in which brim the cold, transparent waters of the Tao, drawn up from the pure reservoir of Being, which has no bottom man can sound. In this connection, the first two lines of the judgment suggested my move from China to America, from Ken Kuan to New York. Indeed the town had changed, but the well — that is, the Source, Tao, "Mother of the manifold existences we see around us, this kaleidoscopic pageant of appearances" — remained the same, eternally. In the light of events, I could not but regard this as a reproach.

The commentary on the judgment said:

> Every human being can draw in the course of his education from the inexhaustible wellspring of the divine in man's nature. But here . . . two dangers threaten: a man may fail in his education to penetrate the real roots of humanity . . . or he may suddenly collapse and neglect his self-development.

The sense of admonition was intensified by what I found in the lines:

> Nine in the second place means:
> At the wellhole one shoots fishes.
> The jug is broken and leaks.

> The water itself is clear, but it is not being used. Thus the well is a place where only fish will stay, and whoever comes to it, comes only to catch the fish. . . .
>   This describes the situation of a person who possesses good qualities but neglects them. . . . As a result he deteriorates in mind.

This image of a polluted or neglected well was only too pointed a reference to the effect of our current mode of use, or abuse, of the oracle. The reference to "shooting fishes" likewise seemed a scathing allusion to our exploitation for personal gain of a resource whose only legitimate use was for "drinking long, cool, satisfying drafts of wisdom from the bucket" drawn up "heavy, spilling over, from the darkness of the human heart." In other words, "shooting fish" meant "picking stocks" — another instance of the oracle's famous irony, which for those familiar with its workings was no laughing matter.

In sum, the *Changes,* by my interpretation, had condescended to offer me a second warning against proceeding with the plan. Not surprisingly, Kahn read it differently. With his hand over the microphone, we conferred vehemently at the back of the dais.

"Feh! Phooey!" he said in response to my reservations. "You're paranoid, kid, that's all. It's *oil* wells. Plain as the nose on your . . . well, *my* face." He grinned. "I've had my eye on that sector for a while. I think there's real potential in it, particularly the domestic industry — oil services, exploration and development — you know, the whole shtick. I've been watching two

companies in particular, both about equally promising — earnings and projected earnings roughly equal when factored as a percentage of share cost
— or so I thought." He grinned portentously.

"What companies?" I asked.

"Sun Oil and *Con*oco," he replied. "Guess which one we're going to buy."

Drawing out the suspense as much as possible, Kahn then took the microphone and, like Bert Parks announcing the winner of the Miss America contest, revealed the identity of our choice. The check was then made out with
all due solemnities in the presence of witnesses, hands shaken, congratulations
exchanged. The order was executed, the shares purchased. Cigars were passed
out and thousands of bottles of seltzer fizzlingly unstoppered in lieu of champagne, which was not only expensive but discouraged by the police. The crowd
then dispersed. From then on all Wall Street was on edge waiting for the Dow
to make a sign, like some great Roman emperor sitting impassively above the
Colosseum floor observing the combatants locked in their life-and-death struggle. Thumbs up, thumbs down — which would it be?

The anxious didn't have long to wait. That very afternoon, not fifteen
minutes after the market closed (the timing carefully worked out to prevent
disrupting activity on the trading floor any more than absolutely necessary)
the management at Conoco (or should I say, *Kahn*-oco?) announced the
discovery of reserves of natural gas in the Beaufort Sea in Canada, larger than
any known to that date in the western hemisphere. The news struck Wall Street
like a thunderbolt. Instead of rushing for taxis to make the early trains out to
Long Island or up to Connecticut, the brokers lingered on the floor, crowding
around the machines, staring in stricken silence at the successive updates,
shaking their heads, sighing, exchanging questioning, portentous looks.

Kahn went temporarily mad with joy, falling to his knees in the middle of
the office, raising his face to heaven and shouting his thanks to God over and
over as the tears streamed down his cheeks. At first I too felt a rush of elation.
But as I watched him there, the same sense of horror that had unsettled me
on the dais recurred, and, after the initial thrill, I was stricken numb with
foreboding. In another part of myself, I sighed and let something go. With this
second vindication of Kahn's initiative, there seemed no alternative but to
acquiesce and see where it would lead.

That afternoon as we left the building, the fatuous superiority that had
greeted us before was replaced by troubled looks which intimated abysses of
misgiving and self-doubt, as though the old certainties had been toppled and
a new order had started to emerge. The traders regarded us as though our faces
shed an unwordly light, like the aura said to shimmer around the bodies of the
Immortals.

Investigations were reopened immediately at the Securities Exchange Commission. Were we in collusion with the management at Conoco? Another
instance of inside information? As the Reader knows, however, this time there
was no poop to be uncovered. If we were trading on the basis of inside

information, it was the ultimate inside information, something at once too powerful and too vague to be regulated by the SEC. No, though some tried to write it off as mere coincidence, a lucky guess, others, many others, believed. Once again Kahn had conned the situation shrewdly, demonstrating his astuteness as a student of human nature. The ordeal proved a masterstroke. Overnight we had achieved a measure of fame and notoriety. We had hit the Street, and America herself, where it lived, touched some tender nerve, appealed to that most primordial longing, "a magic which could master life." If over my head I felt the Damoclean sword of the oracle's admonition hanging by a slender thread, I didn't think about it. After all, had not the oracle itself twice backed us up? No, Reader, the stampede had begun in earnest. The Bull, along with his friendly buckaroos and drovers, Kahn and Sun, was loose, and feeling ornery!

Chapter 11

LOST?
Wandering aimlessly for forty days and nights (forty years?)
in this bear-ren,
inhospitable market?
CONFUSED?
by the mindless chatter,
the contradictory prognoses
of the pharisees and scribes,
the indistinguishable (white) hordes of false market prophets?
DON'T DESPAIR!!!
HELP IS ON THE WAY!!!
THE CAVALRY IS COMING!!!
(Hear the thunder of distant hooves?)
BULL INCORPORATED TO THE RESCUE!!!
Climb up in the saddle, America,
and let us take you for a ride!!!
For more information call us direct. Our number is
BUL-LISH
Operators are standing by! (And what operators!)

This ran as a full-page ad in the *Wall Street Journal,* the *New York Times,*
the *Chicago Tribune,* the *Los Angeles Times,* the *Washington Post,* and dozens of other papers around the country. The General Public ate it up. Needless to say, the furor we failed to excite with our original ad because of a
perceived lack of seriousness erupted now with redoubled virulence. Almost
immediately a countercampaign was launched by our outraged competition.

DON'T TAKE THIS BULL S__ITTING DOWN!!!

one particularly strident ad exhorted. Malicious puns were coined in whispers over morning cups of coffee all along the Street. We were referred to scathingly as "Con and Son," or even worse, "Kahn and Abull."

The pathological virulence of the P.R. reprisals genuinely shocked me. At the same time, my competitive instincts were aroused.

Kahn, on the other hand, was unambiguously elated. As he never tired of pointing out, any and every scrap of publicity, even of the most defamatory sort, was grist to our mill. His condition was improving daily, hourly. His confidence was returning. A light of purpose, perhaps a reflection of that light of divine election he'd once felt himself certain of participating in, shone in his face now, accounting no doubt for his frequent use of Old Testament analogies familiar to him from his childhood. Buoyed up by the successes of the first part of our campaign, he set to work devising a logo for our operation. "Got to have that logo," he assured me with an earnest frown.

I had shown him prints of an old Taoist sage with hunched shoulders and a tattered robe riding on the humped back of a Brahman bull. He decided to use this as a basis for our "brand." Only he changed the sage slightly, adding a ten-gallon Stetson, leather chaps, and spurs in fourteen-karat gold. The bull, too, underwent a transformation, from a mild, inoffensive plow animal docilely submitting to its master's sway, to a ferocious, snorting, rodeo-type beast, kicking his heels up with frisky joy — from an ox, in other words, as in the Chinese version, to a well-heeled Texas Longhorn. This, Kahn asseverated, would keep the basic meaning of the symbol intact, while doctoring it for American tastes. Our competition referred to it as the "Brooklyn Bronco." As this suggests, we came increasingly to be identified — stigmatized, I might say — with the smaller, less affluent investors, not the princelings of high finance. But Kahn turned even this to our advantage, touting Bull as the "Larger Vehicle" (as in the Buddhist Mahayana) of the working class. It was to accommodate this segment of our clientele that we opened the second parallel branch of our service, a mutual fund associated with our management company, all under the spreading aegis of Kahn and Sun Enterprises: Mutual Bull, "a division of Bull Incorporated."

The big boys at the institutions couldn't stand it. Though they looked down their noses at the popular ground swell we'd created and were riding, though they might have had moral qualms about committing their resources to an operator with a past as shadowy as Kahn's, they humbled themselves for the sake of the payola, as Kahn might have said, swallowing their medicine like good little (good old) boys.

Not the least "revolutionary" thing about us, particularly Mutual Bull, which Kahn personally managed, was our novel investment strategy, which he, in honor of his lost youth, spent chasing the elusive ghost of Mark Twain through the stacks at Columbia, christened the "Pudd'nhead Approach." This consisted, quite simply, of "putting (pudd'n) all our eggs in one basket, and *watching that basket!*" In other words, on extrapolating a market application from my manipulation of the coins, Kahn promptly put everything we had, 100 percent of total resources, behind the particular stock. Though contravening practically every principle of sound investment strategy, not to mention the laws of common sense and logic, this had phenomenal success. For while failure to diversify exposed us to total annihilation at each turn, our profits were similarly "undiversified," undiluted, that is, by liabilities incurred. And the oracle, against all hope, continued to perform. *Shih*, "The Army" — defense stocks — for example, provided a particularly timely tip for a trading move in that sector. I could multiply examples, but I fear such redundancy of prosperity might begin to seem obscene.

We had, of course, by this time "expanded shop," hiring a bevy of junior drovers to handle orders, along with the inevitable complement of secretaries and switchboard operators. Deliberately flaunting the Wall Street model, our people came to work in cowboy hats and boots and wore Texas string ties rather than the more conventional variety.

A curious corollary of the Pudd'nhead Approach began to develop. As our resources mounted, we sometimes found ourselves in the unintended, but not ungratifying, position of interfering with liquidity in the market. This was especially true when attacking the smaller, "hotter" companies we — that is, the *I Ching* — seemed to favor. Often the supply of outstanding shares was severely taxed by, if not outright insufficient to meet, our demand. The first few times this happened we mercifully forebore. Yet it did raise the tantalizing possibility of expansion by takeover. Kahn, predictably, was all for it. I demurred, my head already swimming with the suddenness and scope of our success. If we were going to diversify, I wanted it to be cautious and rational, a synergistic expansion into related businesses, not an indiscriminate, conglomerate feeding frenzy. It was around this time, too, that we opted to list on the NYSE.

Bit by bit, with admirable pertinacity, Kahn chipped away at my bias against expansion. Dazzled by our successes, with a sense of virtual omnipotence, he began to chafe under the narrowness of our original inspiration. Why limit ourselves to simple portfolio management, or even a mutual fund? Why not a general financial services organization under the umbrella of Kahn and Sun: brokerage, investment banking, arbitrage, commodities, perhaps a credit card division (Charging Bull?).

Though I had been firm at first, I bristled under his continual allegations of O.C. I might have held out had he not in his ingeniousness come up with an argument which, if not precisely original, seemed inspired to me. This was a modified version of the Social Darwinist apologia for competition in the marketplace, specifically geared to the idea of corporate mergers and spiced up with a few touches of Kahn's inimitable style. Kahn patiently explained to me that, rather than serving immoral, or at best amoral, ends, by actively prosecuting takeovers, we would, in effect, be contributing to the improvement of the corporate ecology of the American marketplace. By acting as "business predators" we were actually "policing the corporate gene pools," insuring the survival of the fittest. No, he vehemently asseverated, competition and predation were not self-aggrandizing, but on the contrary the foundation of a great spiritual discipline, profoundly altruistic at its heart. By a process analogous to natural selection in the wild, where adaptability to nature's ("Tao's," he glossed) changing demands and stresses enables one individual to survive and propogate while weaker members of the species perish without issue, just so in the economic wild adaptability to the demands of competition in a free marketplace insures the survival of healthier generations of businesses, thus assisting the economy in its ascent by slow, inevitable degrees toward perfection.

I was astounded by the sublimity of this vision, whose implications spread far beyond the business sphere. Thinking back to my first discussion with Riley, I wondered if this weren't the answer to the question he'd proposed: How was the Christian to reconcile the existence of evil with the unconditional benignancy of God? Or, alternatively, how did the Taoist reconcile the existence of what was not Tao — which represented an affront to its essential nature, even contradicted it — with the primordial unity of all things *in Tao*? Was it possible that this was the answer? If so, then on both counts the objections were based on a simple narrowness of view. Once the Great Whole was seen, objections flew away like chaff. Evil, then, was the crucible in which the good was tried and proved. The unnatural was the fever which the body suffered internally to purify itself and become well again. The sores and corrupt places of the economic world, as of the larger, were where the Tao had sent the legions of its influence, its platelets and leukocytes, its antibodies and white corpuscles, to eradicate diversity's failed experiments, devouring the excesses of the blood. Diversity was necessary to insure the greatest possible perfection, and if it created a few monstrosities as well, then it also provided for their destruction by natural selection. That was the miracle! Everything was tending toward the good!

That was our function then at Bull, to act as natural de-selectors, culling over (and out) the weaker members of our industry, reconstituting them into simpler elements, corporate fodder, which could then be absorbed and used by the stronger survivors, us! I can hardly exaggerate the impression this argument had on me. It hit me with the force of revelation, the very articulation of a thought I'd been harboring for some time. Only I had lacked the skills to distill it in a coherent form. I rehearsed it over and over in my mind until I'd mastered it completely. For the first time since the decision to embark in Bull Inc., with this opened vista of moral intent, I became engaged in the project at the most intimate personal level, beyond the simple desire to effect my friend's rehabilitation. No longer providing a brake to his initiative, from that time I threw myself into the project with an intensity that rivaled, perhaps even exceeded, his. What we needed, we both agreed, to anchor us and provide a base for further possible diversification, was a bank.

In utmost secrecy we began perusing takeover candidates. I must admit I took pleasure in the search. There was something sinfully voluptuous about our interest — like a couple of old roués examining the members of a chorus line — which might have put me off had I not consoled myself with Kahn's revelation of the deeper altruism of our task. But if one could feel a lecherous delight while exercising a moral function, why not? Taoism had never been particularly sympathetic to ascetic regimens anyway, I reflected, being much more attuned, in essence, to a philosophy of taking things as they came, ebb *and* flow, *yin* and *yang*. Chuang Tzu was often at pains to point out that enforced penury and asceticism were as much at odds with the free give-and-take of life, its alternate abundance and scarcity, as were excessive indulgence and prodigality. I couldn't have agreed more!

Under the tutelage of this inspiration, my new wealth sat more easily on me. I determined to cease my self-flagellation, dispense with remorse, and quietly enjoy. Offering guidance and encouragement in this project in my personal life, as Kahn had on the job, was Li. We began to see a great deal of one another from this time, dining together often, going to shows, museums, parties, even an occasional discotheque. Her instruction in the mysteries of personal enjoyment was as invaluable to me in my private life as Kahn's was in my public one. It wasn't long before we took a lease on a townhouse in Washington Mews, the cobbled, ivy-festooned little street between Fifth Avenue and University Place just above Washington Square Park. I asked her to move in with me, and for all intents and purposes she did, though she kept her old apartment.

I think she viewed the rise of Bull Inc. with the same amazement everyone did. Yet her appraisal of the phenomenon held an element of amusement. Not that she disapproved; far from it. Li never judged. That moral twilight which surrounded her was constant and invariable. It soothed and pacified my conscience, which I suspected Yin-mi might have chafed. I surmised that exposure to a variety of cultures with widely varying attitudes and values had made Li something of a moral relativist, though perhaps, on the contrary, it was her temperament which had drawn her to such studies in the first place.

Even the mania that had attended our brief pursuit of Doe paled in comparison with the excitement of this first takeover. For in the final analysis, that had been mere spectator sport (at least for me, if not for Kahn), like a horse race, where one places his stake on a favored contender, and attends with passionate interest but without visceral connection to the contest itself, observing without participating, in other words. But this was the thing itself, the Hunt. Only, the blood lust was excused for the higher purposes of evolution; the means tended toward a moral end. "Over that art which you say adds to Nature, is an art that Nature makes." Those were the first lines of Western poetry I ever really understood and psychically appropriated. They changed my life forever, that great shibboleth of indiscriminate permission.

"Visceral connection," yes, that goes far toward capturing the sensation.

For here, unlike in the Jane Doe episode, there was a sense of another life, something hidden in the jungle thickets of legal foliage, breathing heavily, warm and afraid, but also tensed to spring, keenly posed to resist our ambush. That sense of otherness became as vivid to me as another human life, only in opposition it acted as a subtle irritant, a seed of antagonistic intention, forever unassimilable. As I became more and more intimate with it, a cold, controlled fury grew within me, a psychic hunger to snap the backbone of its resistance, to taste the warm blood and marrow, to feel it malleable beneath the focus of my will. If its assimilation could come only at the price of its life, then die it must.

All this, too, remorselessly conscious. As I pieced it out, observing my own deliberate acts, I felt not so much horror at what I was doing as a sense of terrible awe. The old prescriptions and proscriptions of the moral life came back to me as scratched recordings of meaningless conversations, schoolboys reciting paradigms by rote, empty catechisms. They didn't apply in this world where we were stalked and stalking. This reaction was, in part, I believe, made possible by my sincere belief in Kahn's talk about a "higher altruism." But even more, the suspension of self-censure was a reflex of my visceral (again that word) conviction that this was right, that I was making progress toward my goal of understanding the Dow. Yes, as Bull Inc. moved into the first takeover, for the first time I felt myself to be in the presence of the thing itself, on the threshold of the sanctum sanctorum of the Dow. My eyes had not yet quite adjusted to the darkness of the inner room, but I could sense that I was there.

In our initial fit of enthusiasm, we ruled out nothing as too large or formidable for our pursuit. Chase, Chemical, Morgan Guaranty — none escaped our scrutiny. For though many of our prospective targets had assets several times larger than those of Kahn and Sun, in the image of corporate mergerdom the banks were no more immune than brontosaurs — gentle grazers, vegetarians, huge, lethargic, and benign — assaulted by the financial Tyrannosaurus Rex of Bull Inc. Our soaring price and prospects for future growth and earnings gave us the leverage we needed to attempt takeovers of institutions many times our size, since we planned to carry it out, if necessary — that is, assuming management resisted, a virtual dead certainty (our certainty, their death) — by the bloody route of a public tender offer, making a direct appeal to shareholders to sell us their holdings at a price substantially higher than the current market for their stock, paying in warrants and debentures, corporate IOUs of various sorts, some of them "convertible," which made them extremely tempting to investors since they contained a privilege to acquire shares of Kahn and Sun at substantial discounts. In the end we opted for a more modest portion, Second Jersey Hi-Fidelity, which, though smaller, was still many times our size.

In the end our fear (or was it our desire?) was realized. Management resisted. In a brief tête-à-tête we apprised them of our intentions and offered them terms of surrender. They refused. I'll never forget the looks on the faces of the executive officers at that parley. In other circumstances they were men I might not have noticed in an elevator or on the street. Their faces were unremarkable for dignity or beauty. But that morning all their anger, all their fear, their vulnerability, their courage, their will to resist, shimmered darkly below the surface, lending their eyes an uncommon brilliancy and depth. I couldn't stop staring at them, impolite as it was. Yet politeness was irrelevant under the circumstances. They peered just as hard at me. After stealthily setting this ambush for them and watching them walk straight into it, deliberately putting their careers, which is to say their lives, at risk, and doing so with cold, deliberate malice, now in the issue I discovered a certain affection for them, a certain pity, though not the impulse to spare them.

As we sat glowering at one another across the conference table, my mind ranged far. I thought back to that afternoon in China on the Gold Sand River, sitting opposite Tsin, listening with fascinated horror as he described battle as "the highest expression of human aspiration, the final truth and end of human life, pushing us beyond our limits into our divinity." "We kill, not out of grim, unwelcome necessity," he'd explained, "but because it refreshes and invigorates us, because the spirit craves it, and because only in the moment of taking life are we truly alive ourselves." Now I understood what he'd meant and, what's more, knew that he was right. The realization struck me so powerfully it almost made me gasp, but I laughed instead, a little wildly perhaps, as at a private joke which no one else understood, or could possibly understand. The others ogled me as though I'd lost my mind. Perhaps I had. But I believe that at a deeper level they understood, understood with the most intimate knowledge of all, that of the prey for the predator, who understands him better than he understands himself. I could tell by the looks on their faces — all one look — suffering without self-pity, acquiescence without capitulation, fatalism without resignation or despair, a look that was almost bland and yet was the opposite of bland, not an intimation of understanding, of knowledge, but the thing itself. It went on and on. I could have lost myself in that look. I think perhaps I did.

Despite the vivid reality of these sensations, a dreamlike quality hovers over this time in memory. Things were happening so fast. Sometimes I wonder if it occurred at all. I remember waking up some mornings with the peculiar sensation of not knowing where I was. I no longer recognized the landscape. A world of natural wonders revealed itself to me: prehistoric swamps and inland seas, spouting volcanoes, steamy sumps and marshes where unknown creatures wallowed ponderously beneath the slime; great rifts appeared where mountain ranges bubbled up and congealed before my eyes, or alternatively toppled and disappeared in silent, slow, stupendous avalanche — and all of it moral and within.

And yet other sensations were quite vividly concrete. Most subtle was a strange alteration in the quality of light. Colors seemed more deeply saturated, the sunlight took on an unaccustomed brilliance, shadows etched themselves more sharply on the stone. At other times, there was an opposite effect of mist, a golden sfumato which dissolved the edges of things. With childlike delight, I waved my hand through the air to see if the mist would swirl and eddy. Sometimes it did.

Even more tangible, if less delightful, were what I came to call the "animalcules," a word which Li taught me. This is what the Western magi called the coiling, squirming shapes they saw in water drops beneath their microscopes. For me, the animalcules glided through the air like tiny germs. Indeed, some of them were shaped very much like bacteria — coccus, spirillum, bacillus — but many more were random and amorphous, a few distinctly shaped like animals, though no animals I had ever seen or heard of in the world, and all no bigger than the head of a pin. When I first told Li about them, she said she'd experienced something similar after poring too long over rows of print in library carrels where the light was bad; on emerging into the sunlight, she could see small alphabets deploying before her eyes, as though the letters had been etched upon her retinas themselves. Perhaps I should see an ophthalmologist, she suggested. I declined at first, but as the phenomenon persisted, at last I took her up on it.

I went on a Saturday. I think perhaps because Li had referred me, and because I was wearing casual clothes, the doctor took me for a student, or perhaps a blue-collar worker, for his politeness was transparently perfunctory. While I described my symptoms, he was hardly able to contain his impatience, proceeding straight to the examination without comment. While prying my lids apart and leaning close over me with the little penlight, he was silent and, I felt, a little brusque. Writing out my prescription for the drops, he delivered his appraisal.

"What did you do, spill something in your eyes?" He stopped writing and glanced up at me with brief interest.

I returned his stare with surprise. "Not to my knowledge."

"Your condition resembles certain chemical burns I've come across, or the effect welders get from looking directly at the torch without their goggles. You aren't a welder, are you?"

I smiled to myself, thinking "only in the corporate mode"; to him, I simply shook my head.

"Well, whatever the cause, there's unmistakably been a deterioration in the cornea, significant, but not sight threatening . . ." — he paused — "I don't think. The damage has been done, though. We'll just have to wait and see." He tore the page off his prescription pad and handed it to me. "These drops should at least soothe the burning. You did say they burned?"

"No," I replied, "I didn't."

"Use them anyway," he counseled. "It can't hurt. It should at least take care of the animal crackers."

"Animalcules," I corrected him.

"Whatever."

He made it clear that I had taken up all the time he could spare. I left the office muttering.

Later it occurred to me that my "baptism" in the East River might have been the cause of this problem. If nothing else, my appointment with the ophthalmologist explained the sensitivity to light I'd been experiencing for some time and my increasing dependency on the dark glasses. Despite his assurances, the animalcules didn't evaporate. The eye drops didn't work. I had my doubts about his prognoses anyway. "A progressive deterioration in the cornea." What made him so confident? Perhaps I was simply seeing something others didn't, couldn't. Maybe the animalcules were the result of an *enhancement* rather than an impairment of vision. I considered the possibility that the black forms I saw gliding through the air were the molecules, the atoms themselves, randomly colliding and rebounding in the void.

That my visions were due to a sharpening of my faculties rather than a deterioration seemed much more logical in light of something that happened to me the morning before our parley with the chieftains of the bank. As I was knotting my tie before the wardrobe mirror in the bedroom of our new townhouse, a curious impulse seized me. I dropped my hands and, furrowing my brow in concentration, stared down at my tie with all my might. At first nothing happened, though it appeared to tremble slightly. I was on the point of giving up when I caught sight of my image in the mirror. The tie had levitated on its own! Springing horizontal in the air, it quivered like an arrow in a block of wood. I was so surprised, so delighted, I gave out an involuntary whoop.

Li stuck her head out from the bathroom. "Did you say something?" Grinning like a bandit, I pointed proudly to the tie. She gave me a quizzical look.

Dropping my eyes, I saw that it had fallen limp again. I debated telling her what had happened, then decided it was better not to. Perhaps it's just as well, for after she went away no effort of concentration could make it rise again.

Yet I *had* done it once. To hell with the eye doctor — this was something else! And lest, Reader, you think I was imagining things, let me tell you that the phenomenon was confirmed by a second occurrence. That morning in the office while waiting for the appointed hour, Kahn and I were too nervous and excited to do any serious work, so we decided to kill time, as we often did, pitching pennies. As we took turns tossing them, horseshoe style, at the wall, I became aware that by concentrating especially hard I was able to warp them in their trajectories. My control was crude and incomplete, but I could see it working. I could even manipulate the side of the coin that came up after the throw, at least half the time. I could tell that Kahn wasn't aware of it: the changes were too slight and occurred too quickly for his eye to catch, like a magician's sleight of hand. I wasn't about to tell him either, not while I was making money! The glee I felt, however, was all the more delicious by virtue of its secrecy.

Chapter 12

Our victory wasn't long in coming. Second Jersey's shareholders came over in droves. The night after passing the 51 percent mark, Kahn and I went drinking to celebrate our victory. In our euphoria we were affectionate and shy with one another. Dozens and dozens of times we repeated the same pat formulas of congratulation, investing them with more and more emotion as we got progressively drunker. Our mutual sabotage of diffidence in buying one another drinks was reminiscent of Lo's and mine, the way we typically foiled, through overzealous application of the laws of etiquette, our worst intentions and main object, which, of course, was simply to get uproariously, unrepentantly shitfaced. Both of us, I think, were anxious to deliver something profound and uplifting on the occasion, but what was there to say? Instead we just beamed and clapped each other on the back. After some hours of this, tipsy and elated, I took a cab up to Washington Square.

Li was waiting for me. When I came in I found her on her tiptoes in the front hall, watering a fern she'd brought from the old apartment with the glass milk bottle from the health-food store which brought the cats their daily allotment of curds and whey. She put it down and came to me smiling, slipping one slim arm around my waist and kissing me with her soft, warm mouth.

My mood changed swiftly and unaccountably. My elation vanished, leaving a strange melancholy, bittersweet, far-seeing. I realized how much things had changed since that first night, and, at another level, how little. Her taking me to the theater then had been like an act of noblesse oblige; or was slumming closer to the mark? In either case, I'd felt unworthy and abashed, like a country cousin, or worse, a country lover, the bumpkin wooing the princess. What was it she'd said? "Ladies of the court pay heavy premiums for the privilege of seducing beggars." There was none of that talk now, not even a hint of the attitude behind it. She was gentle, affable, receptive without exception. And yet, how can I explain? In her presence I still felt a slight compunction, as though I were presuming on her favor. I think it was something constitutional in me, this feeling that I was very tenuously placed in her affections and might at any moment, by a change in the wind, be blown like a feather out again. I wondered if it weren't simply exposure to the rigors of the marketplace that made me feel this way, an intuition of the precariousness and ephemerality of all our surest enterprises, of the inexorability of change, a fundamental paranoia regarding the material world picked up from participation in the Dow — that beautiful female principle, index of mortality — which taught its green disciples the need to get in quick and ride it while it lasts. For nothing lasts forever. Dow.

I contemplated the vista opened by this thought with a poignant sadness. Then I chided myself with the reflection that such crossovers from public to private life were inadmissible evidence. For the Dow was an index of the material fate of the world, where all things must inevitably follow the downward-tending path to ruin. But in the realm of the spirit, I told myself, what was impossible became possible, that the wealth of love, unlike precious metal, would not rust, or be tarnished by time and vicissitude, that the heart's conviction might stand proof against the erosion of the rivers of time. It was this hope that taught me to strive against my feelings of inferiority to try and believe in myself as someone worthy to be loved by her. For whether I was in love with Li, utterly and forever, had ceased even to be a question.

"Hello, sweet boy," she said with her slow, twilight way of drawing out the vowels. "I missed you today. It was like an ache in the pit of my stomach. Here." She took my hands and placed them on her stomach over her womb, like a pregnant mother inviting her husband into the warm precincts of the mystery, her secret, their treasure, only Li's hands circumscribed an emptiness. "I carried your smell in my dress all day," she whispered in my ear, smiling, leaning close. "Like a ghost wandering in an abandoned house, haunting the scene of an old love . . ." — she laughed softly — "or crime. I think of you all the time. I really do." She kissed me again, this time on the forehead. Then she looked at me, her eyes like narrow windows opening on a world of inner riches — the dark, liquid glimmering of mooring lights in a becalmed harbor, the bumping of hulls, the gentle lapping of the waves, so still the reflected stars twinkled on the surface sheen of blackness. She stood slightly stoop shouldered, so that her shirt opened and I could glimpse her breast where it swayed like a moon-drawn tide into the lace cup of her silk brassiere. Then she smiled and yawned, showing her beautiful white teeth. The sight of that voluptuous tenderness in her made my diffidence, my inhibitions, disappear like smoke, replaced by a sweetness so intense it was almost debilitating. God, how she could love! She overwhelmed me with her riches. She was made for it, the rarest vintage I have ever tasted, so subtle and astounding to the palate that the brain could not begin to inventory the magnitudes of pleasure it contained until the savor had already vanished from the lips. My beautiful angel of sex.

"When I look at you," I said, letting the mood take me, "I feel that everything is finished." I gazed into her face, drinking deeply of the gloaming of her soul, its essential twilight. "You are so much my consummate desire that nothing else seems real. Five minutes ago I was elated over something that happened to me at work today. Now I hardly remember what it was. Dow, Tao — I forget the meaning of the words when I'm with you, and I don't care." I spoke with rapt emphasis, despairing of making her understand me, the magnitude of it. "*I don't care*, Li, do you see what that means? I . . ."

"Shhh," she breathed, raising her long, slim finger, with its perfect nail, to her lips. "Don't. You must be careful not to frighten it away."

"What?" I asked.

She smiled but didn't answer.

I almost had to bite my hands to keep from crying out in the agony of sweetness she aroused.

"Sit down." Slipping off my jacket, I let her lead me to the sofa. Her socks made a soft rushing sound gliding across the carpet. Taking the bottle of white burgundy from the nest of opened books and papers on the secretary, she replenished her glass, then poured one for me. "You know, something odd happened today." She eyed the glass, careful not to spill it, as she crossed the floor. Handing it to me, she sank down at the far end of the sofa, curling one foot under her and taking a sip. Her lips puckered slightly, she sat waiting for me to inquire.

"What?"

"I saw Yin-mi."

"Where?" I asked quickly.

"In the park." We traded looks. "I almost panicked. I was sure she was staking out the joint." She laughed with false ease.

"Well?"

She took another sip and shook her head. "I'm pretty sure it was just an accident."

"What was she doing?"

Li shrugged. "How should I know? Probably buying dope."

"Yin-mi?" I returned skeptically. "Come on."

She regarded me closely. "I'm just joking. What's the matter, I suppose you think she's too pure for that sort of thing?"

I pointedly ignored her. "Go on."

"Well, that's basically it. I don't know what she was doing. I could just tell it was innocent."

"How?" I persisted.

"Something in her manner. She was glad to see me. We talked for a while. I regained my confidence." Li laughed nervously, remembering. "I almost blew it though when she asked what I was doing there. I blushed and lost my composure. My mind went blank. I hemmed and hawed a minute before finally managing to stutter that I was on my way to see a friend. When she asked who, all I could think of was Jane Doe. I don't remember what I said. Jane something, Jane Dour maybe. She gave me a funny look, but I don't think it meant anything. For a minute, though, I was really terrified. It's almost funny, don't you think, me afraid of her?"

I shrugged in mildly querulous neutrality.

She smiled with a hint of mischief. "I know it was probably cruel, but I couldn't resist asking if she'd seen you."

"Why would you do that?" I asked sharply. "You know she hasn't."

She shrugged almost happily. "I don't know. I just couldn't help myself. Yin-mi just shook her head and looked sad, staring off into space." Li directed an acute, appraising glance in my direction, which irked me a little, making me feel under observation. "She's in love with you," she pronounced in a quiet voice.

"And I love you," I replied, suddenly understanding that she was jealous, touched by the earnestness of it.

"Shhh," she said again, taking my hand in both hers and placing it against her cheek. "Don't say it, Sun I. It frightens me when you do."

"Why?" I asked, my curiosity numbed partially by an uneasy intimation. "Don't you love me? Can't you?"

Li looked at me then, not unkindly, but with that old remoteness which I knew so well and feared so deeply. Simultaneously embraced and distanced by that look, I fancied a resemblance between Li and some supernatural being, a goddess staring down from heaven, touched to sadness at the sight of a devout petitioner racked by the pangs of his mortality, which she could not share, hovering on the brink of genuine empathy, then drawn back by the irresistible gravity of her privilege. That look was more terrible finally than any conscious cruelty, full of that radical amorality which was the essence of her being, the thing I loved in her more than all else, and despaired of, too, knowing it the implacable enemy to my purpose. It made me sad to acknowledge that we could never share it. And then I thought of Yin-mi's eyes, that great solemnity which had encompassed everything I was and understood it all, too well. Perhaps that was the problem.

"Sooner or later she's going to find out," Li said, drawing me back from where I'd traveled, "one way or another. Perhaps it would be better if we simply told her."

The suggestion surprised me. I frowned.

"Would you rather do it, or should I?" she asked.

I shifted my eyes and gazed off into space, thinking.

"Don't volunteer so fast," she chided with a resentful laugh.

"You think it's absolutely necessary?" I asked.

She shrugged. "It certainly would be more honorable."

I nodded at the justice of it. "Perhaps it would be better if I did then."

To my surprise, she winced slightly. "I'm not so sure. I think maybe I'd prefer doing it myself."

"Why did you ask then?" I demanded, hardly attempting to disguise my irritation.

"I wanted to see what you'd say." She paused. "Do you ever miss her?"

I debated whether to lie, and decided not to, that there was no need. "Sometimes," I admitted. "A little."

She frowned again, more darkly this time. "I'd prefer it if you didn't see her." Her tone was curt, almost peremptory.

"You know I haven't," I replied, "but why? What difference does it make?"

"You do want to then." She spoke with accusatory finality, as though confirming a deep suspicion.

"It's not that," I objected. "I simply wondered why you'd mind."

"Well, if I'm not going to see Peter, I don't see why you should see her," she continued, with a trace of petulance that I found repellent and infuriating.

"Well, by all means let's make sure nobody's cheated in the bargain, that we get our money's worth on both sides," I said. "Damn it, Li, we're talking about seeing her to tell her about us, aren't we? It's not exactly like it's going to be a joyous social occasion, a date. Besides," I added, having worked myself up into legitimate indignation, "I never asked you to promise anything about Peter."

Her expression betrayed hurt, then hardened and grew cold. "All right," she said tersely, deliberately cryptic, deliberately cruel in her ellipsis. She folded her arms and refused to look at me.

Finally I relented. "Okay, I'm sorry. It doesn't matter. You do it. I don't care."

She accepted my capitulation, though not exactly graciously. The whole thing left a bitter taste.

"So," she began again with false brightness, "tell me about your day. When you came in you said you were happy. What happened? Tell me how many millions you made, how your Bull hammered up the dust and left the others behind, blinded in it, sneezing, bellowing with rage." She laughed, growing expansive, though with an edge of mockery in her voice. "Or how you raped the fair Europa of finance, swimming away with her toward Asia, bare breasted, nubile, smiling with fond obliviousness as she wove the garland of flowers for your horns."

"You're making fun of me," I commented matter-of-factly, resigned.

"Oh no!" she protested with an amused laugh.

"Am I so ridiculous?"

The cutting edge was sheathed a moment and she grew milder, though still playful. "Ridiculous?" she echoed. "I can't decide. A little bit perhaps. But even more, astounding. How you've succeeded is impossible, miraculous! A babe among ravenous wolves — or bears — making them lick your hand. Who would have believed it? Sun I" — she took my face between her hands — "you are amazing. Absolutely. My beautiful Chinese kamikaze, like an eagle dive-bombing Wall Street straight from the steppes of Tibet, stooping from your high aerie at the summit of the world — who could have imagined you? If you were fiction you'd be scorned as too outlandish. Yet you are real and true. I know that. If nothing else, that." She kissed me briefly, richly on the lips, the resounding seal of her approval.

All my grievances and misgivings vanished like dew beneath the sunlight of her generosity, extravagant as it was. That was her way. I couldn't resist it, or her.

"But come," she said, "the table's set and I've been holding dinner for you." She loosened my tie and began unbuttoning my vest.

Over dinner she let me talk. I filled her in on the latest in the takeover, the last, climactic act of the drama she'd been following with interest all along. As I spoke, and drank, my spirits revived. Exhilaration returned, followed eventually, and inevitably, by garrulity. I was still talking when we went to bed, and after we'd made love, as we lit the cigarette and passed it. In my enthusiasm I no doubt waxed a little pompous, launching into a long pedantic disquisition on the "higher altruism." It was only at this point that she finally interrupted, and then only to laugh. With my mouth open, finger still poised in the air, I turned to her and blinked. "What?"

She simply smiled, saying nothing, that telltale hint of amusement and provocation in her expression.

"Well?" I persisted, almost indignantly.

"Nothing," she said, raising her hands in playful meekness, begging off. "Only . . . you don't really believe that, do you?"

"Why shouldn't I?" I challenged.

She shrugged. "Oh, I don't know, except, of course, that it's pompous tripe, fatuous, hypocritical, and self-serving."

I stared at her in stunned silence. This was the first time she'd ever said anything even remotely judgmental about our business dealings.

"Don't get me wrong," she continued. "It's not that I disapprove of your taking over a bank. I think it's wonderful that you can pull it off. But let's at least be honest about motives here, all right? I mean, if you're going to stick it to somebody at least have the intellectual decency not to insist it's for his benefit."

"Well, for the benefit of the system as a whole then," I amended.

"Uh-uh," she said, shaking her head. "Even if the evolutionary analogy holds true (and I'm not sure it does; after all, animals kill by instinct, innocently; men are supposed to have free will), still it wouldn't exonerate you *personally*. When you take over someone else's business against his will, the only larger good it serves is your own bank account." She laughed. "Speaking of which, do you suppose I can get free checking?"

I stared at her in pained disbelief. "You mean you think, after all I've told you about my reasons for being here and participating in the market, that my motive is simple self-interest?"

"Well, call it compound self-interest if you will."

"I'm serious, Li! It isn't funny. You really believe I could be so unfaithful to my principles as to pursue profit for its own sake with no higher end in view?"

Narrowing her eyes, she gave me that familiar taunting smile and shrugged her shoulders. "Why not? Everybody else does, me included. What makes you so special? Come on, Sun I, this is the real world now. You're a big boy, all grown up. Isn't that what Bull Inc. and the ordeal have been all about, a rite of passage, leaving childhood behind?"

"But that was Kahn's idea," I protested. "I did it all for him."

A hard light glinted in her eyes. She smiled without mirth. "You consented in your heart to everything."

I was so crushed, so abashed, I didn't even try to defend myself.

"I don't want to hurt you, Sun I," she went on, "but I simply bristle when you take on those self-righteous airs about what is essentially pure, unmitigated capitalist predation. Not that I disapprove of pure, unmitigated capitalist predation, mind you, in fact, I think it's downright jiffy. Just don't try to dress it, or yourself, up in sheep's clothing. What you've done, what you're doing, is incredible, but don't try and sell it as disinterested moral striving, at least not to me. I think you do it because you like it, and because of what it gets you, and nothing you can say is going to convince me otherwise. That's all I'm saying. Just for the record."

"And what does it get me?" I asked in a cynical, disspirited tone.

She raised her hands in the exact gesture I had seen the priest use to invite the congregation to Communion. "This," she said, rolling her head to indicate the bedroom, the surroundings.

I went a step further. "And you?"

She colored violently. "Perhaps," she said in that old tone of voice that seemed to dare me to assess her credibility. "If you like."

I sat silently shaking my head, trying to take it all in.

"It's just a fact of life, Sun I."

Again that phrase. "Like dying?" I asked.

She smiled wearily. "Right. Like dying. And like dying, it's best to accept it gracefully."

"All this time you've been looking on, saying nothing as we've proceeded," I said, trying to comprehend it, "and you've felt nothing in your heart from the beginning but contempt."

"Far from it," she contradicted. "I've been deeply impressed. I admire what you've accomplished. Honestly. I just can't believe you've worked disinterest-edly."

"But that's the whole point!" I cried, flaring up again. "If you don't believe that, you don't believe in me at all — not really, not in what matters."

She didn't flinch. I sighed and looked away.

"You're wrong though, you know," she began again quietly. "I do believe in you. I didn't think I would when I first met you. But now I really am beginning to. Only not in the way you believe in yourself. I don't believe in your priestly role, this glorified image of you as a pilgrim on a religious quest in search of the Holy Grail. That's simply an adolescent fantasy. Maybe you needed it once to make you strong and spur you on. But you've outgrown it.

It's time to put it behind you now." She reached out to where I sat on the edge of the bed, facing away, and laid her hand gently on my shoulder. "I think you're actually something much stronger than that, and better."

I turned and glared at her ironically. "Better?"

"Better to me."

Propping my elbows on my knees, I clasped my hands and stared at my feet, thinking of nothing, aware only of a dull, distant ache. The sight of my naked toes reminded me of those summer nights sitting with Yin-mi on the roof, dangling our feet over the edge, telling her my story, my hopes, as the sun sank by slow degrees into the wilderness beyond the Hudson. *She* had believed. I was filled with a poignant sense of loss. Never before had I regretted her, not since I'd found Li. Now I felt like weeping.

"You look so sad," she observed tenderly, tremulously. "Come here." She drew me toward her, laying my face above her breast. "What can I do?"

I closed my eyes and said nothing, wishing only to dissolve.

"Shall I tell you a story?" she suggested, stroking my hair. "Let's see, what about?" She paused a moment. "I know — Phaëthon. Do you know about him?"

I shook my head like a child, wanting her comfort, and grudging, a little, the desire.

"He's a figure from Greek mythology," she explained.

"Like Oedipus."

"Like Oedipus," she confirmed. "His mother, Clymene, was mortal, but his father was Helios, the god of the sun. They say that from the second month Phaëthon pounded on his mother's womb, crying to get out into the world, 'fate driven,' like Aeneas, like all of them. His curiosity and desire were unappeasable. They say he had 'star-gazing eyes.'" Li studied me curiously before resuming. "His mother reared him, but he became uncontrollable. Doubting his legitimacy, 'mad for the proof,' he sought his father in the palace of the gods on Mount Olympus, and begged Helios to let him drive the chariot of the sun across the heavens for one day in acknowledgment of their bond — a sort of self-imposed ordeal. Helios tried to dissuade him. He described the monsters he would have to face: the Scorpion, the Lion, the Great Bear, Ursa Major, Taurus . . . 'lions and tigers and bears' galore. But Phaëthon was implacable. You know what happens next?"

I shook my head.

"Of course the horses were too powerful. He was blinded by the light of a thousand suns, a thousand galaxies of suns. Hands bleeding from the reins of power, he panicked and lost control. The chariot burned through the heavens, carving the scorched track of the Milky Way, until the universe itself was threatened with conflagration. Zeus had to intervene. He hurled the thunderbolt and struck him down. Phaëthon fell headlong from the sky into the waters of the river Eridanus and vanished from the eyes of men."

"His sin was pride," I commented, more to myself than her.

"Yes, pride, arrogance, presumption. The Greeks had a name which encompassed the whole constellation of traits: hubris."

"Hubris," I repeated carefully, testing the syllables.

She lifted my face in her hands. "You have the same star-gazing eyes," she said.

"You think I'm proud then," I asked, "among all my other failings?"

She smiled and nodded. "Yes, I think so. Proud, and perhaps the least bit disingenuous."

"Disingenuous?"

" 'Disingenuous?' " she repeated mockingly. "I think you know what I mean."

I blinked my eyes.

"Admit it," she said, "you like nice things, what your new life has brought you."

"But I can live without them," I affirmed. "I did before."

"Before you met me," she glossed, drawing the inference.

I made no reply.

"You know you're always free to live that way again," she observed with bluff fatalism, vaguely admonitory. "You might even solicit my little sister's complicity in the undertaking."

"Please don't." I felt the vortex beginning to reassert its gravity. "I thought we'd settled that."

"But understand, Sun I," she continued, ignoring me, "this isn't gratis. *I'm* not." She opened her eyes very wide in a brazen challenge. "That's right. Don't look so surprised. You said it yourself. If it hasn't dawned on you by now, I suggest you go ahead and face it. It's true. You maintain your ultimate motive is some kind of knowledge, that you came here on a pilgrimage in search of purity and truth. And at the same time you say that I'm your consummate desire. Don't you see? There's a contradiction there. You can't have two supreme desires."

"What are you saying?" I moaned in anguish and frustration.

"I simply wonder if the choice arose — and it always does, Sun I, sooner or later, doesn't it? — which you'd sacrifice first?"

"Why do you have to ask such terrible questions?" I felt as though I were being torn apart. "Why do you insist on belaboring the point? I've already broken my vow for you, haven't I? What else do you want?"

"Simply for you to remember, Sun I," she replied, "that despite your protestations of higher altruism and religious purpose, without *it*, without money, you could not have this. . . . And without this, you could not have me."

I moved back to my former exile at the edge of the bed, clinging forcibly to Yin-mi's image, as though it might protect me from this ugliness.

Li edged over and again lifted my face. She wore a look of tenderness and deep remorse. My own indifference surprised me.

"Don't be sad, Sun I," she whispered.

I didn't say "I'm not," but I was tempted.

"It isn't only that. It isn't only money. I simply mean that, no matter what my feelings were, or are, for you, I could never be happy without certain . . . 'things.' Is that so detestable? Money is simply a prerequisite, not the be-all and end-all. Think of the play we saw. No matter how fine and resonant the drama, to do a good production you simply must have money, to show it to its best advantage. It's a fact of life." I winced slightly at this, though I was starting to relent. "You want the spirit to accomplish everything, move mountains. How nice if it could! But that's a dreamworld, Sun I. Reality is better. It may not leave you constantly agape with wonder, awe, amazement . . ." (she caught her breath between each word in playfully demonstrative exaggeration) "that tingly feeling, but there are always good things to eat and wine to drink." She reached for her glass and toasted me. "There is always making love until our bodies slump in exhaustion." Her eyes were vulnerable and sensual at once. "That is better, isn't it?"

Tears were burning in my eyes now. I didn't try to hide them. "Then let me take it as my god," I said, "if you require it."

She smiled with tender sadness as though taking a deep breath inside herself, then stroked my face with the back of her hand. "You are good, Sun I," she said, "too good."

Then I began to cry.

She sighed and moved away, leaving me with my pain. When I turned again, she was sitting propped on the pillows, a look of dreamy absorption on her face. She was playing with a lock of hair, carding it like wool, the motion of her wrist exactly the one with which she habitually twisted and untwisted the chain of hammered gold. I can't explain it, but this gesture shocked me more than anything she'd said, the deep obliviousness of it. In the half-light, a strange aura, cold like the sheen of marble, glowed around her. After a moment she became aware of my scrutiny and dropped the lock. I kept my eyes trained on it, alert with premonition. Trailing down her breast, black against the whiteness of her naked skin, it curved with the contours of her body. Suddenly it twitched, swished swiftly side to side, like a tail. When I looked up, Li was smiling at me from a fox's face.

"What do you want?" I asked in Chinese, cautious with dread, as though speaking to a spirit.

"This," she replied. "You. All of you, including your contradictions, especially those. I want your ambivalence, your paradox." She smiled at me again, and it was gone; the illusion, the insight, whatever it was, vanished.

I released my breath, sighed with resigned exasperation. "Li, Li" — I shook my head — "sometimes I despair of your ever loving me. 'Ambivalence,' 'paradox' — what do I have to do with such things? I know nothing about them."

"I'm not so sure," she differed. "Perhaps you underestimate, or overestimate, yourself. Sometimes I get the feeling that you have only the merest inkling who you are. Maybe I was wrong before. It isn't disingenuousness or hypocrisy. You're as true as you know how. It's simply that you don't know yourself. When you say Dow, or Tao, aren't these simply shorthand ciphers for the undiscovered selves which go to make up who you are, your Authentic Self? Selves rather, for despite what you may say or think, those selves are multiple, *and* contradictory. *That* is your ambivalence. That is your paradox. That's what draws me to you more and more. In you there seem to be two souls inhabiting a single body, each diametrically opposed, yet each childlike, innocently longing to be reconciled. What are they? Your mother and your father, faith and doubt, an instinct toward life and one toward death? I can't answer. Yet I see you stalking in this wilderness, crying out your purity of motive while your hands are wet with blood. If purity is what you wanted, you should never have left. Why did you? Purity isn't here. If it exists at all, it's only there, at places like Ken Kuan, which exist for the sole purpose of keeping it alive. Though only a fragment of the totality, purity is important. Men like the ones you knew there have a legitimate mission as its guardians. I respect what they do. But you're not one of them, Sun I. You spent many years among them, I know; it's hard to give it up. But you were made for this. I think that's why your master let you go, because he knew your fate was in the world, in Dow. And maybe your friend Kahn is right when he says that in its broad extrapolation Dow is the world. You can beat your head against the wall and break your heart, but that's where you belong, and that's why you came to America. Because this country is its apotheosis, Dow's apotheosis, as perhaps China is Tao's. As for the rest of it — the Tao within the Dow — let it go. You'll never find it. It isn't here. It isn't anywhere, except maybe over the rainbow someplace in your dreams and in your heart, and that's not a real place."

"It isn't?"

She shook her head with absolute assurance. "The two are irreconcilable, Sun I, always and forever. 'The delta,' 'the Tao within the Dow' — that's your hieratic formula for your own absolution, for the relaxation of the tension that exists inside you between good and evil. The reconciliation you seek is sophistry, magic. If it occurs at all, it occurs somewhere beyond the vanishing point of this world. It's illusion, superstition. Even if you found what you are looking for, it would repel you. You would go limp in your felicity." She reached down and closed her fist over my flaccid penis, smiling almost apologetically. "You'd cease to be a man and become a saint. You wouldn't matter anymore, Sun I, at least not to me."

She paused to assess the impact of her words. "Poor boy," she consoled, touching my face with her cool fingertips. "You think that somehow, in some mathematical eternity which you believe is real, the parallel lines of your two incompatible destinies, your two incompatible ambitions, will intersect and all the ravages of your personality will be made whole." She whispered, "It isn't so, Sun I. It isn't."

As she concluded, I became aware that for some time I'd been listening to something else, outside on the window casement: the plaintive, desultory strumming of the harp, which she'd brought with her from uptown. "Perhaps you're right," I capitulated in an exhausted, toneless voice. "I don't know anymore."

She came around the bed and knelt beside me, leaning her head on my thigh, rocking it slowly. "Don't worry," she crooned. "It'll be all right."

As I looked down at her dark hair, I felt a sense of irremediable hurt. She had touched me in so deep a place that nothing would ever make it right again; she had wounded something in my heart forever, and done so with intent, though not, I think with malice. And yet I felt no bitterness, no resentment. In fact, my tenderness for her was deeper now than at any time before, deeper than any I'd ever known. My eyes misted over. I stroked her hair musingly. In a while I became aware of a great benignant emptiness in me, a feeling of release. After the cloudburst of passion, the virulence, after the battle, I felt cleansed and whole. I was at peace.

•

That night lying in bed I thought about Yin-mi. My mind drifted wistfully back, replaying a thousand incidents, our innocent delight in one another, the blandness with which we had accepted it. These things were rendered poignant, almost wrenching, in the light of hindsight, which cast deeps and shadows of catastrophes we had not foreseen over the bright fields of memory. I thought of the look she'd given me that first night in her father's kitchen, how it was the same as that last morning when I'd brushed her aside and gone through the door. That look knit together beginning and end, closing the circle of our intimacy. I remembered, too, her animation, the sparkle of interest in her eyes, the nods of gentle encouragement she'd given me as I spoke to Wo (but really to her) at the Ha-p'is' about my higher purpose. Yes, she had believed, believed and empathized so deeply that she had discovered the crystal image of my heart's true intent, lifted it like a jewel from the clear, rushing torrent of my talk and presented it to me with trembling hands. The delta — she had given me that; Li had taken it away.

Li lay beside me on the pillows, asleep. She was so beautiful. My beautiful angel of sex . . . She had given me that, given me my sexuality. That was her gift. That was her delta. ("That's the delta, sweet boy, the only one that matters.") And I had wanted it. But the other one, the Tao within the Dow. "You would go limp in your felicity." I reached down and touched myself under the spread. In a kind of mournful peace, I closed my eyes.

Then suddenly a burst of laughter escaped from deep inside me, one brief, violent *ha!* I was thinking of what Kahn had said to me that day in the Buttonwood Café: "Caught between your *yin* and your *yang.*" Yin-mi, *yang*

. . . I squeezed it hard. He hadn't meant it that way of course, but it hardly mattered. It was perfect. Just as suddenly a deep upwelling of remorse and pain came on as I recalled that night in the rain, the mad dash through the alley. If only I had known my sexuality then; if only Yin-mi had. Had she, I wondered? Perhaps, perhaps. For me, though, desire had been alchemized in the crucible of my unconscious into aversion and mistrust. That, not the debacle at Trinity, was the beginning of our sundering, its real root. I visualized her standing in the vestibule with her hands behind her, her breasts through the wet shirt. I felt a tightness in my throat, and went hard again remembering the way she had looked down at me as I lifted her, almost sad, the way she kissed my mouth, the taste of it. Inconsolable, I closed my eyes and, for the single instant of release I knew that it would give me before the gnawing in the belly started up again, I masturbated. Tsin's face, my father's, the unknown thing with horns in the hold of the *Telemachos,* these images floated through my dreams, together with a peal of mocking, disembodied laughter, wafting with the music of the harp.

Chapter 13

So that was our first fight. And our last one. And all the ones in between. It always came back down to that: her exemplary ethnological relativism, my need for absolutes. The morning after that first one, I felt like I'd been flayed alive, beaten with rubber hoses, a degradation so intense it caused a physical ache. Not just because of the fight, either, but also from the takeover, my "self abuse" — all of it. I felt deeply unclean, disgusted with myself and with my life. Was this what Tsin had meant by the "hangover of battle"? I wondered.

Kahn was still riding the elation of the previous day, blustering about, issuing orders. I avoided him like bad fish, skulking around, hiding in corners. I left the office early. On my way home in the cab I toyed vengefully with the idea of breaking with Li, kicking her out, knowing I wouldn't. I couldn't live without her. Funny, that expression didn't carry its usual romantic associations. My dependency was more like a drug. Another image from the past bubbled up to consciousness and burst: "an insidious and ultimately debilitating parody of the intoxicating bliss of enlightenment," the master's words to Hsiao. He'd meant opium, but I wondered if it didn't apply equally well to Li, to her love as compared with Yin-mi's. "Caught between your *yin* and your *yang*." I laughed bitterly. I was an addict then.

My generosity of spirit was amply rewarded when I got home. Li was sitting in the middle of the living room floor, flipping disconsolately through a stack of magazines. Since she was still wearing her nightgown and robe, it appeared she hadn't been to class. I could tell she'd been crying, for her eyes glowed with a washed-out sheen of tears. At the sight of me, though, a hopeful light broke in her face.

"You're home!" She jumped up and threw her arms around my neck, holding me tightly. Cradling my face between her hands, she leaned back to examine me. She seemed chastened, grave, more sensitive and tender than I'd ever seen her.

"I thought about you all day long," she said with a slight quaver in her voice.

She hugged me again and laid her face on my chest. "I'm so sorry about last night. I want to apologize for what I said. I don't know what came over me." She drew back again and regarded me earnestly. "I want to make it up to you."

"You didn't go to class?" There was something maudlin and cloying in this sudden flood of tenderness that filled me with a vague revulsion. Silently I wondered if she was simply afraid of losing her new affluence, "all this." I loathed myself for thinking it.

"Yes, I went for a little while," she replied. "But it was too awful. Your come kept leaking into my underwear — cold, cold — and I just wanted to cry. I came home and then I cried. And slept. And cried some more."

"What is all this?" I nodded to the magazines scattered on the floor.

"Oh, I stopped by the apartment for a second and brought some boxes." She disengaged herself and went over to them, dropping to her knees. With a musing pout, she began to turn the pages. "I saw something — I don't know if I can find it now — a picture that reminded me of you." She searched a minute, then flipped the magazine shut with a decisive sigh. "Oh well, I'll tell you about it instead. It was an article about South America, Chile, I think, full of glossy photographs: welders spraying blue-white fire, raining sparks through the air; another of a monstrous crater in the desert, the Atacama, with toy-scale yellow dump trucks and bulldozers rolling on their treads; fishing trawlers steaming into port over a dark blue ocean beneath a swirling cloud of gulls; the skyline of Santiago against the outline of the distant mountain, a full moon rising, partially eclipsed by a glass skyscraper. And amid all these scenes of 'progress,' modernization, a curious photograph of a little boy sitting in the snow, chin propped on drawn-up knees" — she demonstrated — "his tiny face tilted to the side as he sleeps uneasily. His dark skin, his facial structure, his long black hair braided into scores of love locks reveal his race: an Indian.

"Struck by something about him, I puzzled over it a long while. He was dressed in skins and feathers; all around him on the snow were the toys he'd been playing with before he fell asleep: a bitch and pups, a llama made of beaten gold, a cocaine spoon." She touched the carpet lightly at each word, placing the imaginary articles around her. "He was wearing a headband tied with a leather thong. In the center of his forehead, like another eye, was a beadwork figure of the sun with rays running out from the periphery, only colored black.

"The expression on his face was what especially touched me, a sort of pout with the bottom lip turned out, his petulance partially relieved by sleep. His brow was furrowed, but his lower face was perfectly relaxed, lips parted slightly. He looked like he'd dozed off while sulking, like he couldn't stick to his resolve to hate whoever left him there.

"I looked closer, and noticed that his arms were covered with strange brown welts. In places his skin was literally peeling off; you could almost see the bones beneath. That's when I read the caption: 'The Inca Boy.' I could hardly believe it — an Inca! Do you know what that means? He was found exactly as he looks in the photograph by a team of meteorologists high up in the Cordillera on a mountain called El Plomo, over seventeen thousand feet. They saw his arm extended from a snowdrift, uncovered by a violent windstorm. He'd been buried for *four hundred years.*" She paused to let this sink in.

"From the arrangement of his hair, the configuration of the headband, the presence of ceremonial objects with the body, the scientists figured that he'd been singled out for sacrifice. The black sun, they said, alluded to an eclipse. A major one occurred around that time, observed in Europe. Apparently the tribe interpreted it as a sign of the sun's displeasure and offered up the child as a human sacrifice to appease their god.

"I cried when I read about it, and thought of you."

"Why?" I asked.

"Because you remind me of that little Inca boy, Sun I, some innocent sacrifice left behind by a vanished culture, starting awake in a modern landscape and trying to apply the principles you were taught to the New World you found surrounding you, still believing in those fierce, unforgiving, primitive gods which we have lost (which I have lost, Sun I), your eyes still bright with some terrible certainty our instruments can't detect and we dismiss as superstition. I thought of you in your ceremonial robes, offered up to a god that progress, science, has deposed, frozen in your suffering, put on display behind a wall of museum glass for curious tourists to gape at and dishonor, forced to reenact the ritual of your agony over and over forever, with no hope of reprieve." She stared at me with tremulous appeal.

I couldn't speak. I was so moved, so wounded. It didn't cancel out what she had said the night before, but it touched the sore with a magic wand and snowflakes drifted down over the raw place. She had such reaches in her, such poetry. She understood my darkness and my pain better than anyone, even as Yin-mi understood my light and wholeness. The past was swept away. We were reconciled. I was in love again.

She was in love too, I think, for the first time. Perhaps that was the only night she ever really loved me, loved me in that deepest place where there is no accounting. The next morning the ledgers would be brought out again, dusted off, and opened back to the old place.

"Then it's right?" she asked with joy, reading my reaction.

I simply returned her look.

"That's all I really meant to say last night," she averred in a rush. "Somehow it just came out wrong, got twisted up and mean."

I knew it wasn't true, but I didn't contradict her. It didn't matter. I was still happy. And she was. We were together, a moment of pure congruence, the most perfect we ever achieved. (Whatever you were, whatever I was, Li, you were my first love. If I found something surer, saner, more healthy later on, it never had that white heat at the core.)

We made love then, wild, keening, sobbing fucking. Afterward in a quiet glow, we ate dinner by candlelight at a little bistro in the neighborhood. "Let's dress up," she'd suggested, and we had. When we'd finished, we walked down Sullivan toward the Soho bars. Passing Bleecker Street, we noticed the marquee of the Public Cinema: NOW PLAYING: *THE WIZARD OF OZ*. We looked at one another, then without a word went to the back of the line that was forming. And it was there, while waiting, that we saw Yin-mi.

She was with two girlfriends, both Chinese, probably from school. Yin-mi was quiet and attentive between them, talking now with one, now with another, laughing sometimes — beautiful, graceful, dignified, young.

She saw us from the opposite side of the street and stopped; her friends went on obliviously. As in a nightmare, it was too late to do anything. Our secret was written all over us. Like two pieces of marble cut from the same quarry, we shared an aura, a sheen — cold like that — as though surrounded by a bubble of unearthly light. In our elegant clothes I fancy we appeared like two enchanted beings returning from a night's revels to their nether world, Fairyland or Emerald City, surprised on the threshold by a pair of mortal eyes, frozen in their power. We both looked at her; I never looked at Li. Discomfiture and shame must have aged our features; but it was as nothing compared to the naked, timeless pain in Yin-mi's face. It could have shattered stone or etched itself in glass. For a moment, forever, she regarded us, took us in. I thought about the ox along the river, its blue-black eyes as it looked up from drinking, how the water, the trees, the world itself had vanished into them an instant, absorbed by the power of that great passivity. Yin-mi's eyes were like that — we, two tiny foam flecks whirling on the lip of the great vortex of her condemnation, which threatened to draw us down forever into darkness.

She started walking toward us. As she crossed the street, she didn't even look at the traffic, never for an instant averting her eyes.

Neither of us moved. Li grimly threaded her arm through mine and drew me tighter. I, too, tensed as though to face a shock. What was I thinking? That she would attack us, spit in our faces?

Yin-mi stopped in front of us. Turning to Li, she put both hands on her sister's shoulders, then pressed her lips silently to her forehead in a soundless kiss. Me she fixed a little longer, before rising to her tiptoes to kiss me on the lips. As she drew away she touched my hand (not squeezed, just touched) and whispered something: "I understand," or "Now I understand," I didn't catch it exactly, though the difference meant everything. Then she returned to her friends.

•

My heart was breaking all through the film, even when I laughed; especially then. And how I laughed, wiping away my tears with my handkerchief. (It would have had to be a magician's handkerchief indeed to wipe away my grief.) Especially the Cowardly Lion, the way he lisped and sputtered, snarling and cowering, strutting and blustering — "If I were king of the *fore-e-est!*" — through Bert Lahr's India rubber face. I had read the book by then two or three times, and in most ways I thought the movie even better. I particularly admired the way the director had given the story a resonance and a history, a doubleness, by making the Land of Oz a wonderful transmogrification of Kansas itself (a reflection in that fey looking glass where Cinderella sees her dream-self in a ball gown and glass slippers, and the naked emperor is wearing clothes) with all the same characters, only changed, and making the whole trip a dream — which wasn't in the book at all, none of it. I even liked the way they fell asleep in the poppy fields and were awakened by Glinda's snow. I remembered Li had said Yin-mi was like Glinda, and I liked that, the coolness and the purity of snow and how it cleared the senses, that was right. I didn't miss the Queen of the Field-Mice, except that without her to rescue the Lion, the Tin Woodman couldn't say: "We must leave him here to sleep on forever, and perhaps he will dream that he has found courage at last." For that was my favorite part of all. They did save him in the end, though. I was glad they saved him, too, even if somehow it interfered. (Interfered with what, I'm not sure; with the truth, with everything.)

•

After the film, keyed up with a smooth, unfrantic energy, remote within ourselves, we ambled through the maze of streets south of Houston almost as far as Chinatown (turning back by tacit agreement before we reached it), a serene and mournful glide. Many times I've tried mentally to retrace the route we took, but always at some point the thread snaps and the labyrinth swallows us.

Most particularly, I've attempted to recall the precise location of a little shop we visited. All I remember now is a reassuring yellow aura bathing the sidewalk of a dark, deserted street awash with garbage on both sides, silent except for the harsh, flat echoes of our footsteps and the cries of two cats fighting or mating in an alley, a series of eerie, plaintive moans, erupting in squalls of violent oaths and hisses. It must have been midnight or a little after by that time; it was odd to find a shop open in an empty street like that. Yet we were glad to find it, both of us a little cold with the walk and not entirely sure where we were. It was run by a Vietnamese man of Chinese extraction, who stood over an upended crate doing computations on an abacus. He eyed us as we entered, then went back to his arithmetic, leaving us to browse.

The place was as much like a warehouse as a shop, filled with the smell of hemp and rattan from stacks of baskets, fans, and wicker chairs, most of it cheap and poorly made, lowering over the narrow corridors through which we walked. At the rear, though, the character of the store changed to that of a curio shop, with expensive items carefully arranged in glass cases. There were exquisite displays of hand-painted bone-earth china, thin and lucent as dogwood petals with the light behind them; wonderful dolls too, and puppets; painstakingly painted paper fans; lanterns juggling overhead, creating a festive atmosphere. What caught my eye immediately, and Li's, was the display of netsuke. There were only a dozen or so, all fine: a peculiar compound beast out of Japanese mythology I didn't recognize, with the head of a dragon and the body of a lion; naturalistic pieces — a mother pig suckling her brood; a cicada, the antennae, the compound eye, the tympanum, the corrugated spiracles on the belly, the ovipositor, all meticulously observed and carved. After a brief survey, we both fixed in unanimous fascination on one particular carving of a monk — at least from one side he appeared to be a monk. The opposite profile revealed something else entirely. In lieu of robes he wore a garment of shaggy, matted hair, strewn with rotten leaves and wisps of straw, only it wasn't a coat at all (or rather, was, but in the primitive sense: one that did not come off) as one saw from the foot, which, unlike its opposite member — a bare human leg shod in a bast sandal — was a furry padded paw with four clawed toes and a dewclaw, hanging sinister and vestigial above the "wrist." His face, too, segued seamlessly into an animal's, a badger perhaps, or a bear, it was impossible to say.

"The changeling," a voice behind us said in Cantonese. "They all come back to that one in particular. I'm not sure what it is about it." Rounding the counter, the owner took his key ring out and unlocked the case. Placing the piece on the glass, he rotated it slowly for our perusal, frowning at it as he did so. "It's supposed to represent a reprobate bonze, one who sold his soul to fairies for superhuman powers. The changelings were blamed for the disappearance of livestock, young girls' pregnancies, and so on." He saw me blush as Li caught my eye. "Oh yes, they were supposed to be quite the seducers, no young girl was safe."

"Are you sure he was a Buddhist?" Li asked mischievously, speaking for my benefit. "His head isn't shaved. Isn't it possible he was a Taoist?"

The owner shrugged indifferently. "For my own part I'd just as soon get rid of it. It's excellent work, but . . . I don't know. I've never liked it." He closed his fist around it and peered at me with a fractional smile. "Are you interested in buying?"

"I'm not so sure I like it either," I replied.

"Oh, but I do!" Li protested.

Her eyes sparkled with such petition and delight that I was swayed. Taking out my wallet, I raised my eyebrows to inquire the price.

At length we found our way back to a main thoroughfare and caught a cab. On the ride back up we sat huddled in the back seat, examining our purchase with wondering fascination.

"Synchronicity," Li pronounced once in a quiet voice, more to herself than me, "our finding it now like that."

My thoughts kept returning to the movie. The bestial foot might as easily have been a lion's as another animal's. I pictured the farmhand Hank, captured in the changeling midway in his transmogrification, halfway between man and animal, straddling the magic looking glass between Kansas and Oz. "Strange," I mused, "that in that purer dreamworld Hank should be an animal, whereas in Kansas he's a man. I can't help feeling it should have been the other way around."

"Maybe that's the point," Li suggested.

We were silent the rest of the way home.

•

To cut the chill we decided to take a shower together. Li knelt down and washed my thighs and calves with scented soap, pressing deeply, soothingly into the warmed muscle as the chrome shower head rained its warm jets over my back. In the heated updraft a fine spray billowed over my shoulders, dampening her thick, heavy tresses, pinned in a loose chignon. A few wisps trailed onto the nape of her neck. Her vertebrae were like a path of stepping-stones in the middle of two braiding rivulets of silver water that flowed in parallel flumes down her back and coursed together as they funneled through the steep ravine her buttocks made. She worked with expert hands, like a masseuse, and as she finished she reached up and took my penis in her soapy fingers, sliding each cupped palm in turn down its length with the motion of a cat pawing at a piece of furniture, sharpening its claws.

After we bathed she rubbed me down with oil until the water beaded on my flesh, then allowed me to anoint her likewise. Her body was soft and flushed with the moist, tropical heat, lightly but firmly muscled under the flesh, lithe, tight, beautiful. I rubbed her breasts with a barely restrained hunger, two small, but ample plenitudes in the deserts of her feral leanness. As she bent down, back to me, drying her feet, I noted the slight, strong wishbone of her pelvis, separating at her thighs and curving inward toward the knee, the empty space through which the reflection from the tiles broke, silver-white, like the glint from a blade, silhouetting the knoll of tangled underbrush between her legs. My old ideas about chastity struck me as vaguely laughable now, like conventions picked up from medieval poetry. What was the point of it all supposed to have been? I could remember everything but that.

Yet sometimes I dreaded making love to her, intimidated by her experience, partly, but even more by the desolation which attended her satiety, a kind of viciousness which preceded her withdrawal into a private place of inconsolable pain. That night was no different. Sitting up against the headboard with one knee propped up, she bit her thumbnail and took the cigarette I passed her in a preoccupied manner. I watched with tender anxiety, no better able to deal with these moods of restive introspection than I had been that first night.

"What's the matter, Li?" I asked gently after a while. "It frightens me and breaks my heart when you withdraw like this. Please talk to me. Tell me what I can do to make you happy."

"I'm just thinking about it," she muttered, taking her thumbnail from between her teeth, examining it critically, avoiding my eyes.

"About what?"

"The way she looked at you, the way she kissed you on the mouth," she replied bitterly.

"Let it go," I implored in a weary tone.

She shrugged, continuing to bite her nail. "Whatever you say."

"Let's talk about something else," I suggested.

She smiled to herself. "All right, I'll tell you a riddle." She dropped her hands in her lap and assumed her well-known air of provocation. "The Scarecrow wants a brain," she began. "The Tinman wants a heart. The Lion wants courage. Which one are you most like?"

I almost said the Lion, but, after considering, changed my mind. "Dorothy perhaps," I suggested.

"Who wanted only to return to Kansas," she observed with a frown, drawing her own inference.

"That isn't what I meant."

"Or Oz," she continued, following her own track, "who wanted everything." She fixed on me. "Oz was a changeling too, in a sense, wasn't he? Remember in the book, 'The Great Humbug'?"

"I don't know what you mean," I said.

"Don't you?" she taunted. "I just mean that the changeling is a better image, truer at any rate."

"Truer than what?"

"Than the Inca boy, for instance." Something mean and spiteful appeared in her face, which quickly changed to earnest fury. "Seducer of young girls. You'd better stay away from her" (her voice became an icy whisper) "*bastard.*"

"Bastard" — the word pierced my heart like the cold tip of an ice pick. The intensity of her hatred was almost pathological. It chilled my blood. All the poetry, all the generosity of motive, all the wordless intimacy of that long afternoon and night . . . shattered with a single blow.

Without responding, I curled up and went to sleep, dreaming of a green sun rising over Oz, the Lion asleep among the scarlet poppies, the blood flowers, never having to wake up.

Chapter 14

If my personal life was foundering in dissatisfaction and unhappiness, in business things had never been running more smoothly. Our power on Wall Street had begun to consolidate. In its first quarter of operation, Mutual Bull outperformed the rest of the funds by an average of over 100 percent. Our more exclusive private portfolio management service scored similar successes. Kahn and Sun Enterprises was the hottest operation on Wall Street. Partial thanks were due of course to Kahn, whose advertising campaign demonstrated consistent brilliance. Our weekly full-length spreads were awaited by the financial community with the same avid hunger with which housewives attend the latest developments in the soaps. My fat friend's talents as an advertising man and capitalist poet had been vindicated. Major thanks, however, were due to the simple, no-nonsense testimony of the company's financial balance sheet, in the final analysis the most eloquent advocate of any capitalist enterprise.

Millions were rolling into our coffers weekly. A spirit of euphoria reigned in the offices. We had expanded our square footage, taking over the whole of the twenty-first floor, hiring new account executives, secretaries, and switchboard operators, who worked in shifts around the clock. The latter expedient became necessary in part because of the volume of calls we were receiving, but also because our clientele was spreading from the East Coast westward. We had to accommodate ourselves to investors on Rocky Mountain and Pacific time. The increase in service was converted into further promotional fodder: "Now You Can Get Bull on the Horn 24 Hours a Day!!!"

Due to the immense popularity of our operations there, we were obliged to open branch offices in Los Angeles. If possible, the craze in that city exceeded even that in New York. A rash of bumper stickers broke out on the chrome posteriors of Mercedes-Benzes all over that city: "Bulls have bigger horns!"; "I'm horny, how about you? (Honk once for 'yes,' twice for curb service)"; "Get a piece . . . of the Horn"; "Bull gets more raw hide!" Ingenuity run amok; Kahn's tic was catching.

The large weekly newsmagazines — *Time, Life, Newsweek, U.S. News and*

World Report — likewise "did" Kahn and me. (The business press — *Fortune, Forbes, Business Week* — by this time had long ago come and gone.) One day, a reporter duly arrived in our offices, a tall, gaunt, elderly man in a wrinkled madras jacket and a polka-dot bow tie, with sunken cheeks and steel wire-rim glasses. These he breathed on, wiping them with his handkerchief, as he looked around waterily with an expression of bilious wonder. Catching sight of him through the two-way mirror, Kahn, who was in my office discussing some reports, nudged me with his sheaf of papers, unconsciously lowering his voice. "See that guy?"

I nodded.

"Take a good look at him. That's Ernest 'Bones' Hackless, the éminence grise of the yellow press."

"Hackless," I repeated musingly. "He's the guy who wrote those articles about my grandfather and my father."

Kahn nodded grimly. "Kid, he's chronicled the fortunes of the Loves from the beginning, always just ahead, like a pilot fish, or just behind, like a vulture. It looks like now he's come for you."

I swallowed hard. "Maybe he doesn't know about the family connection."

"Maybe," Kahn said unencouragingly.

"What do you suppose he wants with me?" I asked.

"What else?" Kahn replied cryptically and started to withdraw.

"No wait, Kahn!" I cried. "Don't leave me alone with him."

Kahn shrugged. "If you need me, kid. I'm not sure it'll help though."

I sat fidgeting in my chair while Kahn went out to fetch him. "Don't tell him!" had been my last request as he went out.

"I've seen a lot of things in my day, Kahn," Hackless was saying as they entered, "but this is truly rare." He pronounced the last word with an ironic emphasis and fixed on me.

I felt the blood rise to my face.

"Never say 'rare,' Mr. Hackless," Kahn bantered, "say 'well done' instead. At Bull Incorporated we like our Bull well done!"

Hackless acknowledged the pleasantry with a slight grimace, then crossed the room to me. "So, you're the little prince," he said, "Love's heir apparent, the next in line." Offering a bony hand, he smiled at me like a death's-head. "I always said Eddie Love was up to no good over there in Asia. You've got a big pair of black bedroom slippers to fill, little man."

As I shook his hand, I looked frantically toward Kahn for support, panicked at the mention of my father's name.

As though distressed to have to leave me to my fate, Kahn shrugged apologetically. "Sorry, kid — I told him. I couldn't help myself."

Hackless seated himself in the chair beside my desk and, taking out a penknife, casually began shaving down the point of a pencil. After a moment, he looked up over his shoulder at Kahn. "If you don't mind, your boss and I would like a word in private."

Though he blushed at the word "boss," Kahn was on the point of meekly obeying until I gripped him ferociously by the wrist. "We're full partners, Mr. Hackless," I said. "We keep no secrets from one another."

"Well, I didn't mean to imply anything derogatory by it," Hackless rejoined, raising his eyebrows.

"Besides," I continued on a more conciliatory note, "you have to remember I'm still a virtual immigrant. Kahn sometimes has to serve as my interpreter."

"Sound fluent enough to me," he remarked.

"Excuse please, could you repeat?"

He shrugged, and, finishing his surgical procedure on the pencil, tested its sharpness with a terse jab on a yellow legal pad supported on his crossed legs. "So then, gentlemen," he said, "what excuse do you have to offer for yourselves to the general public?"

The interview covered a great deal of widely varied ground (all of it, from where I was sitting, decidedly rugged). Most traumatic perhaps — with the possible exception of his allusions to my father, allusions in which the taint of that ugly, hated word "bastard" hovered just beneath the surface — were his repeated needling inquiries about our use of the *I Ching,* which he sensed was a sore spot with me.

"You claim you have in the *I Ching* what every speculator since the Babylonians has dreamed of," he said, in words that found their way unchanged into the finished article, "an infallible method, a speculative perpetual-motion machine, a philosophers' stone for Dowists, *a way of picking stocks that cannot fail.* Well, gentlemen, can you explain to me why not just anyone can use it? Why are people paying heavy premiums for your services when they might just go out, buy a copy of the book, and accomplish the same thing for themselves at home much cheaper? What's your secret anyway?"

I shook my head solemnly. "We have no secret."

He smiled at me indulgently. "You mean to tell me that anyone with three cents and a copy of the book can become a millionaire on Wall Street overnight like you have? Come on now."

"Theoretically, yes," I replied, "assuming they have a small fund of capital to begin with." I held his eyes, insisting silently on my candor, despite his expression of disgust.

Kahn, who was standing just behind my chair, decided it was time to mediate. "You've got the basic picture right, Mr. Hackless," he said, "but there's one important detail you've missed, and it makes all the difference. You see, the successful use of the *I Ching* in forecasting stocks isn't a matter of a secret so much as a simple condition, one that has to be met by the inquiring party. That's why Sonny here is so singularly well qualified to use it." He laid his hand proudly on my shoulder.

"And what 'condition' is that?" Hackless asked, looking not at Kahn but me.

"Purity of heart," my interpreter replied without a trace of irony or hesitation.

I felt the blood drain from my face.

"Sonny?" Hackless asked, managing somehow to plant a barb of irony even in the pronunciation of my name.

Had it been anybody else, I might have found the resolve to deny, deflect, or somehow excuse myself from answering, but this grinning death's-head of a man filled me with such overpowering and irrational hatred that I nodded tersely, then excused myself to the bathroom where I heaved up my breakfast.

To my annoyance, when I came back he was still there, leaning back in the chair, blowing smoke rings toward the ceiling, smiling cryptically to himself. Kahn had disappeared.

"I'm sorry, Mr. Hackless, but I've given you all the time I can spare," I said coldly.

"Oh, that's all right," he replied cheerfully, gathering his things. "I've found out pretty much all I need to know." He paused. "Just one more question." Our eyes met. "What next?"

"We have no plans for further expansion in the foreseeable future," I replied, "if that's what you mean. At Kahn and Sun we're quite happy with what we've achieved already."

"Come on now, that doesn't sound like Eddie Love's son talking," he taunted with a smile that was, despite his antagonism, almost affectionate.

I don't know why, but I smiled back at him — just barely. "Good day, Mr. Hackless," I bade him. And he left.

The next week my face appeared on the cover of *Your Money and Your Life* accompanied by this headline:

A NEW SUN RISES OVER WALL STREET:
SON OF LOVE (EDDIE LOVE)

In a style Kahn characterized as "gossip-column baroque," Hackless threw the details of my parentage like scraps of still-bleeding meat into the scandal-hungry jaws of America. Still, in the issue I found the article filled me not so much with shame as with a defiant pride. Let them talk. They couldn't touch me. I was way beyond the range of Ernest Hackless's turgid prose. That's why the General Public was hungry for the news, the bulletins from the front, from the frontier, the cutting edge. That's where Kahn and I were riding, and that's why Hackless's aspersions didn't compromise, but only enhanced, our power. Because it made us magical and other, outside the reach of law.

The only place where he drew any real blood was in the concluding volley: "Will this Sun outshine his father, or merely prove another gegenschein?" It was like a sly, insinuating whisper meant for my ears alone, and I knew it. "Don't go 'way!" he wrote. "Here at *M&L* we'd bet *Your Money and Your Life* there'll be a sequel. Stay tuned!"

" 'Will this Sun outshine his father?' " For a reason I couldn't satisfactorily explain, that question stuck with me, at first only as a faint echo resounding occasionally in some unfurnished chamber of my brain, but as time went on, more and more as a sort of furious, unconscious tic, like a scratched recording stuck on a single, endlessly repeating note. In the beginning I thought it was the implied question concerning the sincerity of my filial piety that bothered me, and though that answer served in part, the division left a remainder, something undigested.

I had no leisure to puzzle it out though. Not then. We were too involved in trading. By this time our operations had become so large that, to a great extent, our investment predictions had become self-fulfilling prophecies. Not only were we in the position materially to enforce our choices on the market, employing the tremendous weight of our capital assets (there are always limits to how far one can go in this direction); psychologically our leverage had become virtually unbounded, extending as far as the limits of imagination itself, down to the very taproot of human fear and greed. The contrarians who dared to buck our trend were few and far between. For, protected by the magic power of our fetish, we had never yet gone wrong. We were fey, and when we nodded toward a sacrifice or favorite, Wall Street toed the line, bringing the ax or the laurel. As a curious corollary of this state of affairs, the *I Ching*, which had given us our power in the first place, became virtually obsolete, as though in fulfillment of the seventh song from *Ten Bulls:*

> Only on the Bull was he able to Return.
> But, lo, the Bull has disappeared now;
> The Ox-herd sits alone, settling into the long labor
>   of forgetfulness.
> The sun has touched the zenith of a windy sky.
> In the afterglow of an accomplished task, the Ox-herd dreams
>   a cloudless dream.
> The whip and bridle lie abandoned in the empty hut.

> A snare becomes obsolete when the rabbit has been trapped. The
> salmon lies in a golden haze upon the platter, so what use is the net?
> The gold has flowed clear of the smelting dross; the moon has
> broken through the clouds; a beam of virgin light illuminates the
> world.

Yes, the *Changes* was the instrument, the dark web of the seine in which we had brought up the wriggling, flipping, silver gleam of Wall Street's deepest aspiration, and now the instrument was useless; we were in possession of the thing itself. There was a delicious irony in this that Kahn refused to see. When I suggested that we spare ourselves the pains of consultation, he became grave and admonitory, totally unlike himself. Turning and turning the bracelets on his wrists, he insisted that we cling "religiously" to the security of the ritual. I noted with amusement that he had become more the Taoist than I. Though I continued, for his sake, peremptorily going through the motions, in my heart of hearts I had lost interest. For it no longer mattered.

And not only because of our psychological leverage; there was another reason why casting the coins had become superfluous. Since that day in Kahn's office when I first noticed my inexplicable power to warp the pennies in their trajectories, my control had solidified. The last few consultations we had made together were thus a banality for me. For I foresaw the harvest even as I sowed the seed, and, more than that, I actually caused it by a conscious act of will. Kahn, of course, knew nothing of this, the threshold I had crossed within myself, and for reasons of my own I didn't choose to tell him.

Not only did I cultivate this power with regard to individual stocks, I attempted to exercise it in the market as a whole. The necessary concentration eluded me except in moments. But that rare instance of success! How can I explain to the uninitiated the effect such power had on me? Imagine: as though the whole trajectory of creation were compacted down on a financial chart into the single trend-line of the Dow, a black thread trailing from the spinarettes of the Great Black Widow as she constructs the square-ruled grid of her web, which is the universe itself . . .To concentrate and by a conscious effort of the will make her, make *it,* actually change direction — to move the Dow! It was a delight, I sometimes think, too sweet for mortality to bear, putting one's head like that against the bountiful, yielding breasts of that primordial female and *hearing the actual heartbeat of the world,* I have never found anything to equal it.

Coming down off these wild, impossible highs, the sense of degradation returned, blacker and blacker. I renounced all my unholy pleasures with oaths and tears. More and more I was subject to peculiar visionary episodes. Peering in the fountain in the park one day on my way to work, I saw seven pennies arranged like a brazen constellation in the precise configuration of the Bear, and for a moment that wishing well pierced right through the core of the earth, opening into China's night, the eye of darkness in America's light, America, *yang* of the world! Closing my eyes, I felt myself lift from the earth as though tornado borne, whirling through whistling eternities of space and time, cold tears of speed streaming from the corners of my eyes. I heard the sounds, smelled the smells, for an instant was actually there, in China. But there was a catch. When I opened my eyes it disappeared, all except the tears. One day, I promised myself, I wouldn't open them, but like the Lion sleep on and on forever.

Even the thrill of trading didn't really last. Nothing did. Soon we found ourselves plotting further "synergistic" diversification into other financial-service markets. First we allocated funds for a research division, publishing a bimonthly newsletter called the "Hornbook Primer," which examined market strategy in the light of traditional Taoist wisdom. Then we got into arbitrage, calling our foreign currency division "John Bull" at Kahn's insistence. Finally we entered the gold market, importing a team of gnomes from Zurich to head up operations in "Gold Bull-ion, Unlimited." And each of these expansions required the absorption of some new enterprise small or large, run by men of poor, or middling, or decidedly exceptional abilities and great determination, who had spent the best part of their lives serving, or building from the ground up, the businesses we plundered savagely and with impunity.

I was like a great bear smashing into a beehive, breaking the wax seal of their treasure troves, their dark golden honey oozing out onto my paws. Furious as it made them, these industrious honeybees, they could not hurt me, though they could, if they chose, and sometimes did, sting me into a towering rage which in the end only worked to their disadvantage. No, when that rage of destruction was upon me, nothing could save them, not even capitulation. I smashed their tiny lives to splinters with a single swipe of my great paw.

Dropping the terrible bomb of our unprecedented power from a great altitude on the cities they inhabited, I watched with serene fascination as their tiny dollhouses, their factories and farms, whirled up like chaff in the hurricane of the nuclear wind. I saw the conflagration breaking out in the streets, observed the frantic, agitated movements of the tiny black specks (which were the people), heard at a great distance the anxious wailing of the sirens, but from that altitude there was no sense of horror, no tallying of personal costs. From there I could see the larger order unfolding, enfolding them and all their misery, like a kaleidoscope transforming with a logic that was always a surprise, a black time-lapse flower miraculously blooming out of the charred center of the earth. So beautiful. So beautiful. Strange, somehow it never seemed quite real. Perhaps I should have read that as a warning. For I know now that those moments of disembodied, hallucinogenic vision, as I floated like a god above the earth, were when I first — no, not first, but finally — put the wafer of the dark Communion to my lips and drank the blood of sin, which is only, finally, unconsecrated blood shed from an unwilling sacrifice in murder. It requires no Antichrist to mutter over it a spell of dark pollution but bears its own curse, which God himself cannot unloose — irredeemable through all the eternities, forever and forever, hell without end.

Yet at other times, equally vivid, I reveled in a joyous conviction of my own unequivocal salvation. I remember the morning when this first came to me, completely unexpected. Kahn had been showing signs, if not of actual regression, at least of a new restiveness and irritability that I was at a loss to explain. That day he was in my office complaining about one of our new subsidiaries, when it occurred to me that I'd been neglecting him of late, that perhaps what he was really asking for was attention.

"Come on, Kahn," I proposed, "let's get away for a few minutes and take a walk somewhere, like in the old days."

The readiness with which he accepted my proposal made me suspect my guess was right.

"That's just it," he complained as the elevator doors trundled open and we let ourselves be swept with the crowd into the third-floor lounge, "we're so swamped with busywork, all this corporate nurture, we never get a chance to do anything else. I mean, if I'd wanted to have kids, I would have gotten married, right? That's exactly what it's like, raising kids. You always have to go behind them picking up their dirty underwear. Don't think I'm complaining or anything, this is really great, all these takeovers and stuff. But don't you ever feel yourself getting the least bit antsy?"

I nodded paternally as we walked onto the gallery.

"You know what I'd really like, just once?" he said excitedly, like a kid. "To be back out there on the floor again, like the old days, dropping a big block on an uptick." He gazed wistfully down, then turned to me with sudden vehemence. "Hell, kid, I'm not a businessman, I'm a trader. You know that. And you can't teach an old dog new tricks, or an old wolf either, even though we've been pretty successful at giving an old dodge new twists." He grinned, then frowned. "Put in another way, you can lead an old tick to new dogs, but you can't make him drink, right? And that's what some of these operations are, dogs. That's what it's like for me, eating when I'm not hungry. Don't you see, kid, I'm not hungry for it anymore, not this. I'm stuffed. Up to here. What really doesn't agree with me is the continual vigilance. It's like marriage, the 'till death do us part' part. I always preferred my contract with a loophole. That's the chief attraction of floor trading. As it is now, we fuck 'em, then end up paying for it till we drop. Five minutes of fun in the sun and an eternity of housecoats and curlers and rolling pins (rolling pins . . . ah! for Doe and the good old days)." He shrugged apologetically. "I guess I'm just an incorrigible Wandering Jew, kid. I can't help myself. Kid? Hey, kid! You listening to me?"

"Hmm?" I asked, emerging from the trancelike state the motion of the floor had induced. "Oh yeah, Kahn," I said, "I hear you."

The truth was, however, I didn't really, not what he was *really* saying, though I should have. For as I stood staring down at the frantic throng, an odd sensation came over me. Perhaps it was only my eyes, but I became aware that I no longer saw the familiar images I'd catalogued through my experience in Wall Street, no longer saw the teeming Western prairie, or social insects, or a pantomime of human life, but something infinitely deeper — in fact, the thing itself. In a sudden resolution as beneath a microscope — a focus that was simultaneously a blurring, as in a slow-exposure photograph — the faces melted into one another, the bodies all dissolved into a single rushing stream. The activity was like the contraction and dilation of a mystic heart — most mystic, most material — the circulation of the blood from auricle to ventricle in the great heart of America itself. And then even these concrete attributes vanished, and I stood looking down, like God, at the ebb and flow of vast metaphysical tides of Tao, the marketplace become pure spiritual essence. It was then I asked myself for the first time, could it be that I had finally arrived, that this was it, the delta, that I was actually *there*?

Certain signs suggested it. I remembered the words from the *Tao Te Ching:*

> Without leaving his door
> He knows everything under heaven.
> Without looking out of his window

> He knows all the ways of heaven.
> For the further one travels
> The less one knows.
> Therefore the sage arrives without going,
> Sees all without looking,
> Does nothing, yet achieves everything.

"Does nothing, yet achieves everything" — didn't this describe to perfection the mastery I'd achieved over the market? And what was it finally but simple Taoist *wu-wei*, the actionless activity of a sage, *wu-wei*, which in its highest realization merges finally with *Te* itself, the *Te* of *Tao Te Ching*, the Way and its *Power, Te*, proof and vindication of the Taoist's long penance, the wages of enlightenment, an outward and visible sign of an inward and spiritual grace, the triumph over death itself?

And yet, something was lacking. Somehow the change was not as radical as I'd expected, not quite radical enough. In the lull of combat, I looked around and the world appeared the same, same as it ever was. Doubt gnawed at me again, and I questioned my attainment. For I aspired to a higher certainty beyond all doubt, a place where everything had changed and changed forever, somewhere over the rainbow on which my soul was drawn now like a dark arrow, aiming for the sun.

After the spate of takeovers, I began to feel an impatience similar to Kahn's. Only it wasn't trading I craved. An instinctual rage militated against complacency in me, furiously scanning for some possibility of greater stimulation, some further enhancement of life.

I began to have the same recurrent dream I'd had in China before my decision to leave Ken Kuan. Only now it was a full-blown nightmare, and the landscape was an urban one: New York. Now, too, I caught occasional glimpses of the beast, staring up at me through the grate of a sewer, or through the bright reflection on a shop window. A protean creature, sometimes it resembled a tiger, sometimes a bear, sometimes a tiger with the body of a bear. And sometimes, most chillingly of all, it had a man's face. Starting awake once in the middle of the night, I described it all to Li.

To my surprise, she laughed. "A Kalidah," she said.

"A what?"

"A Kalidah, from the *Wizard of Oz* — the book, not the movie — don't you remember?" She reached over to the bedside table and flipped open the copy I kept there to read myself to sleep. "The Kalidahs chased them across a fallen tree spanning a ravine where the Yellow Brick Road came to a sudden halt in the forest," she reminisced. "Remember? The Tin Woodman saved them by chopping it after they'd crossed over. Here it is — 'monstrous beasts with bodies like bears and heads like tigers.'" She closed the book with an air of finality. "You just need to find yourself some different bedtime reading." She grinned. "This is for adults."

But it didn't go away, my Kalidah. And after several days I had become so anxious I couldn't sleep at all. Then Li became more serious. One day she told me a story.

"A professor told us about it in class," she began. "I'd forgotten all about it till now, but I went back in my notes and found the reference. He was describing this tribe in Malaysia — the Senoi, I think they were called — who have a cult centered around dreaming and the interpretation of dreams. One of his examples, a documented case apparently, which makes it all the more remarkable in this connection, was about a little boy who dreamt he was being chased by a tiger and woke up screaming. In the morning his mother took him to the shaman, and the old man told the boy he'd made a serious mistake not to turn on the tiger and fight back, since the animal would sense his fear and return night after night, preying on his spirit, until the boy mastered his fear and confronted it. The old man told the boy to call his friends to help if the tiger proved too strong, but in any case not to stop fighting, since any lapse in concentration could prove fatal. When, and if, he vanquished the dream enemy, the shaman told the boy, he must demand a prize. It could be almost anything — a poem, a dance, the answer to a riddle — only it had to be demonstrably useful in waking life, otherwise no one would believe him.

"Why don't you try it?" she suggested in a quiet voice. "You've got nothing to lose." She smiled. "And don't forget to ask your Kalidah for a prize."

So I did. For several nights I fought with it, writhing, cold-sweat dreams that always ended in the heartbroken stalemate of the dawn, when we uncoupled and he escaped into the forest to lick his wounds. My dream friends spelled me: Wu came with his big bamboo, Scottie kicked the beast with his tennis shoes, poured rum over its head, and tried to light it with a match; the Cowardly Lion came, but mostly supervised from a comfortable distance; and I called for my father, too, but perhaps the dead can't hear us. On the third night, sometime toward morning, I finally prevailed. The Kalidah looked at me with tame, conquered eyes. "What do you want?" it asked me speechlessly, and I said "happiness and truth." It averred that it could bring me only one, and, after hesitating, I chose truth. The Kalidah then disappeared a long time in the forest, and when it returned it bore an apple in its mouth, which it laid tamely at my feet. Then it vanished like the Cheshire cat, leaving nothing but the smile, and that only for an instant, its teeth, like those painted on the nose of the P-40, exactly congruous with the bite imprinted in the fruit, in which, on looking closer, I now saw maggots teeming, flies buzzing their wings and squatting to defecate and lay their eggs.

And that was how the idea first occurred to me of taking over American Power and Light, "the APL of America's eye." The beauty of it ravished me. "Will this Sun outshine his father?" That would be the final test, the assault on the summit.

When I told Kahn about it, he just laughed. "APL? You must be kidding. Who do you think you are anyway, the Sun King, Louis Quatorze or something?" He grinned. "Or rather, the Sun Kid. Sonny Squat-tor-ze, Mafioso hit man, a.k.a. the Sun Kid, armed and dangerous to corporations. That's it — your new nickname, the Sun Kid."

"I'm serious, Kahn," I said in a quiet, deadly voice.

" 'I'm *serious*'!" he burlesqued. "Give me a break, will you? I'm going to get a hernia laughing like this. Before long you'll be running around here in your birthday suit telling everybody you're the emperor."

His irreverence made my blood boil. Kahn wasn't hearing me anymore either, not really. I became conscious of actually loathing him. Mastering my rage, however, I quietly impressed my point upon him. He assumed at last a measure of gravity appropriate to the situation.

"Kid, I ask you to reconsider. I mean, do you have any idea what we're talking about here? *APL.* Do you know how *big* it is? We're not talking just plain old everyday big big here. I mean *large,* stupendous, huge — *bi-ig*! I mean, Bull is big, but this is something else."

"Sure, APL's big, 'stupendous,' if you will," I answered. "But we've taken over corporations larger than ourselves before. The bank, for instance, there's a good analogy there. Like the bank, APL is large, slow, unexcitable, an elephant. The share price never fluctuates outside a narrow range. It pays a good dividend, sure, but it's a stock for grandmothers, on a par with T-bills and passbook savings. Say we go in there and offer twice the current market value, payable in warrants and debentures, with some convertibility. With our current price rising like it is, anyone in his right mind would jump at it. Even those grandmothers. It worked before, why shouldn't it again?"

He shook his head. "We're talking different orders of magnitude here, kid. Not even Bull could pull off a takeover of those dimensions."

"We must," I said.

"We can't," he replied.

"We will," I persisted.

"I'm begging you, Sonny," he impored. "Down on my knees. Put this out of your mind. We've done real well so far, but we're not impregnable. APL is the biggest corporation in America . . ."

" 'And thus, of course, the world' " I said ironically.

"It's . . . it's . . . it's insane, that's what it is! If you insist on this, I'll . . ."

"You'll what?" I asked.

"Why I'll . . ."

I glared at him.

"I'll quit!"

"You wouldn't."

He smiled tauntingly. "Wouldn't I?"

"Kahn," I said, warning, beseeching, "don't do this to me. I've never asked you for anything before. This, I'm asking."

"Why?" he whispered, as though the point of it were totally opaque to him.

"Because I have to."

A look of rare tenderness appeared on his features. "You're that unhappy?"

I recoiled with surprise. "What does unhappiness have to do with it? It's a business proposition."

He shook his head. "This isn't business, kid," he averred. "It's something else, I'm not quite sure what. You can't ask me this."

I stared at him increduously. "Can't ask? *Can't*? After what I've done for you?"

He blushed, then turned pale. His lips trembled as he spoke. "You've been good to me, kid, I admit it. I owe you. Ask me anything, but not this. I beg you. I'll do anything else, but I'm not going to climb aboard your funeral pyre and set myself alight. That may be the way they do things in the East, but as I told you once before, a different protocol is operative in Manhattan."

"But why look at it that way, as a suicidal auto-da-fé?" I protested. "It could just as easily be a triumph."

Kahn's expression suddenly grew doleful. Unconsciously he touched his copper bracelet. "What can I tell you, kid? My little voice says no."

I scoffed. "Your little voice is a squeak, Kahn, distinctly mouselike. You're losing your nerve. Where's your chutzpah? What happened to 'no balls, no glory' — the battle cry of Ashkenazi warriors? What is this, Hasidic Complacency, H.C.?"

"Laugh if you want, kid," he said sadly, "but I'm telling you up front. If you insist on going ahead with this, I'll quit. I mean it."

"After everything . . . ?"

He nodded solemnly. "Try me."

"And what if I *were* unhappy?" I asked. "What if I told you everything for me was riding on it? What then?"

"Ah, kid, kid," he sighed, shaking his head, "don't make me pay for this. Don't do it to me. Don't do it to yourself."

"I'm unhappy, Kahn," I said.

He smiled with wistful sympathy. "Your angst is such an exquisite savor not half a dozen men alive in the world today could appreciate it. Don't throw it away. It's still new to you, but you'll learn. It's an acquired taste."

"Kahn . . ."

"No."

"I'll never forgive you for this."

"Maybe not," he said, "but some day you'll thank me for it."

So I backed down, temporarily. But his resistance only crystallized my resolve. In my heart I seethed and plotted. In utmost secrecy I appointed a few trusted confederates to begin reconnaissance toward the articulation of a comprehensive battle strategy. They began the compilation of a top-secret dossier on APL, which we code-named "The Dowager."

Constrained in my ambitions, my restiveness and frustration carried over into my personal life, or rather, found their perfect mirror image there. Li had begun behaving curiously. I caught flashes of her frustration during the take-over phase but, being too busy to deal with it, dismissed it as unimportant. In the lull now, however, I began to see it more and more. I watched her closely. Sometimes she would become taciturn and introspective for whole days on end. Then her mood would break, and with a vehemence that created its own emotional shock wave she turned on me, accusing me of incoherent sins, saying first that I neglected her, then complaining that my clinging, claustrophobic closeness was smothering her. The phase of the moon shifted again and she lavished me with tenderness, or became possessive and tyrannical. One morning when I came in for breakfast she was sitting with her coffee cup in both hands, blowing it lightly as she peered through the rising steam. She appeared calmer and more settled than I had seen her in some time. "I'll be late coming home tonight," she said. "Don't wait up for me."

I regarded her in solemn inquiry.

"There's a deadline coming up for a thesis draft," she said into her cup. "I've hardly done anything at all these last few weeks."

"You'll be at the library?"

She nodded, blowing her coffee.

I was lying wide awake when she came in. Trying to be very quiet so as not to wake me, she tiptoed to the bed and leaned over me. "Are you awake?" she whispered.

I didn't stir.

She stood watching me for a long time, then I heard her pad across the carpet. The bathroom door clicked shut. I saw the line of yellow light flash on beneath it. The toilet flushed. She turned on the shower. I rolled over on my side facing the wall, sick with grave suspicions.

The next morning she left early, and I rummaged through the wastepaper basket like a thief, with obsessive, greedy, unhappy curiosity. I found a paper carton of douche, with a picture of a gauzy woman dancing happily through spangles of sunlight. "Vinegar and water," it said, "recommended by more doctors." Something turned in my stomach like a horrible secretion: "vinegar and water," I thought bitterly, "gall." Beneath the panic was a current of resignation, as of a loss absorbed already, discounted long ago. But I forced myself to draw back from the irretrievable, to refrain from drawing the conclusion.

The next night I couldn't sleep. I stalked the room furiously, like a caged tiger, waiting for her. On a sudden impulse I threw on my coat and went out. At the curb I hailed a cab and gave the driver the address of her apartment. I checked my keys. Yes, I still had the duplicate she'd had cut for me.

When Ramon looked over from the pay phone and saw me at the door, a fleeting gravity crossed his face. He recovered instantly, but I had seen it. I knew I had. Letting the phone hang, he came and unlocked the door.

"Hey, mon, long time," he said with that air of taunting camaraderie. "Wha's happeneén?"

"Is she here?" I demanded, boring into him with my glance.

"Hey, mon," he said, stepping back and raising his hands, "I don't know *noth*ink, see? Nothink."

I stalked by him to the elevator.

Walking softly down the hall, I lowered my head as though following a trail, listening for voices. Nothing. I stood outside the door, very still, hardly breathing. My heart was racing. I slipped the key in the lock very quietly and turned the knob. The door opened, then caught. The night chain. She was there. She had to be. Maybe she was only studying. "Li," I called. No one answered. She might be asleep, I told myself. "Li," I called again, louder. Still no reply. A sudden fury seized me. "*Li!*" I shouted. "Open the door. I know you're in there." Panting, furious, I paused to listen. I heard bolts slipping up and down the hall. Doors cracked all around me.

"Who is it?" a woman whispered.

"What are you staring at?" I shouted, lunging toward her. "Mind your own business!" Shaking Li's door furiously back and forth against the chain, I kicked it savagely, slammed it, and stormed back to the elevators, not even bothering to lock it. Then I went home to wait for her.

When she came in, I watched her from beneath gathered brows, lowering, furious. "Cunt," I breathed viciously.

"Did you say something?" She looked up from her bag, which she'd been rummaging through.

"I said 'cunt,' " I replied.

She looked over her shoulder, as though perhaps I were addressing someone behind her, then back at me with surprise. "You mean me?" She touched herself.

" 'You mean me?' " I mimicked, scathingly effeminate. "You really think you can pull that shit? I know you were in there."

"What are you talking about?" She abandoned her bag on the floor, beginning to get annoyed. "In where?"

Her ruse was so transparent it disgusted me, adding insult to injury. I averted my eyes, seething, refusing to speak or acknowledge her existence.

"Boy, you must have had a lousy day," she commented hostilely.

"Galling," I said, flashing a triumphant look of vindictiveness at her. "Pure vinegar and water, recommended by more doctors."

She narrowed her eyes, regarding me with a queer expression. "Have you lost your mind?"

"It appears I've lost more than that."

"*What are you talking about?*" she screamed.

I snickered. "A douche box."

"A what?"

"A douche box — I found it in the trash this morning."

"So?" she said.

"Then it wasn't only my imagination?"

"No," she admitted. "I put it there last night. I got my period yesterday."
I glared at her.

"What?" she asked. "Am I missing something here? Have they passed a law making menstruation a capital crime?" She paused. "Punishable by having one's head bitten off in private?"

"Show me," I said.

"Show you what?"

"The blood."

She gazed at me incredulously, then her features contorted in a grimace of disgust. "You're sick," she hissed.

"All right," I conceded grudgingly. "Even if you're telling the truth, how do you explain the night chain?"

"What night chain?"

"Come on, Li, you know what I'm talking about. The night chain in your apartment."

"What about it?"

"How come it was locked *from the inside?*"

She shrugged. "How should I know?"

"You aren't serious?"

"I'm serious," she reiterated. "How should I know?"

"You damn well better know," I said. "You locked it."

She shook her head. "I think I'm beginning to get the picture."

"What picture?"

She flushed, eyes flashing. "You realize of course that a girlfriend of mine has been staying there for the past two weeks."

"Who?" I asked.

"Kay Ellis, from my Ph.D. program. You want to call her? Go ahead. You know the number."

I felt something tighten in my stomach. I looked at the phone, sorely tempted.

"You went there, didn't you?" she demanded furiously. "What did you do, try and break down the door?"

I gazed at her in sullen witlessness, unable to reply.

She laughed bitterly. "You want to know why the night chain was attached? I'll tell you why. She probably left by the fire escape, that's why, thinking she was being attacked by a maniac — which she was. You bastard! Damn you!" Searching frantically for some way to vent her wrath, she spat on the floor in fury, then burst into tears and, snatching up her coat, rushed past me, slamming the door behind her.

I was crushed. But maybe she was lying. No, nobody could act that well. Could they? No! No! No! I thought. No! What's happening to me?

When she came back it was almost dawn. Disheveled, pale, she regarded me gravely.

"I'm so sorry," I said in a quavering voice. Then I broke down and wept with my face in my hands.

Taking one hand out of her coat pocket, she laid it on my head, not stroking it, not playing with my hair, not doing anything. She smiled down at me, very remote, very introspective, very gentle, very cold.

For several days I overwhelmed her with tenderness. I doted on her, I waited on her. I bought her gifts. She accepted everything with that same remote, cold smile.

Then one day, to my surprise and ineffable happiness, sitting at the kitchen table blowing on her coffee, very casually, not even looking at me as she said it, she asked, "Remember that night you said you wanted to take me to Fairyland?"

I nodded.

"You asked me something else." She peered at me furtively over her cup, then took a cautious sip.

"I asked you to marry me," I supplied, my voice trembling with nervous excitement.

She looked up at me. "And do you still feel that way about it now?"

"Yes," I whispered, overjoyed. "Yes, yes, yes."

She took a long, slow sip of her coffee. "All right," she assented quietly.

"You mean it?"

"I mean it."

I was ecstatic for several days. Only the thought of Yin-mi, like a plaintive melody drifting in from another room, occasionally caught me up. It seemed incomprehensible. I had felt things deteriorating slowly. I had thought I was losing Li, and now suddenly . . . And her manner was so odd, that remote composure. But what had I expected? It didn't matter. Nothing mattered!

With her, though, it was as though nothing had changed. The remoteness had settled in like a seasonal change, like winter. And her absences, if anything, became more prolonged.

I wanted to make plans, tell everyone, but she asked me to wait. There were certain things she needed to do, certain things she needed to straighten out. She didn't elaborate, and I didn't ask, wanting to demonstrate my trust. And I did trust her. The only thing she said was, "I think maybe afterward I'd like to move."

"Where?" I asked.

She shrugged. "I don't know. To the country maybe. Can we afford it?" She posed this with tender reticence, almost timidly.

"Of course," I said, taking her hands and staring earnestly into her eyes, almost with pain, as though I'd deprived her. "Of course."

"Maybe the Hamptons," she mused.

It was only some time later that the thought of the estate in Sands Point occurred to me. It would require a lot of work, of course, but . . . Well, it was only an idea. Maybe she wouldn't like it. But certainly there was no harm in taking her there to look it over. It would be nice anyway, I thought. She should see it.

Chapter 15

This time, a parallelism: the upturn in my private fortunes presaged a quickening of interest at work, as, piece by piece, the Horns of the Bull — code name
of my cell of loyal cadres secreted within the larger Corporate Intelligence
Agency of Kahn and Sun (Intelligi-Bull) — began to assemble a clear picture
of the history and inner workings of American Power and Light. Though the
origins of the largest corporation in America (and thus, of course, the world)
were shrouded in mists, like the origins of the nation itself with its mythic ax
and cherry tree, its silver dollar skipped over the Potomac, I willingly suspended disbelief, ravished by the vision their researches opened up to me of
a veritable financial Fairyland, an Oz in the corporate mode. The old joke duly
made the rounds: "And God said, 'Let there be light'; and there was light,"
American Power and Light.

I don't know which thrilled me more: the thought of my upcoming marriage
to Li, or the as-yet unfulfilled dream of corporate connubiality. I played the
jealous lover there as well, phoning every fifteen minutes to check the winsome
Dowager's whereabouts on the Big Board. True love, I knew, was more than
I could hope to have, for APL was a Sphinx, as old and canny-wise as time
itself — two hundred years at least — and posed her fond, foolish suitors a
riddle few had answered. Consequently she'd been widowed many times, so
many, in fact, she'd been christened the Great Black Widow of the Dow. Alas,
my father had been one of her more recent victims. But what deep, soul-
satisfying drafts of pleasure he had surely tasted!

One of the few corporations extant today which was operating in the early
period of the republic, born with America, her twin and spitting image, APL
had not been delivered out of any womb by merely mortal generation, but
immaculately conceived; some maintained the Dowager had sprung full
formed from the craggy brow of Alexander Hamilton himself, like Minerva
from the brain of Jupiter. Hamilton, so this version went, conceived the notion
in an idle hour, returning to it with increasing frequency as the years went on,

until APL became his overriding passion. Far more than such minor projects as the National Bank, the public debt, or the good faith and solvency of the new republic, the corporation benefited from Hamilton's energies in his later years, which he passed in a state of high abstraction, like a man in a waking dream, or a mad scientist — a mad political scientist — drafting its charter and prospectus. But the infant corporation had not died with Hamilton, oh no! It survived, as all true and beautiful ideas survive, under the protection of Hamilton's great friend and patron, George Washington, Father of the Nation (and Uncle of the Corporation), who saw to its incorporation, though admittedly under a different name. Heart and liver of the nation, the corporation could never die, or go into receivership, as long as America itself should last. For it was as indestructible as matter, out of whose purest, most substantial stuff it had been fashioned, containing as little of metaphysical flatulence and the insubstantial gases of the spirit as could be managed.

And at last, after so many reincarnations, shaped by the Loves, it had attained corporate perfection, reborn within our time in its present guise under its present name. American Power and Light: what a fine ring those words had! Indeed, "as true a line of poetry as has ever been written in the New World," as Hackless had once said. The industrial base! There, there, and nowhere else had the greatest genius of America been lavished! Hsiao was right. The arts were little better than crude Neolithic scratchings on the walls of caves by savages with sticks, compared to her fabulous, her incomparable technology!

But enough apostrophe! I've forgotten myself in recollection of the ecstasy which my dream, my obsession, then aroused. Strange, after all that's come to pass, the purchase that vision still has upon my soul. Was I deluded or inspired?

But perhaps, Reader, you have yet to be initiated into the mystery rites of American high finance? Perhaps you pause to demand the black-edged outline of this corporate effulgence which so bedazzled me? In short, what were the assets and liabilities of the corporation (the latter, few and negligible), what its sources of revenue, its past and projected earnings, its prospects for future growth? A fair, indeed, a fundamental, question, and one that might fit more easily within the compass of a volume of American history than in the meager scope of my poor paragraph. Yet, ever your humble servant, I will attempt to enlighten you.

American Power and Light is more than a utility, though utilitarian in the extreme. She pioneered the concept of conglomeration, the original corporate omnivore. As utilities go, however, she is no slouch. In fact, she is the nonpareil of energy, source of that divine incandescence that lights the nation from within and makes America like a beacon and a watch fire to the world. And not light only, but heat as well, the heat that warms the lifeblood of the country. At present, the generators of APL are located throughout the length and breadth of the land, some fired by coal, some by oil, some by nuclear fuel; for, like it or not, though sensitive to public opinion, a repository of democratic virtues, the utility is hardheaded and pragmatic, and stubbornly adheres to what works.

But her holdings go far beyond the scope of the traditional utility. Long before electricity was invented, when America was still lit by spermacetti candles, she began the process of diversification, investing heavily in the whaling industries of New Bedford and Nantucket and synergistically expanding into shipbuilding concerns. On land, to secure her need for raw materials, she bought coal mines in Pennsylvania and West Virginia, and railroads to guarantee access to the mines. The purchase of track right-of-way made the utility proprietor of limitless tracts of virgin timber, oil wells, and more mines — gold and silver, tungsten, copper, iron. In more recent times, APL has invested vast sums in domestic oil exploration. Her offshore rigs probe the sea floor in regions as far apart as the Beaufort Sea north of Canada and the tepid waters of the Gulf of Mexico. From her primordial base in shipbuilding, she also turns out the supertankers necessary to retrieve our quota of Middle Eastern oil from deep-water ports in the Persian Gulf. As domestic steel production is a vital component of her shipbuilding capability, the oily waters of the Great Lakes shimmer murkily with the light of hellish meteors cast off from the furnaces of Buffalo and Gary, where subsidiaries of APL work round the clock, when not on strike, to produce the steel required.

With her holdings of natural resources, her extensive manufacturing plant, her steel and shipbuilding capabilities, it was only natural that American Power and Light diversify into defense production, turning out not only ships but airplanes, tanks, and assorted armored vehicles, not to mention ordnance, high explosives, firearms and ammunition, and other weapons of genocide and mass destruction, which during World War II pushed gross assets to an all-time high and made the corporation the largest in the world.

The production of heavy equipment for the military led APL after the war into the manufacture of cars and trucks, which became competitive with and eventually displaced the railroads, carrying goods to market over the new system of interstate highways, built by construction firms that were subsidiaries of the corporation too. Converting the wilderness into farmland, American Power and Light embarked in agro-business, hauling the timber to her own sawmills where the forests of America were converted into board-feet. This provided an entrée into the housing industry. Expanding her manufacturing capability yet again, she began to produce the dizzying array of tools which served the carpenter. Her automotive subsidiaries made pickup trucks and four-wheel-drive vehicles to haul the wood and tools to remote sites previously cleared of corporation timber, which now went into the corporation housing being thrown up on the spot — cutting down the forests to rebuild them. American Power and Light produced the trucks that hauled the tools she manufactured and the timber she cut and processed, fired them with gasoline she imported or produced, and then went further, acquiring textile mills to clothe the worker, whom she also largely owned, retail outlets to sell the clothes to him, commercial banks and Savings and Loans where he might borrow money to invest in those same trucks, tools, timber, housing, clothes. She took his hard-earned wages and fed him from her farms, and then she created Leisure to relieve him from his labor and send him back to work refreshed.

But Leisure — the American genius for which was expressed in the invention of the weekend — as you, Reader, are undoubtedly aware — only opened up new panoramas of free enterprise to the visionary entrepreneurs and impresarios who sat on the original board of directors of this paragon of corporations, tapping markets scarcely dreamt before!

First there were books, ponderous Bibles and treatises on commerce, devotional manuals, austere, heavy stuff, yet entertainment enough to bring a thin-lipped smile to a grim Puritan Father, sitting in his straight-backed chair of a winter's night in Boston, totaling his accounts receivable, as well as credits and debits in the larger double-entry ledger of his salvation, by a single, penurious spermacetti candle (also supplied by APL). But there soon followed the sweet bloom of lyric poetry, a greenhouse flower brought in fresh from Europe, whose stray grains of gilded pollen floating on the air, finding none of its own to fertilize, mixed with sturdier stuff, with pine and melancholy cedar, to produce a fierce, resistant strain of native song, the short story and the prose romance. This wild bastard, through successive generations, was improved, until it bore the rich, delicious fruit of the American Novel, large and full of meat, able to accommodate the diverse tastes of democratic multitudes, a form which could no more be improved on than the apple (or the APL!), but only tampered with, rendered monstrous, taken out of nature back into the hothouse of the diseased urban imagination, where it lost its firmness of flesh and that strain of virgin wildness, tart and bittersweet, from the days when it grew alone in the forests.

From this point on the types proliferated. Somewhere along the line — the production line, of course — came the institution of the press, an inalienable right on a par with life, liberty, the pursuit of happiness itself, to which it contributed its democratic share. The word was made flesh — very flesh — and newspapers were born (made, not begotten). These soon divided into twelve tribes and were scattered to the ends of the earth (some of them still wandering lost in the wilderness today), among them your *Times*es and your *Tribune*s, your *Sun*s and *Globe*s, your *Dispatche*s, *Gazette*s, *Courier*s, *Journal*s, *Sentinel*s, *Observer*s, *Post*s, *Constitution*s, and *Constitutional*s in all their various permutations, daily, nocturnal, biweekly, weekly (some more weakly than others), monthly, semiannual, annual, perennial, evergreen, millennial, and blessedly occasional. On these the infant populace was teethed, and also taught to read, leading, in addition, to a further Very Important Development.

In those days, the ladies lacked a proper forum for their views, and were forced to resort to the expedient of trading gossip by word of mouth, a slow, tedious, primitive, unscientific, grassroots type of operation ill-befitting the dignity of modern ladies (and difficult to carry out in heels). Thus the magazine was born, catering to the original special-interest group, whose unsurpassed lobbying techniques have been copied with degrees of varying success by all successors (as well as failures). Women's Liberation took its first halting step! And were the men nonplussed? Indeed they were! Grumbling and pouting, starching their own wing collars and ironing irregular creases in their knee-length underwear, they skulked off to work and pirated their wives' idea, creating their own publications on professional topics and sports, as well as magazines which presented Woman in a more nostalgic, more ideal, more desirable incarnation, which is to say, winsome, accommodating, and largely unattired. But a step in time to Forty-second Street, Reader, with its twenty-five-cent movies, its curtained cubicles rocking and groaning, reeking of sweat and something sickly sweet, its racks of bookshelves featuring exotic genitalia, different as the species in a florist's shop. And then, of course, the children wanted in, and out of the think tank of American Power and Light came comic books and *Boy's Life* for the more wholesome types, *Mad Magazine* for nuts and weirdos, and *Popular Mechanics* for whiz kids and budding greasers, not to mention *Teen Luv* for those pining unfulfilled of both genders.

But the printed word could never satisfy the growing appetite for entertainment which increasing Leisure bred. Books were too intellectual, took too much concentration, thought, and effort. After all, the weekend was for fun! Why not some form of popular entertainment that could satisfy the whole being (without taxing the mind)? As usual, American Power and Light came up with the solution. Radio, silent films, and, finally, as technology improved, the talkies! Hollywood! The Little Tramp and Captain Blood, Fred and Ginger, Marlene Dietrich, Garbo, Bette Davis, Citizen Kane and Capra, Cukor, Griffith, Garland, Cary Grant, Gary Cooper, and a cast of thousands impossible to cite without significant and unforgivable omission!

And out of the demise of RKO and MGM, not to mention the social fabric, arose finally the ultimate, the *nec plus ultra* of American entertainment, perhaps the single finest testament to the creativity and ingenuity of the nation — the tube! The box! T.V.!

One hesitates with deep humility before so vast a subject. What is there to say? It leaves us inarticulate with wonder! Is it enough to note that hour after hour night after night we sit with leaden faces (but full of joy inside), basking like monstrous, hydroponic vegetables in the sunlight of our double-wide T.V.s, heedless of the rays in which they bathe us, irradiating our testicles and ovaries with all the lifelike colors of the radioactive rainbow, insuring the viability of future generations by seeing to it that the gene pool doesn't stagnate, but continues to produce strange and wonderful mutations which, in accordance with Darwin's teachings, will either fail in the stiff competition, or else produce a better species, an Overman, who, unimpeded by the general frailty mortality is heir to, will soar up on eagle's wings (bald eagle's wings, America!) into the clear empyrean and there, in an act of glory — with a grin, a shrug, an "O.K." sign for the folks back home — instantaneously overcome himself and be made new into what we cannot even begin to imagine, and what's more, don't care to. O day of glory! Will we be privileged to see it in our lifetimes? *Homo sapiens,* having finally gotten it on the ball (or balls, collectively), will at last transcend himself and all the petty, embarrassing incidents of his parochial history. That old Greek ploy again, Reader, deus ex machina (where the machine is the T.V.). Isn't it always the case that man, poor, silly man, is getting himself into a scrape from which his gods, creaking and lumbering as they descend from the groaning rafters of this theater, the world, crowns and halos partially askew, suspended on block and tackle, must extricate him — us — by some magical suspension of the laws of gravity?

Television, of course, was the great masterstroke of APL's centuries-old campaign to blaze new trails of pleasure through the uncultivated wilderness of American consciousness (building economy motels and family restaurants, convenience stores, fast-food chains, factory outlets, package stores, used-car lots, and, of course, the Mall, enclosing all of the above, and more, a hermetically sealed, subterranean Carnival, only in reverse, with all the normal people locked in glass cages and the freaks let loose to mill and stare, a saturnalian circus for spelunkers, complete with fifty rings, bubbling colored fountains, and gigantic cellophane sculptures suspended from the roof, only cranking along to the sound of Musak rather than a steam calliope).

But the tube was supplemented by other sources, in particular, radio. What American has not at some time relieved those weary summer hours of impassioned boredom on beaches from Malibu to Coney Island with the aid of his faithful transistor radio in its black imitation-leather sheath, slightly wilted from the heat? Yet, even as I write, that great American institution has gone the way of all good things, becoming a technological dinosaur before its time. The transistor radio has lost out in the competition for its technological niche to the hi-tech, digital, push-button, Dolby-compatible radio-cassette deck, more familiarly known as the Third World Briefcase, which can be seen on the streets and subways of New York today carried on shoulder straps (or in small wagons for convenience), a necessity for some to whom the thought of walking a block without music to distract them and short-circuit any introspection resembling the oppression of thought seems intolerable. Thought, it appears, has been revealed as a type of intellectual imperialism invented by the upper classes to enslave the poor, the underprivileged, and minorities. Renouncing rational activity along with the other values which have sponsored the delinquent, imperialistic mentality of the West, the more radical members of these groups have plugged themselves into the jacks of their cassette decks for the duration, until, little by little, their cerebral cortexes atrophy and set them free.

The advances in electronics which led to these exciting possibilities have also yielded fruit for the home stereo, which has evolved from its primitive origins in the Victrola to become as important a part of the American domestic scene as indoor plumbing or a G.E. (subsidiary of APL) toaster-oven. For, to their credit, Americans are a music-loving people. After all, didn't Orpheus tame the wild beasts with his lyre (though it's never specified whether he used the instrument to serenade or bludgeon them to death)? American Power and Light encourages the artists of America to play whatever their genius calls them to, moog synthesizer, hammer dulcimer, Fender Bass or Stratocaster, tuba, pedal-steel, Wurlitzer or Flentrop, banjo, violin, piano, and, of course, that national albatross, the sousaphone, in any and all combinations, shake hands and come out squalling! The corporation pours money into the recording business, hiring producers, engineers, and, of course (guess who?), those corporate hyenas (always laughing, America! — at *you*), the advertising men.

And for less commercially feasible genres, to appease her corporate conscience (and obtain a write-off), out of her profits she hires archivists to reap and press in celluloid the rich wildflower harvest of America's ethnic music: bluegrass from the stony hollows of Appalachia, with its flavor of ancient Irish jigs and reels like the bite of hard, aged cider, and the blacker blues from farther south, played with a pick in Texas or finger-style up in North Carolina, a music created by blind musicians like Will McTell, who wandered the dusty circuit from church to fair, unassuming but presentable in his shiny, threadbare suit and cap, shoes without socks or laces, sitting on the edge of the chair staring with his haunting-haunted marble eyes, as he strummed and sang, lost in some fey parable of sin and dark redemption here on earth. And when the blues turned its eyes heavenward and saw the light of American evangelical Protestantism, the result was gospel, which found a home in Nashville, along with country-Western music, Hank Williams, Wailin' Waylon Jennings, Tammy ("Stand by Your Man") Whine-ette (Why not?). Out of New Orleans, via Chicago, New York, and San Juan, Puerto Rico, came jazz, which combined with elements of all the rest in the Universal Synthesis of Rock 'n' Roll, which enjoyed a brief High Renaissance (short-lived as a generation of laboratory fruit flies) in the sixties not long after I first arrived on these shores, before quickly degenerating into Mannerism with Punk and New Wave, and the mindless, exhibitionistic glitter of disco with its thumping, humping, metronomic, rabbit-mating rhythm. And thanks to APL, all this could, and can, be enjoyed at the push of a button, right in the home!

And then, to help us out of the self-inclusive pleasure domes it had created to amuse us, American Power and Light created nightlife: clubs and coffeehouses, discotheques and concert halls, places where we could escape our happy homes and get relief and needed distraction from our all-consuming Leisure, listening to our favorite types of music live, dancing, drinking to excess, sleeping with one another — and contracting venereal diseases, which opened up a further market in the field of pharmaceuticals, which Eddie Love, of course, had already tapped in timely fashion, anesthetizing the armed forces throughout the ordeal of World War II.

And the field of pharmaceuticals was, of course, unlimited. The corporation began to produce wonder drugs like penicillin, and birth-control technology. From there horizons widened. For with all the nightlife, America was badly in need of drugs, especially amphetamines, for dieters (Keep America Beautiful!) and those who simply found it hard to stay awake after a night's partying. Barbiturates followed as a logical consequence to counteract the speed and help us get to sleep. Then overdose centers had to be created in the hospitals, and APL set up drug rehabilitation clinics staffed with social workers, psychiatrists, psychologists, nurses, counselors, well-meaning people, and dispensers of good advice, setting an example for their patients to get their lives together and learn to use their time constructively.

Thus sports were born in the ghettos out of the insatiable American appetite for good clean fun! APL saw to it that every neighborhood in Harlem received a hoop and backboard made of sequoia, Douglas fir, or giant redwood and thus was linked symbolically with the countryside, the forest, the frontier, representing the unlimited possibilities of social and geographical mobility in America, hinting that every boy could be, with a little practice, if not the president, then Wilt the Stilt, or Havlicek! This created the original demand for sports equipment, so notable today: jogging shoes and elephant rifles, backpacks, bows and arrows, fishing reels and poles, ice picks and carabiners, pitons, and ropes for rappelling off the sides of mountains (or anywhere one damn well chooses!), golf clubs, cleats, tennis rackets, scuba gear, pigskins for the gridiron, pucks and sticks and skates for hockey, BB guns for small furred and feathered species, telescopic sights for long shots (skyscraper fun!), and much more, Reader, much, much more, as Americans pursue their pleasure on land, on sea, and in the air, dirt-biking, mud-wrestling, surfing, skiing, sailing, sinking, sipping, swilling, gliding, hang-gliding, hanging, hand-jiving, flying kites, B-52s, and helicopter gunships, raining incendiaries and .50 caliber machine-gun fire from on high, jumping out with parachutes to raze and terrorize, visiting death and holocaust and destruction on everything in sight! *Yahoo!*

But lest anyone think that American Power and Light squanders undue proportions of her capital on the pursuit of frivolous Leisure, let me hasten to add that in the opinions of many of the leaders of the financial community (who ought to know), the greatest frontiers left to business are within the human mind itself, the last new market to be tapped. More American dollars go toward the purchase of escape than to all other goods and services combined. APL is merely going with the flow, casting off all ballast and sailing into the sunrise of newer industries and a better tomorrow.

Such was the account the Horns, piece by piece, provided me, brought up to date by me for the Reader's convenience. At the time, innocent that I was, I was ravished by what I saw. The more I looked, the more appealing became the prospect of plundering and possessing such a prize — I, who had once been content (duped, Reader, duped — God damn to hell forever complacency and mysticism, which had enthralled me and sapped my natural ambition for a higher standard of living!) with "coarse rice to eat, cold water from the well, and the crook of a bent elbow for a pillow." But after all, I did have 50 percent American blood in my veins, which made it 100 proof, like sour mash corn whiskey or high-test gasoline, and that, combined with my Chinese racial instinct for gambling, produced a highly volatile and explosive mixture, like the fuel that propelled the Apollo astronauts to the moon. And I too dreamed secretly of being launched out of the realms of sublunary existence, landing on the luminous orb of Final Attainment, free at last, enlightened, sitting in the navigator's seat, the swivel chair of the chairman of the board and chief executive officer of American Power and Light, all the universe before me, and the vehicle that could navigate its vastness purring smoothly between my legs, ready to take off at a moment's notice, to travel at the speed of thought, following *him,* my father, to our fierce accounting in the black hole where he'd disappeared without a trace, a place I'd dreamt of darkly, but where I'd never had the spiritual technology to follow him. But I would have it soon!

It was only then, I think, that the idea finally dawned on me that all along, without really knowing it (yet trusting in my heart it must be so), I had been approaching closer and closer to my destination, destination original and final, and that at last, in a way I had not expected and could never in a million years have imagined, I was within striking distance, on the threshold. For suddenly I saw that this last financial conquest, the takeover of American Power and Light, was the final ascent into Enlightenment itself. There was no distinction. They were one. That was the final test and proof. If any knowledge could bring me into that dispensation which I longed for, be it terrible or sublime, this must be it. Beyond that veil, the seventh seal of my investment career, was the delta I had dreamt, where Dow at last flowed out into the vast Pacific of the Tao, mingling its troubled waters with that silent, endless blue. There the road disappeared into the destination, and I was home! It had to be, *had* to!

The joys of meditation ("the deep well-being which quiescence brings"), even sex, were as nothing to the feelings I experienced then, the exquisite tremors of a restless, far-seeing ecstasy, able to contemplate and move markets so vast that worlds could be bought and sold in them. As Columbus must have felt when he set foot in the New World for the first time, the virgin continent spread before him like a new beginning for mankind, so felt I. But one short step from realizing my dream, even now I stood gazing, like Moses from the summit of Mount Abarim, across the last barren mile of wilderness and desert into paradise, the Promised Land, after so long and desperate a journey.

But there was still one obstacle in my path, and thoughts of Moses and Mount Abarim brought it into painful focus. Kahn. What was I going to do with him? Could I really bring myself to cut him loose? Perhaps I'd have to, if he didn't yield. It could hardly be construed as a betrayal now, I comforted myself. His rehabilitation was complete (and then some!). And the emotional cost to me? That didn't count, I told myself. Not here. This was business.

Chapter 16

Having been informed by my secretary that I needed to see him on urgent business, Kahn strode in, took one look at me, and stopped dead in his tracks. Shaking his head, he emitted a susurrant sound halfway between a sigh and a laugh, then smiled a brilliant — too brilliant — smile. "So," he said.

"So, what?" I asked when it appeared he wasn't going to continue, mildly irritated by his manner. "I suppose you think you know why I've called you?"

"Isn't it obvious?" he replied. "All this earnestness and mystery, it's a dead giveaway. Look at your face. You look like the condemned man."

I smiled grimly to myself at the irony of his remark, considering our relative positions. "So what are you, a prophet?"

He shrugged again. "I come from a prophetic people, Sonny. I hardly need to be clairvoyant, though, to see what's been on your mind these last few weeks. You've been like a kid at Christmas with a new toy."

"Don't talk down to me, Kahn," I said.

He smiled at me wistfully. "Let's not make this any more unpleasant than it has to be, kid. I don't want to fight with you." There was something both resigned and imploring in his voice.

"Neither do I," I sighed. I considered what he'd said. "I suppose you're right, it must have been obvious."

He shrugged as though to say, "Can I help it if I'm a fucking genius?"

I smiled. "So."

We studied one another from a core of hard resolve, each set inalterably in his course. Yet as I looked at him, the melancholy pouches underneath his eyes, his sagging jowls, I felt the creeping irritation that lately had begun to poison our relationship start dissolving, pushed clear like silt by the current of the old affection.

"Yeah, kid," he said (feeling it too, I could see that), "the writing has been on the wall for some time now, hasn't it? We just never stopped long enough to read it. It's not just this APL thing. No matter what I said, I was listening when you brought it up. I don't agree with your arguments, but that's only one opinion. It doesn't make you wrong. I think you've got a fighting chance to pull it off. If anybody does, you do. It's just not for me, the whole shtick. Takeover, management, administration — I told you before, I'm a trader, not a businessman. I'm homesick for the trading floor, kid, can't you see that? That day we stood up there on the gallery, I could almost hear it, you know? Like the wolf heard it ringing in the mountains. I want to go back, kid. They'll take me now, if not with open arms with an open purse. You know as well as I do money can buy anything. I've been trying to break it to you for a while now in little ways, but you were too wrapped up in your own thing to notice. I don't blame you. We both were. We both missed a lot of signals. No more semaphore though, kid. I quit. I don't know how to make it any plainer. You don't need me anymore. Maybe you never did, except just at the beginning to give you a little nudge. I've taught you everything I know. I hope it's enough."

He shook his head. "No, you're way past me, Sonny. Nobody else can help you now, or really hurt you either, except yourself. From here on out I'd only be a weight around your neck dragging you down. I know it's something you feel you've got to do, but the guide has gone as far as he can go. This last stretch you've got to navigate on your own. That's the way it should be.

"And you know something else?" I shook my head. "I don't need you anymore either. Don't get me wrong. I don't want to sound ungrateful. I know what you did for me. I mean, if it weren't for you . . ." His voice caught in his throat, and his eyes gleamed with almost ferocious tenderness. "Well, you understand. I owe you all. You put me back on my feet again. I'll never forget it. I'm grateful." His manner suddenly hardened. "But I'm not going to kowtow to you for it, or enslave myself in guilt. Because I know, even if you don't . . ." (he narrowed his eyes as though trying to see in) "yet I think you do, deep down, you must: you also did it for yourself, did it, even, mainly for yourself. It was your ticket to the ball game, to the mysteries." He smiled. "And now you're there. It wasn't even really that hard, was it? *Facilis descensus Averno*, remember? I said one day you'd understand. Maybe now you do."

"Maybe," I said. "Only this isn't hell."

"No," he conceded, pouting thoughtfully, "it isn't." Then he flashed that incisive, predatory grin. "But maybe it's something just as good."

Our eyes met on it for a long moment. "So," I said.

"So." He shrugged his shoulders. "I guess that's it, huh?"

"I guess it is."

He laughed. "I'm kind of disappointed."

"I'm sorry."

"Oh no, not about that," he said. "After all, I was the one who quit, wasn't I? Even if you were going to fire me, or retire me to the back room, or whatever you had in mind. I guess I just sort of expected you to protest a little more, that's all. I mean, after all, am I really that expendable? Who's going to interpret the oracle for you?"

"I don't need that anymore," I answered.

He raised his eyebrows.

I closed my eyes and shook my head. "Not for a long time. All that was for you."

"Oh?"

I picked up the cup on my desk in which I kept the coins, shaking them into my palm. Closing my eyes, I made a fist. "When I hold them now," I whispered, hoarse with passion, "I can see the final pattern of the toss." Steeling myself to the look of disbelief I knew I'd get, I opened my eyes.

"You mean . . . ?"

I nodded. "Before they fall."

There was distinct anxiety in the incredulousness he turned on me. "You're kidding, right?"

I shook my head. "I'm serious, Kahn."

He didn't smile.

"I didn't expect you to believe me."

"Well, you were right, I don't."

"So what point is there in protesting? We've lost our synergy, Kahn. You don't believe in me anymore, and I don't . . ." I caught myself up.

"Go ahead," he insisted, smiling with a trace of bitterness. "Finish it. You don't believe in me. What's the matter, you think I'm too old for such fast action? Or maybe that whole thing with Doe took something out of me, maybe I lost my nerve?"

I blinked noncommittally, cruelly dispassionate. "You said it, not me."

"Yeah, I said it all right." He got up in a huff.

"Maybe it's for the best, Aaron," I observed. "This way I have no one but myself to worry about. If I go down I won't have to drag you with me. You won't have to share the blame."

"Or the profits," he pointed out cynically.

"Or the profits."

"All right," he relented. "At least you admitted it. Now it's out in the open. There's nothing else to discuss."

"Don't go away angry," I said.

"What's the matter," he asked, briefly reverting, "afraid I'll stick it to you on the way out the door?" His eyes flashed, then he repented. "I'm sorry, kid. You don't deserve that. And you don't need to worry. I'll divest myself of my interest in Kahn and Sun discreetly (I guess it'll just be Sun Enterprises now, huh?), so as not to scare down the price. That's the last thing you can afford now, a falling price."

"I appreciate that," I said.

"I don't suppose you'd care to buy my shares yourself?"

I shook my head. "I can't. I'm going to have to plow everything I have into APL if I'm going to get a foot in the door. I would like to know who gets it, though."

"Sure," he promised. "Not to worry. I'll do even better than that. I'll get rid of them slowly in small lots. I owe you that at least."

"Thanks, Kahn."

Having nothing else to say, yet neither of us quite yet wanting to let the other go, we fidgeted in an embarrassed silence.

"What will you do now?"

He shrugged. "Who knows? Take some time off. Do some reading. Maybe visit Israel, look up Herschel. He's probably over there on the West Bank somewhere, a little old long-beared ben Torah in a knitted skullcap, leading a bunch of miniature Herschels complete with beards and earlocks to school, carrying a Talmudic exegesis under one arm and a Uzi under the other. Maybe I'll even enroll in a kibbutz. Can you see it? The new all-natural Kahn. Back to nature. Hell, kid, while I'm about it maybe I'll even enter a Taoist monastery and study the *I Ching* for a few years." He noted my look of amused skepticism. "Okay, so it's a long shot! What's the matter, you think I can't hack it or something? Listen, kid," he confidently averred, "if you can become a Dowist, I can become a Taoist."

"Once a Taoist, always a Dowist," I pronounced ambiguously.

"Right," he replied. "And vice versa."

I laughed.

"One thing I think I will do for certain," he went on musing.

"What?"

He stroked his head. "Get a hair transplant." He appeared ready to pounce on any twinge of judgment.

"A hair transplant?" I asked as neutrally as possible.

"Yeah, you know, for my head."

"Oh." I winced a little as I smiled.

"What's the matter, too unnatural for you?"

"Well . . ." I hedged.

"Don't be bashful. We may as well get it all out now while we've still got the chance. So what were you going to say? I want to hear this."

"Well, since you ask," I began, "I've always thought you'd look more . . . 'distinguished' if you'd stop trying to hide it. It's a natural occurrence after all. I don't understand why it bothers you so much."

He nodded, repeating my phrase, " 'Why it bothers me so much.' You want to know why it bothers me?" he demanded with sudden heat. "Want me to tell you why? Because it's part of me that's dying, that's why." He stabbed his chest with his thumb. "Me, kid. Not you. Me. It's mortality, that's what it is. And it's arrived on the scene prematurely. I'm not ready to start dying yet."

"But it's part of life, isn't it?" I asked quietly.

"Oh, that's profound," he remarked scathingly. "That's positively pythonic. Is that a nugget of Taoist wisdom or something? Here" — he reached toward my desk — "give me a pen and paper. I want to write that down so I won't forget it. 'Dying is a part of life.' Um-hm. Real nice."

"I'm sorry, Kahn," I apologized, "I didn't realize you were so sensitive about the subject."

"Sensitive! I'm not sensitive! What makes you think I'm sensitive?" He couldn't repress a slight smile.

"I saw that," I teased.

"So what are we supposed to do?" he went on, ignoring me, "just lie down, spread our legs, and let entropy fuck us? Is that what enlightenment is? Huh? It is, isn't it? Admit it. In the final analysis, after all is said and done, that's all the Tao is — entropy. And the Taoist motto is, 'You can't win, ergo, don't try,' and beyond that, 'love it,' 'happiness is reveling in your own degradation, thermodynamic rape.' " He snickered. "You still trying to sell me that bill of goods, kid? *You? Now?* What are we talking here? I thought you got out of that line long ago. You still believe it though, don't you, a part of you anyway, that all this was for a higher purpose?"

"I know you don't, Kahn," I rejoined, "so let's just drop it, all right?"

"You're damn right I don't believe it. It's a joke. A bad joke."

"And hair transplants are still unnatural," I fired back, matching spite with spite.

"Unnatural?" He smiled brilliantly. "So are false teeth, kidney transplants, insulin injections" — he leaned across the desk, rubbing his thumb over my lapel — "eight-hundred-dollar suits. Why don't we just run around in our birthday suits, for Christ's sake? *That* would be natural. Come to think of it, kid, maybe that's exactly what you're doing. The only thing is, you're convinced you're the emperor." He shook his head disgustedly. "I didn't want to fight, kid. I hope things work out for you. I really do."

"Thanks, Kahn," I said querulously.

"Well, I guess that about covers it, doesn't it?" He rose from his chair and abruptly started for the door. "See you around, kid," he said without looking back.

"Aaron . . ."

He stopped and wheeled around.

With a supreme effort I held out my hand. "Wish me luck," I petitioned with a vulnerable, imploring smile.

He stepped forward and gripped my hand, looking straight into my eyes. "How about a mazel tov instead?" he offered. "They're cheaper and get better mileage. . . . You shit." Then he turned and strode toward the door, opened it, and disappeared.

It was almost a relief to see him go into the outer office and the outer world (for all intents it might have been outer space). I unfreighted with a sigh, letting go the whole incident.

It was only then, when I had made my decision and executed it (executed him, I almost felt), only when I finally saw my way clear to proceed with the takeover, that a sense of something like peace returned to me, returned for the first time since . . . I could hardly remember when. Since China, it seemed.

I even felt a certain lightness of heart, a gaiety, as I threw myself back into the raging torrent of the Dow, submitting to the inexorable gravity of fate.

And there *was* a sense of fatefulness now, as though on my journey I had crossed the last frontier into the final wilderness. I had followed my father's spoor, that trail of bread crumbs, so deeply into the Dow — a trail broadcast along the treacherous banks of that swift-flowing stream — that there could be no thought of turning back. And there was none. Through all the devious windings in its course, I had put my faith in the logic that at last my journey would lead me to the Source, back to the calm, abiding ocean of the Tao. Here the torrent disappeared around a bend as it circled the base of the biggest obstacle in my path, American Power and Light. Around that bend would it at last debouch into the shining sea of my desire, or would it plunge, like the western cataract, off the edge of the world into the void?

I continued to believe. And yet, the truth was, it no longer really mattered where that swollen stream was taking me. For I no longer had a choice, having made it long before, long, long before, perhaps as long ago as the beginning. The truth was, I had ceased to care. I was in for the duration now, and it was not the destination that I cared for, but only the ride, only that. The rush and tumult, the onward motion had possessed my soul. I was rapt with speed, mesmerized by the scenery flashing past as the stream flowed on, downward from the mountains over the invisible threshold of the fall line, past which there is no return (Where had that been? Like asking where did life begin. Only one answer: at conception), on with the irreversible momentum of gravity into the mystic heartland — most mystic, most material — of America. I couldn't help but go! All things conspired to take me there. And I was mad to go, made to go, mad for the threshing. I had not forgotten the purpose that had led me out of China — so long ago it seemed! How could I? But it was like a dream to me now, a precious relic from another time whose use has been forgotten, sanctified by age and memory. I could only hope that in following the straight course of my necessity it would guide me back, back to the Way. But that was a wish; the decision itself I left to life to arbitrate, real life, life in the world as it is. Because I had no choice.

•

Having cast off the final ballast which Kahn constituted, my first step was to call the Horns together in a preliminary meeting to discuss takeover strategy. A great deal came out in this session. I was further indoctrinated into the mysteries of American Power and Light, in particular, those of its internal organization. And there were mysteries, peculiarities at least, most striking of which the fact that after my father's disappearance, the Board of Directors had, in effect, undergone a radical reorganization by remaining radically the same. That is to say, no one had succeeded Love in the post of chairman of the board, a move which some said was designed to allow its members collectively to exercise supreme power without being personally responsible for it

— more precisely, for its misuse — in the way my father had, the way which had led ultimately to his downfall. This, of course, was sheer speculation, as was a great deal of the received wisdom about the motives, methods, and maneuverings of the board members, which, insofar as practicable, and legal, were kept shrouded by a network of tight security precautions, elaborate even by normal Wall Street standards. To the General Public, the resulting internal balance of power was hyped as a revolutionary attempt to "democratize" corporate rule by the institution of what was touted as "fiduciary republicanism," which they said would inhibit such abuses of power as Love's. "Never again would such enormities take place." Yes, the Board of Directors had actively repudiated my father, in spite of the fact that most, if not all, its members owed their positions to him, and in spite, too, of the fact that they had in effect institutionalized his rule by leaving things exactly as they were at his death, only with the top spot vacant. I leapt eagerly at this. The active repudiation of my father, smacking as it did of ingratitude, only enhanced my eagerness to proceed, sweetening it with an added savor of revenge. It was my chance to vindicate his memory, I told myself, to restore the family honor. In that sense I would be following in his footsteps.

At any rate, for whatever reason, APL was run by what amounted to a corporate politburo, making its decisions by majority rule, an arrangement virtually unprecedented in American business. This junta, as it was sometimes called in the press, was currently made up of eleven members, most of them, as I said, appointees from the epoch of my father's tenure as chairman. It had been a considerable surprise to Wall Street, I discovered, that these men who had come to power on my father's coattails, most of them young at the time and with little or no experience in business, had been able to maintain themselves in power, since they were commonly regarded as a rubber-stamp assembly, mere puppets to his will. Yet somehow they'd survived, even managed to thrive, and thrived to manage.

The Executive Committee of APL, responsible for the day-to-day management of the corporation, was made up of three men, all of whom held positions on the Board of Directors. In a manner analogous to the power sharing of the board, they ruled as a triumvirate, each presiding over a particular domain of the vast inner corporate turf of APL, but each responsible to the other two for his decisions. Despite the impartiality of this inner system of checks and balances, in the general consensus of opinion among analysts on the Street, one man, David Bateson, had managed to promote himself into a position of de facto, if not de jure, preeminence. In APL's dealings with the world, he was the spokesman and intermediary. This fact held a particular interest for me, since Bateson had served with my father under Chennault in China. Several others of the board had also. What was unique about Bateson was that he had been my father's wingman. They had fought together as a team. Consequently, the man possessed an aura for me, a distinctly evil one. To have existed on terms of such intimacy, fighting beside my father in battle, and, in addition, owing his position in the world to him — after that, actively to defame my father's memory, however justly, seemed to me the height of treachery. From the information I received about him, Bateson appeared unremarkable as an individual, possessing no particular personal flair or charisma. "A good team player," "an organization man," that was how the profile I'd commissioned from the Horns described him, something of a good-natured four-flusher. And his very blandness made me hate him even more.

In a way analogous to its management, since my father's day the corporation itself had changed by remaining virtually static. On closer inspection, it began to emerge that APL was not as innovative and dynamic as it had, at first sight, appeared, and as it in fact once had been. Certainly the picture was not as rosy as the balance sheet suggested. The uninterrupted rise in earnings over the years had, of late, been produced not so much by increased productivity resulting from inspired investment decisions as from flights of creative fancy on the part of APL's accountants. Tax windfalls on many of her takeover and merger bids emerged from the murky crucibles of the accountants' brains alchemized into "profits." They exercised a similar (black) magic by encouraging these mergers with companies with smaller price-earnings multiples, a process which, by some obscure necromantic logic, automatically assured APL of an increase in earnings per share, despite the fact that neither she nor the absorbed company increased productivity, or investment, or, in any authentic sense, did more business than each separately would have done. The mere fact of combination had a sacramental effect on the balance sheet, transubstantiating "profits" and "earnings" out of thin air, like manna, Wonder Bread indeed!

This evidence of "creative" accounting was like the film of slime overlying a general stagnation of initiative, hidden or excused by a lurking deviousness. A pattern began to emerge which showed the corporation again and again shying away from investment in the long-term health of her basic industries, such as factory retooling, and turning for her bread and butter to the newer nonproductive "service" industries, and to entertainment. Rather than the bracing, if sometimes ugly, risk-venture capitalism which I had seen in operation on the floor of the Exchange, proceeding unabashedly by the law of the jungle, survival of the fittest, here we found a bureaucratic quagmire filled with timid, retiring creatures whose every step and gesture was minutely reasoned according to a calculus of risk avoidance. No cowboys or gunslingers here; the wilderness was a bog. And not only were their policies timid and contemptible, without breadth or grandeur, but they whiningly insinuated themselves into a position of dependency on government. Government regulation maintained prices at artificially high levels in many sectors. There were government guarantees on credit. When the few risks the corporation did take failed to work out, they were covered by the government in the form of tax write-offs. And the taxes they paid were so small to begin with that they amounted to a virtual government subsidy. Then, of course, there were the government contracts, especially in defense. In all, I found the picture profoundly depressing.

Not that I was naive about such matters. Kahn and Sun had even used some of the accounting gimmicks in its own takeovers, but only as gravy. The underlying core of solid expansion on our track record was in striking contrast to APL's. What was worst was that the Dowager attempted to hide her condition under makeup and stays, like an old whore. A certain deviousness was at work here, an underlying cynicism that was almost shocking. I was even tempted to reconsider. In the end, however, APL's structural malaise only acted as a further spur to my resolve. For I saw that a merger with Rising Sun Enterprises (the new name of the company — I had gone Kahn one better) could be genuinely beneficial to both parties: to us, because it would put unequaled capital reserves at our command; and to the shareholders of APL, because the policies and style of management that had made Bull Inc. so successful would act as a shot in the arm to the sluggish Dowager, a step toward reform. What she needed more than anything was a transfusion of fresh blood, and that is precisely what I had to offer.

Thus, beyond any personal motives, the takeover assumed the nature of a crusade, an aspect the Horns and I planned, when the time came, to use to our advantage in a promotional campaign, selling APL's shareholders on the idea that the merger would be in their best interests. Management, however, would be a different story. They deserved to lose. APL's officers had allowed investments that, when my father and his predecessors in the family had made them, had been on the cutting edge to go shamefully to seed, harvesting without resowing or tending the plot. Fields that had once been on the frontier were now afflicted by urban blight. At the corporation's expense, management had proved the old saw that on Wall Street the surest way to change is by standing still — the surest, and the worst. Yes, they deserved to lose. Yet I wasn't so naive as to suppose the officers of APL would relinquish power easily, even if it was in the best interests of the shareholders. The shareholders' best interests and their own diverged, and I knew that capitalists, even of the most entrenched and conservative sort (especially those) would fight tooth and nail for their turf, preferring to set themselves ablaze in their own house in a suicidal auto-da-fé rather than willingly surrender to a perceived adversary.

This, together with the betrayal of my father's memory, inspired me with an almost pathological hatred of these men whom I had never met. I was fired with a sense of righteous indignation at their crimes, filled anew with a conviction of the moral purpose which I had thought I'd lost. Part knight-errant, part dutiful Chinese son in the Confucian mode, I saw elements of East and West welded indissolubly in my quest, as in my person, as I constituted and commissioned my own *posse comitatus* and set out on a crusade of vengeance essential to the "honor" of both parts, saving face on the one hand, and serving God and country on the other.

So what was the plan? Having had such astounding successes with the public tender offer in the past, I decided, with the concurrence of the Horns, that it would be foolish to alter a winning formula, unless of course APL capitulated without a fight, in which case we would be compelled to show mercy — a prospect I dismissed as unlikely in the extreme. The fact that Second Jersey Hi, the bank we'd taken over, already possessed substantial holdings in American Power and Light, plus my private cache of shares (which I sold to the corporation to consolidate accounts) breezed us a considerable way down the Yellow Brick Road toward fulfillment of our design.

The next step, then, would be to begin the secret purchase of a large number of additional shares of APL in relatively small lots, anywhere from a hundred to eight or nine thousand at a time, on the open market, following Kahn's example and buying through numbered accounts to prevent detection, not by the SEC this time, but by APL herself. At all costs, we wanted to preserve the element of surprise as long as possible, keeping the sluggish Dowager from rousing herself to defensive measures. The Horns calculated that a 4 percent position in APL would give us the needed leverage to proceed with our bid. A 4 percent position in APL, however, was no trifling matter, especially since it had to be paid up front, cash on the hoof. In order to borrow the necessary sums, Rising Sun Enterprises had to go highly leveraged, a second excellent reason for preserving security, since it made us vulnerable to attack from outside. Once we had gotten our foot (or hoof) in the door, however, and could proceed with the actual tender, our position would be relieved, for, as in the past, we intended to offer debt security to APL's shareholders in lieu of cash, which would have been impracticable.

It was our plan to make a bid for 51 percent of all outstanding shares at *twice,* that is, 100 percent above, the current market for American Power and Light. The buying hysteria we were currently enjoying and our high price-earnings multiple relative to APL's gave us the leverage to take over the larger company. As if an instant 100 percent profit weren't inducement enough, we decided to sweeten the offer by including a percentage of warrants and convertible debentures, giving the shareholders of APL a chance to acquire our soaring stock at a significant discount.

All in all, the package we put together was virtually irresistible, a true windfall for American Power and Light shareholders. This generosity, we felt, would more than offset the fact that the payment was in unsecured paper, not in cash. The overwhelming health of Rising Sun Enterprises, however, made our corporate note of hand virtually as good as cash — better in fact, since it was capable of appreciating as our shares appreciated. The final refinement of the plan, and its crowning touch, was a method devised by the Horns which would allow us, after the takeover had been accomplished, to transfer the cost to the books of American Power and Light. This was a delicious inspiration, for it meant making the Dowager finance her own subjugation.

The plan proceeded with almost clockwork precision. While making our anonymous purchases on the open market, I directed my operatives to begin as quietly and unostentatiously as possible steering the reserves of Mutual Bull into APL plus those of our managed private accounts in Bull Inc.

We had reached a position somewhat in excess of 2 percent before the first hitch developed. Whether traceable to a leak in our security, or infiltration on their part, I never discovered, but somehow APL found out. Kahn's name was brought up by the Horns, who still preserved their fierce partisan attitudes from the previous era of joint command when they'd had to work in secret against Kahn's own forces. I preferred to discount the possibility of betrayal, since in any case there was nothing to be done about it. After reexamining our position, it appeared that the blow was in the nature of an inconvenience rather than an insuperable obstacle to continuing. It simply meant that APL would probably resort to buying her own shares defensively, making us pay more dearly for our interest. It threw off our timing a little, made the prospect of the acquisition somewhat more expensive, but we could absorb it. We had wanted to acquire the full 4 percent before going public with the registration statement of our tender offer. Though we were tempted to proceed immediately, after further debate we agreed that the wiser course would be to bide our time as long as possible while continuing to improve our position in APL by stepping up the buying.

Within a day of our discovery of their discovery of us, the plot thickened. Bateson called me on the telephone.

"Hello, Sun I? David Bateson here at APL."

"Yes," I answered as neutrally as possible, "what can I do for you?"

He laughed. "The question is what *are* you doing *to* me, isn't it?" He sounded immensely entertained by the whole thing.

"I wasn't aware that I was doing anything to *you,*" I said, smiling at my cleverness in parrying his inquiry without engaging in an outright lie.

"To us then," he qualified, picking up on my equivocation, his cheerful tone going flat. "Of course, I'm only a cog in the wheel here. Yes, of course, 'us.' Not that I — 'we,' excuse that! — mind, you understand," he continued, regaining his glibness. "I want you to know, we deeply appreciate your vote of confidence in the soundness of the corporation." It was his turn to laugh at his own ironic misconstruction of my motives. "Yes, it means a lot to us to win the respect and trust of the rising generation, especially an individual as outstanding as yourself. You know, we've followed your, well, I guess the only word for it is 'ascent,' with extreme interest. Rooted for you all the way, if I may say so, just like one of our own. Why, for all intents and purposes, you are, considering the family connection. It's almost as if our organizations are related, *blood* relations. It would be a shame for any unpleasantness to arise. Why don't you come down here — oops! I'm forgetting — that's *up* here. Don't mean to talk down to you or anything, but we're right upstairs. Won't even cost you taxi fare. We can have a nice little chat over lunch and see if we can't straighten things out amicably. What do you say? How about tomorrow?"

"All right, Mr. Bateson."

"David, David, by all means! Tomorrow it is!"

I hung up and called my secretary. "I don't have anything scheduled for lunch tomorrow, do I?"

"That meeting with the trustees of the Met about the new China wing," she said with an air of reproach.

"Damn! Well, we'll have to cancel again. Call them about a time next week."

I hung up, pleased with my performance. They had felt impelled to make the first move. That meant they were sweating it. They had been conciliatory. That proved they were scared. Yes, I was very pleased. I had revealed nothing, admitted nothing, in no way committed myself. It was the perfect policy under the circumstances. Watch and listen. The less said the better, less chance of making a mistake. I determined to follow the same plan the next day at the parley.

Chapter 17

In spite of my nervousness, I experienced an unexpected delight on entering the premises of American Power and Light. It was like stepping into another era. Unlike our newly decorated offices, where everything was consistent with a severe minimalist elegance, here a warm, effusive eclecticism made itself felt, an endearing motleyness, one might have said, had it not been for the richness of the pieces. And there were indeed "pieces." Bateson's private secretary's desk was ponderously handsome, a walnut-stained Honduras mahogany that age had darkened almost black. I noted the carved gallery molding around the upper edge and the ball-and-claw feet. Its weight and substance expressed the fine superfluity of a more confident era. On the glass surface was an Art Nouveau Tiffany lamp, and a Chinese famille noire vase filled with an effusion of pale yellow chrysanthemums like exploding suns. As I gazed at them, waiting to be announced, a dreamlike feeling came over me, a sense almost as vivid as the one I'd experienced at Sands Point, that the past had come to life.

"Do you like flowers?"

Bateson was standing at the threshold of his office, smiling and studying me closely. I was surprised at his appearance. Though his hair was silver-white and thinning, he was younger looking than I'd pictured him. It made me reflect that my father, had he been alive, would still have been a relatively young man, in his fifties. Bateson had bright, cold blue eyes that shone with a cheerfulness that was not particularly kind. I had known beforehand from the Horns that he wore a hearing aid in one ear, a souvenir from the war. He pressed it with his index finger from time to time, working it deeper into his ear, as though to improve the reception. Perhaps it simply itched him.

He came over to me and, before even shaking hands, cleanly snipped off one of the flowers with a penknife, clipping backward toward his thumb. "Do you have a pin, Anne?" he asked his secretary, frowning with concentration as he lifted my lapel and threaded the stem through the buttonhole. She opened her drawer and handed him one, and he inserted it, paused to judge, then patted my lapel twice and smiled. "There," he said. "That looks very nice." He turned to the young woman, "Don't you think so?"

She smiled at me too.

"Flowers are a nice touch, don't you think? It definitely adds something." He ushered me politely into his office, then turned back to his secretary. "See we're not disturbed." He closed the door.

"Sit down, sit down," he invited, pointing me to a chair. "Yes, we always keep flowers around here. It's a tradition I understand Arthur Love initiated. And your father maintained it. He was partial to them too, did you know that? In our own small way we try to keep up appearances. Family tradition is important to us here." He sat down and leaned back in his chair. "Yes, you'll find a lot of them here in spirit, the Loves, your father in particular. They made this place what it is. No denying it. In a sense I'm — we're, excuse that — only their executors, appointed proxies continuing the work they started."

At first exposure, Bateson was more charming than I'd expected, almost disarmingly so. Had I not known the duplicity involved in his claims of loyally carrying on the tradition, I might have liked him. As it was, I began to wonder if there weren't something a little monstrous about a man who could lie through his teeth like that. Wanting to establish my authority before he socially usurped my rightful equality as business adversary, I opted to break with my previous strategy and challenge him immediately.

"I don't see how you can even bring yourself to mention my father's name," I bitterly accused.

He looked surprised. "Why, Sun I, your father and I were best friends. We were with Chennault together in China. Didn't you know? I was . . ."

"Yes, yes," I interrupted, "I know. You were his wingman. That's what's inexcusable. I don't see where you get the balls even to allude to it after the way you've betrayed him."

He appeared earnestly concerned. "How have I betrayed him?"

" 'Fiduciary republicanism,' " I replied, pronouncing it scathingly. "He took the rap and then you disowned him, even made a P.R. ploy out of it."

"That's your objection?" He sat back in his chair again. "Don't be naive, Sun I. What choice did we have? We couldn't very well propose his canonization, could we? The corporation had to dissociate itself from the scandal. It was a business decision. Period. That's all. You said it yourself, a P.R. ploy. Your father would have done the same thing. I know he would have. Actually though, behind closed doors we're still quite devoted to him, as I think you'll see. Look around. Nothing has been changed since his tenure. The flowers are just one example. There are many others. You'll see for yourself." He rose to his feet. "In the boardroom, for example. The rest of the directors are waiting for us there now." He politely assisted me up from my chair. "Did you know that when your father was, well, when we lost him, as a gesture of respect the board voted to leave his chair at the center of the table permanently vacant?" He nodded emphatically, as though most anxious to clear up the misunderstanding. "That's part of the reason we've never reinstated the office of chairman. Who could fill his shoes, or seat?" He simpered apologetically.

Though I said nothing, I wasn't particularly impressed by their act of homage, which seemed on a par with retiring an athlete's number or his cleats. I couldn't figure exactly what game Bateson was playing. He appeared to be painfully sincere, so much so that I might have felt inclined to pity him had I not known he was dissembling. He was a very good actor; either that, or he actually believed his own hype, in which case pity was genuinely deserved.

As we entered, the residual complement of the board, ten members, all seated on the far side of a massive oblong conference table surfaced with a slab of black, veined marble, bestirred themselves and rose to greet us. There followed the ritual offering of hands and smiles, some grim, some earnest, some appraising, some nearly sympathetic, and the repeated protest of familiarity, "No, no, call me . . ." with all the relevant first names. I was surprised at the absence of animus. Of course, it was in their best interest not to show their true feelings.

Bateson had not been joking about the chair. Actually there were two vacancies, one of them, I assumed, to be filled by him. The others resumed their places, five on one side of the empty chairs, five on the other. The table was huge; seated, the board members were scarcely within reaching distance of one another. Bateson showed me to my chair — alone on the side opposite them — then began to circumambulate the table. "Gentlemen, I was just telling Sun I about our, well, virtual veneration of his father's memory." He grinned as a thought occurred to him. "You might almost say we're models of Confucian filial devotion." Assuming his place, he leaned over and patted the back of the central chair with confident righteousness. Instantly, however, a look of ugly surprise appeared on his features, and, following his line of sight, I saw, smoking in the ashtray before the "venerated seat," too far to have been conveniently in reach of either Bateson or the director opposite, a lighted cigarette carrying an inch of ash.

I chuckled with genuine pleasure. "Yes, it looks like it's been permanently vacant for at least the last five minutes." I regarded him cynically. "You know, I'm not sure what you're trying to prove or accomplish by this little performance, but you really needn't bother on my behalf. Certainly you don't expect me to be so moved by your piety as to renounce my intentions? Let's end this little masquerade. I promise you, I won't be in the least offended if you want to sit in the 'mystic seat of power,' or whatever you call it."

The board members exchanged dark looks among themselves.

"No, no, you misunderstand," Bateson said. "When I went to meet you, I came from here. I simply left my cigarette there on my way out. Look, there isn't another ashtray on the table." He invited me to verify this with a sweeping gesture of his arm. He took a wincing drag, coughed, then, blushing profusely, stabbed the cigarette out in the ashtray and hurriedly sat down.

There was something exceedingly queer about this little performance. I would have sworn that Bateson had never smoked a cigarette in his life. As I observed the white-gray wisp of smoke peeling up from the extinguished cigarette, the same sense of unreality came over me that I had felt in the outer office gazing at the flowers. Something about it left me with an eerie sensation. The room itself contributed to my sense of being slightly drunk and adrift. The warm, cozy bonhomie which had attracted me in the outer offices was completely lacking here. Indeed, this room was more like Rising Sun Enterprises, with a severe, repellent lucidity. It was extremely sparse, with nothing but that massive table, placed transversely. The two side walls were mirrored from floor to ceiling, as was the wall in which the door was cut, producing a disorienting effect of infinite regress. It made me feel self-conscious and exposed, as though on display, particularly since I knew the directors could see me from behind, whereas I was denied equal advantage; for the back wall, only a few feet behind their seats, was comprised of a single dark-green velvet drape. The effect was disappointing finally, I decided, as soulless and impersonal as a motel lobby.

"I see you're looking at the room," Bateson commented, having regained his composure. "Another of your father's touches."

I regarded him with mild surprise.

He nodded. "The design was his idea. But it doesn't appear to best advantage like this." He reached under the table and I heard a switch click. The curtains began to draw apart mechanically from the center. A starburst exploded brilliantly through the part, glinting off the marble and striking the mirrors with a lucid echo and reverberation, wheeling around and around the room with demonic ecstasy, like a jinni released from an unstoppered bottle. From between the contracting, wimpling panels of fabric emerged the most dazzling view of the skyline of New York and the East River I had ever seen. Suddenly I understood my father's intention and saw its brilliance. The effect was stunning, breathtaking. Everything was ruthlessly sacrificed to that view. The nakedness of the mirrors opened to it gave one the sense of standing on the edge of an abyss and peering over, or rather, of actually floating in it. It was vertiginous and thrilling. We were so high the tower tops of the Brooklyn Bridge appeared below us in a middle distance. The river was like a dark vein of lapis, no thicker than my arm, with the shadows of high clouds floating gray upon it. A tugboat moving upstream against the current resembled the fine tip of a sculptor's chisel, throwing a white shaving in its wake. At the south tip of Roosevelt Island a water main had apparently burst, throwing up a fantastic rooster tail of spray hundreds of feet into the air, raining down in a sheer, dazzling crystal curtain, which the sun, hanging low in the winter sky over Brooklyn, touched to rainbows. And far to the south, in the lower corner of the frame, the Statue of Liberty stood with her back to us, that terrible angel with the roll call of the final judgment in one hand and the torch of the conflagration in the other. I remembered opening my eyes on the Wonder Wheel, taking in the grand low sweep of earth's horizon from the summit. Only now my exhilaration held no trace of fear. This was what I wanted. This was what I stood to gain.

"What do you think?" Bateson asked.

"It isn't at all what I'd expected."

He laughed. "Did you expect cigar smoke and rolled-up sleeves?" He shook his head. "No, Sun I, the air is brisk at the top of the world. It has an alpine quality, a rare, immortal air." He spoke with settled passion, earnest, knowing, a little wistful. "Your father used to love this room. He said it was like flying, or something just as good."

I laughed, because it was. What surprised me most was the fact that the sun no longer hurt my eyes. I smiled to myself, thinking about the ophthalmologist. Yes, something was happening, but it was not a deterioration. My eyes were growing stronger. Opposite me, Bateson's face was framed in the radiance of the corona, and as I watched with profound wonder, his skin began to glow and turn translucent. Suddenly, as in an X-ray, the apparition of his naked skull appeared through his flesh, circled by a network of quivering veins and arteries, the brain like a dark pudding in their midst. Delight transmogrified to horror. I gasped and felt the prickle of a million pores dilating. Yet the vision lasted only a moment; I blinked and it was gone, leaving me disoriented and mildly nauseated. I squinted and shaded my eyes with my hand.

"Too bright for you?" Bateson asked. "Here, I'll close it."

Over the low drone of the motor as the curtains drew together, one of the board members at the far end of the table initiated the parley. "We've watched your progress with great admiration," he said.

I smiled politely, watching the vista incrementally closing as the curtains impinged from either side like the shutter of a camera contracting around the aperture, or an iris around the pupil of an eye.

"And even contributed in a modest way," a second volunteered.

The drapery lips touched and swayed, one side catching up on a heating duct, forming an imperfect seal through which a finger of light searched uncertainly.

"No complaints, I hope?" I bantered, forcing myself to look away from it toward my interlocutor's face. "We try to keep the public happy."

"Public!" another protested gamely. "Surely, Sun I, we're more to you than that? I mean, considering the family ties."

"That's just it, Ted," Bateson answered him, "Sun I insists on viewing us as outsiders. Against all evidence, he persists in regarding our professions of goodwill as disingenuous."

There were murmurs of protest around the table.

"No, no," one corrected, instructing me to orthodoxy, "we hope to play a paternal . . ." — he noticed me wince — "avuncular then, yes, avuncular, call it that, role in your affections."

"Which is to say," Bateson elaborated, "we had hoped for an amicable settlement."

The flicker of light from the curtain danced across my eyes. I squinted to look at him. "Nothing I'd like better," I said, smiling with wicked pleasure. "My terms are simple."

Expressions of approval and relief sounded around the table.

"And what are they?" Bateson asked, not quite so optimistic as the rest.

"I want executive control."

"What!" one blurted.

"Impossible!" said another.

The table buzzed with whispers as they leaned toward one another and conferred. I sat immaculately cool, enjoying the sensation I'd produced, staring directly at Bateson, whose face, for the first time, had turned grave. His color had deserted him. He was almost gray.

"Consider what it would mean," said one, trying an appeal to reason. "The corporation today, as you must see yourself, is virtually unchanged from your father's time."

"That's precisely the problem," I interjected. "It's stagnated. It needs new initiative. The corporation is a swamp."

"A swamp!" he echoed indignantly. "American Power and Light is a historical entity, young man," he tutored me, "and, beyond that, a living monument to your father's memory. Would you destroy that?"

"I don't want to destroy it," I replied, "I simply want to inject new life into it."

"By absorbing it into Rising Sun Enterprises, I presume?" he inferred with a scathing intonation.

I nodded. "Precisely."

"But don't you see that that would be precisely to destroy it?" said another. "The corporation as such would cease to exist. American Power and Light a subdivision of Rising Sun Enterprises!" He laughed contemptuously. "Preposterous!"

"Unthinkable!" said another.

"What bull!" said a third, more archly.

"Precisely what I've been trying to tell him," Bateson said. "To take over APL would not only do violence to a venerable public institution, causing untold distress in the marketplace, it would amount to virtual corporate patricide."

I smiled at his sophistry. "Patricide," I repeated. "You'll forgive me if I'm a little dense, but how does one kill a man who's dead already?"

Bateson narrowed his eyes. "You can murder his memory, Sun I."

"His memory! It would seem to me that after you got through with that there was very little left to kill."

Bateson drew back in his chair with a frown. "I've explained to you already that our repudiation was done for purely business reasons. We continue to venerate him privately. If you can't see that . . ." He threw up his hands. "No, Sun I, Eddie Love's memory is alive with us, and, more important even than his memory, his legacy. That's what this corporation is. And if you dismantle it, you anatomize his spirit. That's why I call it patricide."

I shrugged, unmoved. "I see it differently. I see the takeover as a vindication of his memory and a reestablishment of family honor."

Bateson shook his head and glared at me. "You're very dangerously mistaken on that point, and if you persist in the misconstruction, I'm afraid it will put us at odds, fatally at odds. In which case, I fear for both of us. We aren't oblivious to your power, as you should not be oblivious to ours. I won't conceal from you that we feel threatened by your show of arms, your militancy. The recklessness of your attitude worries me, personally, and I think I speak for the rest in that. You put us in a difficult position. We are not as agile as we once were, as you perhaps are now. But what we lack in nimbleness, we more than make up for in weight. The power of this corporation, if we choose, if we are forced, to marshal it, is awesome. If you force our hand, I have no doubt that we can mount a formidable campaign. Already we have people at work. Ways exist and will be found. There are always ways," he reiterated grimly.

"What ways?" I asked contemptuously. "I too have people at work, and I don't see that you have a great variety of options to pursue."

"Come, come," chided the man at the end of the table, "you don't seriously expect us to reveal our options and give away our strategy, do you?"

"Any more than we expect you to," said another.

"Surprise is the key, Sun I," Bateson averred. "That was your father's forte, surprise."

The sunlight piercing through the crack in the curtain flicked about my face and eyes like a feather, tickling me with sadistic playfulness, making me squint and turn in my chair.

"I will tell you this, though," Bateson went on. "We know that you intend to use convertible debt security to reimburse our shareholders, at least for part of their interest." He studied me as though hoping to read assent or demurral in my expression.

I squirmed, continuing to avoid the light.

He continued, threateningly. "You realize, of course, that such a route will dilute the equity of your own shareholders in Rising Sun Enterprises."

"I don't suppose they'd be particularly pleased to learn about that," suggested another.

"I don't intend to try and hide it," I informed them querulously.

"Yes, but I don't suppose you'll make a point of advertising it either," Bateson pointed out.

"Meaning you might . . ." I inferred.

He smiled and didn't answer.

"What? A form letter to my shareholders?" I scoffed. "How much credence do you think they'll put in your allegations?"

"It'll be the truth," he said.

I frowned. "Well, I believe the long-term advantages that will accrue to the stockholders of Rising Sun will outweigh any temporary disadvantages."

He shrugged in a smug, dismissive manner. "There is also the little matter of Mutual Bull's recent substantial move into APL."

"It's a matter of public record," I replied. "What about it?"

He pursed his lips with false casualness. "Oh, very interesting, that's all."

"Not that we object," someone piped in.

"Or would dream of deprecating our own stock," seconded another.

"It's just that your fund, heretofore, has seemed to prefer — has, in fact, made its reputation through — the purchase of more volatile growth-oriented stocks. APL, of course, is a dividend-oriented income stock. What would the shareholders in your fund think if their assets became tied up in what you yourself call the 'capital swamp' of American Power and Light? How will that affect performance?"

This time I had a more ready answer. "Have you considered that when the takeover is accomplished . . ."

"If," someone qualified admonitorily.

"When," I reiterated with emphasis. "APL will appreciate . . ." — I started to give a figure, but decided to save that as a surprise — "considerably. *And* instantaneously. I'm not prepared to give you an exact figure at this time, but I think I can set your minds at rest, it will constitute what we call in the business 'a respectable trading move.' "

They frowned and exchanged looks.

"It's rather neat, don't you think?" I taunted. "The resources of Mutual Bull and Bull Inc. will help provide the necessary leverage to make the takeover possible, and they in turn will stand to gain a substantial increase in the net asset value per share of their holdings as APL appreciates from the very same takeover they're financing."

No one was smiling now, except me. I laughed. "You see, gentlemen, despite your talk of 'ways,' I don't really think you have a hole to crawl in, in this case. And we haven't even mentioned what should be, from your perspective, the paramount consideration of all: the immense benefit that your own share-holders stand to derive. Notice I say, 'should be.' I realize, of course, that, under the circumstances, from your point of view that's more or less irrele-vant."

"Not irrelevant at all," Bateson corrected, "but a value judgment, certainly. We consider ourselves in a much better position to assess the best interests of our shareholders than you, Sun I. After all, we've spent our lives doing so."

"You may prefer to believe that," I retorted, "but I think differently. And I'll tell you something else," I continued heatedly, "an instantaneous one hundred percent appreciation in the value of their investments is unarguably in the best interests of your, or anybody else's shareholders. If you think you can argue them out of it, I urge you to do so."

"One hundred percent!" someone blurted.

Bateson regarded me grimly.

"That's correct," I said, turning to the man who had spoken. "We plan to offer twice the current market value for your shares."

"In Monopoly money," one said contemptuously.

"Debt security!" another scoffed.

"Corporate flypaper, that's what it amounts to."

I smiled, refusing to lower myself to resent their aspersions. "Call it what you will, gentlemen. If you have any reason to doubt the financial soundness of Rising Sun Enterprises, or why our corporate IOU shouldn't be as good as legal tender, I'd be glad to hear it."

"Isn't there some question about the breadth of your stock?" one man demanded spitefully.

Bateson frowned at him.

"I'm not aware of any," I replied airily. "Weak, gentlemen, weak. You're bluffing."

Suddenly Bateson rocked forward in his chair. "All right," he said, "let's stop this cat fight before it gets out of hand. Does there have to be enmity and bloodshed? Isn't there another way?"

"Your unconditional surrender," I posed, letting the momentum carry me.

"Impertinent boy!" one man said in outrage. "Do you think an ornamental Chinese goldfish can swallow the Leviathan? We'll crush you!"

"Enough!" Bateson said, raising his voice. "Let me finish for Christ's sake!" He turned to me. "All right, Sun I, you know as well as I do that's out of the question. However, we'll regard it as a bargaining position. Fair enough?"

I pouted superciliously.

"But don't answer now. Take a few minutes to think it over. Lunch is ready anyway. Let's break and let the temperature cool a few degrees."

Just then waiters appeared and set our places around the table, followed in short order by others with carts clamorous with the feast.

"We like to eat in here sometimes," Bateson explained, "on special occasions. And this is a special occasion for us, despite what you may think." He smiled winningly. "In celebration of which," he continued, "we've prepared something rather special for you, Sun I. I hope you'll be pleased. Before we serve though, try the bread." He passed me the basket. I unfolded the napkin, and a cloud of earthy, wheaten steam arose. "Crusty French loaves still warm from the oven," he said. "Pierre is a wonderful baker. And the wine . . ." Rising, he took the bottle from the steward and served me himself, presenting the label to me. "Château Lafite-Rothschild, forty-two," he announced. "Your father's favorite. Besides the intrinsic excellence of the vintage, I think your father was partial to it because it commemorated our time in China. He bought several cases at auction once. This is among the last of it." Bateson sighed, remembering. "Eddie used to call it 'Wrath Child,' affecting a kind of nouveau riche Texas oilman bumptiousness. It became a private joke among us." He laughed in a subdued manner and shook his head. "He always ordered it for special occasions. It was the wine we drank at the directors' luncheon after we first came to power. I've had it I don't know how many times since then, yet it never ceases to surprise, never grows old." His eyes misted over with the smoky passion of a connoisseur, a light I knew quite well, having seen it in

Lo's eyes as he discoursed upon the subtleties of wine. "All of which makes it doubly appropriate that we share it together today in honor of our meeting, our 'reunion,' let us call it." He raised his glass to me. "Kan pei," he said with a twinkle in his eye.

"Cheers," I replied, frowning as I clinked his glass.

I had never tasted such wine. It had all the complexity and denseness of a human personality, someone extraordinary, if perhaps a little eccentric, who, upon entering a room, becomes the immediate focus of attention, leaving the others cowed and overawed, not by calculated effect, but simply by some quality of enhanced vitality. I was drunk after one sip, or not drunk so much as in an altered state, altered by the degree and quality of concentration the wine demanded for appreciation. I felt moved to discourse upon its subtleties in the manner of Lo, but noting the looks of sober, satisfied, self-absorbed contemplation on my hosts' faces, wisely managed to throttle the impulse.

Before long the entrée was served, rare prime rib of beef, au jus. The sight of the beef floating red in its own blood with little pools of melted fat shining around it with a pearly iridescence made me slightly queasy. Yet I couldn't take my eyes off it, ineffably, obscenely beautiful.

As the meal progressed and finally concluded, the sense of dreamy, disembodied unreality I'd felt since entering had deepened. Having "buttered me up," so to speak, Bateson patted his lips with his napkin as the dishes were cleared and prepared to get back to business. "Now that we're all feeling better, I'd like to offer you our proposal, Sun I," he began. "We discussed the matter beforehand and came up with what I think you'll agree is an acceptable compromise. All along you've seemed inclined to doubt our good offices. Perhaps this will convince you. You already own a percentage, perhaps one and a half."

"Over two," I cheerfully corrected him.

He raised his eyebrows. Some of the others exchanged glances.

"All right then, two," he conceded. "We've talked it over, and we believe that entitles you to a position on the board. And it's not simply a question of entitlement either: we're *anxious* to have you join us. It's been our plan all along. Perhaps some of your allegations are justified. Maybe we have grown a little complacent, taken on a little midriff bulge. A shot in the arm may be just the thing. And for our part, we may still have one or two tricks left in us that would be worth your while to learn. You, too, may stand to profit from indoctrination into the mysteries of the corporation." He grinned at me suggestively, then suddenly frowned. "But you'll have to put aside all talk of executive control." He clasped his hands on the table. "So then, Sun I, what do you say? A seat on the board — I don't think you can deny it's a generous offer."

"I suppose that is *your* bargaining position," I twitted him.

His face became ashen. "No, Sun I," he replied in a quiet, steady voice, "though our first, it's also our final offer. It's that or face the consequences."

"An ultimatum, in other words," I said, drawing the implication.

He shrugged coolly. "As you wish."

I hesitated. It wasn't a contemptible offer, rather attractive actually, and it was painless. The light flicked through the curtain, riddling my eyes again. I didn't have to ponder long.

"Well, gentlemen," I said, pushing back from the table, "I suppose that concludes our business. You'll forgive me if I eat and run, but I suppose that's in the nature of the corporate predator, isn't it?" I smiled brilliantly, encompassing them all. "Good day."

I left the meeting flushed with triumph, gleeful, feverish, not to mention a little light-headed from the wine. "They're humbugs, humbugs," I kept telling myself, chortling with malicious pleasure. "They don't have a leg to stand on or a card to play. 'There are ways.'" I repeated it contemptuously. It was a bluff. "Humbugs!" The word had a talismanic quality of reassurance.

Yet something had unsettled me a little. Not so much anything they'd said; on that score the parley had proceeded pretty much according to plan, *my* plan. I'd accomplished my initial objectives. But the accumulation of troubling details disturbed me: the flowers, the meal, that business with the cigarette, the boardroom itself, its almost surreal beauty, the sense of weightlessness I'd experienced, as though suddenly released from the pull of gravity, "like flying," the very seating arrangement! And then, too, there was their stupid persistence in claims of loyalty, so transparently specious, and that remorseless-playful probing of the finger of sunlight through the curtain. What did it mean? Was it all in my imagination? Or had it perhaps been staged? Were they attempting to undermine my confidence and resolve through subtle psychological intimidation, subliminal terrorist cues? However it was, it worked in a devilish way on me. But what did it all add up to? Nothing. Absolutely nothing. Maybe the wine was drugged!

"Humbugs!" I concluded with a tinge more bravado than I actually felt. I decided to take the offensive, going public with the registration of the tender offer as soon as possible. Give me ultimatums, would they? That would show them! I wasn't a man to be trifled with. I wouldn't be intimidated!

Unfortunately it was Friday. The Horns convinced me that, rather than go off half-cocked, when everyone was waiting impatiently for the market to close, many already embarked on their weekend pilgrimages upstate or to the Hamptons, it would be better to wait and toss the meat of the initiative to a full circus complement of bright-eyed, eager lions on Monday morning. I reluctantly agreed, not looking forward to the prospect of two idle days in which to feed my own obsession.

Chapter 18

That night I hardly slept. Tossing in bed, I kept waking Li, so that she finally suggested I take a hot shower or a walk around the block. I tried both without success. I brewed a pot of tea and perched at the kitchen table, hands clasped around my cup, brooding and plotting. The next morning, long after light had begun to stream through the windows, Li ambled in in her robe and stretched on the threshold, extending her arms above her head. Still marked by sleep, her face was lax and smooth with a sedated happiness.

"Good morning," she offered.

I glared at her threateningly.

"Umm," she said, deliberately ignoring it, rolling her shoulders, stretching again with her hands in the small of her back, "you look like you've been eating nails."

"I have," I confirmed, showing her mine.

She studied me attentively. "What's wrong? You kept me awake all night."

I smiled ironically. "I can see I did."

She clucked her tongue impatiently. "So what am I supposed to do, stay up and hold your hand?" She set the kettle on the gas. "It's the APL thing, isn't it?"

"I had my first meeting with them yesterday," I said, leaping at the opening.

"You need to take your mind off it, distract yourself a while," she prescribed, parrying my overture.

My enthusiasm doused, I turned inward sullenly.

"I ought to work today," she went on, more to herself than me, as though weighing alternatives, "but I could take off . . ." She turned around. "Why don't we go on an expedition?"

"An expedition?"

She smiled. "Sure, like in the old days, an ethnological field trip. Only this time you get to play the guide."

"Where to?" I asked apathetically.

"We could rent a car and drive out to Long Island," she suggested. "You could show me the house."

I pricked up my ears. "Sands Point?"

She nodded, a little flushed and excited by the felicity of the idea.

"All right," I agreed, understating my enthusiasm. "Why not?"

On the way there, taking advantage of my captive audience, I unfreighted the weight of my concerns. Though Li knew what I was contemplating, we hadn't really discussed the takeover in depth before. Now it poured from me. I described the parley, lingering on the details, scanning her face for a reaction, not wanting to ask outright. She didn't seem to pick up on it. I brooded over her obliviousness, again considering the possibility that I had imagined it all. One detail, however, did produce a reaction, though not one I particularly cared for.

I contemptuously recounted Bateson's remark about "corporate patricide" and how I'd skillfully parried it, exposing his sophistry. I waited for corroboration or approval from her. She didn't volunteer.

"Well?" I asked irritably. "You do agree it was sophistry?"

She studied my face, then looked away. "Actually I think it was rather astute of him," she remarked, almost blandly.

"What do you mean by that?" I had an impulse to slam on the brakes right there in the middle of the expressway and have it out, venting the full violence of my outrage on her.

She shrugged. "It's nothing to get excited about. It's a fairly normal reaction."

"What, murdering one's own father?"

"His memory," she quietly corrected. "Isn't that what he said?"

"I'd like to know where you come up with that," I said, ignoring the qualification.

She turned to me. She wasn't smiling, but there was a faint flicker of amusement in her eyes. "Remember Oedipus?"

It hit me rather hard. "But Oedipus didn't set out deliberately . . ."

"It's rarely deliberate," she interrupted. "Much more frequently unconscious. It's nothing to be ashamed of either, Sun I. It's been around for quite some time, the enmity between fathers and sons. Since Zeus and Cronos at least, or Jupiter and Saturn. Remember Saturn? In a drunken rage he tried to eat his children, but Jupiter, who was protected by his mother, Rhea, escaped. Rhea tricked her husband by giving him a stone instead of a son to devour. He must have been pretty drunk not to notice the difference. An awful business, especially for Jupiter. For me, it's one of the most chilling images in Greek mythology, which doesn't suffer any shortage of gruesome incidents."

She began to elaborate in her typically graphic manner. "I can almost see the boy, squatting in the shadows with a cold sweat dripping down his face, hardly daring to breathe, nursing the slippery sickle in his hands, listening to his father in the next room raging like a wild beast. And then the screams of his brothers and sisters and the sickening, dull thud of their skulls breaking open against the walls, and the crunching of their bones between the monster's teeth. And Jupiter waiting in the shadows for his father's fury to subside, for him to sleep, then disemboweling him with one clean swipe of the blade, hacking away the organ of his ghastly power and deposing him." She examined me for a reaction.

"Pretty awful, I think you'll agree, but old as sin, and just as natural. The father resents the son because of the threat the son poses to his own continued dominance; the son resents the father because he blocks his way to power and full self-expression. Generally the struggle is engaged around the figure of the mother, the primary, and primordial, bone of contention. You can read all about it in Freud. If I remember correctly, he even argues someplace that the unconscious search for immortality, which springs from our natural fear of death, necessarily entails a death wish toward the father, who, as the prior link in the chain of mortality, comes to represent the chain itself, mortality itself — a memento mori, in other words, reminding the son of his own eventual demise, so that he has no choice but to murder his father symbolically, thereby obliterating the whole cycle of mortal causation, simultaneously conquering death and achieving immortality by becoming *father of himself,* eternally self-regenerative. It's really quite fascinating when you think about it." Her face had taken on a flush from the pleasure of working it out.

"I'm sure it is," I said with a tinge of resentfulness. "But what does it have to do with me? I don't hate my father. Why should I?"

"Come on, Sun I," she chided, "everybody has legitimate grievances against their parents. But *you* — your case is classic. I mean, where do you want me to start? Bastardy, desertion, exile to a monastery . . ." She counted them off, thumb, index finger, middle finger, touching each with the ball of her opposite thumb.

"He didn't mean for it to happen," I said, repeating the ritual absolution. "It was circumstance."

She smiled without pleasure, looking straight ahead. "It always is."

I, too, gazed grimly out into the landscape, my eyes burning with tears I refused to let her see. "Maybe he wanted to spare me," I speculated.

She fixed me with an inquisitive glance. "Spare you what?"

I smiled with malicious satisfaction. "This."

She laughed, a short, sharp, violent burst of sound, like a clap. "That's a nice thing to say to your betrothed."

I made no reply.

"Don't misunderstand me, Sun I," she went on. "I'm not judging, him *or* you."

"You never do," I observed bitterly.

"I'd probably feel the same way," she continued, ignoring, or oblivious to, my remark. "Anybody would, anybody normal."

"I love my father," I said, gazing into the farthest distance where the lines of the highway intersected and it disappeared, thinking to myself that neither she nor I nor anyone could see or know that place, and that it was hallowed by its own unknownness. I didn't want to know.

"Of course," she replied. "But there is the other side as well, always. Even if you aren't aware of it."

"How do you presume to know my unconscious motives?" I asked with sudden vehemence. "If you think they're so contemptible, why do you want to marry me, anyway?"

"I don't think your motives are bad," she protested with perfect equanimity. "I didn't mean to imply that. I think they're normal and healthy."

"In other words, 'ambivalent,' " I glossed cynically.

"All right," she conceded, "if you will, ambivalent."

We were silent for a while, and then I asked finally, urgently, "Why must you always take the other side?" It was almost an entreaty.

A look of tenderness softened her features. "I don't mean to," she said gently. "I wasn't taking sides."

"That's right," I agreed bitterly, "you never do, do you? You never take sides, or parts, you just take the center and the whole and the heart of everything and throw the rest away for scrap. What is it you want from me anyway, Li, my money?"

"I don't think that's fair," she said coldly, her eyes hot and bright. "If you don't have the courage of your own convictions, if you don't believe in yourself enough, you can't expect me to take up the slack."

"All right," I conceded. "I grant that. But is it too much to ask for you to see my side of things sometimes, to help me by believing in me? Why must you always see the worst in me?"

"I didn't know I did," she remarked in a surprised, chastened tone. "I'm sorry you feel that way. Nothing I've said was meant in spite. You asked for my opinion, and I gave it. I just told the truth." She smiled bitterly. "Maybe that's the problem."

I kept my eyes trained straight ahead.

"If you feel that way," she said at last, very quietly, "maybe we're making a mistake."

"Maybe we are," I agreed, throwing everything to the winds.

After a few miles of heartbreaking silence, I was unable to bear it any longer. "Li," I said, imploring her, anxiously searching her face, "I'm sorry. Just forget what I said. This APL thing has me out of sorts. I'm not myself today."

She fixed her eyes on me, not in inquiry, acknowledgment, or anything at all really, only a look, then averted them again, gazing without expression into the landscape, her arms crossed resolutely across her stomach.

•

The reticence of our argument hung over us like a pall as we reached the house and began our exploration of the grounds. In the aftermath, the joy I had anticipated for our expedition — this time I played the cicerone as she had done for me that first night, exploring the West Side — was all gone out of it. In such light the observance seemed hollow and pathetic. I mourned the loss inside myself. As if in reflection of the mood, the sky was steely overhead, beyond appeal, a leaden, winter, wood-smoke day, without wind, settled, but a little cold. As we got out of the car, Li put on her hooded sweatshirt and handed me a sweater silently.

No one answered at our knock. Chiang Po was not about, either in the house or in the yard. I suppose I should have regarded this as fortunate, since I had no idea what I'd say to him after the disastrous conclusion of our first inter- view, when he'd forbidden me the house, except perhaps to point out my interest as a potential buyer — my right to be there, in other words, certified by my money. Somehow I doubted the argument would impress him; nor, as I stood holding the brass knocker in my hand, was I sure I put much stock in it myself.

"It isn't very well kept up, is it?" Li commented.

"No, I suppose it isn't," I conceded mournfully.

No one came to the door, so we strolled down the long trough of lawn toward the seawall and the narrow strip of beach beyond. In striking contrast to its summer splendor, the grass was unkempt, brown and withered. The dead stalks of dispersed dandelions stood sentinel irregularly, like the filaments of exploded light bulbs. Climbing the jolted members of black-gray quarry stone, I steadied myself on the wall and reached a hand down to her.

A trancelike state came over me, little by little, as we wandered on the beach, a fey, mystic ecstasy of seeing, simultaneously attracted to and repelled by the common objects in our path. The tide was low and the boulders loomed huge from the water, dark, riddled accretions of grotesque sand-dripped slag, hairy with mussels below the oil-stained waterline. All around the rocks "Dead Man's Fingers" with gas bladders in the fingertips reached from their dark, murky world toward the sun, waving in desultory, wraithlike supplication tempered of all urgency or hope. The stench of oceanic putrefaction hovered over the whole beach in the still air, sweet, rich, and rank in the lungs. The water was glassy calm, like an oil slick, rising against the shore in small wavelets, which cracked like a whip with an abnormal loudness in the motion- less air. In greenish tidal pools overspread with the nacreous sheen of gasoline, fragments of shell and quartz glittered pink and silver, opulent as jewels. The beach was littered with washed-up debris: driftwood, smooth and petrified in graceful contortions; crinkly snares of backlashed fishing line; whelk cases curved and tapered like miniature human spines, and within, perfectly formed shells hardly bigger than a pinhead.

I stopped to pick up the egg case of a skate, like the black silk purse my father gave me, wondering fancifully if it contained a master key which could unlock the mystery of the beach. For indeed there was a mystery here to be deciphered, mystic patterns written in detritus, thin, hollow reeds like harvest stubble, only smaller, jointed like bamboo, broken off and blackening with decay. These spread everywhere in odd configurations that suggested more than randomness. They were like iron filings revealing the presence of some invisible and unsuspected energy, tracing the magnetic fields of the tidal ebb. Where did they come from? There were no reeds here, no marshes. What law governed their arrangement? What did they mean? I didn't know. I could only sense its presence. They were like the yarrow stalks, like the oracle bones themselves, whole and broken lines, nines and sixes, pick up sticks, sevens and eights, open the gate. But what gate? I was left with nothing but the phrase, rolling over and over in my mind, "mystic patterns written in detritus." After a few minutes I noted that Li was similarly absorbed, similarly contemplative. "How are you?" I asked, another code for another, deeper question.

She understood. Smiling vaguely, she directed her gaze over on the vacant water. "It makes me think of Stephen Dedalus on Dublin Beach," she said, not so much to me as to herself, " 'ineluctable modality of the visible, signatures of all things I am here to read.' " She regarded me appraisingly, with a slight frown of doubt.

"What does that mean?"

" 'Ineluctable,' " she glossed, turning away again, "not to be struggled out of, inescapable. 'Modality' . . ." She pursed her lips. "That's the hard one. Maybe it's simply a fancy way of saying 'faculty,' 'capacity.' In which case it means we can't escape our seeing, our own capacity for vision. But 'signatures of all things I am here to read' — signatures, reading — that suggests something more complex. A 'mode' in philosophy is the way in which an invisible substance manifests itself concretely."

Her phrase triggered an association. "An outward and visible sign of an inward and spiritual grace," I recited.

"Yes, like that, like a sacrament. Vision is like a sacrament we celebrate as a way of participating in the deeper, always invisible mystery. That's why there's an undertone of pathos in Joyce's phrase, because the sacrament we celebrate is also a sentence, we must serve. We're doomed to read the world continually, like a tantalizing, but perhaps finally indecipherable, code, in an attempt to reach back beyond all codes to the origin itself, where meaning is simply being. Life: that's the sentence, to know the signer through the signature, continually to read . . ."

"But who is the signer?" I asked.

She pouted again and shrugged. "God, I suppose, isn't that the obvious answer? He is the killer in this murder mystery," she said, smiling as she lapsed into parody, "sowing his clues through the pages of our lives, which we must turn to find him." She laughed softly, "Yea, down to the last page and paragraph, reading, always reading."

"Mystic patterns written in detritus," I thought, again repeating my own talismanic phrase, which was oddly in tune with her musings. Synchronicity. Mystic connection.

A little farther on we found a dead tern, and knelt down over it. A few flies, nervous with the lateness of the year, had lighted. Marching briskly a few steps, abruptly stopping and starting, jerkily moving off in another direction, they looked like distracted men pacing the scene of a catastrophe, trying to decide what to do. The bird, in contrast, appeared quite self-possessed, self-possessed in its bereavement of itself. Through the thinned, ruffled neck-feathers we could see the skin beneath, black as tar paper. Its wings were stretched out on the sand in a feeble parody of flight, even as the slow bacteriological combustion of decay consumed it. Its posture had a calligraphic elegance, poised for flight into the darker mysteries of corruption, back to dust — another hieroglyphic to be read. The look on its face was vague without being vacant, expressive of a kind of peace, I thought, almost smiling, even as the fly squatted deep into the eye to suck.

A sudden noise like thunder broke the silence. The landscape shook.

"What was that?" I cried, my heart beating very fast.

"A sonic boom," she replied matter-of-factly. Jerking herself up from where she knelt in the sand, like a cow lumbering up off its haunches, she dusted off her pants and pulled up the hood of her sweatshirt. It was growing colder. "Look, see the vapor trail?" Shading her eyes with one hand, she pointed up into the sky. As she did so, I noticed her long fingernail, elegant and sinister, tapering to a rounded sharpness like a blade. Perhaps it was the plane screaming overhead, but as she stretched her finger out, I seemed to hear a *screek,* like chalk across a blackboard, only magnified a thousand times, as if she scrawled a rune on a slate as big as the whole sky — "signatures of all things I am here to read." I thought of the Land of Oz and the message that the Wicked Witch traced out in cursive across the emerald sky.

Something was happening. The sky began to melt like ice, swirling and transforming overhead. Strange things frozen in the glacier's heart appeared, moiling and transmogrifying. In another quarter of the sky I saw what looked like a bristling cloud of bees. I thought at first of a tornado, but then I saw more clearly what it was. "Look," I said, pointing now myself.

Still shading her eyes, Li peered upward. "What?"

"Right there!" I thrust vehemently for emphasis.

She squinted and looked hard.

"Don't you see them?"

She dropped her hand and regarded me curiously. "I don't see anything." Her voice had grown distinctly quieter.

I checked again to make sure.

"What do *you* see?"

"The animalcules!" I shouted, throwing my wrist at it repeatedly. "Right there as plain as day!"

The swarm started to rise like a hot-air balloon, dark and semitransparent, gravitating toward the sun, where it dispersed, forming radii around the solar disc, like a crown of thorns, or the rays protruding from the black orb of the

Inca sun. Again I heard the sonic boom. The corners of the Sound quivered like gelatin. A face appeared in the sun, its features coalescing out of the shimmying heat waves. This face was like the Great Oz, at once an enormous head and a raging ball of fire. Its lips were moving, speaking, but I couldn't make out what it was saying. I took off my dark glasses to see more clearly.

"What are you doing?" Li asked.

"Reading," I said without looking at her, smiling to myself, "reading lips."

"Don't do that!" she ordered sharply, struggling with me to cover my eyes. "You'll blind yourself."

I held her wrists firmly pinioned, continuing to stare. "It can't hurt me," I told her reassuringly, as to a child who can't be expected to understand. "The sun blinds only those who can see already, but restores the blind to sight."

"You don't need an ophthalmologist," she said, struggling violently to break away, "you need a shrink!"

Breaking my concentration, I frowned at her, and threw her wrists from me sharply. She stumbled away and fell on her knees in the sand. When I looked back up, the face had vanished. There was only sky.

I turned on her. "Damn you!" I cried furiously. "You made me lose it."

She was squatting on all fours with her face lowered to the sand. Slowly she raised her head: it was the face of a fox that peered out from within the sweatshirt's pointed hood, with a long snout and small white pointed teeth, eyes glowing with ferocious malice. In its mouth it held the dead bird, giving it a shake or two with its whole head, convulsing in silent hilarity. I felt a door open inside me and a cold wind begin to blow from some unfathomable distance. The dark shadow of the wing of madness passed across the ground in front of me, swathing me in its penumbra, covering the whole earth.

•

I don't remember going home. I woke up in bed with a searing headache and a burning sensation in my eyes. The shower was running in the bathroom. Suddenly I felt an urgent need to recall what Oz had said to Dorothy when he materialized before her for the first time as the enormous head on the green marble throne. What was the condition he'd posed for the return to Kansas? I couldn't remember, and it seemed critical. Picking up the book from its place on the nightstand, I opened it to find the place; but as I did so, the letters came alive on the page, like black maggots, seething and boiling — the animalcules. I slammed the cover shut before they spilled over onto the sheets. Hours and moments passed. The water was still running when I fell asleep.

In my dream I was staring into a green velutinous darkness in which nothing was discernible. An incandescent finger of light appeared, violently probing a crack. A dazzling light burst on the scene, only it was not the sun, as I'd expected, but a klieg light, and the parting darkness was a curtain opening on stage, the boardroom of American Power and Light. On the far side of the black marble table eleven figures were seated around an empty chair, five on one side, six on the other, I, the twelfth man, seated opposite on the near side, participating in the drama even as I observed myself from the audience. An enamel-yellow sun with rays protruding unrealistically from its perimeter hung in the sky above the backdrop of Manhattan on a painted scrim, framing my head like a sallow aureole.

The characters on stage appeared to be waiting for something. Occasionally someone scratched his head with a jerky, unnatural motion and looked mechanically from side to side, or Bateson got up woodenly and fretted over the chrysanthemums in the vase, trying to fluff them like a woman's hairdo, leaving them more mussed than before. This went on for an unconscionably long time. I could hear people starting to yawn and fidget in their seats. Suddenly a bloodcurdling howl like a wolf's erupted from offstage. The hair prickled along the back of my neck. Then the howl went up an octave and became a bark, the yap-yap, yap-yap-yap of a rabid and obnoxious feist. A wirehaired terrier bounded in from stage right, skidding to a halt on all fours like a cartoon character, panting blithely toward the audience in expectation of applause. "Toto!" people cheered, and sure enough, it was. The little star stood on his hind paws and turned in a circle, then leapt up onto the black marble table. Only Toto wasn't little; he was as big as the seated men, big almost as the table itself, and consequently clumsy. In performing his trick, he upset the vase, which shattered in a thousand fragments, spilling a red, viscous fluid over the black marble. Bateson leapt up and threw his hands in the air, performing an apoplectic jig, and Toto turned to him, tilted his head quizzically, then bit the director's head off, stretching his neck out to swallow the difficult morsel. The audience stomped in their seats for more. Toto then lowered his head and began contentedly lapping the mysterious effluent, wagging his tail, each pert swipe simultaneously slapping the faces of the entire Board of Directors of American Power and Light, knocking their heads together with a wooden sound like bowling pins. The audience roared. Largely undeterred by his misfortune, Bateson's mutilated remnant produced from out of thin air a loaf of crusty French bread, "still warm from the oven," with which he sopped the fluid, handing it to me. I wrung it into a green bottle marked "Château Snake Oil." Where the vintage should have been it simply said, "Eternal Life."

Intrigued by this detail, I hardly noted the weird change coming over Toto. As he drank, his body began to bulge in some places and contract in others. He simultaneously swelled and shrank. The drum rolled and the cymbals clashed, and when I looked up again he was no longer Toto at all, but Tsin's dog. His glass eye glittered, cold as Sirius in the winter sky. The audience gasped and held its breath as the huge beast reared on its hind legs, performing its model's turn with even less finesse than Toto. When the painful revolution was accomplished, the animal had changed again, as though turned on a mystic lathe, becoming a smiling fox with female dress and carriage.

Then the cymbals clashed again, and once more it was Toto. The sighs of the audience escaped like gases. Exhausted with suspense, but happy, they clapped, becoming more and more vociferous, as little Toto, still on his hind legs, moved now stage right, now stage left, begging and acknowledging the applause. Then suddenly he leapt up for the final act, a death-defying double somersault straight into the window! Oh no! The audience shut its eyes and sucked its breath in through its teeth. Oh yes! The scrim disintegrated with a tremendous sound of ripping fabric, and Toto disappeared into the sun!

Sick with suspense, we waited, sweating. Nothing happened. He was gone! A little boy began to whimper somewhere near the back. Then, like a film run in reverse, the little dog swung back in through the tattered, flapping backdrop, yapping for glory, riding the flying trapeze of his invisible trick wire! The audience went wild! Mothers whistled with their fingers and fathers wept. The children leapt madly up and down in their chairs until the upholstery springs thrummed like an ecstatic chorus of Jew's harps, until it seemed the kingdom of heaven was at hand.

Then a small hand pointed, and one by one the members of the crowd hushed. Behind the tattered scrim, among the wires and pulleys, trying very hard to make himself as inconspicuous as possible, was a man! A giant! And now we knew we'd been watching puppets, except for Toto, the whole stage, the curtain, nothing but a puppet theatre! I too was a puppet, very puppet of very puppets! The giant gathered up his paraphernalia, withdrawing the scaffolding which had held up our painted, magic world, and all the actors, myself included, collapsed like Punch and Judy, faces flat down on the table, torsos slumped double-jointed between still-upright knees. The whispers became outright hisses. The puppeteer smiled nervously, embarrassed and apologetic, tipping his black silk top hat while he packed his gear, so that his black bag of tricks overflowed like a volcano, spewing his tackle over the floor like a trail of breadcrumbs leading nowhere.

Growing belligerent and brave, the audience roundly hooted him, throwing paper airplanes at the stage and crying "Humbug! Humbug!" until I almost felt sorry him. But I should have known; it was all part of the act. The drums rolled and, tipping his top hat again, the giant became a tiger with vertical green eyes like emeralds and a black and orange tail sticking through the vent of his tuxedo. He roared and the whole earth shook with the high-pitched whine, like an electric saw or a P-40 in a power dive. The women fainted and the children caught them. The men were streaming for the exits. The cymbals clashed, he tipped his hat again, and he became a bear, a giant panda, with a white face like a skull and coal-black rings of exhausted self-abuse around his molten honey eyes. Fluttering the top hat, he did a vaudeville stretch-strut off stage, going nowhere fast and always coming back to more and more applause.

When the crowd was almost hoarse with cheering, he returned to take his final bows, and when he rose from his final final bow, it was, of course, my father, Eddie Love, and he was wearing aviator glasses with black-green tear-shaped lenses and smiling that cryptic smile, which suddenly, beyond all codes, I understood. In a burst of blinding light he vanished then amidst a puff of rainbow-colored smoke, leaving a distinctive odor in the air, like wildflowers and dung, or the stench of putrefaction on the beach, only scented with a hint of sulphur. The stage crew killed the lights, the house went dark, and I woke up in a cold sweat.

The water was still running in the bathroom. I reached compulsively for a cigarette. My hands were shaking, but my mind was clear, for the first time in months it seemed, clearer than it had ever been. Now I understood. The dream code shattered all at once. The key turned in the lock, the master key; the door creaked open; inside everything was there: the empty parachute, Mme Chin's mysterious buyer, the incongruous details at the APL parley — the cigarette, the flowers — all of it a farce! He was still there! He was alive! He had been there the whole time, behind it all, like the puppeteer, pulling the strings, like the bogus Oz, the Great Humbug, manipulating the controls of his magnificent stereopticon, his magic lantern. Hun in the Sun on Wall Street indeed! The whole thing had been a monstrous joke, and I had been the butt, since the beginning, since before the beginning, the sperm laughing even as it burrowed head-deep in the egg, drunk as a lord, in a sated rigor mortis of hilarity.

Yes, I had been his dupe, even as I worshipped him like God, throwing away my own salvation to follow him into his putrid mystery. Yes, I was lost. Forever and forever and forever. Hell without end. He had taken me along for the ride in his "descensus Averno." Who knows why? Simply for the hell of it perhaps. The hell of it. Son follows father's footsteps, not out of the enchanted forest, but deeper in, ever deeper into the delicious mystery. And what was the mystery? Sin, Reader, sin, and compromise, and apostasy, and sacrifice of innocence and principle and hope — all those things that lend our souls their mortal tarnish here, living in the world as it is. And I had followed willingly, picking up each crumb behind him, picking up each scrap, each bleeding scrap, eating my way back out — the Way back in — and licking my fingertips! Ha! What a fool I'd been! How I loathed myself. How I loathed *him*. Yes, *him*. Li had been right, and now I knew it. My hatred, dammed up behind the dike of my resistance, held back by a finger plug which I now vehemently withdrew, burst to consciousness with a roar of waters like Grand Coulee Dam collapsing, threatening to drown the world in a renewed diluvial catastrophe. Hatred boiled within me like a crucible.

Yet there was joy, too, in my heart, for he was still alive, still there behind the looking glass! Those mirrors in the conference room; were they two-way mirrors? Of course! And he'd observed it all, reveling in his privileged vantage! But one thing he hadn't seen, couldn't have. He didn't know I knew. "Surprise was his forte." Well, I had followed in his footsteps thus far, like a dutiful son in all other respects, in that too then, by cock! I would revenge myself. "For now we see through a glass darkly; but then, face to face." Yes indeed, face to face. I would have revenge. Pleasure burned so brightly with the pain that chills and fever trembled over me. I felt again the cold wind blowing out of that unfathomable distance, saw the shadow approaching impossibly fast over the ground. I closed my eyes and fought it, grinding my molars and clenching my fists, and it passed on. Opening my eyes again, I shivered like a dog emerging from a cold sea, having retrieved at peril the bobbing toy of my own sanity.

The door of the bathroom opened and Li came out in her robe, toweling her hair. "You're awake!" She studied my face with anxiety. "How do you feel?"

"Wonderful," I replied, slathering the word with irony.

"Hmm," she said. "You sound like your old self again. I was worried about you for a while there. You were acting very strange."

"Just a minor psychotic breakdown," I remarked, "nothing to get worked up about. Happens all the time."

She laughed and came up beside the bed. Standing over me, she lifted my chin. "Your color does seem better," she observed. "Do you really feel all right?"

"I'm fine," I assured her, tossing my head impatiently.

"I think you should see someone," she told me quietly. "In fact, I insist on it."

"Oh, I have every intention of it!" I bantered wryly, thinking with pleasure of a particular rendezvous.

"What is that supposed to mean?"

"Nothing," I replied. "Forget it."

"I won't forget it, Sun I. What happened back there was serious. And it wasn't normal. You had a seizure of some kind. You fainted dead away and were out for several minutes. Do you remember?"

"How did we get home?"

"*You drove,*" she informed me with exasperated incredulity. "Oh my Christ. We're lucky to be alive! You came in here and crashed on the bed and were asleep in fifteen seconds." She checked her watch. "That was three hours ago."

"All right," I conceded, "I'll see someone, okay?"

"Okay." She frowned at me doubtfully. "You know, what happened back there set something ringing in my head. On the way home I remembered what it was. While you were asleep I looked for it." She went into the other room and came back with a book. "I want you to read something." She opened to a marked place.

"Read it to me," I said, a little queasy at the prospect of confronting print.

"Remember we were talking about Freud? This is from one of his case studies, a man named Schreber. Freud talks about the sun as a sublimated symbol for the father. Here it is:

The sun used to speak to him [Schreber] in human language and thus revealed itself to him as a living being. Schreber was in the habit of abusing it and shouting threats at it; he declares, moreover, that when he stood facing it and spoke aloud its rays would turn pale before him. After his "recovery" he boasts that he can gaze at it without any difficulty and without being more than slightly dazzled by it, a thing which had naturally been impossible for him formerly.

It is out of this delusional privilege of being able to gaze at the sun without being dazzled that the mythological interest arises. We read in Reinach that the natural historians of antiquity attributed this power only to the eagle, who, as dweller in the highest regions of the air, was brought into especially intimate relation with the heavens, with the sun, and with lightning. We learn from the same sources, moreover, that the eagle puts his young to a test before recognizing them as legitimate offspring. Unless they can succeed in looking into the sun without blinking, they are cast out from the eyrie. . . .

The procedure gone through by the eagle with his young is an *ordeal* [Li fixed me pointedly], a test of lineage, such as is reported of the most various races of antiquity.

"Fascinating, isn't it?" She closed the book. "Well?" she asked in solemn inquiry.

I didn't answer. I was too absorbed in her hands. Curled around the spine of the closed book, prizing it like claws, her perfect nails flashed white, and I saw that, just below, her fingertips were lined and puckered, shriveled from the water. I spontaneously recalled what I hadn't earlier been able to, Oz's ultimatum to the pilgrims: "Kill the witch," that was what he'd said. "Kill the Wicked Witch of the West"; and then her cries as she melted from the cold water Dorothy doused her with and became a steaming puddle on the floor. Lowering with malignant hatred, I glared at Li. "It's all a game to you, isn't it?"

"What do you mean?" she asked in alarm. "Why are you looking at me like that?" She drew back a step, raising the book to her breast in a gesture of unconscious self-defense.

It wasn't the fox's face I saw then, but, truly, something equally evil. She reminded me of Mme Chin, regarding the world, regarding me, with a glutton's (or connoisseur's, it didn't matter in the end) unhealthy and insatiable appetite. I was a case study for her still and always had been. She was as remote and cold as she had been on that first night, cold and remote as a statue, like the Venus de Milo, only a restored version, with a death's-head smiling in cynical invitation to enjoy the perfect flesh. "You remember the first night we made love," I asked in a low whisper, "you said I'd hate you for it?"

She gaped at me in bewilderment and alarm.

"Well, you were right," I continued. "I do."

"What are you saying?" she cried. "What on earth is going through your mind?"

But I didn't give away my secret. I didn't answer, or pursue her as she quickly walked into the other room. I knew she was plotting against me, against my life. But it didn't matter. She wasn't the real witch. That was American Power and Light, the Dowager. And it wasn't the witch I wanted anyway, not really. It was Oz.

I sat on the edge of the bed for some time, brooding. From the initial phase of frantic mania after the dream, my fury had abated somewhat, or rather been transformed, as if by the touch of a magic wand, into something desperate and settled, cold and malign, like the city in which I found myself — in which I'd lost myself. I had no delusion anymore, not on that score. I was lost. Forever and forever. Hell without end. I smiled. The stream on which I'd ridden all the way had disappeared into the bowels of the earth and flowed through dripping limestone caverns underground, where huge stalactites, breaking off, resounded with an unearthly echo as they fell into the greenish, phosphorescent water. That the stream would issue out into the sunlight and run sparkling through the brightness of the day once more I had believed sincerely once. No more. Now I knew beyond all doubt, beyond all hope, that I had made a terrible mistake. Now I knew the river I was riding was called Phlegethon and issued only at the burning heart of hell, bubbling up black and emerald and red in a chancred font where souls were baptized into an eternity of pain. Yes, I had made a terrible mistake, as terrible as hell, and now I knew. I'd made a gamble, and lost. And the cost was everything. My soul itself was forfeit. Forever and forever. Hell without end.

I laughed, thinking of a story I'd read recently in the papers, not quite understanding, about Alf Landon, a presidential contender from Kansas who always lost. "The Kansas tornado is an old story," he was quoted as saying in the aftermath of one of his defeats, "but let me tell you of one. It swept away first the barn, then the outbuildings. Then it picked up the dwelling and scattered it all over the landscape. As the funnel-shaped cloud went twisting out of sight, leaving nothing but splinters behind, the wife came to, to find her husband laughing. She angrily asked him, 'What are you laughing at, you darned fool?' And the husband replied, 'The completeness of it.' "

And I laughed too, because I understood it now. "The completeness of it." The completeness of my fall and of my reprobation. I had tasted blood, a fitting feast for a Dowist perhaps, but for a Taoist, no redemption. Yes, I was lost.

But the joy of knowing he was still alive consoled me wickedly. I remembered again the passage from Corinthians: "When I was a child, I spoke as a child, I understood as a child, I thought as a child; but when I became a man, I put away childish things." Yes, it was time to put away childish things. The child in my heart was dead. That was the price I'd had to pay. The greatness of the price; the completeness of it. But I would know him now, even as he knew me, in that final intimacy which Tsin alone had tasted, dared to know, "that intimacy, deeper than any other, which exists between the hunter and his prey." I understood now. *I* was the Adversary, *I* was the Hunter in Chung Fu's metaphor, who had hounded him across the earth, tracking his blood spoor into the dead end of this final sanctuary, American Power and Light. There we would meet upon the field of battle and share the only gift that we had left to share with one another, the only gift that we had ever had to share: the ecstasy of combat. It occurred to me that all along, in the name of restoration, I'd unconsciously intended a subtle but devastating revenge against him, posthumously inflicted against his name and memory. Bateson had been right. And he had known because my father knew. The vista opened wider and I saw that at some level, even as a child, I'd always hated him and, like an avenging Fury, followed him across the world, waiting in the fullness of time to revenge my bastarding. Only then did I understand that beyond all specious intimations of transcendence, which albeit had thrilled my soul and stirred belief, there remained the galling impetus of that insidious question: "Will this Sun outshine his father?" And I told myself I would, I vowed it, even at the cost of an eternity of pain; and not as an "ordeal" either, to prove myself worthy of him, not to vindicate his memory or the family honor, but for the simple joy of murder. Yes, it was Oz I wanted, and there was murder in my heart.

"Corporate patricide." I laughed, thinking with what vehement righteousness I'd denied such intent. It seemed curiously tame now. No, "corporate" patricide wasn't enough. I wanted the real thing. I wanted blood. I wanted to wet my hands in him, split him down the middle and scoop out his quivering heart and inner organs and eat them, eat them raw. I wanted . . . But again I saw the dark wing circling, coming close, and I refrained. Suffice it to say, my heart was full of joy.

Chapter 19

The next morning early, Li, who seemed nervous and upset, announced that she was going to the library. "I wish I didn't, but I simply have to get back to my thesis," she said, face slightly averted as she clipped in an earring.

I noticed, in addition, that she was wearing makeup.

"Do you think you'll be all right?" she asked.

I smiled ambiguously and nodded, observing her obliquely. Her features shimmied in the heat wave of my settled malevolence. I knew where she was going. It was all too clear to me now. All. She'd deceived me once. I'd been a fool to believe her. But I wouldn't be duped again. I'd played that role too many times to too many white clowns, shrill and vicious behind their paints. I knew she was seeing him again. The queer. Peter. They were plotting, and it wasn't difficult to see what. "Marriage. Holy matrimony." On my lips the words were like a poisoned sacrament. I knew what came next, and it wasn't "till death do us part." Or perhaps it was. But I didn't think they'd go that far. They didn't have the balls. *I* did — the thought gave me satisfaction — but not them. Besides, they didn't have to. There were other ways. I could see what they were scheming. The scenarios were finite. Divorce. Settlement. That should do them handsomely. Or she might try and have me committed. That thing about Schreber . . . The cogs had already engaged in her mind; the machinery was running. But first I had to step into the springe.

I smiled grimly with the anticipated satisfaction of obstruction. Perhaps some opportunity would even arise of destroying them without risk to myself. Surprise was on my side here as well. But I wouldn't sacrifice my major objective to it, not to them. They were secondary.

•

After she was gone I continued furiously feeding the furnace, shoveling the black coals of my grievance into the flames, stoking the engine of my hatred until the metal smoked and turned red-hot. But I couldn't sustain such enmity;

the blood lust was too consuming. There was a sudden drop in temperature. A slow chill of resolve, like death, spread gradually inward from the extremities toward the core, toward my heart. This was accompanied by a rising panic, in which I could detect faintly, like music heard from a distance, the shrill, witless piping of hysteria.

I rummaged in the medicine cabinet and took a sleeping pill. But it only drugged me. I napped fitfully and woke each time disoriented and in a deepened terror. I stared up from the bed at the undifferentiated plaster of the ceiling, lost in the white sea of myself. I felt a terrible sense of aloneness, like a tiny sail lost between horizons on a shoreless waste of water, tacking and tacking. Craving to be covered, to be swathed, I tried pathetically to assuage the longing with the bedclothes. Getting to my knees, I pulled them over me and buried my face in the pillows, rocking and rocking, emitting a low, inarticulate wail.

How had I arrived here, I asked myself? How? Had the motives of my search been impure? *Had* they? No, I had believed. I could not, *would* not, accuse myself on that score. My quest had been legitimate. Hadn't it? The delta? The Tao within the Dow — was there a hidden seed of evil planted there? Too deep . . . too deep. And if not, then how had I arrived here? How could a man — a child — set out in purity of heart and arrive at such a state of degradation in a world subject to the laws of Tao, a world subject to law at all?

There was no answer. Only the sail, tacking and tacking. But now the sail was black and it tacked on a red ocean. For the river of Dow was a blood river, and here at last at the delta it debouched into a blood sea.

My mind was filled with blood. In a waking dream I inventoried tuns and casks of it, hogsheads and barrels, rivers and lakes, a vast thalassic wilderness of blood, and I was swimming in it without hope, desperately tired, beginning to weaken. It was too thick (so much thicker than water), I could feel myself beginning to drown. My chin slumped toward it, wetted. I could feel the warmth rising from it like a breeze, and the sickening stench. I struggled, but my head sunk lower, lower, until the putrid bubbles formed around my lips and it covered my eyes and my hair lifted above me with a gentle tug, floating like the Dead Man's Fingers.

I screamed awake — a dream. I was frightened. This was not what I had wanted. This was not what I had meant at all. Not this. I had never wanted this.

As I rocked and keened, I gradually became aware of a murmurous voice speaking low in my inner ear, a voice of memory out of my unconscious. I stopped and trained my hearing, listening. Inarticulate at first, bit by bit it grew louder, until finally it crossed the threshold into consciousness and I recognized it. It was Riley's voice, and he was saying, "This is my blood of the New Testament, which is shed for you, and for many, for the remission of sins." Over and over, like a recording. Becoming very still, not even breathing, mesmerized like an animal at night by the glare of headlights, I stared at it, my heart beating very fast.

"For the remission of sins," I repeated wonderingly in a quiet voice as though the words were fragile and might break apart on my tongue, like the wafer, like the body, and with them, their promise. A terrible excitement filled me, terrible because tinged with dread that at the slightest touch or pressure the promise might go away, burst like a bubble.

Then suddenly the beautiful idea broke over me, a wave of light. If I was lost, and damned in it, perhaps the blood could save me, too. "A fitting feast for a Dowist" — the phrase which had erupted from a deep, unconscious irony now filled me with gigantic hope. Not only was it fitting, it was the only feast, my only hope. There was no salvation left to me through Taoism. I had squandered all my Treasures. But perhaps Christianity could save me. Perhaps it wasn't too late after all. Maybe there was still a chance. What did I have to lose? I had taken on all the other trappings of a Dowist, I might as well take the religion too. Blood worship at an altar of blood. Conversion seemed the merest formality. Had I not already tasted the Sacrament? "The remission of sins."

Taking out the Prayer book Riley had given me, I hunted down the passage he'd drawn to my attention: "Grant us therefore, gracious Lord, so to eat the flesh of thy dear Son, Jesus Christ, and to drink his blood, that our sinful bodies may be made clean by his body, and our souls washed through his most precious blood, and that we may evermore dwell in him, and he in us."

Yes, *washed* through his most precious blood. That was it. That was what I wanted. Not to drown in the ordure of it, but to be cleansed in the blood of holy sacrifice. Sacred murder. The idea brought me peace. Feed on him in thy heart, and be thankful. Oh yes. Yes. I would.

I dressed hurriedly and caught a cab. The Avenue of the Americas was almost deserted. I stuck my head out the window and let the cold wind flatten back my hair, heedless of the tears streaming down my cheeks. I gazed up at the blue vista opening between the buildings, the splash of yellow sunlight on the pavement amid the black and white morning shadows, and I was happy, happy. The scene was a restorative, and gave me back myself.

But at the church I lost heart. The sustaining inner logic of it failed me, and the scheme seemed desperate, or even worse, insane. But I didn't leave. I felt ashamed, but I went in, skulked in as I had once before, and hid myself in a rear pew. And when the usher came and soberly nodded his permission, I stood up with the rest and walked in a chastened line toward the altar. Riley was serving with a second priest, each administering half the rail, starting at the ends and working toward the middle. I was near the back, positioned solidly to fall in Riley's lot. Eschewing dignity or prudence, I began walking quickly, shouldering past the others apologetically, so that by the time we'd reached the choir I'd managed to advance my cause considerably. Kneeling with the others, I raised my hands in devout petition and bowed my head low over the rail, sweating and examining the rutted nap of the claret-colored carpet. I could hear them both approaching, their voices drifting in and out of sync, producing a hallucinatory effect as of a single voice mimicked at a higher pitch by its own syncopated echo.

The wafer tickled my palm. It was the other priest. Riley was standing near, almost close enough for me to touch the hem of his robe, but he turned and I escaped. My heart thudded in my chest, and I exhaled. Slowly I dissolved it on my tongue, flipping and flipping it in my saliva. "How thin! How flavorless!" I thought, almost laughing as I recalled Lao Tzu's subtle inverted paean to the savor of the Tao. But the wine was coming soon. That was what I wanted. I could hear them again converging toward the center, whispering the secret antiphony which filled my heart with joy: "This is my blood (*blood*) of the New (*New*) Testament (*ament*), which is shed for you, and for many (*any*), for the remission (*ion*) of sins (*s — s*)." It hissed out like a wave. I closed my eyes and silently repeated the syllables with them, cueing on Riley's voice, listening with pleasure to the second priest as he returned them changed, higher, distilled further toward immaculate whiteness. But suddenly there was only my voice and the echo. Riley had stopped speaking. This time the rhythm had been altered slightly, he had come a little faster. Opening my eyes, I saw him standing motionless in front of me, holding the chalice at my eye level, gleaming gold against the snowdrift furrows of his vestment in his flushed hands, innocent forever of all labor. He tilted it slightly, and the wine washed in a slow swirl against the rear wall of the cup, winking at me in the gloom of candles, a purple almost black. When he didn't move, I raised my face to him, and all my pain. A troubled tenderness showed in his features, warring with chagrin. Handing the chalice to the other priest (who had stopped now too and stood beside him, scrutinizing now my face, now Riley's), he slipped the brass rail back and lifted me gently by the arm, walking me toward the vestry.

In the first moment I had thought I had a chance. But now I saw I'd been mistaken. His tenderness remained, but it was like a treacly condiment on a tray of bitter offerings. His face was red with pained embarrassment and anger. His eyes scintillated like the edges of broken glass. He carefully shut the door, and then he exploded, emitting a great burst of air, too vehement to be called a sigh. He paced with angry deliberateness.

"So that's what you were doing here," he said, as though the idea had just dawned on him, "that afternoon you almost ran me over in the vestibule." He stalked away again, shaking his head as though mortified at his own credulousness. "I don't believe it. I simply don't believe it. How dare you?" He seethed with righteous venom, wheeling on me. "*How dare you?* And we were so cozy, weren't we? Drinking tea, the Love Feast, East meets West."

"Forgive me, Father," I said, lowering my head.

" 'Father'?" he repeated, smiling as though the idea amused him. "Father? Don't you dare 'Father' me, Sun I. Don't you dare try and play the humble penitent to my 'Father.' That dog won't hunt, boy. I'm not your father. This is not your church. What are you, some kind of religious pervert? Do you have on black panties and a hair shirt underneath your suit, a barbed-wire cinch? Or what are you? What? You should know, if anyone does, the gravity of this. Didn't I catechize you on it one whole evening? Are you stupid? Are you an idiot? Hmm?" He tapped his forehead. "What are you doing back? Is it the moth and the flame? Are you a wino? D.T.s? Does sherry give you chills? Or have you forgotten what I told you then? 'For as the benefit is great, if with a true penitent heart and lively faith you receive that holy Sacrament; so is the danger great, if you receive the same unworthily.' Remember? 'So *dangerous* to those who will presume to receive it unworthily; my duty is to exhort you, in the mean season to consider the dignity of that holy mystery, and the great peril of the unworthy receiving thereof; and so to search and examine your own conscience, and that not lightly, and after the manner of dissemblers with God; but so that ye may come holy and clean to such a heavenly Feast, in the marriage-garment required by God in holy Scripture, and be received as a worthy partaker of that holy Table.' Eh? Remember now? Strike a bell? Is it coming back to you?"

"I remember, Father," I said earnestly, not flinching under his angry leer. "It's because I remember that I came back. I'm not sure I recall the words exactly as you have said them, but that doesn't matter. They are right. 'So to come holy and clean to the heavenly Feast, in the marriage-garment required by God in holy Scripture.' Yes, they are right. I am prepared. I wish to wear this garment and approach."

He appeared flabbergasted. "What in God's name are you saying? Are you mad?"

"I'm ready to convert, Father," I said. As he still didn't respond, I clasped my hands together vehemently, fingers interlocking, and bowed my head, beginning fervently to pray. " 'Grant us therefore, gracious Lord . . .' " and I repeated it.

When I looked up again, tears were rolling down Riley's cheeks, though his eyes were still wide with amazement. Covering his face with one hand, he turned away. His voice beseeched me. "Forgive me, Sun I. I've made a terrible mistake."

I smiled gravely. "So have I, Father. So have I."

"I'm so moved." He stared into the air above my head as at the visitation of his wonder. "So moved." He began to weep again.

"You aren't unhappy?"

"No, no," he said, sniffling and blotting his tears on the sleeve of his vestment. "Not that. It's simply that my heart is overflowing with so much happiness for your sake. Do you know, this has never happened to me before? And yet . . ." — he regarded me through narrowed lids, as though adding a sum that didn't quite compute — "I would never have expected it. Not you. You seemed so settled in your faith, so fired." He sighed and shook his head. "But let that pass. There is joy in this church today." He became agitated in a confiding way. "Goodness though, I have to deliver the sermon! I must go back now, Sun I. Father Davis will be frantic. Meet me here after the service and I'll take you myself to the Inquirers' class and introduce you." Radiant with happiness, he took my hands. "I'm so moved, Sun I. So moved. Really."

"And the Communion, Father?" I called after him as he started off. "The cup?"

He pivoted. "You must be baptized first, Sun I," he explained gently, as though repeating a lesson to a wayward but beloved child.

"I realize that, Father," I said. "But can't we forego the formalities, or defer them, just this once, just today?"

"Why are you so anxious?" he asked. "Is something bothering you?"

I bowed my head, conceding silently.

"Sun I, let me refer you once again to the Exhortations." He assumed a firm, authoritative, but not unkindly tone. " 'It is requisite that no man should come to the holy Communion, but with a full trust in God's mercy, and with a quiet conscience; therefore, if there be any of you, who by this means cannot quiet his own conscience herein, but requireth further counsel or comfort, let him come to me, or some other Minister of God's Word, and open his grief; that he may receive such godly counsel and advice, as may tend to the quieting of his conscience, and the removing of all scruple and doubtfulness.' The burden of which, Sun I, is that you must be prepared. Whatever it is that's brought you here today, that's brought you back over and over, whatever it is that's troubling you has got to be worked out" — he smiled — "so you may come, 'holy and clean to the Feast.' Besides, this isn't a step to be taken rashly. You must steep a little first in the thought of it, learn some more about the Church. By Easter, when the bishop baptizes and receives, you should be ready. I admire your enthusiasm, but you must simply wait till then. Believe me, it will mean more to you."

"It will mean nothing," I contradicted harshly. "Easter will be too late. Tomorrow will be too late. It must be now, Father. It has to be today."

"But why?" he asked, reverting to his original perplexed exasperation.

I shook my head. "I don't know, Father. Truly I don't. It just has to." I kept my head bowed. As he said nothing, I went on imploringly. "It satisfied some thirst in me," I confided, hoarse with passion. "It gave me peace."

"But it was deadly sin," he pointed out. "Or if it wasn't then, it would be now."

I stared into his eyes unflinchingly, applying the full weight of my candor, sparing neither him nor myself. "I know."

He recoiled visibly, a shudder of revulsion crossing his features. He seemed to interrogate me silently, and then he said, "You knew that, didn't you, coming here today, that it was deadly sin to partake? And yet you did anyway — tried at least."

I didn't answer.

Starting from his neck and moving upward, a blush spread over his whole face, so that, with his hair, he looked like he was burning, sunstruck. "Now

I think I'm beginning to understand." A poisoned smile overspread his features. "What did you think, that you could save yourself by redoubling your damnation? Or didn't you care? You didn't, did you? You only wanted solace, no thought of anything beyond. You actively willed your own damnation coming here, and conversion was only a ploy. Oh my God . . ." He laughed. "I've made a terrible mistake all right." He looked like he was going to spit in my face. "You disgust me. You're like a dog salivating over a piece of meat, or an old lecher with an itch for a beautiful, chaste girl, trying to entice her into bed with a promise of marriage he doesn't intend to keep, has no intention of keeping. Is that what you did with Yin-mi?" he added viciously.

It was my turn to blush; but I ignored it, choking back the rage his taunt unleashed. "I only know my soul is dying," I said with a tremulous voice, "and I'm asking you for help." A sob escaped from me, and I put my face in my hands and wept unrestrainedly. "And I'll keep this promise, too," I affirmed fiercely through my tears.

He sobered. "I've offered you help already, Sun I," he observed, "on the only terms I'm able."

"Today?" I asked, still weeping.

He rolled in his lips and grimly shook his head.

"It's not enough."

"Then get out," he ordered. "If everything isn't enough, get out. Go on, go." He approached me gesticulating recklessly, as though he would strike me.

An icy calm gripped my heart with the suddenness of a shock, as if I'd plunged into a pool of freezing water. I turned and started out.

"And don't come back," he sputtered with rage.

I stopped at the threshold. "Don't worry, I won't," I spat hatefully.

"If your need, or your fantasy — whatever it is — persists, go to some other priest, some other parish. Only, not here. Whatever you've done, whatever you are, I hope you find forgiveness. But don't come here. I can't minister to you in good conscience. Not now. Not after this. Not having looked into your heart." He narrowed his eyes. "You're lost, Sun I," he whispered hoarsely. "Lost."

"I know," I said, grinning viciously, "and I owe it all to you." Then I winked at him and disappeared.

Outside on the sidewalk I stood peering in at the graveyard. The wrought iron bars bit my hands with cold. I squeezed tighter for the pain. The pain: that was real. Nothing else was. It ran through my veins like electricity, pumping me up, burning. I smiled slowly as I realized that in an oblique, backhanded way, my journey had accomplished its objective. The danger was past. I was no longer afraid. My hate had been restored. Implacable now. Forever and forever.

Chapter 20

Rising Sun opened off a point on Monday morning, rather strange considering our recent performance. Hardly cause for alarm, though. The Horns speculated, and I concurred, that Kahn had simply got impatient and let go a little too many of his holdings at one time. Not to worry. We planned to file the statement of our tender offer that day at noon, projecting that registration would cause a terrific spurt, not only in the share price of American Power and Light, which would be primarily affected, but also, more modestly, in our own. There was much gleeful hand rubbing, winking, and appetite whetting of a general sort among us that morning in anticipation of the furor and confusion our coup de main was sure to excite. I intended to slip inconspicuously down to the Visitors' Gallery to witness the scene and revel in my triumph.

Trading activity proceeded normally for the first ten minutes after I assumed my station. Then a man rushed in from the Members' Smoking Lobby with a lit cigarette in his hand. He ran several steps before realizing he had it, then stopped, regarded it with a vexed expression, wheeled around quickly as though to leave, looked at it again, turned back, took a puff, and threw it down, grinding it out beneath his toe. He then took off for the first post. Before arriving, he met someone he apparently knew and paced off with him in a different direction, gesticulating with his hands. Obviously in a hurry, not listening, the second man nodded perfunctorily and picked up his pace to escape. The first man spun around and grabbed the arm of the next broker he saw. Red in the face, he flailed his arms. The arrested broker looked at him like he was crazy. Something consequential must have passed between them, though, for his listener became attentive and shook his head vehemently, moving his lips — "You're sure?"

The first man nodded his emphatic assent. A third man joined their conversation. Then, before my eyes, the dominoes began to topple. The progression went forward sequentially, tracing curlicues and arabesques and whirligigs around the trading posts, across the threshold into the garage, into the Members' Lobby, public lobby, and through the doors into the Street, leaving behind the most profound silence. Those who had heard were frozen in an attitude of slack-jawed astonishment. The bookkeepers put down their pens and forgot to record new orders in the ledgers, the telephone clerks lapsed into catatonic amazement, and the phones flashed their lights in vain for attention. The pneumatic tube itself went hissing hungry and, deprived of its vital nutriment, the great heart of the organism fluttered, lurched, and finally infarcted. Brain death occurred, and for a moment the tape whirred by on the screen, empty! For perhaps the first and only time in Wall Street history, the trading floor was still, so still one could have heard the scratching of a clerk's pen writing out an order; only there weren't any. Specialists, brokers, bookkeepers, clerks, reporters, squad boys, all alike stood frozen, as though turned to stone by the apparition of the primal terror. And then a deafening roar rose upward. It might have announced either the final launching of the missiles from their silos or the release of thousands upon thousands of parti-colored balloons at some great worldwide festival of peace and brotherhood, for at first no one knew whether the world had ended or the millennium had arrived. Only something great, something unprecedented in its scale, had occurred, that alone was certain.

Then suddenly the crowd bolted like a herd of cattle spooked by thunder, racing madly back and forth without a leader, looking for a precipice. Red-faced brokers elbowed and clawed to get to the pneumatic slots to place their orders first, stampeding underfoot specialists and assorted Exchange personnel who tried to stand in their way maintaining protocol. A few canny individuals were auctioning off floor space before the Dow Jones news wire as the confused and desperate stood trying to absorb the deluge of press releases steaming in over the lines. And it was I, I alone, who had applied the initial leverage which set the pieces falling, as with a tiny fillip of my index finger.

"Sir . . . sir . . ." a meek voice said, breaking in unwelcomely on my meditations.

From beneath beetling brows, I lowered down at an anxious, harried girl who apparently had been tugging unheeded at my elbow for quite some time. I recognized her as the receptionist at the Visitors' Center. "Yes?" I demanded in a severe tone.

"I'm very sorry, sir," she apologized timidly. "But the gallery will be temporarily closed to the general public. You'll have to leave."

" 'General public'? Young lady," I said, assuming a tone of stertorous authority, "do you have any idea to whom you're talking?"

She gave me a queer look, but, not wanting to make trouble either for herself or me, simply reiterated, "I'm sorry, sir, I just work here, I don't make the rules. We always close when there's a panic. The orders come from upstairs, or downstairs — at any rate, from the top."

"A panic, eh?" I squinted down at the trading floor out of one narrowed eye, partially consoled by the sound of the word. "Panic." Yes, it had scope and grandeur. "All right then," I conceded, "you're just doing your job I suppose. I don't want to make it rough on you. I remember myself what it's like working for an hourly wage." And I left peacefully, to her great relief, even eagerly, having hit upon the bright idea of witnessing the "panic," *my* panic, from the firsthand vantage of the floor itself, by the light of the flares and incendiaries and bombs bursting in air.

And so, amid the deepening piles of paper, like the ashes that covered a civilization at Herculaneum or Pompeii, only here pink, yellow, and powder blue, like flower petals strewing the path of a conqueror, I walked out onto the floor amidst the turmoil, the panic, that I had created. Among the raging men and women screaming, weeping, wailing, and gnashing their teeth, I glided as one invisible, like a spirit of the air, in the thick of it, but spiritually high above, as though in the gallery still (still in the gallery of myself), looking down at the spectacle of greed and passion run amok with only the subtlest, the most exquisite melancholy and a scientific interest, like an observer from another planet, or a god, cut off forever from the rout and rut of humankind. If it was not at all what I'd expected, neither was it unpleasant, this feeling of vague wistfulness, this remote satiety, almost like emptiness, only without hunger. Rather like what an astronaut must experience, I conjectured, as he gazes back to earth, his ship hurtling out into the frigid night of space.

I remembered the exultation that had moved me that first day, and so many days since, observing the wonderful spectacle of the trading floor, one of the most thrilling sights there is, one that touches the hearts of all who witness it whether or not they understand. But that exultation had dissolved now, evaporated, leaving only the lingering bouquet of the experience. And, in truth, the bouquet was all I wanted, the wine purposely discarded as too raw, too coarse, too carnal for the palate of a connoisseur so far evolved. And as I thought these thoughts, I wheeled and wistfully surveyed the gallery, high above the trading floor, where I had stood that first morning, and sighed with the knowledge that the market could never more appear to me as it had then, in the glow of my original innocence. It seemed appropriate that that dim, narrow corridor, where one observed without participating, charmed perhaps but untouched finally by the passion of it, should be empty, if *I* could not be there, appropriate that everyone alike should be here on the floor, wrangling like blind sharks in a feeding frenzy. Everyone, including me: for if I had come full circle and observed without participating now, again, it was only because I had carried participation to its highest pitch, because I had fed most deeply and been filled.

But as I looked again, I saw I was mistaken. There *was* someone there! In the reflection of the ceiling lamps, like klieg lights splashing out a dozen equidistant suns in the wall of Plexiglas, a face appeared, coalescing. Was it the receptionist? I couldn't make it out at first, advancing and retreating, fusing and dispersing in the central pool of light — yet it appeared to be a man. Like someone eyeing a painting in a museum, trying to find exactly the right spot to escape the glare on the shiny surface of the oils, I moved a few steps this way, a few steps that way, trying to find my place. When at last I attained it, I stopped stock still, and a chill tingled down my spine.

It was him. Face to face at last, Reader, I squared off against my father and my adversary — Eddie Love. There was no mistake. Out of the heavier face of middle age, which gravity had weighed on for another quarter century almost, as from within a carnal prison, the face of the young man in the photograph peered out at me. I recognized it as infallibly as I would have recognized my own, through a glass darkly, reflected in a funhouse mirror. As if there could be any doubt, he was wearing the dark glasses with the tear-shaped lenses, just as I was, and smiling the mysterious smile that I could never quite pin down. Only now I understood it, understood the smile perfectly, and him by dint of it. For that smile expressed the remote satiety of a man who has lost his appetite for life, transformed the whole into a game, tricking the hours out until he dies, playing at it to amuse himself and stave off the despair that lurks beneath the surface scratching to get out, the gnawing restlessness that comes from final knowledge, final power, tasted illicitly in other's blood, sin original and ultimate, without redemption or the hope of it, forever and forever, hell without end. I understood that smile because it was the mirror image of my own, we two like ultimate players in the ultimate game, who know each other like they know themselves; reading the adversary's mind clairvoyantly, anticipating every move, such a player must rely on something deeper, the deepest thing of all, to win. And so must we, we confirmed silently across the intervening distance, loving and hating one another, smiling that final, secret smile. By mutual consent, we took off our dark glasses then, studying one another in a speechless intimacy beyond either love or hatred, an intimacy in which the unutterable mystery and beauty of the world came home once and forever, the mystery of life and otherness, life as otherness, unassimilable forever, forever free, subject to no compulsion, not even death. And like fishermen, we threw our magic fishes — each a fisherman, each a fish — back into the ocean of the world, awaiting another day when the sport, we knew, would be for keeps.

Gradually I became aware of voices whispering all around me. "It's him, it's him," they said, echoing my own discovery.

I nodded, impatient of the obvious, then turned and zeroed in on a victim in the nearest convenient lot. "Do you have any idea who that man is?" I pointed behind me.

"What man?" he asked innocently.

"Up there!" I shook my hand. "In the gallery!"

The fellow and his companion traded looks.

"It's my father!" I shouted, wheeling around to verify my claim. "See . . . ?" The question died on my lips.

"There's no one there," he observed quietly, bringing up perception's rear once more. Eddie Love had vanished. But of course he had, I thought. Of course.

More and more voices picked it up, whispering the chant, "It's him, it's him." Casting a final glance over my shoulder to be sure, I spun back, realizing they meant me.

Shaken by the incident, I started to depart, and, as I made my way, the crowds parted for me like the waters of the Red Sea when Moses waved his hand, and there was fear and amazement in their eyes. For in that brief span of half an hour, in the eyes of the ordinary investor on the Street, I had been apotheosized, dubbed by the mystic corporate Excalibur something more than human, a god to be appeased and placated, worshipped as the peasant farmers of China worship the Yangtze, beseeching the fickle deity to flood their paddies at the proper season and bring "prosperity to the rice and fishes to the nets," sparing them his greater wrath. I was no longer just another whiz kid, the latest fad, or a seasonal phenomenon. I had been translated, taken my place in that constellation of great speculators which, let him deny who will, is the only pantheon Wall Street will ever acknowledge. I had done what Gould and Harriman and Jessie Livermore himself, the Great Bear, what Diamond Jim and Fisk and all the Loves in turn beginning with A.E., Sr., and going down the line, including even Arthur, by his abdication, and, finally, Eddie, by his reassumption, had done: I had caused a panic. That was the ultimate compliment the old Bitch could ever pay a man, to grow flustered and give way to hysteria at some unexpected action on his part, throwing dignity to the winds and retreating helter-skelter before him. "Will this Sun outshine his father?" That still remained to be seen. But I had equaled him, that at least, already.

And what a panic! The Dow's first response to the news that her weightiest component, the heart and soul of the Average, was under attack, was no less than mortal terror. Within the first two hours it had retreated fifty points. Already the tape lagged behind by forty minutes. It seemed certain that before the day was out a hundred million shares would change hands. The downward plunge was given added momentum by the dire prediction of one of Wall Street's leading analysts, Joseph Pettyville, that a takeover of American Power and Light Corporation by Rising Sun Enterprises might mean "the end of American capitalism and the free-market system as we know it," a prediction that came across the wire preceded by an epigraph from Yeats, "Things fall apart; the center cannot hold."

Just at the darkest hour, however, another guru, with a following equally fervent, equally rabid, as Pettyville's, let it be known that, in his opinion, the proposed merger would be the best thing to happen to the American economy since the Louisiana Purchase, and would pump new blood into the veins of America's corporate mother, jolting her out of her torpor and complacency, forcing her to show some of the old fire and powder which had made her the greatest company in America — a marriage, in other words, of *sunrise* and sunset (or "Lights Out" as APL was sometimes known in New York City, where she owned and operated, through a subsidiary, the commercial power grid; "Old Brownout," less respectfully). With this the Averages bottomed out and began to climb. By the end of the afternoon the market had recovered the fifty points it had previously lost and tacked on thirty more for good measure. This provided a great boost to the reputation of the second analyst and a slap in the face to Pettyville, who was reportedly burned in effigy in major cities around the globe.

For the acute stress wasn't limited to Wall Street, or even the shores of the New World. In London the Financial Times Index dropped more than forty points, closing too early to take advantage of the rebound, only to open to a rally like none seen since the end of the Second World War. The Hang Seng Index in Hong Kong hung ten on the cresting financial tsunami with even more reckless aplomb than usual. A more conservative madness was reflected by the movements of the Crédit Suisse in Zurich, the Commerzbank in Frankfurt, the ANPCBS in Amsterdam, the Bourse in Paris. In Singapore and Sidney, Oslo, Milan, and Toronto, the Averages all took similarly hairy rides, not to mention the Nikkei-Dow in Tokyo, where ancestral swords were unsheathed and cries of bonzai! filled the air.

And within these mad fluctuations in the markets as wholes, individual stocks, too, seemed infected with a case of tarantism or Saint Vitus's dance. Back on Wall Street, APL, like an old mother on a roller coaster, half indignant, half terrified, plummeted like a stone and then, her bosoms bouncing and her corsets flapping in the wind, rebounded, holding down her bonnet with one hand and clutching the safety bar with the other, ending the day up 3½, a rise equal to a business quarter, or even two, of typical activity. Rising Sun Enterprises with its most unstable stable of Bulls common, uncommon, and preferred, kicked and whipsawed like one of its rodeo counterparts. Strangely, however, Rising Sun closed down two, considerably more than one might have expected under the circumstances. Curiouser and curiouser. But this development was easily dismissed as a fluke attending on the temporary chaos which had broken loose following our public bid; the price slide formed only a minor corrective blip in the rising trend line of the major long-term Bull market of our happiness, mine and the Horns'. They suggested, and I concurred, that it was best not to get bogged down worrying over details when, in its large sweep, our campaign had been such an overwhelming and unambiguous success.

For when the dust and dead paper had settled on the floor and been swept up by the janitors to be sent to the incinerator, out of the ashes a new order had started to emerge, something unprecedented in its scale, so vast and so magnificent, beyond the company, beyond the corporation, beyond the multinational — Novus Ordo Seclorum, New Order of the Ages, prophesied by the Founding Fathers! A concept so big the mind boggled at it as before the prospect of infinity! This business monolith, which I proposed to call American Sun — or better yet, All-American Sun — would be to the science of economics what the primal fireball was to astronomers and physicists: the original undifferentiated state, unity, Oneness, and yes, no need to hesitate with false modesty now, Tao! Tao, which, as Riley and I had once discussed, had at some point in the past, for an unknown reason, exploded into multiplicity, the ten thousand things, still hurtling farther and farther apart, like the galaxies thrown off from the fireball, red-shifting in space. That explosion was the central mystery which had spurred the development of all religion; and now at last I saw that it was up to me, to me alone, to heal the rift and make things whole. Lost? Ha! What a fool I'd been! I was found! Saved! Delivered! Guided by faith and Taoist intuition, all along I'd believed that somehow Tao would emerge out of the labyrinth of the Dow. And life had led me true! It was my appointed calling from God, bastard though I was, now at last after all the ages, to reintegrate the howling multiplicity back into the original unity, to shepherd the ten thousand things back into the nurturing, forgiving, motherly embrace of Tao; and the means to accomplish this was the merger of Rising Sun Enterprises, dynamic *yang* of corporations, with the sluggish, but still fertile *yin* of American Power and Light! This purpose reconsecrated all my acts. In it all lesser motives — power, pelf, revenge itself — would be made whole. Thus I conjectured, and the Horns concurred. I was so pleased I gave them hefty bonuses for the good work and took them out for drinks and dinner at Lutèce.

I came home rather late and rather loaded, ready to forgive Li all her trespasses and get down to making serious whoopie. Unfortunately my visions of mutual conquest and surrender were not to be enacted. When I walked into the bedroom, misty-eyed with drink and passion, I found spread out on the king-size mattress not the object I'd anticipated and most ardently desired, but a double-wide suitcase in which my own true love was recklessly flinging the balance of her earthly possessions.

"What are you doing?" I asked, coming up behind Eddie the cat, imitating him as he turned his head from side to side, following the trajectory of nighties, underwear, and other items which had figured in my recent fantasies, back and forth like the feathered birdie in a badminton contest.

"As if you didn't know," she quipped scathingly.

Something hit me in the stomach. I looked down to find myself holding a stuffed toy panda which she'd just fired at me.

"What's that supposed to be?" she asked. "A propitiation offer? A bribe to make me stay?"

"What are you talking about?" I demanded, more and more distressed. "I've never seen this before in my life." I looked at it again. Hmm . . . Or had I?

"You didn't send it?"

I shook my head innocently.

"Well, I'm glad you're not that far gone." She started packing again. "It arrived this morning. Maybe it was a joke."

I dropped it and moved toward her.

"Stay where you are," she warned, drawing back. "Don't touch me. I won't be physically intimidated."

"What are you talking about? What does this mean?" I implored pathetically.

"It means I'm leaving you," she said firmly, challenging me briefly before resuming her activity.

"But why?"

"Why!" she echoed incredulously. "After what you said to me last night? The way you looked at me?" She shuddered, remembering. "I was afraid of you, Sun I, afraid for my life."

"Afraid for your *life*?" I asked with a laugh. "Of *me*?"

She simply returned my gaze.

"That's ridiculous!" I scoffed. "Are you afraid now?"

She shook her head, not as though in answer to my question, but as though denying the whole proposition. "Now is now, then was then," she said. "That's just it. You're not the same from one day to the next, from one minute to the next. You've changed. Something's come over you. You need help."

"If I need help, who better to give it than you?" I demanded. "You're my fiancée, aren't you?"

She looked up sharply, darkly. "Professional help," she qualified pointedly. "You're not well, Sun I. You need to see someone. I'd like to help you, but" — she shook her head — "I'm not going to put myself at risk, not physical risk." She brooded silently, with terrible finality.

"Talk to me," I pleaded. "Can't we even discuss it?"

She shook her head as she folded a sweater. "There's nothing more to discuss. I've made up my mind. Nothing you can say will make me change it. You see somebody, then maybe we can talk." She folded the suitcase brusquely and latched it. Lifting it off the bed with difficulty, she slipped her other arm under her coat, which was folded over a chair back, then confronted me in the doorway. "Get out of my way," she said threateningly. "I'm not kidding. Please don't make this any harder than it is."

I faced her trembling with rage and despair. With the world crumbling under my feet, my confidence annihilated, I had nothing to draw on, no inner resources to match the severity of her resolve and bearing. I stood aside, cowed, and let her go.

"I know where you're going," I called after her in tearful spite.

She stopped.

"Back to him," I said.

She faced me. "Is that what you think?"

I held her gaze unflinchingly. "You won't get a dime," I vowed.

"You're sick, Sun I. *Really* sick." Throwing her keys at my chest, she stormed out, slamming the door behind her. I read her reaction as final, incontrovertible proof of guilt.

It was for the best, I told myself. It didn't matter. Lying on the bed, I closed my eyes, and masturbated to her image. Sobbing as I came, I rolled over to her side of the bed, still redolent with her scent — perfume and sweat, our mingled soils — and cried myself into a drunken sleep. My beautiful angel of sex.

•

It is a great deal easier to hate than to mourn, however, and on the principle of such economy my unconscious implemented its strategy. But though I hated Li and her infidelities, I continued to return a hopeful prognosis, telling myself that everything would work out in the end, that I would "see someone" and she would be appeased, that she would give Peter up and come back to me. Finally, work was my salvation and my escape. For my hatred of Li, to use an old phrase but a good one, was like a candle in the sun to my larger sustaining hatred of *him,* Love.

And as if that weren't enough, some just deity provided me with lesser grievances to nurse for diversion. The éminence grise of the yellow press had been skulking nearby, observing developments with his hideous jackal smile. Later that week in a special edition of *Your Money and Your Life,* Hackless, who had somehow found out about my latest visit to Trinity, burlesqued it in the following terms:

> Having gone public with his tender offer to shareholders of American Power and Light, last weekend, Sonny, a.k.a. the Mandarin Pope, went on to the second stage of his comprehensive plan for financial and religious world domination by attempting a friendly takeover of the Episcopal Church. Apparently counting on a similarity of interests and doctrines to make the merger attractive to the Anglican board of directors, Sonny was surprised to receive a polite but firm no thank you from the Most Rev. and Rt. Hon. Archbishop of Canterbury, declining the invitation "with regrets."

Hackless then proceeded to sow seeds of doubt about the earnings prospects for Rising Sun Enterprises in the upcoming quarter.

> How will faithful shareholders at Rising Sun respond to the "watering of their wine" by the proposed offer of convertible debt security to the infidels at APL as an enticement to convert and be saved (or be damned)? Will they shoulder their cross with Christian meekness? Or is there a cloud of Reformation looming on the horizon of the Sun Church?
>
> What's happening to Bull Inc. and Mutual Bull, anyway? In an earnings report released today, profits last quarter were up a mere 28 percent and 32 percent respectively as compared with 290 percent and 360 percent the previous three months. Not getting too bogged down in APL we hope!

These pointed aspersions, together with the marked hostility in the burlesque, made us wonder if Hackless had perhaps been enticed into the opposition camp by means of a bribe. In any case, his insinuations were bludgeoned home in an APL phone and mail campaign in which both their shareholders and our own were contacted and warned, on the one hand about the alleged "unsoundness" of debt security, and on the other about their dilution of equity. This was only one of a number of "harassment and interdiction" defensive strategies which Bateson and crew used to riddle our flanks. They attempted to cut our communications lines, as it were, by putting on retainer all the major proxy-soliciting firms on the Street, a ploy we got wind of and moved to counter before they were able to implement it. There was talk of a frantic search for a "white knight" to take them over before we could, thus putting antitrust obstacles in the path of our advance; or, if not by means of a white knight, then they might hope to save themselves by taking over in their turn a financial services organization like Rising Sun Enterprises with a similar effect. But all this was so much braggadocio, idle saber rattling. In these maneuverings they had the desperate *tant pis* air of men at wits' end scanning the horizon for a ship or the cavalry. Almost pathetic finally, their efforts did more good in building our confidence than harm in destroying that of our shareholders'.

Far more disturbing than anything their feeble efforts were able to accomplish was the continued inexplicable decline of our own stock on the open market. Like a mysterious leak in a well, or an internal hemorrhage in the corporate body, impossible to stanch because unlocalizable in origin, the shares of Rising Sun continued to bleed away their value, not precipitately, a quarter or an eighth each day, then a half, followed by a slight recovery which failed to regain the ground already lost. Not that we were immediately threatened either as an entity or in our major goal of taking over APL. We began from a position of such superlative advantage that we calculated (the Horns calculated, and I concurred) that even under the inconceivable worst-possible-scenario projection of a drop of 25 or even 30 percent in the value of our shares, our offer would remain attractive to American Power and Light Corporation's shareholders. In fact, a number of them had already come over; after the first week we found ourselves in possession of 15 percent of their outstanding shares, a good start. And, as yet, the decline had consumed barely 5 percent of our substance. Nevertheless, one couldn't be too careful, for in the long run our entire leverage in the takeover was based on three factors: our current high price relative to APL's, the prospects for continued appreciation, and, most important of all, the aura of magical infallibility that surrounded our phenomenal successes. Our appeal to the investor was lodged in a substrate deeper than sober, rational judgment, and in that lay our major strength.

After much deliberation, we agreed that the best method available to accomplish all our objectives — to shore up our own dipping price, reassure our shareholders, and further whet the appetite of APL's to get their hands on some of what we offered — was by a spectacular investment coup such as we had staged so often in the days before Kahn's departure and our heavy investments in APL, which had admittedly depressed earnings somewhat. In other words, an *I Ching* consultation like the original ordeal, duly hyped in the media. A big success might put us once and for all firmly over the line, making our bid for APL unstoppable. Wide publicity, of course, would serve a deeper end as well, for with the psychological leverage we continued to exercise in the marketplace, a buy signal from us could send investors flocking to the company we singled out, assuring a price rise in its shares. This in turn would make our interest in the new company appreciate and help restore the bottom line at Rising Sun.

Only this time an actual consultation was superfluous, as I well knew. I had proven before to my own satisfaction, and events had borne me out, that my command over the oracle was complete, so complete now that the coins, and even the stalks themselves, had become obsolete, an actual encumbrance in their crude physicality. No, this was to be a purely mental act. Purely. It would substantiate and consecrate the vision of the higher purpose that had been vouchsafed to me that morning on the floor, a purpose beyond "higher altruism," a highest altruism, which was working itself out, and had been all along, through me.

The Horns, all committed believers in the efficacy of the *I Ching,* expressed some reservations concerning the soundness of this proposed solo flight, or "consultation sans culottes," as one of them phrased it. But I vetoed them, firm on this point. I argued that success would more than reassure the faithful, it would turn believers into fanatics, creating a wave of mass hysteria that would sweep away all obstacles in its, in our, path. It would constitute my own de facto apotheosis among investors. They agreed it would be a miracle.

So without further ado, a day, the following Monday, was set and all was put in readiness. I felt unsettled and oddly mournful all morning long, even during the crucial moments of the consultation. That was how I later explained to myself the fact that this time, against all expectation, against all certainty, it didn't work. Oh yes, I closed my eyes and one by one the lines appeared, writing themselves across the retina of my inner eye (mystic patterns written in detritus). The hexagram derived was *Ku,* number 18, "Work on What Has Been Spoiled," or simply "Decay" in English. The character *ku* is a pictogram which shows a bowl with food that has gone bad and in which worms or maggots have started breeding. The single moving line was glossed:

> Setting right what has been spoiled by the father.
> In continuing one sees humiliation.

> This shows the situation of someone who is too weak to take
> measures against decay that has its roots in the past and is just
> beginning to manifest itself. It is allowed to run its course. If this
> continues, humiliation will result.

After reading this I seemed to be emerging from a dream. I looked around at the cameras flashing and the reporters anxiously scanning my features for a clue, pens at the ready, and I couldn't remember what I was doing there, what it was for. Briefly I became the same star-struck boy, the Uncarved Block I had been when I arrived from China, my first day on these shores. Was it possible that the little boy wasn't entirely dead in me after all?

I grew terribly afraid, because even as I glimpsed it living, that part of myself started to recede and recede until it was only a tiny speck, and the desk where I was sitting, the offices, the lights and cameras, Rising Sun Enterprises itself, were like some hideous growth, a cancer, which had reproduced around the single healthy cell of what I once had been, swelling and throbbing around it, until my original nature was dwarfed and hopelessly adrift in it. No, it was too late to withdraw. Things had gone too far. It disappeared with a tiny cry, like a snowflake dissolving in the brine.

Recovering from this spell, I took a deep breath, flexed my jaw, and went on. After deliberation, we hit on a particular pharmaceutical firm which had developed a more cost-effective technique for the production of bacteriological cultures for penicillin and related antibiotics, even though it was still some way from production and the drug stocks had been in a period of severe and prolonged disfavor in the marketplace.

Our initial infusion of capital turned it up encouragingly at first, but at the end of the week catastrophe occurred when several of the researchers were shown to have suffered severe and irreversible chromosomal damage from exposure to the experiments and the technique was outlawed by the FDA. The price dropped like a stone. An unqualified disaster. By the time we got out, Mutual Bull and Bull Inc. had suffered paper losses of more than 15 percent of their combined — our clients' combined — net assets. Overnight, Rising Sun dropped by several points.

I was devastated. There was open rebellion among the Horns. They bemoaned my imprudence in abandoning the tried and true consultative techniques. I became listless and whiningly self-pitying, willing to admit to anything. Yes, I had proceeded too cavalierly. Yes, everything would have been all right had I only not abandoned the old ways. Yes, I was willing to mend my ways. But what was to be done? The situation was critical. Shareholders were deserting us in droves. The influx of APL shareholders accepting our bid came to an abrupt halt, and we were still just under 20 percent. The drop in our share price was hardly a mystery now. Drastic action had to be taken. But what?

That is when we hit on the extraordinary plan that put Wall Street in an uproar, the plan which Hackless lampooned, along with the events leading up to it:

MYTH OF INFALLIBILITY EXPOSED AS PAPAL *BULL*!
Sun I's Peking Duck Is Singed (Severely)
Still Positioned — Dicily — to Pounce on APL

The Mandarin Pope — referred to gleefully today by his former colleagues on the floor of the Exchange, the squad boys, in a resounding Bronx chorus, as the Mandarin Slope — in a colossal error of judgment resulting in paper losses rumored to be as high as 25 percent of the net assets of his holdings in Rising Sun Enterprises (parent holding company of the Bull Group), in a move *totally without precedent in Wall Street history,* has reversed the traditional relationship of pastor to flock and applied to his own congregation for an indulgence for remission of his sins, which he concedes to be of staggering proportions.

Apparently carried away temporarily in an epic, and epileptic, transport of megalomania, he now offers to apply all his personal assets, including his own holdings in Rising Sun (rumored to constitute the largest single block of shares) toward the indemnification of shareholders should a second consultation, to be undertaken in the near future, prove equally ill-fated.

This time he promises to followed tried and true procedures as opposed to the late, lamentable, look-Ma-no-hands, now-I-see-it-even-if-you-don't approach. The M.P. has even offered to "rehabilitate" his former comrade, Chairman Kahn, from mothballing on the floor of the Exchange, to help decipher the reading in a separation of powers as per the original prospectus.

In short, a second ordeal! Will the Pope pass muster or take the gas? Will the faithful rally round the cross? And if so, with instruments of the financial, or the blunt and pointed, variety? Stay tuned! The oracle may — or may not — tell, but the market will! It always does!

In the state of self-abasement I had fallen into, I almost welcomed his derision. Regarding the upcoming consultation, which he described extravagantly, but in more or less accurate terms, I had little hope. From the fever pitch of only a few days earlier, after the setbacks, both personal and public, I had suffered, my resolve and confidence were set back virtually to zero. If there ever was a time, a place, an opportunity to reconsider, to think of getting out, this was surely it. The brief intimation of some tiny corner of my soul untouched by the general ruin, still salvageable from the wreckage of my life — that vision which had come to me so briefly during the previous consultation — the hope of saving that was with me almost hourly during that time. It was as if fate, or heaven, had offered me a period of respite from the furious conflagration raging inside me, soothed my ravaged spirit with a breeze of wistful remembrance blowing gently out of some forgotten summer twilight, another, better time. And it was then, on that same breeze, that Yin-mi came to me.

Chapter 21

Though astonished, somehow I was not surprised when my secretary announced Yin-mi over the desk intercom. Looking off in the air, I completely forgot myself, holding my finger on the "talk" button.

"Sir?" Mary had opened the door a crack and stood regarding me with vexation and concern. "What should I tell her?" she whispered, as though afraid of being overheard. "Shall I send her in?"

Panic seized me; I froze up.

"Sir?" she persisted, fidgeting.

"All right," I breathed.

"All right *what?*" she demanded in a militantly imploring tone.

I took a deep breath and sighed it out. "Show her in."

"Miss . . ." Mary uttered aloud in relief, looking back over her shoulder. Holding open the door behind her, she turned sideways and smiled perfunctorily as Yin-mi brushed past. Mary raised her eyebrows slightly as though surprised in her appraisal, perhaps mildly disapproving, then left, towing the door behind her.

"Hello," Yin-mi said.

She was standing there, and I had managed not even to see her, not really, until her voice woke me to remembrance.

Her face startled me, so utterly different from what I had expected. She was smiling, glowing, beaming at me, as though we were two old friends meeting after a long separation, between whom no cloud has ever passed. None of that whetted edge of grievance, that something never forgotten, never forgiven, smoldered in her eyes as it had in Li's the night she left me. The absence of it opened up a broad and restful vista inviting me to enter.

"Cat got your tongue?" she asked a little mischievously.

I winced at her reference to cats; it broke the spell. "Excuse me. Won't you sit down?" I offered with reflexive courtesy, realizing its inappropriateness even as I said it.

She laughed in a clear, happy voice. "My, aren't we formal." She took the chair (so close to me!) and folded her hands in her lap, her features shimmering with animation. "I don't suppose we'll have to go through introductions all over again, will we?" she teased with a coy pout.

I didn't answer.

"You do remember who I am?"

"Yin-mi," I answered with stunned, stupid earnestness.

"Good!" She giggled. "And you're Sun I." She reached out and pressed my lips with the cool tip of her index finger, and at her touch I closed my eyes and began convulsing in a silent fit of tears.

When I looked up again, she was studying me with that great solemnity in her eyes. I wiped my face on the sleeve of my jacket, and a peculiar lightness came over me. "So how are you?" I asked gaily, bouncing up and walking toward the bank of windows.

"How are *you?*" she rejoined in a tone much graver than my own.

I sniffled, took an energetic breath, and faced her again, ignoring her question. "Let me look at you."

There was something wonderfully touching in the mild self-consciousness with which she acquiesced, looking down with a deepened color, not quite a blush, then up again, smiling a little painfully.

I observed her, not hungrily — there wasn't the slightest trace of appetite in me, of *any* sort, not that — but with a deep and nonetheless delicious joy, as one passing a stand of flowers growing wild beside the road some early morning might bend down to inhale their odor and the fresh, cold wetness of the dew.

Magically, clairvoyantly, as if in keeping with my image, she raised her hand from her lap. "I brought you something," she said, smiling beautifully. She presented a chrysanthemum, twirling the stem between her thumb and finger like a tiny parasol.

I experienced a wrenching dissonance, deeply bittersweet. Taking it from her, I frowned into its petals with brooding wistfulness, then carefully laid it down on the edge of the desk. She picked it up and started nervously twirling it again.

After a moment the association ceased to resonate for me and I forgot it. I couldn't get over her — physically, her presence. She was wearing a black chamois skirt, streamlined over her hips, hose, and stylish leather shoes, highly becoming to her. She looked all grown up, a chaster, more classic version of many of the elegant young women one saw along the Street. Only she wore no makeup, and her matching cardigan hung open over a simple white blouse with a round collar, buttoned, in an endearingly vulnerable touch, at the top. She was sitting near the edge of the chair, back straight, knees pressed demurely together, hands settled in her lap twirling the flower. I noted a tense, fragile grace in her attitude and posture, which reminded me of a bow, poised, tensile, waiting to be drawn, and I remembered that it was just so that I had seen her at the first family gathering at her parents' house.

I rememorized her face, compared each feature with the image I had preserved of it. Her hair had grown. It looked nice. It altered her face, contributed to the effect of enhanced maturity. Her eyes remained the same; they always would. And the tiny gold inclusion in her iris, her slightly crooked tooth, made me laugh with joy inside myself, as at the chance discovery of something precious once but lost and eventually forgotten in the press of daily life, then unexpectedly recovered. Yet they were never lost — *she* never was. Seeing her was rather like removing a cherished memento from a box where it has been carefully stored for safekeeping, perhaps for years, examining it again with fresh, vivid eyes. I recognized each feature, but each was somehow new; and beyond the features, beyond the sum of them, a new quality, completely new, behind them in the deep ground of her face and in her presence, new and unknown, something I couldn't put my finger on, something I couldn't read.

"You've changed," I observed.

"You think so?" She reached up and touched her hair, traced it behind her ear with her finger.

I nodded, smiling as I remembered.

She blushed. "So have you." The remark was utterly transparent; she smiled back at me as she said it. But I turned to the windows, lowering darkly at the row of buildings facing opposite.

"I thought you might be hungry," she speculated after a pause. "I brought some lunch." She lifted a white paper bag from the floor beside her purse, holding it up for my perusal. "Actually, Father sent it."

"Lo?" I asked in surprise.

She smiled in acknowledgment.

"How is he?"

"Same as always," she replied. "He said to give his regards to the young dragon." She chuckled.

I ogled her. "You told him you were coming here?"

She nodded. "He said he thought I should."

"You spoke to him about . . . ?" I didn't finish.

She answered with a direct gaze.

"And your mother?"

Her face darkened and she shook her head.

I looked away; there was something wrong. Flowers, lunch — I was astounded by her generosity and tact, grateful for it, unconscious though I knew it was. She mentioned nothing, *nothing,* as though we had just picked up our conversation where we left it after a trifling disturbance. Perhaps that was it: I couldn't accept the settlement. It wasn't *owed.* It was given. I felt the mysterious rankling rising in my heart, like ice crystals forming on a pane. That was it. With Yin-mi it was always given. She always came with mercy. And I wanted justice. Wanted justice on *myself.* Would have it, too. I resented the forgiveness implicit in every inflection of her face and eyes. Not that I didn't feel tremendous tenderness for her. And more than tenderness, a fierce protectiveness. I wanted to protect her savagely — against myself. Not for any harm I intended, but for the past. I simply wanted to do violence to myself on her behalf, for the past, though the past was gone and irretrievable. I knew that, yet I wanted it still because it was owed. Because I owed it. And I would pay. Savagely would.

"Why have you come?" I demanded harshly.

"Do I need a reason?"

I laughed an abrupt, ugly laugh. "Maybe not," I replied. "But I do."

"It's been a long time," she said.

"How long?"

"Too long."

"Three long," I said, cryptically vicious.

"What's the matter, Sun I?" In her tone I detected a trace of vague despair that frightened me, frightened me more than anything else. "If I'm hurting you somehow — I don't mean to, but if I am — I'll go."

"Don't," I said, turning to her quickly with more entreaty than I intended to betray. "Don't go, Yin-mi."

She blinked her eyes. "I spoke with Father Riley."

"Ah." I leaned back in my chair and made a steeple with my fingers, observing it as I spoke. "He told you about our little visit."

"He said you tried to take Communion."

A burst of air exploded through my nostrils — laugh, snicker, sigh. "The sneak thief," I remarked, printing my teeth in the nails and flesh of my two index fingers, the first arch of the steeple. "Cat Burglar of the Sacrament." I grinned at her brazenly.

"It isn't funny," she chided, quiet, earnest. "He said you asked to convert."

I frowned and looked away again. "It was a joke," I proposed in a querulous, resentful tone, not caring whether she believed me, "a practical joke."

"I didn't know you were a practical joker," she remarked, venturing further than she should have.

I directed a taunting smile at her. "There are a lot of things you don't know about me."

"I know," she conceded, blushing and dropping her gaze to the flower, which she covered with one hand in a spontaneous gesture, gently cupping her palm around it like a shield.

Again I felt the rankling. "All this . . ." I said, rocking in my chair, starting on another tack. I held both hands out, palms opened upward — Riley's gesture as he invited the communicants to approach the altar. "Aren't you impressed?"

She didn't turn her eyes an inch in either direction, but kept them firmly fixed on mine. "It's beautiful," she admitted.

I snorted with displeasure and looked away. "It's nothing," I rejoined with surly dissatisfaction.

"If you know that . . ." She didn't finish.

I shook my head. "It doesn't matter. Knowing doesn't help. It was never that, anyway." I turned on her with fierce accusation. "You should know that."

She blushed and dropped her eyes.

"I'm lost, Yin-mi," I said, earnestly, but without self-pity.

She looked up at me, her eyes urgent, contradictory, misted with tears.

I shook my head with knowing finality, all that foregone. "It's true. I know it. I admit it." I stared vacantly out the window. "The only thing I care for now is him."

"Whom?" she asked.

"My father," I replied, surprised she had to ask. "Remember Coney Island?"

"How could I forget?" she said tenderly.

"I told you he was dead?"

She nodded.

I fixed her with the content of my next words heavy in my eyes before I said them. "I saw him."

"Your father?" She leaned toward me with quickened intensity.

I closed my eyes and nodded.

"Where?"

"In the gallery."

"Did you speak to him?"

"I was on the floor," I explained.

"When?"

"During the panic," I replied. "After we made our tender offer public."

She blinked, not understanding the cant. "You're sure it wasn't your imagination?"

I glared at her resentfully. "You think I'm crazy too, don't you?" I demanded shrilly. "Just like Li. You think I need to 'see someone.' " I spat the words with a hateful smile. "You've come to save me," I remarked scathingly.

"I wish I could," she said in a pained, earnest tone. "I'd do anything. Anything." She inhaled deeply and shook her head as she sighed it out. "No, I just think you're in pain," she continued quietly, searching my face as though it were a text she was reading from. "Terrible pain. And I want to help you."

The sob caught in my throat, like a stifled sneeze, and I turned away until I could take it. "I don't need your help," I refused in a cold, flat voice, "and I don't want it."

The sadness in her gaze was beginning to grow remote. I felt a fleeting pang of panic and despair. "Why should you want to help me?" I asked, averting my eyes, wanting to draw her back without compromising what I'd done already to push her away. "I don't deserve it," I said, forgetting her a moment in my earnest self-accusal.

"What do you mean, you don't deserve it?" she asked tenderly, coming back.

"After . . . everything," I explained. "The way I treated you."

"I don't believe you ever once meant to hurt me, Sun I," she affirmed fiercely, as though it were a point she wouldn't compromise. And in a flash I saw where she was blind and weak, and how exactly the same thing, precisely that, made her so formidable. The filament of her inmost life.

"You got caught up in circumstances beyond your control," she said, and it was like an echo of something.

"You think I'm innocent then?" I asked incredulously, accusing her.

"Not entirely. But not entirely guilty either."

I felt a tremor of déjà vu. "On whom then falls the rest of it, the blame?" I asked, repeating the next line like an old actor who has got the role by heart, too deeply ever to forget, though the play has vanished from his memory.

She closed her eyes and shook her head, smiling unhappily.

"The world," I mimed silently, anticipating.

"I don't know" — she surprised me. "Everyone."

The echo flitted through my brain again. Unable to pin it down, I let it wander its own way down the dark corridors of remembrance into the opacity from which it had emerged.

"Ever since the first time I saw you . . ." she went on in a voice that quavered slightly, a voice I knew.

"Don't," I pleaded softly, my eyes still closed, lingering on the echo as it diminished.

"Tanned, healthy," she described, not heeding me, "your hands calloused from those weeks of work on shipboard, your eyes clear, your face as I remember it, as I know it best, serious and intense, yet still and serene, not as it is now, nervous, bitter, desperate, afraid, blue shadows underneath your eyes . . ." She leaned forward and laid her hand against my cheek, rubbing her thumb under my eyes, cool, gentle, soothing. "It almost makes me want to cry to see you this way," she whispered, her face puckering.

" 'Ever since . . .' " I reminded her.

She dropped her hand and sat back. "Your heart was set on dredging up some unimaginable truth from the bottom of the world, where it had sunk and been forgotten. I hardly understood what it was except to know that somehow that truth was the key to your own understanding of yourself, and that you would have gone through any hardship to retrieve it."

"Ever since . . ." I prompted wearily.

"Ever since," she concluded, "I knew that I was meant to love you, and to help you. And that you were meant to love me, too. Someday. Let me."

I looked at her as I had looked back at the little girl from the edge of the forest, knowing she was my only hope of happiness in life, and that I could never have her. Life wouldn't let me, I wouldn't let myself. And I foresaw my future in an instant, searching for her over and over forever, finding her, leaving her, letting her go, grieving for her finally, always that at last, the cycle condensed at last to the terrible succinctness of grief. Forever and forever.

"Let it go, Yin-mi," I said, a terrible pity in my heart for both of us.

"I can't," she replied, her eyes brimming with tears.

I smiled unhappily. "You never could."

She covered her face with the back of her hand and wept.

"You still say this, even after Li." I took it up again, trying it, weighing it in my mind, unable to absorb it. I smiled. "You once accused me of being unworldly. You said I was a dreamer." I laughed. "You're the dreamer, Yin-mi, not me."

She wiped her nose on her sleeve. "My dreams aspire to reality," she said. "Yours to an illusion."

"You could never forgive me," I responded obliquely, "and what's more" — I looked away — "I could never forgive myself."

"Whatever there was to forgive," she offered in a tearful voice, "if there ever was anything, I forgive it now. I forgave it then. That first night. Forever and ever."

"Hell without end," I glossed with despairing irony.

Then I had a change of heart, felt strangely buoyant and uplifted. "Stop crying," I chided her with foolish fondness, like an old friend. "Why are you crying?"

Face lowered, still weeping, she shook her head as though unable to reply. "I don't know," she answered finally with effort.

Our eyes met. A beautiful light shone in her face, through the tears. "Something in my heart."

Stricken with remembrance, I smiled painfully.

"Sun I, listen."

"Don't, Yin-mi," I implored. "If you keep on, you'll make me weep. And I can't weep. I can't."

She returned my look with distress and sympathy.

"I have no more tears."

"What can I do?" she asked. "Tell me what you need."

I shook my head. "I want only to pay," I told her, coming back to it. "Nothing else. Not you. Not anything. Only that. To pay and get it over with, whatever it is, whatever I owe. The price. To be finished. Done."

"You're very tired," she observed. "Tired in a way I've never seen anyone."

"Yes," I agreed simply.

"One day you'll feel different," she suggested, a fine, hopeful promise. "Something will restore you. Life will. You'll feel refreshed. You'll feel new."

"There's nothing to restore," I contradicted without the least trace of self-pity, matter-of-factly. "Only ashes, and what's still burning." I shook my head. "And you know something? I don't even want to be restored." I learned it myself for the first time even as I spoke. "I only want to pay. To pay the price."

"What is the price, Sun I?" she asked, tilting her head to the side and narrowing her eyes.

"Who knows?" I replied, shrugging. "Everything." Suddenly it seemed funny and I laughed.

"I don't believe you," she challenged, suddenly losing her way, making another mistake.

"Thank you." I looked away. "But you're wrong."

"What's happened to you?" she demanded. "Did she do this?"

"Li?" I laughed. "Do you really think she could?"

"The night I saw you" — she stared fixedly, fiercely past me — "it almost broke my heart. You looked like a wild horse that's been caught and broken, sold to the circus, a top hat cut out around his ears, made to perform tricks."

I frowned. "That's most unkind. And rather ugly. It isn't like you."

"I'm sorry," she said, looking down. "I apologize."

"You realize I loved her," I said, letting my anger stoke itself, making no effort to close the furnace door. Cruelly, I emphasized that final "her."

"Did she love you?" she rejoined from a deep blush.

I laughed. "Now we reach the heart of it, don't we? The real, red meat. She gave it to me," I said, turning on her with vicious fury, "and I gave it to her back. And to her front," I added, relishing my pun with obscene joy.

"What?" she asked, imploring me with her eyes and tone to turn the volume down, to come back and be calm. "The jewel in the casket of your life?"

Her allusion struck home, and a trickle of clear blood flowed from the festered sore. "I tried to, I think," I said, pained but grateful for the relief. "But Li never wanted that. She never believed in me, Yin-mi, not like you did."

"I still do," she whispered.

I shook my head in bitterness, refusing. "It doesn't matter. It's too late."

"Why?" she asked. "Why too late?"

"Because I no longer believe in myself."

She simply looked at me, finding nothing to say. There was nothing to say. The fire flared up again. "She gave me sex," I said. "You never did."

"You never asked," she replied immediately, as though the answer had long been ready on her lips. She smiled at me, tender, a little hurt, almost with humor, so direct. Her candor shocked me, actually shocked me. I was surprised that I could still be shocked. She was shockingly beautiful, her youth, her innocence, her intrepidity. Precisely: shockingly beautiful.

"What if I asked you now?" I proposed on sudden impulse, the rankling rising once more.

"Don't, Sun I," she implored.

"No," I persisted, "what if I did? You said before you wanted to save me, that you'd do anything. What if that were it, the price. *Your* price."

She shook her head. "It wouldn't work."

"How do you know? What if I thought it would? What if I said it would?"

She blinked with sad neutrality, neither acceding nor denying. I pressed the button, keeping my eyes fixed on hers, smiling with infatuated surmise. "Mary, no calls. See that we're not disturbed for . . ." — I slipped back my cuff and looked at my watch, then, deliberately, at Yin-mi's face, cruelly debonair — "say, fifteen minutes? Make it half an hour." In that moment I knew that there was something monstrous in my heart, that I was lost beyond redemption. Through all that had passed, never had I felt the presence of actual, active evil alive and crawling in myself, but I did now, and I relished the sensation. It was exhilarating, even as it terrified me, like a carnival ride, like the Wonder Wheel.

"What's the matter," I bullied, "are you afraid?"

"Yes," she replied in a voice that startled me with its calmness, "afraid for you."

I pouted, deprecating her answer. I regarded her over the steeple of my fingers, gnawing the first arch with cool nervous energy, waiting.

A sickening resignation set in her face. Large tears rolled down her cheeks. Then, looking down, she raised her hand slowly, watching it almost as though it were someone else's, her wrist so slim, so white, so supple, and pinched open the top button of her blouse. I can never forget that she was smiling. I can never forget that smile. What did it mean? I was overcome with astonishment and suddenly sobbed, burying my face in my hands. "Get out," I cried, slumping across my blotter and weeping without restraint. "It was just a joke, a practical joke." I was out of control, hysterical, laughing and crying at the same time as the words came back to me.

But when I looked up she was gone. In her chair lay the green stem of the chrysanthemum, which she'd torn to pieces in her lap, the shredded petals scattered across the seat and over the dark pile of the rug.

I felt oddly calm. Noticing the white paper bag, I opened it and peered in. There were two fortune cookies nested in a pile of napkins over the white boxes with their wire handles. I took them out and broke them. The first said: "Even happy turns of fortune often come in a form that at first seems strange to us." I recognized the words from the *I Ching*. The second said: "Beware of what you want; you may get it." I smiled at this, and wondered which one was meant for her, which for me. I thought I knew.

Popping one of the broken pieces into my mouth absently, I brushed the remaining crumbs off the edge of my desk into the wastepaper basket, then turned my attention to something else and completely forgot that she had ever been there.

Chapter 22

I was almost blithe about the second consultation. Its possible consequences for the fate of the takeover, for the future of Rising Sun Enterprises itself, not to mention my own personal fortune, hardly concerned me. Not that I had lost hope or interest, or was incapable of understanding the precariousness of the situation; as the Horns, who were understandably dismayed at my attitude and behavior, lectured me individually and together about these matters, I nodded solemnly, understanding perfectly, acquiescing in their initiatives, promising to reform. But the truth was, in the strict economy of my inner life I had no leisure for such trifles, for I was overwhelmed entirely by a prior obligation: existence, existence itself, which I had inherited fee simple, unasked and from an unknown donor, a gift, a burden, which now, suddenly, required a 100 percent deployment of my time, attention, and resources to dispose. Not that I was harried or distressed, not that any particularly difficult, much less insurmountable, obstacles lay in my path, not that I was consciously suffering or in pain, but simply that life in its most elementary applications — turning a doorknob, walking across a length of open space to my desk, sitting down, finding a sharpened pencil — tasks I could spend minutes of devout concentration in accomplishing and feel the utmost satisfaction and reward in doing so — absorbed me wholly, the past and future become as remote as metaphysics or the moon.

But this was only a temporary phase. I think my psyche was instinctively resting itself in preparation for the final blaze of glory, the fire still smoldering hot beneath the weight of ashes of what had already been consumed, spontaneous combustion in the hold ignited by a gravity of ruin.

It was good to see Kahn again, though. His presence reassured me, seeming to bring with it, and indeed to entail by law and right, the old safety, the relative safety, which had existed during those first hopeful days when we had conceived our idea and incarnated it in Bull Inc., when I had seen him like a withered blossom slowly opening back to life. Good to see him, though he regarded me with that same light in his eyes as during those difficult weeks after his ultimatum and the revelation of the subsequent history of Eddie Love, weeks when I had been in such despair over how to dispose my life and future prospects, a despair which now, in recollection, touched me with its aura of innocence. "When I was a child, I understood as a child" — suffered as a child. I did my best to set his mind at rest concerning my personal and the corporate welfare, but to little effect. He was even more anxious for the initiative to succeed than I was.

If possible, this second consultation was an even bigger production than the first, than the ordeal itself, and it held an air of bigger consequence, bigger stakes riding. The ordeal had been perceived widely as a joke, and people had gathered with eggs and rotten fruit to hoot us down. The preceding consultation, *Ku,* had promised to be simply another in a string of successes that had become monotonous and banal, at least until its disastrous conclusion. But now the string was broken, and this time the Wall Street hordes gathered with red, hungry eyes like scavenging predators around a wounded animal thrashing in a brake. No, there was nothing of the joke about it this time. The smell of hot blood filled the air, and they skulked with obscene eagerness at the perimeter, waiting for some sign, the telltale intonation of a groan, a stiller silence, to close and feed. This woke the anger in my heart and partially restored me to myself. I remembered the faces of all the men we'd crushed, that portentous, lowering, militant despair and hatred; though I tried to suppress it, tried even to smile, I knew the same look had etched itself on my face now. They too had smiled, I remembered, smiled down on me the same fey, harrowed curse which I presently smiled down on others. Yet it rekindled my spirit to life. I remembered what Yin-mi had said — "Something will restore you" — and smiled with morbid irony. "Life will," she'd promised. Hate had. Maybe hate *was* life. And the more I considered this proposition, the more profound the thought became, life like a low-grade rage against inanimacy, against entropy. Bound to lose.

At my manipulation — this time by the book and letter, not even using coins but stalks — the oracle returned the hexagram *Ming I, K'un* over *Li,* "Earth" over "Fire," the "Darkening of the Light."

> Here the sun has sunk under the earth and is therefore darkened.
> The name of the hexagram means literally "wounding of the bright";
> hence the individual lines contain frequent references to wounding.

There were moving lines in the fourth and sixth places:

> Six in the fourth place means:
> He penetrates the left side of the belly.
> One gets at the very heart of the darkening of the light,
> And leaves gate and courtyard.

We find ourselves close to the commander of darkness and so
discover his most secret thoughts. In this way we realize that there is
no longer any hope of improvement.

Six at the top means:
Not light but darkness.
First he climbed up to heaven,
Then he plunged into the depths of the earth.

Here the climax of the darkening is reached. The dark power at first
held so high a place that it could wound all who were on the side of
the good and of the light. But in the end it perishes of its own
darkness, for evil must itself fall at the very moment when it has
wholly overcome the good, and thus consumed the energy to which
it owed its duration.

The fourth line was less than sanguine (or perhaps too much so), but after
the initial portent of disaster, the commentary on the final line — six at the
top — revived my hopes. For who was the "dark power" but my father, Eddie
Love, who had "at first held so high a place," but now, by virtue of my own
ascent, was finally within striking distance? Indeed, "close to the commander
of darkness," I had "discovered his most secret thoughts," I who had all along
been "on the side of the good and of the light." "In the end it perishes of its
own darkness, for evil must itself fall at the very moment when it has wholly
overcome the good, and thus consumed the energy to which it owed its
duration." The prophecy was an unspeakably delicious satisfaction to me, and
I relished its anticipated fulfillment.

Kahn, however, whose business it was to derive a market application, was
not so optimistic. In fact, after half an hour of idle wrangling, we dismissed
the press and adjourned the meeting overnight to give him time to deliberate
further.

"I just can't think, kid," he said, shaking his head in perplexity. "It doesn't
ring a bell." He looked up. "Unless it could be a signal to buy put options on
American Power and Light itself." He grinned. "Get it? The Darkening of the
Light?"

"I get it, Kahn," I said. "Of course it's your baby, but do you really think
it would be wise to buy puts on a stock our own takeover bid is driving *up*?"

"Just a joke, kid. Take it easy. Don't worry, I'll come up with something.
There are a few possibilities I want to scope out before I commit myself. I'll
let you know, probably by eight or nine tonight."

But it was after 9:00 A.M. before I heard from him. Only a few minutes
remained before the market opened. The Horns were frantic. I had been trying
to reach him all night.

I thought he'd been on a binge when he first walked into my office. He had
his jacket suspended on a finger over his shoulder, his sleeves rolled up, tie

slacked down and askew. A blue stubble of beard covered his face almost up to his cheekbones, and his eyes were red in their pouches. Yet he was grinning like a thief.

"Kahn, you're drunk!" I indignantly protested.

A look of righteous offense appeared on his features. "No way, José," he twitted, throwing his jacket down on the desk in front of me.

"Where have you been?" I demanded. "I've been calling all night."

"At Columbia," he said, volunteering as little as possible, as always relishing his advantage.

"Columbia!"

He nodded, yawning and patting his mouth with the back of his hand with false casualness. "The library. Thought I'd go back up there and see if my old carrel was still intact."

"Kahn!" I threatened.

He lifted his jacket and took a folded newspaper from the side pocket, fishing out some bonbons too and offering them around. Everyone declined.

"Sure now? Damn good," he admonished. He dropped the newspaper on the blotter with a deft little wrist flick that spun it right-way round in front of me, then leaned forward, reading upside down from the far side of the desk as he nipped at his sweet.

It was the financial column of the London *Times*.

"London?" I asked.

He nodded. "You owe me, kid," he said. "Or rather . . ." — he raised his eyebrows — "we're even."

Circled with a black felt-tip pen was the obscure designation "TTOAK."

"T-toak?" I asked.

"No, kid," he said snidely, "T-T-O-A-K."

"Oh," I said.

He took something else out of his pocket, a promotional brochure of some sort apparently, perhaps an annual report, and threw it down. On the cover, over a photograph of dozens of Arab women in chadors sitting side by side at rows of sewing machines: "2001: Arabian Knights. Sheik Evening Wear for Men."

"What is this, Kahn, a joke?" I asked indignantly.

"Is this a time for jokes?" he rejoined significantly. "I kid you not, kid. This guy is the hottest thing to hit the English business scene since Cecil Rhodes — almost the only thing."

"Who is he?"

"Yassuh Gamal Hassan Abdullah Tinbad Mohammed Fahd Ali el-Ararat de-Sadat," Kahn said, "also known as Light of the Desert, Sartor of the Suez, Clotheshorse of the Koran, Ugly Duckling of the Aswan, Padded Foot and Shoulder of the East, Elbow Patch of the Imam, Armpit of the Universe, Worster of Worsteds, Bester of Bastings, Cuffer of Cuffs, Double Cross-Stitch of Damned Smiles and Laughter, Yes-er of Yassuhs, Three Ply of Fly-Bys, and

Chief Executive Officer and Chairman of the Board of 2001: Arabian Knights, 'The Sartorial Cartel of the Future.'

"He bought the estate of some baronet in Sussex and converted it into a factory (they call it 'Sartor Resorts' in the press) where they're producing high-fashion evening wear — get it? Darkening of the Light? — at cut-rate prices, using cheap immigrant labor. He defected from South Yemen with his twelve sisters, who are now the factory foremen. After they got going, they started enticing more women over with promises to arrange marriages with foreign workers living in England. After a brief seven years or so of indentured servitude, or what virtually amounts to it, they generally do manage to hook them up one way or another, though Yassuh is also reputed to run an Islamic prostitution ring."

"But Kahn," I protested, "is this operation really on the level? I mean, is it big?"

He tilted his head and arched one eyebrow. "*Big,*" he pronounced portentously. "It could be the biggest thing since Rolls-Royce. I'm serious, kid. This guy is the real goods, an authentic Third World entrepreneur, cut from whole cloth and dyed in the wool" — he grinned — "so to speak. He may look a little unsavory, but he sells to all the best. Been to Macy's lately? You can now buy tuxedos, cummerbunds too, all produced by you know who."

"You think this is really it?" I asked.

"Darkening of the Light," he said with a shrug. "As in 'After Six.'"

"Two Thousand and One: Arabian Knights," I tried out the sound of it. "Sheik Evening Wear for Men."

"There's a joke going around, kid," Kahn said. "Specializing in tall tails and armored tuxedos for Arab oil magnates traveling abroad."

I glared at him threateningly.

"Get it? Arabian Nights: Tall Tales? Knights: Armored Tuxedos?"

"I get it, Kahn," I observed wryly. "If you ask me, the whole thing sounds like a joke. And a bad one."

"Well, excuse me!" he huffed. "I stay up all night trying to get your skinny little Oriental ass out of the frying pan and this is the thanks I get? Remind me to stick to self-abuse in the future. It's safer and more fun."

"All right, Kahn," I said, conciliating, "don't take offense. I appreciate what you've done. I really do."

He nodded, pouting, by way of acceptance.

I turned to the Horns. "Okay, boys, you heard the man. Hit the phones!"

And this time, against all hope, it worked. Within half an hour I got a phone call from an excited Yassuh, who vowed that his descendants would worship me for "a hundred and say-van-*dee*" generations and that he himself, despite his "physical handicap," whose nature he didn't volunteer (nor did I ask), would prostrate himself ten times each day to Wall Street, before and after Mecca. More importantly, later that morning he announced that with the infusion of new capital he was forthwith proceeding with the wholesale importation and forced resettlement of two entire nomadic villages, and bought a further string of bed-and-breakfast castles along the Thames. Before the afternoon was out, TTOAK had appreciated, and our interest along with it, an astounding 22 percent. By the end of the week, nudged along by a timely retreat of the pound against the dollar, Rising Sun Enterprises had regained almost all of its lost ground, APL shareholder acceptances of our tender offer had increased substantially, and my own personal property was timely snatched from the jaws of perdition. The following Monday I took Kahn and the Horns out for a celebratory Islamic luncheon. But our conviviality whiffled out on a skewed note when the troops left manning the fort phoned to tell us that Rising Sun had closed the day down a point, renewing its decline. We all took off our rented turbans and sat glumly around the table for some time before Kahn spoke up.

"Listen," he said, "maybe it's none of my business, but you guys are all young, post-Reformers. You don't remember the prelapsarian — or, perhaps I should say, ultralapsarian — days before the passage of the Securities Exchange Act in thirty-four, floor trading's heyday. Not that I do either really. But I experienced it indirectly after a fashion, secondhand that is, through my uncle Ahasuerus." He paused for effect, and breath.

"Well? What are you saying?"

"Just this, kid," he replied. "This leak you've sprung over there. It has all the earmarks of a classic bear raid."

"A bear raid," mused one of the Horns. "I know what that is. I read about it in a course on business history."

"That's outdated," said a second.

"It's illegal," put in a third.

"He means a multiple flogging," glossed a fourth.

I thought about the toy panda that arrived the night after the parley with APL, and a cold shiver of intimation tingled down my nerves. "What is a bear raid, Kahn?" I asked quietly.

"It's an attack against price by means of sales and short sales over a prolonged period," he replied.

"A multiple flogging," reiterated the same Horn. "It induces an artificial glut which leads to a severe buyer's market! Too much supply for the available demand."

"Is it illegal?" I asked.

"Illegal as hell!" said one of the Horns angrily.

"Stock manipulation!" said a second.

"Not if you don't get caught," said Kahn with a smile of wise, wistful weltzschmerz.

"That's it," I affirmed, suddenly stone cold sober, an icy fury rising in my heart. "The bastards!" I darted a glance at Kahn. "All right, how do we defend against it?"

He rolled in his lips and shook his head. "The only thing I know to tell you is to stimulate demand by buying your own shares defensively. Either that, or expose them."

"How would we do that?" I asked.

"Difficult," he conceded. He surveyed the Horns. "Put some of this talent on it. Maybe they can come up with something."

"The problem is," I continued, more to myself than him, mulling over the first option, buying our own shares, "we're so highly leveraged now, almost one hundred percent."

"You'll have to borrow more," he said. "You own a bank, don't you?"

"How much?"

"Better too much than too little," he replied. "And if I were you, I wouldn't spare my personal assets either."

I questioned him silently.

"Put them up as collateral on a loan," he elaborated. "It'll take a little of the pressure off the company. You don't want Rising Sun to get overextended. That's the worst thing you can do."

"What do you mean?" I asked.

"Just be on the lookout," he answered, obliquely portentous. "Be careful they don't slip in the back door on you."

"You mean take us over instead?"

He nodded.

"If they're executing a bear raid, how're they going to take us over too?" one of the Horns challenged. "I mean, if they're selling us hand over fist, selling us long and selling us short, how're they going to hoard us too?"

"Hmm," Kahn pondered. "You've got a point there. I'm glad to see you're thinking." He turned to me and gestured toward the man with his chin. "Smart kid there. I just want to make sure you're on your toes."

My protégé blushed and preened.

"Okay, I've put in my two cents' worth. I'll butt out now. You guys keep him on the straight and narrow." He turned to me. "See you round, kid. And mazel tov encore, et a fortiori."

•

The next morning one of the Horns brought in a ponderous tome fitted with an antique clasp and bound in black, mildewed leather which emitted a musty smell. Filled with brittle, yellowing folio-sized pages printed in Gothic black-letter type with broad counters and heavy ornamental serifs, all the *s*'s written as *f*'s, this volume was entitled: *Wall Street before the Fall: Usque ad annum Domini MCMXXXIV.* As I opened it, the spine cracked and the leather screamed like a soul in agony. Indeed, within we found what amounted to a virtual medieval torture chamber fully equipped with nailed coffins, cat-o'-nine-tails, thumbscrews, rack and wheel, and other ingenious devices, all in use on the unwitting and uninformed before 1934 (and, if Kahn was right, on us at that very moment). We read of wash sales and pool operations. We read of corners: the first and second Harlem Railroad corners, the Erie raids engineered by Drew, Fisk, and Gould, the Northern Pacific corner, the Stutz and Piggly Wiggly of sacred memory. And secreted away among these treasures, we found a succinct and telling analysis of the technique known as the bear raid and became only more convinced that this was the very rack on which they had us stretched, the very wheel on which we turned, only an improved, updated version, multiple flogging, with rack-and-pinion steering, as it were, for a smoother and more silent writhe.

We mobilized immediately and began countermaneuvers. First I assigned several of the sharpest Horns to a team whose sole mission was to expose and discover any and all evidences of wrongdoing on the part of APL's Board of Directors, including extramarital affairs and sexual deviancy, which I suspected strongly. Second, and more important, I called in the CEO of the Bull Group Bank (formerly Second Jersey Hi-Fi), a man who, because of his reputation for straightness and probity in matters fiduciary, had been retained from the antebellum administration before our takeover, despite a well-known personal testiness and his obvious and openly displayed enmity toward Kahn, an enmity I had become sole beneficiary of since the latter's departure. I explained the situation to him briefly, and was chagrined to see a vindictive smile light his features. He gnashed his molars with predatory satisfaction. I told him that Rising Sun would require further loans to buy its stock defensively, and that I myself would require funds for the same purpose. He then replied that in his opinion the bank was too deeply implicated in the takeover already and that further commitments would constitute an unwise concentration of resources, which, in the case of some unforeseen contretemps, could lead to disaster, even a potential bank failure. Already, he complained, APL's own creditor institutions had begun applying pressure to the bank, making him a virtual pariah and excommunicate in the financial community. Heating up, he then went on to state the obvious fact that as CEO of the parent holding corporation, I was, of course, free to fire him and hire someone more amenable to my designs to fill his chair, but that I could not force him to derogate from what he considered the financial straight and narrow. Having relieved himself of this credo, he went on grudgingly to concede that some further loans could be arranged for the corporation and that, as far as I myself was concerned, he would be more than happy to arrange loans on the same terms of credit that the bank offered its very best commercial customers, but that if I expected him to put himself or his reputation in jeopardy by any illicit practices I was sadly mistaken, and furthermore . . .

I stopped him here and assured him that I expected only minimally preferential treatment, and, as he appeared pacified, I then inquired how much I could expect against the collateral of my shares, and he promptly and unambiguously replied, sixty cents on the dollar. When I expressed my shock and dismay at this figure, he replied that they were standard terms and that the bank must protect itself against all unwise investments. I asked him heatedly if he considered an investment in Rising Sun Enterprises an unwise investment, and he said it was not his job to assay the soundness or lack thereof of any securities whatsoever, that he was a banker not a speculator. I responded by asking did he not realize that the very same future of that very same bank which he so ably headed and, I hoped, would continue to, was tied, tied intimately and inextricably, with the very same soundness of that very same Rising Sun stock, and that furthermore his very own job as chief executive officer of said bank was similarly contingent on the soundness of Rising Sun stock and that he damn well better have faith in it or find some, and he concluded, frowning, that since there was some question as to whether the perceived recent weakness in Rising Sun's share price was intrinsic or artificially induced through the operation of a putative, reprehensible bear raid, a.k.a. multiple flogging, that he was prepared to compromise and offer me the generous and unprecedented terms of sixty-five cents on the dollar, on the understanding, of course, that the loans would be very short term, for periods not in excess of one week, and at substantial rates of interest compensating the degree of risk incurred. I agreed, on the understanding, framed as a "gentlemen's agreement" between concerned parties, that in the event that defensive strategies failed to stabilize and reinvigorate Rising Sun's share price within said period of one week, and further, in the unlikely event that Rising Sun should continue its (temporary) decline, that I would be allowed to service the debt by repledging any and all new shares purchased in Rising Sun in lieu of cash interest payments, and, further, that the repayment of the principal would be for all intents and purposes infinitely reschedulable at my leisure until such time as I should choose to render full and complete satisfaction under the terms of the original agreement, signed and duly notarized that day in the . . . etc., etc.

Chapter 23

The magnitude of the attack APL was carrying out against us came into focus only after we had thus dug in and started returning fire. Despite the considerable resources we mounted for the counterattack, relief was only temporary. The leak in our share value continued, quickening to a rill, then a stream, and nothing we could do seemed to stanch it. The conversion of APL stockholders leveled off again and came to a halt, and still we had managed to amass only a 28 percent position of their outstanding shares. And Rising Sun continued to fall. After the expiration of the initial term of my loan, unable to pay interest out of the expected, but still unmaterialized, reappreciation of Rising Sun shares, I was forced to repledge a percentage of the new shares I had amassed, in lieu of interest payments.

Once again I found myself, not only in my corporate role, but personally, through the erosion in the value of my property, in jeopardy. Of course, there was no danger of losing my shares through being declared in default, since the bank was ultimately, if only indirectly, under my jurisdiction, and I knew, *knew,* that the erosion in the value of our stock was not the result of the "bloodless verdict of the marketplace," but had been artificially engineered by APL, ultimately by *him,* and could not continue indefinitely. No, once we had discovered the hidden pressure point on which they were applying their malign (and, what's more, illegal) leverage, Rising Sun must inevitably explode through the artificial resistance line on the charts, like a geyser artificially dammed by some obstruction, slowly building up pressure, finally to erupt in a fountain of plenty that would see me flush and the stock restored to a fair valuation. No other ultimate outcome was plausible, or indeed, even conceivable.

But the ultimate and the immediate were far removed as yet, and there were slim odds in impassively waiting for some disembodied justice in the heart of things to restore a rightful equilibrium. This was war. We were in the middle of our major offensive now, both sides taking heavy casualties, both driven to exact a furious and implacable retaliation. The Hunt was on in earnest, both parties hunter and hunted, both hit and bleeding copiously.

And there was joy in battle, at times fine and free hearted, at others deeply obscene. For this was the first time in all our maneuvers, our pillage and marauding of other companies, that we had been remotely threatened ourselves as an entity, the first time we had matched ourselves against an equal adversary in the heat of battle, as Tsin had said, and so "come into the higher reaches of the mystery." For they were our equals. *He* was mine. The mastery and audacity of his campaign, its impenetrability, were awesome, and all so clearly marked with his classic signature, surprise, out of the sun, the dark scythe coming to reap.

His signature. How I longed to read it in the open ledger of the debt, there beside my own. Equals. I craved our dark accounting, craved it with every fiber of my being. To pay the price. To pay up and pay out. To strike a fearful, final balance and close the books forever. To ask for no forgiveness of my debts and to forgive nothing. There would be no forgiveness in that place. And that knowledge — the greatness of the price, the completeness of it — made it sweet, the sweetest thing I've ever tasted, as sweet as the Communion wine, as sweet as the blood of a child, the child within my heart which I now sacrificed with full permission of my will, the child in him, in Love, those two children one child, his and mine, which we would now most fearfully cleave in our most strict accounting. There would be no mercy *there,* not in that place, no remorse, no distinction between joy and obscenity, obscenity and religion, all that left far behind, far, far below, half-truths which permit an expedient world to function, but whose righteousness rings hollow in the clear air of the summit I was then approaching, where he had always been, waiting for me since the beginning of the world. Forever and forever. And that is a secret, Reader, which I give as casual alms to you who have followed me into the dark precincts of this mystery: that hell is a summit, not an abyss.

Tsin was vividly with me in those days (that day, that hour, that moment). In my mind I replayed all that he had said, over and over like a record that never ceased to move and awe me. All other masters I had outgrown, their words no longer touched me in the deepest places, the places I needed to be touched; but his voice still resonated, sending chills and fevers of unmistakable authenticity down the live wires of my nerves. He had been there, where I was going, where I was, and now I took him as my mentor and my guide into the heart of the mystery, sanctum sanctorum. "There is a sense of something absolutely real and present which obviates the need for gods. It sates and saturates the sensibilities with a conviction of absolute and unequivocal existence. The consolation of religion, life's meaning, the complexion of the future — these problems and dilemmas reveal their specious nature to us and then disappear. The gnawing, the dissatisfaction in the belly, finally vanishes. We cease to be divided with ourselves. This is the consummation of reality, most intense when one comes face to face with a single adversary in the heat of battle." Face to face. "For we know in part, and we prophesy in part. But when that which is perfect is come, then that which is in part shall be done away. . . . For now we see through a glass darkly; but then, face to face; now I know in part, but then shall I know even also as I am known."

And I did. I knew. Now I knew. And Tsin was right, damnation was a small enough price to pay for the sweetness of such ecstasy, such knowledge. The point seemed academic. Not that I was blind or unaware of the peril I was in. Hourly I tasted the dark fruits of perdition, the agony and suffering together with the impossible exhilaration. I knew vividly, beyond all doubt, beyond all hope, the reality of my damnation, of my eternal loss; and yet it didn't matter. I didn't care. I was in love with my own moral death, in love with the ferocious beauty of the flames. Burning. And knowing this, I accepted, too, in my heart without bitterness or regret that my search had been in vain, a fool's errand, that there was no delta, that the foaming torrent of the Dow never reached the destination I had dreamed and once believed with all my heart it might and must. For there was no place for this, for *this*, Reader, this pristine, immaculate animal rage, or rather, much more so, this quintessential human violence, this joy in killing, in bloodshed — not for meat, for feeding, not for self-defense, not for any of the purposes of survival or necessity, but as a form of play, yes, godlike play, coming momentarily into the presence of the ineffable, experiencing it in all its gorgeousness and power, through the willed destruction of other life (as in the unleashing of the atom's fury, nature only exposing final secrets, final truths under final duress) — *this, this,* no place for this, which Tsin had conjured with the chilling magic of that talismanic phrase, "the ecstasy of combat," no place for this in Tao. Without bitterness or regret then, as I say, I opened my hand and blew from my fingertips the fragile, timid butterfly of my last illusion, my last hope, and I felt unutterably clean and stripped, stripped down to animal leanness, stripped down to the brutal human core. Mighty.

And the shares kept falling, more and more precipitately. My relief seemed to fall into a hole, to feed a hunger, that yawned wider, that grew more voracious, from the feeding and the filling. Within a period of weeks, of *days,* the market price of Rising Sun had dropped below the 25 percent of preraid value which the Horns had earmarked as the red line, the watershed, beneath which our takeover would be threatened, dropped below 30 percent, which they had designated as the line of last resistance, had even briefly touched 35 percent, or sixty-five cents on the initial dollar, and at this point, after an ominous tirade from my banker, I was forced to repledge the last of the new Rising Sun shares I'd purchased with the bank loan to replenish the severe depletion of my original collateral. There was no farther to go. This was it. The first strategy, defensive buying, had proved a failure. Had we not been so highly leveraged when we began, it might have worked. But there was small comfort in reviewing options that had long since expired. Our last chance was exposure.

And it was there, in extremis, that the answer came to me. While the Horns were trying to trace funds through numbered Swiss accounts, I suddenly realized the solution. And the obviousness of it made me want to laugh with both joy and disgust. So obvious. So obvious. It had been there all along, invisible by its very conspicuousness, its banality, like the dark glasses on the revolving rack. The APL directors themselves had suggested it. The chair on the board. *My* chair. Of course! And *then,* when they'd first offered it, I'd had control of only 2 percent. *Now* I had close to 28! I could demand three seats in their cozy little politburo, certainly two, two at least, and a voice in choosing a third, a compromise candidate, a neutral third party, who would serve my purposes just as well. I could undermine them *from within,* if not by voting and majority rule, then by becoming privy to their counsel, privy to their counsel by becoming privy to their council. Yes! I laughed with delight at the thought of it. So obvious! Yet, if it worked, nothing was lost. All the ground we'd given up could easily be regained. And with this inspiration, I knew immediately what I must do. I put through a call to Bateson.

"Ah, Sun I," he said in his unpleasant pleasant voice, "this is a surprise."

"I think we need to meet," I informed him, terse, guarded, resentful.

"Do we?" He fell silent.

"Well?" I prompted impatiently.

"Sorry," he replied as though abstracted, not paying attention, "I was just trying to remember. Last time I called you, I believe, didn't I?" I perceived a faint but unmistakable trace of suppressed glee in his voice. "Nice of you to reciprocate," he went on, barely restraining an outright laugh. "Damned thoughtful! Lunch?"

I almost choked on the rage his glib insinuations triggered, but I bridled it, taking delicious satisfaction, poisonously delicious, in the thought of the revenge I'd wreak on him. "I get your implication, Bateson," I said in a subdued tremulous voice. "You're suggesting that the tables have been turned, that last time, when *I* had leverage, you came to me, but now I have to come to you." He didn't answer, but I could virtually hear him smirk. "Well, aren't you?" I demanded angrily.

"Thou sayest," he replied in a voice gone suddenly quiet and portentous.

"I've got a big surprise in store for you, my friend," I warned.

"Do you? I love presents," he rejoined, returning to his impertinent glibbery. "And isn't that a coincidence? I — oops! excuse that — *we* have one for you."

"I already know all about your little secret, Bateson. You're so subtle, the panda and everything. What is that, like the Sicilians with a fish or something? But then, of course, that wasn't your idea at all, was it? It was *his.* "

"Panda? Fish? *His?* Sorry, I'm afraid I don't follow you. What, and whom, are you speaking of?"

"That's all right, Bateson, I don't expect you to give yourself away. Suffice it to say I know, and have known for quite some time."

"Excuse me, know *what?* "

"About your 'little surprise,' your maneuverings."

"Oh, that. I was beginning to think we were talking on a different wavelength. Well, if you know all about that, Sun I, what purpose is there in a meeting?"

"Don't expect me to tip my hand either, Bateson," I said. "That's precisely what you'll find out in the meeting."

"Well then, I'm all eagerness, counting the minutes, as they say."

"Tomorrow then," I proposed.

"Tomorrow, by all means! One o'clock?"

"One." I started to hang up, but he couldn't resist a final jab.

"Oh, Sun I, before you go, just one last question. I love presents, but I hate surprises. If you know all about what you call our 'maneuverings,' and have known for quite some time, well, let me rephrase it, your 'knowledge' doesn't seem to have altered the complexion of the situation very much, has it? Where are your shares now?" In the pause I heard him punching keys on the desk Quotron I'd seen in his office. "Tut, tut, down again. *Too bad, Sun I.*"

"Couldn't resist a parting shot, could you, Bateson?"

"Never could," he replied.

"You realize, of course, you've just tipped your hand, virtually admitting your manipulation."

"Manipulation!" He laughed. "Is that what you think we're doing down — oops! *up* — here?"

"You just confessed, Bateson," I gloated, and then a brilliant, vicious inspiration seized me, "and this conversation is being recorded," I lied.

His voice became suddenly grim. "I've admitted nothing," he contradicted. "And for your information wiretapping is a federal offense."

It was my turn to laugh. "Touchy about the law all of a sudden, Bateson? Formerly you were less fastidious."

"All right, Sun I," he concluded. "This conversation has outlived its usefulness. I'll expect you tomorrow. One o'clock."

"Counting the minutes!" I twitted, turning his own glibness back on him. "Oh, and Bateson, before you go, just one more thing." I paused for effect.

"Yes?"

"Not only am I going to take you over, not only am I going to oust you and your puppet regime, I'm going to put your ass in jail."

It so thoroughly stumped him that he couldn't speak. "Jail!" he echoed finally, retreating to a hollow levity, a burlesque of his former confidence. "Good heavens! You're overreaching yourself there, aren't you? Exaggerating just a little?"

"Not one jot."

"Well then!" he said. "Something as serious as that we'd best put off till we can get our knives and forks together over it, shouldn't we? Tomorrow."

"Bateson." I held him, drawing out my satisfaction. "Let's make sure we have some of those crusty loaves 'still warm from the oven,' shall we? And some of that wine — what was it called? Wrath Child, wasn't it? You remember. Under the circumstances I think it's apropos."

"You asked for it, you got it," he said tersely, and hung up.

I immediately called my secretary. "Mary? Lunch at one tomorrow at APL."

"I'm sorry, sir," she replied, "you're already scheduled for luncheon with the trustees at the Met. It's the third time you've rescheduled."

"Damn it!" I hissed. "All right, just make it early. Twelve — before, if possible. I'm a busy man. My time is valuable."

"Yes, sir," she agreed. "I know."

Bateson be damned, I thought, hanging up. I didn't want to eat with him anyway.

•

Luncheon at the Metropolitan Museum passed, for me, in a state of high abstraction brought on, of course, by anticipation. Not quite so high, however, that I wasn't able to pick up, and fairly early on, that I had been earmarked as a contributor, benefactor, let us say, to, or of, a projected China wing, then in the development stages, to be added to the museum at an unspecified date in the future, contingent, of course, on the generous support of patrons like myself. Of course. I listened with half an ear to their pitches, forcing myself to look my speaker in the eye occasionally, for form, and trying to refrain from pulling up my sleeve and checking my watch too often. They were quite subtle really, quite sophisticated — charming men. They had done their homework, too. They knew who I was, where I'd come from, what I'd done. There was even an offhand, joking reference to the "merger," which I smiled on icily, causing it to be quickly and discreetly dropped, dropped like a hot potato in fact. They knew how to avoid offense, swiftly bringing the tone back to an intimate reserve I felt more comfortable with. Quite charming really, those men. I had met no one like them before. Not on Wall Street, though I had met cultured men on Wall Street. From such distance they flattered me extravagantly with surgical precision, and without the least trace of obsequiousness, or, on the other hand, of condescension. But they were human too, and they made one mistake, got one detail mixed up.

"You realize, of course," said one of the younger members of the party, a man with thinning hair and flushed cheeks like a girl's, a bit more eager than his elders, the same man who had made the remark about the takeover, "that a great number of religious artifacts will find their way into the wing, assuming it's ever built, of course." They all laughed moderately, or at least smiled. "Take our current exhibit, for example. Have you seen it?"

He caught me with my sleeve up. I raised my head, smiled sourly, and shook my head.

"Perhaps we could arrange a tour?" he suggested. "I myself . . ."

"Some other time," I parried. "I'm in a terrible rush today."

"Of course," he acceded, bowing out like a genie off to perform his master's wishes, or rather returning to the bottle after having been dismissed. "What I meant to say, though, was that I felt, we felt rather" — he was becoming a little flustered and proportionately more flushed — "that you would be especially interested in that fact — about the religious artifacts, I mean." He paused and, feeling rather cruel in my annoyance, I let him hang. His companions cast looks of discrete dismay among themselves.

"Since you were," he persisted with a trace of vehemence, "if I'm not mistaken, formerly a Buddhist, were you not?" His look, the look of a man used to being proud and right, was indignantly imploring.

His error jarred me for the first time during the luncheon into sharp attention, that and his use of the past tense, "formerly," as though my card had expired — which, in a sense, I suppose it had, and long before, but it was not for him, not for this young puppy (though he was older than I) to presume to call me on it.

"Taoist," I corrected curtly, frowning and looking aggressively at my watch. "Gentlemen" — I rose with a chilly smile — "you must excuse me. I have a very important date at one o'clock. I've enjoyed it immensely. You'll hear from me." I was tempted to say, "Don't call me, I'll call you," but appeased myself with the thought.

Rather than take the chauffeured limousine they'd sent for me I hailed a cab on Fifth Avenue "Wall Street," I said as I fell into the seat. But as I spiraled in and down, my eye was suddenly caught by the huge banner fluttering from the entablature above the columns. Despite the spaced holes punched to reduce its wind resistance, it billowed like a spinnaker on a momentary gust. "Wait a minute. Stop," I ordered. I looked up, waiting for it to luff.

I was right. I had seen it. "Here," I said, stuffing more money than I owed him, uncounted, into the glass drawer and climbing out.

I have said the world was full of signs, as full of signs as the nighttime sky was full of stars off the dark coast of Sumatra that summer long ago, or Borneo, I could no longer remember, those nights when Scottie had catechized me on the constellations, the first words of English I had ever learned, and I had seemed to see my fate writ large across the black slate of the universe in runes of glittering chalk, a mystic alphabet that burned as cold and true as diamonds. I was certain the first moment I saw it that this Manjusri was the same one I had seen, Scottie and I, in the hold of the *Telemachos*. For they are all slightly different, with that precious and incalculable difference of the conceiving hand and eye brought to the task by an individual maker, and there was something about this one, even with the approximateness of appliqué, like regatta colors sewn on a great sail, and the hugeness of the banner, which confounded scale, something about the eyes, I think, the two human eyes, smiling, subtle, composed, and the Third Eye of transcendental wisdom in the middle of his forehead, something that convinced me that this was the same figure we had seen. "The Lost Religion of Tibet," the legend read. And beside him, beside Manjusri, balancing the composition, a figure, a great horned figure. . . .

I ran up the steps.

Following the stream of visitors, I bought a catalogue and thumbed it distractedly as I walked. But hardly had I opened it when I arrived at the threshold of the exhibition, where I no longer needed it, no longer needed the description, the words, with the thing itself before me, the signature superfluous in the presence of the signer. Face to face.

Beside Manjusri, the supersubtle boy, Bodhisattva of Transcendental Wisdom, with the lotus and the book balanced on the stigma (ah, but that said it all, the Book of Knowledge on the stigma), and a sword newly honed by the restorer's art, beside him, balancing the composition, fifteen feet tall, and massive, several tons at least, awesome to look at even in representation, loomed a black figure with two great bronze horns, thick as a man's waist at the base and tapering to a tip as sharp as the point of a spear (in the dim light I almost seemed to see the swatch of cloth from my old pea jacket pinned to one of them, the left one, only one of many trophies), horns garlanded not by flowers, like those Europa wove around the horns of Zeus, but human skulls, real ones. An enormous black erection, with ropes of veins like an addict's forearm chiseled in the stone, stood up almost to his solar plexus, big around as my thigh. Among many other implements, all no doubt with esoteric meanings obscure to me, the figure held the hourglass I remembered, once filled with such strange sand (magic sand for magic sleep and dreaming, and he, the Magic Sandman), held it in one of many, literally dozens, of hands, each arranged in a different mudra, each a sacrilege, mudras of power and obscenity I had never even seen. And in the central pair of hands, the four-toed claw of the mang dragon, he held the Wheel of Life itself, the Egg of Chaos, the Great Primal Opposition, *T'ai Chi T'u, yin* and *yang,* the symbol of the Tao itself. Inscribed around the outer edge I read the universal mantra: "Om Mani Padme Hum," the Jewel within the Lotus. But most of all it was the face that drew me, for it was the face of a raging bull, eyes bulging — all three of them — in an expression of obscene surprise and relish, like a cartoon character in some X-rated comic book, rubbing his hands and licking his chops over the tasty morsel of an eight-year-old virgin, mouth partway open, tongue curled up touching the top row of teeth, almost coy, almost hilarious, the bloodred tongue, as the monster opened his arms, the whole lot of them, in a familiar gesture of invitation, Riley's gesture, but an invitation to a darker Communion than Riley had ever celebrated, a blacker mystery than he had even dreamed.

Yama, the Black Lord of Death, Tibetan counterpart of Yen Lo Wang, but with a difference, with a twist, a twist that made all the difference. Yama, balancing the composition, Yama, with the black head of a bull. Yes, here at last I wandered unwittingly around the final corner into the very heart of the labyrinth and found my grinning Minotaur waiting to embrace me like a lover. Yama, Lord of Death. Yama, Lord. Yama. The Bull. Final enlightenment.

Total eclipse. Final enlightenment, total eclipse. "Samsara equals Nirvana."
I remembered the expression and smiled grimly. Well then, Nirvana equals
Samsara. The commutative law, remember? Nirvana is Samsara. Mystic pat-
terns written in detritus.

The label on the wall rounded and closed it:

> From *The Way of the White Clouds,* by Lama Anagarika Govinda:
> "The God of Death (Yama) is represented in his terrible form as a
> bull-headed deity . . ."

"Bull-headed" — I laughed outright. Several people stared.

> According to a popular legend, a saintly hermit, who had been
> meditating for a lifetime in a lonely cave, was about to attain
> complete liberation when some robbers entered his cave with a stolen
> bull and killed it by severing its head, without being aware of the
> hermit's presence. When they discovered that the latter had been a
> witness of their deed, they killed him too by cutting off his head. But
> they had not counted on his supernatural power, which he had
> acquired during his lifelong penance. Hardly had they severed the
> head of the hermit when the latter rose, joined the bull's head to his
> body and thus transformed himself into the ferocious form of Yama.
> Deprived from reaching the highest aim of his penance and seized by
> an insatiable fury, he cut off the heads of the robbers, hung them
> around his neck as a garland and roamed through the world as a
> death-bringing demon, until . . .

But I didn't read the rest. Light as a feather, floating a thousand feet above
the ground, I hardly needed a taxi to take me back downtown. For I emerged
from the museum as Yama, "seized by an insatiable fury," with my eye the
glittering Third Eye right in the middle of my forehead, trained on eleven men
— twelve men, yes, twelve, I mustn't forget that empty chair, him most
important of all — who had robbed me of the fruit of my own penance, twelve
stars soon to be glittering in my crown, a new constellation. Yama, Death. For
I had been good, so very, very good, who now would be most horrid.

Chapter 24

Though it didn't surprise me (nothing could have surprised me) Bateson's tone
was not what I'd expected. There was something grave and almost wistful in
his manner as he greeted me, even, perhaps, far down in the depths of his cold
eyes, a glimmering of tenderness. It was strange, as though the conversation
of the previous day had never occurred, stranger yet because I felt it too. We
talked together in his office for a few minutes, I hardly remember what about,
about nothing at all it seems, about the snow. It had started on my way down
in the taxi, I told him. He raised the venetian blinds and we stood together
absorbed in the mystery of its soundless, soft descent. Then we sat down and
he offered me a cigarette, took one himself, to my surprise. Yes, he did smoke.
Perhaps he'd simply been nervous the time before. He wasn't nervous now.
Nor was I. We smoked in silence, a certain intimacy in our distance then,
feeling under no compulsion to improve the time with speech, like soldiers
before a battle. Only we were enemies, he and I, the battle to be waged between
ourselves. Leaning back my head to sigh up the smoke, I thought again of the
cigarette burning in the ashtray before the empty chair at the conference table
at our first parley. An inexplicable hilarity swept over me and I laughed.
Bateson caught it too at the same instant, and he joined in. And thinking of
that cigarette, and others behind it, a chain smoke stretching all the way back
through the nexus of Li's bedside table no doubt to the Creation itself when
God rested from his labors, I laughed so hard the tears streamed down my
cheeks, and Bateson laughed with me all the way, though he couldn't have had
the slightest inkling what touched off the fuse of my hilarity and kept it
burning. Watching him laugh, even as I myself convulsed (both there and
someplace high above, observing), I had the odd sensation that I was watching
my own reflection in a mirror. On impulse, I stood up from my chair, still
laughing, and passed my hand over his head, as though to bless him, or warm
myself at some tongue of Pentecostal flame burning from the center of his
brain.

He recoiled slightly, as though I'd meant to strike him. "What on earth . . . ?" he uttered in an astonished tone, still smiling.

"Just checking," I said, chuckling to myself, relishing the privacy of the joke.

"Checking what?" he asked, echoing me again and smiling as though he understood.

"To see if there are any wires," I replied, guffawing; and he laughed too, damn him, he laughed too.

I remember that trivial incident almost more vividly than anything else about the parley. I can never get over it. Why did he laugh? He couldn't have known what I was thinking of, my dream of the puppeteer. It wasn't anything I said. No, it was something behind the words. It had to be.

Though I can't say I found him any more attractive as a man than at our prior meeting, a deeper intimacy existed between us then, as though we'd known each other all our lives, a tenderness almost, whose source, I think, can only have been hatred itself. His presence possessed a vividness for me nearly as intense as that which had astonished me on the roof with Yin-mi so long before, when the hairline seam had parted and I had seen her soul, the thing itself, caught a glimpse of it shyly emerging from the forest within her, stepping like a deer, each small hoof quivering poised in the air before she touched it down, then beautifully folding on her cannons to drink at the shining pool of our hope in one another. With her then I had craved no other joy. But with Bateson, I was the hunter waiting at another, darker pool, waiting to slay, and the thing that emerged from the wilderness within him and gazed at me, studied me, was not a deer but a predator like myself, its eyes calm and deep with science and the will of death. It wanted to slay me, too. That was acknowledged between us, and it made it seem all right, almost innocent, as though out of the final rite of darkness a light might shine, a new innocence emerge out of final desecration.

We adjourned to the conference room where I sensed something festive in the atmosphere, inexplicable, like our prior spate of laughter, only held in, frothing slightly at the edges, an undertone of giddiness hinting vaguely at hysteria, but a hysteria born of confidence and power, not helplessness, shimmering out as nervous energy, heat.

I was glad to find them so, radiant with confidence, as up as I was. It took the putrid savor from the act of death, rinsed away the bad taste in my mouth that had been left by those black, harrowed looks in all the other takeovers. No black looks here. Everything bright and terse, all the consequences known, accepted, forgiven in advance, in eagerness for the play. So much better that way. Indeed, we were a gay company. To a casual observer, at first glance, it might have appeared to be an inner-office Christmas party, the bonuses about to be dispensed. Only there was a sharpness in the air, like the crack of a whip, in every look and smile. Deeps opened under the most casual remarks, and we paused to contemplate them in each other, to contemplate *it,* as Bateson and

I had contemplated the silent snowfall, united before it, each moved, each respectful, though *it* was nothing finally but the ineluctable fatality we must exact upon each other, the destruction we would make together, like lovers, one giving, one accepting, in the final coitus of war where consummation brings not rest, but death.

"Well, gentlemen," Bateson said at last, clasping his hands in front of him, his look, his manner, like that of a man who has spent a great deal of time and care preparing a feast, and now, calling the guests to table, does so with a certain sadness and resignation, knowing the meal, however good, will never taste as sweet as his own labors in preparing it. "I suppose we should proceed to business — though I must admit, I'm not exactly sure what our business is." Everybody laughed. "Somehow it seems more like an occasion for pleasure than business, doesn't it? And everybody with surprises! Sun I has surprises. We have surprises. He's promised us a big one. And we hope to reciprocate in our own modest way, don't we, gentlemen?" He nodded around. The others had started sidling toward him, grouping around and behind him, the lines forming almost like a dance, they on one side of the table, I on the other, as before. "Yes, we have a few surprises of our own." He smiled and lapsed into fatuity. "Why, taking all of them together, our surprises, your surprises, the sum of them, we're so rich with surprises one hardly knows where to begin!" He shrugged with outturned palms and frowned, opening his eyes wide, the clown's look of perplexity. Yes, exactly. Like the circus. I could practically hear the roar of laughter and applause. But where was the ringmaster, the emcee, the man in the top hat and the black tuxedo? The mirrors mocked me with my own image, infinitely redoubled, depth after depth, plane after plane, smaller and smaller, until it disappeared within itself. And there at the vanishing point, behind the two-way mirror, he waited. I could sense his presence, almost hear him breathe.

"Since I know yours already," I said, coming to Bateson's relief, but looking into the mirror, into my own eyes, and his behind them, "I suppose the burden falls on me."

He nodded, pursing his lips, both permissive and conceding.

"I was pleased to receive your present in the mail," I began as I'd long planned. "The panda. It's been with me quite a lot of late, day and night in fact. You might almost say I've slept on it" — I smiled into a vacuum — "and it's made me rethink a great number of things, forced me to reconsider how in certain respects I might have misjudged you at our first parley, been inclined to doubt your good faith on certain points, particularly your professions of loyalty to him" — I looked into the mirror and smiled — "to my father, Eddie Love. I'd like to apologize to you on that score, for it's become clear to me how wrong I was, quite clear to me now," I said, smiling at them with ferocious irony, "the depths of your sincerity. An admittedly impressive feat of pres-ti-di-gi-TAY-shun, gentlemen" — I laughed, discovering it suddenly — "your concealment — in both senses, on both *counts* — impressive in every sense." I savored the innuendo, meeting their eyes in turn. "Concerning the gift simply, though," I continued, "to return to that, I'd like to say I appreciate the satisfaction your little joke must have given you, appreciate it deeply. On the other hand, however, I feel bound to add, I sympathize with the lack of discipline that prompted it — unfortunate for you, fortunate for me, since it led me ultimately to the discovery of your plot, your little 'surprise,' as you call it. In short, gentlemen," I said, frowning and growing suddenly stern, "the bear raid you're currently undertaking against the share price of my company's stock. I've come to tell you it must stop. *Now.*"

Murmurs broke out across the table. They leaned together, conferring in whispers. "Bear raid," I heard over and over, uttered as though in surprise or affront.

Bateson exhaled and sat forward, almost a sigh of relief. "Let me get this straight, Sun I," he began. "This is your 'surprise'?" He looked from side to side at the others. "You've come to 'tell us' we must stop?" He snorted, continuing to regard his cohorts with incredulity; then he fixed me pointedly. "Assuming the fall in your shares were the result of manipulation — what did you call it, a bear raid? That's a little old-fashioned, isn't it? — and not simply the result of the free play of market forces, as I suspect, and further assuming that we were behind this alleged manipulation, what incentive would we have to stop? Your telling us to? Surely you haven't come to beg for mercy?" He almost scoffed.

"Correct. I haven't come to 'beg' for anything." I leaned forward across the table on my elbows, keen upon him. "I've come to take, Bateson" — I almost spat his name — "to take what's mine."

"And what is that?" he asked, lowering hatefully at me, his smile like a grimace.

I peered at him a moment, then sat back coolly drawing the bow. "What you offered me at the first meeting," I said casually, raising my eyebrows to examine my cuticles. "Remember?" I grinned at him. "My seat." I paused to watch the dark blur of the arrow traverse the distance. I could almost hear it whistle, delicate and gay, before the brutal, sharp, report, the ugly crunch of splitting bone, as it sank home to its final depth.

"It was quite generous of you to offer it then," I went on, savoring each inflection of discovery in his eyes as he thought ahead, "considering I held only two percent, if that. Above and beyond the call, so to speak." I smiled, and then I didn't. "Now, however, as I don't doubt you're fully aware, I have in excess of twenty-eight percent. Only a start, of course. Short of a majority. But I've reconsidered my position. Why wait? I want to take advantage of what's mine. I don't see how you can fault me on that. After all, it's the American way, isn't it? Twenty-eight percent, let's see . . ." I turned my eyes toward the ceiling and pursed my lips as though figuring, "That entitles me to three seats by my calculations. No, gentlemen, no need to beg what's mine already." I beamed at them in full consciousness of triumph.

"And why have you suddenly become so keen to join us, Sun I," Bateson asked, "when at our first meeting you rejected our offer out of hand?" He glanced at his confederates in a way that seemed to say, "as if I didn't know."

"Let's simply say I want to work within the system," I explained gleefully. "I want to avail myself of your excellent counsel."

"To discover how we operate, in other words," he glossed, taking it up.

"Correct," I said. "And of course to exercise my voting privileges."

"You realize, of course, such privileges entail responsibilities."

I nodded. "Of course."

"We've always enjoyed a certain unanimity of perspective here, enjoyed it, of course, because we've worked for it. And because we've all had the same goal in mind: the ultimate welfare of the corporation and the best interests of the shareholders."

"No doubt," I deprecated. "I believe I expressed my opinion on that at our first meeting."

"We'd require certain assurances of good faith, of course."

I frowned. "I don't think you're in a position to 'require' anything."

He studied me, then shook his head, as though arriving at a decision. "I'm afraid it wouldn't work, Sun I. Unless, of course, you were willing to give up this idea of a takeover. In that case something might be arranged. Otherwise, I'm afraid there'd be too great a conflict of interest on your part. A directorship here — even two — couldn't advance your cause. We operate democratically, as you know. . . ."

"Yes, 'fiduciary republicanism,' " I retorted scathingly.

". . . and you couldn't work your will against the confirmed opinion of the majority, we here" — he nodded to each side — "that such a takeover would be against the best interests of the corporation."

"If I can't vote you down, I can expose you," I blurted, laying it before him. "As a director I'm privy to all corporate secrets, correct? Well, I'll find out how you're doing it, your little sleight of hand, and if you don't desist . . ."

"You'll blow the whistle," he said, completing my thought. "That's what I mean, Sun I, about the conflict of interest. That would be treasonous in a director, to sabotage his own company. I'm afraid we couldn't tolerate it."

"Too bad, Bateson," I consoled. "I guess you'll just have to learn to, won't you? I mean, seeing as you have no choice." I grinned brilliantly.

"What do you mean 'no choice'?"

"Come on, Bateson, don't be obtuse," I chided. "You're spoiling my fun. You know as well as I do you can't keep me out. Accept it gracefully. It's a fact of life, like dying. *You lose.*" I laughed.

"Am I missing something?" he asked, looking around. He caught my eye and held it. "There's one rather major problem with your argument, Sun I. You're *not* a director."

"Don't give me that, Bateson," I lashed out. "You know as well as I do that's merely a formality. You can't keep me out. I control twenty-eight percent of your shares. Goddamn it, I'll *be* a director, and what's more, I'll appoint two others of my choosing to chairs and do anything I damn well please once I'm inside."

"You keep saying 'I,' Sun I. 'I own,' 'I control,' 'I'll appoint.' Correct me if I'm wrong, but it was my impression that Rising Sun Enterprises owned those shares."

"I *am* Rising Sun!" I shouted at him, thudding the table with the heel of my palm for emphasis.

"Please don't raise your voice to me." He sighed and shook his head. "And we'd made such a pleasant start. Perhaps we'd better break for lunch to let things simmer down a little. It seemed to work before, perhaps it will again."

"Damn it, Bateson" (I was furious) "I don't want lunch. I want this straightened out right now."

"Don't deny me — us — the pleasure, Sun I," he replied with a slight pout of petition. "If you're absolutely adamant, then we'll continue while we eat; but wouldn't it be pleasanter if we simply took a little recess to refresh ourselves? Humor me. We have something very special prepared for you."

"Oh yes," I seethed, throwing myself back in my chair, "your luncheons always are quite special, aren't they? I'll grant you that. What are you serving for dessert today, figs arsenic?"

He chuckled. "Oh, let's wait a bit before we start thinking about dessert, shall we? Let that be a surprise." He paused. "We'll eat in here again, shall we? Open the curtain and watch the snow?" He pressed the button and the green velvet drape began to retract and dimple to the low whine of the motor. The snow was falling less heavily than before, though it had been relatively light to begin with. A blue patch of sky had opened over the river. The winter sun hung like a huge white paper lantern over Brooklyn, wreathed in mists which it seemed to be trying to burn away, a white, restless broiling in a cold sky.

I was restless too, beginning to become disgruntled. I realized I had been unrealistic, but somehow I'd expected them to fold at once after I tipped my cards. Of course, Bateson really had no choice, he had to keep on bluffing. I didn't really blame him for it. Still, I was anxious to get it over with, to stop playing games. To pay up and pay out. I wanted my place.

Bateson excused himself, ostensibly to inform the kitchen staff of our plans. But perhaps he'd gone to confer. Maybe that was the game. He was buying time, awaiting new orders. But what was the point? The battle was over. I'd won. I looked at the mirrors, up and down the length of them, as though to find a crack, an eroded patch of silvering I might peer through, as one wipes away the hot condensation of the bath or one's own breath on a mirror to see the face behind. And as I searched, I allowed myself to wonder, just for an instant, if he was really there at all. What if he weren't? It was the first time since the dream, since Coney Island really, that I had even questioned it. The thought that he might not be frightened me much more than that he was. I experienced a momentary vertigo. Coney Island in reverse, a small crisis of faith: I realized that as much as I had needed him there before to love, even if only "mystically present," through "the subtler alchemy which occurs in the believer's heart through faith," just so much I needed him there now, to hate. The thought made me almost sad, and I asked myself if I had truly given all up in my heart, all, and if I ever would give it up, if one ever could. But then, remembering the cigarette, I laughed again as Bateson and I had laughed, only to myself, and I thought of Yama, and the will rose up implacable in me.

They served the meal then, bringing it in again in covered dishes, huge silver bells that rang and jangled as they walked. Waiters in white jackets, two for their side of the table, one for me alone, worked quickly from carts. When all the places had been set, Bateson nodded, and my waiter lifted up the smoking bell with a white cloth.

A huge cloud of swirling steam arose, and from within it two poached eyes stared back at me.

"Oh, my God," I said, wincing with disgust, but leaning closer to look, "what is it?"

Bateson looked at me with a vaguely hurt expression, as though surprised at my reaction. "Tête de veau au beurre noir?" he asked the air in a thin, pained voice. "With tiny new potatoes, baby carrots, celery hearts?" His chin wavered slightly in a palsy of disappointed sensitivity, making him seem momentarily geriatric. "Don't tell me you don't like it."

"It is, isn't it?" I ogled it.

"Is what?"

"*A cow!*"

"Calf," he corrected testily. "What do you think it is? Of course it's a cow, tête de veau."

I gaped at him with skeptical incredulity, unable to believe he wasn't joking. But that expression! He must have practiced it before a mirror. After further reflection, however, I decided not to yield the benefit of the doubt. "Spare me, Bateson," I griped, feeling my way queasily toward righteous indignation. "What is this supposed to be, symbolic? Another touch of gastronomic terrorism?" I continued to gaze at it with fascinated loathing, unable to divert my eyes.

" 'Gastronomic terrorism' — that's a bit strong, don't you think?" he demanded, recovering strength, a little miffed. "I won't deny I ordered it with you in mind, Sun I, like the prime rib, but as a sort of tribute. Bull Inc. . . . ?"

"Yes, Bateson," I replied scathingly, "I think I got it."

"On the other hand," he pointed out, "it is one of our chef's specialties, perhaps his finest dish." He sought corroboration from his fellows. "It's not something we eat every day," he went on indignantly, as though chiding a child for not cleaning his plate, "I can tell you that."

"I don't blame you," I rejoined. "I wouldn't either if I had the choice."

He looked disgusted. They all did.

Suddenly it seemed almost funny. Making a face, I gingerly poked at the boiled eye with my fork. "Do you think you can starve concessions out of me you can't gain otherwise, that you can cow me?" The eye popped and the vitreous humor droozed, a swift gelatinous tear, down onto the snout. I threw back my head and laughed a high queasy laugh, tapering off into a shiver of disgust. "Take it away," I directed, closing my eyes and averting my head as I pushed the plate from me. "Lucky for me I ate before I came." Bateson didn't seem to hear me, testing the doneness, or rareness, of the specimen with his fork. "All right, Bateson, you've had your little joke, as much good as it's done you. Let's get back to business."

"Mmm," he nodded with his mouth full. With an effort he managed to swallow. "You don't mind, do you?" He pointed to his plate with the tip of his knife. "Go ahead. You were saying?" He turned to the man beside him. "Delicious." They nodded to one another as though pumping up the pressure in their internal engines until it was high enough for speech.

"Yes, marvelous," the second finally replied, unable to manage any better eulogy.

"We do like to have our beef," Bateson asseverated. "It keeps us lean and" — he allowed himself the fraction of a grin — "carnivorous, so to speak. I'm sorry it didn't agree with you. From your reaction one would almost think we'd served you a tête de mort rather than tête de veau." He chortled with the others in self-congratulatory amusement.

I observed them feeding, listened to the click of silverware on china, the clatter of dishes, their low, indistinguishable rumble of speech, like articulate digestion noises. Their appetite fascinated and appalled me. Bateson particularly relished his meal. I watched with something amounting to horror as he applied himself to the two boiled nubbins of tender horn protruding through the melting flesh of the forehead. Forcing them with the lever of his knife, he cracked them on his plate, then lifted them in his fingers and tipped them up, sucking the marrow. Noting my scrutiny, he offered one to me like a toast, smiling and nodding with unembarrassed gusto.

"We were discussing my twenty-eight percent," I resumed eventually in a thin voice, forcing myself to look away.

"Right!" he agreed, raising his chin to swallow and his knife to interrupt. "Rising Sun's twenty-eight." He smiled gratuitously.

"What's the difference, Bateson, my shares, Rising Sun's shares? We've been over that before. I told you, I am Rising Sun."

"Right you are," he conceded, nodding and chewing. "So you said." He patted his lips with his napkin and gestured to the waiter to clear. "Bring the second course," he directed in a low murmur.

"You know, Sun I," he said, folding his napkin, not looking at me, "I must say you have a very cavalier attitude toward your position in your company, toward your shareholders." He regarded me pointedly. "Perhaps that's permissible at Bull Incorporated, at Rising Sun, but I — *we* rather — are a bit dismayed by it, quite frankly. That's another reason it would never work, teaming up, I mean, a mutual joining of forces, yours and ours. We would never dream of presuming so far here as to lump together 'our' resources with the corporation's." He frowned and shook his head gravely. "No, I must say, it seems a little irresponsible, a little high-handed."

"Let's leave Rising Sun out of this, shall we?" I asked with acid politeness. "How I run my company is none of your business. It's not an issue here. We're discussing you."

Still folding his napkin and frowning, he shook his head. "No, Sun I, you're wrong. It is an issue. Set it down," he told the waiter who had appeared beside me with a tray.

"I don't care for any." I begged off in a softer voice, smiling up and shaking my head.

"But you haven't even seen it," Bateson protested.

"*Whatever* it is."

"I must insist," he said grimly. "Go ahead." He signaled the waiter with a peremptory backhand flick of the wrist before I could object. The man lifted the cover, and inside, surrounded by sprigs of fresh green parsley, I discovered a thick stack of stock certificates. The engraved logo showed the sun balancing on the horizon, halfway up — a theme borrowed from my mother's robe. Rising Sun.

My heart began to thud. "What is this?" I asked in a quiet voice.

"Dessert," he replied, smiling. "That's all. *Just* dessert."

"Very cute, Bateson," I observed with hollow scorn. "What's it supposed to mean?"

He shrugged, pouting. "Only that we're shareholders too, Sun I, in *your* corporation, and as such have certain rights and interests of our own in how that company is run, particularly in the attitudes and dispositions of its directors and managers, in *your* attitudes and dispositions, Sun I, just as you might be expected to have in ours in a similar situation."

That was it? I felt the arrow whiz past my face and continue on, on, somewhere, it didn't matter. It had missed me. I felt a surge of savage joy, and gazing out the picture window, I saw the sky was suddenly blue and the sun shone.

"That was it," I asked, "the surprise?"

He blinked and nodded. "Precisely. You had only half of it before."

I laughed in his face.

They eyed one another gravely. "I don't think laughter is appropriate under the circumstances, Sun I," he chided.

"No, no, you're right," I agreed, wiping the tears from the corners of my eyes with the back of my wrist. "I'm just so relieved. You frightened me. For a moment there . . ." I shook my head at it. "No, gentlemen, of course you're entitled to your say at Rising Sun. After all, I run my business democratically too. It's the price you pay for going public, isn't it?" They didn't respond to my attempt at corporate weltzschmerz. "Of course, you have the same rights as any other shareholders," I conceded, retreating to an intimate reserve, emulating the trustees at the Met.

Bateson held one finger up to interrupt. "Not quite the same, Sun I," he differed. "I don't think you quite understand."

"What do you mean?"

"Perhaps you'd better count them."

Thwack. Out of nowhere it came back. I felt the world pull out from under me, and I was falling impossibly fast, falling. "Why don't you just tell me," I said, trying not to panic.

"Fifty-three," he pronounced.

"Thousand?"

He smiled pityingly. "Percent."

The arrow hit home. I closed my eyes. Wake up, I thought. "Impossible," I said aloud. "You can't amass a position like that" — I pointed my chin at them, at the certificates — "not like that, and be selling right and left at the same time, selling enough to do the kind of damage you've been doing." I shook my head in vehement denial. "What is this, another joke? What, are they fakes? More psychological terrorism?"

"Have them checked," he suggested. "Check them yourself."

I lifted off the crisp top leaf, ten thousand shares, and held it toward the light. I could see the watermark. I stared past it out the window, over the skyline of Manhattan. Falling, I could hear the wind whistling in my ears. Cold tears seeped from the corners of my eyes and flew upward. Giddy with panic, I began to laugh, threw back my head and howled. And above my laughter, above the whistling of the wind, I could hear another laughter, higher, stranger than my own, like the cry of an osprey, thin, reedy, shrill, not quite human, and with it the droning of an engine. Through the fluttering of my lashes I saw a tiny black speck materializing in the center of the sun, growing larger and larger. But by the time I recognized it, it was too late. I was dead already.

"Ever noticed, Sun I," Bateson was saying, nodding toward the certificate in my hand, "the way it's depicted? One can't tell whether the sun is rising or setting, an ambiguous design."

"*Rising* Sun," I reminded him mechanically before I realized how he'd set me up.

"Setting Sun," he said, "for you."

Then the needle skipped back in the groove, the right groove, repeating. I shook my head. "Impossible," I said. "You couldn't have been hoarding our shares, you were selling, short selling. How could you be hoarding too?"

"That's the sixty-four-thousand-dollar question, isn't it, Sun I? Though sixty-four million would be closer to the mark, and even that would be off by an order of magnitude or so."

"It's a trick, some sleight of hand." I spat my accusations at the mirror.

"How could you have gotten your hands on so much? Just tell me that. Fifty-three percent." I glared at the certificates, chiding them.

He shrugged. "That one isn't hard. There was your initial public offering. We invested quite heavily in that. Our motives were purely benign too, I might add. *Then.* Whatever you may be inclined to believe, whatever you've forced us to now, in the beginning we wished you well. Sincerely." He rolled in his lips and gazed at me earnestly, apologetic and condemnatory at once.

"Liar!" I shouted at him.

"As you prefer," he said. "Secondly, of course, there were purchases over the open market. Those have been stepped up considerably of late. Then there was your friend, Kahn."

"Kahn?" I was flabbergasted. "I don't believe you."

He nodded. "I'm afraid so. Of course, he was unaware who he was selling to. We bought through public brokers, numbered accounts, in relatively small lots, that sort of thing. He wasn't actively in complicity, though he wasn't overscrupulous about who he sold to, either. In the end we managed to come up with pretty much everything he put up for offer. That about covers it I believe." He smiled. "Oh wait — I almost forgot the best part. The last little bit, those last few percent, what is it they say about the last mile?"

"What about them?"

"You gave them to us, Sun I." He beamed.

I touched my chest unconsciously. "I did?"

He nodded. "Your most enticing offer of convertibility, remember? We decided to take advantage of it ourselves."

I stared at him in amazement. "You sold me your own shares while I was trying to take you over?"

"Precisely. So we could get control of you. I hardly need add, those were the sweetest. I believe that about sums it up."

I shook my head. "Not quite. That still leaves the main point unexplained. Assuming what you say is true, how could you be buying shares, buying on that scale, and driving *down* the price?"

Bateson smiled paternally. "It's a moot question isn't it, Sun I? *Now.* The point is we control Rising Sun Enterprises, which means, in addition, that we indirectly control that twenty-eight percent of our own shares which you've gone to so much needless trouble to acquire only to hand back to us, shares which you, rather rashly I must say, spoke just now of 'owning,' which further means that you are entitled to nothing, precisely nothing — no seat on our board, no voting privileges, no privy information — in short, zero. You understand? And what's more, we hereby relieve you of your duties as CEO of Rising Sun Enterprises, effective immediately."

"But you can't," I objected thinly, putting out my hand limply in an attempt to stop the avalanche. "I still own my initial interest in the corporation. I am Rising Sun. I made the corporation."

"Wrong again," he said. "As to your first point, 'we can't': owning a fifty-three percent interest, as you so ably put it just now, we can do 'anything we damn well please.' " There were laughs around the table. They slapped the marble with their palms. "Here, here!"

"As to the second," he went on, "your initial holdings: though any such would be immaterial anyway in light of our majority interest, I think I should remind you that those same holdings were posed by you as collateral for loans to purchase a further position in Rising Sun. Since the price has continued to fall, we know you have been unable to service the loan and so have been forced to repledge the new shares in lieu of interest and to reschedule, quite a few times, I might add, your repayment of the principal."

"That's confidential information," I said furiously. "Where did you find that out?"

He smiled. "We have our sources. There are always ways."

"As if I didn't know," I said. "It doesn't matter anyway. Collateral or no collateral, pledged or not, I still own those shares. And you can't keep them artificially depressed forever. Eventually I'll be able to repay." I smiled acidly. "Or, having voted yourselves directors, do you plan to sabotage Rising Sun? That would be treasonous, you know." I threw his platitude in his face.

Bateson shook his head. "Still wrong, Sun I. Wrong on both counts. We don't have to sabotage Rising Sun to carry out our plans. In fact, what we have in mind — a little necessary pruning, long overdue — should make the corporation grow back fuller than before. And as to that 'eventually,' in your case, I'm afraid 'eventually' will be too late. As of *now,* this minute, controlling the Bull Group Bank along with the rest of the assets of Rising Sun Enterprises, we hereby declare you in default and confiscate your original collateral, plus any and all shares repledged as debt service, plus further shares pledged as secondary collateral, which amounts to . . ." He whisked out a pair of reading glasses from his handkerchief pocket, flicked them open briskly with one hand, and frowned through them at a sheet of paper on the table. Replacing them as brusquely, he examined me with a hard glitter in his eyes. "Which amounts to, why, I believe it comes out pretty much a wash, Sun I," he gloated, pretending to be amazed. (No mercy here.) He exchanged looks of grisly satisfaction with the others. "Yes, precisely — a wash. There is a small debit to your account, but that can be covered quite conveniently by your two weeks' severance pay, and even leave you, I believe, something over and above." He smiled. "So you see? You come out ahead after all. After all and overall. Not by a great deal, of course, not as much, perhaps, as you had hoped. There is certainly no question now of any major position in Rising Sun Enterprises. In fact, no question of any position at all. As of this moment, you are without either interest in or obligation to the corporation. Naked as a newborn babe, as I believe the expression goes."

"Nothing," I repeated, stunned by it, the completeness of it, unable to take it in. "Nothing." I looked up at him. "Nothing?"

"Not nothing, Sun I. A small balance. And of course we're speaking here strictly about the corporation and its assets. A man in your position will of course have other personal holdings, something set aside to tide him over. You needn't worry. We have no interest in, no designs on, anything of that nature. As I said, we consider it a wash."

"But I put everything up as collateral," I explained, "everything — even my personal savings."

Bateson shook his head, a flash of legitimate sympathy in his eyes for an instant, just an instant. "Most unwise, my boy," he chided quietly. "You should have known better. Let it be a lesson to you for the future."

I laughed. "The future." I sat gaping at it. The future. Nothing. So enormous. Suddenly an echo played back through my inner ear. "A wash, you said." I sought confirmation in his face. "You said a wash."

He frowned. "Yes, I believe I did. What of it? Merely a figure of speech."

"That's it," I said, sinking into contemplation. "That's how you did it, how you built up a position in us and at the same time sold us out. A wash." My discovery provided a momentary solace in the general ruin. I could almost hear the leather binding screaming as the tome fell open. "Wash sales. You never really sold us at all, did you? How did you arrange it?" I nodded. "Don't tell me. I can guess. Back and forth between subsidiaries, right? All in the corporation. All in APL. All in the family. The pension fund of one of your manufacturing divisions sells Rising Sun at a loss to one of your other subsidiaries. The price goes down, but the shares remain under APL control. You lose on the share value of your holdings in Rising Sun, but it was worth it. To protect yourself you had to take the loss. That was the price. *Your* price. That's it, isn't it? Wash sales between subsidiary corporations in the APL family group, back and forth, selling us down the drain without ever losing control of a single share. A bear raid and a wash sale at the same time. Ingenious."

"Ingenious indeed," Bateson said with a slight flush of pride. "But fanciful. You have quite an imagination. Perhaps you should go into advertising, even write a novel."

I laughed outright. "It's illegal, Bateson," I said. "You can't get away with it. I won't let you."

"The burden of proof is on you, Sun I," he pointed out, "and it seems to me you've pretty much exhausted your resources. Yours and ours. Rising Sun's, I mean. You have a good group over there. What do you call them, the Horns? Of course, you'll be carrying out any further investigations without their services, as a 'civilian,' a private citizen, member emeritus and a fortiori (which is to say, with a vengeance) of the G.P., or General Public. In other words, you're on your own, Sun I. If you want to carry on your own private vendetta against us, that's your business. But is it really worth it? Do you really think that if they haven't found it collectively, you will by yourself? If there were anything to turn up, wouldn't they have done so?" He shook his head. "Give it up, my boy. Go on to something else. There's nothing more pathetic than a man determined to martyr himself on the cross of a private grievance. Especially when he's brought it on himself, which, forgive me, you most emphatically have."

"It's still illegal, Bateson," I persisted, ignoring his sententiousness. "You may have covered your tracks and your ass — anything's theoretically possible, I know that — but it's still illegal."

He sighed over me, as over a lost cause. "That was always your weakness as an adversary, Sun I, your weakness, and our gain. You played de jure in a de facto game, in a de facto world. There is no law. Not in this place. Not *here.*"

"Did *he* tell you that?" I asked scornfully.

But he didn't hear, or acknowledge it, continuing on the same track. "Did you really think we would let you waltz in here like some Mephisto, some Taoist Mephisto in new patent-leather shoes and take us over, take the girl, the cakes and all, that we wouldn't find a way, find one by hook . . ." He stopped.

"Or crook?"

He blinked his eyes, almost conceding, then sighed through his nose. "I don't think you really had it, my boy."

"Had what?"

"The killer instinct."

I didn't answer. I laughed.

"I almost pity you."

"Give me back what's mine, then," I said virulently. "I made Rising Sun. Give me back my stock."

"Ah!" He raised his eyebrows in a sad smile. "I pity you, but pity doesn't run that deep."

We fell silent.

"Let me see him," I said, not looking at his face.

He cocked his head. "See whom?"

"You know 'whom,' " I replied. "*Him.* What point is there in keeping up the pretense? I know he was behind it. I saw him, that day in the gallery. You may as well confess."

Bateson shook his head. "I'm sorry, Sun I, I'm afraid you've lost me. I don't know what you're talking about. Whom do you mean?"

"Love." I pointed to the mirror. Seeing my own reflection pointing back at me, I quickly dropped my hand. "Please, Bateson," I implored, suddenly very weary, broken from the weight of ruin he'd heaped on me, or I'd heaped on myself — it hardly mattered. "This one thing I'm begging you."

"You mean your father, don't you? *Eddie* Love." He exchanged looks with the others.

I nodded, exhausted.

"You mean to say you think he's *still alive?*"

I just stared.

He snorted. "Preposterous! You must be mad. Where did you come up with such an idea?"

I sadly gathered my things together.

"Eddie Love!" Bateson repeated in a wondering, confidential whisper, soliciting the man beside him. They both burst out laughing. All of them laughed.

Draping my overcoat across my arm and picking up the catalogue from the exhibition, I started toward the door without a word.

"You'll receive your two weeks' severance pay, Sun I," Bateson called after me, almost choking on his hilarity. "The balance of it, that is. Oh, and Sun I, if you're hard up for work?"

I spun and faced him.

"My wife has been after me for some time to get a Chinese houseboy. She thinks it's 'aristocratic.' " He simpered. "I know you have some experience as a cook. Perhaps you could manage *that* — or rather, I should say, perhaps you could *manage* that."

They all burst out in derisive laughter, howling like animals.

"Bastard," I accused in a mournful, apathetic tone, not even hating him.

He leered. "Takes one to know one, doesn't it, Sun I?"

Chapter 25

That was it then. The expressions on their faces told me everything, the final, terrible truth. And not even truth, but simply disabusal of the final illusion. Despite their mockery, their derision, there could be no doubt about it. Not on that point. They really hadn't known what I was talking about. He had never been there. Never. I couldn't get over it. Everything at its face value. At their face value. Face to face. Too terrible to face. No God in the works pulling the strings. Nothing behind the curtain. No mystery. No sacrament, only the outward and visible signs. No signer, only the signatures. No deus, only the remorseless grinding of the machine. The banality of it, the mediocrity of it, was infinitely more horrible than the dream of fey, beautiful killing I had dreamed, the dream I'd dreamed of the deep mystery of sin. No mystery. Not even any sin. Not even that. Bateson at the labyrinth's heart. Bateson, the Minotaur. It was almost hilarious. It was hilarious. It was terribly hilarious. Hilariously terrible. I couldn't get over it. I couldn't take it in. Love wasn't there. He never had been. Not "mystically present." Not present through the "subtler alchemy which occurs in the believer's heart through faith," that hocus-pocus. Not present thus, or otherwise. Bateson was right. I was mad. I had been all along. Since that first moment in the master's cell when I foolishly spoke up and sealed my fate, telling Hsiao to proceed with the tale. Mad even then. Mad to believe. Mad to hope. Mad to love.

"The completeness of it." The phrase kept playing through my mind, like a skipping record, like a tic. I almost laughed. Only I dared not let myself, afraid of the stillness on the other side of laughter when the laughter ceased, and what might open up in it.

Thus, bit by bit, it came home to me, the completeness of it, what I'd lost. Everything. Yes, now at last, everything. And only now, losing him. With that, the slate wiped clean. The account closed. The price paid. The greatness of the price, the completeness of it, only now. Truly stripped down. Stripped down to something more than animal leanness, way beyond that now. The thing itself. This. And there was no dignity in it either, in the loss, nothing ennobling in suffering or sacrifice. Only a drab, ugly prospect stretching out ahead and behind, no grandeur in it, not even any view. Only this moment, this place. Here, now. Where I was. And I could hardly bring myself to look at it, to look around me and observe the world. The New World. What was left. What had always been there. Same as it ever was. The world as it is. Face to face. Too terrible to face.

Forcing it, though, like medicine, I did look around me, queasy at the sight, and when I had, I didn't want to look again. Ever. I'd seen enough. Too much. As much as I cared to. Forever and forever.

That was it then. Nirvana, Samsara, the world as it is, all wrapped up in one. And pinioned on the horns of the last equation, the final dilemma, by the commutative law, I found myself, Sun I. Face to face. "Then shall I know myself even also as I am known." And I did. I knew myself now, at last. And, through myself, I knew the rest, the world as it is. Neither a summit nor an abyss, neither the shout for mastery nor the cry of being overcome, neither singing, nor laughter, nor tears, but only pitiful, ragged things around me like myself, laboratory specimens, shivering in the aseptic light of a fluorescent sun, etiolated, increate, the stones as living as men's eyes, and nothing very.

I thought about the face of the dead tern on the beach at Sands Point, the expression in its eyes, almost smiling. Smiling even as the fly spread out its wings and squatted down to suck. That smile. I couldn't get over it. So that was knowledge. Final knowledge. Only knowledge. That was enlightenment. And everyone could have it. No penance necessary. Everybody would. Most savagely would. Every body.

It came down on me all at once then, crashed down on me all in an instant, once and forever, the completeness of it, the enormity of it, of what I'd done and what I'd lost — my pride, my peace, my hope and happiness, my youth, my innocence, my soul — all given, all paid in a lost cause. Paid up and paid out. That was the price. The price of living in the world as it is. The greatness of the price. All. And I would never enter into that glorious place, the magic Kingdom of Delights that I had dreamt and spent myself pursuing (all my Treasures spent, all squandered), never see that place where the parallel lines of my two incompatible ambitions, my two incompatible destinies, intersected and the steel rails fell in love. Never see it. For the tracks stopped here. Everybody off. Every body.

That was it then. There you were. Here I was. Last stop on the line. The final destination. As far as I would ever go. I had arrived. With a vengeance. I was there. Here. In the world as it is.

I looked around me and, in fact, "here" was an elevator. It seemed as good a place as any. All aboard! Going down. I was at the front, like the conductor, and when we stopped I got shoved out, shouldered out with the crowd, the cattle, the G.P., into the red plush lounge of the Visitors' Center on the third floor. Swept along on the tour, I offered no resistance, having none to offer, none to give. I had given everything already. I had paid the price. Why not take the tour?

And, strangely, it was good to be there with the cattle, strange and good to be there with the cattle and be touched. The concreteness of it worked on me. Memory by memory, rung by rung, I came back down the ladder, down the chain of being out of the bright heaven of despair, and an ordinary, human sadness settled over me, an ordinary man living in the world as it is, having paid the price of admission — everything — just like all the rest, along for the ride on the unguided tour, just like them.

And on the gallery I wept. With relief at first, and release. And then without it, dry heaving, no tears left, no release at all. Just naked pain. Incontinence of weeping. I dropped my coat on the floor and I buried my face in my hands and wept. My tour left without me, and another came. I continued weeping where I stood, there at the very end, unashamed, as the tours went by, one after another, like the generations, son after father, father after son, sons becoming fathers, farther and farther, all the way in both directions, back to the beginning, forward to the end, and I wept for all of them, and for myself, wept without release, without sweetness. I wept there before the spectacle of life, life beyond the glass, life in the world as it is, life unredeemed by mystery. Wept because I was lost in it for the first time, lost in life, ordinary and afraid, like everybody else, afraid because lost, lost because ordinary, just like all the rest. Wept because I had once thought I was different and that a different destiny awaited me, a special destiny, that I would never die. Wept because I had lost my hope, had lost my faith, my love, lost all. The greatness of the price. The completeness of it.

A hand touched me lightly on the shoulder, a human hand. I looked up through my tears, nodding gratefully, an attenuated look, not even seeing, not needing to, because I knew who it was, a man like me, ordinary and afraid, rising above it for an instant to be kind. He gently slipped my coat back on my arm, and patted it.

"Don't cry, son," he consoled in a quiet, unhappy voice. "It isn't worth it."

I nodded, trying to stop. I couldn't help myself. "No," I agreed, "you're right. It isn't."

"And yet sometimes it is."

I could hear the smile in his voice, and I smiled too, though I continued weeping. "Yes," I admitted. "Sometimes it is."

"I don't think we were put here to be happy," he said.

I shook my head, agreeing.

"I used to think so, that we were owed it like a basic right, that it was guaranteed. Not anymore."

"I used to think so too," I said.

"And yet, sometimes we are happy."

I didn't answer this time, because I didn't know if I believed him.

"You will be too again," he promised with the same smile behind the words.

"I've lost everything," I told him, the only truth I knew.

"I know," he replied. "I can see that. I'm sorry." Then he was quiet for a long time, respectful before the fact of it, before the completeness of it.

"Did it mean so much?" he asked finally, when he spoke again.

The question almost shocked me, but I thought about it. I nearly found it in my heart to say, no, perhaps it didn't. But I changed my mind and I said, "Yes, it did."

"Of course," he conceded. "Of course it did." This time his silence seemed a little troubled. "But losing is part of it, isn't it?" he inquired as though trying it with himself.

"Yes," I answered. "It has to be."

"The deeper part I think sometimes," he continued. "Perhaps it's the whole game." The smile came back into his voice. "And that's a secret, isn't it, that winning is small and paltry when placed next to it, almost trivial, that happiness itself is trivial compared to suffering and loss, compared to pain. A mystery," he pronounced, with a very different kind of smile in his voice, colder and brighter and farther away. "And God is merciful after all. Good-bye, young man. Good luck." He placed his hand gently on my shoulder again, and as he did I felt a chill, a tingling, a faint electric shock — the same sensation I had felt when Chung Fu laid his hand over my breast and by some mystic sleight of hand produced the cicada in the temple of the heart and blew it from his fingertips, laughing; and again as he touched me at the monastery gate when we parted for the last time and I went out into the world, this world, the world as it is.

By the time I dried my eyes and looked up, really looked, he was halfway down the corridor. The departing tour swirled around him and swept him up like a bit of flotsam.

"Goodbye!" I called, raising my hand with the impulse to arrest him, to bring him back, troubled by something, gazing after him, squinting to get a better look.

"Thank you!" I cried again, petitioning him, wanting to make him turn.

He didn't, simply raised his hand above his shoulder and picked up the pace. And as he did I noticed he was limping. My heart almost stopped, then lurched again beating impossibly fast. I was weak and sick with excitement, sick with the violence of impossible hope.

"Wait!" I shouted. "Just a minute!"

Reaching the threshold, he stopped, turned, and raised his hand.

A small cry escaped my lips, despair and happiness. It was him. It was Love. He was wearing aviator glasses with the black-green tear-shaped lenses.

Then he was gone, pushed through the door like an obstruction through a funnel, forced by the weight of the crowd dammed up behind like water, like the waters of the earth.

"Wait!" I cried, running after him. But the next tour was coming in like the turning of the tide. I forced my way, pushing and shouldering. Reaching the door, released, I sprinted after him toward the elevators.

He was standing at the very front, the car completely empty otherwise. Hands clasped before him, he was watching the lighted panel blinking overhead.

I almost reached it, almost touched him. He looked down at the last moment, directly in my face, as the doors trundled shut, as the curtain closed, and he smiled at me. I can never forget that smile. I can never get over it.

I watched the lights blinking all the way to the top. It didn't stop at the last floor, at the penthouse, not at APL. Somehow I knew it wouldn't. All the way to the top. Up to the roof. As high as you could go. And I followed him there. Here. Followed him into the final wilderness, into the world as it is.

A rush of cold air and a burst of sunlight greeted me as I pushed through the door onto the roof. I felt an almost unbearable excitement, and a sadness too. The final hunt. Forever and forever. The snow had started melting, patches and puddles in the gravel. No tracks. I couldn't see him. Yet I could sense him there, his presence, almost hear him pant. I walked quickly to the center of the roof and squinted into the wind, peering around. Around the world. Around the earth. Horizon to horizon. Only there wasn't any horizon. There wasn't any earth. Only the sky. Shoreless blueness stretching out and out and up and up. Only wind and sky and light, clear as a block of ice, and the blue shadows, like smoke, on the gravel, like the shadows in a block of ice. I could sense his presence, but he wasn't there. I knew he wasn't, though I searched for him, searched without hope, and without despair.

I heard the hum of the machinery, the remorseless grinding of the machine, a hiss like line spun from a reel, a squeal like locomotive brakes. Sounds of a trainyard. Gears and pulleys working. Wheels. I searched for him there. In the elevator cupola. The door was open. It was warmer. The concrete floor was very clean, swept. Big as a factory. The huge cables glistened, playing in and out, the spools turned and stopped, quivered, started up again, fishing. Fishing in the Well of Sighs. The heart of the machine. Oz's closet. Oz's lazarette. It would have been so right. I searched in every corner, though I knew he wasn't there, knew even as I looked, and before I looked, had known all along that he wouldn't be there, that he couldn't be. And leaning over, peering down into the well, I wondered if that was where he'd gone, back into the heart of the machine. And for a moment, just a moment, I felt it coming back, felt it seeping back, drip by drip, the deathly emptiness, like poison intravenously administered. I felt the pull of gravity, the gravity of ruin, the completeness of it, drawing me to follow him down into the heart of the machine. I entertained the thought of falling, and it was deep and wide. But instead I reached into my pocket, took out a penny, dropped it in, and wished that I might die. Because he wasn't there. Because he wasn't. And I was. Forever and forever. The completeness of it. My being there. His not being. It was all there was. It was all there. Everything. All there was. All there. Suddenly I saw the bucket coming up, rising into light, coming back out of the Well of Sighs. Overflowing with the mystery. The world as it is. And I laughed, because I understood. So many things. Remembered more. Remembered my mother's answer to Hsiao when he'd told her Love would leave. "I know," she'd said, "don't you see? I've always known." He hadn't seen, but I did, now. And I realized she was glad in her heart, even at the end. And I was too, glad because I knew, because I'd always known, like her. Of course he wasn't there. Of course. And I threw back my head and laughed. Then, wiping the tears from my eyes, I turned around and left that place.

And back outside beneath the cold sky in the wind and light, in a blue shadow etched on the gravel like a photograph, I saw the cigarette. Doused in a puddle. Just a cigarette. But my heart beat fast again. And beyond it, closer to the edge, in a patch of snow, the footprint, a single footprint. Just a footprint. Pointing to the edge. The shoreless blue above the rim of the world. I followed it, the track, and looked over. Out and down over the city. Back into the sky. And then I saw it. Saw the vapor trail following the glint of light, the silver winking, the scintilla. Saw the vapor trail, like the slow flight of an arrow shooting toward the sun, lasting forever, and I watched with joy till I grew cold. And shaking out my overcoat, still where he had left it on my arm, I saw something flutter out, a bit of paper, a ticket stub — the price of admission, the greatness of the price — something, fluttering, spinning, twirling, like a dead leaf, like an autumn leaf. Detritus. Only it flew upward. And suddenly I saw it was a moth. It had to be. What else? I watched its aerobatics with amazement and delight. And as it fluttered up the sunlight touched its wings and they lit up like stained glass windows, and the moth became a butterfly. And looking down inside my coat, placed by some mystic sleight of hand, I found the robe. And God was merciful after all.

•

Back out in the streets, I walked like a sleepwalker in a joyous trance, down toward the river, down toward the River East, drawn by the old gravity, the same gravity that drew the melting snowfall gurgling toward the drain, shouting for mastery, crying for being overcome, laughing, laughing toward the drain, the water, the water of all the rivers, the water in the cells, the rivers of the blood, the blood-river, all the tributaries, all, toward the mother stream, toward the ocean, the mystic ocean, drawn by the old gravity of ruin and of hope, drawn by the gravity of loss. I looked down at the water swirling around my feet, and there was blood in it, a pale pink tint of blood, flowing from the fish market, and floating boats of garbage, flowers placed out on the street before a florist's shop, launched on the rivers of the snow, like a flotilla, like a parade, following it down to the gutter, down to the drain. Everything hurrying on the same place I was, drawn by the gravity of loss. Sticks and bits of reed drifted and bobbed in it, small sticks and twigs like those left scattered on the beach at Sands Point. Mystic patterns written in detritus, the force fields of the tidal ebb. Now I understood. The flood consumed itself, erased its tracks into that wilderness of ecstasy where it vanished, where he vanished, and all that remained was this, mystic patterns written in detritus, the bread crumbs of the way back out, magnetic tracings of the ebb, of loss, everything going, everybody. Then the mystery opened deeper, and I glimpsed the jewel within the lotus, and once again I wept, because I saw that I was there, that this was it, the delta — Loss — and everything was going, every body, even the raging torrent of the Dow, even the blood-river, back at last to this, to the delta, the Great Confluence of the Great Divide, back to Loss, the mother ocean, Tao. Back to the Source. Back to the world as it is.

And the words of the ninth song, "Returning to the Source," came to my lips, and I sang.

> Too long the way that led me here,
>   back to the Source of All.
> Blind and dumb from the beginning,
>   better never to have taken that first step.
> Cross-legged in the cell of my Original Nature,
>   indifferent to the world outside,
> The river flows serenely where it must — it always did;
> And the flowers are red in the new dawn.

And they are, Reader. The flowers are blooded, too.

About the Author

David Payne was born in North Carolina and now lives in New York. His first novel, *Confessions of a Taoist on Wall Street*, received the Houghton Mifflin Literary Fellowship Award.